CW00431483

ENCYCLOPAEDIA
OF CULTIVATED ORCHIDS

IA *Ascocentrum ampullaceum* (Ldl.) Schltr. [A.D. HAWKES]

IB *Brassia Lawrenceana* Ldl. [H.R. FOLKERSMA]

ENCYCLOPAEDIA
OF CULTIVATED ORCHIDS

AN ILLUSTRATED DESCRIPTIVE MANUAL

ALEX D. HAWKES

faber and faber
LONDON · BOSTON

First published in 1965
by Faber and Faber Limited
3 Queen Square London WC1N 3AU
Reprinted 1970, 1975, 1977, 1978 and 1987

Printed and bound in Great Britain
by Butler & Tanner Ltd
Frome and London
All rights reserved

© copyright by Alex D. Hawkes 1965

To

the memory of

America's foremost orchidologist,

PROFESSOR OAKES AMES

who encouraged and taught me at an early age,

this volume is dedicated

CONTENTS

PREFACE

HOW TO USE THIS ENCYCLOPAEDIA

This *Encyclopaedia of Cultivated Orchids* is designed for easy use by the orchid collector, whether he is botanically trained or not.

Each genus now considered valid within the Orchidaceae is noted here, in alphabetical sequence. (A complete list, with citations of publication, of all orchid genera—valid and synonymous—is found starting on page 502.) After a discussion of the genus, its allies, distribution, basic appearance, etc., we find a note regarding its hybrids (if any) and presumed genetic relatives. (A list of multigeneric hybrid groups registered in the Orchidaceae—as of the date of completion of this manuscript—is furnished, with pertinent notes and cross-index, commencing on page 527.) This is followed by cultural directions, these generalized to accommodate the greater percentage of the cultivated components in the case of a genus with more than one species in general cultivation. Basic cultural instructions for orchids as a whole are not given, since these are readily available in other books, such as the author's *Orchids—Their Botany and Culture* (Harper and Brothers, New York, 1961).

Then follow brief descriptions of the component species which are in general cultivation and which are more or less available in the contemporary trade. In these descriptive passages, certain abbreviations have been utilized for commonly used terms; these are explained on page 21. At the beginning of each specific entry is its accepted name, followed by essential synonymy (where available). At the end of each descriptive paragraph is a generalized indication of flowering-season, followed by parenthetical letters designating its temperature preference when in our collections (see page 21 for explanation of these). This is followed by an indication of the distribution of the plant under discussion.

In a genus containing more than one species in general cultivation, those species most commonly encountered (and most generally available) are described in some detail. These are followed by a section devoted to more abbreviated descriptions of somewhat rarer species, these again listed in alphabetical sequence.

Phonetic pronunciations for all botanical names utilized in this manual are to be found in the Index at the end of the volume.

Those terms which are of necessity used within the text, but which may be somewhat unfamiliar to readers, are explained—with appended phonetic pronunciations—in the Glossary, commencing on page 533.

All orchids which are generally listed in the trade are included in this manual. Certain species which occur only as isolated specimens in the collections of private persons or those of botanical gardens are in many instances mentioned, but not taken up in particular detail, since they are not available to the average collector. Photographs and drawings accompanying the text have been chosen especially to show genera and species not previously illustrated in the readily accessible literature dealing with orchids.

It is planned to issue periodic supplements to this manual. These will include future important alterations in our knowledge of orchid taxonomy, pertinent illustrations, and discussions of plants which come into general cultivation. I will welcome correspondence from interested persons regarding these points.

It is patently obvious that a work such as this can never be truly 'complete', for scarcely a month passes that an orchid species (or genus) previously not available to the average collector is introduced into the trade. Through international co-operation, however, we can keep this work—and its supplements—up to date, so that they will furnish a comprehensive continuing *Encyclopaedia* of all of the orchidaceous plants in cultivation—and those which come into cultivation.

A. D. H.

Coconut Grove, Florida, U.S.A.

ACKNOWLEDGEMENTS

During the preparation of a study of these dimensions, it is obviously necessary to call on the assistance of a great many persons. I would like at this time to express my especial thanks for favours rendered in many ways to the following orchidists and orchidologists.

Firstly, my thanks must go to

George Fuller, New Plymouth, New Zealand, without whose incredible photos this volume would have been lacking in its present appeal.

The late Paul H. Allen, and Dorothy O. Allen, of the Republic of Honduras

Blanche Ames, and the late Professor Oakes Ames, of Ormond, Florida

Kari Berggrav, of Rutherford, New Jersey

John W. Blowers, Editor of *The Orchid Review*, and Secretary of the Orchid Committee of The Royal Horticultural Society

Jack Brant, Jr., of Miami, Florida

The late W. M. Buswell, of the Buswell Herbarium, at the University of Miami, Florida

Henry P. Butcher, of Volcán, Chiriquí, Republic of Panama

Alex C. Chang, of Honolulu, Hawaii

Charlesworth and Company, Haywards Heath, Sussex, England

Katherine Hawkes Chatham, Coconut Grove, Florida

The Rev. N. E. G. Cruttwell, Papua, New Guinea

Reg S. Davis, San Diego, California

Gordon W. Dillon, Executive Secretary of the American Orchid Society

H. A. Dunn, Panama Canal Zone

G. C. K. Dunsterville, Caracas, Venezuela

The late Dr. and Mrs. David G. Fairchild, 'The Kampong', Coconut Grove, Florida

Edward A. Flickinger, Coconut Grove, Florida

H. R. Folkersma, of Velsen, Netherlands

John Fredericks, of Homestead, Florida

Fred J. Fuchs, Jr., of Naranja, Florida

Jack Grant, of Naples, Florida

Miss M. Hawkes, of Coconut Grove, Florida

A. H. Heller of Monte Fresco, Managua, Nicaragua

The late Federico Carlos Hoehne, of São Paulo, Brazil

R. E. Holttum, of Singapore and Kew, England

Wm. Kirch-Orchids, Ltd., Honolulu, Hawaii

Oscar M. Kirsch, of Honolulu, Hawaii

C. K. Kueh, Kuching, Sarawak

John Lager, of Lager and Hurrell, Summit, New Jersey

Marcel Lecoufle, Boissy-Saint-Léger, France

H. F. Loomis, of Miami, Florida

J. Marnier-Lapostolle, Jardin Botanique 'Les Cèdres', Saint-Jean-Cap-Ferrat, France

The Robert McCue family, of Cutler Ridge, Florida

The late Lester McDonald, of The Orchid Digest Corporation

Dr. and Mrs. Luys de Mendonça e Silva, Rio de Janeiro, Brazil

W. W. G. Moir, of Honolulu, Hawaii

Montréal Botanical Garden, Montréal, P.Q., Canada

Dr. Y. Nagano, of Tokyo, Japan

H. Narramore, of Port Elizabeth, South Africa

Wallace H. Otaguro, of Honolulu, Hawaii
Betty and Tom Powell, of the Horticultural Society of New York
Merle A. Reinikka, of the American Orchid Society
João Rocha, of São Paulo, Brazil
H. Schmidt-Mumm, of Bogotá, Colombia
G. Hermon Slade, Homebush, N.S.W., Australia
F. L. Stevenson, of Chamblee, Georgia
V. S. Summerhayes, of the Royal Botanic Garden, Kew, England

FOREWORD

by

JOHN W. BLOWERS, A.H.R.H.S.

Editor, The Orchid Review
Secretary, Orchid Committee of The Royal Horticultural Society

Trends and fancies in orchids fluctuate, as they do in all modes of life. Wild orchids, gathered from most parts of the world, were introduced by many thousands in the early part of the nineteenth century, to start off a cult that has since increased tremendously in size and momentum. The latter part of the century saw a dramatic change—a swing away from the natural species to the hybrids—a fresh field started by Dominy in 1856. Hybrids almost completely dominated the orchid scene until the middle of this present twentieth century, when orchidists realized that hybrids had their limitations, and that the riches of the orchid world were incompletely appreciated without the species. Consequently, nowadays there is a serious interest in both hybrids and species on the part of every true orchidist—and, indeed, an increasing delight in the marvellous diversity of the 'wild' species of this incredible group of plants.

But all of these changes, and lapse of time, have resulted in a void of a modern, accurate treatise of the cultivated Orchidaceae. Orchid growers' requirements were well provided for in early days by such works as Williams' *Orchid Growers' Manual* (1885), the *Manual of Orchidaceous Plants* by James Veitch & Sons (1894), and the more comprehensive works of *Sanders' Orchid Guide* (1901), and (in German), Schlechter's *Die Orchideen* (1914).

Since then many new species—and genera—have been introduced into cultivation. Numerous alterations and errors, in naming of cultivated orchids, have come to light through continuing critical study. And as a result, orchidists have been severely hampered in their interests through a lack of international collation of these changes. Partial studies have appeared, dealing mostly with the orchid flora of such-and-such a country, or with all or a few members of a given genus—but these have been, largely, all too technical (even though of notable value) for the average collector.

No comprehensive orchid encyclopaedia has been written for fifty years! And now we have one—a study written both for the hobbyist and for the scientific student of these plants.

The contemporary orchid world is lucky in having the brilliant orchidologist, Alex D. Hawkes, to fill this outstanding void with this remarkable volume, *Encyclopaedia of Cultivated Orchids*. Being the most comprehensive and botanically accurate work on the Orchidaceae ever written, it is destined to become the orchid grower's Bible!

It will be essential for the novice, for it gives concise guidance as to where orchids are found, and expertly-done instructions as to how thsee habitats can be simulated in other climates, or in greenhouses, thereby ensuring the successful cultivation of these extraordinary plants. It will help the experienced orchidist in identifying his plants, and in showing to him the amazing scope of the almost seven hundred genera, so that special individual desires may be pursued until completion.

If, for example, a grower has selected Oncidiums as favourites, then from this *Encyclopaedia* he will learn which species and variations are presently in general cultivation, and will be able to add to the value of his collection and enjoyment by tracking them down.

At the same time he will be able to converse with the correct pronunciation of all orchid technical names and terms—a most important and again unique feature of this *Encyclopaedia*. Hybrid interests are also well catered for, including a roster of the multigeneric orchid hybrid groups (plus reference cross-index of component genera), never before available in book form. The wealth of handsome illustrations will, further, lead everyone into paths of additional exploration of the amazing breadth of this orchid world.

This *Encyclopaedia* is recommended for its backing of more than twenty-five years' preparation, from a specialist with a world-wide reputation. Alex D. Hawkes, born in Houlton, Maine, in 1927, commenced working with orchids at the age of eleven years. Such famous botanists as Oakes Ames, Liberty Hyde Bailey, and David Fairchild were among his early influential mentors. At the age of twelve his first article on the subject was published, the forerunner of many thousands of papers on orchids and other largely tropical plants. Dr. Hawkes founded two of the largest orchid societies in existence, and has enriched the literary contributions to the orchid world through editorship of *The Orchid Weekly* and *The Orchid Journal*, and as author of *Orchids—Their Botany and Culture* (Harper & Brothers, 1961), and *Cultural Directions for Orchids* (The Horticultural Publications, 1960). He has also long been a very faithful and regular contributor to all of the reputable orchid magazines of the world. Travels over much of the globe in pursuit of orchids and information about them have further strengthened his reputation as one of the world's foremost orchidologists.

Problems will be solved, and enjoyment immeasurably increased, through this successful closing of a chasm in orchid literature, through this work, *Encyclopaedia of Cultivated Orchids*. It is destined to be the most frequently used source of accurate reference in any library.

In the near future many people will be adding congratulations and appreciation for this indispensable aid to our knowledge of the Orchidaceae.

AN INTRODUCTION TO THE ORCHIDS

Orchids are flowering plants—as opposed to plants such as mushrooms, mosses, and ferns, which do not produce flowers—all of which are members of a single botanical family, the Orchidaceae.

Orchids are members of the great plant grouping called the monocotyledons, which are distinguished by having only a single seed-leaf upon germination of the seed. Plants such as the oak and the poppy have two seed-leaves, hence are relegated to another grouping, this called the dicotyledons.

Although the irises and the lilies, and even the bromeliads and the aroids, are all members of this aggregation of monocotyledons, the orchids are—despite their occasional apparent superficial similarity—only distant relations. In reality, the orchids' closest allies are the Burmannias (members of the family Burmanniaceae), and the Apostasias and Neuwiedias (family Apostasiaceae),[1] both groups of rather insignificant and seldom-seen terrestrial or saprophytic plants, found mostly in tropical areas.

The number of different kinds of orchids which grow wild throughout the world has never been determined with any accuracy, and estimates today range from a low of 7,500 species to a high of more than 30,000. From the evidence at our disposal, it would seem that a figure of approximately 24,000 apparently valid species is a safe and reasonable estimate. In addition to this prodigious quantity of 'wild' orchids, there exist about 32,000 or so—the number increases at the average rate of more than 1,000 per annum—hybrid forms, these hybrids having been produced, for the most part, by man's action. Thus, in the Orchidaceae, we have by far the largest assemblage of flowering plants known to science—at the lowest estimate something in excess of 56,000 distinct kinds, as this book is written!

Orchids are perennial herbs[2] of varying habit. They may be found growing on trees or shrubs, when they are termed epiphytes or 'air-plants', or on rocks, when they are correctly termed lithophytes, or—more archaically—saxicolous plants. The ground-dwelling species are referred to as terrestrials, and certain seldom-seen orchids which derive their nourishment from dead or decaying organic matter in the ground or on rotting logs are called saprophytes. A few orchids grow in the water, as semi-aquatics, under special conditions, and two extremely rare and peculiar genera, the Australian *Cryptanthemis* and *Rhizanthella*, are actually subterranean, with only the small cup-like inflorescences reaching the surface of the ground, and in some cases even these remain underground during their complete life-cycle.

The majority of orchids found in temperate climates are terrestrial in habit, while those from tropical regions are found most frequently on trees and somewhat less commonly on rocks. In so far as is known today, no orchids are true parasites, despite the fact that most of the epiphytic species are believed by lay persons to be parasitic in their mode of growth, such as the mistletoes (Loranthaceae), etc.

Vegetatively the orchids are divided into three basic groups: sympodial, monopodial, and pseudo-monopodial. In the sympodial types, genera such as *Cattleya* and *Epidendrum* for example, the growth of the principal part of the plant, or the axis, ceases at the termination of the flowering-season, to be continued the next season by a different, newly grown axis; thus a series of successive annual axes is in time produced by a single individual plant. The inflorescence or flower-spike in this category is borne either from the apex of the shoot, or from the side of the shoot on a short leafless branch. In the monopodial orchids, such as *Vanda* and *Angraecum* and their myriad allies, the main axis continues to grow and elongate season after season, bearing new leaves at the apex[3] and producing flowers on side shoots arising from the leaf-axils of the older parts of the plant. The small group of pseudomonopodials, the subtribes *Dichaeinae*, *Pachyphyllinae*, and possibly *Pterostemmatinae*,[4] are arbitrary in the extreme, but are generally considered to be

---

[1] Garay has recently (in *Bot. Mus. Leafl. Harv. Univ.*, 19(3), 1960), proposed a new subfamily in the Orchidaceae to accommodate the old Apostasiaceae, but in this treatment we do not follow this suggestion, which we feel requires additional research.

[2] *Zeuxine strateumatica* (L.) Schltr. appears to be the only annual orchid known as yet to botanists, although further research may prove that it does not truly belong in this arbitrary category. Certain other incompletely known terrestrial species may well prove to be of only annual duration under special conditions.

[3] Some genera of this group, the subtribe *Sarcanthinae*, such as *Microcoelia* and *Taeniophyllum*, are essentially leafless when adult.

[4] Including the genera *Dichaea* (Dichaeinae), *Centropetalum*, *Pachyphyllum* (Pachyphyllinae), and possibly *Pterostemma* (Pterostemmatinae).

somewhat intermediate between these two, having stems which elongate season after season, but which also extend in a lateral direction of growth as well. Here the flowers are borne mostly on side shoots, often near the apices of the stems. *Lockhartia*, of the subtribe *Lockhartiinae*, has also been placed in this pseudo-monopodial grouping, but apparently is better considered a true, but somewhat aberrant, sympodially growing genus, closest in its affinity to the *Oncidium* alliance (subtribe *Oncidiinae*).

The terrestrial species of orchids typically have an erect or ascending stem, with one or more leaves either at the base or up the stem, and one or more flowers at the apex. The leaves are for the most part present during the flowering season, although in a percentage of the species they are produced when the plants are not in bloom, or else die down prior to the expansion of the blossoms. A very few terrestrial orchids possess no true leaves of any kind, at any time.

In the terrestrial kinds, leaves—when present—vary from a bract-like sheath to a more or less broad structure, occurring in all possible dimensions from thread-like to rounded, and in textures from very thin and paper- or parchment-like to incredibly thick and coriaceous. Variously folded or plicate leaves are characteristic of many genera, as well as certain individual species within large and polymorphic genera. The veins present in these leaves are parallel—as is typical of monocotyledons—although in a very few genera (e.g., *Epistephium*) noticeable reticulate venation is also found.

The roots of the terrestrial orchids are also variable in form, being found from thin and fibre-like to inordinately fleshy and tuberoid. Often a more or less conspicuous rhizome is produced, from which copious roots are borne; fleshy corms or rounded tubers—usually termed, for ease of definition, pseudo-bulbs—are produced by certain ground-dwelling genera and species.

The saprophytes are commonly dwarf, inconspicuous plants growing in woodland or forest humus, or on decaying fallen trees and the like. Typically a coral-like rhizome is produced, from which the erect, white, brown, or yellow flower-stems arise. Leaves are reduced to tiny sheathing scales on these stems, or in some instances essentially absent. A virtual lack of chlorophyll is one of the principal features of these peculiar orchids. In the saprophytic genus *Galeola*, vines of frequently gigantic dimensions—sometimes clambering in tropical trees to heights of more than forty feet—are found. Because they rely on decaying organic matter in the medium in which they occur, the saprophytes are almost impossible to maintain in a living condition under cultivation, hence they are very little known by enthusiasts, despite the fact that some of them are extremely handsome when in bloom.

Epiphytic and most lithophytic orchids have no permanent main roots. Instead, there are adventive roots produced from the stem-nodes; these roots, familiar in such popular genera as *Cattleya*, *Dendrobium*, and *Oncidium*, attach the plants to the tree or rock on which they grow, and often penetrate for some distance into the mossy or licheny substratum. Certain of the epiphytic orchids, particularly some of the sarcanthads such as *Vanda*, *Aërides*, *Angraecum*, and their multitudinous allies, produce quantities of aerial roots, which generally hang free in the air and aid materially in the absorption of moisture and, to a lesser extent, food-materials. Anatomically, the roots of these epiphytic orchids are remarkable structures, being covered with a greatly thickened epidermis, which is called the velamen; this velamen is a layer of several thicknesses of spongy cells which possess extraordinary qualities of absorption and retention of moisture. The colour of these roots varies considerably, depending on whether they are moist or dry. If wet, they are generally green or greenish, but when desiccated their hue changes to tan, whitish, or dull grey.

The leaves of the epiphytic (and lithophytic) orchids are basically similar to those of the terrestrials, even though, as we have previously mentioned (see footnote 3 on page 17), in a few genera—at least in the adult stage—they are totally absent or at least drastically reduced.

Pseudobulbs are found in a large proportion of the epiphytic orchids whose growth-habit is sympodial; they are unknown in the monopodials or in the pseudomonopodials. Pseudobulbs are not true bulbs, but rather are highly specialized, more or less thickened, secondary stems, made up of one or more internodes, which act as storage structures for moisture and food. Their shape varies tremendously—generally they are globular, pear-shaped, or spindle-shaped—and often serves as an easy means of differentiation of different genera and species. Leaves may be borne either all along the length of these pseudobulbs, or only at or near their apices, and may be solitary or numerous. Many epiphytic orchids possess leaves which are extremely thick and fleshy, and which are covered by a hard cuticle or 'skin' which reduces transpiration materially.

All orchids bear their flowers in an inflorescence which is either a spike, a simple raceme, or a more or less branched panicle; one to very many blossoms may be produced on a single inflorescence, depending upon the species or upon the strength of the individual specimen under consideration. The origin of this inflorescence varies from genus to genus, and often as well from species to species in some of the larger and more polymorphic groups. It may be terminal, pseudo-terminal, lateral, basal, or even pseudo-basal, though such extremes do not occur within a single given generic aggregation, and seldom within a single subtribe.

The flowers of orchids are exceedingly complex structures which, on superficial examination, appear remarkably simplified in construction. One of the most important characteristics of all orchid flowers is that they are zygomorphic, meaning that when they are split into two equal halves on one plane only, the parts are of identical appearance. Most other flowers can be split into two equal halves on *any* plane and still be identical, hence the oddity of the orchids.

These flowers are bisexual (perfect), or, much more rarely, unisexual (as in most Catasetums and the genus *Cycnoches*). The unisexual ones have the male (staminate) and the female (pistillate) sexual parts borne in separate blossoms—often, in fact, on separate inflorescences—while the bisexual ones, comprising the bulk of the Orchidaceae, have both the male and the female organs present in one and the same blossom. The ovary, which is in this family combined with the pedicel (flower-stalk) and is hence known as the pedicellate ovary, is inferior and consists of one or three cells, these called locules by the botanists.

Almost all orchidaceous plants are cultivated principally for their flowers, which may be small and relatively insignificant to large and very spectacular. Abnormal forms—examples of polymorphy, cleisto-gamy, pelory, or teratology—are infrequent, and when they occur, it is usually on the same inflorescence with otherwise normal blossoms. Cleistogamy might be cited as an exception to this statement, for in some tropical (and a few temperate-zone) species, this condition is prevalent throughout the flower-spike in aberrant, usually named forms.

In the orchids both the sepals and the petals are typically coloured, a condition which does not obtain in most other flowers, e.g., the rose (genus *Rosa*), in which the sepals (calyx) are green and bract-like at the base of the prominent, coloured petals (corolla).

The sepals may be free from one another or somewhat united, on occasion forming a definite tube, which is called the sepaline tube (e.g., *Physosiphon*, many Masdevallias). The upper or dorsal sepal is symmetrical and usually differs slightly in shape from the often relatively oblique lower, or lateral, sepals. These lateral sepals may be free from each other or joined together at the base (or, in some instances, to their apices), and often form a mentum or small protruding chin, this condition usually in conjunction with the column-foot.

The inner floral segments, called the petals, are actually three in number, although one of them—termed the lip, or labellum—is typically very much modified and enlarged and is often the most prominent and distinctive part of the flower. The petals are identical to each other and highly variable in shape and degree of development, varying from the broad wavy segments of a *Cattleya* to the tiny wart-like protuberances of certain kinds of *Pleurothallis* and *Bulbophyllum*. In the bud, the lip is the uppermost petal of the blossom, but in almost all orchids it becomes the lowermost one through a remarkable twisting of the pedicellate ovary, a process known as resupination.

The lip (or labellum, as it is often written) may be simple or variously lobed, flattened, sac-like, or tubular, and apically and marginally entire, fringed, toothed, or notched. Its upper surface, called the disc, is typically furnished with various sorts of growths or protuberances, called calli, papillae, or lamellae; these structures on the disc are often diagnostic in various species or genera, and are sometimes—as in many members of the genus *Oncidium*, for example—developed to a remarkable degree of size and complexity. The lip may be elongated at the base to form a more or less prominent spur, in which the nectariferous glands are customarily to be found; in some genera, such as *Habenaria, Angraecum, Aërangis, Plectrelminthus*, etc., this spur reaches extreme lengths and forms a showy part of the blossom.

Orchids may most easily be differentiated from all other kinds of plants by the sexual apparatus, which is borne on a more or less elongated stalk-like or finger-like structure called the column (or, more technically, the gynostemium), which is situated at the centre of the blossom.[5] This column, which varies in size and degree of development in the various genera and species, bears at the summit or on the sides near the summit, one to rarely three movable or rigidly attached anthers; in front, on the ventral surface, is found the stigma or more or less confluent stigmas. A rostellum, which is actually a modified stigma, projects out over the stigmatic surface in many genera; this flap-like structure, which is of great taxonomic importance in certain groups of orchids (notably in the subtribe *Sarcanthinae*), serves primarily to aid in the affixing of the pollinia to visiting insects and to prevent the pollen-masses from falling on the viscid stigmatic surface of the same flower, and thus may be termed an aid (and, at the same time, a deterrent) to pollination. The anther (or anthers) are found behind the rostellum—if it is present—and often lie against it; the shallow or rather deep

[5] A column is also present in the Milkweed family (Asclepiadaceae), but it differs materially in structure from the type found in the orchids.

pit in which they rest is called the clinandrium. Orchid anthers are more or less distinctly 2-celled, and contain either a mass of powdery pollen (as in the *Cypripedium* group and a few genera in other aggregations), or two, four, six, or eight distinct masses of waxy pollen, termed pollinia (singular, pollinium). The number of these pollinia present in a flower is often of critical importance in differentiating one genus from another. This pollen varies in consistency from powdery or granular-mealy to hard and waxy or cartilaginous. The base of the column is frequently extended to form a foot, to the apex of which (in such cases) the lip is usually attached. In some orchids, the lateral sepals are prolonged and are attached obliquely to this column-foot, to form a chin or mentum.

Orchid fruits, or seed-capsules as they are popularly called, are usually dry when ripe and vary in shape from rather egg-shaped to almost globular or cylindrical; three or more angles are sometimes present, the angles being winged to various degrees. In *Dichaea* and a few other genera, prominently developed spine-like excrescences cover the surface of the fruit. Vanilla is distinctive in bearing a rather cylindrical fleshy pod which, when dried and cured, becomes the 'vanilla bean' of commerce, furnishing our commercial extract. Most orchids bear the persistent flower-remains at the apex of the fruit, and in some species these old perianth segments even increase in size and thickness as the fruit forms; a notable example of this condition is found in the popular *Phalaenopsis Lueddemanniana*. When ripe, the dry capsule splits along one, two, three, or six longitudinal sutures, and the valves thus formed usually remain connected at the base and at the apex, the seeds being dispersed through the median openings.

The seeds of almost all orchids are exceedingly small, usually simulating a tiny bit of tan or brown dust rather than the seed of a potentially large plant. They are extremely light and are hence readily dispersed by the wind. Each mature seed-capsule may contain upwards of a million seeds, and it has been authoritatively estimated that a fruit of *Cycnoches ventricosum* var. *chlorochilon* holds as many as 3,770,000 individual seeds! The seeds of the members of the subtribe *Cypripedilinae* are larger and of greater consequence than are those of most other orchids, a condition also occurring in such genera as *Vanilla*, *Sobralia*, *Galeola*, etc.

ABBREVIATIONS AND SYMBOLS USED

In the succeeding pages of this work, abbreviations and symbols are used for words and conditions that are many times repeated in the descriptions. Here is a list of these abbreviations and symbols:

caps. = capsule, or 'seed-pod'
col. = column, or gynostemium
diam. = diameter
dors. = dorsal
fl. = flower
fld. = flowered
fls. = flowers
infl. = inflorescence
infls. = inflorescences
lat. = lateral
lats. = lateral (sepals)
lb. = lobe
lbd. = lobed
lbs. = lobes
lf. = leaf
lvs. = leaves
midlb. = midlobe

pb. = pseudobulb
pbs. = pseudobulbs
pls. = plants
ps. = petals
rac. = raceme
racs. = racemes
rhiz. = rhizome
segm. = segment
segms. = segments
sep. = sepal
sp. = species (singular)
spp. = species (plural)
ss. = sepals
st. = stem
sts. = stems
subvar. = subvariety
var. = variety

The following symbols have also been used in this work: x designates that the plant under discussion is of hybrid origin; × indicates the two (or more) parents of a hybrid.

The letters (C), (I), and (H) designate theoretically ideal temperature requirements for a genus or one of its component species or variants. The symbol (C) indicates that cool conditions should prevail (that is, average night temperatures of 45–50°F. during the cool months); (I) indicates intermediate (55–65°F.); and (H) warm or tropical conditions (65–70°F. or more). Combinations of one or more symbols enclosed parenthetically—as (C, I), (I, H), (C, I, H), etc.—indicate that the temperature requirements of the genus, species, or hybrid under consideration are variable. Individual conditions, especially in the tropics, will determine which range of temperature will best suit the plant.

MONOCHROME PLATES

COLOUR PLATES

THE GENERA AND SPECIES OF CULTIVATED ORCHIDS

ABDOMINEA J.J.Sm.

A member of the subtribe *Sarcanthinae*, this genus contains but a single rare species, **A. minimiflora** (Hk.f.) J.J.Sm. (*Saccolabium minimiflorum* Hk.f., *Abdominea micrantha* J.J.Sm.), which is native in the Malay Peninsula and Java. A dwarf epiphyte, it bears a few fleshy leaves and abbreviated, many-flowered inflorescences of small flowers, with the sepals red-brown, the petals dull reddish-green, and the lip white tinged with green. Strictly of scientific interest, *Abdominea* is not present in contemporary collections.

Nothing is known of the genetic affinities of this group.

CULTURE: Presumably as for the tropical Vandas, etc. (H)

ACACALLIS Ldl.
(*Kochiophyton* Schltr.)

Acacallis contains but a single species of very rare epiphytic orchid, native in Brazil and Colombia, allied to *Aganisia* Ldl. and *Paradisianthus* Rchb.f., but differing from those groups in the structure of the lip and other characters. It is a handsome, rather dwarf plant, occasionally found in particularly choice collections, though its cultivation under artificial conditions is a difficult undertaking.

No hybrids have as yet been produced in *Acacallis*, and nothing is known of its genetic affinities, although it seems probable that hybrids with allied genera of the subtribe *Zygopetalinae* could be effected.

Acacallis cyanea Ldl. [B.S.WILLIAMS]

CULTURE: As for *Aganisia*. Particular care should be taken to keep the compost moist at all times, and a high temperature should always be maintained. (H)

A. cyanea Ldl. (*Aganisia coerulea* Rchb.f., *Aganisia tricolor* N.E.Br., *Aganisia cyanea* Lind. not Bth., *Kochiophyton negrense* Schltr.)
A creeping dwarf epiphyte, one of the 'blue' orchids. Rhiz. slender, prostrate, giving rise to pbs. about 2″ tall at intervals. Pbs. ovoid, glossy green. Lvs. solitary, rarely paired, erect, rather leathery, to 8″ long. Spikes basal, erect or arching, to 12″ tall, slender, with up to 10 proportionately large fragrant fls. to 2½″ across. Ss. and ps. mauve outside, deep sky-blue within, often white apically, oval, the ps. somewhat incurved. Lip white basally, becoming deep indigo-blue above, with a yellow crest. Col. white marked with blue or purple-blue. Summer, especially in May. (H) Brazil; Colombia.

ACAMPE Ldl.

The genus *Acampe* includes about thirteen species of epiphytic or rather rarely lithophytic monopodial orchids, widely dispersed in the Asiatic and African tropics. They for the most part simulate a robust *Vanda* in vegetative appearance, but florally are closer in their alliance to *Sarcanthus* Ldl. The leaves are typically very fleshy and somewhat recurved, and the generally small to medium-sized, fragrant, waxen flowers are borne in dense cylindrical racemes or tight heads. They are often rather nondescript orchids, seldom cultivated, and of interest only to connoisseurs.

A single hybrid has to date been registered which utilizes an *Acampe* in its parentage, this a cross with *Vanda*, to give *Vancampe*. This is an interesting and floriferous plant, as yet rare in collections. Additional intergeneric breeding between Acampes and various allied sarcanthad genera should be attempted, particularly if the compact inflorescences could be made more colourful thereby.

CULTURE: The cultural requirements of this genus approximate those of the tropical and subtropical Vandas. The plants are often grown in baskets rather than in pots, for better aeration of the prominent fleshy roots. (I, H)

A. longifolia (Ldl.) Ldl. (*Vanda longifolia* Ldl., *Saccolabium longifolium* Hk.f., *Acampe penangiana* Ridl.)
Sts. robust, often branched, frequently curving rather gracefully, mostly erect, to 2′ tall (rarely more), usually densely leafy. Lvs. thick, stiffly ascending, to about 8″ long, the tip broader than the basal part, tongue-shaped. Infls. erect, sometimes shortly branched, to 4″ tall, the fls. very crowded, mostly opening successively over a relatively long period. Fls. fleshy, not expanding well, about ¾″ across at most, rather delicately fragrant. Ss. and ps. pale lemon-yellow with narrow crimson cross-bars and spots. Lip white with a few purple spots, with a sac at the base. Summer. (I, H) Himalayas to Malay Peninsula (Penang) and the Langkawi Islands.

A. dentata Ldl. Sts. to about 2′ tall, rather similar in basic habit to *A. longifolia* (Ldl.) Ldl., but the rigidly thick lvs. arching outwards and downwards. Infls. to about 12″ tall (usually less) a lax panicle (rarely a simple rac.), many-fld., the fls. opening successively over a long period. Fls. long-lived, delicately fragrant, heavy in texture, not expanding fully, about ½″ across, yellowish-white, the ss. and ps. with numerous brown blotches, the lip mostly white striped and streaked with dull purple or reddish-purple, rather similar in shape to that of *A. multiflora* (Ldl.) Ldl. Mostly summer. (I, H) India, mostly at rather low elevations.

A. multiflora (Ldl.) Ldl. (*Vanda multiflora* Ldl.) Rather similar in habit to *A. dentata* Ldl., but the sts. smaller, usually under 12″ tall, and less robust in all parts. Lvs. tongue-shaped, to 12″ long and about 2″ wide, fleshy, bilobed apically. Infls. to about 12″ tall (usually less), loosely panicled or not, many-fld. Fls. about 1″ across, very fleshy, faintly fragrant at times, long-lived, the ss. and ps. yellow often spotted with red or dull brown. Lip white streaked with dirty-purple, with a short, blunt, basal, sac-like projection, short lat. lbs., and an ovate, blunt midlb. Autumn–early winter. (I) Southern China; Himalayas; northern India.

A. papillosa (Ldl.) Ldl. (*Saccolabium papillosum* Ldl., *Sarcochilus praemorsus* Spreng.) Rather similar in habit to *A. dentata* Ldl., the thick, recurving lvs. only about 5″ long and 1″ wide. Infls. usually a simple rac., very short, mostly to about 1½″ long, very rarely branched, densely many-fld., the fls. often arranged in a rather compact head. Fls. long-lived, rather sweetly fragrant, heavy-textured, to about ½″ across, the ss. and ps. dark yellow spotted and dotted with dull brown, the lip white, marked on the elongate midlb.—which is longer than the ss.—with rose-red. Mostly autumn. (I) Himalayas to Burma.

ACANTHEPHIPPIUM Bl. ex Endl.
(*Acanthophippium* Bl.)

The name of this genus is customarily misspelled *Acanthophippium*. It includes about fifteen species of terrestrial, rarely epiphytic or lithophytic orchids, related to *Pachystoma* Bl. and *Calanthe* R.Br., distributed in the tropics of the Old World from southern China to the Fiji Islands. The plants have prominent, often furrowed pseudobulbs, and plicate foliage like their allies. The extraordinary bottle- or cup-shaped, fleshy, usually heavily fragrant flowers are produced in short erect racemes simultaneously with the new growths. The Acanthephippiums are at this time rare orchids in our collections, but all of them are most interesting plants, and the group should be better known by connoisseurs.

No hybrids have as yet been produced in this genus, but interspecific breeding should prove most interesting, and it seems possible that *Acanthephippium* will prove genetically compatible with allied genera, such as *Phaius*, *Calanthe*, *Spathoglottis*, and the like.

CULTURE: These singularly interesting and attractive orchids should be grown in well-drained pots, in a mixture such as that suggested for *Phaius*, with a liberal addition of leaf-mould and gritty sand. They benefit by regular applications of fertilizers, and should be transplanted as infrequently as possible, though they are very intolerant of stale conditions at the roots. When the new growths have completed (and, in almost all of the species, the flowers have faded), the plants should be given a definite period of rest, for about three or four

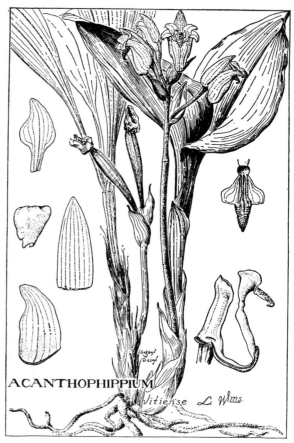

Acanthephippium vitiense L.O.Wms. [GORDON W. DILLON]

weeks, in a somewhat cooler situation than usual. Semi-shade is required for best results, as the foliage is subject to burning through excessive exposure. (I, H)

A. bicolor Ldl.

Pbs. egg-shaped, fleshy, often flushed with purple, becoming deeply furrowed with age, to about 2″ tall. Lvs. several, to 12″ long and 4″ wide, folded, elliptic-lanceolate, acute to acuminate, eventually deciduous. Racs. short, erect, with prominent bracts, bearing up to 6 fls. Fls. to 2″ long, cup-shaped, waxen in texture, extremely fragrant of candy, pale yellow, more or less prominently streaked with red or red-brown, the complex lip borne in the floral cup, bright lemon-yellow. Spring. (I, H) South China; India; Ceylon.

A. javanicum Bl.

Pbs. almost conical, rather irregular, to 10″ tall and 2″ in diam., often flushed with purple, becoming furrowed with age. Lvs. usually 3–4, borne near top of pb., short-stalked, heavy in texture, sometimes purple-flushed beneath, to 2′ long and 6″ wide, strongly plicate, eventually deciduous. Infls. borne from median nodes of the pbs., to about 5″ tall, the rachis with large bracts and few fls. Fls. about 2″ long, heavily fragrant, the sepaline tube dull yellow or pale pink with red-purple stripes and spots, the sep.-tips free; ps. projecting slightly beyond the sep.-apices, similar to them in colour. Lip 3-lbd., with large, erect lat. lbs. with rounded tips, white with red marginal spots; midlb. smaller, convex, white with rows of blood-red spots. Summer. (H) Malay Peninsula; Sumatra; Java; Borneo.

A. Mantinianum Lind. & Cgn. Pbs. about 2″ tall, usually dark purple. Lvs. narrowed into a stalk towards base, to 12″ long and 5″ wide, rather heavy in texture, strongly folded, usually purple underneath. Racs. to 10″ tall, with up to 5 fls. Fls. about 2″ long, fleshy, very fragrant, yellowish, more or less striped with dull red, the lip complex, usually pale yellow to vivid golden-yellow. Summer. (I, H) Philippines.

A. striatum Ldl. Rather similar in habit to *A. bicolor* Ldl., but smaller in all vegetative parts. Racs. abbreviated, erect, prominently bracted, usually 2–3-fld. Fls. heavy-textured, fragrant, cup-like, about 1½″ long, white, whitish, or creamy-yellow, streaked and flushed with dull red. Ss. and ps. almost equal in length, oblong, acute. Lip 3-lbd., small, borne in sepaline tube, fleshy, with numerous red-purple wart-like protuberances on disc, these extending onto midlb. Spring. (I) Nepal; Himalayas.

A. sylhetense Ldl. Similar in habit to *A. bicolor* Ldl., but somewhat more stout in all parts. Fls. heavily waxen, very fragrant, long-lasting, about 2″ long, cup-shaped, cream-yellow to dirty-yellow, streaked and spotted with dull purple. Ss. and ps. oblong-lanceolate, acute. Lip 3-lbd., lat. lbs. small; midlb. fleshy, tongue-shaped, with 3 fringed calli on the disc. Spring–summer. (I) Himalayas.

ACERAS R.Br.

This is a genus of a single species, an interesting terrestrial plant which is native over much of Europe, certain of the Mediterranean islands, and in North Africa. Closely allied to *Himantoglossum* Spreng. and to *Serapias* L., it is on occasion found in choice collections specializing in such ground orchids. Because of the structure of the small flowers, the common name of 'Man Orchid' has been applied to it.

Several natural hybrids between *Aceras* and *Orchis* have been noted in the wild in Europe, being known by the generic name of *Orchiaceras*.

CULTURE: As for *Orchis* and the temperate Habenarias. (C, I)

A. anthropophora (L.) R.Br. (*Aceras anthropomorpha* Sm., *Orchis anthropophora* L., *Serapias anthropophora* L., *Loroglossum anthropophorum* A.Rich.)
Tubers ovoid. St. rigidly erect, 6–16″ tall, with several broad lvs., these upright at first, later spreading outwards. Infl. very dense, bracted, the fls. somewhat hanging. Fls. very small, yellow or greenish-yellow with the segms. often margined or streaked with red or reddish. Ss. and ps. forming a hood over the dull yellow lip, which is 4-lbd., the divaricate lbs. of the midlb. shorter than the lat. ones. Apr.–June. (C, I) Great Britain to Greece, Cyprus, Rhodes; North Africa.

ACERATORCHIS Schltr.

Two apparently valid species of *Aceratorchis* are known to science, these rather inconsequential terrestrial orchids of the subtribe *Habenarinae*, which are possibly better referred to *Orchis* [Tournef.] L. They are native to China, and at this time are unknown in our collections.

Nothing has been ascertained regarding the genetic affinities of this rare group.

CULTURE: Possibly as for *Orchis*, the temperate-zone Habenarias, etc. (C, I)

ACIANTHUS R.Br.

A genus of about twenty species, *Acianthus* is virtually unknown in contemporary collections outside of its native haunts—Australia, New Zealand, and New Caledonia—although they are unusual and interesting terrestrial orchids, well worthy of attention by connoisseurs. Their common Australian names of 'Pixie-Caps', 'Gnat Orchid', and 'Mosquito Orchid' are apt indeed, and give us an immediate clue to the delightful elfin structure of the flowers. *Acianthus* has small, globular, subterranean tubers, from which arise the flower-stems, bearing a single heart-shaped, roundish, or kidney-shaped leaf near their base, and a few small flowers in a terminal raceme. These flowers are rather less complex in structure than many of the ground orchids of this alliance, but are still sufficiently complicated to warrant close inspection.

No hybrids are reported in *Acianthus*, and nothing is known of the genetic affinities of the genus.

CULTURE: As for *Caladenia*. (C, I)

A. fornicatus R.Br. (*Acianthus Brunonis* FvM)
St. slender, often dull red-brown, including the infl. 2½–12″ tall. Lf. cordate, basal or about 1½″ above the ground-surface, often distinctly but not deeply 3-lbd., pale reddish underneath. Fls. 1–10, usually pale reddish-brown, sometimes darker, rarely green, variable in size, but mostly about 1″ long, not opening fully. Dors. sep. ovate-lanceolate, usually hooded over the col., the tip acuminate or ending in a filament; lat. ss. linear, almost as long as the dors. one, often minutely notched just below the tip, slightly deflexed under the lip, nearly parallel or sometimes partly connate. Ps. half as long as ss., narrowly lanceolate. Lip slightly longer than ps., sessile or almost so, oblong-lanceolate, acute, usually darker than other parts, erect and concave at base with 2 calli, then spreading horizontally, with 2 longitudinal papillose ridges along the middle. Spring–autumn. (C, I) Australia.

A. reniformis (R.Br.) Schltr. (*Cyrtostylis reniformis* R.Br., *Caladenia reniformis* Rchb.f.) St. very slender, 2–11″ tall. Lf. sessile at st.-base, reniform, orbicular, or cordate, hoary below, prominently reticulate. Infl. 1–8-fld. Fls. pale reddish-brown, or darker, rarely pale yellowish-green. Lip sessile, almost as long as the ps., broadly oblong, almost horizontal, the 2 basal calli often produced into 2 obscure parallel ridges along the middle. May–Oct. (C, I) Australia.

ACINETA Ldl.

(*Luddemania* Rchb.f., *Lueddemannia* Rchb.f., *Luedemannia* Bth., *Neippergia* C.Morr.)

Acineta contains about twelve species of robust epiphytic or rarely lithophytic orchids in the American tropics, ranging from southern Mexico to Ecuador and Venezuela. They are allied to *Peristeria* Hk., but the floral structure—especially that of the lip—is more like

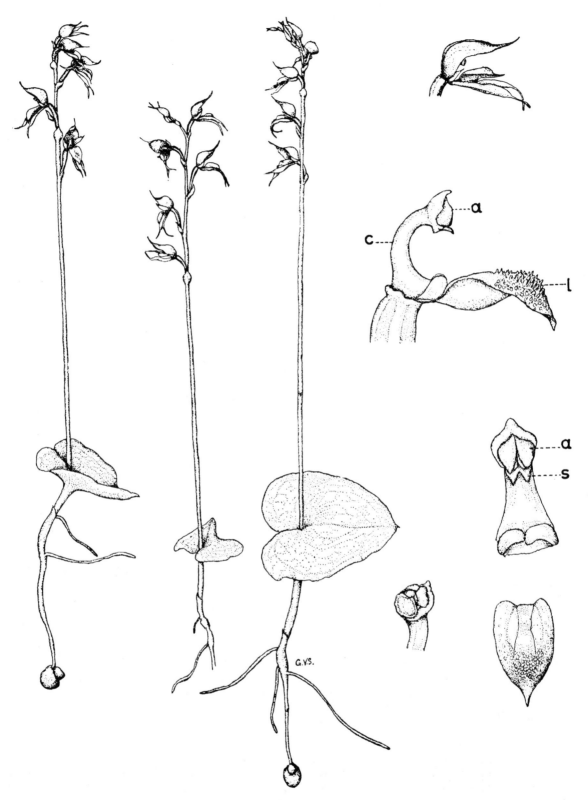

Acianthus fornicatus R.Br. [Rupp, *Orchids of New South Wales*]

that of *Stanhopea* Frost. The usually rather large, egg-shaped to cylindrical, often strongly furrowed pseudo-bulbs bear a couple of folded, heavy-textured leaves to several feet in length, and produce basal, sharply pendulous racemes to three feet and more long, which are usually rather densely set with big cup-like flowers of strange hues and exotic fragrances. Although among the most splendid of all orchidaceous plants, the Acinetas are regrettably very scarce in contemporary collections.

The breeders have not as yet taken the Acinetas in hand, although interspecific crossing seems to offer some fascinating possibilities, and hybrids with allied groups of the subtribe *Gongorinae* should produce some extraordinary progeny.

CULTURE: As for *Stanhopea*. Because of the strictly pendulous inflorescences, these fantastic plants must be grown in baskets or on rafts or tree-fern slabs. They are often rather refractory in the collection. (I, H)

A. chrysantha (C.Morr.) Ldl. & Paxt. (*Neippergia chrysantha* C.Morr., *Acineta densa* Ldl., *A. sellaturcica* Rchb.f., *A. Warscewiczii* Kl.)
Very robust pls., the clustered pbs. ovoid or subconic, somewhat laterally compressed, more or less strongly furrowed, to 5″ long. Lvs. 3–4, to almost 2′ long, heavy-textured, plicate, oblanceolate, acute. Infls. elongate, pendulous, to 3′ long (usually less), rather densely few- to many-fld. in apical third or so. Fls. fleshy, waxy, highly fragrant, cup-like, to more than 2″ in diam., rather long-lived, the ss. usually bright yellow, the ps. yellow spotted with red or crimson towards base and margins, the lip golden-yellow more or less spotted and marked with red and reddish-brown. Ss. fleshy, concave, the dors. obtuse, the lats. shortly and broadly acute. Ps. membranaceous, obovate, acute. Lip very fleshy, 3-lbd., the basal hypochil broadly concave or almost sac-like, terminating in a short, erect, fleshy horn; lat. lbs. erect, subreniform; epichil (apical lobe) short, concave or spreading, squarish or rhombic-obovate, acute; disc with a broad, erect, prominent callus with 2 small, lateral, subfalcate wings, the projecting carinate apical margin with short fleshy teeth. Col. stout, fuzzy, the apex with narrow lat. wings. Spring. (I) ? Guatemala; Costa Rica; Panama.

A. superba (HBK) Rchb.f. (*Anguloa superba* HBK, *Peristeria Humboldtii* Ldl., *Acineta Colmani* hort., *A. fulva* Kl., *A. Humboldtii* Ldl.)
Habit as the above-noted sp. Fls. to 3″ in diam. and more, spicily fragrant, very heavily waxy, not opening fully, variable in colour from pale yellow to reddish-brown, more or less densely spotted on all segms. with brownish-purple or red. Lip very fleshy, gibbous, 3-lbd., the basal hypochil rectangular-linear, concave, the lat. lbs. erect, broadly triangular, the apical epichil elongate, carinate, obovate, obtuse; disc with a very conspicuous, erect, oblong-squarish, fleshy callus with 2 identical, divergent, forked processes arising from a common restricted base, one pointing towards the apex and the other towards the base of the lip. Col. stout, fuzzy, subterete below, narrowly winged above, the wings confluent and forming at the apex a hood over the clinandrium. Mostly spring. (I, H) ? Panama; Colombia; Venezuela; Ecuador; Peru.

A. Barkeri Ldl. (*Peristeria Barkeri* Batem.) Rather similar to the other spp. in vegetative appearance. Infls. sharply pendulous, to about 1½′ long, 10–15-fld., the glossy bracts greenish-brown. Fls. waxy, heavily fragrant, cup-shaped, to about 1½″ in diam., vivid golden-yellow, the ps. usually sparsely red-spotted near base, with a large blood-red blotch on the lip. Lip 3-lbd., very fleshy, the lat. lbs. large, incurving, broadly halberd-shaped, with a large fleshy disc between them; midlb. much smaller than lat. ones, narrowly oblong, retuse, concave, keeled beneath. Col. fuzzy, with a very narrow wing on each side of the stigma. Spring. (I) Mexico.

ACOSTAEA Schltr.

This is a genus of two known species, one apparently restricted to Costa Rica, the other found as well in Panama. Neither of the Acostaeas appears to be present in contemporary collections, but they are remarkably interesting dwarf epiphytic pleurothallids (allied to *Lepanthes* Sw. and to *Pleurothallis* R.Br.) which may eventually be grown by connoisseurs. Vegetatively they resemble a small *Lepanthes*, but they are immediately differentiated on floral characters.

Nothing is known genetically of this rare genus.

CULTURE: Presumably as for the high-elevation species of *Pleurothallis*. (C, I)

ACRIOPSIS Reinw.

This is a genus of six or more species of mostly dwarf epiphytic orchids in the Asiatic tropics, superficially resembling a miniature *Cymbidium* in habit, although the generic alliance is with *Thecostele* Rchb.f.

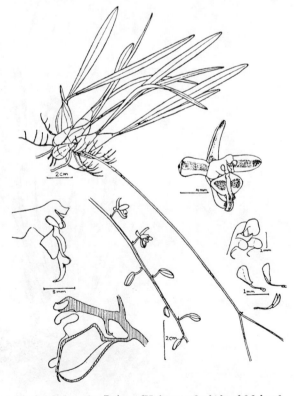

Acriopsis javanica Reinw. [Holttum, *Orchids of Malaya*]

Typically the egg-shaped or globular pseudobulbs are less than two inches tall, and bear two leaves about three inches or more long at the apex. The small to minute, intricately constructed flowers are borne on branching panicles which may reach a height of a foot or more.

No hybrids have as yet been attempted in *Acriopsis*, and nothing is known of its genetic alliances.

CULTURE: These charming little orchids should be treated like the small, tropical species of *Bulbophyllum*. (H)

A. javanica Reinw. (*Spathoglottis trivalvis* Wall., *Acriopsis Griffithii* Rchb.f., *A. crispa* Griff.)

Habit as in the genus. Pbs. to 2″ tall, egg-shaped, with 2–5 lvs. to 7″ long which are linear, blunt apically, and rather fleshy. Infls. erect or arching panicles, proportionately large, to 2′ tall, many-fld. Fls. about ½″ across, light yellow-green or violet-green, veined with white, with a darker purple blotch often present at the apex of each segm. Lip purple or violet, with a whitish margin and a pair of raised keels on the disc. Summer. (H) Burma and Sumatra to the Philippines and New Guinea.

A. latifolia Rolfe Similar to *A. javanica* Reinw., but with larger foliage and differently-shaped fls. Fls. about ¼″ across, yellowish-white, striped with dull red, the lip with reddish protuberances at the middle of the disc. Spring. (H) Sumatra; Malay Peninsula.

A. Ridleyi Hk.f. Similar to the preceding sp., but smaller in all parts. Panicle with 12 or more minute fls. (less than ¼″ across) which are greenish marked with purple. Lip rather complex in structure. Winter. (H) Malay Peninsula.

ACROLOPHIA Pfitz.

This is a genus of about nine or more species of terrestrial orchids of the subtribe *Polystachyinae*, which in basic appearance simulate certain kinds of Eulophias, although they are not particularly allied to that group. All inhabit southern Africa, and their mostly dull, usually brown flowers offer little of interest to collectors. *Acrolophia* is apparently unknown in cultivation at this time.

Nothing is known of the genetic affinities of this incompletely studied group.

CULTURE: Presumably as for the tropical Eulophias. (I, H)

Ada aurantiaca Ldl. [VEITCH]

Aceras anthropophora (L.) R.Br. [GEORGE FULLER]

Acampe multiflora (Ldl.) Ldl. [GEORGE FULLER]

Acineta chrysantha (C.Morr.) Ldl. & Paxt. [*The Orchid Journal*]

Aërangis biloba (Ldl.) Schltr. [J. MARNIER-LAPOSTOLLE]

Aërangis articulata (Rchb.f.) Schltr. [GEORGE FULLER]

Aërides falcatum Ldl. var. *Houlletianun* (Rchb.f.) Veitch [GEORGE FULLER]

ADA Ldl.

Ada contains two medium-sized epiphytic or litho-phytic orchids in the Colombian Andes, allied to *Odontoglossum* HBK, and occasionally cultivated for their spectacularly colourful flowers. The plants recall an *Odontoglossum* in habit, but the cinnabar-orange or red blossoms, bell-shaped and usually nodding on a dense spike, are widely divergent from the members of that genus, both in structure and superficial appearance.

Two artificially produced hybrid genera, *Adaglossum* (*Ada* × *Odontoglossum*) and *Adioda* (*Ada* × *Cochlioda*) are registered. Additional hybridization with other allied groups of the subtribe *Oncidiinae*—to which *Ada* belongs—should prove most interesting.

CULTURE: The cultural requirements of *Ada* are those of the high-elevation species of *Odontoglossum*. (C)

A. aurantiaca Ldl. (*Mesospinidium aurantiacum* Rchb.f.)
Pbs. clustered, narrowly ovoid-oblong, compressed, becoming furrowed with age, 3–4″ long. Lvs. 1–2, linear-ligulate, acute, 7–12″ long. Infls. to almost 20″ long, gracefully arching, furnished with sheathing bracts, the dense apical rac. 7–12- or more-fld. Fls. about 1″ long or more, bright cinnabar-red, expanding only from above the middle. Ss. and ps. linear-lanceolate, very acute, with a sunken median line on the face, the ps. shorter and narrower and with a purple streak on the median line. Lip half as long as the ss., narrowly oblong, acuminate, with 2 short keels at base. Col. very short, concave below the stigmatic surface. Winter–early spring. (C) Colombia.

A. Lehmanni Rolfe Similar to the other sp. in habit, but more rigid. Lvs. linear, acute, leathery, dark green more or less marbled with grey, 8–12″ long. Infls. erect, rather shorter than the lvs., the rac. 5–8-fld. Fls. about 1″ long, bright cinnabar-orange, the ss. and ps. linear-lanceolate, acute, rather fleshy. Lip oblong-lanceolate, acuminate, with incurved undulate margins and recurved apex, about ¾ as long as ss., white except for the very fleshy, linear callus which is deep orange and extends from the base to near the apex, and on each side of which is a recurved white hook. Col. short, dull yellow. Summer. (C) Colombia.

ADENOCHILUS Hk.f.

A member of the subtribe *Caladeniinae*, *Adenochilus* consists of two species of rather handsome terrestrial orchids, one in New Zealand (**A. gracilis** Hk.f., which is not in cultivation), the other in Australia (**A. Nortoni** Fitzg., described below). Like most Australian ground orchids, they are very scarce in collections, and difficult to keep in good condition for any length of time. *Adenochilus Nortoni* grows, in New South Wales, in wet rock-crevices or in sphagnum moss at an elevation above 3000 feet, in the Blue Mountains and Barrington Tops region.

Nothing is known of the genetic affinities of this genus, and no hybrids are on record.

CULTURE: As for *Caladenia*. (C, I)

A. Nortoni Fitzg.
Rhiz. fleshy, subterranean or buried in moss. St. slender, glabrous, to 8″ tall. Lf. solitary, either sessile on the st. or on a long petiole arising from the rhiz., ovate to cordate. Fl. solitary, opening widely, to 1¾″ across, white, the lip and col. red-spotted, the calli of the lip yellow. Dors. sep. broad, acute, more or less hooded, the lat. ss. narrower, acuminate, slightly longer than the dors. one, all ss. with a few short marginal cilia. Ps. narrower and shorter than ss., sparsely ciliate marginally. Lip clawed, 3-lbd., the surface covered with calli except at the tip. Col. erect, with large wings that are crenulate-dentate on top. Autumn–winter. (C, I) Australia: N. S. Wales.

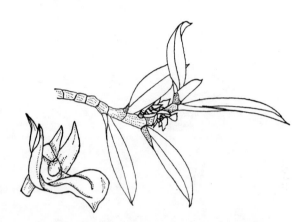

Adenoncos sumatrana J.J.Sm. [A.D.HAWKES, AFTER HOLTTUM]

ADENONCOS Bl.

This is a genus of about ten species of epiphytic sar-canthad orchids, generally considered to be somewhat allied to *Luisia* Gaud., and apparently not present in even the most comprehensive of contemporary collec-tions, despite their unique botanical interest. They in-habit the Malayan-Indonesian region from the Malay Peninsula and Lower (Peninsular) Thailand to New Guinea. The primarily green flowers, though small, are of unusual structure, and the plants are rather attractive in vegetative appearance.

No hybrids are known in *Adenoncos*, and nothing is known of its genetic alliances.

CULTURE: Presumably as for the tropical Vandas. (H)

ADRORRHIZON Hk.f.

Adrorrhizon is a genus containing a single highly aberrant species of epiphytic orchid in Ceylon and southern India, which has been placed in a subtribe (*Adrorrhizinae*) near either the *Coelogyne* group or the *Dendrobium* alliance. **Adrorrhizon purpurascens** (Thw.) Hk.f. (*Coelogyne purpurascens* Thw.) is a small pseudo-bulbous epiphyte with two-flowered racemes, the in-tricate blossoms purple in colour. Its only allied genus is the little-known *Josephia* Wight, also native in Ceylon. *Adrorrhizon* is apparently unknown in contemporary collections, but is sufficiently unusual and attractive to warrant attention from specialists.

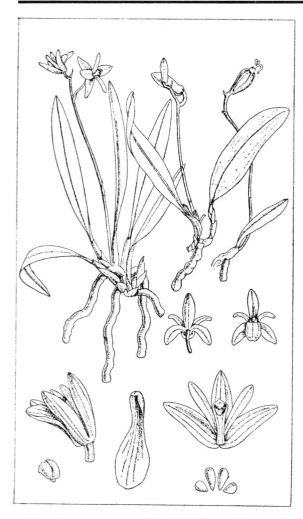

Adrorrhizon purpurascens (Thw.) Hk.f. [*Icones Plantarum*]

Nothing is known of the genetic affinities of this group.

CULTURE: *Adrorrhizon* requires cultural conditions similar to those afforded the dwarf tropical species of *Dendrobium* and *Bulbophyllum*. (H)

AËRANGIS Rchb.f.
(*Radinocion* Ridl.)

Some seventy species comprise this attractive and interesting genus, which is a member of the very complex angraecoid group of the subtribe *Sarcanthinae*. It is a segregate, in part, from *Angraecum* Bory, a genus which most of the component species superficially simulate; *Aërangis* differs from the other aggregation in technical characters of the flowers, notably the pollinia-accoutrements. A few of these fine, primarily epiphytic orchids—which inhabit tropical Africa, Madagascar, and adjacent insular areas—are today to be encountered in choice collections, but further attention needs to be paid to the genus, which offers a wealth of showy species of considerable horticultural potentialities. Mostly rather small plants, they are highly diverse both vege-

tatively and florally, though the flowers for the most part are rather star-shaped, furnished with spurs of variable length, waxen in texture, and usually white in colour; most *Aërangis* blossoms give off a heavy aroma, particularly towards evening.

A single natural hybrid has been registered to date in this genus, namely *Aërangis x primulina* H.Perr. (*A. citrata × A. hyaloides*), a native of Madagascar. Additional breeding within the genus should prove most interesting, and experimental hybridization with allied groups—*Angraecum, Jumellea, Plectrelminthus*, etc.—promises some fascinating and valuable results.

CULTURE: As for *Angraecum*, depending upon the individual and its place of origin. Most of the Aërangis inhabit relatively low elevations, but certain of the East African species are found at considerable heights in the mountains of that area. (I, H)

A. articulata (Rchb.f.) Schltr. (*Angraecum articulatum* Rchb.f., *Angraecum descendens* Rchb.f.)

St. rather thick, to about 6″ tall, with rather few lvs. Lvs. very leathery, dark green, oval or obovate-oblong, emarginate or obliquely 2-lbd. at apex, to 5″ long, to about 1½″ wide at most. Infls. with rather stout, strong-jointed, pale green peduncle, pendulous, 9–18″ long, racemose from near the base, very densely many-fld. Fls. 1¼–1½″ across, fragrant, waxy, long-lived, pure glittering white, on short, pale orange-red pedicels, the spur 3–4″ long. Dors. sep. and ps. oblong-elliptic, acute, the lat. ss. similar but narrower, all spreading. Lip larger than the other segms., oval or oval-oblong, acute. Summer, usually Mar.–July. (H) Madagascar.

A. biloba (Ldl.) Schltr. (*Angraecum bilobum* Ldl., *Angraecum apiculatum* Hk.)

St. rather slender, usually 3–5″ tall. Lvs. leathery, obovate-oblong, unequally 2-lbd. at apex, 4–6″ long, to about 1″ wide. Infls. drooping to pendulous, to more than 12″ long, rather loosely 7–15-fld. Fls. 1–2″ across, waxy, fragrant, rather long-lasting, on reddish-brown pedicels, pure white, rarely sparsely dotted with pale pinky-rose, the slender spur to about 2″ long, brownish or pale orange-red. Ss. and ps. spreading, elliptic-lanceolate, acute or acuminate. Lip similar but slightly broader. Col. short, vaguely triangular. Spring. (H) Tropical West Africa.

—var. **Kirkii** (Rchb.f.) Schltr. (*Angraecum bilobum* Ldl. var. *Kirkii* Rchb.f., *Aërangis Kirkii* Krzl.)

Differs from the type in several respects, perhaps better treated as a distinct sp. Lvs. narrower than in typical *A. biloba* (Ldl.) Schltr., and slightly dilated at the apex. Infls. racemose, with fewer fls. (usually only 3–5) than in the type, these fls. with somewhat narrower segms. Spring. (H) Zanzibar; Moçambique.

A. citrata (Thou.) Schltr. (*Angraecum citratum* Thou.)

St. short, usually less than 4″ tall, rather thick. Lvs. rather few (averaging 6–10), leathery, deep glossy green, ovate to ovate-oblong, slightly unequally 2-lbd. at apex, or acute, 3–6″ long, to about 1½″ broad. Infls. gracefully down-arching or pendulous, 8–20″ long, densely many-fld. Fls. ¾–1″ across, waxy, fragrant, on short pedicels, all turned upwards and facing the same way, crowded, cream-white to pale straw-colour (rarely citron-yellow), the slender, curved spur usually pale yellow, about 1″ long. Ss. broadly obovate to oval, obtuse, the lats. usually larger than the dors. one. Ps. elliptic-oblong, obtuse or acutish. Lip short-clawed, the blade roundish to cordate, emarginate, flattened. Col. very short and thick. Late winter–spring. (H) Madagascar.

A. Ellisii (Rchb.f.) Schltr. (*Angraecum Ellisii* Rchb.f.)
St. to 10″ tall (rarely more), more than ½″ in diam. Lvs. very heavily leathery, narrowly oblong, the apex emarginate or unequally 2-lbd., 5–8″ long, usually about 2″ broad. Infls. arching at first, becoming pendulous in time, to 2′ long, bearing 12–25 fls. in apical two-thirds, these on greenish pedicels which arise from a small protuberance on the rachis, with a small, scale-like, brown bract at base of each. Fls. waxy, fragrant of gardenias, long-lived, the apical ones to 2½″ across, the basal ones somewhat smaller, snow-white, the slender, awl-shaped, twisted spur 6–8″ long, flushed apically with brownish or pale orange-red. Ss. and ps. similar, subequal, elliptic-oblong, acute, the dors. sep. inflexed at the tip, the ps. and lat. ss. reflexed. Lip similar to other segms. but broader. Summer, mostly July–Sept. (H) Madagascar.

A. Kotschyana (Rchb.f.) Schltr. (*Angraecum Kotschyanum* Rchb.f., *Angraecum Kotschyi* Rchb.f., *Angraecum semipedale* Rendle & Rolfe, *Aërangis Kotschyi* Rchb.f.)
St. abbreviated, emitting numerous stout, flexuose, greyish-brown roots often several feet long. Lvs. few, variable in size and shape, the largest ones obovate-oblong, 5–7″ long, unequally 2-lbd. at apex and very leathery, the smaller ones narrowly oblong, 3–4″ long, subacute or emarginate apically. Infls. strictly pendulous, or with the peduncle erect and the rac. pendulous, to more than 1′ long, rather densely 7–12-fld. Fls. fragrant, waxen, lasting well, to 1½″ in diam., borne on elongate pale red-brown pedicellate ovaries, pure white. Dors. sep. and ps. ovate-oblong, acute, reflexed, the lat. ss. longer and narrower, lanceolate, acute, spreading. Lip with a broad claw and a sub-rhomboidal, apiculate blade; spur very long for the size of the fl., slender, inflated apically, twisted, 8–10″ long, pale red-brown. Autumn, especially Sept.–Oct. (H) Tropical Africa, where it is widespread.

A. cryptodon (Rchb.f.) Schltr. (*Angraecum cryptodon* Rchb.f.)
St. 1–3″ tall, profusely rooting. Lvs. usually only 3–4 at a time, to 3″ long, leathery, obovate-oblong. Infls. pendulous, to 12″ long, the rachis bright russet-brown, few-fld. Fls. fragrant, to 1½″ in diam., on abbreviated reddish pedicels, all segms. at first reflexed, becoming spreading with age, the ss. pale orange-red to reddish, the ps. and lip white, the slender spur pale orange-red or reddish-brown, twisted, to 5″ long, the col. white. Ss. and ps. similar, linear-lanceolate, rather acuminate. Lip oblong-cordate, shortly apiculate. Summer. (H) Madagascar.

A. fastuosa (Rchb.f.) Schltr. (*Angraecum fastuosum* Rchb.f.)
Dwarf, the st. at most 2″ tall, obscured by the lf.-bases. Lvs. 3–5, rather rigidly fleshy, oval-oblong, the midvein prominently depressed, apically emarginate to unequally 2-lbd., 2–3″ long, to 1″ wide. Infls. very short, the peduncle stout,

greenish, 2–4-fld. Fls. waxy, fragrant, to 1½″ across, long-lived, pure dead white, the slender spur to 3″ long, often flushed towards apex with reddish or brownish. Ss. and ps. similar, narrowly elliptic-oblong, acute. Lip broader than other segms., obovate-oblong, obtuse, with raised midvein. Autumn. (H) Madagascar.

A. fuscata (Rchb.f.) Schltr. (*Angraecum fuscatum* Rchb.f.)
Rather closely allied to both *A. articulata* (Rchb.f.) Schltr. and *A. Ellisii* (Rchb.f.) Schltr., differing from them in technical details. St. short, usually about 3″ tall. Lvs. leathery, oblong-cuneate, obtuse or unequally 2-lbd. at apex, 4–5″ long, about 1½″ wide. Infls. to 8″ long, flaccid, hanging, many-fld., the rachis russet-brown flushed with green, the pedicels arising from a cushion-like growth as in *A. Ellisii* (Rchb.f.) Schltr. Fls. very fragrant, waxy, 1–1½″ across, usually cream-white, the spur slender, about 3″ long, often brownish. Ss. and ps. similar, subequal, lanceolate, acute. Lip broader than the other segms., oblong to beyond the middle, then rather abruptly acuminate. Summer. (H) Madagascar.

A. hyaloides (Rchb.f.) Schltr. (*Angraecum hyaloides* Rchb.f.)
A very small sp., the st. usually less than 1″ tall. Lvs. 5–7, spreading, leathery, oval-oblong, obtuse or unequally 2-lbd. at apex, usually less than 2″ long. Infls. slightly longer than the lvs., spreading horizontally, densely 10–20-fld. Fls. distichously arranged, to almost ½″ across, transparent pure white, on short, white pedicels, the spur slender, as long as the pedicels. Ss., ps., and lip similar, subequal, oval-oblong, acute, the ss. somewhat the narrowest. Spring. (H) Madagascar.

A. modesta (Hk.f.) Schltr. (*Angraecum modestum* Hk.f., *Angraecum Sanderianum* Rchb.f.) St. erect, to about 8″ tall, densely leafy throughout, very freely rooting. Lvs. rather leathery, dark green, narrowly oblong to narrowly obovate-oblong, subacute or obliquely emarginate, to 7″ long, about 2″ broad. Infls. sharply down-curving to pendulous, to 20″ long, the peduncle and rachis brownish-green, densely many-fld., the fls. arranged in 2 alternating ranks, all pointing in the same direction. Fls. about 1″ across, fragrant, waxy, long-lived, pure white, the pedicels short, pale orange-red, the slender spurs 2½–3″ long, white. Ss. lanceolate, acute. Ps. broader, ovate-lanceolate, acute. Lip broadly ovate, apiculate. Col. very short and blunt. Spring, mostly Apr.–May. (H) Madagascar; Comoro Islands.

A. rhodosticta (Krzl.) Schltr. (*Angraecum rhodostictum* Krzl.)
St. usually pendulous, short. Lvs. about 8 in number, all in one plane, narrowly strap-shaped, somewhat falcate, bright green, to 6″ long, 2-lbd. at apex. Infls. usually hanging, to 15″ long, 6–25-fld., the fls. forming 2 rows in a single plane. Fls. flat, long-lived, about 1–1¼″ long, the rounded ss. and ps. varying from white or greenish-white to cream or pale sulphur-yellow, the column vivid scarlet or vermilion. Autumn–spring. (I, H) Cameroons eastward to Ethiopia, Kenya, and Tanganyika.

AËRANTHES Ldl.

This is a genus of about thirty species of seldom-seen but most unusual monopodial epiphytes and lithophytes of the subtribe *Sarcanthinae*, confined in their distribution to Madagascar and adjacent islands. Typically stemless, the plants consist of several large, leathery leaves, and give rise to mostly sizeable, brilliant green or white, fragrant flowers, borne on generally lengthy, wire-like spikes. The members of this genus are very

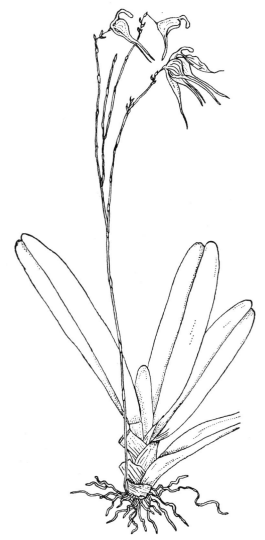

Aëranthes ramosus Rolfe [A.D.HAWKES, AFTER *Flore de Madagascar*]

ps. broadly ovate, very long-acuminate. Lip similar to the dors. sep. in shape and size. Spur produced from the col.-foot, basally conic-cylindric, becoming long and narrow, about ¾″ long. Summer–winter, often more than once annually. (H) Madagascar.

A. arachnitis (Thou.) Ldl. (*Dendrobium arachnitis* Thou.) Lvs. to 8″ long, about 1″ wide, leathery. Spikes mostly hanging, bearing a few fls. in succession at the apex, to 8″ long, wire-like. Fls. about 2″ across, fragrant, yellow-green, the lip very complex. Summer–autumn. (H) Madagascar.

A. ramosus Rolfe. (*Aëranthes vespertilio* Cgn.) Similar to *A. grandiflorus* Ldl., but slightly smaller, the spike 2′ long, with one or two fls. about 3″ across. Fls. olive-green, very complex, the spur short. Autumn. (H) Madagascar.

AËRIDES Lour.
(*Aeëridium* Salisb., *Aëridium* Pfeiff., *Dendrorkis* Thou., *Orxera* Raf.)

This popular genus contains more than sixty species of often spectacular monopodial epiphytes or lithophytes, in vegetative appearance basically simulating Vandas. Many of the Aërides, however, are easily distinguished from Vandas—even when not in flower—by the presence of a peculiar cinnamon-brown or reddish-brown suffusion on the old stems and remnants of leaf-bases, a characteristic not found in the other genus. These handsome orchids are natives of the tropical parts of Asia, Indonesia, etc., ranging from China and Japan to New Guinea, with many of the commoner species occurring in the Himalayas, Burma, the Philippines, and Indonesia. These are widely grown by enthusiasts, and because of the unique formation of the inflorescences of many of the species are often known as 'Fox-Tail Orchids' (a name which is also applied to *Rhynchostylis*). The lovely waxen flowers, typically possessed of a heady fragrance, are borne in large numbers (in most species) in elongate pendulous racemes which are more or less cylindrical in shape; for the most part, all of the blossoms are open at once, thus giving to the inflorescence an elegance scarcely equalled in any other group of the Orchidaceae. Floral colour in *Aërides* is variable, ranging primarily through shades of green, magenta, and white in various combinations. The flowers are usually of characteristic formation, with spreading sepals and petals; the lateral sepals are mostly broader than the dorsal one, and adnate basally to the column-foot, to which the frequently complex lip is also attached. This organ is generally freely movable, and often of great beauty, with fringed margins and ornate colour-scheme. The column, which has a prominent foot, is frequently so shaped as to resemble a diminutive bird's head, set neatly in the middle of the blossom, thus adding even more to its interesting beauty.

Hybridization between the component species of *Aërides* has as yet been negligible (one of the most recently registered crosses—*A. x Hermon Slade*, the product of breeding *A. Lawrenceae* with *A. Fieldingii*—is, however, the most magnificent and floriferous plant in the entire genus!), and much additional work remains to be done in this respect. *Aërides* is freely inter-fertile with many of the allied groups, and such artificial aggregations as *Aëridovanda* (× *Vanda*), *Aëridopsis* (× *Phalae-*

rare in contemporary collections, but are well worth attention by connoisseurs.

The breeders have not as yet taken *Aëranthes* in hand, though it seems probable that it will prove genetically compatible with at least some of its angraecoid allies.

CULTURE: Aëranthes should be grown like the tropical Angraecums or Vandas, preferably on tree-fern slabs or in baskets because of the often horizontal or pendulous inflorescences; they require abundant water and heat at all times. Perfect drainage of the potting-compost is essential, since these orchids are prone to rot if allowed to become stale at the roots. If grown in pots, firmly packed osmunda or shredded tree-fern fibre should be used. (H)

A. grandiflorus Ldl.
Lvs. to 12″ long or more, glossy-green, leathery, linear-falcate, unequally bilobed at the tip. Fls. large, about 8″ across, solitary or paired, borne on short basal spikes, brilliant green, fragrant and long-lived. Ss. and

nopsis), *Aëridachnis* (×*Arachnis*), *Renades* (× *Renanthera*), etc., have thus far been produced, giving promise of many fabulous things to come in the future.

CULTURE: Aërides delight in basket-culture, for these airy containers give their rampant roots ample access to the outside, which is important; they may also, of course, be grown in pots, but these must be of considerable dimensions, to afford expansion of the roots. A rather loose, well-aerated compost should be utilized. Chunks of tree-fern fibre, or shredded tree-fern fibre (with or without the addition of some gravel or pieces of broken crock) are admirable for this purpose. Perfect drainage is essential, as these orchids—which grow throughout the year, and require quantities of moisture at all times—are highly intolerant of staleness at the roots. They also dislike disturbance, and when being repotted should be handled carefully to avoid undue injury to the brittle root-system. Warm, humid conditions, with abundant free-moving air, are required at all times (the very few species from high elevations naturally need somewhat cooler temperatures), and a reasonably bright situation—short of burning of the succulent foliage—is best, and induces profuse flowering. Offshoots (commonly known by their Hawaiian name of *keikis*) are produced by many mature Aërides, and may be removed from the parent specimen when they have reached sufficient size to possess two or three roots of their own. These orchids may be fertilized with regularity, as Vandas and similar monopodials. (I, H)

A. crassifolium Par. & Rchb.f. (*Aërides expansum* Rchb.f.)

Sts. robust, usually not very tall. Lvs. very close together on the st., to 7″ long (rarely more), rigidly leathery, to 2″ broad, usually dull green, unequally bilobed at the tip. Infls. to 2′ long, arching to sharply pendulous, rather loosely many-fld. Fls. about 1½″ across, very fragrant, heavy-textured, long-lasting, vivid rose-purple or purplish-red, the segms. usually somewhat paler at base. Ss. oblong, obtuse, the lats. the broadest. Ps. oval-oblong. Lip 3-lbd., the lat. lbs. semilunate or crescent-shaped, the midlb. broadly ovate, obtuse, often darker coloured than the other floral parts, with 2 basal keels that are divergent at the front. Spur bent, compressed, greenish at the tip. Summer. (I, H) Burma.

A. crispum Ldl. (*Aërides Brookei* Batem., *A. Lindleyanum* Wight, *A. Warneri* hort.)

St. considerably more elongated than other spp., to 5′ tall, often dull purple or brownish-violet, the lvs. rather distant from one another. Lvs. spreading, 5–8″ long, 1½–2″ broad, bilobed at the apex, with a small mucro between the lobes. Infls. horizontal to arching, often paniculate, to more than 3′ long, rather loosely many-fld. Fls. about 2″ across, with an odour of pineapple or sassafras, the ss. and ps. white lightly flushed with rose-purple behind, and with a faint flush of the same hue near the apex in front, oval-oblong, obtuse, the lat. ss. larger and the ps. smaller than the dors. sep. Lip 3-lbd., the lat. lbs. white streaked on the inside with rose-purple, small, erect, roundish-oblong; midlb. rich amethyst-purple, broadly ovate, saddle-like, marginally serrate, with a white grooved callus at the

spur-entrance, the spur small, horn-like, compressed. Col. white, the anther-cap yellowish. Summer. (I, H) India; Himalayas.

A. falcatum Ldl. (*Aërides Larpentae* Rchb.f., *A. Mendelii* hort.)

An attractive and variable sp., which may attain heights in excess of 6′ in old specimens. Lvs. 6–14″ long, to 1½″ broad, linear-ligulate, bilobed at tip, rather glaucous above, striated with dark lines beneath. Infls. to 20″ long, pendulous or arching, loosely or densely many-fld. Fls. handsome, fragrant, waxen in texture, 1–1¼″ long, the ss. and ps. white with a small light amethyst-purple apical blotch, broadly oval, the lat. ss. broader and the ps. narrower than the dors. sep. Lip 3-lbd., the lat. lbs. light amethyst-purple, falcate or crescent-shaped, spreading; midlb. rich amethyst-purple, broadly obovate, somewhat saddle-shaped, emarginate, the margin denticulate with 2 shallow median keels above. Spur short, compressed, greenish. Mostly summer. (I, H) India; Burma; Thailand; Laos.

—var. **Houlletianum** (Rchb.f.) Veitch (*Aërides Houlletianum* Rchb.f., *A. Picotianum* hort.)

Lvs. slightly longer and narrower than the typical sp. Racs. shorter and considerably more dense. Fls. smaller in all parts, light tawny-yellow with an apical orange-brown spot on each segm., the margin of the midlb. of the lip fimbriate rather than denticulate, the median keels shorter. Spring. (I) Viet-Nam.

—var. **Leoniae** (Rchb.f.) Veitch (*Aërides expansum* Rchb.f. var. *Leoniae* Rchb.f., *A. Leoniae* Godefr.)

Lvs. more distant from one another than in the typical sp. Fls. larger, the midlb. of the lip somewhat broader; ss. and ps. white with a small amethyst-purple apical spot, and some dots of this colour towards the base of the ps, and lat. ss. Lip with the lat. lbs. dotted and marked with light amethyst-purple, the median and apical parts of the midlb. darker purple, the remainder white dotted like the other segms. Spring. (I) Burma.

A. Fieldingii Jennings (*Aërides Williamsii* Warn.)

St. rather abbreviated, densely leafy. Lvs. 7–10″ long, to 1¾″ broad, the lower ones deflexed, the upper ones spreading or slightly ascending. Infls. usually sharply pendulous, to 2′ long, usually racemose, but sometimes with a branch or two near base, very densely many-fld. Fls. about 1–1½″ across, fragrant, waxy, the dors. sep. and ps. amethyst-purple suffused with white, sometimes with the basal half white dotted with purple, rarely pure white, obovate, obtuse; lat. ss. white with a pale purple spot, rarely pure white, broadly oval. Lip amethyst-purple mottled with white, deltoid to trowel-shaped, very acuminate, slightly compressed laterally, with 2 small basal lbs. rolled inwards over the mouth of the small, funnel-like, whitish spur. Summer, mostly May–June. (I) Himalayas.

A. Lawrenceae Rchb.f.

St. robust, eventually to 5′ tall, when old typically branching from near base. Lvs. 9–12″ long, 1½–2″ broad, thick and leathery, curving, unequally bilobed at tip. Infls. arching, usually several produced at once, to 2′ long, densely many-fld. Fls. very thick and waxy, highly

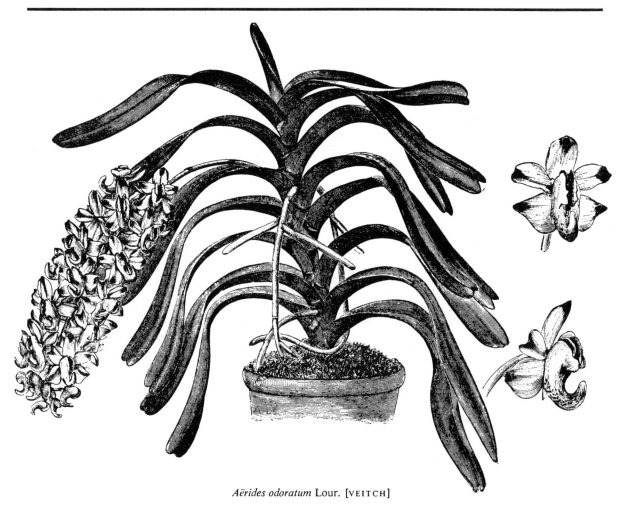

Aërides odoratum Lour. [VEITCH]

fragrant, about 1¾″ long (rarely larger), long-lived. Ss. and ps. white or cream-white, tipped with crimson-purple or vivid magenta, the dors. sep. and ps. oval-oblong, obtuse, the lat. ss. much broader, broadly oval. Lip prolonged at base into a horn-like, incurved, emerald-green spur, deeply 3-lbd., the lat. lbs. somewhat hatchet-shaped, the margins denticulate, white; midlb. oblong, marginally dentate, rich amethyst-purple or brilliant magenta, the colour sometimes prolonged between the lat. lbs. as far as the green spur-tip. Autumn–early winter. (I, H) Philippines: Mindanao.

A. multiflorum Roxb. (*Aërides affine* Wall., *A. Godefroyanum* Rchb.f., *A. roseum* Paxt., *A. trigonum* Klotzsch)
St. usually rather short, but in aged specimens becoming elongate. Lvs. to about 9″ long, to almost 1″ broad, very leathery, curved. Infls. longer than the lvs., pendulous or arching, very densely many-fld., to 12″ long. Fls. handsome, fragrant, waxy, about ¾–1″ long, the dors. sep. and ps. basally white with 2–3 or more purple spots, the apical area light amethyst-purple, oval-oblong, acutish; lat. ss. broader, suborbicular, white with a pale purple stain. Lip light amethyst-purple, darker along the middle, cordate, obtuse, slightly convex above. Spur short, straight, compressed laterally.

Col. with 2 rounded auricles on the foot. Summer. (I, H) Himalayas; Burma; Mergui Archipelago; Thailand; Laos; Cambodia; Viet-Nam.

—var. **Lobbii** (hort.) Veitch (*Aërides Lobbii* hort.)
St. usually much shorter than the typical sp., the lvs. very crowded, lying almost flat one upon another. Infls. usually longer than in the typical form, to 16″ long, usually with 1–3 basal branches. Fls. more numerous and more richly coloured. A very distinctive variant. Summer. (I, H) Burma.

—var. **Veitchii** (De Puydt) Morr. (*Aërides Veitchii* De Puydt)
Differing from var. *Lobbii* (hort.) Veitch in having the lvs. more distant from one another and more spreading, the racs. shorter with more branches, the fls. paler in colour, the ss. and ps. white dotted apically with rose, the lip pale rose-purple. Summer. (I. H) Burma.

A. odoratum (Poir.) Lour. (*Epidendrum odoratum* Poir., *Orxera cornuta* Raf., *Aërides Dayanum* hort., *A. nobile* Warn., *A. suavissimum* Ldl., *A. virens* Ldl.)
The commonest *Aërides* in cultivation, highly variable, to 5′ tall, profusely branching and often rather strongly pendulous in old specimens. Lvs. to 10″ long and 1¾″

broad, leathery, rather yellowish-green in many instances, linear-ligulate, unequally bilobed at the tip. Infls. usually several at once, arching to sharply pendulous, to 2′ long (usually much shorter), more or less densely many-fld., cylindrical. Fls. 1–1¾″ long, very fragrant, waxy, viscid in bud, the ss. and ps. white with an amethyst-purple or magenta apical blotch (but variable), oval-oblong, obtuse, the lat. ss. broader, the ps. narrower than the dors. sep. Lip funnel-shaped, prolonged at base into a horn-like spur, 3-lbd., the lat. lbs. erect, roundish-oblong, white, sometimes with a faint light purple flush, and some scattered purple spots; midlb. small, white with a broad purple median band, linear-oblong, the margin minutely denticulate or entire. Mostly autumn, especially Sept.–Nov. (I, H) China; Himalayas; Burma; Thailand; Laos; Cambodia; VietNam; Philippines; Malay Peninsula; Indonesia; New Guinea.

A. quinquevulnerum Ldl. (*Aërides album* Sander, *A. Farmeri* Boxall, *A. Fenzlianum* Rchb.f., *A. marginatum* Rchb.f., *A. Thibautianum* Rchb.f.)
St. stout, in old specimens to 5′ tall, often rather profusely branched. Lvs. usually glossy light green, 9–12″ long, 1–1½″ broad, folded at base, unequally bilobed at apex. Infls. to 1½′ long (rarely longer), arching or sharply pendulous, densely many-fld. Fls. 1″ long or less, rather similar to those of *A. odoratum* (Poir.) Lour. in shape, very fragrant, lasting two weeks or more, the dors. sep. and ps. similar, almost equal, oval-oblong, obtuse, white with a bright amethyst-purple apical blotch and some purple dots usually scattered over the remaining area; lat. ss. oblique, broadly oval or suborbicular, similar in colour. Lip 3-lbd., prolonged at the base into an incurved, horn-like, green spur; lat. lbs. erect, triangular-oblong, rotund in front, white faintly dotted with purple; midlb. dark amethyst-purple, oblong, the margins revolute, denticulate. Col. white. Mostly Aug.–Nov. (I, H) Philippines: Luzon.

—var. **purpuratum** Rchb.f.
Similar to the typical sp., but with burgundy-red fls. which give off a pervading spicy fragrance and which have a differently shaped lip. Apr.–May. (I, H) Philippines: Luzon, Mindoro.

A. vandarum Rchb.f.
Sts. slender, somewhat flexuose, terete, to several feet in length, branching mostly at or near the base to form tangled clumps. Lvs. terete, slender, 6–8″long, acuminate, with a shallow sunken line on the upper side, rather similar to those of *Vanda teres* (Roxb.) Ldl. Fls. solitary or in short 2–3-fld. racs., about 2″ across, fragrant, rather long-lived, white, the lip usually flushed with yellow in the centre. Ss. and ps. semi-transparent in texture, the ss. obovate-oblong, very undulate, the ps. much broader, spreading, sub-rhomboidal, undulate and somewhat crisped. Lip 3-lbd., the lat. lbs. linear-falcate, acuminate, unequally toothed at apex, bearing a small toothed lobe near the inner base; midlb. bent downwards, broadly obcordate with crenulate margins, clawed, the claw with 3 raised short plates. Spur subulate, terete, ¾″ long. Spring. (I) China; Himalayas; Northern India.

A. cylindricum Ldl. Rather similar in all parts to *A. vandarum* Rchb.f., but typically pendulous, the terete lvs. only 3–4″ long. Infls. very abbreviated, 1–2-fld. Fls. about 1″ across, often not lasting well, fragrant, the ss. and ps. white, the lip marked with violet or pale magenta, with 3 yellow keels on the disc. Summer. (H) Southern India; Ceylon.

A. Emerici Rchb.f. Rather similar in habit to *A. odoratum* (Poir.) Lour., differing chiefly in its longer infls. of smaller fls. of different shape and coloration. Lvs. to 12″ long and 1½″ broad, leathery. Infls. mostly about as long as the lvs., arching to pendulous, the rachis viscid. Fls. about 1″ long, on pale purple pedicellate ovaries, the ss. and ps. white with an apical light amethyst-purple blotch, broadly obovate-oblong. Lip 3-lbd., the lat. lbs. white with some purple spots inside at the basal end, rounded, erect; midlb. dark amethyst-purple, very small, narrowly oblong, acute. Spur funnel-shaped, incurved. Col. very short. Summer. (H) Andaman Islands.

A. Huttoni (Hk.f.) Veitch (*Saccolabium Huttoni* Hk.f.) St. to 12″ tall or more, the few lvs. fleshy, linear-ligulate, obliquely bilobed apically, to 10″ long and 1″ broad. Infls. pendulous, to 14″ long, densely many-fld. Fls. 1–1¼″ long, waxy, very fragrant and handsome, the pedicellate ovaries pale pink, the ss. and ps. rose-purple, the lip much darker rose-purple. Ss. and ps. similar, broadly oblong, rounded at apex. Lip with a stout, incurved, funnel-shaped spur, at the mouth of which are 3 erect lbs., of which the middle one is the narrowest. Col. short, with a yellow anther-cap. This is perhaps not correctly placed in *Aërides*. Autumn. (H) Celebes.

A. japonicum Rchb.f. Stemless or almost so, rather simulating a *Phalaenopsis* in vegetative appearance. Lvs. few, leathery, 3–4″ long, about 1″ broad, linear-oblong to ovate-oblong, blunt and bilobed apically. Infls. arching, to 7″ long, with up to 12 proportionately large and handsome fls. which last for several weeks in perfection. Fls. 1–1½″ long, fragrant, waxy, white or greenish-white with some light purple or red-purple transverse bars on the basal halves of the lat. ss., the lip white spotted or stained with amethyst-purple, the disc usually dark purple. Ss. and ps. oval-oblong, the ps. slightly the smaller. Lip with 2 erect lobules at the base, first oblong, then broadly obovate with crenulate margins, concave with a median raised ridge. Spur funnel-shaped, half as long as the lip. Summer. (I) Japan.

A. Jarckianum Schltr. Similar in vegetative appearance to *A. odoratum* (Poir.) Lour., but generally smaller in all parts. Infls. hanging, to 9″ long, densely many-fld. to rather loose. Fls. about ¾″ long, fragrant, waxen in texture, bright purple-red to burgundy-red, the large complex lip dark wine-purple. Spring. (I, H) Philippines: Luzon.

A. maculosum Ldl. (*Saccolabium speciosum* Wight, *Gastrochilus speciosus* O.Ktze., *Aërides illustre* Rchb.f.) Somewhat similar in vegetative habit to *A. crispum* Ldl., but usually smaller and less robust. Lvs. to 9″ long and almost 2″ broad, leathery. Infls. longer than the lvs., arching, usually branched basally, many-fld. Fls. about 1½″ long, waxy, fragrant, the oval-oblong ss. and ps. white at base, the remaining area stained and spotted with amethyst-purple or magenta. Lip with a broad claw, on each side of which is a small auricle; lamina almost flat, ovate-oblong, obtuse, entire, amethyst-purple, paler marginally, with 2 small white basal tubercles; claw and auricles white with purple streaks. Spur short, horn-like, incurved, tipped with green. Col. white, with a yellowish anther-cap. Summer. (H) Peninsular India, especially Travancore.

—var. **Schroederi** Henfr. (*Aërides Schroederi* hort.) Differs from the type in the more robust stem of greater height, the lvs. more distant and longer, the infls. with stouter peduncles, more profusely branched, the ss. and ps. narrower, with the apical stain larger and brighter, the midlb. of the lip longer and dark amethyst-purple in colour. Summer. (H) Peninsular India, in the southern part.

A. mitratum Rchb.f. Almost stemless. Lvs. 3–5 (rarely more) in number, semi-terete, whip-like, 5–18″ long, deeply channelled on upper side. Infls. usually produced from below the lvs., ascending or rigidly erect, to 6″ tall, very densely many-fld., cylindrical. Fls. ½–¾″ long, fragrant, on short pedicellate ovaries, the ss. and ps. white tinged apically with mauve-purple, subequal, broadly oval-oblong. Lip amethyst-purple or magenta-red, with a horn-like projection on each side at base, broadly trulliform, obtuse. Spur short, very compressed, projecting backwards, mitre-shaped. Spring. (I, H) Burma; Thailand; Laos.

A. radicosum A.Rich. (*Aërides rubrum* hort., *Gastrochilus Wightianus* O.Ktze., *Saccolabium ringens* Ldl., *Saccolabium rubrum* Wight, *Saccolabium Wightianum* Ldl.) A dwarf, rare species. Lvs. rigidly leathery, to 10″ long and 1¼″ broad. Infls. with stout peduncle, erect or ascending, rarely branched, the rachis dull purple and furrowed, to 8″ tall, densely many-fld. Fls. fragrant, on pale rose-purple pedicellate ovaries, less than 1″ across, the ss. and ps. pale rose-purple spotted with dark purple, broadly oval, the lat. ss. the largest. Lip 3-lbd., the lat. lbs. very small, round, erect, coloured like the ss. and ps.; midlb. oblong, acute, dark rose-purple. Spur horn-like, short, laterally compressed. Col. with 2 small rounded whitish wings below the stigmatic surface. Summer. (H) Peninsular India: southern part.

AGANISIA Ldl.

This genus consists of a single species of rather small epiphytic orchid, native in northern South America and as yet extremely rare in cultivation. It is allied to *Acacallis* Ldl. and to *Zygopetalum* Hk., differing from those groups in technical details of the flowers. The plant is of unusual appearance, and its flowers are sufficiently attractive to make it of interest to the specialist collector.

A single hybrid is on record between *Aganisia* and *Zygopetalum*, to produce the artificial group *Zygonisia*. Additional experimental breeding should be attempted in this alliance, and also with the related subtribe *Lycastinae*.

CULTURE: *Aganisia* should be cultivated either on tree-fern slabs, or else in shallow fern-pans, in a compost of about equal parts of shredded tree-fern fibre and chopped sphagnum moss. It must be kept in a moist fresh atmosphere, and care must be taken that the compost does not become stale, or the plants will quickly deteriorate. Warm, humid conditions are required, and a semi-shaded spot is most suitable for their successful care. (H)

A. pulchella Ldl.
Rhiz. slender, creeping, closely covered with overlapping brown scale-like sheaths. Pbs. borne at intervals along the rhiz., ovoid, about 1″ long, dull green. Lf. solitary, oval-oblong to lanceolate-elliptic, acute, 4–5″ long, narrowed below into a slender petiole. Infls. erect to pendulous, 4–8-fld., to about 5″ long. Fls. 1–1½″ across, fragrant or not, the white ss. and ps. ovate-oblong, acute, almost equal. Lip shorter than the ss., 2-parted, the basal hypochil roundish, concave, spotted

with red; epichil much larger, broadly ovate, entire, with a yellow disc and white margin, the basal glandular crest golden-yellow. Col. 2-winged apically. Mostly late spring. (H) British Guiana; Northern Brazil (Amazonas).

AGLOSSORHYNCHA Schltr.

A member of the subtribe *Glomerinae*, this genus consists of about six species of very rare and little-known epiphytic orchids, all native in New Guinea, none of which appears to be present in contemporary collections. The plants rather simulate the species of *Glossorhyncha* Ridl. in vegetative appearance, but differ in minor details and also in floral characteristics. All of the known Aglossorhynchas produce yellow or yellowish flowers of small dimensions.

Nothing is known of the genetic affinities of this rare genus.

CULTURE: Presumably as for *Glomera*. (I, H)

AGROSTOPHYLLUM Bl.

This is a genus of somewhat more than sixty species of epiphytic and lithophytic orchids of the subtribe *Glomerinae*, native over an immense area, extending from the Seychelles Islands and Malaya throughout Indonesia to Samoa, with the largest number of representatives occurring in New Guinea. The species of *Agrostophyllum* are apparently unknown in cultivation outside of their native lands, though their often elongate, densely leafy, frequently pendulous stems and peculiar inflorescences—mostly tightly bracted and ball-like—make them of unique interest to the specialist collector.

Nothing is known of the genetic alliances of this odd genus of orchids.

CULTURE: As for the tropical Dendrobiums. The species with pendulous stems naturally should be affixed to tree-fern slabs, or else grown in baskets. Some of the New Guinean members of the group occur at rather high elevations. (I. H)

ALAMANIA LaLl. & Lex.

A single member of *Alamania* is known to science, this an exceptionally handsome and rare member of the subtribe *Laeliinae*, somewhat allied to *Epidendrum* L., but differing from that group in technical details of habit and floral structure. For many years, this dwarf epiphyte from Mexico was considered a 'lost' orchid, but several collections made in recent years show that it is actually relatively frequent in a few restricted areas in that country. It is today very rare in cultivation, but its clusters of *Sophronitis*-like blossoms, borne on a diminutive, most interesting plant, make it of considerable interest to the connoisseur orchidist.

As yet no hybrids have been made with *Alamania*, although it seems possible that it will prove, through experimentation, to be compatible genetically with at least certain of the allied genera of the subtribe. The results which should be obtained promise some fascinating colours and forms, on a small, profusely flowering plant.

CULTURE: *Alamania* is far from easy to maintain in good condition under cultivation, but with some extra attention to its wants, the plants will grow and flower well in the cool greenhouse. Small, perfectly drained pots, tightly filled either with osmunda or a mixture of shredded tree-fern fibre and chopped sphagnum moss, kept in a moist, shaded spot in the collection will suit the little plants well. They should never be allowed to become overly wet, and yet must never dry out, either. Disturbing the roots should be avoided, unless absolutely necessary. (C)

A. punicea LaLl. & Lex. (*Epidendrum puniceum* Rchb.f.)

Pbs. narrowly cylindrical, usually less than 1″ tall, curving, borne at intervals along the creeping rhiz., often flushed with dull purple. Lvs. 1–3, rigidly leathery, oblanceolate, acutish, usually about as long as the pbs., often purple-flushed. Infls. terminal from a leafless pb., the abbreviated rac. densely few-fld. Fls. opening well, lasting well, about ¾″ in diam., varying in colour from vivid vermilion to scarlet, usually with a whitish area around the lip-base. Ss. and ps. subequal, narrow, spreading or somewhat incurving. Lip adnate to the col., the lamina similar in shape to the ss. Spring. (C) Central and South-Central Mexico, mostly at rather high elevations.

ALLOCHILUS Gagnep.

Allochilus consists of a single recently described species of terrestrial orchid, of the subtribe *Phaiinae*, native in Viet-Nam. It is not completely known at this time, and is not present in contemporary collections.

Nothing is known of the genetic affinities of this odd genus.

CULTURE: Presumably as for the tropical species of *Phaius*. (I, H)

ALTENSTEINIA HBK
(*Aa* Rchb.f., *Myrosmodes* Rchb.f.)

Altensteinia is a genus of more than twenty species of rather unusual terrestrial orchids, of the subtribe *Cranichidinae*, which reach their greatest development in the Andes of South America, with outlying representatives extending to Brazil and Argentina. Unknown in collections today, when in bloom they are rather attractive, with dense racemes of intricate flowers subtended by large, usually coloured bracts.

Nothing is known of the genetic alliances of this genus.

CULTURE: Presumably as for the high-elevation *Erythrodes* and other thick-rooted terrestrials. (C, I)

AMBLOSTOMA Scheidw.

This is a genus consisting of about three rather polymorphic species of not very impressive epiphytic or lithophytic orchids, indigenous to the Andean regions of South America, and to Brazil. Rather closely allied to *Epidendrum* L. and to certain other components of the subtribe *Laeliinae*, they are today very scarce in cultivation, although the species noted below is occasionally encountered in a very few specialized collections.

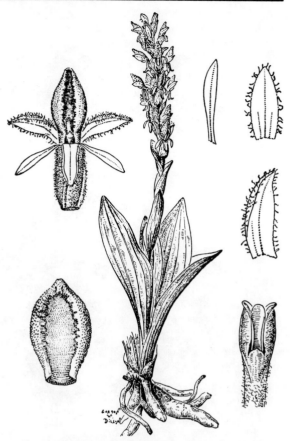

Altensteinia elliptica C. Schw. [GORDON W. DILLON]

No hybrids have as yet been made in *Amblostoma*, and nothing is known concerning its genetic affinities.

CULTURE: These slim-bulbed plants require, generally speaking, the cultural treatment of the tropical, pseudobulbous Epidendrums. They thrive in well-drained pots, grown in bright light, in a compost of firmly packed osmunda or shredded tree-fern fibre, or can be mounted on tree-fern slabs. They benefit by a month-long rest upon completion of the new growths, and should be fertilized with regularity for best flower-production. (I, H)

A. tridactylum Scheidw.

Pbs. rather clustered, usually bright yellowish-green, narrowly spindle-shaped, to about 8″ tall. Lvs. several, borne near apex of pb., usually erect or ascending, to about 10″ long, narrow, thin-textured. Infls. erect, racemose or rarely paniculate, rather densely many-fld., to about 6″ tall. Fls. about ¼″ in diam., fragile in texture, usually yellowish-white, the ss. and ps. spreading, the lip 3-lbd., the midlb. smaller than the lat. ones. Mostly summer. (I. H) Brazil.

AMBRELLA H.Perr.

But a single species of *Ambrella* is known to date, this, **A. longituba** H.Perr., an excessively rare epiphytic orchid of the *Angraecum* alliance of the subtribe *Sarcanthinae*, endemic to Madagascar. It is placed in the group

Amblostoma tridactylum Scheidw. [Hoehne, *Flora Brasilica*]

surrounding *Angraecum* Bory and *Oeoniella* Schltr., and is a small plant with proportionately large, green, very complex blossoms. *Ambrella* is unknown in cultivation at this time.

Nothing is known of the genetic alliances of this rare group.

CULTURE: Probably as for the smaller-growing, tropical Angraecums. (H)

AMITOSTIGMA Schltr.
(*Mitostigma* Bl.)

This is a genus of about twenty-four species, all of them slender, rather dwarf terrestrial orchids, native in the Himalayas and China. A member of the subtribe *Habenarinae*, *Amitostigma* is unknown in contemporary collections, though several of the described species appear to be rather showy little plants.

Nothing is known of the genetic affinities of this genus.

CULTURE: Presumably as for *Orchis*, etc. (C)

AMPAROA Schltr.

Two species of *Amparoa* are known to date, both extremely rare and incompletely described epiphytic orchids native in Costa Rica. The genus is a member of the subtribe *Oncidiinae*, and is very close in its alliance to *Odontoglossum* HBK, with which it will perhaps eventually be united. Neither of the Amparoas are present in our collections at this time.

Nothing is known of the genetic affinities of this group.

CULTURE: Presumably as for the medium-elevation Odontoglossums, Oncidiums, etc. (I)

AMPHIGENA Rolfe

This is a little-known genus of two species of reed-like terrestrial orchids in South Africa, often included in *Disa* Berg, but differing in technical characters of the flowers. The Amphigenas are virtually unknown in contemporary collections, and are of interest primarily to the specialist, since their blossoms are small and rather dull coloured, though produced in large numbers on elongate spikes.

No hybrids are known in this genus, and its genetic affinities have not been established as yet.

CULTURE: As for *Disa*. (C, I)

A. tenuis (Ldl.) Rolfe (*Disa tenuis* Ldl.)
Slender pls. to $1\frac{1}{4}'$ tall when in fl., the st. usually curved, with 2–3 short basal sheaths. Basal lvs. 2–4, to 4″ long, linear, withered at time of flowering; st.-lvs. small, brown, bract-like, acuminate. Infl. erect, elongate, many-fld. Fls. not opening well, about $\frac{1}{2}″$ across, greenish with a few purple spots, or the lower half of the fls. greenish, the upper half deep brown. Ss. free, with bristle-like tips, the dors. one hooded, with a very short, ascending, obtuse spur; lat. ss. narrow, spreading. Ps. erect, the tips incurved, oblong, obtuse, short, the front margins serrulate. Lip as long as the ps., linear, acute, the margins entire. Spring. (C, I) South Africa.

ANACAMPTIS A.Rich.

Anacamptis consists of a single species of very handsome terrestrial orchid, native in Central and Southern Europe, where it usually inhabits the montane regions, growing in grassy fields and meadows. It resembles a slender *Orchis* in habit, and is indeed related to that genus, as well as to *Neotinea* Rchb.f. and to *Himantoglossum* Spreng. It is rare in cultivation outside of its native haunts.

Several natural hybrids with *Anacamptis* are on record, primarily with *Orchis*, which gives the group *Anacamptorchis*. The rare hybrid between *Anacamptis* and *Gymnadenia conopsea* (R.Br.) R.Br., found in England has been noted under the name *Gymnanacamptis x anacamptis* (Wilms) Aschers. & Graebn.

CULTURE: Though difficult to keep alive under artificial conditions, this attractive plant may sometimes be grown successfully if given the culture required by *Orchis* and *Ophrys*. (C)

A. pyramidalis (L.) A.Rich. (*Orchis pyramidalis* L., *Orchis bicornis* Gilib., *Orchis condensata* Desf., *Aceras pyramidalis* Rchb.f.)
A slender terrestrial orchid to 2′ tall, with rather narrow foliage. Racs. mostly egg-shaped, very densely many-fld., with numerous small subtending bracts. Fls. variable in colour, typically bright red, sometimes pale carmine-red, about $\frac{1}{4}″$ long or more. Lip usually darker than the other segms., longer than them. Summer, especially June. (C) South and Central Europe.

ANAPHORA Gagnep.

But a single species of *Anaphora* is known to date this, **A. liparidioides** Gagnep., a rare terrestrial plant of the subtribe *Liparidinae*, which has been collected on a few occasions in Viet-Nam and Cambodia. A relatively insignificant plant with tufts of lanceolate leaves, the very small white flowers—which are rather complex in structure—are borne in an erect, very dense raceme. At this time *Anaphora* is not in cultivation.

Nothing has been ascertained regarding the genetic affinities of this group.

CULTURE: Possibly as for the tropical *Phaius*. (H)

ANCISTROCHILUS Rolfe

This is a strange and aberrant genus of two species of handsome epiphytic orchids, native in tropical West Africa. They are allied to *Pachystoma* Bl. and to *Ipsea* Ldl., and at previous times have been placed in those groups, though they are now considered worthy of full generic rank. At least one of the species is occasionally encountered in choice collections today, but both of them must be classed among the rarest of cultivated orchids.

No hybrids have been produced in *Ancistrochilus*, and nothing is known of its genetic affinities.

CULTURE: As for the tropical, evergreen Dendrobiums and Bulbophyllums. A rich compost, perfectly drained, is a prime requisite for success with these handsome but sometimes refractory orchids. (H)

Ancistrochilus Thompsonianus (Rchb.f.) Rolfe [VEITCH]

A. Thompsonianus (Rchb.f.) Rolfe (*Pachystoma Thompsonianum* Rchb.f., *Ipsea Thompsoniana* Pfitz.)

Pbs. borne at short intervals on a creeping rhiz., roundish, to 1½″ tall, usually covered with fibrous brownish sheaths. Lvs. 1–3, stalked, folded, lanceolate, acuminate, rather heavy-textured, to 8″ long. Infls. 1–2 from base of each pb., erect or ascending, to about 9″ tall, loosely 2–4-fld. Fls. to 3½″ across, rather heavily fragrant, long-lived, the ss. and ps. snow-white, lanceolate, acute, the dors. sep. the broadest, the lat. ss. narrower and falcate. Lip 3-lbd., the lat. lbs. erect, squarish, greenish, densely spotted with deep purple on the inner side; midlb. triangular, elongated, tapering to a recurved point, traversed by 5 raised longitudinal purple lines which gradually coalesce towards the apex. Col. arched, semi-terete, green spotted with red. Summer–early autumn. (H) Tropical West Africa.

ANCISTRORHYNCHUS Finet
(*Cephalangraecum* Schltr.)

Twelve species of *Ancistrorhynchus* are presently known, all of them very rare epiphytic orchids from tropical Africa. Somewhat vaguely allied to *Angraecum* Bory, they are rather variable in vegetative structure, and often bear peculiarly clustered masses of very complex blossoms. Although of considerable potential value to the specialist collector, they appear to be unknown in cultivation at this time.

Nothing is known of the genetic affinities of *Ancistrorhynchus*.

· CULTURE: Presumably as for the tropical Angraecums. (H)

ANDROCORYS Schltr.

Androcorys, the only known genus of the subtribe *Androcorydinae*, consists of four species of relatively small and insignificant terrestrial (or rarely lithophytic) orchids, indigenous to the Himalayas, China, and Japan, where they usually grow at rather high elevations. The single species now grown, *Androcorys gracilis* (King & Pantl.) Schltr., was formerly included in *Herminium* L., but the present group is apparently well differentiated from that genus on technical details of the flowers. In our collections at this time, *Androcorys* is exceptionally rare, and in any event, these orchids are principally of scientific importance.

Nothing is known of the genetic affinities of this group, and no hybrids have as yet been registered.

CULTURE: As for *Orchis*, although constantly cool conditions are required. (C)

A. gracilis (King & Pantl.) Schltr. (*Herminium gracile* King & Pantl.)

Tubers fusiform, with thickened accessory fibres. Lf. solitary, basal, obovate or oblong, short-pointed, to about 1½″ long. Infl. erect, slender, naked, 4–6″ tall, with a few scattered small fls. Fls. about ⅛″ across, pale green. Dors. sep. elliptic or orbicular, forming with the ps. an elliptic hood; lat. ss. elliptic, deflexed, concave, blunt. Lip narrowly ovate, blunt, the tip deflexed. Mostly July. (C) Sikkim, at high elevations.

ANGRAECOPSIS Krzl.

Angraecopsis is, according to a relatively recent (1951) revision by Summerhayes, a genus of fourteen species, native principally in tropical Africa, with outlying members in the western islands such as São Thomé and Fernando Pó, and the eastern groups of the Comoros, Madagascar, and the Mascarene Islands. They are dwarf epiphytic orchids, technically allied to *Mystacidium* Ldl., with short, leafy stems and long inflorescences of often very small, spidery flowers of complex structure. Two of the known species are occasionally encountered in choice collections today, but they must be classed as rare orchids and of primarily technical importance.

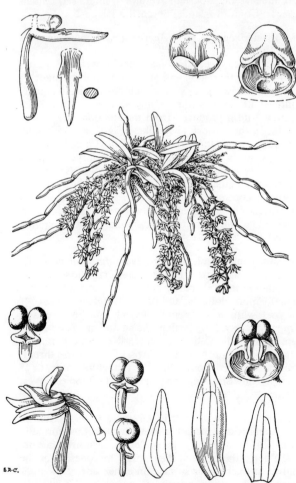

5.R-C.

Angraecopsis breviloba Summerh. [*Icones Plantarum*]

No hybrids are known in *Angraecopsis*, and as yet nothing has been ascertained concerning its genetic affinities.

CULTURE: As for the tropical Angraecums. (H)

A. ischnopus (Schltr.) Schltr. (*Angraecum ischnopus* Schltr.)

St. abbreviated, leafy. Lvs. ligulate, 1½–4″ long, rather leathery. Infls. loosely 4–10-fld., to about 5″ long. Fls. less than ¼″ across, yellowish, the lip 3-lbd., the spur to almost ½″ long. Late winter–spring. (H) Sierra Leone; French Guinea; British Cameroons.

A. tenerrima Krzl. (*Angraecum amaniense* Krzl., *Angraecum tenerrimum* Schltr.)

Similar in habit to *A. ischnopus* (Schltr.) Schltr., but about twice as robust, with the fls. to ¾″ across, white in colour, with a spur to almost 2¾″ long. Spring. (H) Tanganyika Territory.

ANGRAECUM Bory
(*Aërobion* Kaempf., *Angorchis* Spreng., *Angorkis* Thou., *Macroplectrum* Pfitz., *Monixus* Finet, *Pectinaria* Cordem.)

The genus *Angraecum*, despite the fact that it contains more than two hundred species—many of which are exceptionally handsome and showy—is by and large only moderately popular with contemporary orchidists. This is doubtless due to the relative unavailability of all but a very few species in the trade, though through importations from the wild, a tremendous variety is made accessible to the connoisseur. *Angraecum* is, botanically, among the more difficult genera of the subtribe *Sarcanthinae*, having been used in the past as a convenient repository for a large number of only vaguely related plants, which are now relegated to segregate genera, such as *Aërangis* Rchb.f., *Diaphananthe* Schltr., *Mystacidium* Ldl., etc. Angraecums are of highly diverse vegetative appearance, and somewhat so in floral construction, but in general (if a generality may be drawn for such a varied aggregation) they have short or lengthy monopodial stems, set mostly with plane fleshy leaves, and bear short or elongate racemes of several (rarely solitary) small to large, often handsome flowers. These blossoms typically occur in shades of white and green, and are in many instances rather star-shaped; the lip is furnished with a spur, which in the remarkable *A. sesquipedale* Thou. reaches the astonishing length of upwards of one foot! Distribution of this fascinating genus is primarily in tropical Africa and adjacent insular groups, although outlying species are to be found as far away as the Philippines and Ceylon. Despite its having been established as long ago as 1804, *Angraecum* still contains many serious taxonomic problems, and a critical revision of the entire group of genera surrounding it—which are commonly called, for reasons of convenience, the angraecoid orchids—is sadly needed.

To date, only two hybrids have been recorded in this genus, peculiarly enough. *Angraecum x Veitchii* (*A. eburneum* × *A. sesquipedale*)[1] is an old cross, dating

[1] See 'Notes on *Angraecum x Veitchii*', in *The Orchid Weekly* 4: 133–134, 1963, for some pertinent comments regarding this plant and its parentage.

from 1899, while *A. x Alabaster* (*A. eburneum* × *A. x Veitchii*) is a modern hybrid registered by Oscar M. Kirsch, of Honolulu, Hawaii. Additional experimental hybridization, both within *Angraecum* itself, and with its presumed allies, should certainly be followed, for some fascinating possibilities come to mind.

CULTURE: The cultural requirements of *Angraecum* vary almost as much as do the component species themselves. Robust plants, such as *A. eburneum* and *A. sesquipedale*, delight in pot- or basket-culture, in a perfectly drained compost of rather tightly packed osmunda or tree-fern chunks. The dwarf species, such as *A. distichum*, *A. Scottianum*, etc., do best in small pots, filled with tight-packed osmunda, shredded tree-fern fibre, or a mixture of the latter with chopped sphagnum moss. The various bark preparations have not proved to be acceptable for use with Angraecums, or with other angraecoid orchids. Certain of the small, climbing species can to good advantage be mounted on tree-fern slabs or 'totem-poles'. Most of them require rather diffused light, and all must have quantities of fresh, free-moving air. While the plants are in active growth—which is generally almost throughout the year—they should be watered heavily (assuming drainage is perfect), and may to good advantage be fertilized regularly. Temperature requirements fluctuate from species to species, but the majority of the commonly grown Angraecums originate in warm, humid regions. (I, H)

A. distichum Ldl. (*Aëranthus distichus* Rchb.f., *Limodorum imbricatum* Sw., *Macroplectrum distichum* Finet, *Mystacidium distichum* Rchb.f.)

Sts. clustered, often forming dense entangled masses, branching basally and upwards, normally entirely clothed with lvs., to 6″ tall. Lvs. very fleshy, glossy bright green, imbricately distichous, vaguely triangular-ovate, blunt, usually about ¼″ long, persistent for many years. Infls. very abbreviated, 1-fld., produced mostly from the more recent portions of the leafy sts., often very numerous at one time. Fls. inverted, fragrant of narcissus, glittering pure white, about ¼″ in diam., lasting for about two weeks. Ss. and ps. oblong, obtuse, the ps. somewhat the smaller and narrower. Lip helmet-shaped, the tip somewhat compressed, extending into a rather elongate, cylindric, pure white spur. Usually autumn–winter, but almost ever-blooming when well grown. (I, H) Tropical West Africa.

A. eburneum Bory (*Limodorum eburneum* Willd., *Angorchis eburnea* O.Ktze., *Angraecum virens* Ldl.)

Very robust, to more than 6′ tall, on occasion branching from near base and forming huge clumps. Lvs. thickly set, very rigidly leathery, to more than 3′ long and 3″ broad, unequally bilobed at apex, gracefully arching or horizontally arranged. Infls. often several at once, ascending or horizontal, stout, to 4′ long, densely many-fld., the fls. inverted, neatly arranged in 2 ranks. Fls. long-lived, very fragrant, heavily waxy, to 3″ long, the ss. and ps. greenish-white or almost emerald-green, the large lip white, with or without 2 basal green suffusions, the elongate spur with a greenish tip or not. Ss. and ps. down-thrust, ligulate, shortly acute. Lip concave, almost rounded, with a prominent apicule at tip, the

spur awl-shaped, to 4″ long. Mostly autumn–early winter. (H) Mascarene Islands.

—var. **giryamae** (Rendle) A. D. Hawkes (*Angraecum giryamae* Rendle)

Differing principally from typical *A. eburneum* Bory in its distribution and in details of the fls. Fls. numerous, crowded, usually 2¼″ long, pale green, the lip glistening-white, heavily waxen, suffused near col. with green. Lip almost rectangular, broader than long, deeply concave, 1½″ broad × 1″ long, the apicule short and recurved. Spur conical, straight or lightly curved, 1¾–2″ long. Winter–spring. (H) Kenya; Tanganyika; Zanzibar; Pemba Island; almost always near the shore, usually on coral-rock cliffs as a lithophyte.

—var. **superbum** (Thou.) A.D.Hawkes (*Angraecum superbum* Thou., *A. Brongniartianum* Rchb.f. ex Lind., *A. comorense* Krzl., *A. comoroense* hort., *A. Voeltzkowianum* Krzl., *A. eburneum* Bory ssp. *superbum* H.Perr.)

Differs from the typical species in its range, and in the larger fls., of which the ss. and ps. are white, the lip almost 3-lbd. apically, the lat. lbs. rounded, the apicule very prominent and acute, and the basal callus more prominent and 2-parted. Autumn–winter. (H) Madagascar; Comoro Islands; Seychelles Islands.

A. Eichlerianum Krzl. (*Angraecum Arnoldianum* De Wild.)

Sts. pendulous or climbing, sparsely branched, rather compressed, to 5′ long and more. Lvs. rather distant on the sts., in 2 ranks, 4–5″ long, oblong-elliptic, unequally bilobed at apex, rather thinly leathery. Infls. 1-fld. (rarely 2-fld.), produced from the sts. opposite the lf.-bases, rather short, wire-like. Fls. heavy-textured, fragrant, rather long-lived, to about 3″ across, the ss. and ps. green or yellowish-green, the large lip white with an emerald-green area in the throat. Ss. and ps. spreading, ligulate, acute. Lip very broadly rhombic-cordate, concave, keeled basally; spur funnel-shaped basally, becoming much narrower towards tip, bent in the middle, obtuse at tip, to 1¾″ long. Mostly summer. (I, H) Tropical West Africa.

A. infundibulare Ldl. (*Mystacidium infundibulare* Rolfe)

Closely related to *A. Eichlerianum* Krzl. and somewhat resembling it in all parts, but the lvs. smaller, the sts. usually more elongate, and the fls. larger (to almost 3½″ across), with a differently shaped lip. Fls. solitary, fragrant, waxy, long-lasting, the ss. and ps. pale yellow-green, spreading, linear, acute, the broadly funnel-shaped lip white with a yellowish flush in the throat; spur awl-shaped from a broadly funnel-like base, to 5″ long, yellowish. Autumn–winter. (H) Tropical West Africa.

A. Leonis (Rchb.f.) Veitch (*Aëranthus Leonis* Rchb.f.)

St. abbreviated, usually almost obsolete. Lvs. normally very few in number, rigidly fleshy, ensiform, falcate, 5–10″ long, the blade vertical from the cohesion of the halves at their upper surface on either side of the mid-nerve. Infls. stout, horizontal or erect, 3–7-fld. Fls. fragrant, long-lasting, the compressed, ancipitous,

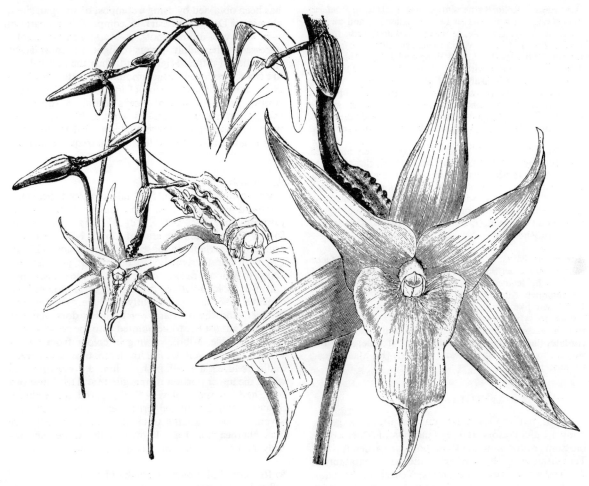

Angraecum sesquipedale Thou. [VEITCH]

narrowly winged pedicellate ovaries 3″ long (including the short 6-ribbed ovary), waxy, 2–3″ in diam., the ss. and ps. white or yellowish, the large lip pure ivory-white. Ss. and ps. lanceolate, acuminate, recurved, keeled behind, the ps. slightly shorter and broader than the ss. Lip cordate, cuspidate, concave, produced at the base into a flexuose spur 5–6″ long, this funnel-shaped and compressed in upper part, with a short elevated plate at its aperture, the dilated half white, the distal slender half green. Col. very short, the rostellum produced in front into 2 rounded plates. Winter. (H) Comoro Islands; Madagascar.

A. Scottianum Rchb.f.

Sts. branching, ascending to pendulous, slender, rarely to 2′ long, leafy throughout, or after the lvs. fall clothed with brown sheaths. Lvs. terete, spreading and recurved, deeply grooved on upper side, 3–4″ long. Infls. slender, 1–2-fld., to about 4″ long, usually ascending. Fls. inverted, waxy, fragrant, to about 2″ in diam., the ss. and ps. pale straw-yellow changing to white, similar, linear, acute, the ps. slightly the narrower. Lip pure white, transversely oblong, concave, with a mucro on the anterior edge, and prolonged at the base

into a slender, pale reddish-brown spur about 4–5″ long. Col. very short, with a pair of small hatchet-shaped wings in front. Mostly autumn. (H) Comoro Islands.

A. sesquipedale Thou. (*Aëranthes sesquipedalis* Ldl., *Angorchis sesquipedalis* O.Ktze., *Macroplectrum sesquipedale* Pfitz., *Mystacidium sesquipedale* Rolfe.)

St. usually solitary, seldom more than 3′ tall, woody below, leafy above. Lvs. closely arranged, dark green, often rather glaucous, leathery, ligulate-oblong, folded and sheathing at base, unequally 2-lbd. at apex, wavy-margined, to about 12″ long and 1½–2″ broad. Infls. usually horizontal to down-arching, stout, 2–4-fld., to about 12″ long, the keeled bracts brownish. Fls. very fleshy, heavily waxy, fragrant, long-lived, to 7″ in diam., ivory-white, star-shaped, the ss. and ps. broad at base, narrowing towards apex, the ps. contracted at base and narrower than the ss.; lip broader than the other segms., cordate at base, then oblong and irregularly serrated, terminating in a reflexed acuminate tip; spur greenish, to almost 12″ in length, flexuose towards the tip. Col. very short and thick, the rostellum produced into 2 squarish lobes that almost conceal the stigma. Mostly winter. (H) Madagascar.

A. birrimense Rolfe. Rather similar in all parts to *A. Eichlerianum* Krzl., but with smaller fls., a smaller lip, and an erect spur. St. rather elongate, to several feet in length, the lvs. strictly 2-ranked, leathery, rectangular or elliptic-rectangular, apically obliquely 2-lbd., 4–5″ long and 1–1¼″ broad. Infls. 1-fld., the peduncle wire-like, about 1¼″ long. Fls. waxy, fragrant, long-lived, to about 2¾″ across, the linear-lanceolate, acuminate ss. and ps. greenish-yellow, the ovate lip white with a green basal blotch, apically triangular and acuminate; spur curving, erect, to 1¼″ long, funnel-shaped, the apical part compressed and awl-shaped. Autumn. (H) Ghana.

A. erectum Summerh. St. erect, simple or sparsely branched, freely rooting, to 2′ tall. Lvs. numerous, borne close together, to 3½″ long, rather fleshy, deeply and unequally 2-lbd. at apex. Infls. numerous, normally 1-fld., short. Fls. inverted, about ½″ long, fleshy, varying from white to yellowish or pale salmon-colour, the spur slender, slightly curved. Almost throughout the year. (I, H) Uganda; Kenya; Tanganyika; Northern Rhodesia.

A. ramosum Thou. (*Angraecum Germinyanum* Hk.f., *Macroplectrum ramosum* Finet). St. elongate, to 1½′ tall, branched. Lvs. rigidly leathery, closely arranged, oblong, unequally and obliquely 2-lbd., 1¾″–2¾″ long, to almost 1″ broad. Infls. 1-fld., wire-like, about ¾″ long. Fls. fragrant, waxy, long-lasting, to 3½″ long, white, usually inverted, the ss. and ps. from a lanceolate base long-acuminate. Lip almost square-cordate, the tip long-acuminate, keeled at base; spur awl-shaped, to 4″ long. Spring–early summer. (H) Madagascar; Comoro Islands.

ANGULOA R. & P.

About ten species make up this fabulous genus, known by collectors as the 'Tulip Orchids', since the blossoms rather simulate those popular garden flowers. Terrestrial or epiphytic in habit, they are inhabitants of the Andean regions of Colombia, Venezuela, Ecuador, and Peru, and are closely related to *Lycaste* Ldl., which the plants vegetatively resemble. The typically large, waxy, solitary blooms are cup-shaped, the sepals forming a structure in which the petals, lip, and column are borne. Colour varies considerably from species to species, with a large number of horticultural variants being on record. Anguloas are unfortunately very uncommon in contemporary collections, although they are among the finest of American orchids.

Several extremely handsome natural and artificial hybrids are known in *Anguloa*, and the genus has also been successfully bred with *Lycaste*, to give *Angulocaste*. It seems logical that it will prove genetically compatible with at least some others of the subtribe *Lycastinae*, and possibly also the subtribes *Zygopetalinae* and *Huntleyinae*.

CULTURE: Anguloas are easily grown, even by the rank amateur, and never fail to prove a delight when brought into flower. Mostly high-elevation plants, they are in theory best suited to the cool *Odontoglossum-Miltonia* house, though an intermediate temperature is not detrimental to most of the species and hybrids. Cultivation in pots is preferred, in a very well-drained compost of about 3 parts of good rich loam or sifted soil, 1½ parts slightly chopped osmunda fibre, about ½ part fresh sphagnum moss, and a rather small quantity of dried, shredded leaves. In recent years, some success

has been obtained by using a compost of straight, sifted, chunks of Douglas fir bark or comparable preparation —in very well-drained pots. A·bright and airy spot is necessary—the adult plants delight in considerable quantities of diffused light—and when the new growths are being produced, large amounts of water should be given, but upon maturation of the pseudobulbs a strict resting-period of several weeks' duration (until new root-action again occurs) is absolutely essential for proper production of flowers. Heavy feeders, Anguloas may to good advantage be fertilized at frequent intervals. (C, I)

A. Clowesii Ldl.

Pbs. cylindric-oblong, 5–6″ tall, clustered, becoming furrowed with age. Lvs. deciduous in time, broadly obovate-lanceolate, acute, 18–24″ long, prominently folded. Infls. often several at once, 1-fld., set with numerous overlapping loose bracts, to almost 12″ tall. Fls. with a rather medicinal odour, subglobose, very waxy, to 3″ long, rather compressed on the sides, bright citron- or golden-yellow, the ss. and ps. elliptic-oblong, concave, the lat. ss. slightly oblique, shorter and broader, and the ps. narrower than the dors. sep. Lip complex, almost boat-like, jointed with the col.-foot and freely movable, 3-lbd., varying in colour from cream-white to orange-yellow; lat. lbs. large, triangular, erect; midlb. reduced, a small, fleshy, 2-lipped, hairy funnel of which the upper portion is emarginate and the lower one acute and reflexed. Col. very thick, curved, terete above, concave with 2 rounded processes below the stigma. Several colour variants (including the extremely rare fma. *eburnea* hort.) are known in the trade. Spring–early summer. (C, I) Colombia; Venezuela.

A. Rueckeri Ldl. (*Anguloa Ruckeri* hort.)

Similar in vegetative appearance to *A. Clowesii* Ldl., but the vegetative parts smaller, the infls. shorter, and the fls. larger and of heavier texture. Fls. very fragrant, almost 3½″ long, greenish-brown outside, yellow densely red-spotted inside. Ss. and ps. elliptic-oblong, the lat. ss. slightly oblique, shorter and broader, and the ps. narrower than dors. sep. Lip 3-lbd., the lat. lbs. erect, oblong, rounded at the apex, the midlb. as in *A. Clowesii* Ldl. Col. short, thick, swollen below the stigma on each side of the deep furrow that extends thence to the base. Highly variable in the inner colour of the fls., ranging from pure glittering white to almost entirely blood-red. Spring–summer. (C, I) Colombia.

A. uniflora R. & P. (*Anguloa virginalis* Lind.)

Pbs. angular, rather elongate, ovoid-oblong, 4–7″ tall. Lvs. broadly lanceolate, acute, prominently folded, to 2′ long and more. Infls. erect, 6–10″ tall, often very numerous from a single growth. Fls. rather open for the genus, rather objectionably candy-scented, very waxy and long-lived, to 4″ long and wide, cup-shaped, in the typical phase waxen white or cream-white, usually flushed and dotted inside with pale or bright pink or rose-pink. Ss. ovate, acute, concave. Ps. smaller, elliptic-oblong, acute. Lip 3-lbd., the lat. lbs. roundish, rolled inwards into a tube; midlb. very small, linear, reflexed, with a 2-parted thick plate at its base. Col. club-shaped.

Aërides vandarum Rchb.f. [GEORGE FULLER]

(RIGHT) *Anacamptis pyramidalis* (L.) A. Rich. [GEORGE FULLER]

Agrostophyllum sp., an unidentified species, from the Philippines [REG S. DAVIS]

Angraecum distichum Ldl. [GEORGE FULLER]

Angraecum infundibulare Ldl. [GEORGE FULLER]

Anguloa Clowesii Ldl. [GEORGE FULLER]

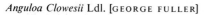

Ania Elmeri (Ames) A.D.Hawkes [REG S. DAVIS]

IIA   *Bulbophyllum Lobbii* Ldl. [KARI BERGGRAV]

IIB   *Catasetum Oerstedii* Rchb.f. [H.A.DUNN]

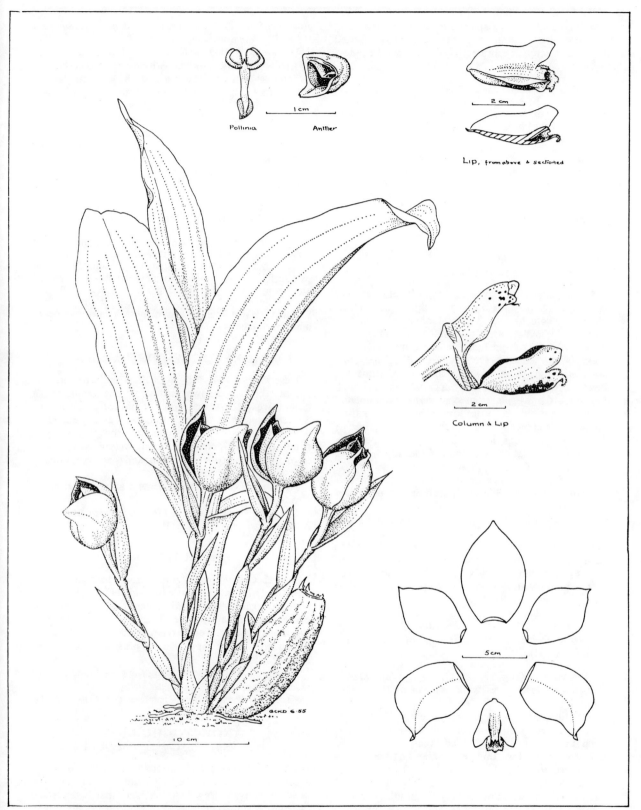

Pollinia

Anther

1 cm

LIP, from above & sectioned

2 cm

Column & Lip

2 cm

5 cm

10 cm

GCKD 6-55

Anguloa Rueckeri Ldl. [G.C.K.DUNSTERVILLE]

with 2 narrowly oblong apical auricles. A variable sp., with completely white and very distinctly spotted variants. Mostly early spring. (C, I) Colombia; Ecuador; Peru.

A. brevilabris Rolfe. Similar in all parts to *A. Rueckeri* Ldl., and perhaps best considered a variant of it. Fls. mostly smaller than those of that sp., less brilliantly coloured, the formation of the lip somewhat at variance. Summer. (C, I) Colombia.

A. Cliftoni Rolfe. Similar in habit to the other described spp. Fls. very large, to almost 3½" across and long, waxy, highly fragrant, pale yellow, shading at the base of the sepaline cup to a very dark butter-yellow, the ss. and ps. usually more or less marked at their bases with purple-brown. Spring-summer. (C, I) Colombia.

ANIA Ldl.
(*Ascotainia* Ridl.)

Ania contains about six or more species of often very handsome terrestrial (rarely lithophytic on mossy, damp rocks) orchids, which inhabit the region extending from the Himalayas to the Malay Peninsula and Indonesia. Formerly included in the genus *Tainia* Bl. (which is now placed in the subtribe *Collabiinae*), *Ania* is a member of the subtribe *Phaiinae*. Unfortunately, they are at this time very rare in our collections, although they are attractive plants of considerable ornamental value which should be better known by the specialist.

Nothing is known concerning the genetic affinities of *Ania*. It seems probable that it will prove genetically compatible with at least certain of the allied genera, such as *Phaius*, *Calanthe*, *Plocoglottis*, etc.

CULTURE: Best grown under intermediate temperatures, the Anias thrive in well-drained pots in a compost consisting of about equal parts of fibrous loam, leaf-mould, sharp white sand, chopped tree-fern fibre, and chopped sphagnum moss. While actively growing, the plants require copious quantities of water, but upon maturation of the new pseudobulbs, a rest-period of almost one month should be given them, during which only enough moisture is supplied to prevent shrivelling of the vegetative parts. The Anias seem to benefit by annual repotting, and also thrive when fertilized at regular intervals. Because of the rather fragile foliage, they will become sunburned if kept in too bright a situation. (I, H)

A. Hookeriana (King & Pantl.) Tang & Wang (*Tainia Hookeriana* King & Pantl., *Ascotainia Hookeriana* Ridl.)
Pbs. clustered, egg-shaped, prominently ribbed, to 3" tall and about 2½" in diam., usually bluish or greyish-green. Lf. solitary, strongly folded, eventually deciduous, to 2½' tall, with a long thin petiole about half as long as the lamina. Infls. basal, erect, to 3' tall, wand-like, the rac. to almost 2' long, loosely 10–25-fld. Fls. about 2" across, yellow with numerous longitudinal brown stripes on the rather narrow ss. and ps., the iip white tinged with yellow, with some tiny reddish dots round the front keels on the disc, the spur brownish. Spring. (I) Himalayas; Sikkim; Northern Thailand.

A. penangiana (Hk.f.) Summerh. (*Ascotainia penangiana* Ridl., *Tainia penangiana* Hk.f.)
Pbs. ovoid to flagon-shaped. 1–2" tall, usually about 1" in diam, at base, clothed with brown fibrous sheaths. Lf. solitary, with a slender stalk to 8" long, the lamina folded, to 14" long and 2¾" wide. Infls. to 2½' tall, with few to several fls. in a loose apical, erect rac. Fls. almost 2" across, lasting well, the spreading ss. and ps. pale yellow with 5–7 slender red or purple longitudinal lines, the lip 3-lbd., the erect rounded lat. lbs. white, the midlb. ovate, acute, white with a yellow blotch and 3 yellowish keels, the spur small. Spring. (I, H) Malay Peninsula.

A. Elmeri (Ames) A.D.Hawkes (*Tainia Elmeri* Ames, *Tainia inamoena* Krzl., *Ascotainia Elmeri* Ames). Pbs. clustered, pear-shaped, to 1½" tall, the solitary lf. with slender petiole, to 12" long, the often undulate-margined blade narrow and thin-textured. Infl. erect, to 2' tall, with several fls. in a lax rac. Fls. pretty, faintly fragrant, to under 1" long, the ss. and ps. usually brownish-yellow, often flushed darker, ascending and flaring outwards at tips. Lip 3-lbd., with a small basal spur, white, marked on the middle of the disc with dull red. Spring. (I, H) Philippines: Luzon and Mindanao, at low to medium elevations in forests.

ANKYLOCHEILOS Summerh.

Described in 1943, **Ankylocheilos Coxii** Summerh. is to date the only known member of the genus, this a diminutive leafless epiphytic orchid of the subtribe *Sarcanthinae* from Africa's Ghana. Vaguely allied to *Microcoelia* Ldl., it differs materially from that group in details of the tiny, complex, orange-yellow flowers. It is as yet unknown in our collections, and is an exceptionally rare orchid even in herbaria.

Nothing is known of the genetic affinities of *Ankylocheilos*.

CULTURE: Presumably as for *Polyrrhiza* and other tropical leafless epiphytes. (H)

ANOCHILUS Rolfe

Two species of *Anochilus* are known to date, both of these formerly included in *Pterygodium* Sw. of the subtribe *Disperidinae*, from which genus they are segregated on technical details of the rather small, but complex, racemose flowers. Terrestrial orchids, from southern Africa, they do not appear to be present in our collections at this time.

Nothing is known concerning the genetic affinities of *Anochilus*.

CULTURE: Presumably as for *Disa* and *Caladenia*. (I)

ANOECTOCHILUS Bl.
(*Anecochilus* Bl., *Chrysobaphus* Roxb.)

The genus *Anoectochilus* contains an estimated twenty species of scarce and very refractory orchids, known collectively as the 'Jewel Orchids'.[1] Primarily terrestrial (a few of them sometimes are found on heavily mossy rocks or on the bases of moss-hung trees) in habit,

[1] Members of several other orchid genera which possess variegated or mottled foliage are also often called by this name.

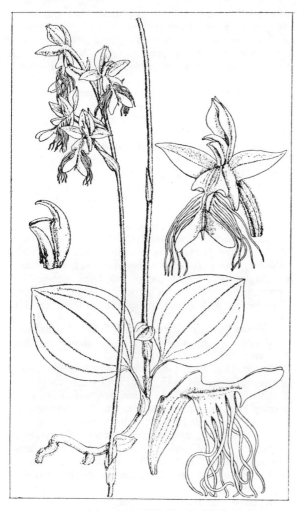

Anoectochilus elatior Ldl. [*Icones Plantarum*]

they are native over a huge region, extending from the Himalayas of India to New Caledonia, with large numbers of species in Indonesia. Unlike the vast majority of orchids, these plants are not cultivated for their flowers—which are typically rather small and insignificant—but rather for the magnificent, variegated, velvety foliage. Allied to such genera as *Zeuxine* Ldl., *Hetaeria* Bl., *Vrydagzynea* Bl., *Dossinia* E.Morr., *Macodes* Bl., and *Haemaria* Ldl., they are today among the rarest—and at the same time most desirable—of cultivated orchids. Within the past few years, however, considerable interest has been shown in them, and several of the more important and showy species are now to be encountered in a few particularly choice collections.

Anoectochilus Roxburghii has been crossed with *Haemaria discolor* Ldl., to produce the rare and delightful *Anoectomaria x Dominyi*.

CULTURE: The cultural requirements of this genus are difficult to formulate briefly, since almost every component species seems to require slightly different treatment. The principal requisites, however, appear to be the following: (1) A perfectly-drained compost, as rich and porous as possible; (2) High temperatures and humidity

at all times; (3) Shade from direct sun-exposure; and (4) Disturbance of the root-system as infrequently as possible. A compost consisting of equal parts of shredded osmunda or tree-fern fibre, sphagnum moss, porous pea-size gravel or crushed pumice, and leaf-mould, has been recommended as satisfactory. Greenhouse culture is obligatory except in tropical countries, and many authorities suggest growing these highly fragile and excessively temperamental plants under bell-jars to assure adequate humidity and protection from abrupt temperature changes. The members of this genus are not recommended for the amateur hobbyist, but the mere fact that they have been in cultivation for more than one hundred years indicates that, with a little extra caution and attention on the part of the collector, their rather peculiar cultural wants may be met and the full beauty of the plants realized. (H)

A. albolineatus Par. & Rchb.f.

Similar in habit to *A. geniculatus* Ridl. Lvs. velvety, dark purplish, the intricate branching veins red, about $2\frac{1}{2}''$ long and $1\frac{1}{2}''$ wide, few in number, forming a rather ascending rosette, sharp-pointed. Infl. to about 5″ tall, usually about 3–5-fld. Fls. about $\frac{1}{4}''$ long or more, white, with reddish hairs on the outside of the ss., the lip fimbriate marginally, very complex in structure. Spring–summer. (H) Burma; Malay Peninsula.

A. geniculatus Ridl.

St. short, rather stout, with about 4 lvs. in a loose rosette. Lvs. velvety, very dark green with an intricate branching network of gold or reddish veins, about $2\frac{1}{2}''$ long and $1\frac{1}{2}''$ wide, sheathing the st. basally. Infl. to about 6″ tall, with a few-fld. rac. at the apex. Fls. about $\frac{1}{2}''$ across, white, with reddish hairs on the outside of the ss., the lip with 2 pink spots, fimbriate marginally. Spring–summer. (H) Malay Peninsula: Penang to Singapore.

A. regalis Bl. (*Satyrium repens* L., *Anoectochilus setaceus* Ldl. not Bl.)

Lvs. few, forming a rather loose rosette, to 2″ long and $1\frac{1}{2}''$ wide, very dark velvety-green with an extremely complex branching network of golden-yellow veins. Infl. about 12″ tall, with a few-fld., rather dense rac. at the apex. Fls. less than $\frac{3}{4}''$ long, the ss. and ps. greenish, the complex fringed lip white, long-spurred. Spring. (H) Southern India; Ceylon.

A. Reinwardtii Bl.

Rather similar to *A. regalis* Bl., but the lvs. velvety reddish-black-green, with extremely prominent, copper-gold veins in an intricate network. Infl. about 12″ tall, with a few-fld. dense rac. in the apical portion. Fls. less than $\frac{3}{4}''$ long, the ss. and ps. grey-green with brownish tips, the fringed lip white, the ss. hairy outside. Spring–early summer. (H) Sumatra; Java.

A. Roxburghii (Wall.) Ldl. (*Chrysobaphus Roxburghii* Wall.)

Similar in appearance and dimensions to *A. regalis* Bl., but with a distinct golden velvety zone in the median part of each lf., and with a reddish suffusion towards each margin. Fls. rather similar to those of the other sp. in colour, but with a differently-shaped lip. Summer. (H) Himalayas.

A. setaceus Bl.

Similar in appearance and size to *A. regalis* Bl., but with the lvs. velvety greenish-black with an intricate network of branching and re-branching silver-white veins. Fls. about ¾″ long, the ss. and ps. greenish with brown-red tips, the fringed lip white or whitish. Summer. (H) Java.

A. sikkimensis King & Pantl.

Lvs. few, to 2½″ long by 1¼″ broad, very dark red with velvety sheen and strong gold veins, underneath dull red. Infl. erect, to 9″ tall, the peduncle fuzzy. Fls. intricate, ¾″ long, olive-green and white, the toothed lip white, the teeth and spur green. Col. green. Autumn. (C, I) Sikkim, at 3000–5000 feet elevation.

ANSELLIA Ldl.

This is a genus made up of a single highly variable species of epiphytic or lithophytic orchid which is widespread and often very common in tropical and South Africa. Peculiarly enough a member of the subtribe *Polystachyinae*, *Ansellia* is not as yet particularly frequent in cultivation, although the facility with which the plant is brought into flower, its attractive appearance even

Ansellia africana Ldl. [B.S.WILLIAMS]

when not in bloom, and the spectacular show put on by its branching inflorescence all make it ideally suited to the amateur or professional's purpose. The blotched, sleek markings of the large and long-lasting flowers has given this genus the common name of 'Leopard Orchid'.

Hybrids between several of the forms of *Ansellia africana* have been made in Hawaii, and are now often more readily available in the trade than is the true original—and variable—species.

CULTURE: *Ansellia* is easily grown, even by the amateur hobbyist, provided he can provide the plant with the heat and humidity of the greenhouse—unless, of course, he resides in a warm climate. Strictly tropical in origin, the plant does best in a bright spot in a perfectly-drained, rather large pot. It thrives either in straight tight-packed osmunda fibre, or in a mixture of equal parts of chopped tree-fern fibre and dust-free bark preparation. While in active growth, it benefits by liberal applications of water, but a slight lessening of moisture and humidity should be afforded as the pseudobulbs mature, for optimum flower-production. Heavy feeders, the specimens benefit by frequent applications of fertilizer. (H)

A. africana Ldl. (*Ansellia confusa* N.E.Br., *A. congoensis* Rodig., *A. gigantea* Rchb.f., *A. nilotica* N.E.Br., *Cymbidium Sandersoni* Harv.)

Pbs. st.-like, almost cylindrical in most specimens, sometimes club-shaped or spindle-shaped, to more than 2′ tall, often yellowish. Lvs. borne mostly near pb.-apex, usually 7 or so, thinly leathery, gracefully arching, to about 12″ long and 1¼″ wide. Infls. terminal, often very stout, to 3′ long, rather loosely many-fld., typically branching. Fls. about 2½″ long in the largest phases, spreading, rather delicately fragrant during the hot hours of the day, long-lasting, the ss. and ps. varying in colour from almost green to bright yellow, more or less spotted, blotched or transversely barred with pale or dark chocolate-brown. Lip 3-lbd., the lat. lbs. erect around the col., all parts yellow or yellowish with dark or pale brown veins, the disc with several yellow keels. Spring–summer. (H) Tropical and South Africa.

ANTHOGONIUM Wall. ex Ldl.

Anthogonium contains a single species of relatively seldom-grown terrestrial or rock-dwelling orchid from the Himalayan regions of India and China, which is allied to *Spathoglottis* Bl., and rather simulates a small member of that genus in vegetative and floral structure. Leaves, numbering but one or two in most cases, are stalked and customarily deciduous during at least part of the year.

No hybrids have as yet been effected in this genus, and nothing is known of its genetic affinities.

CULTURE: As for *Bletia* and *Phaius*, though the species is generally more hardy than those orchids. (C, I)

A. gracile Ldl. (*Anthogonium Griffithii* Rchb.f.)

Pbs. ovoid, to ¾″ long, produced on a slender creeping rhiz. Lvs. 1–3, deciduous, stalked, narrowly lanceolate, to 10″ long. Infls. erect, slender, to almost 18″ tall, with a branched or simple, rather dense rac. at the apex.

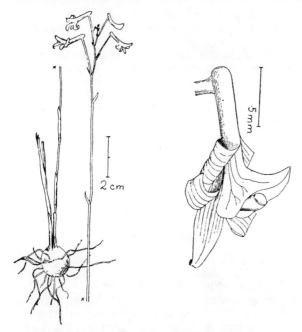

Anthogonium gracile Ldl. [*Orchids of Thailand*]

Fls. to 1″ long, usually not fully opening, rose-pink, the lip customarily with some bright scarlet spots; bracts and pedicellate ovaries usually pink-flushed. Ss. connate to form a narrow tube, which is swollen basally and free apically, the dors. one linear and thrust forward, the lats. oblong and revolute. Ps. borne within the sepaline tube, linear. Lip narrow basally, the lamina flabelliform. Autumn. (C, I) India; China.

APHYLLORCHIS Bl.

This is a genus of about twelve species of little-known, rare, saprophytic orchids, widespread in the region extending from Ceylon and northern India throughout Malaya and Indonesia to New Guinea. A member of the subtribe *Cephalantherinae*, *Aphyllorchis* is apparently not present in contemporary collections, and it seems doubtful that its peculiar cultural requirements would allow the plants to be grown for more than a single season in any event.

Nothing is known of the genetic affinities of this strange group.

CULTURE: Presumably as for *Corallorrhiza* and other saprophytes, though tropical temperatures must naturally prevail. (H)

APLECTRUM Torr.

This is a genus of a single species, native in temperate North America, in Canada and a large portion of the United States. Allied to *Cremastra* Ldl. and to *Tipularia* Nutt., the plants are terrestrial in habit (they apparently have a saprophytic stage early in life as well), and commonly inhabit moist, rich spots in woodlands or in swamps. Not common in collections, they transplant readily from the wild and are sufficiently attractive and

interesting—whether in flower or not—to warrant attention by specialists.

Nothing is known of the genetic ties of this genus.

CULTURE: A perfectly drained, loose, rich compost of wood loam and gritty sand, in pots, seems to suit these plants best. Shady conditions and a rather distinct resting-period after completion of the new growth will generally assure flowering, although *Aplectrum* does not, in every case, bloom annually. (C, I)

A. hyemale (Muhl. ex Willd.) Torr. (*Cymbidium hyemale* Muhl. ex Willd., *Aplectrum spicatum* BSP)
Rootstock usually consisting of several almost globular corms which are connected by slender stolons. Lf. solitary, appearing in autumn, decaying before the fls. are produced (in spring), stalked basally, broad above, dark green with whitish nerves or stripes, sometimes purple-tinged, to about 7″ long and 3″ wide. Infls. erect, sheathed in basal part, with a loose rac. in the

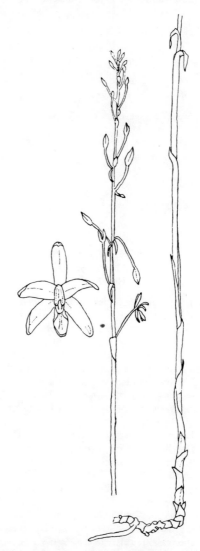

Aphyllorchis unguiculata Rolfe ex Downie [A.D.HAWKES, AFTER *Orchids of Thailand*]

upper portion. Fls. about 1″ across, varying from greenish or yellowish to almost pure white, the lip white marked with magenta, not opening widely in most instances. Spring. (C, I) Eastern Canada; United States (west to Arizona).

APOROSTYLIS Rupp & Hatch

But a single species of *Aporostylis* is known to date, this **A. bifolia** (Hk.) Rupp & Hatch, a rather rare and not well-known terrestrial orchid native to New Zealand. In the past it has been known as *Caladenia bifolia* Hk. and as *Chiloglottis Traversii* FvM., but it differs from both of those groups (and from all other genera of the subtribe *Caladeniinae*) in critical details of the flowers. At this time, *Aporostylis* does not appear to be present in cultivation.

Nothing is known regarding the genetic affinities of this peculiar genus.

CULTURE: Presumably as for *Caladenia*. (C, I)

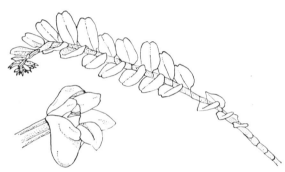

Appendicula reflexa Bl. [A.D.HAWKES, AFTER HOLTTUM]

APPENDICULA Bl.

(*Conchochilus* Hassk., *Metachilum* Ldl., *Scoliochilus* Rchb.f.)

The more than forty species of *Appendicula* are today virtually unknown in any collections save the choicest ones, being of almost exclusively 'botanical' interest. Generally bearing very small, rather dull-coloured flowers in short inflorescences, they can scarcely be classed as showy plants, although many of them are vegetatively very handsome, the densely leafy, often pendulous stems resembling some kind of fleshy fern rather than an orchid. Native principally in Indonesia, outlying members of the group extend to as far away as the Himalayas, the Philippines, and New Caledonia. The genus is allied to *Chilopogon* Schltr. and to *Cyphochilus* Schltr., and is a member of the subtribe *Podochilinae*.

Nothing is known of the genetic affinities of this interesting group.

CULTURE: As for the tropical species of *Dendrobium* and *Bulbophyllum*. Basket-culture is recommended for the erect species, but rafts or tree-fern slabs should be utilized for those of pendulous or arching habit, for best effect. (I, H)

A. cristata Bl. (*Conchochilus oppositiflorus* Hassk., *Appendicula longepedunculata* Rolfe, *Podochilus cristatus* Schltr.)

Pls. to about 4′ long, usually semi-pendulous. Sts. flattened, thickly covered with lvs. Lvs. to 2″ long, fleshy, deep green. Infls. both lateral and terminal, the peduncle to 12″ long, densely 10–20-fld. Fls. less than ¼″ long, greenish-yellow with brown nerves. Lip golden-yellow, with some intricate calli on the disc. May–June. (H) Java; Borneo.

A. lucida Ridl. (*Podochilus lucidus* Schltr.)

Pls. to about 10″ long, most erect, sometimes arching, the sts. densely leafy. Lvs. about ½″ long, glossy polished green, rather thickly fleshy. Infls. lateral, short, few-fld. Fls. less than ¼″ across, whitish, the lip complex. Spring. (H) Malay Peninsula; Borneo.

A. reflexa Bl. (*Appendicula cordata* Hk.f., *A. robusta* Ridl., *A. viridiflora* Teijsm. & Binn., *Podochilus reflexus* Schltr.)

Pls. to about 2′ tall, the sts. erect, densely leafy. Lvs. about 1½″ long, oblong, obtuse, glossy bright green. Infls. lateral, short, dense, racemose. Fls. rather simulating those of *A. lucida* Ridl., but larger (about ¼″ across), greenish-white. Lip broadly oblong, white, reflexed apically. Spring–autumn. (H) Malay Peninsula and Sumatra to New Guinea.

ARACHNIS Bl.
(*Arachnanthe* Bl.)

The genus *Arachnis* consists of about seventeen species, widespread in the area extending from the Himalayas to New Guinea and the Solomon Islands, with particularly large development in Indonesia and Malaya. Allied to *Vanda* R.Br., *Renanthera* Lour., and *Dimorphorchis* Rolfe, these are very popular orchids with enthusiasts especially in the tropics, and are among the showiest of the monopodial groups. In the wild, they are found as epiphytes, as lithophytes, or as terrestrials, often in boggy places, from which their copiously rooting clambering stems extend up neighbouring trees. Vegetatively, the members of *Arachnis* exhibit considerable variance in structure, ranging from tall vines many feet in length to plants with abbreviated, close-leaved stems less than a foot tall. The leaves are typically abundant and persist for many years; shape of foliage varies from species to species, and is sometimes diagnostic. The flowers are mostly produced in considerable quantities, on simple racemes or branching panicles, and typically are sufficiently large and showy to offer much in the way of horticultural value. Colour-range is considerable, though greens, yellows, browns, and purples predominate; the sepals and petals are generally blotched or otherwise marked with a different hue from that of the lip, and their formation in some species gives rise to the common name of 'Scorpion Orchid'.

The Malayan *Arachnis x Maingayi* has been shown to be a natural hybrid. In addition, artificially induced hybridization in *Arachnis* has been extensive in recent years, particularly in Malaya and Hawaii. Some magnificent products have been raised through interspecific breeding within the genus itself, and in multigeneric crosses with allied groups such as *Vanda*, *Renanthera*, *Aërides*, *Vandopsis*, etc. Despite these efforts, however, considerable additional experimental breeding yet remains to be done, particularly in the multigeneric field.

CULTURE: The tall-growing, vine-like Arachnis do best if grown in specially prepared, raised beds, in a perfectly-drained compost made as rich as possible, this to include shredded osmunda (or tree-fern fibre), sphagnum moss, gritty white sand, and manure or other fertilizing materials; addition of loam, leaf-mould, and perhaps even portions of the bark preparations may also be made in moderation, with good effect. Full sun-exposure is required in most cases for proper production of flowers, and water should be given in large quantities at all times. If grown in pots, under glass, the plants must be subjected to as much sun as possible, and even then they usually will not flower until they have reached a considerable size; large pots should be used to accommodate the rampant root-system, with copious drainage. Liberal, regular applications of fertilizers prove beneficial to these robust, heavy-feeding orchids. The short-stemmed species thrive when grown like the tropical Vandas. (I, H)

A. Cathcartii (Ldl.) J.J.Sm. (*Vanda Cathcartii* Ldl., *Esmeralda Cathcartii* Rchb.f., *Arachnanthe Cathcartii* Bth.)

Sts. usually pendulous, sometimes branching at base, to 6′ long and more, leafy throughout. Lvs. linear-oblong, to 8″ long and 1½″ wide, with a distinctly unequally bilobed apex, very leathery, recurved. Infls. rather stout, pendulous or horizontal, 3–6-fld., to 10″ long. Fls. 3–3½″ across, very waxy, highly fragrant, long-lived, the similar ss. and ps. pale yellow, transversely barred with numerous wavy, often confluent red-brown bands, orbicular-oblong, concave. Lip 3-lbd., the lat. lbs. incurved, white streaked with red, small, roundish-oblong; midlb. yellow, reniform, marginally obscurely toothed, the centre very thick with a crenate margin; callus 2-parted, basal, fleshy, pale yellow spotted with red. Col. very thick, buff-yellow flushed round the stigmatic surface and anther with red-brown. Spring-summer. (I, H) Himalayas.

A. Clarkei (Rchb.f.) J.J.Sm. (*Arachnanthe Clarkei* Rchb.f., *Esmeralda Clarkei* Rolfe.)

Sts. elongated, rather thick, often pendulous or arching, to 6′ long and more, mostly leafy thoughout. Lvs. very thick and leathery, linear-oblong, to 6″ long and 1½″ wide, unequally bilobed at apex. Infls. ascending to pendulous, to 8″ long, loosely 2–4-fld. Fls. about 3″ across, fleshy, very fragrant, long-lived. Ss. and ps. bright chestnut-brown with yellow transverse stripes, the ss. linear-oblong, cuneate at base, the lats. falcately curved; ps. slightly narrower than ss. Lip almost as long as ps., 3-lbd., the erect lat. lbs. light yellow, often almost white, streaked with red, roundish; midlb. chestnut-brown with 7–9 radiating white keels, of which the central one is broadest, broadly roundish with a small lobule at the apex. Summer–autumn. (I, H) Himalayas.

A. flos-aëris (L.) Rchb.f. (*Epidendrum flos-aëris* L., *Limodorum flos-aëris* Sw., *Renanthera flos-aëris* Rchb.f., *Renanthera moschifera* Hassk., *Renanthera arachnites* Ldl., *Aërides arachnites* Sw., *Arachnis moschifera* Bl., *Arachnanthe flos-aëris* Rchb.f., *Arachnanthe moschifera* Bl.)

Sts. stout, climbing, to more than 15′ tall, often branching, the lvs. rather distant. Lvs. to 7″ long and 2″ wide, narrowed gradually towards the 2-lbd. apex, curved and slightly twisted, the edges smooth and not recurved at base. Infls. simple or branched, ascending or drooping, to about 4′ long, the fls. rather numerous but widely spaced. Fls. to more than 4″ long and 3½″ wide, fleshy, glossy, with a strong musky odour, long-lived. Ss. and ps. pale yellow-green with broad and irregular dark purple-brown bars and spots, the ps. typically down-curving, the lat. ss. incurving. Lip pale yellow-green, purple-brown, and dull-purple, complex, the midlb. with a low keel (thus differing from *A. x Maingayi* (Hk.f.) Schltr., which has a narrow midlb. with a high keel). Mostly during the autumn months, but often ever-blooming in the tropics. (H) Malay Peninsula; Sumatra; Java; Borneo.

A. Hookeriana (Rchb.f.) Rchb.f. (*Renanthera Hookeriana* Rchb.f., *Arachnanthe alba* Ridl., *Arachnis alba* Schltr.)

Rather similar in habit to *A. flos-aëris* (L.) Rchb.f., but the lvs. closer together, stiff, obliquely ascending, to 3½″ long, widest near base, the edges decurved, the frilled base slightly toothed. Infls. erect, simple, to 2′ tall, the rachis purplish. Fls. 6–8, about 2½″ tall and 2¼″ wide, fleshy, fragrant, long-lived. Ss. and ps. creamy-white, yellowish towards the widened tips, with very small purple spots mainly in the middle third. Lip mostly purple or whitish with purple stripes. Summer-autumn. (H) Malay Peninsula; Riauw Archipelago; Borneo.

A. x Maingayi (Hk.f.) Schltr. (*Arachnanthe Maingayi* Hk.f.)

Natural hybrid between *A. Hookeriana* (Rchb.f.) Rchb.f. and *A. flos-aëris* (L.) Rchb.f., rather similar in all parts to the latter parent. Sts. turning red-brown when old. Lvs. stiff, nearly straight, the edges recurved and slightly toothed near the base, about 5″ long. Infls. and fl.-shape much as in the other sp., the fls. slightly smaller. Ss. and ps. whitish or faintly pinkish with bands and blotches of pink or light purple. Lip whitish or pinkish. Mostly summer. (H) Malay Peninsula; Borneo.

A. annamensis (Rolfe) J.J.Sm. (*Arachnanthe annamensis* Rolfe, *Renanthera annamensis* Rolfe). Rather similar in habit to *A. flos-aëris* (L.) Rchb.f., the sts. to several feet in length, rather densely leafy. Lvs. to 3″ long and ¾″ wide, shortly 2-lbd. at the apex. Infls. erect, to 2′ tall, the rac. loosely many-fld. Fls. about 1½″ long, the ss. and ps. yellow with red spots and marks, the ps. with a distinct pale red blotch near the apex. Lip pale scarlet-red. Spring. (H) Viet-Nam.

A. breviscapa (J.J.Sm.) J.J.Sm. (*Arachnanthe breviscapa* J.J.Sm.) Sts. relatively short, fleshy, the lvs. rather close together. Lvs. about 8″ long, to 2½″ wide, unequally bilobed at the apex. Infls. usually several at once, from the sts. opposite the lf.-junction, to 2″ long, 2–6-fld. Fls. very waxy, fragrant, almost 3″ across and long, the ss. and ps. wider than most of the other spp. of the genus, undulate marginally, cream-white or yellow-white, with large irregular deep or pale brown markings. Lip small, whitish or cream, with a slender upcurving tip. Summer. (H) Borneo.

ARETHUSA [Gronov.] L.

Two species of *Arethusa* are known to date, one widespread in temperate North America, the other in Japan. The latter does not seem to be in contemporary cultivation, but **Arethusa bulbosa** L. is occasionally seen in choice collections, and is certainly among the most handsome of the boreal American orchids. Found principally in bogs and dense swamps, often growing in beds of sphagnum moss, its large solitary flower, produced in spring and summer, is of remarkable beauty and intricacy, and readily attracts the attention of all who see it, whether in the wild or in the garden.

Nothing is known of the genetic affinities of *Arethusa*.

CULTURE: The cultural requirements of this genus are not readily met, but some enthusiasts have notable success with it in their collections. An extremely porous, well-drained compost—as intensely acid as possible—is obligatory. Growing primarily in shaded, cool, very moist spots, these conditions must be emulated under cultivation as well. Since the root-system consists of but a single corm, its constitution is rather delicate, and it must be treated with care at all times. (C)

A. bulbosa L.

Corms bulbous, subterranean, less than ¾″ in diam. Scape slender, erect, developed prior to the lf., which is grass-like, solitary, and attains a length of as much as 9″. Fls. solitary (very rarely paired), to 2″ long, very handsome and fragrant, the ss. and ps. light or dark rose-purple. Lip large, the forward part sharply downthrust, mostly whitish or pale rose-purple, basally yellow, purple-tipped, the intricate fringed medial area sometimes with purple blotches or spots. Spring–summer. (C) Canada; United States (south to North Carolina).

ARETHUSANTHA Finet

Arethusantha bletioides Finet, the only known member of the genus, is an extremely rare and very incompletely-known terrestrial orchid which has apparently been collected on only a single occasion. Native of 'the Indies' (presumably what is now called Indonesia), the vegetative portions of the plant somewhat resemble a *Bletia*, while the flowers superficially simulate those of *Arethusa*. It is probably best placed in the subtribe *Bletillinae*, and is of course not present in our collections at this time.

Nothing is known of the genetic ties of *Arethusantha*.

CULTURE: Unknown, but possibly as for *Bletia*, with tropical temperatures requisite. (H)

ARMODORUM Breda
(*Arrhynchium* Ldl. & Paxt.)

This is a genus of three known species, two of which are present in contemporary collections, although they must be classified as very rare orchids. *Armodorum* is a member of the oft-confused '*Vanda* alliance' of the subtribe *Sarcanthinae*, and its components have in the past been relegated to several other genera, as is evidenced by the synonymy indicated below. They are principally epiphytic plants, rather simulating *Arachnis* in habit, distributed from Assam and Burma to Siam, Sumatra, and Java. The rather large flowers are produced in relatively lengthy racemes, and are sufficiently conspicuous to be of importance to collectors and breeders of fine orchids.

At this time *Armodorum* has been utilized by the hybridists on only one or two occasions, having been crossed with *Arachnis* to produce *Armodachnis*. It seems entirely possible that the members of the group will prove, upon further experimental breeding, to be freely compatible genetically with at least certain of the allied genera of the subtribe *Sarcanthinae*.

CULTURE: As for *Arachnis* and *Vanda*. (H)

A. labrosum (Ldl.) Schltr. (*Arrhynchium labrosum* Ldl., *Arachnanthe bilinguis* Hk.f., *Arachnis labrosa* J.J.Sm., *Renanthera bilinguis* Rchb.f., *Renanthera labrosa* Rchb.f.)

St. clambering, elongate, rather vine-like in time, to several feet in length, rather slender. Lvs. produced at rather distant intervals, or distichous and close together, linear to linear-ligulate, unequally 2-lbd. at apex, keeled below, rigidly leathery, to 8″ long and ¾″ wide. Infls. to about 8″ long, horizontal or ascending, usually with about 3–6 rather distant fls., these usually all open at once. Fls. long-lasting, waxy, fragrant, to about 1½″ in diam., the ss. and ps. yellow blotched and margined with brown or red-brown. Ss. and somewhat smaller ps. narrowly oblong, obtuse. Lip 3-lbd., with very small lat. lbs., the midlb. oblong, obtuse, white or yellowish, with 3 brownish raised keels near the base; spur cylindric, curved towards the front, somewhat shorter than the lip. Spring–summer. (H) Assam; Burma; ? Java.

A. Sulingii (Bl.) Schltr. (*Aërides Sulingii* Bl., *Arachnis Sulingii* Rchb.f., *Armodorum distichum* Breda)

St. rather robust, elongate, to about 4½′ long. Lvs. rather closely placed, ligulate, apically 2-lbd., thickly leathery, dark green, 7–14″ long, to 2″ broad. Infls. about 6-fld., to almost 8″ long. Fls. fleshy, lasting well, fragrant, about 1¼″ in diam., the ss. and ps. greenish-yellow outside, brown inside, spreading, linear-lanceolate, obtuse. Lip rather small, 3-lbd., the erect lat. lbs. pale yellow streaked inside with brown, the midlb. thickly fleshy, convex, obtuse, pale yellow sparsely blotched with dark brown. Summer. (H) Sumatra; Java.

ARNOTTIA A.Rich.

A small genus of two known species, both restricted in their distribution to the Mascarene Islands, *Arnottia* is not present in contemporary collections, although both **A. inermis** S.Moore and **A. mauritiana** A.Rich. are rather attractive terrestrial plants, somewhat simulating a small *Cynorkis*, to which genus they are allied.

Nothing is known of the genetic affinities of this group.

CULTURE: Presumably as for *Cynorkis*. (I, H)

ARPOPHYLLUM LaLl. & Lex.
(*Arophyllum* Endl.)

A member of the subtribe *Ponerinae*, the genus *Arpophyllum* contains, according to most recent studies, but two species, both of which are in cultivation today, though they are far from common orchids in our collections, albeit very desirable ones. Exceedingly spectacular, epiphytic, lithophytic, or terrestrial plants, their range extends from Mexico to Colombia. Highly variable in both vegetative and floral dimensions, they are readily identified—generically at least—by their slender, stem-like pseudobulbs (sometimes more than a foot tall), topped by a single fleshy, narrow, usually erect leaf. The small, vividly hued flowers are borne in very dense, elongate, cylindrical racemes, which make the species singularly handsome when in bloom, and give them their vernacular name of 'Hyacinth Orchids'.

Hybridization has not, as yet, been attempted in *Arpophyllum*, and nothing is known of its genetic affinities.

CULTURE: Generally as for the pseudobulbous, tropical Epidendrums. The Arpophyllums do best in perfectly drained pots, filled with a compost consisting of equal parts of chopped sphagnum moss and chopped tree-fern fibre. Though they should be kept moist at all times, they are highly intolerant of stale or sour conditions at the roots, and will soon perish if such are permitted to persist. They do best in an airy, semi-shaded position in the greenhouse. Moderately weak applications of fertilizer are beneficial at frequent intervals. (I, H)

A. alpinum Ldl. (*Arpophyllum medium* Rchb.f.)

Pbs. arising at intervals from a stout creeping rhiz., to more than 12″ tall, usually less than ½″ in diam., mostly concealed by several large, spathe-like, warty sheaths. Lf. solitary, rigidly fleshy, linear-ligulate, acute to subobtuse, to almost 2′ long, less than 1½″ wide. Infls. rather long-stalked, the rac. cylindrical, very densely many-fld., to 6″ long and more than 1½″ in diam., the pedicellate ovaries of the fls. dark brown-purple. Fls. less than ¾″ across, purplish-pink, the lip uppermost, often paler in colour. Spring. (I, H) Mexico; Guatemala; Honduras.

A. spicatum LaLl. & Lex. (*Arpophyllum cardinale* Lind. & Rchb.f., *A. giganteum* Hartw. ex Ldl., *A. jamaicense* Schltr., *A. stenostachyum* Schltr.)

Pls. to almost 4′ tall in robust phases, rather similar to the other sp., but the pb.-sheaths smooth, the pedicellate ovaries sparsely furnished with black hispid glands (not dark brown-purple), and the lip smaller. Fls. slightly smaller than those of *A. alpinum* Ldl., varying in hue from rose-red to purple-pink or rose-pink. Spring. (I, H) Mexico; Guatemala; Honduras; Costa Rica; Colombia; Jamaica.

ARUNDINA Bl.

This is a small genus (possibly consisting of only a single highly variable entity), widespread in the region extending from southern China and the Himalayas, throughout Malaysia, Indonesia and adjacent areas to the Pacific Islands. Closely allied to *Dilochia* Bl., it is generally placed in the small subtribe *Thuniinae*. Tall-growing terrestrial plants, rather reminiscent of *Sobralia* in general vegetative appearance, Arundinas are popular with orchidists, particularly in the tropics, where they are often used as stately ornamentals in the garden. In certain areas, notably the Hawaiian Islands, **A. graminifolia** (D.Don) Hochr. has become naturalized, and may be found growing 'wild' with more or less freedom.

Hybrids have not as yet been made within this genus, although critical breeding of some of the finer forms should prove productive. Holttum has suggested that bigeneric crosses with *Dilochia* should give a more open and attractive inflorescence.

CULTURE: Grown out of doors, Arundinas are of singularly easy cultivation; if confined in pots in a greenhouse, flowers are not always produced with the ease otherwise attained. Since, as individuals, the plants are generally not particularly free-flowering, it is recommended that they be grown in quantity, preferably in specially-prepared outdoor beds (provided, of course, that climatic conditions are sufficiently equable to permit this). Since perfect drainage is essential, the bed should be dug out to a depth of about eight inches, and a one- or two-inch layer of broken crock or other drainage material added to it. The remainder of the bed should then be filled with a mixture consisting of the following ingredients, in about equal proportions: rich loam, chopped osmunda or tree-fern fibre, shredded leaves, and dried manure or commercial orchid fertilizer. The plants should not have their bases buried in the compost, and if they are top-heavy, should be supported by sticks and ties. A sunny spot, with liberal applications of water and fertilizer while the plants are in active growth—which is virtually throughout the year in the tropics—plus temperatures as warm as possible, suits these handsome orchids well. If grown in pots under glass, the above-noted compost should prove satisfactory, and when the warm summer months

Arundina graminifolia (D.Don) Hochr. [B.S.WILLIAMS]

arrive, the plants should be set outside, to facilitate flowering. Large, well-drained pots should be used. (H)

A. graminifolia (D.Don) Hochr. (*Bletia graminifolia* D.Don, *Arundina bambusifolia* Ldl., *A. speciosa* Bl., *A. revoluta* Hk.f., *A. densa* Ldl.)

Sts. close together on the rhiz., to 8′ tall in robust specimens, slender, erect, leafy throughout, the lf.-sheaths overlapping. Lvs. linear, rather grass-like, sharp-pointed, to 12″ long, usually not more than 1½″ wide. Infls. terminal, usually simple, prominently bracted, gradually elongating and producing a succession of fls. 1 or 2 at a time, the fls. lasting about 3 days apiece. Fls. to 2½″ long (rarely more), rather simulating those of a small *Cattleya*, but with the lat. ss. close together behind the lip, with a delicate fragrance. Ss. and ps. white to pale rose-mauve, of a handsome glittering texture. Lip tubular at base (thus enclosing the col.) usually bright rose-purple at apex, the throat paler, veined with purple, with a yellow patch on the disc. The pure white, yellow-throated fma. **alba** hort. is sometimes encountered, but it is rare. Throughout the year, often almost ever-blooming. (H) South China and the Himalayas throughout Malaysia, Indonesia, and adjacent areas to the Pacific Islands (Tahiti).

ASCOCENTRUM Schltr.

Allied to *Vanda* R.Br. and to *Ascoglossum* Schltr., four of the nine known species of *Ascocentrum* are present in contemporary collections, almost always being grown under the erroneous name of *Saccolabium*. Typically dwarf, compact-growing monopodial epiphytes (rarely lithophytes), their range extends from southern China (Yunnan), Formosa, and the Philippines to Java and Borneo. Producing their myriads of small, extremely bright-hued long-lived flowers in stiffly erect, cylindrical racemes, the Ascocentrums are among the most delightful of the sarcanthad orchids, and are heartily recommended to the orchidist, whether amateur or professional.

To date, registered hybrids in which *Ascocentrum* figures include *Ascocenda* (× *Vanda*) and *Ascofinetia* (× *Neofinetia*), both of these charming groups. Additional experimental breeding with allied groups of the 'Vanda alliance' is being carried out, and soon we will have other representatives of this fascinating assemblage available for cultivation.

CULTURE: As for the tropical Vandas. (I, H)

A. ampullaceum (Ldl.) Schltr. (*Aërides ampullaceum* Ldl., *Gastrochilus ampullaceus* O.Ktze., *Saccolabium ampullaceum* Ldl.)

Sts. to 10″ tall, generally much shorter, densely leafy throughout, the basal lvs. falling with age. Lvs. linear, deeply and irregularly cut and toothed at the apex, keeled beneath, 5–6″ long and ¾″ wide, rather thickly leathery. Infls. short-stalked, stiffly erect, often more than one produced simultaneously, to 6″ tall, very densely many-fld. Fls. about ½″ across (sometimes slightly larger), long-lived, deep rose or rose-magenta, the lip sometimes paler, the col. white, and the anther yellow.

Ss. and ps. similar, almost equal, obovate, spreading. Lip shorter than the other segms., linear, reflexed, produced at the base into a cylindric, compressed spur longer than the lamina, at the entrance of which are 2 rounded protuberances. Spring–early summer. (I, H) Himalayas; Burma.

A. curvifolium (Ldl.) Schltr. (*Saccolabium curvifolium* Ldl., *Gastrochilus curvifolius* O.Ktze.)

Rather closely allied to, and somewhat simulating *A. miniatum* (Ldl.) Schltr. Sts. seldom more than 5″ tall, stout, woody, covered with lf.-bases. Lvs. very rigid and fleshy, to 10″ long, about 1″ wide, linear, typically down-curving, irregularly cut and furnished with 2 sharp teeth at the apex. Racs. erect, very dense, to 6″ tall. Fls. about ½″ long, slightly less in horizontal expansion, extremely variable in hue, ranging from purple orange-scarlet through vivid vermilion to rich cinnabar-red, the lip with a pale orange median keel and 2 rather prominent tubercles at the base, the col. short, cinnabar-red, the anther purple or violet. May–June. (I, H) Himalayas.

A. Hendersonianum (Rchb.f.) Schltr. (*Saccolabium Hendersonianum* Rchb.f.)

Sts. usually less than 3″ tall, densely leafy. Lvs. few (usually 4–5), to 5″ long, thickly leathery, somewhat down-curving, narrowly ligulate, the apex subacute. Infls. racemose, stiffly erect, to 6″ tall, with up to 30 fls. Fls. about 1″ across, rather delicately fragrant, borne on pale green pedicellate ovaries, the ss. and ps. brilliant magenta-rose, the lip and spur mostly somewhat lighter. Spring. (H) Borneo.

A. miniatum (Ldl.) Schltr. (*Saccolabium miniatum* Ldl., *Gastrochilus miniatus* O.Ktze.)

Sts. usually less than 4″ tall, thick, woody, obscured by the persistent lf.-bases. Lvs. linear, very fleshy, rigid, 3–8″ long, usually less than ½″ wide, strongly keeled beneath, obliquely truncate or unequally 2-lbd. at apex. Infls. erect, to 5″ tall, very densely many-fld., cylindrical. Fls. about ¾″ across, variable in hue from bright orange through orange-yellow to brilliant vermilion-red. Ss. and ps. ovate-oblong, acute. Lip linear-oblong, obtuse, recurved, produced at base into a slender cylindric spur longer than the lamina, on each side of the opening of which are 2 small auricles. Col. very short, with a purple anther. Spring–early summer. (H) Himalayas to the Malay Peninsula, Java, and Borneo.

ASCOCHILOPSIS Carr

Ascochilopsis contains but a single species, a rather rare epiphytic monopodial orchid inhabiting the Malay Peninsula and Sumatra. Holttum (in *Fl. Malaya* 1: 701. 1953.) remarks concerning this unusual plant, which is evidently unknown in contemporary collections outside of its native haunts: 'It has the appearance of a small *Sarcochilus*, with roughened erect scape and thickened rachis bearing many very small flowers in succession close together, a few open at the same time; but the flowers lack a column-foot, and the lip consists

58

Ascocentrum Hendersonianum (Rchb.f.) Schltr. [VEITCH]

almost entirely of a spur joined immovably to the base of the column. The stipes of the pollinia is rather long, and the disc narrow.'

The single species of *Ascochilopsis* has not been utilized by the hybridists as yet, and nothing is known of its genetic affinity.

CULTURE: As required by the tropical epiphytic sarcanthads, such as Vandas, etc. (H)

A. myosurus (Ridl.) Carr. (*Saccolabium myosurus* Ridl.) Sts. to 3″ long, very branched, leafy apically. Lvs. 10 or so, to 8″ long and less than 1″ wide, linear-lanceolate, narrowed at base, apically narrowed and unequally biloped. Infls. often several together, erect, to 2″ long, the rachis very fleshy, distinctly roughened, set near apex with a few very small fls. which open successively. Fls. lasting one day, pale yellow, the lip white, the col. yellow, about $\frac{1}{4}$″ across, very insignificant. Summer. (H) Malay Peninsula; Sumatra.

ASCOGLOSSUM Schltr.

This is a genus of two known species of remarkably showy, monopodial epiphytes, allied to *Renanthera* Lour. and to *Ascocentrum* Schltr., native in New Guinea and the Moluccas. They are, unfortunately, today extremely rare in cultivation, but are so spectacular when in full bloom that further attention to them should be paid. Vegetatively simulating a *Renanthera* of rather small stature, the extremely numerous, rather sizeable flowers —produced in large, branching panicles—are among the most highly coloured of any of the sarcanthad orchids.

As yet, no hybridization experiments have been attempted with *Ascoglossum*, but it is to be assumed that members of the genus are freely inter-fertile with allied groups, such as *Vanda, Renanthera, Arachnis*, etc., and the resultant progeny from any such crosses should certainly prove of great interest and beauty.

CULTURE: As for the tropical Vandas. (H)

A. calopterum (Rchb.f.) Schltr. (*Saccolabium calopterum* Rchb.f., *Saccolabium Schleinitzianum* Krzl., *Cleisostoma cryptochilum* FvM.)

Sts. robust, often curving, to 2′ long, thickly leafy. Lvs. rigidly stiff, linear, unequally bilobed at apex, to 10″ long and 1″ wide. Infls. slender, erect or horizontal, to 2′ long, usually profusely branched, densely many-fld. Fls. about 1″ long, variable in colour from bright rose-magenta to light purplish, the lip with a distinct spur. Spring–early summer. (H) New Guinea.

ASPASIA Ldl.
(*Trophianthus* Scheidw.)

Aspasia contains about ten species of showy, epiphytic or lithophytic orchids in the American tropics, ranging from Guatemala to Brazil, several of which are today reasonably frequent in choice collections. Allied to several groups of the complex subtribe *Oncidiinae*, these mostly medium-sized plants possess prominent, often basally-stalked pseudobulbs and bear erect or arching inflorescences of a few showy, often remarkably handsome and long-lived flowers. They are easily grown, and as a group are particularly recommended to the amateur hobbyist because of the facility with which the blossoms are produced.

Several hybrids utilizing *Aspasia* have been registered

Aspasia epidendroides Ldl. [GORDON W. DILLON]

to date, these mostly by Moir in Hawaii, with other genera of the *Oncidium* alliance. These are by and large very attractive and give ample evidence of spectacular future productions, since the genus seems freely interfertile with many other groups.

CULTURE: The Aspasias, as noted above, are very easily grown. They thrive equally well when tightly mounted on tree-fern slabs or cubes, or when potted either in osmunda or tree-fern fibre (the latter preferably shredded or in small chunks) in well-drained pots. They require warm temperatures and abundant moisture while actively growing, but benefit by a rest-period of upwards of one month upon the termination of flowering. *A. principissa* delights in a very bright situation, and like other members of the group benefits by liberal applications of fertilizer on a regular schedule. (I, H)

A. epidendroides Ldl. (*Aspasia fragrans* Kl., *Odontoglossum Aspasia* Rchb.f.)

Pbs. stalked, laterally compressed, usually ellipsoidal in shape, to almost 6″ long and 2″ broad, covered by bracts (which are usually lf.-like) at the base. Lvs. paired, rather leathery, lanceolate to ligulate, acute, to almost 12″ long and 2″ broad. Infls. often 2 per growth, erect, few-fld., to 10″ tall. Fls. 1½″ long, not as wide, faintly fragrant at times during the heat of the day, the ss. greenish with broad transverse bands of brown or brownish-lavender, the ps. pale lavender to greenish-brown, the lip white, with conspicuous purple or lavender markings in the centre, the disc yellow, the col. and anther tinged with lavender. Summer. (I, H) Guatemala; Honduras; Nicaragua; Costa Rica; Panama; Colombia.

A. principissa Rchb.f. (*Aspasia Rousseauae* Schltr., *A. epidendroides* Ldl. var. *principissa* P.H.Allen.)

Vegetatively similar to *A. epidendroides* Ldl., but usually less robust and with larger fls. Fls. about 3″ long or less, not as wide, faintly fragrant, the ss. and broader ps. pale green or yellow-green with longitudinal brown or tan stripes. Lip undulate marginally, wide-spreading, creamy-white ageing to pale yellow, more or less marked on the disc with darker yellow. Late spring–summer. (I, H) Costa Rica; Panama.

A. lunata Ldl. (*Odontoglossum lunatum* Rchb.f., *Trophianthus zonatus* Scheidw.) Pbs. oval, about 2″ tall, fleshy, laterally compressed. Lvs. 1 or 2, ligulate, acute, to 8″ long. Infls. 1–2-fld., to 3″ tall. Fls. about 1½″ long, the ss. and ps. green, spotted and barred with dull or rather bright brown. Lip white with an irregular violet blotch in the middle. Spring. (I, H) Brazil.

A. variegata Ldl. (*Odontoglossum variegatum* Rchb.f.) Similar in habit to *A. epidendroides* Ldl., but smaller, the lvs. only about 6″ long. Infls. 1–3-fld., to about 4″ tall. Fls. about 2½″ long, fragrant, long-lasting, the ss. and ps. green with transverse brown or purple-brown bars mostly towards the base, the lip 3-lbd., white dotted with violet. Late winter–spring. (I, H) Brazil; Guianas; Trinidad.

AUXOPUS Schltr.

This is a genus of two known species, both diminutive saprophytic orchids of the subtribe *Gastrodiinae*, one native in the Cameroons, the other in Madagascar. They are unknown in contemporary collections, and in any event are primarily of botanical importance. The entire plant, including the flowers, is usually dull brownish or yellowish-brown.

Nothing is known of the genetic affinities of this singularly rare genus.

CULTURE: Possibly as for *Corallorrhiza*, although their successful maintenance for more than a single season in the collection is certain to be difficult. (H)

BAROMBIA Schltr.

Barombia gracillima Schltr., the only known member of this very rare and incompletely understood genus of the subtribe *Sarcanthinae*, is a native of the Cameroons of West Africa, and is not present in contemporary collections. It appears to be a connecting-link between the genera *Aërangis* Rchb.f. and *Plectrelminthus* Raf., bearing large yellowish flowers with a spur almost ten inches in length.

Nothing is known of the genetic affinities of *Barombia* at this time.

CULTURE: As for the tropical Angraecums. (H)

BARTHOLINA R.Br.

Three species of *Bartholina* are known, native in South Africa, and today very scarce in collections, although they were formerly rather popular with specialists in England and on the Continent, where the common name of 'Spider Orchids' was given to them in reference to the extraordinarily dissected lip of the showy flowers. A member of the subtribe *Habenarinae*, the genus is near in its alliance to *Holothrix* Ldl.

No hybrids have been made in *Bartholina*, and nothing is known of its genetic affinities.

CULTURE: As for *Cynorkis*, though a perfectly drained, sandy compost is needed, and moistly cool temperatures must prevail at all times, except after the foliage has died down, when a strict resting-period should be afforded the tubers, until action once again commences. (C, I)

B. Ethelae Bolus

Tubers subterranean, small, roundish. Lf. solitary, fleshy, almost round, basal, usually lying prone on the ground, about 2″ across at most. Infl. erect, 1-fld., to 4″ tall. Fls. about 1¼″ long, the white ss. and ps. small, the lip round, white, with elongated intricate fringed processes, the spur cylindric, rather long. Spring. (C, I) South Africa.

BASIPHYLLAEA Schltr.
(*Carteria* Small)

Basiphyllaea is a peculiar genus of three species of rare and incompletely known terrestrial (rarely lithophytic) orchids of the subtribe *Laeliinae*. The plants have been collected on a very few occasions in South Florida, the Bahamas, and Cuba, and recently plants from Puerto Rico have appeared which seem to be referable here. An aberrant genus in its subtribe, *Basiphyllaea* has a cluster of subterranean tuberous roots, a solitary rather fleshy leaf, and an erect spike of small, scarcely opening, dull-coloured blossoms of some complexity. None of the species appears to be in cultivation at this time. According to some authorities, they do not blossom annually, as do most orchids, remaining dormant for periods of several years' duration.

Nothing is known of the genetic affinities of this distinctly odd group.

CULTURE: Possibly as that afforded *Bletia*. (I, H)

BASKERVILLEA Ldl.

Baskervillea is a genus of but two known species, one apparently endemic to Peru (**B. assurgens** Ldl.), the other rather widespread in Central Brazil (**B. paranaensis** (Krzl.) Schltr.). The group is a member of the subtribe *Cranichidinae*, and is vaguely allied to *Ponthieva* R.Br., though it differs radically from that genus in the elongate inflorescence and very distinct, numerous, small flowers. Neither of the species has as yet been introduced into cultivation, though they are rather showy terrestrials, well worthy of attention by the specialist.

Nothing is known of the genetic affinities of *Baskervillea*.

CULTURE: As for the tropical Habenarias, etc. (I, H)

BATEMANIA Ldl.

Batemania (often misspelled *Batemannia*) contains two species of showy, uncommon epiphytic orchids in Colombia, the Guianas, and Trinidad. Similar in habit to the somewhat allied genus *Bifrenaria* Ldl. (although a member of the subtribe *Zygopetalinae*), they differ in the two-leaved pseudobulbs, the pendulous or nodding inflorescences, and in technical details of the flowers. Both of the known species are present in contemporary collections, albeit rarely, and are exceedingly handsome and unusual orchids which should be better known by connoisseurs.

Batemania Colleyi has already been utilized by the breeders, in the production of the delightful and excessively scarce bigeneric hybrid, *Zygobatemania x Mastersii* (× *Zygopetalum crinitum*), which was produced by Linden as long ago as 1899. Since the genus is presumably freely inter-fertile with members of both the subtribes *Zygopetalinae* and *Lycastinae* (and possibly also the *Huntleyinae*), additional experimental hybridization along these lines is to be encouraged.

CULTURE: As for *Bifrenaria*. (I, H)

B. armillata Rchb.f. (*Zygopetalum chloranthum* Krzl.)

Pbs. laterally compressed, ovoid, rather shiny green, to 2″ tall, clustered. Lvs. paired, rather broad, acute apically, leathery, to 8″ long. Infls. racemose, pendulous, loosely 3–6-fld., to 8″ long. Fls. about 2″ across, waxy, fragrant, the spreading, oblong ss. and ps. greenish-white. Lip pale greenish-white with a brownish suffusion, 3-lbd., the lat. lbs. small, obtuse, erect, the midlb. roundish, broadly rhombic. June–Aug. (I) Colombia.

B. Colleyi Ldl. (*Maxillaria Colleyi* Batem.)

Pbs. ovoid, 4-sided, to 3″ tall, tightly clustered. Lvs.

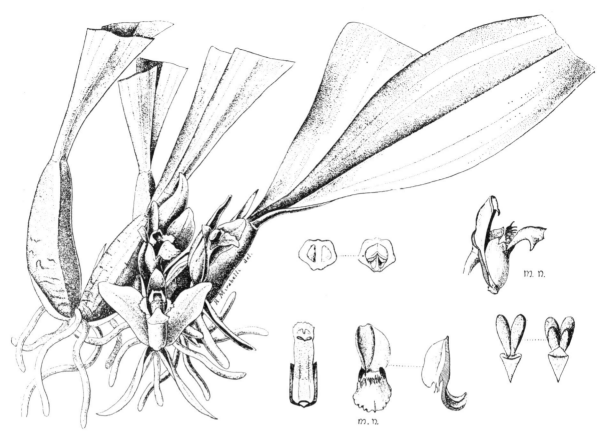

Batemania Colleyi Ldl. [Hoehne, *Flora Brasílica*]

in pairs, glossy, leathery, oblong-elliptic to lanceolate, acute, narrowed towards the base, 7–10″ long and 3″ wide. Infls. racemose, loosely 4–7-fld., to 8″ long, usually pendulous, rarely ascending. Fls. usually all pointing in the same direction, about 3″ in diam., fleshy, fragrant, long-lived, the dors. sep. and ps. similar, almost equal, deep wine-purple to brownish-red flushed with brown, often with greenish tips, elliptic-oblong; lat. ss. narrowly oblong, falcate with the inner margin folded in, the margin green, the remaining area wine-purple flushed with brown, often with greenish tips. Lip white with a reddish flush at the base of the midlb., appressed to the col., 3-lbd., the lat. lbs. round, the midlb. almost square, emarginate, the callus brown-purple, 2-parted, toothed at front. Col. semi-terete, white with red spots, the anther hooded. Autumn–winter. (I, H) Guianas; Trinidad; ? Northern Brazil.

BENTHAMIA A.Rich.

Benthamia is a genus of about twenty-six species, most of them endemic to Madagascar, with a few extending to the Mascarene Islands. The group is a member of the subtribe *Habenarinae*, and despite their attractive appearance, none of the component species are present in collections at this time. The usually small flowers are white for the most part, and are borne in dense erect racemes.

Nothing is known of the genetic affinities of this group.

CULTURE: As for *Cynorkis* or the tropical Disas. (H)

BIERMANNIA King & Pantl.

But a single species of *Biermannia* is known to date, this an extremely rare and relatively uninteresting epiphytic member of the subtribe *Sarcanthinae*, indigenous to the Himalayas. **Biermannia bimaculata** (King & Pantl.) King & Pantl. (*Sarcochilus bimaculatus* King & Pantl.) is a dwarf monopodial plant with small, fugacious, almond-scented flowers, these white with two brown blotches on the lip-calli. The genus is closest in its alliance to *Sarcochilus* R.Br., and is not presently in cultivation.

Nothing is known of the genetic affinities of this very scarce genus.

CULTURE: Possibly as for the smaller-growing, epiphytic Vandas, etc. (I)

BIFRENARIA Ldl.

With the segregate genera *Rudolfiella* Hoehne and *Stenocoryne* Ldl. now removed from it, *Bifrenaria* consists of about eleven apparently valid species (plus several varieties) of often very spectacular orchids, all endemic to Brazil. The genus is a component of the sub-

Benthamia Bathieana Schltr. [*Flore de Madagascar*]

fascinating field for future endeavour, since it now seems apparent that Bifrenarias are not only 'crossable' with members of the subtribe *Lycastinae* (to which they belong), but also with the allied subtribes *Zygopetalinae* and *Huntleyinae*. In days to come, we may look forward to a wealth of orchids manufactured from the handsome components of this fine genus by enterprising breeders.

CULTURE: Generally speaking, the Bifrenarias are easily grown, even by the novice hobbyist, hence they should be far better known by all orchidists. Their basic cultural requirements approximate those afforded to the warm-growing Lycastes. Best kept in the intermediate or warm greenhouse, they will stand considerable quantities of rather bright light, and while actively growing should be given as much water and humidity as possible, short of souring the compost. Upon completion of the new pseudobulbs, a rest-period of several weeks' duration should be allowed—preferably in a slightly cooler and shadier spot—for the best production of the lovely flowers. Repotting should be attended to only when absolutely necessary, as these orchids are singularly intolerant of disturbance. (I, H)

B. Harrisoniae (Hk.) Rchb.f. (*Dendrobium Harrisoniae* Hk., *Colax Harrisoniae* Ldl., *Lycaste Harrisoniae* G.Don, *Maxillaria Harrisoniae* Ldl., *Maxillaria pubigera* Kl., *Maxillaria spathacea* Ldl., *Stanhopea Harrisoniae* G.Don)

Pbs. clustered, broadly ovoid, vaguely or strongly 4-angled, 2–3″ tall, often suffused with red-brown, especially near the apex. Lf. solitary, oblong-elliptic, acute, leathery, rather rigid, glossy, to 12″ long and 5″ broad. Infls. usually paired from the latest formed pb.-bases, 1–2-fld., usually about 2″ tall. Fls. about 3″ in diam., very waxy, heavily fragrant, long-lasting, very handsome, the chin formed by the lat. ss. very prominent, spur-like, about 1½″ long, fl.-colour variable, but usually with the ss. and ps. ivory-white (sometimes yellowish or greenish-yellow, apically flushed with reddish). Ss. and ps. spreading, oval-oblong, obtuse, the dors. sep. concave, the lat. ss. larger, slightly falcate, adnate to the col.-foot. Lip 3-lbd., large, rich wine-purple to magenta-red, usually with darker veins, the lat. lbs. oblong, incurved, the midlb. almost square, emarginate, wavy marginally, hairy above, the disc very hairy, yellow or orange-yellow. Col. clavate, curved, large, white. Spring–early summer. (I, H) Brazil.

B. inodora Ldl. (*Bifrenaria fragrans* B.-R., *B. Fuerstenbergiana* Schltr., *Lycaste inodora* hort.)

Rather similar in habit to *B. Harrisoniae* (Hk.) Rchb.f. Fls. heavily waxy, fragrant or odourless, long-lasting, to 3″ in diam., the ss. apple-green or yellow-green, oblong, obtuse, the lats. with a mucro at apex; ps. much smaller than ss. but more vividly coloured, sub-rhomboidal. Lip 3-lbd., white, yellow, or pale rose, often suffused with darker colour, the erect lat. lbs. sub-triangular, the midlb. broadly oval, hairy, reflexed, crisped and undulate marginally; disc a fleshy grooved plate that is toothed and projecting in front; spur sub-cylindric, half as long as pedicellate ovary. Col. curved, concave below stigmatic surface, white or greenish-yellow. Late winter–summer. (I, H) Brazil.

tribe *Lycastinae*, and in the wild its members often are rather frequent on trees and rock-outcroppings, where they often form huge masses of angular pseudobulbs and leathery foliage. The flowers are in this genus usually large and of handsome appearance. They are produced singly or a few at a time in abbreviated inflorescences which arise from the pseudobulb-bases, and often vary markedly in colouration in a given species. Unfortunately, at this time, Bifrenarias are scarce orchids in our collections, though because of their attractive appearance and ease of cultivation, almost all of them should be better known by enthusiasts.

Bifrenaria has only recently been utilized by the breeders, notably in the production of the remarkably beautiful *Lyfrenaria x Darius* (*Lycaste virginalis* × *Bifrenaria Harrisoniae*). This opens up to us an incredibly

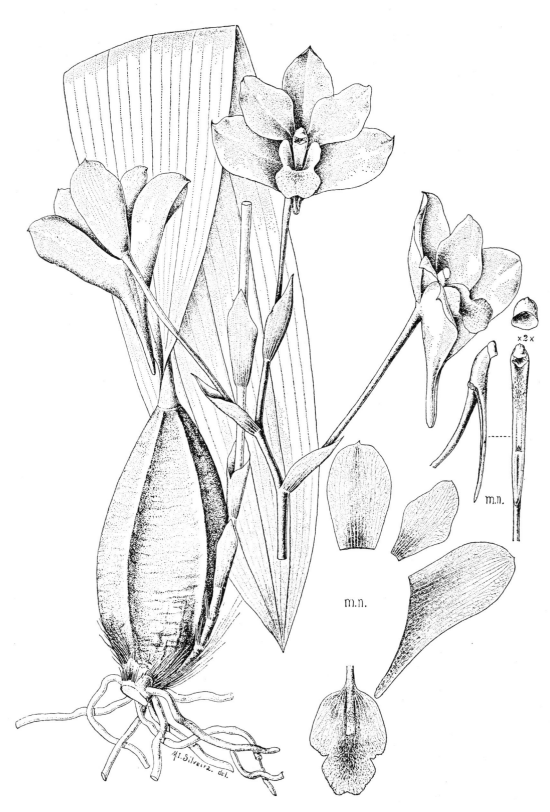

Bifrenaria tyrianthina (Loud.) Rchb.f. var. *magnicalcarata* Hoehne [*Flora Brasílica*]

IIB   *Epidendrum tampense* Ldl.   [A.D.HAWKES]

IIIA   *Cattleya guttata* Ldl.   [EDWARD A. FLICKINGER]

B. atropurpurea (Lodd.) Ldl. (*Maxillaria atropurpurea* Lodd.) Pbs. egg-shaped, 4-angled, to 3″ tall. Lf. solitary, to 10″ long, oblong-lanceolate, acute, rather leathery, dark green. Infls. 3–5-fld., to about 3″ long, usually horizontal. Fls. fleshy, fragrant, about 2″ in diam., the ss. and ps. wine-red, flushed more or less with yellowish medially, the lip whitish or rose-red. Summer. (I, H) Brazil.

B. tetragona (Ldl.) Schltr. (*Lycaste tetragona* Ldl., *Maxillaria tetragona* Ldl.) Pbs. clustered, ovoid, distinctly 4-angled, to 3½″ tall. Lf. solitary, fleshy, elliptic-oblong, to 18″ long. Infls. 3–4-fld., to about 3″ long. Fls. about 2″ in diam., fleshy, heavily fragrant, long-lasting, the ss. and ps. greenish streaked with brown or purplish-brown, the lip 3-lbd., flushed with violet-purple towards the base. Col. whitish. Summer. (I, H) Brazil.

B. tyrianthina (Loud.) Rchb.f. (*Lycaste tyrianthina* Loud., *Maxillaria tyrianthina* hort., *Bifrenaria Dallemagnei* hort.) Similar in almost all respects to *B. Harrisoniae* (Hk.) Rchb.f., but more robust and with fls. to 3½″ in diam., these with the ss. and ps. violet-purple, paler basally, the lip 3-lbd., dark violet-purple, the midlb. thickly hairy, white in the throat. Spring–early summer. (I, H) Brazil.

BINOTIA Rolfe

This is a genus of a single species of uncommon epiphytic (rarely lithophytic) orchid in Brazil, very closely allied to *Cochlioda* Ldl. and differing from it primarily in the structure of the lip, which has a long claw, attached by its margins to the foot of the column. Unlike the bright scarlet and red hues present in the blossoms of the other genus, *Binotia* has greenish and brown flowers with a white, often rose-flushed callus on the lip. The solitary species is present in choice collections, but must be classed as a very rare orchid.

Binotia has not yet been utilized by the hybridists, although it is presumably inter-fertile with such allied genera as *Oncidium*, *Odontoglossum*, *Miltonia*, *Brassia*, and *Cochlioda*.

CULTURE: As for the tropical, pseudobulbous Oncidiums. (I, H)

B. brasiliensis (Rolfe) Rolfe (*Cochlioda brasiliensis* Rolfe)
Pbs. ovoid, rather compressed, wrinkled with age, about 1½″ tall. Lvs. paired, lanceolate-ligulate, acutish, to 5″ long, rather leathery. Infls. loosely 6–13-fld., gracefully arching, often branched, about 18″ long. Fls. less than 2″ across, opening widely, greenish-white flushed with brownish, the lip white or whitish, green-tipped, the calli usually rose-flushed. Ss. and ps. narrowly lanceolate, acute. Lip with a long claw that is attached to the col.-foot, 3-lbd., the lat. lbs. obtuse, the midlb. oblong, obtuse, the disc with 2 papillose calli. Summer. (I, H) Brazil.

BIPINNULA Ldl.

This is a remarkable genus of the subtribe *Chloraeinae*, rather closely allied to *Chloraea* Ldl., but differing in the bizarre structure of the handsome flowers. About eight species are known, all of them terrestrials, inhabiting Chile, Uruguay, Argentina, and southern Brazil. Despite their unique interest, none of them appears to be present in contemporary collections.

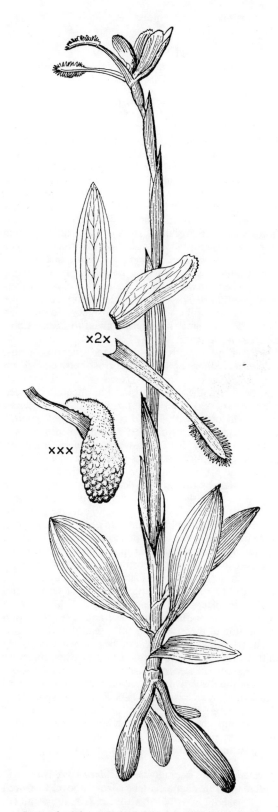

x2x

xxx

Bipinnula Gibertii Rchb.f. [Hoehne, *Flora Brasilica*]

Nothing is known of the genetic alliances of this genus.

CULTURE: As for *Disa* or *Caladenia*. (C, I)

BLETIA R. & P.

(*Bletiana* Raf., *Gyas* Salisb., *Jimenesia* Raf., *Regnellia* B.-R., *Thiebautia* Colla)

This is a genus of an estimated fifty species, all natives of the Americas, ranging from Florida and Mexico (where the centre of dissemination occurs) to Brazil. Relatively infrequent in contemporary collections, *Bletia* contains a remarkable number of showy and handsome terrestrial (rarely semi-epiphytic or lithophytic) species of singularly facile cultural requirements, hence the group should be better known by orchidists. With several folded leaves arising from a typically partially subterranean pseudobulb-like corm, the inflorescences are produced on a lateral leafless branch from (usually) the side or apical part of the corm. The often very spectacular flowers are borne successively over a long period of time in most species, in a simple or branched raceme, and are frequently very numerous (rarely solitary). They vary in colour from rose-purple to greenish or white, and in many instances do not open fully. *Bletia* is somewhat vaguely allied to *Phaius* Lour. and *Spathoglottis* Bl.

As yet no hybrids are registered for this genus, although seedlings of a supposed cross between a *Bletia* and a *Spathoglottis* are now growing in South Florida, and seem to show characteristics intermediate between the two genera. It does seem probable that the present genus will breed with *Phaius, Calanthe, Spathoglottis,* etc. Interspecific hybridization should also prove fascinating, and should help to answer some of our questions regarding taxonomic alliances within the genus itself.

CULTURE: Bletias are, for the most part, readily grown, even by the novice. They thrive in pots in the greenhouse or lath-house, or in specially prepared beds (such as those suggested for *Arundina*) outside, provided the climate is sufficiently equable to permit this. In pots, these handsome terrestrials thrive in a compost of about equal parts of rich loam, leaf-mould, gritty white sand, and shredded or chopped osmunda or tree-fern fibre, with manure or other fertilizing ingredient added. The pots need to be perfectly drained for best results, and while the plants are in active growth they require quantities of moisture, humidity, and warmth. Upon maturation of the new corms (or 'pseudobulbs', as they are usually called), water should be stopped completely until the racemes have started to open, when moisture may be recommenced, gradually and still in moderation. Most of the Bletias will stand almost total sun-exposure, and indeed, seem to profit if kept in a sunny spot. They should be fertilized regularly for good production of growths and flowers. Repotting should be done annually, as these orchids are heavy feeders, and soon exhaust the compost in which they are grown. (I, H)

B. catenulata R. & P. (*Bletia sanguinea* P. & E.)
Pbs. to 3″ in diam., flattened from above, furrowed and considerably wrinkled with age. Lvs. long-stalked, 4–6 in number, to 2′ long, about 4″ wide at the broadest point, almost linear, acute, folded. Infls. to 3′ tall, rather loosely 3–8-fld. Fls. about 2″ across, showy, opening wider than those of most of the spp., the ss. and ps. rose-magenta, the lip deep rose-magenta, the margins crisped and wavy, often paler, the crests usually whitish or cream-white. Spring–summer. (I, H) Peru; Brazil.

B. florida (Salisb.) R.Br. (*Limodorum floridum* Salisb., *Bletia Shepherdii* Hk.)
Pbs. often rather egg-shaped, more commonly flattened-globose, about 1–1½″ in diam., sometimes borne on the surface of the ground. Lvs. few, long-stalked, narrowly lanceolate to broadly oblanceolate, acuminate, to 2′ long and 4″ wide at broadest point. Infls. erect or slightly arching, with an elongate, many-fld. rac. in the upper third, the fls. produced over a period of several months, successively. Fls. to about 1½″ across, showy, very long-lasting for the genus, the ss. and ps. rich rose-purple, the lip slightly deeper, with 5 white irregular crests down the disc. Spring–summer. (I, H) Cuba; Jamaica.

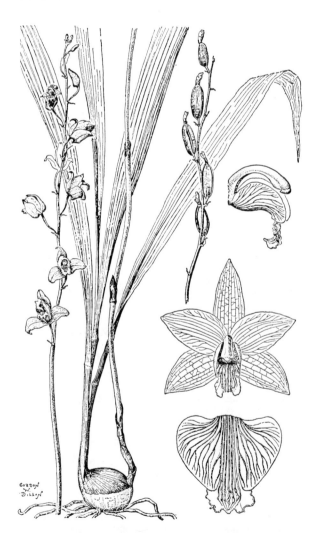

Bletia purpurea (Lam.) DC [GORDON W. DILLON]

B. gracilis Lodd.

Pbs. purplish, about 1½″ in diam., furrowed with age. Lf. solitary, elliptic to lanceolate, usually acuminate, purplish on under-surface, rather fragile in texture, to 12″ long. Infls. with a purplish rachis, wire-like, to 1½′ tall, 1–8-fld. Fls. about 1½″ across, the ss. and ps. varying from greenish-yellow to purple or purple-rose, the lip green, veined with dark red and purple, rose-coloured basally, yellowish-green in front, furnished with lamellae on the disc. Summer. (I) Mexico; Guatemala.

B. patula Hk.

Pbs. clustered, globose or rather flattened from the top, annular, to 2″ in diam., often yellowish. Lvs. to 2′ long, linear-lanceolate, narrowed below into a channelled stalk. Infls. usually rigidly erect, slender, few-fld., to 3′ tall. Fls. showy, often nodding, not opening fully, to 2½″ across, lilac-magenta or rose-magenta, the deeply 3-lbd. lip with several prominent white, irregular keels on the disc. Mostly summer–autumn. (H) Cuba; Hispaniola; Puerto Rico.

B. purpurea (Lam.) DC (*Limodorum purpureum* Lam., *Limodorum tuberosum* L. in part, *Limodorum verecundum* Salisb., *Limodorum trifidum* Michx., *Cymbidium verecundum* Sw., *Bletia verecunda* R.Br., *B. alta* Hitchc. in part, *B. tuberosa* Ames, *B. acutipetala* Hk., *B. havanensis* A.Rich., *B. Pottsii* S.Wats.)

Pbs. compressed from above, about 1½″ in maximum diam., often produced in rather long chains, either subterranean or partially exposed. Lvs. few, stalked basally, linear to narrowly elliptic-lanceolate, long-acuminate, folded, to 3′ long, usually less than 2″ wide, often yellowish-green. Infls. to 5′ tall, a simple or branching rac. at the apex, few- to many-fld., the fls. usually opening successively over a period of more than a month. Fls. about 2″ across in the largest phases, varying in colour from pink to rose-purple (rarely with the ss. and ps. white), not opening fully, the ps. usually lying parallel alongside the col., forming an open hood over the lip. Lip usually deeper in colour than other segms., with 5–7 yellowish lamellae on the disc. Mostly spring–early summer. (I, H) Florida; West Indies; Mexico; Central America; northern South America.

B. reflexa Ldl. (*Limodorum Lankesteri* A. & S., *Bletia Lankesteri* AHS, *B. amabilis* C.Schweinf.)

Extremely variable. Pbs. very small for the size of the pl., which attains heights in excess of 3½′ when in blossom. Lvs. 2 or more, folded, narrowly sword-shaped to broadly lanceolate, long-acuminate, to 2½′ long, about 2″ wide at maximum point. Infls. to 3½′ tall (rarely more), with a 2–12-fld. rac. or panicle at apex, the fls. opening successively. Fls. often almost 3″ across, rather long-lived for the genus. Ss. and ps. purple-rose or pinkish-purple. Lip deep purple apically, usually whitish-green in the throat, with 5 parallel lamellae in the centre. Col. purple. Autumn–winter. (I) Mexico to Panama and possibly northern South America.

BLETILLA Rchb.f.

This genus of about seven known species is restricted in its distribution to the region encompassing China,

Japan, and Formosa (with perhaps certain of the adjacent insular areas). A single terrestrial species is a very common orchid in contemporary cultivation, being widely offered by plantsmen throughout the world, almost always as a *Bletia*, a genus to which *Bletilla* is not even closely allied. The plants consist of rather compressed, roundish, corm-like pseudobulbs—typically borne below the surface of the ground—which give rise to several stalked, folded, sometimes variegated, glossy leaves about a foot in height. The erect, few-flowered inflorescences typically arise from the centre of the expanding new shoots, and bear rather sizeable, rose-magenta to white flowers of interesting shape and attractive appearance in the spring and early summer months. The remaining six species of *Bletilla* are apparently unknown in collections at this time, though several of them are handsome orchids well worthy of our attention.

No hybrids have been made in this genus, and nothing is known of its genetic affinities.

CULTURE: *Bletilla striata* is one of the easiest of all orchids to grow, and is almost completely hardy, even in temperate regions. The plants are most successful when kept confined to big pots (about eight- or nine-inch size), perfectly drained, in a compost consisting of rich garden soil, loam, rotted leaves, and gritty white sand, with some manure added rather liberally. Often the plants will not blossom until they become pot-bound, hence they should be disturbed only when absolutely essential. They need to be kept moist while actively growing, but upon withering of the foliage, water should be withheld until the new shoots begin to appear in the spring. They also do well in out-of-door beds, to be treated much in the manner of garden bulbs—tulips, narcissus, etc.—although they should not be dug up during the winter. (C, I, H)

B. striata (Thunb.) Rchb.f. (*Limodorum striatum* Thunb., *Bletia hyacinthina* R.Br., *Bletia gebina* Ldl., *Bletilla hyacinthina* Rchb.f., *Bletia hyacinthina* hort.)

Pbs. roundish, compressed, wrinkled with age, typically subterranean. Lvs. tightly stalked at base, folded above, light or dark green, sometimes variegated with white or cream-white, to 12″ tall, rarely to 2′ tall. Infls. solitary, appearing from the middle of the expanding shoots, to 2′ tall in robust specimens. Fls. to 12 (generally fewer), opening successively, 1–2″ across, rather nodding on the stalk, usually not opening fully. Ss. and ps. typically rose-purple or magenta-purple. Lip darker, with very deep purple, raised, median keels, the throat cream-white or glossy yellow. In the rare fma. **alba** (hort.) A.D.Hawkes (*Bletilla striata* (Thunb.) Rchb.f. var. *alba* hort.) the entire fl. is white, except for the throat of the lip, which is pale yellowish. Mostly June–July. (C, I, H) China; Japan.

BOGORIA J.J.Sm.

Bogoria consists of three known species—**B. Raciborskii** J.J.Sm., **B. papuana** Schltr., and **B. taeniorrhiza** Schltr.—the first from Java, the second from New Guinea, and the third from Sumatra. None of these appears to be present in contemporary collections, and because of their typically short-lived, rather small flowers, they are of potential interest only to specialists. A member of the subtribe *Sarcanthinae*, the genus is intermediate in alliance between *Thrixspermum* Lour. and *Sarcochilus* R.Br., and even in the wild state, the plants appear to be exceptionally scarce.

Nothing is known of the genetic affinities of this group.

CULTURE: Presumably as for the tropical Vandas. (H)

BOLLEA Rchb.f.

This delightful genus of South American (primarily Colombian) epiphytic orchids contains six known species, of which five are today present in collections, although they must be classed as rare and difficult plants, because of their peculiar cultural requirements. Allied to *Chondrorhyncha* Ldl. and other members of the subtribe *Huntleyinae*, they simulate those orchids in vegetative appearance, and somewhat so in floral structure, although the technical characters of the column and lip readily serve to differentiate them from their allies.

To date, only one hybrid in which a *Bollea* figures has been registered, this an extremely rare and unusual bigeneric natural hybrid from Colombia, known as *Chondrobollea x Froebeliana* Rolfe (*Bollea coelestis* × *Chondrorhyncha Chestertoni*). Interspecific breeding offers some fascinating possibilities, as does critical hybridization with presumably allied genera.

CULTURE: As for *Chondrorhyncha*. All of the species are native in high-elevation 'cloud forests', hence require constantly moist, cool conditions for any degree of success to be anticipated. (C)

B. coelestis (Rchb.f.) Rchb.f. (*Zygopetalum coeleste* Rchb.f., *Bollea pulvinaris* Rchb.f.)
One of the finest of American orchids, one of the 'blue'-flowering species. Lvs. forming a more or less loose fan, 6–10 per growth, oblong-lanceolate, acuminate at tip, 6–12″ long, 1½–2″ broad, rather fragile in texture. Scapes rather stout, suberect or nodding, shorter than the lvs., with a small sheathing bract at each joint, 1-fld. Fls. 3–4″ in diam., very fleshy, highly fragrant, long-lived. Ss. and ps. wide-spreading, varying from deep violet-blue to almost sky-blue, the wavy margins and basal parts usually olive-green or yellowish-green, often yellowish at tips; dors. sep. broadly obovate, bent forwards; lat. ss. oval-oblong; ps. similar to dors. sep., but more widely spreading. Lip shorter than other segms., which it simulates in colour, with a large buff-yellow, semicircular crest occupying ¾ of the area, this deeply grooved longitudinally into numerous rounded ridges, the small ovate blade recurved marginally and apically. Col. broad, arching, convex and bluish-violet above, concave and yellow in front, hairy and red-spotted towards base. Summer. (C) Colombia.

B. Lalindei (Rchb.f.) Rchb.f. (*Zygopetalum Lalindei* Rchb.f.)
Rather similar in habit to *B. coelestis* (Rchb.f.) Rchb.f., but with fewer, narrower lvs. with 5 prominent longitudinal nerves. Scapes to about 4″ long, mostly nodding. Fls. solitary, 2½–4″ across, very fleshy and fragrant, long-lasting, the ss. and ps. spreading and apically recurved, pale rose, the upper half of each segm. usually deep rose-red, often tipped with straw-yellow, broadly ovate-oblong in ss., the lats. of which often have lower margins straw-yellow, the ps. oblong, obtuse, sometimes rose-coloured with white margins. Lip large, fleshy, brilliant golden-yellow, ovate-hastate, the margins and tip recurved, the latter obtusely pointed; disc with 13 grooves, with raised, close-pressed, smooth lamellae. Col. broader than raised lip-disc, arching, rose-coloured, or sometimes white at base. Summer–fall. (C) Colombia.

B. Lawrenceana (Rchb.f.) Rchb.f. (*Zygopetalum Lawrenceanum* Rchb.f.)
Simulating *B. coelestis* (Rchb.f.) Rchb.f. in habit, and of about comparable size. Scapes to about 8″ tall, mostly suberect. Fls. solitary, to about 4″ across, fragrant, waxy, long-lived, the ss. and ps. wide, white, with a violet-purple blotch at the apex of each segm., the ps. rather wavy-margined. Lip white basally, the apical part deep violet-purple, the crest with 11 blunt keels. Col. pale yellow, with a dark violet anther. Summer. (C) Colombia.

B. Patini (Rchb.f.) Rchb.f. (*Zygopetalum Patini* Rchb.f.). Similar in habit to *B. coelestis* (Rchb.f.) Rchb.f. Infls. arching or pendulous, bearing a solitary, very fleshy, highly fragrant, long-lasting fl. about 4″ across. Ss. and ps. pale rose, blunt apically, the lat. ss. somewhat darker than other segms. Lip golden-yellow, the very large and fleshy crest flesh-pink. Summer. (C) Colombia.

B. violacea (Ldl.) Rchb.f. (*Huntleya violacea* Ldl., *Zygopetalum violaceum* Rchb.f.) Similar in habit to *B. coelestis* (Rchb.f.) Rchb.f. Fls. about 3″ across, very waxen in texture, fragrant, deep violet-purple, the ss. and ps. with white margins, the lip extremely dark violet, with a yellow, 13-keeled crest. Col. broad, arching, violet. Summer. (I, H) Guianas.

BOLUSIELLA Schltr.

Bolusiella is a genus of about six apparently valid species, all indigenous to tropical Africa, where they are usually epiphytic, or more rarely lithophytic. A segregate from *Angraecum* Bory, they are complex in floral structure and seem to offer much to connoisseurs, although at this time they are unknown in our collections. All of the species were previously placed in *Angraecum* Bory, *Listrostachys* Rchb.f., or *Rhaphidorhynchus* Finet.

Nothing is known as yet regarding the genetic affinities of *Bolusiella*.

CULTURE: Presumably as for the tropical Angraecums, etc. (H)

BONATEA Willd.

About twenty species of terrestrial orchids of the complex subtribe *Habenarinae* make up this interesting genus. Its members occur from Arabia southward through East Africa to South Africa's Cape Province. Tuber-bearing plants with leafy stems and erect racemes of often large and showy, usually white or greenish, long-spurred flowers, they are very rare in our collections at this time, albeit most desirable orchids.

No hybrids have been made utilizing the Bonateas, and nothing is known of their genetic affinities.

CULTURE: As for the tropical Habenarias. (I, H)

B. ugandae Rolfe

Tubers elongate, clustered. St. stout, erect, 2–3¼′ tall, leafy. Lvs. to 5″ long and 2½″ broad, rather heavy-textured, broadly lanceolate. Infl. rather lax, with up to 30 fls. Fls. to more than 2″ long, very complex, strongly fragrant of cloves, pale green, the large and ornate multi-parted lip white, the spur to almost 6″ long. Summer. (I, H) Uganda; Kenya; Tanganyika.

BONNIERA Cordem.

Two extremely rare epiphytic orchids of the subtribe *Sarcanthinae*, **Bonniera appendiculata** Cordem. and **B. corrugata** Cordem., make up this interesting and unique genus. Somewhat allied to and resembling *Angraecum* Bory, these orchids differ from that group in technical details of the flowers, especially in the absence of a spur on the lip. Both are native in the Mascarene Islands, and neither is present in our collections at this time.

Nothing is known of the genetic affinities of *Bonniera*.

CULTURE: Presumably as for the tropical Angraecums. (H)

BOTHRIOCHILUS Lem.

Four species of spectacular epiphytic or lithophytic orchids make up this genus, all of which are present in choice collections today, though none of them are common in cultivation. Allied to *Coelia* Ldl.—in which they were formerly contained—the species inhabit Mexico and Central America. Pseudobulbous plants with folded, rather narrow leaves, they produce their very numerous or few, often large and brightly hued flowers from the base of the pseudobulbs.

The breeders have not as yet taken these orchids in hand, but interspecific crossing seems to offer some fascinating possibilities. Nothing is known of the genetic alliances of *Bothriochilus*, which is a member of the polymorphic subtribe *Ponerinae*.

CULTURE: The members of this genus grow best in very well-drained, proportionately small pots, tightly packed in either osmunda or shredded tree-fern fibre. A bright spot (shaded from the direct rays of the sun) in the intermediate house should be found for them. Re-potting should be done only when absolutely essential, since these orchids are very intolerant of being disturbed. High humidity is necessary at all times, and the plants should be kept moist at the roots (though never wet!) at all times for success. (I, H)

B. bellus Lem. (*Coelia bella* Rchb.f.)

Pbs. egg-shaped to globular, somewhat compressed, to 2″ long, extended above into a short terete stalk. Lvs. several, clustered, linear-lanceolate, long-acuminate, folded, to 2′ long, very narrow, rather glossy. Infls. to 6″ tall, clothed with shiny tan sheaths, 2–6-fld. Fls. to more than 2″ long, nearly erect, rather fragrant, tubular below and funnel-shaped above, yellowish-white with the segms. tipped with rose-purple, the midlb. of the

Bonatea Kayseri (Krzl.) Rolfe [*Flora of the Belgian Congo*]

lip orange. Summer. (I, H) Mexico; Guatemala; Honduras.

B. densiflorus (Rolfe) A. & C. (*Coelia densiflora* Rolfe)

Rather similar to *B. bellus* Lem. in habit, the pbs. to 3″ long, the lvs. slightly wider. Infls. to about 3″ tall, erect, heavily furnished with sheaths, with a short, dense, many-fld., egg-shaped rac. of 150–200 fls. arranged in spiral rows round the rachis. Fls. less than ½″ long, rather fragrant, semi-translucent, pure white. Summer. (I, H) Guatemala; Honduras.

B. guatemalensis (Rchb.f.) L.O.Wms. (*Coelia guatemalensis* Rchb.f.)

Pbs. conical, extended above into a short stalk, with dark brown sheaths, to 2″ long. Lvs. shorter than those of the other spp., rather fleshy, strongly nerved. Infls. to 8″ tall, sheathed by several inflated bracts, several-fld. Fls. about ¾″ long, the ss. and ps. white, often marked apically with blush-pink, the lip with a fleshy thickening in the middle below the tip, coloured like the other segms. Summer. (I, H) Guatemala.

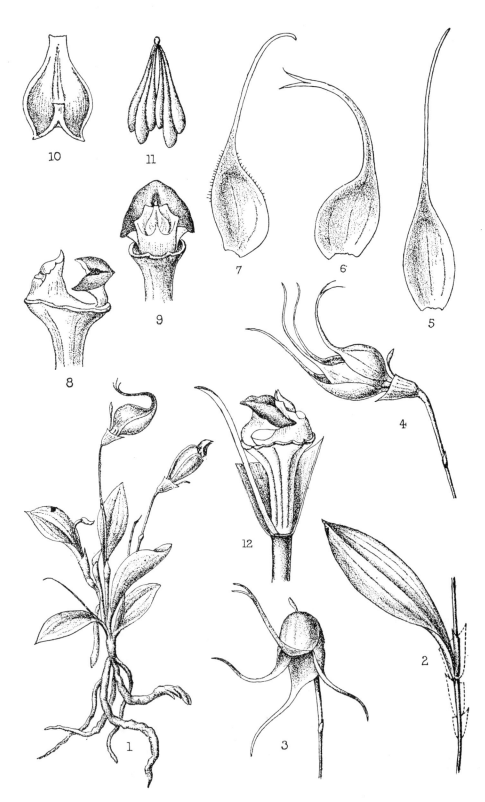

Brachionidium Sherringii Rolfe [Fawcett & Rendle, *Flora of Jamaica*]

B. macrostachyus (Ldl.) L.O.Wms. (*Coelia macrostachya* Ldl.)

Pbs. globular to egg-shaped, extended above into a slender stalk, brown-bracted, to 4″ tall, clustered. Lvs. usually 3, linear-lanceolate, long-acuminate, rather fleshy, folded, to 3′ long, about 1″ wide; lf.-sheaths strongly toothed apically when the lf. falls. Infls. erect, to 2′ tall, heavily sheathed, with a cylindrical, densely many-fld. rac. 6″ long at the apex. Fls. fragrant, about ⅛″ long, crystalline-pink or pinkish-white, sometimes rose. Lip with a small globular, somewhat 2-lbd. sac at the base. Summer. (I, H) Mexico; Guatemala; Honduras; Costa Rica; Panama.

BRACHIONIDIUM Ldl.

This is a genus of about six species of rare epiphytic orchids with a peculiarly disjunct distribution, occurring in the Colombian and Bolivian Andes, on Mount Roraima in British Guiana, and in the West Indies. Allied to *Lepanthes* Sw. and other members of the subtribe *Pleurothallidinae*, the Brachionidiums are very rare in contemporary collections, though one species, noted below, is occasionally encountered.

Nothing is known regarding the genetic affinities of this unusual aggregation.

CULTURE: As for *Pleurothallis*. (I, H)

B. Sherringii Rolfe

Pls. very small, less than 2″ tall at most, the minute secondary sts. arising from a long prostrate often branching rhiz. which is more or less covered with sheaths. Lf. solitary, 3-toothed at the apex, to 1¼″ long, narrowed basally, fleshy. Infls. thread-like, exceeding the lvs. in length, with a proportionately large, solitary fl. at the apex, furnished with inflated sheaths. Fls. not opening widely, more than 1″ long, the ss. and ps. long-tailed, claret-purple, the ss. sometimes flushed with tawny-yellow, the small lip purple. Autumn–early winter. (I, H) Jamaica; Lesser Antilles.

BRACHTIA Rchb.f.

Brachtia is a genus of about four species of very rare and little-known epiphytic orchids of the subtribe *Brachtiinae* (formerly incorporated in the *Ionopsidinae*), which inhabit the chilly woods in the high Andes of Ecuador and Colombia. Unknown in contemporary collections, they are dwarf pseudobulbous plants with small yellowish or greenish flowers of considerable complexity.

Nothing is known concerning the genetic affinities of *Brachtia*.

CULTURE: Probably as for the highland Odontoglossums, etc. (C, I)

BRACHYCORYTHIS Ldl.

This is a genus of the subtribe *Habenarinae*, comprising about ten species of seldom-seen terrestrial orchids native in tropical and South Africa, with a single outlying representative in Madagascar, which also occurs on the African mainland. Although the flowers are not particularly large, they are borne in sufficient quantities to be showy, and when the plants are well grown they form a handsome addition to the specialized collection.

Nothing is known of the genetic alliances of this group.

CULTURE: As for *Cynorkis*. (I, H)

B. pleistophylla Rchb.f. (*Brachycorythis pulchra* Schltr., *B. Perrieri* Schltr.)

Tubers subterranean, fuzzy, elongate, numerous. Flowering sts. to 2½′ tall. Lvs. very abundant, clasping the erect st., sessile, lanceolate, about 2″ long, acuminate, the upper ones becoming bract-like. Infls. racemose, cylindrical, about 7″ long, densely many-fld., the subtending bracts equalling the fls. in length in many cases. Fls. about ½″ across, purple or rose-purple, the lip complex in structure. Winter. (I, H) Tropical East Africa; Madagascar.

BRACISEPALUM J.J.Sm.

A solitary species of *Bracisepalum* is known to date, this an excessively rare epiphytic orchid from Celebes, called **Bracisepalum selebicum** J.J.Sm. It is a rather aberrant member of the subtribe *Coelogyninae*, with very complex flowers in which the sepals and petals are reddish-yellow, and the lip dark golden-yellow. A medium-sized pseudobulbous plant, it appears to be of potential interest to connoisseurs, but has not as yet made its appearance in our collections.

Nothing is known of the genetic affinities of *Bracisepalum*, but they are presumably with *Coelogyne*, *Dendrochilum*, and other members of the subtribe.

CULTURE: Presumably as for the tropical, epiphytic Coelogynes. (H)

BRASSAVOLA R.Br.
(*Lysimnia* Raf., *Tulexis* Raf.)

The Brassavolas, numbering about fifteen species, are very popular, showy, mostly epiphytic (occasionally lithophytic) orchids, which are closely allied to *Laelia* Ldl. Two of the most commonly grown species, known by most collectors as *B. Digbyana* Ldl. and *B. glauca* Ldl., are now referred to the segregate group *Rhyncholaelia* Schltr. The genus, as now delimited, extends from Mexico and Jamaica to Brazil, Bolivia, and Peru. It contains orchids with cylindrical, stem-like pseudobulbs which are topped by a solitary, also terete, fleshy leaf. The flowers, numbering one to several per raceme, are borne from the junction of the leaves with the pseudobulbs (except in the rare *B. acaulis* Ldl. & Paxt., in which they are produced from specialized, leafless basal shoots directly from the rhizome), and are typically green, yellowish, or white in colour. For the most part, they are very easily grown, and hence are thoroughly recommended to the amateur collector.

With *Brassavola Digbyana* and *B. glauca* removed from the genus, it seems evident that proportionately little breeding has been done here, almost all of it centring round the very popular and handsome *B. nodosa*. For horticultural purposes, however—in order to avoid undue and exasperating confusion—we must consider the two first-named species as components of

71

Brassavola; these have been very extensively utilized in the production of artificial hybrids, giving rise to such aggregations as *Brassocattleya* (× *Cattleya*), *Brassolaeliocattleya* (× *Laeliocattleya*), *Brassolaelia* (× *Laelia*), *Brassodiacrium* (× *Diacrium*), *Brassoepidendrum* (× *Epidendrum*), *Brassophronitis* (× *Sophronitis*), *Lowiara* (× *Sophrolaelia*), *Potinara* (× *Sophrolaeliocattleya*), and *Rolfeara* (× *Sophrocattleya*). A few hybrids have been registered within the genus *Brassavola* itself.

CULTURE: In general similar to that required by *Cattleya*, etc. The species do not benefit by too frequent division, hence they are best grown as specimen plants, either in pots or baskets. Abundant supplies of water and strong, relatively undiffused light should be given them while in active growth, but upon maturation of the new stem-like pseudobulbs, water should be withheld for a couple of weeks, to allow a rest-period. Perfect drainage is always required for success in growing the Brassavolas, in whatever sort of container or compost. Species such as *B. nodosa*, *B. cordata*, and *B. cucullata* thrive best when exposed to almost full sun, and *B. acaulis*—because of its sharply pendulous habit—must be grown on an osmunda-filled raft or tree-fern slab for best success. (I, H)

B. acaulis Ldl. & Paxt. (*Brassavola lineata* Hk.)

Pendulous, epiphytic pl. to 2½′ long, often forming huge masses. Sts. cylindrical, 1-leaved. Lf. to more than 2′ long, terete, fleshy, often flushed with purple. Infls. produced from the rhiz., 1-4-fld., much shorter than the lvs. Fls. fragrant, very heavy-textured, rather hooded, to about 4″ across. Ss. and ps. green, greenish-white, or tan, linear, acute. Lip pure white, basally somewhat tubular, the tube short, the lamina very broad, prominently veined. Summer–autumn. (I) Guatemala; Costa Rica; Panama.

B. cordata Ldl. (*Brassavola subulifolia* Rolfe)

Sts. to 7″ tall, sheathed, jointed, the apical sheaths spathe-like. Lf. solitary, fleshy, to 1¼′ long, terete, semi-erect to almost pendulous. Infls. bearing a few- to many-fld. rac. Fls. fragrant, long-lasting, about 1¾″ across, similar in basic shape to those of *B. nodosa* (L.) Ldl., but smaller and more numerous, the ss. and ps. pale green or greenish-yellow, the large white lip with a long serrate claw which enfolds the col. Summer–autumn. (I, H) West Indies (particularly Jamaica), and Lesser Antilles.

B. cucullata (L.) R.Br. (*Epidendrum cucullatum* L., *Cymbidium cucullatum* Sw., *Bletia cucullata* Rchb.f., *Brassavola appendiculata* A.Rich., *B. cuspidata* Hk., *B. odoratissima* Regel)

Sts. to 5″ tall, terete. Lf. solitary (rarely paired), terete, whip-like, acute, fleshy, to almost 2′ long, mostly pendulous or arching downward. Fls. solitary (rarely paired or in 3's), fragrant, long-lasting, to 7″ across in robust forms when the ss. and ps. are held out, the ss. and ps. usually pendulous, varying from white or yellowish with white margins to greenish-white, sometimes red-flushed at apex, linear, very long-acuminate. Lip white or whitish, cordate, fimbriate basally, where it is sometimes marked with reddish, the apex linear, acute to long-acuminate. Pedicelate ovary with its stalk

to as much as 8″ long. Throughout the year, but mostly in winter. (I, H) West Indies; Mexico; Central America to northern South America.

B. flagellaris B.-R.

Sts. to 12″ long, terete, very slender. Lf. solitary, to 1½′ long, terete, fleshy, sharply acute at the apex. Infls. rather loosely 3-8-fld. Fls. about 2½-3″ in diam., fragrant, long-lasting, yellow-white, the lip white or yellowish-white, usually with some emerald-green in the throat. Ss. and ps. linear, acute to acuminate, widely spreading. Lip elliptic to narrowly elliptic, with a small apicule at the tip. Spring–early summer. (I, H) Brazil.

B. nodosa (L.) Ldl. (*Epidendrum nodosum* L., *Cymbidium nodosum* Sw., *Bletia nodosa* Rchb.f., *Bletia venosa* Rchb.f., *Bletia rhopalorhachis* Rchb.f., *Brassavola grandiflora* Ldl., *B. nodosa* (L.) Ldl. var. *rhopalorhachis* Schltr., *B. rhopalorhachis* Rchb.f., *B. scaposa* Schltr., *B. venosa* Ldl.)

Pl. erect to pendulous, high variable in vegetative and floral dimensions, and, to a lesser degree, in shape, the pls. in large forms to 15″ tall. Sts. terete, to 6″ tall. Lf. solitary, mostly erect, linear to linear-elliptic, acute to acuminate, very fleshy, grooved on the upper surface, to more than 12″ long and 1″ wide (usually much narrower and sometimes sub-terete). Infls. to 8″ long, 1-6-fld. Fls. to 3½″ across, very fragrant at night, long-lived, the ss. and ps. varying from pale green or yellowish to almost pure white, the large, basally tubular lip white, often with some purple spots on the inside of the tube. Throughout the year, often almost ever-blooming. (I, H) West Indies; Mexico through Central America to Venezuela and Peru.

B. Cebolleta Ldl. (*Bletia Cebolleta* Rchb.f.) Very similar in all parts to *B. Perrinii* Ldl., differing principally in the fewer fls. produced per infl. Fls. fragrant, about 2″ across, the ss. and ps. yellowish or greenish-yellow, the lip white. Summer (H) Brazil.

B. Martiana Ldl. (*Bletia Martiana* Rchb.f., *Bletia angustata* Rchb.f., *Brassavola angustata* Ldl., *Brassavola surinamensis* Focke) Rather similar to *B. cucullata* (L.) R.Br., but generally somewhat smaller in vegetative dimensions. Fls. often rather numerous per infl., to about 3″ across, very fragrant, especially at night, long-lasting, the ss. and ps. yellowish-white, linear, the lip white or yellowish-white, sometimes with an apple-green blotch in the throat, serrate basally. Summer. (H) Brazil; Guianas.

B. Perrinii Ldl. (*Bletia Perrinii* Rchb.f., *Brassavola fragrans* Lem.) Similar in habit to *B. flagellaris* B.-R., the terete st.-like pbs. to 6″ long. Lf. solitary, terete, usually deeply grooved above, to 10″ long. Infls. 3-6-fld., short-stalked. Fls. fragrant at night, long-lasting, about 2½-3″ across, often not opening fully, the linear ss. and ps. yellowish or greenish-yellow, the elliptic lip pure white, sometimes with an apple-green area deep in the throat. Spring. (I, H) Brazil.

B. tuberculata Hk. (*Bletia tuberculata* Rchb.f., *Brassavola Gibbsiana* Wms., *Tulexis bicolor* Raf.) Rather similar to *B. Perrinii* Ldl. in all parts, differing principally in the red-spotted yellowish ss. and ps. Lip white, widely spreading, sometimes with a green area deep in the throat. Summer. (I. H) Brazil.

BRASSIA R.Br.

The genus *Brassia* contains about thirty or more species, these widespread in the American tropics from South Florida, Mexico, and the West Indies, to Peru, Bolivia, and Brazil. The group is very closely allied to *Oncidium* Sw., from which it is technically inseparable, although the majority of the cultivated members are easily distinguished from that genus by the often amazingly elongate lateral sepals and, to a somewhat lesser degree, the other floral segments. It is from these attenuated flower-parts that the common name of 'Spider Orchid' applied to these plants has been derived. Several of the large-flowered species are rather commonly cultivated, being readily brought into spectacular bloom even by the amateur hobbyist. Typically, the Brassias possess large, relatively flattened pseudobulbs, borne rather close together on a creeping rhizome; one to three large and leathery leaves are produced at the apex of each pseudobulb, and leaf-like sheathing bracts may also appear at their bases. The flower-spikes of these orchids arise from the pseudobulb-bases, or in some species from the leaf-axils of the flushes of new growth; they often attain considerable lengths, and bear a few to rather numerous typically large and handsome flowers. Blossoms whose over-all length exceeds twelve inches are not infrequent in this fascinating genus, and almost all of the commonly grown species produce flowers at least five or six inches long. Colour in the flowers of this group is variable, although yellows, greens, and browns predominate. Almost all of the Brassias bear flowers which give off a pervading and pleasant fragrance, especially during the warm daytime hours.

The Brassias have only during the past few years come under the notice of the orchid-breeders, although the group appears to offer a tremendous wealth of potential material to the enterprising hybridist. Most of this work has to date been done in Hawaii, where a wonderful series of splendid creations utilizing *Brassia* in combination with allied genera of the subtribe Oncidiinae have been made. Many additional, experimental crosses in this group are now being grown, and will in time grace our collections.

CULTURE: Generally speaking, Brassias require conditions similar to those afforded *Cattleya*, etc. For the most part very easily grown, they are highly recommended to all collectors of orchidaceous plants. They do well in perfectly drained pots, these tightly filled with osmunda or shredded tree-fern fibre, or firmly mounted on tree-fern slabs. The use of the various bark preparations has generally been found to be unsatisfactory in reference to these orchids. Since virtually all of the species are epiphytic, tropical plants, considerable warmth and moisture is required at all times; a rest-period of about two weeks' duration following maturation of the new growth is often helpful. Most Brassias thrive in a fairly sunny spot where air-circulation is good. They should be repotted whenever stale conditions exist at the roots, as they are singularly intolerant of poor compost. All of the species benefit from regular applications of fertilizers. (I, H)

B. Alleni L.O.Wms.

Highly aberrant vegetatively for the genus, without pbs., the pls. almost exactly simulating those of *Huntleya meleagris* Ldl., with which it often occurs in the wild. Pls. consisting of a fan of imbricating lvs., growing to a length of about $1\frac{1}{2}'$, with a width of about $1\frac{1}{2}''$, linear-ligulate to lanceolate, usually subfalcately acuminate at the apex, not very heavy in texture, often yellowish-green in colour. Infls. erect or arching, arising from the upper lf.-axils, 5–8-fld., crowded, to about 8″ long. Fls. somewhat variable in colour, to 3″ long, very fragrant of honey, the ss. usually reddish-tan to olive-ochre, shading to cinnamon-buff at the base, the ps. similar in colour, with a triangular bright yellow basal area, the lip yellow, with a semicircular band of reddish-brown surrounding the white disc. Ss. and ps. considerably shorter than in most of the spp. Autumn. (I) Panama, mostly at moderately high elevations.

B. caudata (L.) Ldl. (*Epidendrum caudatum* L., *Malaxis caudata* Willd., *Oncidium caudatum* Rchb.f., *Brassia Lewisii* Rolfe, *B. longissima* (Rchb.f.) Schltr. var. *minor* Schltr.)

Extremely variable in size and shape of all parts. Pbs. compressed, to 6″ tall and $1\frac{1}{2}''$ wide, oblong-elliptic, usually glossy, often yellowish-green. Lvs. 2–3, oblong-elliptic to oblong-lanceolate, obtuse to acute, rather leathery, folded at base, to more than 12″ long and $2\frac{1}{2}''$ wide. Infls. often paired per growth, to $1\frac{1}{2}'$ long, usually gracefully arching, 3–12-fld., the rac. rather loose to dense. Fls. 5–8″ long, fragrant, rather waxy, the often very elongate ss. and ps. yellowish, greenish, or yellow-green with more or less numerous light or dark brown spots and bars, especially towards the bases of the segms. Lip apically acuminate, mostly yellowish or greenish-yellow, with some dull brown spots and marks near the base; calli fuzzy, broken up into teeth at the front. Autumn–early winter; occasionally more than once annually. (I, H) South Florida; Cuba; Mexico to northern South America.

B. Gireoudiana Rchb.f. & Warsc. (*Oncidium Gireoudianum* Rchb.f.)

Rather similar in habit to *B. caudata* (L.) Ldl., often somewhat more robust and typically with larger and more handsome fls., the segms. of which are rigid rather than flaccid and somewhat drooping. Fls. numerous, very fragrant, lasting for several weeks, to more than 12″ long in certain phases, the ss. and ps. greenish-yellow, blotched mostly near the base with very dark, shiny brown or almost blackish-brown. Lip large, pale yellow with sparse brown spots and blotches, the apical half conspicuously broader than the basal half, the calli thickened into broad plates at the front. Late spring–summer. (I, H) Costa Rica; Panama.

B. longissima (Rchb.f.) Nash (*Brassia Lawrenceana* Ldl. var. *longissima* Rchb.f.)

Similar to *B. caudata* (L.) Ldl. in basic vegetative appearance, but the pbs. usually much more compressed, of a paler colour, and with a solitary apical lf. Lf. to almost 2′ long and 3″ wide, with a distinct basal stalk. Infls. erect or arching, few- to many-fld., to $1\frac{1}{2}'$ long. Fls. occasionally measuring as much as 21″ from tip to tip, fragrant, rather long-lived, the segms. very long-attenuated and thread-like, the ss. yellow to greenish-yellow, spotted and blotched basally with reddish-brown; ps. shorter than the dors. sep., similar in colour. Lip pale yellow to greenish-white, with a few reddish basal spots, the base somewhat concave with erect margins. Spring. (I, H) Costa Rica; Panama; Colombia; ? Ecuador; Peru.

B. maculata R.Br. (*Brassia guttata* Ldl., *B. Wrayae* Skinner, *Oncidium Brassia* Rchb.f.)

Often rather similar to *B. caudata* (L.) Ldl. in basic habit, the pbs. sometimes 1-leaved, to 6″ long, usually more robust and often more curving medially than the other sp., mostly yellow-green. Lvs. larger and broader than the other sp. Infls. from the typically bare bases of the pbs., the rachis customarily flecked with brownish-purple, few- to many-fld., usually rather dense and with the fls. tightly arranged in 2 vertical ranks. Fls. waxy, fragrant, long-lasting (upwards of 1½ months), usually 5–8″ in total length, the segms. rigid. Ss. and ps. greenish or greenish-yellow, flecked and barred with purple, bright brown, or reddish-brown, the ps. antrorsely erect. Lip yellowish, mostly spotted with purple or brown-purple, dilated near the middle to form a rather triangular apical part, the margins wavy, recurved, the callus entire, pubescent, yellowish or bright orange. Autumn–spring; occasionally twice annually. (I, H) Cuba; Jamaica; British Honduras; Guatemala; Honduras.

B. verrucosa Ldl. (*Brassia aristata* Ldl., *B. brachiata* Ldl., *B. coryandra* Morr., *B. longiloba* DC, *B. odontoglossoides* Kl. & Karst., *Oncidium brachiatum* Rchb.f., *Oncidium verrucosum* Rchb.f.)

Pbs. narrowly egg-shaped, compressed, usually somewhat furrowed, to 4″ tall, to about 2″ wide and about ½″ thick or more, mostly dull dark green, with several typically lf.-like sheaths at base. Lvs. (apical) 2, oblong-elliptic to lanceolate, acute, leathery, folded at base, to 15″ long and 2″ wide. Infls. often with a purple rachis, produced from the pb.-base, to more than 2′ long, the loose rac. 5–8-fld. Fls. to 8″ long in largest forms, fragrant, waxy, long-lived, pale green spotted with dark green or reddish, the lip whitish, furnished especially on the lower half with prominent black-green warts, sometimes red-spotted basally, the callus yellowish, 2-parted. Spring–early summer. (I, H) Mexico; Guatemala; El Salvador; Honduras; Venezuela.

B. chlorops Endr. & Rchb.f. (*Brassia parviflora* A. & S.) Pbs. rudimentary, slender, ellipsoidal, usually completely concealed by the folded lf.-bases. Lf. (apical) solitary, lanceolate, shortly acuminate, rather leathery, to 12″ long and 1″ broad, the folded base often forming a short, narrow petiole. Infls. erect or arching, produced from the upper lf.-axils, 3–7-fld., to 10″ long, usually shorter. Fls. less than 2″ long, waxy, only faintly fragrant, the ss. and ps. rather fleshy, green with darker spots or brown with yellow markings, the lip rather fleshy, green or yellow with some deep green or brown spots. Summer. (I) Costa Rica; Panama.

B. Keiliana Rchb.f. (*Brassia cinnamomea* Lind., *Oncidium Keilianum* Rchb.f.) Similar in basic habit to *B. caudata* (L.) Ldl., but the pbs. only about 2″ tall. Lvs. paired, rather leathery, to 10″ long. Infls. mostly erect, to 1½′ tall, loosely 10–20-fld. Fls. to about 6″ long, fragrant, waxy, the ss. and

ps. greenish-yellow, spotted with brown, the lip white, with a brown-flecked callus. Summer. (I) Colombia.

B. Lanceana Ldl. (*Brassia macrostachya* Ldl., *B. pumila* Ldl., *Oncidium suaveolens* Rchb.f.) Pbs. oblong, compressed, clustered, rather yellowish, to 5″ tall. Lvs. paired, not especially heavy, lanceolate-ligulate, acute, to 12″ long. Infls. to 2′ tall, erect or horizontally spreading, loosely or rather densely 7–12-fld. Fls. to 5″ long, fragrant, the relatively long-acuminate ss. and ps. light greenish-yellow to almost orange, mostly spotted with dark brown or cinnabar-brown in the lower half, the lip whitish-yellow, the basal callus 2-parted, brown-spotted. Autumn. (I, H) Venezuela; Guianas.

B. Lawrenceana Ldl. (*Brassia augusta* Ldl., *B. cochleata* Kn. & Westc., *Oncidium Lawrenceanum* Rchb.f.) Similar in habit to *B. Lanceana* Ldl., usually somewhat more robust in vegetative parts. Infls. to more than 2′ tall, usually rather rigidly erect, densely many-fld. Fls. to about 7″ long, fragrant, waxy, long-lasting, the ss. and ps. pale yellow, spotted more or less copiously with brown, the lip pale yellow, the callus pubescent, 2-parted, unspotted. Spring–summer. (I, H) Brazil; Guianas.

BROMHEADIA Ldl.

The genus *Bromheadia*, a member of the subtribe *Polystachyinae*, consists of about eleven rather confused terrestrial or epiphytic species, distributed from Sumatra to New Guinea and Australia, with the centre of development apparently in the Malay Peninsula. They are rather rare in cultivation outside of Malaya, although the relatively handsome *B. Finlaysoniana* (Ldl.) Rchb.f. is sometimes seen in choice collections elsewhere. 'The flowers are very much alike in all species, differing chiefly in size and small details of colouring; most are pale yellowish with purple and yellow markings. The vegetative form of the plants varies much more than the flowers. . . . There are two very distinct groups in the genus. One has normal oblong leaves with blades spreading more or less horizontally; the other has leaves laterally compressed, so that they are all in one plane with the stem, exactly as in the strange *Aporum* section of *Dendrobium* which they resemble so closely that when not flowering they can easily be confused with *Dendrobium*. . . . A character which all Bromheadias share is the short life of their flowers, which open in the morning and are fading by noon.'[1] Despite their short-lived flowers, the species of *Bromheadia* are in most instances well worthy of cultivation, at least by connoisseurs of the more unusual orchids.

As yet, no hybridization has been attempted within the genus, and nothing has been ascertained regarding its genetic affinities.

CULTURE: As for *Arundina*. The rare epiphytic species require treatment such as that suggested for *Dendrobium*, being best grown in osmunda-filled pots. (H)

B. Finlaysoniana (Ldl.) Rchb.f. (*Grammatophyllum Finlaysonianum* Ldl., *Bromheadia palustris* Ldl.)

Terrestrial orchids, the sts. close together, commonly more than 3′ tall, sometimes to 7′ tall, the basal part with green sheaths, above these 6 pairs or more of lvs. in two rows, then an apical part bearing green sheaths only, below the infl. Lvs. rather leathery, to 5″ long and slightly more than 1″ wide, mostly ligulate, obtuse.

[1] R. E. Holttum in *Fl. Malaya* (*Orch. Malaya*) 1: 536, 537. 1963.

Infls. erect, sometimes branched, usually about 4″ long, bearing 1 (rarely 2) fls. at a time, at intervals of about 10 days. Fls. extremely variable in size, to almost 3″ across in the largest phases, white or cream, sometimes tinted with mauve, the lip with purple-veined lat. lbs., the median part of the midlb. yellow with some purple spots near the base. Mostly spring–autumn, but often almost ever-blooming. (H) Malay Peninsula; Sumatra; Borneo.

BROUGHTONIA R.Br.

This genus contains but a single species, this a remarkably showy and handsome epiphytic or lithophytic orchid which is evidently confined to Jamaica. Rather frequently encountered today in collections, it is one of the most delightful of the species of the subtribe *Laeliinae*, and is sometimes confused with members of the allied genera *Cattleyopsis* Lem. and *Laeliopsis* Ldl., which it rather resembles vegetatively.

A few hybrids have been made with *Broughtonia* in recent years, the most notable are the crosses with *Cattleya* (= *Cattleytonia*) and *Diacrium* (= *Diabroughtonia*). Considerable additional experimental hybridization seems in order, with such closely allied groups as *Cattleyopsis*, *Laelia*, *Epidendrum*, *Brassavola*, *Rhyncholaelia*, *Sophronitis*, etc.

CULTURE: Once established, these pretty plants do best if grown on rafts tightly packed with osmunda fibre, or on slabs of tree-fern fibre. If confined to pots, flowering usually does not occur as readily as if other arrangements are utilized. Conditions of almost full sun, a rather scanty water-supply, and high temperatures suit them well. They are highly susceptible to bacterial rot and other ills, if improper drainage exists. They are, further, extremely difficult to import from their native island, being almost invariably killed by the fumigation which accompanies their entry into the United States and other areas. They dislike being disturbed, hence should be transplanted only when absolutely essential. When properly grown, *Broughtonia* is almost ever-blooming. (I, H)

B. sanguinea (Sw.) R.Br. (*Epidendrum sanguineum* Sw., *Dendrobium sanguineum* Sw., *Broughtonia coccinea* Hk.)

Pbs. tightly clustered, often prostrate against one another, usually greyish-green, to about 2″ tall, varying from almost globular to somewhat cylindrical, becoming furrowed with age. Lvs. paired, rigid, oblong, acutish, to 8″ long. Infls. to almost 2′ long, slender, wiry, rarely branching, with a loose, 8–15-fld. rac. at the apex. Fls. flattened out when opened fully, to 1″ across (very rarely to 2″), variable in colour, but usually a vivid crimson (very rarely yellow), the ps. often with slightly paler median veins, the lip broader than long, roundish, slightly toothed on the margins, yellowish or whitish at base, with vivid rose-purple veins. Autumn–spring. (I, H) Jamaica.

BROWNLEEA Harv.

This is a genus of more than ten species of often very handsome, principally terrestrial orchids of the subtribe

Disinae, native for the most part in eastern South Africa, with outlying representatives in Madagascar and tropical Africa. Closely allied to *Disa* Berg. and certain of its segregates, *Brownleea* differs from them in technical characteristics. Like Disas, the often brilliantly-hued blossoms are complexly formed, with the dorsal sepal hooded and labelloid in appearance, while the true lip is considerably reduced in dimensions. A few of the species are present in collections at this time, but they must be classed as very rare orchids in cultivation.

Nothing is known of the genetic affinities of *Brownleea* —although it is presumed that they lie with *Disa*, etc.— and no hybrids have as yet been attempted.

CULTURE: As for *Disa*, depending upon the place of origin of the particular specimen. The Brownleeas are often rather difficult to maintain in good condition in the greenhouse for more than a single season. (C, I)

B. coerulea Harv. (*Disa coerulea* Rchb.f.)

Tubers usually solitary, sessile. St. rather slender, $\frac{1}{2}$– $1\frac{1}{4}′$ tall. Lvs. cauline, ovate or elliptic-ovate, 2–6″ long, becoming bract-like upwards. Rac. loosely many-fld., 1–3″ long. Fls. about $\frac{3}{4}$″ in diam., lilac-blue or purple-blue more or less spotted (especially on the dors. sep.) with rich purple. Dors. sep. hood-like, ovate-lanceolate, somewhat recurved, the spur cylindrical, slightly curved, about 1″ long. Lat. ss. elliptic-lanceolate. Ps. oblong-lanceolate, oblique. Lip tiny, very short, linear. Mostly Mar. (C, I) Cape Colony; Tembuland; Natal; Transvaal.

B. recurvata Sond. (*Disa recurvata* Rchb.f.)

Tuber usually solitary, ovoid, sessile. St. rather slender, 12–15″ tall. Lvs. cauline, stalkless, linear-lanceolate or lanceolate, rather small. Rac. rather loosely many-fld., 2–3$\frac{1}{2}$″ long. Fls. about $\frac{3}{4}$″ across, pale pink, sometimes more or less streaked with purple, the conspicuous anther reddish-brown. Dors. sep. hooded, ovate-lanceolate, its spur cylindrical, somewhat curved, blunt, $\frac{3}{8}$″ long. Lat. ss. ovate-lanceolate. Ps. falcate-oblong, oblique, somewhat undulate on outer margins. Lip tiny, erect, linear. Feb.–Apr. (C, I) Cape Colony; Tembuland; Basutoland.

B. alpina (Hk.f.) N.E.Br. (*Disa alpina* Hk.f., *Disa Preussii* Krzl.) Tuber small. St. rather stout, to about 2′ tall. Lvs. cauline, broadly linear or linear-lanceolate, pointed, becoming bract-like above, 3–9″ long. Rac. narrow, densely many-fld., crowded, to 3″ long. Fls. about $\frac{1}{4}$″ across, erect, white and pink. Dors. sep. hooded, the lat. ss. subfalcate-oblong, marginally incurved. Ps. narrow, forming a hood with the dors. sep. Lip tiny, linear, blunt. Mar.–May. (C, I) Cameroons.

B. Nelsoni Rolfe. St. rather slender, to about 8″ tall. Lvs. cauline, lanceolate or lanceolate-oblong, stalkless, 2–3$\frac{1}{2}$″ long. Rac. usually about 9-fld., loose. Fls. about $\frac{5}{8}$″ across, rosy-purple. Dors. sep. hooded, ovate-lanceolate, its spur cylindrical, somewhat curved, about $\frac{3}{16}$″ long. Lat. ss. elliptic-ovate. Ps. ovate-lanceolate, oblique. Lip tiny, erect, 3-lbd. Mostly Mar. (C, I) Transvaal.

BUCHTIENIA Schltr.

Evidently confined to the high Andes of Bolivia and Peru, but a single species of *Buchtienia* is known to date, and this is a very rare terrestrial orchid, which has not been introduced into our collections. A member of the subtribe *Spiranthinae*, **Buchtienia boliviensis** Schltr. is a stout plant growing to about three feet in height, leafy at the base, with an elongate raceme of rather small, fleshy, rose-coloured or greenish blossoms. It has apparently been collected on only two occasions to date.

Nothing is known of the genetic affinities of *Buchtienia*.

CULTURE: Presumably as for *Spiranthes*, although cool conditions should be necessary for any degree of success. (C)

BUESIELLA C.Schweinf.

A member of the subtribe *Bulbophyllinae*, *Buesiella* consists of but a single known species, this an excessively rare epiphytic orchid, **B. pusilla** C.Schweinf., apparently known only from a single herbarium specimen from the Department of Cuzco, in Peru. A small plant, pseudobulbous, with narrow foliage and racemes of tiny blossoms, it appears to be of interest only to botanists or to the specialist collector; it is, obviously, not in cultivation at this time.

Nothing is known of the genetic affinities of *Buesiella*.

CULTURE: Possibly as for *Ornithocephalus* and other relatively fragile 'botanical' orchids. The plant has a creeping rhizome, which would necessitate some sort of 'totem-pole' of tree-fern fibre or other materials, up which it could clamber. (I)

BULBOPHYLLUM Thou.

(*Anisopetalum* Hk., *Bolbophyllaria* Rchb.f., *Bolbophyllum* Spreng., *Cirrhopetalum* Ldl., *Cochlia* Bl., *Didactyle* Ldl., *Diphyes* Bl., *Epicranthes* Bl., *Epicrianthes* Bl., *Gersinia* Neraud., *Henosis* Hk.f., *Lyraea* Ldl., *Macrolepis* A.Rich., *Malachadenia* Ldl., *Megaclinium* Ldl., *Odontostyles* Breda, *Osyricera* Bl., *Oxysepalum* Wight, *Sestochilos* Breda, *Taurostalix* Rchb.f., *Tribrachia* Ldl., *Xiphizusa* Rchb.f.)

The genus *Bulbophyllum* is without a doubt the largest assemblage of species in the entire Orchidaceae, the most recent estimate putting the total number of component taxa at approximately two thousand. This extraordinary aggregation of orchids is widespread in all tropical and most subtropical parts of the globe, being particularly well developed in tropical Asia and environs, and in Africa and near-by insular areas. The centre of dissemination is in New Guinea, where more than six hundred species occur. In the Americas, *Bulbophyllum* contains only about one hundred species, most of them indigenous to Brazil, with outlying representatives as far away as South Florida, Cuba, and Mexico. The principal genus of the subtribe *Bulbophyllinae*, it is vaguely allied to *Dendrobium* Sw. (subtribe *Dendrobiinae*), through the strange group *Epigeneium* Gagnep., which appears to form a connecting-link between the two subtribal groupings. Because of the extremes of variance which occur within *Bulbophyllum*, it has been split into a number of distinct segregates by some orchidologists; horticulturists often recognize at least two of these genera—*Cirrhopetalum* Ldl. and *Megaclinium* Ldl.—for the sake of convenience, but botanically these intergrade perfectly with the larger group, hence are here considered as synonymous. A brief generic characterization of *Bulbophyllum* is difficult to make, because of the tremendous number of entities involved, and their diversity, both vegetatively and florally. A great many of the cultivated species, however, possess more or less prominent, often angular, one-leaved pseudobulbs which are borne at varying distances from each other on a creeping rhizome. The leaves are typically rather fleshy and highly diverse in shape and dimensions. In most of the commonly seen species the inflorescences arise from the rhizome, at or near the base of the pseudobulbs, and produce from one to very numerous small to rather large flowers. In many of these the sepals (particularly the laterals) are more or less joined and are considerably larger than the often complicated petals and lip. Oftentimes they are furnished with a strong scent, sometimes pleasant, and sometimes foetid and almost suffocating in its intensity. Colours range through virtually every hue imaginable, from pure white to almost black; green, brown, red, and yellow are particularly frequent shades. A very large number of Bulbophyllums have been in sporadic cultivation in the past; today they are far from common orchids in our collections, but quite a few of them are still to be encountered in greenhouses devoted to the odd and unusual orchids. Their often extremely complex flowers are among the most remarkable of all orchidaceous plants.

Thus far the hybridists have largely passed this immense genus by. To date of this writing only three crosses have been made within the group, and two of these have been registered under the now synonymous name *Cirrhopetalum*, namely *Bulbophyllum x Fascination* (*B. fascinator* × *B. longissimum*) and *B. x Louis Sander* (*B. longissimum* × *B. ornatissimum*). The third hybrid is the rare and very handsome *Bulbophyllum x David Sander* (*B. Lobbii* × *B. virescens*). Further experimental breeding within the genus seems definitely in order, with some truly fantastic results to be anticipated. Nothing is known concerning the intergeneric compatibility of *Bulbophyllum*, as yet; it seems, however, entirely possible that it will cross with *Epigeneium*, and probably with certain other groups of this alliance.

CULTURE: In a genus of this size, it is very difficult to set up a definite system of cultural directions, since almost every species—and often every individual of a given species with a wide distribution—requires slightly different conditions than its relatives. Generally speaking, however, the following basic requirements seem to apply to the majority of the cultivated Bulbophyllums: (1) Temperature requirements depend upon the place of origin of the species under consideration, those from high elevations naturally requiring much cooler conditions than the lowland, tropical types. Certain Bulbophyllums have wide ranges, extending from constantly hot to mostly cool altitudes; in such instances, therefore, it is most essential that the grower know precisely where his individual plant comes from, to best attend to its temperature wants. (2) Most of the members of this genus in common cultivation possess more or less elongate rhizomes, which rapidly outgrow the confines of the average pot. Because of this, once they are well rooted, the plants seem to do best if grown on tree-fern slabs or in sizeable, rather shallow baskets, over the surface of which the rhizomes may ramble as they wish. If grown in sufficiently large pots, especial care must be paid to the drainage supplied, and only a relatively small proportion of the container should be filled with compost. (3) Compost for these orchids must be very well drained and porous, since they are exceedingly intolerant of stale conditions at the roots, and will soon perish if such a state is permitted to persist for very long. In the past, either straight osmunda fibre, or chopped tree-fern fibre, was utilized in most cases, and the recently recommended bark preparations have been so unsuccessful that no change seems to be warranted. A mixture of chopped sphagnum moss and shredded tree-fern is very acceptable by some of the smaller, more delicate tropical species. No matter what potting-medium is utilized, it should be packed round the mostly small root-systems rather tightly, for best results. (4) While actively growing—which in most species is throughout the year—copious quantities of water should be given, and relatively high humidity maintained. Upon completion of the new growths in species from areas in which they are naturally allowed a dry season (e.g., Burma, Himalayas, China), moisture should be somewhat curtailed for a couple of weeks, to permit ripening of the new pseudobulbs. Virtually all of the tropical species need no such rest-period under cultivation. (5) Most Bulbophyllums require a rather shaded situation in the collection, as the fleshy foliage and pseudobulbs are very liable to sunburn if given too bright light. (6) Repotting should be done as infrequently as possible, since these orchids are intolerant of disturbance. Conversely, however, they must be transferred immediately from any container in which the compost shows even the slightest sign of staleness. Most of the species do well if allowed to grow into 'specimen' plants, though naturally these require a certain amount of extra special attention at all times. (7) Frequent and regular applications of weak fertilizing solutions seem most beneficial, provided the plants are well rooted, and the potting-material is sufficiently fresh. (8) When new growths or flower-spikes appear, one should be very careful not to let water lodge in the opening leaves or buds, or rotting may occur. (C, I, H)

B. Amesianum (Rolfe) J.J.Sm. (*Cirrhopetalum Amesianum* Rolfe)

Pbs. borne at rather close intervals on a creeping rhiz., prominently 4-angled, to a maximum of about 1″ tall. Lf. solitary, about 6″ long and 1½″ wide, stalked towards the base, oblong, blunt apically, fleshy. Infls. stalked, about 8″ tall, with a 5–10-fld. umbel at the apex. Fls. about 1″ long, rather foetid-scented, mostly very short-lived, the dors. sep. blackish-purple, elliptic, long-ciliate marginally; lat. ss. yellowish-red, joined together into a narrow, linear segm. Ps. and lip very small, reddish or purplish-red. Summer. (I, H) Philippines.

B. barbigerum Ldl.

Pbs. clustered, broadly oval, flattened, to 1½″ long and almost as much in diam. Lf. solitary, leathery, rather rigid, to 3″ long and about 1″ wide, oblong, blunt at the apex. Fls. borne in a 2-ranked rac., 8–14 in number, the peduncle to about 6″ long. Fls. horizontally spreading, about 1″ long (including the lip), rather foul-smelling, lasting rather well, the lanceolate, acute ss. dirty-purple, the ps. so reduced as to be scarcely noticeable, the lip tongue-shaped, thickly furnished with oscillating deep purple hairs which move even when there is a scarcely perceptible breeze, green with brownish or purplish-brown veins. Late spring–summer. (H) Tropical West Africa.

B. Beccarii Rchb.f.

The largest sp. in the genus, one of the most remarkable of all orchids! Rhiz. sometimes as much as 8″ in diam., encircling the trees on which it grows like a great snake. Pbs. distant, egg-shaped, about 2″ long and wide. Lf. solitary, to almost 2′ long and 8″ wide, very thick and rigidly leathery, stiffly erect, usually yellowish-green, elliptic, acute, somewhat folded together near the base. Infls. borne from the rhiz., near the pbs., short-stalked, pendulous, to 9″ long and 4″ in diam., cylindrical, composed of several hundred small fls. Fls. excessively foetid,[1] not opening widely, about ½″ across, the ss. oblong, yellowish intricately netted inside with red, the ps. smaller, lanceolate, yellow, with a red median line, the lip small, tongue-shaped, golden-yellow with red stripes. Autumn. (H) Borneo.

B. biflorum Teijsm. & Binn. (*Bulbophyllum geminatum* Carr, *Cirrhopetalum biflorum* J.J.Sm.)

Pbs. rather distant on the rhiz., sharply 4-angled, usually yellow, about 1½″ tall. Lf. solitary, to 5″ long and 1¼″ wide, oblong, blunt apically, shortly narrowed at base. Infls. erect, 2-fld., to 4″ tall. Fls. almost 3″ long, rather foul-smelling, fleshy. Dors. sep. with a wide blade which is concave at the base and then reflexed, the tip with a slender, thick-tipped tail about ½″ long, brown-purple; lat. ss. about 3″ long, narrow, the upper edges joined almost throughout their length, and the lower edges also in the apical half, which is gradually narrowed, yellow-green, the basal half purple-spotted, with 5 rows of spots towards the base on the lower surface. Ps. asymmetric, small, the blunt tip with a small tail, brown-purple. Lip small, bent at a right angle, dull yellow with some purple spots. Summer. (H) Malay Peninsula; Sumatra; Java.

B. Binnendijkii J.J.Sm.

Rhiz. prominently jointed, elongate, the pbs. borne at intervals, cylindrical, somewhat laterally compressed, to 5″ long. Lf. solitary, rather rigidly leathery, bright glossy green, elliptic, acute, to 12″ long and 5″ wide. Infls. slightly arching, to 6″ long, with a 10–15-fld. umbel about 10″ in diam. at the apex. Fls. to almost 4″ long, foetid-smelling, rather waxy, the ss. yellow-green with brown spots, the lat. ones often spirally twisted, the ps. smaller, coloured like the ss., the lip tongue-shaped, yellow, red frontally, very thick, about 1″ long, the col. short, yellowish, dotted with red. Spring. (H) Java.

B. bracteolatum Ldl. (*Bolbophyllaria bracteolata* Rchb.f.)

Pbs. egg-shaped, 4-angled, less than 1″ tall. Lvs. paired, thick and rigid, ligulate, obtuse, about 2″ long

[1] It is on record that persons studying this foul-smelling orchid in a confined space have been rendered unconscious by its overpowering stench—this likened to 'a herd of very dead elephants'!

Bulbophyllum barbigerum Ldl. [VEITCH]

and ½″ wide. Infls. with a very fleshy, cylindrical rachis, to 6″ tall, usually stiffly erect, the fls. sessile on the rachis. Fls. about ¼″ long, not opening well, fleshy, yellowish flushed with reddish, the intricate lip very small, yellow, purplish in front. Summer. (H) Guianas; Brazil.

B. campanulatum (Rolfe) Rolfe (*Cirrhopetalum campanulatum* Rolfe, *Cirrhopetalum auratum* Ridl.)

Pbs. rather distant on the rhiz., egg-shaped, grooved, dark olive-green, about 1″ tall. Lf. solitary, purplish, rather fleshy, to 5″ long and 1″ wide, with a bluntly pointed apex, the base narrowed into a stalk. Infls. to 6″ tall, the rachis purplish, bearing about 8 fls. in a whorl, the fls. all drooping so that the whole structure forms a bell. Fls. fragrant, short-lived, about 1½″ long, the dors. sep. small, fringed on the margins, yellow with crimson veins, the lat. ss. very pale yellow with pink veins and innumerable pink dots, free at the base, then joined to form an oblong blade, the apex slightly back-curved, the ps. similar to the dors. sep. but narrowed basally, the lip dark crimson. Autumn. (H) Malay Peninsula; Sumatra.

B. chinense (Ldl.) Rchb.f. (*Cirrhopetalum chinense* Ldl.)

Pbs. rather distant on the rhiz., about 1¼″ tall, egg-shaped, somewhat angular. Lf. solitary, leathery, to about 5″ long and 1″ wide, elliptic, blunt apically. Infls. shorter than the lvs., mostly erect, about 4″ tall, with a 10–12-fld. umbel at the apex. Fls. about 2″ long, vaguely fragrant, the elliptic, concave dors. sep. with a short apical point, yellowish, the tip red; lat. ss. mostly free, tongue-shaped, yellowish; ps. yellowish, oblong, with a series of warts on the margins; lip greenish-yellow, freely mobile. Summer–autumn. (I) South China.

B. cocoinum Batem.

Pbs. clustered or rather distant, egg-shaped, 4-angled, to 2″ tall. Lf. solitary, rather rigidly leathery, narrowly ligulate, to 5″ long and about 1¼″ wide. Infls. arching to almost pendulous, to 10″ long, the rac. very dense, many-fld. Fls. about ½″ long, heavily fragrant, all segms. white with rose or rose-red tips, the ss. long-acuminate, the ps. small and linear, the lip small, densely ciliate. Winter. (H) Tropical West Africa.

B. comosum Coll. & Hemsl.

Pbs. egg-shaped, about 1½″ tall. Lvs. paired, rather papery, deciduous prior to flowering-time, fragrant of sweet-hay when dried, broadly tongue-shaped, blunt at apex, to 8″ long and 1½″ wide. Infls. mostly erect, to 8″

tall, with a very dense, cylindrical rac. Fls. about $\frac{3}{4}''$ long, highly fragrant, rather long-lasting, yellowish-white. Ss. with small hair-like marginal cilia. Ps. very tiny. Lip tongue-shaped, butter-yellow. Winter. (I, H) Burma; Thailand.

B. coriophorum Ridl. (*Bulbophyllum compactum* Krzl., *B. crenulatum* Rolfe, *B. mandrakanum* Schltr., *B. robustum* Rolfe)

Robust sp., to almost 2' tall when in fl., the pbs. oval, 4-angled, to 3" tall. Lvs. paired, heavily leathery, to 7" long and 2" wide, oblong, blunt apically, slightly narrowed towards the base. Infls. erect or arching, to about 2' tall, the rachis very fleshy, the rac. erect or nodding, very densely many-fld., cylindrical, about 1" in diam. Fls. inserted in cavities on the rachis, about $\frac{1}{4}''$ long, not opening fully, yellow with reddish veins, the outside of the ss. covered with tiny wart-like protuberances. Autumn–spring. (H) Madagascar; Comoro Islands.

B. crassipes Hk. (*Bulbophyllum Careyanum* Wall. not Hk.)

Pbs. often 4" or more apart on the rhiz., ellipsoidal, about 3" tall at most, about $1\frac{1}{2}''$ in diam. Lf. solitary, thickly leathery, tongue-shaped, blunt apically, to 9" long and 2" wide. Infls. short-stalked, horizontal or somewhat hanging, to $2\frac{1}{2}''$ long, the fls. very numerous and tightly packed together in a dense cylindrical rac. to 1" in diam. Fls. less than $\frac{1}{2}''$ long, rather sour-smelling, the ss. yellow or ochre-yellow, more or less densely spotted with purple-brown, the lat. ss. cohering into an elliptic, short-acuminate segm. Ps. very small, long-acuminate, mostly yellow, sometimes with a median brownish line. Lip broadly tongue-shaped, dull brownish or purplish-brown, fuzzy. Spring. (I, H) Himalayas; Burma; Thailand.

B. Dayanum Rchb.f.

Pbs. egg-shaped, about $1\frac{1}{2}''$ tall, usually clustered. Lf. solitary, very fleshy, rigidly erect, oblong, narrowed or somewhat stalk-like basally, to 4" long, about 2" broad, usually reddish or purplish underneath. Infls. almost stalkless, the fls. 2–4 in number, borne from the pb.-bases. Fls. about $1\frac{1}{2}''$ in diam., foul-smelling, the ss. green, streaked with lines of purple or red-purple spots, furnished with long hairs, the much smaller ps. blood-red with yellow margins, the lip green, the disc furnished with blood-red ridges or warts. Spring–summer. (I, H) Burma.

B. Dearei Rchb.f. (*Bulbophyllum Godseffianum* Weathers, *Phyllorchis Dearei* O.Ktze., *Sarcopodium Dearei* hort., *Sarcopodium Godseffianum* hort.)

Pbs. egg-shaped, clustered, to 2" tall, rather glossy. Lf. solitary, rather rigidly leathery, tongue-shaped, acute, to 6" long and about $1\frac{1}{2}''$ wide. Infls. rather short to as long as the lvs., 1-fld., erect. Fls. about 3" across, heavy-textured, long-lasting, fragrant, the dors. sep. ovate-lanceolate, tawny-yellow spotted with red; lat. ss. lanceolate, falcate, dilated and saccate at the base, tawny-yellow with some purple or red-purple markings on both sides; ps. linear-lanceolate, shorter than the ss., tawny-yellow with deeper veins and some reddish-

purple spots; lip whitish or yellowish, articulated with the col.-foot by a flexible claw, hence almost constantly mobile, triangular with the lateral angles turned upwards, and the anterior one reflexed; calli U-shaped, whitish mottled with purple; col. very short, dark tawny-yellow margined with red. Spring–early summer. (I, H) Philippines; Borneo.

B. fascinator (Rolfe) Rolfe (*Cirrhopetalum fascinator* Rolfe)

Pbs. clustered, almost globular, about 1" tall, glossy. Lf. solitary, leathery, narrowly elliptic, blunt, to 2" long and about $1\frac{1}{2}''$ wide. Infls. about 4" tall, usually erect. Fl. solitary, about 9" long. Dors. sep. ovate-lanceolate, acuminate, thickly hairy on the margins, about $1\frac{1}{4}''$ long, greenish with dark purple spots; lat. ss. about $7\frac{1}{2}$–9" long, joined together and greenish basally with numerous reddish warts, the very long tails brownish-green, thread-like. Ps. very fuzzy marginally, greenish to reddish. Lip small, reddish. Autumn. (I, H) Viet-Nam; Laos.

B. gracillimum (Rolfe) Rolfe (*Bulbophyllum psittacoides* J.J.Sm., *Cirrhopetalum gracillimum* Rolfe, *Cirrhopetalum psittacoides* Ridl.)

Pbs. about $\frac{3}{4}''$ apart on the rhiz., egg-shaped, to 2" tall. Lf. solitary, rather leathery, to 5" long and 1" wide, elliptic, blunt apically. Infls. slender, the rachis purple, to 12" long, usually arching under the weight of the 8–10-fld. umbel. Fls. fragrant, to about $2\frac{1}{4}''$ long, mostly brilliant crimson. Dors. sep. ovate, hooded, with a long slender tail, the basal part fringed with red marginally; lat. ss. to almost 2" long, both edges joined together in the basal part (without a gap for the lip), the long-tailed curved ends free. Ps. lanceolate, acuminate, fringed. Lip very small, purple-violet. Summer–autumn. (I, H) Thailand; Malay Peninsula to New Guinea.

B. lemniscatum Par. (*Bulbophyllum lemniscatum* Par. var. *tumidum* Par. & Rchb.f.)

Pbs. almost globular, clustered, glossy, tubercled, $\frac{1}{2}$–$\frac{3}{4}''$ in diam. (rarely more). Lvs. $1\frac{1}{2}$–2" long, in a tuft of 3–4 from the base of the pb., ligulate to elliptic-lanceolate, acute, deciduous prior to flowering-time. Infls. very slender, the rachis somewhat thickened above the middle, to 7" tall, the rac. pendulous or nodding, very densely many-fld. Fls. about $\frac{1}{8}''$ across, rather globular in shape, the ss. deep purple or reddish-purple, basally green, with a long slender pendulous angular appendage, banded with red, at the apex of each of the three segms., this appendage deciduous as the fl. expands, the sep.-margins long-hairy; ps. very small, linear-lanceolate, white with a reddish or purplish median streak; lip small, broadly ovate, recurved, convex, dark blue-purple. Summer. (I) Burma.

B. leucorhachis (Rolfe) Schltr. (*Megaclinium leucorhachis* Rolfe)

Pbs. egg-shaped, often somewhat angular, about 2" tall. Lvs. paired, leathery, rather rigid and erect, tongue-shaped, blunt at the apex, to 8" long. Infls. mostly erect, to about 10" long, the flattened, whitish rachis about $\frac{1}{2}''$ wide, bearing a rather large number of small fls. in a line down the middle of the flat portion. Fls.

foul-smelling, about ½" long, golden-yellow, the ss. and ps. fleshy, with warts on the outside; lip very small, brilliant golden-yellow. Spring. (H) Tropical West Africa: Nigeria; Cameroons.

B. Lindleyi Schltr. (*Megaclinium maximum* Ldl. in part)

Pbs. rather egg-shaped, to 2½" tall, often somewhat elongated and neck-like in upper part. Lvs. paired, rather heavily leathery, tongue-shaped, blunt apically, to 6" long and 1" wide. Infls. erect or arching, to 12" tall, the flattened, incised rachis about ½" wide, bearing the rather numerous fls. in a line down the centre of the flat portion. Fls. about ½" long, often not lasting well, olive-green, spotted with dull red, the small lip mobile. Summer. (II) Tropical West Africa: Sierra Leone to Cameroons.

B. Lobbii Ldl. (*Bulbophyllum Henshallii* Ldl., *B. Lobbii* Ldl. var. *siamense* Rchb.f., *B. siamense* Rchb.f., *Sarcopodium Lobbii* Ldl. and var. *Henshallii* Henfr., *Sestochilos uniflorus* Breda)

Pbs. about 3" apart on the stout rhiz., the sheaths of which split into persistent, often yellowish fibres, egg-shaped, usually yellow-green, 1–2" long, narrowing upwards. Lf. solitary, rather leathery, to 10" long and 3" wide, oblong, the apex with a blunt point, stalked basally. Infls. produced from any node of the rhiz., to 5" tall, usually arching because of the weight of the solitary fl. Fls. widely opening, 3–4" across, very fragrant, waxy, long-lived, pale yellow or buff-yellow spotted and flushed with purple and rosy-purple, all the segms. broad. Ss. lanceolate, acuminate, the lats. falcate. Ps. similar to the dors. sep. but smaller. Lip shorter than the other segms., cordate, acute, reflexed, mobile, yellow or yellowish, more or less finely spotted with purple and with a small orange mark at the base, narrowed to a sharp apical point. Col. short, broad, yellow spotted with purple. Mostly late spring–summer. (I, H) Thailand; Malay Peninsula; Sumatra; Java; Borneo.

B. longiflorum Thou. (*Cirrhopetalum longiflorum* Schltr., *Cirrhopetalum Thouarsii* Ldl., *Cirrhopetalum umbellatum* Frapp. ex Cordem., *Phyllorchis longiflora* O.Ktze.)

Pbs. borne at intervals on the creeping, roughened rhiz., egg-shaped, 4-angled, about 1½" tall, often almost hidden by the numerous fibrous remains of the sheathing basal bracts. Lf. solitary, leathery, rather rigidly erect, oblong, narrowed and stalk-like basally, distinctly incised at apex, to 6" long and 1¼" wide. Infls. erect or arching, to 10" long, with a rather loose, mostly hanging umbel of 6–12 fls. at the apex. Fls. about 2" long, rather foul-smelling, light yellow, the lip golden-yellow. Dors. sep. with a long, apically thickened bristle at the apex; lat. ss. joined for more than half of their length, then slightly flaring, the tips acutish. Ps. very sharp-pointed, hairy. Lip rather small, the upper surface with hair-like papillae. Autumn–spring. (H) Madagascar; Mascarene Islands.

B. longissimum (Ridl.) J.J.Sm. (*Cirrhopetalum longissimum* Ridl.)

Pbs. about 2" apart on the creeping rhiz., to 2" tall, egg-shaped, often vaguely angular, glossy. Lf. solitary, leathery, rather rigid, oblong, blunt apically, to 6" long and 2" wide. Infls. mostly erect, about 8" tall, with a 5–10-fld. umbel at the apex. Fls. to about 11" long, fragrant, short-lived, the dors. sep. ciliate, acuminate, whitish-green, streaked with red, about ¾" long; lat. ss. mostly pendulous, joined basally, the apical parts extended into tails about 8–10" long, pale rose-red with deeper veins. Ps. very small, reddish. Lip small, green. Winter. (H) Thailand.

B. macranthum (Ldl.) Ldl. (*Sarcopodium macranthum* Ldl.)

Rather similar in habit to, and allied to *B. Lobbii* Ldl. Pbs. about 1" tall, the lvs. to 12" long and 4" wide, the apex blunt and 2-lbd. Infls. about 2" tall. Fls. opening widely, solitary, the dors. sep. and ps. whitish with dense purple spots, the lat. ss. ochre-yellow spotted with purple towards the base on the halves away from the lip only, their adjacent edges close together except for a gap at the base, through which the mobile, yellowish lip can swing. Spring. (H) Malay Peninsula; Sumatra; Java; Borneo.

B. Makoyanum (Rchb.f.) Ridl. (*Cirrhopetalum Makoyanum* Rchb.f.)

Pbs. about ¾" tall, broadly egg-shaped, ridged with age. Lf. solitary, to 2½" long and about ¾" wide, tongue-shaped, the apex rounded and cleft, narrowed to a very short stalk. Infls. with a purple rachis, to about 8" long, the 5–10 apical fls. forming a fan or almost perfectly circular umbel. Fls. fragrant, about 1½" long, the dors. sep. small, the apex thread-like, reddish with darker spots and veins, marginally yellow-hairy; lat. ss. narrow, fringed with yellow hairs, pale yellow with purple spots in the basal half and a few towards the tip, both edges joined for most of their length. Ps. somewhat longer than the dors. sep., fringed with yellow hairs, coloured like the dors. sep. Lip tongue-shaped, small, yellowish spotted with purple. Winter. (H) Singapore.

B. maximum (Ldl.) Rchb.f. (*Megaclinium maximum* Ldl., *Megaclinium purpuratum* Ldl.)

Pbs. oblong, 4-angled, to 4" tall. Lvs. paired, leathery, linear or tongue-shaped, blunt at the apex, to 7" long and 1½" wide. Infls. mostly erect, the flattened, rather wavy-margined rachis about 1" wide, blotched with very deep brown or blackish-brown, to 12" tall, the fls. borne along the flat sides in a line from top to bottom. Fls. rather foetid-smelling, about ½" long, yellow, striped outside with red, inside spotted with pale red, the small mobile lip dull red. Summer. (H) Tropical West Africa: Sierra Leone to Cameroons.

B. medusae (Ldl.) Rchb.f. (*Cirrhopetalum medusae* Ldl.)

Rhiz. stout, the pbs. borne at rather distant intervals along it, to 1½" tall, conical, angled, often yellowish. Lf. solitary, rather rigidly leathery, to 8" long and 2" wide, oblong, the apex blunt and slightly cleft, short-stalked at base. Infls. erect or arching, to 8" tall, with several loose sheathing bracts and a mop-like head of many long-tailed fls., the bracts conspicuous, cream-coloured, sometimes reddish-spotted. Fls. to 6" long, rather musty-smelling, white, cream-white, or variously pink- or red-spotted, the lip usually yellowish. Lat. ss. to 5" long, the

Anoectochilus sikkimensis King & Pantl. [H. R. FOLKERSMA]

Arachnis Hookeriana (Rchb.f.) Rchb.f. [GEORGE FULLER]

Arachnis × *Maggie Oei*, a hybrid of this genus [C. K. KUEH]

Arpophyllum spicatum LaLl. & Lex. [GEORGE FULLER]

Bollea coelestia (Rchb.f.) Rchb.f. [H. SCHMIDT-MUMM]

Bletilla striata (Thunb.) Rchb.f. [SAMUEL C. C. CHEN]

basal blade less than $\frac{1}{2}''$ long, the remainder a very slender, thread-like tail. Autumn–winter. (H) Malay Peninsula; Sumatra; Borneo.

B. ornatissimum (Rchb.f.) J.J.Sm. (*Cirrhopetalum ornatissimum* Rchb.f.)

Pbs. 4-sided, egg-shaped, about 2″ apart on the rhiz., to about $1\frac{1}{2}''$ tall. Lf. solitary, leathery, to 6″ long and $1\frac{1}{2}''$ wide, oblong, blunt apically. Infls. about 6″ tall, with a 3–5-fld. fan-like umbel at the apex. Fls. about 4″ long, fragrant, the dors. sep. rhombic-lanceolate, yellow, red-streaked, with hair-shaped appendages on the margins, the lat. ss. narrowly lanceolate, acute, yellowish, veined with reddish, about 3″ long. Ps. small, yellow, striped with red, with apical pendulous appendages. Lip small, purple- or magenta-red. Autumn–early winter. (I, H) India; Himalayas.

B. pachyrrhachis (Rchb.f.) Griseb. (*Bolbophyllaria pachyrrhachis* Rchb.f., *Bulbophyllum vinosum* Schltr.)

Pbs. borne at considerable intervals on the creeping rhiz., usually yellow-green, to about 1″ tall, subconical, strongly 4-angled. Lvs. paired, leathery, usually glossy, linear-lanceolate, acute or acuminate, to 8″ long and almost 1″ broad. Infl. erect or arching from pb.-base, 8–14″ long, the apical fl.-bearing rachis usually dull red and very inflated, bearing the scattered fls. in shallow pits. Fls. small, not opening well, often foul-smelling, about $\frac{1}{4}''$ long, greenish-yellow more or less spotted with purple, or entirely wine-red with darker spots. Col. with a long foot, to which the mobile lip is attached. Dec.–Feb. (H) South Florida; West Indies; Mexico to Panama.

B. picturatum (Ldl.) Rchb.f. (*Cirrhopetalum picturatum* Ldl.)

Pbs. clustered, egg-shaped, sometimes becoming furrowed with age, to 2″ tall, often yellowish-green. Lf. solitary, leathery, usually rather rigid, linear-oblong, rounded at tip, to 7″ long and 1″ wide. Infls. erect, the rachis with red spots, to 10″ tall, with an 8–10-fld. umbel at the apex. Fls. about $2\frac{1}{2}''$ long, slightly fragrant, rather short-lived; dors. sep. yellow-green or purple, red-spotted, with a red club-shaped apical bristle; lat. ss. about 2″ long, olive-green to purple, spotted with deep red or purple-red near the base. Ps. small, mostly greenish, with red tips. Lip dark red, mobile. Spring. (I, H) Burma.

B. purpureorhachis (DeWild.) Schltr. (*Megaclinium purpureorhachis* DeWild.)

Pbs. usually clustered, oblong, smooth (at least when young), to 3″ tall. Lvs. paired, leathery and rather rigid, oblong, obtuse, to 6″ long and 2″ broad. Infls. about 12″ tall, arching, the rachis flattened, about 8″ long, to $1\frac{1}{2}''$ wide, green, densely spotted with violet-purple, the fls. borne in a longitudinal row on the flat sides. Fls. about $\frac{1}{2}''$ long, deep brown or purplish-brown, the outside of the ss. thickly hairy, the small, fleshy, freely mobile lip yellow-brown, spotted with dark brown. Autumn–winter. (H) Belgian Congo.

B. reticulatum Batem.

Pbs. rather distant on the creeping rhiz., oblong to ovoid, about $1\frac{1}{2}''$ tall. Lf. solitary, stalked, ovate-cordate, acuminate, to 5″ long and 3″ wide, rather soft-textured and flaccid, many-nerved, the longitudinal and transverse dark green nerves producing a beautiful network on the paler green background. Infls. short, usually 2-fld., covered with large sheathing bracts. Fls. to 3″ across, fleshy, fragrant, whitish or yellowish striped with red-purple, the stripes sometimes broken up into spots. Dors. sep. ovate-lanceolate, acuminate; lat. ss. much broader at the base, falcate and decurved. Ps. like the dors. sep., but smaller and more pointed. Lip fleshy, yellow, mostly spotted with purple-red, trowel-shaped, recurving. Autumn. (H) Borneo.

B. robustum (Rolfe) J.J.Sm. (*Cirrhopetalum robustum* Rolfe, *Cirrhopetalum graveolens* F.M.Bail.)

Pbs. clustered, egg-shaped, sometimes slightly compressed, to 3″ tall. Lvs. paired, leathery, rather rigid, glossy dark-green, elliptic-oblong, acuminate, to 12″ long and 3″ broad. Infls. robust, about 3″ tall, with an umbel of about 10 fls. at the apex. Fls. spreading in an almost perfect circle, to 3″ long, foul-smelling, fleshy, the ss. yellow, shaded basally with brownish-red, the lat. ones blunt apically. Ps. small, acute apically, yellowish-brown. Lip short and thick, dark red. Spring. (H) New Guinea.

B. suavissimum Rolfe

Pbs. egg-shaped or elongately so, sheathed basally, about 1″ long. Lf. solitary, rather thin in texture, deciduous prior to expansion of the fls., 4–5″ long, narrowly oblanceolate, blunt apically. Infls. very dense, arching, mostly 1-sided racs. to 10″ long. Fls. pendulous or horizontally arranged, about $\frac{1}{3}''$ long, extremely fragrant, the ss. and ps. primrose-yellow, pale rose, or whitish, the small lip golden-yellow. Summer. (I) Burma.

B. tripetaloides (Roxb.) Schltr. (*Dendrobium tripetaloides* Roxb., *Bulbophyllum auricomum* Ldl., *B. foenisecii* Par. & Rchb.f.)

Pbs. egg-shaped, clustered, about 1″ long, glossy. Lvs. paired, falling before the appearance of the fls., very fragrant when dried, tongue-shaped, rather blunt apically, to 8″ long and 1″ wide. Infls. arching or pendulous, to 10″ long, very densely many-fld. Fls. in a single rank, very fragrant, about $\frac{1}{2}''$ long, white or golden-yellow, the ps. very small, ciliate, the small lip golden-yellow, its upper surface furnished with warts. Summer. (I, H) Burma.

B. umbellatum Ldl. (*Cirrhopetalum guttulatum* Wight)

Pbs. fairly distant on the rhiz., narrowly ovoid to oblong-ovoid, $1\frac{1}{2}$–2″ tall. Lf. solitary, leathery, oblong, blunt apically, narrowed into a stalk basally, to 8″ long and $1\frac{1}{2}''$ wide. Infls. erect, slender, to 8″ tall, with a terminal 5–8-fld. umbel. Fls. 1–$1\frac{1}{2}''$ long, rather foul-smelling, pale yellow spotted with red or very dark purple, the lip white with a purple blotch and some smaller purple spots. Ss. and ps. oval, the lat. ss. the largest, the ps. the smallest, the dors. sep. intermediate in size; lip very small, cordate-oblong, emarginate, reflexed. Col. very short, winged, with a small horn on each side of the anther. Autumn. (I) Nepal; Himalayas.

B. uniflorum (Bl.) Hassk. (*Ephippium uniflorum* Bl., *Bulbophyllum galbinum* Ridl., *B. Reinwardtii* Rchb.f.) Pbs. about 4″ apart on the creeping rhiz., to 4″ long and ½″ in diam., somewhat flattened, rather cylindrical. Lf. solitary, to 12″ long and 3½″ wide, heavily leathery, broadly elliptic, the tip shortly pointed, the base narrowed into a rather long stalk. Infls. about 5″ long, with several conspicuous sheaths, with 1 or 2 fls. (more— up to 5—in var. **pluriflorum** Carr). Fls. not opening fully, to 3½″ long, fleshy, foul-smelling, the colour varying from yellow with lines of red spots to reddish spotted with dark red at base of the ss. and ps., the lip usually red with some yellow at the base and apex. Spring–summer. (H) Malay Peninsula; Sumatra; Java.

B. Weddellii (Ldl.) Rchb.f. (*Didactyle Weddellii* Ldl.) Pbs. egg-shaped, prominently 4-angled, to 2″ tall. Lf. solitary, rather rigidly fleshy, oblong, obtuse, to 4″ long and 2″ broad. Infls. erect, about 12″ long, the rac. apical, pendulous, dense, about 6″ long. Fls. about 1″ long, the ss. greenish-yellow spotted inside near the base with red, the much smaller ps. similar in colour, the rather large lip white spotted with dark purple. Autumn. (I, H) Brazil.

B. Bittnerianum Schltr. Allied to, and rather simulating *B. crassipes* Hk. in the shape and dimensions of the vegetative and floral parts, but with yellow fls. Infls. erect, to 4″ tall, the peduncle furnished with large, rather inflated, overlapping, scarious sheaths, usually tinged with brownish, the rac. about 2″ long, the fls. virtually hidden by the very large, lanceolate, whitish bracts (typically inrolled) which subtend them. Spring–early summer. (H) Thailand.

B. calamarium Ldl. Pbs. egg-shaped, 4-angled, to 1½″ tall. Lf. solitary, leathery, ligulate, blunt apically, narrowed towards the base, to about 5″ long and 1″ wide. Infls. with very slender peduncles, to almost 2′ tall, the rac. about 4″ long. Fls. rather resembling those of *B. barbigerum* Ldl., but smaller, only about ¾″ long, the ss. brownish-yellow, the much smaller ps. brownish, the linear lip deep purple, furnished with numerous purple, readily oscillating hairs round the margin. Spring–summer. (H) Tropical West Africa.

B. Careyanum Hk. (*Anisopetalum Careyanum* Hk., *Tribrachia purpurea* Ldl., *Pleurothallis purpurea* D.Don, *Bulbophyllum Careyanum* Hk. var. *ochraceum* Hk.) Very closely allied to, and simulating *B. crassipes* Hk. to large degree, differing from it in its somewhat more robust habit (pbs. to 3½″ tall), longer racs. (to 4″ long), and fls. more strongly spotted with brown-red, the lip of which differs in shape. Winter–spring. (I, H) Himalayas; Burma.

B. Collettii (Hemsl.) King & Pantl. (*Cirrhopetalum Collettii* Hemsl.) Rhiz. very stout, creeping, the pbs. rather distant, less than 1″ tall, ovoid. Lf. solitary, rigidly leathery, to 5″ long and 1″ wide, ovate to elliptic-oblong, stalkless. Infls. very stout, to 6″ tall, with a many-fld. umbel at the apex. Fls. to 6″ long, fragrant, whitish, basally rose-red, the lip golden-yellow. Lat. ss. with long tails, the dors. one hooded, narrowed into a long fringed tail, the ps. ciliate marginally. Spring, (I, H) Burma.

B. corolliferum J.J.Sm. (*Bulbophyllum Curtisii* J.J.Sm. not Ridl., *Cirrhopetalum Curtisii* Hk.f.) Pbs. distant on the creeping rhiz., about ¾″ tall, ovoid, strongly angular. Lf. solitary, rigidly leathery, stalked at the base, tongue-shaped, apically blunt and slightly lobed, to 7″ long. Infls. to 4″ tall, bearing an irregular umbel of 12–15 fls. at the apex. Fls.

about ¾″ long, entirely purple, the lip yellowish, or white with more or less coalescent veins, or rose-mauve and white. Winter. (H) Thailand; Malay Peninsula; Borneo.

B. cupreum Ldl. Very similar to *B. crassipes* Hk., but the rhiz. and scape very slender, the copper-yellow, unspotted fls. fewer, less densely crowded, about ½″ long, not opening fully, with divergent structural details. Spring. (I, H) Burma.

B. Ericssoni Krzl. Very closely allied to and resembling *B. Binnendijkii* J.J.Sm., but the fls. only about 2″ long, pale yellowish-green, the lip acutish, yellowish, dark purple at the apex. Autumn. (H) Moluccas.

B. falcatum (Ldl.) Ldl. (*Megaclinium falcatum* Ldl., *Megaclinium endotrachys* Krzl.) Similar in all parts to *B. maximum* (Ldl.) Rchb.f., but smaller, the rachis very polished, the fls. about ½″ long, yellowish-brown, the lip purple-brown, foul-smelling. Spring–summer. (H) Tropical West Africa: Sierra Leone to Cameroons.

B. Mastersianum (Rolfe) J.J.Sm. (*Cirrhopetalum Mastersianum* Rolfe). Pbs. egg-shaped, becoming furrowed with age, to 2″ tall. Lf. solitary, rather rigidly leathery, oblong to ligulate, to 8″ long and 2″ wide. Infls. to 12″ tall, the 6–10-fld. umbel usually causing it to arch gracefully. Fls. about 2″ long, yellow with brownish spots, the lip brown. Spring. (H) Moluccas.

B. Pechei Bull. Very closely allied to *B. crassipes* Hk. and *B. Careyanum* Hk., but differing in the unspotted, yellow-brown fls., in the very short, sharp teeth on the apex of the col., and in the toothed flaps on the sides of the lip. Winter. (I, H) Burma.

B. platyrhachis (Rolfe) Schltr. (*Megaclinium platyrhachis* Rolfe). Pbs. oblong, about 3″ tall, often flushed with purple. Lvs. paired, rigidly erect, heavily leathery, ligulate, blunt apically, to 6″ long. Infls. erect, the rachis about 10″ long, to 2″ wide, flattened, yellow-brown, yellow in the centre, where the numerous small, foul-smelling fls. are borne. Fls. about ¾″ long, yellowish, striped and flecked with reddish. Summer–autumn. (H) Nyasaland.

B. rhizophorae Ldl. (*Megaclinium lasianthum* Krzl.) Pbs. egg-shaped, about 3″ tall. Lvs. paired, rather heavily leathery, tongue-shaped, to 4″ long. Infls. erect, the flattened rachis about 3″ long, purple, the fls. borne on the flat portions in longitudinal rows. Fls. less than ½″ long, brown-red, yellow inside, hairy on outside of the ss. Spring–autumn. (H) Tropical West Africa, on mangroves along the coast.

B. saltatorium Ldl. Closely allied to and somewhat resembling *B. barbigerum* Ldl. in vegetative appearance, the fls. rather simulating those of *B. calamarium* Ldl., the rac. pendulous, to 3″ long, the fls. about ¾″ long. Winter. (H) Sierra Leone.

B. virescens J.J.Sm. Simulating *B. Binnendijkii* J.J.Sm. in habit, the pbs. prominently furrowed. Fls. about 5½″ long, rather strongly foul-smelling, greenish-yellow, the lip yellow with a rose-red spot at the base, apically narrowed and sharp-pointed. Summer. (H) Moluccas.

BULLEYIA Schltr.

Bulleyia yunnanensis Schltr., the only described member of this rare and little-known genus of the subtribe *Coelogyninae*, is a rather odd and not particularly attractive epiphytic orchid inhabiting the mountains of Yunnan, in China. Not present in our collections at this time, it is a rather robust plant, somewhat resembling a *Coelogyne* in habit, with smallish white or yellowish flowers in a loose, two-ranked raceme.

Nothing has been ascertained regarding the genetic affinities of *Bulleyia*.

CULTURE: Presumably as for the high-elevation Coelogynes. (C, I)

BURNETTIA Ldl.

This is a genus of a single very rare terrestrial species, native in the States of Tasmania, Victoria, and New South Wales in Australia, which appears to be unknown by contemporary collectors. A member of the subtribe *Acianthinae*, it has been placed in synonymy under *Lyperanthus* R.Br. in the past, but most modern students consider it a valid genus. It is a dwarf plant with a few flowers which are large for the size of the vegetative parts, and of rather unusual structure.

No hybrids are known in *Burnettia*, and nothing is recorded concerning its genetic alliances.

CULTURE: As for *Caladenia*, etc. (C, I)

B. cuneata Ldl. (*Caladenia cuneata* Rchb.f., *Lyperanthus Burnettii* FvM.)

Tubers small, globular, subterranean. Lvs. solitary or paired, basal, usually absent at flowering-time, ovate-lanceolate. St. to 4″ tall when in fl., with 2–5 proportionately large fls., 1–2-bracted, the bracts loosely clasping. Fls. thick in texture, reddish or purplish-brown outside, white within, with conspicuous dark veins. Dors. sep. broadly lanceolate, concave, the lat. ss. and ps. as long as the dors. one, not expanding widely, the ps. the narrower. Lip sessile, short, simple, erect at base, recurved towards the tip, truncate or obscurely sinuate, sometimes fringed, with 2 longitudinal ridges or raised plates which become broken up into calli above the middle. Autumn–early winter. (C, I) Australia.

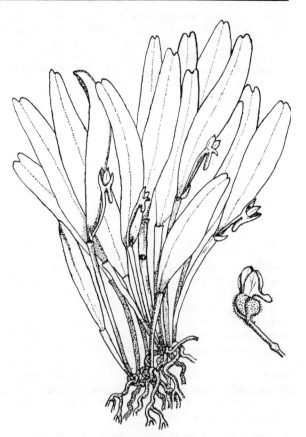

Cadetia heteroidea (Bl.) Schltr. [A.D. HAWKES, AFTER KRAENZLIN]

CADETIA Gaud.

This is a genus of about sixty species of epiphytic or rarely lithophytic orchids, all of which are today very rare in collections. Allied to *Dendrobium* Sw., they are often included in that group, but their vegetative appearance (rather simulating a *Pleurothallis* in many cases) and technical characters of the very small flowers readily serve to distinguish them. Mostly indigenous to New Guinea, a few members of *Cadetia* extend into Australia, the Moluccas, New Caledonia, and the Solomon Islands.

Nothing is known of the genetic affinities of this strange genus.

CULTURE: As for the tropical species of *Bulbophyllum*. (H)

C. Taylori (FvM) Schltr. (*Bulbophyllum Taylori* FvM, *Dendrobium Taylori* Fitzg.)

Pbs. very slender, st.-like, about 4″ long. Lf. solitary, fleshy, rigid, linear, blunt at the apex, to 2″ long. Infls. usually 1-fld., produced at the lf.-base, at its junction with the st.-like pb. Fls. very short-lived (often withering after a few hours' expansion), less than ¾″ across, cream-white, the lip often with some brownish or reddish

marks near the middle, the ss. and ps. very narrow, blunt apically. Summer. (H) Australia: Queensland.

CALADENIA R.Br.

Caladenia is a genus of more than seventy species, the vast majority of which are terrestrial orchids in Australia, with a very few outlying representatives in Indonesia, New Caledonia, and New Zealand. Rare in collections and rather difficult to maintain in good condition for more than a single season, these often spectacular, mostly large-flowered and showy plants should be better known by enthusiasts, despite their rather refractory temperaments. They represent a large number of primarily Australian genera of terrestrial orchids which are but little-known by contemporary orchidists, which would form admirable additions to our collections if their cultural requirements could be mastered. Producing a subterranean, mostly globular tuber, the erect stems bear a solitary, usually basal, often hairy leaf, and one or a few extremely complex, often long-tailed blossoms, the lip of which is typically freely movable. Colour in *Caladenia* is variable (often within a given species), but the flowers are usually of bright and attractive hues.

No artificial hybrids have as yet been produced in *Caladenia*; some presumed natural ones are known in

Australia. Intergeneric breeding with allied groups of the subtribe *Caladeniinae* should prove most interesting.

CULTURE: The cultivation of Caladenias (and many other of the Australian genera of ground orchids) is not a particularly easy matter, but the following recommendations may assist the enthusiast. A perfectly-drained, rather rich compost is obligatory in all cases; staleness at the roots will rapidly prove fatal to these often fragile plants. Quantities of freely-moving air and moisture are needed while the plants are in active growth, but they must receive a rest-period (often of several months' duration) after flowering, when the shoots die down; water should be resumed when the new growths begin to appear at the surface of the compost, though of course, the potting-medium should not be permitted to become excessively desiccated and hard. A rather sunny spot suits them best, and fairly good results have been obtained by growing the plants in shallow pans (such as are used for ferns), with about half of the depth filled with broken crock, gravel, or crushed brick. The remainder is filled with a mixture of about equal parts of shredded tree-fern fibre, leaf-mould, crumbled loam, and sharp gritty white sand; some chopped sphagnum moss may also be added to good advantage. The tubers should be only slightly buried, and the compost around them not packed overly firm. Water should be increased gradually for the first few weeks after the tubers are planted, or when the new shoots appear at the surface. Repotting of these orchids should, in most cases, be done annually or at least every two years, as they rapidly exhaust the compost. (C, I)

C. alba R.Br. (*Caladenia carnea* R.Br. var. *alba* Bth.)

Rather similar in all respects to *C. carnea* R.Br. and often confused with it, the sts. to 12″ tall, with a rather long, linear, fuzzy lf. at the base. Fls. usually solitary, about 2″ across, pure white with an orange or yellow tip to the lip, the lip-calli sometimes tipped with yellow, the lip and col. never barred with red as in *C. carnea* R.Br. A form with pink fls. is sometimes encountered in the wild, but apparently has never been cultivated. Late summer–autumn. (C, I) Australia.

C. carnea R.Br. (*Arethusa catenata* Sm., *Caladenia alata* R.Br.)

Highly variable, the sts. typically slender, to 10″ tall, with a linear, basal, fuzzy lf. of varying length. Fls. 1–4, apical, usually pink (rarely white), fragrant or not, about 1½″ across in largest forms, the lamina of the lip and the col. barred with conspicuous transverse red lines. Autumn–winter. (C, I) Australia.

CALANTHE R.Br.

(*Amblyglottis* Bl., *Aulostylis* Schltr., *Calanthidium* Pfitz., *Centrosis* Thou., *Ghiesbreghtia* A.Rich. & Gal., *Limatodis* Ldl., *Preptanthe* Ldl., *Styloglossum* Kuhl & v.Hass.)

This very popular genus contains upwards of one hundred and fifty species of primarily terrestrial or lithophytic (very rarely epiphytic) orchids with a huge area of dispersal, extending from South Africa and Madagascar, and China and Japan throughout tropical Asia, Indonesia, and Australia to Tahiti, with a single outlying representative in tropical America. Vegetatively the genus is divided into two groups, one with evergreen foliage and rather insignificant corm-like pseudobulbs, the other with deciduous foliage and very prominent, often large, more or less angular pseudobulbs. All Calanthes bear rather sizeable, usually distinctly folded leaves, and produce erect or arching inflorescences—often to several feet in length—with a few to many typically showy flowers. These blossoms occur in almost every imaginable colour combination, though white, pink, and yellow are perhaps predominant. The customarily equal sepals and petals typically are exceeded in size by the colourful, often several-lobed lip, which may be furnished with intricate protuberances and callosities.

Many hybrids have been made within the genus *Calanthe*, and quantities of these are often grown commercially for cut-flower purposes in various parts of the world. A few multigeneric hybrids have also been made, notably with *Phaius* (= *Phaiocalanthe*) and *Gastorchis* (= *Gastocalanthe*). Additional experimental breeding with allied genera, such as those listed above and other members of the subtribe *Phaiinae*, as well as further interspecific crosses, should be attempted.

CULTURE: Calanthes should, culturally speaking, be treated in two ways, depending upon the vegetative characteristics of the plant. The evergreen ('non-pseudobulbous') types require conditions such as those afforded *Phaius*, which see. The deciduous species with prominent pseudobulbs should be grown in pots, in a rich, perfectly-drained compost, much like the others, but with the addition of gravel or crushed volcanic pumice to assure adequate drainage, which is most essential. As long as the plants are actively growing (prior to flowering), manure-water or other fertilizing ingredients should be given with frequency and in relatively large amounts, since these orchids are very heavy feeders. The foliage falls when the pseudobulbs are mature, and the inflorescence appears; water should then be reduced considerably, or may be stopped altogether while the plants are in bloom, without adverse results. After flowering, the pseudobulbs should be removed from their pots, divided into single individuals, trimmed of all old roots, cleaned, and set away—on their sides—bare-rooted, in a dry cool place until the new growths have attained a length of about two inches, when repotting may again be attended to. Calanthes of this pseudobulbous section in general require division and repotting every year to assure proper production of flowers. Temperature requirements fluctuate from species to species (certain of the Japanese and Chinese species are perfectly hardy in most temperate areas), and most of the tropical members with prominent pseudobulbs will thrive under rather cool conditions; the evergreen species, however, almost all require intermediate or warm temperatures. A rather sunny spot is favoured by all of the cultivated Calanthes, and all should be given as much fertilizer as convenient while growing. (C, I, H)

C. brevicornu Ldl.

Evergreen sp. Lvs. oblong-elliptic, stalked, to about 12″ long and 3″ wide, folded. Infls. to almost 2′ tall, with a loosely many-fld. rac. at the apex. Fls. about 1″ in diam., the ss. and ps. spreading, brown shading to pale yellowish-tan in the middle, oblong, acute. Lip 3-lbd., rather fiddle-shaped, purple-red with a whitish margin, the base with 3 golden-yellow keels, the spur very short. Spring. (C, I) Nepal; Sikkim; Bhutan; Assam.

C. discolor Ldl.

Similar in habit to *C. brevicornu* Ldl., but the rac. shorter, with fewer fls. about 1½″ across, the ss. and ps. violet-purple, narrowly elliptic, spreading around the large whitish-rose lip, which is strongly 4-lbd. and has 3 high keels near the base. Spring. (C, I) Korea; Japan.

C. labrosa (Rchb.f.) Rchb.f. (*Limatodis labrosa* Rchb.f., *Calanthidium labrosum* Rchb.f.)

Pbs. to 5″ tall, pale brownish or grey-green, strongly constricted near the middle, swollen at the base. Lvs. to 2′ long and about 5″ wide, broadly lanceolate, rather fragile in texture, prominently ribbed, deciduous. Infls. hairy, to 2′ tall, with a rather loose, many-fld. rac. at the apex, gracefully arching. Fls. about 1″ across, the ss. and ps. yellow outside, rose-purple within, the lip roundish, crisped, pale purple with some dark purple spots near the base, the spur longer than the ss., pink or purple. Autumn. (I, H) Burma.

C. masuca (D.Don) Ldl. (*Bletia masuca* D.Don)

Evergreen sp., the stalked, rather tightly folded lvs. to 2′ long, numerous, narrowly elliptic, acuminate apically. Infls. arising from the centre of the new growths, to 2½′ tall, usually rigidly erect, the numerous fls. in a very dense, compact, head-like rac. Fls. variable in size and colour, sometimes to 1⅓″ in diam., the ss. and ps. usually violet-red or magenta-red, the 3-lbd. lip very dark magenta-red with some golden-yellow warts on the disc, the spur curved, magenta or purple. Summer–autumn. (C, I) Himalayas.

C. natalensis (Rchb.f.) Rchb.f. (*Calanthe silvatica* Ldl. var. *natalensis* Rchb.f.)

Rather similar in habit to the preceding sp., often more robust vegetatively. Infls. very slender, to 4′ tall, the rac. usually many-fld., dense, head-like. Fls. about 1″ across, the ss. and ps. pale violet or lilac-purple, the tips darker. Lip 3-lbd., violet or mauve, the disc with some pale yellow warts; spur about 1½″ long, slightly curving, usually lilac. Summer. (I, H) Natal; Transvaal.

C. pulchra (Bl.) Ldl. (*Amblyglottis pulchra* Bl., *Calanthe curculigoides* Ldl.)

Evergreen sp., the lvs. lanceolate, acute, folded, to 2½′ long and 4″ wide. Infls. to about 2′ tall, the fls. densely crowded at the apex, rather numerous, the bracts deciduous. Fls. not opening fully, usually less than 1″ across, dark orange-yellow with an orange-red lip. Ss. and ps. oblong, acutish. Lip broadly fiddle-shaped, the spur strongly hooked at the end. Winter. (I, H) Southern India; Sumatra; Java; Malay Peninsula; ? Borneo.

C. rosea (Ldl.) Bth. (*Limatodis rosea* Ldl.)

Similar in habit to *C. labrosa* (Rchb.f.) Rchb.f., rather more robust in all parts, the pbs. to 8″ tall, usually greyish-green. Lvs. broadly lanceolate, to 1½′ long,

Calanthe veratrifolia R.Br. [VEITCH]

deciduous. Infls. finely hairy, to 2½′ tall, the 7–15 fls. rather loosely arranged in a rac. Fls. about 2½″ across, bright rose-pink, the lip flat, oval, large for the fl., rose-pink, the lat. lbs. white, inrolled over the col., the throat white surrounded by a ridge of dark rose. Autumn. (I, H) Burma.

C. veratrifolia R.Br.

Evergreen sp., highly variable in all parts, sometimes to 7′ tall when in bloom. Lvs. to 4′ long and 8″ wide, somewhat or prominently stalked at base, numerous, narrowly elliptic, acuminate, distinctly folded, dark green to silvery, slightly fuzzy underneath. Infls. to 7′ tall, more or less velvety-hairy, the rac. extending over a period of several months, rather head-like and dense at first, many-fld. Fls. about 1″ long (sometimes longer), white except for the red or yellowish wart-like callus at the base of the lip, the lip often turning yellowish with age. Ss. and ps. lying almost in one plane, facing obliquely downwards, more or less fuzzy on the reverse surface. Lip very deeply 4-lbd., the lbs. widely spreading. Pedicellate ovary white. Spring–autumn. (I, H) South China, and India throughout Malaya and Indonesia to Australia, New Guinea, and the Pacific Islands.

C. vestita Ldl. (*Cytheris Griffithii* Wight, *Preptanthe vestita* Rchb.f.)

Pbs. to 8″ tall, conical-egg-shaped, prominently angled, silvery green. Lvs. deciduous, to 3′ long and 4″ wide, folded, usually yellowish-green, lanceolate, acute. Infls. to 3′ long, usually gracefully arching, fuzzy, the 6–15-fld. rac. occupying the upper third. Fls. long-lived, of rather fragile texture, extremely variable in colouration, sometimes 2½–3″ long (usually smaller),

Calanthe vestita Ldl. var. *Williamsii* (Moore) A.D.Hawkes [B.S.WILLIAMS]

white, sometimes with a rosy-pink flush, the lip-callus varying from yellow to orange to red, sometimes the whole lip rose-pink. Ss. and ps. elliptic, acute, usually widespreading, sometimes rather incurved. Lip deeply 4-lbd., the basal callus rough, the spur curving, about 1" long. Winter. (I, H) Burma; Viet-Nam; Lower Thailand; Malay Peninsula; Borneo; Celebes.

—var. **Regnieri** (Rchb.f.) Veitch (*Calanthe Regnieri* Rchb.f.)

Differs from the typical sp. in the longer pbs. of more cylindrical shape, and in the fls. being only about 1½" long, the lip rose-red with a dark purple-rose blotch on the disc. Winter. (H) Viet-Nam.

—fma. **rubro-oculata** (Paxt.) A.D.Hawkes (*Calanthe vestita* Ldl. var. *rubro-oculata* Paxt.)

Differs from the typical sp. in its longer, more drooping, white-hairy infls. Fls. to 2" long, the ss. and ps. white, the lip white with a blotch of very rich crimson at the centre. Best considered a horticultural form of this variable species. Autumn–winter. (I, H) Burma.

C. angustifolia (Bl.) Ldl. (*Amblyglottis angustifolia* Bl.) Habit rather similar to that of *C. veratrifolia* R.Br., the lvs. sheathed basally, slender. Infls. about 2' tall, the rac. rather few-fld. Fls. about 2" long, white, the lip sometimes yellowish with a dark butter-yellow callus, the lat. lbs. of the lip almost square, the spur club-shaped. Summer. (H) Sumatra; Java; Malay Peninsula; Philippines.

C. cardioglossa Schltr. (*Calanthe Fuerstenbergiana* Krzl.) Pbs. oblong, about 3" tall, often constricted near the middle. Lvs. lanceolate, acute, to 12" long and 3" wide, folded, deciduous. Infls. finely hairy, loosely 10–20-fld., to 2½' tall. Fls. about 1" across, the ss. and ps. dark rose-red or yellowish-rose, the lip broadly heart-shaped or kidney-shaped, rose-red with dark purple spots. Autumn. (H) Thailand.

C. Ceciliae Rchb.f. Evergreen sp., the lvs. stalked (stalk about 6" long), the lf.-blade about 12" long and 4" wide, folded. Infls. to 18" tall, the short, rather few-fld. rac. crowded. Fls. about 2" across, white, tinted or flushed with violet, the long spurs pointing upwards. Autumn. (H) Sumatra; Java; Malay Peninsula.

C. densiflora Ldl. Similar in habit to *C. pulchra* (Bl.) Ldl., but the infls. only about 6" tall. Fls. less than 1" across, in a dense, compact head-like rac., pale yellow, the lip almost square, the spur rather long, awl-shaped. Autumn. (I, H) Himalayas.

C. Foerstermannii Rchb.f. (*Calanthe Scortechinii* Hk.f.) Evergreen sp., the vegetative habit reminiscent of *C. veratrifolia* R.Br. Infls. with a stout peduncle, about 18" tall, with a short dense rac. at the apex, the buds protected by large, deciduous bracts. Fls. about ½" across, dull yellow, the lip with 2 small basal keels. Autumn. (I, H) Himalayas to Malay Peninsula.

C. furcata Batem. ex Ldl. (*Alismorchis furcata* O.Ktze., *Calanthe triplicata* Ames). Very closely allied to, and perhaps synonymous with *C. veratrifolia* R.Br., differing principally in the shape of the lip-lbs., which are somewhat narrower and more spreading than in that sp. Fls. turning black with age. Summer–autumn. (I, H) Philippines.

C. herbacea Ldl. Pbs. short, vaguely fusiform, annular, to 1¼" tall. Lvs. to 12" long and 4" broad, long-stalked, broadly elliptic. Infls. erect, to 2' tall, with a lax rac. Fls. to 1½" long,

the ss. and ps. green, or yellow and green. Lip longer than the ss., 3-lbd., pure white, with a triangular warty yellow callus at base. June–July. (C, I) Sikkim.

C. madagascariensis Rolfe Lvs. few, to 4" long, short-stalked at base, elliptic, acute, folded. Infls. about 8" tall, with several large bracts, the 10–20-fld. rac. head-like, compact, apical. Fls. about 1½" across, violet or white flushed more or less with rose-red, the lip 4-lbd., purple-red or golden-yellow. Autumn. (H) Madagascar.

C. rubens Ridl. (*Preptanthe rubens* Ridl.) Rather similar in habit to *C. vestita* Ldl., but mostly smaller in all parts, the pbs. to about 4" tall. Lvs. deciduous, short-stalked, folded, to 1½' tall and 6" wide. Infls. hairy, to 1½' tall, the rachis many-fld., gradually elongating over a period of several months. Fls. about 1½" long, pink with a crimson stripe down the middle of the lip (rarely pure white), the midlb. fan-shaped, again 2-lbd. Autumn. (H) Langkawi Islands; Thailand.

C. silvatica (Thou.) Ldl. (*Centrosis silvatica* Thou., *Centrosis Auberti* A.Rich., *Bletia silvatica* Bojer, *Alismorchis centrosis* Steud., *Calanthe Warpuri* Rolfe, *C. silvatica* (Thou.) Ldl. var. *pallidipetala* Schltr.) Rather similar in habit to *C. masuca* (D.Don) Ldl. Infls. about 6" tall, with a very dense, compact, head-like rac. at the apex. Fls. about 1" across, dark violet-purple, the lip very dark purple, with some orange-red warts on the disc. Spring. (I, H) Madagascar; Comoro Islands; Mascarene Islands.

C. striata (Banks) R.Br. (*Limodorum striatum* Banks, *Calanthe Sieboldii* Regel). Similar in habit to *C. discolor* Ldl. Fls. about 1½" across, the ss. and ps. golden-yellow, flushed medially with brown, the lip differently shaped than the other sp., the disc with 3 red-margined keels. Spring. (C, I) Korea; China; Japan.

CALEANA R.Br.
(*Caleya* R.Br.)

Five species of *Caleana* are known to date, native in Australia and New Zealand. Very rare in collections even in their native haunts, they are rather dull little terrestrial plants of interest primarily to botanists. The genus is somewhat allied to *Spiculaea* Ldl. and other members of the subtribe *Drakaeinae*, but differs in technical details of the flowers.

No hybrids are known in *Caleana*, and its genetic affinities have not been ascertained.

CULTURE: As for *Caladenia*. (C, I)

C. major R.Br. (*Caleya major* R.Br.)
Very slender, rather variable pls., to almost 2' tall, the subterranean tubers oblong. Lf. solitary, basal, red-brown underneath, broadly linear to lanceolate, to 4" long. Infl. loose, 1–4-fld., erect. Fls. inverted, deep red-brown (rarely green), about ¾" long. Dors. sep. channelled, curving closely behind the col., the lat. ss. slightly longer, reflexed, channelled for the basal half, then rather abruptly contracted and tubular or filiform for distal half. Ps. narrowly linear, shorter than ss., erect alongside the col.-wings. Lip with a long lorate claw, the lamina ovate, peltate on the claw, smooth, the centre inflated and hollow, the cavity open below. Spring–summer. (C, I) Australia.

C. minor R.Br. (*Caleya minor* Sweet)
Very slender, to 7" tall. Lf. solitary, basal, red-brown underneath, narrowly linear, 1½–5" long. Fls. 1–4,

about ½" across, green or dull reddish-brown, complex. Dors. sep. slightly incurved, the lat. ss. slightly channelled, not as long as the dors. one. Ps. shorter than the ss., filiform. Lip with a long lorate claw, the lamina ovate, peltate on the claw, produced on the columnar side into a bifid gland-tipped appendage, and at the other end into a triangular pointed process with a spur on each side; centre inflated and hollow; upper surface and margins tuberculate except at the base. Spring–summer. (C, I) Australia; New Zealand.

CALOCHILUS R.Br.

Calochilus is a genus of about ten species of unusually handsome terrestrial orchids, native in Australia, New Zealand, New Caledonia, and New Guinea. They are very scarce in contemporary collections, but are among the most delightful of ground-dwelling groups, and should be better known by enthusiasts. Robust or slender plants arising from ovoid subterranean tubers, they bear solitary basal leaves and rather few-flowered racemes of complex and beautiful flowers which are characterized by a particularly large lip. The generic name (meaning 'beautiful lip') is derived from the lustrous metallic

Calochilus caeruleus L.O.Wms. [GORDON W. DILLON]

hairs which cloak this organ in most of the species. In Australia they are commonly known as 'Beardies'. *Calochilus* is a member of the subtribe *Thelymitrinae*.

No hybrids are known in this genus, and nothing has been ascertained concerning its genetic affinities.

CULTURE: As for *Caladenia*. (C, I)

C. campestris R.Br.

Robust, 8–30" tall. Lf. basal, solitary, thick, to 9" long, deeply channelled, triangular in cross-section. Infls. with 2 bracts which are sometimes copper-coloured, as are also the bracts of the lower fls.; rac. rather loose, 2–15-fld. Fls. less than 1" long, the ss. green with brownish stripes, the ps. yellowish-green with dark green stripes, the lip with the upper surface yellowish-green, clothed with sparse rather long copper-red or reddish-blue hairs, except for a smooth plate towards the base, with or without several longitudinal ridges, the plate and ridges usually dark blue; lip-apex acuminate to prolonged into a short, bare, ribbon-like process extending beyond apical hairs. Col. marked with brown and red-brown. Sept.–Nov. (C, I) Australia; New Zealand.

CALOPOGON R.Br.
(*Cathea* Salisb.)

According to most recent estimates, *Calopogon* consists of four species of handsome terrestrial orchids, native mostly in the south-eastern United States, with one extending into eastern Canada. Occurring primarily in bogs, wet spots, in meadows or savannahs in often intensely acid soil, their cultural requirements are not readily met by the collector, although they are of sufficient beauty to warrant attention by the specialist. With grass-like leaves and an often tall inflorescence arising from a subterranean mostly globular corm, the Calopogons bear proportionately large, intricate flowers in which the lip is uppermost, differing in this respect from most of the North American orchids. The lip is furnished with beard-like hairs and papillae on its midlobe, these often being of a different hue than the other floral parts.

No artificially-produced hybrids are known in *Calopogon*, although natural ones occur.

CULTURE: As for *Arethusa*. (C, I)

C. barbatus (Walt.) Ames (*Ophrys barbata* Walt., *Limodorum parviflorum* Nash, *Limodorum graminifolium* Small, *Calopogon parviflorus* Ldl., *C. pulchellus* (Salisb.) R.Br. var. *graminifolius* Ell., *C. graminifolius* Ell. ex Weatherby & Griscom)

Corm subterranean, mostly globose, with a tuft of roots at one end and usually the remnants of the old stalks at the other. Sts. erect, often tinged with reddish-brown, to 1½' tall. Lvs. 1–2, basal, narrowly linear, grass-like, to 7" long, less than ¼" wide. Infls. slender, the rac. short, 3–8-fld., dense. Fls. about 1¼" across, usually rose-pink (rarely white), mostly all open at once, the segms. spreading, the lip with the disc bearded on the central portion with club-shaped hairs, the basal and central hairs deep rust-red, the apical ones gradually reduced to pale lavender papillae, the col. with prominent wings. Winter–spring. (C, I) South-eastern United States.

Calopogon pallidus Chapm. [BLANCHE AMES]

CALYMMANTHERA Schltr.

Five species of *Calymmanthera* are known to science, all of them very rare epiphytic orchids of the subtribe *Sarcanthinae*, endemic to New Guinea. Rather close in their systematic affinities to *Chamaeanthus* Schltr., they are small plants with racemes of tiny yellowish flowers, hence are of interest primarily to specialists. None of the Calymmantheras is in cultivation at this time.

Nothing is known of the genetic ties of this rare genus.

CULTURE: Presumably as for the small, tropical Vandas, etc. (I, H)

CALYPSO Salisb.
(*Cytherea* Salisb., *Norna* Wahlb., *Orchidium* Sw.)

Calypso bulbosa (L.) Oakes, the only known member of the genus, is an extremely handsome terrestrial orchid whose range extends virtually throughout the North Temperate Zone, in North America, Europe, and Asia. Several of the geographic races of this fine plant have in the past been given distinct names, but they now all seem referable to a single, highly variable species. *Calypso* is very rare in collections, and rarely survives under cultivation for more than a couple of years, but its remarkable flowers make it one of the most highly desirable of all indigenous North American orchids. The genus is a member of the subtribe *Calypsoinae*.

Nothing is known of the genetic affinities of this peculiar genus.

CULTURE: Best kept in perfectly-drained pots in a cool spot, *Calypso* may sometimes be induced to live a few years if potted in a moist, porous soil with a high degree of humus present. A shady situation is necessary, and the buried corms should be disturbed as infrequently as possible. (C)

C. bulbosa (L.) Oakes (*Cypripedium bulbosum* L., *Cytherea bulbosa* House, *Cytherea occidentalis* Heller, *Cytherea borealis* Salisb., *Limodorum boreale* Sw., *Orchidium americanum* Steud., *Orchidium arcticum* Sw., *Orchidium boreale* Sw., *Norna borealis* Wahlb., *Cymbidium boreale* Sw., *Calypso occidentalis* Heller, *Calypso borealis* Salisb., *C. japonica* Maxim., *C. bulbosa* (L.) Oakes var. *japonica* Mak.)
Corm subterranean, globose to ellipsoid, more or less sheathed, to 1″ long. Lf. solitary, produced late in the first season and persisting through the winter, long-stalked, the total length to about 5″, the lamina usually heart-shaped, folded, often bluish-green. Scape fleshy, often stout, pale yellowish-purple to brownish-purple, with 2 or so loose sheaths near the base, 1-fld. (very rarely 2-fld.). Fls. pendent, heavy-textured, fragrant, very showy, about 1½″ long, the ss. and ps. purplish (rarely white), often twisted, usually ascending. Lip very large, slipper-shaped, complex, whitish or yellowish to pale reddish-brown, with vivid reddish-brown spots or lines inside, with 3 rows of golden-yellow or brown-spotted hairs on the frontal part, more or less purple-spotted. Spring–summer. (C) North Temperate Zone.

CALYPTROCHILUM Krzl.

Allied to *Ancistrorhynchus* Finet and to *Diaphananthe* Schltr., this genus includes about six species, native in tropical Africa and Madagascar. All are epiphytes, somewhat like some of the Angraecums in basic floral structure, though the critical details are distinctive. Two members of *Calyptrochilum* are present in collections at this time, both of these very rare orchids.

Nothing has as yet been ascertained concerning the genetic affinities of this genus, and no hybrids have been made from its components.

CULTURE: As for the tropical Angraecums. The plants are generally grown firmly affixed to slabs of tree-fern fibre. (H)

C. Christyanum (Rchb.f.) Summerh. (*Angraecum Christyanum* Rchb.f., *Angraecum Moloneyi* Rolfe, *Calyptrochilum mombasense* Schltr., *C. orientale* Schltr.)
Sts. usually pendulous, to 2′ long, woody, freely rooting. Lvs. numerous and dense, strap-shaped, leathery, almost succulent, 2¼–3¼″ long, to ¾″ broad, almost rectangular, with 2 pointed lobes at apex, often olive-green in colour. Infls. numerous, shorter than the lvs., densely many-fld. Fls. ½″ long, faintly fragrant, white. Ss. and ps. elliptic, acutish, the ps. barely falcate. Lip proportionately large, 3-lbd., the lat. lbs. rounded, much shorter than the midlb., which is oblong and notched at the rounded apex. Spur green, ⅝″ long, sharply bent. Summer. (H) Liberia to Angola, across Africa to Kenya, Uganda, and Tanganyika.

C. imbricatum (Ldl.) Schltr. (*Angraecum imbricatum* Ldl., *Calyptrochilum Preussii* Krzl., *Saccolabium Barbeyae* Krzl.)
Sts. pendulous, robust, to 2′ long, densely leafy. Lvs. oblong, unequally and bluntly 2-lbd. at apex, fleshy, to 4″ long and more than 1½″ broad. Infls. numerous, to about 3½″ long, densely many-fld., the fls. usually arranged in two distinct ranks. Fls. not opening widely, about ½″ long, rather fleshy and long-lived, white with a greenish-yellow spur about ¼″ long. Autumn. (H) Tropical West Africa.

CAMAROTIS Ldl.

Camarotis contains about fourteen species of climbing, long-stemmed epiphytes (rarely terrestrials or lithophytes) in the region extending from the Himalayas and Burma throughout Malaya, Indonesia, and the Philippines to Australia (Queensland) and New Guinea. Vegetatively they rather simulate a *Sarcanthus* or a *Trichoglottis*, but are readily distinguished when in bloom, since the lip always points towards the apex of the inflorescence, thus generally making the flowers appear inverted. Only a single species of *Camarotis* appears to be at all frequent in contemporary collections, but there are several other members of the genus which deserve attention by enthusiasts.

No hybrids are known in this genus, though, in theory at least, *Camarotis* is genetically compatible with such allied genera as *Trichoglottis*, *Vanda*, *Aërides*, etc., and some interesting results would doubtless be obtained through critical experimental breeding along these lines.

CULTURE: Camarotis is best treated in the manner afforded *Renanthera* and *Arachnis*, because of the typically elongate stems. (I, H)

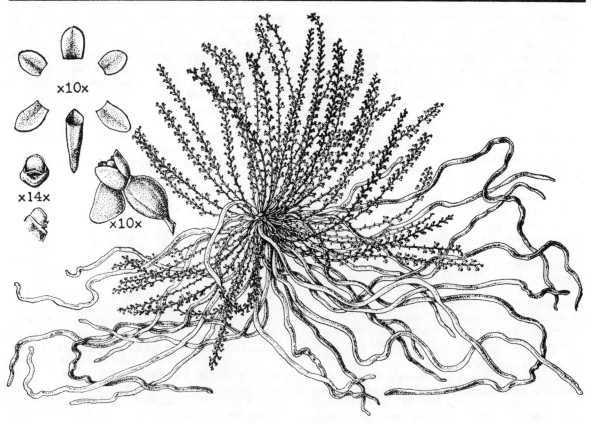

Campylocentrum Burchellii Cgn. [Hoehne, *Flora Brasilica*]

C. rostrata (Roxb.) Rchb.f. (*Aërides rostratum* Roxb.,
   Camarotis purpurea Ldl.)

Sts. clambering, often branching near the base,
erect, to 8′ tall or more, usually densely leafy throughout.
Lvs. fleshy, to 5″ long and ¾″ wide, oblong-linear,
bilobed at the apex. Infls. horizontal to gracefully
pendulous, to 10″ long, very densely many-fld. Fls.
about 1″ across, the lip uppermost, heavy-textured,
fragrant, long-lasting, very deep rose-crimson, the
spreading oblong ss. and ps. pale rose or whitish-rose.
Mostly spring. (I, H) Himalayas.

C. philippinensis Ldl. St. rather stout, erect, 1–4′ tall, leafy.
Lvs. rather numerous but not too close together, horizontally
spreading in 2 ranks, to 8″ long, linear-ligulate, heavily
leathery. Infls. erect or ascending, to almost 12″ tall, the
rachis thick, 15–20-fld. Fls. inverted, waxy, about ¾″ in diam.,
pearl-white more or less tinged with purple, the ss. and ps.
recurved, the lip sac-like, not spurred. Col. with an elongate
curved appendage, much like an elephant's trunk. Mostly
Aug.–Sept. (I) Philippines: Luzon, Leyte.

CAMPYLOCENTRUM Bth.
(*Todaroa* A.Rich., *Harrisella* F. & R.)

This is a remarkable genus, the principal one of the
subtribe *Campylocentrinae* (formerly included in the
Sarcanthinae), whose members extend from Central
Florida and Mexico to Argentina, with most of them
occurring in Brazil. About sixty-five epiphytic or lithophytic species are presently recognized, but very few of
these are grown to any degree today, since the plants
are not readily acquired, and—at least certain of them—
are very difficult to keep in good condition in collections.
The genus consists of two radically different sections:
one, consisting solely of a minute woody stem and a
cluster of round or flattened roots (which are furnished
with chlorophyll), and completely without leaves; the
other consists of relatively short, often profusely
branching stems which are furnished with numerous
two-ranked, usually fleshy leaves, and large stout roots.
The short inflorescences arise either from the centre of
the root-cluster or from the sides of the stems, and bear
a few to very many extremely small, two-ranked,
spurred flowers, usually greenish or yellowish in colour,
and often furnished with oddly-formed spurs.

Hybridists have not as yet worked with the members
of *Campylocentrum*, which contains very few species of
more than scientific interest.

CULTURE: The leaf-bearing species may be grown in
the manner afforded the tropical Vandas and their
allies; it is very important that they never be permitted
to become dry at any time. The leafless species are more
difficult to maintain in good condition, because removal
of the fleshy roots from their tree-hosts is often fatally
injurious. If possible, the plants should be kept on their
original 'host' branches, disturbing them as little as
possible. A bright, well-ventilated spot in the intermediate or warm house suits them well, and they must

never be permitted to become dry, due to the absence of moisture-storing structures or foliage. If removed from the tree on which they originally grew, it is sometimes possible to re-establish them on slabs of bark or tree-fern fibre, or on small hardwood branches, by cautiously pinning down the rambling roots against the moisture surface with wire or threads. It is thought that for successful cultivation of certain of these aphyllous Campylocentrums, a living tree is essential, but no research has been done in this matter as yet. (I, H)

C. micranthum (Ldl.) Rolfe (*Angraecum micranthum* Ldl., *Angraecum brevifolium* Ldl., *Angraecum Lansbergii* Rchb.f., *Aëranthus micranthus* Rchb.f., *Aëranthus Lansbergii* Rchb.f., *Campylocentrum panamense* Ames, *C. peniculus* Schltr.)

Sts. curving, pendulous to erect, to 2′ long, often rather profusely branching, furnished with lvs. and large fleshy roots. Lvs. to 4″ long and $\frac{3}{4}$″ wide, broadly ligular to elliptic-oblong, apically blunt and unequally 2-lbd., leathery. Infls. to 1$\frac{1}{2}$″ long, very densely many-fld., often several produced at once, from the st.-sides just below the point of emergence of the roots. Fls. 2-ranked, all pointing upwards, less than $\frac{1}{2}$″ long, white or yellowish-white, with a large, pendulous, sac-like spur. Mostly autumn. (I, H) Cuba and Mexico to Brazil and Peru.

C. pachyrrhizum (Rchb.f.) Rolfe (*Aëranthus pachyr-rhizus* Rchb.f., *Aëranthus spathaceus* Griseb.)

Leafless and essentially stemless, consisting of a radiating cluster of usually flattened, grey to orange-flushed roots to several ft. long and less than $\frac{1}{4}$″ across. Infls. produced from the centre of the root-cluster, erect, to 1$\frac{1}{2}$″ tall, prominently bracted, the bracts usually reddish-brown, densely many-fld. Fls. inverted, 2-ranked, yellow-green, less than $\frac{1}{4}$″ long, the lip with a slightly curved, sac-like spur. Late winter–spring. (H) Southern Florida; Cuba; Jamaica; French Guiana; Trinidad; Brazil.

C. porrectum (Rchb.f.) Rolfe (*Aëranthus porrectus* Rchb.f., *Harrisella porrecta* F. & R., *Harrisella Amesiana* Cgn.)

Leafless and essentially stemless, very small epiphytes, the roots often hanging partially free, round in cross-section, flexuous, to 6″ long and less than $\frac{1}{64}$″ in diam. Infls. arising from the centre of the root-cluster, to 3″ tall, the stalk thread-like, zig-zag, bearing 2 or more minute fls. near the apex. Fls. not opening fully, less than $\frac{1}{4}$″ across, yellow-green, the lip with the spur constricted below, globose above. Autumn–early winter. (H) Central and South Florida; Cuba; Jamaica; Puerto Rico; Mexico; El Salvador.

C. Barrettiae F. & R. Rather similar in habit to *C. micranthum* (Ldl.) Rolfe, but the sts. much shorter, usually only 3–4″ tall, the lvs. closer together, and usually oblong in shape. Infls. produced opposite the lvs., sometimes paired, densely many-fld., to 1$\frac{1}{4}$″ long. Fls. about $\frac{1}{4}$″ long, rather tubular, yellowish-green, 2-ranked, the spur slightly club-shaped, somewhat constricted at base. Autumn–winter. (H) Jamaica.

CAPANEMIA B.-R.

Twelve species of *Capanemia* are known to date, all of them endemic to Brazil, where they are often rather frequent in the moist tropical forests, growing on mossy trees. Despite this fact, none of the members of this attractive and interesting genus of the subtribe *Capanemiinae* appear to be present in collections at this time outside Brazil, although most of them are of considerable potential interest to the connoisseur hobbyist. Dwarf, pseudobulbous epiphytes with smallish but often rather dense racemes of tiny but handsome white or greenish flowers, the Capanemias are charming 'botanical' orchids, which we hope to see at some time in future in our greenhouses.

Nothing is known of the genetic affinities of this odd genus, at this time.

CULTURE: As for *Ornithocephalus*. (I, H).

CATASETUM L.C.Rich.
(*Catachaetum* Hoffmsgg., *Clowesia* Ldl., *Cuculina* Raf., *Monacanthus* G.Don, *Monachanthus* Ldl., *Myanthus* Ldl., *Warczewitzia* Skinn.)

Catasetum contains an estimated one hundred and ten species of mostly epiphytic (rarely lithophytic or terrestrial) orchids in the American tropics, distributed from Mexico to Peru, with the centre of dissemination in Brazil. This genus includes some of the most unusual and handsome of all orchidaceous plants, and a rather large number of them have found favour with contemporary collectors. Botanically, the genus consists of two distinct sections, one (*Clowesia*) bearing perfect (hermaphroditic) flowers, and the other (*Orthocatasetum*) producing unisexual and only very rarely perfect flowers. In the latter group, the male (staminate) or female (pistillate) blossoms are remarkably dissimilar, and are often borne on separate inflorescences, or even at different seasons. This sexual dimorphy has resulted in an extreme amount of nomenclatural confusion within the genus, confusion which largely persists even to the present day. Catasetums are allied to *Mormodes* Ldl. and to *Cycnoches* Ldl., and, like them, bear large, fleshy pseudobulbs which, in this genus, are usually spindle-shaped, roundish, or almost conical. These have large, folded, deciduous leaves, and produce arching or erect inflorescences—often many-flowered—from their bases, sometimes more than once annually. Floral form and colour is varied in the genus, and most of the species bear blossoms of sufficient size and brightness to warrant their cultivation.

Few hybrids as yet are known in *Catasetum*. One is the attractive natural hybrid *C.* x *splendens* Cgn. (*C. macrocarpum* × *C. pileatum*), from Venezuela. Moir, in Hawaii, has registered a couple of apparently handsome crosses, as well. Because of the rarity of the female or perfect flowers in the most commonly-cultivated species, breeding is difficult. Additional experimental hybridization within the genus should definitely be attempted, however, and orchidists should also try their hand with intergeneric crossing, although little is known concerning the genetic compatibility of *Catasetum*.

CULTURE: Catasetums are very easily grown, even by the beginner, and are hence recommended to all hobbyists. They do particularly well in perfectly-drained

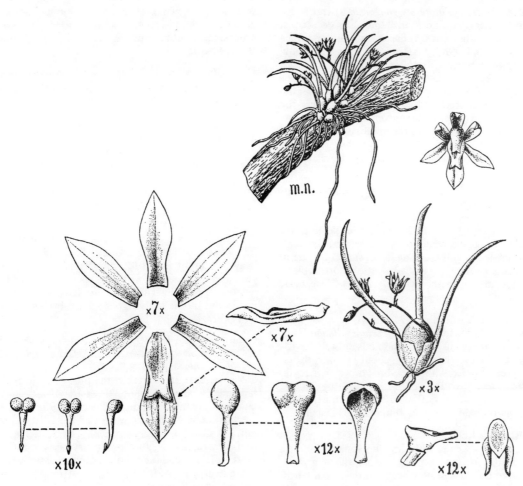

Capanemia micromera B.-R. [Hoehne, *Flora Brasílica*]

pots, tightly packed either in osmunda or shredded tree-fern fibre; smallish chunks of the latter material can also be used. While actively growing, they benefit by quantities of moisture, humidity, and heat, but upon maturation of the new pseudobulbs, water should be almost completely withheld for at least two weeks, to afford a needed rest. In the wild, many Catasetums grow almost fully exposed to the sun, and under cultivation a bright, well-ventilated spot suits them well. When the new shoots are just expanding, care must be taken that water does not lodge inside them, or rotting may occur. Snails and slugs are particularly fond of the succulent flower-spikes, and precautions against their depredations must be taken as these appear. Repotting should be done whenever needed, and the plants must never be kept in overly large containers, as they are intolerant of sour conditions at the roots. Regular applications of fertilizers are recommended, and normally assist in marked increases in growth and flower-production. Almost all of the Catasetums—particularly those with pendulous inflorescences—do well in osmunda-filled baskets, or mounted on large tree-fern slabs. (I, H)

C. atratum Ldl.[1] (*Catasetum adnatum* Steud.)

Pbs. spindle-shaped, to 5″ tall. Lvs. 2–4, to 12″ long, elliptic, acuminate, folded. Infls. pendulous or arching, to 12″ long, with a dense 12–15-fld. rac. Fls. about 2″ long, fragrant, waxy. Ss. and ps. green, thickly spotted with black-brown, oblong, acutish. Lip helmet-shaped, with a white apex, yellow-green, dotted and spotted with black-brown. Spring. (I, H) Brazil.

C. barbatum (Ldl.) Ldl. (*Myanthus barbatus* Ldl., *Myanthus spinosus* Hk., *Monachanthus viridis* Schomb., *Catasetum spinosum* Ldl.)

Habit as in the genus. Infls. pendulous, to 1½′ long, loosely few-fld. Fls. about 2″ long, fleshy, fragrant, the ss. and ps. greenish with black-purple flecks, oblong, acute. Lip oblong, concave in the middle, greenish, the margins with numerous linear, blunt projections. Spring. (I, H) Guianas; Brazil.

[1] All species included in this treatment are members of the section *Orthocatasetum*, unless perfect flowers are indicated in the descriptions. The male (staminate) flowers of the Orthocatasetums are described, since the female (pistillate) ones are seen so seldom, and often rather simulate each other in the different species.

C. bicolor Klotzsch (*Catasetum gongoroides* Krzl.)

Pbs. subconical or cylindric, to 4″ long. Lvs. deciduous, rather small for the genus. Infls. arching or pendulous racs., to 6″ long, few-fld. Fls. fragrant, about 3½″ long, the ss. brownish-green, purplish, flesh-pink, or deep red-brown, the ps. usually green, purplish-green, or flesh-pink. Ss. free, lanceolate, acute, erect and closely approximating the dors. sep., the 3 segms. arching over the col. Lip white or pale yellow, the margins of the midlb. red-brown, the lat. lbs. and inner surface of the sac-like base irregularly splotched with red-brown. Summer. (I, H) Panama; ? Colombia.

C. callosum Ldl. (*Myanthus callosus* Beer, *Myanthus grandiflorus* Beer)

Habit as in the genus. Infls. loosely 10–15-fld., to 12″ long. Fls. inverted, about 2″ long, the ss. and ps. brownish, lanceolate, acute, the lat. ss. erect, the dors. sep. and ps. together, extending downwards. Lip green with red dots, ovate, blunt apically, with a short, conical, obtuse sac at the base. Winter. (I, H) Venezuela; Colombia.

C. cernuum (Ldl.) Rchb.f. (*Myanthus cernuus* Ldl., *Monachanthus viridis* Ldl., *Catasetum trifidum* Hk.)

Habit as in the genus. Infls. pendulous, loosely 10–15-fld., about 12″ long. Fls. nodding, about 1½″ long, the ss. and ps. green spotted with black-brown, oblong, acute. Lip green, very broadly wedge-shaped, 3-lbd. in the front part, the lat. lbs. triangular, the short, blunt midlb. also triangular. Spring–summer. (H) Brazil.

C. Christyanum Rchb.f.

Habit as in the genus. Infls. arching, loosely 5–8-fld., to 1½′ tall. Fls. fragrant, about 4″ across, the ss. and ps. greenish-red dotted and blotched with deep red, lanceolate, acuminate. Lip brownish-rose with a short, white sac, oblong, 3-lbd., the midlb. shortly acuminate, oval. Col. brownish-rose. Winter. (H) Brazil.

C. discolor (Ldl.) Ldl. (*Monachanthus discolor* Ldl., *Monachanthus Bushnani* Hk., *Catasetum roseo-album* Hk.)

Habit as in the genus. Infls. to 1½′ tall, rather densely many-fld., erect, robust. Fls. inverted, about 1½″ long, fleshy, very fragrant. Ss. and ps. greenish, the former oblong, the latter linear-lanceolate. Lip opening widely, helmet-shaped, almost hemispherical, with 6–8 hair-like projections on each side near the base, apically acute, whitish with some reddish marks. Spring. (I, H) Brazil.

C. fimbriatum Ldl. (*Myanthus fimbriatus* Morr.)

Habit as in the genus. Infls. arching, loosely 7–15-fld., to about 1½′ tall. Fls. fleshy, spicily fragrant, about 1½″ across, the ss. and ps. lanceolate, acuminate, yellowish with numerous small reddish flecks and spots. Lip fan-shaped, yellow, sometimes flushed with greenish, with a short wide sac-like depression near the base, the basal callus 3-sided, lobe-like. Spring–summer. (I, H) Brazil.

C. globiflorum Hk.

Habit as in the genus. Infls. erect, rather loosely 10–15-fld., to 1½′ tall. Fls. not opening widely, rather globular in shape, fleshy, fragrant, the ss. and ps. yellow-green

with large brown blotches, oval, blunt. Lip almost globular, bluish-green, brown-spotted inside and around the mouth of the opening. Spring–early summer. (I, H) Brazil.

C. longifolium Ldl. (*Monachanthus longifolius* Ldl.)

Pls. pendulous, the pbs. spindle-shaped, to 12″ long, rather slender. Lvs. hanging, rather fragile in texture, to 2′ long, about 1½″ wide, very deep green, linear-ligulate, acute. Infls. mostly hanging, rather loosely few-fld., to about 1½′ long. Fls. about 1½″ across, the ss. and ps. greenish-yellow tipped with crimson, oblong, reflexed, the lip helmet-shaped, with a fringed membrane of rich yellow colour under the lamina, otherwise deep wine-purple. Autumn. (H) Guianas; North Brazil.

C. luridum (Lk.) Ldl. (*Anguloa lurida* Lk., *Catasetum abruptum* Ldl.)

Habit as in the genus. Infls. erect, rather loosely 5–10-fld., about 12″ tall. Fls. somewhat nodding, fleshy, heavily fragrant, about 1½″ long. Ss. and ps. greenish or yellow-green, spotted with blackish-brown, oval, apiculate. Lip helmet-shaped, golden-yellow, spotted inside and on the margins with black-brown. Autumn. (I, H) Brazil.

C. macrocarpum L.C.Rich. (*Monachanthus viridis* Ldl., *Catasetum tridentatum* Hk., *C. Claveringii* Hk., *C. floribundum* Hk.)

Very robust and variable, the pbs. sometimes to 1½′ tall and 5″ in diam. Lvs. to 3′ long and 4″ wide, oblong-lanceolate, acute or acuminate, deciduous in time. Infls. erect or arching with the weight of the 5–10 fls., to 1½′ tall. Fls. about 3″ long, not opening fully, fleshy, rather foul-scented, the ss. and ps. incurving, greenish with more or less abundant red dots, oblong, acuminate. Lip ovate-helmet-shaped, very large and thick, yellow or greenish-yellow, the midlb. 3-tipped. Mostly autumn–winter. (I, H) South America, where it is widespread.

C. Oerstedii Rchb.f. (*Catasetum Brenesii* Schltr., ? *C. maculatum* Kth., *C. rostratum* Klinge)

Robust sp., rather similar in habit to *C. macrocarpum* L.C.Rich. Infls. to almost 2′ tall, 4–12-fld., usually arching due to the weight of the fls. Fls. 2″ long or more, very fleshy, heavily scented, the lip uppermost. Ss. and ps. green or greenish-brown, usually marked with purple or red-brown, all of them incurving over the col. and forming a concave trough. Lip very fleshy, somewhat conical, green or yellow, usually marked or spotted with purple or red-brown, the lat. margins fimbriate. Autumn. (I, H) Nicaragua; Costa Rica; Panama; ? Colombia.

C. pileatum Rchb.f. (*Catasetum Bungerothii* N.E.Br.)

Probably the finest sp. in the genus, the National Flower of Venezuela. Pbs. usually more nearly round than most of the other spp., to 9″ tall and 3″ in diam. Infls. to 12″ long, gracefully arching, 4–10-fld. Fls. opening flat, to more than 4″ across, very heavy in texture, extremely fragrant, usually pure ivory-white (rarely pale yellow), the ss. and ps. oblong, acuminate. Lip 2½″ in diam., transversely oblong to almost round, deeply concave or almost flat, pure ivory-white, with a cone-like sac below the middle which is sometimes orange-coloured. Autumn. (I, H) Venezuela; ? Colombia; Ecuador.

C. purum Nees (*Catasetum inapertum* Hk., *C. semiapertum* Hk.)

Habit as in the genus. Infls. erect, densely 18–25-fld., to 1½' tall. Fls. fleshy, about 1½" long, fragrant, the ss. and ps. yellow-green, oblong, acutish. Lip shortly helmet-shaped, green, fleshy, oval, the lat. lbs. slightly toothed, the midlb. very short. Autumn. (I, H) Brazil.

C. Russellianum Hk. (*Catasetum calceolatum* Lem.)

Pbs. rather smaller than most of the spp., to about 4" tall, roundish-conical, usually grey-green, the lvs. to 20" long. Infls. pendulous, 15–20-fld., including the rather long stalk up to 15" long. Fls. perfect, to 2½" across, delightfully fragrant, not as heavy-textured as most other members of the genus, grey-green to nearly white marked with deep green, sometimes net-branching longitudinal stripes, the dors. sep. and ps. forming a rather open hood over the col., the lat. ss. flaring and outstretched. Lip inflated, slipper-shaped, complex, fimbriate marginally (the teeth usually whitish), with a winged, toothed callus extending on the top of the slipper almost to its apex. Autumn. (I, H) Mexico; Guatemala; El Salvador; Honduras; Nicaragua; Panama.

C. tabulare Ldl. (*Catasetum rhamphastos* Krzl.)

Habit as in the genus. Infls. erect, loosely 2–6-fld., to 1½' tall. Fls. about 4" across, opening widely, very fleshy and excessively fragrant, the ss. and ps. yellowish-white, more or less flushed and dotted with reddish, narrowly oblong, acute. Lip whitish flushed with dull red, with a rather large egg-shaped callus on the disc, basally with a small, blunt sac. Spring–autumn. (I, H) Colombia; Brazil.

C. trulla Ldl.

Habit as in the genus. Infls. arching to almost pendulous, to 12" long, rather densely many-fld. Fls. about 2" across, fragrant, the ss. and ps. whitish-green, narrowly elliptic, shortly acuminate. Lip triangular, whitish-green with a brown apex, marginally fimbriate. Autumn. (I, H) Brazil.

C. viridiflavum Hk. (*Catasetum serratum* Ldl.)

Robust sp., identical in vegetative appearance to *C. Oerstedii* Rchb.f. Infls. erect or arching, to 2½' long, 2–12-fld. Fls. to almost 4" across and long, fleshy, fragrant, often not opening fully, the lip uppermost; ss. and ps. pale green aging to yellow, the dors. sep. and ps. concave and forming a hood over the col. Lip very fleshy, globose, with an abrupt, conical basal constriction, the outside yellow, the lat. margins minutely ciliate, pale green aging to yellow, the inside usually dull orange. Spring–summer. (H) Panama.

C. Warscewiczii Ldl. & Paxt. (*Catasetum scurra* Rchb.f.)

Rather dwarf sp., the egg-shaped pbs. to less than 4" tall, becoming very ridged and wrinkled with age, the 4–6 lvs. to 1½' long and 3" wide, deciduous in time. Infls. sharply or somewhat pendulous, to 12" long, usually dense, few- to many-fld. Fls. perfect, about 1½" or less across, very fragrant, long-lived, the ss. and ps. white or greenish-white striped longitudinally with pale green, the dors. sep. and ps. forming a slight hood above the col. Lip white or greenish-white, striped with pale green, 3-lbd., the fleshy base sac-like, the lat. lbs. erect, with fimbriate margins, the midlb. with a strongly bearded apex. Mostly summer–autumn, sometimes more than once annually. (I, H) Costa Rica; Panama; Colombia; Venezuela.

C. Gardneri Schltr. (*Monachanthus fimbriatus* Gardn.) Rather similar in all respects to *C. discolor* Ldl., but the infls. to more than 2' tall and the more numerous fls. of different shape. Fls. about 1½" long, yellow-green, the lip with a yellow base, marginally furnished with numerous hair-like appendages. Spring. (H) Brazil.

C. Garnettianum Rolfe. Very closely allied to, and simulating *C. barbatum* (Ldl.) Ldl., but somewhat smaller in all parts, and with fewer fls. in an infl. less than 8" tall. Fls. about 2" across, fleshy, fragrant, the ss. and ps. whitish-green with large red blotches, the lip white, slightly fringed marginally. Winter. (H) Brazil.

C. integerrimum Hk. (*Catasetum maculatum* auth. not Kth., *C. Wailesii* Hk.) A robust sp., rather simulating *C. macrocarpum* L.C.Rich. in basic appearance. Infls. erect, 3–10-fld., to 15" tall. Fls. very fleshy, fragrant, about 3" long, not opening fully, yellowish-green to purplish, often spotted with deeper colour, the helmet-shaped lip rigid, laterally compressed, uppermost. Autumn. (I, H) Mexico through Central America to Nicaragua; Venezuela.

C. Lemosii Rolfe. Dwarf sp., the almost globular pbs. usually less than 4" tall. Infls. erect, loosely 6–10-fld., about 6" tall. Fls. about 1½" across, the lanceolate-elliptic, acuminate ss. and ps. green, the helmet-shaped lip yellow-green outside, inside yellow, rose towards the base. Spring. (I, H) Brazil.

C. naso Ldl. Allied to *C. macrocarpum* L.C.Rich. Fls. inverted, pendulous, about 3" long, very fleshy and heavily fragrant, the ss. and ps. green with small brownish flecks, the hooded lip 3-lbd., green spotted with brownish-red, the midlb. ligulate, obtuse. Autumn. (I, H) Venezuela; Brazil.

CATTLEYA Ldl.
(*Maelenia* DuMort.)

The genus *Cattleya* contains about sixty-five species, literally innumerable varieties and forms, and many thousands of hybrids, both natural and artificially produced. This huge aggregation of orchids is, without a doubt, the most popular and widely-grown in the entire Orchidaceae, and its members are, to all of us, synonymous with the very word 'orchid' itself. Since a large percentage of the known species of *Cattleya* are in contemporary cultivation, we will at this time devote considerable space to a discussion of the genus. Botanically, *Cattleya* is a member of the subtribe *Laeliinae*, and is closest in its alliance to *Epidendrum* L.; in fact, Reichenbach, the great German orchidologist, reduced the present genus to synonymy under *Epidendrum*, an action which, while logical (considering the close ties which exist between the two groups), would result in such terrible confusion among horticulturists that most contemporary students have not followed his proposals. Even when not in flower, most Cattleyas are readily distinguishable from the allied genera (although a few of them do simulate certain kinds of Laelias and even some Epidendrums, such as *E. ciliare* L.); vegetatively, the genus is conveniently divided—horticulturally at least—into two sections. The first, and larger, of these sections is termed the 'bifoliate' group by orchidists; it consists of typically two-leaved (rarely more or less) plants, with cylindrical, often stem-like pseudobulbs of varying heights. The flowers produced by these species are generally smaller, of heavier texture, and more numerous than those of the second section. This second group, called the 'labiate' or 'unifoliate' section, comprises *Cattleya labiata* Ldl., its multitudinous variants, and a few allied species with typically solitary leaves, spindle-shaped or club-shaped, fleshy pseudobulbs, and producing (per inflorescence) one to a very few large and spectacular flowers. Today, most of the Cattleyas in cultivation belong to the latter category, and the vast majority of contemporary hybrids in this genus have been derived from them. A few species, such as *Cattleya citrina* (LaLl. & Lex.) Ldl., etc., cannot conveniently be placed in either of the two sections, which in any case are of little botanical significance. Floral structure in this genus is basically rather simplified, the typically spreading, wide sepals and mostly broader, frilled or crisped petals standing out away from a large, usually differently-coloured, often very ornate lip. In most Cattleyas, the basal part of this lip is rather tube-shaped, thus simulating many Laelias, Sobralias, and members of other genera. The species of *Cattleya* are widespread in the American tropics, with two centres of dissemination: one, the Andean regions of northern and western South America, and the other (the larger) in Brazil, principally in the coastal regions. Outlying representatives of *Cattleya* occur in Mexico, Central America, Panama, Trinidad, and in several other South American countries not noted previously. Despite its extreme popularity, the exact taxonomic delimitations of many of the component entities are not yet established, and a critical revision of the genus is sorely needed.

More hybrids are registered for *Cattleya* than for any other genus of the Orchidaceae, the current total extending well into the thousands. Most of the cultivated species of this genus (and hundreds of their hybrids) have also been crossed with a great many of the allied groups of the subtribe *Laeliinae*, with which they are largely freely inter-fertile. Some of the recent productions in this alliance, made most notably in Hawaii, are extravagantly beautiful and diverse orchids, only now coming into general cultivation. Considerable additional work yet remains to be done in this field, and many of our contemporary hybridists are devoting much of their effort to it at this time.

CULTURE: Cattleyas are included in the easiest of all orchids to grow, and are because of this among the most satisfactory types for the amateur to have as a basis for his collection. Most of them will stand considerable neglect and poor cultural conditions, though, naturally, flowering will not be as profuse under such treatment. Because of their popularity, a tremendous amount has been written regarding their culture; directions given here are a summary of the most usual methods, though a certain degree of individual variation will naturally be expected in different climatic regions and with the different species, variants, and hybrids.

Cattleyas will grow in almost any compost, provided that it will allow sufficient air to reach the fleshy, white roots, and that it does not become stale through excessive moisture-retention. Media such as osmunda, tree-fern fibre, and the bark preparations are most commonly used, although materials like gravel, volcanic pumice or cinders, or even sharp white sand have been utilized with notable success by many growers. They may be kept in pots, in baskets, hung on rafts, slabs, or pieces of tree-fern, or even on branches cut from hardwood trees. All Cattleyas require rather large amounts of light at all times, and some—such as *C. labiata* var. *Warscewiczii* and var. *Percivaliana*, *C. guttata*, and a few others—do not thrive unless they are grown under conditions of almost total exposure to the sun's rays. All Cattleyas (with the exception of *C. citrina*—which requires rather cool conditions) do well in warm or intermediate temperatures, although excessively high or low ones must naturally be avoided, since these are basically tropical plants native in areas with little natural temperature flux. While in active growth, they require quantities of water at the roots; because they are intolerant of stale compost, a potting medium must be utilized which will permit this water to drain off rapidly, or both vegetative and flower production will be seriously curtailed. When the new pseudobulbs have reached maturity—and have, in most instances, expanded their flowers—water should be cut down for a period of two weeks or so, until the new growths have had an opportunity to ripen. By this time the basal 'eyes' (incipient new growths) have usually started to swell, and a few tiny, green-tipped roots may have begun to appear at the base of the previous pseudobulb. Watering may then be resumed, preferably with a regular application of fertilizing materials given with it, since Cattleyas are heavy feeders, and benefit by liberal nutrients during the active period of growth. These orchids should be repotted (and divided) whenever necessary, that is, when the growths have exceeded the limits of the container in which they are grown, or are in stale or old compost. (C, I, H)

C. Aclandiae Ldl. (*Epidendrum Acklandiae* Rchb.f., *Epidendrum Aclandiae* Rchb.f., *Cattleya Acklandiae* J.E.Planch., *C. Auclandii* Beer)

Pbs. mostly cylindrical, sometimes slightly swollen above, to 4″ tall. Lvs. 2, rigidly leathery, broadly elliptic, blunt apically, to 4″ long and 1″ wide. Fls. solitary or in pairs, to 4½″ across, very fragrant, heavy-textured, glossy, long-lived, the ovate-oblong, obtuse ss. and ps. usually green or yellowish-green with large purple-brown blotches and spots, the ps. typically undulate. Lip very large, 3-lbd., not embracing the col., the small lat. lbs. usually pale magenta-red, the almost roundish, undulate midlb. brilliant magenta, golden-yellow at the base. Col. very wide, usually whitish or rose-white. Summer–autumn. (I, H) Brazil, in the North.

C. aurantiaca (Batem. ex Ldl.) P.N.Don (*Epidendrum aurantiacum* Batem. ex Ldl., *Epidendrum aureum* Ldl.)

Often grown as an *Epidendrum*. Pbs. rather spindle-shaped to cylindrical, furrowed with age, often yellowish-green, to 15″ tall, sheathed basally. Lvs. 2, often rather

Bothriochilus macrostachyus (Ldl.) L.O.Wms. [*Botanical Magazine*]

Brassavola cucullata (L.) R.Br. [MONTREAL BOTANIC GARDEN]

Brassavola nodosa (L.) Ldl. [H. R. FOLKERSMA]

Brassia Alleni L.O.Wms. [H. A. DUNN]

Brassia caudata (L.) Ldl. [H. A. DUNN]

recurved, rigidly fleshy, to 7" long and 2" wide, mostly broadly ovate, retuse apically. Infls. subtended by a large, often spotted sheath which sometimes conceals the stalk, to 4" long, few- to many-fld. Fls. often not opening fully, rather heavy-textured, expanded about 1½" across, bright orange-red, orange, or orange-yellow, sometimes with brownish or purplish streaks or spots on the mostly ovate lip. Summer–autumn. (I, H) Mexico; Guatemala; El Salvador; Honduras; Nicaragua.

C. bicolor Ldl. (*Epidendrum bicolor* Rchb.f.)

Similar in habit to *C. guttata* Ldl., the pbs. sometimes to 4½' tall, usually very slender and cylindrical. Infls. mostly short, 1–4-fld., furnished with a large sheath. Fls. to 4" across and more, highly fragrant, very heavy-textured, lasting for several weeks in perfection, the ss. and wider ps. usually pale green flushed with copper-brown or tawny-yellow, oblong, obtuse, the ps. usually undulate marginally. Lip with a long, narrow claw at the base (called an 'isthmus' by orchidists), then abruptly flaring to a more or less crisped, toothed apex, rich crimson-purple, rather rough near the col.-apex; lat. lbs. absent. Col. large, wide, usually pink. Autumn–winter. (I, H) Brazil.

C. Bowringiana Veitch (*Cattleya Skinneri* Batem. var. *Bowringiana* Krzl.)

Rather similar in habit to *C. Skinneri* Batem., differing in the strongly swollen bases of the much taller (to 3') pbs. and in floral characters. Infls. long-stalked, erect or arching under the weight of the fls., which number up to 15 per spike in robust specimens. Fls. usually less than 3" across, similar to those of *C. Skinneri* Batem., rose or purple, with a beautiful glittering appearance, the tubular lip with a white disc, the flaring midlb. typically much darker than other floral parts. Autumn. (I, H) British Honduras; Guatemala.

C. citrina (LaLl. & Lex.) Ldl. (*Sobralia citrina* LaLl. & Lex., *Cattleya Karwinskii* Mart., *Epidendrum citrinum* Rchb.f.)

Pendulous sp., rather small to medium-sized, with egg-shaped, usually grey or greyish-green pbs. about 2" long. Lvs. 2, pendulous, glaucous greyish-green, rather soft-textured, to 8" long and 1" wide, ligular or ligulate-lanceolate, acutish apically. Fls. pendulous, very long-stalked, solitary (very rarely paired), not opening fully, waxen in texture, very fragrant, persisting for several weeks in perfection, about 3–3½" long, the oblong, obtuse ss. and ps. bright citron-yellow, the ps. broader, undulate marginally. Lip large, beautifully frilled on margins, often white there, and deep golden-yellow in the middle and throat. Autumn–spring. (C, I) Mexico.

C. Forbesii Ldl. (*Maelenia paradoxa* DuMort., *Cattleya vestalis* Hoffmsgg., *Epidendrum Forbesii* Rchb.f.)

Pbs. cylindrical, rather slender, to 12" tall, furrowed with age. Lvs. 2, narrowly elliptic, obtuse, to 6" long and 2" broad, rather rigidly leathery. Infls. erect, to 4" tall, 1–6-fld. Fls. to 4½" across, waxy, rather heavily fragrant, long-lived, highly variable in hue, but in the typical phase with olive-green or yellowish-green ss. and ps., the down-curved lip dirty white often flushed with rose on the outside of the lat. lbs., inside with a yellow throat which has red veins, the undulate midlb. dull red

with a white margin. Ss. and ps. oblong-ligulate, the ps. often rather undulate marginally. Lip 3-lbd., the roundish lat. lbs. embracing the col., the roundish midlb. flaring, usually very crisped on margins. Summer–autumn. (I, H) Brazil.

C. granulosa Ldl. (*Epidendrum granulosum* Rchb.f.)

Rather similar in habit to *C. guttata* Ldl., the st.-like pbs. to more than 2' tall, the paired, rigidly leathery lvs. to 7" long, oblong-lanceolate, obtuse. Infls. rather short, 5–8-fld., with a large sheath. Fls. very glossy and thick, highly fragrant, long-lived, to 6" across, rather variable in colour, the ss. and ps. usually olive-green with more or less numerous rich brown spots, the lip white on the sides and apically, dull orange and crimson medially, the central part very rough. Ss. mostly undulate marginally, the dors. one oblong-elliptic, obtuse to acute, the lats. strongly falcate, elliptic-lanceolate, mostly acute. Lip deeply 3-lbd., the rather triangular lat. lbs. embracing the col., the midlb. distinctly clawed at base, then abruptly dilated into a fan-shaped lamina which is strongly crisped or even fringed marginally. Autumn–early winter. (I, H) Brazil; ? Guatemala.

—fma. **Schofieldiana** (Rchb.f.) A.D.Hawkes (*Cattleya granulosa* Ldl. var. *Schofieldiana* Rchb.f., *Cattleya Schofieldiana* Rchb.f.)

The most frequently seen variant of the sp., differing from it only in floral colour: ss. and ps. pale tawny-yellow, flushed with purple and sometimes also with green, densely spotted with crimson-purple; lip very large, the lat. lbs. white tinged with rose, the midlb. brilliant magenta, very rough. Autumn. (I, H) Brazil.

C. guttata Ldl. (*Cattleya elatior* Ldl., *C. guttata* Ldl. var. *Leopoldii* Lind. & Rchb.f., *C. Leopoldii* Versch., *C. granulosa* Ldl. var. *Russeliana* Ldl., *C. guttulata* Ldl., *C. sphenophora* Morr., *Epidendrum elatius* Rchb.f., ? *Epidendrum elegans* Vell.)

Pbs. st.-like, cylindrical, furrowed with age, to 5' tall in robust forms. Lvs. typically paired, rigidly leathery, broadly lanceolate, obtuse apically, to 8" long and 2½" wide. Infls. often very large, long-stalked, the total to as much as 1½' tall (usually shorter), 5–30-fld. Fls. highly variable in size and colour (especially in the degree and size of the spots), 2–4" across, very waxy and heavy-textured, fragrant, short- or long-lived, the ss. and ps. usually green with more or less numerous brown-red spots and dots, the lip with rose or whitish lat. lbs., the somewhat flaring, rough midlb. usually bright magenta, often with a white margin. Ss. and ps. oblong, obtuse, the latter usually somewhat wider and undulate marginally. Lip strongly 3-lbd., the lat. lbs. embracing the col., ovate, blunt, the midlb. narrowed basally and then flaring, often undulate or vaguely toothed marginally. Mostly autumn–winter. (I, H) Brazil.

—fma. **Prinzii** (Rchb.f.) A.D.Hawkes (*Cattleya amethystoglossa* Lind. & Rchb.f., *C. guttata* Ldl. var. *Prinzii* Rchb.f., *C. purpurina* B.-R., *Epidendrum amethystoglossum* Rchb.f., *Epidendrum elatius* Rchb.f. var. *Prinzii* Rchb.f.)

Differing from the sp. only in the colour of the fls., which typically are about 4" in diam. and produced in

Cattleya intermedia R.Grah. [VEITCH]

many cases in large numbers. Ss. and ps. typically white or blush-white ground-colour, more or less copiously spotted with bright magenta. Lip with white lat. lbs., the rough, flaring midlb. brilliant magenta, more or less suffused with paler colour, usually with some white or cream-yellow markings in the throat. Autumn–winter. (I, H) Brazil.

C. intermedia R.Grah. (*Cattleya amabilis* hort., *C. amethystina* Morr., *C. candida* hort., *C. Loddigesii* Ldl. var. *amethystina* hort., *Epidendrum intermedium* Rchb.f.)

Similar in habit to *C. Forbesii* Ldl., often slightly more slender and with longer pbs. Infls. 3–7-fld., short- to long-stalked. Fls. to 5″ across, very fragrant, heavy-textured, long-lasting, somewhat variable in colour, the ss. and ps. typically blush-white, the lightly 3-lbd. lip typically with a rich magenta-rose midlb., the lat. lbs. enfolding the col. Ss. and ps. oblong, obtuse, the latter broader and usually undulate marginally. Lip with oblong, blunt lat. lbs. and a roundish, usually crisped midlb. Mostly spring–summer. (I, H) Brazil, particularly in the South; Paraguay; Uruguay.

C. labiata Ldl. (*Cattleya labiata* Ldl. var. *vera* Ldl., *Epidendrum labiatum* Rchb.f.)

Doubtless the most variable and widely-grown sp. in the genus; only the major variants are listed below. Pbs. mostly strongly club-shaped, furrowed with age, to 10″ long. Lf. solitary, rather rigidly leathery, oblong, obtuse, to 10″ long and 3½″ wide. Infls. typically 2–5-fld., in a short-stalked rac. which is furnished at base with a large, rather leathery spathaceous sheath. Fls. to 7″ across (larger in some variants), the ss. and ps. rose or whitish-rose, the ss. narrowly oblong, obtuse to acutish, the much broader ps. elliptic, often reflexed apically, usually very crisped and frilled marginally. Lip very large, ovate-oblong, obscurely 3-lbd., the lat. lbs. with entire margins, forming a large tube around the col., outside the same colour as the ss. and ps.; midlb. spreading, deeply emarginate, with a crisped or frilled margin, rich magenta-purple bordered with rosy lilac, with a pale yellow blotch which is streaked and veined with reddish-purple in the throat. Usually Oct.–Nov. (I, H) Brazil.

—var. **Dowiana** (Batem. & Rchb.f.) Veitch (*Cattleya Dowiana* Batem. & Rchb.f.)

Vegetatively scarcely distinguishable from typical *C. labiata* Ldl. Fls. 5–6 per spike, to 6″ across, highly fragrant, often not lasting well, the ss. and very large frilled ps. nankeen-yellow (the ps. occasionally veined and/or flushed with magenta or red-magenta), the midlb. of the very large lip broader and more wide-spreading than the type, velvety, very rich crimson-purple, with golden-yellow veins radiating from the centre to all margins and with 3 prominent golden-yellow streaks down the centre. Summer–autumn. (I, H) Costa Rica.

—subvar. **aurea** (Lind.) Veitch (*Cattleya aurea* Lind., *C. Dowiana* Batem. & Rchb.f. var. *aurea* T.Moore)
A geographic variant, differing from var. *Dowiana* (Batem. & Rchb.f.) Veitch in its place of origin, and in the intricately branching and re-branching, richer-coloured veins on the lip. Summer–autumn. (I, H) Colombia.

—var. **Eldorado** (Lind.) Veitch (*Cattleya Eldorado* Lind., *C. virginalis* Lind. & André, *C. trichopiliochila* B.-R., *C. Wallisii* Lind. & Rchb.f., *C. MacMoorlandii* Nichols., *C. crocata* hort.)
Vegetatively usually smaller and more slender than typical *C. labiata* Ldl., the fls. usually 1–3 on a very short infl. Fls. usually about 5″ across, fragrant, often not opening well, the ss. and ps. generally narrower than in the type, pale rosy-lilac to white or white faintly flushed with pink. Lip more tubular than in the type, the midlb. less spreading and hence not as large, the disc (at throat-apex) rich orange-yellow or golden-yellow, surrounded by a wide white zone, which on the anterior side is either bordered with purple or blotched with purple on a pale rose ground which fades off on the sides to pale rose-lilac, the tube either white outside or coloured like the ss. and ps. The pbs. of this distinct variant are typically more rounded and smooth than the type, and the lvs. are generally very rigid and stiffly erect. Mostly July–Aug. (H) Brazil: Amazon Basin.

—var. **Gaskelliana** (Sand.) Veitch (*Cattleya Gaskelliana* Sand.)
Highly variable, often difficult to identify, vegetatively approximating var. *Mendelii* (Backh.) Rchb.f. or even var. *Warneri* (T.Moore) Veitch, florally often rather close to var. *Mossiae* (Hk.) Ldl., particularly in the shape of the lip. Fls. usually less than 5″ across, fragrant, the ss. and ps. mostly pale amethyst-purple flushed with white, rarely deeper amethyst-purple and without the suffusion, occasionally (particularly the ps.) with a strong white median band. Lip with the tubular lat. lbs. usually paler than the ss. and ps.; midlb. marginally crisped, pale rose-mauve, the disc rather saddle-shaped, orange, tawny-yellow, deep yellow, or even lemon-yellow, typically streaked with magenta, with a large white blotch on each side, and a mottled blotch of rich amethyst-purple in front of it. Mostly June–Aug. (I, H) Venezuela.

—var. **Lueddemanniana** (Rchb.f.) Rchb.f. (*Cattleya Lueddemanniana* Rchb.f., *C. speciosissima* Anders., *C. Dawsoni* Warn., *C. Bassettii* hort., *C. Mossiae* Hk. var. *autumnalis* hort.)
Differing from the type in the more nearly cylindrical, smoother pbs., topped by a single, narrower, rigidly erect, often greyish-green lf. which is usually longer than in typical *C. labiata* Ldl. Fls. 3–5, to 8½″ across (sometimes larger), very fragrant, the ss. and ps. usually

delicate purplish-rose suffused with white, the ps. nearly 3 times as broad as the ss., somewhat or strongly un-dulated, chiefly in the apical half, sometimes slightly toothed there. Lip usually with a narrow, often some-what compressed tube, of the same colour as the ss. and ps.; midlb. almost completely circular, more or less distinctly crisped, emarginate, rich or light amethyst-purple, with two pale yellow (sometimes white) blotches at the tube-entrance, between which are lines of deep amethyst-purple gradually diverging from the lip-base. Sept.–Oct. (I, H) Venezuela.

—var. **Mendelii** (Backh.) Rchb.f. (*Cattleya Mendelii* Backh.)
Variable, though not so much so as many other variants, the vegetative habit rather approximating that of var. *Trianaei* (Lind. & Rchb.f.) Duch., sometimes not as robust. Fls. 2–5, to 7″ across, fragrant, opening well and long-lived, the ss. and ps. white, often flushed with delicate rose, this colour usually more developed in the ps., which are often minutely toothed and very undulate in the apical half. Lip with the tube coloured like the ss. and ps.; midlb. broad and spreading, often almost round but generally longer than broad, marginally very in-dented and crisped, apical half or so rich crimson-purple, this area separated from the bright or dull yellow disc (which is often streaked with reddish or crimson) by an almost straight line of demarcation. Mostly May–early June. (I, H) Colombia.

—var. **Mossiae** (Hk.) Ldl. (*Cattleya Mossiae* Hk., *C. labiata* Ldl. var. *atropurpurea* Paxt., *C. labiata* Ldl. var. *picta* Van Houtte)
Usually very similar vegetatively to typical *C. labiata* Ldl., the pbs. sometimes more oblong. Fls. 2–7 per spike, to 8″ across, very fragrant, extremely variable (par-ticularly in the colour of the midlb. of the lip), the ss. and very large, undulate ps. pale or dark rose-lilac to white. Lip larger than any other variant except var. *Warscewiczii* (Rchb.f.) Rchb.f., the tube usually the same colour as the ss. and ps. on the outside, inside obliquely streaked with purple and pale lilac; midlb. very broad, marginally crisped, deeply cleft medially, highly variable, but almost always with a central band of yellow which extends from the disc to the base, the remaining apical part rich velvety magenta or magenta-purple, mottled and irregularly veined with lilac, with a broad lilac marginal area. May–June. (I, H) Venezuela.

—fma. **Reineckiana** (Rchb.f.) A.D.Hawkes (*Cattleya Reineckiana* Rchb.f., *C. Mossiae* Hk. var. *Reineckiana* hort., *C. labiata* Ldl. var. *Mossiae* (Hk.) Ldl. subvar. *Reineckiana* Veitch)
Differs from the var. *Mossiae* (Hk.) Ldl. only in floral colour, the ss. and ps. being pure white, the lip very crisped marginally, the midlb. lilac-mauve, the disc bright yellow more or less veined with crimson-purple. May–June. (I, H) Venezuela.

—fma. **Wageneri** (Rchb.f.) A.D.Hawkes (*Cattleya Wageneri* Rchb.f., *C. Mossiae* Hk. var. *Wageneri* hort., *C. Mossiae* Hk. var. *alba* hort., *C. labiata* Ldl. var. *Mossiae* (Hk.) Ldl. subvar. *Wageneri* Veitch)
Differs from the var. *Mossiae* (Hk.) Ldl. only in floral colour, the ss., ps., and lip being pure white,

except for a small bright or pale yellow disc on the lip. May–June. (I, H) Venezuela.

—var. **Percivaliana** (Rchb.f.) Rchb.f. (*Cattleya Percivaliana* Rchb.f.)

Similar to typical *C. labiata* Ldl. in vegetative habit, the few fls. to a maximum of 5″ across (usually smaller), giving off a peculiar, rather objectionable, musty odour, often not lasting well. Ss. and ps. rosy-lilac often flushed with amethyst-purple, the ps. usually more deeply coloured than the ss. Lip with the tube the same colour as the ss. and ps., often suffused with tawny-yellow; midlb. crimson-magenta shaded with maroon or yellowish-maroon, the margin pale lilac and frilled; disc and basal part of lat. lbs. rich tawny-yellow, orange, or brownish-orange, usually streaked with red and purple, this area variable in size and degree of intensity. Mostly Jan.–Feb. (I, H) Venezuela, almost always growing on rocks.

—var. **quadricolor** (Ldl.) A.D.Hawkes (*Cattleya quadricolor* Ldl., *C. chocoensis* Lind. & André, *C. labiata* Ldl. var. *Trianaei* (Lind. & Rchb.f.) Duch. var. *chocoensis* Schltr., *C. labiata* Ldl. var. *Trianaei* (Lind. & Rchb.f.) Duch. subvar. *chocoensis* Veitch)

Readily distinguished from typical *C. labiata* Ldl. (and from allied var. *Trianaei* (Lind. & Rchb.f.) Duch.) by its smaller fls. which never open fully—usually remaining almost bell-shaped—with extremely heavy fragrance. Ss. and ps. usually pure white, sometimes tinted with pale lilac, the ps. sessile. Lip with the tube pale amethyst-purple, the disc orange-yellow, with a small purple blotch in front of it. Dec.–Feb. (I, H) Colombia.

—var. **Rex** (O'Brien) Schltr. (*Cattleya Rex* O'Brien)

Vegetatively much like typical *C. labiata* Ldl. Fls. variable, fragrant, to 7″ across in the finest forms, the ss. and very wide ps. cream-white or yellowish (very rarely butter-yellow), usually flushed with butter- or lemon-yellow. Lip with a deep yellow tube, the throat often marked with reddish-brown or magenta-brown, the beautifully crisped and frilled, large midlb. bright yellow mottled and marked with magenta, the margins usually white. Mostly July–Aug. (I, H) Peru; Amazonian Brazil.

—var. **Trianaei** (Lind. & Rchb.f.) Duch. (*Cattleya Trianaei* Lind. & Rchb.f., *C. bogotensis* hort., *C. Lindigii* Karst.)

Usually misspelled 'Trianae'. Extremely variable, usually approaching typical *C. labiata* Ldl. in vegetative appearance, but often larger and more robust. Fls. to 8″ across, highly variable, especially in the degree of coloration of the midlb. of the lip. Ss. and the broader ps. varying from pure white or delicate rose-white to deep amethyst-purple, the ps. usually crisped marginally. Lip usually with the tube the same colour as the ss. and ps., rather narrow; midlb. not opening as widely as most other variants, often longer than wide, often not crisped or only slightly so, usually rich magenta-crimson, sometimes as pale as the ss. and ps.; disc broad, usually orange-yellow, often prolonged to the base of the lip in the form of a broad band, sometimes streaked with pale purple, lilac, or white. Dec.–Feb. (I, H) Colombia.

—subvar. **Schroederae** (Rchb.f.) A.D.Hawkes (*Cattleya Schroederae* Rchb.f., *C. Trianaei* Lind. & Rchb.f. var. *Schroederae* hort.)

Differs from the var. *Trianaei* (Lind. & Rchb.f.) Duch., in the following respects: the fls. are usually larger and more highly perfumed; the ps. are broader; the tube of the lip is broader and the midlb. much larger and more frilled marginally; the disc is very large and bright or dull orange; apical part of midlb. either pale or bright rose-purple, the ss. and ps. usually rather pale lilac. Mar.–July. (I, H) Colombia.

var. **Warneri** (T.Moore) Veitch (*Cattleya Warneri* T.Moore)

Very closely allied to typical *C. labiata* Ldl., and often scarcely distinguishable from it, the fls. appearing, however, at a different season. Fls. very fragrant, to 8″ across, highly variable, the ss. and ps. usually pale rose more or less shaded with deeper amethyst-rose. Lip with the tube coloured like the ss. and ps.; midlb. not paler on the margins, usually rich magenta-purple, sometimes with deeper veins; disc tawny-yellow or orange-yellow streaked with pale lilac or white. June–July. (I, H) Brazil.

—var. **Warscewiczii** (Rchb.f.) Rchb.f. (*Cattleya Warscewiczii* Rchb.f., *C. gigas* Lind. & André, *C. Sanderiana* hort., *C. imperialis* hort.)

Variable, but not so much so as many other phases of the sp., the fls. to 11″ across in rare cases (usually 7–9″), fragrant, very handsome, the ss. and broader ps. usually delicate rose. Lip with the tube mostly the same colour as the midlb., the latter part rather fiddle-shaped, the apical part broader and more spreading than the basal part, very deeply cleft at the apex, mostly rich crimson-purple, sometimes mottled and bordered with paler crimson-purple; disc golden-yellow, often with 3 or more parallel red-purple lines that are prolonged to the base of the lip, from which shorter lines radiate obliquely on both sides; on each side of the disc is a large white or pale yellow blotch. Mostly July–Aug. (I, H) Colombia.

C. Lawrenceana Rchb.f.

Rather similar in vegetative appearance to *C. labiata* Ldl., but the pbs. usually reddish-brown, to 15″ long, and not as distinctly club- or spindle-shaped. Lf. solitary, narrower than that of the other sp. Infls. 5–8-fld., short-stalked, usually stiffly erect, the sheath usually brownish-purple. Fls. to 5″ across, fragrant, long-lived, the ss. and ps. white, rose or pale rose-violet, the lip with a very long, slender tube, the midlb. brilliant rose-purple, often mottled with pale brownish, the throat white. Ss. narrowly ligular, obtuse. Ps. narrowly elliptic, obtuse, undulate on the margins, slightly wider than the ss. Lip with the lat. lbs. forming a very long, thin tube around the col., the flaring midlb. deeply bilobed again, usually not crisped marginally. Spring–early summer. (H) Guianas, especially around Mount Roraima; Venezuela; ? Northern Brazil.

C. Loddigesii Ldl. (*Cattleya ovata* Ldl., *C. maritima* Ldl., *C. Arembergii* Scheidw., ? *C. vestalis* Hoffmsgg., *Epidendrum violaceum* Lodd., *Epidendrum Loddigesii* Rchb.f.)

Rather similar in habit to *C. Forbesii* Ldl., often somewhat larger and more robust. Infls. short, 2–6-fld., with a rather small sheath at the base. Fls. to 4½″ across, waxy, fragrant, long-lived, rather variable, the oblong, obtuse ss. and broader, undulate-margined ps. usually blush-white, sometimes flushed with deeper rose (especially on the ps.). Lip slightly 3-lbd., the lat. lbs. curving over the col., oblong; midlb. broad, almost square, usually crisped marginally, light or deep rose or lilac-rose, the disc almost smooth, cream-white or cream-yellow. Aug.–Sept. (I, H) Brazil; Paraguay.

—var. **Harrisoniana** (Ldl.) Veitch (*Cattleya Harrisoniana* Ldl., *C. Harrisoniae* Paxt., *C. Harrisonii* P.N.Don, *C. intermedia* R.Grah. var. *variegata* Hk., *C. Papeinsiana* C.Morr., *Epidendrum Harrisoniae* Rchb.f.)

Differs from the type in having mostly longer, more slender, st.-like pbs., the lvs. not as rigid and lighter-coloured; fls. more flattened; disc of the lip corrugated and deep yellow or orange-yellow, the side margins of the midlb. reflexed. Autumn. (I, H) Brazil.

C. luteola Ldl. (*Cattleya flavida* Klotzsch, *C. Meyeri* Regel, *C. modesta* Meyer, *C. epidendroides* hort., *C. Holfordii* hort., *C. Ursellii* hort., *Epidendrum luteolum* Rchb.f., *Epidendrum Cattleyae* hort.)

Pbs. ovoid, slightly compressed, furrowed with age, to 4″ long. Lf. solitary, elliptic-oblong, emarginate or obtuse at apex, to 5″ long and ¾″ wide, rather rigidly leathery. Infls. shorter than the lvs., 2–6-fld. Fls. about 2″ across, waxy, long-lived, delightfully fragrant (or odourless), pale lemon- or butter-yellow, the margins of the midlb. of the lip usually white or whitish, the tube of the lip often streaked with dull purple or red inside. Ss. and ps. similar (the ps. sometimes slightly broader), oblong-lanceolate, the tips usually recurved. Lip 3-lbd., suborbicular when spread out, the lat. lbs. forming a tube around the col.; midlb. spreading or somewhat so, crisped and often toothed marginally. Mostly Nov.–Dec., sometimes more than once annually. (I, H) Brazil: Amazon Basin; Peru.

C. maxima Ldl. (*Epidendrum maximum* Rchb.f.)

Pbs. usually almost cylindrical, sometimes club-shaped in upper part, 4–15″ long, usually becoming somewhat compressed and furrowed with age. Lf. solitary, to 10″ long and 2½″ wide, oblong or ligulate-oblong, obtuse apically, usually rigidly leathery. Infls. erect or arching, 3–15-fld., sometimes as much as 12″ tall. Fls. to 5″ across (often smaller), fragrant, long-lived, somewhat heavy-textured, the ss. and ps. pale glossy rose, the tube of the lip the same colour, its midlb. spreading, crisped marginally, pale rose or whitish with a citron-yellow band traversing the entire length of the tube, on either side of which are numerous branching purple lines running obliquely from it. Ss. lanceolate, acuminate. Ps. oval-oblong, acute, undulate marginally, usually twice as broad as the ss. Lip ovate-oblong in

general outline, the lat. lbs. angular, the midlb. roundish. Autumn–winter. (I, H) Colombia; Ecuador; Peru.

C. Skinneri Batem. (*Cattleya Patinii* Cgn., *C. Skinneri* Batem. var. *parviflora* Ldl., *Epidendrum Huegelianum* Rchb.f.)

Somewhat variable vegetatively, the usually club-shaped, slightly compressed pbs. mostly less than 1½′ tall, sheathed basally when young. Lvs. 2, oblong, obtuse, rather rigidly leathery, to 8″ long and 2½″ wide. Infls. usually erect, up to 5½″ tall, 4–12-fld., the fls. often not all open at once. Fls. faintly fragrant in some forms, to 3½″ across, glittering rose or true purple, the midlb. of the lip typically darker, the disc whitish. Ss. linear-lanceolate or elliptic-lanceolate, obtuse, acute or apiculate, the lat. ones slightly oblique. Ps. broadly oval, rounded to apiculate at the tip, rather undulate marginally, wider than the ss. Lip slightly 3-lbd., or vaguely fiddle-shaped when expanded, the basal portion forming a tube around the col., the apex emarginate or obtuse, with a small ridge down the middle. Spring–early summer. (I, H) Mexico; British Honduras; Guatemala; Honduras; Costa Rica; Colombia; Venezuela; Trinidad.

—var. **autumnalis** P.H.Allen

Differs from the typical sp. in its different flowering-time, the deep purple throat and disc of the lip, and the generally smaller fls. Sept.–Oct. (I, H) Panama.

C. velutina Rchb.f. (*Cattleya alutacea* B.-R., *C. alutacea* B.-R. var. *velutina* B.-R., *C. fragrans* B.-R.)

Rather similar in habit to *C. bicolor* Ldl., but usually smaller and the pbs. often more thickened in their upper parts. Infls. 4–7-fld., rather short, usually less than 5″ tall. Fls. very glossy and heavy-textured, highly fragrant, to almost 4″ across (often smaller), the ss. and ps. light orange or yellow-orange more or less densely spotted with deep purple or brownish-purple, the lip whitish with magenta streaks down the middle, and a golden-yellow disc. Ss. and ps. oblong, rather blunt apically, the ps. somewhat broader than the ss., usually very crisped. Lip 3-lbd., the lat. lbs. short, roundish, the midlb. broadly heart-shaped, furnished with numerous rough projections. May–July. (I, H) Brazil.

C. violacea (HBK) Rolfe (*Cymbidium violaceum* HBK, *Epidendrum violaceum* Rchb.f., *Epidendrum superbum* Rchb.f., *Cattleya superba* Schomb., *C. Schomburgkii* Lodd. ex Ldl., *C. odoratissima* P.N.Don)

Pbs. spindle- or club-shaped, usually flushed with reddish or magenta-red, to 10″ long, very glossy, furrowed with age. Lvs. 2, ovate-oblong, rigidly leathery, often red-flushed, to 6″ long. Infls. rather stout, 3–7-fld., short, the stalk usually reddish. Fls. very fragrant, opening out very flat, rather heavy-textured, long-lived, to 5″ across, the ss. and ps. bright rose-purple (sometimes suffused with white), the 3-lbd. lip with the lat. lbs. magenta-purple, the midlb. brilliant crimson-purple or magenta-red, the yellow disc with a white, purple-streaked blotch on each side. Ss. oblong-lanceolate, acute. Ps. broader above the middle than below, often vaguely undulate, usually wider throughout than the ss. Lip with sharply triangular lat. lbs. which cover the col., the midlb. transversely oblong, slightly down-curved, emarginate, minutely toothed on the margin. Mostly June–Aug. (H) Colombia; Venezuela; Guianas; Brazil; Peru.

C. Walkeriana Gardn. (*Cattleya bulbosa* Ldl., *C. Gardneriana* Rchb.f., *C. princeps* B.-R., *C. nobilior* Rchb.f., *Epidendrum Walkerianum* Rchb.f.)
Pbs. often borne at some intervals from each other on the stout, rather zigzag rhiz., spindle-shaped, often reddish, to 5″ long, stalked basally. Lvs. 1–2, to 5″ long, elliptic-oblong, usually rather rigidly leathery, often red-flushed. Infls. short, slender, leafless shoots arising from the rhiz. near the base of the pbs., 1–2-fld., to 3″ tall. Fls. to 4½″ across, fragrant, rather heavy-textured, opening flat, varying from bright rose-purple to soft pinkish-lilac, the outside of the lip-tube the same colour as the ss. and ps., the midlb. bright amethyst- or magenta-purple, streaked with darker purple, the disc white or pale yellow. Ss. lanceolate, acute. Ps. ovate, blunt to acutish, twice as broad as the ss. Lip 3-lbd., fiddle-shaped when spread out, the lat. lbs. suberect and partially enclosing the col. at their base; midlb. spreading, kidney-shaped to almost round, emarginate, crisped or frilled marginally. Mostly Feb.–May. (I, H) Brazil.

C. Brownii Rolfe. Rather approximating *C. Loddigesii* Ldl. and its var. *Harrisoniana* (Ldl.) Veitch in all parts, differing in lip-characters, usually slightly more robust vegetatively, the fls. to 3½″ across, fragrant, heavy-textured, the ss. and ps. rose-purple. Lip with whitish lat. lbs. which are usually flushed with rosy-mauve, the midlb. bright rosy-purple, with a yellowish-white, slightly roughened disc. Nov.–Dec. (I, H) Brazil.

C. x dolosa Rchb.f. (*Cattleya Walkeriana* Gardn. var. *dolosa* Veitch, *C. eximia* B.-R., *Epidendrum dolosum* Rchb.f.) Natural hybrid between *Cattleya Walkeriana* Gardn. and *C. Loddigesii* Ldl. var. *Harrisoniana* (Ldl.) Veitch. Vegetatively rather similar to *C. Walkeriana* Gardn., the pbs. not as swollen, to 6″ tall, the lvs. usually paired, rigid, to 5″ long, 1½″ wide, elliptic-oblong, obtuse or slightly emarginate apically. Infls. borne from the apex of the pb. (not from the rhiz.-shoots, as in *C. Walkeriana* Gardn.), usually 1-fld. Fls. to 5″ across, fragrant, heavy-textured, the ss. and ps. dark rose or magenta-rose, the lip pale rose basally, light rose at the tip, the disc yellow, the margins often veined with deep violet-purple. May–June. (I, H) Brazil.

C. elongata B.-R. (*Cattleya Alexandrae* Lind. & Rolfe, *C. Nilsoni* hort.) Similar in habit to *C. bicolor* Ldl., the pbs. to 2′ tall and more. Infls. 2–10-fld., the stalk to 2′ tall. Fls. about 3″ across, variable in colour, heavy-textured, fragrant, long-lived, the ss. and ps. varying from copper-brown to bright green or purplish-brown, spotted or not with deep purple-brown, the lip usually completely rich magenta or red-magenta. Ss. and ps. linear-oblong, obtuse, very crisped marginally. Lip 3-lbd., the lat. lbs. partially covering the col., oblong, often pale rose; midlb. slightly clawed, then sharply dilated, broadly kidney-shaped, apically retuse or emarginate, margined with paler colour. Mostly spring. (I, H) Brazil.

C. x guatemalensis T.Moore (*Cattleya x guatemalensis* T.Moore var. *Wischhuseniana* Rchb.f., ? *C. Deckeri* Klotzsch, *Epicattleya x guatemalensis* Rolfe) Natural hybrid between *Cattleya aurantiaca* (Batem. ex Ldl.) P.N.Don and *C. Skinneri* Batem. Vegetatively most like the latter parent, the fls. rather numerous, to 2″ across, fragrant, variable in colour, but usually orange-yellow more or less flushed with bright rose, the lip tubular, often marked in the throat with brownish-purple streaks, the midlb. not expanding widely. Mostly Feb.–Mar. (I, H) Guatemala; perhaps elsewhere in Central America.

C. x Hardyana Wms. Natural hybrid between *Cattleya labiata* Ldl. var. *Warscewiczii* (Rchb.f.) Rchb.f. and *C. labiata* Ldl. var. *Dowiana* (Batem. & Rchb.f.) Veitch subvar. *aurea* (Lind.) Veitch. Vegetatively similar to the first-named parent. Fls. 1–4, to 8″ across, very fragrant, the ss. and ps. deep rose-purple, the ps. very large and beautifully undulate and crisped. Lip to 3″ across, very crisped and frilled marginally, brilliant velvety magenta-crimson, the throat and upper part veined with golden-yellow; a large bright yellow 'eye' is present on each side of the throat-entrance, and is margined with particularly vivid magenta-crimson. This natural hybrid is, of course, technically merely a variant of the polymorphic *C. labiata* Ldl. Autumn. (I, H) Colombia.

C. porphyroglossa Lind. & Rchb.f. (*Cattleya amethystoglossa* Lind. & Rchb.f. var. *sulphurea* Rchb.f., *C. Dijanceana* hort., *C. granulosa* Ldl. var. *Dijanceana* Veitch, *Epidendrum porphyroglossum* Rchb.f., *Epidendrum porphyroglossum* Rchb.f. var. *sulphureum* Rchb.f.) Allied to and rather resembling *C. granulosa* Ldl., the pbs. to more than 2′ tall. Fls. 7–8, to 3″ across, very fragrant, heavy-textured, long-lived, the ss. and ps. varying from yellowish-brown to greenish (rarely clear yellow), the ps. especially rather undulate. Lip 3-lbd., the lat. lbs. whitish flushed with magenta, the midlb. shortly and narrowly clawed, brilliant magenta-purple, toothed marginally, furnished with radiating crested veins. Summer. (I, H) Brazil.

C. Schilleriana Rchb.f. (*Cattleya Regnellii* Warsc., *Epidendrum Schillerianum* Rchb.f.) Similar in habit to *C. Aclandiae* Ldl., the pbs. to 5″ tall, the paired lvs. often deep purplish-green, rigid, to 5″ long. Infls. 1–2-fld., very short. Fls. to 4½″ across, very waxy, fragrant, long-lived, the ss. and ps. dark green or brownish-green, densely blotched with deep brown or purple-brown, sometimes reddish-mahogany without spots. Lip light reddish-purple, the midlb. darker with very deep magenta veins, the disc yellow, with a thin yellow stripe extending from it to the apex of the lip. July–Oct. (I, H) Brazil.

CATTLEYOPSIS Lem.

Cattleyopsis is a genus of three species of handsome, brilliantly-flowered epiphytic or lithophytic orchids in the Antilles (especially Cuba) which are now becoming rather frequent in choice collections. Allied to *Broughtonia* R.Br. and to *Laeliopsis* Ldl., both of which the plants vegetatively simulate, they are among the most delightful and free-flowering of the smaller members of the '*Cattleya* group'. The dwarf to medium-sized plants consist of globular to rather elongate pseudobulbs, rigidly leathery leaves with unique saw-toothed margins, and give rise to often very long racemes or panicles of rather small but bright-coloured blossoms which last in perfection for several weeks. The genus *Cattleyopsis* differs from its allies in technical floral details.

A few hybrids have been produced recently by crossing *Cattleyopsis* with such allied genera as *Cattleya, Broughtonia, Laelia*, etc., mostly in Hawaii and South Florida. Considerable additional experimental breeding with these delightful orchids is to be encouraged.

CULTURE: As for *Broughtonia*. (I, H)

C. Lindeni (Ldl.) Cgn.

Pbs. small, usually less than 3″ tall, prominently ringed, grey-green, varying from globular to stoutly cylindric. Lvs. 2, rigid, thick, grey-green, about 5″ long, toothed on the margins. Infls. to 3′ long (rarely more), arching or erect, with up to 12 fls. at the apex, rarely branching. Fls. rather delicate in texture, to 2″ across, pale blush-rose, the lip large, vivid rose or pinky-rose, with complex wavy lines of crimson and a yellowish throat. Spring–autumn. (I, H) Bahamas; Cuba.

C. Ortgiesiana (Rchb.f.) Cgn.

Rather similar in habit to *C. Lindeni* (Ldl.) Cgn., typically smaller in all parts. Infls. to 3½′ long, many-fld., rarely branched. Fls. opening successively over a long period, more flattened than in the other sp. noted, brilliant rose-magenta to pale rose, the lip roundish, darker, marked with still more intense purple-magenta and bright yellow or whitish. Late winter–spring. (I, H) Bahamas; Cuba.

CAUCAEA Schltr.
(*Abola* Ldl.)

Caucaea contains but a single exceedingly rare epiphytic species, **C. radiata** (Ldl.) Schltr. (*Abola radiata* Ldl.), native in the high Andes of Colombia. A member of the subtribe *Oncidiinae*, this group, which considerably simulates a *Gomesa*, is not present in our collections at this time, and is in any event primarily of scientific interest.

Nothing is known of the genetic affinities of *Caucaea*.

CULTURE: Presumably as for the highland Odontoglossums, etc. (C, I)

CAULARTHRON Raf.
(*Diacrium* Bth.)

This is a small genus of about six (or possibly fewer) very closely allied species, native in the area extending from Guatemala to Trinidad and Venezuela. Generally known as Diacriums, these orchids are allied to *Epidendrum* L. (with which the group has been combined in the past). At least two of them are rather frequent in contemporary collections, and one of these, *C. bicornutum* (Hk.) Raf., is often considered to be among the finest of all American orchids. These plants, usually epiphytic or lithophytic in habit, have fleshy, typically hollow pseudobulbs which bear a few rigidly leathery leaves at the summit. The terminal inflorescences are often rather lengthy, and bear a few to rather numerous large and showy or relatively small blossoms at the apical portion. Both of the Caularthrons in contemporary cultivation have white or creamy-white flowers. In the wild, the plants often grow in nests of fire-ants, hence their collection is fraught with difficulty.

Caularthron bicornutum has been used on several occasions by the hybridists, under the now-synonymous name of *Diacrium* with other members of the subtribe *Laeliinae*. For the large part, these multigeneric hybrids are scarce in collections, though all of them are of considerable beauty and should be better known. The genus is presumably genetically compatible with still other groups of the subtribe *Laeliinae* than those which have thus far been utilized, and additional experimental breeding should definitely be attempted.

CULTURE: Generally speaking, the Caularthrons should be given the cultural conditions such as those afforded the 'labiate' Cattleyas, though they seem to do best if kept in pots, tightly filled with osmunda or tree-fern fibre. Both of the cultivated members of the genus delight in large quantities of bright light, and while in active growth benefit by liberal applications of fertilizers, as they are heavy feeders. The Caularthrons are usually very intolerant of division, hence this should be done only when absolutely necessary. (I, H)

C. bicornutum (Hk.) Raf. (*Epidendrum bicornutum* Hk., *Diacrium amazonicum* Schltr., *Diacrium bicornutum* Bth.)

The magnificent 'Virgin Orchid', among the finest of American orchids. Pbs. hollow, clustered, elongately spindle-shaped, with prominent nodes, the lf.-sheaths persistent, to 9″ long and 1½″ in diam., narrowed and vaguely stalked at the base, typically with some small openings there. Lvs. from upper parts of pbs., rigidly leathery, glossy, few in number, oblong-lanceolate, obtuse, to 8″ long. Infls. loosely or rather densely 5–20-fld., erect, slender, to more than 12″ tall. Fls. to almost 3″ in diam., opening flat, fragrant, waxy, long-lived, pure ivory-white (sometimes tinged with pinkish or lavender on the reverse sides of the ss.), the lip with some crimson or magenta spots, these mostly towards the base, the disc yellow. Ss. and ps. elliptic, shortly acuminate, the ss. sometimes rather concave. Lip small, 3-lbd., the lat. lbs. short, erect; the larger midlb. elongately lanceolate, acuminate. Mostly spring. (I, H) Colombia; Venezuela; Trinidad; Tobago; Br. Guiana; Brazil: Amazonas.

C. bilamellatum (Rchb.f.) R.E.Schultes (*Epidendrum bilamellatum* Rchb.f., *Epidendrum bigibberosum* Rchb.f., *Diacrium bigibberosum* Hemsl., *D. bilamellatum* Hemsl., *D. indivisum* Broadway, *D. venezuelanum* Schltr.)

Rather similar in vegetative appearance to *C. bicornutum* (Hk.) Raf., usually less robust. Infls. occasionally branched, erect, very long-stalked, to 3′ long, few- to many-fld., the rachis often tinged with purple. Fls. about 1½″ in diam. (usually much smaller), sometimes not opening but self-fertilizing prior to anthesis, white typically tinged outside with pink or lavender, the disc of the lip yellow. Ss. and ps. elliptic, obtuse to apiculate, the ss. concave, the ps. short-clawed. Lip vaguely 3-lbd., the lat. lbs. reduced to teeth or almost absent, the apical part rather triangular, mostly long-tipped; disc with 2 large fleshy triangular plate-like calli on the lower part, with 2 pits on the under side. Mostly late winter–spring. (I, H) Guatemala; British Honduras; Nicaragua; Costa Rica; Panama; Colombia; Venezuela; Trinidad.

CENTROGENIUM Schltr.

This is a genus of about fifteen species of often handsome terrestrial orchids in the American tropics, the range extending from South Florida to Brazil. Little-known by collectors, they have fleshy, clustered, subterranean roots, large leathery, often mottled foliage, and erect inflorescences of rather showy green, purple, white, or brown blossoms of interestingly complex structure and attractive appearance. Allied to *Spiranthes* L.C.Rich.—and included in that genus by some orchidologists—they should be better known by enthusiasts, since their cultural requirements are rather easily met and they are almost without exception very handsome plants.

No hybrids are known in this genus, and nothing has been ascertained concerning its genetic affinities.

CULTURE: As for *Bletia*. (I, H)

C. setaceum (Ldl.) Schltr. (*Pelexia setacea* Ldl.)
Roots rather stout, clustered. Lvs. 1–2, long-stalked, basal, the stalk usually purple, the blade elliptic-oblong to narrowly elliptic-lanceolate, acute, the entire structure to more than 12″ long (often much shorter), usually more or less mottled with dull purple. Infls. erect, to 2′ tall, loosely few-fld. above, sheathed below, fuzzy. Fls. not opening fully, faintly fragrant, rather long-lived, to 2½″ across, greenish-white or greenish with a white lip which is toothed towards the sharp apex, the lat. ss. forming a spur-like mentum which is attached to the pedicellate ovary for about half its length. Late winter-spring. (I, H) South Florida through the West Indies to Trinidad, Colombia, and Brazil.

CENTROGLOSSA B.-R.

This genus consists of seven species, all Brazilian, except for one which occurs in Peru. The plants are dwarf epiphytes, with small flowers of unique structure. The group differs markedly from the only other member of the subtribe *Trichocentrinae—Trichocentrum* itself. None of the Centroglossas appears to be present in collections at this time outside of their native lands, and in any event they are principally of botanical interest.

Nothing is known of the genetic affinities of this group.

CULTURE: As for *Ornithocephalus*. (H)

CENTROPETALUM Ldl.
(*Nasonia* Ldl.)

A member of the small subtribe *Pachyphyllinae*, *Centropetalum* consists of about seven or more species of rare dwarf epiphytic orchids, native in the high Andes of Colombia, Ecuador, and Peru. They are attractive little plants, with abbreviated, densely leafy stems, the leaves imbricated and very fleshy, and proportionately large, mostly red or scarlet flowers of interesting structure. Unfortunately none of the Centropetalums appears to be present in cultivation today, although they offer some intriguing potentialities to the specialist.

Nothing has been ascertained regarding the genetic ties of this genus.

CULTURE: As for the high-elevation Odontoglossums. Because of the habit of the plants, they should doubtless be grown mounted on tree-fern slabs. (C)

CENTROSTIGMA Schltr.

Now comprising about six species in tropical Africa, the genus *Centrostigma* is a member of the exasperatingly complex subtribe *Habenarinae*, differing from its immediate allies in technical details of the often rather showy, usually white or green flowers. Terrestrial orchids, they are relatively rare in the wild, apparently, and have not as yet been introduced into our collections.

Nothing is known of the genetic affinities of *Centrostigma*.

CULTURE: Probably as for the tropical species of *Habenaria*. (I, H)

CEPHALANTHERA L.C.Rich.
(*Dorycheile* Rchb.)

About a dozen species of *Cephalanthera* are known to date, these primarily terrestrial orchids (there is one saprophytic member), widespread in the Temperate Zones, and extending into North Africa and the southern Himalayas. Exceptionally rare in contemporary collections, several of them are sufficiently handsome, leafy plants, to warrant attention by connoisseurs. The often complex flowers—mostly white, red, or green in colour—are produced in frequently elongate racemes at the tops of robust, heavily-leaved stems, these arising from a creeping subterranean rhizome. *Cephalanthera* is a member of the subtribe *Cephalantherinae*, being closest in its taxonomic alliance to *Epipactis* Sw.

No hybrids seem known in this genus, and nothing has been ascertained regarding its genetic affinities. Interspecific hybrids seem to offer some interesting potentials.

CULTURE: As for *Orchis*, etc. Cephalantheras are usually not particularly easy to maintain in good condition in the collection for very long. (C, I)

C. erecta (Thunb.) Bl. (*Serapias erecta* Thunb., *Epipactis erecta* Wettst., *Limodorum erectum* O.Ktze.)
Tubers paired, irregular, subterranean. St. slender, 12–15″ tall, leafy below, clothed with sheaths above. Lvs. cauline, usually about 3 in number, ovate-lanceolate, plicate, clasping the st., acutish, 1½–2″ long. Infl. short, rather loose, usually about 8-fld. Fls. about ¾″ long, green and white, the dors. sep. ovate-lanceolate, concave, acutish, the lats. similar but obtuse. Ps. lanceolate, acutish. Lip entire, more or less erect, ovate-lanceolate, concave, acutish, the spur saccate, very blunt, slightly curving. Spring–early summer. (C, I) North China; Japan.

C. pallens (Willd.) L.C.Rich. (*Epipactis pallens* Willd., *Cephalanthera Damasonianum* Druce, *C. grandiflora* Bab.)
Rhiz. creeping, subterranean, rooting freely. St. stout, usually slightly sinuous, leafy, 9–24″ tall. Lvs. cauline, numerous, ovate or ovate-lanceolate, acutish, becoming bract-like above, 2–4″ long. Rac. loosely few-fld., 4–8″ long. Fls. almost 1″ long, yellowish-white or cream-coloured. Dors. sep. ovate-lanceolate, the lats. lanceolate, slightly curved at the tip. Ps. similar to dors. sep. Lip 3-lbd., the lat. lbs. small, triangular, blunt, the midlb.

elliptic, the disc covered with lines of fine hairs. Summer. (C, I) Europe; Asia Minor; Caucasus Mts.

C. rubra (L.) L.C.Rich. (*Serapias rubra* L., *Cymbidium rubrum* Sw., *Epipactis rubra* All.)

Rhiz. short, creeping, emitting numerous black, fleshy fibrous roots. St. erect or vaguely zigzag, 9–24″ tall, leafy to the apex. Lvs. numerous, lanceolate, acute, spreading, 2–4″ long. Infl. about 6–12-fld., rather loose, to 4″ long. Fls. about ¾″ long, opening only partially, the ss. and ps. pinkish-red to pale violet-red, the lip white with a narrow red apical margin. Ss. lanceolate, the lats. tapering to a fine elongate point. Ps. lanceolate, long-pointed. Lip small, cordate. Mostly May–June. (C, I) Europe; Asia Minor to Iran.

C. xiphophyllum (L.f.) Rchb.f. (*Serapias xiphophyllum* L.f., *Cymbidium xiphophyllum* Sw., *Cephalanthera acuminata* Ldl., *Cephalanthera ensifolia* L.C.Rich., *Cephalanthera longifolia* Fritsch)

Rhiz. subterranean, with stout, fleshy, fibrous roots. St. rather stout, erect, 6–18″ tall. Lvs. mostly on basal part of the st., plicate, rich green, oblong or lanceolate, becoming linear upwards, 3–8″ long. Infl. loosely many-fld., 4–8″ long. Fls. about ¾″ long, white, sometimes marked with butter-yellow on the lip. Ss. lanceolate, acutish. Ps. elliptic, obtuse. Lip small, erect basally, embracing the col., the apical part recurved. Spring–early summer. (C, I) Europe; North Africa; North Asia to the Himalayas.

C. falcata (Sw.) Ldl. (*Epipactis falcata* Sw., *Cephalanthera platycheila* Rchb.f.) Rhiz. slender, creeping, the roots numerous, short. St. slender, leafy, 9–15″ tall. Lvs. about 4–6 in number, broadly lanceolate, acutish, plicate, suberect, 2–3″ long. Infl. loosely 9–18-fld., to about 6″ long. Fls. about ⅝″ long, white or green flushed with white, fragrant. Ss. lanceolate, acutish, the lats. spreading. Ps. oblong-elliptic, falcate, obtuse, incurving. Lip ovate, narrow below, 3-lbd., the lat. lbs. ovate-triangular, diverging, blunt, the midlb. oblong, acutish. Mostly May–July. (C, I) China: Yunnan.

CERATANDRA Eckl.
(*Callota* Harv.)

Ceratandra, as now restricted, contains only two species of terrestrial orchids in South Africa; segregate genera, such as *Ceratandropsis* Rolfe and *Evota* Rolfe, have been removed from it, apparently with good reason. These are unusual plants of the subtribe *Disperidinae*, extremely rare at this time in cultivation, but well worthy of further attention by enthusiasts.

No hybrids are known in *Ceratandra*, and its genetic affinities have not been deduced.

CULTURE: As for *Caladenia*. (C, I)

C. atrata (L.) Dur. & Schinz (*Orchis atrata* L., *Ceratandra chloroleuca* Eckl. ex Bauer)

Lvs. numerous, basal and on the st., ascending, minutely fringed, to 3″ long. Infl. erect, to more than 12″ tall, few- to many-fld., the spike rather dense. Fls. to 1½″ long, with an unpleasant soap-like scent, yellow-green, the ss. sometimes tipped with pink or red-brown, the ps. and lip yellow. Winter. (C, I) South Africa, especially Cape Peninsula.

CERATANDROPSIS Rolfe

The genus consists of a single species, **Ceratandropsis globosa** (Ldl.) Rolfe (*Ceratandra globosa* Ldl.), a rare South African terrestrial orchid which is at this time unknown in cultivation. *Ceratandropsis* differs from *Ceratandra* Eckl. in not possessing a lip-appendage, and in the white flowers. It is incompletely understood.

Nothing is known of the genetic affinities of this strange genus.

CULTURE: Presumably as for *Caladenia*. (I)

CERATOCHILUS Bl.

Ceratochilus biglandulosus Bl., the only described member of this genus, is a native of the higher mountains of Java and Sumatra, where it grows epiphytically on mossy trees. Unknown in cultivation, it is a dwarf member of the subtribe *Sarcanthinae*, somewhat allied to *Hymenorchis* Schltr., with proportionately large, complex flowers produced from a small, densely leafy monopodial plant.

Nothing is known regarding the genetic ties of the genus *Ceratochilus*.

CULTURE: Presumably as for the smaller *Vanda* relatives from tropical areas. (I)

CERATOSTYLIS Bl.
(*Ritaia* King & Pantl.)

Ceratostylis is a genus of the little-known subtribe *Glomerinae*. Very few of the more than seventy described species are grown by orchidists, although some of them are unusual and certainly handsome enough to warrant attention. Distribution of the genus extends from the Himalayas of India throughout Indonesia and Malaya to New Caledonia, with a particularly rich representation occurring in New Guinea. Many of the species resemble nothing more than a large or small rush or tuft of grass when not in flower, hence are of interest as being of most 'un-orchid-like' appearance. The usually small blossoms are often brightly coloured, and are sometimes produced in considerable abundance on well-grown plants.

Hybridization has not yet been attempted in *Ceratostylis*, and nothing is known of its genetic affinities.

CULTURE: As for the tropical species of *Bulbophyllum*. Certain of these plants, because of their sharply pendulous habit, must be grown on rafts or slabs. (I, H)

C. rubra Ames
Sts. clustered, covered by large brownish papery bracts. Lvs. very fleshy, semi-terete, grooved above, to 5″ long and ½″ wide, mostly curving, usually dull green. Fls. solitary or paired, short-stalked, lasting about a week, opening flat, glossy brick-red, about 1″ across, the ss. and ps. similar, the lip very small, often yellowish or whitish. Several times throughout the year. (I, H) Philippines.

C. subulata Bl. (*Appendicula teres* Griff., *Ceratostylis teres* Rchb.f., *C. cepula* Rchb.f., *C. gracilis* Rchb.f., *C. malaccensis* Hk.f.)
Sts. terete, closely tufted, to 6″ long, less than ⅛″ in diam., dark green. Lf. solitary, subterete, broadly

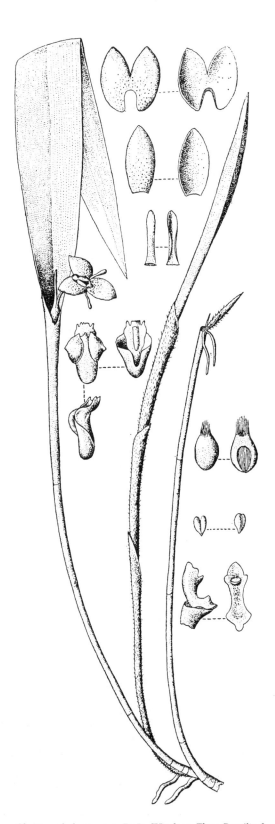

Chaetocephala punctata B.-R. [Hoehne, *Flora Brasílica*]

grooved on one side, about 1½″ long, rounded apically. Fls. appearing singly on very short stalks from a tuft of small chaff-like bracts, not opening fully, less than ⅛″ long, dull purple-red with a yellow lip, the lip enclosed in the hairy mentum formed by the lat. ss. Mostly autumn. (I, H) India, Malaya, and Sumatra to the Philippines and Borneo.

C. pendula Hk.f. Rhiz. pendulous, profusely branched, to 1½′ long, covered by overlapping ribbed brown sheaths. Lvs. about ½″ apart, to 1½′ long, thickly fleshy, acute, partly covered at base by the rhiz.-sheaths. Fls. almost stalkless, borne from a dense tuft of bracts at the lf.-bases, white, about 1/16″ long. Autumn. (H) Malay Peninsula.

CHAENANTHE Ldl.

This is a genus of but a single rare species, **Chaenanthe Barkeri** Ldl. (*Diadenium Barkeri* Schltr.), a member of the subtribe *Comparettiinae*. It is a small Brazilian epiphyte which somewhat resembles *Comparettia* P. & E., but differs from that group in floral structure. It is apparently unknown in contemporary collections.

Nothing is known of the genetic affinities of this obscure plant.

CULTURE: Presumably as for *Ornithocephalus*. (H)

CHAETOCEPHALA B.-R.

Two species of *Chaetocephala*, **C. lonchophylla** B.-R. and **C. punctata** B.-R., are known at this time, neither of which appears to be present in cultivation. Rare and very unusual members of the subtribe *Pleurothallidinae*, they are vaguely allied to *Pleurothallis* R.Br., but differ materially in structural details of the peculiar flowers. Both of the Chaetocephalas are epiphytic plants, inhabiting the rather dry woods of the interior parts of the Serra do Mar, in Brazil.

Nothing is known of the genetic affinities of this group.

CULTURE: Presumably as for *Pleurothallis*, etc. (I, H)

CHAMAEANGIS Schltr.

About eight species of *Chamaeangis* are known to date, distributed in tropical East Africa, Madagascar, the Comoro Islands, and the Mascarene Islands. Somewhat allied to *Aërangis* Rchb.f. of the subtribe *Sarcanthinae*, these are rather small epiphytic orchids with dense racemes of very small but highly intricate flowers, usually white or yellowish in colour. At this time, none of the Chamaeangis is present in our collections.

Nothing is known of the genetic affinities of this incompletely-studied genus.

CULTURE: As for the small-growing, tropical Angraecums. (H)

CHAMAEANTHUS Schltr.

This is a genus of about eight known species, distributed from Malaya and Java to New Guinea and New Caledonia. A member of the subtribe *Sarcanthinae*, it is nearest in its relationship to *Sarcochilus* R.Br., but differs from that group in floral details. In *Chamaeanthus*, the inconspicuous plants, bearing only a few leaves on short stems, also produce very small inflorescences.

hence they are of little interest save to the specialized collector. No members of the genus are known in contemporary collections.

Nothing is known of the genetic affinities of this peculiar genus.

CULTURE: Presumably as for the tropical species of *Vanda*. (H)

CHAMAEGASTRODIA Mak. & Maek.

This is a very odd genus, consisting of but a single known species, C. **shikokiana** (Mak.) Mak. & Maek. (*Gastrodia shikokiana* Mak.), indigenous to Japan, and not present in cultivation at this time. Although presently placed in the subtribe *Gastrodiinae*, it has been suggested that it would be better relegated to the *Physurinae*, because of technical details of structure. A smallish saprophytic orchid, it is as yet incompletely known by botanists.

Nothing is known of the genetic affinities of *Chamaegastrodia*.

CULTURE: Possibly as for *Corallorrhiza*, though scant success can be anticipated in growing it for more than a single season. (I)

CHANGNIENIA Chien

The genus *Changnienia* was described in a rather obscure Chinese publication, to which we have been unable to gain access, hence we are unable to furnish any details regarding this orchid, or its generic affinities.

CHASEËLLA Summerh.

Established as a genus in 1961, *Chaseëlla* consists of a single species of very rare epiphytic orchid known to date only from South Rhodesia. C. **pseudohydra** Summerh. somewhat resembles a *Bulbophyllum* in appearance, but differs from that group in floral structure and in the remarkable vegetative parts, noted by Summerhayes as follows: 'The fleshy ovoid pseudobulb and bunch of radiating narrow green leaves at its apex are remarkably reminiscent of the coelenterate genus *Hydra*, on a much larger scale, and the specific epithet is chosen in view of this similarity.' *Chaseëlla* is apparently best placed in the subtribe *Bulbophyllinae*.

Nothing is known of the genetic affinities of this very scarce plant.

CULTURE: Presumably as for the tropical species of *Bulbophyllum*. (H)

CHAUBARDIA Rchb.f.

A single species of *Chaubardia* is known to date, this C. **surinamensis** Rchb.f., a very rare terrestrial or semi-epiphytic orchid of the subtribe *Huntleyinae*, known only from Suriname. Rather simulating a *Chondrorhyncha* in vegetative appearance, it differs from that genus in the divergent structure of the smallish flowers, which are borne in a few-flowered raceme. The genus is not present in collections today, and is largely of scientific interest, in any case.

Nothing is known of the genetic affinities of *Chaubardia*.

CULTURE: Presumably as for *Chondrorhyncha*, although warmer temperatures should prevail at all times. (H)

CHAULIODON Summerh.

Containing but a single species, **Chauliodon Buntingii** Summerh., this extraordinary genus of the complex angraecoid section of the subtribe *Sarcanthinae* is as yet not present in our collections. A dwarf epiphyte, completely leafless like the allied group *Microcoelia* Ldl., it bears tiny brownish-rose fls. in slender racemes from the centre of the mass of clambering roots. It has been detected on only a very few occasions, in Liberia and southern Nigeria.

Because of its exceptional rarity, nothing is known of the genetic affinities of the genus *Chauliodon*.

CULTURE: Presumably as for *Polyrrhiza* and other aphyllous epiphytic orchids. (H)

CHEIRADENIA Ldl.

A rare and little-known genus of the subtribe *Huntleyinae* from the Guianas, *Cheiradenia* contains two terrestrial, rather nondescript members which greatly resemble *Koellensteinia graminea* (Ldl.) Rchb.f. in habit, but which bear entirely different flowers, these of small dimensions and produced in elongate, wand-like racemes. The genus is unknown in contemporary cultivation.

Nothing is known of the genetic alliances of *Cheiradenia*.

CULTURE: Presumably as for *Phaius*. (H)

CHEIRORCHIS Carr

Cheirorchis is a genus of five known species, none of them present in contemporary collections. Native in Thailand and the Malay Peninsula, they are typically epiphytic on small trees. The group is somewhat allied to *Sarcochilus* R.Br., but differs from that genus in technical details of the small flowers.

Nothing is known of the genetic alliances of *Cheirorchis*.

CULTURE: Presumably as for the tropical Vandas and other epiphytic monopodial orchids. (H)

CHEIROSTYLIS Bl.

Cheirostylis is a genus of about fifteen species of mostly insignificant terrestrial orchids of the complex subtribe *Physurinae*, native over a huge region which extends from tropical Africa to Australia and New Guinea. Closely allied to *Zeuxine* Ldl., the group differs from it in technical details of the diminutive flowers. *Cheirostylis* is unknown in contemporary cultivation.

Nothing is known of the genetic affinities of this odd group.

CULTURE: Probably as for *Anoectochilus*. (H)

CHELONISTELE Pfitz.

Five species of *Chelonistele* are known, these variously epiphytic or lithophytic orchids found from the Himalayas through Burma to Borneo and Java. Closely

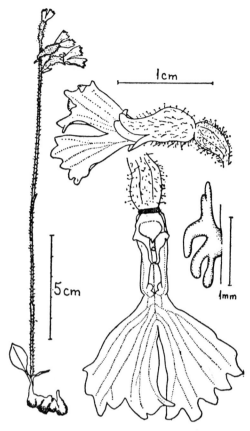

Cheirostylis sp. (Thailand) [*Orchids of Thailand*]

allied to *Coelogyne* Ldl., they are possibly more correctly referred to that genus, although the structure of the column and lip is aberrant. Pseudobulbous plants with racemes of medium-sized, usually white or yellowish flowers, they are unknown in our collections at this time.

Nothing is known of the genetic affinities of *Chelonistele*, although they presumably approximate those of *Coelogyne*, *Dendrochilum*, etc.

CULTURE: Probably as for *Coelogyne*, depending upon the place of origin of the particular species or individual involved. (I, H)

CHILOGLOTTIS R.Br.

A member of the subtribe *Drakaeinae*, *Chiloglottis* contains about ten species of uncommon, rather showy terrestrial orchids in Australia and New Zealand. Little-known by collectors, they are handsome plants well deserving of a place in the greenhouse, though, like most of their ilk, they are somewhat refractory orchids whose cultural requirements are not easily met. As in a few other orchidaceous genera (e.g., *Didymoplexis* Falc.), the pedicellate ovary elongates considerably after fertilization of the flower.

Nothing is known of the genetic affinities of *Chiloglottis*, and no hybrids have been reported.

CULTURE: As for *Caladenia*. (C, I)

C. Gunnii Ldl. (*Caladenia Gunnii* Rchb.f.)

Tubers subterranean, globose or ovoid. St. very short at flowering-time (usually less than 1″), but after fertilization elongating to as much as 8″. Lvs. paired, basal, more or less prostrate, ovate to broadly lanceolate, to 3″ long. Infls. 1-fld. Fls. widely expanding, to 1½″ across, varying from light or dark red-brown to greenish, rather complicated in structure. Winter. (C, I) Australia.

C. reflexa (Labill.) Druce (*Epipactis reflexa* Labill., *Chiloglottis diphylla* R.Br.)

St. slender, when flowering to 5″ long, often much longer when in fruit. Fl. solitary, about 1″ long, similar in colour to *C. Gunnii* Ldl., the dors. sep. usually incurved and following the contour of the col., the lip long-clawed at base. Late summer–autumn. (C, I) Australia.

CHILOPOGON Schltr.

Chilopogon is a genus of about three known species, segregated from *Appendicula* Bl., to which it is closely allied, differing only in technical details of the small flowers. All three species are extremely rare and incompletely-known botanically. They are epiphytes, inhabiting the mossy montane forests of New Guinea, and are not present in our collections at this time.

Nothing is known of the genetic affinities of *Chilopogon*.

CULTURE: Presumably as for *Appendicula*. (I)

CHILOSCHISTA Ldl.

Chiloschista consists of three or possibly four species of dwarf, leafless epiphytes of the complex subtribe *Sarcanthinae*, one of which is today found in a few particularly choice collections. Indigenous to the Himalayas, India, Burma, South-east Asia, and Indonesia, they consist of entangled masses of roots, from the centre of which arise graceful elongate inflorescences bearing leaf-like bracts and small but rather showy, very intricate flowers.

Nothing has as yet been ascertained regarding the genetic affinities of this peculiar genus of orchids.

CULTURE: As for *Polyrrhiza* and other leafless epiphytic orchids. (I, H)

C. lunifera (Rchb.f.) J.J.Sm. (*Sarcochilus luniferus* Bth. ex Hk.f., *Thrixspermum luniferum* Rchb.f.)

Roots densely tufted, numerous, elongate, flexuose. St. obsolete. Infls. racemose, elongate, 3–6″ long, many-fld. Fls. ½″ in diam., yellow spotted with purple. Ss. spreading, oblong, obtuse. Lip complex, 3-lbd., the lat. lbs. linear-oblong, obtuse; midlb. truncate, emarginate, the disc pubescent. Col. very short. Autumn. (I, H) Sikkim to Burma: Tenasserim.

CHITONANTHERA Schltr.

This is a rare and little-known genus of about seven species, all dwarf epiphytic plants of considerable botanical interest, native in the montane forests of New Guinea. A member of the subtribe *Thelasinae*, the genus is closest florally to *Octarrhena* Thw., and none of its component species is to be found in cultivation at this time.

Nothing is known of the genetic affinities of this strange little group.

CULTURE: As for the tropical Bulbophyllums. (H)

CHITONOCHILUS Schltr.

A member of the subtribe *Glomerinae*, the single known species of *Chitonochilus*, **C. papuanus** Schltr., is a native of New Guinea, and is unknown in our collections at this time, although it is a rather handsome member of the aggregation to which it belongs. The genus is apparently closest in its alliance to *Agrostophyllum* Bl., but differs from it in the structure of the small white flowers.

Nothing is known of the genetic affinities of this rare genus.

CULTURE: As for the tropical Bulbophyllums. (H)

CHLORAEA Ldl.
(*Bieneria* Rchb.f., *Geoblasta* B.-R., *Ulantha* Hk.)

Chloraea is a complex genus of an estimated one hundred species (many of which are little-known botanically, and which may not be valid taxa), native in the southern half of South America, mostly in Chile and Argentina. They are typically handsome terrestrial (rarely litho-

phytic) orchids, but unfortunately are virtually absent from contemporary collections. Bearing solitary or racemose, large, brightly-coloured flowers above a loose basal rosette or cluster of leaves (which are produced from a group of finger-like, subterranean tubers), the Chloraeas do not resemble any other types of orchids in particular, except possibly some of the closely allied genera *Asarca* Ldl. or *Bipinnula* Comm., neither of which has cultivated members. The below-noted *Chloraea* is present in a few choice collections today.

No hybrids are on record in this genus, and nothing is known of its genetic ties.

CULTURE: As for *Caladenia*. (C, I)

C. penicillata Rchb.f. (*Asarca Arechavaletae* O.Ktze., *Geoblasta Teixeirana* B.-R., *Chloraea Bergii* Hieron., *C. Arechavaletae* Krzl., *C. Teixeirana* Cgn.)

Lvs. forming a rosette at the base of the infl., usually 2–5, oblong-oval, glabrous, to 2″ long and ¾″ wide, rather fleshy. Infl. about 12″ tall, with a few lf.-like sheathing bracts, 1-fld. (rarely 2-fld.). Fls. to about 3″ across, greenish-white, the ps. greenish, more or less veined with reddish or magenta-red, the large lip red or wine-red, the gland-like projections covering the oval midlb. varying from greyish-red to brilliant wine-red. Winter. (C, I) Patagonia to southern Brazil.

CHLOROSA Bl.

A member of the subtribe *Cryptostylidinae*, *Chlorosa* contains two known species, both very rare and unusual terrestrial orchids, neither of which is present in our collections at this time. **Chlorosa Clemensii** A. & S. is known from the vicinity of Mt. Kinabalu, in Borneo, and **C. latifolia** Bl., is recorded from Java. They are rather nondescript plants with smallish but very complex, usually green flowers, and are primarily of scientific importance.

Nothing is known of the genetic affinities of *Chlorosa*.

CULTURE: Possibly as for *Anoectochilus*. (H)

CHONDRORHYNCHA Ldl.
(*Kefersteinia* Rchb.f., *Warczewiczella* Rchb.f., *Warscewiczella* Rchb.f., *Warszewiczella* Bth. & Hk.f.)

This fascinating genus of epiphytic (rarely lithophytic) orchids contains about twelve species which are widespread in the region extending from Mexico and Cuba to Brazil, with perhaps the greatest concentration occurring in the Andes of Colombia. Several of them are in more or less sporadic cultivation today, often under the synonymous name of *Warscewiczella*, and all of the known species are handsome enough to warrant attention by enthusiasts. A relatively recent article by Schultes and Garay has proposed the resurrection of Rafinesque's old name *Cochleanthes* for some of these plants, but I do not believe that this course should be followed, at least at this time. The Chondrorhynchas, allied to *Bollea* Rchb.f. and to *Huntleya* Ldl., are largely inhabitants of highland 'cloud forests', and require relatively cool conditions under cultivation. Consisting of a more or less loose fan of rather fragile leaves, from the bases of which the horizontal, erect, or pendulous,

C. *gracilis* L. W.ms   C. *filiformis* L. W.ms

CHITONANTHERA *Brassii* L. W.ms

Chitonanthera (3 spp., from New Guinea) [GORDON W. DILLON]

one-flowered peduncles arise, these plants bear blossoms which are often of extraordinary beauty and structure, and are heartily recommended to all orchidists who are able to afford them the somewhat specialized cultural conditions which are required.

Chondrorhyncha has to date been successfully crossed with *Bollea* (= *Chondrobollea*, one member of which occurs as a natural hybrid in Colombia), *Zygopetalum* (= *Chondropetalum*), and *Pescatorea* (= *Pescarhyncha*). Additional experimental hybridization with allied genera should produce some exceptionally interesting and handsome results, and is to be encouraged.

CULTURE: Chondrorhynchas and their allies grow best in perfectly-drained open baskets (rather than in pots, which they often appear to resent!) in a rather loose compost of either straight osmunda or shredded tree-fern fibre, or the same ingredient with some chopped sphagnum moss mixed in. Because these marvellous orchids do not possess water-storing pseudobulbs, or even particularly fleshy foliage, they must never be permitted to become dry. A shady, very airy spot is required, and excessively high temperatures should be avoided, since most of these plants are indigenous to areas of considerable elevation, where they are constantly cool and bathed in mists or fogs. When the new growths are expanding, or the sheathed flower-spikes start to appear, care must be taken that water does not lodge in them, or rotting may occur. Repotting should be attended to only when absolutely necessary, as Chondrorhynchas are highly intolerant of disturbance. While actively growing, periodic applications of weakened fertilizer are beneficial. Most orchidists have encountered serious difficulties with these plants, when growing them in the various bark preparations, hence these should be avoided. (C, I)

C. amazonica (Rchb.f. & Warsc.) A.D.Hawkes (*Zygopetalum amazonicum* Rchb.f. & Warsc., *Zygopetalum Lindeni* Rolfe, *Warscewiczella Lindeni* hort., *Warscewiczella amazonica* Rchb.f.)

Lvs. to almost 12″ long, forming a rather tight fan. Scapes to 3″ tall, usually erect. Fls. about 2″ across, 3″ long, fragrant, waxen in texture, the ss. and ps. white, lanceolate, acutish or acute. Lip white nerved with angular purple-red markings, large, shortly ovate, apically emarginate, the lat. lbs. small; callus square, grooved, fleshy. Winter–early spring. (I) Venezuela; Brazil.

C. Chestertoni Rchb.f.

Lvs. linear, rather flaccid in texture, obtuse, to 6″ long and ¾″ wide. Scapes about 3″ tall, usually horizontal or somewhat pendulous. Fls. about 3″ across, fleshy, very fragrant, greenish-white, the lip sometimes ·greenish-yellow. Ss. and ps. lanceolate, acute, the ps. slightly broader. Lip about 1½″ long, roundish, marginally furnished with a large fringe. Summer. (C) Colombia.

C. discolor (Ldl.) P.H.Allen (*Warrea discolor* Ldl., *Warscewiczella discolor* Rchb.f., *Zygopetalum discolor* Rchb.f.)

Lvs. rather pale green, thin in texture, to 2′ long and about 2″ wide, mostly linear or linear-lanceolate, acutish. Scapes usually several from base of each new growth, mostly nodding or horizontal, 1-fld., to 5″ long. Fls. about 3″ across, strongly fragrant, waxy, long-lived. Ss. white, sometimes flushed with pale yellow or cream-yellow towards the tips, oblong, acutish. Ps. white flushed with violet or purple, similar in shape to the ss., thrust forward over the lip and col. Lip very deep violet-purple to almost blue-purple, with a large complex white or yellowish-white callus, sometimes with a white margin. Late spring–autumn. (I) Cuba; Costa Rica; Panama.

C. flabelliformis (Sw.) A.D.Hawkes (*Epidendrum flabelliforme* Sw., *Cymbidium flabelliforme* Griseb., *Eulophia cochlearis* Steud., *Warscewiczella cochlearis* Rchb.f., *Warscewiczella flabelliformis* Cgn., *Zygopetalum cochleare* Ldl.)

Rather similar in habit to *C. discolor* (Ldl.) P.H.Allen, although generally not as robust and with wider foliage. Scapes to about 4″ long, usually almost erect. Fls. about 3″ across, fragrant, rather short-lived, waxy, the lip extremely fleshy. Ss. and ps. white or greenish-white, spreading, narrowly elliptic, acutish. Lip rich violet or purplish-violet with deeper veins or stripes, concave and rather shell-shaped, lightly 3-lbd., emarginate at apex, the callus very fleshy, grooved, almost square, blunt apically. Summer. (I) West Indies.

C. Lendyana Rchb.f.

Lvs. to 12″ long and almost 2″ wide, linear-lanceolate to oblanceolate, abruptly acute to acuminate, rather fleshy. Scapes to 6″ tall, erect. Fls. to about 2″ long, yellowish or white with a yellow flush, distinguished from the allied spp. by the recurving, wide-spreading lat. ss., which are narrowly elliptic to lanceolate and somewhat concave, as are the ps. Lip tubular, undulate-crisped on the apical margins, the callus flat, triangular-squarish, 2-several-toothed. Summer. (I) Mexico; Guatemala; Costa Rica; Panama.

C. aromatica (Rchb.f.) P.H.Allen (*Zygopetalum aromaticum* Rchb.f., *Warscewiczella aromatica* Rchb.f., *Zygopetalum Wendlandii* Rchb.f., *Bollea Wendlandiana* hort., *Warscewiczella Wendlandii* Schltr.) Lvs. tufted, rather compressed towards base, lanceolate, to 10″ long and 1½″ broad, rather stiffly ascending. Scapes 3–4″ long, mostly erect. Fls. 3½–5″ across, very fragrant, heavy-textured, long-lived, the ss. and ps. greenish or greenish-white, sometimes suffused with whitish, lanceolate, somewhat twisted. Lip ovate, cordate, undulate and frilled marginally, white with a median violet-purple flush, the apex revolute; callus semicircular, violet-purple, grooved. Col. white, lined underneath with violet. Mostly Aug.–Sept., sometimes more than once annually. (C, I) Costa Rica; Panama.

C. fimbriata (Lind. & Rchb.f.) Rchb.f. (*Stenia fimbriata* Lind. & Rchb.f.) Similar in habit to *C. Chestertoni* Rchb.f., and sometimes confused with it, but with the lip differently shaped and the ps. with very prominent marginal fringes. Fls. about 3″ across, fragrant, pale yellow, the lip strongly frilled, marked with red or reddish. Summer–autumn. (C) Colombia.

C. marginata (Ldl.) P.H.Allen (*Huntleya marginata* hort., *Warrea marginata* Ldl., *Warrea quadrata* Ldl., *Warscewiczella velata* Rchb.f., *Warscewiczella marginata* Rchb.f., *Zygopetalum fragrans* Lind., *Zygopetalum velatum* Rchb.f., *Chondrorhyncha Lipscombiae* Rolfe). Simulating *C. flabelli-*

formis (Sw.) A.D.Hawkes in habit, but not quite as robust and generally with shorter infls. Fls. about 3″ across, fragrant, fleshy, long-lived. Ss. and ps. white, elliptic, acute. Lip white, pale violet marginally, striped medially with deep purple, the almost square, grooved callus streaked with pale purple, the entire lip rather rhombic, blunt towards the apex. Summer–autumn. (C, I) Panama; Colombia.

C. Wailesiana (Ldl.) A.D.Hawkes (*Warrea Wailesiana* Ldl., *Warrea digitata* Lem., *Warscewiczella Wailesiana* E.Morr., *Zygopetalum Wailesianum* Rchb.f.) Resembling *C. flabelli-formis* (Sw.) A.D.Hawkes in general habit, but with longer infls. and a distinctly shorter pedicellate ovary. Fls. about 2½″ across, fragrant, heavy-textured, white. Ss. and ps. narrowly elliptic, acute, somewhat reflexed. Lip white flushed with violet-purple, and with some deep violet-purple stripes down the middle, the callus 7-keeled, striped with violet-purple. Spring–summer. (I) Brazil.

CHRONIOCHILUS J.J.Sm.

Two species of *Chroniochilus* appear to be known at this time, one (**C. Godefroyanus** (Rchb.f.) L.O.Wms.) native to the Fiji Islands, the other (**C. minimus** (Bl.) J.J.Sm.), from Java and Borneo. The group is a member of the subtribe *Sarcanthinae*, and both of the component species have in the past been placed in several other genera, such as *Thrixspermum* Lour., *Sarcochilus* R.Br., etc., although they seem distinct, by reason of details of the flowers. Often very robust epiphytic plants, neither of the Chroniochilus is in cultivation at this time.

Nothing is known regarding the genetic affinities of this group.

CULTURE: Presumably as for the tropical Vandas, etc. (H)

CHRYSOCYCNIS Lind. & Rchb.f.

Two or so species of *Chrysocycnis* are known to science, these excessively rare and little-known epiphytic orchids of the subtribe *Maxillarinae*, native in the high Andes of Colombia. They are strange plants of unique vegetative habit, and bear complex flowers with a singularly elongate arching column (rather like that of *Cycnoches*), and do not appear to be closely allied to any other genera of the subtribe. They are unfortunately unknown in contemporary collections.

Nothing is known of the genetic affinities of this unusual group.

CULTURE: Presumably as for the high-elevation Odontoglossums. (C)

CHRYSOGLOSSUM Bl.

This is a genus of about ten species of often rather handsome terrestrial orchids, native in a huge region which extends from Ceylon to the Fiji Islands. A member of the subtribe *Collabiinae*, *Chrysoglossum* is closest in its alliance to *Diglyphosa* Bl., but is distinguished from it by technical characters, mostly of the flowers. A single species is known in cultivation, but it must be classed as a rare orchid.

No hybrids have been attempted in *Chrysoglossum*, and nothing is known of its genetic affinities.

CULTURE: As for *Phaius*. (H)

C. ornatum Bl.

Rhiz. creeping, about ¼″ thick, with short sheathing lvs. at intervals, also producing pbs. about 1½″ tall which are mostly obscured by a large sheath. Lf. (solitary per pb.) stalked, plicate, to 15″ long and 4½″ wide, elliptic, with prominent nerves. Infls. erect, borne from the rhiz., to almost 2′ tall, smooth, purplish, few-sheathed basally, the many-fld. rachis elongating to about 8″ long in time. Fls. complex, about 1½″ long, the ss. and ps. olive-green with small red-brown spots arranged in longitudinal rows, purple-flushed basally, the dors. sep. concave, the lats. bent downwards; lip white or pale yellow with some purple spots, the lat. lbs. erect, the midlb. concave. Mostly summer. (H) Malay Peninsula; Sumatra; Java; Celebes.

CHUSUA Nevski

Two species of *Chusua* are known, both of these segregated from *Orchis* [Tournef.] L. of the subtribe *Habenarinae*, perhaps on rather tenuous differences of floral structure. Rather small terrestrial orchids indigenous to the far reaches of the U.S.S.R., they are not present in our collections at this time, and in any event are primarily of botanical importance.

Nothing is known of the genetic ties of *Chusua*.

CULTURE: Possibly as for the cool-growing Habenarias. Orchis, and the like. (C)

CHYSIS Ldl.
(*Thorvaldsenia* Liebm.)

According to a recent revision of the genus, *Chysis* now consists of two variable and widespread epiphytic (rarely lithophytic) orchids whose range extends from Mexico to Venezuela. Although not common in collections, both of the known species, and several of their forms and varieties, are in cultivation, and, when well-flowered, are among the handsomest of American orchids. The prominent pseudobulbs are fleshy, rather club-shaped, typically pendulous, and bear several folded leaves which are eventually deciduous. The waxy blossoms are borne in short racemes, produced concurrently with the flush of new growth, and are long-lived, often rather large, and highly aromatic. The sepals and petals are somewhat concave, while the large, fleshy lip is complexly excavated and often of a different colour. The more or less prominent, often red-tipped calli on its disc give rise to the rather unpleasant common name of 'Baby Orchids' for the members of this genus, the name being derived from the supposed similarity of these calli to the budding teeth of an infant!

Three hybrids are registered in the genus *Chysis*, all of them produced by Veitch in the period from 1874–1896. Since two of them—*C. x langleyensis* and *C. x Sedeni*—are the result of breeding variations of what is now considered a single species, *C. aurea* Ldl., the name *C. x Sedeni* must be utilized, and *C. x langleyensis* reduced to varietal status under it. The third hybrid is *C. x Chelsoni*, a cross between *C. aurea* Ldl. var. *bractescens* (Ldl.) P.H.Allen and *C. laevis* Ldl., and was registered by Veitch in 1874. All of these extraordinarily handsome hybrids seem to have been lost to cultivation, and should be re-made by some enterprising breeder. Little or nothing is known about genetic compatibility of *Chysis*, with supposedly allied genera, such as *Phaius* Lour., *Calanthe* R.Br., *Cymbidium* Sw., etc., and some interesting experimental hybridization might profitably be attempted along these lines.

CULTURE: Chysis prefer cultivation in baskets rather than in pots, since their rampant root-systems delight in an abundance of readily obtainable air, and the large pseudobulbs are typically pendulous. Perfect drainage is a necessity, and some pieces of broken crock may with advantage be scattered through the compost itself to assure this. Straight fresh osmunda, cut into rather small pieces, is generally used as a potting-medium; shredded tree-fern fibre is also highly satisfactory for this purpose. These orchids flower best if grown in a rather sunny spot, though care must be taken to avoid burning of the thin foliage. While the plants are in active growth —typically during the summer months—water must be given in large quantities, but upon completion of the new pseudobulbs the plants should be removed to a somewhat cooler situation and watering lessened. In the following spring, the new growths will appear, whereupon the plants should be moved back to a warm location and moisture gradually increased. The racemes of flowers are produced when the new shoots are a few inches long, and when these have faded heavy watering and higher temperatures should be continued until the pseudobulbs reach maturity. Repotting should be carried out when absolutely necessary only, as Chysis do not like to be disturbed any more than essential. Regular applications of fertilizer are beneficial. (I, H)

C. aurea Ldl.

Pbs. pendulous, elongately spindle-shaped, stalked, sheathed when young, often greyish, to $1\frac{1}{2}'$ long. Lvs. deciduous, jointed with the sheaths, oblong-lanceolate, acuminate, wavy, rather soft-textured, to $1\frac{1}{2}'$ long and 2″ wide. Infls. produced from the lower axils of the flush of new growth, 6–12-fld., to about 12″ long (usually shorter), long-stalked. Fls. very waxy and fragrant, long-lived, to 3″ across, highly variable in coloration (and somewhat so in size and shape of floral segments), usually lemon-yellow or pale yellow, the whitish lip marked with maroon or dull brown, the disc of the lip with 3–5 yellowish velvety keels extending from the base to the midlb.-base. Mostly summer. (I, H) Mexico to Venezuela and Peru.

—var. **bractescens** (Ldl.) P.H.Allen (*Chysis bractescens* Ldl., *Thorvaldsenia speciosa* Liebm.)
Distinguished from the typical phase primarily in having the floral bracts usually more than an inch long (instead of shorter than that size). Summer. (I, H) Mexico; British Honduras; Guatemala.

—fma. **Lemminghei** (Lind. & Rchb.f.) P.H.Allen (*Chysis Lemminghei* Lind. & Rchb.f., *C. aurea* Ldl. var. *Lemminghei* Hk.)
Differs from the type in having the ss. and ps. marked with purple. Summer. (I, H) Mexico.

—fma. **maculata** (Hk.) P.H.Allen (*Chysis aurea* Ldl. var. *maculata* Hk.)
Differs from the type in having the ss. and ps. marked with reddish-brown. Summer. (I, H) Costa Rica; Panama; Colombia.

C. laevis Ldl. (*Chysis costaricensis* Schltr., *C. tricostata* Schltr.)
Vegetatively much like *C. aurea* Ldl. and its variants, but differing in the colour of the fls. and in that the disc of the lip has 3 very prominent fleshy keels. Pbs. to about 15″ long, pendulous. Infls. 8–12-fld. Fls. to 3″ across (often smaller), very waxy and fragrant, long-lived, the ss. and ps. yellow in the basal half, with a large orange spot often covering the apical half or so. Lip yellow, spotted and blotched with crimson, the lat. lbs. falcate, the midlb. roundish, strongly undulate marginally. Spring–early summer. (I, H) Mexico to Costa Rica.

CHYTROGLOSSA Rchb.f.

A member of the subtribe *Ornithocephalinae*, *Chytroglossa* consists of three rare species of dwarf epiphytic orchids, all native in Brazil. Dwarf, fan-shaped plants, they bear racemes of small but exceedingly complex and attractive flowers, in the structure of which they differ materially from the allied *Ornithocephalus* Hk. They are very rare in collections today, but are of sufficient charm to warrant attention from the connoisseur.

Nothing is known of the genetic affinities of *Chytroglossa*.

CULTURE: As for *Ornithocephalus*. (I, H)

C. Marileoniae Rchb.f.
Lvs. arranged in a fan, ligulate, somewhat 3-toothed at the tip, narrowed basally, to about $1\frac{1}{2}″$ long. Infls. loosely 4–6-fld., to about 2″ long, the rachis very slender. Fls. almost $\frac{1}{2}″$ across, golden-yellow with some dark brown spots on the very complex lip. Spring. (I, H) Brazil.

CIRRHAEA Ldl.
(*Sarcoglossum* Beer, *Scleropteris* Scheidw.)

Cirrhaea is a genus of about four species of often handsome, strange, epiphytic or lithophytic orchids native in the central and southern parts of Brazil, where they are sometimes rather frequent and form large colonies in the forests. The group is allied to *Gongora* R. & P. and to *Polycycnis* Rchb.f., and is as yet little known in cultivation, although the typically bright flowers of extraordinary structure, borne in long pendulous racemes, are attractive and interesting to the connoisseur.

This genus has not yet been taken in hand by the breeders, although it is presumably genetically compatible with allied groups of the subtribe *Gongorinae*.

CULTURE: As for *Gongora*. (I, H)

Broughtonia sanguinea (Sw.) R.Br. [ROD MCLELLAN CO.]

Bulbophyllum ornatissimum (Rchb.f.) J.J.Sm. [GEORGE FULLER]

Bulbophyllum purpureorhachis (De Wild.) Schltr. [GEORGE FULLER]

Caladenia pectinata R.S.Rog. [W. H. NICHOLLS]

Camarotis philippinensis Ldl. [REG S. DAVIS]

A leafy species of *Campylocentrum*, *C. micranthum* (Ldl.) Rolfe [BLANCHE AMES]

Catasetum pileatum Rchb.f., showing a raceme of male flowers at the left, and two hooded female flowers below another male on the right [G. C. K. DUNSTERVILLE]

Cattleya labiata Ldl. var. *Trianaei* (Lind. & Rchb.f.) Duch. [H. A. DUNN]

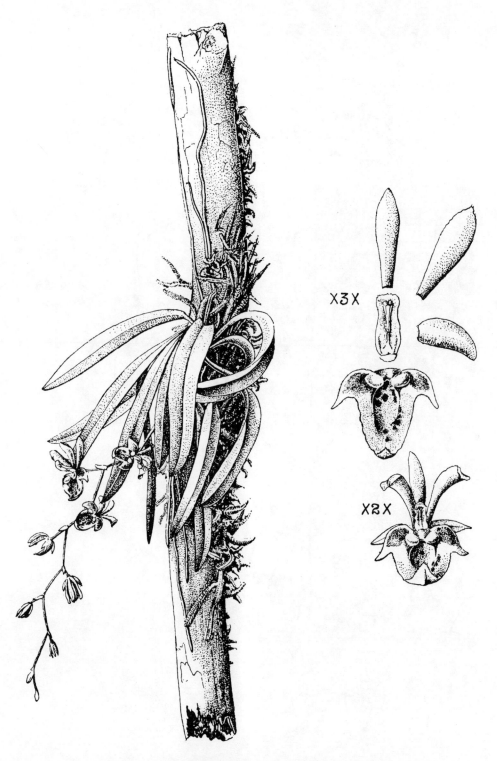

Chytroglossa Marileoniae Rchb.f. [Hoehne, *Flora Brasilica*]

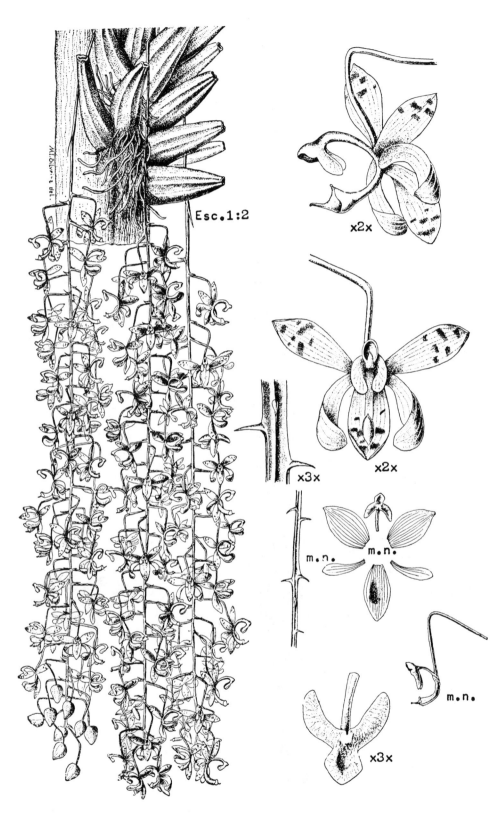

Cirrhaea longiracemosa Hoehne [Hoehne, *Flora Brasílica*]

114

C. dependens (Lodd.) Rchb.f. (*Cymbidium dependens* Lodd., *Gongora viridipurpurea* Hk., *Sarcoglossum suaveolens* Beer, *Cirrhaea fuscolutea* Ldl., *C. Hoffmannseggii* Heynh., *C. livida* Lodd., *C. Loddigesii* Ldl., *C. tristis* Ldl.)

Pbs. egg-shaped, to 3″ tall, strongly furrowed and rather angular in many cases. Lf. solitary, folded, rather heavy-textured, to 12″ tall, stalked basally. Infls. sharply pendulous, with up to 20 fls., to 1½′ long. Fls. about 2″ across, long-lived, delicately fragrant, rather waxy, extremely variable in colour, facing upwards, not opening fully. Ss. and ps. varying from apple-green or ochre-yellow to rich brown-red, spotted or barred (or not) with chocolate-brown, dull red, or orange-red, the lip (and sometimes the ps.) usually barred, sometimes rich wine-purple, the col. usually white or whitish. Summer. (I, H) Brazil.

CLADERIA Hk.f.

A genus of two species of semi-terrestrial or epiphytic orchids of the subtribe *Thuniinae*, one native in Malaya, the other in New Guinea, *Claderia* is very little-known botanically. Neither of the component species appears to be present in collections today. Vaguely resembling a dwarf *Arundina* in vegetative appearance, these plants produce erect leafy shoots at long intervals from a creeping rhizome, and bear medium-sized green flowers on slender inflorescences.

Nothing is known of the genetic affinities of this group.

CULTURE: Presumably as for *Arundina*, though the plants probably will do better in pots. (H)

CLEISTES L.C.Rich.

This is a genus of some eighty species which has been reduced to synonymy under *Pogonia* Juss. by some authorities, but it seems to be distinct enough, on technical details, to warrant recognition as a valid taxon. Although *Cleistes* contains some very handsome terrestrial species, it is virtually unknown by contemporary collectors. This is perhaps due to the relative unavailability of the plants, and the short-lived character of the blossoms, which in many cases wither after a few hours' time. Native in temperate, sub-tropical, and tropical America from New Jersey in the United States southward, with the vast majority of the species inhabiting Brazil, the plants typically bear fibrous, often fuzzy roots and a more or less shortened rhizome, from which the leaf-bearing, flowering stems arise. The blossoms, borne singly or in few-flowered racemes, are mostly rather large and brightly-coloured, and somewhat superficially resemble a *Sobralia* in certain respects. Coloration in *Cleistes* is variable, though whites, pinks, yellows, greens, and browns perhaps predominate.

No hybrids are as yet known within this genus, although it seems possible that critical inter-specific breeding should produce some exceptionally handsome results. Nothing is known of the genetic affinities of the group.

CULTURE: As for *Caladenia*. (I)

C. divaricata (L.) Ames (*Arethusa divaricata* L., *Pogonia divaricata* R.Br.)

Sts. erect, slender, when in fl. to more than 2′ tall, the lf. solitary, borne above the middle of the st., oblong-lanceolate to elliptic-oblong, blunt to acuminate, glaucous, to 8″ long. Fls. solitary, subtended by a lf.-like, large bract, to almost 5″ across, fragrant, the spreading, linear-lanceolate, acuminate ss. brownish or purple, the ps. magenta-pink to white, joined to the lip and forming a tube, the lip vaguely 3-lbd., mostly pale pink, often with some dark pink markings on the roughened crest of the disc. Spring–early summer. (I) Eastern and Central United States.

C. rosea Ldl. (*Pogonia rosea* Rchb.f., *Pogonia Moritzii* Rchb.f.)

St. slender, erect, 1–3′ tall, with a few lvs. mostly near apical, usually solitary fl., erect, rather heavy-textured, usually amplexicaul, to almost 5″ long and 1¼″ broad. Fls. often not opening well, short- or long-lived, to 4½″ across if expanded, the mostly erect ss. rose, the broader ps. similar in colour, usually thrust forward over the lip and col., the tubular lip mostly darker rose, with a median flattened plate that becomes a series of serrulate ridges towards apex, often yellow-suffused. Autumn, but sporadically throughout the year. (I, H) Panama and northern South America (including Trinidad) to Brazil.

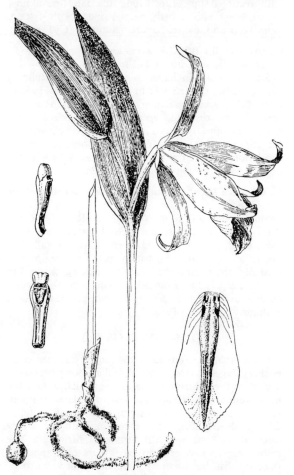

Cleistes rosea Ldl. [BLANCHE AMES]

COCHLIODA Ldl.

Five species of *Cochlioda* are known to date, three of which are sometimes seen in choice contemporary collections. Native in the Andean regions of Peru, Ecuador, and Colombia, they are epiphytic plants rather simulating certain types of *Odontoglossum* in vegetative habit, but producing flowers of distinct structure and, typically, of brilliant scarlet coloration. The blossoms are rather large and are borne in dense, gracefully arching racemes of great beauty.

Cochliodas have been extensively utilized by the breeders, since the members of this genus are freely inter-fertile with several other groups, notably *Odontoglossum*, *Oncidium*, and *Miltonia*. When crossed with these genera, the results are, respectively, *Odontioda*, *Oncidioda*, and *Miltonioda*.

CULTURE: As for the high-elevation Odontoglossums. (C)

C. Noetzliana (Rchb.f.) Rolfe (*Odontoglossum Noetzlianum* Rchb.f.)

Pbs. ovoid, somewhat flattened, grooved and wrinkled with age, to 3″ tall. Lf. solitary, rather soft-textured, linear, obtuse, about 10″ long. Infls. arching, densely many-fld., to 1½′ long. Fls. opening widely, to almost 2″ across, brilliant scarlet, the ss. and ps. elliptic, obtuse, with recurved tips. Lip 3-lbd., the lat. lbs. almost round, the midlb. shortly heart-shaped, with 4 long, hairy keels on the disc. Summer–autumn. (C) Peru.

C. rosea (Ldl.) Bth. (*Mesospinidium roseum* Rchb.f., *Odontoglossum roseum* Ldl.)

Rather similar in habit to *C. Noetzliana* (Rchb.f.) Rolfe, the lvs. rather wider in most cases. Infls. loosely many-fld., gracefully arching, to 1½′ long. Fls. about 1½″ across, dark rose-red, opening widely. Ss. and ps. narrowly elliptic, obtuse. Lip 3-lbd., shortly clawed, the lat. lbs. rhombic, the midlb. ligulate-oblong, obtuse, much longer than the lat. lbs., the disc with a short, oblong callus. Spring–summer. (C) Peru.

C. vulcanica (Rchb.f.) Bth. (*Mesospinidium vulcanicum* Rchb.f.)

Similar in habit to *C. Noetzliana* (Rchb.f.) Rolfe, the lvs. linear, obtuse, about 6″ long and ¾″ wide. Infls. erect, loosely 6–18-fld., slender, to 15″ tall. Fls. about 1¾″ across, opening widely, rose-red, the lip paler medially, the ss. and ps. lanceolate-oblong, acute. Lip 3-lbd., the lat. lbs. roundish or squarish, the midlb. cordate-ovate, the disc with 4 oblong, rough keels. Autumn–winter. (C) Peru.

CODONORCHIS Ldl.

Codonorchis Lessoni Ldl., the single member composing this genus, is a delightful, rather showy terrestrial orchid of the subtribe *Caladeniinae*, which enjoys the most southerly distribution of any orchidaceous plant. It inhabits the chill, wind-swept pampas of southern Chile and Argentina, even extending into the highly inhospitable terrain of the Straits of Magellan. The rather large, white, red-spotted flowers offer much to the specialist, but this rare plant does not seem to be present in contemporary collections.

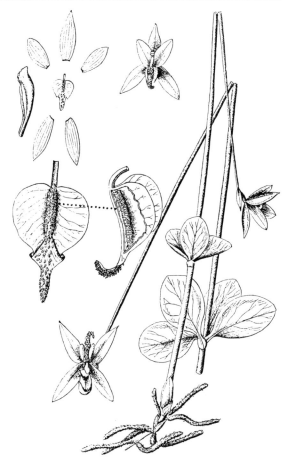

Codonorchis Lessoni Ldl. [Hoehne, *Flora Brasilica*]

Nothing is known regarding the genetic ties of *Codonorchis*.

CULTURE: Presumably as for *Caladenia*, although perpetually moist and chilly conditions will be required for any hope of success. (C)

CODONOSIPHON Schltr.

Three species of *Codonosiphon* are known to science, one—**C. codonanthum** Schltr.—native in Celebes, the others—**C. campanulatum** Schltr. and **C. papuanum** Schltr.—inhabiting New Guinea, where the plants are epiphytic in the high montane forests. Allied to *Bulbophyllum* Thou. and to *Tapeinoglossum* Schltr., they are extremely rare orchids, none of which is present in contemporary collections.

Nothing is known of the genetic affinities of this odd group.

CULTURE: As for the high-elevation New Guinean Dendrobiums, probably. (C, I)

COELIA Ldl.

Only a single species of *Coelia* is recognized today, namely **C. triptera** (Sm.) G.Don ex Steud. Several additional orchids have, in the past, been called Coelias, but these are now considered referable to the genus

Bothriochilus Lem. *Coelia* is a rather attractive plant, which is sometimes encountered in choice collections. Native in Mexico, Guatemala, and the West Indies, in the wild it is found as a true epiphyte high in trees, growing terrestrially under bushes on rocky hillsides, on rotting logs, or sometimes even on rock outcroppings. Where it occurs, it is often very abundant, forming large colonies of hundreds of plants.

The genus has not been utilized by the hybridists as yet, but intergeneric breeding with *Bothriochilus* should prove most interesting.

CULTURE: As for *Bothriochilus*. (I, H)

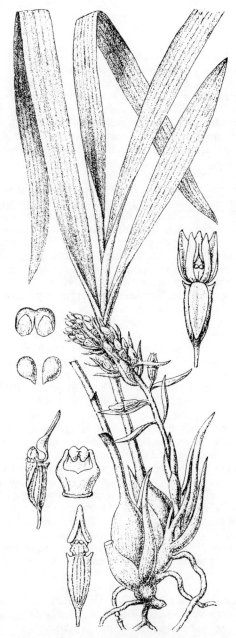

Coelia triptera (Sm.) G.Don ex Steud. [Fawcett & Rendle, *Flora of Jamaica*]

C. triptera (Sm.) G.Don ex Steud. (*Epidendrum tripterum* Sm., *Cymbidium tripterum* Sw., *Coelia Baueriana* Ldl.)

Pbs. egg-shaped to almost round, extended above into a short terete st., to 2″ long. Lvs. several, the basal stalks forming a st., mostly arching, linear-lanceolate, folded, rather leathery, to 15″ long, about 1″ wide or less. Infls. from the base of the pbs., to 7″ tall, the rac. loosely or densely many-fld., furnished with large mostly brown sheath-like bracts. Fls. scarcely opening, very fragrant, about ½″ long, white, the pedicellate ovaries very prominently winged. Winter–early spring. (I, H) Mexico; Guatemala; West Indies.

COELIOPSIS Rchb.f.

The only species of *Coeliopsis* known to date is a very attractive epiphyte, which is unfortunately very rare in contemporary collections, though it is among the most charming of the small-flowered members of the subtribe *Gongorinae*. Its cultural requirements are readily met, and it should decidedly be better known by enthusiasts. The genus is somewhat allied to *Eriopsis* Ldl., but is immediately distinguishable from that group, even when not in flower, by the different vegetative appearance of the plants.

Coeliopsis has not been taken in hand as yet by the breeders, and nothing is known of its relative genetic compatibility with allied genera.

CULTURE: As for *Acineta*. (I)

C. hyacinthosma Rchb.f.

Pbs. mostly long-egg-shaped, often wrinkled and yellowish, to 4″ long. Lvs. 3–4, to 2′ long and 3″ wide, folded, with prominent veins. Infls. produced from the base of the pbs., extending down through the compost (in the manner of *Acineta* and *Stanhopea*), to 3″ long, basally enveloped in papery, brown bracts, with up to 15 fls. arranged in a dense roundish head. Fls. about 1″ across, not opening fully, very fragrant, heavily waxen in texture, ivory-white, the lip with an orange blotch near the base, the col. with a purple dot at the base. Spring. (I) Costa Rica; Panama.

COELOGLOSSUM Hartm.

About four species of *Coeloglossum* are known, these rather insignificant mostly green-flowered terrestrial plants in North America, Europe, and northern Asia. Occasionally included in *Habenaria* Willd., the genus appears to be distinct on the basis of floral details. The 'Frog Orchid', described below, is an infrequent inhabitant of specialists' outdoor gardens in Europe.

Natural hybrids between *Coeloglossum viride* and several species of *Orchis* are known as *Orchicoeloglossum*, while *Gymnaglossum* is a natural cross between *Coeloglossum* and *Gymnadenia*.

CULTURE: As for *Orchis*. (C, I)

C. viride (L.) Hartm. (*Satyrium viride* L., *Gymnadenia viridis* L.C.Rich., *Habenaria viridis* R.Br., *Orchis viridis* Crantz, *Platanthera viridis* Ldl.)

Tubers several, lobed, about 1½″ long. Lvs. basal and cauline, ovate below, becoming lanceolate and bract-like on upper part of st., 1–2″ long. Infl. 3–13″ tall, slender, the rather loose, many-fld. rac. 2–5″ long. Fls. ⅜–½″ long, hooded, pale green usually with reddish margins on segms., fragrant. Dors. sep. ovate, the lat. ss. falcately lanceolate, the ps. falcately linear, small. Lip greenish-yellow (rarely red-flushed), cuneate, bifid at the tip with a tooth in the sinus; spur greenish-yellow, tiny, almost globular. May–Aug. (C, I) Iceland across Europe and Asia to Siberia; eastern North America.

COELOGYNE Ldl.
(*Acanthoglossum* Bl., *Chelonanthera* Bl., *Bolborchis* Ldl., *Gomphostylis* Wall., *Hologyne* Pfitz., *Ptychogyne* Pfitz.)

The Coelogynes form a genus of extremely desirable and, for the greater part, ornamental orchids which have long found favour with enthusiasts. About one hundred and twenty-five species are now known for the group, these ranging over a tremendous area which extends from China and the Himalayas throughout South-east Asia, Indonesia, the Philippines, and the Pacific Islands to the Fijis. The principal cultivated species occur in Indonesia, the Philippines, and the Himalayas, where they are mostly epiphytes, though some of them grow as terrestrials in grassy meadows or rocky places, and still others are typically found on rock-outcroppings, as lithophytes. *Coelogyne* is a genus sufficiently distinct from almost all other orchids to be recognized with but little difficulty, even, in most cases, when the plants are without flowers. Pseudobulbs are always present, and in some species attain very large dimensions; they may be closely grouped on an abbreviated rhizome, or produced at rather distant intervals along a lengthy rhizome. The usually few apical leaves (generally numbering one to four per pseudobulb) are extremely variable in size, shape, and texture, ranging from flaccid and thin to extremely leathery, rigid, and stiffly erect. Many Coelogynes have folded (plicate) leaves, which, with the frequently angular pseudobulbs, give to the plants a most characteristic appearance. The flowers in this genus are produced singly, in pairs or threes, or—more commonly—in long multiflorous racemes, which may be rigidly erect, gracefully arching, or sharply pendulous. Typically fragrant, the small to relatively large blossoms —which are often produced in tremendous numbers on well-grown specimens—vary in coloration from white to brown, yellow, or green, often with intricate mottlings or blotchings of yellow, brown, orange, or almost black on the complexly keeled and callused lip. The sepals are usually larger than the petals and generally about equal among each other in size and shape. The petals may (rather rarely) be like the sepals, or extremely narrow and almost thread-like. The typically large lip varies from entire to deeply three-lobed, is sometimes sac-shaped basally, and is occasionally joined to the base of the column. This segment is usually rather concave and bears two or more intricately crested longitudinal veins down its centre, and often some additional crests on the upraised lateral lobes. The column is arched or erect, free or adnate to the lip-base, membranaceously marginate at the apex, and bears a movable anther inserted below its apex. This anther contains four waxy pollinia. The stigma is prominent, two-parted and deeply sunken, and it is from this characteristic that the generic name is derived. *Coelogyne* is allied to *Pholidota* Ldl., *Pleione* Don, and other genera of the subtribe *Coelogyninae*, and many of its members are rather common inhabitants of our collections today, being among the most highly prized of Old World orchids.

Few hybrids are as yet registered within *Coelogyne*, and additional experimental breeding is definitely recommended to enterprising collectors. The only recent hybrid is *C. x Mem. William Micholitz* (*C. Lawrenceana* × *C. Mooreana*), registered in 1950; it is among the finest of all Coelogynes. Almost the only commonly-grown hybrid in this group is *C. x Stanny* (*C. asperata* × *C. pandurata*), usually grown under the erroneous, synonymous name of *C. x burfordiense*. Seven additional hybrids are registered to date. Possible breeding with *Pholidota*, *Pleione*, *Otochilus*, *Dendrochilum*, and other allied groups should be attempted.

CULTURE: This large genus is divided into three groups, based on temperature requirements: those which need warm conditions at all times, those which need more intermediate temperatures, and those from high elevations which thrive under rather cool conditions. Most of the warm-growing Coelogynes do not require a rest-period, continuing to grow throughout the year. These tropical species are evergreen plants (certain other members of the genus have deciduous foliage) which may be grown in pots, in baskets, or on rafts or tree-fern slabs with comparable success. Perfect drainage, no matter what container or mount is used, is essential, since none of these handsome orchids will tolerate stale conditions at the roots. Most growers today utilize straight osmunda as compost for these epiphytic species, though in some areas tree-fern fibre may form an excellent medium. Species with elongate rhizomes, on which the pseudobulbs are borne at intervals, are naturally better accommodated in baskets or on tree-fern poles, since confining them to pots is often not feasible. Repotting should be done no more often than absolutely necessary, since Coelogynes are intolerant of disturbance and frequently require several years to become sufficiently re-established to bloom again. If re-potting is necessary for any reason, it should be attended to just before the new growths start to appear. Because many of these warm-growing Coelogynes are almost constantly active, particular attention must be paid to them should the need for repotting arise, as the period when this may be best done is a brief one indeed. When these tropical Coelogynes are actively growing, abundant supplies of water must be given at the roots; moisture may be slightly reduced should any apparent cessation of growth occur, but the plants must never dry out completely. When the new growths are forming and have opened at the apex into a leafy tube or funnel, especial caution must be exercised that no water lodges there, or rotting may occur. These tropical representatives of the genus thrive in temperatures always above 60 degrees Fahrenheit at night (minimum); maximum temperatures may go as high as available provided of course that sufficient humidity is maintained in conjunction. Most Coelogynes—whether from the tropics or from high mountainous areas—do best in rather bright, but diffused light; harsh, direct sunlight should for the most part be avoided, as the foliage is singularly prone to burning or spotting through excesses of exposure. The intermediate species are cultivated best under almost the same conditions as are the tropical, 'warm' Coelognes, though extremes of high temperatures often prove disadvantageous; minimum night temperatures (particularly during the cool winter months) may drop to 45–50 degrees Fahrenheit for brief periods without difficulty. A short resting period should generally be provided for these plants after maturation of the new growths. Difficulty is sometimes experienced by orchidists when dealing with the high-altitude, 'cool' Coelognes, but through attention to a few cultural details, most problems may easily be overcome. Generally speaking, these orchids are not recommended for cultivation in warm or tropical climates, since even when kept in cool greenhouses their success cannot be guaranteed. Mostly native in the Himalayas, these Coelognes are frequently found at elevations exceeding 10,000 feet, in situations where for at least part of the year they are subjected to freezing temperatures, and where they may even be covered with snow for a time! Maximum temperatures should, therefore, be kept as moderate as possible, although for brief periods these may exceed 70–80 degrees Fahrenheit without injurious effects. A long and strict resting period is absolutely essential for flower production in these species; in most cases water must be stopped altogether after the maturing of the new growths, and not recommenced until root-action again starts, a period sometimes of several months' duration. Should excessive shrivelling of the pseudobulbs and foliage take place, spraying with a fine mist of water once or twice weekly should suffice to keep the plants in good health until growth starts. The few Coelognes which, in nature, occur as terrestrials or on rocks should, under cultivation, be treated as epiphytes, though they should not be potted as firmly as their tree-dwelling relatives. All Coelognes benefit materially by liberal and rather frequent applications of fertilizers. (C, I, H)

C. asperata Ldl. (*Coelogyne Lowii* Paxt.)

Pbs. clustered, somewhat compressed, strongly furrowed, rather broadly conical, to 6″ tall, to 2″ in diam. Lvs. 2, elliptic, acutish, folded, stalked basally, widest near the tip, to 2′ long and 5″ wide. Infls. produced from the middle of the new growths, arching to pendulous, to 1½′ long, rather densely many-fld. Fls. lasting about 5 days, fragrant, rather heavy-textured, to 3″ across, the ss. and ps. creamy-white, the lat. lbs. of the lip white veined with light brown, the midlb. irregularly marked with darker brown, warty, thick, the keels mostly yellowish. Ss. ovate-oblong, acutish. Ps. much narrower, lanceolate, acute. Lat. lbs. of the lip erect at sides of col., the midlb. curving downwards. Spring–summer. (H) Malay Peninsula and Sumatra to New Guinea.

C. barbata Griff.

Pbs. ovoid to almost round, pale green, clustered, about 4″ tall at most. Lvs. 2, oblong-lanceolate, stalked, leathery, to 1½′ long and 2″ wide. Infls. erect or arching, densely few-fld., the fls. opening successively, the infl.

rather zigzag in upper portion, to 1½′ long, with large bracts. Fls. 2–3″ across, lasting well, musk-scented, the ss. and ps. pure white, the lip white fringed with pale sepia-brown projections, with 3 deep sepia-brown, fringed crests down the centre. Ss. oblong, acutish. Ps. linear-lanceolate, acutish. Lip 3-lbd., the lat. lbs. short, ovate, erect, the midlb. roundish. Autumn–winter. (I) Himalayas: Nepal, Bhutan, Khasia Hills.

C. carnea Hk.f. (*Coelogyne radicosa* Ridl.)

Pbs. about 2″ apart on the rhiz., the slender base becoming swollen and rather flattened in apical half, finely grooved with age, to 3″ tall. Lvs. 2, variable in shape, stalked, to 8″ long and 2″ wide, rather leathery. Infls. with a flat stalk and rachis, to 15″ long, the rachis elongating as the fls. open, the bracts deciduous. Fls. rather numerous but appearing in succession, to almost 2″ across, pale dull salmon-pink or white, the lip veined with brown on the lat. lbs. and tall, smooth, median keels which are brown at the highest point. Dors. sep. arching over the col., the lat. ss. spreading. Ps. filiform, acutish. Lip 3-lbd., the large lat. lbs. erect, their tips free, roundish, the midlb. almost round, blunt at tip. Autumn. (I, H) Malay Peninsula.

C. chloroptera Rchb.f.

Pbs. ellipsoidal, 4-angled, to 1½″ tall, rather glossy. Lvs. 2, narrowly lanceolate, rather leathery, to 6″ long and 2″ wide. Infls. loosely 4–8-fld., arching, to 6″ long. Fls. about 1″ across, fragrant, waxy, the ss. and ps. pale yellowish-green, the lip paler yellowish-green with red-brown veins on the lat. lbs. and brownish-yellow keels on the midlb. Ss. oblong, acute. Ps. elliptic, acute. Lip 3-lbd., the lat. lbs. erect at the sides of the col. Spring. (I, H) Philippines.

C. corymbosa Ldl.

Pbs. oblong or ovoid, sheathed at the base with dark brown, papery cataphylls, about 2″ long. Lvs. 2, short-stalked, to 6″ long and 1½″ wide, rather leathery. Infls. produced from the middle of the expanding new growth, erect, loosely 3–5-fld., about 8″ tall. Fls. to 2″ across, fragrant, heavy-textured, the ss. and ps. cream-white, the lip white with a pair of bright yellow spots near the middle which are surrounded by brown, the throat irregularly streaked with brownish-yellow. Ss. narrowly lanceolate, acutish. Lip 3-lbd., the small lat. lbs. erect, the midlb. ovate, acute. Summer–autumn. (C) Himalayas, at rather high elevations.

C. cristata Ldl. (*Cymbidium speciosissimum* D.Don)

Pbs. clustered, almost round, often yellowish-green, wrinkled with age, to 2½″ long. Lvs. 2, rather soft-textured, often wavy-margined, linear-lanceolate, acutish, to 12″ long and 2″ wide. Infls. from base of last season's pbs., gracefully arching to pendulous, to 12″ long, 3–8-fld. Fls. fragrant, crystalline in texture, to 4″ across, all parts beautifully wavy, snow-white, the lip with 5 large golden-yellow keels down the middle. Ss. and ps. narrowly elliptic, the tips usually reflexed, blunt. Lip 3-lbd., the lat. lbs. blunt, usually spreading, the midlb. blunt at the tip and often somewhat reflexed there. Winter–spring. (C) Himalayas, at high elevations.

C. Cumingii Ldl.

Rhiz. elongated, bearing the pbs. about 1″ apart, clothed with brownish sheaths. Pbs. ovoid, becoming wrinkled with age, often yellowish, about 2″ long. Lvs. linear-lanceolate, acutish, narrowed to a short stalk, glossy, to 6″ long and 1½″ wide. Infls. produced from middle of the new growths, erect or arching, loosely 3–5-fld., slender, about 6″ long, the bracts deciduous. Fls. to 2½″ across, fragrant, lasting well, the ss. and ps. white, the lip veined with yellow or orange on the erect, blunt lat. lbs., the midlb. with 5 yellow or orange keels, 2 of which are shorter than the others. Ss. and ps. elliptic-lanceolate, acute, the ps. slightly narrower. Lip with short lat. lbs., the midlb. broadly elliptic, crisped marginally. Spring–summer. (I, H) Thailand; Malay Peninsula; Sumatra; Borneo.

C. Dayana Rchb.f. (*Coelogyne quadrangularis* Ridl.)

Pbs. strongly ribbed, narrowly conical, to 10″ tall. Lvs. 2, short-stalked, rigidly leathery, folded, mostly erect, narrowly elliptic, acute, to 2′ long and 4″ wide. Infls. sharply pendulous, to 3¼′ long, very densely many-fld., the fls. mostly arranged in 2 ranks, the bracts persistent. Fls. about 2½″ across, musk-scented, long-lived, the ss. and ps. pale yellowish or yellowish-tan, the lip similar, the keels white, the margins white, veined on the midlb. with chocolate-brown. Ss. and ps. oblong, acutish, the ps. narrower. Lip 3-lbd., the midlb. with 2 keels from the base to apex, with 3 short keels on the sides, all distinct and not coalescing into a warty mass as in the allied *C. Massangeana* Rchb.f. Spring–summer. (H) Peninsular Thailand; Malay Peninsula; Sumatra; Java; Borneo.

C. elata Ldl.

Pbs. almost cylindrical to narrowly ovoid, angular, to 6″ tall. Lvs. 2, stalked, narrowly lanceolate, acutish, rather heavy-textured, prominently veined, to 12″ long and 2½″ wide. Infls. terminal, erect, to almost 2′ tall, the 4–10-fld. rac. drooping. Fls. more than 2″ across, fragrant, lasting well, waxy, pure white, the lip white with a forked yellow central band and 2 longitudinal deep orange, crisped keels on the disc. Ss. and ps. lanceolate. acutish, rather narrow. Lip 3-lbd., the lat. lbs. rather short, blunt, the midlb. much larger. Spring. (C) Himalayas, at rather high elevations.

C. fimbriata Ldl. (*Broughtonia linearis* Wall.)

Pbs. borne about 1½″ apart on a very slender rhiz., ellipsoid, often not compressed, to 1½″ tall. Lvs. 2, rather thinly leathery, often somewhat yellowish, linear-lanceolate, to 5″ long and ¾″ wide. Infls. erect from the apex of latest pb., 1–2-fld., to 2″ tall, with some papery bracts at the base. Fls. scented of musk, rather long-lived, about 1½″ across, the ss. and ps. greenish-yellow to tan, the lip mostly yellowish streaked with reddish-brown or with intricate sepia-brown veins. Ss. oblong, acutish. Ps. linear, reflexed. Lip 3-lbd., the lat. lbs. erect at the sides of the col., the midlb. almost square, fine-fringed marginally, the keels on the disc irregularly crisped. Autumn. (C, I) China; Northern India: Thailand; Viet-Nam.

C. flaccida Ldl.

Pbs. narrowly spindle-shaped, 2-lvd., to 3″ tall, with some brownish-black sheaths at the base. Lvs. stalked, rather glossy, leathery, narrowly lanceolate, to 12″ long and 1¼″ wide. Infls. arching to sharply pendulous, to 10″ long, loosely few- to many-fld., the fls. usually all opening at once. Fls. waxy, highly fragrant (rather objectionably so), about 1½″ across, long- or rather short-lived, the ss. and ps. white, the middle of the lip golden-yellow, with 3 keels which become orange-brown towards the tips. Ss. oblong. Ps. almost linear. Lip with short, obtuse, erect lat. lbs. and an elliptic, acute midlb. that is twice as long. Spring–early summer. (C, I) Himalayas, at rather high elevations.

C. flexuosa Rolfe (*Coelogyne bimaculata* Ldl., *Ptychogyne bimaculata* Pfitz. & Krzl., *Ptychogyne flexuosa* Pfitz. & Krzl.)

Pbs. clustered, ovoid, to almost 3″ tall and about 1¼″ in diam. basally, ridged. Lvs. 2, about 10″ long and 2″ wide, oblong, acute or acuminate, short-stalked, rather leathery. Infls. produced from the fully mature pb., erect, about 15″ tall, the flexuous rachis bearing about 15 fls. which all open at once. Fls. not expanding well, about 1″ across, white, with a yellow area across the middle of the midlb. of the lip and continuing back along the base of the lat. lbs., which are erect and rounded. Spring–early summer. (H) Sumatra; Java; ? Malay Peninsula.

C. Foerstermanni Rchb.f. (*Coelogyne Kingii* Hk.f.)

Pbs. borne at intervals of about 4½″ on the creeping, heavily dark-sheathed rhiz., narrowly cylindrical, grooved in age, to about 4½″ tall. Lvs. rigid, closely folded, stalked basally, the blade to 12″ long and more than 1½″ wide, lanceolate, rather heavy-textured. Infls. erect or arching, to 1½′ long, arising from near the base of old pbs., with about 15 fls. which mostly open all at once. Fls. showy, fragrant, almost 3″ across, white, the lip with a central yellow area near the apex and 3 keels extending from the base almost to the apex. Often several times throughout the year, following about 3 months after dry weather. (H) Malay Peninsula; Sumatra; Borneo.

C. fuliginosa Ldl.

Pbs. borne at intervals of about ¾–1½″ apart on the creeping rhiz., narrowly ellipsoidal, about 2″ tall. Lvs. paired, narrowly elliptic or almost ligulate, 4–6″ long, about 1¼″ wide. Infls. produced from the mature pbs., erect, 2–3-fld., shorter than the lvs., with some sheathing bracts at base. Fls. about 2″ across or more, translucent brownish-yellow, the lip with sepia-brown veining. Ss. oblong. Ps. narrowly linear, reflexed. Lip 3-lbd., the lat. lbs. almost circular, large, the midlb. vaguely fringed marginally, with 2 large keels on the disc. Winter. (C, I) Himalayas.

C. graminifolia Par. & Rchb.f.

Pbs. ovoid, about 1½″ tall, closely clustered, ribbed in age. Lvs. 2, to about 1½′ long and usually less than ½″ wide, linear, acute. Infls. arching, about 2–4-fld., to 6″ long. Fls. fragrant, about 2″ across, white, the lip white except for the orange-yellow base of the midlb. and tips of the lat. lbs., with some dark brown veins on the lat. lbs. and 3 crisped dark brown median keels on the disc. Mostly summer. (I, H) Assam; Burma; Thailand; Malay Peninsula.

C. Huettneriana Rchb.f.

Rather similar in habit to *C. graminifolia* Par. & Rchb.f. in habit, the fls. to more than 2″ in diam. or so, white, the disc of the lip citron-yellow, the midlb. ovate. Fls. scented of musk, rather objectionably so. Spring–early summer. (I, H) Burma; Thailand.

—var. **lactea** (Rchb.f.) Pfitz. (*Coelogyne lactea* Rchb.f.)
Differs from the type in its smaller ps. and white lip. Summer. (I, H) Burma.

C. Lawrenceana Rolfe

Pbs. ovoid, becoming somewhat wrinkled with age, clustered, to 4″ tall and almost as thick. Lvs. 2, lanceolate, acuminate, leathery, glossy, to 10″ long and 1¼″ wide. Infls. arching, 1–3-fld., to about 10″ long. Fls. about 4″ across, waxy, fragrant, brownish-white, the lip with brown-veined lat. lbs., a large brown blotch at the base of the midlb., and a golden-yellow blotch on the disc. Ss. oblong. Ps. narrowly linear, acute. Lip with a very large midlb., the keels densely warty. Spring. (I, H) Viet-Nam.

C. lentiginosa Ldl.

Pbs. ellipsoidal, somewhat compressed laterally, bluntly 4-angled, to 3″ tall. Lvs. 2, short-stalked, lanceolate, acute, to 7″ long, leathery. Infls. loosely 4–6-fld., arching, to about 8″ long. Fls. about 2″ across, musk-scented, straw-yellow, the lat. lbs. of the lip margined with brown and the midlb. with an orange-yellow blotch. Ss. lanceolate. Ps. much smaller, linear-lanceolate. Spring–early summer. (I) Burma; Thailand.

C. Massangeana Rchb.f. (*Coelogyne densiflora* Ridl., *C. tomentosa* Ldl. var. *cymbidioides* Ridl., *C. tomentosa* Ldl. var. *Massangeana* Ridl.)

Rather similar in habit to *C. Dayana* Rchb.f., the pbs. about 3–4″ long, narrowly ovoid, when young with 2 opposite longitudinal ridges only; in age becoming yellow-green and considerably wrinkled. Lvs. 2, the stalk about 4″ long, the blade narrowly elliptic, acute, strongly folded, to about 1½′ long and 3″ wide (often smaller). Infls. sharply pendulous, up to 20-fld., to more than 15″ long, the bracts persistent. Fls. about 2¼″ across, fragrant, pale yellowish, the lat. lbs. of the lip brown inside with white veins, the midlb. brown and pale yellow, with 3 keels extending throughout the length of the lip, and additional shorter ones on either side, these all warty and so close together as to partially coalesce. Mostly summer. (I, H) Peninsu'ar Thailand; Malay Peninsula; Sumatra; Java; Borneo.

C. Mayeriana Rchb.f.

Pbs. 2–4″ apart on the thick creeping rhiz., to 2½″ tall, ribbed, slightly flattened, rather broadly conical. Lvs. 2, stalked, narrowly elliptic, to 8″ long and 1¼″ wide, acute, rather heavy-textured. Infls. and fls. similar to those of *C. pandurata* Ldl., but the fls. less than 3″ across, and the midlb. of the lip widening abruptly from

its base; ends of keels on midlb. covered with many white warts. Autumn. (H) Malay Peninsula; Sumatra; Java; Borneo.

C. miniata (Bl.) Ldl. (*Chelonanthera miniata* Bl., *Coelogyne Lauterbachiana* Krzl., *Hologyne Lauterbachiana* Pfitz., *Hologyne miniata* Pfitz.)

Pbs. borne about ¾–1¼″ apart on the creeping rhiz., cylindric, to 1½″ tall, very thin. Lvs. 2, elliptic, rather thin-textured, to 5″ long and 1¼″ wide. Infls. produced from the centre of the new growths, to 3″ tall, few-fld. Fls. about 1″ across, pale orange-red, the apical part of the lip 5-sided, with 2 prominent keels on the disc, these usually deep red. Summer–autumn. (H) Sumatra; Java; Lesser Sunda Islands.

C. Mooreana Sand.

Pbs. clustered, ovoid, oblong, furrowed with age, glossy-green, to 3″ tall. Lvs. 2, very glossy, heavy-textured, linear-lanceolate, acute, 8–15″ long, to 1½″ wide. Infls. erect, loosely 3–8-fld., to 15″ tall. Fls. fragrant, extremely handsome, about 3″ across, snow-white, the lip with a golden-yellow blotch on the disc. Ss. oblong. Ps. elliptic. Lip 3-lbd., the lat. lbs. short, the midlb. large, ovate, obtuse, with some hairy keels on the disc. Spring–early summer. (I) Viet-Nam.

C. nervosa A.Rich. (*Coelogyne corrugata* Wight)

Pbs. angled, ovoid, about 2½″ tall. Lvs. 2, stalked, narrowly elliptic, acute, to 6″ long and 1¼″ wide. Infls. produced from between the unfolding lvs., loosely 7–12-fld., erect, to about 6″ tall. Fls. about 2″ across, fragrant, white, the lip veined with yellow and furnished on the disc with 3 slightly wavy brownish-orange keels. Ss. and ps. elliptic. Midlb. of the lip ovate, acutish. Summer–autumn. (I, H) India, mostly in the Neilgherry Hills.

C. nitida (Roxb.) Hk.f. (*Cymbidium nitidum* Roxb., *Coelogyne ocellata* Ldl.)

Similar in all parts to *C. corymbosa* Ldl., but differing in details of the infl. and in the smaller fls. which have a shorter, broader lip, the less bright yellow venation, and the broadly ovate, obtuse midlb. Late winter–spring. (C, I) Himalayas; Bhutan, Upper Assam, and Khasia Hills, at high elevations; Thailand.

C. ochracea Ldl.

Similar in habit to *C. corymbosa* Ldl., the pbs. cylindric, to 4″ tall. Lvs. 2, narrowly lanceolate, acutish, stalked, about 8″ long and 1″ wide. Infls. produced from the unfolding lvs., loosely 6–10-fld., erect, about 8″ tall. Fls. like those of the other sp., but smaller, white, with 4 yellow orange-red-flushed keels on the smaller and shorter midlb. of the lip. Spring–summer. (C, I) Himalayas, at high elevations.

C. odoratissima Ldl.

Pbs. ovoid or almost roundish, 1¼–1½″ tall. Lvs. 2, linear, acute, to 3½″ long and about ½″ wide. Infls. arising with the unfolding young lvs., loosely 2–5-fld., about 4″ tall. Fls. fragrant, waxy, about 1½″ across, white, with a median yellow stripe down the lip. Ss. oblong. Ps. somewhat smaller. Lip 3-lbd., with short lat. lbs. and a broadly elliptic midlb. Spring–early summer. (I, H) Ceylon; India, especially in the southern part.

C. ovalis Ldl. (? *Coelogyne pilosissima* Planch.)

Similar in all parts to *C. fimbriata* Ldl., but more robust. Fls. almost 1″ across, scented of musk, the lip differently-shaped than the other sp. Summer. (I) Himalayas, and Thailand, usually at medium elevations.

C. pandurata Ldl.

One of the famed 'Black Orchids'. Pbs. rather distant on the robust creeping rhiz., oblong, somewhat or strongly flattened, often somewhat curved, to about 5″ tall and almost 3″ wide. Lvs. narrow basally, the blade elliptic-lanceolate, rather heavy-textured, to 1½′ long and 2½″ wide, widest just above the middle. Infls. as in *C. asperata* Ldl., arching gracefully, but the fls. more widely spaced and fewer. Fls. more than 3″ across, very fragrant, clear pale green, with some irregular almost black markings on the lip. Lip very narrowed in the middle at the base of the midlb., with 2 high thin keels between the lat. lbs. and warts on the midlb., which is crisped marginally. Autumn. (H) Sumatra; Borneo; Malay Peninsula.

C. Parishii Rchb.f.

Pbs. almost cylindrical, angled, about 4″ tall. Lvs. 2, elliptic, to 6″ long and 2″ wide. Infls. borne from the apex of the mature pbs., 2–4-fld., erect, to 4″ tall, furnished with some sheathing basal bracts. Fls. about 3″ across, fragrant, green, the lip blotched and veined with brownish-black. Ss. lanceolate, acute. Ps. almost linear. Lip fiddle-shaped, warty apically. Spring–early summer. (I, H) Burma.

—var. **brachyptera** (Rchb.f.) Pfitz. (*Coelogyne brachyptera* Rchb.f.)

Differs from the type in its smaller fls., these with a white, brown-spotted lip. Spring–early summer. (I, H) Burma.

C. Rhodeana Rchb.f.

Pbs. ovoid, about 2″ tall. Lvs. 2, linear, to more than 12″ long, about 1¼″ wide. Infls. appearing with the unfolding young lvs., loosely 3–5-fld., about 4″ tall. Fls. more than 1″ across, fragrant, white, the lip with brown lat. lbs. and 2 yellow streaks down the midlb. Ss. oblong. Ps. smaller than ss. Autumn. (I) Burma; Thailand; Cambodia.

C. Rochusseni DeVr. (*Chelonanthera cymbidioides* Teijsm., *Coelogyne macrobulbon* Hk.f., *C. plantaginea* Ldl.)

Pbs. about 1½″ apart on the rhiz., narrowly cylindrical, to 8″ tall, strongly ribbed, slightly narrowed upwards and abruptly contracted at the top. Lvs. 2, stalked, oval to oval-elliptic, widest near the apex, which is abruptly narrowed to a short point. Infls. borne from near base of past pb., slender, many-fld., to more than 1½′ long. Fls. very fragrant, shaped rather like those of *C. Dayana* Rchb.f., lemon-yellow, the lip with yellow keels, the inside of the lat. lbs. with prominent brown stripes. Early winter, usually in Nov. (I, H) Philippines; Peninsular Thailand; Malay Peninsula; Sumatra; Java; Borneo.

C. Rossiana Rchb.f.

Similar in all parts to *C. Rhodeana* Rchb.f., differing

in the bracts of the infl. and the shortly fiddle-shaped midlb. of the lip. Fls. about 1″ across, white, the lat. lbs. of the lip yellowish-brown, the apex of the midlb. yellowish-brown. Autumn. (I) Burma.

C. Sanderae Krzl.

Pbs. narrowly ovoid, 1¼–3″ tall. Lvs. 2, narrowly elliptic, glossy, rather wavy-margined, to 6″ long and 2″ wide. Infls. erect, borne from the apex of the mature pb., loosely 4–7-fld., about 12″ tall, with prominent overlapping bracts just below the fl.-bearing portion. Fls. about 3″ across, fragrant, rather waxen in texture, white, the lip deep orange-yellow, with 3 brown keels on the disc. Ss. oblong. Ps. linear, sharply outstretched. Lip with short obtuse lat. lbs. and an almost round, vaguely fringed midlb. Later summer–autumn. (I, H) Burma.

C. sparsa Rchb.f.

Pbs. ovoid, about 1½″ tall, becoming grooved with age. Lvs. 2, short-stalked, oblong-lanceolate, to 4″ long and 1½″ wide. Infls. about 2–3″ tall, with the loosely 3–5-fld. rac. arching. Fls. rather reminiscent of those of *C. Rhodeana* Rchb.f., about 1″ across, white slightly flushed with greenish, fragrant, the lat. lbs. of the lip brown, the disc bearing 3 yellow keels. Ss. oblong. Ps. linear, obtuse. Lip with very short lat. lbs., the midlb. almost round. Summer. (I, H) Philippines.

C. speciosa (Bl.) Ldl. (*Chelonanthera speciosa* Bl.)

Pbs. ovoid, clustered, rather glossy, about 2″ tall. Lvs. 2, glossy-green, narrowly elliptic, to 10″ long and 2½″ wide. Infls. produced with the unfolding lvs., loosely 2–3-fld., slender, abbreviated. Fls. musk-scented, rather long-lived, to more than 3″ across, the ss. and ps. usually almost translucent greenish-yellow or greenish-tan, the large lip chestnut-brown inside, veined and blotched darker, with 2 long deep brown keels on the disc and one shorter one. Ss. oblong. Ps. almost thread-like, curled and reflexed. Lip fringed on the margin of the midlb. Spring–summer, often very floriferous. (I, H) Sumatra; Java; Lesser Sunda Islands.

—var. **salmonicolor** (Rchb.f.) Schltr. (*Coelogyne salmonicolor* Rchb.f.)

Differs from the type principally in colour, the ss. and ps. being pale flesh-coloured, the lip darker, with almost white keels. Perhaps better treated as a mere form. Spring. (I, H) Sumatra; Java.

C. sulphurea (Bl.) Rchb.f. (*Chelonanthera sulphurea* Bl., *Coelogyne Crookewittii* Teijsm. & Binn.)

Pbs. cylindric or somewhat spindle-shaped, about 4″ tall. Lvs. 2, stalked, elliptic-lanceolate, to 10″ long and 1½″ wide. Infls. arising with the young lvs., loosely 7–15-fld., erect, about 8″ tall. Fls. about 1¼″ across, fragrant, greenish-yellow, with an orange-red blotch on the disc. Ss. oblong, acute. Ps. narrowly linear, acute. Spring. (H) Sumatra; Java.

C. testacea Ldl.

Pbs. clustered, ovoid, ribbed, to about 3″ tall. Lvs. 2, stalked, narrowly elliptic-lanceolate, to 1½′ long and 2½″ wide. Infls. arising from the new unfolding lvs., arching to pendulous, loosely 7–10-fld., about 8″ long, the rachis almost glabrous, the pedicellate ovaries somewhat fuzzy. Fls. about 2″ across, somewhat fragrant, varying from dull buff to flesh-colour, the lip with brown lat. lbs. and additional brown markings, the 4 white keels strongly fringed or toothed. Ps. somewhat smaller than the ss. Spring–summer. (H) Malay Peninsula; Sumatra.

C. tomentosa Ldl.

Similar in habit to *C. Dayana* Rchb.f. and to *C. Massangeana* Rchb.f., differing mostly in technical details of the fls. Infls. to about 1½′ long, strongly pendulous, the rachis shortly but densely hairy. Fls. almost 2″ across, musk-scented, light orange or salmon-coloured, the lip brown with paler veins and yellow keels, the 3 principal ones extending throughout the entire length of the lip, with 2 additional short ones on either side of midlb., all distinctly separate and finely warty. Spring. (I, H) Peninsular Thailand; Malay Peninsula; Sumatra; Borneo.

C. venusta Rolfe

Pbs. ellipsoidal, about 2–3″ tall. Lvs. 2, short-stalked, lanceolate, to 10″ long and 1¼″ broad. Infls. pendulous, loosely many-fld., to about 15″ long. Fls. about 1″ across, white, the lat. lbs. of the lip yellow, the disc of the midlb. with a yellow blotch and 4 brown keels. Ss. oblong-ovate. Ps. broadly linear. Lip with an almost rectangular midlb. Winter–spring. (C, I) China: Yunnan, in the mountains.

C. viscosa Rchb.f.

Pbs. narrowly ovoid or spindle-shaped, 3″ tall. Lvs. 2, short-stalked, linear-lanceolate, to 12″ long and 1¼″ broad, rather leathery. Infls. loosely 3–7 fld., erect or arching, about 6″ tall, the rachis glandular. Fls. about 1½″ across, fragrant, white, the lat. lbs. of the lip veined with brown, the midlb. with a yellow blotch on the disc, and 3 white keels. Ss. oblong-lanceolate. Ps. linear-lanceolate. Midlb. of lip shortly and broadly ovate. Summer. (I) Himalayas, at medium elevations.

C. annamensis Rolfe Rather rare in collections, but a most desirable sp. Pbs. spindle-shaped, about 3½″ tall. Lvs. 2, short-stalked, elliptic-ovate, to 8″ long. Infls. usually 8-fld., arching, about 10″ long, furnished with sheathing bracts. Fls. more than 3″ across, pale yellow, the lip much darker yellow with intricate brown nerves on the lat. lbs., the nerves on the midlb. orange-brown. Winter. (I) Viet-Nam.

C. Beccarii Rchb.f. Pbs. ovoid, about 2″ tall, clustered. Lvs. 2, lanceolate, to 10″ long and 2″ wide. Infls. arising with the new growths, loosely 3–5-fld., slender, naked, erect or slightly arching. Fls. more than 3″ across, yellowish-white, the lip with 5–7 flat, reddish-yellow keels on the disc. Almost throughout the year, often more than once annually. (H) New Guinea.

—var. **Micholitziana** (Krzl.) Schltr. (*Coelogyne Micholitziana* Krzl.) Differs from the type primarily in the confluent keels on the lip, which form near the middle of the disc a broad red-yellow protuberance. Summer–autumn. (H) New Guinea.

C. borneensis Rolfe Pbs. spindle-shaped, clustered. Lvs. 2, shortly ovate-oblong, about 6″ long. Infls. erect, loosely few-fld., exceeding the lvs. in length. Fls. about 2″ across, fragrant, light chocolate-brown, long-lived, the lip darker chocolate-brown, somewhat veined with dull white. Summer–autumn. (H) Borneo.

C. breviscapa Ldl. Pbs. narrowly ovoid, 2″ tall. Lvs. 2, narrowly lanceolate, short-stalked, about 6″ long and ½″ wide. Infls. slightly arching, loosely 4–6-fld., about 4″ long. Fls. about ½″ long, white with yellow veins on the lip, the disc with 2 deep golden-yellow median keels. Spring. (I, H) Ceylon.

C. carinata Rolfe Pbs. ellipsoidal, about 1¼″ tall. Lvs. lanceolate, paired, 4–5″ long, 1¼″ wide. Infls. arising with the new growths, loosely 4–8-fld., about 8″ long, arching. Fls. almost 1″ across, greenish-white, the lip greenish-white with 3 brown keels and brown-veined lat. lbs. Summer. (H) New Guinea.

C. cinnamomea Teijsm. & Binn. (*Coelogyne angustifolia* Ridl., *C. cinnamomea* Teijsm. & Binn. var. *angustifolia* Pfitz. & Krzl., *C. stenophylla* Ridl.) Pbs. borne at intervals on the creeping rhiz., yellow-green, ovoid, about 3½″ tall. Lvs. 2, stalked, to more than 1½′ long, narrow. Infls. about 6-fld., at flowering-time about 4″ long, elongating gradually as the fls. expand. Fls. with a noxious odour, about 2″ across, cream-coloured, the lat. lbs. of the lip brown, the midlb. cream-coloured at base, the apical part with a brown central patch, the keels all vaguely warty. Summer. (H) Peninsular Thailand; Malay Peninsula; Java.

C. cuprea Wendl. & Krzl. Pbs. ovoid or almost cylindric, 2–3″ tall. Lvs. 2, narrowly elliptic, to 12″ long and 2″ wide. Infls. borne from the apex of mature pbs., loosely 3–7-fld., usually with only a single fl. open at once. Fls. about 1¼″ across, salmon-brown, the lip with darker veins and keels. Spring–summer. (H) Sumatra.

C. fragrans Schltr. Pbs. borne at intervals on the creeping rhiz., narrowly ovoid or oblong, to 3½″ tall. Lf. solitary, elliptic, acuminate, stalked, with the stalk to more than 1½′ long. Infls. erect, loosely 2–4-fld. Fls. usually all open at once, fragrant, almost 3″ across, light yellowish-white, the lip beautifully veined with chocolate-brown, the col. apically golden-yellow. Autumn–winter. (I) New Guinea, mostly in the mountainous areas.

C. integra Ames Similar in all parts to *C. chloroptera* Rchb.f., differing in the more elongate infls. (to 10″ long), with more fls. Fls. about 1″ across, fragrant, rather waxy, the ss. and ps. white, the lip veined with golden-yellow, oblong, acute. Spring–early summer. (I, H) Philippines.

C. lamellata Rolfe Similar in all parts to *C. Beccarii* Rchb.f. Infls. 3–5-fld., usually with only one fl. open at a time, slender. Fls. about 3″ across, greenish-white, the lip white, 3-lbd., with 9–11 keels on the disc. Summer. (H) New Hebrides.

C. Mossiae Rolfe. Pbs. ovoid, about 2″ tall, clustered. Lvs. 2, narrowly elliptic, 6–7″ long, about 1¼″ wide. Infls. arising with the new growths, loosely 8–10-fld., arching, about 8″ long. Fls. about 2½″ across or less, fragrant, white, with 2 yellow-brown blotches on the midlb. of the lip. Spring–early summer. (I) Upper India.

C. peltastes Rchb.f. Pbs. ellipsoid, often almost disc-shaped, laterally flattened, about 3½″ tall, to 2″ wide. Lvs. 2, stalked, shortly ovate-elliptic, about 12″ long, to 2½″ broad. Infls. arising with the new growth, loosely 4–6-fld. Fls. about 3″ across, fragrant, whitish- or greenish-yellow, the lip white veined with yellow-brown. Summer–autumn. (H) Borneo.

C. prasina Ridl. Pbs. borne at considerable intervals on the narrow, very elongate rhiz., to 4″ tall, ovoid, tapering to the narrow apex. Lvs. 2, to about 11″ long, folded, stalked. Infls. slender, several- to many-fld., but usually with only one fl. open at a time, the rachis very irregular. Fls. about 1″ across, uniform pale green or olive-green. Summer. (I, H) Malay Peninsula.

C. Sanderiana Rchb.f. Pbs. spindle-shaped, 2–4″ tall. Lvs. 2, oblong, acute, to 15″ long. Infls. erect, 5–9-fld., about 12″ tall. Fls. more than 3½″ across, fragrant, very showy, white, the lip with brown-veined lat. lbs., a yellow disc, and 5 strong longitudinal yellow keels down the middle. Spring. (H) Sumatra; ? Java.

C. Swaniana Rolfe Pbs. clustered, 4-angled, to 4″ tall. Lf. solitary, to 10″ long and 2¼″ wide. Infls. pendulous, to 1½′ long, rather densely many-fld. Fls. 2″ across, white, the lip light brown, veined with white and with dark brown keels. Allied to and rather resembling *C. Massangeana* Rchb.f. Summer–autumn. (H) Malay Peninsula; Sumatra; Borneo; ? Philippines.

C. Veitchii Rolfe Similar in habit to *C. Dayana* Rchb.f. Infls. pendulous, loosely many-fld., to 2′ long. Fls. very showy, about 2″ across, snow-white, the lip concave basally, with 3 keels on the disc. Summer–autumn. (H) New Guinea.

C. xyrekes Ridl. Pbs. clustered, ovoid, about 2″ tall. Lf. solitary, to 12″ long and 3½″ wide, stalked. Infls. few-fld., the fls. opening singly, the scape slender, about 6″ long. Fls. almost 4″ across, pale salmon-pink, the lip large, salmon-pink, partly mottled with warm or dark brown, with 2 very dark brown, very wavy, minutely warty keels from base to apex. Summer. (I, H) Peninsular Thailand; Malay Peninsula, in the mountains.

COHNIELLA Pfitz.
(*Cohnia* Rchb.f.)

But a single species of *Cohniella* is known to date, this one of the rarest and most obscure of all orchidaceous plants. **Cohniella quekettioides** (Rchb.f.) Pfitz. (*Cohnia quekettoides* Rchb.f.) is a very incompletely known epiphytic orchid of the subtribe *Capanemiinae*, which has been ascribed to both Guatemala and Nicaragua, but does not appear to have been collected in either country. The genus superficially resembles *Quekettia* Ldl., and is unknown in our collections at this time.

Nothing is known of the genetic affinities of *Cohniella*.
CULTURE: Possibly as for *Ornithocephalus*. (I)

COILOCHILUS Schltr.

A single excessively rare terrestrial orchid, **Coilochilus neocaledonicus** Schltr., makes up this little-known genus of the subtribe *Cryptostylidinae*, native in New Caledonia. It bears a dense raceme of greenish-yellow flowers of intricate structure, rather reminiscent of *Cryptostylis* R.Br., to which the genus is allied.

Nothing is known of the genetic affinities of this odd group, which does not appear to be in cultivation at this time.
CULTURE: Presumably as for *Caladenia*. (I)

COLAX Ldl.

This is a genus of three species of epiphytic or rarely semi-terrestrial orchids, indigenous to south-central and southern Brazil. Often relegated to synonymy under *Zygopetalum* Hk., *Colax* seems to be sufficiently distinct from that genus to warrant retention, differing in structural details of the flowers, and particularly of the

pollinia-appendage. Only a single species of *Colax* is present in collections today, and despite its great beauty, it must be classed as a very rare plant.

This genus has been crossed successfully with *Zygopetalum*, to give *Zygocolax*. Additional breeding with that group, and with other allied aggregations in the subtribe *Zygopetalinae* (as well as the subtribes *Huntleyinae* and *Lycastinae*) should be attempted.

CULTURE: As for the epiphytic Zygopetalums. (I, H)

C. jugosus (Ldl.) Ldl. (*Maxillaria jugosa* Ldl., *Zygopetalum jugosum* Schltr.)

Pbs. clustered, elongate-ovoid, rather glossy, 2–3″ long. Lvs. 2, broadly lanceolate, acuminate, rather leathery, 6–9″ long, to 1½″ wide, very dark glossy green. Infls. erect or arching, to 8″ tall, 2–4-fld., sheathed by pale green, acute bracts. Fls. fleshy, 2–3″ across, fragrant, long-lasting, the oval-oblong, obtuse ss. pale cream-white, the obovate-oblong ps. white or cream-white with numerous transverse blotches and spots of rich deep chocolate-purple, violet-purple or rose-purple. Lip shorter than the other segms., shortly clawed, fleshy, 3-lbd., the lat. lbs. rounded, erect, cream-white streaked with deep chocolate-purple or violet-purple; midlb. semicircular, with numerous fleshy, pubescent, radiating keels, cream-white streaked and blotched with rich-chocolate-purple or violet-purple. Col. rather stout, bent towards apex, hairy in front, spotted with chocolate-purple or violet-purple, often tinged basally with greenish. May–June. (I, H) Brazil.

COLLABIUM Bl.

This is a genus of about five known species of interesting terrestrial (rarely semi-epiphytic) orchids of the subtribe *Collabiinae*, native from the Himalayas throughout Indonesia to the Fiji Islands. It is allied to *Chrysoglossum* Bl., but differs in structural details of the rather showy flowers. Several of the species, such as **Collabium nebulosum** Bl., have the broad leaves attractively blotched with yellow. Despite their ornamental appearance, even when not in bloom, the Collabiums have not as yet been introduced into our collections.

Nothing is known of the genetic affinities of this genus.
CULTURE: As for the tropical species of *Phaius*. (H)

COMPARETTIA P. & E.

This is a genus of about twelve species which reach their greatest development in the Andes of Colombia and Ecuador; a single member, *Comparettia falcata* P. & E., extends to the West Indies and Mexico. Placed today in the subtribe *Comparettiinae*, this genus is vaguely allied to *Trichocentrum* P. & E. and to *Ionopsis* HBK, and its components are today very scarce in collections, although most of the known species are handsome, showy little orchids—usually epiphytic in habit—well worthy of attention. They have very small pseudobulbs and proportionately large, leathery leaves; the inflorescences are either simple or branched, and arise from the pseudobulb-bases, bearing a few often proportionately large and brilliantly-coloured flowers. The floral structure is unique in that the lip bears two

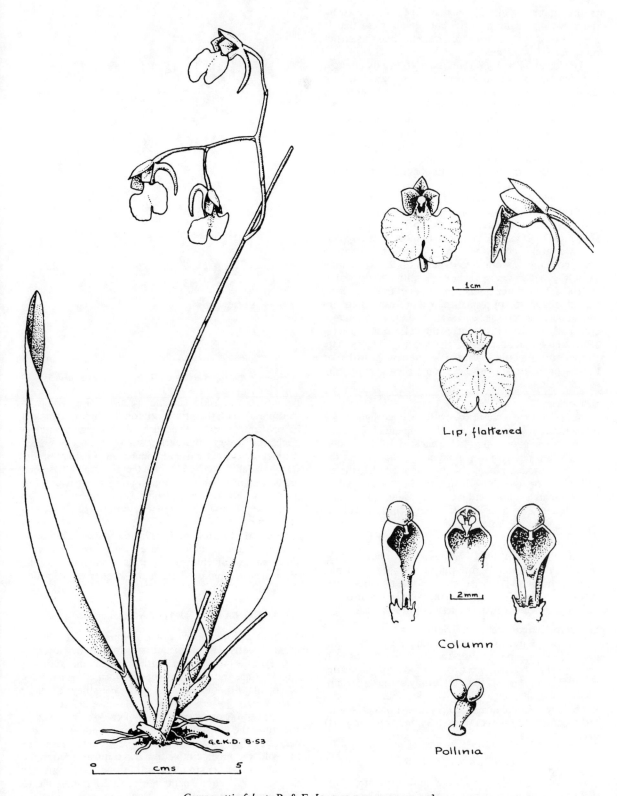

1cm

Lip, flattened

2mm

Column

Pollinia

Comparettia falcata P. & E. [G.C.K.DUNSTERVILLE]

tail-like spurs at its base, which are in turn enclosed by the very long mentum of the lateral sepals, so that it appears as if three spurs were present, when this structure is closely examined.

Hybridization with *Comparettia* is still in its infancy, but seedlings in flasks offer promise of some fascinating things to come. The lovely and very floriferous crosses between this genus and *Rodriguezia*, called Rodrettias, are now available, notably from Hawaiian sources.

CULTURE: Comparettias are variously grown as pot-plants, or—perhaps more preferably—on pieces of tree-fern fibre, to which their copious root-systems can attach themselves and grow with abandon. If confined in pots, these should be proportionately small and very well-drained. Various composts have been suggested by different authoritative growers, though a mixture of about equal parts of shredded tree-fern fibre and chopped sphagnum moss has been found to be most advantageous under average conditions. A top-dressing of fresh sphagnum moss is often used, since these often some-what fragile plants must never be permitted to dry out at the roots. If mounted on slabs or cubes of tree-fern fibre, the initial addition of a smallish pad of fresh sphagnum moss under the roots is beneficial. A shaded, humid and constantly rather moist spot in the collection is neces-sary, and for almost all of the species, intermediate temperatures should prevail. When new growths or flower-spikes are starting, caution to avoid injury by snails or slugs is necessary. (I)

C. coccinea Ldl.

Pbs. very small, clustered, with a single ligulate or oblong, acute, leathery lf. to 4″ long and 1½″ wide, bright green above, purplish beneath. Infls. slender, erect, with a nodding to pendulous 3–8-fld. rac. at the apex. Fls. about 1″ long, pale or bright scarlet, the ss. and ps. narrowly elliptic, acute, the lip usually yellow outside, scarlet within, flattened, obcordate, the mentum of the lat. ss. (which encloses the double lip-spurs) about ½″ long. Autumn–winter. (I) Brazil.

C. falcata P. & E. (*Comparettia rosea* Ldl.)

Similar in habit to *C. coccinea* Ldl., but the fls. slightly smaller and rose-purple or violet-purple. Mentum about 1″ long, enclosing the two lip-spurs. Autumn–winter. (I) Mexico and the West Indies through-out Central America to northern South America.

C. macroplectron Rchb.f. & Triana

Similar in habit to *C. coccinea* Ldl. Pbs. very small, oblong, blunt, compressed, the angles rounded. Lf. solitary, bright green, erect, oblong to ligulate, acute, about 5″ long at most. Infls. gracefully arching, 5–8-fld. Fls. about 2″ long, light violet with deep purple spots in more or less abundance, the lip proportionately large, the mentum 2″ long or more. Summer–autumn. (I) Colombia.

CONSTANTIA B.-R.

Four species of *Constantia* are known to date, all of them delightful but very rare epiphytic orchids, endemic to limited localities in Brazil. Somewhat allied to *Sophronitis* Ldl., they differ from that genus in the diminutive dimensions of the plants (which often in-

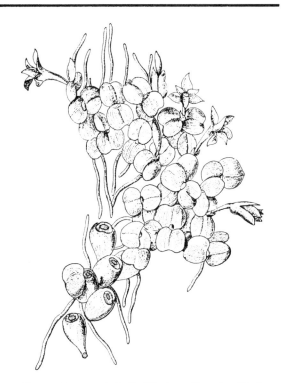

Constantia rupestris B.-R. [Hoehne, *Flora Brasílica*]

habit trunks of Vellozias, and are almost impossible to transplant), with their tiny pseudobulbs tightly arranged in prostrate masses, peculiarly vivid-green, granular-appearing leaves, and little usually green flowers of distinct structure. **Constantia cipoensis** C.Porto & Brade, from the Serra do Cipó, Minas Gerais, Brazil, has been introduced into our collections on several occasions, but it quickly perishes under artificial conditions.

Nothing is known of the genetic affinities of *Constantia* at this time.

CULTURE: Possibly as for *Ornithocephalus*, although somewhat drier conditions at all times seem requisite. Their successful cultivation seems almost impossible, once they are removed from the host-trees on which they grow. (I, H)

CORALLORRHIZA [Haller] R.Br.

About a dozen species of *Corallorrhiza* are known, these mostly inconspicuous, saprophytic orchids native for the most part in North America, but extending into Mexico, and into Europe and Northern Asia. Very odd plants without well-developed leaves, they bear their often showy flowers at the top of a usually succulent brown, yellow, or purple flower-spike. Very complex in structure, the blossoms vary in hue depending upon the degree of light to which they are subjected, whether in the wild or under cultivation. Like most saprophytic orchids, they are extremely rare in our collections, for their cultural requirements are virtually impossible to approximate artificially. The genus is a member of the subtribe *Corallorrhizinae*, somewhat allied to *Hexalectris* Raf., from which it differs in critical details of the complex flowers.

No hybrids are known in this genus, and nothing has been ascertained regarding its genetic alliances.

CULTURE: Sometimes these very refractory plants may be transplanted from the wild for a season or two, but their permanent place in the collection can seldom be assured. Since they derive their basic nourishment from dead and decaying organic matter—which usually cannot be transpotted intact without disturbing the delicate root-systems and their accompanying fungal associations—they are to be classified as strictly transient plants in the collection. According to certain authorities, they may be raised from seed under ideal conditions, generally flowering in five to ten years. (C, I)

C. maculata Raf. (*Corallorrhiza multiflora* Nutt.)

Pl. varying from slender to robust, erect, leafless, madder-purple or yellowish, 6–30″ tall, the succulent st. provided with several tubular elongate sheaths. Rac. loosely few- to many-fld., very variable in size, the fl.-bracts translucent. Fls. on stout pedicellate ovaries, to more than ½″ long, the ss. and ps. crimson-purple or rarely greenish, the lat. ss. concave. Lip deeply but unequally 3-lbd., whitish or white, often spotted with magenta-crimson. Col. yellow with magenta spots on ventral surface, strongly curved, compressed. Mostly summer–autumn. (C, I) Canada; United States; Mexico; Guatemala.

CORDANTHERA L.O.Wms.

A single species of *Cordanthera* is known to date, this an extremely rare dwarf epiphytic orchid, **C. andina** L.O.Wms., which has apparently been collected on only one occasion in the montane forests of Colombia. The group is a member of the subtribe *Ornithocephalinae*, and is not present in cultivation at this time.

Nothing is known of the genetic affinities of *Cordanthera*.

CULTURE: Presumably as for *Ornithocephalus*. (C, I)

CORDIGLOTTIS J.J.Sm.

But a single species of *Cordiglottis* is known to date, this a very rare epiphytic orchid, **C. Westenenki** J.J.Sm., which has apparently been found on only one occasion in Sumatra. The group is a member of the subtribe *Sarcanthinae*, and is not present in our collections at this time.

Nothing has been ascertained regarding the genetic affinities of *Cordiglottis*.

CULTURE: Presumably as for the tropical Vandas and their relatives. (H)

CORUNASTYLIS Fitzg.
(*Anticheirostylis* Fitzg.)

This genus consists of but a single extremely rare terrestrial species, native in New South Wales, Australia, and unknown in contemporary collections. It is an insignificant plant, somewhat allied to *Prasophyllum* R.Br., but differing from it in technical details of the flowers.

Nothing is known of the genetic affinities of this odd genus.

CULTURE: Presumably as for *Caladenia*. (C, I)

C. apostasioides Fitzg. (*Anticheirostylis apostasioides* Fitzg., *Prasophyllum apostasioides* FvM.)

Very slender pls. to about 12″ tall, with several oblong subterranean tubers. Lf. solitary, reduced to a sheathing bract high up the st. Infl. rather densely many-fld., erect. Fls. reversed, brownish-yellow, less than ½″ across. Ss. narrowly lanceolate, concave, the dors. one with ciliate anterior margins. Ps. shorter than the ss., narrowly linear, unequally and deeply 2-parted. Lip shortly clawed, linear-lanceolate, fimbriate, the upper surface with sparse reversed hairs, except along the middle. Summer. (C, I) Australia: New South Wales.

CORYANTHES Hk.
(*Corynanthes* Schlecht., *Corythanthes* Lem., *Meliclis* Raf., *Panstrepis* Raf.)

This extraordinary genus of orchids consists of about fifteen species of epiphytic (very rarely lithophytic) plants in the American tropics, native in the region extending from British Honduras and Guatemala to

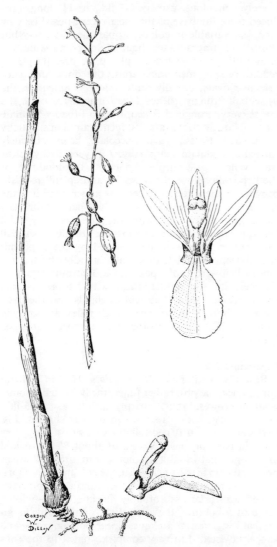

Corallorrhiza Williamsii Correll [GORDON W. DILLON]

Brazil and Peru. They are related to *Stanhopea* Frost and somewhat simulate that genus in vegetative appearance, though the pseudobulbs of many of the species are more elongate and deeply grooved longitudinally, and the flowers are radically different. These blossoms, virtually unique in the entire Orchidaceae for complexity of formation, are especially remarkable for their unusual pollination mechanism. They are borne in sharply pendulous racemes arising from the base of the pseudobulbs, and are few in number (sometimes solitary), fleshy (at least in part, the sepals and petals frequently being very fragile), and typically give off a very strong and penetrating odour. Colours in *Coryanthes* are variable even within the same species, though cream-white or green, often spotted with lurid purples and reds, predominate. The entire flower is of exceedingly complicated design, but the formation of the lip in particular can scarcely be explained in mere words (see page 129). Coryanthes are rare in cultivation today, but their strange structure makes them most desirable to all orchidists. Because of the shape of the lip, the common name of 'Bucket Orchid' has often been applied to members of this incredible aggregation.[1]

[1] P. H. Allen, writing in Woodson & Schery's *Flora of Panama* 3 (4): 66–67, 69, 1949, has some interesting and pertinent comments to make regarding this genus, from which we quote: '. . . [Coryanthes] usually occur as a conspicuous element in the unique arboreal myrmecophilous gardens, in the nests of ants of the genera *Camponotus* and *Azteca*, the association often including a purple- or orange-flowered, erect, tufted *Epidendrum* and several apparently specialized succulent-leaved non-orchidaceous plants, among the most frequent being *Peperomias* and members of the Gesneriaceae. The flowers are probably the most complex and fascinating of the entire Orchidaceae, every detail of the floral structure having been profoundly modified to attract insects and to assure cross-fertilization. To accomplish insect attraction, the flowers, although lasting only 3–4 days, are usually brightly colored, large, and strongly fragrant, secreting some substance on the inner margins of the epichile which is extremely attractive to hymenopterous insects. The sepals, although born, soon wither, the direction of the insect's path being left almost entirely to the intricate contrivances of the marvelous labellum. This organ is unique in the Orchidaceae, the apical lobe or epichile resembling an inverted helmet or waxy cup, on one side prolonged below the apex of the column into a short, usually 3-cornute spout-like channel. The column, in its turn, is sharply reflexed at the apex, which rests precisely over the channel, exposing the anther and stigmatic surface to any insect seeking a way out from the interior of the lip. It would seem that the broad expanse of the mouth of the epichile would provide ample space for an insect to take flight, with only an occasional individual choosing the lateral exit. If the flowers were of longer duration, this might have been left to pure chance, but since time is also an important factor, this possibility of escape by flight has been ingeniously circumvented by the plant in the following manner. Above the cup, on the base of the column, 2 fleshy glands have been developed. When the flowers are fully open and numbers of bees have been attracted to gnaw at the inner margins of the cup, these glands begin secreting a clear liquid, drop by drop, filling the bottom of the cup to the level of the apical channel. Any bee that loses its footing in the competing swarm on the upper margins is precipitated into this liquid, and once its wings have been wet, it has no other choice than to force its way out through the narrow channel below the stigma and anther. Thus the first bee to make the circuit receives the pollinia firmly cemented to its back, to be inserted on the stigma of this or another flower, on the next turn through. . . . In Panama the plants [of *Coryanthes maculata* Hk.] are frequently found in the tops of slender trees, in ants' nests, often associated with *Epidendrum imatophyllum*. They are well protected by the belligerent ants and are painful subjects to collect, and still more painful to transport. Moreover, they seldom thrive in cultivation, possibly from lack of some essential element contributed by the ants in their natural association. . . .'

No hybrids are on record as yet within this genus, although their production should certainly be encouraged. *Coryanthes* is, presumably, freely inter-fertile with allied groups of the subtribe *Gongorinae*, such as *Stanhopea*, *Gongora*, etc. Multigeneric breeding should be tried by enterprising collectors, since the resultant progeny promises to be fantastic in the extreme!

CULTURE: As for *Stanhopea*. Because of the strongly pendulous inflorescences, cultivation in baskets, or on rafts or slabs, is obligatory. As noted by Allen (cf. footnote on this page), these fantastic orchids often do not thrive in collections. (I, H)

C. maculata Hk. (*Coryanthes Albertinae* Karst., *C. Hunteriana* Schltr., *C. Powellii* Schltr., *C. splendens* B.-R.)

Pbs. clustered, elongate, subcylindric, tapering upwards, strongly ridged (often somewhat angular), to 6″ tall and 1½″ thick. Lvs. 2, rather rigidly leathery, plicate, prominently veined, lanceolate, acute to acuminate, to 2′ long and 4″ wide. Infls. very slender, elongate, sharply pendulous, usually 2–3-fld., to 1½′ long, produced from the base of the most recent pbs. Fls. very complex, variable in colour, in part heavily waxy but short-lived, fragrant, to about 4″ long and wide. Ss. clear yellow with sparse purple spots, pale purple or reddish-brown, membranaceous, the dors. one suborbicular-ovate, broadly acute, minutely apiculate, the upper half strongly reflexed, lateral margins revolute, the lat. ss. very strongly deflexed, from a broadly lobulate base, obliquely subfalcate. Ps. membranaceous, usually coloured like the ss., ligular-lanceolate, the tips obliquely subacute, undulate marginally. Lip very fleshy, clear waxy yellow, pale purplish spotted with blood-red, or the hypochil yellow, the mesochil and epichil reddish-brown on the outer surfaces, the inner epichil white spotted with red-brown, complexly 4-parted, the claw semiterete, continuous with the col.-base; hypochil broadly galeate, obtuse or subacute apically; mesochil canaliculate, the basal half covered by the hypochil; epichil deeply cucullate or galeate, broadly obtuse, prolonged below the col.-apex into a 3-cornute spout or channel. Col. subterete, footless, with 2 broad, lateral, subfalcate or obliquely auriculate glands near the base, the apex shortly winged and strongly reflexed. Mostly in spring. (I, H) Panama; Colombia; Venezuela; Guianas; Brazil.

C. speciosa Hk.

Basically similar to *C. maculata* Hk. in general appearance, the pbs. rather fuller, the lvs. usually somewhat narrower. Infls. sharply pendulous, 2–5-fld., rather robust, with a few brown tubular sheaths. Fls. borne on stout scurfy pedicellate ovaries to 4″ long, very waxy in part, not lasting well, to about 5″ across and long, somewhat variable in colour, most often yellowish-brown, the lip usually yellowish, the col. greenish. Dors. sep. suborbicular-flabellate to rhombic, apiculate, rather waxy; lat. ss. broadly falcate, ovate-oblong, acute to subobtuse, the apex slightly thickened, longitudinally striate. Ps. oblique, linear-oblong, wavy and vaguely twisted. Lip very complex, joined to the col.-base by a narrow slightly compressed claw; hypochil

Catasetum viridiflavum Hk., a male inflorescence [H. A. DUNN]

Cattleya Skinneri Batem, var. *alba* Rchb.f. [WM. KIRCH—ORCHIDS LTD.]

Cephalanthera Austinae (A. Gray) Heller
[AMERICAN ORCHID SOCIETY]

Caularthron bilamellatum (Rchb.f.) R.E.
Schultes [G. C. K. DUNSTERVILLE]

Chelonistele sulphurea (Bl.) Pfitz. [GEORGE FULLER]

IVA   *Cycnoches ventricosum* Batem. var. *Warscewiczii* (Rchb.f.)
P. H. Allen [H.A.DUNN]

IVB   *Dendrobium Parishii* Rchb.f. [H.R.FOLKERSMA]

Coryanthes speciosa Hk. [Hoehne, *Flora Brasílica*]

helmet-shaped or obliquely hemispherical, puberulent outside; mesochil arising from within the hypochil, broadly semicylindrical, dorsally pubescent, the margins strongly inrolled to form a tube, slightly sulcate on back; epichil pendent from the mesochil, galeate-hemispherical, deeply cleft in front with 3 projecting teeth at the base of the cleft, each tooth provided with a small wart near the base, the sac large, the lat. teeth uncinate-incurved and acute, the median tooth larger, linear and obtuse. Col. fleshy, almost terete, with narrow lat. wings near the truncate, abruptly recurved apex, with a pair of short recurved glandular horns at base. Summer. (I, H) Guatemala; Honduras; Northern South America to Trinidad and Brazil.

C. macrantha (Hk.) Hk. (*Gongora macrantha* Hk.) Similar to the other spp. in habit, the pbs. often more ovoid, sometimes almost spindle-shaped, to 5″ tall. Infls. almost always 2-fld., sharply pendulous, to 8″ long or more, the pedicellate ovaries very elongate. Fls. heavily scented, variable in colour, about 5″ long, the ss. usually yellowish with numerous red oblong spots, the ps. yellowish, often flushed with flesh-pink, basally red-spotted, the very fleshy lip with a dark purple, fleshy claw, the hypochil hemispherical, greenish-purple, the mesochil contracted, vivid blood-red, the margins turned back and marked with 4–5 deep sharp-edged plaits; epichil broadly conical, rather sharp-pointed, yellow streaked and spotted with light crimson-red. Winter–spring. (H) Venezuela; Guianas; Trinidad; North Brazil; Amazonian Peru.

CORYBAS Salisb.
(*Corysanthes* R.Br.)

This is a large genus, of more than sixty species, with a huge range, extending from the foothills of the Himalayas eastward to the Philippines, southeast through Malaysia to New Guinea, Australia, New Zealand, and certain insular groups in Micronesia and Melanesia. Very rare in cultivation, they are small to extremely small terrestrial plants, and despite their diminutive stature are of great interest and unusual beauty, even when not in bloom. Corybas bear a solitary, heart-shaped to roundish leaf—which is often borne flat on the ground—from one or more small, subterranean, globular tubers. The single, proportionately large flower arises from the base of this leaf, and is typically almost stalkless. Its shape gives to the members of this genus their common name of 'Helmet Orchids', since in most of the species the dorsal sepal is considerably developed and forms a hood over the large lip and often minute petals and lateral sepals. Structure of the lip in *Corybas* is frequently very complex, with fringing of various degrees occurring in many of the species. Like certain other orchids (*Didymoplexis* Griff., for example), the inflorescence and pedicellate ovary elongate remarkably after fertilization.

No hybrids are known in *Corybas*, and nothing is known of its genetic alliances.

CULTURE: As for *Caladenia*. The members of this enchanting genus are usually very difficult to maintain in good condition for more than a single season. (C, I)

C. pruinosus (Cunn.) Rchb.f. (*Corysanthes pruinosa* Cunn.)
Lf. roundish-heart-shaped, green above and below,

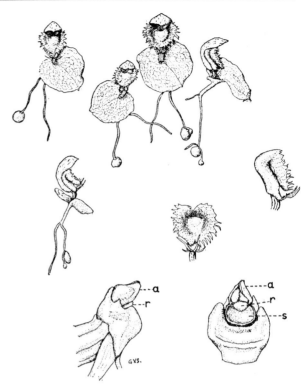

Corybas pruinosus (Cunn.) Rchb.f. [Rupp, *Orchids of New South Wales*]

sometimes vaguely lbd., about 1½″ in diam. Fl. solitary, rather erect, sometimes to almost 1″ long, purple with translucent patches except for the dors. sep., which is grey-green with dark spots, the lip with a pale green central depression, the long marginal fringes purple. Dors. sep. hooded, rather narrow; lat. ss. filiform, very small. Ps. filiform, very small. Lip tubular at base, the lamina spreading and fringed. Spring–summer. (C, I) Australia: New South Wales.

CORYCIUM Sw.

About eight species of *Corycium* are known to date, all of these native in South and South-central Africa, where they are usually found growing as terrestrials or on rocks. Rather robust plants with erect spikes of small, intricate flowers, the Coryciums are at this time unknown in collections. They are closely allied to *Pterygodium* Sw. of the subtribe *Disperidinae*, differing from it in technical details of the flowers.

Nothing is known of the genetic affinities of this rare genus.

CULTURE: Presumably as for *Caladenia*. (I)

CORYMBORCHIS Thou. ex Bl.
(*Corymbis* Thou., *Macrostylis* Rchb.f.)

Corymborchis is an unusually interesting terrestrial genus, since its members usually simulate a robust ginger or a grass rather than an orchid. About 18 species are known, widespread in virtually all tropical

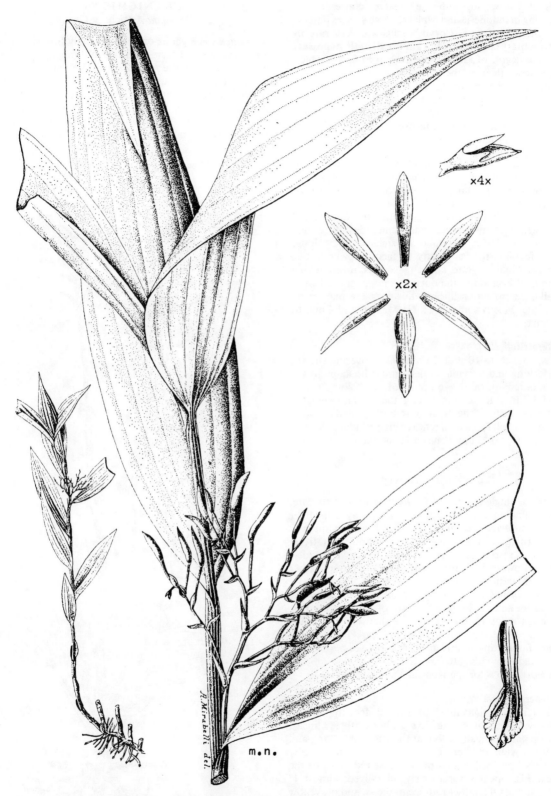

Corymborchis flava (Sw.) O.Ktze. [Hoehne, *Flora Brasilica*]

131

parts of the world, with the greatest concentration occurring in Indonesia and Malaysia; two species inhabit the American tropics. Corymborchis are very rare in contemporary cultivation, but almost all of them possess a certain degree of attractiveness when in flower which recommends them to the connoisseur.

This genus has as yet not been utilized in hybridization, and nothing is known of its genetic compatibility.

CULTURE: As for *Arundina*, although more shade should be given the plants, in order to successfully induce flower-production. (I, H)

C. forcipigera (Rchb.f.) L.O. Wms. (*Macrostylis forcipigera* Rchb.f., *Corymborchis cubensis* Acuña)

Robust pls. to 6' tall. Lvs. crowded in upper parts of the terete sts., to 15" long and 3" wide, elliptic-lanceolate to narrowly lanceolate, long-acuminate, folded and prominently many-nerved. Infls. sometimes more than one per st., loose, corymbose panicles, to 5" long, rather few-fld., the fls. mostly all facing upwards. Fls. greenish-white or white, about 1½" across, the ss. with a prominent keel along the outside, the ps. crisped marginally, the lip with a linear callus near the margin on each side. Mostly summer. (I, H) Mexico and Cuba to Panama.

C. veratrifolia Bl.

Sts. robust, to 10' tall. Lvs. almost covering the st., to 15" long and 6" wide, rather similar in shape to the other noted sp. Infls. 4–6-branched, to 4" long, rather few-fld. Fls. to more than 2" long, the ss. pale green, the ps. white, the lip white. Ss. and ps. both dilated apically, the ps. crisped. Lip with a reflexed crisped blade. Mostly summer. (I, H) Malay Peninsula; Indonesia.

COTTONIA Wight

Only a single species of *Cottonia* is known to date, this an uncommon but very unusual epiphytic member of the subtribe *Sarcanthinae*, native in Ceylon and Southern India. The genus is allied to and vegetatively somewhat resembles *Trichoglottis* Bl., but its very oddly-shaped flowers differ materially from the group, rather more simulating a *Luisia*.

Cottonia has not as yet been taken in hand by the breeders, and nothing is known of its genetic ties, although it seems entirely possible that it is 'crossable' with at least certain other genera of the *Vanda* group. Some fascinating multigeneric hybrids seem potential here, and should be attempted.

CULTURE: As for the tropical Vandas, etc. (H)

C. macrostachya Wight

Sts. rather elongated, to several feet in length, densely leafy, clambering. Lvs. rather leathery, linear, obtuse and unequally 2-lbd. at the apex, to 9" long and about ½" wide. Infls. erect, to more than 5' long, usually sparsely branched, with a rather dense rac. towards the apex. Fls. opening successively, long-lived, almost 1" long, giving off a rather foul scent, the ss. and ps. yellow with brown streaks, the large, complex, hairy lip dark brown- or blackish-purple with a yellow centre. Spring. (H) Ceylon; Southern India.

CRANICHIS Sw.
(*Ocampoa* A.Rich. & Gal.)

Cranichis is a genus of approximately fifty species of mostly very small terrestrial (rarely lithophytic or epiphytic) orchids in the American tropics and subtropics, as yet little known in cultivation, but sufficiently attractive to warrant attention. The leaves are typically borne in a basal rosette, from the centre of which arises a frequently rather tall inflorescence bearing a dense many-flowered raceme of tiny, usually white or green

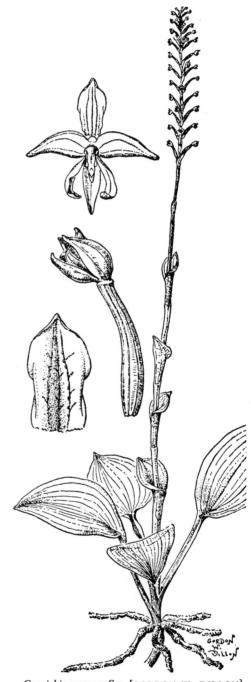

Cranichis muscosa Sw. [GORDON W. DILLON]

blossoms at the top. These flowers are very complex, are handsome when inspected closely, and are unique in generally having beautifully fringed petals. A member of the subtribe *Cranichidinae*, the genus is perhaps closest in its alliance to *Fuertesiella* Schltr. and *Ponthieva* R.Br.

No hybrids are to date known in *Cranichis*, and nothing has been ascertained concerning its genetic affinities.

CULTURE: As for *Anoectochilus*, although most of the species of the present genus do not require such excessive conditions of heat and high humidity as are needed by the 'Jewel Orchids'. Some of them occur at relatively high elevations. (I, H)

C. muscosa Sw.

Variable in size, from about 4″ to more than 12″ tall when in fl. Roots fleshy, clustered, subterranean. Lvs. 4–6, forming a rather compact or loose rosette, stalked, smaller above, to 4″ long, varying from almost heart-shaped to oblong, obtuse or acute, rather soft-textured. Infls. erect, to more than 12″ tall, the rachis usually purple-tinged, the densely few- to many-fld. rac. mostly cylindrical, to 5″ long. Fls. white, the lip white spotted with green, wavy-margined, the disc slightly rough-thickened. Mostly autumn. (H) South Florida and Mexico throughout the West Indies and Central America to Trinidad and Venezuela.

CREMASTRA Ldl.
(*Hyacinthorchis* Bl.)

This small genus of two terrestrial orchids—one native in the Himalayas, the other in the mountains of Japan—is a member of the subtribe *Cyrtopodiinae*, and is apparently not represented in our collections today. Allied to *Oreorchis* Ldl., the Cremastras are small insignificant plants of interest primarily to specialists or botanical students.

Nothing is known of the genetic affinities of this little-known group.

CULTURE: Presumably as for *Orchis* and the temperate zone Habenarias. (C)

CRYBE Ldl.

Crybe contains a single seldom-seen terrestrial orchid of considerable beauty, native in Mexico, Guatemala, Honduras, and Nicaragua. Allied to *Bletilla* Rchb.f., it rather simulates a *Bletia* in most characters, bearing nodding, inch-long purplish-red flowers which make it of interest to collectors. The roundish, green corms are usually partially or entirely buried in the ground. The leaves—which are stem-like at the base—and the inflorescences are borne at different points from these corms. In some cases the flowers of this rare little orchid do not open well, and they almost invariably produce seed-capsules without assistance.

Nothing is known of the genetic compatibility of *Crybe*, but it is presumably 'crossable' with certain allied groups, and possibly also with *Bletia*.

CULTURE: As for *Bletia*. (I, H)

C. rosea Ldl. (*Bletia purpurata* A.Rich. & Gal., *Arethusa rosea* Bth. ex Hemsl., *Arethusa grandiflora* S.Wats.)

Corm typically subterranean, green, roundish. Lvs. 2, stalked basally, with a basal lf.-like sheath, folded, oblong-elliptic to linear-lanceolate, acute or acuminate, strongly veined, eventually deciduous, to 15″ long and 2½″ wide. Infls. 3–6-fld., slender, erect, sheathed, to 1½′ tall. Fls. purplish-red, the lip usually brighter, often whitish in the throat, about 1″ long, nodding, often not opening well. Ss. often purple-spotted above the middle, roughened outside, oblanceolate, acute or acuminate, apically recurved. Ps. oblanceolate, obtuse to acutish, curving, often white tinged with purplish. Lip forming a tube around the col., the margins crisped, the disc with 3 crest-like veins. Autumn. (I, H) Mexico; Guatemala; Honduras; Nicaragua.

CRYPTANTHEMIS Rupp

With the allied genus *Rhizanthella* R.S.Rog., *Cryptanthemis* forms a group of almost unbelievable orchids, since they are *subterranean* in habit. The late Rev. H. M. R. Rupp states, in his *Orchids of New South Wales* (105. 1943.): 'The specimens obtained by Kesteven and Rupp established the point that this remarkable orchid actually develops and matures its flowers below the surface of the soil. The method of fertilization is still doubtful, but it is certainly effective, for in capitula with flowers past maturity most of the ovaries contain seeds. Apparently *after* fertilization the capitula are pushed up just level with the ground-surface, presumably to ensure seed-distribution, but in the specimens cited the tops of the capitula with perfect flowers were not less than 2 cm. below ground-level.' The single species, Australian in origin, was discovered accidentally, and is saprophytic on various types of tree- or bush-roots (evidence of at least partial parasitism seems possible here). It is a unique plant, but one which is not in cultivation, since it seems logical that its peculiar requirements could not be met in the collection.

Nothing is known concerning the genetic affinities of *Cryptanthemis*.

CULTURE: Possibly that of *Corallorrhiza* and other saprophytes, though its successful cultivation seems very dubious. (H)

C. Slateri Rupp

Rhiz. stout, to 6″ long, often several-branched, more or less clothed with white or dingy fleshy imbricating bracts, the uppermost bracts elongated, subtending the slightly swollen capitula of fls., these capitula consisting of 15–30 small crowded fls. on irregularly 4-angled pedicellate ovaries. Fls. less than ¼″ across, facing inwards, the outer ones larger than the inner, waxy-white when disinterred, but slowly darkening to dull purplish-brown when exposed to light. Dors. sep. concave, hooded over the col., the lat. ss. larger, broad and concave to about the middle, then tapering to a long point. Ps. acute, the margins minutely toothed. Lip entire, ovate or sometimes almost cordate, acute, thick and fleshy, with a slender claw, the lamina densely papillose, dark reddish-purple, with a smooth median plate towards the base, the marginal papillae slightly elongate. Spring. (H) Australia.

Cryptarrhena lunata R.Br. [D.E. TIBBITS]

CRYPTARRHENA R.Br. ex Ldl.
(*Clinhymenia* A.Rich. & Gal., *Clynhymenia* A.Rich. & Gal., *Orchidofunckia* A.Rich. & Gal.)

This is a genus of about three species of rare and infrequently-grown, dwarf, epiphytic orchids, inhabiting the region which extends from Mexico and Jamaica throughout Central America and parts of the West Indies to Brazil. *Cryptarrhena* is allied to *Notylia* Ldl., but differs in the structure of the flowers, and even in their superficial vegetative appearance Two of these orchids may be present in particularly choice collections today, though they must be classed as rarities.

Nothing has been ascertained regarding the genetic affinities of *Cryptarrhena*.

CULTURE: As for *Notylia*. (I)

C. guatemalensis Schltr.
Dwarf, cluster-forming pls., the ovoid, compressed pbs. about $\frac{1}{2}''$ long, subtended and almost concealed by sheathing lf.-bases. Lvs. 1–2 at apex of pb., also at its base, to $3\frac{1}{2}''$ long, linear-ligulate to linear-oblanceolate, obliquely acute. Infls. basal, slender, mostly erect, few- to many-fld., to 6'' long. Fls. about $\frac{1}{2}''$ across, pale green. Lip shortly clawed, 4-lbd., the lower pair of the lbs. linear-falcate, acuminate, the upper pair linear, somewhat erect; claw with an erect flap-like callus. Summer. (I) Guatemala; Costa Rica; ? Panama; Colombia; British Guiana.

C. lunata R.Br. (*Clinhymenia pallidiflora* A.Rich. & Gal., *Clynhymenia pallidiflora* A.Rich. & Gal., *Cryptarrhena pallidiflora* Rchb.f., *Orchidofunckia pallidiflora* A.Rich. & Gal. ex Rchb.f.)
Pls. from a short creeping rhiz., forming clusters, without pbs., to more than 12'' tall. Lvs. distichous, linear to narrowly oblanceolate, oblique, rather leathery, the basal sheaths folded. Infls. from lf.-axils, slender, with a slender, cylindrical, loosely many-fld. rac. Fls. small, fleshy, green-yellow, about $\frac{1}{2}''$ across, the ss. and ps. green, the lip yellow, 4-lbd., complex. Summer. (I) Mexico and Jamaica to Costa Rica, Northern South America, and Trinidad.

CRYPTOCENTRUM Bth.
(*Anthosiphon* Schltr., *Pittierella* Schltr.)

About fifteen species of extraordinary epiphytic orchids in tropical America—ranging from Costa Rica to Peru—make up the genus *Cryptocentrum*, which is closely allied to *Maxillaria* R. & P., but which is readily distinguishable both vegetatively and florally from that group. The plants, typically without pseudobulbs, rather simulate a monopodial orchid, such as a dwarf *Vanda*, than a sympodial one, since the short, often solitary stems bear 2-ranked, leathery leaves. The solitary flowers are produced on basal, erect to horizontal, prominently sheathed scapes, the uppermost concealing the pedicellate ovary and leaving only the perianth segments exposed. Usually small and dull-coloured, these blossoms are far from attractive, but their unusual structure and the remarkable appearance of the plants make the Cryptocentrums of singular interest to the connoisseur.

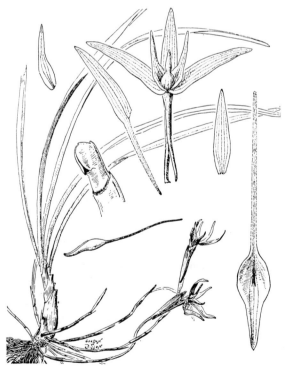

Cryptocentrum inaequisepalum C.Schw. [GORDON W. DILLON]

134

Nothing is known of the genetic alliances of this odd genus of orchids.

CULTURE: As for *Ornithocephalus*. (I, H)

C. latifolium Schltr.

Without pbs., the pls. variable in size, sometimes to 10″ tall, rather resembling a monopodial orchid, such as a dwarf *Vanda*. Sts. woody, covered with the persistent, brown, imbricating lf.-bases, often rooting above the base. Lvs. usually few, leathery, 2-ranked, close together, broadly ligular, rounded apically, to 9″ long and ¾″ wide. Infls. 1-fld., erect or arching, to 6″ long, the peduncles completely covered by tubular, papery sheaths. Fls. to 3″ across, fleshy, greenish-olive to greenish-tan. Ss. widely spreading in apical half, narrowly ligular-lanceolate, acute, the margins mostly revolute, the lat. ss. oblique, the bases joined and forming a long spur which is pressed against the pedicellate ovary. Ps. obliquely lanceolate, acute. Lip joined to the col.-base, the free part lanceolate, acute, the base long-tubular, the tube contained within the sepaline spur. Summer. (I, H) Costa Rica; Panama.

CRYPTOCHILUS Wall.

This genus, containing six species, is distributed from Tibet and the Himalayas to the Moluccas, where the plants grow as epiphytes or as lithophytes on rock outcroppings at medium or high elevations. Rare in collections, two species of *Cryptochilus* are present in a few choice assemblages of orchidaceous plants today. The genus is allied to *Eria* Ldl., but may readily be distinguished from that group by the strange cup-shaped flowers, the parts of which are of different shape from those of *Eria*.

No hybrids utilizing *Cryptochilus* have been made as yet, and nothing is known of its genetic alliances.

CULTURE: As for the small, highland Dendrobiums. (C, I)

C. luteus Ldl.

Pbs. cylindrical, to about 3½″ tall. Lvs. paired, rather leathery, lanceolate-ligulate, acute, narrowing towards the base, to 7″ long. Infls. arising with the new lvs., terminal, densely many-fld., the fls. all facing in one direction, subtended by large bracts. Fls. about ¼″ long cup-shaped, yellow throughout, the lip somewhat darker than other parts. Summer. (C) Himalayas (particularly Sikkim), mostly above 4500 feet elevation.

C. sanguineus Wall.

Pbs. egg-shaped, to about 2½″ tall. Lvs. 1–2, broader than those of the other sp., to 10″ long, acute. Infls. with the bracts shorter than the fls. (rather than longer, as in *C. luteus* Ldl.). Fls. almost 1″ long, light or dark red or scarlet. Summer. (C, I) Nepal and other parts of the Himalayas, usually lower than 4500 feet elevation.

CRYPTOPHORANTHUS B.-R.

This is an extraordinary genus of about twenty species, native in the region extending from Cuba and Jamaica to Brazil. A member of the subtribe *Pleurothallidinae*, *Cryptophoranthus* consists of mostly dwarf (rarely medium-sized) epiphytic or lithophytic plants which vegetatively rather simulate certain kinds of *Pleurothallis*. Florally, however, the group is completely distinct from that group, and approximates *Masdevallia* in basic structure. The blossoms of these orchids— typically produced singly or in small fascicles at the junction of the secondary stems with the leaf-blades— are mostly purple, red or brown in colour, and are structurally among the most unusual of any found in the Orchidaceae. The large sepals (in the majority of the species) are joined together at the base and apex, opening only along a median slit, thus showing a tiny aperture through which pollinating insects may reach the sexual apparatus on the column within. The considerably reduced petals and lip are also borne within this sepaline structure, and may be viewed through the aperture. It is from this peculiar characteristic that these plants receive their common name of 'Window Orchids'. These species of *Cryptophoranthus* are very rare in contemporary collections, but their remarkable appearance makes them of unique interest to connoisseurs.

No hybrids have as yet been attempted with the 'Window Orchids', and nothing is known of their genetic affinities.

CULTURE: The cultural requirements of this genus are those of allied groups, such as *Pleurothallis* and *Masdevallia*, dependent in large part upon the original habitat

Cryptophoranthus atropurpureus (Ldl.) Rolfe [Hoehne, *Flora Brasilica*]

of the particular species or individual specimen involved. They prefer pot-culture, in a perfectly-drained compost made up of equal parts of chopped sphagnum moss and shredded tree-fern fibre. Since no pseudobulbs are present, they must never be allowed to become completely dry at the roots. They are highly intolerant of stale conditions in the compost, which must never be permitted to become soggy, even for a brief period. A warm, moderately shady spot in the greenhouse suits them well, and frequent repotting should be avoided. (I, H)

C. atropurpureus (Ldl.) Rolfe (*Specklinia atropurpurea* Ldl., *Pleurothallis atropurpurea* Ldl., *Masdevallia fenestrata* Ldl. ex Hk.)

Sts. clustered, erect, to 2″ tall, 5–7-jointed, covered with sheaths, the sheaths increasing in size from the base upwards, dilated at the mouth, glabrous. Lf. solitary, rather rigidly leathery, obovate-elliptic, tapering below into a short stalk, to 3½″ long and 1¼″ wide. Infls. solitary or few in a tight cluster, 1-fld., very abbreviated. Fls. about ½″ long, dark crimson or purplish-red, structure as noted for the genus. Lip hastate, the lat. lbs. folded in front, with a minute ear-like lb. at each side at the base. Aug.–Dec. (I, H) Cuba; Jamaica.

C. lepidotus L.O.Wms.

Sts. clustered, ¾–2¾″ tall, covered with 4–5 papery, funnel-shaped sheaths which soon disintegrate. Lf. solitary, rather leathery, oblanceolate to narrowly obovate, obtuse or acutish, distinctly petioled at base, 1¼–4″ long. Infl. consisting of 1–6 long-peduncled fls., these furnished with short funnel-shaped sheaths. Fls. about ¾″ long or less, apically down-curving, dark dull reddish-purple, fleshy, each sepal with a median verrucose ridge. Lip hastate, clawed, the lamina verrucose or lepidote, with 2 longitudinal, lamellate calli extending from the auricles to about the middle. Summer. (I, H) Panama.

CRYPTOPUS Ldl.
(*Beclardia* A.Rich.)

This is a genus of three known species, all unusual epiphytic orchids of the subtribe *Sarcanthinae* in Madagascar and the Mascarene Islands, as yet extremely rare in our collections. Somewhat allied to *Oeonia* Ldl., they are plants of considerable potential value to connoisseurs, for the very complex and beautiful mostly white flowers, these borne in graceful racemes. **C. elatus** (Thou.) Ldl. has recently been introduced into cultivation, but the rare and desirable **C. brachiatus** H.Perr. and **C. paniculatus** H.Perr., both from Madagascar, as yet appear to be unknown outside of their native island.

Nothing is known of the genetic affinities of this rare angraecoid genus.

CULTURE: As for the tropical species of *Angraecum*, *Aërangis*, and the like. (H)

C. elatus (Thou.) Ldl. (*Angraecum elatum* Thou., *Beclardia elata* A.Rich.)

Sts. slender, often branched, sinuous, rather lengthy. Lvs. rather distant or close together, 2–3″ long, leathery, dark green, oblong-elliptic, emarginate and obtuse at

apex. Infl. to 2′ long, usually pendulous or hanging, mostly densely 7–15-fld. Fls. very widely opening, white turning to pale yellow with age, of remarkably intricate structure, to almost 2½″ across and slightly more in length. Ss. spatulate, the ps. almost twice as long, clawed and with an irregularly 4-lbd. apical part. Lip as long as ps., 4-lbd., the basal ones small, narrow, falcate, the apical ones conspicuously larger and more or less conspicuously 2-lbd. in turn; a flush of yellow or orange sometimes occurs on the tiny apicule between these final lobes. Mostly spring to early summer. (H) Mascarene Islands: Mauritius; Réunion.

CRYPTOSTYLIS R.Br.
(*Zosterostylis* Bl.)

Cryptostylis is a genus of about twenty species of unusually attractive, but very seldom cultivated terrestrial orchids. All of the described entities are rather similar, and more critical study may prove that at least some of them should be reduced to synonymy under the others. Even when not in bloom, these rather robust ground orchids are handsome, due to the foliage, in most cases, being more or less variegated, spotted, or bearing dark veins on a paler background; the leaves arise separately from the subterranean rhizome, near the base of the flowering-stem, and do not clasp the base of that stem, as is the case in many leafy terrestrial orchids. *Cryptostylis* ranges from North India, Ceylon, Formosa, and the Philippines throughout South-east Asia and Indonesia to Australia, New Guinea, New Caledonia, and certain of the Polynesian insular groups. In Australia, considerable research has been done in the fantastic partnership between various species of this genus and the male ichneumon-wasps of the species *Lissopimpla semipunctata*, a remarkable occurrence termed pseudocopulation taking place.

Nothing is known of the genetic affinities of *Cryptostylis*, and no hybrids are registered as yet.

CULTURE: As for the tropical species of *Phaius*. (I, H)

C. arachnites (Bl.) Hassk. (*Zosterostylis arachnites* Bl.)

Rhiz. fleshy, creeping under the surface, with several very hairy, thick roots. Lvs. from the rhiz., 1–4, the blade to about 7″ long and 3″ wide, pale green with a more or less distinct network of darker veins, ovate, acute, rounded basally, the stalk slender, to 6″ long, purple-spotted. Infls. erect, to 2′ tall, rather many-fld., the fls. opening gradually over a long period, the base of the scape sheathed, the floral bracts rather large. Fls. inverted, to 1½″ long, the ss. and ps. greenish (sometimes flushed with dull red), the lip purplish-red basally, the upper part (apical part) pale with deep red or purplish spots, this portion velvety-hairy. Dors. sep. pointing straight downwards, very narrow, the margins inrolled; lat. ss. spreading almost horizontally, about the same size as the dors. one. Ps. spreading, narrow. Lip erect, concave at base, almost flat above, narrowed gradually to an acute tip. Mostly summer. (H) Malay Peninsula; Sumatra; Java.

C. erecta R.Br.

Lvs. 1–3, usually darker underneath than above, long-stalked, the length very variable, broadly to narrowly lanceolate. Infls. erect, slender, to almost 3' tall, 2–10-fld., the fls. opening successively. Fls. inverted, about 2" long, the ss. and ps. green, the lip red-brown. Dors. sep. linear, spreading; lat. ss. slightly shorter, otherwise similar. Ps. about half as long as ss., filiform, Lip large, strongly contracted just above the broad base, enclosing the col., then suddenly erect and very broad, deeply concave, conspicuously striped and more or less reticulate-veined with deeper red-brown, with a vertically broad ridge running down the middle. Autumn–spring. (I) Australia.

C. leptochila FvM. ex Bth.
    Similar in habit to *C. erecta* R.Br., but seldom more than 15" tall when in fl. Lvs. often almost ovate, acute. Fls. 4–15, inverted, about 1½" long, green, the lip red-brown. Ss. and ps. filiform. Lip enclosing the col., suddenly contracted into an oblong-linear, thick, channelled lamina, this pubescent, recurved in front, the margins much depressed, with a row of 6–9 stalkless calli on each side. Autumn-spring. (I) Australia.

C. subulata (Labill.) Rchb.f. (*Malaxis subulata* Labill., *Cryptostylis longifolia* R.Br.)
    Similar in habit and foliage to *C. erecta* R.Br., the lvs. less often dark underneath. Fls. 2–14, to almost 2½" long, green, the lip bright red-brown. Dors. sep. wider at base than the lats. (which approximate it in length), spreading, the lats. divergent. Ps. narrower than the ss., about half as long. Lip oblong, the margins depressed or reflexed along the middle part, with the upper surface narrow and convex; lamina traversed for more than half its length, anteriorly, by 2 thick beaded ridges and 2 parallel finer ones, all ending in a conspicuous, dark, 2-lbd. glandular apical process. Autumn-spring. (I) Australia.

CYANAEORCHIS B.-R.

    A single very scarce and little-known terrestrial orchid, **Cyanaeorchis arundinae** B.-R., makes up this genus of the subtribe *Polystachyinae*. Somewhat allied to *Bromheadia* Ldl., it inhabits southern Brazil and Paraguay, and bears loosely arranged racemes of rather small but interestingly complex flowers at the top of a few-leaved, slender stem.
    Nothing is known of the genetic ties of *Cyanaeorchis*. CULTURE: Presumably as for *Bletia*. (I, H)

CYCNOCHES Ldl.
(*Cycnauken* Lem.)

    The fabulous 'Swan Orchids', genus *Cycnoches*, are among the most handsome and justifiably prized of American species grown today. Of singularly easy cultivation, they are attractive plants even when not in flower, and the remarkable blossoms are of great beauty and notably long-lived. 'Unlike most orchids, in which the male and female elements are both present in the column, the flowers of this genus are uni-sexual and dimorphic. The normal production of separate staminate and pistillate flowers, either on separate scapes or in mixed inflorescences would be bewildering enough,

Cyanaeorchis arundinae B.-R. [Hoehne, *Flora Brasilica*]

without further complicating factors such as the extreme floral dimorphism in the more advanced section of the genus [*Heteranthae*], with little structural resemblance between the male and female flowers. To further compound the confusion, the staminate forms in this section are often, almost usually, variable in structure, so that it is difficult to find two specimens exactly alike. On rare occasions perfect (hermaphroditic) flowers may be produced, but these also are sometimes found to differ one from the other. It is considered doubtful if a more perplexing group could be found in nature, yet they have a peculiar charm and fascination that remains forever new.'[1] All species of *Cycnoches* are rather similar in vegetative appearance, consisting of often very large, more or less cylindrical pseudobulbs which are furnished with few to many, deciduous, rather thin, folded leaves. The erect, arching or pendulous inflorescences usually arise from the upper nodes of the pseudobulbs, and bear one to several dozen uniquely handsome, typically

[1] P. H. Allen in *The Orchid Journal* 1: 174. 1952.

waxy and fragrant flowers.⸱ In the § *Eu-Cycnoches*, both the staminate (male) and the pistillate (female) flowers are large and showy, bearing rather similar broad sepals and petals and a large, often very thick lip which is not divided. In the § *Heteranthae* the staminate and pistillate flowers are remarkably dissimilar in both size and shape, the pistillate ones being rather like those of § *Eu-Cycnoches*, and the much commoner staminate ones—which are produced in long, multiflorous, pendulous racemes—have the small lip more or less reduced to a disc, furnished (or not) with finger-like projections, which are sometimes enlarged at the tips. The arching, elongate column in all of the sex forms gives rise to the vernacular name, since it supposedly simulates the graceful neck of a swan, with its head the anther-bearing apex. Ranging from southern Mexico to Peru and Brazil, seven species and several variants are recognized at this time in *Cycnoches*.

Cycnoches has to date produced only one registered hybrid within the group (this incorrectly identified in the registry), and an unusual cross with *Mormodes*, to give the group *Cycnodes*. Additional breeding within the group, and with *Catasetum* as well as *Mormodes* is to be recommended, for its fascinating potentials.

CULTURE: As for *Catasetum*. Particular care must be taken not to over-water the plants at any time, as the fleshy pseudobulbs are prone to rotting. (I, H)

C. Egertonianum Batem. (*Cycnoches Amparoanum* Schltr., *C. densiflorum* Rolfe, *C. glanduliferum* A.Rich. & Gal., *C. guttulatum* Schltr., *C. pachydactylon* Schltr., *C. pauciflorum* Schltr., *C. peruvianum* Rolfe, *C. Rossianum* Rolfe, *C. stelliferum* Lodd., *C. stenodactylon* Schltr., *C. ventricosum* Batem. var. *Egertonianum* Hk.)

§ *Heteranthae*. Habit as in the genus, the pbs. usually rather slender and short. Staminate fls. in long, mostly dense, pendulous racs. to 1½′ long, to 2½″ across (often considerably smaller), the ss. and ps. green or greenish-tan, sometimes flushed with purple on the front surfaces, or spotted with red-brown, maroon, or purple, the apical half of the ss. and ps. often sharply reflexed. Lip varying from green tinged with purple to pure white, the middle concave disc ovate to orbicular, the teeth elongate, rounded, club-shaped or rarely forked. Pistillate fls. relatively large, fleshy, similar to those of § *Eu-Cycnoches*. Mostly autumn–winter. (I, H) Mexico and Guatemala to Colombia, Peru, and Brazil.

—var. **aureum** (Ldl.) P.H.Allen (*Cycnoches aureum* Ldl.)
Staminate fls. to 3½″ in diam., the ss. and ps. pale yellowish-green, sometimes veined with darker green, or sometimes almost white, with tiny rose dots. Lip ovate or triangular, white, often obscurely green-striped, the marginal teeth mostly forked. Late summer–autumn. (I, H) Costa Rica; Panama.

—var. **Dianae** (Rchb.f.) P.H.Allen (*Cycnoches Dianae* Rchb.f., *C. albidum* Krzl., *C. Powellii* Schltr.)
Staminate fls. to 2″ across, the ss. and ps. rosy-pink with white shadings. Lip with a distinct basal claw, the middle concavity white, orbicular, the lateral margins crenate or with more or less distinct, sometimes club-shaped teeth. Late summer–autumn. (I, H) Panama.

C. pentadactylon Ldl. (*Cycnoches Amesianum* Sandw., *C. Cooperi* Rolfe, *C. Espiritosantense* Brade)
§ *Heteranthae*. Habit as in the genus, the pbs. to 1½′ long. Staminate fls. in arching or pendulous rac., to 12″ long (rarely longer), numerous, to almost 4″ across, fragrant. Ss. and ps. green blotched and spotted with chocolate-brown. Lip green or white, spotted with reddish or chocolate-brown, fleshy, with a long, slightly curved basal claw, with an arching, finger-like appendage on the dorsal surface; blade divided into a 4-lbd. mesochil, the epichil linguiform to lanceolate, the acute apex mostly recurved. Spring–summer. (I, H) Brazil; Peru: Amazonian region.

C. ventricosum Batem.
§ *Eu-Cycnoches*. Habit as in the genus. Staminate and pistillate fls. almost identical, except for the structure of the col., to almost 5″ across, fragrant, waxy, long-lived, the ss. and ps. green, aging yellow, spreading or more often strongly reflexed, the lat. ss. often falcate. Lip white, with an elongate basal claw which is sometimes slightly winged, the basal callus rounded, not projecting, the surrounding area dark green, blotched, lunate in shape, not depressed. Summer–early autumn. (I, H) Mexico; Guatemala; Honduras; ? Panama.

—var. **chlorochilon** (Klotzsch) P.H.Allen (*Cycnoches chlorochilon* Klotzsch)
Distinguished from typical *C. ventricosum* Batem. by the much larger fls. (to almost 7″ long), the not-clawed lip, and the triangular, projecting basal callus. Spring–summer. (I, H) Panama; Colombia; Venezuela; Guianas.

—var. **Warscewiczii** (Rchb.f.) P.H.Allen (*Cycnoches Warscewiczii* Rchb.f., *C. Tonduzii* Schltr.)
The commonest *Cycnoches* in cultivation, typically grown as *C. chlorochilon*, which is correctly the extremely rare *C. ventricosum* Batem. var. *chlorochilon* (Klotzsch) P.H.Allen, found in only a very few of the most comprehensive of collections. Variable, but differing from the type primarily in the much shorter basal lip-claw, and the differently proportioned and more strongly projecting basal callus, the surrounding depressed area often almost black-green. Fls. varying in size to more than 5″ across. Spring–summer. (I, H) Costa Rica; Panama.

C. Haagii B.-R. (*Cycnoches versicolor* Rchb.f.) § *Eu-Cycnoches*. Fls. about 2¼″ across, in arching or pendulous racs. to 8″ long, the staminate ones yellowish-green with a white or pale rose lip irregularly spotted with red-brown. Col. green, densely spotted with red-purple on the lower half. Summer. (H) Brazil.

C. Lehmanni Rchb.f. (*Lueddemannia Lehmanni* Rchb.f.) § *Eu-Cycnoches*. Staminate fls. about 5″ across, yellow-green, the apex of the basal callus elongate, tongue-shaped, conspicuously projecting. Summer. (I, H) Ecuador.

C. Loddigesii Ldl. (*Cycnoches cucullata* Ldl.) § *Eu-Cycnoches*. Staminate fls. to 5″ long, 9 or more in an arching or pendulous rac., the ss. greenish-brown blotched with brown, the ps. greenish-brown. Lip fleshy, varying from white to pale pink, or with the apical half yellowish, with sparse reddish spots, apparently without a basal callus. Autumn–early winter. (H) British Guiana; Suriname; Brazil; Venezuela; Colombia.

C. maculatum Ldl. § *Heteranthae*. Staminate fls. 5–7 in a pendulous rac., to 3¼″ across, the ss. and ps. yellowish heavily spotted with reddish-brown. Lip white spotted with reddish-brown. Col. with the apex dilated, heavily red- or purple-spotted. Autumn. (I, H) Venezuela.

CYMBIDIELLA Rolfe
(*Caloglossum* Schltr.)

Three species of *Cymbidiella* are known to science, all of them rare and very remarkable epiphytic or terrestrial orchids, endemic to the island of Madagascar. Customarily known in horticulture as Cymbidiums, these plants are, to be sure, allies of that group, but are closer in their affinity to *Eulophiella* Rolfe. Robust orchids with typically creeping elongate rhizomes, the long pseudobulbs bear a fountain of mostly narrow foliage, and basal sheathed racemes or panicles of a few to rather numerous large and highly spectacular flowers. Opening widely, these blossoms last in perfection for some time, and are among the showiest of any produced in the subtribe *Cymbidiinae*. In their native haunts, the Cymbidiellas exhibit a marked predilection for particular 'host' plants, *C. rhodochila* (Rolfe) Rolfe being almost invariably found growing upon the masses of one of the 'Stag-Horn' ferns (*Platycerium* sp.), which in turn grows as an epiphyte, mostly on tall trees of *Albizia fastigiata*; *C. Humblotii* (Rolfe) Rolfe apparently grows only on the upper parts of the stems of the palm, *Raphia Ruffia*; the third member of the genus, *C. flabellata* (Thou.) Rolfe, is generally a terrestrial in boggy spots along rivers and streams. Today extremely rare in our collections, the Cymbidiellas have been sporadically grown for some time, and should be more widely known by enthusiasts, for their spectacular appearance.

As yet, despite the attempts of several breeders, no hybrids have been produced which utilize these orchids. From casual experimentation, it seems rather evident that the Cymbidiellas are not genetically compatible with true *Cymbidium*, although it is possible that a suitable 'connecting link' may be found elsewhere in the subtribe, possibly *Eulophiella* Rolfe. Interspecific breeding within *Cymbidiella* seems to offer some fascinating potentialities, and should be attempted.

CULTURE: Although the Cymbidiellas are not in general difficult plants to grow, under our conditions, rather special attention must be paid to their wants, for any degree of success to be attained. The two epiphytic species, *C. rhodochila* and *C. Humblotii*, do best when grown in hanging pots or baskets, these perfectly-drained and rather tightly filled with osmunda, or a mixture of shredded tree-fern fibre and medium tree-fern chunks. *C. flabellata*, which customarily grows as a terrestrial, thrives under conditions such as those afforded the tropical species of *Phaius*. All three plants need constantly hot, humid temperatures, with copious water given at the roots throughout the year; it follows, perforce, that adequate drainage of the compost is extremely important. They need a semi-shaded spot for best results (the rather heavy foliage is very susceptible to sunburn), and benefit by frequent applications of fertilizing materials. Repotting and/or division should be done only when absolutely necessary, as the Cym-

bidiellas are very intolerant of being disturbed, and often require several years to become sufficiently re-established to flower again. (H)

C. flabellata (Thou.) Rolfe (*Limodorum flabellatum* Thou., *Cymbidium flabellatum* Spreng., *Caloglossum flabellatum* Schltr., *Cymbidiella Perrieri* Schltr.)
Rhiz. elongate, creeping. Pbs. borne at intervals of up to 4″, ovoid-cylindric, rather narrow, the nodes furnished with persistent remains of lf.-bases. Lvs. 6–8, narrowly ligulate-lorate, acute, rather heavily leathery, strongly veined, to almost 2′ long and ¾″ broad, gracefully arching. Infls. to almost 4′ tall, long-peduncled, bearing about 10–15 large fls. in a customarily branched panicle. Fls. to 2″ long, long-lived, rather heavy-textured, the ss. and ps. yellow-green, the ps. sometimes with a few protruding red spots, the lip spotted and bordered with bright red. Lip 3-lbd., the small lat. lbs. erect, obtuse, the large midlb. obovate-flabellate, incised and vaguely 2-lbd. at apex, the margins strongly undulate-crisped. Autumn–winter. (H) Madagascar.

C. Humblotii (Rolfe) Rolfe (*Cymbidium Humblotii* Rolfe, *Caloglossum Humblotii* Schltr., *Caloglossum magnificum* Schltr.)
Pbs. usually few in number, clustered, cylindric-ovoid, narrowing gradually from base to apex, to about 12″ tall. Lvs. very numerous (up to 40 per pb.), arranged in a large, graceful fan, lorate-lanceolate, the upper ones to 2′ long and 2″ broad, rather heavy-textured. Infls. erect, the peduncle sheathed, to about 3′ tall, the many-fld. panicle profusely branched. Fls. long-lasting, to 3″ long, the ss. and ps. yellow-green, unspotted, the large lip yellow-green with a wide border of black-purple, and some median spotting of the same hue. Winter, mostly Dec.–Jan. (H) Madagascar.

C. rhodochila (Rolfe) Rolfe (*Cymbidium rhodochilum* Rolfe)
Pbs. clustered, oblong-conoidal, to about 5″ tall, becoming dark purple with age. Lvs. distichously arranged, usually about 5–10 in number, lorate, acutish, dark green, to about 3½′ long and 2″ broad. Infls. borne from base of matured pbs., erect, sheathed, to about 3½′ tall, usually a simple rac. with 20 or more fls. Fls. long-lasting, heavy-textured, to 4″ in diam. (often slightly smaller), the reflexed ss. pale or yellowish-green, the rather erect ps. pale-green or yellowish-green with a number of large dark olive-green blotches; lip 3-lbd., the lat. lbs. coloured like the ps., the large midlb. glossy crimson, with a yellow stripe down the middle, this spotted with olive-green. Mostly Nov.–Dec. (H) Madagascar.

CYMBIDIUM Sw.
(*Iridorchis* Bl., *Jensoa* Raf.)

Cymbidium is today one of the best-known and most widely popular of all of the myriad genera of the Orchidaceae. It consists of only about seventy species, but from these (or at least from a few of these) have been derived a positively incredible series of artificially-produced hybrids, these now numbering well into the thousands! The principal aggregation of the subtribe

Cymbidiinae, Cymbidium contains highly variable plants which are variously terrestrial, lithophytic, or epiphytic in habit. They range from Korea, Japan, and China throughout the Himalayas, Formosa, the Philippines, and South-east Asia to New Guinea and Australia. Even though almost all of them are of attractive—and often spectacular—appearance, but a remarkably small percentage of the known species have as yet been introduced into our collections. The Himalayan and Burmese members of the genus have long been popular with orchidists, but it is only within the past decade or so that the many Japanese, Chinese, Formosan, and Indonesian Cymbidiums have come to the attention of connoisseurs. Largely pseudobulbous plants, they bear thin-textured or notably leathery foliage, often of pretty structure, and pendulous to arching or erect racemes of one to very many small, medium-sized, or very large flowers. Floral shape is rather diversified in *Cymbidium*, as is also coloration, although green, yellow, brown, and pinkish perhaps prevail as hues. These fine orchids are among the most widely grown of any members of the family in contemporary collections; they are raised on a commercial scale in many parts of the world, both for sale as plants, and for the production of cut-flowers, the handsome blossoms being widely utilized in the preparation of corsages, ornamental bouquets, etc.

As noted before, several thousand hybrids have thus far been produced (mostly by man—although there are a few natural crosses on record), through interspecific breeding within *Cymbidium*. The genus has also been crossed successfully with *Phaius* (= *Phaiocymbidium*), with *Grammatophyllum* (= *Grammatocymbidium*), and with *Cyperorchis* (= *Cyperocymbidium*). Considerable additional experimental breeding yet remains to be attempted, with allied—and supposedly allied—genera of the *Cymbidiinae, Phaiinae*, etc.

CULTURE: Volumes have been written through the years regarding the cultural requirements of Cymbidiums. There is, in fact, even a periodical (the *Cymbidium Society News*), appearing at frequent intervals, which is almost entirely devoted to this aspect of the genus. Because of this wealth of often contradictory information, it is rather difficult to concisely indicate basic cultural needs for the genus; the present discussion will, therefore, be a brief résumé of the most generally accepted methods utilized by experts who specialize in these plants. The vast majority of Cymbidiums grown today are treated as semi-terrestrials, whether they adopt that habit in the wild or not. For the most part robust, copiously-rooting plants, they need proportionately large, well-drained pots for best results. A multitude of composts have been proposed through the years, but in general these are porous, rapid-draining mixtures consisting of approximately equal parts of such materials as fibrous loam, chopped tree-fern fibre (or osmunda), chopped sphagnum moss, gritty white sand (or turkey grit), and possibly also dust-free bark preparation. The addition of manure or other fertilizing material to the compost is often advocated, and since these orchids are very heavy feeders, can certainly do no harm; additional accessory feeding, at frequent intervals, is strongly recommended for robust vegetative

growth and strong floral production. While in active growth, Cymbidiums require large amounts of water at the roots, and reasonably high humidity, but upon the maturation of the new pseudobulbs, a strict rest-period —often of several weeks' duration—should be given to assure proper development of the inflorescences, which arise from the bases of the mature pseudobulbs in most instances. During this rest-period, only enough water is given the plants to avoid undue shrivelling of the pseudobulbs or foliage. A rather brightly sunny situation in the collection suits most Cymbidiums well, although caution should always be exercised that the leaves do not become sunburned. Certain of the tropical species (e.g., *C. Finlaysonianum, C. simulans*, etc.) have strongly pendulous inflorescences, hence should be kept in hanging pots or slatted baskets, either in a compost such as the one suggested above, or in tightly-packed straight osmunda fibre. Temperature requirements fluctuate considerably within this genus, the majority of the large, showy, contemporary hybrids (and many of the species as well) requiring relatively cool conditions, while others (such as those from Formosa) need intermediate temperatures, and the Indonesian and Australian species need warm temperatures. Repotting and/or division of Cymbidiums should be done whenever needed; many growers successfully split their specimens into single pseudobulbs from time to time, thus materially augmenting their stock; such single-bulb propagations usually require about two to four years to flower, under ideal conditions, after division. (C, I, H)

C. Devonianum Paxt.

Pbs. almost obsolete, in old specimens usually hidden by persistent lf.-bases. Lvs. about 3–5 per growth, broadly lorate-lanceolate, rather obtuse, narrowed below into a grooved petiole about ¼ as long as the blade, 7–14″ long, rather heavily leathery. Infls. sharply pendulous, stout, to more than 12″ long, densely many-fld., the peduncle basally with a few brown boat-shaped bracts. Fls. heavy-textured, long-lasting, 1–1½″ in diam., rather variable in colour, the ss. and ps. similar, ovate-lanceolate, olive-green spotted with purple, or buff-yellow streaked with wine-purple, the ps. usually shorter and more acute than the ss. Lip shorter than the other segms., vaguely lobed, broadly ovate or subcordate, the lamina reflexed, dark sanguine-purple, or sometimes pale rose-purple with a darker area near each lateral margin. Col. curved, with two small rounded wings near apex, greenish-yellow, usually with some red apical spots. May–July. (C, I) Himalayas; Khasia Hills.

C. eburneum Ldl. (*Cymbidium syringodorum* Griff.)

Pbs. rather obscure and usually hidden by the long-persistent lf.-bases, clustered. Lvs. about 9–15 per growth, narrowly linear, acute, not very heavy-textured, to 2′ long and ½″ broad. Infls. about 12″ tall, erect, prominently sheathed, usually 1–2-fld. Fls. waxy, very fragrant, long-lasting, to 3″ in diam., ivory-white, the lip with some additional colour. Ss. and somewhat narrower ps. similar, oblong or ovate-oblong, acute, the dors. sep. concave and apiculate, the ps. often subfalcate. Lip broadly ovate-oblong, 3-lbd., the lat. lbs. incurved towards the col., ivory-white, the midlb.

crisped and undulate marginally, ivory-white, often with scattered purple or magenta-purple spots and dots around the yellow disc; crest an oblong, fleshy, grooved, pubescent, yellow plate, thickened at the apex, with 3 raised lines extending the entire length. Col. clavate, 3-angled, with 2 narrow wings, white above, concave in front, stained with purple. Mostly Apr.–May. (C, I) Himalayas: Sikkim; Khasia Hills; Burma.

—var. **Parishii** (Rchb.f.) Hk.f. (*Cymbidium Parishii* Rchb.f.)

Essentially without pbs. Lvs. broader and shorter than the typical form of the sp. (to about 1½' long and 1" broad), striated, distichously imbricating at base. Infl. rather short, erect, usually about 3-fld. Fls. very fragrant, to about 3" in diam., the ss. and ps. ivory-white, almost equal. Lip 3-lbd., very broad, quadrate-retuse, undulate and crisped marginally, the disc orange-yellow spotted with purple, the marginal area on each side also purple-spotted. The lip-callus does not have the velvety line characteristic of the species. Spring. (C, I) Burma.

C. erythrostylum Rolfe

Pbs. clustered, oval-oblong, to about 2" long or more. Lvs. rather few in number, to about 15" long and ¾" wide, linear, acute, rather thin-textured. Infls. erect or arching outward, sheathed, to almost 2' long, loosely 4–7-fld. Fls. to almost 4½" long, the spreading ss. white, the ps. thrust forward over the col. and lip, white usually with some purple or violet-purple dots arranged in lines towards the middle base. Lip 3-lbd., shorter than the ps., heavily marked and lined with dark crimson-purple on a yellow ground, the lat. lbs. enfolding the col., the midlb. proportionately small, only slightly reflexed apically. Col. short, dark red-violet. Later summer–autumn. (I) Viet-Nam.

C. Finlaysonianum Ldl. (*Cymbidium aloifolium* Ldl., *C. pendulum* Bl., *C. tricolor* Miq., *C. Wallichii* Ldl.)

A robust epiphytic sp., with short, stout sts., scarcely pseudobulbous. Lvs. very thick and rigidly leathery, ensiform, obtuse and retuse apically, furrowed, 2–3¼' long, to 2" broad. Infls. racemose, very long, 2–4½' long, sharply pendulous, rather loosely many-fld. Fls. to 1½" in diam., the rather heavy-textured ss. and ps. dull yellowish-green tinted with olive, subequal. Lip 3-lbd., not saccate, the lat. lbs. rose streaked with wine-purple, the midlb. white, wine-purple-marked at apical notch, basally dark yellow, the two parallel basal lamellae amber-yellow. Col. reddish, with an amber-yellow anther. Spring–summer. (I, H) Burma; Laos; Cambodia; Viet-Nam; Thailand; Malay Peninsula; Philippines; Sumatra; Java; Borneo; Celebes.

C. giganteum Ldl. (*Iridorchis gigantea* Bl.)

Pbs. clustered, rather ovoid, somewhat compressed, 4–6" long. Lvs. linear-ligulate, acute, to 3' long, convolute into a tube and yellowish to 3–4" from the base, distinctly keeled on the underside. Infls. stout, as long as or longer than the lvs., furnished below with brown, membranous, rather large bracts, bearing 7–12 fls. in an apical rac. Fls. rather distant, 3–4" in diam., lasting rather well, faintly fragrant, the ss. and ps. light yellow-green striped longitudinally with red, the former

oblong, acute, the latter narrower, linear-oblong, acute, subfalcate. Lip 3-lbd., oblong, the lat. lbs. erect, coloured like the ss. and ps., the midlb. fuzzy above, reflexed, with undulate, ciliate margins, yellow more or less densely spotted with red, the disc with 2 ciliated lamellae that are confluent at their apices. Col. clavate, arched, terete, pale yellow above, concave and streaked with dull red below the stigmatic surface. Autumn, especially Sept.–Oct. (C, I) Himalayas, from Nepal to Bhutan and the Khasia Hills and Sikkim.

C. grandiflorum Griff. (*Cymbidium Hookerianum* Rchb.f.)

Rather similar in habit to *C. giganteum* Ldl. Lvs. usually about 2' long or slightly more, ligulate, acute, dilated below into ribbed and grooved sheaths which are striated with two shades of green. Infls. very stout, sheathed below, to more than 2½' long, with a usually nodding, 7–12-fld. apical rac. Fls. to 5" in diam., fragrant, long-lasting, the similar and subequal ss. and ps. green, oblong, acute, the ps. usually slightly the narrower. Lip 3-lbd., triangular, acute, ciliolate on the margins, light yellow with lines of red-purple dots on the inner side, the cordate midlb. crisped and fringed marginally, yellow spotted with red-purple, the basal lamellae paired, ciliate, rather elongate. Col. terete and green above, spotted with red below the stigmatic surface. Early winter, mostly Nov. (C, I) Nepal; Sikkim; Bhutan.

C. insigne Rolfe (*Cymbidium Sanderi* hort. Sand.)

Rather similar in habit to *C. erythrostylum* Rolfe. Lvs. linear-oblong, to 3' long and usually less than ½" broad. Infls. sheathed, usually erect, to almost 4' tall, with about 8–12 rather loosely-arranged fls. at apex. Fls. spreading, about 3½" in diam., the oblong ss. and ps. pale rose-red, often with darker median basal streaks. Lip 3-lbd., rose-red, more or less densely spotted and marked with dark purple-red, the lat. lbs. erect at the sides of the col., the disc with a pair of obtuse, bright yellow lamellae. Spring, especially Mar.–May. (I) Viet-Nam, usually as a terrestrial.

C. Lowianum (Rchb.f.) Rchb.f. (*Cymbidium giganteum* Ldl. var. *Lowianum* Rchb.f.)

Rather similar in habit to *C. giganteum* Ldl. Infls. stout, arching, to about 3' long, with a rac. of 15–25 fls. at the apex. Fls. about 3–4" across, fragrant or not, long-lasting, the ss. and ps. similar, greenish-yellow with more or less prominent reddish veins, oblong-lanceolate, acute, the ss. vaguely keeled behind, the ps. slightly the narrower. Lip 3-lbd., the erect lat. lbs. roundish-oblong, pale buff-yellow, the midlb. deltoid, reflexed, the margins slightly undulate, velvety-pubescent, dark red-crimson with a pale buff-yellow edge, white towards the base, the disc with 2 lamellae that converge towards their apices. Col. vaguely triangular, arching, concave below the stigmatic surface, yellow spotted with red. Late winter–spring. (C, I) Khasia Hills; Burma.

C. Tracyanum Rolfe

Rather similar in habit to *C. giganteum* Ldl. Infls. 3–4' long, arching or sometimes almost erect, the rather dense rac. usually about 15–20-fld. Fls. 4–5" in diam., the ss. and ps. greenish-yellow with longitudinal lines of red-crimson dots and streaks, the ss. oblong, acute, the ps. similar but considerably narrower. Lip 3-lbd., the erect lat. lbs. roundish-oblong, light yellow, obliquely striated with red-crimson, the midlb. broadly oblong, reflexed, crisped and somewhat fringed marginally, cream-white spotted with red-crimson. Col. greenish spotted with red. Autumn, mostly Oct.–Nov. (I) Burma.

C. **Aliciae** Quis. Pl. stemless, terrestrial, erect. Lvs. 8–10 in number, tufted, subcoriaceous, pale green, curving, elongate, linear, channelled at base, tapering to the acute apex, to 2' long and ½" wide. Infls. erect, few-fld., to 8" tall. Fls. slightly fragrant, to 2" long, the ss. and ps. greenish-yellow except the tips of the ss., which have a very slight tinge of purple. Lip 3-lbd., the erect lat. lbs. wine-purple, the midlb. white with a few blotches of pale wine-purple, the basal lamellae vivid yellow. Col. and anther dull green-yellow. Summer. (I) Philippines: Luzon.

C. aloifolium (L.) Sw. (*Epidendrum aloifolium* L., *Aërides Borassi* Smith, *Cymbidium crassifolium* Wall., *Cymbidium Mannii* Rchb.f.) Virtually without pbs., often confused with the group of spp. around *C. pendulum* (Roxb.) Sw., etc. Lvs. very fleshy, rather rigid, linear to linear-ligulate, obtuse, 12–18" long. Infls. sharply pendulous, to 2½' long, loosely many-fld. Fls. spreading, to about 1¾" across, the ss. and ps. pale brownish-yellow, ligulate. Lip 3-lbd., reddish-brown with a white-margined midlb. which has a pale yellow centre and with 2 obtuse lamellae extending from the base to the bottom of the midlb. Summer–autumn. (H) Ceylon; Peninsular India.

C. canaliculatum R.Br. Pbs. clustered, often almost ovoid, 1–3" long. Lvs. dull green, rigid and rather thick, deeply channelled above, linear to linear-lanceolate, acute, 12–18" long, to 1¼" wide. Infls. often rather numerous per growth, densely many-fld., to 1½' long. Fls. rather waxy, to 1½" in diam., highly variable in colour, the equal ss. and ps. lanceolate, spreading, brown or green outside, inside dull or golden-green usually heavily blotched, flaked, or spotted with purplish-brown or red. Lip white with small purple or red markings, somewhat variable in shape, but usually ovate-lanceolate, with an acute apex, the lat. lbs. small but very distinct. Col. about half as long as the lip, stout, slightly incurved. Spring. (I, H) Australia.

C. chloranthum Ldl. (*Cymbidium sanguinolentum* Teijsm. & Binn.) Pbs. small, clustered. Lvs. usually about 6 in number, rather thin-textured, ensiform, curving, to 15" long and more than 1" wide, the tips rounded, folded along midrib near base. Infl. rather stout, erect, to 15" tall, with about 15–20 fls. disposed along upper half. Fls. about 2" in diam., pale green, turning to light crimson after pollination, the ss. and narrower ps. spreading, oblong, obtuse. Lip 3-lbd., the erect rounded lat. lbs. shorter than the col., more or less spotted with purple on a green ground, short-hairy inside, the broad midlb. curved down but the tip not reflexed, notched, greenish medially, the margins white, with a few purple spots. Col. semiterete, pale greenish or yellowish stained or spotted with purple or red. Summer. (H) Malay Peninsula; Sumatra; Java; Borneo.

C. Dayanum Rchb.f. (*Cymbidium acutum* Ridl., *C. eburneum* Ldl. var. *Dayanum* Hk.f., *C. Simonsianum* King & Pantl.) Pl. terrestrial, without pbs., grass-like. Lvs. 5–6 per growth, tufted, subcoriaceous, pale green, elongate-linear, stalkless, channelled towards the base, acute and suboblique at apex, to 2¾' long and ½" broad. Infls. erect, usually about 10-fld., to about 9" long, furnished with purplish-pink or white sheaths.

Fls. fragrant, to 1¾" in diam., the ss. and ps. white with a crimson central line which does not extend to their apices. Lip rich red-purple with oblique white and whitish-yellow lines on the erect lat. lbs., the midlb. turned under, with a broad central basal yellow area, the lamellae continuous, thickened at tips, yellow or white. Col. blackish red-purple, with a sulphur-yellow anther. Summer. (I, H) Sikkim and Assam south to Malay Peninsula, and Sumatra, east to Celebes and Philippines.

C. ensifolium (L.) Sw. (*Epidendrum ensifolium* L., *Cymbidium micans* Schau., *C. sinense* Willd., *C. xiphiifolium* Ldl.) Without pbs., the grass-like lvs. few in tufts, linear, acutish, to about 12" long and usually less than ½" broad. Infls. erect, to 12" tall, about 3–7-fld. Fls. fragrant, lasting rather well, to 2" long or more, highly variable in colour, usually the ss. and shorter ps. pale green, often with 5 lines of red, especially on the spreading ss. Lip broadly ligulate, obtuse, pale green or greenish-yellow with or without red veins on the lat. lbs. and some similarly-coloured spots on the midlb. Usually spring, especially May–June. (C, I) China and Japan southward through Indochina to Sumatra and Java.

C. Forrestii Rolfe. Pbs. absent. Lvs. tufted, usually 6–7 in number, narrowly linear, acutish, minutely denticulate, 12–15" long, usually under ½" broad. Infls. with a few sheaths, 6–9" long, erect or arching, 1–2-fld. Fls. about 1½" in diam., green or yellowish-green, often with some white markings on the lip, very fragrant and lasting rather well. Ss. and ps. spreading, oblong, rather blunt. Lip 3-lbd., the lat. lbs. suborbicular, rounded at tip, the midlb. suborbicular, undulate marginally, concave. Mostly Feb.–Mar. (C, I) China: Yunnan, at moderately high elevations.

C. Gonzalesii Quis. Pbs. produced in old specimens only, ovoid, approximate, rather small. Lvs. persistent for some time, erect, somewhat leathery, dark green, narrowly linear, acute, to 14" long and about ½" broad. Infls. few-fld., erect, to about 9" tall. Fls. odourless, to 1½" across, the somewhat spreading ss. and ps. light yellowish-green, flushed at tips with greenish-yellow and lined with maroon. Lip almost white, washed with very pale yellow, the lbs. barred or spotted with red-purple, the basal part citron-yellow, the lamellae vivid yellow. Col. citron-yellow. Summer. (I) Philippines: Luzon.

C. lancifolium Hk. (*Cymbidium Gibsoni* Paxt.) Pbs. st.-like, cylindric or fusiform, to about 5" tall, basally covered with thin sheaths. Lvs. 3–5, borne near apex of pbs., with a stalk about 2½" long, the blade rather tough but thin, elliptic, acute, to about 8" long and 1¾" wide. Infls. erect, to more than 12" long, usually with about 5–6 rather distant fls. Fls. fragrant, rather long-lasting, about 2" long or more, the short-pointed ss. pale green, the shorter ps. pale green with broken purple median line and some scattered purple spots. Lip white, the low rounded lat. lbs. shorter than the col., with purple edges and markings, the broad midlb. apically down-curved, with transverse purple marks near the base and 2 longitudinal ones near the tip, the lamellae paired, very short, fleshy, basal. Col. greenish marked with purple. Spring–early summer. (I, H) India to Japan, southward to Malaya and Java.

C. madidum Ldl. (*Cymbidium iridifolium* Cunn., *C. albuciflorum* FvM.) Sts. stout and short, forming with the lf.-bases rather distinct pbs. with age. Lvs. more flaccid than those of the somewhat similar *C. canaliculatum* R.Br., shining-green, not deeply channelled, to 2' long. Infls. 1–2' long, mostly rather pendulous or down-arching, loosely few- to rather many-fld. Fls. fleshy-textured, to 1" in diam., brownish on outside, inside usually olive-green, fragrant. Lip with very small lat. lbs. and a large, very obtuse, yellowish midlb., the lamina with a glossy glandular-sticky median line. Col. truncate, angular in front. Winter, mostly Nov.–Dec. (I, H) Australia.

C. pendulum (Roxb.) Sw. (*Epidendrum pendulum* Roxb., *Cymbidium aloifolium* Hk.f.) Pl. eventually forming vague pbs. 2–3″ long, these clustered, sheathed by the bases of the lowermost lvs. Lvs. broadly linear, distichous, equitant at base, 12–20″ long or more, very fleshy and rigid, suberect, obliquely 2-lbd. at apex. Infls. shorter than the lvs., pendulous or strongly down-curving, many-fld. Fls. 1½–2″ in diam., the ss. and ps. light yellow with a wine-purple median stripe, this often striated or broken up into irregular streaks, narrowly oblong, acute, the ps. somewhat shorter and more acute than the ss. Lip elliptic-oblong, obscurely 3-lbd., dark plum-purple with pale yellow longitudinal lines, the lat. lbs. narrow, erect, the midlb. small, almost square, reflexed, the lamellae paired, bilobed, yellow, basal. Col. wine-purple, with a yellow anther. Summer, mostly June–July. (I, H) Southern China and the Himalayas (from Nepal to Sikkim and Assam), southwards to Burma, Thailand, and the Andaman Islands.

C. pubescens Ldl. Similar in habit to *C. Finlaysonianum* Ldl., but the lvs. to only about 1½′ long and ½″ broad, the sheath below its joint to 3″ (instead of to 5½″). Infls. pendulous, usually under 10″ long, many-fld. Fls. to about 1½″ long, the ss. and ps. pale greenish or buff, medially with a broad dark purple stripe. Lip short-hairy at inner base, the lat. lbs. with free ends shorter than the col., pale yellowish with numerous purple-brown spots, midlb. with apex recurved, pale yellow marked with purple, the lamellae yellow, interrupted in the middle, the basal parts curving. Col. dark purple on back, in front pale yellow with purple spots. Summer, especially July. (H) Malay Peninsula; Sumatra; Java; Borneo.

C. pumilum Rolfe Pbs. clustered, small, about 1″ tall, ovoid. Lvs. usually 3–5 in number, elongate-linear, rather curving, acutish, 6–12″ long. Infls. suberect, furnished with a few lanceolate sheaths near base, rather many-fld., 4–5″ tall. Fls. about 1¼″ in diam., lasting well, somewhat variable in colour, the ss. and ps. usually reddish-brown medially, with yellow margins, the lip white, with some reddish-brown spots on the midlb. and some tiny dots of the same colour on the lat. lbs., the disc bright yellow, with 2 rather vague longitudinal lamellae down the centre. Ss. spreading, oblong, blunt. Ps. narrowly elliptic-oblong, rather incurving towards one another, blunt. Lip suberect, 3-lbd., the lat. lbs. erect, oblong, blunt, the midlb. oblong, blunt, recurved. Autumn, especially Aug.–Sept. (C, I) China; Japan.

C. simulans Rolfe (*Cymbidium aloefolium* Lodd.) Very similar and often confused with *C. pubescens* Ldl., but the lat. lbs. of the lip as long as the col., all of the lobes striped (not spotted), and usually with a longer infl. Summer. (H) Burma; Sumatra; Java.

C. tigrinum Par. Pbs. clustered, ovoid, 1–1½″ long. Lvs. 3–5, rather leathery, oblong-lanceolate, recurving, 3–6″ long. Infls. horizontally ascending to suberect, slender, longer than the longest lvs., usually 3–5-fld., the fls. distant. Fls. to almost 4″ across in largest forms, the ss. and ps. usually olive-green, paler marginally and with some red basal spots, linear-oblong, acute, the ps. occasionally paler and more spotted than the ss. Lip oblong, 3-lbd., the lat. lbs. roundish, erect, yellow striped obliquely with broad red-brown bands, the midlb. almost square, apiculate, reflexed, white with short brown-purple transverse streaks, the lamellae basal, paired, raised, white. Col. clavate, arching, pale olive-green above, spotted below the stigmatic surface with red. Mostly May–June. (I) Burma, especially near Tenasserim, growing almost invariably on rocks.

CYNORKIS Thou.
(*Amphorchis* Thou., *Amphorkis* Thou., *Barlaea* Rchb.f., *Bicornella* Ldl., *Cynorchis* Thou., *Cynosorchis* Thou.)

This is a remarkable genus of more than one hundred and twenty-five species, with the centre of distribution in Madagascar; representatives also occur in tropical Africa, the Comoro Islands, the Mascarenes, and the Seychelles. A member of the complex subtribe *Habenarinae*, *Cynorkis* is very little known in contemporary collections, although it contains a wealth of species admirably suited to cultivation by connoisseurs. Mostly handsome leafy terrestrial plants (a few of the species are epiphytic or lithophytic) they produce often large heads of showy, frequently brightly-coloured flowers of considerable lasting qualities. The group is somewhat allied to *Habenaria* Willd., but differs in technical details of the flowers, particularly in the structure of the rostellum. In this genus the lip is usually much more developed than the other floral segments.

A single artificially-produced hybrid is on record, this being *Cynorkis x kewensis* (*C. Lowiana* × *C. purpurascens*), registered by the Royal Botanic Gardens at Kew in 1903. Some fascinating additional experimental breeding seems possible in this genus.

CULTURE: These orchids are best grown in rather shallow, perfectly-drained pots or pans, filled with a porous compost of shredded osmunda, fibrous loam, gritty sand, and chopped sphagnum moss. Most of the Cynorkis have somewhat tuberous roots, and are at least partially deciduous. Although they require quantities of water while in active growth, when the foliage starts to become yellow and wither, moisture should be virtually stopped. Care must be taken, however, that the compost never dries out completely, or the tubers may become overly desiccated. When the new shoots again appear at the surface, water should be resumed. A semi-shaded spot suits them well, they benefit by periodic applications of weak fertilizer, and warm temperatures should prevail at all times. Should the potting-medium become stale, the plants should be repotted in fresh compost at once, since they are very intolerant of sour conditions at the roots. (I, H)

C. compacta Rchb.f.
Pls. 3–6″ tall, with a solitary elliptic lf. sheathing the base of the infl., which is loosely 4–10-fld. Fls. about ½″ long or less, the ss. and sickle-shaped ps. white, the 3-lbd. lip white spotted with violet-red. Spur short, conical. Spring–summer. (H) Natal.

C. Lowiana Rchb.f.
Pls. 4–8″ tall. Lf. solitary, basal, lanceolate, acute, to 4″ long. Infl. slender, 1-fld. Fls. long-lived, about 1½″ long, the ss. and ps. greenish flushed with rose-red. Lip proportionately large, 4-lbd., carmine-red, with a long spur. Winter–early spring. (H) Madagascar.

C. purpurascens Thou. (*Cynosorchis calanthoides* Krzl., *C. praecox* Schltr., *Gymnadenia purpurascens* A.Rich., *Orchis purpurascens* Sprgl.)
Pls. 10–16″ tall when in fl. Lf. solitary, basal, oblong, to 12″ long and 4″ broad, rather flaccid in texture. Infl. densely 5–25-fld. Fls. about 1½″ long, opening widely,

light violet-red, long-stalked, with a long awl-shaped spur. Summer–autumn. (H) Madagascar; Mascarene Islands.

C. uniflora Ldl. (*Cynosorchis grandiflora* Ridl., *Gymnadenia uniflora* Steud.)

Pls. 8–10″ tall. Lvs. 2, basal, linear, to 7″ long. Infl. 1-fld., with several lf.-like sheaths at the nodes. Fls. fragrant, about 1½″ long, yellow-green spotted with red, the ss. and ps. forming a hood, the lip 4-lbd., proportionately large, with an awl-shaped, very long spur. Summer–early autumn. (H) Madagascar.

CYPEROCYMBIDIUM A.D.Hawkes

One *Cyperocymbidium* is known to date, this a rarely cultivated bigeneric natural hybrid from Sikkim. It has been known as a *Cymbidium* in the past, but with the recognition of *Cyperorchis* Bl. as a valid genus, its true complex identity becomes recognized. It is a notably showy plant when in full flower, rather more like the *Cyperorchis* parent than the other, and should be more widely appreciated by the connoisseur collector.

Insofar as we are aware, only one hybrid in which *Cyperocymbidium x Gammieanum* figures has as yet been registered. This, of course, becomes a *Cyperocymbidium*, under our accepted nomenclatural rules, rather than true *Cymbidium*. Additional experimental breeding should prove unusually interesting.

CULTURE: As for the 'cool-growing' species of *Cymbidium*. The plant occurs, mostly as an epiphyte, at elevations of 5000 to 7000 feet. (C)

C. x Gammieanum (King & Pantl.) A.D.Hawkes (*Cymbidium Gammieanum* King & Pantl.)

A natural hybrid between *Cyperorchis elegans* Bl. and *Cymbidium longifolium* D.Don, rather like the former in vegetative appearance. Lvs. narrowly linear, acuminate, somewhat dilated at equitant base, 2–3′ long, about ¾″ broad. Infl. from base of pseudo-stem, decurved, shorter than foliage, loosely sheathed upwards, with a loose or dense, 15–20-fld. apical rac. Fls. bell-shaped, usually nodding, 1¾″ long and 2–3″ across when expanded, pale yellow or dull yellow flushed with brown and with brown lines. Lip 3-lbd., about as long as the ss., yellow, the lat. lbs. small, acute, lined with brown, midlb. almost orbicular, undulate, puberulous, separated from lat. lbs. by a sinus; lamellae 2, pubescent, meeting and ending abruptly with the lat. lbs. opposite the ciliolate sinus, otherwise parallel. Col. slender, slightly winged. Mostly Sept.–Oct. (C) Sikkim, where it is rather common.

CYPERORCHIS Bl.

This is a genus of about six species of rather infrequently-seen epiphytic, lithophytic, or terrestrial orchids in the Himalayas, South-east Asia and Malaya, and in Indonesia, which are usually included in *Cymbidium* Sw., though they are distinct in floral structure and in the fact that the blossoms are bell-shaped and produced (generally) in very dense racemes or head-like clusters. Vegetatively the members of this genus simulate many Cymbidiums. The flowers are often extremely showy and produced in considerable quantities.

Both *Cyperorchis elegans* Bl. and *C. Mastersii* (Griff.) Bth. have to date been crossed with members of *Cymbidium*, to give some unusually interesting and attractive hybrids, including at least one produced by natural agents in the wild. I have proposed the name *Cyperocymbidium* to accommodate these.

CULTURE: As for *Cymbidium*. (C, I, H)

C. elegans Bl. (*Limodorum cyperifolium* Buch.-Ham., *Cymbidium elegans* Ldl.)

Pbs. absent. Lvs. clustered, gracefully arching, leathery, linear, acute, to 2′ long and ¾″ wide. Infls. arching to pendulous, produced from the lower lf.-axils, to 2′ long, very densely many-fld. Fls. opening only at the tips, about 1½″ long, pale tawny-yellow, the midlb. of the lip typically spotted with blood-red. Ss. and ps. ligulate, acute, the tips sometimes reflexed or spreading. Lip 3-lbd., the basal part long and narrow, the midlb. roundish, much shorter than the basal clawed part. Autumn. (C, I) Himalayas: Nepal, Bhutan, Sikkim.

C. Mastersii (Griff.) Bth. (*Cymbidium Mastersii* Griff., *Cymbidium micromeron* Ldl.)

Pbs. absent. Lvs. tufted, distichous, linear or ensiform, acute, rather leathery, gracefully arching, to 2½′ long and ¾″ wide. Infls. erect, 4–10-fld., sheathed, to 12″ tall. Fls. not opening widely, about 2″ long, fragrant of almonds, white, the disc of the lip yellow with red-purple spots, the markings usually continuing onto the round midlb. Ss. and ps. ligulate, obtuse. Lip 3-lbd., not as long as the ps. Autumn–winter. (C, I) Himalayas.

C. cochlearis (Ldl.) Bth. (*Cymbidium cochleare* Ldl.) Pbs. absent. Lvs. linear, tufted, distichous, to 3′ long and ½″ wide, gracefully arching. Infls. arching to almost pendulous, to about 2′ long, loosely rather many-fld. Fls. 2″ long, the ps. reflexed, the ss. forming an open tube, all brownish-green, the lip with a golden-yellow midlb., the lat. lbs. paler yellow, more or less spotted with red. Ss. and ps. linear, acutish. Lip 3-lbd., the lat. lbs. small, the midlb. roundish, with a 2-parted median callus. Autumn. (C, I) Himalayas.

C. rosea (J.J.Sm.) Schltr. (*Cymbidium roseum* J.J.Sm.) Pbs. small, clustered. Lvs. 8 or more, linear, apically obliquely pointed, to 12″ long and ¾″ wide. Infls. erect, usually 3-fld., about 12″ long. Fls. about 2½″ across, white becoming pink-tinged with age, the lip with 2 orange-yellow keels on the disc, the erect, blunt lat. lbs. with irregular spots and streaks of purple, the shortly fuzzy, concave midlb. yellow at base, otherwise white with scattered purple spots. Ss. and ps. forming a hollow cone at base, the apical halves widely flaring, the ps. slightly the narrower. Autumn. (I, H) Malay Peninsula; Sumatra; Java.

CYPHOCHILUS Schltr.

Seven epiphytic members make up the very rare and little-known genus *Cyphochilus*, all of them endemic to the forests of New Guinea. None of them is present in contemporary collections, and the group is not completely understood by orchidologists. It is a member of the subtribe *Glomerinae*, although the plants much resemble *Appendicula* Bl., of the subtribe *Podochilinae*.

Nothing is known of the genetic affinities of *Cyphochilus*.

CULTURE: Presumably as for *Appendicula*. (I, H)

Va   *Epigeneium amplum* (Ldl.) Summerh.   [H.R.FOLKERSMA]

Vb   *Laelia harpophylla* Rchb.f.   [H.R.FOLKERSMA]

CYPRIPEDIUM L.
(Arietinum Beck, *Calceolus* Adans., *Corisanthes* Steud., *Criosanthes* Raf., *Fissipes* Small, *Hypodema* Rchb., *Sacodon* Raf.)*

This genus contains the true temperate-zone (with a very few subtropical species) 'Lady's-Slippers'. The name *Cypripedium*, unfortunately, is much more commonly applied in horticultural circles to the tropical Asiatic species, which are in reality known correctly as Paphiopedilums. To further compound the confusion connected with this generic epithet, it is also often used in reference to *Phragmipedium* Rolfe (the members of which, in turn, may be even more confusedly known as Selenipediums, which they are not!). The true Cypripediums number about fifty species, and are widespread in the North Temperate Zone, with a few outlying representatives extending into warmer areas, such as Mexico, Guatemala, parts of the tropical Himalayas, etc. They are considered—together with the three other genera comprising the subtribe *Cypripedilinae* (*Paphiopedilum* Pfitz., *Phragmipedium* Rolfe, and *Selenipedium* Rchb.f.)—to be the most primitive of orchids, and represent a section isolated from the rest of the Orchidaceae, without any intermediate or connecting links surviving in modern times. In the past, several authorities have suggested that the *Cypripedium* group could well form a distinct family, because of its aberrant floral structure (the two fertile stamens are unique, among other characters) and the lack of relatives elsewhere in the Orchidaceae. Cypripediums are commonly terrestrial orchids (very rarely lithophytic or epiphytic on mossy rocks or tree-trunks) with a short or rather elongated rhizome, from which fibrous roots arise, and which produces an erect stem, bearing the sheathing, folded, strongly ribbed leaves and an apical flower or raceme of flowers. These blossoms are usually showy—often very distinctly so—and of various, frequently unusual colour combinations. Basic structure of these flowers is much the same as that found in other genera of the subtribe *Cypripedilinae*, the sepals being spreading, and either all free, or with the lateral pair united to form a synsepal behind the lip. The spreading petals are usually narrower and smaller than the sepals. The stalkless lip is inflated, and sac-shaped or pouch-shaped; usually is of a different hue from the other floral segments. The short column bears a pair of fertile stamens on the sides, hidden by a thick roundish staminode (sterile stamen); the pollen is granular, and the terminal stigma is vaguely 3-lobed. Many members of this genus are present in choice collections today, mostly as valued ornamental plants in the out-of-door garden in temperate areas. Their cultural requirements are usually met with ease, and both their handsome plicate foliage and delightful flowers make them of unique value to orchidists. The magnificent *Cypripedium Reginae* Walt. is the State Flower of Minnesota, U.S.A.

A rather large number of natural hybrids are known in this genus, but no artificially-produced ones seem to be on record. The interesting and provocative possibility that Cypripediums may be genetically compatible with other genera of this alliance has apparently not been explored, although two crosses between *Phragmi-* *pedium* and *Paphiopedilum* are registered. Critical experimental breeding in this genus is to be encouraged.

CULTURE: Generally of rather readily-met cultural requirements, the Cypripediums vary markedly from species to species in individual necessities for treatment. Some of them inhabit swamps or bogs, where they grow in highly acid soils; others are found on dry outcroppings in relatively alkaline soils; and still others are encountered on wooded slopes with comparatively neutral soils. Certain of the North American Cypripediums require highly specialized conditions, and these are generally indicated when the plants are purchased from dealers in native rarities. The European and Asiatic species do well, for the most part, in well-drained pots, filled with a compost consisting of rich leaf-mould, gritty sand, and shredded sphagnum moss. This compost should, ideally, be replenished on an annual basis. While in active growth, all of the Cypripediums delight in copious supplies of water, but as the shoots flower and begin to wither, moisture should be somewhat curtailed, and a definite resting-period given until the new sprouts once again commence to appear at the surface of the compost. Most of these true Cypripediums are perfectly hardy, under normal conditions, in temperate climes, but a few—from the more southerly areas of the genus' range—should be protected against excessively low temperatures. Virtually without exception, all members of this entrancing group of orchids do best in heavy or semi-heavy shade. (C, I)

C. acaule Ait. *(Cypripedium humile* Salisb., *Fissipes acaulis* Small)*
Lvs. 2 (very rarely 3), opposite and sheathing the scape-base, usually broadly elliptic to oblong-elliptic, strongly ribbed, silvery beneath, dark green above, 4–9″ long and 1–5½″ wide. Infl. 1-fld. (very rarely 2-fld.), subtended by a foliaceous bract, to 15″ tall. Fl. nodding, showy, to about 2″ long or more, the ss. and ps. yellowish-green to greenish-brown, often with purple or brown streaks, the lip velvety, crimson-pink to rarely pure white, rose-veined on outer surface. Ss. and ps. down-arching over the lip, the wavy-margined ps. somewhat spreading, the lat. ss. entirely united in a synsepal. Lip an inflated ovoid pouch, fissured in front with the edges folded in and downwards, densely pubescent on the inner surface at the base with the hairs directed forward. Apr.–July. (C, I) Newfoundland west to Alberta and Minnesota, south to Georgia, Tennessee, and Alabama.

C. arietinum R.Br. *(Criosanthes arietina* House)*
Rhiz. slender, giving off a musky odour. St. slender, erect to rather twisted, provided below with several brown tubular sheaths, leafy at or about the middle. Lvs. 3–5, narrowly elliptic to ovate-lanceolate, obtuse to acute, plicate, bluish-green to dark green, 2–4″ long, to 1¼″ wide. Infl. with a rather glandular-pubescent peduncle, the entire st. to about 14″ tall, with a solitary large bract subtending the solitary, nodding fl., which is fragrant and notably short-lived. Fls. about 1″ long or slightly more, the all free ss. and ps. dark purplish-brown or madder-purple, margined or streaked with green, somewhat pubescent on outer surface and margins, the lip whitish or pinkish-white, strongly

netted with crimson or madder-purple. Lip saccate, much inflated at the base, prolonged downward into a blunt conical pouch, with the mouth of the orifice and inner surface along the base of the sac silky-pubescent. May–June. (C, I) Eastern and Central Canada, south to Minnesota and Connecticut; also Western China.

C. Calceolus L. (*Calceolus alternifolius* St.Lager, *Calceolus marianus* Crantz)

Much like the commoner var. *pubescens* (Willd.) Corr., differing in range, the shape of the staminode, and in the size and coloration of the flowers, which are very fragrant. Usually May–July. (C, I) Great Britain across Europe to Siberia, south to the Pyrenees.

—var. **pubescens** (Willd.) Corr. (*Cypripedium pubescens* Willd., *C. flavescens* DC, *C. parviflorum* Salisb., *C. veganum* Cockerell & Barker)

Pl. erect, more or less glandular-pubescent throughout, 4–26″ tall. Lvs. 3–5 (rarely paired), elliptic to ovate or ovate-lanceolate, acute to acuminate, plicate, 2–8″ long, to 4″ wide at middle. Infl. 1–2-fld., each fl. subtended by a large lf.-like bract. Fls. highly variable in size and somewhat so in colour, in largest forms to 6½″ long if dors. sep. is spread out, usually considerably smaller, the ss. and ps, varying from greenish-yellow to madder-purple, the large lip dull cream-colour or rarely whitish to golden-yellow, usually veined or spotted with magenta-purple on the inner surface. Lat. ss. united almost to apex, 2-toothed at tip. Ps. narrow, linear-lanceolate, acuminate, down-thrust, spirally twisted or sometimes flat, to 3½″ long. Lip pouch-shaped or slipper-shaped; staminode bright yellow, spotted with madder-purple. Apr.–Aug. (C, I) Quebec and Newfoundland south to Georgia, west to New Mexico and Arizona.

C. guttatum Sw. (*Cypripedium orientale* Spreng., *C. variegatum* Georgi, *C. Yatabeanum* Mak.)

Pl. 5–14″ tall, softly glandular-pubescent with brownish jointed hairs, the rhiz. slender, elongate, repent, the st. slender, more or less flexuous, provided below with 3 or so clasping tubular sheaths. Lvs. 2, borne about the middle of the st., erect-spreading, ovate-elliptic to elliptic-lanceolate, obtuse to subacuminate, plicate, sparsely pilose, ciliate, 2¾–6″ long, 1–2½″ wide. Infl. 1-fld., the peduncle usually curved, with a ciliate foliaceous bract subtending the fl. Fls. white more or less densely blotched with purple. Ss. more or less pubescent on outer surface and margins, the dors. one deeply concave, spreading over the col., the lat. ss. united almost to apex. Ps. spreading, oblique, dilated below the middle, lightly undulate marginally. Lip obovoid, somewhat pendent, with a broad orifice with involute margins, pilose on the inner surface. June–Aug. (C, I) West Canada to Alaska and the Aleutian Islands; Japan; China; Manchuria; Siberia to Central Russia (Moscow).

C. montanum Dougl. ex Ldl. (*Cypripedium occidentale* S.Wats.)

Pl. erect, 10–25″ tall, more or less glandular-pubescent throughout, the rhiz. short, stout, the st. rather stout, leafy, somewhat flexuous. Lvs. usually 4–6, clasping the st., spreading-ascending, broadly ovate to elliptic-lanceolate, obtuse to abruptly short-acuminate,

glandular-pubescent on the veins, becoming smaller above, plicate, 2–6½″ long, 1–3″ wide. Infl. 1–3-fld., the fls. rather distant, subtended by foliaceous bracts. Fls. to about 5″ long from tip to tip, the ss. and ps. spreading, brownish-purple or dark green, suffused with purple, the globose lip white tinged with purple. Dors. sep. ascending, undulate marginally, the lats. united almost to apex, concave, bidentate at tip. Ps. linear to linear-lanceolate, down-thrust, acuminate, twisted, pilose inside at base. Lip pilose on inner surface. Staminode yellow with purple dots. May–July. (C) Montana and Wyoming west to California, north to Alaska.

C. Reginae Walt. (*Cypripedium album* Ait., *C. canadense* Michx., *C. spectabile* Sw.)

Pl. erect, the leafy st. often twisted, glandular-hirsute throughout,[1] 14–30″ tall. Lvs. usually 3–7, closely sheathing the st. at base, ovate to elliptic-lanceolate, acute to acuminate, strongly ribbed and plicate, 4–9½″ long, 2½–6″ wide. Infl. 1–2- (rarely 3–4-) fld., short-pedicellate in the axils of erect lf.-like bracts. Fls. to almost 4″ long, rather variable in colour, the ss. and ps. normally waxy-white, the large lip white, crimson-magenta, or rose-pink in front, with shallow vertical white furrows, often purple- or rose-veined. Dors. sep. ovate-orbicular, the lats. entirely united. Ps. spreading, oblong-elliptic to ovate-lanceolate, obtuse to acute. Lip pouch-shaped, to 2″ long. This is the State Flower of Minnesota. May–Sept. (C, I) Newfoundland west to Saskatchewan, south to Missouri and Tennessee; Western China.

C. californicum A.Gray Pl. slender or stout, 1–4′ tall, the lvs. 5 or more, alternate, erect-spreading, plicate, broadly ovate to ovate-lanceolate, obtuse to acute, 3–6½″ long and ½–2¾″ wide. Infl. 3–12-fld., the floral bracts large, foliaceous. Fls. to about 1½″ long, the ss. dull brownish-yellow, the ps. dull yellow, the lip white or somewhat rose-coloured, spotted with pale brown. Dors. sep. erect, concave, the ps. spreading, the lip obovoid, with the margins of the orifice deeply infolded. May–July. (C, I) Oregon; California.

C. candidum Muhl. ex Willd. Pl. rigidly erect, 6–15″ tall. Lvs. 3–4, crowded at about the middle of the st. when in full flower, almost erect, rather rigid, plicate, elliptic-lanceolate to lanceolate, acute to acuminate, 3–7½″ long. Infl. 1-fld. (very rarely 2-fld.), with an erect foliaceous bract. Fls. slightly fragrant, to about 3½″ from tip to tip, the ss. and ps. greenish or greenish-yellow, sparingly or heavily streaked or spotted with madder-purple, the obovoid lip waxy-white, polished outside, spotted with purple on edge of orifice and purple-veined inside at base, silky-pubescent inside. Staminode yellow spotted with purple. Apr.–June. (C, I) Ontario west to Nebraska and the Dakotas, southward to Missouri and Kentucky.

C. fasciculatum Kell. ex S.Wats. (*Cypripedium Knightae* A.Nels., *C. pusillum* Rolfe) Pl. 2½–14″ tall, the slender st. grooved. Lvs. 2, subopposite, at st.-summit, orbicular-ovate to oblong-elliptic, broadly rounded to obtuse, membranaceous, 1½–4½″ long and 1–3″ wide. Infl. short when young, elongating with age, brownish, bearing 2–4 fls. in a short corymbose rac., furnished with large bracts. Fls. to about 2″ long, the ss. and ps. dark purple or light yellow,

[1] The hairs which cover this plant are capable of causing severe cases of dermatitis on susceptible persons handling it incautiously.

veined with brownish-purple, the small globose lip green-yellow, the orifice-margin deeply infolded and purplish, abruptly turned out and reflexed at the base. Dors. sep. erect, the ps. horizontally spreading, the lat. ss. united for most of their length, down-thrust. Mostly Apr.–Aug. (C, I) Montana, Idaho and Wyoming west to Washington, Oregon, and California.

C. fasciolatum Franch. Pl. to 1½′ tall, rather stout. Lvs. 3–5, oblong, covered with tiny hairs, about 4½″ long and 1½″ wide. Infl. 1-fld., the peduncle pubescent. Fls. to 4½″ across, the ss. and ps. dull yellow veined and streaked with purple (very rarely reddish-purple veined with black-purple), the short, globular lip with a contracted orifice, purplish-rose veined with dark purple-rose. Ps. linear or linear-lanceolate, twisted towards tip. Mostly June. (C, I) Western China.

C. japonicum Thunb. St. essentially absent, the paired lvs. springing directly from the rhiz., suberect, very broadly ovate, tightly folded, almost fan-like in appearance, to about 6″ long. Infl. to 12″ tall, slender, hairy, 1-fld. Fls. about 3¾″ in diam., the ss. and spreading ps. pale green more or less marked near base with crimson, the ovoid, inflated lip to 2½″ long, white more or less marbled with bright pink. May–June. (C, I) China; Japan.

C. luteum Franch. St. 9–18″ tall, erect, stout, downy, leafy to apex, the sheathing lvs. pointed, folded, downy, 5–6 in number, 2½–9″ long. Infl. 1-fld. Fls. 2½–3½″ in diam., the ss. and ps. clear yellow, the lip vivid yellow, usually more or less spotted or blotched with orange-brown. Lat. ss. joined together behind the lip, pointed. Ps. narrower than dors. sep. June. (C, I) South-west China, usually at rather high elevations.

C. macranthum Sw. St. 1–1½′ tall, usually very stout, downy. Lvs. several on the st., ovate to lanceolate-elliptic, acute, downy, undulate, sheathing, 3–6″ long. Infl. 1–2-fld., with large foliose bracts. Fls. to 3″ across and 2½″ long, rose-purple or salmon-pink, usually tessellated with dark purple. Dors. sep. concave, usually curving over the col. Ps. spreading, drooping slightly but rarely twisted. Lip large, inflated, ovoid, corrugated around the orifice. May–July. (C) North Europe; North Asia to Siberia.

C. margaritaceum Franch. St. obsolete, the paired lvs. basal, oblong, opposite or subopposite, deeply folded, dark green blotched with purple-maroon, beneath covered with purple hairs, to about 5″ long. Infl. erect, 1-fld., usually about 8″ tall. Fls. without a subtending bract, to about 2″ in diam., very brittle and waxen in texture, the ss. and ps. yellowish-green spotted with purple, the ovoid, inflated, pointed lip pale yellow spotted with purple and with purplish glandular hairs. June–July. (C) China: Yunnan, at high elevations, growing in limestone in coniferous forests.

CYRTIDIUM Schltr.

Two exceedingly rare epiphytic orchids make up this little-known genus from the mountains of Colombia. Neither **Cyrtidium rhomboglossum** (Lehm. & Krzl.) Schltr. (*Chrysocycnis rhomboglossa* Lehm. & Krzl.) nor **C. tripterum** (Schltr.) Schltr. (*Chrysocycnis triptera* Schltr.) are known in our collections at this time, although they are very interesting plants of the subtribe *Maxillarinae*, rather simulating in vegetative habit a member of the section *Camaridium* of *Maxillaria* R. & P., but differing markedly from all related genera in the structure of the lip and column.

Nothing has been ascertained regarding the genetic affinities of *Cyrtidium*.

CULTURE: Possibly as for the intermediate and high elevation species of *Maxillaria*. (C, I)

CYRTOGLOTTIS Schltr.

Cyrtoglottis consists of but a single member, this the excessively scarce **C. gracilipes** Schltr., an epiphytic orchid native in the highlands of Colombia. Somewhat allied to *Mormolyca* Fenzl of the subtribe *Maxillarinae*, it is a unique plant of considerable botanical interest, but unfortunately one which is not present in collections at this time.

Nothing is known of the genetic affinities of this obscure genus.

CULTURE: Presumably as for the highland Maxillarias, etc. (C, I)

CYRTOPODIUM R.Br.
(*Tylochilus* Nees)

About thirty-five species of very large to rather small epiphytic, lithophytic, or terrestrial orchids make up the genus *Cyrtopodium*. They are indigenous in virtually all parts of the American tropics, from South Florida and Mexico southward, with the largest representation in Brazil. Vegetatively the genus consists of two basic sections: species allied to *C. punctatum* (L.) Ldl. have medium-sized to immense, spindle-shaped pseudobulbs (sometimes to five feet and more tall and weighing several pounds apiece!), while many of the Brazilian species bear pseudobulbs rather like those of a stout *Catasetum*. The often highly-coloured flowers are produced in erect, usually tall, sometimes branching inflorescences, and are generally yellow, red, or brown in colour, frequently with blotches or markings of darker hues. In certain of the species the large floral bracts are strikingly coloured and spotted, and often are almost as showy as the flowers which they subtend. Cyrtopodiums are relatively frequent in contemporary cultivation, and, in the larger species at least, of such impressive appearance, that they may be unequivocally recommended to all enthusiasts. The genus is a member of the subtribe *Cyrtopodiinae*, and is somewhat allied to *Eulophia* R.Br. and to *Govenia* Ldl.

To date only one hybrid has been registered within this genus, this the very handsome *Cyrtopodium x Dr. Harold Lyon* (*C. Andersoni × C. punctatum*), bred by Oscar M. Kirsch, of Honolulu. The possibility of crossing some of the small Brazilian species amongst themselves—as well as with the larger-growing plants—is a fascinating prospect. Nothing is known concerning the genetic compatibility of *Cyrtopodium* with other genera of orchids.

CULTURE: The cultural requirements of these spectacular orchids are, in general, rather simply met. They should be grown in pots, preferably of sufficient dimensions so that several growths may be made before re-potting becomes necessary. The epiphytic (or lithophytic) types, such as *C. punctatum*, *C. Andersoni*, etc., are usually grown in straight osmunda or tree-fern fibre, which should be packed around the roots rather tightly; perfect drainage is essential, as these orchids are highly intolerant of a stale compost. The terrestrial species (*C. paludicolum, C. virescens*, etc.) seem to prefer a medium similar to that used for Cymbidiums and again the drainage must be thoroughly attended to. Some growers have had notable success by keeping both types in a compost such as that recommended for *Phaius* and the evergreen Calanthes. Both groups of species appreciate abundant water and heat while actively growing, and almost full exposure to rather strong sunlight (though care must be taken to avoid burning of the foliage) is usually necessary to induce flowering. When a pseudobulb of mature size has been made, and the next new growths start to appear, water should be completely stopped until the flower-spikes arise, this generally when the new growth is a couple of inches long. Water may be given then, and gradually increased as the inflorescence expands and the growth elongates. Cyrtopodiums are all very heavy feeders, and do not thrive in most cases unless fertilized regularly. Manure or other fertilizing materials may with benefit be mixed directly into the compost in which they are planted. (I)

C. Andersoni (Lamb ex Andr.) R.Br. (*Cymbidium Andersoni* Lamb ex Andr., *Epidendrum polyphyllum* Vell., *Tylochilus flavus* Nees, *Cyrtopodium glutiniferum* Raddi, *C. flavum* Lk. & Otto, *C. Godseffianum* hort.)

Pbs. clustered, erect, spindle-shaped, narrowed at both ends, to 4′ tall (rarely more). Lvs. deciduous, leaving their spiny, sharp sheaths attached to the pbs., elongate, linear-lanceolate, acuminate, prominently nerved, often yellowish-green, to 2½′ long. Infls. erect, mostly branched, to 6′ tall, robust, many-fld., the lower bracts undulate, to 2″ long, often yellow. Fls. to 2″ across, fragrant, rather waxy, long-lived, the ss. yellow shaded apically with green, the ps. citron-yellow flushed with green apically, the lip citron-yellow with the disc usually almost orange-yellow, the disc thickened and grooved longitudinally. Mostly spring. (I, H) West Indies to Brazil.

C. gigas (Vell.) Hoehne (*Epidendrum gigas* Vell.)

Almost identical vegetatively with *C. palmifrons* Rchb.f. & Warm., differing in the size and structure of the fls. Infls. erect, branched, the fls. less clustered than those of the above-noted sp., to 3½′ tall, the large bracts yellow spotted and blotched with red. Fls. about 1¼″ across, yellow with prominent red marks, especially on the ss., the lip mostly red, the disc with a roughened callus that gradually becomes a series of roughened lines extending to the base of the claw. Autumn. (I, H) Central Brazil.

C. palmifrons Rchb.f. & Warm.

Rather similar in habit to *C. punctatum* (L.) Ldl., the pbs. often more swollen medially, the lvs. usually more regularly down-arching. Infls. branched, more compact than those of the above-noted sp., to 5′ tall. Fls. about 1½″ across, fragrant, the ss. very wide-spreading, slightly concave, oval-rounded, very undulate, reddish-blotched on a yellow-green ground; ps. yellow with numerous small spots of red, oval-rounded, rounded at tip or almost truncate, slightly undulate marginally; lip shorter than the lat. ss., semicircular, the claw long and narrow,

yellow with numerous red blotches and flushes, the disc with a many-warted yellow callus, red marginally. Autumn–winter. (I, H) Central and South Brazil.

C. paludicolum Hoehne

Terrestrial in wet places (often in bogs and marshes). Pbs. robust, spindle-shaped, to 15″ tall, narrowed towards the ends. Lvs. deciduous, large, smooth, rather heavy-textured, linear-lanceolate, acutish, somewhat stalked at base, to 3½′ long, mostly ascending. Infls. simple (rarely branched), erect, to 7′ tall, with up to 40 fls. which open successively over a long period. Fls. sometimes rather nodding, to 1½″ across, clear yellow with a few red spots on the lat. lbs. of the lip, the col. greenish-yellow. Winter. (H) Brazil: Mato-Grosso, São Paulo.

C. punctatum (L.) Ldl. (*Epidendrum punctatum* L.)

Pbs. erect, clustered, elongately spindle-shaped, to 4′ long (rarely more, often less), to 2″ in diam. near the middle. Lvs. leaving their spine-like midrib parts attached to the upper portion of the pbs. when they drop, linear to linear-elliptic, acute to long-acuminate, folded, drooping gracefully, to 2½′ long. Infls. basal, produced concurrently with the new growths, erect, stout, many-fld., branching, to 5′ tall (usually less), furnished with large wavy bracts which are greenish-yellow spotted and blotched with red or maroon-red. Fls. to 1½″ across, the ss. greenish-yellow irregularly blotched and spotted with red, maroon-red, or madder-purple, the ps. somewhat undulate-crisped marginally, bright yellow with fewer spots than the ss., usually clawed at base. Lip clawed, 3-lbd., the lat. lbs. erect and arching over the col., mostly reddish-brown, yellow at base; midlb. much broader than long, reddish-brown or madder-purple with a yellow centre, the apical margin crisped and roughly toothed, the disc with a fleshy grooved callus. Spring–early summer. (I, H) South Florida and Mexico throughout tropical America to Argentina.

C. virescens Rchb.f. & Warm.

Terrestrial, the pls. rather resembling a robust *Catasetum*. Pbs. clustered, conical-ovoid, long-attenuate at tip, to 4″ tall and 1½″ in diam. near the middle, at first clothed with lf.-like sheaths, later prominently jointed. Lvs. deciduous, linear-lanceolate, acutish, to 1½′ long, folded, rather heavy-textured. Infls. robust, erect, to 4′ tall, many-fld., branching above. Fls. wide-spreading, long-lived, to 1¼″ across, pale green or yellowish spotted with brown, the lat. lbs. of the lip erect and somewhat incurved, often dull red, the disc with many calli that are multi-grooved. Spring. (H) Brazil; Paraguay; ? Uruguay.

C. Aliciae L.Lind. & Rolfe. Rather similar in habit to *C. punctatum* (L.) Ldl., differing primarily in the smaller fls. (about 1″ across), the lip with a very short midlb., the ps. very strongly clawed. Autumn. (I, H) Brazil; ? Paraguay; Uruguay; Argentina.

C. paranaense Schltr. Closely allied to and simulating *C. palmifrons* Rchb.f. & Warm., but differing in the colour of the fls. and the midlb. of the lip, which is not emarginate at the apex, and in the 3-parted callus. Fls. about 1″ across, the ss. greenish-yellow, the ps. and lip golden-yellow. Autumn–winter. (I, H) Coastal Brazil, especially in the south.

Cyrtopodium punctatum (L.) Ldl. [BLANCHE AMES]

C. parviflorum Ldl. Terrestrial in rather wet places. Pbs. often partially buried, egg-shaped to conical, to 3″ tall. Lvs. thick, erect, linear-lanceolate, acutish, to 2′ long, deciduous. Infls. erect, branched, rather many-fld., to 3′ tall. Fls. less than 1″ across, yellowish-green densely spotted with greyish- or brownish-red, the base of the lip golden-yellow. Winter. (H) Guianas; Brazil; Bolivia.

CYRTORCHIS Schltr.

This is one of the numerous segregates from the genus *Angraecum* Bory, a group containing about fifteen known species, all of these native in the African tropics. *Cyrtorchis* comprises some very handsome epiphytic (rarely lithophytic or terrestrial) plants, but few of which are present in contemporary collections, though their floriferous habit, ease of cultivation, and strongly fragrant, usually white, star- or bell-shaped blossoms recommend them to all enthusiasts. Most closely allied to *Diaphananthe* Schltr. and to *Listrostachys* Rchb.f., this genus is differentiated by technical characters of the flowers, which typically have the lip identical in appearance to the petals, and which are furnished with a proportionately long and prominent spur.

No hybrids are as yet known in *Cyrtorchis*, but it is presumably genetically compatible with at least some of its generic relations, such as *Angraecum*, etc.

CULTURE: As for the tropical Angraecums. (H)

C. arcuata (Ldl.) Schltr. (*Angraecum arcuatum* Ldl., *Listrostachys arcuata* Rchb.f.)
St. robust, thick. Lvs. stiffly leathery, thick, oblong, obliquely bilobed at apex, to 6″ long and 1″ wide. Infls. arching or horizontal, densely 10–20-fld., to 8″ long. Fls. about 1½″ across, waxy, very fragrant, pure white. Ss. and ps. oblong, recurving, the ps. slightly the shorter, acuminate. Lip lanceolate, recurving, acuminate, the spur slightly curving, towards the apex becoming smaller, about 1¼″ long. Spring–summer. (H) South Africa: Kaffirland, Natal, Transvaal.

C. Chailluana (Hk.) Schltr. (*Angraecum Chailluanum* Hk., *Listrostachys Chailluana* Rchb.f.) Rather similar to *C. arcuata* (Ldl.) Schltr. in habit, the st. to 8″ tall, the lvs. oblong-ligulate, unequally bilobed at tip, to 8″ long and 2″ wide. Infls. rather densely 6–12-fld., about 8″ long. Fls. similar in shape to those of the other sp., to 3″ across, pure white, fragrant, the spur about 4½″ long. Spring–early summer. (H) Tropical West Africa.

C. hamata (Rolfe) Schltr. (*Listrostachys hamata* Rolfe) Resembling *C. Chailluana* (Hk.) Schltr. to large degree, the lvs. smaller, the fls. about 3″ across, the spur green, 2¼″ long, hook-shaped, bent inwards. Winter. (H) Tropical West Africa.

C. Monteirae (Rchb.f.) Schltr. (*Listrostachys Monteirae* Rchb.f.) St. thick, to 2′ tall, leafy throughout. Lvs. oblong-ligulate, to 7″ long and 2¼″ wide, rigidly leathery. Infls. loosely 10–15-fld., arching, to 8″ long. Fls. about 1½″ across, waxy, fragrant, brownish-white. Ss. and ps. lanceolate, acuminate, recurving. Lip similar, recurving, the spur slightly curved, to 2″ long, brownish-yellow at the tip. Spring. (H) Tropical West Africa: Nigeria to Angola.

CYSTOPUS Bl.

Cystopus is a genus of an estimated sixteen species, widespread in the region extending from the Himalayas throughout Malaysia and Indonesia to New Guinea and Samoa. Terrestrial orchids of the subtribe *Physurinae*, the group is allied to *Anoectochilus* Bl., from which it differs in details of the small flowers. Their foliage is often handsomely variegated (thus placing them in the category of the 'Jewel Orchids'), but they do not appear to be present in our collections at this time.

Nothing is known of the genetic affinities of this genus. CULTURE: Presumably as for *Anoectochilus*. (H)

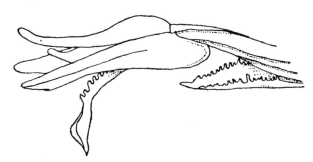

Cystopus fimbriatus J.J.Sm. [A.D.HAWKES, AFTER J.J.SMITH]

CYSTORCHIS Bl.

A member of the complex and seldom-cultivated subtribe *Physurinae*, *Cystorchis* contains about eight species in Malaya and Indonesia, with one representative in China. Vegetatively, they resemble most other genera of this alliance (though one of them, **C. aphylla** Ridl., from the Malay Peninsula and the Sunda Islands, is a saprophyte), with a few variegated leaves in a more or less loose rosette at the base of the inflorescence, which supports a raceme of small, complexly shaped flowers of no special beauty. Because of this, these plants are placed among the group known as the 'Jewel Orchids', being grown only for their unusually attractive foliage rather than for the insignificant blossoms. *Cystorchis* differs primarily from its allies in the presence of two small bladder-like vesicles on either side of the mostly abbreviated spur.

No hybrids are known in this genus, though we may assume that it is genetically compatible with at least some other members of the *Physurinae*.

CULTURE: As for *Anoectochilus*. (H)

C. variegata (Miq.) Bl. (*Hetaeria variegata* Miq.)
Lvs. mostly basal, forming a vague loose rosette, about 6 in number, short-stalked, the blade to 3″ long and 1″ wide, asymmetric, light green, veined with intricately branching deep green veins, elliptic, acute. Infl. erect, hairy, to 10″ tall, the rac. about 7–12-fld., short. Fls. not opening fully, about ½″ long, the ss. pinkish-brown, basally becoming greenish-yellow, the ps. white, the lip white and orange, complex in structure. Autumn. (H) Malay Peninsula; Sumatra; Java; Borneo.

—var. **purpurea** Ridl. (*Cystorchis javanica* Bl.)

Pls. in fl. to only about 6″ tall, smaller in all parts than the typical form, the lvs. deep purple-brown, the principal veins paler, the blade about 1¼″ long and ½″ wide. Fls. as in the type. Autumn. (H) Malay Peninsula.

DACTYLORHYNCHUS Schltr.

Dactylorhynchus flavescens Schltr., the only known member of the genus, is an extremely rare small epiphytic orchid, native in the high mountain forests of New Guinea. Scarce even in herbaria, it is unknown in collections at this time. Closely allied to *Bulbophyllum* Thou., it differs from that genus in technical details of the flowers.

Nothing is known of the genetic affinities of this obscure group.

CULTURE: As for the high-elevation Bulbophyllums, etc. (C, I)

DENDROBIUM Sw.

(*Aclinia* Griff., *Aporum* Bl., *Bolbidium* Ldl., *Callista* Lour., *Dichopus* Bl., *Ditulima* Raf., *Grastidium* Bl., *Latouria* Bl., *Macrostomium* Bl., *Onychium* Bl., *Ormostema* Raf., *Oxystophyllum* Bl., *Pedilonum* Bl., *Pierardia* Raf., *Stachyobium* Rchb.f., *Thelychiton* Endl., *Thicuania* Raf., *Tropilis* Raf.)

The genus *Dendrobium* is doubtless the second largest in the entire Orchidaceae, being exceeded in number of species-components only by *Bulbophyllum* Thou. Today upwards of sixteen hundred distinct Dendrobiums are considered to be valid, these with a gigantic range which extends from Korea and Japan throughout the Indo-Malayan region and Indonesia to Australia, New Zealand, and certain of the insular groups of Polynesia. The largest assemblage of species exists in New Guinea, where more than three hundred and fifty species occur. These multitudinous orchids range from steamy hot sea-level areas to snow-swept mountain heights, and, as may be expected, the genus exhibits a tremendous diversity of structure—both vegetative and floral—and necessarily of cultural requirements. *Dendrobium* is among the more complex of orchid genera, due in part to the tremendous number of entities contained within it, and to the extremes of variation which occur in a single taxon. As a genus, it was monographed in 1910 by Fritz Kraenzlin, but his work was at best fragmentary, and so many species have been added since that date (notably by Schlechter, J.J.Smith, *et al.*) that the only extant revision is essentially useless, save as a basic reference. A critical, modern study of the genus—and its several close allies, as well—is sorely needed, but no contemporary orchidologist seems willing to attack the seemingly insuperable difficulties attendant on such a work. A member of the subtribe *Dendrobiinae*, *Dendrobium* is allied to *Eria* Ldl., *Porpax* Ldl., *Pseuderia* Schltr., and naturally to several segregates from the group itself, such as *Cadetia* Gaud., *Diplocaulobium* (Rchb.f.) Krzl., *Epigeneium* Gagnep., *Flickingeria* A.D.Hawkes, and *Inobulbon* Schltr. & Krzl. In dealing

with a group of this immense size, it is difficult to give a concise characterization of the genus as a whole, because of the extremes of variability encountered within it. Like many large orchid aggregations, *Dendrobium* is divided into a large number of theoretically-allied species-sections, these based on a combination of vegetative and floral characters. The vegetative proportions of the Dendrobiums vary from plants with clustered, dwarf, pseudobulbs less than one inch tall, to the gigantic 'canes' produced by *D. violaceoflavens* J.J.Sm. and a few of its allies, these among the largest of all pseudobulbous orchids. The foliage varies from plane to terete, or peculiarly flattened and grooved as in *D. linguaeforme* Sw. The inflorescences are typically terminal or sub-terminal, and bear from one to several dozens of flowers of extremely diverse dimensions, colours, and size. Four pollinia are always present, thus differentiating the genus from many of its close allies—*Eria* Ldl., for example. *Dendrobium* is today extremely popular with orchidists throughout the world, and a large number of the species are cultivated, though this number is of course only a tiny percentage of the total components of the genus.

There are now several hundred hybrids on record within the genus *Dendrobium*. Perhaps the largest number of these have been produced by breeders in the Hawaiian Islands and in Malaya, though certain American hybridists (and a few in England and on the Continent) have played an important role in the development of these fine crosses. Regrettably, because of the taxonomic and nomenclatural difficulties attendant in this genus, many of the species used as parents in these hybrids have been mis-named, so that the state of *Dendrobium* hybrids in general is excessively confused. As yet, we do not know sufficient concerning the genetic barriers which exist within the genus, and certain seemingly 'impossible' hybrids have in recent years been produced. No hybrids are registered with allied genera at this writing, though a tremendous and fascinating field is open in this respect.

CULTURE: Dendrobiums are, for the most part, among the easiest grown of all orchids, hence they are heartily recommended to all collectors, from novice to professional. Because the species range from steaming lowland jungles to the snow-swept heights of the Himalayas, temperature requirements naturally fluctuate from plant to plant, and often from individual to individual. Those Dendrobiums related to *D. nobile*, etc., which mostly inhabit relatively high elevations, are extremely popular with collectors at this time. They may be grown either in pots or baskets, these very well-drained (no Dendrobiums will tolerate stale conditions at the roots, hence drainage is an extremely important factor in their successful cultivation), and filled with any one of a variety of composts, from straight osmunda or chopped tree-fern fibre to mixtures of different sorts. While actively growing, these 'cool' Dendrobiums require copious quantities of moisture, bright light, and will take as much heat (without its being abnormal) as is available; upon maturation of the new growths, however, the plants must be removed to a considerably cooler spot in the collection, and water all but stopped, in order to harden the pseudobulbs and induce formation of the flower-buds. Like all Dendrobiums, these plants benefit by frequent and liberal applications of fertilizers, though naturally such additives should be ceased during their resting-period. These 'cool'-growing Dendrobiums are often called the 'deciduous' species, but this is a misnomer, since many of them—even when at rest—retain at least a portion of their foliage under cultivated conditions. Species such as *D. densiflorum*, *D. Farmeri*, etc. require approximately the same conditions, though at no time should they be subjected to as cool temperatures as are afforded the members of the *D. nobile* aggregation, and while at rest (a period of only a couple of weeks, instead of a month or more as in the other plants), should be lightly sprayed with water from time to time, to avoid excess desiccation of the pseudo-bulbs and foliage. The principal tropical species grown are *D. bigibbum*, its var. *Phalaenopsis*, *D. discolor* (long known by the homonymic epithet *D. undulatum*), and their myriad allies. These are known collectively as the 'evergreen' Dendrobiums, since at all times they bear at least some leaves; all are from warm regions, and hence require constant high temperatures. They grow continuously, and should not be permitted a resting-period. For the most part, they do best in proportionately small containers, seemingly producing their majestic flowers with great profusion if root-bound. In Hawaii, South Florida, and other warm areas, they are often grown out-of-doors in specially-prepared beds such as those suggested for *Arachnis* or *Arundina* (which see), in full sun. The 'nigro-hirsute' group contains such magnificent plants as *D. formosum*, etc. (*D. Dearei*, *D. Sanderae*, and *D. Schuetzei*, though not strictly of this group, require comparable cultural conditions). They do best in medium-sized pots, the compost very tightly packed around their roots, in a rather sunny spot, with quantities of water at all times. Certain of the dwarf, creeping Dendrobiums are best treated as Bulbophyllums, while those with pendulous habit (e.g. *D. anosmum*, *D. Pierardii*) must be grown in hanging pots or baskets, so that their typically elongate pseudobulbs may hang down. (C, I, H)

D. aemulum R.Br.

Pbs. usually spindle-shaped, to 12″ tall. Lvs. 2–4, ovate to almost lanceolate, usually glossy-green, rigidly leathery, to 4″ long. Infls. 1–3 per pb.-apex, loosely 4–6-fld., to 4″ long. Fls. not opening widely, about 1½″ across, fragrant, white, the lip with some purple marks. Ss. and ps. linear, acuminate. Lip 3-lbd., the midlb. with an acute or obtuse point, the lamina with 3 parallel ridges between the lat. lbs., converging into a single undulate, fuzzy, yellow-crested ridge. Autumn–early winter. (I) Australia: New South Wales, Queensland.

D. aggregatum Roxb. (*Dendrobium Lindleyi* Steud.)

Pbs. clustered, usually yellowish, furrowed and wrinkled with age, angular, to 2½″ tall, oblong-ovoid. Lf. solitary, oblong, obtuse, rigidly leathery, to 2½″ long, usually deep dull green. Infls. produced from the upper nodes of the pbs., loosely 5–15-fld., mostly arching to sharply pendulous, to 6″ long (often shorter). Fls. about 1¾″ across, very fragrant of honey, deep golden-yellow, the disc of the lip orange-yellow. Ss.

small, ovate, obtuse. Ps. much broader, ovate, obtuse. Lip shortly clawed at base, transversely oblong, the pubescent disc concave, the margin minutely fringed. Mostly spring. (I) South China to Burma, Thailand, and Laos.

—var. **Jenkinsii** (Wall.) Ldl. (*Dendrobium Jenkinsii* Wall.)

Differs from the type in the considerably smaller vegetative habit, smaller fls. (to 1″ across), and in the kidney-shaped, retuse lip, which is not as fuzzy as in the typical form. Spring. (I) Burma.

D. amboinense Hk. (*Callista amboinensis* O.Ktze.)

Pbs. club-shaped basally, narrowing upwards, to 8″ tall. Lvs. 2–3, apical, to 6″ long, lanceolate, usually acute, rather leathery. Infls. short-stalked, 2–4-fld., mostly at apex of pbs. Fls. to almost 7″ across, the ss. and ps. very narrow, long-acuminate, white, the lip about 1″ long, acuminate, white, veined with red and orange-yellow, margined with red. Summer. (H) Moluccas.

D. amoenum Wall. ex Ldl. (*Dendrobium aphyllum* Roxb., *D. Egertoniae* Ldl., *D. mesochlorum* Ldl.)

Pbs. st.-like, mostly arching to pendulous, to 2′ long, slender, the nodes slightly swollen. Lvs. rather soft-textured, to 5″ long, linear-lanceolate, acuminate, undulate marginally, eventually deciduous. Infls. 2–3-fld., produced from the leafless pbs., abbreviated. Fls. to 2½″ across, fragrant of violets, rather variable in colour, the ss. and ps. pure white tipped with magenta, the lip white with a deep magenta-purple apex, marked with 3 deep purple veins, the concave, rather tubular basal part yellow, velvety. Spring. (I) Himalayas to Burma.

D. anosmum Ldl. (*Dendrobium leucorhodum* Schltr., *D. macranthum* Hk., *D. macrophyllum* Ldl., *D. Scortechinii* Hk.f., *D. superbum* Rchb.f., *D. superbum* Rchb.f., var. *anosmum* Rchb.f., *Callista anosma* O.Ktze., *Callista Scortechinii* O.Ktze.)

Pbs. st.-like, pendulous, to 12′ long (usually much shorter), often yellowish or greyish, the nodes only slightly swollen. Lvs. rather fleshy, glossy-green, oblong-lanceolate, acutish, to 5″ long, flattened and borne in 2 ranks, deciduous. Infls. usually 2-fld., almost stalkless, borne on the leafless pbs. Fls. to 4″ across, often not opening widely, extremely fragrant (of raspberries or rhubarb) or not, variable in colour, the typical phase with mauve-purple ss. and ps. and a lip with 2 deep purple blotches in the throat, the flaring part of this segm. veined with deeper purple. (A rare pure white variant is sometimes seen under the name of var. **Huttoni** hort., and one with white ss. and ps. and a bright yellow lip-throat is often called var. **album** hort.; both are best relegated to the status of forms.) Ps. broader than the ss., often undulate marginally. Lip tubular, fuzzy to rough-textured, broadly ovate. Mostly late winter–spring. (I, H) Laos, Viet-Nam, Malay Peninsula, and the Philippines throughout Indonesia to New Guinea.

D. Aphrodite Rchb.f. (*Dendrobium nodatum* Ldl.)

Pbs. branching, the joints very swollen, to 12″ tall. Lvs. few, deciduous, to 3″ long, oblong, obtuse, rather fleshy. Fls. solitary from the nodes of the leafless pbs., to 3″ across, delicately fragrant, the ss. and ps. white, the lip white in the throat, often purple-blotched there, further out turning bright orange, with a broad marginal area of pale yellowish-white. Ss. and ps. oblong, obtuse, the ps. the wider. Lip with the lat. margins incurved over the col., the midlb. large, almost round, acute. Spring. (I) Burma; Thailand.

D. arachnites Rchb.f.

Pbs. yellow, usually swollen apically, glossy, roundish, to 4″ tall. Lvs. usually 2–3, linear-lanceolate, acute, to 5″ long, glossy. Fls. usually paired from the apical part of the pbs., to 2½″ across, the ss. and ps. cinnabar-red, the lip darker, sometimes veined with dull purple. Ss. and ps. very narrow, acute apically. Lip rather fiddle-shaped, slightly clawed, somewhat recurved at apex, the disc with 2 ridges at the extreme, basal point. Spring. (I) Burma.

D. atroviolaceum Rolfe (*Dendrobium Ashworthiae* O'Brien, *D. Forbesii* Ridl.)

Pbs. narrow basally, becoming club-shaped above, to about 8″ tall in robust phases, sometimes flushed with purplish. Lvs. 2–4, apical, rather rigidly leathery, often yellowish-green, elliptic, to 7″ long and 2″ broad. Infls. 10–20-fld., erect, rather dense, to 8″ tall. Fls. to 2½″ across, fragrant, heavy-textured, very long-lasting, nodding, the ss. and ps. cream-white with deep purple blotches. Lip 3-lbd., green outside, rich dark violet-purple within. Spring. (H) New Guinea.

D. barbatulum Ldl.

Pbs. st.-like, slender, usually erect, to 1½′ long. Lvs. lanceolate, acuminate, to 4″ long. Infls. 8–15-fld., produced from near the apex of the pbs. Fls. about ½″ across, whitish, the lip ovate, hairy on the disc, with a small lobule on each side of the basal part. Spring. (H) Lower India.

D. bellatulum Rolfe

Pbs. clustered, ellipsoidal, about 2″ tall. Lvs. usually paired, about 1½″ long, vaguely oblong, the sheaths short, black-hairy. Fls. usually solitary from the upper pb.-nodes, about 1½″ across, fragrant, lasting well, the ss. and ps. white, the large somewhat tubular lip very deep purple at the apex, the mentum formed by the lat. ss. large. Spring. (I) South China; Himalayas; Thailand; Viet-Nam.

D. Bensoniae Rchb.f. (*Dendrobium signatum* Rchb.f.)

Rather similar in habit to *D. crystallinum* Ldl., the pbs. st.-like, almost erect or more commonly pendulous, to 3′ long, the nodes rather swollen. Lvs. deciduous, linear, acute or emarginate, to 5″ long or less. Infls. borne from upper nodes of the leafless pbs., solitary or sometimes paired, 1–3-fld., to 2″ long. Fls. about 2½″ across, fragrant, the ss. and ps. cream-white, the lip orange with 2 large black-purple blotches at the base. Ss. oblong-lanceolate, acutish. Ps. roundish or oblong, obtuse. Lip concave, tomentose, orbicular, forming a tube at the base. Spring. (I, H) Burma; Thailand; Laos; Cambodia.

D. bifalce Ldl. (*Bulbophyllum oncidiochilum* Krzl., *Doritis bifalcis* Rchb.f., *Latourea oncidiochila* Krzl., *Dendrobium breviracemosum* F.M.Bail., *D. chloropterum* Rchb.f. & Moore)

Pbs. clustered, narrowly stalked basally, becoming fusiform above, sulcate, usually bright yellow, to 12″ tall. Lvs. 2–3, apical, leathery, oblong, obtuse, to 6″ long and 2½″ broad. Infls. borne from lf.-axils, usually multiple per growth, to 15″ long, the rather loose rac. few-fld. Fls. waxy, lasting rather well, about ¾″ in diam., yellowish or greenish, more or less streaked with dark purple or purple-brown, the lip usually brownish-yellow, very complicated, with the lat. lbs. enfolding the col., the large midlb. pandurate, sinuate apically, with a fleshy 2-parted callus on the disc. Mostly summer. (H) Timor; New Guinea; New Britain; Solomon Islands.

D. bigibbum Ldl.

Pbs. st.-like, cylindrical (sometimes slightly swollen near middle or above), to 1½′ tall. Lvs. mostly apical, rather narrow, to 4″ long, leathery, rather rigid, oblong-lanceolate, acutish. Infls. apical, 4–12-fld., arching, to about 12″ long. Fls. to 2″ across, variable in colour, long-lived, rather heavy-textured, the ss. and ps. usually rose-mauve (rarely white), the lip usually much darker. Ss. oblong, acute. Ps. much broader than ss., oblong, acutish. Lip with the midlb. blunt, notched; disc thickened and papillose, white or whitish in most phases. Mostly spring. (H) Australia: Queensland, Cape York Peninsula; Thursday Island; New Guinea.

—var. **Phalaenopsis** (Fitzg.) F.M.Bail. (*Dendrobium Phalaenopsis* Fitzg.)

Highly variable, more common in cultivation than the typical sp. Similar in habit to typical *D. bigibbum* Ldl., but much more robust in all parts, the pbs. to 4′ tall and more, the lvs. larger. Fls. to 3½″ across (rarely more), varying from pure white to rosy-mauve or rich purple, the lip usually the darkest colour. Midlb. of lip pointed, the disc not thickened, only minutely papillose. Mostly spring, but sometimes more than once annually. (H) Timor to Australia (Queensland) and New Guinea.

D. Brymerianum Rchb.f.

Pbs. terete, rather swollen medially, to 1½′ tall, furrowed with age. Lvs. mostly apical, few, oblong, acute, rather leathery, to 5″ long, eventually deciduous. Infls. produced from near the apex of leafless pbs., 2–3-fld., rather short. Fls. about 3″ across, very fragrant, often not lasting well, golden-yellow, the midlb. of the lip greenish-yellow fringed with a long beard-like area of branching processes, the short, broad lat. lbs. deep orange, shortly fringed. Ss. ovate-lanceolate, acutish. Ps. linear-oblong, acutish. Lip triangular-cordate, very large. Spring. (I) Burma; Thailand.

D. candidum Wall. ex Ldl. (*Dendrobium spathaceum* Ldl.)

Similar in habit to *D. aduncum* Wall., but the infls. very short, 2-fld. Fls. about 1″ across, slightly fragrant, the ss. and ps. white, the oblong lip also white, but olive-green in the wider median parts, the mentum also olive-green, large. Spring–early summer. (C, I) Himalayas, at rather high elevations.

D. chrysanthum Wall. (*Dendrobium Paxtoni* Ldl.)

Pbs. st.-like, usually pendulous, to 7′ long, terete. Lvs. eventually deciduous, somewhat twisted, rather leathery, ovate-lanceolate, acuminate, to 7″ long. Infls. usually produced while the pbs. are still in growth, 2–3-fld., rather short. Fls. lasting about 2 weeks, very fragrant, rather fleshy, intense dark yellow, the lip with 2 large blotches of rich red-purple on the disc. Ss. oblong, obtuse. Ps. obovate, broader than the ss., obtuse. Lip toothed marginally, roundish, concave, velvety especially on the disc. Mostly spring, but often sporadic throughout the year. (I, H) India, Nepal, and the Himalayan region to Burma and Thailand.

D. chryseum Rolfe (*Dendrobium aurantiacum* Rchb.f.)

Pbs. st.-like, very slender, to about 2′ tall. Lvs. narrowly lanceolate, acute, to 4″ long. Infls. 2–3-fld., pendulous, short. Fls. very fragrant, rather short-lived, to 2″ across, golden-yellow, the lip velvety on the disc (where it is usually orange), the margins slightly fimbriate. Spring–early summer. (I) Himalayas; Burma.

D. chrysotoxum Ldl. (*Dendrobium suavissimum* Rchb.f.)

Pbs. clustered, club-shaped or spindle-shaped from a slender base, ribbed with age, to 8″ tall. Lvs. 2–3, apical, leathery, oblong, to 5″ long and 1½″ wide, eventually deciduous. Infls. rather loosely few- to many-fld., to about 12″ long, gracefully arching. Fls. about 1½″ across (rarely to 2″), very fragrant, lasting well, golden-yellow or orange-yellow, the disc of the lip with a curved band of rich orange or deep brown, the lip fringed marginally, rather crisped. Autumn–spring. (I, H) South China and the Himalayas to Burma, Thailand, and Laos.

D. crepidatum Ldl. (*Dendrobium Lawanum* Ldl., *D. roseum* Dalz.)

Pbs. st.-like, drooping to sharply pendulous, striped with purple or magenta-purple, terete, to 12″ long (rarely longer). Lvs. oblong, acute, rather leathery, to about 4″ long, eventually deciduous. Infls. short, usually 2-fld., borne from the nodes of the leafless pbs. Fls. very long-lived, fragrant, about 1″ across, the ss. and ps. white with pink or magenta-pink tips, the lip white margined with pink or magenta-pink, the disc rich yellow. Ss. and ps. oblong, acutish, glossy. Lip roundish to heart-shaped, pubescent, the basal part folded in on each side. Spring. (I) India; Himalayas; Upper Burma; Thailand; Laos.

D. cretaceum Ldl.

Pbs. clustered, pendulous, terete, striped with purplish, the sheaths whitish, to 2′ long, furrowed with age. Lvs. deciduous, lanceolate, acute, to 4″ long, rather leathery. Fls. solitary, produced from the nodes of the leafless pbs., very long-lived, to 2″ across, fragrant, dull opaque white, the ss. and ps. often tipped with pale yellow, the roundish, concave, pubescent, marginally fimbriate lip white on the edge, the remainder pale yellow with some crimson streaks. Summer. (I, H) Himalayas; Burma; Andaman Islands,

D. crumenatum (Rumph.) Sw. (*Angraecum crumenatum* Rumph., *Onychium crumenatum* Bl., *Callista crumenata* O.Ktze., *Dendrobium caninum* Merr.)

Pbs. spindle-shaped at base, often yellowish, becoming furrowed with age, prolonged above into a long, often branching, whip-like, jointed stalk to 5′ long, erect or arching. Lvs. eventually deciduous, rather rigidly leathery, borne in upper part of stalk-like portion of pbs., oblong, sessile, to 5″ long and ¾″ wide. Fls. solitary or paired, produced from the chaffy bract-clusters along the upper parts of the stalk-like pb.-portions, all (usually) opening on the same day and persisting for only a single day, but often flowering several times throughout the year, faintly to rather strongly fragrant, about 2″ across, pure glittering white, the lip with a bright yellow disc. Throughout the year. (H) South China, Ceylon, Burma, and the Philippines throughout Southeast Asia and Indonesia to New Guinea.

D. crystallinum Rchb.f.

Pbs. st.-like, pendulous, terete, the nodes not swollen, to 2′ long. Lvs. deciduous, to 6″ long, rather soft-textured, falcately lanceolate, acute. Infls. 1–3-fld., produced from the leafless pbs., very short-stalked. Fls. about 2″ across, very fragrant, the ss. and ps. white tipped with magenta or rose-purple, the lip orange on the disc, with a small magenta tip. Ss. and much broader ps. oblong-lanceolate, acute. Lip shortly clawed, roundish, the disc rough, forming a slight tube at the base. Mostly summer. (I) Himalayas; Burma; Thailand; Laos; Cambodia; Viet-Nam.

D. Dearei Rchb.f.

Pbs. st.-like, rather stout, sometimes slightly swollen above, to 3′ tall. Lvs. persisting in apical part of pbs., falling below, to 3″ long, rather dull green, oblong-ligulate, emarginate, rather close together and distichous. Infls. both apical and lateral, produced from both the old and new pbs., 3–6-fld., rather short. Fls. about 3″ across, long-lived, pure white with a green throat in the lip. Ss. and broader ps. oblong, acuminate. Lip 3-lbd., the lat. lbs. incurved over the col., the midlb. blunt apically. Mostly spring. (I, H) Philippines.

D. densiflorum Wall. (*Dendrobium Schroederi* hort.)

Pbs. distinctly 4-angled, green, club-shaped, to 15″ tall. Lvs. 3–5 at the apex of the pbs., persistent, rather stiffly leathery, to 6″ long, elliptic, acutish. Infls. borne from the upper nodes of the pbs., very densely many-fld., sharply pendulous, cylindrical, to 8″ long and 3″ in diam. Fls. to 2″ across, delicately fragrant, usually lasting only 4–6 days, bright butter-yellow, the round, very hairy lip orange-yellow, the margin not fringed. Spring. (I) Himalayas to Burma.

D. Devonianum Paxt. (*Dendrobium pictum* Griff. ex Ldl.)

Pbs. st.-like, often branching, slender, pendulous, to 5′ long. Lvs. few, fragile in texture, deciduous, linear-lanceolate, acuminate, to 5″ long. Infls. 1–2-fld., very short-stalked, produced from the nodes of the leafless pbs. Fls. rather long-lived, fragrant, to 3″ across, the ss. usually cream-white with some pinkish suffusions (rarely blotched with rich magenta at the tip), the ps. white or pale yellow with a magenta blotch at the apex, the lip white with a blotch of rich orange on each side of the disc, the emarginate apex with a large magenta blotch, the margin deeply fimbriate, the fringe rather pendulous. Spring–early summer. (I) China and Himalayas to Burma, Thailand, and Viet-Nam.

D. discolor Ldl. (*Dendrobium undulatum* R.Br. not Pers.)

Pbs. to 10′ tall (often shorter), frequently yellowish, cylindrical or more or less definitely swollen at or above the middle, tapering at both ends, prominently ringed with the old lf.-scars. Lvs. partially persistent, rigidly leathery, often yellowish, oblong-lanceolate, acutish or rounded apically, sometimes unequally bilobed there, to 4″ long and ¾″ wide. Infls. apical from the upper pb.-nodes, few- to many-fld., to 2′ long, horizontal or gracefully arching. Fls. extremely variable in colour, to 3″ across, honey-scented, waxy, long-lived, the ss. and ps. usually yellowish-brown, oblong, very crisped and undulate. Lip 3-lbd., usually the same colour as the other segms., the disc often whitish with bright yellow keels, marginally undulate and crisped. Mostly spring. (H) Northern Australia; Torres Straits Islands; New Guinea.

D. draconis Rchb.f. (*Dendrobium Andersoni* J.Scott, *D. eburneum* Rchb.f.)

Pbs. slightly spindle-shaped, to 1½′ tall, mostly covered by the persistent lf.-sheaths, which are densely clothed with small black hairs. Lvs. rather leathery, lanceolate, obliquely obtuse at the apex, to 3″ long, persistent. Infls. apical or axillary, very short, 2–4-fld. Fls. to 3″ across, waxy, very long-lived, fragrant of tangerines, pure ivory-white except for the throat of the lip, which is rich vermilion or orange-red (rarely orange-yellow or yellow). Ss. and ps. lanceolate, acute or acuminate, the mentum long and straight, the ps. often undulate marginally. Lip lanceolate, the small lat. lbs. rounded, incurved around the col., the midlb. long, oblong, obtuse or acuminate, often crisped marginally. Spring–summer. (I, H) Burma; Thailand; Laos; Cambodia; Viet-Nam.

D. Falconeri Hk. (*Dendrobium Wardianum* Warn. var. *assamicum* Jenn.)

Pbs. st.-like, very slender, profusely branching, pendulous, often rooting from the nodes which are small and knot-like, to 4′ long, forming dense thickets of interwoven pbs. Lvs. few on the growing shoots, quickly deciduous, linear or narrowly lanceolate, acuminate, to 4″ long. Fls. solitary from the nodes of the older pbs., to 4½″ across, fragrant, white or blush-white, all segms. with an apical rich magenta-purple blotch, the lip with a broad orange disc which has a median deep purple blotch. Lip somewhat tubular at base, the throat-apex undulate, the margins recurved, fuzzy, fringed. Spring–early summer. (I) Himalayas to Burma and Thailand.

D. Farmeri Paxt. (*Dendrobium densiflorum* Wall. var. *Farmeri* Regel)

Rather similar in vegetative habit to *D. densiflorum* Wall., the pbs. to about 12″ tall, strongly 4-angled in upper part. Lvs. 3–4, apical, to 6″ long. Infls. drooping, densely many-fld., to 8″ long, rather cylindrical. Fls. about 2″ across, the ss. and ps. delicate lilac-mauve or white, the almost round, hairy lip yellow. Mostly spring. (I, H) Himalayas to Malay Peninsula (Pahang).

D. fimbriatum Hk. (*Dendrobium Paxtoni* Paxt.)

Pbs. st.-like, slender, terete, usually erect or arching, to 6′ tall, swollen at base. Lvs. very deep green, lanceolate, acuminate, not very leathery, to 6″ long. Infls. loosely 8–15-fld., produced from the old (typically leafless) pbs., drooping, to 8″ long. Fls. to 3″ across, rather sour-scented, bright butter-yellow to orange-yellow, the lip with a very rich orange-yellow disc. Ss. and ps. broadly elliptic, obtuse, the ps. typically toothed marginally. Lip roundish, very beautifully fringed marginally, the disc velvety. Spring. (I) Himalayas to Burma, Thailand, Viet-Nam, and Malay Peninsula.

—var. **oculatum** Hk. (*Dendrobium oculatum* hort.)

More frequent in cultivation than the type, from which it differs in its often more robust stature, usually somewhat larger fls. (to 3½″ across), wider ps. which are often not toothed marginally, and the presence of two blackish-brown, velvety blotches on the disc of the lip. Spring. (I) Burma.

D. Findlayanum Par. & Rchb.f. (*Callista Findlayana* O.Ktze.)

Pbs. st.-like, to 2′ tall, usually erect, the nodes very swollen, grooved, formed above the sheathing, persistent, brownish lf.-bases. Lvs. deciduous, oblong-lanceolate, acute, unequally toothed apically, to 4″ long. Infls. usually 2-fld., rather short, produced from the old leafless pbs. at the nodes, the pedicellate ovaries very long. Fls. to 3″ across, fragrant, rather long-lived, the ss. and ps. varying from blush-white to lilac, the apices often deeper or even with a definite dark lilac-purple blotch. Lip pale lilac marginally, the disc yellow, with a rich magenta-purple blotch on the claw. Winter–early spring. (I, H) Burma; Thailand.

D. formosum Roxb.

Pbs. erect or pendulous, to 1½′ tall, often slightly spindle-shaped, furrowed with age, clothed with the persistent black-hairy lf.-sheaths. Lvs. leathery, oblong or ovate, obliquely emarginate, to 5″ long. Infls. terminal or axillary, 2–4-fld., rather short. Fls. variable in size, to 5″ across in the best forms, pure white except for the yellow or orange-yellow throat on the lip. Ss. oblong-lanceolate, acuminate. Ps. much broader, often undulate marginally, frequently almost round, cusped apically. Lip with very small, rounded lat. lbs. which embrace the col., the dilated midlb. retuse, apiculate, the disc with 2 rough ridges. Winter–early spring. (I, H) Himalayas and Burma to Peninsular Thailand and the Andaman Islands.

D. Gibsoni Paxt. (*Dendrobium fuscatum* Ldl.)

Pbs. st.-like, erect to pendulous, cylindrical, to 4′ long, slender, the nodes not appreciably swollen. Lvs. eventually deciduous, lanceolate to ovate-lanceolate, acuminate, to 6″ long. Infls. loosely 6–12-fld., produced from near the apex of the older pbs., pendulous. Fls. about 2″ across, lasting for two weeks, very fragrant, saffron-yellow to orange-yellow, the lip with 2 black-brown blotches on the pubescent disc. Differs from the allied *D. fimbriatum* Hk. in its shorter, more slender pbs., smaller fls., ps. without toothed margins, and broader lip, the margins of which are only vaguely fringed. Autumn. (I) South China (Yunnan) and Himalayas to Burma.

D. Gouldii Rchb.f.

Pbs. st.-like, stout, to about 4' tall (sometimes to 7' tall). Lvs. rather few, distichous, ovate-elliptic, obtuse, rigidly leathery, to 6" long. Infls. apical and lateral, 6–25-fld., erect or arching, to 2' long. Fls. to 2¾" across, the ss. yellowish stained with purple-brown mostly above the middle, the ps. yellowish at base, otherwise deep purple or chestnut-brown, the lip yellowish, the keels of the midlb. stained with purple or blue-purple. Lip 3-lbd. above the middle, the lat. lbs. rounded at tip, semi-elliptic, the midlb. elliptic, obtuse, with 5 prominent keels which are dilated near the apex, the median one slightly exceeding the others and curved forward into a sharp point. Mostly autumn. (H) Solomon Islands.

D. Haniffii Ridl. (*Dendrobium tortile* Ldl. not A.Cunn.)

Pbs. club- or spindle-shaped, erect, furrowed, to about 12" tall, grooved and ribbed with age. Lvs. recurved, rather leathery, deciduous, linear, retuse, to 4" long. Infls. 2–6-fld., borne from the nodes of the leafless pbs., short. Fls. to 3½" across, very fragrant, rather long-lived, the ss. and ps. white tinged faintly with pale rose or lilac, very undulate, more or less twisted spirally; lip large, pubescent, shell-shaped, lemon-yellow with some purple streaks at the base. Spring. (I, H) Burma; Peninsular Thailand; Andaman Islands; Malay Peninsula; Viet-Nam.

D. Harveyanum Rchb.f.

Allied to and rather simulating *D. Brymerianum* Rchb.f. Pbs. spindle-shaped, furrowed, to 6" tall. Lvs. 2–3, ovate-oblong, rather leathery, about 3" long. Infls. axillary, 3–5-fld., about 6" long. Fls. 2" across, with the odour of honey, bright canary-yellow, with a pair of orange blotches on the disc of the lip, differing from the other sp. principally in having the ps. (as well as the lip) with a wide, intricate, marginal fringe. Lip rough-surfaced, with an obscure callus near the base. Spring. (I) Burma; Thailand.

D. heterocarpum Wall. (*Dendrobium atractodes* Ridl., *D. aureum* Ldl., *D. minahassae* Krzl., *D. rhombeum* Ldl., *Callista aurea* O.Ktze., *Callista heterocarpa* O.Ktze.)

Variable in all parts. Pbs. erect to sharply pendulous, often yellowish, cylindrical to vaguely club-shaped in upper parts, to 5' long. Lvs. deciduous in time, oblong-lanceolate, acute, to 5" long, rather leathery. Infls. 2–3-fld., produced from the nodes of the leafless pbs., short. Fls. to 2½" across, long-lived, fragrant or odourless, cream-white to yellow, sometimes suffused with green or greenish, the lip golden-yellow or white with a yellow disc which is usually streaked and veined with crimson or dull magenta. Lip ovate-lanceolate, acute, often somewhat recurved, the base with incurved sides, the disc pubescent. Spring–autumn, often more than once annually (I, H) India and Ceylon throughout Southeast Asia, Indonesia, and the Philippines to the Moluccas.

D. Hildebrandii Rolfe

Pbs. fleshy, rather st.-like, slender, to 2' tall. Lvs. eventually deciduous, rather leathery, lanceolate, acutish, to 4" long. Infls. usually 2-fld., produced from the leafless pbs., short. Fls. to 3" across, fragrant, rather long-lived, variable in colour, the sometimes twisted ss. and ps. usually greenish-white, the velvety, basally tubular lip white, the disc pale yellow with 2 brown or chocolate-brown blotches. Spring. (I) Burma; Thailand.

D. Hookerianum Ldl. (*Dendrobium chrysotis* Rchb.f.)

Pbs. st.-like, usually pendulous or arching, to 7' long, the nodes rather swollen, often yellowish, elongating for many years. Lvs. persistent for several years, rather papery in texture, dark green, oblong-lanceolate, acuminate, to 6" long, often undulate marginally. Infls. 6–9-fld., mostly produced from near the apices of the older parts of the previous year's pbs., drooping, to 6" long. Fls. to 4" across, fragrant, dark rich yellow, the lip apricot-yellow with 2 purple-black blotches on the disc, fringed marginally. Autumn. (I) India; Himalayas.

D. infundibulum Ldl. (*Dendrobium moulmeinense* hort. Low ex Warn. & Wms.)

Allied to and rather simulating *D. formosum* Roxb., the pbs. more slender, to 2' tall. Fls. to 4" across (usually smaller), pure white, the lip white with a large blotch of golden-yellow in the funnel-shaped throat, the lat. lbs. larger and more distinct than in the other sp. Spring–early summer. (I) Burma and Thailand, at rather high elevations.

—var. **Jamesianum** (Rchb.f.) Veitch (*Dendrobium Jamesianum* Rchb.f.)

Differs from the type in its stouter pbs. and in the lip, which has differently shaped lat. lbs., roughened on their inner surface, and a cinnabar-red disc. Spring. (I) Burma.

D. Johannis Rchb.f.

Pbs. densely clustered, fusiform, often brownish, to more than 12" tall, usually about ½" in diam. Lvs. few, apical, lanceolate, acuminate, apically 2-lbd., to 4" long, very thick and fleshy. Infls. usually erect, slender, often several at once, to 12" long, rather loosely few-fld. Fls. waxy, fragrant, long-lasting, about 1½" long, somewhat variable in colour, but usually with brown or dark brown ss. and ps., the lip yellow streaked on rhombic, rounded lat. lbs. with purple. Dors. sep. and ps. erect, linear, obtuse, twisted. Lat. ss. similar but spreading downwards, usually not twisted. Lip-midlb. ovate-triangular, shortly acute, with 3 roughened calli on disc. Autumn. (H) Northern Australia.

D. Johnsoniae FvM. (*Dendrobium MacFarlanei* Rchb.f., *D. monodon* Krzl., *D. niveum* Rolfe)

Among the finest in the genus. Pbs. slender, club-shaped, to 10" tall. Lvs. 2–3, apical, persistent, rather thickly leathery, elliptic or oblong, subacute apically, to 6" long. Infls. apical or sub-apical, erect, to 12" tall, with 2–12 fls. in a loose rac. at the apex, the stalk long, wiry. Fls. to 5" across, fragrant, snow-white, the lip marked with purple or magenta-red on the inside, the midlb. purple basally, the col. bordered with purple around the stigmatic cavity. Ss. oblong-lanceolate, acute. Ps. much broader, sub-rhombic, acuminate. Lip 3-lbd., the lat. lbs. roundish, erect at the sides of the col., the midlb. cuneate-oblong, acute, the tongue-shaped, furrowed callus usually purple. Autumn–early winter. (I) New Guinea, in the mountains.

D. Kingianum Bidw. ex Ldl.

Very variable, the pbs. either stout or stout only at base and st.-like above, to 12″ tall, often producing offshoots at the top, club-shaped, furrowed, the nodes constricted. Lvs. persistent, 3–6, not very thick, lanceolate, acutish, to 4′ long. Infls. 2–9-fld., apical, usually erect. Fls. fragrant, about 1″ across, not opening fully, varying from pure white (rarely) through various shades of pink to dark mauve, the more or less fan-shaped midlb. of the lip usually splashed with mauve. Autumn–winter. (I) Australia: New South Wales, Queensland.

D. lasianthera J.J.Sm. (*Dendrobium Stueberi* Stueber ex Zurow.)

Rather similar in habit to *D. discolor* Ldl., the pbs. to 10′ tall, the lvs. to 6″ long. Infls. 10–20-fld., to about 1½′ long, produced near the apex of the pbs. Fls. to 2½″ long, the ss. twisted once, glossy dark brown with a red glow, bordered with yellow, the ps. similar but without the yellow margins. Lip with 5 simple ribs ending on the midlb., the middle part clear purple, the lat. lbs. white with purple veins at the base, entirely dull purple upwards, midlb. with basal edges recurved, the disc deep purple, shading to light purple, the margin yellow. Summer. (H) New Guinea.

D. leporinum J.J.Sm.

Allied to and rather simulating *D. stratiotes* Rchb.f., the pbs. to almost 3′ tall. Infls. to 8″ long, 4–6-fld. mostly. Fls. about 2½″ long, the ss. suffused with pale mauve, the veins purple, margins crisped, the ps. narrow, stiffly erect and much twisted, dark purple, sometimes greenish at tips, the lip with greenish lat. lbs., purple-streaked on the outside, the midlb. almost white with purple veins, the 5 keels greenish. Mostly summer–autumn. (H) Moluccas; New Guinea.

D. lineale Rolfe (*Dendrobium Augustae-Victoriae* Krzl., *D. Cogniauxianum* Krzl. ex Warb., *D. Imperatrix* Krzl., *D. veratrifolium* Ldl. ex Hk. not Roxb.)

Pbs. to 10′ tall, often swollen near the base, narrowing at both ends. Lvs. persistent, rigidly leathery, oblong or oblong-lanceolate, usually obtuse, to 6″ long, purple-tinged when young. Infls. many-fld., to 3′ long, produced from the apex or upper nodes of the old pbs., usually gracefully arching. Fls. 2–3″ long, fragrant, heavy-textured, long-lived, variable in colour, the ss. usually violet-mauve, curved backwards, crisped and slightly twisted, the ps. obliquely erect, straight, slightly twisted, not crisped, pale violet-mauve, occasionally flushed with yellow. Lip with 5 white ridges with violet borders, raised and flattened at their apices on the midlb.; lat. lbs. minutely toothed marginally, white veined with violet, greenish towards the base; midlb. small, pale violet, the apex reflexed. Autumn–winter. (H) New Guinea; New Ireland; Solomon Islands.

D. linguaeforme Sw. (*Dendrobium linguiforme* Smith)

Rhiz. creeping, branched. Pbs. very small. Lf. solitary, very thick and tough, ovate to ovate-lanceolate, conspicuously ribbed longitudinally, usually less than 1″ long. Infls. erect or arching, to 5″ tall, the rather numerous fls. densely racemose. Fls. not opening fully, about 1″ long, fragrant, the very narrow ss. and ps. white or rarely pale yellow, the very short lip with some faint purple or lilac marks mostly on the midlb. Autumn–winter. (I) Australia: New South Wales, Queensland.

D. lituiflorum Ldl. (*Dendrobium Hanburyanum* Rchb.f.)

Pbs. clustered, pendulous, slender, usually yellow, to 3′ long, the base very swollen, upper parts terete. Lvs. quickly deciduous, oblong-lanceolate, acutish, rather fragile in texture, to 4″ long. Infls. 2–5-fld., produced from the nodes of the leafless pbs., short, with very large bracts. Fls. to 2½″ across, variable in colour, usually long-lived, fragrant, the ss. and ps. either dark purple or white, sometimes flushed with purplish towards tips, the lip turned up like a trumpet, the broad disc deep violet-purple surrounded by a velvety yellowish band, the margins purple. Spring. (I) India and the Himalayas to Burma and Thailand.

D. Loddigesii Rolfe (*Dendrobium pulchellum* Lodd. not Roxb., *D. Seidelianum* Rchb.f.)

Pbs. st.-like, branching, terete, prostrate or pendulous, grooved and sometimes striped with purplish, usually white-sheathed, to 8″ long. Lvs. quickly deciduous, oblong-lanceolate, acutish, about 3″ long, glossy. Fl. solitary from the nodes of the leafless pbs., about 2″ across, fragrant, rather long-lived, the ss. and ps. pale rose-purple (sometimes white flushed with that colour), the lip almost round, concave, the disc orange, surrounded by a zone of white, with a purple apex, the margin fringed. Late winter–spring. (C, I) China; Hainan Island.

D. longicornu Ldl. (*Dendrobium flexuosum* Griff., *D. Fredianum* hort., *D. hirsutum* Griff.)

Rather similar in habit to *D. formosum* Roxb., but not as robust. Pbs. slender, to 1½′ tall, often rather zigzag, covered by the black-hairy, persistent lf.-bases. Lvs. ovate-lanceolate, obliquely acute, rather leathery, to 4″ long. Infls. 1–3-fld., apical, very short, almost stalkless. Fls. about 1½″ across, fragrant, waxy, long-lived, white except for the often yellowish lip which has an orange-yellow throat; mentum very elongated. Autumn. (I) Himalayas; Burma.

D. Lowii Ldl.

Similar in habit to *D. formosum* Roxb., the pbs. more slender, about 12″ tall. Infls. 2–7-fld., borne from the sides of the pbs. near their apex, rather short. Fls. to 2″ across, fragrant, long-lived, bright yellow, the lip deeper yellow with 6 red veins near the base, the disc red-hairy. Summer–early winter. (H) Borneo.

D. luteolum Batem.

Pbs. rather fleshy, erect, furrowed with age, often striped with dull purple, to 12″ tall. Lvs. stalkless, linear-oblong, acute, rather leathery, to 4″ long. Infls. very numerous from the upper part of the leafy pbs.,

2–4-fld., short-stalked. Fls. to 2½″ across, fragrant, long-lived, rather heavy-textured, pale primrose-yellow, the pubescent disc of the lip deeper yellow with a few red streaks. Ss. oblong, subacute. Ps. much broader, obtuse. Lip broadly ovate-oblong, the lat. lbs. rounded, crisped marginally, enfolding the col., the midlb. un-dulate, ovate, subacute, the disc with 3–5 ridges. Winter–spring. (I) Burma; Malay Peninsula.

D. Macarthiae Thw. (*Dendrobium MacCarthiae* Pfitz.)

Pbs. st.-like, usually pendulous, to 2′ long, greyish-white, the nodes blackish, slightly swollen. Lvs. few, confined to the upper parts of the pbs., to 4″ long, linear-lanceolate, acute. Infls. 2–3-fld., pendulous, pro-duced from the uppermost nodes of the pbs. Fls. rather flattened, when spread out to 4″ across, the ss. and ps. pale rosy-mauve with white suffusion, the broader ps. sometimes striped with amethyst-purple along the middle. Lip delicate mauve-purple, striped and flushed with deep purple, the disc maroon-purple, surrounded by a zone of white, forming a tube at the base. Spring–summer. (H) Ceylon.

D. macrophyllum A.Rich. (*Dendrobium ferox* Hassk., *D. sarcostemma* Teijsm. & Binn., *D. Veitchianum* Ldl.)

One of the finest of Dendrobiums, very variable. Pbs. club-shaped, often somewhat flattened, usually yellow-green or flushed with purple-brown, strongly ribbed, to 12″ tall. Lvs. 2–3, apical, persistent, to 12″ long and 5″ wide, leathery, elliptic, acute or somewhat obtuse, usually glossy yellowish-green. Infls. erect or arching, with a large sheath at the base, apical, 4–20-fld., to 12″ tall or more. Fls. rather sour-smelling, heavy-textured, to 2″ across, variable in colour, typically with the ss. (which are glandular-hairy outside, as is the pedicellate ovary) pale yellow-green, the brighter yellow ps. more or less purple-spotted outside, the lip pale green or yellow-green, the lat. lbs. very large, forming a shallow cup around the col., purple-veined, the midlb. widened from a narrow base, wider than long, more or less marked with rows of purple spots, fleshy, the margins sometimes incurving, the basal callus white. Mostly spring–early summer. (H) Java and the Philippines to New Guinea.

D. macrostachyum Ldl.

Pbs. st.-like, rather fleshy, to about 2′ long, usually more or less erect. Lvs. to 4″ long, lanceolate, acute, eventually deciduous. Infls. usually 2-fld., short, pro-duced from the older leafless pbs. Fls. about 1″ across, the ss. and somewhat wider ps. yellowish, the tubular, rather compressed lip deeper yellow, veined with dull or bright red, broadly oval, undulate marginally. Spring–early summer. (H) Ceylon; India, in the southern and central parts.

D. Mirbelianum Gaud. (*Dendrobium prionochilum* FvM. & Krzl.)

Highly variable in both vegetative and floral dimen-sions. Pbs. somewhat spindle-shaped, to 4′ tall or more (often not more than 2′ tall), the upper part leafy. Lvs. rigidly leathery, to 4″ long, mostly oval, obtuse. Infls. 8–15-fld., produced from near the apex of the old or new pbs., to 12″ long, usually horizontal or gracefully arching. Fls. to 2″ across, glossy, waxy, heavy-textured, light yellow-green to olive-green, the ss. and slightly twisted ps. often with some tiny brown-purple spots, the lip 5-keeled, green, veined with dark violet-brown, the midlb. acute. Almost throughout the year, often more than once annually. (H) Moluccas; Timor; Halmahera; Alor Islands; New Guinea; New Britain.

D. monile (Thunb.) Krzl. (*Epidendrum monile* Thunb., *Onychium japonicum* Bl., *Ormostema albiflora* Raf., *Dendrobium catenatum* Ldl., *D. japonicum* Ldl., *D. moniliforme* Sw.)

Pbs. clustered, terete, the nodes slightly swollen, usually pendulous, to 1½′ long (often shorter). Lvs. deciduous, linear-lanceolate, obtuse, about 5″ long, rather glossy. Infls. usually 2-fld., very short, produced from the leafless pbs. Fls. about 1½″ across, extremely fragrant, pure white except for some purple or red-purple spots or marks in the typically greenish tube of the lip. Spring. (C, I) Japan; Korea.

D. moschatum (Willd.) Sw. (*Cymbidium moschatum* Willd., *Thicuania moschata* Raf.)

Pbs. arching or pendulous, strongly striped with dull brownish-purple, terete, to 8′ long. Lvs. oblong to oblong-ovate, strongly veined, leathery, acuminate, to 7″ long, eventually deciduous. Infls. 5–10-fld., pendulous, produced from near the tips of the old pbs., about 8″ long. Fls. to 3½″ across, heavy-textured, lasting about a week, musk-scented, creamy-buff flushed with rose, the slipper-shaped lip pale yellow, deeper basally, with a large black-purple blotch on each side within, very pubescent. Spring–early summer. (I, H) Himalayas to Burma, Thailand, and Laos.

—var. **cupreum** (Herb.) Rchb.f. (*Dendrobium cupreum* Herb.)

Differs from the type in its smaller vegetative stature, more numerous but smaller (to 3″ across) fls. which have apricot-yellow ss. and ps. and a rich golden-yellow lip which has a large orange blotch on each side within the slipper. Summer. (I, H) Himalayas; ? Thailand.

D. mutabile (Bl.) Ldl. (*Onychium mutabile* Bl., *Ony-chium rigidum* Bl., *Dendrobium rigidum* Ldl., *D. rigescens* Miq., *D. triadenium* Ldl., *Callista mutabilis* O.Ktze.)

Pbs. rather slender, erect, striped with reddish when old, furrowed, to 3′ tall. Lvs. persistent, lanceolate, blunt apically, fleshy, to 4″ long, becoming smaller upwards. Infls. 4–15-fld., often branching, apical, to 7″ tall, usually erect. Fls. about 1¼″ across, lasting about 2 weeks, variable in colour, white or white flushed with rose, the lip deeply emarginate or obcordate, 3-crested on the disc, the crests blunt apically and tinted with yellow or orange. Throughout the year, often more than once annually. (I, H) Ryukyu Islands; India; Sumatra; Java; Moluccas.

D. nobile Ldl. (*Dendrobium Lindleyanum* Griff.)

Probably the most widely grown of Dendrobiums, extremely variable in floral colour and dimensions. Pbs. st.-like, erect, furrowed with age, often yellowish, clustered, terete, the nodes usually somewhat thickened, somewhat compressed, often thickened and club-shaped upwards, to 2' tall, frequently rather zigzag. Lvs. distichous, deciduous, oblong, obliquely emarginate, rather softly leathery, to 4" long. Infls. 1–3-fld., short, produced from the upper nodes of the old leafless pbs. Fls. to 3" across (often smaller), rather waxy and heavy-textured, long-lived, very fragrant, highly variable, often not opening fully, in the typical phase the oval ss. and much wider, wavy-margined ps. white with rose tips, the basally tubular lip downy, cream-white with a rose tip, the throat deep crimson or crimson-purple. Several dozens of horticultural variants have been described, based mostly on divergencies in floral colour. Mostly spring–early summer. (C, I) South China; Nepal; Himalayas; Thailand; Laos; Viet-Nam; Formosa.

D. ochreatum Ldl. (*Dendrobium cambridgeanum* Paxt.)
Pbs. usually yellowish, rather stout, cylindric, to 12" long, arching or pendulous, the nodes strongly swollen. Lvs. deciduous, 2–4" long, ovate-lanceolate, acute, rather leathery. Infls. produced from the nodes of the young leafy pbs., usually 2-fld., very short. Fls. to 3" across, long-lived, fragrant, the elliptic-oblong ss. and ps. rich golden-yellow, the basally tubular lip deeper yellow with a dark maroon-purple blotch on the disc, the apical part velvety. Spring. (C, I) India; Himalayas, often at high elevations; Thailand.

D. palpebrae Ldl.
Simulating *D. Farmeri* Paxt. in habit, but the infls. less dense, the fls. smaller, white with an orange-yellow disc on the lip, and produced at a different season. Infls. loosely 6–10-fld., produced from the joints just below the lvs. Fls. about 1½" across, with a fragrance of hawthorn, the lip downy above and with a fringe of long hairs near the base. Late summer. (I) China: Yunnan; Burma; Thailand.

D. Parishii Rchb.f.
Pbs. usually prostrate or pendulous, cylindrical, thick, curving, to 2' long, often yellowish. Lvs. deciduous, oblong-lanceolate, notched apically, rather soft-leathery, to 5" long. Infls. 2–3-fld., produced from the leafless pbs., mostly in the upper part, short. Fls. to 2" across, fragrant of rhubarb, rather long-lived, the ss. and ps. usually rose-purple, the downy lip lighter in colour at the middle, with a deep purple blotch on each side of the throat. Lip with the expanded part small in comparison to the large, rather inflated tube. Spring–summer. (I) China (Yunnan) and Burma to Thailand, Laos, Cambodia, and Viet-Nam.

D. Pierardii Roxb. (*Limodorum aphyllum* Roxb., *Cymbidium aphyllum* Sw., *Dendrobium cucullatum* R.Br., *Pierardia bicolor* Raf.)
Pbs. very slender, st.-like, pendulous or drooping, to 6' long (rarely longer). Lvs. deciduous, rather soft-textured, to 4" long, sessile, lanceolate, acuminate. Infls. 1–3-fld., short-stalked, produced from the old leafless pbs. Fls. to 2" across, fragrant, rather short-lived, very fragile in texture, often semi-transparent, the ss. and ps. pale blush white or rosy-blush, the lip usually pale yellow, with the tubular part typically furnished

with some dull or bright purple streaks. Spring–early summer. (I, H) India and China and the Himalayas to Burma, Thailand, and Perak in the Malay Peninsula.

D. primulinum Ldl. (*Dendrobium nobile* Ldl. var. *pallidiflorum* Hk.)
Pbs. clustered, rather slender, mostly pendulous or arching, to 12" long and ½" in diam., the nodes slightly swollen. Lvs. deciduous, rather leathery, oblong, obtuse or obliquely emarginate, to 4" long, becoming smaller towards the tops of the pbs. Infls. produced from the nodes of the leafless pbs., usually 1-fld., short. Fls. to 2½" across, very fragrant, lasting well, the ss. and ps. white with pink tips, the large downy lip pale sulphur-yellow or primrose-yellow, the basal sides forming a tube, streaked with purple. Ss. and ps. almost equal, oblong to linear-oblong, obtuse. Lip with a short claw, pubescent, round or vaguely kidney-shaped, the margins fringed. Spring. (I) China; Himalayas; Burma; Thailand; Viet-Nam; Malay Peninsula.

D. pulchellum Roxb. (*Dendrobium Dalhousieanum* Wall.)
Pbs. rather slender and st.-like, to 8' tall (rarely more), terete or somewhat swollen medially, the internodes striped with bright or dull reddish-magenta or reddish-brown, mostly erect or somewhat arching. Lvs. often persisting for several years, to 8" long, rather leathery, linear-oblong or oblong, heart-shaped at the base, obtuse apically. Infls. 5–12-fld., borne from near the apex of the old leafless pbs., to 12" long (often shorter). Fls. to 5" across, rather musk-scented, usually lasting less than a week, the ss. and ps. varying from cream-yellow or lemon-yellow to almost white with a more or less definite rosy suffusion, the large, concave, velvety lip cream-white, basally pale yellowish, with a large magenta-maroon or reddish-maroon blotch on each side of the disc. Mostly spring. (I, H) Himalayas to Burma, Thailand, Viet-Nam, and Malay Peninsula.

D. regium Prain
Pbs. st.-like, rather fleshy, usually erect or slightly arching, to 1½' tall. Lvs. mostly deciduous, lanceolate, rather blunt apically, to 4" long. Infls. usually 2-fld., produced from near the pb.-apex, very short. Fls. to 3" across, fragrant, long-lived, rather heavy-textured, the ss. and ps. rosy-red with white bases, the lip darker rose-red, the tube margined with white, the disc yellow. Ss. oblong, obtuse, the broader ps. elliptic, obtuse. Lip 3-lbd., the lat. lbs. forming a tube, the midlb. rather small. Summer. (H) Lower India.

D. rhodostictum FvM. & Krzl. (*Dendrobium Madonnae* Rolfe)
Pbs. slender, club-shaped, to 8" tall. Lvs. 2–3, apical, leathery, persistent, oval, obtuse, to 2½" long. Infls. produced near pb.-apex, loosely 2–3-fld., about 3" long. Fls. to 2" across, waxy, fragrant, white, the throat of the lip veined with green, the margin of the midlb. with some reddish flecks. Ss. and ps. triangular, acute, the ps. often almost rhombic, somewhat narrowed towards the base. Lip 3-lbd., the lat. lbs. forming a tube around the col., the midlb. almost round. Spring–early summer. (H) New Guinea.

D. rupicola Rchb.f. ex Krzl. (*Dendrobium ciliatum* Par. ex Hk.*)

Pbs. st.-like, terete, sometimes thicker in upper half than below, to 2′ tall. Lvs. persisting (especially above), leathery, glossy bright green, to 5½″ long, oblong to almost lanceolate, acutish. Infls. both apical and axillary, usually arching or horizontally spreading, rather loosely 5–25-fld., to 12″ long. Fls. about 1″ across, cream- or greenish-yellow, the lat. lbs. of the lip veined and sometimes marked with dull reddish-brown. Ss. and ps. rather narrow, mostly erect, the lat. ss. sometimes falcately decurved. Lip cuneate-oblong, the lat. lbs. incurved over the col., the small, ovate, fimbriate midlb. with long club-shaped processes on the nerves. Autumn–early winter. (I) Burma.

D. Sanderae Rolfe

Allied to and rather simulating *D. Dearei* Rchb.f., but the fls. larger (to almost 4″ across), white, the tube of the lip dull or rather bright red, the colour extending onto the midlb. in several irregular streaks. Midlb. of lip broadly ovate, retuse apically, the outside of the tube around the col. often flushed with reddish. Mostly autumn–winter. (I, H) Philippines: Luzon.

D. sanguinolentum Ldl.

Pbs. erect, rather fleshy, to 1½′ tall. Lvs. purplish when young, the sheaths veined with purple, lanceolate, acute, to 3″ long, persistent. Infls. 2–6-fld., dense, produced mostly from the upper nodes of the pbs. Fls. about 1″ across, waxy, deep cream-white or yellowish-white, all segms, with or without crimson-purple tips, the lip-claw with a right angle bend near the base, with an orange spine-like appendage attached to it, which is in close contact with the col.-foot. Summer–autumn. (H) Peninsular Thailand; Malay Peninsula; Sumatra; Borneo.

D. scabrilingue Ldl. (*Dendrobium alboviride* Par., *D. hedyosmum* Batem. ex Hk.f.)

Pbs. club-shaped above, slender below, rather like those of *D. infundibulum* Ldl., but shorter (to 12″ tall, usually less), and more densely clustered, the lf.-sheaths covered with short black hairs. Lvs. persistent, rather leathery, ligulate-oblong, unequally emarginate, to 3″ long. Infls. usually 2-fld., very short, produced from both the old and new pbs. Fls. about 1½″ across, very fragrant, long-lived, waxy, at first green or greenish-white, later turning pure white, the lip with erect, acute lat. lbs. which are green streaked with purple, the longer, recurved midlb. yellow with deep orange grooves down the disc, where it is also striped with crimson or magenta-crimson. Spring. (I, H) Burma; Thailand; Malay Peninsula.

D. Schuetzei Rolfe

Simulating *D. Dearei* Rchb.f. in habit, but the pbs. more robust and usually somewhat shorter. Fls. flat, about 3″ across, fragrant, waxy white, the tube of the lip green, with some purple spots at the extreme base. Lip 3-lbd., very large, the midlb. transversely oblong to almost round or ovate. Autumn. (I, H) Philippines: Mindanao.

D. Schuleri J.J.Sm.

Vegetatively rather similar to *D. discolor* Ldl., the pbs. cylindrical or slightly swollen near the middle or above, to 6′ tall (rarely more), the rigidly leathery lvs. to 7″ long. Infls. many-fld., usually horizontal or arching, to 1½′ long. Fls. to 2½″ across, very pale brownish-green, the ps. narrow basally, widening markedly above, scarcely twisted, the lip with 5 slightly waxy keels, greenish-white with violet markings with abruptly raised ends on the midlb., the lat. lbs. yellow-green with brownish veins. Mostly autumn. (H) Northern New Guinea.

D. secundum (Bl.) Ldl. (*Pedilonum secundum* Bl., *Dendrobium bursigerum* Ldl., *D. secundum* (Bl.) Ldl. var. *bursigerum* Ridl., *Callista bursigera* O.Ktze., *Callista secunda* O.Ktze.)

Pbs. erect to semi-pendulous, usually curving, to 6′ long, rather thick, tapering at both ends, becoming furrowed with age. Lvs. persistent, rather rigidly fleshy, lanceolate, acutish, to 5″ long. Infls. from the uppermost nodes of the pbs., to 5″ long, with very many densely placed fls. all facing upwards. Fls. not opening fully, waxy, glossy, to about ½″ long, bright mauve-pink (rarely white), with an orange lip which forms a spur-like mentum at the base of the col.-foot. Spring–early summer. (I, H) Burma, Thailand, and Viet-Nam through Malaysia to the Philippines, Sumatra, Java, and Borneo.

D. senile Par. & Rchb.f.

Pbs. spindle-shaped, to 4″ tall (usually shorter), covered with short white hairs. Lvs. persistent, 2–3, apical, to 3″ long, flat, rigidly leathery, obovate, acutish, covered with short white hairs. Fls. solitary or paired from the upper pb.-nodes, long-stalked, very fragrant of lemons, waxy, long-lived, about 2″ across, bright yellow, the 3-lbd. lip with a green blotch on each side of the orange or orange-yellow disc. Spring–summer. (I) Burma; Thailand; Laos.

D. speciosum Sm.

Very robust, the pbs. to 3′ tall, variable, usually very swollen basally and narrowing above, ribbed, usually deep green, sometimes flushed with brown or purple-brown. Lvs. 2–5, apical, persistent, rigidly leathery, to 10″ long, broadly to narrowly ovate, acutish or obtuse at apex. Infls. erect or arching, often several produced at once, terminal or from upper lf.-axils, very densely many-fld. (almost cylindrical), to 1½′ tall. Fls. variable in size, very fragrant, not opening widely, about 3″ across when spread out, white, cream, or yellow, the ss. and ps. linear to very narrowly lanceolate, the lat. ss. more or less falcate. Lip very short, 3-lbd., streaked or dotted with purple or red. Col. short, often red- or purple-spotted. Autumn–early winter. (I, H) Australia; New Guinea.

—var. **Hillii** (Hk.f.) F.M.Bail. (*Dendrobium Hillii* Hk.f.)

Differs from the type in being taller, the pbs. more slender, and the lvs. larger. Fls. white or yellow, the segms. more slender and smaller than in the sp. Autumn. (I, H) Australia: New South Wales, Queensland.

Chloraea penicillata Rch b.f.
[F. C. MUELLER-MELCHERS]

Chondrorhyncha aromatica (Rchb.f.)
P.H.Allen [GEORGE FULLER]

Chysis aurea Ldl. [P. H. ALLEN]

Cochlioda Noetzliana (Rchb.f.) Rolfe [GEORGE FULLER]

Coelogyne Dayana Rchb.f. [J. E. DOWNWARD]

Coelogyne cristata Ldl. [*The Orchid Journal*]

D. spectabile (Bl.) Miq. (*Latouria spectabilis* Bl., *Dendrobium tigrinum* Rolfe ex Hemsl.)

Similar in habit to the allied *D. macrophyllum* A.Rich., but larger, the pbs. often more than 2′ long, the infls. with fewer, larger fls. (to 3″ across), in which the ss., ps., and the lip all have long narrow apices and edges strongly crisped towards the base, the colour somewhat brighter than that of the other sp., ss. and ps. cream to pale greenish marginally, with mottled dull purple veins; lip almost white towards the base, yellowish apically, strongly veined with dark purple, the lat. lbs. like those of the other sp., but proportionately smaller, with irregularly crinkled margins, the base of the lip between the lat. lbs. with a large complexly lbd. callus, shining-white with a polished surface, conspicuously 3-lbd. in front. Col. massive, very short, the anther-cap green. Winter–early spring. (H) New Guinea; Solomon Islands.

D. stratiotes Rchb.f.

Pbs. rather like those of *D. discolor* Ldl., to 6′ tall (rarely more). Lvs. rigidly leathery, persistent for several years, the lowest ones to 5½″ long, the upper ones gradually smaller. Infls. 7–15-fld., mostly horizontal, produced from the median and upper nodes or lf.-axils, to 8″ long. Fls. about 3″ tall, the ss. white, curved backwards, the margins somewhat undulate; ps. stiffly erect, twisted, very narrow, light green, more than 2″ long. Lip large, white, the lat. lbs. densely streaked with purple, the midlb. more or less rounded, pointed, strongly purple-veined, 5-keeled, the 2 side keels short. Summer–autumn. (H) Celebes; ? New Guinea.

D. strebloceras Rchb.f. (*Dendrobium Dammerboeri* J.J.Sm.)

Similar in habit to *D. stratiotes* Rchb.f. Infls. 5–10-fld., mostly horizontal, to 1½′ long. Fls. fragrant, about 2″ tall, the ss. and ps. yellowish with dark violet-brown streaks, the ss. curved back, twisted and with wavy margins, the ps. stiffly erect, twisted, about 1¾″ long. Lip with 5 white, violet-bordered keels, the lat. lbs. light yellowish with violet veins, the midlb. widened from a narrow base, abruptly pointed, white with a violet edge and a few violet markings. Mostly autumn. (H) Halmahera.

D. sulcatum Ldl.

Allied to and rather simulating *D. densiflorum* Wall., differing in the flattened, furrowed pbs. and shorter racs. of smaller, short-lived fls. Pbs. club-shaped, to 10″ long, compressed and deeply furrowed, slender below. Lvs. 2–3, apical, ovate-oblong, acute, leathery, to 4″ long. Infls. 10–15-fld., dense, produced from the upper lf.-axils, pendulous. Fls. about 1″ across, very short-lived, orange-yellow, the lip dark orange, broadly ovate, forming a tube around the col. at the base, where there are some reddish streaks. Late winter. (I) Himalayas to Burma, Laos, and ? Thailand.

D. x superbiens Rchb.f. (*Dendrobium Fitzgeraldii* FvM., *D. Goldiei* Rchb.f.)

Natural hybrid between *D. discolor* Ldl. and *D. bigibbum* Ldl. var. *Phalaenopsis* (Fitzg.) F.M.Bail. Variable in habit, usually approximating the latter parent, the pbs. to 5′ tall. Infls. apical or from upper lf.-axils, erect to gracefully arching, to 3′ long, with up to 20 fls. which open in succession over a long period. Fls. to 3″ across, the ss. usually deep rose shaded and reticulated with magenta-purple, whitish on the back, with a narrow pale rose or whitish margin; ps. less than twice as wide as the ss., slightly twisted, deep rose shaded and mottled with magenta-purple. Lip magenta-purple, the 5-keeled disc very rich magenta-purple, usually somewhat recurved apically. Mostly autumn–early winter. (I, H) Northern Australia; Torres Straits Islands; New Guinea.

D. taurinum Ldl. (*Callista taurina* O.Ktze.)

Pbs. often strongly spindle-shaped, usually narrowing both at base and apex, to 6′ tall. Lvs. usually at least partly persistent, mostly near middle of pbs., to 5″ long, very thick and leathery, broadly oblong, unequally bilobed at apex. Infls. 8–20-fld., mostly erect, usually borne from the apex of the old pbs., to 1½′ tall. Fls. about 2½″ across, waxy, long-lived, the ss. yellowish-green, the apices rolled back; ps. very long, erect, twisted, deep purple or brown-purple. Lip oblong, whitish, purple-violet at tip, the 3 keels on the disc usually purplish, marginally very crisped and wavy. Autumn–winter. (I, H) Philippines.

D. teretifolium R.Br. (*Dendrobium calamiforme* Lodd. ex Ldl.)

Variable, the rhiz. elongate, creeping, profusely branched, Pbs. st.-like, very slender, wiry, usually pendulous, branching freely, to 9′ long (usually shorter). Lvs. persistent, numerous, slender, terete, pendulous, to 2′ long, sharp-pointed. Infls. many-fld., often numerous, produced from the lf.-bases or directly from the rhiz., often branched, to 12″ long. Fls. 1–4″ across, often not opening widely, fragrant, the narrowly linear ss. and ps. white, cream-white, or yellow, the lip sometimes with the lat. lbs. red-dotted, the midlb. fringed marginally, red-dotted. Summer–autumn. (I, H) Australia; Torres Straits Islands; New Guinea.

D. tetragonum A.Cunn. ex Ldl.

Pbs. sharply 4-angled, narrowed at both ends, swollen and rather club-shaped medially, to 1½′ tall. Lvs. 2–5, apical, persistent, very glossy, rigidly thin, obovate to lanceolate, usually with wavy margins, to 4″ long. Infls. 2–4-fld., borne from the upper lf.-axils, very short. Fls. very fragrant, varying in size from 2–6″ long, the ss. and ps. yellowish-green flushed or marked with brown, red, or purple, the ss. broad basally, becoming almost thread-like above, the ps. narrowly linear, about ⅔ as long as the ss. Lip yellowish with brown, crimson, or pale red markings, the midlb. with 3 parallel ridges which converge into one at the apex. Mostly spring, sometimes almost throughout the year. (I, H) Australia.

D. thyrsiflorum Rchb.f. (*Dendrobium amabile* O'Brien, *Callista amabilis* Lour.)

Similar in habit to *D. densiflorum* Wall., but the club-shaped pbs. without angles or with several slight ridges. Infls. as in the other sp., pendulous, densely many-fld. Fls. about 2″ across, fragrant, the ss. and ps. white, the lip yellow or orange-yellow. Winter–spring. (I) Himalayas to Burma; Thailand.

D. transparens Wall. (*Dendrobium Henshallii* Rchb.f.)

Pbs. erect to pendulous, slender, cylindrical or slightly swollen at the nodes, to 1½′ long. Lvs. eventually deciduous, 3–4″ long, linear-lanceolate, acute, rather soft-textured. Infls. usually 2-fld., produced mostly from the older leafless pbs., short. Fls. about 1½″ across, delicately scented, not lasting well, the ss. and ps. pale transparent purplish-lilac or pink with whitish bases, the lip oblong, slightly fringed marginally, whitish, with a dark blood-red or dark purple blotch in the throat which extends onto the midlb. in fine streaks or lines. Spring–early summer. (I) Himalayas to Burma, usually at rather high elevations.

D. uniflorum Griff.

Pbs. cylindrical or slightly swollen above the middle, often red-striped, to 4′ long, erect or pendulous. Lvs. to 5″ long, rather softly leathery, oblong, acutish, eventually deciduous. Fls. solitary from the nodes of the old pbs., about 1½″ long, heavy-textured, long-lived, cream-white when fresh, turning dull yellowish or greenish-yellow, the lip with 2 longitudinal orange, crimson, or dull magenta streaks. Ss. and ps. usually recurved, much smaller than the thrust-out lip. Spring. (H) Philippines; Malay Peninsula; Borneo.

D. Victoriae-Reginae Loher (*Dendrobium coeleste* Loher)

Pbs. st.-like, very slender, profusely branching, cylindrical, the nodes swollen and tapering down to the apex of the next node, more or less furnished with a greyish fibrous sheath which gradually breaks down into filaments, to 4′ long, forming an entangled mass. Lvs. deciduous, glossy, oblong-lanceolate, acute, to 3″ long. Infls. 1–5-fld., produced from the nodes of the older, leafless pbs. Fls. often not opening widely (or opening out flat), slightly more than 1″ across, variable in colour, the typical phase with white ss. and ps. furnished with an irregular apical blotch which is sky-blue to violet-blue. Lip flattened or concave, coloured like the other segms., the disc often yellowish or orange. Almost throughout the year. (C, I) Philippines, at rather high elevations.

D. violaceoflavens J.J.Sm.

Pbs. slender, usually cylindrical, sometimes slightly swollen medially, to 18′ tall, mostly erect. Lvs. rigidly leathery, mostly persistent, to 9″ long and 5″ wide, unequally bilobed at the apex. Infls. many-fld., mostly erect or horizontal, to 2′ long, produced from the apex or upper nodes of the older pbs. Fls. 2″ across, the ss. and ps. yellow more or less spotted with dark violet, the ps. wider apically than at base, scarcely twisted. Lip with 5 keels, the lbs. veined with rich violet. This is the largest of the Dendrobiums, vegetatively, and one of the tallest-growing of all pseudobulbous orchids. Mostly autumn–early winter. (H) New Guinea.

D. Wardianum Warn. (*Dendrobium Falconeri* Hk. var. *Wardianum* Hk., *D. album* Wms.)

Pbs. erect or arching, stout, terete, the nodes rather thickened, to 4′ tall. Lvs. deciduous, linear-lanceolate, acute, to 4″ long, glossy, rather leathery. Infls. 1–3-fld., short, produced from the upper nodes of the old leafless pbs. Fls. fragrant, long-lived, to 4″ across, variable, the

ss. and ps. white tipped with magenta, the very large, concave or hooded, pubescent lip white tipped with magenta, the disc very large, rich orange, often with a reddish blotch on each side. Spring. (I) Himalayas to Burma and Thailand.

D. Williamsoni Day & Rchb.f.

Rather similar to *D. infundibulum* Ldl. in habit, but somewhat more robust, the black-hairy, somewhat spindle-shaped pbs. to 1½′ tall. Lvs. numerous, leathery, oblong-ligulate, unequally bilobed at apex, to 4″ long, persistent, velvety with short black hairs. Infls. usually 2-fld., apical or from uppermost lf.-axils, very short, black-hairy. Fls. about 3″ across, waxy, long-lived, fragrant, cream-white, the disc of the lip with a cinnabar-red blotch. Ss. and ps. oblong, acute. Lip 3-lbd., the lat. lbs. enfolding the col. Spring. (I) Himalayas to Thailand.

D. xanthophlebium Ldl. (*Dendrobium marginatum* Batem. ex Hk.)

Pbs. st.-like, less than ¼″ in diam., to 1½′ tall, somewhat angular. Lvs. deciduous, linear-lanceolate, obliquely emarginate, rather soft-textured, to 4″ long. Infls. usually 2-fld., produced from the nodes of the leafless pbs., short. Fls. to 2½″ across, fragrant, rather waxy, short-lived, the ss. and ps. white, the 3-lbd. lip with large, erect, white, orange-veined lat. lbs., the crisped, downy, roundish midlb. orange-yellow bordered with white, the coloured part sometimes veined with brownish. Spring. (I) Burma.

D. aduncum Ldl. Pbs. st.-like, straggling, slender, often zig-zag, to 2′ long. Lvs. deciduous, thin-textured. Infls. 3–5-fld., short, produced through the scarious pb.-sheaths just above the nodes. Fls. rather long-lived, fragrant, about 1″ across, the ss. and ps. white tinged with pink or pale lilac-violet, the lip similar in colour, the anther-cap dark purple. Summer. (I) Himalayas to Burma.

D. affine (Decne.) Steud. (*Onychium affine* Decne.) Pbs. narrowly spindle-shaped, mostly covered with grey, fibrous sheaths, to 2′ tall. Lvs. usually persistent only near tops of pbs., rigidly leathery, curving, ovate-lanceolate, acute to acuminate, to 5″ long. Infls. 10–30-fld., the fls. opening successively over a period of more than a month, from the upper nodes or apex of both old and new pbs., to 2′ long, arching or horizontal. Fls. often not opening fully, rather long-lived, to 1¼″ across, pure dead white, the mentum bright green, the lip with the lat. lbs. folded over the col., greenish, the midlb. greenish at base, with 3 long and 2 lateral short pale magenta lines extending well out, often with a very faint pale magenta streak extending to the sharp apex, which is down-curved. Ps. almost 3 times as broad as ss., rather curved back. Autumn. (H) Moluccas; Timor; New Guinea.

D. albosanguineum Ldl. & Paxt. (*D. atrosanguineum* E.Morr. & DeVos). Pbs. clustered, erect, st.-like, cylindrical, the nodes rather swollen, to 15″ tall. Lvs. deciduous, narrowly lanceolate, to 6″ long, few in number. Infls. produced from the leafless pbs., usually 2-fld., sometimes to 7-fld., short. Fls. 2–3″ across, rather fleshy, long-lived, fragrant, the ss. and ps. creamy-white, the large lip flat, white with a crimson blotch on each side near the base. Ss. and ps. ovate-lanceolate, acutish, the ps. broader. Lip roundish to almost square, not forming a tube. Spring. (I) Burma.

D. aloefolium (Bl.) Rchb.f. (*Macrostomium aloefolium* Bl., *Aporum serra* Ldl., *Dendrobium serra* Ldl.) Sts. thin, flattened, to about 1½′ long, usually erect, the basal and apical portions with bract-like lvs., the median part with thick, fleshy, laterally flattened, oblique, acute lvs. to 1″ long which are strongly jointed at base. Infls. producing the fls. in succession from a cluster of small chaff-like bracts. Fls. about ¼″ across, short-lived, white, with a green anther-cap. Ss. and smaller ps. reflexed. Lip straight, the sides upcurved, truncate at tips, the midlb. not widened, deeply bilobed. Autumn. (H) Thailand; Viet-Nam; Malay Peninsula; Sumatra; Java; Borneo.

D. amethystoglossum Rchb.f. (*Callista amethystoglossa* O.Ktze.) Pbs. st.-like, erect or arching, to 2½′ long, cylindrical, often rather zigzag. Lvs. deciduous, lanceolate, rather fleshy, to about 4″ long. Infls. often more than one simultaneously, to about 6″ long, 15–20-fld., drooping. Fls. about 1½″ across, fragrant, lasting rather well, white, the lobed lip pale lavender-purple, the ss. and ps. somewhat reflexed. Autumn-winter. (C, I) Philippines: Luzon, at high elevations.

D. anceps Sw. (*Aporum anceps* Ldl.) Sts. rather robust, flattened, to 3′ long and ½″ broad, densely leafy. Lvs. to 3″ long, triangular to ovate-lanceolate, acute. Infls. densely clustered, terminal and lateral, short, the pedicellate ovaries very short. Fls. fleshy, faintly fragrant, about ½″ long, not opening well, greenish or yellowish, the lip with a purple margin. Ss. and ps. rather similar, the tips usually incurved, the mentum longer than the ss. Lip faintly 3-lbd., cuneately oblong, membranous, veined, the edges crisped. Spring-autumn. (I) India and the Himalayas to Burma, Thailand, and Viet-Nam.

D. antennatum Ldl. Rather similar in habit to *D. stratiotes* Rchb.f. in all parts, but the pbs. to only about 2′ tall and the lvs. considerably narrower. Infls. mostly arching or horizontal, about 10-fld., to about 10″ long. Fls. about 3″ long, rather similar to those of the other noted sp. in shape but more slender with a narrow lip which has 5 keels, the central one of which is much the longest, the midlb. ovate from a narrow base, concave, with a short point. Ss. whitish, the ps. yellow-green, the lip whitish with red-violet veins. Summer. (H) New Guinea; New Ireland.

—var. **d'Albertisii** (Rchb.f.) J.J.Sm. (*Dendrobium d'Albertisii* Rchb.f.) Differs from the type primarily in its smaller stature, thicker pbs., less twisted ps. and in having the midlb. of the lip convex. Summer. (H) Southern New Guinea.

D. Aries J.J.Sm. (*Dendrobium aeries* hort.) Somewhat simulating *D. discolor* Ldl. in habit, the pbs. st.-like, to about 5′ tall. Lvs. to 6″ long and 3″ wide. Infls. to 8″ long, many-fld., the fls. often all open at once. Fls. long-lasting, heavy-textured, about 2″ long and wide, the broad triangular ss. yellow outside, brown within, the margins narrow, lemon-yellow, the base yellow and violet; ps. narrower than ss., twisting and curving, glittering chestnut-brown, almost 1½″ long; lip with 3 violet keels, the middle one much raised at its forward end, the midlb. round, light brown at base, the apex yellow-green. Autumn. (H) New Guinea.

D. bracteosum Rchb.f. (*Dendrobium chrysolabium* Rolfe, *D. Dixsoni* F.M.Bail., *D. Novae-Hiberniae* Krzl., *D. trisaccatum* Krzl.) Pbs. st.-like, pendulous, thickly cylindrical, furrowed with age, to 10″ long. Lvs. narrowly ligulate, to 3½″ long, rather leathery, glossy. Infls. 3–8-fld., short, usually pendulous. Fls. about 1″ across, waxy, fragrant, rose-red or white, the ligulate lip orange-yellow. Spring. (H) New Guinea; New Ireland.

D. Bullenianum Rchb.f. (*Dendrobium erythroxanthum* Rchb.f., *D. topaziacum* Ames). Pbs. st.-like, fleshy, furrowed with age,

usually erect, to 1½′ tall. Lvs. oblong, leathery, about 2″ long. Infls. about 2½″ long, very dense, egg-shaped, many-fld. Fls. about ¾″ long, waxy, orange-yellow with red longitudinal stripes, not opening fully, the lip spatulate. Spring. (I, H) Philippines.

D. cruentum Rchb.f. Pbs. st.-like, erect, cylindrical, to 12″ tall. Lvs. deciduous, rather leathery, obliquely oblong, emarginate, to 5″ long. Infls. short, 1–2-fld., axillary. Fls. to 2½″ across, heavy-textured, faintly fragrant, lasting well, pale green, the lip with erect, oblong, crimson lat. lbs., the ovate apiculate midlb. green with a warty scarlet crest and 3 red ridges. Autumn. (I) Burma; Thailand; Northern Malay Peninsula.

D. cucumerinum Macleay Rhiz. branched, creeping, fibrous, emitting copious white roots. Pbs. absent. Lvs. solitary, to more than 1″ long and about ¾″ in diam., resembling tiny gherkins, matte-green. Infls. about 1″ long, few-fld., set with papery bracts. Fls. about ⅝″ long, with a foetid odour, the ss. and ps. narrow, recurving in apical halves, green-white more or less streaked with dark red mostly near bases. Lip 3-lbd., white marked with dark wine-red, the very crisped, down-curving midlb. white with very crisped magenta keels and scattered magenta dots and blotches. Col. stout, whitish. Spring. (I, H) Australia: New South Wales, Queensland.

D. Cunninghamii Ldl. (*Dendrobium biflorum* A.Rich., *D. Lessoni* Colenso) Pbs. wiry, st.-like, very slender, profusely branching, to 2½′ long, often forming tangled masses, the few linear, glossy lvs. mostly on the new growing tips, to 2″ long. Infls. 2-fld., short-stalked, borne mostly on the older parts of the leafless pbs. Fls. about 1″ wide, pure white, the lip sometimes with a yellow flush in the throat, 3-lbd., with 5 short keels on the disc. Winter. (C, I) New Zealand.

D. epidendropsis Krzl. Pbs. st.-like, slender, cylindrical, to 2′ tall. Lvs. oblong-lanceolate, acute, to 3″ long, rather leathery. Infls. about 15-fld., slender, with a slim stalk, pendulous, to about 4″ long. Fls. (including the mentum, which is sometimes 2″ long) about 2½″ long, greenish-yellow, the lip larger than the other segms., the lamina almost square. Summer-autumn. (I, H) Philippines; Java.

D. Friedericksianum Rchb.f. Somewhat like *D. Bensoniae* Rchb.f., but more slender, and with smaller fls. Fls. 2–4 per infl., to more than 1½″ across, pale yellow, the vaguely funnel-shaped lip with or without a median dark purple blotch. Spring. (I, H) Thailand.

D. Fuerstenbergianum Schltr. Very similar in all parts to *D. bellatulum* Rolfe, but twice as large, the lvs. smaller, the fls. larger (about 2″ across), white, the midlb. of the lip orange-yellow. Autumn. (H) Thailand.

D. Fytchianum Batem. Pbs. st.-like, to 1½′ tall, slender, erect, cylindrical. Lvs. deciduous, 3–4″ long, oblong-lanceolate. Infls. terminal, 5–10-fld., arching, to 8″ long. Fls. long-lasting, to 2″ across, pure white or white flushed with pale rose, the lat. lbs. of the lip rose-red. Ss. and ps. roundish-obovate, blunt at tips. Lip 3-lbd., bearded at tubular base, the lat. lbs. small, incurved, oblong, the midlb. obcordate, apiculate, about as large as the ps., white. Winter–spring. (I) Burma; ? Thailand.

D. gratiosissimum Rchb.f. (*Dendrobium Bullerianum* Batem.) Pbs. st.-like, usually pendulous, striped longitudinally with purplish, to 3′ long, cylindrical, somewhat thickened at the nodes. Lvs. linear-ligulate, 2-toothed at apex, rather leathery, deciduous, to 4″ long. Infls. short-stalked, 2–3-fld., produced from the leafless pbs. Fls. about 2½″ across, white or lilac with rose-purple tips on the segms., the lip white tipped with rose-purple, the disc with a large roundish, yellow, orange-striped blotch. Ss. and wider ps. oblong-lanceolate, acute. Lip entire, broadly ovate, wavy-margined, glabrous. Spring. (I) Burma; Thailand.

D. Hasseltii (Bl.) Ldl. (*Pedilonum Hasseltii* Bl., *Callista Hasseltii* O.Ktze.) Pbs. st.-like, fleshy, to 4′ long, arching. Lvs. narrowly lanceolate, to 4″ long, rather fragile in texture. Infls. very short, 2–4-fld., produced from the upper parts of the pbs. Fls. about 1″ across, the mentum an additional 1″, deep violet-red, the lip orange-yellow in its apical part, linear-ligulate. Summer–autumn. (H) Sumatra; Java.

D. Hendersoni Hawkes & Heller (*Dendrobium fugax* Schltr. not Rchb.f.) Allied to *D. crumenatum* (Rumph.) Sw. and somewhat resembling it, the sts. to 2½′ tall, the swollen basal part 2-winged, distinctly flattened (*i.e.*, the two wings in one plane much narrower than those in the plane at right angles to it), to about 2″ long. Lvs. and lf.-sheaths purplish when young, about 1″ apart, to 3″ long. Infls. usually 1-fld., very short, produced from the clusters of chaff-like bracts on the st.-like portion of the pbs. Fls. about 1″ long, very fragile, white with a faint pink blush, sometimes with definite pink veins on the lat. lbs. of the lip, the middle part of the lip with 3 low rounded yellow ridges, the acute tip turned down, the ps. narrow. Throughout the year, often more than once annually. (H) Peninsular Thailand; Malay Peninsula; Sumatra; Borneo.

D. histrionicum (Rchb.f.) Schltr. (*Dendrobium Brymerianum* Rchb.f. var. *histrionicum* Rchb.f.) Differs from *D. Brymerianum* Rchb.f., to which it is closely allied, in the spindle-shaped pbs., smaller fls. (to only about 1½″ across), and the fringeing of the lip, which is either very slight or entirely absent. Spring. (I) Burma; Thailand.

D. kentrophyllum Hk.f. (*Dendrobium albicolor* Ridl., *D. capitellatum* J.J.Sm.) Pbs. st.-like, very thin, leafy throughout (often leafless at apex), to 8″ long. Lvs. oblique, flattened, slightly curved backwards, acute, to 1¼″ long. Infls. terminal, the fls. solitary, but often several borne close together. Fls. to ¾″ across, not opening fully, rather waxy, pale greenish-yellow, sometimes flushed outside with pink, the mentum about ½″ long, curved, the ps. narrower than the ss., the lip without distinct lat. lbs., the midlb. cleft, with a median yellow stripe. Autumn. (H) Burma; Thailand; ? Laos; Malay Peninsula; Sumatra; Borneo.

D. Kuhlii (Bl.) Ldl. (*Pedilonum Kuhlii* Bl.) Very closely allied to and simulating *D. Hasseltii* (Bl.) Ldl., but distinguished by the smaller fls., these only about ¼″ long at most, the ss. and ps. deep violet-red, the lip broader than other segms., rosy-purple. Spring. (H) Sumatra; Java.

D. lamellatum (Bl.) Ldl. (*Onychium lamellatum* Bl., *Dendrobium compressum* Ldl.) Pbs. to about 5″ long and 1¼″ wide, flattened and very thin, sheathed at nodes. Lvs. 2–3, broad, rather rigidly leathery, to 3″ long. Infls. borne near apex of pbs., about 4-fld., pendulous, short. Fls. almost 1″ long, not opening fully, the ss. and ps. white with a faint median greenish tinge when young, turning yellowish in age, the lip mostly yellowish, with a dull patch of greenish and 3 low keels, these usually yellow, on the disc. Mostly summer. (H) Burma; Thailand; Malay Peninsula; Sumatra; Java; Borneo; Philippines.

D. linearifolium Teijsm. & Binn. Similar in habit to *D. crumenatum* (Rumph.) Sw., but with smaller, narrower lvs. to 2″ long, the pls. to 2′ tall and more, the pbs. oval, about 1¼″ tall. Fls. similar to the other sp., slightly more than ¼″ long, about ⅛″ wide, white, lasting only 1 day. Spring–early summer. (H) Sumatra; Java.

D. lobatum (Bl.) Miq. (*Aporum lobatum* Bl.) Pbs. st.-like, elongated, to more than 3′ long, pendulous, branched, entirely leafy. Lvs. about 1″ wide, flattened, equitant, flushed with pale purple when young. Infls. borne from any node, few-fld., the fls. appearing successively. Fls. about ¼″ across, pale greenish-yellow, flushed with purple in the middle of the ps. and under the lip-claw, the callus formed of 2 forward-curving horns. Throughout the year, often more than once annually. (H) Malay Peninsula; Sumatra; Java; Borneo.

D. Moorei FvM. Similar in habit to *D. aemulum* R.Br., but more slender, the infls. longer. Fls. about ½″ long, fragrant, white, the lip often marked with purple. Ss. and ps. narrowly lanceolate. Lip rhombic, the lat. lbs. very small. Spring–summer. (I) Lord Howe Island.

D. Odoardi Krzl. Similar to *D. discolor* Ldl. in habit. Infls. many-fld. Fls. 1½″ across, the ss. curved backwards, about 1″ long, basally white, the upper part lemon-yellow suffused with chestnut-brown; ps. longer than the ss., narrow basally, widening abruptly in upper half to almost ½″ wide, twisted, shining-brown suffused with yellow. Lip broad, the lat. lbs. pale green with brown veins, the midlb. lemon-yellow with brown veins, with 5 violet ridges on the disc, the central one much raised at its apical end. Mostly summer. (H) Northern New Guinea.

D. pendulum Roxb. (*Dendrobium crassinode* Bens. & Rchb.f.) Pbs. stout, erect or arching, 6–24″ long, the closely-set nodes swollen into globe-like knots often almost 1″ in diam. Lvs. deciduous, thin, linear-lanceolate, to 5″ long. Infls. 1–2-fld., short, borne from near the tips of the leafless pbs. Fls. 2–2½″ across, fragrant, long-lived, variable in colour, waxy, the ss. and ps. typically white with magenta-purple tips, the large velvety lip white with a magenta-purple tip and a large orange-yellow basal blotch. Winter-spring. (I) Burma; Thailand.

D. planibulbe Ldl. (*Dendrobium tuberiferum* Hk.f.) Rather similar in habit to *D. Hendersoni* Hawkes & Heller, the sts. to 2′ long, the swollen part of the pbs. of 2 internodes, to about 1½″ long, with a low ridge in the middle of each face. Lvs. when young (and sheaths) purple-flushed, to 2″ long. Fls. solitary, very short-lived, about ½″ long, white veined with crimson in all parts, with a yellowish 2-lbd. callus at base of midlb. on lip. Mostly summer. (H) Malay Peninsula; Sumatra; Java; Borneo; Philippines.

D. revolutum Ldl. (*Dendrobium refractum* Teijsm. & Binn., *D. tonkinense* DeWild.) Rather similar in all parts to *D. uniflorum* Griff., differing in its larger size (to 2′ tall), longer lvs. and in floral structure. Fls. solitary, about 1″ long, white, the dors. sep. and ps. back-curved, the lip dull orange on the down-curved sides, with 3 bright orange keels on the midlb. Early summer. (I, H) Burma; Thailand; Laos; Viet-Nam; Malay Peninsula; Borneo; ? New Guinea.

D. rhodopterygium Rchb.f. (*Dendrobium polyphlebium* Rchb.f.) Similar in habit to *D. Parishii* Rchb.f. Infls. 1–3-fld., borne from the leafless pbs. Fls. to 3″ across, fragrant, rather long-lived, the ss. and ps. rather pale rose-purple, sometimes mottled with white, the lip tubular at base, the midlb. roundish, fringed, basally streaked with purple, with a broad or narrow pale yellow border, the disc roughened, the col. white, with a purple anther. Spring. (I) Burma.

D. spectatissimum Rchb.f. Very similar in all parts to *D. formosum* Roxb., but with larger fls. (to 5″ across and more), these snow-white, heavy-textured, with a golden-yellow blotch on the disc of the midlb. Mentum very short, blunt. Summer–autumn. (H) Borneo.

D. spurium (Bl.) J.J.Sm. (*Dendrobium euphlebium* Rchb.f., *Dendrocolla spuria* Bl.) Rhiz. growing downwards, the successive pbs. arising below each other but erect, in age becoming horizontal to arching, to 12″ long, thickly green-sheathed when young, thickened upwards from a slender base. Lvs. 2–3 at apex of pbs., drooping, about 4–5″ long. Infls. 1-fld., arising from the bare pbs. below the lvs. Fls. lasting one day only, flowering over an interval of several weeks or months, about 1¼″ across, the spreading ss. and ps. white, the lip-blade almost round, concave, cream or pinkish with conspicuous purple-brown veins and a median orange flush. Throughout the year. (H) Malay Peninsula; Sumatra; Java; Borneo; Philippines; New Guinea.

D. strepsiceros J.J.Sm. Similar in habit to *D. discolor* Ldl. and its allies, to about 2′ tall, the pbs. relatively thick. Infls. about 12-fld., erect, to 12″ tall. Fls. more than 2″ high, the ss. and ps. light yellow-green, the ss. marked with brownish, the dors. sep. and ps. twisted. Lip with rounded, light green, dark violet-veined lat. lbs. that are warty inside, the midlb. large, white, streaked basally with violet, within 5 white, violet-streaked keels. Throughout the year, often more than once annually. (H) Moluccas.

D. striolatum Rchb.f. (*Dendrobium Milligani* FvM., *D. schoeninum* Ldl.) Rhiz. loosely branched, st.-like. Pbs. almost absent. Lvs. solitary, terete, fleshy, to 4″ long. Infls. 1–2-fld., loose, rather short. Fls. often not opening fully, about ½″ long, whitish, more or less streaked with red-brown. Ss. and ps. linear, acute. Lip 3-lbd., the disc of the midlb. with several yellow calli. Autumn. (I) Australia.

D. trigonopus Rchb.f. (*Dendrobium velutinum* Rolfe). Pbs. fleshy, furrowed, to 8″ tall. Lvs. leathery, narrowly oblong, obtuse, to 3½″ long. Infls. very short, 2–4-fld., borne from the pb.-sides. Fls. about 2″ across, fragrant, with a strongly 3-angled pedicellate ovary, yellow, the lip somewhat darker, with very small lat. lbs. that are velvety-warty. Spring. (C, I) China: Yunnan; Burma; Thailand; Laos.

D. trilamellatum J.J.Sm. Similar in habit to a small *D. discolor* Ldl., the pbs. to about 2′ tall. Infls. to 1½′ long, few-fld., arching to semi-erect. Fls. about 2″ long, waxy, long-lived, the ss. and ps. light yellow or greenish-yellow, with 3–6 dark brown lines, narrow, twisted, the ps. crisped. Lip with the lat. lbs. yellow with violet veins, the midlb. sulphur-yellow, with 3 darker keels which are very prominent. Throughout the year. (H) New Guinea.

D. Wattii Rchb.f. Pbs. st.-like, fleshy, cylindric, the sheaths shortly black-hairy, to 12″ tall. Lvs. leathery, to 4″ long. Infls. shortly-stalked, 2–3-fld., borne at the pb.-apex. Fls. about 2″ across, white, the disc of the lip golden-yellow, warty-thickened. Spring. (H) India: Bengal, Munipore; Thailand.

DENDROCHILUM Bl.
(*Acoridium* Nees, *Platyclinis* Bth.)

The genus *Dendrochilum* (almost universally and incorrectly known by orchidists as *Platyclinis*) contains about one hundred and fifty species of epiphytic or lithophytic—very rarely terrestrial, mostly pseudobulbous, often very handsome orchids, a few of which are found in contemporary collections. Distributed in a huge region extending from Burma and Sumatra to New Guinea, these plants are particularly abundant in Borneo, Sumatra, and the Philippines, where many of them are known only from a single valley or mountain-

top, thus giving evidence of extreme endemism in the genus. Despite the large size of the group, proportionately few species occur in common cultivation at this time, due doubtless to their general unavailability in the trade, as well as to the often small size of the flowers. These blossoms, however, are customarily produced in considerable numbers in long, very dense, often distinctly two-ranked, gracefully arching or rigidly erect racemes, and are usually sufficiently showy to warrant a place in our collections. The genus is allied to *Coelogyne* Ldl. and to *Pholidota* Ldl., but is both vegetatively and florally rather distinctive, the pseudobulbs (if present) being mostly small and elongate-ovoid to cylindrical, the solitary leaves rather leathery and usually with a prominent petiole, and the inflorescences customarily produced from the centre of the unfolding new growths. The flowers, too, differ from both allied genera in technical details.

Dendrochilum has not, as yet, been taken in hand by the breeders, although interspecific hybridization seems to offer some most intriguing possibilities, as does crossing with allied groups, such as *Coelogyne, Pholidota, Pleione*, etc., providing, of course, that the several genera prove to be genetically compatible.

CULTURE: Generally as for the warm-growing species of *Coelogyne*. Notable success has been enjoyed in the cultivation of these plants of late, by keeping them in well-drained, proportionately rather small pots, filled with a compost consisting of equal parts of chopped sphagnum moss, and shredded tree-fern fibre. Many of them also do very well when tightly mounted on tree-fern slabs. Principally tropical in origin, the Dendrochilums in general grow throughout the year, hence no appreciable rest-period need be given them. They delight in a semi-shaded situation, with abundant free-moving fresh air, and benefit by frequent and rather liberal applications of fertilizing materials. They are highly intolerant of stale conditions at the roots, and must immediately be removed from a compost which has deteriorated. With careful attention to their cultural wants, they may be grown into highly spectacular 'specimen' plants, with dozens of their handsome sprays of small, mostly highly fragrant flowers. (I, H)

D. Cobbianum Rchb.f. (*Acoridium Cobbianum* Rolfe, *Platyclinis Cobbiana* Hemsl.)
Pbs. tightly clustered, elongate-ovoid to subconical, angled, mostly furrowed, dark dull green, 1–2″ tall. Lf. solitary, long-petioled, rather softly-leathery, elliptic-lanceolate to narrowly lanceolate, rather wavy, to about 6″ long and 1½″ wide. Infls. long-peduncled (to about 12″), the rac. sharply pendulous, to 8″ long, very densely many-fld., the fls. in tortuous, twisted, paired ranks. Fls. rather strongly fragrant, short- or long-lived, about ¾″ across at most, white to pale straw-yellow, the lip yellow or orange-yellow, the col. white apically, greenish below. Ss. and ps. elliptic-oblong, acute. Lip flabellate, slightly retuse at apex. Mostly Sept.–Oct. (I, H) Philippines.

D. filiforme Ldl. (*Platyclinis filiformis* Bth.)
Pbs. clustered, ovoid, somewhat elongated, to 1¼″ long, becoming grooved with age. Lf. solitary, rather

long-stalked, broadly linear, 5–8″ long, usually rather rigidly erect or ascending. Infl. with the naked slender peduncle arching, to 12″ long or more, the very densely many-fld. (up to 100 fls.) rac. sharply pendulous, often of comparable length, the fls. arranged in 2 ranks. Fls. more than ¼″ across, fragrant, often rather short-lived, yellowish-white to yellow, the lip often almost golden-yellow. Ss. and ps. oval. Lip shorter than the other segms., obcordate, emarginate. Spring–early summer. (I, H) Philippines.

D. glumaceum Ldl. (*Platyclinis glumacea* Bth., *Acoridium glumaceum* Rolfe)

Pbs. ovoid, to about 2″ tall, the juvenile ones furnished at base with reddish sheathing bracts, clustered. Lvs. rather long-petioled, narrowly lanceolate, vaguely plicate, to about 10″ long and 1½″ wide, often wavy-margined. Infls. filiform, the arching to pendulous, very densely 2-ranked, many-fld. rac. occupying the apical half or more, overall to more than 12″ long. Fls. about ½″ in diam., often rather short-lived, fragrant of sweet hay, the ss. and ps. whitish or straw-coloured, the lip with a greenish or yellowish suffusion on the disc. Ss. and ps. linear-oblong, acuminate. Lip 3-lbd., the lat. lbs. acute; midlb. roundish with 2 rather thick lamellae on the disc. Mostly Mar.–May. (I, H) Philippines.

D. abbreviatum Bl. (*Platyclinis abbreviata* Hemsl.) Pbs. clustered, to about 2″ tall. Lf. solitary, long-petioled, narrowly lanceolate, rather undulate marginally, to 14″ long. Infl. to 12″ long and more, loosely many-fld., somewhat arching. Fls. about ½″ in diam., pale green, the lip brownish in the middle, on the disc. Summer. (H) Java.

D. aurantiacum Bl. Pbs. borne at intervals of about 1–3½″ along a creeping rhiz., cylindric, to 1¼″ tall. Lf. solitary, rather long-petioled, 3–4½″ long. Infl. borne from a specialized growth near the pb.-bases, loosely many-fld., short-peduncled, to 5″ long. Fls. very fragrant, about ¼″ in diam., orange-red. Summer, mostly June–July. (H) Sumatra; Java.

D. cornutum Rchb.f. (*Platyclinis cornuta* Bth., *Acoridium cornutum* Rolfe). Pbs. usually very narrow, cylindrical, rising one above the other from the creeping rhiz., to about 2″ long. Lf. solitary, petioled, narrowly lanceolate, to 8″ long. Infl. very slender, gracefully arching, to 8″ long. Fls. about ¼″ in diam., yellow-green, the disc of the lip sometimes dark green. Summer–early autumn. (I, H) Sumatra; Java.

D. latifolium Ldl. (*Platyclinis latifolia* Hemsl., *Acoridium latifolium* Rolfe) Much like *D. glumaceum* Ldl., but markedly more robust, with longer, broader lvs. Infl. with a long, naked peduncle, gracefully arching, densely many-fld., the fls. arranged in 2 ranks. Fls. fragrant, about ½″ in diam., yellow-green. Ss. oblong, acute. Lip shorter than the other segms., apically rather reflexed. Spring, mostly Mar.–Apr. (I, H) Philippines.

D. longifolium Rchb.f. (*Platyclinis longifolia* Hemsl., *Acoridium longifolium* Rolfe). Similar in habit to *D. glumaceum* Ldl., but considerably more robust, the lvs. similar but somewhat broader. Infl. very slender, long-peduncled, gracefully arching, the rac. rather densely many-fld., the fls. borne in 2 ranks. Fls. about ½″ in diam., very fragrant, the ss. and ps. greenish-yellow, lanceolate, very acute, the lip suffused with sepia-brown on the disc. Mostly May–July. (I, H) Sumatra; Java.

D. uncatum Rchb.f. (*Platyclinis uncata* Bth., *Acoridium uncatum* Rolfe) Rather similar in habit to *D. filiforme* Ldl., but somewhat less robust. Infls. with slender, elongate peduncles, gracefully arching outwards and downwards, to 6″ long, with a rather densely many-fld., 2-ranked rac. at the apical half or so. Fls. about ⅜″ in diam., fragrant, yellowish-white, the ss. and ps. oblong, the apically blunt lip brownish or ochre-brown. Mostly Oct.–Nov., sometimes also during the summer months. (I, H) Philippines.

DENDROPHYLAX Rchb.f.

The genus *Dendrophylax*, a member of the subtribe *Campylocentrinae*, contains about five very remarkable species, all natives of the West Indies. Closely allied to *Polyrrhiza* Pfitz., they are characterized by possessing no leaves in the adult plants (minute leaf-like bracts are borne on the seedlings), very short, woody stems, and a rather large number of spreading, roundish or flattened, chloroplast-bearing roots. The only species in contemporary cultivation, **D. varius** (Gmel.) Urb., is a completely charming epiphyte, but unfortunately one whose cultural requirements are met with difficulty, and it is but barely kept alive for more than a year or so after being transported from the wild.

Nothing is known of the genetic affinities of this rare genus.

CULTURE: As for the leafless species of *Campylocentrum*. (H)

D. varius (Gmel.) Urb. (*Orchis varia* Gmel., *Aëranthus hymenanthus* Griseb., *Dendrophylax flexuosus* Urb., *D. hymenanthus* Rchb.f., *Limodorum flexuosum* Willd.)

Roots often to 12″ long, flattened, greyish-green with innumerable tiny darker spots over the entire surface. Infls. arising from the centre of the root-cluster (where a very minute abortive st. may be seen in old specimens), to almost 12″ tall, usually simple but occasionally with a few short branches, bearing up to 8 showy fls. which open successively over a period of several weeks. Fls. about ¾″ across, pure white, with a tiny blotch of vivid yellow on the disc of the lip, the ss. and ps. considerably reduced in size. Mostly spring. (H) Cuba; Hispaniola.

DEROEMERIA Rchb.f.

Deroemeria is a member of the subtribe *Habenarinae*, and all of its three terrestrial species inhabit South or South-central Africa. They are complex plants allied to *Holothrix* Ldl., and none of them appears to be present in cultivation at this time, although they are of sufficient interest to warrant attention by specialists.

Nothing is known of the genetic affinities of this rare group.

CULTURE: Presumably as for *Stenoglottis*. (I)

DIADENIUM P. & E.

This is a very rare and incompletely known genus of the subtribe *Comparettiinae*, with but a single recorded species known to date. **Diadenium micranthum** P. & E., indigenous in Peru, is a small epiphytic plant rather

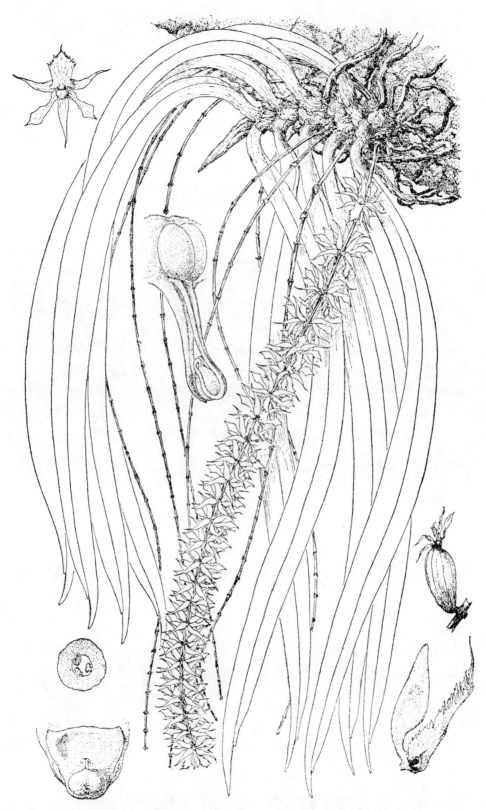

Diaphananthe fragrantissima (Rchb.f.) Schltr. [*Flora of the Belgian Congo*]

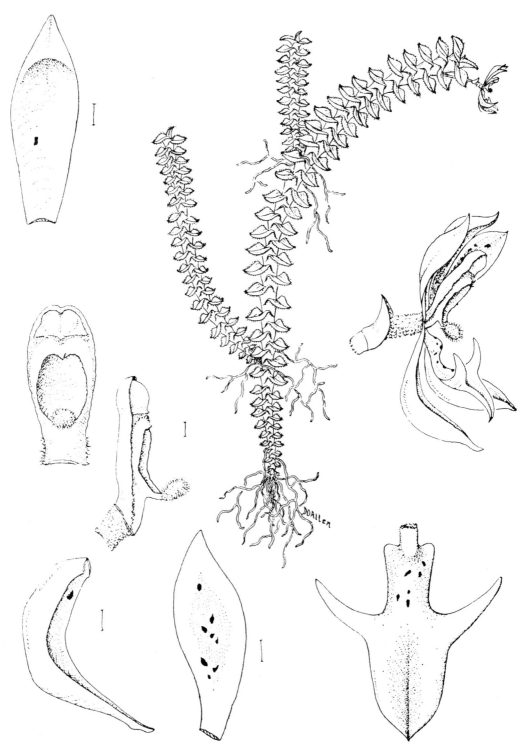

Dichaea ciliolata Rolfe [DOROTHY O. ALLEN]

simulating *Comparettia* P. & E., but differing in technical details of the flowers. It is not in cultivation at this time, and is in any case of primarily scientific interest.

Nothing is known of the genetic affinities of *Diadenium*.

CULTURE: As for *Ornithocephalus*, though cooler temperatures must prevail. (C, I)

DIAPHANANTHE Schltr.

This is a genus—a segregate from *Angraecum* Bory—which now contains about twenty-five species of rather scarce epiphytic (rarely lithophytic) orchids, native mostly in tropical Africa, but with outlying representatives in such areas as the Mascarene Islands, Abyssinia, etc. Allied to *Listrostachys* Rchb.f., from which it differs in characters of the lip and column, the Diaphananthes are typically rather robust plants with leathery or somewhat soft-textured leaves and generally elongate, very densely many-flowered, sharply pendulous inflorescences. Though small, the blossoms of this genus are produced in sufficient quantities, and are often so delightfully fragrant, that they recommend the group to all enthusiasts.

No hybrids have as yet been produced in *Diaphananthe*, and nothing is known of its genetic affinities.

CULTURE: As for the tropical Angraecums. (H)

D. bidens (Afz.) Schltr. (*Limodorum bidens* Afz., *Listrostachys bidens* Rchb.f.)

Sts. elongate, typically pendulous, to 2′ long and more, leafy throughout. Lvs. spreading, leathery, oblong-elliptic, strongly 2-lbd. at the apex, sharply narrowed basally, to 5″ long and 1½″ wide. Infls. pendulous, densely many-fld., to 6″ long. Fls. transparent yellowish-pink, about ½″ long, fragrant. Ss. and ps. oblong, obtuse. Lip broadly ovate, 3-keeled, the spur, slightly longer than the lamina. Summer. (H) Sierra Leone.

D. pellucida (Ldl.) Schltr. (*Angraecum pellucidum* Ldl., *Angraecum Althoffii* Krzl., *Angraecum Thonnerianum* Krzl., *Listrostachys pellucida* Rchb.f.)

Sts. short, often branching near base, usually less than 6″ tall. Lvs. very gracefully arching, rather soft-textured, drooping, oblong, unequally 2-lbd. at the apex, glossy bright green, to 1½′ long and 3½″ wide. Infls. pendulous, very densely many-fld., the fls. arranged in two ranks, to 12″ long and more. Fls. about ½″ across, fragrant, transparent white, glittering, the lip studded and bordered with tiny crystalline projections. Ss. and ps. spreading, ligulate, acutish. Lip almost square, the spur thickened medially, about as long as the lamina. Autumn–winter. (H) Sierra Leone to the Belgian Congo.

D. vandaeformis (Krzl.) Schltr. (*Listrostachys vandaeformis* Krzl., *Diaphananthe vandiformis* Schltr.)

Robust sp., the sts. usually simple, erect, to 1½′ tall, densely leafy. Lvs. very thick and leathery, ligulate, obliquely 2-lbd. at apex, to 1½′ long and 1½″ wide. Infls. pendulous, densely many-fld., about 12″ long. Fls. about ½″ long, fragrant, transparent yellow. Ss. and ps. spreading, lanceolate-ovate, acute. Lip almost square, constricted medially, apiculate, fine-ciliate marginally, the spur rather long, blunt. Autumn. (H) Cameroons.

D. lorifolia Summerh. St. pendulous, to 6″ long, the few leathery arching lvs. usually all arranged in a single plane, to 10″ long. Infls. several at once, sharply pendulous, loosely 10–16-fld. Fls. almost ¾″ across, varying from white to pale yellow or pale salmon-pink-coloured, the lip proportionately larger than other segms. Winter–late spring. (I) Sudan and Uganda to Kenya and Tanganyika.

DICERATOSTELE Summerh.

Consisting of but a single known species, **Diceratostele gabonensis** Summerh., this very odd terrestrial genus of the subtribe *Sobraliinae* has apparently been collected on only a single occasion. A native of Gabon, it vegetatively simulates a *Corymborchis*, but differs markedly in structure of the rather small white flowers. It is unknown in cultivation at this time.

Nothing is known of the genetic affinities of *Diceratostele*.

CULTURE: Possibly as for *Sobralia*. (H)

DICHAEA Ldl.
(*Dichaeopsis* Pfitz., *Epithecia* Kn. & Westc.)

A member of the peculiar pseudomonopodial group of orchids (and of the subtribe *Dichaeinae*), *Dichaea* contains approximately forty often rather confused species of handsome epiphytic or lithophytic plants in tropical America, ranging from Cuba and Mexico to Peru and Brazil. Unfortunately little-known in collections today, they are grown as much for their unusually attractive foliage as for the unique, often brightly-hued and highly fragrant flowers. Pendulous, erect, or creeping plants, they frequently branch profusely, and consist of often elongate stems which are closely covered by flattened, two-ranked leaves, which may be persistent for many years, or may be gradually deciduous in the lower portions of the specimen. These leaves are often tinged with brownish or purplish, and when the plants are well-grown, form a most handsome and exotic plant, even when the blossoms are not in evidence. The flowers—which are typically small and of remarkable complexity—are produced singly from the leaf-axils along these stems, and for their size give off an amazingly powerful perfume, frequently like that of chocolate or cocoa. Colour in the blooms of *Dichaea* is variable, and certain of the species have floral parts which are of a particularly entrancing bright blue shade. Dichaeas are generally conceded to be among the more highly evolved of all orchidaceous plants.

A single natural hybrid, native in Mexico and Central America, is on record for *Dichaea*. Artificial interspecific breeding seems to offer some fascinating possibilities in this genus of 'foliage' orchids.

CULTURE: Once imported from the wild, Dichaeas are often rather difficult to re-establish, since the transportation and the fumigation which they typically receive upon their arrival in the United States, has a deleterious and frequently fatal effect on them. They are best rooted in small, perfectly-drained pots, in a mixture of about equal parts of chopped sphagnum moss and shredded tree-fern fibre, preferably with a top-surfacing of sphagnum moss. The plants should be kept in a relatively shaded, moist, very humid spot, although if too much water is given the plants until they have a sufficiently active root-system, they may rot rapidly. When rooting is active, they may be transferred to sphagnum-covered tree-fern slabs, and kept in a slightly brighter, but still constantly moist spot in the greenhouse. Since they have no moisture-storing structures, they must never be allowed to dry out, even for a few days. They should be disturbed as seldom as possible, since repotting sets them back, and often results in a total lack of flowers for several years. The erect, non-branching species (*e.g. D. glauca*) do well when kept in pots such as suggested above. Frequent applications of weakened fertilizing solution have proven to be most beneficial. (I, H)

D. glauca (Sw.) Ldl. (*Epidendrum glaucum* Sw., *Cymbidium glaucum* Sw., *Epithecia glauca* Schltr., *Dichaeopsis glauca* Schltr., *Dichaea Willdenowiana* Krzl.)

Robust for the genus, erect or somewhat arching downwards, the sts. clustered, more or less concealed by the persistent lf.-sheaths at base, to 2′ tall, slightly compressed, rather stout. Lvs. 2-ranked, thin, ascending or almost horizontally arranged, eventually deciduous, linear-oblong to oblong-elliptic, the rounded apex cuspidate, usually very glaucous, to almost 3″ long. Infls. from upper lf.-axils, slender, about 1″ long, 1-fld. Fls. fragrant, heavy-textured, to ¾″ across (usually smaller), white or greyish-white, more or less spotted with lavender and yellow, especially on the lip. Spring. (I, H) West Indies; Mexico to Costa Rica.

D. Morrisii F. & R. (*Dichaea Bradeorum* Schltr., *Epithecia Morrisii* Schltr.)

Sts. erect or more commonly pendulous, branching, to 1½′ long, the persistent lf.-sheaths very broad, conduplicate, distichously imbricating. Lf.-blades jointed to lf.-bases and eventually deciduous, elliptic-oblong to broadly ligular, obtuse and minutely apiculate, vaguely coriaceous, to 2¾″ long and ½″ wide. Infls. 1-fld., very short, produced from upper lf.-axils, the peduncle provided at apex with 2 large spathaceous bracts which completely envelop and conspicuously exceed the pedicellate ovary. Fls. large for the genus, to almost 1″ in diam., often not opening fully, the ss. and ps. pale green striped with dark lavender, the lip dark lavender. Ss. and ps. slightly ciliate marginally. Lip fleshy, clawed at base, the blade dilated and 3-lbd., more or less anchor-shaped. Spring. (I, H) Hispaniola; Jamaica; Nicaragua; Costa Rica; Panama.

D. muricata (Sw.) Ldl. (*Cymbidium muricatum* Sw., *Dichaea latifolia* Ldl., *D. Moritzii* Rchb.f., *D. verrucosa* A. & S.)

Sts. elongate, pendulous, usually profusely branched, to 2′ long (rarely longer), often forming a dense mat on mossy trees or rocks. Lvs. not deciduous, not jointed, elliptic-oblong to ligular, obtuse to acute, with entire margins, the under-surface distinctly keeled, terminating at the apex in a minute to relatively elongate apicule, the blades often rather obliquely ascending, to ¾″ long. Infls. 1-fld., slender, to ¾″ long, produced from upper lf.-axils. Fls. about ½″ in diam., often cup-shaped and not opening fully, fragrant, the ss. and ps. yellowish or greenish-yellow, the ps. usually sparsely spotted with blue, the lip mostly blue. Lip 7-nerved, shortly clawed, obovate-rhomboid, the outer angles with a recurved, long, acuminate lb., the apex tapering, long-mucronate. Caps. densely covered with long bristles which are only slightly swollen just at the base. Winter. (I, H) Cuba to Lesser Antilles; Mexico to Brazil.

D. panamensis Ldl. (*Dichaeopsis panamensis* Schltr., *Epithecia panamensis* Schltr.)

Sts. clustered, usually unbranched, erect or ascending, often rather flexuose, 1½–7″ tall. Lvs. 2-ranked on the st., narrowly linear-lanceolate, acute and apiculate or acuminate, vaguely coriaceous, often glaucous, usually in alternating groups of unequal length, the blades jointed to the sheathing bases and eventually deciduous below, ¼–1½″ long. Infls. thread-like, 1-fld., short, produced from upper lf.-axils. Fls. translucent, usually short-lived, about ⅜″ in diam., usually cup-like, white more or less densely spotted with pink or purple on all segms. Lip sagittate to obovate-spatulate in outline when spread out, the ligular claw slightly arcuate in profile, the blade abruptly dilated, 3-lbd., the midlb. broadly triangular, shortly acute with a short central keel on the lower surface at apex. Summer–autumn. (I, H) Mexico; British Honduras; Guatemala; Honduras; Nicaragua; Costa Rica; Panama.

DICKASONIA L.O.Wms.

The genus *Dickasonia*, a rather recent addition to the Orchidaceae, consists of a single extremely rare epiphytic member, **D. vernicosa** L.O.Wms., from Burma. The group is a member of the subtribe *Coelogyninae*, being somewhat allied to *Panisea* Ldl., but differing from that group in critical details of the smallish, racemose flowers. It is unknown in our collections at this time, and in any event—because of its rather nondescript appearance—is primarily of scientific importance.

Nothing has been ascertained regarding the genetic affinities of *Dickasonia*.

CULTURE: Presumably as for the middle-elevation Coelogynes. (I)

DIDICIEA King & Pantl.

A member of the subtribe *Calypsoinae*, **Didiciea Cunninghamii** King & Pantl. is the only species of this genus known to science, this small terrestrial orchid, rather reminiscent of and allied to *Tipularia* Nutt. It inhabits restricted areas in the Himalayas, usually growing at elevations in excess of 10,000 feet, and is unknown in collections today.

Nothing is known of the genetic affinities of this strange plant.

CULTURE: Possibly as for *Corallorrhiza*. (C)

DIDYMOPLEXIS Griff.
(*Apetalon* Wight, *Epiphanes* Rchb.f., *Leucorchis* Bl., *Leucolaena* Ridl.)

This is a genus of about ten species of very small but unusually interesting saprophytic orchids of the subtribe *Gastrodiinae*, which inhabit the region extending from India throughout Malaysia and Indonesia to the Philippines, New Caledonia, and the Fiji Islands. Virtually unknown in collections and very difficult to keep alive for more than a single season (as are all saprophytic plants), they are of interest for the tremendous elongation of the pedicellate ovaries and rachis which occurs after fertilization. In most of the species the flowers are almost stalkless, but when the fruits have formed, the capsules attain lengths in excess of five inches.

Nothing is known of the genetic alliances of this odd genus.

CULTURE: As for *Corallorrhiza*. (H)

D. pallens Griff. (*Apetalon minutum* Wight, *Arethusa bengalensis* hort., *Arethusa ecristata* Griff., *Epiphanes pallens* Rchb.f., *Leucorchis sylvatica* Bl.)

Rhiz. fleshy, narrowed apically. Sts. erect, leafless, to 5″ tall, with a few fls. at the apex, furnished with a few triangular bracts. Fls. about ½″ long, erect, pale olive-brown or pinkish, the lip yellowish-white with a row of yellowish warts down the middle. Dors. sep. joined to ps. for half its length, the lat. ss. joined and partially connected to the ps. Lip almost triangular. Winter. (H) India to Java and the Philippines.

DILOCHIA Bl.

Dilochia is a genus of about five species, none of them at all frequent in cultivation, of terrestrial, lithophytic, or epiphytic orchids in Malaysia, ranging from the Himalayas to Sumatra, Java, and Borneo in Indonesia. Closely allied to *Arundina* Bl., they are included in that group by some authorities, but differ in technical floral details, and in the conspicuous bracts of the inflorescence. Robust plants, they bear leafy stems much in the manner of *Arundina*, rather wide rigid foliage, and apical usually branching panicles of smallish but attractive flowers of short duration.

No hybrids are as yet known in *Dilochia*, though Holttum has suggested that 'it [**D. Cantleyi** (Hk.f.) Ridl.] would be well worth hybridizing with the larger-flowered varieties of *Arundina*, to produce a large-flowered plant with branched inflorescence'.[1]

CULTURE: As for *Arundina*. (H)

D. Cantleyi (Hk.f.) Ridl. (*Arundina Cantleyi* Hk.f.)

Sts., clustered, robust, rather bamboo-like, to 7′ tall, leafy. Lvs. rather stiff, with a narrow point, to 6″ long. Infls. bearing a succession of fls. for several months, rather compact, several-branched, erect to drooping, to about 12″ long; bracts cream-coloured, cup-shaped, large, the rachis purple. Fls. on purplish pedicellate ovaries, about 1½″ across, not lasting well, white or pale lemon-yellow, the ss. purplish medially on the outside, the lip mostly yellow flushed with brown-orange. Dors. sep. arching over the col., the ps. and lat. ss. more or less curved backwards. Lip 3-lbd., the lat. lbs. erect, triangular at apex, the midlb. oblong, dilated, yellow and 2-lbd. at tip, with 5 irregular white keels. Autumn. (I, H) Malay Peninsula; Sumatra; Borneo.

[1] In *Fl. Malaya* (*Orch. Malaya*)1: 189. 1953.

DIMORPHORCHIS Rolfe

The genus *Dimorphorchis* contains two species of extraordinary epiphytic orchids from Borneo, both generally considered members of the allied group *Arachnis* Bl. Because of their remarkable structure, floral dimorphy, and technical characters, however, it seems best to consider them in this rather than in the older genus, as proposed by Rolfe. **Dimorphorchis Rohaniana** (Rchb.f.) Rolfe (*Vanda Rohaniana* Rchb.f.) is apparently not in contemporary cultivation, but the highly spectacular *D. Lowii* (Ldl.) Rolfe is present in certain choice collections today, and is one of the most prized of all orchidaceous plants.

No hybrids have as yet been made with this incredible genus, although it seems logical to assume that intergeneric breeding with allied groups of the *Vandeae*—particularly with *Arachnis*, *Vanda*, *Renanthera*, *Vandopsis*, etc.—would be possible, and would certainly offer some most fascinating progeny.

CULTURE: As for the tropical Vandas. Because of the exuberant stature of the plants, when mature, some form of support is necessary. (H)

D. Lowii (Ldl.) Rolfe (*Vanda Lowii* Ldl., *Arachnanthe Lowii* Bth., *Arachnis Lowii* J.J.Sm., *Renanthera Lowii* Rchb.f.)

Sts. often multiple from the base, erect or gracefully arching, to more than 7′ tall in old specimens, densely leafy throughout. Lvs. ligulate, rather heavy, unequally bilobed at the apex, to almost 3′ long and 2¼″ wide. Infls. sharply pendulous, to 12′ long in some cases, loosely many-fld., rather slender. Fls. of two distinct forms, the 2–3 basal ones like the others to 3″ across and more, the ss. and ps. bright tawny-yellow finely dotted with cinnabar-brown, broader, shorter, and more fleshy than those of the other fls.; remaining fls. with the ss. and ps. deep red or chocolate-brown, with some light yellow spaces chiefly towards and at the apex, linear-oblong, wavy-margined. Lip identical in structure in both forms, much shorter than the other segms., somewhat slipper-shaped with the toe much contracted, on which is an incurved horn, and behind which is a short fleshy plate, the central area light purple, the remainder yellow spotted with purple, except the apex and horn which are wholly yellow. Col. very short and thick, greenish spotted with purple above, white dotted with rose in front. Mostly autumn–early winter. (H) Borneo, especially Sarawak.

DINKLAGEËLLA Mansf.

The extremely rare genus *Dinklageëlla* consists of but a single known species, **D. liberica** Mansf., an epiphytic monopodial angraecoid orchid from Liberia. It is indicated as being somewhat allied to *Oeonia* Ldl. and to *Oeoniella* Schltr., of the very technical subtribe *Sarcanthinae*, from which it differs markedly in critical details of the rather small, white flowers. Insofar as we are able to ascertain, *Dinklageëlla* has not as yet been introduced into our collections.

Nothing is known of the genetic ties of this odd plant.

CULTURE: Presumably as for the tropical Angraecums, etc. (H)

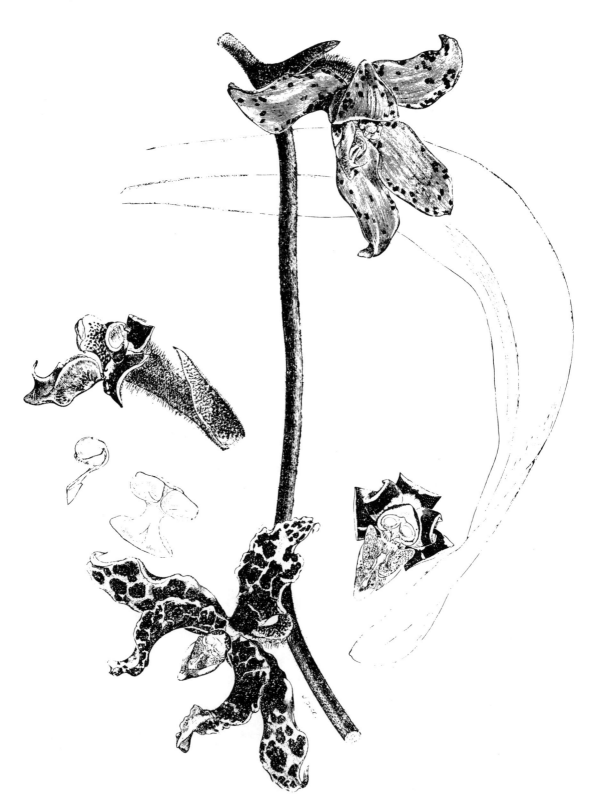

Dimorphorchis Lowii (Ldl.) Rolfe [VEITCH]

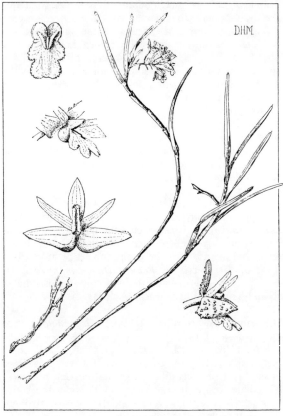

Diothonaea exasperata C. Schweinf. [Schweinfurth, *Orchids of Peru*]

DIOTHONAEA Ldl.
(*Gastropodium* Ldl., *Hemiscleria* Ldl.)

Diothonaea is a small genus of about five species of epiphytic orchids, native principally in the high Andean regions of Colombia, and unknown in contemporary collections. The genus is allied to *Orleanesia* B.-R. of the subtribe *Ponerinae*, and is rather an interesting one, albeit incompletely known and delimited botanically.

Nothing is on record regarding the genetic affinities of this group.

CULTURE: As for the high-elevation Epidendrums. (C, I)

DIPLACORCHIS Schltr.

A single species, **Diplacorchis disoides** (Ridl.) Schltr. (*Habenaria disoides* Ridl., *Brachycorythis disoides* Krzl.) makes up this rare and little-known genus of terrestrial orchids of the subtribe *Habenarinae*. Endemic to Madagascar, it is a rather attractive plant with purple, rose, or whitish-rose flowers, unfortunately not in cultivation at this time.

Nothing is known of the genetic alliances of this genus.

CULTURE: As for *Disa*. (I)

DIPLOCAULOBIUM [Rchb.f.] Krzl.
(*Dendrobium* Sw. § *Diplocaulobium* Rchb.f.)

Diplocaulobium consists of about fifty species of very unusual, mostly rather small epiphytic or lithophytic orchids of the subtribe *Dendrobiinae*. The range of the genus extends from the Malay Peninsula and Indonesia through Melanesia to the Fiji Islands, with the centre of development in New Guinea. In this group the pseudobulbs are ordinarily dimorphic, those bearing flowers differing rather markedly from the sterile ones; this is virtually a unique occurrence in the Orchidaceae. A solitary leaf is produced at the apex of each pseudobulb, and the small to rather large, spidery flowers (usually in shades of white, yellow, or reddish) are borne singly but in succession over a long period from an apical sheath at the leaf-base. These blossoms rather simulate in superficial structure those of *Thrixspermum* Lour. in the subtribe *Sarcanthinae*, and are extremely fugacious, often lasting for only a few hours after anthesis. The Diplocaulobiums are today very scarce in our collections, but they are peculiar little plants of considerable potential interest to the connoisseur orchidist.

No hybrids are known as yet in this genus, and nothing has been ascertained regarding its genetic ties.

CULTURE: As for the smaller, tropical Bulbophyllums and Dendrobiums. Rather fragile orchids, they are often difficult to maintain in good condition for very long. (H)

D. nitidissimum (Rchb.f.) Krzl. (*Dendrobium nitidissimum* Rchb.f., *Dendrobium Mettkeanum* Krzl.)

Pbs. densely clustered, usually strongly 6-grooved longitudinally, usually curving, to 2″ long, very long-lageniform; flowering pbs. slender from a swollen grooved base, with papery basal sheaths, the peduncle from the sheath about 6–7″ long, bearing a succession of very short-lived fls. Lf. usually solitary, rather thinly leathery, linear, narrowed basally, apically slightly 2-lbd., to 6″ long. Fls. about $1\frac{1}{4}$″ in diam., pale rose, the ss. and ps. very long-caudate, the lip crisped marginally. Mar.–June. (H) Admiralty Islands; New Ireland.

DIPLOCENTRUM Ldl.

Two species of *Diplocentrum* are known to date—**D. recurvum** Ldl. and **D. congestum** Wight—neither of which is present in contemporary collections. They are monopodial epiphytes, native in the Himalayan regions of India, and are somewhat allied to *Camarotis* Ldl., which they resemble, except for details of the rather small flowers.

Nothing is known of the genetic affinities of this rare group.

CULTURE: Presumably as for the high-elevation Vandas, etc. (C, I)

DIPLOLABELLUM Mak.

Diplolabellum consists of a single very rare and little-known species of saprophytic orchid from Japan, not present in our collections today. A member of the subtribe *Corallorhizinae*, its exact affinities have not been clarified as yet.

Nothing is known of the genetic alliances of this rare genus.

CULTURE: Presumably as for *Corallorrhiza*. (I)

DIPLOMERIS D.Don
(*Diplochilus* Ldl., *Paragnathis* Spreng.)

Four species of *Diplomeris* are known to date, but unfortunately none of them seems to be present in contemporary collections, though they are among the more unique of terrestrial orchids. A member of the subtribe *Habenarinae*, these plants are all inhabitants of the mountains of North India and China, where they typically grow on exposed rock-outcroppings. They bear large, roundish leaves, these prostrate on the substratum, and erect, one-flowered inflorescences. The flowers are typically of considerable size, great intricacy of structure, and unique beauty.

Nothing is known of the genetic ties of this charming and neglected genus.

CULTURE: As for *Caladenia*, in all probability. (C, I)

DIPLOPRORA Hk.f.

This is a genus of five species of rather nondescript epiphytic monopodial orchids of the *Vandeae* group of the subtribe *Sarcanthinae*, native in the Himalayas, Burma, Siam, China, Formosa, and Hong Kong, very little known in cultivation, and of interest primarily for the intricate structure of their small flowers. **Diploprora Championi** (Ldl.) Hk.f. has on occasion been grown by connoisseurs, and may still be present in choice collections.

No hybrids have as yet been made with *Diploprora*, but the genus is closely allied to *Vanda*, *Luisia*, *Aërides*, and the like, and some unusual crosses could doubtless be produced through critical breeding.

CULTURE: As for the tropical Vandas. (I, H)

D. Championi (Ldl.) Hk.f. (*Cottonia Championi* Ldl., *Luisia bicaudata* Thw., *Vanda bicaudata* Thw.)
St. rather slender, ascending, to 3″ long. Lvs. few, to 4″ long and ¾″ wide, rather thin-textured, falcately lanceolate to ovate, acute to acuminate, rigid. Infls. erect or arching, stout, 5–6-fld., to 5″ long, the rachis irregular. Fls. fleshy, ½–¾″ across, fragrant, pale or brownish-yellow, the lip white, the lat. lbs. streaked with dull red or dull purple. Ss. and ps. spreading, ovate to obovate, broad, the ss. keeled outside. Lip 3-lbd., as long as the ps., connate with the col.-base, the lat. lbs. quadrately rounded, the midlb. projecting at right angles to them and tapering to a finely 2-tailed tip; disc with a large, cushion-like, oval callus. Spring. (I) Himalayas; Burma; Hong Kong.

DIPODIUM R.Br.
(*Leopardanthus* Bl., *Wailesia* Ldl.)

Dipodium is a most remarkable genus, consisting of some twelve known species, which are widely distributed from China throughout the Philippines, Southeast Asia, Malaya, and Indonesia to New Guinea, New Caledonia, and Australia. They are extremely diverse in vegetative habit, some of them being leafless terrestrial herbs, others leafy terrestrials, while still others bear long climbing stems, heavily clothed with leaves, which continue to grow (indefinitely, in theory) at the apex, bearing roots throughout and branching irregularly,

This last category of Dipodiums thus rather simulates the monopodial growth habit of *Vanda*, *Aërides*, etc., though the genus is a member of the subtribe *Cymbidiinae*! The flowers are usually rather showy and produced in relatively large numbers; certain of the species are unique in bearing prominent spots on the outside of the sepals and petals, which may, in some instances, show through to the inner surfaces.

No hybrids have as yet been made in *Dipodium*, and nothing is known of its genetic affinities, though it seems possible that it will prove 'crossable' with certain allied genera, such as *Cymbidium*, *Grammangis*, *Grammatophyllum*, etc. A potentially fascinating field of breeding seems evident here, and is one which should be critically explored.

CULTURE: The leafless, ground-dwelling species are evidently saprophytes, and should therefore be treated like *Corallorrhiza*, *Galeola*, etc., though their successful cultivation is a difficult accomplishment. The leafy, terrestrial members of the genus should be grown like the tropical species of *Phaius*. *Dipodium pictum*, *D. parviflorum*, and other species with 'monopodial' habit should be treated like *Arachnis*. (I, H)

D. paludosum (Griff.) Rchb.f. (*Grammatophyllum paludosum* Griff., *Wailesia paludosa* Rchb.f.)
Pbs. st.-like, tufted, erect, to more than 3′ tall, completely covered by the overlapping lf.-bases. Lvs. light green, erect or ascending, somewhat curved, narrowly lanceolate, acute, to 12″ long and 1″ wide, the blade with a strong keel on the reverse side, the sheaths strongly ribbed. Infls. lateral, ascending, to 1½′ tall, loosely 8–15-fld., the fls. well spaced on the rachis. Fls. to almost 2″ across, rather heavy-textured, the ss. and ps. pale yellowish, the crimson blotches on the back showing through faintly in front, the upper surface of the lip striped or with rows of purple spots on a white ground. Ss. and ps. spreading, narrowly oblong, obtuse. Lip narrowly elliptic, about the same size as the ss., but the apex narrower, the lat. lbs. very small, basal, the midlb. hairy. Summer–autumn. (H) Malay Peninsula; Sumatra; Borneo.

D. pictum (Ldl.) Rchb.f. (*Wailesia picta* Ldl.)
Sts. not particularly thickened, elongate, climbing, rooting at any point, densely leafy (the lvs. gradually dying away from the basal portion, which often rots off and makes the plant become an epiphyte on tree-trunks). Lvs. ensiform to linear-lanceolate, closely 2-ranked, the bases overlapping, the blades curving outwards, to 10″ long and ¾″ wide, with a strong keel on the reverse surface. Infls. erect, from the lf.-axils near the apex of the pl., the bare scape to 8″ long, the fl.-bearing part as long, 10- or more-fld., the floral bracts short. Fls. rather heavy-textured, to 2″ across, opening well, the ss. and ps. pale yellowish, the crimson blotches on the reverse sides showing vaguely through on the frontal surfaces, the lip striped with purple on the upper surface, hairy in the apical half, the hairs long and white. Ss. and ps. similar, narrowly oblong, obtuse, the lat. ss. extended only a little below the horizontal. Lip as long as the other segms., its base narrow, the lat. lbs. short and broad, close to the col.-sides, the midlb. widening

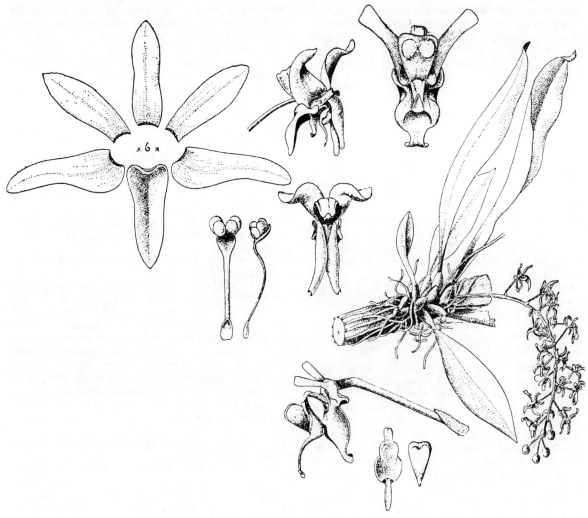

Dipteranthus pellucidus (Rchb.f.) Cgn. [Hoehne, *Flora Brasílica*]

and ending in a broad point. Col. short and broad, hollow and hairy at the frontal base. Summer–autumn. (H) Malay Peninsula; Sumatra; Java.

D. punctatum (Sm.) R.Br. (*Dendrobium punctatum* Sm.)
Rhiz. rather extensive, subterranean, thickly tuberous. St. leafless, robust or slender, to 3′ tall, reddish-spotted, the sheathing bracts at the base few or numerous, closely set, acute, with 6–50 fls. in a loose apical rac. Fls. opening successively, to 1¾″ across, pink with red spots, mauve without spots, or rarely entirely deep purplish-red, the lip always whitish. Ss. and ps. equal, oblong-lanceolate to linear, spreading or recurved. Lip with the lat. lbs. very much shorter and narrower than the ovate-lanceolate midlb., which bears 2 short longitudinal ridges from near the base, converging into a pubescent keel which expands to a woolly patch near the apex. Mostly summer. (I, H) Australia.

D. Hamiltonianum F.M.Bail. (*Dipodium punctatum* (Sm.) R.Br. var. *Hamiltonianum* F.M.Bail.) Similar in most respects to *D. punctatum* (Sm.) R.Br., but usually robust and less than 2′ tall. Sts. greenish, dull red-spotted, the basal bracts thick,

obtuse. Fls. to 2″ across, bright yellow to dull yellowish-green, with red spots or streaks, the lip pink or whitish. Lip with the lat. lbs. linear-subulate, the midlb. ovate-oblong, with 2 short ridges near the base, not converging into a pubescent keel, but the whole lamina pubescent for nearly half its length from the apex. Autumn–winter. (I, H) Australia.

D. parviflorum J.J.Sm. Similar in habit to *D. pictum* (Ldl.) Rchb.f., the infls. longer, about 18-fld. usually. Fls. about 1″ across, dull yellow with crimson blotches on both surfaces, the lip with the lat. lbs. nearly white, the upper surface of the midlb. almost covered with white hairs. Ss. concave, boat-shaped. Ps. slightly concave. Lip 3-lbd. from the base, the lat. lbs. narrow, lying close to the col. and slightly longer than it, the tips rounded; midlb. with an acute tip, margins somewhat reflexed, hairy, with 2 rows of shorter hairs between the lat. lbs. at base. Summer. (H) Malay Peninsula; Java.

DIPTERANTHUS B.-R.

A member of the subtribe *Ornithocephalinae*, *Dipteranthus* consists of three or so species of dwarf epiphytic orchids, all inhabiting the wet forests of Brazil. Most unusual little plants, they bear clusters of tiny pseudobulbs, each with a small tongue-shaped leaf, and minute intricate blossoms in short racemes. The flowers are usually transparent white or greenish, and though very small, are produced in such profusion as to be rather attractive. Regrettably, the genus is apparently unknown in contemporary collections.

Nothing is known of the genetic affinities of this rare genus.

CULTURE: As for *Ornithocephalus*. (I, H)

DIPTEROSTELE Schltr.

A single extremely rare species of *Dipterostele* is known at this time, **D. microglossa** Schltr., which has evidently been collected on only one occasion, on Mt. Chimborazo, in Ecuador, at about 3000 metres elevation. A rather small epiphytic orchid, somewhat reminiscent of *Trichoceros* HBK in vegetative appearance, it bears flowers more like those of *Stellilabium* Schltr. A member of the subtribe *Telipogoninae*, *Dipterostele* is not in cultivation at this time.

Nothing is known of the genetic affinities of this rare group.

CULTURE: Presumably as for *Telipogon*. (C)

DISA Berg.

Approximately two hundred species of *Disa* are known to science, the vast majority of these native to tropical and South Africa, but with four endemic to Madagascar, and one in the Mascarene Islands. The principal genus of the subtribe *Disinae*, certain groups have been segregated from *Disa* proper on technical details, these including *Forficaria* Ldl., *Monadenia* Ldl., *Herschelia* Ldl., etc. Terrestrial or very rarely lithophytic orchids, several members of the genus are now in cultivation, though they are far from common. One of the finest of all orchidaceous plants belongs here, this the very lovely *D. uniflora* Berg., which has long been a prized member of a few specialized collections. Bearing subterranean tubers on a stoloniferous root-system, the erect leafy stems produce one to rather numerous small to very large, complex flowers at the apex. The structure of these blossoms is very unusual. In most species, the predominant part of the floral segments is not the lip (as is typical of most orchids), but rather the dorsal sepal which is frequently ornately-formed, labelloid in shape, and very intricate. The lateral sepals are also usually well-developed, while both petals and lip are in most of the Disas remarkably reduced in dimensions. Formerly popular with collectors, these fine orchids should regain their proper place in our contemporary greenhouses, through further introduction of the available species from their native haunts.

Several hybrids in *Disa* are on record in the official registry lists, most of these made in the late nineteenth century in England, and now presumably lost to collectors. It is to be hoped that additional hybrids be made in the group, and that its affinities with allied genera be more fully ascertained by experimenters.

CULTURE: Many of the Disas are well-known because of the supposed difficulties attending their successful cultivation; in fact, the fabulous *D. uniflora* has long laboured under the reputation of being one of the world's most difficult orchids! Since the numerous members of the genus occur under a variety of natural conditions, and elevations ranging from near sea-level in hot areas to high in the cool mountains, considerable variations quite normally occur in their specialized cultural requirements. The species from warm areas should be grown much like the tropical Habenarias, etc., but unfortunately the cultivated Disas are usually from higher elevations, and most of the hybrids are likewise cool-growing orchids. A compost such as that suggested for *Cynorkis* is recommended for these plants, provided a top-dressing of fresh sphagnum moss is added. Constant moisture at the roots while in active growth seems obligatory, although when the flowering-stems die down, the subterranean tubers need a rather protracted rest-period. Applications of weakened fertilizing solution seem to be beneficial in all cases studied. (C, I, H)

D. crassicornis Ldl. (*Disa macrantha* Hemsl., *D. megaceras* Hk.f.)

St. 1–3′ tall, stout, leafy. Lvs. radical and cauline, oblong-lanceolate, acutish, rather fleshy, 3–12″ long. Infl. rather dense or loosely-fld., 4–10″ long, with leafy bracts subtending the fls. Fls. to 1¾″ in diam., fragrant, long-lived, white, cream-coloured, or yellow, more or less spotted and mottled with dark purple or dull red. Dors. sep. hooded, broadly ovate, the stout curved spur to 1¼″ long; lat. ss. narrowly ovate, oblique. Ps. broadly ovate, oblique. Lip oblong-lanceolate, obtuse. Autumn–early winter. (C, I) Eastern South Africa, often at rather high elevations.

D. draconis (L.f.) Sw. (*Orchis draconis* L.f., *Satyrium draconis* Thunb.)

St. rather stout, to almost 2′ tall. Lvs. few in number, forming a basal or sub-basal rosette, 3–9″ long, linear to oblong-linear. Infl. sheathed, usually many-fld., 2–5″ long. Fls. to 1½″ in diam., cream-white to straw-yellow, usually with median rose-red nerves on the larger segms. Dors. sep. vaguely hooded, obovate or obovate-oblong, somewhat reflexed, the spur filiform, to 2¼″ long; lat. ss. oblong, spreading. Ps. oblong or sub-falcate-oblong, recurved. Lip linear, obtuse. Winter, especially Nov.–Dec. (C, I) Cape Colony of South Africa.

D. laeta Rchb.f. (*Disa Culveri* Schltr.)

St. to 1½′ tall, sheath-clothed above. Lvs. basal in a rosette, 4–9″ long, linear or linear-lanceolate. Infl. oblong, densely many-fld., 3–4″ long. Fls. more than ⅝″ in diam., white or pale pink, fragrant. Dors. sep. hooded, broadly triangular-ovate, the spur cylindrical, curved near the base, ⅜″ long; lat. ss. ovate-oblong. Ps. narrowly ovate-oblong. Lip subspatulate-linear, rather obtuse. Winter. (I) Natal; Transvaal.

D. longicornu L.f.

St. slender, curved, to 8″ tall. Lvs. basal and cauline. the basal ones 3–5, green, spreading, lanceolate or oblong-lanceolate, acute to acuminate, 1¼–4″ long, the few cauline ones sheath-like. Fl. usually solitary, to 2″ long, lilac-blue, the anther red. Dors. sep. hooded, broadly ovate, obtuse or apiculate, somewhat funnel-

Colax jugosus (Ldl.) Ldl. [JOÃO ROCHA]

Cryptopus elatus (Thou.) Ldl. [MARCEL LECOUFLE]

Cryptochilus sanguineus Wall. [J. MARNIER-LAPOSTOLLE]

Cryptostylis arachnites (Bl.) Hassk. [REG S. DAVIS]

Cycnoches Egertonianum Batem., with a male (staminate) inflorescence [H. A. DUNN]

Cycnoches ventricosum Batem., with male (staminate) flowers [H. A. DUNN]

Cymbidium canaliculatum R.Br. [GEORGE FULLER]

shaped behind, with a tapering blunt spur to $1\frac{1}{2}''$ long; lat. lbs. oblong, obtuse or apiculate. Ps. linear, acuminate, with an elongate recurved lobe below the middle. Lip similar to the lat. ss. but smaller. Winter. (C, I) Cape Colony of South Africa.

D. nervosa Ldl.

St. slender, to 2′ tall, clothed with sheaths. Lvs. cauline, rather fleshy, linear or narrowly oblong-linear, 4–8″ long. Infl. oblong, rather densely many-fld., 4–6″ long. Fls. almost $1\frac{1}{2}''$ in diam., fragrant, dark pink or rose-purple, very showy. Dors. sep. hooded, oblong or elliptic-oblong, the margins incurved, the spur cylindrical, curved, $\frac{3}{4}''$ long; lat. ss. oblong, obtuse. Ps. falcate-oblong, obtuse. Lip filiform, apically thickened. Autumn–winter. (C, I) South-east Africa, especially Natal.

D. porrecta Sw. (*Disa Zeyheri* Sond.)

St. rather stout, to $1\frac{1}{2}'$ tall, sheathing above. Lvs. basal, numerous in a rosette, elongate, linear, 5–7″ long. Infl. oblong, rather densely many-fld., $2-3\frac{1}{2}''$ long. Fls. more than $1\frac{1}{4}''$ long, rather fleshy, spicily fragrant, dark rich vermilion to orange-red, with the outside of segms. often paler. Dors. sep. hooded, very broadly ovate, wavy-margined, the slender, narrowly conical, upcurved spur to $1\frac{1}{4}''$ long; lat. ss. elliptic-roundish, concave. Ps. almost square, obtuse. Lip oblong to lanceolate-oblong. Autumn–spring. (C, I) Eastern Cape Colony; Transkei; Basutoland.

D. sanguinea Sond. (*Disa Huttoni* Rchb.f.)

St. stout, to 15″ tall, upwards clothed with sheaths. Lvs. cauline, rather fleshy, oblong-lanceolate, imbricating, 1–3″ long. Infl. very densely many-fld., cylindrical, to $1\frac{1}{4}''$ long. Fls. about $\frac{1}{4}''$ in diam., vivid crimson outside, pale rose inside, not opening fully. Dors. sep. hooded, broadly ovate or semihemispherical, the spur oblong, abbreviated; lat. ss. broadly oblong, keeled. Ps. falcate-linear, hidden within the sepaline hood. Lip rhomboid-ovate, with an odd apical gland. Winter. (C, I) Cape Colony.

D. tripetaloides (L.f.) N.E.Br. (*Orchis tripetaloides* L.f., *Disa excelsa* Sw., *D. venosa* Ldl., *Satyrium excelsum* Thunb.)

St. rather stout, to $1\frac{1}{2}'$ tall, upwards clothed with sheaths. Lvs. basal, in a tuft-like rosette, $1\frac{1}{4}-4''$ long, lanceolate or oblong-lanceolate. Infl. loosely many-fld., 2–5″ long. Fls. to about 1″ in diam., pale pink to white, usually more or less spotted on the ss. with carmine or red-purple. Dors. sep. hooded, broadly ovate or rounded-ovate, the spur broadly conical or oblong, to $\frac{3}{8}''$ long; lat. ss. ovate-oblong or ovate-elliptic. Ps. falcate-oblong, obtuse. Lip linear or oblong-linear, obtuse. Winter–late summer. (C, I) Eastern South Africa; Natal.

D. uniflora Berg. (*Disa Barellii* Puydt, *D. grandiflora* L.f., *Satyrium grandiflorum* Thunb.)

St. leafy, rather stout, to $2\frac{1}{2}'$ tall. Lvs. mostly in a basal rosette, becoming sheathing and bract-like above, lanceolate or elongately linear, rather softly fleshy, 3–8″ long. Infl. 1–5-fld. Fls. rather variable, among the showiest of all terrestrial orchids, to 4″ in

Disa uniflora Berg. [*Gardeners' Chronicle*]

diam., very vivid scarlet, the dors. sep. usually strongly veined with darker hue, the lip often marked with yellow or orange-yellow. Dors. sep. hooded, broadly ovate, the narrowly conical spur to $\frac{1}{2}''$ long; lat. ss. broadly ovate, spreading, abruptly pointed. Ps. obovate or obovate-oblong, the apices incurved. Lip small, linear-lanceolate. Autumn–spring. (C, I) Cape Colony of South Africa.

D. capricornis Rchb.f. (*Disa gladioliflora* Bolus) St. slender, sheathed, to 15″ long. Lvs. basal, grass-like, 3–8″ long. Infl. many-fld., loose, to 4″ long. Fls. about $\frac{5}{8}''$ in diam., rose-red or pink-red. Dors. sep. hooded, ovate-oblong, the spur slender, curved, short; lat. ss. oblong. Ps. falcate-oblong, with a short roundish basal lobe in front. Lip spatulate-ovate, obtuse. Winter. (C, I) Cape Colony; Griqualand East.

D. chrysostachya Sw. (*Disa gracilis* Ldl.) St. usually very stout, to $3\frac{1}{2}'$ tall, clothed with imbricating sheaths. Lvs. numerous, ligulate-linear-oblong below, oblong above, passing into bracts, 9–12″ long. Infl. cylindrical, densely many-fld., 6–18″ long. Fls. about $\frac{1}{4}''$ long, the ss. vivid orange, the ps. and lip yellow. Dors. sep. hooded, elliptic-obovate, the inflated spur elliptic-oblong, $\frac{3}{16}''$ long; lat. ss. elliptic, obtuse. Ps. obovate, obtuse. Lip linear, small. Winter, mostly Nov.–Dec. (C, I) South Africa.

D. Cooperi Rchb.f. St. very stout, to 2' tall, upwards clothed with broad imbricate sheaths. Lvs. cauline, 1–3" long, when found, on st. ovate-oblong, the basal ones from a distinct bud lanceolate, 4–16" long, plicate. Infl. densely many-fld., 6–10" long. Fls. about 1½" long and 1" in diam., white rather strongly flushed with rose-red, the large lip yellow or olive-green. Dors. sep. hooded, very broadly ovate, the spur ascending, curved, about 1½" long; lat. ss. ovate, obtuse. Ps. broadly oblong, inserted in the sepaline hood. Lip large for the genus, broadly rhomboid-ovate, crisped marginally. Autumn–winter. (C, I) South and South-east Africa.

D. cylindrica (Thunb.) Sw. (*Satyrium cylindricum* Thunb., *Disa bracteata* Ldl., *Monadenia bracteata* Dur. & Schinz) St. stout, leafy, to 12" tall. Lvs. numerous, becoming bract-like above, 1½–4" long. Infl. densely many-fld., cylindrical, to more than 4" long. Fls. less than ½" long, dull yellow. Dors. sep. hooded, ovate-oblong, the spur saccate, oblong, tiny; lat. ss. ovate-oblong, recurved. Ps. obliquely ovate. Lip linear-oblong, small, recurved. Autumn–early winter. (C, I) South-west Africa.

D. ferruginea (Thunb.) Sw. (*Satyrium ferrugineum* Thunb.) St. rather stout, to 15" tall. Lvs. radical and cauline, the basal ones few, linear and grassy, to 10" long, the cauline ones several, sheathing, membranous, smaller. Infl. densely many-fld., abbreviated. Fls. vivid orange-red, about ¾" long. Dors. sep. hooded, acuminate, concave and tapering into a slender horizontal or ascending spur about ¾" long; lat. ss. oblong, acute, cusped apically. Ps. borne in sepaline hood, falcate, acuminate, broad and rounded basally. Lip lanceolate, acuminate. Winter–spring. (C, I) Cape Colony of South Africa.

D. hamatopetala Rendle. St. slender, to 1½' tall, clothed with many membranous sheaths. Lvs. borne near base, linear-filiform, 4–6" long. Infl. loosely 1–7-fld. Fls. about ⅛" in diam., blue to purple-blue, often marked darker. Dors. sep. hooded, ovate, the spur stout, obtuse, $\frac{3}{16}''$ long; lat. ss. oblong, concave, obtuse, spreading. Ps. broad basally, narrow medially, dilated and toothed apically. Lip broadly oblong, deeply fringed. Mostly Aug.–Sept. (I) East Africa, especially Tanganyika.

D. polygonoides Ldl. (*Disa natalensis* Ldl.) St. rather stout, to almost 2' tall. Lvs. basal, paired or in 3's, linear-lanceolate, rather flaccid in texture, 8–12" long. Infl. very densely many-fld., with lf.-like sheathing bracts, to 3" long. Fls. about ¼" in diam., pale orange-red. Dors. sep. oval, acutish, the spur pendulous, narrowly cylindric, short. Ps. small, ligulate. Lip small, ligulate, obtuse. Summer–early autumn. (C, I) Eastern South Africa.

D. racemosa L.f. (*Disa secunda* Sw., *Satyrium secundum* Thunb.) St. rather stout, to 2' tall. Lvs. green, the basal 5–6 spreading or semi-erect, lanceolate, acute, 1½–4" long, the few cauline ones closely sheathing the st., distant, acute, smaller. Infl. rather elongate, loosely 3–6-fld., with large bracts. Fls. to about 2" long, vivid rose-pink with darker veins, the ps. purplish in front, the inner margins yellow. Dors. sep. arched or vaguely hooded, shorter than lats., rounded or obovate, concave, with a short obtuse pouch near middle; lat. ss. oblong or ovate-oblong, obtuse, mucronate. Ps. obliquely oblong, incurved. Lip linear, acute. Winter. (C, I) Cape Colony of South Africa.

DISPERIS Sw.

(*Dipera* Spreng., *Diperis* Wight, *Dryopaeia* L., *Dryopeia* Thou., *Dryopria* Thou., *Dryorkis* Thou.)

This is a genus of upwards of fifty species, all confined to continental Africa (especially the southern part), except for a very few which extend to adjacent insular groups—Madagascar, etc. A member of the subtribe *Disperidinae*, its mostly unusually attractive components are at this time essentially unknown in collections. The complex flowers vary in size from very small to rather large, but all are of sufficient beauty and complicated structure to warrant attention by specialists.

Nothing is known of the genetic affinities of *Disperis*. CULTURE: As for *Disa* and *Caladenia*. (C, I)

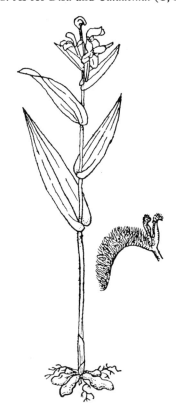

Disperis Hildebrandtii Rchb.f. [A.D.HAWKES, AFTER *Flore de Madagascar*]

DIURIS Sm.

Diuris contains almost forty species of typically very handsome terrestrial orchids, all native in Australia except for one in Java and another in Timor. Very scarce in contemporary collections outside of their native lands, these 'Double-Tails'—as they are known in Australia—are almost without exception beautiful plants which should be better known by enthusiasts who are prepared to attend to their peculiarized cultural wants. Tuberous orchids, with grassy leaves, they bear tall racemes of very complex blossoms, often brightly coloured, the petals of which are typically long-clawed and erect or ascending. The genus is a member of the subtribe *Diuridinae*.

No artificially-produced hybrids are as yet known in *Diuris*, though natural breeding may occur.

CULTURE: As for *Caladenia*. (C, I)

D. alba R.Br.

Tubers subterranean, ovoid. Lvs. 2–3, basal, grass-like, erect, about 6″ long, acuminate. Infls. erect, to 1½′ tall, 2–6-fld., sheathed. Fls. to more than 3″ long, fragrant, white, sometimes with some violet or lilac flushings towards the centre, especially on the lip. Dors. sep. much shorter than the linear lat. ss. Ps. erect or ascending, long-clawed, the claws rather wide. Lip 3-lbd. from the base, the midlb. narrow below with 3 longitudinal ridges or raised lines which end where it suddenly broadens out into a fan-shaped, smooth blade. Autumn–winter. (C, I) Australia: Queensland, New South Wales, Victoria.

D. aurea Sm.

Similar in habit to *D. alba* R.Br., the lvs. mostly paired. Infls. to 2′ tall, 2–5-fld., rigidly erect. Fls. about 2″ long, golden-yellow flushed or marked with brown, the lat. lbs. of the lip blotched with purple-brown, not half as long as the midlb., obliquely oblong, the upper margins rather crisped or toothed. Ps. short-clawed, the claws usually brown-spotted, the blades broadly lanceolate or almost round. Dors. sep. recurved; lat. ss. often greenish, sometimes dilated apically and crossing each other. Autumn. (C, I) Australia: Queensland, New South Wales.

DOMINGOA Schltr.

Two species of *Domingoa* are known to date, both small but strangely attractive epiphytic orchids of the subtribe *Laeliinae*, one, **D. nodosa** (Cgn.) Schltr. (*Octadesmia nodosa* Cgn.) a rare Hispaniolan endemic which is apparently not in cultivation at this time, the other, **D. hymenodes** (Rchb.f.) Schltr., a Cuban, Hispaniolan, and Puerto Rican plant which is being grown today in a few specialized collections. Vegetatively these orchids rather simulate some member of the *Pleurothallidinae*, but when their proportionately large, rather oddly attractive flowers are produced, their true generic affinity at once becomes apparent.

A single hybrid has been registered utilizing a *Domingoa* as of this writing, this the peculiar *Epigoa x Olivine* (*Domingoa hymenodes* × *Epidendrum Mariae*), produced by the indefatigable Mr. W. W. G. Moir, of Honolulu. It seems entirely possible that the genus will prove genetically compatible with at least certain other members of the alliance to which it belongs.

CULTURE: These rather delicate little orchids are often slightly refractory under the conditions of the collection. Generally they require treatment such as that afforded the tropical, pseudobulbous Epidendrums, although they benefit materially if they are grown—in smallish, perfectly-drained pots—in a compost made up of equal parts of chopped sphagnum moss, and shredded tree-fern fibre. Since they possess no appreciable water-storing structures, no rest-period should be afforded them. A rather bright, but not excessively sunny spot is needed, and periodic applications of weakened fertilizer solution seem advantageous. They are highly susceptible to damage from a stale compost, and should be repotted at once whenever such a condition seems to be evident. (I, H)

D. hymenodes (Rchb.f.) Schltr. (*Epidendrum hymenodes* Rchb.f., *Epidendrum haematochilum* Rchb.f., *Epidendrum broughtonioides* Griseb.)

Pbs. st.-like, vaguely angular, to 1½″ long, narrowing basally. Lf. solitary, rather papery in texture, lanceolate-elliptic or lanceolate-ovate, acute or obtuse, dark green. 1¼–3½″ long, to about ½″ wide. Infl. terminal, completely bract-covered, to about 6″ long, slender, the few-fld. rac. subcorymbose, the fls. usually opening successively over a rather long period. Fls. almost translucent in texture, faintly fragrant, to about 1″ in diam. or more, the ss. and ps. usually whitish-green, often with longitudinal purplish lines, the lip usually dark brownish-purple in centre. Ss. and ps. lanceolate-ovate, acute, more or less spreading. Lip free, obovoid in outline, retuse apically, the disc with 2 calli. Col. slender, 2-winged at apex, dilated into a foot at base; clinandrium membranous, tridentate. Mostly winter. (I, H) Cuba; Hispaniola; Puerto Rico.

DONACOPSIS Gagnep.

A single species of *Donacopsis* has been detected to date, this the excessively rare and little-known **D. laotica** Gagnep., which has apparently been collected on only one occasion in Laos. It is an odd apparently terrestrial orchid which somewhat simulates a *Cymbidium* in general appearance, although the exact generic affinities of the group do not seem to have been ascertained as yet.

Nothing is known of the genetic affinities of *Donacopsis*.

CULTURE: Unknown.

DORITIS Ldl.

As currently understood, *Doritis* consists of a single extremely variable epiphytic or lithophytic orchid ranging from Burma to Sumatra, which is frequent in choice contemporary collections, and has been utilized to a considerable extent in modern hybridization. It has long been included in *Phalaenopsis* Bl., but most authorities now consider it to be a distinct genus, on the basis of floral structure. In its largest phases, *Doritis pulcherrima* is a spectacular orchid, while certain of the small-flowered forms are of interest solely to the connoisseur.

Doritis has been successfully hybridized on a number of occasions with true *Phalaenopsis*, these crosses now being known as *Doritaenopsis*. Additional critical breeding with supposedly allied genera of the subtribe *Sarcanthinae* would seem to offer some exceptionally interesting potentials.

CULTURE: As for *Phalaenopsis*. (I, H)

D. pulcherrima Ldl. (*Phalaenopsis antennifera* Rchb.f., *P. Buyssoniana* Rchb.f., *P. Esmeralda* Rchb.f., *P. pulcherrima* J.J.Sm.)

St. often rather elongate, to 6″ tall, freely-rooting. Lvs. to 12 in number, usually strictly spreading in a horizontal arrangement, to more than 6″ long, rather stiffly rigid, often purple-flushed, especially beneath.

Infls. erect, rigid, slender or stout, to almost 3′ tall, with a rather dense rac. of 10–20 fls. near the apex which open successively over a long period, the rachis gradually elongating. Fls. extremely variable in colour and size, ½–2″ across, usually pale rose-purple or magenta-rose, the lip darker, the lat. lbs. usually deeper in hue than the midlb., which is marked around the disc with yellow or cream-white. Ss. and ps. spreading to sharply reflexed, oblong-oval, obtuse, the ps. usually much the smaller. Lip with erect, oval lat. lbs. and an ovate-elliptic midlb. which is often veined with pale lavender in the middle and has a 2-pointed callus on the disc, the midlb. margins reflexed. Autumn–winter. (I, H) Burma; Thailand; Laos; Cambodia; Viet-Nam; Malay Peninsula; Sumatra.

DOSSINIA Morr.

This genus contains but a single species, one of the fabulous 'Jewel Orchids', which are grown primarily for their extraordinarily handsome foliage, rather than for the typically insignificant flowers. Closely allied to *Anoectochilus* Bl., it is a native of Sarawak and possibly other areas in Borneo, and is today uncommon in cultivation, although it is among the finest of this remarkable group of terrestrial orchids.

Dossinia has been crossed with *Haemaria*, to give the handsome group, *Dossinimaria*, now evidently lost to cultivation.

CULTURE: As for *Anoectochilus*. (H)

D. marmorata (Bl.) Morr. (*Macodes marmorata* Bl., *Anoectochilus Lowii* Bl., *Anoectochilus marmoratus* Ldl., *Cheirostylis marmorata* Bl.)
Lvs. usually not more than 5 at a time, forming a rather loose rosette, to 3″ long, often almost as wide, broadly elliptic to almost round, rather sharp-pointed, velvety deep green, with an extremely intricate branching network of golden-yellow veins. Infls. rigidly erect, to 1½′ tall, the upper half occupied by a loose, many-fld. rac. Fls. about ¾″ long, pale brown, the segms. tipped with white or pinkish-white. Summer–autumn. (H) Sarawak, in Borneo.

DRAKAEA Ldl.

Four species of terrestrial orchids, confined to Western Australia, make up the rare and little known genus *Drakaea*. Allied to *Caleana* R.Br. and to *Spiculaea* Ldl., they bear highly complicated, rather attractive flowers in racemes, and should be of interest to specialists, though their cultural requirements are a bit difficult.

Nothing is known of the genetic affinities of this rare group.

CULTURE: As for *Caladenia*. (C, I)

DRYADORCHIS Schltr.

The genus *Dryadorchis* consists of two excessively rare species, both small epiphytic monopodial orchids, **D. barbellata** Schltr. and **D. minor** Schltr., native to the high mountain forests of New Guinea. Somewhat allied to *Saccolabium* Bl., neither of them are to be found in our collections at this time, and in any event they are principally of scientific importance, being rather insignificant in appearance.

Nothing is known of the genetic affinities of *Dryadorchis*.

CULTURE: Probably as for the dwarf, high-elevation *Vanda* relatives. (I)

DRYMODA Ldl.

Drymoda consists of two species of remarkable, very small, rare epiphytic orchids of the subtribe *Genyorchidinae*, one in Burma, the other endemic to Thailand. The live pseudobulbs of *D. siamensis* Schltr. 'are covered with $CaCO_3$-incrusted papillae when alive, which give them a white, mealy appearance; the dead pseudobulbs are glossy green-yellow' (Seidenfaden & Smitinand, *The Orchids of Thailand*, part 3: 457. 1961). They somewhat simulate a sort of weird *Bulbophyllum*, and though they are very small, they are of sufficient intricacy to warrant the attention of the connoisseur. Both of the Drymodas are today exceedingly rare in our collections.

Nothing is known of the genetic affinities of this peculiar genus.

CULTURE: As for the medium-elevation Bulbophyllums. The plants should be grown tightly mounted on tree-fern slabs for best results, and are very difficult to maintain in good condition in the average collection. (I)

D. picta Ldl.
Pbs. disc-like, closely appressed against the bark of the trees on which they grow, less than ½″ in diam. Lf. solitary, stalkless, ovate, acute, quickly deciduous, to ½″ long. Infls. basal, thread-like, 1-fld., to 2″ tall. Fls. ½″ long, very complex, the ss. yellow-green striped with purple, the lip dark red-purple, the col. green spotted with purple. Lat. ss. much larger than the dors. one, borne at the end of the naked column-foot. Ps. tiny, roundish. Lip very small, sac-like basally. Col. with 2 decurved wings and a very elongate naked foot. Summer. (I) Burma.

D. siamensis Schltr.
Pbs. soon becoming very wrinkled, disc-like, borne in erratic rows, less than ½″ in diam. Lf. tiny, very quickly deciduous. Infls. erect, set with transparent

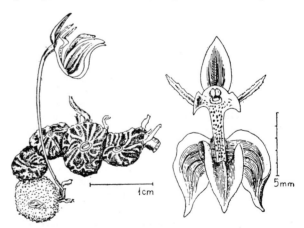

Drymoda siamensis Schltr. [*Orchids of Thailand*]

sheaths, to 2″ tall, 1-fld. Fls. much like those of *D. picta* Ldl., yellowish with more or less definite central red-brown suffusions on the ss., the ps. linear, serrate-margined, the lip tongue-like, much larger than that of the other sp., its tip down-curved. Spring. (I) Thailand.

DRYMONANTHUS Nicholls

Drymonanthus consists of but a single species of extremely rare epiphytic orchid of the subtribe *Sarcanthinae*. Unknown in contemporary collections, it inhabits the warmer parts of Queensland, Australia.

Nothing is known of the genetic affinities of this scarce genus.

CULTURE: Presumably as for the tropical Vandas, etc. (H)

DUCKEËLLA Porto & Brade

Duckeëlla Adolphi Porto & Brade, the only known member of this rare genus, is apparently restricted to the Amazon region of Brazil. Allied to *Epistephium* Kth. by reason of its floral structure, it differs materially in bearing basal, linear foliage and in other details. It is an extremely rare orchid, one as yet unknown in cultivation.

Nothing is known of the genetic alliances of this group.

CULTURE: Presumably as for *Sobralia*. (H)

EARINA Ldl.

About seven species of *Earina* are known to science, these distributed in the region extending from New Zealand to Samoa and the Tonga Islands. A member of the subtribe *Glomerinae*, these attractive epiphytes bear erect or sometimes pendulous, thickly leafy stems and small, usually white flowers of unusual structure. They are regrettably unknown in contemporary collections, though they offer much to the connoisseur.

Nothing is known of the genetic affinities of this genus.

CULTURE: As for the tropical Bulbophyllums. (I, H)

EGGELINGIA Summerh.

Two species of *Eggelingia* are known to date, distributed in tropical Africa from Ghana to western Uganda, with both members relatively common in the Belgian Congo. It is a newly established genus, dating from 1951, and a member of the large and highly complex subtribe *Sarcanthinae*. Neither of the species, **E. clavata** Summerh. and **E. ligulifolia** Summerh., which are allied to *Tridactyle* Schltr., are present in collections at this time.

Nothing has been ascertained regarding the genetic affinities of this genus.

CULTURE: Presumably as for *Angraecum*. (H)

ELEORCHIS Maekawa

Two species of *Eleorchis* are known to date, both of them endemic to Japan. The group is a member of the subtribe *Bletillinae*, with the principal member of the genus, **E. japonica** (A.Gray) Maekawa, having been described previously as *Arethusa japonica* A.Gray and *Bletilla japonica* Schltr. Apparently rather attractive terrestrial orchids, neither this nor **E. conformis** Maekawa appear to be in cultivation at this time.

Nothing is known of the genetic affinities of *Eleorchis*.

CULTURE: Presumably as for *Arethusa*. (C)

ELLEANTHUS Presl
(*Evelyna* P. & E.)

Elleanthus is an extremely complex genus of almost seventy species of primarily epiphytic (rarely lithophytic or terrestrial) orchids in the American tropics, widespread from Cuba and Mexico southward, with the greatest concentration of representatives in the Andes of South America. Vegetatively almost identical to Sobralias in most instances, *Elleanthus* at once is distinctive when in flower, since the small (sometimes minute) blossoms are not produced singly—as are those of most Sobralias—but rather either in dense elongate racemes or in tight ball-like heads. In all cases the flowers are subtended (and often almost obscured) by large bracts, which in certain species are as colourful as the

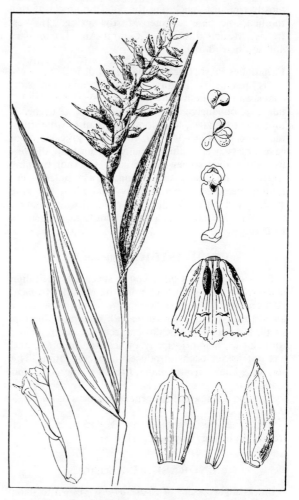

Elleanthus trilobatus A. & S. [BLANCHE AMES]

blossoms themselves. Some species of this genus are dwarf, grass-like plants, while others attain heights in excess of eight feet, forming large thickets in their native haunts.

Hybridization has not as yet been tried with this group, although some fascinating results could theoretically be obtained through critical interspecific breeding. Presumably the genus is genetically compatible with the allied *Sobralia*.

CULTURE: As for *Sobralia*. (C, I, H)

E. capitatus (P. & E.) Rchb.f. (*Evelyna capitata* P. & E., *Bletia capitata* R.Br.)

Pls. highly variable, to as much as 10′ tall, the leafy sts. stout, simple or branching above, covered by the lf.-sheaths. Lvs. rigidly papery, to 9″ long and 3″ wide, prominently nerved, elliptic-lanceolate to narrowly lanceolate, long-acuminate. Infls. terminal, a hemispherical dense head of many fls., the entire structure usually covered with a glue-like fluid, to 3½″ long and 2″ in diam., the bracts large, usually purplish, with the fls. somewhat exserted from the median ones. Fls. tubular, to ¾″ long, rose-purple, the lip with 2 roundish white calli at the base. Ss. oblong-elliptic, obtuse to apiculate. Ps. linear to linear-oblanceolate, obtuse. Lip mostly roundish, enclosing the col., the apical margin toothed, the base saccate. Mostly spring. (I) West Indies; Mexico throughout Central America to Peru and southern Brazil.

E. linifolius Presl (*Isochilus linifolius* Ldl.)

Pls. resembling a grass, clump-forming, the roots coarse and very fleshy, the sts. very leafy, slender, to 15″ tall. Lvs. obliquely erect, linear, not thick, unevenly 3-toothed at the apex, to 6″ long, less than ⅛″ wide. Infls. racemose, short, to 1″ long, the strongly keeled, concave bracts overlapping, usually longer than the few fls. which they somewhat obscure. Fls. not opening widely, white, less than ¼″ long. Lip completely enfolding the col., the margins wavy and ciliate, the base sac-like and with 2 small ovoid calli. Mostly summer. (C, I) West Indies; Mexico throughout Central America to Peru.

ENCHEIRIDION Summerh.

Consisting of but a single known species, **Encheiridion macrorrhynchium** (Schltr.) Summerh., this rare tropical African epiphyte is a leafless plant somewhat vaguely allied to the genus *Microcoelia* Ldl. Bearing numerous small, but very complex flowers from the centre of the root-cluster, it is principally of scientific interest, and has not as yet been introduced into cultivation. The species is known from Ghana, French Cameroons, and Gabon.

Nothing is known of the genetic alliances of *Encheiridion*.

CULTURE: Presumably as for *Polyrrhiza* and other tropical aphyllous epiphytes. (H)

ENDRESIELLA Schltr.

But a single species of *Endresiella* is known to date, this the excessively rare and incompletely described

E. Zahlbruckneriana Schltr., which has apparently been found only once in Costa Rica. A member of the subtribe *Gongorinae*, this unusual epiphyte is unknown in collections at this time.

Nothing is known of the genetic affinities of this genus.

CULTURE: Possibly as for *Gongora, Stanhopea*, etc. (I)

EPHIPPIANTHUS Rchb.f.

To date only a single species of *Ephippianthus* is known—**E. sachalinensis** F.W.Schmidt (*E. Schmidtii* Rchb.f.)—a dwarf terrestrial orchid native in Japan and Korea. Allied to *Cremastra* Ldl. and to *Didiciea* King & Pantl., of the subtribe *Corallorrhizinae*, it is unknown in collections today, and is, in any event, insignificant and primarily of botanical consequence.

Nothing is known of the genetic affinities of *Ephippianthus*.

CULTURE: Probably as for *Corallorrhiza*. (C)

EPIBLASTUS Schltr.

This is a genus of about twenty species, most of them native in New Guinea, but with outlying representatives in Celebes and the Philippines. A member of the subtribe *Glomerinae*, it is closest in its affinity to *Mediocalcar* J.J.Sm., and bears tiny, usually reddish flowers of great intricacy. None of the epiphytic orchids comprising *Epiblastus* are present in collections at this time.

Nothing is known of the genetic affinities of this rare group.

CULTURE: Presumably as for the tropical and medium-elevation Bulbophyllums. (I, H)

EPIBLEMA R.Br.

Epiblema, a member of the subtribe *Thelymitrinae*, contains a single species, **E. grandiflorum** R.Br., which is a rare terrestrial orchid in south-western Australia. Unknown in cultivation, it is a rather insignificant plant which differs from *Thelymitra* R.Br. in technical details of the flowers.

Nothing is known of the genetic ties of this obscure group.

CULTURE: Presumably as for *Caladenia*. (C, I)

EPIDANTHUS L.O.Wms.

This is a genus of three species of scarce, insignificant, epiphytic orchids which were formerly included in *Epidendrum* L., but which actually show little affinity to that group. The range of *Epidanthus* is a rather small one, the plants being confined to Mexico and Central America as far south as Panama. Because of the small size of the plants, the diminutive dimensions and rather dull coloration of the blossoms, and the rarity of the species, these orchids are virtually unknown in contemporary collections, and are of interest only to the scientifically inclined enthusiast.

Nothing has been ascertained regarding the genetic affinities of *Epidanthus*.

CULTURE: As for the cool-growing Masdevallias. (C, I)

E. paranthicus (Rchb.f.) L.O.Wms. (*Epidendrum paranthicum* Rchb.f.)

Pls. profusely branching, often forming dense masses, erect or almost prostrate, the individual sts. to 10″ long, often rather zigzag, leafy, concealed by striped lf.-sheaths, usually rooting at the branch-points. Lvs. pale green, erect-spreading or recurved, distichous, fleshy, usually terete, to 1″ long and less than $\frac{1}{16}$″ in diam. Infls. loose, few-fld., zigzag, short. Fls. fleshy, erect, about $\frac{1}{8}$″ long, yellow, greenish-yellow, or white, often marked with purple. Ss. and ps. more or less spreading or reflexed. Lip with the lamina deeply 3-lbd., the disc with a fleshy central callus. Mostly summer. (C, I) Mexico throughout Central America to Panama.

EPIDENDRUM L.

(*Amphiglottis* Salisb., *Anacheilium* Hoffmsgg., *Anacheilus* Hoffmsgg. ex Schltr., *Anocheile* Hoffmsgg. ex Rchb.f., *Auliza* Salisb., *Aulizeum* Ldl. ex Stein, *Barkeria* Kn. & Westc., *Caularthron* Raf., *Coilostylis* Raf., *Didothion* Raf., *Dimerandra* Schltr., *Dinema* Ldl., *Diothilophis* Raf. ex Schltr., *Dothiolophus* Raf., *Doxosma* Raf., *Encyclia* Hk., *Encyclium* Neum., *Epicladium* Small, *Epithecia* Kn. & Westc., *Epithecium* Kn. & Westc. ex Bth., *Exophya* Raf., *Hormidium* Ldl., *Larnandra* Raf., *Nanodes* Ldl., *Neolehmannia* Krzl., *Nidema* Britt. & Millsp., *Nychosma* Raf. ex Schltr., *Nyctosma* Raf., *Oerstedella* Rchb.f., *Phaedrosanthus* Post & Ktze., *Prostechea* Kn. & Westc. ex Schltr., *Prosthechea* Kn. & Westc., *Pseudepidendrum* Rchb.f., *Psilanthemum* Klotzsch, *Psychilis* Raf., *Seraphyta* Fisch. & Mey., *Spathiger* Small, *Spathium* Ldl., *Sulpitia* Raf., *Tritelandra* Raf.)

Epidendrum is among the largest genera of the Orchidaceae, the total number of component taxa commonly being estimated to be in excess of one thousand. These are exclusively American (except for *E. nocturnum* Jacq., which appears to have been introduced into tropical West Africa, probably by natural agencies), ranging from North Carolina and Mexico throughout the West Indies and Central America to the Galápagos Islands and Argentina. Centres of development occur in Mexico, the Andes of Colombia, and in Brazil. These diverse plants are among the most popular of cultivated orchids, though a remarkably small percentage of the total known species are present in contemporary collections in any quantity. Commercially, almost the only important types are the magnificent and variable hybrids of the 'reed-stem' group (§ *Euepidendrum*), which form a sizeable cut-flower crop in Hawaii and elsewhere in tropical climes. In a genus of this size, it is extremely difficult to give an accurate and yet concise description of its components, since many of them exhibit extremes of vegetative and floral diversity. The Epidendrums vary from truly epiphytic plants to rather rarely terrestrials, with not a few species being found almost habitually on rock-outcroppings, as lithophytes. They may be excessively small or very large (clambering vines in many instances), either with or without a conspicuous rhizome. The stems are either more or less prominently thickened into mostly globular pseudobulbs, or are slender, simple or branched, with leaves at intervals throughout their lengths. The leaves are diverse in shape and vary from flattened to terete. With only a very few exceptions, the inflorescence is terminal; this may be simple, or profusely branched, erect to somewhat pendulous, and bear from one to very many flowers, which are usually of medium to relatively large dimensions in the most frequently cultivated members of the genus. In most Epidendrums, the perianth-parts are spreading, and the petals narrower than the sepals. The lip may be slightly adnate to the column or, more frequently, adnate to the latter organ up to its apex; this labellum is either simple or three-lobed (in varying degrees) and is smooth or furnished with varying types of callosities. The winged or wingless column is short to elongate, and bears four equal pollinia in a terminal anther. *Epidendrum* is very closely allied to *Cattleya* Ldl. (particularly through *Cattleya aurantiaca* (Batem. ex Ldl.) P.N.Don), and the latter genus is technically referable to synonymy under the present one, though no particular purpose would be served by doing so, and the resultant confusion would be too great to warrant it.

Though a number of *Epidendrum* hybrids have long been known on the official register, it is only within the past decade that the breeders' interest in this diverse and valuable genus has started to become evident in our collections. These include a remarkable number of crosses within the genus itself, together with some truly splendid hybrids with allied groups of the subtribe *Laeliinae*, with which *Epidendrum* appears to be largely freely inter-fertile. Despite recent advances in this productive field, however, a tremendous amount of additional experimental hybridization yet remains to be done, even with some of the very commonest of cultivated representatives of this assemblage.

CULTURE: The cultural requirements of all Epidendrums are basically rather like those of the allied genus *Cattleya*, though naturally considerable variation exists in a group of such vast geographic distribution and such specific diversity. The species (and hybrids) with prominent pseudobulbs (members of the § *Encyclium*) thrive if treated like the tropical Cattleyas—though this depends in large part on the place of origin of the particular species or individual—in pots or baskets, or on slabs of tree-fern fibre or hardwood bark. These Epidendrums require a rather firmly-packed compost at the roots, preferably of osmunda or shredded tree-fern fibre (or chunks thereof). When in active growth, most of them require abundant moisture at the roots and relatively high humidity, but watering should be somewhat curtailed upon maturing of the new pseudobulbs. The 'reed-stem' types (§ *Euepidendrum*), because of their frequently elongate, leafy stems, do best if planted in specially-prepared beds, much in the manner of *Arachnis* or *Renanthera* (which see). Some of them, however, do not attain large dimensions under average conditions, hence do very well if grown in well-drained pots filled with osmunda or a compost such as that recommended for *Arachnis*. These 'reed-stem' types, for the most part viney in basic habit, require moist conditions at the roots at all times, rather more so than the pseudobulbous ones noted previously. They will stand virtually full exposure to sunlight (once established), and will both grow and flower better if given liberal applications of fertilizer at regular intervals. The one or two members of the rare § *Dimerandra* (*E. stenopetalum* Hk. is the major one) do best if treated like these 'reed-stem' types, being grown in pots. The species making up the § *Barkeria* (*E. elegans* (Kn. & Westc.) Rchb.f., *E. Lindleyanum* (Batem.) Rchb.f., etc.) do best if kept in very small pots, these tightly packed with fresh osmunda fibre. During active growth, they require quantities of water, light, and heat, but when the new stem-like pseudobulbs have matured, they must be given a very strict and protracted resting-period, often of several months' duration, to induce flowering. Temperature requirements for *Epidendrum* fluctuate from species to species, and often from individual to individual, dependent upon the source of the specimen. Epidendrums range from sea-level to elevations in excess of 13,000 feet in the Colombian Andes. (C, I, H)

E. alatum Batem. (*Epidendrum belizense* Rchb.f., *E. calocheilum* Hk., *E. formosum* Klotzsch, *E. longipetalum* Ldl. & Paxt., *Encyclia alata* Schltr., *Encyclia belizensis* Schltr.)

Robust sp., the pbs. usually pear-shaped, to 5″ tall, sheathed when young. Lvs. 2 or more, stalked and tubular at base, rather rigidly leathery, linear-lanceolate, to 1½′ long and 2½″ wide. Infls. a loose rac. or compound panicle, few- to many-fld., to 3½′ long. Fls. variable in colour, size, and in the shape of the lat. lbs. of the lip, spicily fragrant, usually about 2–2½″ across, the ss. and ps. usually yellowish-green marked (mostly medially) with purple or purplish-brown, the 3-lbd. lip usually dirty white with some brownish or purple suffusions or marks. Midlb. of lip with the central part bearing some raised purple lines which pass into broken warts apically. Spring–autumn. (I, H) Mexico to Nicaragua.

E. anceps Jacq. (*Amphiglottis anceps* Britt., *Amphiglottis lurida* Salisb., *Epidendrum amphistomum* A.Rich., *E. ensatum* A.Rich. & Gal., *E. fuscatum* Sm., *E. Galeottianum* A.Rich. & Gal., *E. musciferum* Ldl., *E. Schenckianum* Krzl., *E. secundum* Sw., *E. virescens* Lodd., *E. viridipurpureum* Hk.)

Extremely variable, to almost 3′ tall (very rarely more), the compressed, often yellowish sts. usually concealed by tubular sheaths. Lvs. distichous, linear-elliptic to oblong or elliptic, usually rounded at apex, rather rigid, sometimes purple-tinged, to 8″ long and 2″ wide. Infls. variable, usually long-stalked, with a few- to many-fld., typically head-like rac. at the apex; peduncle usually producing fls. for several years. Fls. fleshy, with an odour of stale broomstraw, about ½″ across, the ss. and ps. varying from light greenish-brown (or greenish-white) to dull red or tawny-yellow, the lip often flushed with reddish, pink, or dark brown, more or less distinctly 4-lbd. Throughout the year—almost ever-blooming. (I, H) South Florida and Mexico throughout tropical America to Brazil, Ecuador, and Peru.

E. arachnoglossum Rchb.f.

Sts. clambering, typically branching near the base, to several feet long, slender, densely leafy throughout. Lvs. to 4″ long, blunt apically, oblong, rigidly leathery. Infls. erect, very long-stalked, with a gradually elongating, often almost head-like rac. at the apex, sheathed below,

to 4′ long or more. Fls. about 1″ across. magenta, the disc of the lip orange-red. Ss. and ps. spreading, narrowly elliptic, acute. Lip 3-lbd., the lbs. strongly lacerate, the disc with 4 orange-yellow or orange-red calli and 2 white, lateral ones. Spring–autumn. (I) Colombia.

—fma. **candidum** (Rchb.f.) A.D.Hawkes (*Epidendrum arachnoglossum* Rchb.f. var. *candidum* Rchb.f.)

More frequently grown than the type, from which it differs only in the pure white fls., these with the basal lip-calli bright butter-yellow. Mostly summer. (I) Colombia.

E. armeniacum Ldl.

Sts. rather spindle-shaped, to 8″ tall, with 3–5 lvs. at the apex. Lvs. about 5″ long, rather leathery, narrowly lanceolate, acute. Infls. with a densely many-fld. rac., erect or arching, to 5″ long. Fls. less than ⅛″ across, yellowish, the 3-lbd. lip usually orange. Summer. (H) Guianas; Brazil.

E. aromaticum Batem. (*Epidendrum incumbens* Ldl., *E. primuloides* hort. ex Stein, *Encyclia aromatica* Schltr., *Encyclium aromaticum* Ldl. ex Stein)

Pbs. almost round, to 2″ tall, usually deep green or dark purplish-brown. Lvs. 1–2, linear-ligulate, obtuse to subacute, often dark purplish-brown, leathery, to 10″ long and 1½″ wide. Infls. erect or arching, a compound, many-fld. panicle, to almost 3′ long, with a long stalk. Fls. to 1½″ across, objectionably heavy-scented, long-lived, whitish or cream-yellow, the deeply 3-lbd. lip veined with brownish-red, the col. tinged with reddish-purple. Summer–autumn. (I) Mexico; Guatemala.

E. atropurpureum Willd. (*Cymbidium cordigerum* HBK, *Encyclia atropurpurea* Schltr., *Encyclium atropurpureum* Ldl. ex Stein, *Epidendrum Duboisianum* Brongn. ex A.Rich., *E. atropurpureum* Willd. var. *Randii* hort., *E. atropurpureum* Willd. var. *roseum* hort. not Rchb.f., *E. auropurpureum* Ldl., *E. macrochilum* Hk.)

Pbs. conical to cylindrical, often purple-flushed, to 5″ long and 2½″ in diam. Lvs. 2, linear-lanceolate, obtuse to acute, rigidly leathery, to 1½′ long and 2″ broad. Infls. typically a simple rac., 2–10-fld., to 2′ long, including the long peduncle. Fls. to almost 3″ long, highly variable in colour and dimensions, heavy-textured, fragrant, long-lived, the often apically recurved ss. and ps. purplish-green to brownish, the deeply 3-lbd. lip pure white to white with a basal magenta or red-magenta blotch, the lat. lbs. embracing the col., the midlb. very large, usually more or less crisped marginally. Mostly spring–early summer. (I, H) Mexico and Cuba to Peru and Brazil.

—fma. **roseum** (Rchb.f.) A.D.Hawkes (*Epidendrum atropurpureum* Willd. var. *roseum* Rchb.f., *E. macrochilum* Hk. var. *roseum* Batem.)

Differing from the type in floral coloration only, the ss. and ps. being purplish- or chocolate-brown, the very large lip bright rose-magenta, usually with a deeper magenta blotch at the base. Mostly summer. (I, H) Mexico; Costa Rica; Panama.

E. Boothii (Ldl.) L.O.Wms. (*Maxillaria Boothii* Ldl., *Cattleya micrantha* Klotzsch, *Dinema paleacea* Ldl., *Epidendrum auritum* Ldl., *E. Lindenianum* A.Rich. & Gal., *E. paleaceum* Rchb.f., *E. sarcoglossum* A.Rich. ex Rchb.f., *Nidema Boothii* Schltr.)

Pbs. short-stalked, to 2½″ tall, borne at intervals on a creeping rhiz., ellipsoid-cylindrical, somewhat laterally compressed, usually yellowish-green. Lvs. 1–2, bright glossy-green, linear to narrowly lanceolate, obtuse, thinly rigid, to 10″ long and ½″ wide. Infl. a few-fld. rac., to 6″ long, the peduncle compressed, furnished with scarious sheaths. Fls. fragrant, about 1″ wide at most, greenish-white to yellowish-white, the lip white-margined, the median calli bright yellow. Ss. and ps. mostly sharply reflexed. Spring. (I, H) Mexico and Cuba to Suriname.

E. Brassavolae Rchb.f. (*Encyclium Brassavolae* Ldl. ex Stein)

Vegetatively rather similar to *E. prismatocarpum* Rchb.f., often more robust in all parts. Infls. erect, rather long-stalked, to 1½′ tall, 6–9-fld., with a large brownish sheath at the base. Fls. faintly fragrant, rather fleshy, to 4″ across (usually smaller), the ss. and ps. (which are usually reflexed above the middle) deep yellowish-brown to greenish, the ps. often filiform-elongate above the middle. Lip entire, with a long, linear-oblong claw, the lamina white with a magenta or purple-red apex. Col. dilated above, usually green with purple spots or marks. Summer–autumn. (I, H) Mexico; Guatemala; Honduras; Nicaragua; Costa Rica; Panama.

E. ciliare L. (*Auliza ciliaris* Salisb., *Aulizeum ciliare* Ldl. ex Stein, *Coilostylis emarginata* Raf., *Epidendrum ciliare* L. var. *minor* hort. ex Stein, *E. cuspidatum* Lodd., *E. luteum* hort. ex Planch., *E. viscidum* Ldl., *Phaedrosanthus ciliaris* O.Ktze.)

Highly variable in vegetative structure (often simulating a *Cattleya*), and somewhat so in floral size and proportions, the pbs. usually stalked, spindle-shaped or cylindrical, somewhat compressed in many cases, sometimes grey-green, borne on a creeping rhiz., to 6½″ tall (rarely taller). Lvs. 1–2, elliptic-oblong, obtuse, rigidly leathery, usually glossy, to 12″ long and 3½″ wide. Infls. often produced before the new growth has matured, terminal, the rac. loosely few-fld., to 12″ long, furnished with large papery viscid bracts. Fls. 3–7″ across, fragrant, rather long-lived, waxy, the narrow ss. and ps. usually pale green or yellowish-green (rarely yellow or flushed with purplish), thread-like apically. Lip white, the disc usually bright yellow, the whole structure deeply 3-lbd., with fringed lat. lbs. and a sharp, needle-like midlb. Autumn–spring, often more than once annually. (I, H) Mexico and the West Indies throughout tropical America to Colombia, the Guianas, and Brazil.

E. cinnabarinum Salzm.

Rather similar vegetatively to *E. arachnoglossum* Rchb.f., but usually considerably more robust in all parts, to 6′ tall, branching basally. Infls. very long-stalked, with a loose or rather compact, few- to many-fld. rac. at the apex, to 6′ tall, the fls. opening successively over a long period of time. Fls. to 2½″ across, vermilion

or coral-red, fading to crimson or purplish-crimson, the disc of the lip yellow, spotted with red on the lamellae. Closely allied to, and often confused with, *E. Mosenii* Rchb.f. Mostly spring, but often almost throughout the year. (I, H) North-eastern Brazil.

E. clavatum (Raf.) Ldl. (*Didothion clavatum* Raf.)

Pbs. club-shaped, narrowing at both ends, to 6″ tall, becoming grooved with age. Lvs. 2, apical, narrowly elliptic, leathery, to 5″ long and 1″ wide. Infls. terminal, short-stalked, loosely 4–10-fld., the fls. opening successively. Fls. about 2″ across, fragrant, greenish, the lip white. Ss. and ps. linear, acute, spreading. Lip deeply 3-lbd., the lat. lbs. rhombic, spreading, the midlb. lanceolate-rhombic, acute, somewhat longer than the lat. ones. Summer. (H) Venezuela; Guianas.

E. cochleatum L. (*Anacheilium cochleatum* Hoffmsgg., *Epidendrum cochleatum* L. var. *costaricense* Schltr., *Phaedrosanthus cochleatus* O.Ktze.)

Pbs. clustered, stalked at base, compressed, often yellowish-green, ovoid or narrowly ellipsoid, 1–3-lvd., to 8″ tall and 1½″ wide. Lvs. slightly leathery, glossy, oblong-lanceolate to linear-lanceolate, more or less sharp-pointed, to 15″ long (usually shorter) and 2½″ wide. Infls. rarely branched, long-stalked, erect or arching, few-fld., the fls. opening successively over a long period, to 1½′ tall (usually shorter), with a large spathe at the base. Fls. inverted, long-lived, to 3½″ long, highly variable in degree of expansion and somewhat so in colour, the ss. and ps. usually greenish-yellow, with some purplish spots near base, the lip rich deep purple (almost black-purple), the basal central part whitish, with conspicuous purple radiating veins, the 2 calli at disc-base yellow. Ss. and ps. spreading or sharply down-thrust, more or less twisted, long-acuminate. Lip spreading from the middle of the col., entire, broadly roundish-cordate, cochleate, deeply concave, marginally rather wavy. Almost throughout the year, essentially ever-blooming. (I, H) Mexico and Cuba throughout tropical America to Brazil.

—var. **triandrum** Ames

Differs from the type in having 3 anthers (instead of 1); usually less robust and with smaller fls. than the typical form. Almost throughout the year. (I, H) South Florida; Dominican Republic; Puerto Rico.

E. condylochilum Lehm. & Krzl. (*Epidendrum Deamii* Schltr., *E. tessellatum* Batem. ex Ldl., *Encyclia tessellata* Schltr.)

Pbs. stalked, obliquely spindle-shaped, ovoid or ellipsoid, compressed, 2–3-lvd., to 3″ tall, usually yellowish-green, sheathed when young. Lvs. glossy, linear-lanceolate, acute or acuminate, to 12″ long and ¾″ wide. Infls. simple or branched, usually rather many-fld., erect or arching, very variable in length. Fls. not opening well, to ¾″ across, the ss. and ps. greenish-yellow outside, brown inside with darker brown streaks, the lip pale yellow with purplish streaks, the col. reddish-brown above, yellowish beneath. Ss. and ps. fleshy-thickened at the apex. Lip with the disc thickened along the middle below, between the lat. lbs. with a spongy-thickened pubescent callus which disintegrates into numerous warty calli on midlb. Mostly summer. (I, H) Mexico to Panama, Colombia, and Venezuela.

E. conopseum R.Br. (*Amphiglottis conopsea* Small)
Pls. without pbs., forming mats or clusters. Sts. very slender, compressed, to 8″ tall (usually less), 1–3-lvd., with rather large sheaths. Lvs. apical, rigidly leathery, usually glossy, often purple-flushed, narrowly oblong to linear-lanceolate, acute or cusped, stalkless, to 3½″ long. Infls. terminal, sheathed, usually simple, loosely or densely few- to many-fld., mostly erect, to 6½″ tall. Fls. very fragrant, lasting well, to about ¾″ across, greyish-green, usually tinged with purple or pale magenta. Ss. with the margins involute. Lip shallowly 3-lbd., the disc with 2 short fleshy calli at the base. Spring–autumn. (C, I) South-eastern United States, with a poorly-defined variety (var. **mexicanum** L.O.Wms.) in Mexico.

E. Cooperianum Batem.
Sts. thick, erect or ascending, leafy throughout, to 3½′ tall. Lvs. rigidly leathery, ligulate, acute, to 5″ long. Infls. densely 10–25-fld., to 5″ long, pendulous, apical. Fls. about 1¼″ across, yellow-green, the lip yellow-green, the disc pale rose with yellow calli. Ss. and ps. spreading, oblong, acutish, the ps. slightly shorter than the other segms. Lip 3-lbd., the lat. lbs. broadly roundish, the midlb. short, emarginate. Spring. (I, H) Brazil.

E. coriifolium Ldl. (*Epidendrum coriifolium* Ldl. var. *purpurascens* Schltr., *E. fuscopurpureum* Schltr., *E. magnibracteatum* Ames, *E. palmense* Ames, *E. subviolascens* Schltr.)
Extremely variable in all parts. Sts. clustered, forming large clumps, stout, somewhat compressed, with several large compressed sheaths, to 1½′ tall (usually less), often flushed with purple. Lvs. mostly near top of sts., often purple-flushed, few, erect-spreading, oblong-elliptic to linear-oblong (rarely almost semiterete), obtuse and obliquely retuse at apex, rigidly leathery, to 10″ long and 2″ wide. Infls. apical, more or less zigzag, rather few-fld., to 10″ long, the peduncle concealed by large imbricating closely appressed bracts, which are often purple-flushed or red-spotted. Fls. fleshy, to 1½″ across, lasting well, greenish or purplish-green to reddish-green, the lip usually darker. Lip with the lamina strongly convex, cordate-reniform, the disc with a fleshy keel terminating in the sinus-apicule. Autumn–winter. (I, H) Mexico to Peru.

E. criniferum Rchb.f.
Sts. clustered, densely leafy, to 15″ tall. Lvs. linear-lanceolate, acute, about 4″ long. Infls. erect, loosely 3–7-fld., short-stalked, the peduncle covered with overlapping, long-pointed sheathing bracts, compressed. Fls. about 2½″ across, fragrant, long-lived, showy, yellow more or less densely spotted with brown or reddish-brown, the lip white, with deeply lacerated lat. lbs. and a linear midlb. Ss. linear-lanceolate. Ps. narrowly linear. Winter. (I, H) Costa Rica; Panama; Colombia.

E. dichromum Ldl. (*Encyclia dichroma* Schltr.)
Pbs. fleshy, to about 4″ tall, ovoid. Lvs. usually paired, leathery, ligulate, obtuse, to 12″ long and 1½″

wide. Infls. erect or arching, loosely many-fld., to more than 3½′ long. Fls. fragrant, long-lived, very handsome, more than 2″ across, rose-red or pinkish-red, the large lip dark purple with a white margin. Ss. and ps. elliptic-spatulate, obtuse, spreading. Lip 3-lbd., the midlb. almost kidney-shaped. Autumn–early winter. (I, H) Brazil.

E. difforme Jacq. (*Amphiglottis difformis* Britt., *Auliza difformis* Small, *Epidendrum umbellatum* Sw.)
Pls. pendulous, erect, or ascending, highly variable in all parts. Sts. often rather zigzag, more or less densely leafy, to more than 12″ long, often shorter. Lvs. oval to oblong-lanceolate, rigid and very fleshy to rather thin-textured, to more than 4″ long, often yellowish-green, usually very glossy. Infls. almost stalkless, umbelliform, 1- to many-fld. Fls. very variable in size, at most to about 1¼″ across, fragrant, somewhat translucent, pale green or whitish, the lip almost square to kidney-shaped, with 2 erect calli on the basal disc, the nerves more or less thickened. Almost throughout the year, but mostly in autumn months. (I, H) South Florida and Mexico throughout the West Indies and Central America to Brazil and Peru.

E. diffusum Sw. (*Seraphyta diffusa* Pfitz., *S. multiflora* Fisch. & Mey.)
Highly variable, from 3–15″ tall when in fl. Sts. slender, more or less leafy, somewhat flattened, often red-tinged. Lvs. rigid, often flushed with purple or purple-red, oval, obtuse, to about 3″ long. Infls. erect or arching, very many-fld., loose, a rac. or diffuse panicle, to 12″ long. Fls. usually less than ½″ across, translucent green or yellowish-green, usually turning red when dry. Ss. and ps. linear, acute. Lip ovate, with an apicule, the disc with 2 obtuse keels. Mostly autumn–winter. (I, H) Mexico and the West Indies to Colombia, Suriname, and Brazil.

E. elegans (Kn. & Westc.) Rchb.f. (*Barkeria elegans* Kn. & Westc.)
Sts. tightly clustered, erect, cylindrical or somewhat swollen above, to 7″ tall, leafy especially towards the apex. Lvs. lanceolate, acute, to 2½″ long, rather flaccid, soon deciduous. Infls. to 12″ long, loosely 3–7-fld., rarely branched, the peduncle slender, sheathed. Fls. about 2¾″ in diam., very handsome, the ss. and ps. dark or pale rosy-red, the large lip pale rosy-red to almost white, with a broad apical blotch of deep rose-red. Winter–early spring. (I) Mexico.

E. ellipticum Ldl. (*Epidendrum crassifolium* Hk.)
Similar in habit to *E. elongatum* Jacq., but with obtuse lvs. and larger purple-violet fls. about 1″ across, the lozenge-shaped thickening on the lip-disc golden-yellow. Ss. and ps. strongly spreading. Spring–summer. (I, H) West Indies; Brazil.

E. elongatum Jacq.
Rather similar in habit to *E. arachnoglossum* Rchb.f., but the sts. shorter and more slender, to about 1½′ tall, leafy throughout, the lvs. about 3″ long, rigidly leathery. Infls. long-stalked, few- to many-fld. Fls. about ¾″ across, light scarlet-red, the lip-callus often yellow or orange-yellow. Ss. and ps. lanceolate, acutish. Lip 3-lbd.,

all of the lbs. fringed or lacerated, with a short lozenge-shaped thickening on the disc. Spring–summer. (I, H) West Indies; Brazil.

E. Endresii Rchb.f.

One of the most charming sp. in the genus. Sts. tightly clustered, erect, rigid, to 10″ tall, leafy throughout, the lf.-sheaths warty. Lvs. elliptic, obtuse, about 1½″ long, very rigid, fleshy. Infls. erect, loosely 4–10-fld., about 3–5″ tall. Fls. about 1″ across, fragrant, the ss. and ps. flushed with pale rose-red outside, white inside, the lip white with a rose-red centre and a deep or rather pale violet-purple blotch on the disc, the col.-apex and anther violet-purple. Lip 4-lbd., larger than the other segms. Winter. (I) Costa Rica; Panama.

E. erubescens Ldl. (*Encyclia erubescens* Schltr.)

Pbs. mostly spindle-shaped, rather thick, to about 3″ tall. Lvs. usually paired, leathery, to 4″ long, ligulate, obtuse. Infls. erect, loosely many-fld., usually branched, to almost 2′ tall. Fls. very fragrant, to about 1½″ across, long-lived, variable in colour, but usually reddish-yellow, the lip mostly darker. Ss. oblong. Ps. elliptic, obtuse. Lip with a very broad midlb. Spring–early summer. (C) Mexico: Oaxaca, at high elevations.

E. floribundum HBK

Sts. rather slender, somewhat compressed, to about 1½′ tall, densely leafy. Lvs. variable in shape, elliptic to lanceolate, to 6″ long, usually rather heavy-textured. Infls. erect or arching, rather loosely many-fld., sometimes branched, to 5″ long. Fls. about 1″ across, yellowish-green, the lip white with some red spots. Lip 3-lbd., the midlb. almost linear. Autumn–winter. (I, H) Colombia; Venezuela; Brazil.

E. fragrans Sw.

An extremely variable sp. Pbs. usually ellipsoidal, yellowish- or deep-green, to 3″ tall and more. Lf. solitary, ligulate to almost oval, obtuse or acutish, to 4″ long and more. Infls. short-stalked, loosely 2–8-fld., to 5″ long. Fls. inverted, very fragrant (often rather objectionably so), to about 1½″ across, usually yellowish- or greenish-white, the lip white or cream-white, with more or less prominent violet or dull purple radiating streaks from the base. Ss. and ps. narrowly lanceolate, acute to acuminate. Lip broadly cochleate, acute or acuminate apically. This sp. is often confused with *E. ionophlebium* Rchb.f. and *E. radiatum* Ldl. Winter–spring. (I, H) Mexico and the West Indies to Ecuador, Peru, and Brazil.

E. fucatum Ldl. (*Epidendrum affine* A.Rich., *E. hircinum* A.Rich., *E. Sagraeanum* A.Rich., *Encyclia fucata* Schltr.)

Pbs. forming large clusters, ovoid, to about 3″ tall, becoming furrowed with age. Lvs. 2–3, rather leathery, linear, acutish, to 12″ long. Infls. erect or arching, rather loosely or densely 10–40-fld., often paniculate, to 2½′ long. Fls. faintly fragrant, long-lived, about 1¼″ across (usually less), somewhat variable in colour, usually yellowish or butter-yellow, the lip white streaked with red. Ss. and ps. oblong, obtuse. Midlb. of lip shortly cordate, the lat. lbs. enfolding the col. Mostly autumn–winter. (I, H) Cuba; ? Bahamas.

E. ibaguense HBK (*Epidendrum pratense* Rchb.f., *E. radicans* Pav. ex Ldl., *E. rhizophorum* Batem. ex Ldl.)

Highly variable in all parts, among the most common and widespread of American orchids. Sts. often extremely lengthy, sometimes to 30′ long, branching and forming numerous offsets, usually vine-like and forming dense masses, rooting at the nodes, leafy. Lvs. ovate-oblong to oblong-elliptic, broadly rounded to obtuse, clasping the st. at the base, often yellowish-green, rigidly fleshy, to 4″ long. Infls. very long-stalked, a typically densely many-fld., simple rac. which gradually becomes elongated, the fls. opening gradually over a long period of time. Fls. about 1¼″ across at most, varying in colour from orange, red, or yellow to scarlet, vermilion, or orange-red, the lip with a large yellow median blotch, lat. lbs. of lip more or less fringed, the midlb. separated from them by a rather distinct sinus. Throughout the year, essentially ever-blooming. (I, H) Mexico throughout Central America to South America.

E. imatophyllum Ldl. (*Epidendrum lorifolium* Schltr., *E. palpigerum* Rchb.f.)

Pls. usually growing in ants' nests, variable in vegetative habit, forming dense clumps often several ft. in

Epidendrum ibaguense HBK [B.S.WILLIAMS]

diam., the individual sts. 10–80″ tall, with very copious matted roots, slender or stout, leafy, the lf.-sheaths yellow-green, often purple-spotted. Lvs. erect-spreading, distichous, ligulate to linear-lanceolate, obtuse, rigidly fleshy, to 8″ long. Infls. a simple or several-branched rac., densely many-fld., the fls. opening over a long period, to 6″ long. Fls. showy, long-lived, to about 1″ across, light lavender to deep purple, the disc of the lip usually whitish. Lat. lbs. of lip almost entire to deeply and irregularly lacerate, the midlb. usually entire marginally. Almost throughout the year. (I, H) Mexico throughout Central America to Brazil and Peru.

E. ionophlebium Rchb.f. (*Epidendrum Hoffmanni* Schltr., *E. pachycarpum* Schltr.)

Allied to and rather resembling *E. fragrans* Sw., differing in bearing 2-lvd. pbs. and in the almost square, fuzzy callus on the lip-base. Pbs. ovoid to spindle-shaped, compressed, 2-lvd., to 3″ long, usually rather greyish-green. Lvs. ligulate, narrowly obtuse, leathery, to more than 12″ long. Infls. short, stout, 2–7-fld., erect. Fls. inverted, fragrant, about 2″ across at most, greenish-yellow or greenish-cream-coloured, the lip with some mostly dull purplish radiating streaks, cochleate, concave. Winter–spring. (I, H) Mexico to Panama.

E. ionosmum Ldl. (*Encyclia ionosma* Schltr.)

Pbs. ovoid, about 1½″ tall, clustered. Lvs. usually paired, linear, about 4″ long. Infls. densely 4–10-fld., to about 12″ tall. Fls. strongly fragrant of violets, about 1¼″ across, greenish-brown, the lip yellow veined with dull or bright red. Ss. and ps. shortly ovate, concave. Lip 3-lbd., the midlb. oblong, emarginate. Spring. (H) Guianas.

E. Laucheanum Rolfe ex Bonhof

Sts. cluster-forming, to 3′ tall, slender, erect, concealed by tubular lf.-sheaths. Lvs. linear-lanceolate to narrowly lanceolate, acuminate, usually almost horizontal, to about 7½″ long. Infls. arching to pendulous, few- to many-fld., simple, including the stalk to 1½′ long. Fls. thin to very fleshy-thickened, waxy, pinkish-brown, purple, or purplish-green, about 1″ across, the narrow ps. reflexed, the lip with a folded lamina. Mostly summer. (I, H) Guatemala; Honduras; Nicaragua; Costa Rica; Colombia.

E. Lindleyanum (Batem. ex Ldl.) Rchb.f. (*Barkeria Lindleyana* Batem. ex Ldl., *B. melanocaulon* A.Rich. & Gal., *B. spectabilis* Batem. ex Ldl., *Epidendrum melanocaulon* Rchb.f., *E. spectabile* Rchb.f., *E. Whartonianum* C.Schweinf.)

Pls. cluster-forming, usually small, highly variable in all parts, the sts. cylindrical or somewhat spindle-shaped, to 6″ long, concealed by whitish lf.-sheaths. Lvs. mostly near the apex of sts., distichous, linear-lanceolate to oblong-lanceolate, acute to acuminate, rather fleshy, to 6″ long, often streaked with purplish, quickly deciduous. Infls. loosely few- to many-fld., rarely branched, to 2′ long, but usually shorter. Fls. nodding, about 2–3″ across at most, highly variable in colour and lip-shape, the colour ranging from almost white to deep purple, the lip often spotted with reddish-purple, the

disc with 3–5 keels along the middle, the keels more pronounced apically. Winter–spring. (I, H) Mexico; Guatemala; Honduras; Costa Rica.

E. Mariae Ames

Pbs. clustered, usually narrowly pyriform, more or less grey-green, to almost 2″ long. Lvs. usually 2, olive-green or greyish-green, to 7″ long, erect or not. Infls. usually arching, 1–5-fld., the peduncle slender, grey-green. Fls. to 3″ long (very rarely more), long-lasting, very beautiful, the broad ss. and ps. lime-green to almost olive-green, glossy, the immense flaring basally tubular lip frilled, dead-white, emarginate, with a prominent basal dull yellow or green mark. One of the loveliest of all of the Epidendrums! Summer. (I) Mexico, at moderately high elevations.

E. Mosenii Rchb.f.

Very similar to and often confused with *E. cinnabarinum* Salzm., differing in the orange or yellow fls., fading to crimson, usually smaller in size, and with some dark red spots around the lip-calli. Ps. usually somewhat toothed towards the apical margins. Mostly autumn, but often almost ever-blooming. (I, H) Brazil, where it is common and widespread.

E. moyobambae Krzl. (*Epidendrum benignum* Ames, *E. subpatens* Schltr.)

Pls. stout, pendulous or ascending, to 2′ tall, the sts. leafy. Lvs. distichous, oblong-elliptic to linear-lanceolate, obtuse to acute, rather leathery, to 6″ long, the margins often saw-toothed. Infls. usually pendent, loosely 10–35-fld., to 1½′ long, the rachis often zigzag. Fls. fleshy, fragrant, about 2″ across at most, the ss. and ps. brownish-green, the lip white. Lip deeply 3-lbd., the midlb. 2-lobulate, the disc with a pair of calli in front of the col. Summer. (I, H) Guatemala; Costa Rica; Panama; Colombia; Trinidad; Peru; Brazil.

E. nemorale Ldl. (*Epidendrum verrucosum* Ldl. not Sw., *Encyclia nemoralis* Schltr.)

Pbs. ovoid, often very robust, to 5″ tall and almost as much in diam., clustered, often rather greyish. Lvs. linear-lanceolate, acutish, to 12″ long, heavily leathery. Infls. to 3′ long, rather loosely few- to many-fld., the fls. often arranged in regular planes. Fls. very fragrant, long-lived, widely spreading, to almost 4″ across, dusty rose-red, the large, broad midlb. of the lip deep rose-red or magenta-red, veined with deep purple, the area around the basal calli usually whitish. Summer, especially during July. (I, H) Mexico.

E. nocturnum Jacq. (*Amphiglottis nocturna* Britt., *Auliza nocturna* Small, *Epidendrum discolor* A.Rich. & Gal., *E. nocturnum* Jacq. var. *panamense* Schltr., *Nyctosma nocturna* Raf., *Phaedrosanthus nocturnus* O.Ktze.)

Highly variable, especially as to vegetative stature and details, to 3′ tall, usually shorter, the sts. clustered, terete below, compressed above, papery-sheathed, bearing lvs. mostly near the apex when mature. Lvs. glossy, distichous, oval-elliptic to lanceolate, broadly rounded to acutish, leathery, to 7″ long. Infl. a very compact, often branched rac. producing 4–5 fls. or more over a period of several months, usually only one open at a time, frequently producing fls. for more than one season. Fls. opening well or not, very fragrant (especially at night), variable in size and colour, usually about 3–5″ across, the ss. yellowish- or greenish-white, the thread-like ps. whitish, the large lip white, with a large bright yellow blotch on the disc around the 2 elongate parallel lamellae. Lip deeply 3-lbd., the lat. lbs. oval, the midlb. thread-like or filiform, often irregular. Throughout the year, but mainly summer–autumn. (I, H) South Florida and Mexico throughout tropical America to Ecuador, Peru, and Brazil; apparently introduced into tropical West Africa.

E. oncidioides Ldl. (*Epidendrum guatemalense* Klotzsch, *Encyclia oncidioides* Schltr.)

Pbs. ovoid, narrowly pear-shaped to almost cylindrical, to about 4″ long, with sheaths at the base. Lvs. 2–3, linear-ligulate to oblong-linear, obtuse to acute, rather fleshy, to 2′ long and more than 1½″ wide. Infls. usually branched, the branches short and spreading, few- to rather many-fld., to 3′ long and more. Fls. extremely variable, faintly fragrant, long-lived, often very handsome, to 2″ across (rarely larger), the ss. and ps. usually yellowish-brown or greenish-yellow, often flushed medially with brown, the lip white, yellow, cream-coloured, or variously mottled and marked with dull brown or purplish-brown. Col. stout, gently reflexed at about the middle. Mostly autumn–winter. (I, H) Mexico to Honduras, Trinidad, and northern South America.

E. osmanthum B.-R. (*Epidendrum Cappartianum* L.Lind., *E. Godseffianum* Rolfe, *Encyclia osmantha* Schltr.)

Pbs. ovoid, very robust, to 5″ tall and more. Lvs. 2–3, tongue-shaped, obtuse, to 1½′ long, heavily leathery, rather rigid. Infls. usually profusely branched, to 3′ long, loosely many-fld., the fls. opening gradually over a long period. Fls. very fragrant, about 2″ across, the ss. and ps. yellow-green veined with dull red or brownish-red, the large lip 3-lbd., white, veined with red, the midlb. cordate. Autumn–winter. (I, H) Brazil.

E. paniculatum R. & P. (*Epidendrum isthmi* Schltr., *E. piliferum* Rchb.f., *E. reflexum* A. & S., *E. resectum* Rchb.f., *E. turialvae* Rchb.f.)

Exceedingly variable in all parts, especially in the fls. and shape of the lip. Pls. often very robust, to 8′ tall, usually much shorter. Sts. clustered, erect, slender to stout, concealed by lf.-sheaths. Lvs. rather thin to leathery, elliptic-ovate to linear-lanceolate, acute to long-acuminate, often purplish on lower surface, to 10″ long. Infls. usually greatly exceeding the lvs., to several ft. in length, simple or more commonly branched, few- to many-fld., the fls. opening gradually over a long period. Fls. lasting well, very variable in size and colour, usually about 1″ across or less, greenish-white to rosy-purple, the lip often pure white, ranging from almost simple to 3- or 4-lbd., the disc with several complex calli. Mostly summer, but often more than once annually. (I, H) Mexico throughout Central America to Ecuador, Peru, Bolivia, Brazil, and Argentina.

E. Parkinsonianum Hk. (*Epidendrum aloifolium* Batem. not L., *E. falcatum* Ldl., *E. falcatum* Ldl. var. *Zeledoniae* Schltr., *E. lactiflorum* A.Rich. & Gal., *E. Parkinsonianum* Hk. var. *falcatum* AHS)

Pls. strongly pendulous from trees, often extremely large and forming clumps to 7′ long and more. Pbs. clustered, curved-ascending, slender, terete, to 4″ long, concealed by translucent, often rough sheaths. Lvs. 1-more per pb., linear-lanceolate to narrowly lanceolate, acute to long-acuminate, often almost cylindrical on superficial observation, very fleshy, flaccid, deep green often tinged with purple, to 1½′ long, to 1″ thick. Fls. borne on short peduncles from the new growth, 1–3, showy, fragrant, long-lived, to more than 6″ across, often smaller, widely spreading, the ss. and ps. pale yellow or yellowish-green, often tinged outside with mauve or purplish-bronze, the large 3-lbd. lip white, with a more or less distinct yellow or yellowish-orange blotch on the disc, where there are two flap-like obtuse keels, just in front of the col. Mostly summer–autumn, often more than once annually. (I, H) Mexico; Guatemala; Honduras; Costa Rica; Panama.

E. patens Sw.

Rather similar in all respects to *E. moyobambae* Krzl., too closely allied perhaps for segregation as a distinct taxon, since both spp. are variable. Sts. clustered, slender, arching to pendulous, to 2′ long, leafy. Lvs. lanceolate-oblong, acute, to 4″ long. Infls. rather sharply pendulous, loosely or densely few- to many-fld., to about 5″ long. Fls. fragrant, waxy, long-lived, about 1¼″ across, the ss. and ps. greenish-yellow, the large lip white or cream-white. Ss. and ps. narrowly oblong, acutish. Lip 3-lbd., the midlb. oval, obtuse. Mostly summer. (I, H) West Indies, especially Jamaica; Brazil.

E. pentotis Rchb.f. (*Epidendrum Beyrodtianum* Schltr., *E. confusum* Rolfe, *E. fragrans* Sw. var. *megalanthum* Ldl.)

Pbs. narrowly cylindrical or somewhat spindle-shaped, somewhat compressed, 4–11″ tall. Lvs. 2 (rarely 1), linear-elliptic to lanceolate, obtuse to acuminate, leathery, to 12″ long. Infls. erect, usually 2–3-fld., prominently sheathed at base, to about 2½″ tall. Fls. inverted, very fragrant, to 3″ long, the pedicellate ovaries roughly warty, the ss. and ps. pale greenish-yellow to cream-white, more or less spreading, the lip usually white with some radiating nerves, these purplish in colour, on the disc. Mostly summer. (I, H) Mexico; Guatemala; El Salvador; Honduras; Nicaragua; Brazil.

E. polyanthum Ldl. (*Epidendrum bisetum* Ldl., *E. colorans* Klotzsch, *E. heteroglossum* Krzl., *E. pergameneum* Rchb.f., *E. quinquelobum* Schltr., *E. Stallforthianum* Krzl., *E. verrucipes* Schltr.)

Extremely variable, a polymorphic sp. Sts. clustered, 1–4′ tall, leafy, concealed by the membranaceous lf.-sheaths. Lvs. erect-spreading, often rather thin-textured, linear to elliptic-lanceolate, to 8½″ long and 2½″ wide. Infls. a simple or compound many-fld. rac., to 1½′ long, sheathed. Fls. with slender warty pedicellate ovaries, to about ¾″ across, varying from yellowish-white, orange-yellow, or greenish-yellow to brownish-yellow or reddish, the lip either lighter or darker. Ps. thread-like to filiform-spatulate, often recurved. Lip deeply 3-lbd., the disc with 2 thickened nipple-like calli at the base in front of the col. Mostly summer, often more than once annually. (I, H) Mexico throughout Central America to Venezuela and Brazil.

E. polybulbon Sw. (*Bulbophyllum occidentale* Spreng., *Dinema polybulbon* Ldl.)

Pls. dwarf, forming large flat masses on trees and rocks. Rhiz. slender, creeping, brown-sheathed, bearing the ovoid to cylindric-ellipsoid pbs. at intervals, the pbs. to 1¼″ tall, usually much smaller. Lvs. 2, ovate-elliptic to narrowly elliptic-oblong, leathery, shiny green, to 3″ long, usually much smaller. Fls. 1 (rarely 2), fragrant, long-lived, borne at the apex of the pbs., large for the plant, about 1¼″ across or more, the ss. and ps. greenish-yellow or dull yellow with a brown flush or with reddish streaks below the middle, the lip yellowish-white or cream-white, short-clawed, the lamina roundish to heart-shaped, marginally crisped and wavy. Winter–spring. (I, H) Cuba; Jamaica; Mexico; Guatemala; Honduras.

E. prismatocarpum Rchb.f. (*Epidendrum maculatum* hort., *E. Uro-Skinneri* hort.)

Pbs. clustered or borne a short distance apart on the stout rhiz., often yellowish, narrowly ovoid, often attenuated above, to 6″ tall and 2″ in diam., becoming wrinkled with age. Lvs. 2–3, ligulate to oblanceolate-oblong or narrowly ovate, obtuse, leathery, often yellowish-green, to 15″ long and 2½″ wide. Infls. erect, loosely or densely few- to many-fld., with a prominent sheath at the base, to 15″ tall. Fls. about 2″ across, fragrant, waxy, long-lived, somewhat variable in colour, usually sulphur-yellow spotted with dark sepia-brown or dull magenta, the lip cream-yellow to rosy-red. Ss. and ps. broadly linear, acute, the ps. arching downwards. Lip clawed, the lat. lbs. very short, ear-like, the midlb. lanceolate, fleshy. Summer–autumn. (I, H) Costa Rica; Panama.

E. Pseudepidendrum Rchb.f. (*Pseudepidendrum spectabile* Rchb.f.)

One of the finest of the genus. Sts. clustered, robust, to 3′ tall and more, leafy. Lvs. narrowly lanceolate, acute, to 6″ long. Infls. loosely 3–5-fld., to about 6″ long. Fls. about 2½–3″ long, the apple-green ss. and ps. reflexed, the large brilliant orange or orange-red lip protruding ahead of them. Ss. ligulate-spatulate, acute. Ps. linear, the apex broader. Lip with the midlb. almost round, undulate, finely fringed marginally, with 5 yellow, thick keels on the disc. Col. orange-red at the thickened apex. Summer–autumn. (I) Costa Rica; Panama.

E. radiatum Ldl. (*Epidendrum marginatum* Lk., Kl. & Otto, not L.C.Rich.)

Often confused with *E. fragrans* Sw. and *E. ionophlebium* Rchb.f. Pbs. clustered, stalked, obliquely ovoid-ellipsoid to narrowly spindle-shaped, compressed, strongly ribbed, often yellowish-green, to 5″ tall. Lvs. 2–3, linear-ligulate to linear-lanceolate, obtuse to acuminate, leathery, to 12″ long, often rather yellowish-green. Infls. erect or arching, few- to many-fld., rather

dense, to 4″ long. Fls. inverted, very fragrant (often objectionably so), heavy-textured, to 1″ diam., ss. and ps. pale greenish-white or yellowish-green, the lip the same colour, with radiating purple or dull red-purple veins from the base. Ss. and ps. obtuse to rarely acute, never acuminate. Lip not sharp-pointed. Spring–summer. (I, H) Mexico to Costa Rica; Venezuela; ? Brazil.

E. Schumannianum Schltr.

Sts. clustered, erect or arching, to 7′ tall, rather slender to reasonably stout, leafy above, the lf.-sheaths densely dark-purple-warty. Lvs. glossy, rather thinly leathery, lanceolate to elliptic-oblong, obtuse or acutish, to 4″ long and more than 1″ broad. Infls. usually rigidly erect, simple or laxly branched, mostly very many-fld., to 2′ tall (usually somewhat shorter). Fls. fragrant, long-lived, to about 1″ in diam. at most, the rather concave ss. and ps. outside rich lavender, inside burnt sienna more or less densely spotted with dark brown, the lip dark lavender to almost blue-lavender. Lip large, clawed, deeply 3-lbd., the smallish lat. lbs. oblong, obtuse, spreading, the midlb. obovate-cuneate, 2-lbd. or deeply bifid, the apical margins often crenulate. Late spring–summer. (I) Costa Rica; Panama, at moderately high elevations.

E. selligerum Batem. ex Ldl. (*Epidendrum atrorubens* Rolfe, *E. diotum* Ldl., *E. Hanburyi* Ldl., *E. insidiosum* Rchb.f., *E. violodora* Gal. ex Ldl., *Encyclia diota* Schltr., *Encyclia Hanburyi* Schltr., *Encyclia selligera* Schltr.)

Closely allied to and rather simulating *E. alatum* Batem., differing principally in that the col. is not winged on each side at the apex. Infl. a loosely many-fld. panicle, to more than 3′ long. Fls. fragrant, long-lived, about 1½″ across, the ss. and ps. greenish-brown or yellow flushed with brown, the lip white or yellowish with purple veins, deeply 3-lbd. Summer–autumn. (I, H) Mexico; Guatemala; Honduras.

E. Skinneri Batem. ex Ldl. (*Barkeria Skinneri* Ldl., *Barkeria Skinneri* Ldl. var. *major* Paxt., *Epidendrum Fuchsii* Regel)

Pls. clustered, to 1½′ tall, the sts. narrowly spindle-shaped, 2–5½″ tall, concealed by the papery lf.-sheaths. Lvs. several, mostly near the apex, fleshy, elliptic to elliptic-lanceolate, acute to acuminate, to 6″ long and ¾″ wide. Infls. erect, long-stalked, few- to many-fld., simple or rarely branched, to about 12″ tall. Fls. to 1½″ across, rather long-lived, lilac-purple, rose-purple, or red-magenta, the lip-disc with 3 central yellowish keels, these more thickened and higher near the base. Autumn–winter. (I) Mexico: Chiapas; Guatemala.

E. Stamfordianum Batem. (*Epidendrum cycnostalix* Rchb.f.)

Pbs. clustered, stalked, spindle-shaped, tapering below into a long jointed stalk, to 10″ tall (rarely more) and ¾″ in diam. Lvs. 2–4, apical, leathery, linear-oblong to oblong-elliptic, obtuse, to 10″ long. Infls. arising from the base of the pbs., many-fld., often branched, to 2′ long. Fls. fragrant, long-lived, to more than 1½″ long, the ss. and ps. usually yellow or greenish-yellow, more or less spotted with red, the lip yellow, deeply 3-lbd., the lat. lbs. large, recurved, the midlb. fringed. Winter–spring. (I, H) Mexico to Panama; Colombia; Venezuela.

E. stenopetalum Hk. (*Dimerandra stenopetala* Schltr., *Epidendrum lamellatum* Ldl.)

An aberrant sp., highly variable. Sts. clustered, fleshy-thickened, tapering above and below, often rather zigzag, usually purple-striped lengthwise, 4–15″ tall, mostly leafy throughout. Lvs. erect-spreading, somewhat leathery, linear-oblong to linear-lanceolate, obtuse and oblique at the apex, 1–5″ long. Infl. a short few-fld. corymb-like rac., usually less than 1″ long, heavily bracted. Fls. opening one or more at a time over a long period, to more than 1″ across, often not opening fully, or opening very flat, rose-pink to rose-violet, the lip usually darker, with a square, roughened, yellowish-white or cream-white callus at the base. Lip mostly roundish or wedge-shaped, very rarely lobulate. Winter–spring. (I, H) Mexico and Jamaica throughout Central America to Panama, Trinidad, and northern South America.

E. tampense Ldl. (*Encyclia tampensis* Small)

Pbs. forming huge mats, closely clustered, ovoid to almost round, shining, green, often flushed with purple, 1¼–3″ long, sheathed when young. Lvs. 1–3, linear to linear-lanceolate, acutish, rigidly leathery, to more than 15″ long and about ½″ wide. Infls. simple or branched, 1- to many-fld., to 2½′ long. Fls. long-lived, fragrant, to 1½″ across (usually smaller), highly variable in colour, the ss. and ps. yellowish-brown to yellowish-green or apple-green, more or less veined and suffused with brown or madder-purple, especially towards the tips, the lip white, with a more or less definite magenta-purple blotch on the midlb. Lip with the midlb. separated from the lat. lbs. (which arch over the col.-sides) by an isthmus. Spring–winter. (I) Florida; Bahamas, with a variety (var. **Amesianum** Corr.) in Cuba.

E. varicosum Batem. ex Ldl. (*Epidendrum chiriquense* Rchb.f., *E. leiobulbon* Hk., *E. Lunaeanum* A.Rich. ex Ldl., *E. phymatoglossum* Rchb.f., *E. quadratum* Klotzsch, *E. Ramirezzi* Gajón Sánchez, *Encyclia varicosa* Schltr.)

Pbs. clustered, ovoid-spindle-shaped at base, extending into a more or less long neck above, 1½–7″ tall. Lvs. 2–3, glossy, usually rather leathery, oblong-elliptic to ligulate-lanceolate, obtuse to acuminate, to more than 12″ long. Infls. erect or arching, few- to many-fld., 1½–20″ tall. Fls. fragrant, rather long-lived, often very glossy-textured, usually about 1″ across, the ss. and ps. tan to greenish-brown, the lip yellowish-white, often purple- or red-dotted, deeply 3-lbd. Mostly summer. (I) Mexico to Panama.

E. verrucosum Sw.

Sts. clustered, reed-like, to ¾″ in diam., to 6′ tall, leafy above, the lf.-sheaths more or less covered with black or brown rough spots. Lvs. narrowly lanceolate to oblong-lanceolate, rather fleshy, often curved upward, 3–9″ long. Infls. erect, usually a branched panicle, many-fld., somewhat pyramidal in outline, to 1½′ tall. Fls. fragrant, about ½″ across or more, long-lived, white,

the disc with a grooved yellow basal callus. Lip deeply 3-lbd., appearing 4-lbd., the midlb. fringed apically. Summer. (I, H) Mexico; Guatemala; Honduras; Nicaragua; Colombia; Jamaica.

—var. **myrianthum** (Ldl.) A. & C. (*Epidendrum myrianthum* Ldl.)

Differs from the type in the lilac-scented fls. which are pure white to deep ruby-red or purplish-red, the callus 2-lbd. at apex instead of 3-lbd. Summer. (I, H) Mexico; Guatemala; Honduras.

E. virgatum Ldl. (*Epidendrum amabile* Lind. & Rchb.f., *E. icthyophyllum* Ames, *E. punctulatum* Rchb.f., *E. sphaerobulbon* A.Rich. & Gal., *E. virgatum* Ldl. var. *pallens* Rchb.f., *Encyclia amabilis* Schltr., *Encyclia virgata* Schltr.)

Pbs. clustered, ovoid or pear-shaped, often rather greyish- or bluish-green, to 3″ tall, sheathed at base. Lvs. 2–3, elliptic-lanceolate to ligulate, obtuse to shortly acuminate, to 2′ long and 2½″ wide. Infls. loosely many-fld., branched, the branches obliquely ascending, to 4½′ tall. Fls. to about 1″ across (often smaller), fleshy, long-lived, the ss. and ps. reddish-brown or greenish-brown, the lip fleshy, yellowish-white, usually with some purple dots, the disc with a large cushion-like callus between the lat. lbs. Summer–autumn. (I) Mexico; Guatemala; Honduras.

E. vitellinum Ldl.

Pbs. clustered, ovoid-conical, compressed, ¾–2½″ tall. Lvs. 2–3, rather glaucous, linear-lanceolate to oblong-ligulate, obtuse to acute, leathery, to 12″ long and 2″ wide. Infls. usually erect, loosely few- to rather many-fld., sometimes branched, to 1½′ tall. Fls. long-lived, to about 1½″ across, orange to deep scarlet, the disc of the lip yellow or whitish. Ss. and ps. broad, spreading. Lip entire, rather narrow. Autumn–winter. (C, I) Mexico; Guatemala; ? Costa Rica.

E. Wallisii Rchb.f.

A magnificent orchid, the sts. clustered, erect, to 2½′ tall, leafy throughout. Lvs. oblong-lanceolate, obtuse, leathery, glossy, to 3″ long. Infls. arching to pendulous, about 5–12-fld., about 6″ long, stalked. Fls. very waxy, long-lived, fragrant, to 1½″ across (rarely larger), the ss. and ps. yellow or somewhat orange-yellow more or less densely spotted with deep red or red-purple, the lip large, white, with small red or red-purple warts. Lip 4-lbd. Autumn–early winter. (I) Panama; Colombia.

E. xanthinum Ldl.

Similar in habit to *E. arachnoglossum* Rchb.f., to more than 4′ tall. Infls. rather densely many-fld., head-like, on a long peduncle. Fls. about ½″ across, pale or rather bright yellow, the lip-disc scarlet-red. Ss. and ps. narrowly elliptic. Lip 3-lbd., the lbs. fringed, the disc with about 8 prominent keels. Spring–summer. (I, H) Brazil; Colombia.

E. adenocarpon LaLl. & Lex. (*Epidendrum papillosum* Batem. ex Ldl., *Encyclia adenocarpa* Schltr.) Pbs. ovoid, about 3″ tall. Lvs. 2–3, linear, to 12″ long. Infls. loosely 8–15-fld., to 1½′ long, usually branched. Fls. about 1½″ across, the ss. and ps. yellowish-green with reddish-brown shading and nerves, the lip white with 3 lavender-pink stripes on the disc.

Summer–autumn. (I, H) Mexico; Guatemala; El Salvador; Honduras; Nicaragua.

E. ambiguum Ldl. (*Encyclia ambigua* Schltr.) Similar in habit to *E. alatum* Batem. Fls. very numerous, fragrant, about 1¾" across at most, the ss. and ps. cream-yellow or greenish-yellow, the lip darker, spotted and veined with mostly dull red. Midlb. very crisped, the veins warty. Summer. (I, H) Mexico; Guatemala.

E. arbuscula Ldl. (*Epidendrum magnificum* Schltr., *E. Nubium* Rchb.f.) Pbs. robust, branched, sometimes scandent, to 7' tall, the sts. concealed by loose whitish sheaths, sometimes rooting at the nodes, to ¼" in diam. Lvs. several, clustered at summit of each branch, to 6" long, rather heavily leathery, often purple-flushed. Infls. pendulous, terminating the branches, loosely many-fld., to 8" long. Fls. to more than 1" across, rust-red to yellowish-green, the lip down-curved, 3-lbd. Winter. (I) Mexico; Guatemala; Honduras.

E. Boothianum Ldl. (*Epicladium Boothianum* Small, *Epidendrum bidentatum* Ldl., *E. erythronioides* Small). Pbs. tightly clustered, roundish, very compressed, smooth, glossy yellow-green, to 1¼" tall. Lvs. 1–3, thin, rigid, often twisted, 3–6½" long. Infls. erect, loosely few-fld., to 12" tall (usually much shorter), sheathed. Fls. to about ¾" across, long-lived, waxy, the ss. and ps. yellow blotched with reddish-brown to magenta-purple, the lip small, very complex, greenish-yellow and white, sometimes marked with magenta, the col. blotched with purplish-brown. July–Nov. (I, H) South Florida; Bahamas; Cuba; Mexico; British Honduras.

E. bractescens Ldl. (*Epidendrum aciculare* Batem. ex Ldl., *E. linearifolium* Hk., *Encyclia acicularis* Schltr.) Pbs. conical, wrinkled, clustered, to 1½" tall, usually shorter. Lvs. 2, linear to linear-lanceolate, rigid, glossy, to 10" long. Infls. 5–20-fld., simple or branched, to 15" long. Fls. fragrant, long-lived, about 1" across, the ss. and ps. greenish-yellow with reddish-brown nerves to brick-red, the lip with deep magenta lat. lbs., the midlb. yellowish-white with numerous purplish nerves. Spring. (I) Mexico; British Honduras; Guatemala; Honduras; ? Bahamas.

E. Candollei Ldl. (*Epidendrum cepiforme* Hk., *E. meliosmum* Rchb.f., *Encyclia Candollei* Schltr., *Encyclia meliosma* Schltr.) Pbs. clustered, globose to ovoid, to 3" tall, prominently sheathed. Lvs. 2–3, ligulate to narrowly lanceolate, leathery, to 15" long and 1½" wide. Infls. loosely many-fld., to about 2' long. Fls. about 1" across, the ss. and ps. yellowish-green, the lip white or yellowish with dull purple streaks, prominently veined. Summer. (I, H) Mexico; Guatemala.

E. chinense (Ldl.) Ames (*Barkeria nonchinensis* Schltr., *Barkeria Palmeri* Schltr., *Broughtonia chinensis* Ldl., *Epidendrum nonchinense* Rchb.f., *E. Palmeri* Rolfe, *E. strophinx* Rchb.f., *Laeliopsis chinensis* Ldl. ex Rchb.f.) Originally described in error from Hong Kong, hence the peculiar epithet! Sts. clustered, usually leafless when in fl., spindle-shaped, to 6" tall, more or less concealed by whitish lf.-sheaths. Lvs. soon deciduous, linear to oblong-lanceolate, to 5½" long. Infls. to 5" long, 1- to many-fld., simple or branched, the rachis usually reddish-brown. Fls. about 1" across at most, often not opening well, the ss. and ps. cream-white or pinkish, the lip pale yellow with purplish or brownish-red markings, the nerves on the disc vaguely warty. Mostly winter. (I) Mexico; Guatemala; El Salvador; Honduras; Nicaragua; Costa Rica.

E. chloroleucum Hk. (*Encyclia chloroleuca* Neum.) Pbs. narrowly ovoid, to 2" tall, clustered. Lvs. 2, linear, obtuse, to 8" long. Infls. loosely 7–10-fld., to 12" long. Fls. fragrant,

waxy, long-lived, about 1¼" across, the ss. and ps. spreading, green, the 3-lbd. lip white. Autumn. (H) Guianas.

E. Clowesii Batem. ex Ldl. (*Epidendrum chlorops* Rchb.f., *E. flavovirens* Rchb.f. not Regel, *E. piestocaulos* Schltr.) Sts. mostly stout, somewhat compressed above, to 2' tall, concealed by tubular lf.-sheaths. Lvs. largest near the apex of st., to 6" long, rather leathery. Infls. simple or branched, loosely many-fld., to about 12" tall. Fls. less than 1" across, yellowish-white, the lip white, distinctly 3-lbd., the col. green basally. Closely allied to *E. polyanthum* Ldl., differing in the smooth ss. (outside) and in the smooth rather than warty pedicellate ovaries. Mostly spring–summer. (I, H) Mexico; Guatemala; El Salvador.

E. cnemidophorum Ldl. (*Epidendrum affine* Rchb.f., *E. macrobotryum* Ldl. ex Rchb.f., *Encyclia affinis* Schltr.) Sts. stout, to 1¼" in diam., clustered, leafy, to 6' tall. Lvs. dark green, lanceolate, acuminate, glossy, to 12" long and 2" wide. Infls. many-fld., simple or branched, arching, to 6" long. Fls. with whitish pedicellate ovaries, fleshy, fragrant, about 1½" across, the ss. and ps. rose-purple to white outside, yellow mottled with reddish-brown inside, the lip cream-white flushed with rose, 3-lbd. Summer. (I, H) Guatemala; Honduras; Nicaragua; Costa Rica.

E. cristatum R. & P. (*Epidendrum raniferum* Ldl.) Highly variable in all parts, often very large and robust, the sts. to 7' tall, prominently sheathed, leafy above. Lvs. erect-spreading, leathery, to 10" long, narrowly oblong-elliptic to elliptic-lanceolate. Infls. a simple rac. or several simple racs. at top of st., stalkless or long-stalked, recurved-pendent, to 2' long. Fls. numerous, to 2" across, fragrant, rather long-lived, the ss. and ps. yellowish or greenish, striped or spotted with red, purple, or lavender, the lip usually yellowish with some purple spots, often 6-lbd., the lat. lbs. usually deeply fringed. Summer–autumn. (I, H) Mexico; Guatemala; Venezuela; Trinidad; British Guiana; Brazil; Peru; Bolivia.

E. eburneum Rchb.f. (*Epidendrum leucocardium* Schltr.) Sts. to 20" tall, sheathed, slender. Lvs. few, mostly near top of sts., elliptic to lanceolate, glossy, to 5½" long. Infls. short, usually less than 3" long, the rachis zigzag, bearing the few fls. successively. Fls. about 2–2½" across, fragrant, waxy, the ss. and ps. narrow, yellowish or cream-yellow, the broadly heart-shaped lip white. Autumn–winter. (I, H) Panama.

E. evectum Hk.f. Similar in habit to *E. arachnoglossum* Rchb.f., but more robust, the lvs. to 5½" long, rigidly leathery. Fls. numerous, in a dense head-like rac., to 1½" across, purple, the disc of the lip usually whitish. Lip 3-lbd., the lat. lbs. lacerate, the midlb. separated from them by an isthmus, fringed. Spring–summer. (I) Colombia.

E. Friederici-Guilelmi (Ldl.) Rchb.f. (*Spathium Friederici-Guilelmi* Ldl.) Sts. clustered, to 12" tall, leafy. Lvs. ligulate, obtuse, leathery, to 6" long. Infls. erect, to 8" tall, the rac. many-fld., rather dense. Fls. long-stalked, to almost 4" across, light carmine-red. Lip 3-lbd., the midlb. ligulate, acute. Summer. (I) Peru.

E. glumaceum Ldl. (*Aulizeum glumaceum* Ldl.) Pbs. ovoid, clustered, to 2½" tall. Lvs. 2, ligulate, to 4" long, rather leathery. Infls. rather densely 6- to 12-fld., erect, to 6" tall. Fls. inverted, fragrant, about 2" across, the ss. and ps. white with some red streaks towards the base, the lip white streaked with rose-red, elliptic, acuminate. Summer–autumn. (I, H) Brazil.

E. gracile Ldl. (*Encyclia gracilis* Schltr.) Pbs. erect, to 12" tall, elongate-ovoid, often dull brownish, the lvs. long, rather narrow, leathery. Infls. rigidly erect, to almost 4' tall, the

Cymbidium Devonianum Paxt. [GEORGE FULLER]

Cymbidium ensifolium (L.) Sw. [GEORGE FULLER]

Cynorkis species, possibly undescribed, from Madagascar [J. MARNIER-LAPOSTOLLE]

Cyperocymbidium × *Gammieanum* (King & Pantl.) A.D.Hawkes [J. MARNIER-LAPOSTOLLE]

Cyrtorchis arcuata (Ldl.) Schltr. [GEORGE FULLER]

(LEFT) *Cypripedium acaule* Ait. [BLANCHE AMES]

Dendrobium Dearei Rchb.f. [WM. KIRCH—ORCHIDS LTD.]

numerous fls. scattered. Fls. more than 1″ across, very fragrant, the ss. and ps. usually greenish-yellow flushed with brown, the crisped lip 3-lbd., yellowish more or less veined with dull red. Autumn–winter. (H) Bahamas, where it is often terrestrial.

E. Harrisoniae Ldl. Very similar in all parts to *E. patens* Sw., differing principally in the obtuse lvs., the more prominent sheaths on the infl., the obtuse ss. and ps. of the green, white-lipped fls., and the oblong midlb. of the lip. Perhaps not distinct from its ally. Summer–autumn. (I, H) Brazil.

E. Hodgeanum A.D.Hawkes (*Epidendrum altissimum* Batem., *Encyclia altissima* Schltr.) Pbs. rather slender, often almost cylindric-ovoid, frequently yellow-green, to 3″ tall. Lvs. 2–3, to more than 12″ long, rather narrow, heavily leathery. Infls. rigidly erect, to more than 4′ tall, branched, few- to many-fld. Fls. to more than 1″ across, fragrant and long-lasting, butter-yellow, sometimes the ss. and ps. flushed with brownish, the sides of the large midlb. of the lip usually down-curved. Winter–spring. (I, H) Bahamas, often growing in sand as a terrestrial.

E. lockhartioides Schltr. A most unusual sp., the sts. densely covered with the equitant lvs., to 10″ tall at most, clustered. Lvs. ¼–1¼″ long, laterally compressed, usually pale green. Infls. borne from the upper lf.-axils, 1- to more-fld., very short. Fls. often not opening fully, fleshy, about ½″ across, greenish-yellow or green, the lip clawed. Summer. (I) Costa Rica; Panama.

E. Loefgreni Cgn. A very strange sp., sharply pendulous from trees. Sts. clustered, to 12″ long, densely leafy, especially above. Lvs. blue-green, elliptic, to 3″ long, folded and forming a pendent semi-tubular structure in which the almost stalkless infls., these several-fld., are borne. Fls. about ¼″ across, greenish or whitish-green, short-lived. Spring–summer. (I) Brazil.

E. longicolle Ldl. Sts. leafy, clustered, to 12″ tall. Lvs. linear-lanceolate, acute, to 5″ long, rather leathery. Infls. few-fld., short. Fls. long-stalked, waxy, fragrant, about 2½″ across, the ss. and ps. yellowish or cream-yellow, the lip similar to that of *E. Parkinsonianum* Hk., but smaller, white, the disc with 2 yellow keels. Winter. (H) Guianas.

E. longifolium B.-R. (*Encyclia longifolia* Schltr.) Similar in habit to *E. Candollei* Ldl., but the infls. erect, shortly branched, many-fld. Fls. about 1¼″ across, the ss. and ps. green or yellow-green, the 3-lbd. lip white with some intricate reddish veins on the midlb. Flowers at various times. (H) Brazil.

E. medusae (Ldl.) Bth. (*Nanodes medusae* Ldl.) Sts. clustered, pendulous, densely leafy, to 8″ long. Lvs. lanceolate, acutish, very thick and fleshy, blue-green often somewhat flushed with dull purple, to 3½″ long. Infls. 1–3-fld., very abbreviated. Fls. heavy-textured, to more than 3″ across, fantastic, the spreading ss. and ps. yellow-green flushed with brown, the large lip kidney-shaped, purple-brown, intricately fringed and lacerate marginally. Mostly July–Aug. (I) Ecuador.

E. ochraceum Ldl. (*Epidendrum pachyriferum* Schltr., *E. papyriferum* Schltr., *E. panthera* Rchb.f., *E. triste* A.Rich. & Gal., *Encyclia ochracea* Ldl., *Encyclia panthera* Schltr.) Highly variable, especially in the size of all parts. Pbs. somewhat distant on the rhiz., usually obliquely ascending, elongated, narrowly ovoid-cylindrical, to 5″ tall, usually considerably shorter. Lvs. 2–3, not very thick, to 11″ long (or as short as 2″), rather narrow. Infls. typically a densely many-fld., simple rac., usually longer than the lvs. Fls. often not opening fully, fleshy, often rather cup-shaped, to ¾″ across when spread out (usually smaller), brown-yellow, greenish, or

almost orange, the lip-callus single basally, becoming a series of warts on the midlb. Spring–summer. (I, H) Mexico; Guatemala; El Salvador; Honduras; Nicaragua; Costa Rica.

E. odoratissimum Ldl. (*Encyclia odoratissima* Schltr., *Encyclia patens* Hk.) Similar in habit and fls. to *E. gracile* Ldl. Infls. loosely 5–15-fld., sparsely branched, about 10″ tall. Fls. very fragrant, long-lived, rather heavy-textured, to more than 1″ across, the ss. and ps. greenish, the lip yellowish veined with red. Ss. and ps. oblong-spatulate. Lip 3-lbd., the lat. lbs. oblong, obtuse, the midlb. only slightly larger. Summer. (I, H) Brazil.

E. phoeniceum Ldl. (*Epidendrum oblongatum* A.Rich., *Encyclia phoenicea* Neum.) Pbs. ovoid, robust, to 2″ tall, becoming furrowed with age, sometimes flushed with purplish. Lvs. 2, linear-ligular, acutish, rather heavily leathery, to 12″ long and 1¼″ broad. Infls. erect or arching under the weight of the fls., usually branched, many-fld., the fls. opening successively over a long period of time, to 3′ long. Fls. very fragrant of chocolate, to almost 2″ in diam., the spreading ss. and ps. rather heavy-textured, purple-red, often flushed with darker colour, the lip bright rose-purple, usually marked with darker purple. Ss. oblong, the ps. spatulate, obtuse. Lip roundish, the midlb. distinctly 2-lbd., longer than the ss. In cultivation this sp. is often confused with *E. plicatum* Ldl., differing in floral colour and in the conspicuously 2-lobed midlb. of the lip, which is longer than the ss. Spring–early summer. (I, H) Cuba; ? Bahamas.

E. plicatum Ldl. (*Encyclia plicata* Britt. & Millsp.) Pbs. clustered, robust, ovoid, to more than 3″ tall. Lvs. 2, rigid, linear-ligulate, acute, to 10″ long and 1″ broad. Infls. simple or few-branched, to 2¼′ long, few- to rather many-fld. Fls. fragrant of chocolate, heavy-textured, long-lasting, longer than wide, to about 2½″ long, the oblanceolate, acuminate ss. and ps. greenish or green flushed with tan, with the apical portions more or less suffused with purple or wine-purple, the lip several shades of very vivid magenta-purple. Lip 3-lbd., about as long as the ss., the midlb. obtuse or rarely rounded or retuse at apex. Spring–early summer. (I, H) Cuba; Bahamas.

E. pygmaeum Hk. (*Epidendrum pseudopygmaeum* Finet, *E. uniflorum* Ldl., *Hormidium pygmaeum* Bth. & Hk.f., *H. tripterum* Cgn., *H. uniflorum* Heynh.) Variable in vegetative stature, creeping, mat-forming, the rhiz. elongated, giving rise to ellipsoid, spindle-shaped, or cylindrical pbs. at intervals, the pbs. 1–4″ tall, usually glossy yellowish-green. Lvs. mostly 2, oval to linear, rather leathery, ½–5½″ long. Infls. extremely short, 1- to several-fld. Fls. usually not opening well, 1/16–½″ long, greenish or brownish-green, often tinged with lavender, or white, the lip cup-shaped at base, white with a median purple blotch. Mostly summer–autumn. (H) South Florida and Mexico throughout tropical America to Peru, Bolivia, and Brazil.

E. pyriforme Ldl. (*Encyclia pyriformis* Schltr.) Pbs. roundish to almost pear-shaped, about 1″ tall at most, clustered. Lvs. 2, narrowly ligulate, rigid, to 4½″ long. Infls. loosely 1–2-fld., usually shorter than the lvs., erect. Fls. about 2¼″ in diam., fragrant, long-lived, the ss. and ps. greenish, flushed towards the tips with brown, the large lip cream-white, red-veined, the midlb. almost round, undulate marginally. Winter. (I) Cuba.

E. ramosum Jacq. (*Epidendrum flexicaule* Schltr., *E. modestiflorum* Schltr.) Extremely variable in all parts, the pls. erect, creeping, or pendulous, simple to profusely branched, in extreme cases to 3′ tall or long. Sts. usually slender, often rather irregular, few- to many-lvd. Lvs. usually fleshy, often yellow-green, linear-ligulate to oblong-elliptic, ¼–5″ long.

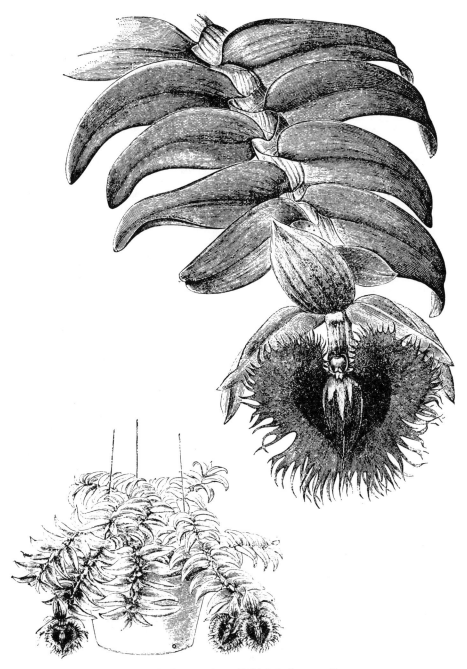

Epidendrum medusae (Ldl.) Bth. [VEITCH]

Infls. terminal at the end of main sts. and branches, 2-several-fld., usually short. Fls. not opening well, about ¼–1″ long, usually rather fleshy, varying in colour from cream-white to yellow-green, often tinged with dark red or bronze, the lip usually simple. Mostly spring. (I, H) South Florida, Mexico and Cuba throughout tropical America to Brazil.

E. rigidum Jacq. (*Spathiger rigidus* Small) Rhiz. creeping, often branched and forming large mats, giving rise to scattered erect or ascending sts. from 4–12″ tall. Lvs. usually glossy yellow-green, narrow or rather wide, very fleshy, 1–5″ long. Infls. few- to many-fld., usually erect, the fls. mostly almost hidden by the large bracts, to 6″ long. Fls. almost stalkless, often not opening well, leathery in texture, to ½″ across, green or yellowish-green, inconspicuous. Throughout the year, but mostly in winter–spring. (I, H) South Florida and Mexico throughout tropical America to Brazil and Peru.

E. sceptrum Ldl. Pbs. spindle-shaped, to 6″ tall. Lvs. 2–3, broadly linear, leathery, to 10″ long. Infls. erect, loosely many-fld., the rac. cylindrical, to almost 2′ tall. Fls. slightly more than 1″ across, fragrant, the ss. and ps. yellow spotted with sepia-brown, the lip broadly rhombic, yellow with sepia-brown spots. Autumn. (I, H) Venezuela.

E. Schlechterianum Ames (*Epidendrum brevicaule* Schltr., *E. congestoides* A. & S., *Nanodes discolor* Ldl.) Pls. dwarf, densely clustered, often very branched, to 2½″ tall, the sts. densely leafy, completely concealed by the imbricated lf.-sheaths. Lvs. distichous, very equitant, very fleshy, convex, to about 1¼″ long, the margins reddish or transparent. Fls. usually solitary at the apex of st., stalkless, erect, to about 1¼″ across, yellow-green or reddish-green to pale pinkish-purple, not opening fully. Mostly summer. (H) Mexico and the West Indies to Peru, Brazil, and Suriname.

E. Schomburgkii Ldl. (*Epidendrum ibaguense* HBK var. *Schomburgkii* C.Schweinf., *E. splendens* Schltr.) Very robust sp., rarely to as much as 6′ tall, the st.-sheaths often purple-spotted. Lvs. throughout length of st., or just in upper part, very thick and rigid, horizontally spreading, to 8″ long and 2″ broad. Infl. with an elongate sheathed peduncle to several ft. long, erect, the apical rac. 5–30-fld., the fls. mostly facing upwards. Fls. long-lived, to 1½″ long, opening out flat, varying from brick-red to vivid orange, the lip with coarsely-toothed lat. lbs., the midlb. coarsely-toothed, its apical margins usually upturned, vivid orange or orange-red to almost purple, the area around the crest usually rich yellow. Col. elongate, purple or dark red basally, usually shading to yellow towards tip. This stately species is very distinctive from *E. ibaguense* HBK, not branching nor producing *keikis* as does that plant. It is either terrestrial (commonly) or epiphytic in the wild. Mostly winter. (H) Colombia, Venezuela, and the Guianas southward to Peru and Amazonian Brazil.

E. Sophronitis Ldl. Pbs. roundish, closely clustered, less than ½″ tall. Lvs. 2, oblong, acute, about 2¾″ long, blue-green with red margins. Infls. few-fld., very short. Fls. fleshy, about 1½″ across, the ss. and ps. yellow with a network of purple-red veins, the lip dark brown, the disc thickened, mottled with yellow. Spring–summer. (I) Peru.

E. spondiadum Rchb.f. Similar to *E. sceptrum* Ldl. in habit, but the pbs. 1-lvd. Infls. loosely 3–6-fld., apical, erect, to 6″ tall. Fls. about 1½″ across, the ss. and ps. greenish-yellow, brownish in the apical half, the lip brown with greenish-yellow edges. Winter. (I) Jamaica.

E. stellatum Ldl. (*Encyclia stellata* Schltr.) Rather similar in habit to *E. gracile* Ldl., but somewhat more robust and taller, the linear lvs. to 12″ long. Infls. to about 1½′ long, few-fld., the fls. mostly all open simultaneously. Fls. about 1¼″ across, very fragrant, long-lived, green, the lip whitish. Ss. and ps. narrowly oblong. Lip with a roundish midlb., the disc with 3 thickened nerves. Summer. (I, H) Venezuela.

E. strobiliferum Rchb.f. Pls. small, forming branching clumps, often pendulous, to about 10″ long at most, the sts. often rather zigzag, concealed by purplish or greenish lf.-sheaths. Lvs. widely spreading, rigidly leathery, to 1½″ long. Infls. composed of compact, few-fld. racs. at the tips of the branches, to 1¼″ long, with large, often purplish-brown, ribbed bracts mostly obscuring the fls. which they subtend. Fls. scarcely opening, less than ¼″ long, green, white, or yellowish-white, sometimes streaked with reddish. Mostly spring. (H) South Florida and Mexico throughout tropical America to Peru, Brazil, and the Guianas.

E. syringothyrsus Rchb.f. Similar in habit to *E. verrucosum* Sw., to more than 4′ tall. Lvs. elliptic, acute, to 6″ long. Infls. long-stalked, the rac. densely many-fld., about 6″ long and 4″ in diam. Fls. long-stalked, to more than 1″ across, violet-magenta, the lip-callus golden-yellow. Lip 3-lbd., the lat. lbs. roundish, the midlb. almost square, with an apicule. Spring (I, H) Bolivia.

E. teretifolium Sw. (*Cymbidium teretifolium* Sw., *Epidendrum subuliferum* Schltr., *E. teres* Rchb.f. not Thunb., *Isochilus teretifolium* Ldl.) Sts. clustered, erect, to 10″ tall, leafy throughout. Lvs. distichous, erect-spreading, gently recurved, usually terete, rigid, to 2″ long. Fls. usually solitary at the top of a slender compressed stalk, stalkless, fleshy, with 1 or 2 large bracts at the base, about ½″ across, yellowish-green, the lip deeply concave basally. Summer. (I, H) Mexico and the West Indies to Panama and Venezuela.

E. Vespa Vell. (*Epidendrum crassilabium* P. & E., *E. rhab-dobulbon* Schltr., *E. rhopalobulbon* Schltr., *E. variegatum* Hk.) Pbs. extremely variable in form, from almost round (to 2½″ × 2″) to very elongate (to 8″ × ¾″), sheathed basally and usually somewhat compressed. Lvs. normally 2, bright green, moderately heavy, to 10″ long and 2″ broad, often smaller and proportionately broader. Infls. erect, many-fld., to 12″ tall. Fls. inverted, heavily waxy, fragrant or not, to ¾″ in diam. (often smaller), green or yellowish-green more or less spotted and/or blotched with red-purple or brown-purple, the ps. spatulate, the margins of the ss. usually reflexed. Lip very thick, small, white or yellowish more or less marked with pink or magenta, with a blunt 3-notched basal callus. Col. thick, usually pale green. Mostly spring. (I, H) Cuba and Costa Rica southward to Brazil and Peru.

E. virens Ldl. (*Epidendrum ochranthum* A.Rich., *E. Wageneri* Kl., *Encyclia virens* Schltr.) Pbs. clustered, ovoid, to 3″ tall. Lvs. 2–3, linear, obtuse, leathery, to 1½′ long. Infls. loosely many-fld., branched, to more than 4′ tall, mostly erect or arching. Fls. fragrant, long-lived, about 1½″ across or more, the ss. and ps. green or apple-green, the lip white, the midlb. streaked with rose-red medially. Spring–summer. (I, H) West Indies; Venezuela; ? Guatemala.

E. viridiflorum Ldl. (*Encyclia viridiflora* Hk.) Similar in habit to *E. gracile* Ldl., but with a very slender, branched infl. only about 12″ tall. Fls. fragrant, about 1″ across, the ss. and ps. brownish-green, the lip greenish, the midlb. undulate. Winter, mostly in Feb. (H) Brazil.

E. volutum Ldl. & Paxt. (*Epidendrum Radlkoferianum* Schltr.) Pbs. stalked basally, spindle-shaped, to 5″ tall. Lvs. 2–4, apical, leathery, ligulate, to 4″ long. Infls. arising from the middle of the expanding new growths, erect or gracefully arching, loosely many-fld., to about 6″ long, strongly bracted. Fls. fragrant, about 1″ across, semi-translucent greenish, long-lived. Mostly winter–spring. (I) Panama.

E. xipheres Rchb.f. (*Epidendrum yucatanense* Schltr., *Encyclia Purpusii* Schltr., *Encyclia xipheres* Schltr.) Pbs. densely clustered, ovoid, to 1″ long. Lf. solitary, narrowly linear, erect, rigidly leathery, to 10″ long, less than ¼″ wide. Infls. loosely few-fld., sometimes branched, to more than 12″ long. Fls. long-lived, the pedicellate ovaries densely echinate, to ¾″ across, the ss. and ps. reddish-brown, usually margined or marked with yellow or greenish-lavender, the deeply 3-lbd. lip dingy yellow with fine lavender stripes. Spring–early summer. (I, H) Mexico; Guatemala; Honduras.

EPIGENEIUM Gagnep.
(*Katherinea* A.D.Hawkes, *Sarcopodium* Ldl. & Paxt.)

About thirty-five species of *Epigeneium* are known to date, all of them rare but unusually interesting epiphytic or lithophytic orchids of the subtribe *Dendrobiinae*, in the past known as *Sarcopodium*. Their distribution ranges from China, India and the Philippines through Formosa, South-east Asia, and Indonesia to New Guinea. Peculiar plants with angular pseudobulbs (often borne at considerable intervals from each other on the creeping rhizome), they bear terminal or pseudo-terminal racemes of often rather large and showy blossoms, these making them of considerable potential importance to the orchidist. Although today very rare in our collections, a few of the Epigeneiums are nonetheless known to be in cultivation at this time.

Nothing appears to be known regarding the genetic affinities of *Epigeneium*, which seems to be somewhat of a connecting link between the subtribes *Dendrobiinae* and *Bulbophyllinae*. Some fascinating hybrids could doubtless be obtained through utilization of the components of this genus, with other groups—such as *Dendrobium* and the large-flowered species of *Bulbophyllum*, assuming that they are genetically compatible.

CULTURE: Because of their typically creeping, elongate rhizome-growth, these orchids are best kept in baskets or in sizeable shallow fern-pans. Perfect drainage is most necessary for their successful cultivation, and we have found that a compost made up of about equal parts of shredded tree-fern and chopped sphagnum moss is ideal for them. Tree-fern slabs are also most suitable. They grow throughout the year, never requiring a rest-period, and should be kept moist at all times, providing that the compost drains thoroughly after each watering. They do best in a semi-sunny spot (although care must be taken that the fleshy foliage does not burn through over-exposure), under constantly warm, highly humid conditions. The Epigeneiums benefit by liberal and rather heavy applications of fertilizing materials. They are very susceptible to stale or sour conditions at the roots, and although division of the specimens often sets them back for a while, they should be transplanted immediately when such conditions are found to exist. (C, I, H)

E. acuminatum (Rolfe) Summerh. (*Dendrobium acuminatum* Rolfe, *Sarcopodium acuminatum* Krzl., *Katherinea acuminata* A.D.Hawkes)
Pbs. ovoid or ovoid-conical, vaguely angled, borne at some distance from each other on the stout, creeping, bracted rhiz., glossy bright-green, to almost 2″ tall. Lvs. paired, very leathery, elliptic-oblong, obtuse, 4–6″ long, to 1¼″ broad. Infl. terminal or sub-terminal, erect to strongly arching, with the 6–20 fls. borne some distance apart. Fls. opening well, very showy, fragrant, long-lasting, to almost 4″ in diam., the ss. and ps. yellowish-white, more or less flushed with magenta-rose, the lip darker magenta-rose or magenta-purple. Ss. and ps. oblong-linear, attenuate upwards and acuminate at apex. Lip deeply 3-lbd., the midlb. ovate, somewhat recurved and very acuminate apically; lat. lbs. broadly triangular-ovate, subacute, usually orange-yellow with regular dark brown stripes. Spring. (I) Philippines: Luzon.

E. cymbidioides (Bl.) Summerh. (*Desmotrichum cymbidioides* Bl., *Dendrobium cymbidioides* Ldl., *Sarcopodium cymbidioides* Rolfe, *Katherinea cymbidioides* A.D.Hawkes)
Pbs. clustered on the short creeping rhiz., ovoid to oblong-ovoid, angled, the angles usually 4–5, to 2″ tall, more or less sheathed basally with membranaceous scales.

Lvs. 2, erect-spreading, leathery, oblong, obtuse or rather retuse, to about 4½″ long. Infls. terminal from pb.-apex, erect, about 5–12-fld., to about 8″ tall. Fls. long-lasting, faintly fragrant, heavy-textured, to more than 1¼″ in diam., the spreading ss. and ps. yellow or cream-yellow, linear-oblong. Lip much shorter than the ss., oblong-cordate, white sprinkled near the base inside with dark purple, linear blotches, 3-lbd., bearing on the disc tubercles arranged in 2 or 3 lines or series; lat. lbs. short, obtuse, incurved; midlb. ovate, obtuse, tumid or convex. Col. short, spotted on the front face with purple. Spring. (H) Malay Peninsula; Sumatra; Java.

E. Lyonii (Ames) Summerh. (*Dendrobium Lyonii* Ames, *Sarcopodium Lyonii* Rolfe, *Sarcopodium acuminatum* Krzl. var. *Lyonii* Krzl., *Katherinea acuminata* (Rolfe) A.D.Hawkes var. *Lyonii* A.D.Hawkes)
Closely allied to *E. acuminatum* (Rolfe) Summerh., differing from it in its much larger stature in all parts, the much more prominently purple-hued, broader-segmented fls. to 5″ in diam., and the much more prominently developed, flaring lat. lbs. of the larger lip. At the apex of the pb., after the lvs. have fallen, there is a distinct tooth-like point, this feature being absent in the allied sp. Spring. (C, I) Philippines: Luzon, in the mountains to 5000′.

E. amplum (Ldl.) Summerh. (*Dendrobium amplum* Ldl. ex Wall., *Sarcopodium amplum* Ldl., *Bulbophyllum amplum* Rchb.f., *Katherinea ampla* A.D.Hawkes) Rather similar in habit to *E. Coelogyne* (Rchb.f.) Summerh., differing in the structure of the usually solitary, rather short-lived fls., which measure up to 3″ in diam., the contorted ss. and ps. being greenish-white with definite emerald-green and magenta suffusions. Lip proportionately large, 3-lbd., mostly magenta, with some suffusions of greenish-white, and some very dark purple spots in the vicinity of the calli on the disc, the lat. lbs. erect at the sides of the broad, curving, greenish-white col. Winter. (I, H) India.

E. Coelogyne (Rchb.f.) Summerh. (*Dendrobium Coelogyne* Rchb.f., *Sarcopodium Coelogyne* Rolfe, *Katherinea Coelogyne* A.D.Hawkes) Pbs. borne at considerable intervals from each other on the scale-clothed elongate rhiz., ellipsoid, prominently 4-angled, to about 2½″ tall. Lvs. paired, leathery, glossy, oblong, obliquely acutish, about 4″ long. Infl. normally 1-fld., terminal, rather abbreviated. Fl. powerfully fragrant, heavy-textured, long-lasting, about 4″ across when expanded the dors. sep. and ps. considerably narrower than the lat. ss., all these segms. more or less twisted and reflexed, outside bright or dull yellow, inside tan-yellow more or less spotted with purple. Lip very large, prominently 3-lbd., the erect lat. lbs. cream-yellow with some purple markings, the corrugated midlb. almost black-purple. Autumn. (I, H) Burma; Thailand.

EPIPACTIS [Zinn, in part] Sw.
(*Epipactum* Ritg.)

About twenty-five species of *Epipactis* are known to date, many of them scantily delineated, with the result that the genus is in a state of considerable taxonomic confusion. Usually large terrestrial orchids, they are found in the temperate zones of Asia and Europe, with two species in North America. A member of the subtribe *Cephalantherinae*, it is somewhat allied to *Cephalanthera* A.Rich., from which it differs in structural details

Epipactis africana Rendle [*Flora of the Belgian Congo*]

of the mostly rather large and showy, racemose, large-bracted flowers. Although they are handsome ground-orchids, at this time the Epipactis are notably rare in our collections.

A few natural hybrids are known in this genus, mostly among the European species; none of these appears to be in cultivation at this time. No artificial hybrids appear to have been made as yet, although critical interspecific breeding seems to offer certain interesting possibilities. The genetic ties of *Epipactis* are unknown.

CULTURE: As for *Cephalanthera*. (C, I)

E. gigantea Dougl. ex Hk. (*Epipactis americana* Ldl., *Helleborine gigantea* Druce, *Peramium giganteum* Coulter, *Scrapias gigantca* A.A.Eaton)

St. stout, often purple-tinged basally, when in fl. to more than 4' tall. Lvs. clasping the st. or with a short tubular petiole, plicate, erect-spreading, broadest upwards, ovate to narrowly lanceolate, 2–8" long. Infl. elongate, loosely about 12-fld., with large lf.-like bracts. Fls. opening rather well, long-lasting, to about 2" in diam., the deeply concave ss. greenish to rose with purple or dull red nerves, the erect ps. pale pink to rose with red or purple nerves. Lip deeply and unequally 3-lbd., complex, strongly veined and marked with red or purple, the midlb. often yellowish. Spring–autumn. (C, I) Western United States south to northern Mexico.

E. Helleborine (L.) Crantz (*Serapias Helleborine* L., *Serapias latifolia* Huds., *Epipactis latifolia* All.)

St. stout, usually slender, 1–4', leafy. Lvs. variable, clasping the st. or with short channelled petioles, roundish to narrowly lanceolate, plicate, broadest at about the st.-middle, 1½–7" long. Infl. loose or dense, few- to many-fld., often secund, with large floral bracts, the rachis fuzzy. Fls. broadly bell-shaped, to about 1" when expanded, greenish flushed with purple or rose-red, the lip greenish and purplish, dark purple on lower half. Summer–early autumn. (C, I) Europe; Asia; scattered in North America.

EPIPOGUM [Gmel.] L.C.Rich
(*Epipogon* Sw.)

Epipogum is a genus of about five species of unusual, saprophytic orchids of the subtribe *Epipogoninae*, found in Europe, Asia, Africa, and from the Malayan area to Australia. Unknown in contemporary collections, their cultural requirements would seem to be extremely complex—as is characteristic of all saprophytic plants—and they are hence of interest primarily to botanists. A fleshy, often coral-like rhizome gives rise to a thick, scaly, essentially leafless stem, on which are borne a few to rather many relatively large and complex flowers, usually white or pale greenish, but sometimes flushed with pink.

No hybrids are registered for *Epipogum*, and nothing is known of its genetic alliances at this time.

CULTURE: Presumably that required by *Galeola*, *Corallorrhiza*, and other saprophytic orchids. (I, H)

E. roseum (D.Don) Ldl. (*Limodorum roseum* D.Don, *Galera nutans* Bl., *Epipogum nutans* Rchb.f., *E. Guilfoylei* FvM.)

Rhiz. an ovoid, horizontal, subterranean tuber, to

about 2" long and 1½" thick, composed of many short internodes. Sts. to 2' tall, hollow, fleshy, brownish at base, becoming almost white above, with a few bract-like sheaths. Infls. to 8" long, many-fld., the floral bracts broad, rather large. Fls. fleshy, very intricate, white (sometimes pink-tinged), inverted, about 1" long. Ss. and ps. narrowly linear, not spreading. Lip about as long as the ss., the blade ovate, acute, the sides raised at the base, the margins rather irregular, the upper surface minutely warty in 2 rows, the spur broad, pointing backwards below the pedicellate ovary. Autumn–early winter. (H) Tropical Africa; India; Burma; Thailand; Malay Peninsula; Java; Timor; Australia.

EPISTEPHIUM Kth.

Epistephium is a most fascinating genus of about twenty species of the subtribe *Vanillinae*, all restricted to South America (mostly Brazil), with a single species occurring in adjacent Trinidad. Extremely scarce in contemporary collections, they are beautiful, principally terrestrial orchids which would well benefit by further attention from the specialist. Even when not in flower, the foliage of many of the species is striking, with its prominent anastomosing venation (quite unlike that of most orchids), and the usually large—though short-lived—blossoms are sufficiently attractive to warrant their cultivation.

No hybrids are known in *Epistephium*, and nothing has been deduced concerning its genetic affinities, though it seems logical that it will breed with *Sobralia*.

CULTURE: As for *Sobralia*. (I, H)

E. lucidum Cgn.

Sts. clustered, erect, leafy, to 3¼' tall, very glossy. Lvs. leathery, oval-oblong to oval-elliptic, very prominently branch-veined, very glossy, deep green, becoming black when dry. Infls. erect or arching, to 1½' tall, 8–25-fld., the fls. opening successively over a long period. Fls. about 3" across, often not expanding fully, brownish, the lip more or less marked with dull purple, tubular. Winter–spring. (I, H) Brazil.

E. Williamsii Hk.f.

Similar in habit to the other noted sp., usually slightly shorter and more robust, the largest lvs. mostly apical. Infls. erect, 5–8-fld., often with several fls. open at once, to 6" long. Fls. to 3" in diam., somewhat fragrant, clear rosy-purple, the lip rather tubular at base, flaring apically, crisped marginally, mostly brilliant magenta-purple, the throat usually yellow or cream-yellow, with white blotches on the lat. lbs., the margin usually whitish. Spring. (I, H) Guianas; Brazil.

ERIA Ldl.
(*Aggeianthus* Wight, *Alwisia* Ldl., *Bryobium* Ldl., *Callostylis* Bl., *Ceratium* Bl., *Conchidium* Griff., *Cylindrolobus* Bl., *Dendrolirium* Bl., *Erioxantha* Raf., *Exeria* Raf., *Lichenora* Wight, *Mycaranthes* Bl., *Octomeria* D.Don, *Pinalia* Buch.-Ham., *Trichosia* Bl., *Trichosma* Ldl., *Trichotosia* Bl., *Tylostylis* Bl., *Xiphosium* Griff.)

The genus *Eria* is one of the larger of orchidaceous aggregations—current estimates of the number of components ranging as high as five hundred and fifty—but it

Epistephium Williamsii Hk.f. [Hoehne, *Flora Brasilica*]

is also among the less frequently seen genera in contemporary cultivation, despite the fact that it contains a remarkably large number of showy and handsome members. Closely allied to *Dendrobium* Sw., this is a genus characterized, like its ally, by extremes of vegetative and floral diversity. Some of the species (most of which were formerly included in a separate genus, *Trichotosia* Bl.) consist of often very lengthy, cylindrical, leafy stems, which in certain kinds are covered with a thick carpet of hairs of varying hues. Others simulate a *Bulbophyllum*, with prominent, usually roundish pseudobulbs produced from a more or less creeping rhizome, and still others resemble certain types of *Dendrobium*. The flowers are generally rather distinctive in shape, and are at once differentiated from *Dendrobium* in possessing eight pollinia instead of four. Many of the Erias have their blossoms in rather dense racemes, and are subtended by large, often brightly-coloured bracts which add considerably to the attractiveness of the inflorescence. These orchids are primarily epiphytic, though certain of them occur on rock outcroppings as lithophytes or even as terrestrials. The range of the genus extends from China, the Himalayas, Ceylon, and India throughout the immense region to Samoa and the Fiji Islands; a particularly large number is found in Indonesia and New Guinea. Because of the ease with which they are grown, and the beauty of many of the species when they are in full bloom, this genus is heartily recommended to all enthusiasts.

No hybrids have as yet been produced in *Eria*, although some fascinating potentialities seem to present themselves through critical inter-specific breeding. The genus is presumably genetically compatible with at least some of the Dendrobiums (and doubtless other genera of the subtribe *Dendrobiinae*), and such experimental hybridization should be attempted.

CULTURE: In a genus as large and diversified as *Eria*, it is difficult to give a simplified set of cultural directions. Generally speaking, their basic needs are those afforded *Dendrobium*, though the dwarf pseudobulbous types with elongate rhizomes do better if grown in the fashion of the tropical Bulbophyllums. The long-stemmed 'Trichotosia' section (including such species as *Eria vestita* Ldl., *E. velutina* Lodd. ex Ldl., etc.) should be grown in baskets, so that their gracefully arching or pendulous, leafy stems may hang naturally; a compost of rather tightly-packed osmunda or tree-fern fibre, with copious supplies of drainage materials, seems to suit this group especially well. All of the Erias require quantities of moisture while in active growth, but upon completion of the new stems or pseudobulbs, a slight resting period (of a couple of weeks' duration) should be allowed. Almost without exception, these fine orchids do best in a rather shaded spot in the collection. Fertilizing moderately seems beneficial, and repotting should be attended to only when absolutely essential, as they are intolerant of disturbance. When possible, large 'specimen' plants should be grown for best flower-production. The temperature requirements of the different species vary markedly, since the genus ranges from hot, sea-level areas to high in the Himalayas. Some of the highland species are sufficiently hardy to be grown out-of-doors even in temperate zone areas. (C, I, H)

E. albido-tomentosa (Bl.) Ldl. (*Dendrolirium albido-tomentosum* Bl.)

Rhiz. elongate, bearing the pbs. 2–2½″ apart. Pbs. distinctly flattened, roundish, to 2½″ tall and 1½″ wide. Lvs. 3–4, curving outwards, to 8″ long, linear-lanceolate, acutish, rather leathery. Infls. arising from the base of the pbs., with a few scale-like bracts, covered with white wool, to 12″ tall, usually erect, rather loosely 8–15-fld., the large bracts pale green. Fls. 1¼″ across, pale green turning yellowish with age, the lip white and dull purple, the backs of the ss. hairy. Ps. much smaller than the ss. Lip 3-lbd., the lat. lbs. small, rounded, erect, the midlb. as long as wide, blunt, wavy-margined, the median part fleshy with 3 short parallel white ridges. Autumn. (I, H) Burma; Thailand; Laos; Cambodia; Viet-Nam; Malay Peninsula; Sumatra; Java.

E. barbarossa Rchb.f. (*Trichotosia barbarossa* Krzl.)

Pbs. st.-like, erect, leafy, to about 12″ tall, the sheaths thickly brown-hairy. Lvs. lanceolate, acute, to 3″ long, the under-surfaces thickly brown-hairy, rather leathery. Infls. densely 6–10-fld., short, the bracts rather large. Fls. about ½″ across, whitish or flesh-pink, outside densely covered with red-brown hairs. Lip spatulate, shortly 3-lbd. Autumn. (H) Malay Peninsula.

E. barbata (Ldl.) Rchb.f. (*Tainia barbata* Ldl., *Eriodes barbata* Rolfe)

Pbs. egg-shaped, 2-lvd., about 2″ tall. Lvs. narrowly elliptic, rather fleshy, stalked, to 1½′ long. Infls. branched, loosely many-fld., to 3½′ tall, the rachis hairy. Fls. on very slender pedicellate ovaries, yellowish striped with brownish-purple, the lip brownish, about 1¼″ across, faintly fragrant. Ss. spreading, almost triangular, acute. Ps. much smaller. Lip ligulate, bent downwards. Autumn. (C, I) Himalayas, mostly at rather high elevations.

E. biflora Griff. (*Eria choneana* Krzl.)

Pbs. st.-like, rather vaguely club-shaped, clustered, narrower towards base, somewhat compressed, to 7″ tall, the internodes very short. Lvs. 2–4, at apex of pbs., narrowly ligulate, rather fleshy, to 3″ long. Infls. lateral, 2-fld., very short, the 3 bracts about ¼″ long, broad, yellow. Fls. ¼″ across, not opening well, whitish-yellow, the lip usually dark yellow. Ss. oblong-lanceolate, obtuse. Ps. linear-oblong, obtuse. Lip with 2 broad short keels on the disc. Autumn. (I, H) Himalayas; India; Burma; Thailand; Malay Peninsula; Sumatra; Java.

E. bractescens Ldl. (*Eria Dillwyni* Hk., *E. litoralis* Teijsm. & Binn., *Pinalia bractescens* O.Ktze.)

Pbs. cylindrical or somewhat compressed, usually elongate-ovoid, mostly covered by the persistent lf.-sheaths, to 3″ long. Lvs. 2–3 at apex of pbs., narrowly elliptic, blunt, leathery, to 5″ long. Infls. produced from upper nodes of pbs., erect, to 6″ tall, loosely many-fld., the large bracts cream-white or greenish. Fls. about 1″ across, white or faintly flushed with pink, the lat. lbs. of the lip pale purple, the midlb. cream with pinkish keels, papillose. Ss. almost triangular, not too much recurved, the ps. thrust forward. Summer. (I, H) Sikkim; Burma; Andaman Islands; Thailand; Laos;

Cambodia; Philippines; Malay Peninsula; Sumatra; Java; Borneo.

E. coronaria (Ldl.) Rchb.f. (*Coelogyne coronaria* Ldl., *Eria cylindropoda* Griff., *E. suavis* Ldl., *Trichosma coronaria* Ldl., *Trichosma suavis* Ldl.)

Pbs. cylindric, rather slender, to 6″ tall. Lvs. 2 at pb.-apex, lanceolate or oblong, acute, rather leathery, to 7″ long. Infls. erect or arching, loosely 3–6-fld., terminal, to 6″ long. Fls. slightly nodding, fragrant, waxy, about 2″ across, the ss. and ps. white, the lip with deep-purple-veined lat. lbs. that are oblong and obtuse, the midlb. golden-yellow, with 5 vague keels down the disc. Ss. and ps. oblong, obtuse, the ps. somewhat the smaller. Winter–spring. (C, I) Himalayas, usually at rather high elevations; Burma; Thailand; Malay Peninsula.

E. densa Ridl.

Pbs. st.-like, elongate, very stout and fleshy, some-what flattened, to 12″ tall and 1½″ in diam., with large sheaths. Lvs. 3–6, apical, to 12″ long and 1½″ wide, oblong-lanceolate, acute, rather leathery. Infls. spreading horizontally or somewhat ascending, densely many-fld. to the base, to 8″ long in largest forms, the bracts small. Fls. about ½″ across, white or pale pink, the ss. edged with deep pink, the top of the col. and the anther dark red. Dors. sep. very broad, hooded, the lat. ss. gaping slightly and exposing the lip. Ps. spreading, narrow. Lip 3-lbd., the lat. lbs. deeply bilobed, with 2 acute diverging points, the midlb. short-pointed, broad. Autumn. (I, H) Malay Peninsula; Sumatra; Borneo.

E. extinctoria (Ldl.) Oliver ex Hk. (*Dendrobium extinctorium* Ldl., *Eria capillipes* Par.)

Pbs. round, often somewhat depressed at top, densely clustered, about ¼″ high and thick. Lf. solitary, deciduous, ovate, acute, about ½″ long, borne at centre of pb. Infls. 1-fld., produced from centre of pbs. after lvs. have fallen, about 2″ tall. Fls. about ½″ long, white flushed with pink, the 3 papillose ridges of the lip and the disc orange-yellow flushed with pink, the inner base of the col. yellow, the mentum greenish, the anther blotched with deep purple-red on the sides. Spring. (I) Burma.

E. ferruginea Ldl.

Pbs. cylindrical, slender, borne about 2″ apart on the creeping rhiz., to 8″ tall. Lvs. 2–4 at apex of pbs., elliptic-oblong, blunt, rather leathery, to 6″ long. Infls. borne from the median nodes of the pbs., erect, loosely 8–15-fld., to 8″ tall, hairy. Fls. about 1½″ across, hairy outside, the ss. olive-brown with darker stripes, the ps. elliptic, white with a rose-red blush, the 3-lbd. lip white becoming pale violet-rose in the throat, with irregular keels on the disc. Spring. (C, I) Himalayas.

E. floribunda Ldl. (*Pinalia floribunda* O.Ktze.)

Pbs. st.-like, narrowly spindle-shaped, to 1½′ tall. Lvs. 5–6 at apex of pbs., lanceolate to elliptic, acute, thin in texture. Infls. often several at once, spreading horizontally from the nodes of the upper half of the pbs., to about 8″ long in the largest phases, densely many-fld. to the base, pale brown-hairy. Fls. about ¼″ across, white faintly tinged with pink, the top of the col. and the stigma deep purple, shaped much as in *E. densa*

Ridl., from which it differs in the narrower pbs., the slightly smaller fls. and in the lbs. of the basal lip-blade being rounded instead of acute. Spring–summer. (I, H) Burma; Peninsular Thailand; Viet-Nam; Malay Peninsula; Sumatra; Java; Borneo; Philippines.

E. hyacinthoides (Bl.) Ldl. (*Dendrolirium hyacinthoides* Bl., *Eria Endymion* Ridl.)

Pbs. spindle-shaped, cylindrical, to 4″ tall. Lvs. 2 at apex of pbs., narrowly lanceolate, acuminate, stalked towards base, to 10″ long. Infls. white-hairy, erect, to 6″ tall, rather loosely many-fld. Fls. about ½″ across, fragrant, white, the lip with violet-purple lat. lbs. Ss. and ps. oblong, obtuse, the lat. ss. spreading, the ps. as wide as the dors. sep. Lip with high, erect, narrow lat. lbs., the midlb. turned down, cordate, the base with a raised fleshy area on each side and 2 low keels in the middle. Spring. (I, H) Malay Peninsula; Sumatra; Java.

E. javanica (Sw.) Bl. (*Dendrobium javanicum* Sw., *Dendrolirium rugosum* Bl., *Eria rugosa* Ldl., *E. stellata* Ldl., *E. vaginata* Bth., *E. striolata* Rchb.f., *Tainia stellata* Pfitz., *Sarcopodium perakense* Krzl., *Katherinea perakensis* A.D. Hawkes)

Rhiz. elongate, creeping, the pbs. about 2″ apart. Pbs. erect, egg-shaped, to almost 3″ tall, 1-jointed, the lf.-sheaths fused to apical parts, with several cataphylls on the sides and near the base. Lvs. 2, erect, fleshy, to 1½′ long and 2½″ wide, lanceolate-ligulate, acute, the sheathing bases joined to the pbs., narrowed and folded basally. Infls. from near top of pbs., erect, to 2′ long, bearing rather distant but numerous fls. almost to the base, the stalk and bracts usually somewhat hairy. Fls. about 1½″ across, facing in all directions, white to pale yellowish, often purple-veined (sometimes purple-striped), the median one of the 3 prominent ridges down the lip-centre yellow. Ss. and ps. linear-lanceolate, acute. Lip 3-lbd., the short lat. lbs. erect, the long midlb. oblong, short-tipped. Mostly spring–summer, sometimes more than once annually. (I, H) Southern China; India; Burma; Laos; Thailand; Malay Peninsula; Sumatra; Java; Borneo; Celebes; Moluccas; New Guinea.

E. latifolia (Bl.) Rchb.f. (*Mycaranthes latifolia* Bl., *Eria bidens* Ridl., *E. iridifolia* Hk.f., *E. longispica* Rolfe)

Pbs. st.-like, stout, to 12″ tall. Lvs. mostly apical, to 10 in number, close together, to 1½′ long and 2″ wide, oblong-elliptic, acutish, stiff. Infls. 3–4 at once, to 12″ long, covered with short brownish hairs, very densely many-fld., the buds dark purplish. Fls. to almost ½″ across, the ss. greenish at base, more or less pink-spotted, sometimes dark red at tips, the ps. greenish-yellow with red spots, the lip pale green-yellow with pink to red-brown spots, the powdery keel and calli white. Dors. sep. hooded, not as wide as the spreading lat. ss. Ps. smaller than ss. Lip forward-pointing, the sides rising gently to form a broadly channel-shaped blade, the midlb. with a powdery keel from base to apex which ends in a powdery callus at midlb.-base. Autumn. (I, H) Sumatra; Java; Borneo; Malay Peninsula, usually on rather high mountains.

E. marginata Rolfe

Pbs. narrowly club-shaped, narrowing towards base, to 8″ tall. Lvs. 3–4 at apex of pbs., linear-oblong, acutish, to 6″ long, rather leathery. Infls. very short, 2-fld., with ovate yellow bracts. Fls. about 1¼″ across, white flushed with pink, the lip pale yellow with a red margin. Ss. triangular, acuminate. Ps. oblong, obtuse. Lip 3-lbd., the lat. lbs. much shorter than the rounded crenate papillose midlb. Autumn–winter. (I) Burma.

E. Merrillii Ames

Somewhat similar to *E. javanica* (Sw.) Bl., the larger, strongly angular pbs. usually greyish-green, clustered or borne at intervals on the creeping rhiz., this robust. Lvs. heavily and fleshily leathery, usually bright green, paired, strongly veined, to 12″ long and 1¾″ broad. Infls. borne from near pb.-apex, erect, bracted, to 15″ tall, with rather numerous crowded or scattered fls. which open in flushes, a few at a time, over a period of a month or more. Fls. faintly fragrant, short-lived, to about 1″ in diam., the narrow, sharp-pointed, somewhat recurved ss. and ps. pale cream-white or ivory-white, often lined with dull purple on inner surfaces. Lip narrow, white or cream-white, yellow on the disc. Spring–summer. (I, H) Philippines.

E. myristicaeformis Hk.f.

Pbs. ellipsoidal, shaped like nutmegs, streaked, to about 1¼″ tall. Lvs. 2–3 at the apex, oblanceolate, acute, leathery, to 7″ long. Infls. erect, loosely 8–12-fld., to 5″ tall. Fls. about 1″ across, fragrant, white, the midlb. of the lip yellow with 2 pale violet keels down the disc, the midlb. ovate, warty. Ss. ovate, acute. Ps. oblong, acutish. Autumn. (I) Burma.

E. neglecta Ridl.

Pbs. st.-like, somewhat thickened towards base, covered with dull brown sheaths, to 6″ tall. Lvs. 3–5, mostly apical, to 8″ long, not very heavy-textured, oblong-lanceolate, acute. Infls. 1-fld., produced from a small terminal sheath, the sheath thin and pale in colour. Fls. about 1″ across, white flushed with pink, the midlb. of the lip and the anther cream. Dors. sep. blunt, hooded. Ps. concave. Lip curved, with the keel on the midlb. thickened and irregularly warty, the sides of the midlb. wavy, folded, very thin. Autumn. (H) Malay Peninsula; Borneo.

E. obesa Ldl. (*Eria Lindleyana* Griff.)

Rather similar to *E. bractescens* Ldl. in habit, but the pbs. often stouter, the lvs. smaller and acute. Pbs. to 3″ tall, silvery-green, the sheaths scarious. Infls. lateral, 4–6-fld., the bracts large, pale whitish. Fls. about ½″ across, almost colourless, becoming greenish at base. Ss. and ps. broadly linear-ligulate, obtuse. Lip vaguely 3-lbd., broadly ligulate, very blunt at apex, with 2 or 3 keels on midlb. Spring. (I) Burma.

E. ornata (Bl.) Ldl. (*Dendrolirium ornatum* Bl., *Eria armeniaca* Ldl., *Pinalia ornata* O.Ktze.)

Similar in habit to *E. albido-tomentosa* (Bl.) Ldl., but more robust, the pbs. often to 5″ tall and 1½″ thick, usually more elongate than in the other sp. Lvs. 4–5, yellow-green, fleshy, the sheaths yellow-veined, elliptic, acutish, stalked at base, to 8″ long. Infls. erect or arching, to 1½′ long, covered with red-brown hairs, the large bracts (to 3″ long and 1″ wide) orange or cinnabar-brown, the fls. rather numerous but not showy. Fls. not opening well, about ¾″ across, the ss. greenish-yellow, the ps. pale greenish with a red median stripe, smaller than the ss., the lip reddish with darker crisped margins. Mostly summer. (I, H) Himalayas; Thailand; Malay Peninsula; Sumatra; Java; Borneo; Philippines.

E. pannea Ldl.

Rhiz. slender, the young parts covered with white-hairy sheaths. Pbs. absent, the sts. to 2″ apart, not fleshy, losing their lvs. when old. Lvs. 2–3 on each shoot, to 6″ long, about ¼″ wide, slightly flattened laterally, fleshy, somewhat incurving, linear, acutish. Infls. short-stalked, about 1″ long, 1–3-fld., erect. Fls. strongly fragrant of vanilla, about ½″ across, pale yellow-green, the lip dark purple. Ss. sharp-pointed, vaguely triangular. Ps. much narrower. Lip fleshy, the basal and apical thickened areas not connected. Spring. (C, I) Southern China and Himalayas to Malay Peninsula and Sumatra.

E. pilifera Ridl. (*Eria bracteolata* Krzl.)

Rather similar in habit to *E. neglecta* Ridll., the pbs. drooping, to about 1½′ long. Lvs. thin-textured, to about 3″ long, tapering towards the apex. Fls. usually solitary, with 3–4 narrow pale orange-yellow bracts subtending them, white with lemon-yellow warts covering the midlb. of the lip about ½″ across. Lip curved, the lat. lbs. erect, narrow, ending abruptly at the base of the short midlb. Summer. (I, H) Malay Peninsula; Sumatra; Java.

E. polyura Ldl. (*Pinalia polyura* O.Ktze.)

Pbs. narrowly club-shaped, to 7″ tall. Lvs. 5–6, mostly apical, narrowly ligulate, acutish, to 8″ long, narrowed basally, rather thin-textured. Infls. pendulous, densely many-fld., to 6″ long. Fls. about ¼″ across, white, the lip pale violet-purple with a yellow apex. Ss. and ps. narrowly elliptic, acutish, spreading. Lip small, with 2 short keels on the disc. Autumn. (I, H) Philippines.

E. rhodoptera Rchb.f. (*Eria Laucheana* Krzl., *E. bractescens* Ldl. var. *latipetala* Leavitt)

Allied to and simulating to a great degree *E. bractescens* Ldl., often more robust. Infls. from upper nodes of the pbs., erect or arching, rather densely many-fld., to 6″ tall, furnished with large, blunt, yellowish or whitish bracts. Fls. about ½″ long, yellowish-white, the lip with magenta-red lat. lbs., the disc with 3 keels. Mostly spring. (I, H) Philippines.

E. Ridleyi Rolfe (*Eria callosa* M.R.Henderson, *E. Kingii* Hk.f., *E. larutensis* Ridl., *E. major* Ridl., *E. tahanensis* Ridl.)

Allied to *E. latifolia* Rchb.f. and somewhat resembling it in habit, the st.-like pbs. to 1½′ tall, the internodes to 1½″ apart. Lvs. variable, sometimes long and narrow, more often to 8″ long and 1¼″ wide. Infls. 2–4 at once, to 15″ long, mostly horizontal, very densely many-fld., shortly brown-hairy. Fls. about ½″ across, the ss. and ps. very pale yellow-green, the lip glossy pale yellow or white with dark red-purple spots, the powdery keel and calli white. Lat. lbs. of the lip together forming a crescent with the ends pointing forward, the midlb. widening from a narrow base, the margins uneven, reflexed. Autumn. (I, H) Philippines; Malay Peninsula; Sumatra; Java.

E. rigida Bl.

Pbs. st.-like, to more than 3′ long, curving, pendulous, leafy. Lvs. rather tough and thick, deep green, to 5″ long and ½″ wide, linear-lanceolate, acute, often pendulous. Infls. lateral, numerous, very short, usually 1-fld., the 5 bracts dull red, narrowing from a broad base to the tip, flattened or somewhat concave. Fls. usually solitary, not opening well, white, the lat. ss. tinged with pale yellow outside and on lower edges, the callus on the col.-foot broad, flattened, covered with orange, club-shaped papillae. Dors. sep. strongly hooded, the lat. ss. turned out above the middle. Ps. concave, as wide as the ss. Lip not clawed, the lat. lbs. erect, obtusely angled, the midlb. with a more or less deeply cleft apex. Throughout the year, often more than once annually. (I, H) Peninsular Thailand; Malay Peninsula; Sumatra; Borneo.

E. Scortechinii Hk.f.

Pbs. st.-like, to 4½′ long, slender, leafy throughout. Lvs. rather thin, oblanceolate, acutish, widest near base, to 5″ long. Infls. terminal, branched, the main branch to about 7″ long, the alternate lateral branches often re-branching, furnished with broad white concave bracts, the fls. rather numerous, the pedicellate ovaries shorter than the bracts, red-brown-hairy. Fls. about ½″ across, white, all segms. with pink edges, the outside of the ss. red-brown-hairy, the high narrow erect lat. lbs. of the lip deep pink or purplish, the short broad midlb. sharply turned down in front, the median part with a longitudinal keel bearing fine spreading lilac hairs along its crest, with 2 shorter smooth keels, one at the base of each lat. lb. Summer. (I, H) Malay Peninsula, in the mountains at 5000–6000 feet elevation.

E. spicata (D.Don) Hand.-Mazz. (*Octomeria spicata* D.Don, *Octomeria convallarioides* D.Don, *Pinalia alba* Buch.-Ham., *Eria convallarioides* Ldl.)

Pbs. oblong or thickly spindle-shaped, mostly covered by the persistent lf.-sheaths, to 8″ tall, sometimes to 1″ in diam. Lvs. 3–4, mostly apical, thickly leathery, lanceolate-elliptic, acute, to 7″ long. Infls. about 4–6″ tall, the peduncle about half that length, usually nodding, very densely many-fld., elongate-egg-shaped, with prominent membranous bracts. Fls. very fragrant, about ½″ across, not opening fully, pure translucent white or straw-yellow, the lip usually golden-yellow at the front, the outside of the ss. either glabrous or conspicuously glandular-hairy. Ss. very broad, obtuse, 5–7-nerved, the ps. 3-nerved, much smaller. Lip cuneate, truncate at apex, usually warty in the middle. Mostly spring. (C, I) Himalayas to southern Burma, Thailand, Laos, and Viet-Nam, at various elevations up to more than 5000 feet.

E. stricta Ldl. (*Mycaranthes stricta* Ldl., *Octomeria secunda* Wall. ex Ldl., *Eria secundiflora* Griff.)

Pbs. narrowly cylindric, to 5″ tall. Lvs. 2 at the apex, oblong, acute, leathery, to 4″ long and ¾″ wide. Infls. erect, produced from near the tops of the pbs., densely many-fld., the fls. all on one side, to 5″ tall. Fls. about ⅛″ across, the ss. white-hairy outside, white, the lip sometimes pale yellow, concave, obtuse, shorter than the other segms. Spring. (I) Himalayas; Burma; Thailand; Viet-Nam.

E. Teysmanni J.J.Sm. (*Trichotosia Teysmanni* Krzl.)

Pbs. st.-like, pendulous, to 7′ long, leafy throughout (except at base), the lf.-sheaths sparsely covered with pale brown hairs. Lvs. linear-lanceolate, acutish, to 8″ long and 2″ wide, covered (even on the lamina) with short pale brown hairs. Infls. limply pendulous, to 15″ long, many-fld., covered with pale brown hairs, the bracts about ½″ long, hairy. Fls. not opening widely, about ½″ across, white, brown-hairy outside, the lip with erect sides which are not definitely lbs., the midlb. wider than long, with a forward-pointing triangular thickening. Autumn. (I, H) Malay Peninsula; Sumatra; Borneo.

E. vestita (Wall.) Ldl. (*Dendrobium vestitum* Wall., *Trichotosia vestita* Krzl.)

Allied to and simulating in large degree *E. Teysmanni* J.J.Sm., but covered with red-brown hairs, the lvs. smaller, to 5½″ long and 1¼″ wide, the infls. somewhat shorter, and the fls. much larger, to more than 1″ across, white, the midlb. of the lip with red margins. Summer. (H) Malay Peninsula; Sumatra; Borneo.

E. xanthocheila Ridl.

Pbs. spindle-shaped to almost cylindrical, covered with the old lf.-sheaths, to 8″ tall, sometimes more than ½″ thick. Lvs. 3–4, apical, thin-textured, rather evenly elliptic, acutish, to 8″ long and 1½″ wide. Infls. usually several at once, spreading horizontally from upper parts of pbs., to 3″ long, densely many-fld. to base, the broad reflexed bracts pale greenish. Fls. about ½″ across, cream-yellow, the lat. lbs. of the lip purple, the midlb. lemon-yellow. Dors. sep. hooded, the lat. ss. wide-spreading. Ps. narrower than ss., rather recurved. Lip 3-lbd., the small lat. lbs. erect, the midlb. bent at the middle, notched at apex, with 3 keels in basal part. Summer. (H) Thailand; Malay Peninsula; Sumatra; Borneo; Java.

E. Braddoni Rolfe (*Eria latibracteata* Ridl.)

Pbs. st.-like, rather slender and irregular, to 8″ long, sheathed. Lvs. 3–4, apical, narrowing to both ends, to 8″ long and 2″ wide. Infls. horizontal, to 3½″ long, the bracts sulphur-yellow, to 1″ long, somewhat concave, the rac. rather few-fld., the fls. usually all facing upwards. Fls. about ¾″ across, whitish, the ss. and ps. veined with red towards base, the lip with the midlb. pale yellow with a red-brown patch towards the base, the lat. lbs. pinkish, the middle part white with deep red keels. Autumn. (H) Malay Peninsula; Borneo.

E. euryloba Schltr.

Pbs. somewhat spindle-shaped, to 1½′ tall, mostly cylindrical, sheathed. Lvs. 3–4 at apex, to 7″ long and almost 2″ wide, leathery, oblanceolate, acutish. Infls. arching downwards from apex of pbs., to 8″ long, very

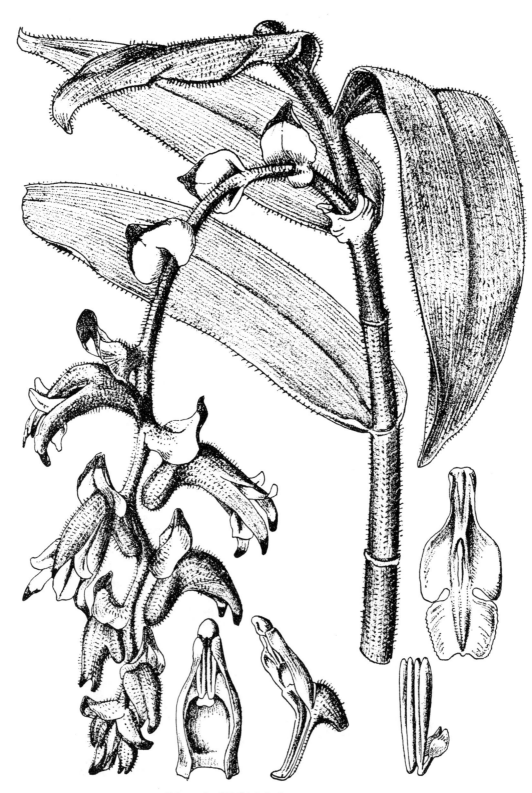

Eria vestita (Wall.) Ldl. [FRITZ KRAENZLIN]

densely many-fld., cylindrical. Fls. fragrant, about $\frac{1}{2}''$ across. white with rose-red veins, the anther bright purple. Spring. (H) Sumatra.

E. ferox (Bl.) Bl. (*Trichotosia ferox* Bl., *Trichotosia pyrrhotricha* Ridl., *Eria pyrrhotricha* Ridl.) Similar in habit to *E. vestita* Ldl., but the hairs longer (to almost $\frac{1}{8}''$ long) and stiffer, the infls. shorter (to 4″ long), the fls. white, about $\frac{3}{4}''$ across. Lip with erect lat. lbs., the broad midlb. extending only slightly beyond them, its apex turned down and cleft, the disc with 3 more or less distinct lines of hairy warts down the middle. Autumn. (H) Malay Peninsula; Sumatra; Java; Borneo.

E. gracilis Hk.f. (*Trichotosia gracilis* Krzl., *Trichotosia oligantha* Krzl., *Eria oligantha* Hk.f.) Pbs. st.-like, erect or arching, to 8″ long, leafy. Lvs. stiff, oblanceolate, narrowing to the obliquely 2-lbd. apex, to 2″ long, hairy on the edges and front of the lf.-sheaths only. Infls. short, 1–3-fld., lateral, the bracts rather small, sparsely hairy. Fls. to $\frac{1}{2}''$ long, creamy-white, the apex of the lip yellow-orange, the margins purple, the anther black. Summer. (H) Malay Peninsula.

E. latibracteata Rolfe. Pbs. narrowly ovoid, furrowed with age, to 2″ tall. Lvs. 2, oblong-elliptic, acute, to 4″ long. Infls. from sides of pbs., rather loosely 8–15-fld., to 4″ tall, the bracts rather long and wide. Fls. not opening well, about $\frac{1}{2}''$ long, brownish-white, the lip 3-lbd., with broad yellow lat. lbs. and a deep rose, obtuse, midlb. Summer. (H) Borneo.

E. microphylla (Bl.) Bl. (*Trichotosia microphylla* Bl.) Rhiz. slender, elongate, bearing erect leafy st.-like pbs. at intervals of about 5″. Sts. to 4″ tall, with 10 or more small fleshy lvs. arranged in 2 rows, about $\frac{1}{2}''$ long and less than $\frac{3}{8}''$ wide. Fls. solitary, white, about $\frac{1}{2}''$ across, the ss. very hairy outside, the lip simple, tongue-shaped, with a conical projection beneath near the tip. Autumn. (H) Malay Peninsula; Sumatra; Java; Borneo.

E. nutans Ldl. Rather like *E. neglecta* Ridl. in habit, but more robust, the st.-like pbs. covered with red-brown sheaths. Lvs. 3–5, to 8″ long and $1\frac{1}{2}''$ wide, the secondary veins prominent on lower surface. Fls. solitary, from axil of short terminal sheath, with a dull purplish-pink bract about $\frac{1}{2}''$ long, the fls. opening to about 1″ wide, the ss. tinged with pink apically, the ps. tinged with greenish-yellow at tips, the lip medially flushed with greenish-yellow, with a vaguely roughened brownish callus at the end of the col.-foot. Summer. (H) Malay Peninsula; Sumatra; Borneo.

E. poculata Ridl. (*Trichotosia poculata* Krzl.) Similar in habit to *E. gracilis* Hk.f., but the st.-like pbs. to more than 3′ long, the lvs. about 5″ long. Infls. very short and dense, usually less than $\frac{1}{2}''$ long. Fls. on the outside green with red hairs, cream-coloured within, the lip orange at base, white apically, about $\frac{1}{4}''$ across. Summer. (H) Malay Peninsula; Sumatra; Borneo.

E. porphyroglossa Krzl. Pbs. rather zigzag, spindle-shaped, sheathed, to $2\frac{1}{2}''$ tall. Lvs. 4–5, mostly apical, leathery, to 6″ long and 1″ wide, oblanceolate, acutish, glossy deep green. Infls. erect or arching, densely many-fld., cylindrical, to 6″ long. Fls. about 1″ across, yellow-green veined with red, the lip purple. Spring. (H) Sumatra.

E. rhynchostyloides O'Brien. Pbs. ovoid, to $3\frac{1}{2}''$ tall. Lvs. 2–3 at apex of pbs., almost linear-ligulate, acute, to 15″ long. Infls. pendulous or arching, densely many-fld., cylindrical, about $1\frac{1}{4}''$ in diam., stalked, to 8″ long. Fls. about $\frac{1}{2}''$ across, white, the anther scarlet-red. Summer. (H) Java.

E. robusta (Bl.) Ldl. (*Dendrolirium robustum* Bl., *Eria brunnea* Ridl., *E. falcata* J.J. Sm., *E. linearifolia* Merr., *E.*

lorifolia Ridl.) Pbs. st.-like, clustered, about 3″ long, thick, almost cylindrical. Lvs. 1–3 at apex of pbs., to 12″ long, linear, acutish, to 2″ wide, rather fleshy. Infls. from near apex of pbs., erect, densely brown-hairy, the stalk long, the fls. very numerous and crowded. Fls. about $\frac{1}{2}''$ long, cream-coloured, with short rust-red hairs on the outside of the ss. and on the pedicellate ovary, the lip entire. Summer. (I, H) Philippines; Peninsular Thailand; Malay Peninsula; Sumatra; Java; Borneo; Fiji Islands.

E. tenuiflora Ridl. Pbs. st.-like or somewhat thickened medially, to 7″ long, pale green with very thin close sheaths. Lvs. 3–4, apical, evenly elliptical, to $6\frac{1}{2}''$ long, thin-textured. Infls. spreading horizontally below the lvs., about $2\frac{1}{2}''$ long, very slender, together with the fls. (which measure about $\frac{1}{2}''$ across and are very fragile in texture) and the small bracts, pale cream-colour, the only difference being the basal part of the lip, which is deep purple. Summer. (H) Malay Peninsula; Sumatra; Borneo.

E. velutina Lodd. ex Ldl. (*Trichotosia velutina* Krzl.) Pbs. st.-like, slender, mostly erect, to $1\frac{1}{2}'$ long, covered densely with short red-brown hairs. Lvs. very fleshy, obliquely oblanceolate, acutish, the apices somewhat reflexed, to 4″ long and $1\frac{1}{4}''$ wide, all surfaces covered with short red-brown hairs. Infls. less than 1″ long, about 2-bracted, entirely hairy, with a solitary fl. usually. Fls. more than $\frac{1}{2}''$ long, not opening well, densely hairy outside, cream or pale pink, the lip pink basally, the midlb. white or yellowish. Summer. (H) Burma; Thailand; Malay Peninsula; Sumatra; Java; Borneo.

ERIOCHILUS R.Br.

Like so many of the unusual genera of terrestrial orchids indigenous to Australia, the five known species of *Eriochilus* are today virtually unknown in collections outside of their native land. In this instance, at least one of the described members of the genus is rather common in the wild, and is an attractive slender plant which should be cultivated, hence the attention paid to it here. The group is rather closely allied to *Caladenia* R.Br., but differs in the clawed lateral sepals and the densely hairy midlobe of the lip.

Nothing is known of the genetic alliances of this strange genus.

CULTURE: As for *Caladenia*. (C, I)

E. cucullatus (Labill.) Rchb.f. (*Epipactis cucullata* Labill., *Eriochilus autumnalis* R.Br.)
Very slender, erect pls., the subterranean tubers globose. Lf. solitary, often not present with the fls., ovate, acute, basal, small. Infls. to 10″ tall, 1–3-fld., the stalk fuzzy. Fls. about 1″ long, white or pale to bright pink, the recurved lamina of the lip furnished with short red hairs. Dors. sep. usually undulate marginally, erect, slightly concave; lat. ss. spreading horizontally or slightly reflexed, with a slender claw, elliptic-lanceolate. Ps. linear. Lip usually slightly 2-lbd. at base, glabrous, the midlb. hairy, the hairs often borne in transverse ridges. Winter–spring. (C, I) Australia.

ERIOPSIS Ldl.
(*Pseuderiopsis* Rchb.f.)

This is a genus of about six species, ranging from Costa Rica to Peru and Brazil, where they are mostly epiphytes at relatively high elevations. The cultivated species of *Eriopsis*, when well-grown, are among the most handsome and unusual of the members of the subtribe *Gongorinae*. Even when not in flower, their peculiar, tightly wrinkled, often almost black pseudobulbs and clean foliage make them extremely attractive, and when the graceful spikes of uniquely-coloured blossoms are produced, they form a welcome addition to even the most comprehensive of orchid collections.

No hybrids are on record within the genus. Experimental breeding with allied groups should be attempted by some enterprising orchidist, and inter-specific crossing also seems to offer some fascinating prospects.

CULTURE: Mostly native at high elevations, Eriopsis require cultural conditions of cool (or intermediate) temperatures, moisture at the roots at all times (though soggy composts must be studiously avoided), and rather subdued light exposure. General cultural directions are those afforded *Gongora* or *Stanhopea*, though the present plants should be grown in pots rather than in baskets. Addition of an amount of chopped sphagnum moss to a compost of chopped osmunda or shredded tree-fern fibre forms a most suitable potting-medium for these delightful orchids. (C, I)

E. biloba Ldl. (*Pseuderiopsis Schomburgkii* Rchb.f., *Eriopsis Schomburgkii* Rchb.f.)

Pbs. egg-shaped, rather narrowing upwards, to 8″ tall, furnished with innumerable inter-connecting wrinkles when mature. Lvs. 2, elliptic, acutish, leathery, glossy, to 1½′ long and 4″ wide. Infls. erect, to 2½′ tall, densely many-fld., the rac. almost cylindrical, to 2½″ in diam. Fls. about 1″ across, waxy, fragrant, the ss. and ps. golden-yellow with brown-red margins. Lip basally almost kidney-shaped, the apical part much smaller, also kidney-shaped, golden-yellow, spotted with red. Autumn. (I) Brazil; Guianas; Peru.

E. rutidobulbon Hk.

Pbs. almost black, covered with numberless fine wrinkles, to 7″ tall, pear-shaped. Lvs. 2–3, glossy green,

Eriopsis rutidobulbon Hk. [B.S.WILLIAMS]

broadly lanceolate, acute, rather fleshy, with prominent veins. Infls. usually densely many-fld., erect or arching, to 1½′ tall. Fls. about 1½″ across, fragrant, waxy, the ss. and ps. dull orange-yellow with red-purple markings. Lip with the lat. lbs. rounded, dull orange-red spotted with dark purple; midlb. spreading, emarginate or 2-lbd. at apex, white spotted with dark purple; the disc with erect, fleshy keels. Col. greenish. Summer–autumn. (C, I) Costa Rica; Panama; Colombia; Peru.

E. Fuerstenbergii Krzl. Similar to *E. rutidobulbon* Hk., but the ps. darker in colour and the ss. with a more acute apex. Perhaps referable to varietal status under that sp. Summer. (C) ? Colombia.

E. Helenae Krzl. Pbs. almost cylindric, to 10″ tall. Lvs. 3–4, to 2′ long and 1½″ wide, leathery. Infls. erect, densely many-fld., to 2½′ tall. Fls. about 2″ across, fragrant, waxy, the ss. and ps. yellow with red margins. Lip white, spotted and blotched with red. Summer. (C) Peru.

ERYCINA Ldl.

Two members of *Erycina* are known, both of them rare epiphytic orchids native in Mexico which are today extremely scarce in cultivation, though both have been grown in the past to some extent. Closely allied to *Oncidium* Sw. and to *Leochilus* Kn. & Westc., it differs from the latter group in having the lip conspicuously 3-lobed, though it shares with that genus the character of having the anther extended in front into a membranaceous appendage which is longer than the locule. Small-flowered, rather inconspicuous orchids, the Erycinas are primarily of scientific interest.

No hybrids are known in *Erycina*, though the genus may prove genetically compatible with certain of the allied groups of the subtribe *Oncidiinae*.

CULTURE: As for the small-growing pseudobulbous Oncidiums. (I)

E. echinata (HBK) Ldl. (*Oncidium echinatum* HBK, *Erycina major* Schltr.)

Rhiz. ascending or erect, short, producing the pbs. at some intervals from each other. Pbs. shortly stalked, often brownish, about 1″ tall, oval, 1-lvd., with about 4 sheathing lf.-like bracts at the base. Lf. usually soon deciduous, oblong, apiculate, rather rigidly leathery, to 2″ long and ½″ wide. Infls. erect or arching, loosely 5–9-fld., to 5″ tall, the rac. arching or pendulous. Fls. cup-shaped, about ½″ across, green, the proportionately large lip golden-yellow or yellow. Ss. and ps. ovate, acuminate, incurved. Lip with fan-shaped blunt lat. lbs., the midlb. short-stalked, oval, the entire lip about ¾″ long and ½″ wide. Spring. (I) Mexico.

ERYTHRODES Bl.
(*Physurus* L.C.Rich.)

A member of the subtribe *Physurinae*, *Erythrodes* consists of somewhat more than one hundred species of highly technical and often misinterpreted terrestrial orchids, these widespread in the tropics and subtropics of both hemispheres. Often rather handsome plants with variegated foliage, certain of them fall into the horti-

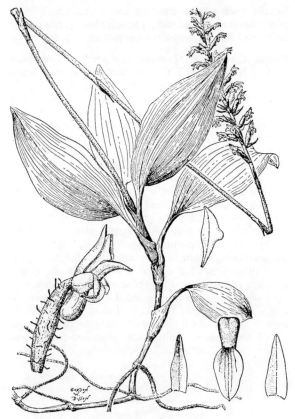

Erythrodes ovatilabia A. & C. [GORDON W. DILLON]

cultural category of the 'Jewel Orchids', and as such, a few of them are occasionally encountered in choice specialized collections. Small-flowered, the blossoms are of great complexity and are often difficult to describe. The genus is allied to *Hylophila* Ldl. and to *Kuhlhasseltia* J.J.Sm., but differs from them in technical floral characters.

No hybrids are as yet known in *Erythrodes*, and nothing has been deduced concerning its genetic affinities, although crosses with allied groups seem possible and should prove most interesting.

CULTURE: As for *Anoectochilus*, though certain of the species do not require the conditions of extreme heat and high humidity mandatory for that group. (I, H)

E. latifolia Bl. (*Physurus latifolius* Bl.)

Pls. in fl. to 2′ tall, with a few lvs. at the base. Lvs. stalked, the stalk to 2″ long, the blades ovate, acute, to almost 5″ long and 2½″ wide, green. Scape short-hairy, the elongating rachis hairy, with numerous rather distant fls., these opening successively over a long period. Fls. less than ½″ long, hooded, the ss. and ps. pinkish-brown, the lip with white margins. Summer. (H) Malay Peninsula; Sumatra; Java.

E. querceticola (Ldl.) Ames (*Goodyera querceticola* Chapm., *Physurus querceticola* Ldl., *Physurus Sagraeanus* A.Rich.)

Pls. slender or stout, to 15″ tall, stoloniferous. Lvs. distant on the st., light green or yellowish or brownish-

green, short-stalked, the stalk sheathing the st., the blade ovate to narrowly lanceolate, prominently veined, to 3″ long. Rac. few- to many-fld., dense or loose, to 4″ long. Fls. yellowish-green or white, less than ¼″ long, tubular, with a sac-like spur on the lip. Throughout the year. (I) Florida; Louisiana; Texas; Mexico; Central America; West Indies; Northern South America.

EUANTHE Schltr.

Euanthe consists of but a single species, this an extremely popular epiphytic orchid from the Philippines which is typically grown under its synonymous name of *Vanda Sanderiana* Rchb.f. One of the most magnificent of all orchidaceous plants, it vegetatively simulates many Vandas, but differs from that group materially in the structure of the huge, flattened flowers, in particular the formation of the lip, which is quite unlike anything found in true *Vanda*.

Euanthe Sanderiana has been utilized by the breeders on a large number of occasions, both with true Vandas, and with members of many allied genera, such as *Renanthera*, *Vandopsis*, *Arachnis*, etc. Except for those hybrids registered by Malayan growers, most of the *Euanthe* hybrids to date are designated as *Vanda* hybrids; most hybridists in Singapore and elsewhere in the area, however, indicate *Euanthe* × *Vanda* crosses, for example, as *Vandanthe*. A revision of this nomenclatural system is sorely needed.

CULTURE: As for the tropical Vandas. In the wild, *Euanthe* usually grows on trees close to the sea—often overhanging the waves, in fact—generally fully exposed to the tropical sun. (H)

E. Sanderiana (Rchb.f.) Schltr. (*Vanda Sanderiana* Rchb.f., *Esmeralda Sanderiana* Rchb.f.)

St. mostly solitary, sometimes rather copiously branching from near base, rooting freely, leafy throughout or with basal lvs. more or less deciduous in time. Lvs. numerous, rather closely arranged, lorate, complicate at base, truncate and cuspidate apically, sometimes unequally 2-lbd. there, to more than 15″ long, to about 1″ broad. Infls. stout, erect or ascending, to about 12″ long, usually with about 4–10 large, well-spaced or somewhat crowded fls. Fls. variable in dimensions and colour, fragrant, long-lived, usually 3½–4½″ in diam., often longer than wide, flattened or with the ss. and ps. somewhat reflexed marginally, with prominently 6-ribbed pedicellate ovaries that are pale brown basally and become purplish upwards. Ss. broadly obovate, the dors. one delicate rose-colour suffused with white, the lats. divergent, somewhat larger than the dors. one, tawny-yellow with brownish-red-net-branching prominent veins. Ps. rhomboid-ovate, smaller than the ss., coloured like the dors. sep., with a tawny-yellow blotch spotted with dull red on the side next to the lat. ss. Lip small in proportion to the other segms., bipartite, fleshy, the basal hypochil transversely oblong, deeply concave, with an inflexed anterior margin, variable in colour, but usually dull tawny-yellow streaked with red on the inner side; epichil with a short claw, roundish-oblong, strongly recurved at apex, with 3 prominent ridges on the disc, reddish-brown, often somewhat suffused with tawny-yellow. Col. very short, buff-yellow. Autumn, mostly Sept.–Nov. (H) Philippines; South-east Mindanao, near Davao.

EUCOSIA Bl.

A member of the subtribe *Physurinae*, *Eucosia* consists of three known species of rather dwarf terrestrial orchids, one native in Java, one in New Guinea, and the third in New Caledonia. Vegetatively, the plants rather simulate an *Anoectochilus*, but they differ in critical details of the small flowers. None of them is in cultivation at this time.

Nothing is known of the genetic affinities of this odd group.

CULTURE: Presumably as for *Anoectochilus*. (H)

EULOPHIA R.Br.
(*Cyrtopera* Ldl., *Lissochilus* R.Br., *Hypodematium* A.Rich., *Orthochilus* Hochst., *Platypus* Small & Nash, *Triorchos* Small & Nash)

As now interpreted, *Eulophia* includes somewhat more than three hundred species of mostly terrestrial (rarely epiphytic or lithophytic) orchids, which are widespread in virtually all tropical and subtropical regions of the globe, with the greatest development in Central Africa. Other species occur in the American tropics, ranging from North Florida to Argentina, and still others inhabit almost all parts of Asia, Indonesia, and the Pacific Islands. The genus is placed in the subtribe *Eulophiinae*, and all recent students have included *Lissochilus* R.Br., long considered distinct, in the synonymy of *Eulophia*. A variable aggregation, most of these orchids possess relatively prominent, somewhat angular pseudobulbs, usually with two or more apical, leathery or plicate leaves. The inflorescences are basal, and bear from a few to very many often showy flowers, which usually open successively over a rather long period of time. In many species (mostly those formerly included in *Lissochilus*), the petals are conspicuously larger and broader than the sepals and form the most prominent part of the flower; these petals are often of a different colour from the sepals, but agree in hue with the lip. The lip may be spurred or spurless, and is attached to the foot of the short or elongate column; its blade may be distinctly three-lobed or entire. Two poilinia are present, these attached to a short broad stipes. Several of the tropical African species—e.g. *E. gigantea* (Welw.) N.E.Br., *E. Horsfallii* (Ldl.) Dur. & Schinz, etc. —are among the most robust of all orchidaceous plants, their inflorescences not infrequently attaining heights in excess of fifteen feet!

No hybrids are registered as yet in *Eulophia*, though the field of critical inter-specific breeding seems to offer some extremely fascinating prospects and should be explored. Nothing is known of genetic affinities, but the genus is presumably compatible with at least some of the allied groups.

CULTURE: The terrestrial species of *Eulophia*—which form the bulk of the genus—should be treated in the manner suggested for *Phaius*. Like that genus, they benefit materially by frequent and liberal applications of fertilizers of various sorts. The epiphytic species should be treated like the tropical Dendrobiums. (I, H)

E. alta (L.) F. & R. (*Limodorum altum* L., *Dendrobium longifolium* HBK, *Cyrtopodium Woodfordii* Sims, *Cyrtopera Woodfordii* Ldl., *Cyrtopera longifolia* Rchb.f., *Eulophia Woodfordii* Rolfe, *E. longifolia* Schltr., *Platypus altus* Small)

Rhiz. tuberous, usually made up of roughly triangular, conical, corm-like annual parts. Lvs. deciduous, few in number, erect, to 6′ tall and 4″ wide, plicate, strongly veined, lanceolate, acuminate, forming a st.-like stalk below. Infls. erect, to 7′ tall, few- to many-fld., the fls. opening successively for a long time. Fls. extremely variable in colour and size, usually about 1½″ across, waxy, long-lived, rather fragrant, the ss. and ps. greenish, bronze-yellow, or dull yellow (rarely almost maroon), the lip darker than the other segms., marked with purple. Ss. ascending, mostly elliptic-oblong, acute to acuminate, often somewhat dilated above middle. Ps. extending above the col. and lip, broadly oblong-spatulate to oblanceolate, obtuse to rounded. Lip usually brownish-green with veins and flushings of deep purple, 3-lbd., saccate at base, the lat. lbs. embracing the col., the disc with 2 erect flap-like calli, midlb. undulate-crisped and

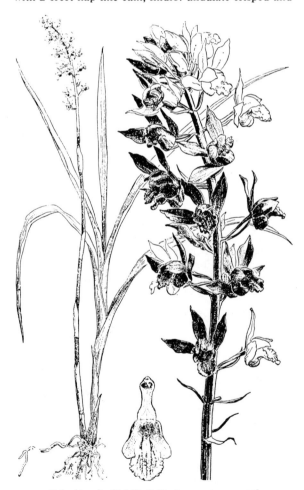

Eulophia alta (L.) F. & R. [BLANCHE AMES]

208

Dendrobium Pierardii Roxb. [Courtesy WALLACE H. OTAGURO]

(ABOVE) *Dendrochilum glumaceum* Ldl.
[H. R. FOLKERSMA]

(LEFT) *Dendrobium linguaeforme* Sw. [G. HERMON SLADE]

(CENTRE) *Domingoa hymenodes* (Rchb.f.) Schltr.
[*The Orchid Journal*]

(BELOW) A species of *Dipodium* (*D. elatum* J.J.Sm.?) growing wild in the hills of Papua [REV. N. E. G. CRUTTWELL]

(BOTTOM) *Diuris longifolia* Rupp [W. H. NICHOLLS]

VIA *Macodes Sanderiana* (hort.) Rolfe [G.HERMON SLADE]

VIB *Maxillaria tenuifolia* Ldl. [MISS M.HAWKES]

cut marginally. Autumn–winter. (I, H) South Florida and Mexico throughout the West Indies and Central America to northern South America; also tropical Africa.

E. bella N.E.Br. (*Lissochilus bellus* Schltr., *Lissochilus milanjianus* Rendle)

Pbs. mostly subterranean, ovoid, clustered, about 3″ tall and 1″ thick. Lvs. paired, linear, acute, rather leathery, to 12″ long, gracefully arching. Infls. slender, erect, loosely 6–10-fld., to almost 2′ tall. Fls. waxy, delicately fragrant, about 2″ across, the ss. greenish, the ps. and lip golden-yellow outside, light red inside, the midlb. of the lip golden-yellow. Ss. reflexed, ovate, obtuse. Ps. much larger than the ss., almost round, basally clawed. Lip 3-lbd., the spur conical, obtuse. Spring–autumn, sometimes more than once annually. (H) Nyasaland.

E. bicarinata (Ldl.) Hk.f. (*Cyrtopera bicarinata* Ldl.)

Pbs. subterranean, variable in shape, usually roundish, white-coloured, bearing the circular bases of the scale-lvs. Lvs. to 2¼′ long and ½″ wide, linear, acute to acuminate, plicate, rather heavy. Infls. to 12″ tall, 8–12-fld., the bracts narrow, the pedicellate ovaries lengthy. Fls. about 1¼″ across, the ss. pale green with 5 brown veins on the reverse surfaces, the ps. pale mauve apically, the basal two-thirds greenish, the lip with green, purple-veined lat. lbs., the midlb. pale mauve with deeper veins, the basal and median parts white with irregular warts. Dors. sep. curved over the col., ps., and lip; lat. ss. larger than the dors. one, spreading. Ps. widest near the blunt apex, extended above the col. and lip. Lip distinctly 3-lbd., the lat. lbs. upturned at col.-sides, the midlb. down-turned, wider than long, vaguely 2-lbd., with 2 prominent mauve keels from base of lip to base of midlb., with a third low keel between, the spur small. Col. pale green, the foot purplish. Mostly summer. (H) India to Australia.

E. ensata Ldl.

Pbs. corm-like, roundish, fleshy, about 2″ in diam., subterranean. Lvs. 2–3, linear, acute, 8–12″ long, less than ½″ wide. Infls. to about 10″ tall, 10–20-fld., the rac. dense and short. Fls. about 1″ across, light yellow, the lip with the midlb. orange-yellow in its centre. Ss. and ps. ligulate, blunt apically. Lip as long as the ss., the lat. lbs. upturned at the sides of the col., the midlb. papillose, the spur shortly cylindric, obtuse. Spring. (H) South Africa.

E. epidendroides (Retz) Schltr. (*Serapias epidendroides* Retz, *Limodorum epidendroides* Willd., *Limodorum virens* Roxb., *Eulophia virens* Ldl.)

Pbs. buried or partially exposed, roundish-ovoid, to 2½″ tall, about 1″ thick usually. Lvs. 2–3, to 1½′ long, narrowly linear, acute or acuminate. Infls. slender, loosely 10–15-fld., to 2′ tall. Fls. rather waxy, about 2″ across, fragrant, white, the lip with violet keels on the disc. Ss. and ps. oblong, obtuse, spreading more or less, the tips reflexed. Lip 3-lbd., the spur cylindric, slightly curved. Spring–early summer. (H) Ceylon; India; Burma.

E. euglossa (Rchb.f.)Rchb.f.(*Galeandra euglossa* Rchb.f.)

Pbs. narrowly cylindric, to about 8″ tall, wrinkled with age, often purplish-flushed. Lvs. 2–3, long-stalked, to 12″ long and 3″ wide, narrowly elliptic, acutish or acuminate. Infls. to 1½′ tall, rather densely many-fld., the fls. opening successively over a long period of time. Fls. pendent, not opening fully, about 1½″ long, green, the lip white with green lat. lbs. which are veined with red, and a midlb. which is veined with violet-purple on the disc. Ss. and ps. narrowly ligulate, acute. Lip 3-lbd., the midlb. roughened. Spring–early summer. (H) Tropical West Africa.

E. gigantea (Welw.) N.E.Br. (*Lissochilus giganteus* Welw.)

Pbs. irregular in shape, rather corm-like, to about 8″ in diam. in some specimens, usually partially or entirely subterranean. Lvs. stalked at base, the stalk very robust, elliptic, acute or acuminate, plicate, heavy-textured, to more than 8′ tall. Infls. to 16′ tall, very robust, densely 20–50-fld., the fls. opening successively over a long period of time. Fls. to 5″ in diam. (often only about 3″ across), variable in colour, but usually light rose-purple, the ps. and lip somewhat darker than the ss. Ss. reflexed, proportionately small. Ps. oval from a clawed base, widely spreading. Lip large, 3-lbd., the spur broadly conical. A most remarkable orchid, one of the largest known. Summer. (H) Belgian Congo; Angola.

E. graminea Ldl.

Pbs. ovoid-ellipsoid, tapering upwards, bright green, to 6″ long and about 2″ in diam. Lvs. grass-like, narrowly linear, acute to acuminate, rather flaccid in texture, to 15″ long and ¾″ wide, few in number. Infls. erect, slender, often branched, to almost 3′ tall, usually many-fld., the fls. opening successively over a long period. Fls. to about 1½″ across, long-lived, the ss. and ps. pale green with a complex network of red-brown veins, the lip with green, red-brown-veined lat. lbs., the midlb. white or pinkish with 5 purple-red hairy ridges. Ss. oblanceolate, acutish, the lats. with their tips recurved. Ps. thrust forward above the col. and lip, shorter and wider than the ss., the tips curved outwards. Lip as long as the ss., the lat. lbs. with blunt tips, the midlb. rounded, marginally wavy, with 3 keels in the basal part, the spur narrowly cylindric, slightly curved. Mostly spring. (I, H) India; Burma; Thailand; Viet-Nam; Malay Peninsula; Java; Philippines.

E. guineensis Ldl.

Pbs. ovoid, clustered, to 2″ tall and about ¾″ in diam. Lvs. 2–3, narrowly elliptic, acute, stalked at base, rather heavy-textured, to 1½′ long and 2½″ wide. Infls. erect, to almost 2′ tall, loosely 5–15-fld. Fls. about 2″ in diam., waxy, fragrant, greenish or brownish, the lip white, the disc rose-red or the entire midlb. rose-red with darker veins. Ss. and ps. ligulate, acutish. Lip 3-lbd., the lat. lbs. inrolled to form an open tube, the midlb. roughened, the spur prominent. Autumn–early winter. (H) Tropical West Africa.

E. Horsfallii (Ldl.) Dur. & Schinz (*Lissochilus Horsfallii* Ldl.)

Similar in habit to *E. gigantea* (Welw.) N.E.Br., but

often even more robust, the lvs. stalked at base, to more than 8′ tall, to 12″ wide or more. Infl. erect, to 15′ tall and more, very robust, the apical part more slender, bearing a densely many-fld. rac. Fls. 3–5″ in diam., fragrant, very handsome, the smallish ss. reflexed, dark purple, the larger ps. broadly oval, bright rose-red. Lip 3-lbd., the lat. lbs. green veined with dark red, the dark violet-purple midlb. with paler keels on the disc. Spur short, conical, obtuse. Spring–early summer. (H) Tropical West Africa.

E. Krebsii (Rchb.f.) Bolus (*Lissochilus Krebsii* Rchb.f.)

Pbs. usually half-buried in the soil, oblong, becoming rather grooved and wrinkled with age, to 2″ tall. Lvs. lanceolate, acute, folded, rather heavy-textured, to 1½′ long and 2½″ broad. Infl. rather loosely 10–20-fld., to almost 3′ tall. Fls. about 1½″ in diam., the reflexed ss. green blotched with brown, the larger, broadly oval ps. bright golden-yellow. Lip 3-lbd., golden-yellow, with a short obtuse spur. Winter–early spring. (I, H) Natal; Transvaal.

E. macrostachya Ldl. (*Graphorchis Blumeana* O.Ktze., *Graphorchis macrostachya* O.Ktze.)

Pbs. not buried, cylindric, tapering upwards, to about 5″ tall, to ¾″ in diam. Lvs. 2–3, stalked, prominently 3-veined, elliptic, acuminate, to 12″ long, the blade to 3″ broad. Infl. slender, to 2½′ tall, the mostly cylindrical, densely many-fld. rac. to about 8″ long. Fls. to about 1″ in diam., rather long-lasting. Ss. and ps. rather similar, green to greenish-white, acute. Lip concave, yellow with reddish veins, 2-lbd. towards the apex, basally with a short 2-lbd. callus, the spur short squarish or roundish. Winter. (I, H) Mascarene Islands; India, Ceylon, Malaysia and the Philippines to Australia.

E. nuda Ldl.

Pbs. roundish, often not buried or only partially so, to 1½″ in diam., clustered. Lvs. usually paired, acuminate, stalked basally, to 15″ long and 3″ broad, plicate. Infl. arising simultaneously with the new growths, loosely 8–12-fld., to 2′ tall. Fls. fragrant at times, to 2¾″ in diam., vivid rose-red, the lip dark rose-red, the disc golden-yellow. Ss. erect, ligulate. Ps. twisted, oblong, rather smaller than the ss. Lip oval, emarginate at apex, crisped and undulate marginally, usually 7-keeled on the disc, the spur conical, acutish, about ¾″ long. Spring, mostly in April. (I, H) Nepal, South China, and India to Thailand and Cambodia.

E. purpurata (Ldl.) N.E.Br. (*Limodorum cristatum* Sw., *Lissochilus purpuratus* Ldl., *Eulophia cristata* Steud., *E. longibracteata* Dur. & Schinz)

Pbs. ovoid, to 3″ tall, clustered, usually not buried. Lvs. usually 2, plicate, to 2′ long and 2″ broad. Infl. very slender, loosely 10–15-fld., to 4′ tall. Fls. fragrant, the segms. spreading, to 1¼″ across, the oblong ss. and ps. pale violet. Lip 3-lbd., the lat. lbs. green veined with violet-brown, the oblong midlb. violet-blue, the keels on the disc darker violet-blue, warty. Spur short, obtuse. Spring. (H) Tropical Africa, usually in grasslands.

E. rosea (Ldl.) A.D.Hawkes (*Lissochilus roseus* Ldl.)

Rather similar to *E. gigantea* (Welw.) N.E.Br. in habit, but considerably smaller and less robust in all parts.

Infl. many-fld. towards apex, erect, to 5′ tall. Fls. to 2½″ across, fragrant, long-lasting, the reflexed ss. brownish, the considerably larger broadly oval ps. rose-red. Lip 3-lbd., the lat. lbs. greenish, the midlb. rose-red, with 3 yellow keels on the disc. Spur short, conical. Winter–spring. (H) Sierra Leone.

E. sanguinea (Ldl.) Hk.f. (*Cyrtopera sanguinea* Ldl., *Cyrtopera rufa* Thw.)

Pbs. rather tuber-like, oblique, rhomboidal, usually buried, to 2″ long, clustered. Lvs. absent at flowering-time. Infl. rigidly erect, 8–15-fld., to 1½′ tall, stout. Fls. rather heavy-textured, to 2″ in diam. or more, the brown ss. and ps. elliptic-lanceolate, acuminate. Lip 3-lbd., margined with whitish-red, the median part brown, with very· numerous thickened, comb-like veins, the spur short, conical, obtuse, greenish. Spring. (I, H) Himalayas.

E. squalida Ldl. (*Cyrtopera squalida* Rchb.f., *Eulophia elongata* Bl., *E. mucronata* Bl.)

Pbs. tuber-like, subterranean, almost round, clustered, to 1¼″ in diam. Lvs. 3–4, often absent at flowering-time, stalked, the stalk about 6″ long, the folded lamina to almost 2′ long and 2″ broad, prominently 7-veined. Infl. to more than 3′ tall, stout, bearing a loosely 4–10-fld. rac. in apical portion. Fls. about 1½–2″ long, rather fleshy, long-lasting, the ss. and ps. green to brown or olive-green, the lip white, yellow or pale red. Ss. ligulate, acute, ascending or erect. Ps. over-arching the col., with upcurved tips, often pure white, or basally greenish and red. Lip with a broad flattened spur pointing downwards, between the divergent halves of the col.-foot, the lip-blade bent at right angles to the spur, its sides upcurved but scarcely distinguished as lobes, sometimes pale mauve, medially white or cream, veined with mauve and brown. Spring. (I, H) India, Sumatra, and the Malay Peninsula throughout Indonesia to New Guinea and the Philippines.

E. streptopetala (Ldl.) Ldl. (*Lissochilus streptopetalus* Ldl.)

Simulating *E. Krebsii* (Rchb.f.) Bolus in large degree, but more slender, the lvs. narrower, usually only about ¾″ wide. Fls. about 1¼″ across, coloured like the other noted sp. Spring. (I, H) South Africa.

E. stricta (Presl) Ames (*Bletia stricta* Presl, *Eulophia exaltata* Rchb.f., *E. ensiformis* Schltr., *E. Warburgiana* Krzl.)

Pbs. subterranean, tuber-like, flattened, 2–4″ long. Lvs. grass-like, linear, acute or acuminate, strongly plicate, stalked basally, to 5′ tall, several in number. Infls. erect, rather stout, to more than 6′ tall, with a few- to rather many-fld. apical rac. Fls. fragrant, rather long-lived, to 1½″ in diam., opening rather well, the ss. and ps. outside canary-yellow, white inside. Lip 3-lbd., large, the midlb. canary-yellow, the upturned lat. lbs. whitish, all margins strongly crisped and undulate. Spring. (I, H) Philippines; Java; Celebes.

E. Zollingeri (Rchb.f.) J.J.Sm. (*Cyrtopera Zollingeri* Rchb.f.)

Pbs. large, subterranean, with many thick roots. Lvs. absent, reduced to scale-like bracts on the infl., this stout, to 2' tall, the bracts about 1" long, narrow, the rac. rather few-fld. Fls. not opening widely, to about 1" across or less, dull red-brown. Ps. shorter and broader than the ss., ascending with the dors. sep. Lip at an acute angle to the col.-foot and making with it a saccate base, the lat. lbs. erect on either side of the col., with rounded incurved tips; midlb. slightly down-turned, concave, broad, bluntly pointed. This species is apparently saprophytic in habit. Winter. (I, H) India through Malaysia to New Guinea.

E. Andersoni (Rolfe) A.D.Hawkes (*Lissochilus Andersoni* Rolfe) Pbs. subterranean, irregularly ovoid, rather large. Lvs. usually paired, linear, acute, folded, to 12" long. Infl. slender, loosely 6–8-fld., to 1½' tall. Fls. about 2" in diam., the ss. and ps. yellowish-green or whitish-green, acute, the latter twice as broad as the ss. Lip 3-lbd., about 1¼" long, white with 5 violet keels on the disc, extending onto the midlb., the spur short, yellow apically. Col. white with a red anther. Spring, mostly April. (H) Ghana.

E. angolensis (Rchb.f.) Summerh. (*Cymbidium angolense* Rchb.f., *Lissochilus angolensis* Rchb.f., *Lissochilus ugandae* Rolfe) Variable in all parts. Pbs. buried, rather large, to about 4" in diam., irregular. Lvs. erect, folded, heavy-textured, to more than 3½' long, to about 1¼" broad. Infls. to 5' tall, densely 20–30-fld., rather stout. Fls. nodding, to 2" across, long-lasting, very variable in colour. Ss. spreading, yellow, red or brown, or yellow-green tipped with brown-red, the ps. broader, somewhat reflexed, similar in colour, or yellow when ss. are red or brown. Lip 3-lbd., the lat. lbs. usually whitish veined with green (or magenta), the very large midlb. golden-yellow (or purple). Mostly spring. (H) Tropical Africa and South Africa, widespread and often common.

E. Keithii Ridl. Pbs. clustered, ovoid, covered by the remnants of the lf.-bases, to 4" long, shining green. Lvs. about 5, deciduous, to 12" long and ¼" wide, thin, narrowed towards the base and to the acutish tip. Infl. produced from the leafless pbs., erect, 10–15-fld., to 15" tall. Fls. more than 1" across, long-lasting, the ss. and shorter ps. green, the lat. ss. spreading horizontally. Lip pale green on the lat. lbs. and edges of midlb., the remainder almost white with brown veins and 3 white warty keels on the basal part; lat. lbs. erect, rather small, scarcely overlapping the col; midlb. broad and reflexed with crisped edges. Spur with a narrow base, the apex swollen. Col. short and thick, its foot long. Autumn. (H) Langkawi Islands; Thailand; Malay Peninsula: Kedah.

E. Mahoni (Rolfe) A.D.Hawkes (*Lissochilus Mahoni* Rolfe) Rather similar to *E. gigantea* (Welw.) N.E.Br., but with smaller fls. in a more elongate rac. Fls. to 3½" in diam., the reflexed ss. green striped with brown, the almost round ps. pale rose-red. Lip 3-lbd., the lat. lbs. green striped with brown, the midlb. violet with darker veins, the disc with prominent yellow keels. Spur conical, acutish. May–Aug. (I, H) Uganda.

E. porphyroglossa Rchb.f. (*Lissochilus porphyroglossus* Rchb.f.) Pbs. obsolete. Lvs. 3 to 6 per growth, to 2½' long and 10" broad, sword-shaped, deeply plicate. Infl. stout, erect, 4–10' tall, many-fld., the fls. opening gradually over a very long period. Fls. heavy-textured, to 2¼" long, the broad ss. bronze-purple, the roundish ps. bright magenta outside, white inside, spreading horizontally. Lip 3-lbd., the erect rounded lat. lbs. greenish with dark purple veins, the midlb. frilled marginally, light purple with 3 irregular keels that become yellow beyond

dark purple basal parts. Summer. (I) Congo, Uganda, and Kenya, in mountain swamps at 6000–8000 ft. elevation.

E. pulchra (Thou.) Ldl. (*Limodorum pulchrum* Thou.) Similar in all parts to *E. macrostachya* Ldl., the fls. to about 1" in diam., the ss. and ps. green flushed with violet-brown, the lip whitish, veined with violet-red. Spring. (H) Madagascar; Mauritius.

E. Sandersoni (Rchb.f.) A.D.Hawkes (*Lissochilus Sandersoni* Rchb.f.) Similar in habit to *E. Horsfallii* (Ldl.) Dur. & Schinz, the fls. 3–5" in diam., the small ss. dark purple, the large ps. white, the lip 3-lbd., with grass-green lat. lbs., the midlb. violet-purple, the disc-keels bright yellow. Spring–early summer. (H) Natal.

E. stylites (Rchb.f) A.D.Hawkes (*Lissochilus stylites* Rchb.f.) Pbs. subterranean, rather large, irregularly ovoid. Lvs. folded, heavy-textured, to 3½' tall and 2" broad. Infl. loosely 4–8-fld., erect, to more than 4' tall. Fls. very handsome, long-lasting, to 2½" in diam., the reflexed ss. greenish with a rose-red overlay, the much larger ps. rose-red, broadly oval. Lip almost square, vaguely 4-lbd., rose-red, densely red-spotted on a yellow ground in the throat, with 2 keels. Spur curved, broad, short, very blunt. Summer, mostly in June. (H) Tropical Africa.

E. Zeyheri Hk.f. (*Eulophia bicolor* Rchb.f. & Sond.) Pbs. subterranean, rhomboidal, about 2" in diam. Lvs. narrowly lanceolate, acute, petioled at base, to 1½' long. Infl. about 12" tall, with a short, densely many-fld. rac. at apex. Fls. about 1½" long, the oblong, apiculate ss. and ps. soft pale yellow. Lip 3-lbd., the lat. lbs. almost black-purple, the midlb. roundish, soft pale yellow, the disc veined with red, 2-keeled, with papillae. Spur cylindric, short. Spring–early summer. (I, H) Kaffirland; Natal; Transvaal.

EULOPHIDIUM Pfitz.

Eulophidium is a genus of about ten species of mostly terrestrial (rarely epiphytic) orchids which, though long considered to be members of *Eulophia* R.Br., are now generally placed in a separate subtribe, the *Eulophidiinae*, closest in alliance to the *Maxillarinae*. Rare in cultivation today, they have a remarkably disjunct distribution, with a single species in Brazil, the remainder in tropical Africa and Madagascar. These are primarily 'foliage' orchids—the leaves in most species being beautifully marbled and blotched with white on a dull green ground —since the flowers are small and relatively insignificant.

Nothing is known of the genetic affinities of this aberrant genus.

CULTURE: As for *Phaius*. (I, H)

E. Ledieni (Stein) Schltr. (*Eulophia Ledieni* Stein) Pbs. clustered, ovoid, about 1" tall, often flushed with purple. Lf. solitary, rigidly leathery, to 6" tall and 2" wide, narrowed basally and folded there, dull green with irregular, mostly transverse blotches of white or silvery-white, oblong, obtuse. Infls. loosely 6–15-fld., to 12" tall, erect, produced from the base of the current pb. Fls. not opening widely, about ¾" across, the narrowly ligulate, acute ss. brownish, the smaller ps. whitish, the lip yellowish-white with a dull red median blotch, fiddle-shaped, 2-keeled on the disc, the rather large spur curved, thickened apically. Mostly autumn– early winter. (I, H) Tropical West Africa.

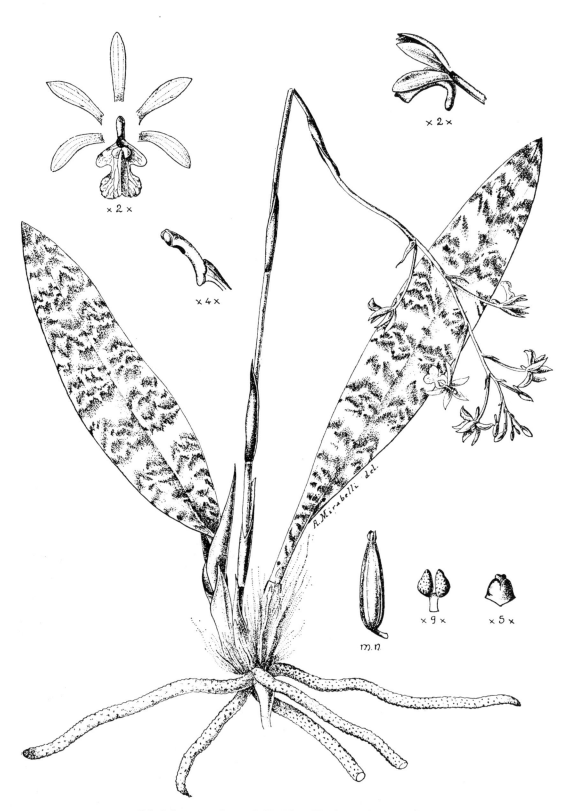

×2×

×2×

×4×

×9×

×5×

m.n

Eulophidium maculatum (Ldl.) Pfitz. [Hoehne, *Flora Brasilica*]

212

E. maculatum (Ldl.) Pfitz. (*Oeceoclades maculata* Ldl., *Eulophia maculata* Rchb.f.)

Similar in all parts to *E. Ledieni* (Stein) Schltr., but the pbs. more flattened, the lvs. longer and acute, the ss. and ps. broader. Fls. about ¾″ across, brownish or pinkish-brown with a white or pale pink lip. Autumn. (I, H) Brazil.

EULOPHIELLA Rolfe

Four species of *Eulophiella* are currently known to science, all of them endemic to the island of Madagascar, where they appear to be rather rare. Highly specialized epiphytes, they are normally found growing only on certain trees, e.g., *E. Roempleriana* (Rchb.f.) Schltr. is apparently invariably discovered on a species of *Pandanus*, and on no other sort of tree. The genus is oddly placed in the subtribe *Cyrtopodiinae*, although upon further research it may prove to be referable to an aggregation of its own. Large, pseudobulbous plants with creeping rhizomes and very elongate plicate foliage, the basal inflorescences (which are sometimes branched) bear a large number of sizeable, ornate, colourful flowers which many experts consider to be among the most enchanting of any orchid! Although they have been in cultivation for a considerable period of time, today the Eulophiellas are excessively rare in our greenhouses; they are, however, to be strongly recommended to all enthusiasts who are intrigued by the rare and unusual.

A single hybrid is known in this genus, this the very lovely *Eulophiella x Rolfei*, a cross between *E. Roempleriana* (indicated in the official registry as *E. Peetersiana*) and *E. Elisabethae*; it was registered by Messrs. Charlesworth & Co. in 1917, and is present in a few choice contemporary collections. Additional interspecific breeding is highly recommended, as well as crossing with theoretically allied groups.

CULTURE: Eulophiellas have often had the reputation of being difficult orchids to maintain in good condition, but if a few rules are adhered to, considerable pleasure may be derived from their extravagant flowers. Since they are native in tropical, humid Madagascar, a warm moist situation is required at all times. The plants must never be permitted to become dry at the roots, though the drainage must be such that souring of the compost does not occur. A suitable potting-medium is made up of about equal parts, fully mixed, of chopped tree-fern fibre and chopped sphagnum moss. Since the rhizomes of these plants are often very elongate, with the growths being produced at considerable distances from each other, they need to be kept in large, flat, slatted baskets for best results. Strong sunlight and sharp draughts of chill air must be strictly avoided at all times, although excessive shade is also to be frowned upon. Despite their rampant growing habits, these orchids are rather intolerant of being disturbed, hence should be divided and/or repotted only when absolutely necessary. (H)

E. Elisabethae Lind. & Rolfe

Rhiz. elongate, covered with sheathing bracts which break up into fibres. Pbs. borne some distance apart, oblong-fusiform, to 6″ long and 1″ in diam., sheathed when young. Lvs. 4–5, narrowly lanceolate, acuminate, plicate, to 2′ long and ¼″ broad. Infls. basal, erect or ascending, to 15″ long, 12–15-fld., the floral bracts and pedicellate ovaries wine-red. Fls. opening well, fragrant, waxy, more than 1½″ in diam., the ss. and ps. white flushed with rose mostly near apex, the white lip with a large vivid yellow blotch on the disc. Ss. and ps. elliptic, very obtuse, somewhat concave. Lip 3-lbd., the lat. lbs. erect, obtuse, the midlb. almost round, slightly crisped and incised marginally; disc with several prominent keels. Col. white, the anther-cap pale yellow. Mostly spring. (H) Madagascar.

E. Roempleriana (Rchb.f.) Schltr. (*Grammatophyllum Roemplerianum* Rchb.f., *Eulophiella Hamelini* Baillon, *E. Peetersiana* Krzl.)

Pl. very large and robust, the creeping elongate rhiz. to 2½″ in diam., covered with large sheaths which become fibres with age. Pbs. borne at intervals from one another, cylindric to ovoid-fusiform, 3–11″ long, 1–1½″ in diam. Lvs. 4–8, lanceolate, plicate, attenuated towards both ends, the base petioled, the apex acute, to 4′ long and 4″ wide. Infls. basal, erect to horizontal, often branched sparsely, robust, to 4½′ long, the apical rac. (or panicle) usually 15–30-fld., the fls. opening successively over a long period. Fls. waxy, fragrant, long-lasting, to almost 4″ in diam., the ss. and ps. pale rose-pink, usually whitish towards bases, the lip rich violet-rose, whitish in the throat, the disc vivid yellow. Ss. and ps. broadly elliptic, very blunt apically, somewhat concave. Lip 3-lbd., the lat. lbs. erect, the disc with several keels. Mostly Apr.–June. (H) Madagascar.

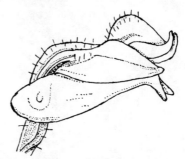

Eurycentrum obscurum (Bl.) Schltr. [A.D.HAWKES, AFTER J.J.SMITH]

EURYCENTRUM Schltr.

A member of the complex subtribe *Physurinae*, *Eurycentrum* contains four very rare and little-known terrestrial orchids in New Guinea, none of which is present in collections today. Allied to *Kuhlhasseltia* J.J.Sm., these plants have handsome variegated foliage, small, intricate blossoms, and are of potential interest to those who specialize in the 'Jewel Orchids' group.

Nothing is known of the genetic alliances of this group.

CULTURE: Presumably as for *Anoectochilus*. (H)

EURYCHONE Schltr.

Two species of *Eurychone* are known to date, both of them very rare and apparently unknown in contemporary collections outside of their native haunts.

E. Rothschildiana (O'Brien) Schltr. (*Angraecum Roth-schildianum* O'Brien) is a native of Uganda, and is a dwarf epiphytic monopodial rather resembling a *Phalaenopsis*, but bearing racemes of relatively showy white flowers, with some green and purplish-brown in the trumpet-shaped lip. The other species, **Eurychone galeandrae** Schltr., is from the Belgian Congo. The genus is a member of the very complex angraecoid group of the subtribe *Sarcanthinae*, and is at this time relatively little-known, even by botanists.

Nothing is known of the genetic ties of this attractive group of orchids.

CULTURE: Presumably as for the smaller-growing Angraecums. (H)

EURYSTYLES Wawra
(*Pseudoeurystyles* Hoehne)

This is a genus of about seven or so species of diminutive epiphytic (rarely lithophytic) orchids of the subtribe *Spiranthinae*, all apparently restricted in their distribution to Brazil, where they grow principally in the damp forests near the coast. Somewhat allied to *Lankesterella* Ames, the plants consist of a rosette of very thin, little leaves, from the centre of which arises an abbreviated inflorescence of one or more small but

Eurystyles Standleyi Ames [BLANCHE AMES]

very intricate, mostly greenish flowers. Peculiarly enough, *Eurystyles* was originally placed in the Ginger Family (Zingiberaceae), so aberrant is its structure. None of the species is in collections today, and their successful cultivation is problematical.

Nothing is known of the genetic affinities of *Eurystyles*.

CULTURE: Probably as for *Ornithocephalus*. The plants must be kept continuously moist, and in a rather shaded spot in the highly humid greenhouse. (I, H)

EVOTA Rolfe

Evota is a segregate from *Ceratandra* Eckl., and consists of a very few, little-known terrestrial orchids from South Africa, none of which appears to be present in contemporary collections. Their solitary or few flowers are often rather peculiarly coloured, and are typically strongly odoriferous; it is noted that **E. Harveyana** (Ldl.) Rolfe (*Ceratandra Harveyana* Ldl.) has 'a pleasant soap-like scent'.

Nothing is known of the genetic affinities of this rare genus.

CULTURE: Presumably as for *Caladenia*. (C, I)

EVRARDIA Gagnep.

Evrardia Poilanei Gagnep., the only known member of this genus of the subtribe *Cephalantherinae*, is apparently endemic to Annam, in Viet-Nam. Unknown in cultivation, it is a dwarf saprophytic orchid, somewhat allied to *Aphyllorchis* Bl., and is not well-understood at this time.

Nothing is known of the genetic ties of this recently-established genus.

CULTURE: Possibly as for the species of *Corallor-rhiza*, etc. (I)

FLICKINGERIA A.D.Hawkes
(*Desmotrichum* Bl.)

About thirty-five or more species make up this peculiar genus of the subtribe *Dendrobiinae*, these epiphytic or lithophytic orchids which are today extremely rare in our collections, although some of them are attractive when in full bloom. Formerly known as *Desmotrichum* Bl., this name proved to be a homonym of an earlier genus (of algae), hence the new epithet was established in 1961 (in *The Orchid Weekly* 2: 451. 1961). With a pendulous or ascending rhizome, the Flickingerias bear their fusiform or subcylindric pseudobulbs at intervals along it. The mostly rather small, very ephemeral, white, greenish, or yellow flowers are produced singly or in fascicles from the upper leaf-axils, hence often appearing to be terminal, though in actuality this is not the case, being pseudo-terminal as in *Diplocaulobium* [Rchb.f.] Krzl. and *Epigeneium* Gagnep. The range of this remarkable genus extends from the Himalayas throughout South-east Asia and Indonesia to New Guinea.

No hybrids have been effected in *Flickingeria*, and nothing is known of its genetic affinities, though they presumably lie with at least certain sections of *Dendrobium*.

CULTURE: These primarily tropical plants should be grown in the manner recommended for the pseudo-bulbous Dendrobiums, etc. Pot-culture usually suits them best, though they are often difficult to keep in good condition for very long in the collection. (I, H)

F. fimbriata (Bl.) A.D.Hawkes (*Desmotrichum fimbriatum* Bl., *Dendrobium fimbriatum* Ldl., *Dendrobium Macraei* Ldl., *Dendrobium plicatile* Ldl.)

Rhiz. pendulous to erect, to 3′ long, usually profusely branching. Pbs. fusiform, borne at intervals along rhiz., to 3″ long, usually smaller, often somewhat compressed. Lvs. solitary or paired, sessile, ligular or lanceolate, obtuse, to 8″ long. Fls. clustered, produced successively, very short-lived, fragrant, to about 1″ in diam., white,

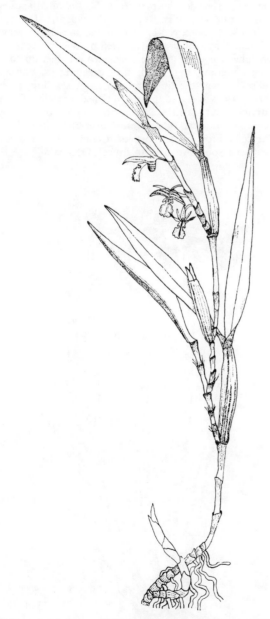

Flickingeria fimbriata (Bl.) A.D.Hawkes [A.D.HAWKES, AFTER KRAENZLIN]

the lip usually yellow or yellow only at base, with tiny purple or magenta spots. Ss. and slightly shorter ps. spreading or incurving. Lip 3-lbd., the lat. lbs. small, cuneate, the much larger midlb. contracted medially, flabellate apically, beautifully crisped and undulated on margins. Almost ever-blooming. (I, H) Himalayas, India, and Ceylon throughout South-east Asia and the Philippines to Sumatra, Java, Borneo, and Celebes.

FORBESINA Ridl.

The single known species of *Forbesina*, **F. eriaeformis** Ridl., is an extremely rare epiphytic orchid which has apparently been found on only one occasion, in the forests of Sumatra. A member of the subtribe *Coelogyninae*, it is perhaps closest in its relationship to *Pholidota* Ldl., but differs from that group in several critical details. It is a rather unusual plant, but not present in cultivation.

Nothing has been ascertained regarding the genetic affinities of *Forbesina*.

CULTURE: Presumably as for the tropical Coelogynes. (H)

FORFICARIA Ldl.

Forficaria is a genus consisting of a single species of unusually interesting terrestrial, reed-like orchid, closely allied to *Disa* Berg., native in South Africa. It is very scarce in our collections today, but is of sufficient beauty to warrant further attention from enthusiasts, though—like many ground-dwelling orchids of this type—its cultural requirements are not easily met. Large, oblong tubers give rise to slender, reedy stems bearing several grassy basal leaves and brown, bract-like, cauline ones. The rather few flowers are produced in an elongate raceme, and are of complex and intriguing structure.

Nothing is known of the genetic affinities of *Forficaria*, though we should presume that it will prove 'crossable' with at least some of the Disas, and allied groups.

CULTURE: As for *Disa*. (C, I)

F. graminifolia Ldl. (*Disa Forficaria* Bolus)

Pls. to 15″ tall, rather slender. Basal lvs. linear, grassy, to 10″ long; cauline lvs. brown, bract-like, acuminate. Infls. to 15″ tall, the fls. rather few, furnished with bristle-tipped bracts. Fls. about ¾″ long, the ss. yellow or greenish-yellow and purple, the ps. and lip bright purple. Dors. sep. roundish, shortly acute, concave, without a spur; lat. ss. narrower than the dors. one, oblong, acute. Ps. lying on the dors. sep., narrow, bent at the middle, the inner surface and margins pubescent with short gland-tipped hairs. Lip short, wide, truncate, convex. Jan.–Feb. (C, I) South Africa.

FRACTIUNGUIS Schltr.

This genus consists of two species of rare epiphytic orchids with slender, branched stems, somewhat simulating certain kinds of *Scaphyglottis* in habit, but differing from that group radically in floral structure, so much so that it is placed in the subtribe *Laeliinae* (not subtribe *Ponerinae*). Neither of the known species—**Fractiunguis reflexa** (Rchb.f.) Schltr. (*Hexisea reflexa*

Rchb.f.), from the West Indies and the Guianas, and **F. brasiliensis** Schltr., from Brazil—is in cultivation at this time, and in any event, they are rather nondescript orchids primarily of scientific interest.

Nothing is known of the genetic affinities of *Fractiunguis*.

CULTURE: Presumably as for the pendulous species of *Scaphyglottis*, etc. (I, H)

FUERTESIELLA Schltr.

About three species of *Fuertesiella* are known, all of them exceptionally rare and little-known terrestrial orchids of the subtribe *Cranichidinae*, indigenous to the West Indies. Somewhat allied to *Ponthieva* R.Br., the Fuertesiellas differ materially in structural detail of the smallish, complex flowers, which are borne in erect spikes above a loose rosette of leaves. None of the species is present in our collections at this time.

Nothing is known of the genetic affinities of this uncommon genus.

CULTURE: Possibly as for the tropical *Spiranthes*, etc. (I, H)

GALEANDRA Ldl.
(*Corydandra* Rchb.)

Galeandra is a genus of about twenty-five species which are widespread in the region extending from South Florida and Mexico to Brazil; most of the known taxa occur in the last-named country. Formerly popular with enthusiasts, these fine, often very robust plants have today largely passed out of vogue, although several of the species are among the most spectacular of American orchids. The genus consists of two distinct sections, one of them (including *G. Beyrichii* Rchb.f.) with tuberous roots, erect inflorescences, and apparently, no leaves at any time; the other (including all of those noted below except *G. Beyrichii* Rchb.f.) with more or less prominent, globular to stem-like pseudobulbs, slender, folded leaves, and terminal racemes of large, showy flowers. Most Galeandras have spreading sepals and petals arranged in a circle around the lip, which typically is much larger than the other segments and produced into an elongate, more or less funnel-shaped spur.

No hybrids have as yet been produced in this delightful genus; interspecific breeding should be attempted. It also seems probable that *Galeandra* is genetically compatible with at least certain other members of the subtribe *Polystachyinae*.

CULTURE: Galeandras vary from strictly epiphytic to terrestrial or lithophytic in habit, but under cultivation thrive when grown as semi-terrestrials. Well-drained pots should be used, filled with a loosely-packed compost of about equal parts of shredded osmunda, rich leaf-mould, sifted loam, and dried crumbled manure; a part of chopped sphagnum moss may be added with benefit. While the plants are actively growing they need quantities of moisture, sun, and humidity, and should be fertilized regularly and with some frequency, since they are heavy feeders. Upon completion of the new

growths, however, water should be largely withheld and slightly cooler temperatures should prevail, until root-action again commences, when the plants may be moved back to the warmer, sunnier spot. Care must be taken at all times to avoid getting water in the expanding tops of the growths, or rotting of both the growing apex and the incipient inflorescence may result. (I, H)

G. Baueri Ldl. (*Galeandra Batemani* Rolfe, *G. cristata* Ldl.)

Pbs. spindle-shaped, slightly zigzag, or simulating a robust *Catasetum*, usually partially concealed by the persistent lf.-bases, to 11″ long (often considerably shorter). Lvs. rather numerous, eventually deciduous, linear to linear-lanceolate, acute to acuminate, to 9″ long and ¾″ wide, the persistent sheaths often spotted with red-brown. Infls. to about 12″ tall, the stalk furnished with loose, red-brown-spotted sheaths, the few-fld. rac. simple or branched, often producing accessory branches for more than a single season. Fls. up to 3″ long, fragrant, long-lived, the spreading ss. and ps. yellow-brown, the lip purple in front shading in the throat to white and purple, crisped marginally, the curving spur tapering from the broad base, long. Summer–autumn, often almost ever-blooming. (I, H) Mexico throughout most of Central America and northern South America to French Guiana.

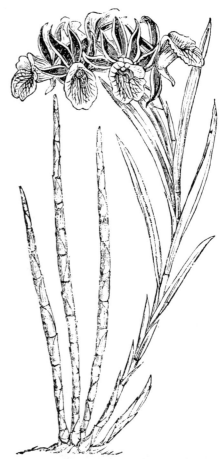

Galeandra Devoniana Ldl. [B.S.WILLIAMS]

G. Devoniana Ldl.

Pbs. 2–6' tall, cylindrical or slightly swollen medially. Lvs. numerous, deciduous, lanceolate, acute, folded, to 12" long and 1½" wide. Infls. a few-fld. terminal rac., nodding or pendulous. Fls. to 3" long, fragrant, long-lived, rather heavy-textured, the linear, acute ss. and ps. somewhat reflexed, deep purple or brown-purple with green or yellow-green margins. Lip large, broadly obovate, the sides forming a tube around the col., white, the crisped apical part with numerous intricate magenta-purple stripes and marks, the large recurved spur green. Usually summer, but sometimes more than once annually. (H) Colombia; Guianas; Brazil.

G. Beyrichii Rchb.f. Terrestrial, apparently leafless sp., the infls. produced from a corm-like pb. beneath the surface. Infls. stout, to 4' tall (usually shorter), the 10–12 fls. in a rather loose apical rac. Fls. about 1–1½" across, delicately fragrant, the ss. and ps. linear-oblong, acutish, green or greenish, the tubular lip white or greenish-white with some bright magenta stripes in the throat, these sometimes extending out onto the flaring, crisped midlb. Autumn. (I, H) South Florida throughout most of tropical America.

G. Claesiana Cgn. (*Galeandra Claesii* hort.) Rather similar in habit to *G. Baueri* Ldl., but more robust in all parts, the pbs. to 1½' long, the persistent lf.-sheaths usually greyish with dull brown spots. Infls. pendulous, about 9" long, few-fld. Fls. about 2½" across, the ss. and ps. green flushed with wine-purple, the large lip wine-purple apically, becoming greenish-yellow towards the base, outside covered with purplish bands. Summer. (H) Brazil.

G. pubicentrum C.Schweinf. Pbs. clustered, slender-fusiform, to 6" tall, sheathed, striped longitudinally. Lvs. few, borne almost all length of pbs., erect-ascending, to 6½" long and less than ½" broad, narrowly linear, acute. Infls. paniculate, to almost 6" long, bracted, few-fld. Fls. to 2" long, lasting well, delicately fragrant, variable in colour, usually with tan or brownish-green ss. and ps., the proportionately very large lip white to cream-white with a more or less prominent apical, lilac area. Ss. and ps. reflexed. Lip with a very large funnel-like spur, the lamina tubular-concave, the keeled disc with a central, hairy band in front. Mostly winter, sometimes almost ever-blooming. (I, H) Amazonian Peru.

GALEOLA Lour.
(*Cyrtosia* Bl., *Erythrorchis* Bl., *Haematorchis* Bl., *Ledgeria* FvM., *Pogochilus* Falc.)

Galeola consists of more than eighty species of extraordinary, virtually leafless, saprophytic, vine-like orchids, whose distribution extends from Japan and Malaya throughout Indonesia to Australia, New Guinea, and New Caledonia. A member of the subtribe *Vanillinae*, very few of the species have ever been in cultivation, since—like most saprophytes—they are almost impossible to keep alive for any appreciable period under artificial conditions. In the case of this genus, this is particularly unfortunate, since *Galeola* contains some of the most spectacular and unusual of all orchidaceous plants. In many of the species, for example, the elongate vine-like stems attain lengths in excess of sixty or even one hundred feet, and when in full flower, produce immense panicles of literally thousands of rather handsome blossoms!

No hybrids are known in this group, and nothing has been ascertained concerning its genetic affinities as yet.

CULTURE: Galeolas may be kept alive for a year or so through carefully transplanting a large surrounding section of the soil in which they naturally grow, into well-drained, very large pots, with as little disturbance of the root-system as possible. A rather sunny spot, high temperatures and humidity, and copious water at all times seem necessary, but scant success can be expected with these gigantic saprophytic vines for more than a single season under artificial conditions. Perhaps additional experiment will solve many of the problems attendant in the cultivation of the saprophytic genera of the Orchidaceae. (I, H)

G. cassythoides (A.Cunn.) Rchb.f. (*Dendrobium cassythoides* A.Cunn., *Ledgeria aphylla* FvM.)
Sts. brownish, to as tall as 20', freely branching, clambering on shrubs and trees. Bracts of the sts. small, broad, acute. Fls. about ½" long, produced in very large paniculate infls., these in robust specimens containing upwards of 1000 fls. Ss. and ps. yellow flushed with brown, oblong-lanceolate, the ps. slightly shorter. Lip whitish with transverse brown or reddish streaks, complex, the surface mostly furnished with calli and patches of fuzz. Autumn–winter. (H) Australia: New South Wales, Queensland.

GASTORCHIS Thou.
(*Gastrorchis* Schltr.)

Six species of *Gastorchis* are known to date, five of them endemic to Madagascar, the sixth found only in the Mascarene Islands. Two of them are present in our collections at this time, but they are extremely rare and most desirable orchids. In the wild, they are variously epiphytic or terrestrial, certain of the species often being found exclusively on a single species of tree, such as *Pandanus*. The Gastorchis are usually erroneously called *Phaius* in horticulture, and although they are allied to that group, are completely distinct generically. *Gastorchis tuberculosa* (Thou.) Schltr. has on occasion been referred to as one of the finest and most spectacular of all orchidaceous plants.

Gastorchis has been successfully crossed with *Phaius*, to give *Gastophaius*, and with *Calanthe*, to give *Gastocalanthe*, although the hybrids resultant are now excessively rare in cultivation. H. Perrier de la Bâthie notes that natural hybrids between *G. Françoisii* Schltr. and *G. Humblotii* (Rchb.f.) Schltr. (the first-named species does not appear to be in cultivation at this time) have been detected in Madagascar. Considerable additional experimental breeding utilizing these very fine orchids seems to offer some fascinating potentials.

CULTURE: Both of the cultivated Gastorchis are terrestrial plants in nature, hence should be treated much in the manner of the tropical species of *Phaius*. Although they are magnificent orchids, they are regrettably often rather refractory under cultivation, and in many instances deteriorate rapidly after a few years, no matter how ideal the cultural conditions may supposedly be. (H)

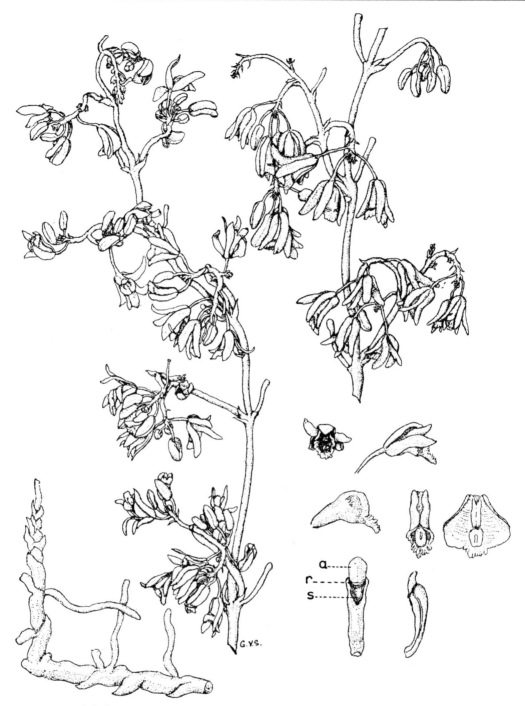

Galeola cassythoides (A.Cunn). Rchb.f. [Rupp, *Orchids of New South Wales*]

G. Humblotii (Rchb.f.) Schltr. (*Phaius Humblotii* Rchb.f.)

Pbs. tightly clustered, sub-globose, about 1½″ in diam., with 2–3 prominent rings after the lvs. have fallen. Lvs. several, deciduous in time, broadly lanceolate, acuminate, plicate, rather heavy-textured, to 2′ long and 4″ broad, narrowed below into channelled, winged petioles. Infls. erect, robust, to 2′ tall and more,

the apical rac. 7–12-fld., the fls. opening successively over a long period of time. Fls. to more than 2″ in diam., long-lasting, light rose-purple more or less suffused with white, the large, complex lip variable in colour. Ss. and ps. spreading, similar and subequal, broadly obovate-elliptic, acutish or with the ps. sometimes retuse. Lip broadly panduriform, the margins all crisped and undulate; lat. lbs. spreading up around the col., notched at the edge, reddish-brown passing to crimson marginally; midlb. flaring, rose-purple with a whitish centre, on which are 2 large inwardly pointing bright yellow teeth. Col. slender, gracefully arching, terete and greenish above. Winter–spring. (I, H) Madagascar.

G. tuberculosa (Thou.) Schltr. (*Limodorum tuberculosum* Thou., *Phaius tuberculosus* Bl., *Phaius tuberculatus* Bl., *Phaius Warpuri* Weath.)

Pbs. fusiform, strongly ringed, prostrate or slightly ascending, 2–4″ long. Lvs. several, heavy-textured, oblong-lanceolate, acuminate, 10–15″ long, in time deciduous. Infls. erect, stout, to 2′ tall, sheathed with a whitish bract at each joint, with a 5–7-fld. rac. at the apex, the fls. opening successively over a rather long period. Fls. to almost 3″ in diam., very handsome and long-lived. Ss. and ps. white, spreading, elliptic-oblong, acuminate, with a depressed line above, slightly carinate beneath. Lip 3-lbd., the lat. lbs. large, suborbicular, meeting above the col. and forming a wide-mouthed funnel, orange-yellow copiously spotted with red-purple and studded with white bristly hairs; midlb. sub-quadrate, emarginate, with a crisped margin and dark yellow callus on the disc consisting of 3 broad toothed ridges, white blotched with rose; below the callus is a dense tuft of sulphur-yellow hairs. Col. club-shaped, arching, white above, purplish on anterior face. Autumn. (I, H) Madagascar.

GASTROCHILUS D.Don

Gastrochilus is a genus of about fifteen species of epiphytic (very rarely lithophytic) orchids native in the region extending from Japan and the Himalayas to Indonesia. Several of the component members are present in collections today, almost invariably being grown under the erroneous and confusing name *Saccolabium*, which applies to an entirely distinct genus of the subtribe *Sarcanthinae*. They are usually rather dwarf monopodial plants with but a few leathery leaves, and produce few-flowered inflorescences (often more than one per node at a given season) of small to rather large, often spectacular flowers. The genus is most closely allied, apparently, to *Sarcochilus* R.Br., but is distinguished from all related groups by technical details of the flowers.

A single natural hybrid has been recorded and may be in cultivation, namely *Gastrochilus x bellino-bigibbus* (*G. bellinus* × *G. bigibbus*), native in Burma. Additional critical interspecific breeding should produce some intriguing results, and multigeneric hybridization with allied groups (e.g., *Vanda*, *Aërides*, *Phalaenopsis*, *Renanthera*, etc.) opens up an entirely new and potentially fascinating field to the enterprising enthusiast.

CULTURE: As for *Vanda*, depending upon the species and its place of origin. (I, H)

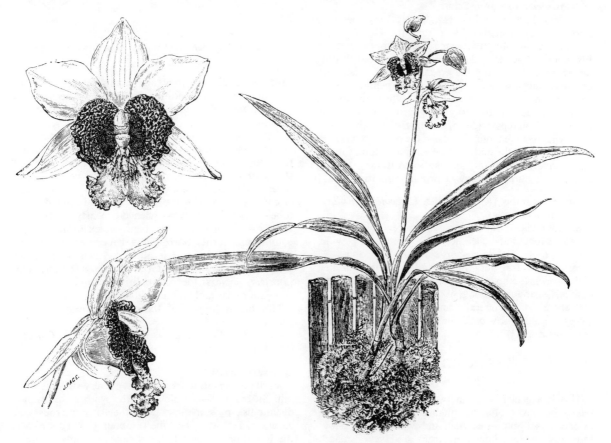

Gastorchis tuberculosa (Thou.) Schltr. [VEITCH]

G. bellinus (Rchb.f.) O.Ktze. (*Saccolabium bellinum* Rchb.f.)

Sts. very short and stout, usually less than 2″ tall, rooting freely. Lvs. usually 6–8, narrowly ligulate, unequally 2-lbd. at tip, rigidly leathery, to 8″ long and 1¼″ wide. Infls. usually erect, densely 4–7-fld., the scape robust. Fls. fragrant, waxy, long-lived, about 1½″ across, the ss. and ps. greenish-yellow with purple spots and blotches, the lip white spotted with dull or bright red. Ss. and smaller ps. oblong, obtuse, often rather concave. Lip complex, the middle part with a large tuft of filiform hair-like processes on each side, the centre bright yellow, the base sac-like. Late winter-spring. (I) Burma.

G. bigibbus (Rchb.f.) O.Ktze. (*Saccolabium bigibbum* Rchb.f.)

St. very short, stout. Lvs. few, ligulate to linear-oblong, unequally 2-lbd. at apex, bright green, leathery, to 5″ long and 1½″ wide. Infls. drooping, short-stalked, densely 10–20-fld., the blossoms arranged in a corymb. Fls. about 1″ across, waxy, long-lived, fragrant, the ss. and ps. golden-yellow, paler towards the base, the lip white with a yellow centre. Ss. and ps. oblong, obtuse, wide-spreading. Lip with the middle part broadly tri-angular, the margins fringed, the spur very broad and blunt. Autumn. (I) Burma.

G. calceolaris D. Don (*Saccolabium calceolare* Ldl., *Gastrochilus sororius* Schltr.)

St. very short, stout. Lvs. 3–6, ligulate, very unequally 2-toothed at tips, leathery, to 7″ long and ¾″ wide. Infls. very short, few-fld., the scape purple-spotted, stout. Fls. about ¾″ across, waxy, somewhat fragrant, lasting rather well, the ss. and ps. greenish or yellowish with brown or purplish spots, the sac of the lip yellow outside, with brown spots, the small lat. lbs. white, the midlb. with fringed edges and a fleshy orange central part, the col. purplish. Ss. and ps. wide-spreading, the ss. particularly somewhat recurved, blunt apically, the ps. narrower. Lip with a large sac, the midlb. twice as wide as long, almost semicircular, hairy on all parts. Autumn. (I, H) Himalayas; Burma; Malay Peninsula; Sumatra; Java.

G. platycalcaratus (Rolfe) Schltr. (*Saccolabium platy-calcaratum* Rolfe)

St. abbreviated, rather robust. Lvs. few, oblong, unequally 2-lbd. at apex, leathery, to 2″ long and ¾″ wide. Infls. densely 6–9-fld., short-stalked. Fls. about ½″ across, waxy, fragrant, the ss. and ps. yellow flecked with brown, the lip white with a greenish callus in the middle. Ss. and ps. oblong, obtuse, wide-spreading. Lip with the basal part laterally compressed, the upper part almost round, finely papillose on upper surface. Late winter-spring. (I) Burma.

GASTRODIA R.Br.
(*Gamoplexis* Falc.)

This is a genus of about twenty species of seldom-seen saprophytic orchids, inhabiting the region which extends from South-east Asia and Malaya throughout Indonesia to New Guinea, Australia, and New Zealand. Like most members of this peculiar group of orchids

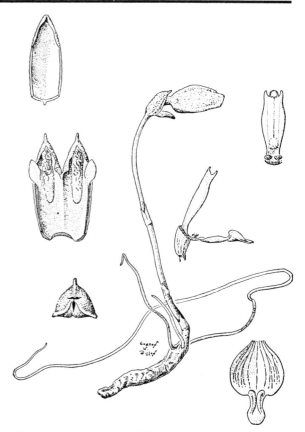

Gastrodia crassisepala L.O.Wms. [GORDON W. DILLON]

called saprophytes, they are virtually impossible to maintain in good condition beyond a single season's growth, but their unique appearance and strange floral structure make them of singular interest to every connoisseur. Growing on decaying organic matter, the Gastrodias typically have roughened, superficially tuberous rhizomes, from which elongate, scaly-bracted stems arise. These, in turn, give rise to an apical raceme of a few flowers which are almost unique in the Orchidaceae in having the sepals and petals united into a tube—which is usually roughened or warty on its outer surface—within which the rather complex lip and lengthy column are borne. *Gastrodia* is a member of the sub-tribe *Gastrodiinae*, and is allied to such little-known groups as *Didymoplexis* Griff., *Auxopus* Schltr., etc. Like *Didymoplexis*, the fruiting structures of these orchids elongate remarkably after fertilization.

Nothing is known of the genetic affinities of this genus.

CULTURE: Presumably as for *Corallorrhiza*, *Galeola*, etc. (I, H)

G. sesamoides R.Br.

Variable in stature from robust to very slender, to 2′ tall. St.-bracts 3–4, scale-like. Rac. with a few rather distant fls., or sometimes with the fls. numerous and crowded. Fls. with the tube to about ½″ long, whitish, the lbs. short or broad. Lip yellow or orange, with a dilated claw, oblong, very blunt, the margins strongly undulate, the blade with a single longitudinal ridge bordered by calli, ending in a multiple gland. Autumn–late winter. (I, H) Australia; New Zealand.

GEISSANTHERA Schltr.

About seventeen species of *Geissanthera* are known to date, the vast majority of them native in the high, mossy 'cloud forests' of New Guinea, with outlying representatives in the Philippines, the Caroline Islands, and Samoa. A member of the subtribe *Sarcanthinae*, these typically very small epiphytic orchids are unknown in contemporary collections, and are primarily of botanical interest. The genus was at one time reduced to synonymy under *Microtatorchis* Schltr., but it has been proven to be distinct.

Nothing is known of the genetic alliances of *Geissanthera*.

CULTURE: Probably as for *Ornithocephalus* and other moisture-loving orchids. (I, H)

GENNARIA Parlat.

A single species of *Gennaria* is known, this an unusual terrestrial orchid of the subtribe *Habenarinae*, widespread in the Mediterranean region, and in Madeira and the Canary Islands. Formerly placed in *Gymnadenia* and *Coeloglossum*, it differs in its odd habit and the *Habenaria*-like stigmas. It is a rare plant in cultivation at this time.

Nothing is known of the genetic affinities of this orchid. CULTURE: As for *Habenaria*. (I)

G. diphylla (Link) Parlat. (*Satyrium diphyllum* Link, *Orchis cordata* Willd., *Gymnadenia diphylla* Link, *Coeloglossum diphyllum* Fiori & Parlat.)

Tubers oblong. St. 6–12″ tall, with 2 lvs. in upper part. Lvs. narrowly ovate, acute, the upper one the smaller. Infl. erect, the rac. to 4″ long, many-fld. Fls. small, yellow-green. Ss. and ps. oblong, obtuse. Lip deeply 3-lbd., with a short rounded spur. Feb.–Mar. (I) Southern Spain and Portugal; Sardinia; North Africa; Madeira; Canary Islands.

GENYORCHIS Schltr.

The typical genus of the small subtribe *Genyorchidinae*, *Genyorchis* consists of about five very rare epiphytic orchids in the tropical parts of Africa, only one of which is present in collections at this time, and this a very rare plant. Somewhat allied to *Monomeria* Ldl., the genus is a distinctive one, vegetatively simulating a *Bulbophyllum*, but with floral characters approaching those of a *Polystachya*.

No hybrids are known in *Genyorchis*, and nothing has been ascertained concerning its genetic affinities.

CULTURE: As for the tropical Bulbophyllums. (H)

G. pumila (Sw.) Schltr. (*Dendrobium pumilum* Sw., *Bulbophyllum pumilum* Ldl., *Bulbophyllum apetalum* Ldl., *Polystachya bulbophylloides* Rolfe)

Rhiz. elongated, creeping, slender. Pbs. borne at intervals along the rhiz., oblong, about ¼–½″ tall. Lvs. paired, ligulate, rather fleshy, to ¾″ long. Infls. loosely 5–12-fld., erect or arching, to about 2″ tall at most.

Fls. less than ¼″ long, white, with a red blotch on the lip. Ps. diminutive, white with red margins. Spring–early summer. (H) Tropical Africa, mostly in the Congo region.

GEODORUM Jacks.
(*Cistella* Bl., *Otandra* Salisb.)

Geodorum is a genus of about ten species of rarely cultivated but unusually attractive terrestrial orchids, native over a huge area extending from India throughout South-east Asia, Malaya, Indonesia, the Philippines, and adjacent insular areas to Australia and New Guinea. They are placed in the subtribe *Eulophiinae*. Almost round, somewhat compressed pseudobulbs are borne under the ground, from which arise a few broad, stalked, folded leaves, and the erect, often elongate inflorescences. In *Geodorum*, the medium-sized, not widely-opening flowers are borne in a dense head-like raceme which is sharply pendulous, thus giving the inflorescence a most unusual appearance. The blossoms usually do not last well, though the waxy texture, delightful fragrance, and charmingly delicate colour-schemes presented by the different species offer much to the connoisseur.

No hybrids are as yet known in this genus, and its genetic compatibilities have not been explored.

CULTURE: Geodorums are not difficult to grow, if treated much in the same manner as the tropical species of *Phaius*. Perfect drainage, a rather shady spot, rich compost, a large container, and abundant fertilizer seem requisite for best growth. When the new pseudobulbs have matured, and the flower-spikes have withered, a brief resting-period (of about two weeks' duration) should be given, when water is strictly withheld, and humidity cut down. Annual division and repotting seem necessary for good flowering and large growths. (I, H)

G. candidum Wall. (*Geodorum attenuatum* Griff.)

Pbs. subterranean, roundish, somewhat compressed. Lvs. usually deciduous after one season, erect, folded, stalked basally, to 1½′ tall, the blade about 12″ long and 3″ wide, elliptic, acute or acuminate, strongly 5–7-veined, the bases sheathing. Infls. erect, to about 12″ tall, the rather dense rac. sharply pendulous, the fls. clustered, the cluster roundish apically, opening a few at a time over a rather long period. Fls. fragrant, waxy, ascending or erect, about 1½″ across, fragrant, the ss. and ps. milk-white, the lip white veined with red and yellow. Lip with a crisped apex. Summer. (I) Burma.

G. citrinum Jacks.

Similar in habit to *G. candidum* Wall., the lvs. usually wider, to about 5″ broad. Fls. opening well, about 1½″ in diam., the ss. and ps. white or pale yellow, the lip yellowish with more or less definite red veins over its entire surface. Lip-margins somewhat down-curved, the base with a small sac. Summer. (I, H) Burma; Thailand; Malay Peninsula.

G. pictum (R.Br.) Ldl. (*Cymbidium pictum* R.Br.)

Rhiz. fleshy, the basally thickened sts. to 15″ tall. Lvs. 1 or 2, to 15″ long, the midrib very prominent. Infl. robust, with several loose sheaths, the rac. at first erect,

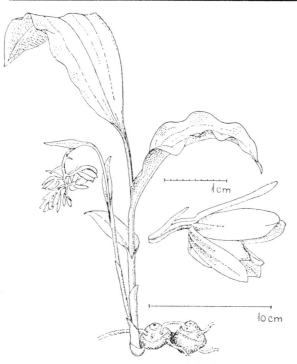

Geodorum purpureum R.Br. [*Orchids of Thailand*]

GLOMERA Bl.

Despite the fact that it is the type genus of the large and very intricate subtribe *Glomerinae*, and contains more than fifty species, *Glomera* is evidently unknown in contemporary collections. The members of the genus inhabit for the most part the montane forests of New Guinea, and are often rather common orchids there. Primarily smallish in stature, they are odd plants, often most 'un-orchidaceous' in appearance, producing head-like inflorescences of small but complex, often brightly-hued flowers. They seem to offer some intriguing potentials for the specialist in the more delicate 'botanical' orchids.

then gradually bending over until mature; rather numerous fls. face downwards; after fertilization this part again straightens and becomes erect. Fls. less than 1″ in diam., usually not opening well, pink, the lip veined or streaked with purplish-red. Lip very broad across the wavy-margined basal lbs. Summer. (I, H) Australia; New Guinea; New Caledonia; Fiji Islands.

G. purpureum R.Br. (*Geodorum dilatatum* Wall., *Limodorum nutans* Roxb., *Malaxis nutans* Willd.)

Similar in general habit to *G. candidum* Wall., but usually more robust, the peduncle of the infl. thick, the rachis elongating, bearing a succession of many fls., a few open at one time. Fls. about ¾″ in diam., waxy, fragrant, not expanding fully, pink or white, the lip pink with a wide yellow median area, the remainder veined with dark pink. Lip fleshy, concave, the blade narrowed to a slightly cleft tip. Summer. (I, H) Burma and Thailand through Malaya and Indonesia to New Guinea, New Caledonia and Northern Australia (Queensland).

GIULIANETTIA Rolfe

Two New Guinean species of *Giulianettia* have been described—**G. tenuis** Rolfe and **G. viridis** Schltr.—neither of which is present in even the most specialized of collections at this time. They are allied to *Glossorhyncha* Ridl. of the subtribe *Glomerinae*, but differ from that genus in technical details of the small, insignificant flowers. The group is principally of scientific interest, and is very incompletely known at this time.

Nothing is known of the genetic affinities of *Giulianettia*.

CULTURE: Presumably as for *Glomera*. (C, I)

Glomera keytsiana J.J.Sm. [J.J.SMITH AND NATA-DIPURA]

Nothing is known concerning the genetic affinities of the genus *Glomera*.

CULTURE: Presumably as for *Ornithocephalus*, although somewhat cooler conditions would seem necessary than for most of those orchids. (C, I)

GLOSSODIA R.Br.

Glossodia is a member of the subtribe *Caladeniinae*, with five known species, all endemic to Australia. Very handsome and showy terrestrial plants, they are extremely scarce in cultivation today, and, like most of the Australian ground orchids, are singularly difficult to grow and maintain in good condition for more than a single season. The genus is somewhat allied to *Eriochilus* R.Br. and to *Caladenia* R.Br., but differs in technical details of the flowers.

Natural hybridization between the two species noted below has been suggested by Rupp (*Orch. N.S.Wales* 72. 1943). Nothing is known of the genetic affinities of *Glossodia*, but it is conceivably inter-fertile with at least some other members of the subtribe to which it belongs.

CULTURE: As for *Caladenia*. (C, I)

G. major R.Br. (*Caladenia major* Rchb.f.)

Tubers small, ovoid, subterranean. St. very slender, to 15″ tall, with a solitary lf. near the base that is prostrate on the ground in most cases, this lf. oblong or lanceolate, to 6″ long, hairy, when dry vanilla-scented. Fls. 1–2 (rarely 3), to 2½″ across, purplish to pure white, the basal part of the lip white, the anterior part purple, the base with a large erect callus (2 calli fused into 1) with 2 yellow heads. Ss. and ps. lanceolate, obtuse to acutish, the reverse surfaces paler. Lip ovate-lanceolate, contracted at base, straight, the basal part pubescent, dilated laterally into 2 bosses with a median furrow, the anterior part glabrous. Autumn. (C, I) Australia.

G. minor R.Br. (*Caladenia minor* Rchb.f.)

Similar in habit to *G. major* R.Br., but smaller in all parts, to 7″ tall. Lf. and lower part of st. very hairy, the lf. broadly lanceolate, prostrate on the ground, to 1¾″ long. Fls. 1–2, about 1¼″ across, deep violet-blue, rarely white, the lip not white at the base, as in the other-named sp. Ss. and ps. broadly lanceolate, the reverse surfaces paler, bluntish apically. Lip ovate, acute, straight, the surface similar to that of the other-noted sp., the base with 2 linear clavate calli that are connate at their bases. Col. erect, the anther acute. Summer–autumn. (C, I) Australia.

GLOSSORHYNCHA Ridl.

Glossorhyncha is, like most of the members of the little-known subtribe *Glomerinae*, unfortunately not present in contemporary collections, although many of its more than sixty component species offer much of interest to the specialist in the 'botanical' orchids. These epiphytic or lithophytic (very rarely terrestrial) plants are native for the most part in New Guinea, though a few species extend as far afield as the Caroline Islands. They simulate in large degree *Glomera* Bl., but differ in their more slender leafy stems, the fringed sheaths, and the secund, larger, white flowers, which are of distinctive structure.

Nothing is known of the genetic affinities of *Glossorhyncha* at this time.

CULTURE: Presumably as for *Glomera* and *Bulbophyllum*. Some of the Glossorhynchas inhabit the high-elevation 'cloud forests' of New Guinea, hence will require constantly cool and moist conditions, much as those suggested for the alpine Odontoglossums, etc. (C, I, H)

GOADBYELLA R.S.Rog.

Goadbyella consists of a single known species, this a very scarce and not well-delimited orchid of the subtribe *Prasophyllinae*, native in Australia. It is a terrestrial plant, not present in our collections at this time, and is in any event principally of scientific interest and importance.

Nothing is known of the genetic affinities of this rare group.

CULTURE: Presumably as for *Caladenia*. (C, I)

GOMESA R.Br.
(*Gomesia* Spreng., *Gomeza* Ldl., *Gomezia* Bartl.)

Gomesa is a genus of about ten species of rather dwarf, singularly attractive epiphytic or lithophytic orchids in Brazil. Closely allied to *Oncidium* Sw. and to *Hellerorchis* A.D.Hawkes, they are but little known in contemporary collections outside of their native land, though their floriferous habits and ease of cultivation assuredly recommend them to all enthusiasts. Pseudobulbous plants, they give rise to arching or pendulous, densely many-flowered racemes of unusually-shaped, fragrant, greenish-yellow, yellow, or whitish blossoms with great lasting qualities. The lateral sepals in this genus's flowers are typically joined behind the lip, and all of the narrow floral segments are attractively wavy. The general conformation of the blossoms gives to this genus the common name of 'Little Man Orchids'.

No hybrids have as yet been produced in *Gomesa*, although the genus is presumably inter-fertile with at least some of the allied groups of the subtribe *Oncidiinae*.

CULTURE: Generally as for the tropical, pseudobulbous Oncidiums. These rather small epiphytes do equally well mounted on tree-fern slabs, or in well-drained pots tightly filled with osmunda or shredded tree-fern fibre. They normally grow throughout the year, and delight in a rather bright spot in the collection. Periodic applications of fertilizers are most beneficial. (I, H)

G. crispa (Ldl.) Kl. & Rchb.f. (*Rodriguezia crispa* Ldl., *Odontoglossum crispulum* Rchb.f.)

Pbs. oblong, compressed, usually dull yellow-green, tightly clustered, to 4″ tall. Lvs. 2, ligulate, acutish, rather soft-textured, to 8″ long and 1½″ wide. Infls. gracefully arching to almost pendulous, densely many-fld., to 8″ long. Fls. fragrant, about ¾″ long, yellow-green, all the segms. very crisped and undulate. Ss. and ps. oblong, obtuse, widespreading, the lat. ss. joined at the base, the tips spreading. Lip oblong, obtuse, simple, with 2 blunt keels on the disc. Spring–early summer. (I, H) Brazil.

G. planifolia (Ldl.) Kl. & Rchb.f. (*Rodriguezia plani-folia* Ldl., *Odontoglossum planifolium* Rchb.f.)
Similar in habit to *G. crispa* (Ldl.) Kl. & Rchb.f. Infls. to 10″ long, densely many-fld., arching gracefully. Fls. about ¾″ long, fragrant, greenish-yellow, the segms. rather crisped marginally, the lat. ss. joined for about two-thirds of their length, the lip ovate-oblong, with a short apicule at tip. Summer. (I, H) Brazil.

G. recurva (Ldl.) R.Br. (*Rodriguezia recurva* Ldl., *Gomesa densiflora* Hoffmsgg., *Odontoglossum re-curvum* Rchb.f.)
Similar to the above-noted spp. in habit, the racs. more dense, the ss. and ps. not undulate nor crisped, spatulate, the lat. ss. longer, the lip ovate, obtuse, with 2 broad, rather prominent keels on the disc. Spring–autumn. (I, H) Brazil.

G. laxiflora (Ldl.) Kl. & Rchb.f. (*Rodriguezia laxiflora* Ldl., *Gomesa chrysostoma* Hoffmsgg., *Odontoglossum laxiflorum* Rchb.f.) Similar in habit to *G. crispa* (Ldl.) Kl. & Rchb.f., the pbs. to 2½″ tall, the lvs. acuminate. Infls. loosely many-fld., to 12″ long, arching to pendulous. Fls. smaller than the above-noted sp., the ss. and ps. not undulate, the lat. ss. joined almost throughout, the lip ovate-oblong, with 2 prominent keels on the disc. Spring–summer. (I, H) Brazil.

G. sessilis B.-R. Similar to the other sp. in habit, the lvs. acute. Infls. to more than 12″ long, rather densely many-fld., differing from the other spp. in the essentially stalkless fls. Fls. about ½″ long, fragrant, yellow-green, the ss. and ps. ligulate, acute, the lat. ss. joined almost throughout, the lip ovate-oblong, with 2 large keels on the disc. Spring–summer. (I, H) Brazil.

GOMPHICHIS Ldl.

Gomphichis consists of about ten species of rather nondescript, large-growing, terrestrial orchids of the subtribe *Cranichidinae*, mostly natives of the mountainous areas of northwestern South America. The genus is very closely allied to *Stenoptera* Presl, and has been included within it in the past. None of them is in cultivation at this time, and in any event because of the diminutive dimensions of the blossoms, they are primarily of scientific interest.

Nothing is known of the genetic affinities of *Gomphichis*.

CULTURE: Presumably as for *Spiranthes*, *Habenaria*, and the like. (C, I)

GONATOSTYLIS Schltr.

Gonatostylis is an extremely rare and incompletely-known genus of the subtribe *Physurinae*, containing but a single species, **G. Vieillardii** Schltr., a terrestrial orchid as yet unknown in our collections. It is one of the 'Jewel Orchids', with variegated foliage and tiny but complex blossoms, and appears to be endemic to New Caledonia.

Nothing is known of the genetic affinities of *Gonatostylis*, though it seems logical that it will prove genetically compatible with at least certain of its allied genera.

CULTURE: Presumably as for *Anoectochilus*. (H)

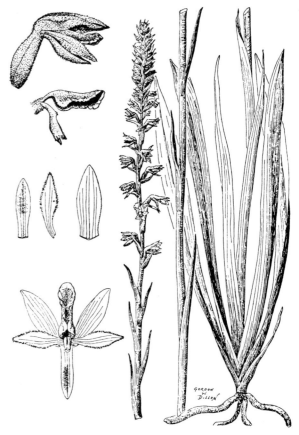

Gomphichis Macbridei C.Schw. [GORDON W. DILLON]

GONGORA R. & P.
(*Acropera* Ldl.)

Although many more names have been proposed, it now seems evident that only about twelve or so valid species (and several well-defined variants) of *Gongora* are known to science. These range from Mexico to Peru and Brazil, and are among the most extraordinary of all American orchids. Usually found growing on trees (rarely on rocks or in soil on rocky hillsides), they have clustered, ovoid, strongly ridged pseudobulbs with two or three apical, plicate leaves much like those of the allied Stanhopeas. The inflorescences are typically elongate (sometimes to three feet and more) pendulous racemes, borne from the pseudobulb-bases, with a few to very many amazingly intricate and fascinating, often highly coloured and strongly-scented flowers. Two distinct sections of the genus have been established by Pfitzer: *Acropera* (formerly considered a separate genus), and *Eugongora*. In section *Acropera*, the pedicellate ovaries are usually strongly curving; the lateral sepals are about as broad as long, spreading or somewhat reflexed, and the sepals and petals are all somewhat connivent at the base; the lip has a narrow, short or elongate, ligulate basal claw; the mesochil is conspicuously lobed or inflated and saccate but rarely has apical horns or antennae; the epichil is elongate, lanceolate and acuminate and sometimes reduced to an

VIIA *Mormodes Hookeri* Lem. [H.A.DUNN]

VIIB *Neocogniauxia monophylla* (Griseb.) Schltr. [JOHN LAGER]

obscure apicule, or divided and two-parted at the tip; the column is slender and somewhat arching, dilated at the tip, sometimes narrowly winged and obscurely two-horned, and has a foot at the base. In section *Eugongora*, the pedicellate ovaries are nearly straight; the lateral sepals are usually almost twice as long as broad, strongly reflexed, the apex acuminate, the margins strongly reflexed, the bases inserted on the column-foot; the dorsal sepal and petals are inserted on the upper part of the column, and their bases are not connivent with those of the lateral sepals; the lip is very fleshy, often laterally compressed, complexly 2-parted, with both a well-developed hypochil and epichil; the base of the hypochil is either with or without short, lateral, rounded, ligulate or ear-like callosities, and the apical margin usually has two slender, erect antennae; the epichil usually has a gibbous or conical, basal projection above the basal constriction; the column is slender and somewhat curving, semiterete below and dilated above, without lateral wings, but with the inserted petals resembling stelidia. As may be deduced from the comments given above, floral structure in *Gongora* is indeed complex, and it is often very difficult to describe lucidly the various parts in mere words. These intriguing orchids are not common in collections today, but several of the species and their variants are grown by some enthusiasts, and the genus as a whole should be better known. When well-grown, certain of the Gongoras will flower more than once annually, and certain phases of *G. maculata* Ldl. seem to be almost everblooming, thus making them of unique value to the collector.

The breeders have not as yet taken *Gongora* in hand, though interspecific crossing should prove most interesting, and the possibility of multigeneric hybrids with allied genera of the subtribe *Gongorinae* should be explored by enterprising experimenters. Although at this time nothing is known concerning the genetic alliances of this group of orchids, it seems logical to assume that at least some of the *Gongorinae* will prove 'crossable' with *Gongora* itself. The resultant progeny should be unusual in the extreme!

CULTURE: Generally as for *Stanhopea* and *Acineta*, although—because of the not strictly pendulous inflorescences (they usually arch outward from the base of the plant, and then downwards)—they may also be grown in hanging pots, rather than slatted baskets. A compost such as that suggested for the other noted genera is suitable, and the plants need humid, moist conditions at all times, although a brief resting-period upon completion of flowering seems advantageous in most species. Regular and frequent applications of fertilizing materials are recommended. Some difficulty is occasionally encountered in making the almost mature floral buds remain on the spray. This seems best controlled by placing the plants (when at this stage of development) in a cooler, shadier spot in the collection, and stopping all water at the roots until after the expansion of the flowers. Moisture on either the buds or the open flowers often causes spotting or premature falling. In most cases, the blossoms of this genus remain in good condition for a week or more. (I, H)

G. armeniaca (Ldl. & Paxt.) Rchb.f. (*Acropera armeniaca* Ldl. & Paxt., *Acropera cornuta* Kl.)

Habit as in the genus, the pbs. to about 2″ long, the lvs. paired, to 9″ long and about 2″ broad. Infls. of variable length, few- to many-fld., arching downward to strongly pendent. Fls. rather waxy, fragrant of apricots, somewhat variable in structure, to about 2″ long, inverted (the lip uppermost), the ss. yellow, orange, or salmon-coloured, sometimes spotted with purple-brown, the ps. pale salmon or orange, the lip usually similar in colour but darker, the mesochil waxy yellow. Ss. membranaceous, the bases all connivent, the dors. one erect, concave, elliptic-oblong and acute to broadly rectangular and obtuse or shortly apiculate; lat. ss. spreading or reflexed, their bases inserted on the col.-foot, obliquely ovate, acute or obtuse and short-apiculate. Ps. membranaceous, lanceolate, abruptly acuminate, sometimes subfalcate, the attenuate tips usually recurved, the bases broadly spreading and connivent with the sepal-bases. Lip with a short, ligulate, basal claw, the mesochil inflated, subcalceiform, the apex broadly obtuse, with a short or elongate, erect, linear-lanceolate, acuminate projection. Col. erect, dilated and almost club-shaped above. Summer–autumn. (I, H) Nicaragua; Costa Rica; Panama.

G. atropurpurea Hk. (*Acropera atropurpurea* Ldl., *Cirrhaea atropurpurea* hort. ex Stein, *Gongora Heisteri* hort. ex Rchb.f.)

Similar to the genus in habit, the pbs. strongly ridged, to almost 3″ long and 1¼″ in diam., the lvs. to 1½′ long. Infls. usually sharply pendulous, the peduncle and rachis usually reddish, to 2¼′ long, the rac. rather loosely many-fld. Fls. fragrant, about 1½″ long, variable in colour, but usually dark red or purplish-red, often with more or less dense spotting of darker colour on all segms. Ss. acuminate, the dors. erect, narrowly oval-oblong, concave, narrowed basally, the lats. narrowly oval-trapezoidal, very oblique, spreading or reflexed, convex, with recurved margins. Ps. inserted near the middle of the col., oval-lanceolate, apically obliquely acuminate, basally decurrent on the col. Lip much shorter than the lat. ss., with a long, slender basal claw, depressed on the hypochil but enlarging apically, with horn-like projections on each side; epichil vertically compressed, sub-sagittate, recurved and mucronulate at apex. Col. slender, very incurved, clavate towards tip. Summer. (H) Venezuela; Trinidad; Guianas; Northern Brazil (Amazonas).

G. bufonia Ldl. (*Gongora irrorata* Hoffmsgg.)

Habit as for the genus, the pbs. strongly ridged and somewhat angular-winged with age, to 1½″ tall and 1″ in diam., the paired lvs. to 1½′ long and 2⅓″ broad, rather heavily leathery, strongly plicate. Infls. pendulous, the rachis angular and sinuous, densely many-fld., to almost 3′ long (often shorter). Fls. inverted, nodding, membranaceous (except for the lip), rose-red or rich-red more or less dotted and spotted with darker red or brownish-red, about 2″ long at most, fragrant. Dors. sep. erect, narrowly ligulate-oblong, inserted on the middle of the col., the lats. larger, obliquely triangular-oblong, reflexed somewhat, somewhat falcate. Ps.

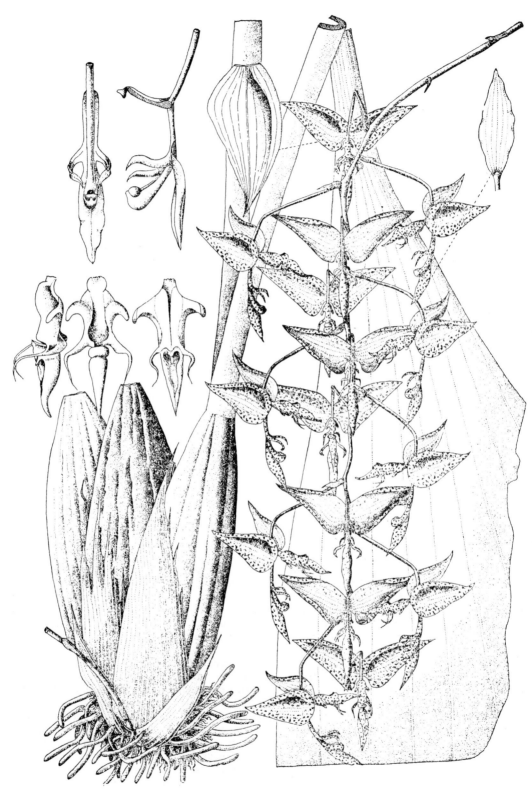

Gongora maculata Ldl. [Hoehne, *Flora Brasílica*]

narrowly linear-ligulate, apically narrowly and obliquely acuminate, basally long-decurrent by the sides of the col. Lip slightly longer than the lat. ss., almost sessile, basally obtuse, the hypochil fleshy, sometimes pubescent outside, usually without appendages; epichil triangular-acuminate, strongly uncinate, angular on lower base, fleshy. Col. clavate, narrowing and almost terete towards the base. Autumn–winter. (I, H) Brazil.

G. maculata Ldl. (*Gongora Boothiana* hort., *G. Jenischii* hort., *G. leucochila* Lem., *G. nigrita* Ldl., *G. odoratissima* Lem., *G. unicolor* Schltr.)

Pbs. clustered, ovoid to cylindric-ovoid, strongly ridged and sulcate, to $2\frac{1}{2}''$ tall and $1\frac{1}{2}''$ in diam., with 2–3 fibrous bracts at base. Lvs. 2–3, glossy, rigidly leathery, usually undulate marginally, lanceolate to elliptic-lanceolate, acute or acuminate, plicate, to 15″ long and $4\frac{1}{2}''$ wide. Infls. elongate, pendulous, many-fld., to more than 3′ long, slender. Fls. strongly fragrant (usually of spices), extremely variable in colour, and somewhat so in size and structure, to $1\frac{1}{2}''$ long, the lip uppermost. Ss. membranaceous, pale yellow, variously spotted or banded with reddish-brown, to rich mahogany-red, the dors. one inserted about halfway up the col., the lats. strongly reflexed. Ps. similar in colour to the ss., their bases inserted on the col., somewhat recurved at the tips, much smaller than the ss. Lip fleshy, pale yellow marked with reddish-brown, ranging to dark reddish-brown or mahogany-red, with a short claw at the base, then a sac-like hypochil with 2 erect lat. lbs. which have an erect lengthy antenna on each side; epichil laterally compressed, vaguely sac-like above the constriction, the tip elongate, recurved. Col. dilated above the point of insertion of the dors. sep. and ps. Almost throughout the year, often more than once annually. (I, H) Mexico to Brazil and Ecuador.

G. quinquenervis R. & P.

Often somewhat more robust than most other spp., otherwise similar vegetatively, the pbs. to more than 3″ tall, the lvs. to $1\frac{1}{2}'$ long and 4″ broad, rather heavily leathery. Infls. pendulous, to 2′ long (rarely more), the rachis slender, usually dark red, the many-fld. rac. rather loose. Fls. inverted, fragrant, membranaceous (except for the rather fleshy lip), usually bright yellow more or less dotted with dark red, the dots often arranged into erratic lines, to about 2″ long at most (often smaller). Ss. acuminate, the dors. one erect, linear-ligulate, concave, narrowed basally, the lats. triangular-lanceolate, subfalcate, reflexed or more or less divaricate, the margins strongly reflexed. Ps. emerging from middle of the col., linear, obliquely acuminate at the tips, with a sinuous, thread-like point, basally decurrent on the col., plane but sinuous. Lip noticeably shorter than the lat. ss., subsessile, basally obtuse, with calli at the base of the hypochil that are appressed or ascending, the sinus of the mesochil small. Col. very strongly arcuate, strongly attenuate towards base. Autumn. (I, H) Colombia; Venezuela; Guianas; Trinidad; Ecuador; Peru.

G. cassidea Rchb.f. (*Acropera Batemanni* Ldl. ex Rchb.f.) Similar in habit to *G. armeniaca* (Ldl. & Paxt.) Rchb.f. Infls. loosely few-fld., to 12″ long, pendulous, the peduncle usually

brown. Fls. fragrant, waxy, about 2″ in diam., greenish-brown or pinkish-brown, the lip usually more waxen and brighter in colour. Lip with 2 distinct lobes at apex, these lobules linear-lanceolate, obtuse. Autumn. (I, H) ? Mexico; Guatemala; Honduras; Nicaragua.

G. galeata (Ldl.) Rchb.f. (*Maxillaria galeata* Ldl., *Acropera Loddigesii* Ldl., *Cirrhaea Loddigesii* Ldl.) Rather similar in habit to *G. armeniaca* (Ldl. & Paxt.) Rchb.f., but with the infls. usually only about 6–8″ long, the pedicellate ovaries more out-thrust. Fls. about 2″ long (often smaller), fragrant, usually rather long-lived, brownish-yellow. Ss. oval, concave, spreading. Lip similar to the other noted sp., but the epichil considerably shorter, apically almost hook-shaped, recurving. Col. rather short. Summer–early autumn. (I, H) Mexico.

G. portentosa Lind. & Rchb.f. Similar in habit to *G. armeniaca* (Ldl. & Paxt.) Rchb.f., but more robust in all parts, the infls. to 2′ long (rarely longer), densely many-fld. Fls. spicily fragrant, about $2\frac{3}{4}''$ long, rather long-lasting, flesh-coloured. Ss. very acuminate, the dors. one inserted about the middle of the col. Ps. small, long-acuminate, inserted near base of the col. Lip fleshy, the hypochil often spotted with purple, with 2 recurving, fleshy antennae above the middle; epichil almost awl-shaped. Col. slender, arching, spotted with red. Spring. (I) Colombia.

G. truncata Ldl. (*Gongora Donckelaariana* Lem.) Similar in habit to *G. atropurpurea* Hk., the infls. pendulous, to about $2\frac{1}{4}'$ long, many-fld. Fls. almost 2″ in diam., fragrant, whitish with more or less numerous reddish blotches and a yellowish lip. Ss. oval, recurved. Ps. very short, with tiny apicules at tips. Lip very concave, the hypochil at its middle with 2 fleshy, erect protuberances; epichil almost erect, oblong, concave, obtuse. Col. slender, lightly arching, white spotted with red. Summer. (I, H) Mexico.

GOODYERA R.Br.

(*Cionisaccus* Breda, *Cordylostylis* Falc., *Elasmatum* Dulac, *Epipactis* Hall., *Geobina* Raf., *Georchis* Ldl., *Gonogona* Lk., *Leucostachys* Hoffmsgg., *Peramium* Salisb., *Tussaca* Raf., *Salacistis* Rchb.f.)

A member of the very complex subtribe *Physurinae*, *Goodyera* contains upwards of twenty-five species of terrestrial (very rarely lithophytic) orchids, these widespread in almost all parts of the terrestrial globe, except Africa. In the United States, where several of them are native, they are customarily called 'Rattlesnake Plantains', this name doubtless being given because of the often handsomely reptile-like mottlings of the foliage, which in many species is borne in basal rosettes, much like the temperate Plantains (genus *Plantago*). *Goodyera* is rather closely allied to several other genera of the subtribe to which it belongs, but differs from them in technical details of the usually smallish flowers, which are borne in more or less erect, rather dense racemes. Certain of the tropical representatives of this genus are in more or less sporadic cultivation for their variegated foliage, being classified among the delightful 'Jewel Orchids'.

Some ill-defined natural hybrids are known in *Goodyera*, principally in the United States, but otherwise no breeding has been done with the group, and its precise genetic affinities are unknown at this time.

CULTURE: The temperate Goodyeras will sometimes thrive under conditions in the outdoor garden or cool greenhouse such as those suggested for *Cypripedium*, while those from warmer climes require conditions as for *Anoectochilus*, etc. (C, I, H)

G. colorata (Bl.) Bl. (*Neottia colorata* Bl.)

Lvs. in a basal rosette, about 6 in number, narrowly ovate, the blade to 2½″ long and 1″ broad, acute, usually almost black, the red veins fading with age, stalked and sheathed at base. Infl. to about 6″ tall, the rac. rather elongate, many-fld., the peduncle short-hairy. Fls. not opening widely, about ¼″ long, the ss. red-brown with white tips, the ps. and lip white; lip swollen and bristly inside, the sharply deflexed apex acute. Summer–early autumn. (H) Sumatra; Java; Malay Peninsula.

G. oblongifolia Raf. (*Goodyera decipiens* Hubbard, *Goodyera Menziesii* Ldl., *Peramium decipiens* Piper, *Peramium Menziesii* Morong)

Lvs. in a basal rosette, usually oblong-elliptic, obtuse to acute, dark green, plain or partly net-veined with white, mostly near the mid-nerve, basally with a broad stalk, to almost 4½″ long. Infl. 4–20″ tall, the sharply secund or spiraled rac. densely many-fld. Fls. about ½″ long or less, hooded, not opening widely, white, streaked or flushed with green, the ps. connivent with the dors. sep. and forming a hood over the col. and lip. Summer–early autumn. (C, I) North America, where it is widespread; Mexico.

Goodyera pubescens (Willd.) R.Br. [BLANCHE AMES]

G. pubescens (Willd.) R.Br. (*Neottia pubescens* Willd., *Epipactis pubescens* A.A.Eaton, *Peramium pubescens* Salisb.)

Lvs. in a basal rosette, about 3–8 in number, ovate to ovate-lanceolate, bluish-green, with several white nerves and numerous thin net-branched white veins, to 3½″ long, with a rather broad short petiole. Infls. densely pubescent above, erect, 4–15″ tall, the cylindrical rac. densely many-fld. on all sides. Fls. globular, white, less than ¼″ long, glandular-pubescent outside, complex in structure. Spring–autumn. (C, I) Northern and Central United States, south to Georgia and Alabama.

G. repens (L.) R.Br. (*Satyrium repens* L., *Peramium repens* Salisb.)

Lvs. in a basal rosette, several in number, ovate to oblong-elliptic, obtuse to subacute, dark green with darker veins, ½–1¾″ long, with rather short broad petioles. Infl. erect, glandular-pubescent above, 3–14″ tall, loosely rather many-fld., strongly secund. Fls. not opening widely, about ¼″ long or less, white tinged with green, or sometimes suffused with brownish-pink. Mostly summer. (C, I) Western North America, south to New Mexico and Arizona; Eurasia.

—var. **ophioides** Fern. (*Goodyera ophioides* Rydb., *Peramium ophioides* Rydb.)

Differing principally from the typical form of the sp. in having the lf.-veins conspicuously bordered with white, instead of being dark green. Summer–early autumn. (C, I) North America; Eurasia.

G. rubicunda (Bl.) Ldl. (*Neottia rubicunda* Bl., *Goodyera rubens* Bl.)

Lvs. in a rather loose basal rosette, several in number, green, the lamina to 7″ long and 2″ broad, elliptic, oblique, acute at the apex, the basal stalk about 2″ long. Infl. about 2′ tall, the hairy floriferous part about half that length, furnished with woolly floral bracts, many-fld. Fls. with woolly pedicellate ovaries, about ¾″ long, usually not opening widely, red-brown, the lip swollen, hairy inside, white. Autumn. (H) Sumatra and Malay Peninsula to New Guinea.

G. tesselata Lodd. (*Epipactis tesselata* A.A.Eaton, *Peramium tesselatum* Heller)

Lvs. in a basal rosette, several in number, spreading, suborbicular-ovate to oblong-lanceolate, rounded or subacute at apex, with short broad petiole, dark green with strong or vague white net-veining, ¾–3¼″ long. Infls. 5–14″ tall, loosely or densely many-fld., secund or spiraled to rarely cylindrical. Fls. about ⅜″ long, not opening well, white, the ss. puberulent on outer surface, the ps. connivent with dors. sep. and forming a hood over the lip and col. Summer–early autumn. (C, I) Newfoundland and Nova Scotia south to New York and Maryland, west to Wisconsin and Minnesota.

G. fusca (Ldl.) Hk.f. (*Aetheria fusca* Ldl., *Cystorchis fusca* Bth.) Lvs. in a basal rosette, broadly ovate, dark green with a paler median nerve, rather pointed, leathery, to 2″ long. Infl. erect, robust, 6–12″ tall, many-fld., dense, secund. Fls. about ⅜″ across, greenish-white often flushed with purple, the falcate ps. swollen at base. Autumn. (C, I) Himalayas, at elevations up to 14,000 ft.

G. Henryi Rolfe (*Epipactis Henryi* A.A.Eaton). Lvs. borne on a partially sprawling rhiz., few in number, ovate, narrowed basally, clasping at the stalked base, dark green, to about 2½″ long. Infl. mostly erect, to 12″ tall, rather densely many-fld. Fls. about ⅝″ in diam., the ss. and ps. green, the complex lip white. Summer–autumn. (C, I) Western China, mostly in Hupeh.

G. hispida Ldl. Lvs. in a basal rosette, usually 4–6 in number, green more or less flushed with pink, with a white or pink network of veins, pointed apically, stalked at base, the lamina to 3″ long and more than 1″ wide. Infl. to 8″ tall, short-hairy, the rac. very densely many-fld. Fls. opening fairly well, about ¼″ long or less, the ss. greenish tipped with white, the ps. almost white, the lip white, with many stiff hairs inside, the reflexed apical part acute. Summer. (C, I) Himalayas to Malay Peninsula.

G. pusilla Bl. Lvs. in a basal rosette, about 4–5 in number, the lamina ovate, acute, to 1¼″ long and ½″ broad, vaguely wavy-margined, velvety dark brown-purple with an intricate network of red veins, paler medially, stalked basally. Infl. to under 5″ tall, short-hairy, rather few-fld. Fls. about ¼″ long or less, glabrous outside, the ss. brown with whitish tips, the ps. yellowish, the lip yellow with white edges. Summer. (H) Sumatra; Java; ? Malay Peninsula.

G. Schlechtendaliana Rchb.f. (*Georchis Schlechtendaliana* Rchb.f., *Goodyera japonica* Bl., *Goodyera similis* Bl.) Lvs. in a basal rosette, few in number, ovate, rather long-petioled, dark green with somewhat lighter veins, ¾–1½″ long. Infl. slender, 3–7″ tall, slender, the few- to many-fld. rac. usually abbreviated. Fls. mostly secund, about ³⁄₁₆″ long, pale green, hooded. Summer. (C, I) China, mostly in Yunnan.

G. secundiflora Ldl. Lvs. mostly basal, in a vague rosette, few in number, ovate or rarely elliptic, pointed, short-stalked, rich dark green with silvery-white net-veins, 1½–2″ long. Infl. erect, glandular-pubescent above, 6–10″ tall, the secund rac. loosely few-fld. Fls. about ½″ across, pubescent outside, white, the ps. subfalcate, crisped on outer margins. Summer. (C, I) Eastern India; Himalayas; China.

G. vittata (Ldl.) Bth. (*Georchis vittata* Ldl.) Lvs. basal and extending rather far up the infl., rich dark green, more or less veined with silvery-white, ovate, rather fleshy, to 3″ long, stalked basally. Infl. to 6″ tall, the rather numerous fls. mostly secund or somewhat spiraled. Fls. about ⅝″ in diam., white tipped with pink, the ss. and ps. pointed. Summer–early autumn. (C, I) Himalayas, especially Sikkim.

GORGOGLOSSUM F.C.Lehm.

This is a genus consisting of but a single species, this an extremely rare epiphytic member of the subtribe *Gongorinae*, apparently endemic to a small area in the Cauca Valley of Colombia. The group is somewhat allied to *Sievekingia* Rchb.f., but differs materially in technical details of the flowers. *Gorgoglossum* is an attractive orchid, and is present in a very few specialized collections at this time.

Nothing is known of the genetic affinities of this genus, and as yet no hybrids have been produced. It seems possible that *Gorgoglossum* will prove inter-fertile with at least certain other members of the aggregation to which it belongs; the resultant progeny should be of extreme scientific, as well as horticultural, interest.

CULTURE: As for *Stanhopea*. (I)

G. Reichenbachianum (Rolfe) F.C.Lehm. (*Sievekingia Reichenbachiana* Rolfe)

Pbs. clustered, ovoid, about ¾″ tall. Lvs. usually paired, narrowly elliptic, acuminate, folded, about 6″ long and 1¼″ broad, narrowed basally into a stalk which is typically spotted with dull red. Infls. sharply pendulous, about 5-fld., to 4″ long. Fls. about 2″ across, the ss. yellowish-green, the ps. greenish flushed with orange-yellow, the lip greenish, densely purple-spotted on the disc, flushed with orange-yellow and with small orange-yellow keels. Col. orange-yellow. Summer. (I) Colombia: Cauca Valley.

GOVENIA Ldl.
(*Eucnemia* Rchb., *Eucnemis* Ldl.)

Govenia contains, according to a recent revision by Donovan S. Córrell, eight species and varieties in Central and South America, with one representative in the West Indies. Very little known by collectors, they are generally rather attractive terrestrial, sometimes pseudobulbous orchids which have been sporadically grown by enthusiasts for more than a hundred years. The plants consist of subterranean tuber-like pseudo-bulbs (which may be absent) from a fibrous rhizome, and one or two rather large, leathery, handsome, stalked, sheathing leaves. The erect inflorescences—bearing a relatively dense, many-flowered raceme at the apex—typically arise from within the basal sheaths. The blossoms are hooded, of rather simplified structure, and vary tremendously in colour even within a single species. The genus *Govenia* is somewhat distantly allied to *Cyrtopodium* R.Br.

No hybrids are known as yet in *Govenia*, and its genetic affinities are uncertain.

CULTURE: As for the tropical Bletias. Considerable success has been had growing these unusual plants in a mixture of chopped sphagnum moss and shredded tree-fern fibre, in rather small, perfectly-drained pots. They are extremely susceptible to rotting through stale conditions at the roots. (I, H)

G. superba (LaLl. & Lex.) Ldl. ex Lodd. (*Maxillaria superba* LaLl. & Lex., *Govenia fasciata* Ldl., *G. lagenophora* Ldl., *G. platyglossa* Schltr., *G. stictoglossa* Schltr., *G. sulphurea* Rchb.f., *G. utriculata* (Sw.) Ldl. var. *lagenophora* Griseb.)

Habit as in the genus, the paired lvs. to 1½′ long and 6″ wide, mostly widely elliptic, usually sharp-pointed apically, rather leathery, with some inflated sheaths towards the base. Infls. to 3½′ tall, the rac. about 15″ long, loosely many-fld., prominently bracted. Fls. about 1½″ long, hooded, fragrant, yellow often flushed with brown or green, the lip with some reddish-brown spots on upper part, sometimes all parts flushed and marked with reddish-brown, the pedicellate ovaries purplish, slender. Dors. sep. linear-oblanceolate, obtuse; lat. ss. falcate-lanceolate, obtuse to acute. Ps. obliquely elliptic-oblanceolate, obtuse to acutish. Lip curved, broadly ovate to ovate-elliptic, rounded to pointed at tip, simple, without a callus. Autumn. (I, H) Mexico to Colombia and Venezuela.

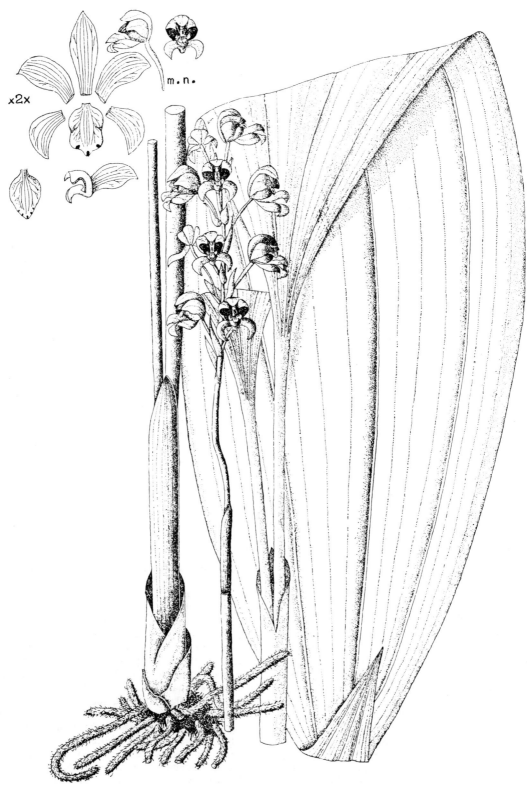

Govenia utriculata (Sw.) Ldl. [Hoehne, *Flora Brasilica*]

230

G. utriculata (Sw.) Ldl. (*Limodorum utriculatum* Sw., *Cymbidium utriculatum* Sw., *Eucnemis brevilabris* Ldl., *Govenia boliviensis* Rolfe, *G. brevilabris* Hemsl., *G. Ernstii* Schltr., *G. Gardneri* Hk., *G. Powellii* Schltr., *G. Sodiroi* Schltr.)

Rather similar in all parts to *G. superba* (LaLl. & Lex.) Ldl. ex Lodd., differing in the colour of the fls. and shape of floral segms.; certain forms of both spp. intergrade. Fls. white or light cream-coloured, often tinged with light purple or lilac outside and furnished inside with reddish-brown spots and transverse bands and lines of light purple, the slender pedicellate ovaries purplish, the fls. usually somewhat larger than the other sp. Ps. usually much broader than the lat. ss. (not about equal). Infls. usually short and congested (not long and loose). Autumn. (I, H) Mexico throughout Central America to Argentina in South America; West Indies.

GRAMMANGIS Rchb.f.

This remarkable genus, once included in *Grammatophyllum* Bl., contains five known species, at least two of which are today encountered in a very few comprehensive collections of rarities. They are robust, exceptionally handsome epiphytic orchids with a peculiar disjunct range, four of the species being endemic to Madagascar, the other found in Malaya and Indonesia. Plants with large pseudobulbs and attractive leathery foliage, the Grammangis produce arching to sharply pendulous, densely many-flowered racemes of sizeable, strikingly coloured blossoms of unique structure, which are often furnished with a pervading scent. Barred or otherwise marked with reddish- or chocolate-brown or purplish on a green or yellow ground, the flowers are quite unlike other orchids in general appearance, and are sufficiently handsome and long-lived to warrant future attention from enthusiasts.

No hybrids have as yet been registered with the members of this genus, but it is presumably compatible genetically with allied groups such as *Grammatophyllum*, and possibly *Cymbidiella* and *Cymbidium*. Critical experimental breeding should produce some fascinating progeny.

CULTURE: The species of *Grammangis* all inhabit tropical areas, and hence require heat and relatively large amounts of moisture and humidity at all times. Best grown in ample pots or sizeable slatted baskets, with perfect drainage essential, rather tightly packed with osmunda or tree-fern fibre, they delight in liberal applications of fertilizers at regular intervals while in active growth, and should be kept in a semi-shaded situation in the collection. These robust orchids should not be disturbed except when absolutely necessary, as they are highly intolerant of being moved. (H)

G. Ellisii (Ldl.) Rchb.f. (*Grammatophyllum Ellisii* Ldl.)

Pbs. spindle-shaped, 4-angled or not, to 8″ tall, narrowing basally. Lvs. 3–4, leathery, oblong, acutish, to 2′ long and 5″ broad, glossy dark-green. Infls. usually arising with the new growths, to 3′ long, densely 20–40-fld., arching or pendulous. Fls. long-stalked, with large subtending bracts, to 3½″ across, waxy, heavily fragrant, long-lived, variable in colour, usually with the ss. yellow copiously barred and streaked with reddish-brown or chocolate-brown, the ps. white or whitish with a rose-red apex, the lip white or whitish striped with red. Ss. spreading, the dors. one usually arching over the ps. and col., oblong, acute, very undulate marginally. Ps.

Grammangis Ellisii (Ldl.) Rchb.f. [B.S.WILLIAMS]

much smaller, ovate, obtuse, at the sides of the col. Lip shorter than the ps., 3-lbd., the apex recurved or downcurved. This plant has been confused in horticulture with the very rare *G. fallax* Schltr. Summer. (H) Madagascar.

G. stapeliiflora (Teijsm. & Binn.) Schltr. (*Cymbidium stapeliiflorum* Teijsm. & Binn., *Cymbidium Huttoni* Hk.f., *Cymbidium Stephensi* Ridl., *Grammangis Huttoni* Bth., *Grammatophyllum stapeliiflorum* J.J. Sm.)

Pbs. oval, rather compressed laterally, glossy green, to 6″ long and 2½″ broad. Lvs. 2–3, narrowing to both ends, oblong-lanceolate, acute, to 1½′ long and 3″ broad, leathery. Infls. gracefully arching or pendulous, densely 5–15-fld., the fls. all facing in the same direction (usually downwards), to 1½′ long. Fls. about 2″ across, rather foul-smelling, waxy, long-lived, the ss. and ps. curved at base to form a bell, their tips spreading, the ss. pale greyish or greyish-yellow densely spotted with purple or brownish-purple, the ps. basally coloured like the ss., the apical part dark black-purple, the lat. lbs. of the lip coloured like the ss., the midlb. whitish with dark purplish-grey spots, the col. dark purple-grey. Ss. wider at base than above, acute. Ps. smaller than the ss., acute. Lip 3-lbd., the erect lat. lbs. rounded, obtuse, the midlb. round, convex, warty. Summer. (H) Malay Peninsula; Sumatra; Java; Celebes.

GRAMMATOPHYLLUM Bl.
(*Gabertia* Gaud., *Pattonia* Wight)

About eight rather confused species of often prodigious orchids make up the genus *Grammatophyllum*. Mostly epiphytic (rarely lithophytic) plants, they range from Burma, the Malay Peninsula, and the Philippines throughout Indonesia to New Guinea, the Solomon Islands, and the Fiji Islands. Three species now appear to be present in our collections, one of these being the fabulous 'Giant Orchid' or 'Queen Orchid', *G. speciosum* Bl., which is generally conceded to be the largest of all pseudobulbous orchids, its bulbs on occasion reaching lengths in excess of twenty-five feet! All of the Grammatophyllums are exceptionally spectacular plants, with huge erect or arching racemes densely set with very many large, long-lasting, varicoloured, more or less spotted flowers of great beauty. Apparently in all of the species, peculiar abnormal (dimorphic) blossoms are borne at the base of the normal inflorescence. The genus is a member of the subtribe Cymbidiinae, and is generally placed in closest alliance to *Grammangis* Rchb.f. *Grammatophyllum* is readily divided into two sections, viz., *Gabertia*, with the pseudobulbs ellipsoidal or ovoid and proportionately short, and *Pattonia*, with often tremendously elongated, frequently pendulous or down-curving, cylindrical or fusiform pseudobulbs. The two sections do not differ from one another appreciably in floral characters, hence are largely utilized for horticultural differentiation.

No *Grammatophyllum* hybrids have as yet been registered by the contemporary registrars, although many years ago, in a German orchid periodical, note was briefly made of the flowering of a *Grammato-*

cymbidium, a cross between a member of this genus and one of *Cymbidium*. Several different Grammatocymbidiums have since been made by modern breeders, but insofar as we are able to ascertain, none of these have been brought into bloom, although in some instances they are very old plants, and are obviously bigeneric hybrids. Considerable additional experimental hybridization utilizing the members of this attractive genus should be tried, interspecific crosses within the genus, in particular, offering notable potentialities. Hybrids between *Grammatophyllum* and *Grammangis*, or *Dipodium*, should also be attempted by enterprising breeders of oddities.

CULTURE: Under the artificial conditions of our collections, the Grammatophyllums are often—outside of their native haunts, at least—rather difficult to maintain in good condition for very long periods. With their fleshy pseudobulbs, they seem highly susceptible to bacterial and virus ailments of many sorts, and huge specimens will rot and perish within an incredibly short period if they become afflicted. The species such as *G. Measuresianum* and *G. scriptum* do best, under average greenhouse conditions in rather large, perfectly-drained pots, tightly packed with straight osmunda, or medium-size chunks of tree-fern fibre. Strictly tropical plants (as are all members of the genus), they require hot, humid conditions at all times, and should be watered heavily while actively growing; a rather brief resting-period may with benefit be given them upon the termination of flowering. They need a very sunny spot (short of burning of the heavy foliage), with quantities of fresh, freely-moving air, and should be liberally fertilized during the period of most active growth. Particular attention must be paid at all times to the state of the compost in which they are grown, and if necessary, they must be repotted whenever any indication of stale conditions at the roots appears. *Grammatophyllum speciosum*, because of its huge size, is very difficult for the average greenhouse orchidist, although it has on a few occasions been brought into flower under such an arrangement. It requires a very large container, filled with a compost such as that suggested for the other species, and conditions of humid, sticky heat at all times, without a rest-period of any sort at any time. This species seems to have to be of very large dimensions, and advanced age before it produces its gigantic inflorescences, which have been aptly likened to 'lamp-posts set with a multitude of blossoms'! In tropical climates, this 'Giant Orchid' is usually grown out-of-doors in specially-prepared, raised beds, much like those recommended for *Arachnis*, *Arundina*, and the like, although here again particular attention must be paid to drainage and to the fresh condition of the compost. (H)

G. Measuresianum Weathers (*Grammatophyllum grandiflorum* hort.)

Pbs. clustered, ellipsoidal to ovoid, slightly furrowed with age, somewhat compressed laterally, to 12″ long, 3″ broad, and about 2½″ thick, usually bearing about 5 basal and apical lvs. Lvs. leathery, elliptic-oblanceolate, obtuse to acutish, narrowed below, to 2′ long and almost 5″ broad, with a prominent stiff midrib. Infls. stiffly erect or ascending, to more than 8′ long (often shorter), the loose or rather dense rac. with up to 50 fls., these expanding gradually over a long period. Fls. rather waxy in texture, faintly fragrant at times, about 2″ in diam. (wider when ps. are spread out), cream-yellow with irregular spots and blotches of dark blackish-brown, with single big blotches at sepal-apices. Dors. sep. thrust forward over col. and lip, almost touching erect lat. lbs. of the lip, apex and upper edges retrorse, undulate, concave below; lat. ss. very undulate, apex retrorse, like the dors. one apically acute or acuminate. Ps. with outer third reflexed, somewhat undulate, slightly falcate, narrowed at base. Lip 3-lbd., the lat. lbs. erect and enfolding the col., the midlb. pendulous and thrust forward slightly, the lat. lbs. pubescent below, yellowish, with usually 6 light brown apically branching veins, edged with light brown, spotted inside with dark brown; midlb. with a basal whitish callus, pubescent basally, white with 3 dark brown curved lines, the median one of which branches towards apex. Col. curving, white marked and spotted with red-purple. Mostly summer. (H) Philippines.

G. scriptum (L.) Bl. (*Epidendrum scriptum* L., *Cymbidium scriptum* Sw., *Vanda scripta* Spreng., *Gabertia scripta* Gaud., *Grammatophyllum Boweri* FvM., *G. Guilielmi-Secundi* Krzl., *G. leopardinum* Rchb.f., *G. multiflorum* Ldl. and var. *tigrinum* Ldl., *G. Seegerianum* hort.)
Extremely variable in all parts. Pbs. rather similar to those of the previous sp., often yellowish-green, to 8″ tall and 2½″ broad. Lvs. mostly apical, 2–5, leathery, venose, wavy, to 1¾′ long and to more than 3″ broad at middle, narrowed somewhat towards base. Infls. erect to strongly arching or pendulous because of weight of fls., to more than 4′ long, usually rather densely many-fld., with up to 100 fls., these opening over a period of some weeks. Fls. rather heavy-textured and waxy, usually rather campanulate, to about 1¾″ across (wider when ps. are spread out), highly variable in colour, but generally greenish-yellow with irregular dark brown blotches on inner surface, outside more greenish, the blotches only partially visible. Dors. sep. concave, somewhat arched over col. and lip, acutish, the apex slightly upturned, marginally somewhat undulate; lat. ss. thrust forward, slightly falcate, more greenish than other segms. in most cases. Ps. spreading, rather falcate, almost obtuse, obscurely undulate, with the blotches more spot-like and regular than sepaline markings. Lip strongly 3-lbd., the lat. lbs. partly enclosing col., erect, whitish-yellow, with several anastomosing brown veins, pubescent below; midlb. with a basal grooved, pubescent callus, this white and yellow with vague brown dots and lines, the segm. pendulous or down-curving, pubescent above, yellowish-white with 3 dark brown median veins which become thickened apically, and a single similar line on each edge, apex yellow. Col. arching, white marked on both faces with red-brown. Mostly summer. (H) Borneo; Celebes; Moluccas; Philippines; New Guinea; Solomon Islands.

G. speciosum Bl. (*Pattonia macrantha* Wight, *Grammatophyllum fastuosum* Ldl., *G. giganteum* Bl., *G. macranthum* Rchb.f., *G. Sanderianum* hort., *G. Wallisii* Rchb.f.)

Highly variable in all parts, probably the largest of all pseudobulbous orchids. Pbs. rather st.-like, sub-cylindric, sometimes vaguely fusiform, gradually tapering upwards, erect to strongly pendulous, varying in length from 5 to more than 25′, often elongating for several years, to about 3″ in maximum diam., bearing 2-ranked lvs. mostly along upper (or apical) third. Lvs. distichous, rather heavy, gracefully arching, linear-ligulate, acute or acutish, to 2½′ long, sheathing and sharply keeled at base. Infls. usually rigidly erect, to 10′ tall (often shorter), very stout, becoming narrower upwards, with a loose or very dense multiflorous rac. along upper one-third or more, the fls. opening over a long period of time. Fls. very heavy-textured, long-lasting, fragrant or not, 5–8″ in diam., variable in colour (especially in degree of spotting and/or blotching), usually with yellow or greenish-yellow ss. and ps. spotted and blotched with dark red-brown or dark red-purple, the proportionately small lip white marked with yellow and red-brown or red-purple. Ss. and ps. widely spreading, more or less undulate marginally, broadly oblong or subobovate, apically rather blunt. Lip 3-lbd., the lbs. small, the lat. ones more or less enfolding the col.; midlb. ovate, acutish, the disc furrowed with 3 plates which are more elevated in the middle, marked with fringed reddish lines. Col. curved, semiterete, somewhat spotted with red or purplish. Mostly autumn. (H) Burma; Thailand; Laos; Viet-Nam; Malay Peninsula; Sumatra; Java; Borneo; Philippines; Moluccas; New Guinea.

GRAPHORKIS Thou.
(*Eulophiopsis* Pfitz.)

In 1953 Dr. Victor S. Summerhayes reinstated the old genus *Graphorkis* of du Petit-Thouars, to include the plants previously incorporated in Pfitzer's group *Eulophiopsis*, of the subtribe *Eulophiinae*. Five species are now known, and one of these has recently been introduced into a few choice American collections from West Africa; a couple of these odd plants are native in Madagascar as well. Rather simulating smallish or robust Catasetums, they produce branching, erect panicles of small, but oddly attractive flowers of interesting structure. In the wild they are normally epiphytic.

Nothing is known of the genetic affinities of *Graphorkis*, and no hybrids have as yet been attempted.

CULTURE: These interesting plants do best when treated like Catasetums, in a perfectly-drained compost (in pots) of equal parts of shredded tree-fern fibre and chopped sphagnum moss. They delight in copious applications of fertilizer, water, and high humidity, and seem able to stand a large quantity of bright light without injury. They appreciate a brief resting-period upon completion of the new growths. (H)

G. lurida (Sw.) O.Ktze. (*Limodorum luridum* Sw., *Eulophia lurida* Ldl., *Eulophiopsis lurida* Schltr.)
Pbs. clustered, ovoid to oblong, becoming strongly furrowed with age, usually rather bright yellow, to 2½″ long and 1¼″ in diam., the midribs of the lvs. leaving spine-like protuberances at the pb.-apex. Lvs. sheathing, linear to narrowly elliptic, strongly plicate, bright green, deciduous, to 12″ long and 1¼″ wide. Infls. usually

erect, loosely branched, to 12″ tall and 6½″ broad, rather pyramidal, many-fld. Fls. to ½″ across, the oblong, obtuse ss. and ps. brownish-purple, the ps. usually somewhat paler. Lip 3-lbd., the lat. lbs. erect, whitish, the midlb. broadly ovate, vaguely 2-lbd., golden-yellow. Spur curving forward, 2-lbd. at tip. Mostly winter. (H) Tropical West Africa, usually growing on palm-trunks.

GROBYA Ldl.

About four species of *Grobya* are known to date, all of them very unusual and often attractive epiphytic orchids of the subtribe *Grobyinae*, endemic to Brazil, where they are reasonably common in the humid forests. Pseudobulbous plants, with narrow foliage and pendulous or arching racemes of very complex, usually pretty blossoms, the Grobyas are regrettably at this time unknown in our collections, although they appear to offer much to the connoisseur collector.

Nothing has been ascertained regarding the genetic affinities of this odd genus.

CULTURE: As for *Catasetum.* (I, H)

GYMNADENIA R.Br.

About fifteen species of *Gymnadenia* are known to science, these often included in *Habenaria* Willd., from which they are separated by technical details. The root-system consists of two or more tubers at the base of the stem, with a few fleshy roots above them. The rather juicy stems are furnished towards the base with a few vivid-green leaves, and terminate in a raceme of very attractively showy flowers, which vary in hue from pink to purple and sometimes white. Usually dwarf alpine orchids, growing in the wild mostly in wet grasslands, they are seldom in contemporary collections, but as a group offer much to the connoisseur.

Some natural hybrids within the genus *Gymnadenia* are on record. A rare natural hybrid with *Anacamptis* is known as *Gymnanacamptis.*

CULTURE: As for *Caladenia* and other terrestrial orchids, although most of the Gymnadenias, because of their habitat in temperate areas, require rather cool temperatures at all times. (C, I)

G. albida (L.) L.C.Rich. (*Satyrium albidum* L., *Orchis albida* Scop., *Habenaria albida* Sw., *Platanthera albida* L.C.Rich., *Bicchia albida* Parlat.)

St. to 1½′ tall, leafy, tapering in diam. from base to summit. Lvs. few, 1–4″ long, oblong to lanceolate, acute, becoming bract-like above. Rac. spire-like, 1–3″ long, many-fld., but not particularly dense. Fls. about ⅕″ long, white, greenish or pale yellow, often secund on the spike, the ss. and ps. all forming a hood over the col. and vaguely 3-lbd., triangular lip. Mostly summer–autumn. (C) North and middle Europe, usually in the higher mountains.

G. conopsea (R.Br.) R.Br. (*Orchis conopsea* R.Br., *Habenaria conopsea* Franch.)

Tubers usually 2, palmately-lobed, to 1½″ long. Lvs. mostly basal, few, linear-lanceolate, suberect, to 4″ long. Infl. slender, to 2′ tall, furnished with a few sheath-like bracts, the cylindrical, rather loosely many-fld. rac. 2–3″ long. Fls. about ⅜″ long exclusive of the spur, varying in colour from pink or lilac through several shades of pale purple to pure white, very fragrant, the dors. sep. and ps. forming a hood over the col., the curved lat. ss. lanceolate, spreading, the lip usually cuneate, shallowly 3-lbd. at tip; spur cylindrical, curved, to ¾″ long. June–Aug. (C, I) Europe; Northern Asia to Japan.

G. odoratissima (L.) Rchb.f. (*Orchis odoratissima* L., *Gymnadenia suaveolens* Rchb.)

Tubers 2, irregular, divided at tip into 2–4 finger-like lbs., about 1¼″ long. Lvs. mostly basal, linear to linear-oblong, pointing, 3–8″ long, becoming bracteose above. Infl. 9–15″ tall, rather slender, frequently flexuous, the cylindrical, dense, often sinuous rac. 2–4″ long. Fls. about ¼″ long, highly fragrant, varying from pale lilac or pale purple to white, the ss. and ps. forming a loose hood over the col. and cuneate, 3-lbd. lip; spur cylindrical, curved, ¼″ long. June–July. (C, I) Europe.

G. cucullata Rchb.f. Lvs. paired, usually opposite, basal, ovate, to 1½″ long. Infl. 6–9″ tall, slender, curved, naked or with a solitary bract, the loosely few-fld., secund rac. to 2½″ long. Fls. about ⅜″ long, pink, lilac or pale purple, the ss. and ps. forming a hood over the col. and lip, the hood with recurved tip. Lip cuneate, 3-lbd., linear or lanceolate, the midlb. the largest. Spur curved, stout, to ⅛″ long. July–Aug. (C) Eastern Europe throughout Asia to China, usually in the high mountains.

G. decipiens (Ldl.) Schltr. (*Neolindleya decipiens* Krzl., *Platanthera decipiens* Ldl.) Tubers large, oblong or ovoid. Lvs. 5–6, oblong or almost round, 3–4″ long. Infl. 8–20″ tall, very leafy, thickly fleshy, the usually many-fld. rac. 4–6″ long. Fls. about ⅜″ across, yellowish-green, the ss. and ps. narrowly ovate, acute to acuminate; lip cuneate, with 3 teeth at tip; spur small, conical, incurved. July–Aug. (C) Siberia; Kamchatka Peninsula; Japan.

G. Delavayi Schltr. Tubers usually paired, palmately-lobed. Lvs. 4–5, borne on the st., ligulate-lanceolate, acute, 3–4″ long. Infl. about 9–10″ long, rather leafy, the densely many-fld., cylindrical rac. about 2½″ long. Fls. about ⅝″ long, bright pink to vivid red, the dors. sep. oblong, concave, the lats. obliquely oblong, blunt, the ps. similar but smaller; lip broadly rhomboid-cuneate, 3-lbd., the lat. lbs. short, rounded, the midlb. longer, almost square, very blunt. Spur filiform, pointed, pendulous, about ⅝″ long. July–Aug. (C) China: Yunnan, at very high elevations.

G. graminifolia Rchb.f. (*Ponerorchis graminifolia* Rchb.f.) Tubers 2, irregular. Lvs. basal and cauline, linear, suberect. 2–4″ long. Infl. to 1½′ tall, sheathed, the short, many-fld. rac. congested. Fls. about ⅜″ across, lilac-pink to rosy-red, the ps. and dors. sep. forming a hood over the col. and cuneate, vaguely 3-lbd. lip, the spur cylindrical, curved, blunt, ⅜″ long. May–July. (C, I) Japan.

G. himalaica Schltr. Tubers usually paired, divided into 4 fusiform lobes. Lvs. 5–7, oblong-ligulate to lanceolate, pointed or blunt apically, to 6″ long. Infl. stout, leafy, to 20″ tall, the densely many-fld., cylindrical rac. to 4½″ long. Fls. about ½″ long, bright violet-rose, the dors. sep. oblong, erect, concave, the lats. obliquely oblong, blunt, spreading; ps. obliquely ovate, blunt; lip cuneate, 3-lbd., the lat. lbs. obliquely triangular, blunt, the midlb. broadly triangular, blunt; spur filiform, pointed, pendulous, about ½″ long. July–Aug. (C) North-west Himalayas, at elevations of 12,000 to 15,000 ft.

G. monophylla Ames & Schltr. Tubers 2, subglobose. Lf. solitary, basal, narrowly lanceolate, sheathed at base, to 2" long. Infl. to 5" tall, slender, erect or slightly twisted, the secund, many-fld. rac. to 1½" long. Fls. about ⅜" long, bright red, the dors. sep. lanceolate, pointed, erect, the lat. ss. lanceolate, falcate at tip, forming a loose hood with the ps. over the col., the ps. subfalcate-linear, pointed; lip deeply 3-lbd., cuneate at base, lat. lbs. linear, blunt, the midlb. broadly ligulate, blunt; spur swollen at base, incurved, 3/16" long. Usually Aug. (C) China: Szechuan, at high elevations.

GYMNOCHILUS Bl.

This is a genus of two extremely rare species of terrestrial orchids, closely allied to *Cheirostylis* Griff. and certain other members of the subtribe *Physurinae*, which inhabit the island of Madagascar. They differ from their allies principally in technical details of the small flowers, and are at this time unknown in cultivation.

Nothing has been ascertained regarding the genetic affinities of *Gymnochilus*.

CULTURE: Presumably as for *Anoectochilus*. (H)

GYNOGLOTTIS J.J.Sm.

But a single member of *Gynoglottis* has been described to date, this an extremely rare epiphytic orchid inhabiting the montane forests of western Sumatra. A member of the subtribe *Coelogyninae*, **Gynoglottis cymbidioides** (Rchb.f.) J.J.Sm. (*Coelogyne cymbidioides* Rchb.f., *Coelogyne xylobioides* Krzl.) rather resembles many Coelogynes in habit, but bears smallish white flowers of distinctive structure in an elongate, multiflorous raceme. It is unknown in collections today, and is apparently very scarce even in the wild.

Nothing is known of the genetic affinities of *Gynoglottis*.

CULTURE: As for the tropical species of *Coelogyne*. (H)

HABENARIA Willd.

(*Acrostylia* Frapp., *Ate* Ldl., *Bicchia* Parl., *Bilabrella* Ldl., *Blephariglottis* Raf., *Centrochilus* Schau., *Choeradoplectron* Schau., *Cybele* Falc., *Diphylax* Hk.f., *Dissorhynchium* Schau., *Glossaspis* Spreng., *Glossula* Ldl., *Gymnadeniopsis* Rydb., *Habenella* Small, *Hemihabenaria* Finet, *Hemiperis* Cordem., *Limnorchis* Rydb., *Lindblomia* Fries, *Lysias* Salisb., *Macrocentrum* Phil., *Mecosa* Bl., *Montolivaea* Rchb.f., *Neolindleya* Krzl., *Perularia* Ldl., *Piperia* Rydb., *Ponerorchis* Rchb.f., *Sieberia* Spreng.)

Habenaria is one of the largest genera of orchidaceous plants, an estimated seven hundred and fifty species being known to date, and more are constantly being added as botanical exploration in certain little-known regions where these plants occur is continued. Habenarias inhabit virtually all parts of the globe, but are particularly abundant in such regions as Brazil, tropical Africa, and the North Temperate Zone. Most of these orchids are terrestrial in habit, though some adopt an epiphytic mode of existence, others live on rocks as lithophytes, and a few even thrive in streams or bogs, as semi-aquatic plants. They have fleshy or tuber-like roots, and erect, simple stems, with a few to rather many basal- or cauline-leaves. The flowers—which are few or numerous, and insignificant to rather showy in appearance—vary tremendously in structure and colour, though most of them possess a rather characteristic conformation by which they are readily recognized. Despite this, the taxonomic status of many of the component entities is (and has long been) confused, and by reference to the above-noted list of generic synonyms, some idea can be gathered of the varying interpretations of different orchidologists throughout the years. In this *Encyclopaedia*, we have attempted to follow a median path in our discussions of the components of this exasperatingly complex subtribe *Habenarinae*, with the result that only a few of the segregate genera from *Habenaria* Willd. are here recognized as distinct. In many species of true *Habenaria*, the dorsal sepal is erect or forms a hood over the column, while the lateral sepals are usually spreading or sometimes reflexed. The petals—which are often proportionately very large, when compared with the other floral segments—are usually joined at least in part to the dorsal sepal, and vary in form from simple to intricately toothed and/or lobed; in some species the petals make up the most distinctive and prominent part of the blossom. The spurred lip may be simple, variously lobed or toothed, or cut into distinct divisions like the petals. The members of this genus, although their numbers are legion, are but little known by collectors, due to the relative difficulty with which most of them are obtained, and their often somewhat specialized cultural requirements. Some of the most attractive of terrestrial orchids exist in *Habenaria*, however, and the group as a whole should be better known by enthusiasts.

Hybridization in this large genus has, oddly enough, not been extensive, though several natural hybrids are known (mostly indigenous to temperate North America), and two artificially-produced crosses are on record. These are *Habenaria x l'Avenir* (*H. rhodocheila* × *H. x Regnieri*) and *H. x Regnieri* (*H. carnea* × *H. rhodocheila*), both of which were produced by A. Regnier during the period of about 1910–12. An additional bigeneric hybrid with *Pecteilis* is discussed there. These apparently handsome orchids have seemingly disappeared from cultivation today, but the crosses should certainly be remade. Additional critical breeding among some of the large-flowered Habenarias is to be encouraged, since some fascinating possibilities are open to exploration. Like most terrestrial orchids, maturation and the consequent production of flowers from seed is remarkably rapid in this genus, sometimes as soon as ten months after sowing.

CULTURE: The cultural requirements of the Habenarias are as varied as are the species themselves, depending primarily upon the place of origin of the particular individual involved. A rich, porous compost, such as that suggested for *Phaius* and the like, is recommended, and in most cases it is suggested that the plants be grown in pots, rather than in the ground, unless a particularly well-set-up outdoor garden is available. Very perfect drainage is absolutely essential for any degree of success with these plants, and as a rule, they should be repotted and the subterranean tubers divided on an annual or at least biennial basis, for best results. Most of the Habenarias in cultivation today do well in a rather brightly lighted situation in the greenhouse, or—during sufficiently warm weather—when set outside, in their containers. While they are in active growth, they benefit by liberal applications of water and fertilizing materials, but upon the cessation of flowering—when the leafy shoots commence to die back (for all of these orchids are normally deciduous annually)—moisture should largely be withheld, and fertilizing stopped, in order to allow the tuberous roots to ripen properly. During this rest-period (which will often continue for a period of several months), only enough water should be given the plant that the compost in which it is growing does not become excessively dry and hard-baked. When the parts of the plant above ground have withered thoroughly, the tubers may be removed and divided, being thereupon repotted and watered only very slightly until the new shoots once again appear above the surface. (C, I, H)

H. achalensis Krzl.

Tubers small, ovoid or oblong, with attached fibrous roots. St. erect, rounded or angular, leafy below, sheathed above, 1–2′ tall. Lvs. clasping the st., lanceolate, acutish, erect, rather thin-textured, 3–5″ long, decreasing in size upwards. Infls. few- to many-fld., 3–6″ long. Fls. about ⅜″ in diam., fragrant, white or pale greenish. Dors. sep. ovate, acutish, the lats. obliquely ovate, acutish, deflexed. Ps. very deeply 2-lbd., the lbs. linear, the outer one falcate apically. Lip deeply 3-lbd., the lat. lbs. linear, deflexed, the midlb. ligulate, the spur filiform, apically clavate. Mostly Feb.–Mar. (C, I) Argentina.

H. Aitchisoni Rchb.f. (*Habenaria brachyphylla* Aitch.)

Tubers thick, fleshy, rather large. St. extremely variable in size and stoutness, 9–18″ tall. Lvs. opposite, rounded, cuspidate, inserted above the base of the st., 1–3″ long. Infl. rather slender, densely many-fld., furnished with a few small sheaths, 3–6″ long. Fls. secund, about ½″ in diam., pale green, fragrant. Dors. sep. oblong-ovate, erect, the spreading lats. oblong-ovate. Ps. about as long as the ss., ovate-lanceolate. Lip straight, deeply divided almost to the base into 3 narrow lbs.; spur filiform, about ¼″ long. Autumn, especially August. (C, I) Afghanistan through the Himalayas to Sikkim.

H. arietina Hk.f. (*Habenaria pectinata* Ldl.)

Tuber usually solitary, large, oblong, irregular in shape. St. stout, very leafy, 1–2′ tall. Lvs. ovate-lanceolate, rather large, the upper ones sheathing the st. Infl. densely many-fld., 3–7″ long. Fls. about 2″ in diam., fragrant, lasting rather well, green and white. Dors. sep. lanceolate, erect, the lats. ovate-lanceolate, spreading. Ps. linear-falcate, obtuse. Lip about as long as the ss., divided into 3 narrow lbs., lat. lbs. lacerate to the middle or inner margin; midlb. linear; spur subclavate, about ⅝″ long. Mostly autumn. (C, I) Himalayas; Khasia Hills, usually at high elevations.

H. carnea N.E.Br.

Tubers rather large, ovoid. St. rather stout, erect, to 10″ tall. Lvs. several, all near base of st., to 4″ long and 1½″ broad, olive-green with pale almost white spots. Infl. with up to 15 fls., these crowded. Fls. entirely pale pink, very lovely, almost 1½″ in diam., long-lasting. Dors. sep. and ps. forming a hood, the lat. ss. larger than the other segms., spreading, with a broad base. Lip very large, 3-lbd., widening abruptly from the base to the broadly rounded lat. lbs.; midlb. widening from its base, the apex rounded, cleft; spur to more than 2″ long. Winter. (I, H) Langkawi Islands and Peninsular Thailand, growing on limestone rocks at low elevations.

H. ceratopetala A.Rich.

Tuber usually solitary, oblong. St. rather stout, leafy, 9–18″ tall. Lvs. cauline, elliptic to oblong, rather blunt, numerous, 1–4″ long. Infl. densely many-fld., 2–9″ long. Fls. about 1¾″ in diam., green and white, fragrant, lasting rather well. Dors. sep. hooded, elliptic-oblong, blunt, the lats. falcate-oblong, acutish, slightly oblique at apex. Ps. very deeply 2-lbd., the upper lb. linear-filiform, the inner lb. more than 1″ long, broader than the upper one, very curved or circinnate at tip. Lip with 3 narrow, linear lbs.; spur filiform, clavate, more than 3″ long. Autumn. (I, H) Ethiopia.

H. ciliosa Ldl.

Tubers several, oblong. St. stout, leafy, to 1¾′ tall. Lvs. fleshy, dark green usually barred with black, linear-oblong to oblong-lanceolate, becoming bract-like upwards and forming basal sheaths, acutish, 2–4″ long. Infl. densely many-fld., 2–5″ long. Fls. about ½″ in diam., fragrant, not lasting well, pale green. Dors. sep. broadly ovate or ovate-oblong, obtuse, fringed; lat. ss. obliquely ovate or ovate-oblong, obtuse, fringed. Ps. obliquely semiovate-oblong, obtuse. Lip 3-lbd., the lat. lbs. linear-oblong, obtuse; midlb. linear, obtuse, like the lats. rather fleshy; spur ¾″ long. Winter, especially Jan.–Feb. (I) Natal; Griqualand East; Tembuland; Transkei.

H. cornuta Ldl.

Tubers several, ovoid. St. stout, leafy, 1–1½′ tall. Lvs. numerous, rather leathery, elliptic-oblong or oblong-lanceolate, dark rich green, 1½–4″ long, becoming smaller upwards. Infl. densely many-fld., 3–5″ long. Fls. about ⅝″ in diam., fragrant, green and white, lasting well. Dors. sep. elliptic-ovate, the lats. obliquely semiovate, rather obtuse, spreading. Ps. with two apical, cleft lbs., the upper one narrowly linear, the lower one incurved, twice as long. Lip 3-lbd., the lbs. tapering; spur ½″ long. Autumn–winter. (I) South Africa, especially Natal, usually in marshy areas.

H. Delavayi Finet (*Habenaria yunnanensis* Rolfe)

Tubers usually paired, small, ovoid or oblong. St. slender, smooth, covered with sheaths, to 1½′ tall. Lvs. cauline and basal, few to numerous, becoming sheath-like above, 2–4″ long. Infls. few- to many-fld., 2–6″ long. Fls. about ¼″ in diam., fragrant, the ss. and ps. green, the lip white. Ss. lanceolate, acutish, the ps. linear-lanceolate, acutish. Lip very deeply 3-lbd., the lbs. fringed, the midlb. linear, acutish; spur pendulous, thickened at the tip. June–July. (C, I) China: Western Yunnan, at high elevations in the mountains.

H. digitata Ldl. (*Bonatea benghalensis* Griff., *Bonatea herbacea* Wall., *Bonatea punduana* Ldl., *Habenaria trinervia* Wight)

Tuber usually solitary, ovoid. St. leafy, rather slender, 1–2′ tall. Lvs. numerous, varying from roundish to lanceolate, acutish, 2–5″ long. Infls. many-fld., 4–7″ long. Fls. about ¾″ in diam., fragrant, pale green. Dors. sep. roundish, the lats. ovate, acutish. Ps. divided into 2 lbs., the upper one the broader. Lip divided almost to the base into 3 linear lbs.; spur subclavate, often inflated. Mostly summer, especially June–July. (I) Himalayas.

H. longifolia Buch.-Ham. (*Gymnadenia longifolia* Ldl.)

Tuber usually solitary, rather large, ovoid. St. slender, leafy, 9–18″ tall. Lvs. scattered, erect, linear, acutish, 3–5″ long. Infls. loosely few-fld., 2–3″ long. Fls. narrow, elongate, about ¾″ long, pure white, the lip much the largest segm. Dors. sep. narrowly oblong-lanceolate, the lats. larger, oblong-lanceolate. Ps. ovate, concave basally. Lip about 3 times as long as ss., very broadly oblong, divided into 3 deep segms., the outer segms. roundish, quite entire, the median one linear; spur slender, almost 1½″ long. Summer–autumn. (C, I) Himalayas.

H. macrantha Hochst.

Tuber solitary, oblong. St. rather stout, leafy, 1–2½′ tall. Lvs. cauline, ovate or ovate-lanceolate, acutish, 2–6″ long. Infls. many-fld., 3–7″ long. Fls. fragrant, more than 1½″ in diam., white and green, very showy. Dors. sep. ovate, acutish; lat. ss. subobliquely ovate-oblong, acutish. Ps. lanceolate-oblong, rather acutish. Lip 3-lbd., narrow at base, the lat. lbs. broad, divided into 8–10 filiform segms., the midlb. linear, rather acutish; spur cylindrical, curved, 1½″ long. Mostly Sept.–Oct. (I) Arabia; Ethiopia, growing in marshy places.

H. pectinata (Smith) D.Don (*Orchis pectinata* Smith, *Habenaria ensifolia* Ldl., *H. Gerardiana* Wall.)

Tuber usually solitary, rather large, ovoid. St. stout, very leafy, 1–2′ tall. Lvs. ovate-lanceolate, mostly sheathing, 4–6″ long. Infl. densely many-fld., 3–8″ long. Fls. about 2″ in diam., fragrant, cream-white, flushed with pale green, handsome. Dors. sep. lanceolate, erect; lat. ss. ovate-lanceolate, spreading. Ps. linear-falcate, somewhat dilated on outer margin. Lip 3-lbd., cut and lacerate along inner margin, the midlb. linear; spur slender, subclavate, ¾″ long. Autumn, especially Aug. (C, I) Himalayas to western China, usually at rather high elevations.

H. quinqueseta (Michx.) Sw. (*Orchis quinqueseta* Michx., *Habenaria macroceratitis* Willd.)

St. variable, slender or robust, 8″–3′ tall. Lvs. gradually becoming smaller and bract-like towards the fl.-bearing part, oblong-lanceolate to oblong-obovate, broadly rounded to acuminate at apex, 2–10″ long. Infl. loosely few- to many-flowered, 3–10″ long. Fls. fragrant, long-lived, variable in size, but to 1½″ long, the ss. and ps. greenish, the lip usually ivory-white. Ps. 2-lbd., both lbs. very long, the upper one included in the hood formed by the dors. sep. Lip 3-lbd., the lat. lbs. filiform, curved, the midlb. larger, with revolute margins; spur 1½–7″ long. Autumn–winter. (I, H) South-east United States

and Mexico throughout West Indies and Central America to northern South America.

H. rhodocheila Hance (*Habenaria militaris* Rchb.f., *H. pusilla* Rchb.f.)

Rather similar in habit to *H. carnea* N.E.Br., the st. 8–12″ tall. Lvs. about 6 in number, basal or almost so, to about 4½″ long, becoming smaller and bract-like above, green with an intricate network of darker veins. Infls. usually about 10-fld., about 2′ long. Fls. very handsome, about 1½″ in diam., long-lasting, varying from yellow or orange to vivid scarlet, the ss. and ps. often green. Dors. sep. and ps. forming a hood, the lat. ss. spreading, twisted. Lip very large, widening gradually from the base, deeply 3-lbd., the lat. lbs. large, slightly longer than wide, with rounded ends; midlb. widening from a narrow base, deeply 2-lbd., rounded; spur 2″ long. Winter. (I, H) South China and Viet-Nam southward to Penang, usually lithophytic on mossy rocks.

H. sagittifera Rchb.f. (*Habenaria linearifolia* Maxim.)

Tubers usually paired, small, ovoid. St. rather slender, to 2½′ tall. Lvs. few, narrowly linear, acutish, 3–4″ long. Infls. loosely 8–12-fld. Fls. fragrant, about ½″ in diam., purple. Dors. sep. ovate, acutish, the lats. semi-ovate, deflexed, suboblique. Ps. simple, ovate, blunt. Lip 3-lbd., the lat. lbs. linear, toothed at apex; midlb. linear, obtuse; spur cylindrical, obtuse, about ⅝″ long. Summer–autumn. (C, I) North China; Manchuria; Japan.

H. uliginosa Rchb.f.

Tubers several, narrowly oblong, about ½″ long. St. rather stout, leafy, to 2′ tall. Lvs. becoming spathaceous bracts above, linear-lanceolate, acutish, 3–4″ long. Infls. densely many-fld., 3–6″ long. Fls. about ½″ in diam., fragrant, pale green and white. Ss. ovate-triangular, acutish. Ps. 2-lbd., the lbs. linear-falcate. Lip deeply 3-lbd., the lat. lbs. subfalcately lanceolate, the midlb. lanceolate, acutish; spur cylindrical, pendulous, clavate apically, about ⅝″ long. Autumn–winter. (I, H) South Brazil to Chile and Argentina.

H. altior Rendle Tubers several, ovoid. St. rather stout, leafy below the middle, to 15″ tall. Lvs. basal and cauline, linear-lanceolate, amplexicaul, acutish, becoming bract-like above, 2–3″ long. Infl. ovoid, densely many-fld., abbreviated. Fls. about ⅝″ in diam., pale green and white. Dors. sep. narrow basally, spatulate at tip; lat. ss. very obliquely ovate. Ps. divided almost to base into 2 lbs., the upper lb. filiform, the lower one lanceolate-subulate, both hairy. Lip deeply 3-lbd., the lat. lbs. linear, rather pointed; midlb. similar but blunt; spur dilated medially and somewhat twisted, ¾″ long. Mostly Sept.–Oct. (C, I) Tanganyika Territory.

H. anguiceps Bolus Tubers several, large, ovoid-oblong. St. leafy, to 9″ tall. Lvs. becoming bract-like above, sessile, oblong-lanceolate, fleshy, to 1½″ long. Infl. about 3″ long, rather dense and broad. Fls. about ⅜″ in diam., pale green and white, fragrant. Dors. sep. concave, broadly ovate, obtuse; lat. ss. obliquely semiovate-oblong, obtuse. Ps. semiovate-oblong, obtuse. Lip linear-oblong, fleshy, obtuse; spur rather thick, inflated apically, ⅜″ long. Winter. (I) Cape Colony; Natal; Orange Free State.

H. Davidii (Finet) Franch. (*Habenaria pectinata* (Smith) D.Don var. *Davidii* Finet). Tubers usually paired, oblong. St.

rather stout, leafy, to 2′ tall. Lvs. very crowded at st.-base, rounded, becoming broadly lanceolate and amplexicaul upwards, acute, erect, 3–4″ long. Infls. erect, 8–12-fld., rather crowded. Fls. about ½″ across and 1¼″ long, faintly fragrant, dull yellow. Ss. and ps. narrowly ovate, acutish, fringed on margins. Lip divided for ⅔ of length into 3 linear segms., the lat. lbs. deeply fringed, midlb. entire; spur cylindrical, thickened at tip, pendulous, almost 3″ long. Mostly July–Aug. (C, I) West China, at rather high elevations.

H. decorata Hochst. Tuber solitary, oblong or ovoid. St. rather stout, leafy, to 9″ tall. Lvs. dark green, cauline, ovate-lanceolate to oblong-lanceolate, acutish, 1–3″ long. Infl. short, loosely 2–7-fld. Fls. more than ⅝″ in diam., white and pale green, fragrant. Dors. sep. ovate, blunt, fuzzy; lat. ss. ovate-oblong, suboblique, acutish. Ps. subobliquely ovate-oblong, rather obtuse. Lip deeply 3-lbd., the lat. lbs. sub-falcate-oblong, divaricate with the tip, split into 5 filiform segms., the midlb. triangular-linear, rather obtuse; spur cylindrical, 1¼″ long. Mostly Sept.–Oct. (C, I) Ethiopia, in the high mountains.

H. Galpinii Bolus Tubers several, rather large, oblong. St. rather stout, leafy, to 9″ tall. Lvs. 6–9 in number, rich dark green, lanceolate, sessile, 3–4″ long, gradually becoming bract-like up the st. Infls. rather loosely many-fld., 4–6″ long. Fls. about ⅜″ in diam., pale green, faintly fragrant. Dors. sep. ovate-elliptic, concave, acutish; lat. ss. semiobovate-oblong, with an oblique pointed tip. Ps. cleft at tip, the upper lb. linear, the lower one lanceolate-linear, longer than the upper one. Lip divided into 3 linear or bristle-shaped lbs., the median one half as long again as the lat. ones; spur slender, ¾″ long. Spring. (I) Transvaal.

H. glaucifolia Franch. Tubers several, oblong. St. to 12″ tall, fuzzy, slender. Lvs. paired, opposite, glaucous grey-green, transversely elliptic, acutish, to 2½″ long. Infl. loosely few-fld., about 3–4″ long. Fls. about 1″ in diam., fragrant, white to green, or sometimes white with a green lip and spur. Dors. sep. oblong, obtuse; lat. ss. semi-ovate. Ps. 2-parted, the segms. linear or triangular. Lip clawed, 3-lbd., the lbs. linear, the median one longer than the lats.; spur filiform, pendulous, inflated at the apex. Summer, especially July. (C, I) China: Szechuan, at high elevations in pine woods.

H. Mairei Schltr. Tubers paired, small, oblong. St. erect or somewhat flexuous, leafy, to 15″ tall. Lvs. usually 5–6 in number, narrowly elliptic, acutish, suberect, cauline, about 3″ long. Infl. loosely few-fld., 3–5″ long. Fls. about ¾″ in diam., fragrant, pale green, rather handsome. Dors. sep. erect, narrowly ovate; lat. ss. spreading, narrowly ovate, falcate at tip. Ps. narrowly oblong, obtuse, marginally fringed. Lip divided almost to the base into 3 narrow lbs., the lat. lbs. fringed, the midlb. linear, obtuse; spur cylindrical, pendulous, incurving, ¾″ long. Mostly Aug. (C, I) China: Yunnan, at high elevations.

H. pachycaulon Hk.f. Rhiz. branching, emitting a few thick fleshy fibres. St. very robust, with a few large sheaths upwards, to 6″ tall. Lf. solitary, near st.-base, oblong, obtuse, rather leathery, 2½–3½″ long. Infl. laxly few-fld., very slender, to 2″ long. Fls. about ¼″ in diam., fragrant, purple, the segms. thickly fleshy. Ss. linear-oblong, the about equal ps. ovate-oblong. Lip ovate-lanceolate; spur short, clavate. Aug.–Sept. (C, I) Sikkim, at high elevations.

H. praestans Rendle Tuber usually solitary, rather large, ovoid. St. to about 6″ tall. Lvs. cauline, ovate-lanceolate, or oblong, rather obtuse, becoming bract-like above, 2–6″ long. Infl. densely many-fld., 5–6″ long. Fls. about 1¼″ in diam., fragrant, pale green and white. Dors. sep. ovate, rather obtuse; lat. ss. ovate-lanceolate, obtuse. Ps. lanceolate-

oblong, subfalcate, rather obtuse. Lip 3-lbd., very narrow at base, the lat. lbs. almost 1″ long, divided into about 12 thread-like segms.; midlb. linear, rather obtuse; spur cylindrical, slightly thickened above, more than ¾″ long. Spring–summer. (I) East and Central Africa, mostly high in the mountains.

HAEMARIA Ldl.
(*Dicrophyla* Raf., *Ludisia* Bl., *Myoda* Ldl.)

Haemaria consists of but a single highly variable species of handsome terrestrial orchid, one of the 'Jewel Orchids', native over a huge area extending from southern China and Burma to Sumatra, Java, and other islands of Indonesia. Allied to *Macodes* Bl. and to *Anoectochilus* Bl., it is one of the most frequently seen of the alliance in collections at this time. Not only is its foliage of singular beauty, but the charming white flowers are considerably larger and more showy than those of most related groups of the subtribe *Physurinae*.

Haemaria has been crossed with *Macodes* (= *Macomaria*), *Dossinia* (= *Dossinimaria*), and *Anoecto-chilus* (= *Anoectomaria*), but it is extremely doubtful whether any of these very attractive hybrids are present in collections any longer.

CULTURE: As for *Anoectochilus*. In the warm, humid greenhouse, *Haemaria* need not be kept under a bell-jar or other such structure, as is usually essential for its more delicate allies. (H)

H. discolor (Ker-Gawl.) Ldl. (*Goodyera discolor* Ker-Gawl., *Ludisia discolor* A.Rich., *Ludisia odorata* Bl., *Ludisia Furetii* Bl.)
Sts. erect or procumbent, leafy, short, usually less than 6″ long, fleshy and brittle, usually reddish or dull purplish. Lvs. mostly less than 6, whorled, stalked basally, the blade to more than 3″ long and usually only about ¾″ broad, green above sometimes with white or silvery-white longitudinal markings, rich red-purple underneath. Infls. to 12″ tall (rarely more), short-hairy, with 3 or more pale sheathing bracts below the rather dense, green-bracted apical rac. Fls. fragrant, very showy for the aggregation, about ¾″ across, white with a vivid yellow anther-cap, the lip very complicated in structure. There are several named horticultural variants, other than the distinctive one listed below, these based primarily on foliar coloration. Autumn–winter. (H) South China and Burma to Indonesia.

—var. **Dawsoniana** (Low) A.D.Hawkes (*Anoectochilus Dawsonianus* Low, *Anoectochilus Ordianus* hort., *Goodyera Dawsonii* Boxall, *Haemaria Dawsoniana* Hassl.)
Leaf-blades to 3½″ long and 1¼″ broad, rich dull red or velvety-red above, with more or less intricate net-veins of paler red or yellow, underneath pale pinkish-red to dark purplish-red. Infls. to more than 12″ tall, the bracts of the rac. usually pink. A very handsome orchid. Autumn–winter. (H) Burma.

HAKONEASTE Mak.

The genus *Hakoneaste* contains but a single described species, this the rare and little-known **H. sawadana** Mak., which has apparently been found on only one occasion in Japan. It is a member of the subtribe *Calypsoinae*, and is not in cultivation at this time.

Nothing is known regarding the genetic ties of this odd group.

CULTURE: Unknown.

HAMMARBYA O.Ktze.

Consisting of but a single species, the genus *Hammarbya* is often included in the group *Malaxis* Soland. ex Sw., from which it differs in the production of true pseudobulbs, and in several details of the small flowers. Typically growing in bogs or other perpetually moist spots, it is an insignificant orchid, primarily of botanical interest. A member of the subtribe *Liparidinae*, it is extremely scarce in cultivation at this time.

Nothing is known of the genetic affinities of this orchid.

CULTURE: Normally growing in bogs, in association with *Sphagnum* mosses, under very acid conditions, *Hammarbya paludosa* is a difficult orchid to maintain under the artificial arrangements of our collections. Some degree of success, however, is sometimes obtained by giving the plant the cultural conditions of *Calypso*, etc. (C)

H. paludosa (L.) O.Ktze. (*Ophrys paludosa* L., *Malaxis paludosa* Sw.)

Pbs, usually paired, one of the current year, the other of previous season, about the size of a garden-pea, usually obscured by lf.-bases, the roots reduced to tiny hairs. Lvs. 2–4, oblong, rather fleshy, to 1¼″ long, often bearing tiny bulb-like thickenings at tips, these giving rise to new plantlets when disengaged. Infl. erect, 1–5″ tall, with a many-fld. rather dense rac. at tip. Fls. about ⅛″ long, complex in structure, the lip at top of the fl., brought there by a twisting of the pedicellate ovary of 360°, pale yellow to greenish-yellow, the lip broad, rather blunt. July–Sept. (C) British Isles throughout northern and central Europe to Siberia and Japan.

HANCOCKIA Rolfe

Hancockia uniflora Rolfe, the only detected species of this group to date, is a native of Yunnan in China and Viet-Nam, and is as yet unknown in our collections. The genus is placed in the subtribe *Collabiinae*, and is somewhat allied to *Nephelaphyllum* Bl., but differs from that group in technical details of the rather small flowers, particularly in the elongate cylindrical spur.

Nothing is known of the genetic affinities of *Hancockia*.

CULTURE: Presumably as for *Phaius*. (I, H)

HARAËLLA Kudo

Two species of rare and very incompletely known epiphytic orchids of the general *Saccolabium* alliance of the subtribe *Sarcanthinae* comprise this genus. Both appear to be endemic to the island of Formosa (Taiwan), and at this time have not made their way into our collections.

Nothing is known of the genetic affinities of *Haraëlla*.

CULTURE: Presumably as for the smaller epiphytic Vandas, etc. (I, H)

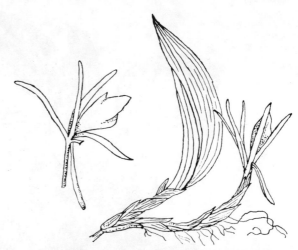

Hancockia uniflora Rolfe [A.D.HAWKES, AFTER F. GAGNEPAIN]

HELCIA Ldl.

Two species of *Helcia* are known to science, one of them now being grown in a very few particularly choice collections. The genus is a segregate from *Trichopilia* Ldl. on technical details, and is incorporated in that group by certain students. Rather unusually attractive epiphytic plants from Colombia and Ecuador, they bear proportionately large flowers on neat, pseudobulbous plants which are quite distinctive even in superficial appearance from the allied *Trichopilia*.

No hybrids have as yet been made utilizing the Helcias, and nothing is perforce known regarding their genetic affinities.

CULTURE: Usually inhabiting rather high elevations, these handsome orchids must for best results be kept in the cool-house, or at least the cooler portion of an intermediate-house. They thrive when grown in smallish, well-drained pots, in a mixture of equal parts of shredded tree-fern fibre and chopped sphagnum moss. While actively growing, they delight in quantities of water and high humidity, but a rather strict rest-period of about three weeks' duration should be afforded them upon maturation of the new pseudobulbs. A semi-shaded spot is necessary, else the rather coriaceous foliage may burn. Regular applications of weakened fertilizer solution seem beneficial. (C, I)

H. sanguinolenta Ldl. (*Trichopilia sanguinolenta* Rchb.f.)

Pbs. tightly clustered, usually rather dull bluish-green, ovoid or oblong, slightly compressed, to about 2″ long. Lf. solitary, leathery, usually wavy-margined, oblong-elliptic, acute, narrowed into a short stalk at the base, to 6″ long and 1¼″ wide, usually dull green. Infls. numerous, 1-fld., hanging or horizontal, to 3½″ long. Fls. fragrant, heavy-textured, long-lasting, to about 3″ across, the spreading ss. and ps. usually yellowish-olive-green with transverse bands of brownish-crimson, the bands sometimes arranged into roundish blotches, the flattened, crisped and incised lip white, with radiating veins that are marked in the lower part with broken lines of crimson or purple-red. Winter. (C, I) Ecuador.

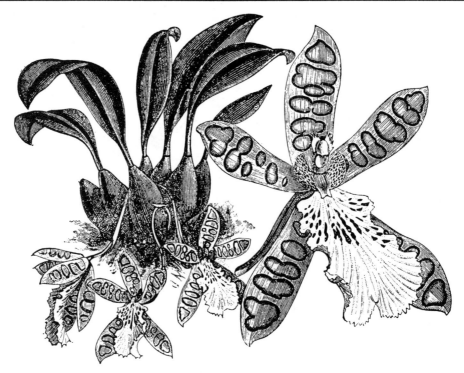

Helcia sanguinolenta Ldl. [B.S.WILLIAMS]

HELLERORCHIS A.D.Hawkes
(*Theodorea* B.-R.)

A segregate from *Gomesa* R.Br., this recently re-named genus (formerly known by the homonymic *Theodorea* B.-R.) consists of six rather rare but singularly attractive smallish epiphytic orchids, native to Brazil. They differ from *Gomesa* in the secund inflorescences of flowers which differ widely in technical structure. Very seldom seen in collections at this time, the Hellerorchis are charming little plants, and are highly floriferous when well-grown.

Nothing is known of the genetic affinities of *Hellerorchis*, although it seems highly logical that it will prove compatible with at least certain other members of the subtribe *Oncidiinae*.

CULTURE: As for the warm-growing, pseudobulbous Oncidiums. (I, H)

H. gomezoides (B.-R.) A.D.Hawkes (*Theodorea gomezoides* B.-R., *Gomesa Theodorea* Cgn.)

Pbs. clustered, ovoid, somewhat compressed laterally, to about 2″ tall. Lvs. usually paired, linear-lanceolate, acuminate, to 6″ long and ½″ broad. Infls. almost erect, secund, about 10-fld. (rarely to 20-fld.), the fls. nodding. Fls. about 1½″ long, fragrant, the ss. and ps. brown, the lip very complex, brown apically, white or yellowish-white in basal half, with 2 hairy calli at base. Summer–autumn. (I, H) Brazil.

HEMIPILIA Ldl.

About eight species of *Hemipilia* are known to date, all of them singularly attractive terrestrial (rarely litho-phytic) orchids of the subtribe *Habenarinae*, native in the mountainous regions of China, northern India, Burma, and Thailand. A single species is sometimes encountered in particularly choice collections at this time, but it must be classed as a rare orchid. The genus is vaguely allied to *Brachycorythis* Ldl., though the flowers more closely simulate, superficially at least, some sort of *Habenaria*.

Nothing is known of the genetic alliances of *Hemipilia*.

CULTURE: As for *Cynorkis*, though considerably cooler temperatures must prevail at all times. (C, I)

H. calophylla Par. & Rchb.f.

. Tuber ovoid, subterranean, small. Lf. solitary, to about 3″ long, ovate, acute, rather heavy-textured, glossy, deep lustrous green marbled with purple-red, usually purplish on undersurface. Infls. erect, 5–6-fld., to about 8″ tall. Fls. distant in a rac., about 1″ long, white to pink, with a dark violet lip which is undulate and crisped marginally. Dors. sep. forming a hood with the ps., the lat. ss. reflexed. Spring–summer. (C, I) Burma and Thailand, on limestone rocks in the mountains.

HERMINIUM R.Br.
(*Chamaeorchis* Koch, *Chamaerepes* Spreng., *Chamorchis* A.Rich., *Cybele* Falc., *Thisbe* Falc.)

Herminium is a genus of upwards of twenty known species of mostly small-flowered, relatively insignificant, terrestrial orchids, native in Europe and in subtropical and tropical Asia. Very rare in cultivation outside of their native haunts, these allies of *Habenaria* Willd. are rather attractive when well-grown, and should be better

Epidendrum Stamfordianum Batem.
[G. C. K. DUNSTERVILLE]

(BELOW) *Epigeneium acuminatum*
(Rolfe ex Ames) Summerh.
[CHARLES MILLER]

Eria javanica (Sw.) Bl. [GEORGE
FULLER]

(ABOVE) *Euanthe Sanderiana* (Rchb.f.) Schltr. [ALEX C. CHANG]

(ABOVE RIGHT) *Eulophia Quartiniana* A. Rich. [GEORGE FULLER]

(RIGHT) *Gastrochilus bellinus* (Rchb.f.) O.Ktze. [GEORGE FULLER]

(BELOW) *Eulophiella* × *Rolfei*, a rare hybrid characteristic of this fascinating genus [GEORGE FULLER]

Hemipilia calophylla Par. & Rchb.f. [A.D.HAWKES, AFTER *Orchids of Thailand*]

known by enthusiasts who specialize in the multitudinous 'ground orchids'.

No hybrids are registered in *Herminium*, though the genus is presumably allied, genetically, to at least some members of the subtribe *Habenarinae*, and hybridization could theoretically occur between them.

CULTURE: As for the temperate species of *Habenaria* and *Orchis*. (C, I)

H. alpinum (L.) Ldl. (*Ophrys alpina* L., *Chamaeorchis alpina* L.C.Rich., *Chamaerepes alpina* Spreng., *Epipactis alpina* Schm., *Orchis alpina* Schrk., *Orchis graminea* Crantz)
Tubers ovoid, subterranean, smallish. Lvs. 5–8, basal, narrowly linear, 2–4″ long. Infls. densely 8–15-fld., erect, to 5″ tall. Fls. usually less than ¼″ long, green flushed with brown, the lip yellowish. Lip shortly 3-lbd. apically, the spur absent. Spring–summer. (C) Central and Northern Europe, in the higher mountains.

H. Monorchis (L.) R.Br. (*Orchis Monorchis* L., *Herminium clandestinum* Gren. & Godr., *Orchis chonorchis* All., *Satyrium Monorchis* Pers.)
Tubers ellipsoidal, subterranean, small. Lvs. 2, basal, narrowly oblong, to 3″ long or less. Infls. erect, to 8″ tall, bearing rather numerous fls. in a fairly dense rac., most of the fls. facing in the same direction. Fls.

about ¼″ long, yellow-green, the lip 3-lbd. near the apex, basally concave. Spring–summer. (C, I) Europe; Northern Asia to North China.

HERPYSMA Ldl.

The genus *Herpysma* contains two species at this time, neither of which is present in our collections today. These are **H. longicaulis** Ldl., a native of the Himalayas, and **H. Merrillii** Ames, from the Philippines. Placed in the very difficult subtribe *Physurinae*, nearest in their alliance to *Eurycentrum* Schltr., they are robust terrestrial orchids with somewhat larger and showier flowers than many of their congeners, thus making them of some potential value to connoisseurs of the 'Jewel Orchids'.

Nothing is known of the genetic affinities of *Herpysma*. CULTURE: As for *Anoectochilus*. (H)

HERSCHELIA Ldl.

Like many of the genera which have been segregated from *Disa* Berg., *Herschelia* is virtually unknown in contemporary collections, despite the fact that it contains some very lovely and unusual terrestrial (rarely lithophytic) species. About nineteen of these are known to date, native mostly in South Africa, with a few representatives extending up into central Africa. The Herschelias are slender, reedy plants, the stems arising from subterranean, ovoid, irregular tubers; two types of foliage are present, the basal leaves being linear and grass-like, the ones on the inflorescence-stem few in number, brown, and bract-like. The flowers—often very brightly coloured and attractive—are produced in relatively small numbers in a loose raceme. Their structure is uniquely complex, and several of the species seem to be somewhat more amenable to cultivation than most of their allies. Here belongs one of the handsomest of the 'Blue Orchids', *Herschelia graminifolia* (Ker-Gawl.) Dur. & Schinz.

No hybrids are known in *Herschelia*, but it is presumably genetically compatible with *Disa* and other members of the subtribe *Disinae*. Some unusual and doubtless most attractive crosses seem potential here.

CULTURE: As for *Disa*. (C, I)

H. graminifolia (Ker-Gawl.) Dur. & Schinz (*Disa graminifolia* Ker-Gawl., *Herschelia coelestis* Ldl.)
Basal lvs. 4–6, grass-like, shorter than the st.; cauline lvs. several, membranous, short, acute, brown. Infls. to 2′ tall, 3–6-fld., erect. Fls. very fragrant and handsome, to more than 1″ long, somewhat variable in colour, the ss. bright blue, the lower part of the ps. mauve, the upper part green, the lip pale blue or whitish edged with deep blue or purple (a form with pure white fls. has been recorded, but is apparently exceedingly rare). Dors. sep. hooded, with a small conical spur, emarginate or shortly acute; lat. ss. spreading, oblong, obtuse, with an apical mucro. Ps. much smaller than the ss., included within the sepaline hood, sharply bent above the middle, the upper part erect, rounded, the lower part dilated at the base into a rounded frontal lb. Lip large, oblong or ovate, recurved, the margins slightly wavy. Feb.–Mar. (C, I) South Africa.

Herschelia graminifolia (Ker-Gawl.) Dur. & Sch.
[B.S.WILLIAMS]

H. purpurascens (Bolus) Krzl. (*Disa purpurascens* Bolus) Basal lvs. 6–8, shorter than the st.; cauline lvs. several, membranous, short, acute, brownish Infls. to 1½′ tall, 1–3-fld., the floral bracts brown. Fls. very fragrant, about 1½″ long, the ss. bright blue or purple-blue, the lip and lower half of the ps. purple, the upper half of the ps. green. Dors. sep. broadly ovate, acute; lat. ss. oblong, acute. Ps. curved, the upper part dilated, rounded and minutely toothed, the lower part rounded, joined to the col. Lip ovate, with involute short-toothed margins. Oct.–Nov. (C, I) South Africa.

HETAERIA Bl.
(*Aetheria* Endl., *Cerochilus* Ldl., *Etaeria* Ldl., *Rhamphidia* Ldl., *Rhomboda* Ldl.)

A member of the subtribe *Physurinae*, and closest in its affinity to *Vrydagzynea* Bl., from which it differs in structural details of the very small flowers, *Hetaeria* contains about thirty species of terrestrial or lithophytic (rarely semi-epiphytic) orchids. These are indigenous in South-east Asia and Indonesia, with a single outlying representative in tropical Africa. One of the genera known collectively as the 'Jewel Orchids', the Hetaerias are virtually unknown in contemporary collections, although several of them have very handsome, coloured foliage which makes them worth a place in the warm greenhouse.

Nothing is known of the genetic affinities of *Hetaeria*.
CULTURE: As for *Anoectochilus*. (H)

H. oblongifolia Bl.

St. rather fleshy, erect or procumbent, leafy to beyond the middle, to about 14″ tall. Lvs. narrowly elliptic, acuminate, stalked, the lamina about 4″ long, glossy-green, with a lustrous red sheen, rather fragile in texture. Infl. a very short, rather densely many-fld. rac. Fls. inverted, about $\frac{1}{16}$″ long, reddish-green to whitish, the lip yellow. Summer–autumn. (H) Sumatra; Java; Borneo.

HEXALECTRIS Raf.

Hexalectris is a genus of about six species of unusual and often rather attractive saprophytic orchids, native in the United States and Mexico, with a single representative (**H. parviflora** L.O.Wms.) extending into Guatemala. Most of the known entities in this genus have been described during the past decade or so, and the centre of dissemination is obviously in Mexico. A single *Hexalectris* may be present in specialized collections at this time, but, like all saprophytes, its cultural requirements are met only with great difficulty. The genus is a member of the subtribe *Corallorrhizinae*.

Nothing is known of the genetic affinities of *Hexalectris*.
CULTURE: As for *Corallorrhiza*. (C, I)

H. spicata (Walt.) Barnh. (*Arethusa spicata* Walt., *Bletia aphylla* Nutt., *Hexalectris aphylla* Raf., *H. squamosa* Raf., *Corallorrhiza arizonica* S.Wats., *Corallorrhiza spicata* Tidestr.)

Highly variable, from slender to very stout, erect, to more than 3′ tall (usually much shorter). St. flesh-coloured to pale madder-purple, the lvs. reduced to sheathing scale-like bracts along the st., broadly ovate, acute. Rac. apical, loosely few- to several-fld., 2–14″ long, with purplish bracts. Fls. usually rather nodding, to about 2″ across, the ss. and ps. yellowish with purplish-brown stripes, the lip yellowish-white with purple stripes. Ss. oblong-elliptic, obtuse to subacute, the lats. oblique. Ps. oblong-elliptic to narrowly oblong-spatulate, obtuse, somewhat falcate. Lip shallowly 3-lbd., concave, recurved; lat. lbs. entire, the apex broadly rounded to obtuse, incurved and clasping the col.; midlb. roundish-ovate, subtruncate to notched at the tip, the margins undulate-crisped; disc with the 5–7 nerves crested with longitudinal fleshy ridges extending from the lip-base nearly to the apex of the midlb., with 3 additional fleshy-ridged nerves spreading out onto the lat. lbs. June–Oct. (C, U) South-east United States to Arizona and New Mexico; Mexico.

HEXISEA Ldl.
(*Euothonaea* Rchb.f.)

This is a genus of about six species—several of which are incompletely known botanically—of unusual epiphytic or lithophytic orchids in Mexico, Central America, and northern South America. Apparently allied to several genera of the subtribe *Laeliinae*, the exact confines of *Hexisea* are not as yet understood, and only one species appears to be presently in cultivation; this is uncommon, too, although it is one of the most delightful and showy of the so-called 'botanical' orchids. **Hexisea bidentata** Ldl., described below, combines the fortunate characteristics of floriferousness (often blossoming more than once annually) with compact habit, unusual vegetative appearance, and remarkable brilliance of floral colour. Because of these features, plus its readily met cultural requirements, it is a plant which can happily be recommended to all orchidists, whether amateur or professional.

Although as yet no hybrids utilizing *Hexisea* have been registered, the below-mentioned species has been successfully crossed with *Cattleya*, *Laelia*, and *Epidendrum*. Additional experimental breeding would seem to be very much in order in future.

CULTURE: Hexiseas may be readily grown if treated much in the manner of *Cattleya*, the pseudobulbous Epidendrums, etc. Since they grow virtually throughout the entire year, no rest-period is needed, however. In the wild occurring usually in rather exposed situations, they benefit by considerable light under cultivation, short of burning of the foliage. Fertilizers, applied on a regular schedule, are beneficial. They do well mounted on tree-fern slabs, or potted in well-drained containers, either in firmly-packed osmunda or shredded tree-fern fibre. (I, H)

H. bidentata Ldl. (*Diothonaea imbricata* Ldl., *Diothonaea oppositifolia* Rchb.f., *Euothonaea imbricata* Rchb.f., *Euothonaea oppositifolia* Rchb.f., *Epidendrum oppositifolium* A.Rich. & Gal., *Hexisea imbricata* Rchb.f., *H. oppositifolia* Rchb.f.)

Pbs. clustered, eventually to 1½′ tall, the sts. (pbs.) composed of alternate elongated swollen parts and shorter conspicuously constricted sections, the swollen ones made up of 1 or more internodes, to 3½″ long and often almost ½″ in diam., spindle-shaped, grooved in age; constricted parts consisting of several short internodes with imbricating sheaths at the nodes. Lvs. 2, at the apex of each swollen st.-section, stalkless, opposite, rather leathery, linear to linear-lanceolate, obliquely 3-toothed apically, to 4½″ long. Infls. terminal, to 1½″ long, 2–6-fld., with several rather large sheaths and bracts at

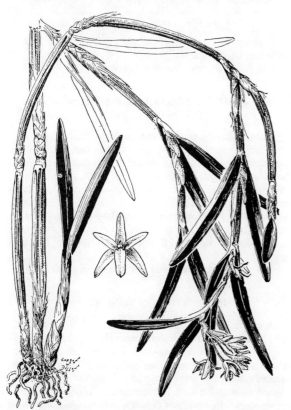

Hexisea bidentata Ldl. [GORDON W. DILLON]

base. Fls. not opening well or opening out flat, to 1″ across (often smaller), varying in hue from vermilion or orange to scarlet, the vaguely elongate-triangular callus on the lip often yellowish, whitish-yellow, or dull reddish-purple. Ss. elliptic-lanceolate, obtuse to acute, the lats. oblique. Ps. obliquely oblanceolate to narrowly elliptic, blunt or acute. Lip united with the col.-base and forming a cup, with a fleshy callus-like thickening in front of the col., the lamina oblong-elliptic, obtuse or acute apically. Mostly summer, but often flowering at intervals throughout the year. (I, H) Mexico to northern South America.

HIMANTOGLOSSUM Spreng.
(*Barlia* Parl., *Loroglossum* L.C.Rich.)

About four species of *Himantoglossum*, the so-called 'Lizard Orchids', are known to date, two of them very rare plants from the Caucasus and Turkey, the other two less uncommon and occasionally found in specialized contemporary collections. The genus is somewhat allied to *Orchis* [Tourn.] L., but differs in technical details of the incredibly complicated, vaguely reptilian flowers, which are produced in dense racemes from a subterranean series of large tubers. The blossoms are notably larger than many of the allied groups, and because of their extraordinary structure always evoke comment when they appear.

No hybrids seem to be known which utilize *Himantoglossum*. The genetic ties of the group are presumably with *Orchis*, etc.

CULTURE: As for *Orchis*. (C, I)

H. hircinum (L.) Spreng. (*Satyrium hircinum* L., *Aceras hircina* Ldl., *Loroglossum hircinum* L.C.Rich.)

Tubers usually paired, ovoid to elongate-ovoid, rather large. St. 9–36″ tall, stout, sheathed, the sheaths loose. Lvs. mostly basal, rather few in number, broad, blunt, fleshy, dark green, 2–5″ long, usually withering as the infl. grows. Infl. 4–12″ long, densely few- to many-fld., sometimes with as many as 80 fls., these mostly all open at once. Fls. more than 2″ long, giving off a strong goat-like odour, usually purplish-green with a peculiar greyish tinge, the elongate lip whitish towards base spotted and blotched with red, the remainder dull green, more or less purple-tinged on the lat. lbs. Ss. and ps. proportionately small, forming a tight hood over the col. Lip to 2″ long, narrow, ribbon-shaped, the midlb. when young rolled up to form a vague coil, expanding into a tongue-like organ that remains spirally twisted several times, the lat. lbs. much smaller, vaguely coiled. Spur short, conical, at extreme base of lip. May–July. (C, I) Central and Southern Europe; Asia Minor.

H. longibracteatum (Biv.) Schltr. (*Orchis longibracteata* Biv., *Aceras longibracteata* Rchb.f., *Barlia longibracteata* Parl., *Loroglossum longibracteatum* Moris.)

Tubers paired, large, irregularly ovoid. St. rather slender, to about 2′ tall. Lvs. cauline and basal, oblong, pointed, wavy-margined, degenerating upwards into broad lanceolate sheaths, 6–9″ long. Infl. densely many-fld., 4–6″ long. Fls. to 1¼″ long, pale purple, the margins of the lip dark purple-brown. Ss. lanceolate, forming a hood, enclosing the lanceolate ps. Lip oblong, 3-lbd., the lat. lbs. irregular in shape, the midlb. always emarginate; spur stout. Jan.–May. (C, I) Mediterranean region, from Spain to Greece; Algeria; Canary Islands.

HINTONELLA Ames

A single rare epiphytic member of *Hintonella* is thus far known, this the very diminutive **H. mexicana** Ames, which has been encountered on a couple of occasions in Central Mexico. A component of the subtribe *Ornithocephalinae*, it is placed by Ames in closest proximity to *Phymatidium* Ldl. and *Chytroglossa* Rchb.f., both from Brazil. Bearing minute pseudobulbs, ensiform foliage, and usually 2-flowered inflorescences of very small presumably yellowish flowers, it is of interest primarily to the connoisseur of the 'botanical' orchids, and is not at this time in cultivation.

Nothing is known as yet of the genetic affinities of *Hintonella*.

CULTURE: Possibly as for *Ornithocephalus* and its allies. (I)

HIPPEOPHYLLUM Schltr.

A genus of four known species, distributed from Sumatra and the Malay Peninsula to New Guinea, *Hippeophyllum* is closely allied to *Oberonia* Ldl., differing from that group in the mostly pendulous stems being placed at some distance from each other on the creeping rhizome, and in the slightly larger flowers with a slender (not short and squat) column. Like the Oberonias, these orchids bear extremely small blossoms, but their mode of arrangement on the inflorescence, the unique vegetative structure of the plants, and their attractive shape when viewed with a lens make them of interest to connoisseurs.

Nothing is known of the genetic affinities of *Hippeophyllum*.

CULTURE: As for the tropical Bulbophyllums with creeping rhizomes. (H)

H. Scortechinii (Hk.f.) Schltr. (*Oberonia Scortechinii* Hk.f.)

Rhiz. prostrate, slender, creeping. Sts. about 2″ apart on the rhiz., rooting freely, short. Lvs. about 4, often pendulous, fleshy, rather close together, linear, acuminate, to 8″ long and ¾″ wide. Infls. short-stalked, mostly pendulous, very densely many-fld., the fls. borne in whorls, bracted, to 12″ long. Fls. less than ¼″ across, pale greenish with a yellow lip. Ss. slightly reflexed, the margins recurved. Ps. narrow, thrust forwards. Lip concave basally, the lat. lbs. erect, the midlb. reflexed. Autumn. (H) Malay Peninsula; Sumatra; Java.

HOEHNEËLLA Ruschi

This is a genus of three known species, all extreme rarities and endemic to Brazil. A member of the complex subtribe *Huntleyinae*, *Hoehneëlla* rather simulates a small *Chondrorhyncha* in vegetative appearance, but bears flowers of divergent structure. They are attractive little epiphytes, but none of them is in cultivation at this time.

Hoehneëlla Heloisae Ruschi [Hoehne, *Flora Brasilica*]

Nothing has been ascertained regarding the genetic affinities of *Hoehneëlla*.

CULTURE: As for *Chondrorhyncha*. (I, H)

HOFMEISTERELLA Rchb.f.
(*Hofmeistera* Rchb.f.)

Hofmeisterella eumicroscopica Rchb.f. is a very rare epiphytic orchid, the only known member of its genus, native in Brazil, and a member of the subtribe *Oncidiinae*. A very small, stemless plant with linear, fleshy, equitant foliage, it bears its small citron-yellow blossoms, these with a red spot on the lip, on a flattened, abbreviated inflorescence. It is unknown in cultivation at this time, and is incompletely understood botanically.

Nothing is known of the genetic affinities of this odd group.

CULTURE: Presumably as for *Ornithocephalus*. (I)

HOLCOGLOSSUM Schltr.

A single rare species of this genus is known to date, this **Holcoglossum quasipinifolium** (Hay.) Schltr. (*Saccolabium quasipinifolium* Hay.). It is a member of the subtribe *Sarcanthinae*, and has apparently been collected on only one occasion in its native island of Formosa. A dwarf plant with little slender terete foliage and small greenish-white, complex flowers, it is not in cultivation at this time.

Nothing is known of the genetic affinities of *Holcoglossum*.

CULTURE: Possibly as for the dwarf, epiphytic Vandas, etc. (I, H)

HOLOPOGON Kom. & Nevski

A single species of *Holopogon* is known to date, this the very rare saprophytic **H. ussuriensis** Kom. & Nevski, a native of Eastern Siberia. A rather small, white-flowered plant with essentially leafless stems, it is unknown in our collections at this time, and is in any event primarily of scientific interest. The genus is indicated as being somewhat allied to *Neottia* L.

Nothing is known of the genetic affinities of this incompletely-known genus.

CULTURE: Possibly as for *Corallorrhiza*, but like most saprophytic plants, scant success can be anticipated when growing it in the collection. (C, I)

HOLOTHRIX L.C.Rich.
(*Bucculina* Ldl., *Monotris* Ldl., *Saccidium* Ldl., *Scopularia* Ldl.)

Holothrix is a genus containing upwards of twenty species of terrestrial orchids of the subtribe *Habenarinae*, native in tropical and South Africa. The group is somewhat allied to *Deroemeria* Rchb.f., but differs in technical details of the mostly small yet highly complex flowers. Several of the species, such as **H. Lindleyana** Rchb.f., **H. orthoceras** Rchb.f., and **H. Schlechteriana** Krzl., have been cultivated in the past, but now seem to have disappeared from our collections. They are unusual little orchids, well worthy of attention by specialists in most cases, with typically hairy leaves in a basal rosette that closely hugs the ground (much like *Bartholina*), and usually fragrant flowers of varying hue.

Nothing is known of the genetic affinities of *Holothrix*.

CULTURE: As for *Cynorkis*. (I, H)

HOMALOPETALUM Rolfe

This is an exceptionally interesting genus of about four species of very dwarf epiphytic orchids, with proportionately large flowers, occurring in Cuba, Jamaica, Mexico, Guatemala, Costa Rica, and possibly adjacent areas. Somewhat allied to *Meiracyllium* Rchb.f., of the subtribe *Laeliinae*, they are extremely rare in our collections at this time. Though diminutive plants, their unusual pseudobulbs—usually very regularly arranged along the rhizome in alternating rows—and showy little flowers combine to make the Homalopetalums highly desirable to all connoisseurs.

No hybrids have as yet been registered utilizing *Homalopetalum*, though it seems a possibility that it would prove genetically compatible with at least some of the allied genera of its subtribe.

CULTURE: Though difficult to bring through fumigation, once introduced successfully into the collection, they are not overly refractory in their requirements. They do best either mounted on small tree-fern slabs, or loosely potted in small, perfectly-drained containers, in a mixture of shredded tree-fern fibre and chopped sphagnum moss. They must never be permitted to dry out completely, nor yet can they ever become sodden at the roots. A bright, moderately sunny spot in the warm or intermediate greenhouse is ideal, and they should be disturbed as seldom as possible. (I, H)

H. pumilio (Rchb.f.) Schltr. (*Brassavola pumilio* Rchb.f., *Bletia pumilio* Rchb.f., *Pinelia Tuerckheimii* Krzl.)
Rhiz. thread-like, bearing the tiny pbs. at regular alternate intervals, cluster-forming. Pbs. usually purple-tinged, to ½″ long, recurved-ascending, obliquely ovoid to oblong-cylindric. Lf. solitary, erect, ovate to linear, usually purplish, very fleshy and thick, obtuse to acute, to 1″ long. Infls. 1-fld., thread-like, from apex of pbs., to 3″ tall, with several sheaths. Fls. to almost 2″ across, transparent pale greenish (often purple-tinged), sometimes not opening fully. Ss. and shorter ps. spreading-erect, recurved, linear-lanceolate, long-acuminate, the ps. rather falcate. Lip shortly clawed, simple, oval-elliptic to elliptic-lanceolate, acute to acuminate; disc with a thickened flap-like ridge on each side at the base, the claw with a small triangular wing on each side. Spring. (I, H) Mexico; Guatemala; Costa Rica.

H. vomeriforme (Sw.) Fawc. & Rendle (*Epidendrum vomeriforme* Sw., *Brassavola vomeriformis* Rchb.f., *Homalopetalum jamaicense* Rolfe)
Rhiz. slender, creeping, the pbs. regularly ranked at intervals along it. Pbs. cylindrical to globose, to ¼″ long. Lf. solitary, ovate-oblong to oblong, keeled, blunt at apex, heavily fleshy, to ¾″ long. Infls. erect, 1-fld., to 2½″ long, jointed. Fls. very thin-textured, often not opening fully, about 1½″ across when expanded, pale rose-pink, often flushed with greenish. Ss. and ps. linear-lanceolate, acuminate, the ps. shorter and narrower. Lip as long as the ps., elliptic, short-acuminate, the disc smooth. Winter–spring. (I) Cuba; Jamaica.

HOULLETIA Brongn.

This is a group of about ten species of variously terrestrial, lithophytic, or epiphytic, often extremely handsome orchids, native in South America (particularly in Colombia and Brazil), with a single outlying representative extending as far north as Guatemala, and others in Panama. The species of *Houlletia* are mostly robust pseudobulbous plants, the often large solitary leaf being heavily leathery, distinctly stalked, and plicate. The basal inflorescences are erect in some species, sharply pendulous in others, and bear a few to rather numerous large, fleshy flowers of unique construction and typically most attractive coloration. The genus is somewhat allied to *Paphinia* Ldl., but differs from it in characters of the floral parts as well as in vegetative habit. Like most of the members of the subtribe *Gongorinae*, the lip of the flowers in this genus is singularly complex, and difficult to describe in mere words. Several of the Houlletias were at one time very popular and in frequent cultivation, but they have largely passed out of vogue in our time, and must today be classed as scarce though eminently desirable orchids.

No hybrids are known as yet which utilize *Houlletia*, but the genus seems to offer some most intriguing possibilities, particularly in the realm of breeding with its allied genera within the subtribe, and possibly also with members of other related aggregations.

CULTURE: The species of *Houlletia* with pendulous inflorescences should be grown in the manner suggested for *Stanhopea* and *Acineta*. Those with erect inflorescences, normally terrestrial in the wild, should be treated like the tropical species of *Phaius*, in a rich but well-drained compost. A rest-period has been suggested in the published literature, but does not seem to be necessary for these fine orchids when properly cultivated, since they reside in regions where they grow throughout the entire year. High humidity is essential,

and fertilization at intervals while in active growth is recommended. (I, H)

H. Brocklehurstiana Ldl.

Pbs. clustered, ovoid-oblong, 2–4″ tall, almost as much in diam. towards the base, smooth, becoming strongly furrowed and wrinkled with age. Lf. solitary, long-stalked (this 12–15″ long), the blade plicate, rather heavy-textured, lanceolate-oblong to elliptic, acute or acuminate. 1½–2′ long and about 3″ wide. Infls. robust, erect, dull purple mottled with pale green, 5–12-fld., rather loose, to more than 1½′ tall. Fls. opening widely, to 3″ in diam., heavy-textured, fragrant, long-lived, the

Houlletia odoratissima Ldl. [VEITCH]

broad ss. and ps. light or dark red-brown streaked with pale or bright-yellow, usually spotted with darker red-brown on basal half, the lat. ss. with a blood-red suffusion on the inner side. Lip very complex, shorter than the other segms., jointed at the middle, the hypochil white densely spotted with blackish warts, transversely oblong at base, then narrowly oblong, produced laterally at its junction with the epichil into 2 ascending curved horns which are whitish streaked with red-purple; epichil broadly trowel-shaped, reflexed at the apex and prolonged at the lateral angles into short cusps, the entire section covered with blackish-purple wart-like protuberances and light orange or yellowish-orange net-like veinings. Col. large, club-shaped, light tawny-yellow spotted with red. Winter. (I, H) Brazil.

H. Lansbergii Lind. & Rchb.f.

Pbs. small for the genus, about 1″ tall, dark green, ovoid, bluntly angled. Lf. pale green, rather rigid, mostly elliptic, acute, to 12″ long and 4″ wide. Infls. pendulous, the peduncle stout, about 4″ long, tinged with reddish or brownish, sheathed, 2–4-fld. Fls. about 2½″ long, not as wide, waxy, fragrant, the ss. reddish-orange with round brown-red spots, the ps. similar but darker in colour, the lip with the basal hypochil white with several cross-bars of blood-red, the epichil white, the central part furnished with numerous violet-purple warts, the col. golden-yellow marked with red. Autumn. (I) Guatemala; Costa Rica; Panama; Venezuela; Brazil.

H. odoratissima Ldl.

Similar in almost all parts to *H. Brocklehurstiana* Ldl., differing from it in the handsome fls. Fls. waxy, long-lasting, fragrant, to 3″ in diam., dark chocolate-red or chocolate-brown, except certain white parts of the lip. Lat. ss. broader than the dors. one, concave. Ps. considerably smaller, linear-spatulate, acute. Lip with a subquadrate hypochil, with 2 slender horn-like appendages that are bent backwards; epichil hastate, produced at the lateral angles into 2 short horns. Col. slender basally, dilated upwards. Autumn. (I, H) Panama; Colombia.

H. chrysantha André Resembling *H. Brocklehurstiana* Ldl. in habit, but with smaller foliage and a shorter, few-fld. infl. Fls. about 2″ in diam., very waxy, headily fragrant, light yellow with pale red spots and marks, wide-spreading. Lip very complex in structure. Autumn. (I) Colombia.

H. picta Lind. & Rchb.f. Similar in habit to *H. Brocklehurstiana* Ldl. Infls. erect or pendulous, rather densely 7–10-fld., to almost 2′ long. Fls. to almost 4″ in diam., waxy, fragrant, widely opening, the ss. and ps. yellow in lower half, with dense brown spots, the upper half glossy brown. Lip rather like that of *H. Lansbergii* Lind. & Rchb.f. in shape, yellow densely marked with blackish-brown. Summer–autumn. (I) Colombia.

HUEBNERIA Schltr.

Only a single species of *Huebneria* is known at this time, this the extremely rare **H. yauperiensis** (B.-R.) Schltr. (*Orleanesia yauperiensis* B.-R.), which has been found on a very few occasions in northern Brazil, where it grows as an epiphyte in the humid forests. A rather nondescript plant of the subtribe *Ponerinae*, it is unknown in our contemporary collections.

Nothing is known of the genetic affinities of *Huebneria*.

CULTURE: Possibly as for the epiphytic, pseudobulbous *Epidendrums*, although it would seem evident that no rest-period should be afforded the plants upon completion of the new growths. (H)

HUNTLEYA Batem. ex Ldl.

Only a single species of *Huntleya* (out of an estimated four for the genus) appears to be present in contemporary collections, where it is justly prized as one of the most magnificent of New World orchids—and, incidentally, one of the most difficult to maintain in good condition! Huntleyas are pseudobulbless, usually tufted orchids (rarely with very elongate rhizomes, on which the leaf-clusters sit at intervals), with glossy, rather loose leaves which form a fan, much as in the related genera *Bollea* Rchb.f., *Chondrorhyncha* Rchb.f., etc. The solitary, sometimes very large flowers are produced on slender, usually erect or ascending scapes which arise from near the bases of the leaf-fans; they are of extraordinarily handsome formation and colour, delightfully fragrant, waxy—as if they had been lacquered—and persist in good shape for more than a month. It is interesting to note that in Panama, where *Huntleya meleagris* Ldl. is a rare epiphyte in the wet highland forests of certain areas, growing in deep shade at elevations above 2500 feet, it is commonly associated with *Brassia Alleni* L.O.Wms., a species which it completely simulates vegetatively, but with which it has not the vaguest botanical alliance. A *Maxillaria* (*M. chartacifolia* A. & S.) also grows intermingled with these two plants in many instances, and simulates both the *Brassia* and the *Huntleya* to a large degree. *Pescatorea cerina* (Ldl. & Paxt.) Rchb.f. also grows in this area, and yet again it resembles the *Huntleya*! It is therefore very difficult to collect the Huntleyas (which are infinitely more desirable than any of the others except, possibly, the *Pescatorea*) when they are not in flower and gain any positive idea of their identity. The genus ranges from Costa Rica to Brazil, and its components are extremely variable and rather confused taxonomically.

Huntleya has not as yet been utilized by the breeders, though it is presumably genetically compatible with several genera, such as *Bollea*, *Pescatorea*, *Chondrorhyncha*, and possibly even *Lycaste*, *Anguloa*, *Aganisia*, *Colax*, and *Zygopetalum*. A large and certainly provocative field of endeavour is open to some enterprising hybridist here, and should be explored.

CULTURE: Since they inhabit relatively high elevations in most cases, Huntleyas are best grown under moderately cool conditions, such as those required by the alpine Odontoglossums, Miltonias, etc.; they will sometimes thrive, however, if given the temperatures afforded Cattleyas and other intermediate category orchids, provided full attention is paid to the humidity and fresh air around them. They do best in pots, the drainage of which must be perfect, since these orchids are highly intolerant of the slightest degree of staleness at the roots. A compost made up of equal parts of shredded tree-fern fibre and chopped sphagnum moss, with a top-dressing of fresh sphagnum moss, is most acceptable. Care must be

Huebneria yauperiensis (B.-R.) Schltr. [Hoehne, *Flora Brasilica*]

248

taken that the base of the plant rises slightly above the compost-level, or rapid rotting may ensue. Copious water is required at all times, coupled with high humidity. Rather diffused light—but not dense shade—is also requisite. Periodic applications of fertilizer are beneficial. (C, I)

H. meleagris Ldl. (*Batemania Burtii* Endr. & Rchb.f., *Zygopetalum meleagris* Bth., *Zygopetalum Burtii* Bth. & Hk.f., *Huntleya Burtii* Rolfe)

Without pbs., the lvs. forming a loose fan, to 12″ long, linear-lanceolate to elliptic-lanceolate, acute, rather pale green in many cases, prominently venose. Scapes often several at once, 1-fld., to 6″ tall, erect to almost pendent, produced from the lower axils of the lf.-fan. Fls. highly variable in size and colour, to 5″ across in largest forms, very waxy, fragrant, long-lived. Ss. with the apical $\frac{2}{3}$ lacquered red-brown, usually with some yellow spots, the basal $\frac{1}{3}$ white or pale yellow, elliptic-lanceolate, acute to acuminate, undulate marginally. Ps. similar in hue to the ss., with purple blotches or streaks at the base near insertion on the col.-foot, broadly elliptic-lanceolate, acuminate, undulate marginally. Lip basally white or yellowish, the frontal half of the apical lobe usually rich red-brown or brown-purple; base of lip abruptly contracted, with a conspicuous claw which forms a geniculate angle with the col.-foot, the basal callus with an erect, semicircular, fringed crest, the midlb. obscurely 3-lobulate, acute to acuminate, con-

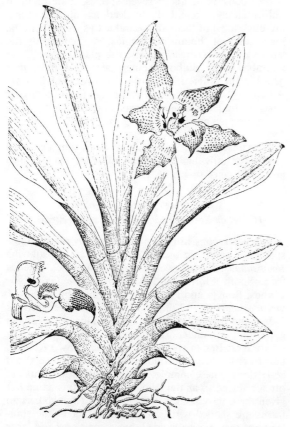

Huntleya meleagris Ldl. [DOROTHY O. ALLEN]

tracted at base and jointed with apex of callus-plate. Summer–autumn. (C, I) Costa Rica; Panama; Colombia; Brazil.

HUTTONAEA Harv.
(*Hallackia* Harv.)

About five species of *Huttonaea* are known to science, none of them present at this time in cultivation, apparently. A member of the subtribe *Huttonaeinae*, these South African terrestrial orchids are interesting with their large, usually white, fringe-lipped flowers, and offer some potentials to connoisseurs. They appear to be rather rare even in their native haunts.

Nothing is known of the genetic affinities of *Huttonaea*. CULTURE: As for *Cynorkis*. (I, H)

HYALOSEMA [Schltr.] Rolfe
(*Bulbophyllum* Thou. § *Hyalosema* Schltr.)

When any members of this genus occur in contemporary collections, they are grown almost invariably under the name *Bulbophyllum*, from which the present group was segregated by R. A. Rolfe in 1919. Naturally closely in alliance with *Bulbophyllum* Thou., *Hyalosema* was initially established as a section of that tremendous aggregation of orchids by Schlechter, but Rolfe pointed out certain important critical discrepancies between the two, and *Hyalosema* is now recognized as a distinct genus. Vegetatively similar to many Bulbophyllums, these extraordinary orchids—of which about twenty are known—are primarily epiphytic plants occurring in the area extending from Sumatra, the Malay Peninsula and Borneo to New Guinea and the Solomon Islands. Several of them (notably *H. grandiflorum* (Bl.) Rolfe, which appears to be the only one currently in our collections) have exceedingly large flowers—to more than seven inches long—which are certainly among the most grotesquely spectacular of all orchidaceous blossoms. The Hyalosemas are regrettably very scarce in collections today, though they are sufficiently large and showy to be worthy of more attention by connoisseurs.

No hybrids utilizing members of this genus have as yet been registered, although it seems to present some intriguing potentials for the enterprising breeder. *Hyalosema* is presumably genetically compatible with at least some of the Bulbophyllums.

CULTURE: As for the tropical Bulbophyllums. Because of the elongate rhizomes of many of the species, cultivation in baskets or large fern-pans is almost obligatory. (H)

H. grandiflorum (Bl.) Rolfe (*Bulbophyllum grandiflorum* Bl., *Bulbophyllum burfordiense* Rolfe, *Ephippium grandiflorum* Bl.)

Rhiz. creeping, the pbs. produced at intervals of about 2″, oblong, usually rather strongly 4-angled, 2–3″ tall. Lf. solitary, usually rigidly erect, oblong, obtuse, narrowed towards the base, 6–8″ long, to $2\frac{1}{2}$″ wide, bright green, heavily leathery, fleshy. Infls. 1-fld., erect or horizontal, to 10″ long. Fls. to 7″ long, rather long-lived, fantastically contorted, usually foul-smelling, the large dors. sep. green or brownish-green with white, semi-transparent blotches, the lat. ss. similar but smaller, incurved, brownish-green. Ps. almost triangular, very small, greenish. Lip small, greenish with brown spots, the margins often somewhat fringed. Autumn. (H) Sumatra; Celebes; Moluccas; New Guinea.

HYBOCHILUS Schltr.

Hybochilus consists of a single very rare epiphytic, dwarf orchid of the subtribe *Capanemiinae*, native to the Guianas, and not present in collections at this time. A peculiar little plant, somewhat allied to *Sanderella* O.Ktze. and to *Capanemia* B.-R., it is incompletely understood botanically, and has only been found on a very few occasions by scientists in the wild.

Nothing is known of the genetic affinities of *Hybochilus*.

CULTURE: Possibly as for *Ornithocephalus*. (H)

HYLOPHILA Ldl.
(*Dicerostylis* Bl.)

About five very little-known and almost never-cultivated terrestrial orchids of the subtribe *Physurinae* make up the génus *Hylophila*, these native in Burma, the Philippines, the Malay Peninsula, Indonesia, and New Guinea. Like so many of the physurids, or 'Jewel Orchids', these orchids are of interest more for their foliage than for the minute blossoms, which in this genus scarcely expand at all.

Nothing is known of the genetic affinities of *Hylophila*.

CULTURE: Presumably as for *Anoectochilus*. (H)

HYMENORCHIS Schltr.

About seven species of *Hymenorchis* are known to date, all extremely scarce epiphytic members of the subtribe *Sarcanthinae*, inhabiting the montane forests of New Guinea, except for the Javanese **H. javanica** Schltr. None is present in our collections at this time, although they are interesting dwarf plants with rather large, complex flowers, usually white or yellowish-white, mostly with a green lip-disc. The fleshy leaves are unusual in being furnished with marginal hairs, a rare occurrence in the Orchidaceae.

Nothing is known regarding the genetic affinities of the genus *Hymenorchis*.

CULTURE: As for the tropical Vandas, etc. (C, I)

IMERINAEA Schltr.

Imerinaea madagascarica Schltr., the only known member of the genus, is a very rare medium-sized terrestrial or lithophytic orchid of the subtribe *Liparidinae*, native in Madagascar. Bearing small clustered pseudobulbs, erect leaves, and slender racemes of complex yellowish-white flowers, it is a most unusual plant, rather intermediate between its subtribe and the *Polystachyinae*. *Imerinaea* is unknown in cultivation at this time.

Nothing is known of the genetic affinities of this rare genus.

CULTURE; Presumably as for the tropical Bulbo-phyllums. (H)

INOBULBON Schltr. & Krzl.

Two species of *Inobulbon* are known at this time, both of them extremely rare epiphytic orchids endemic to the island of New Caledonia, neither of which appears to be in cultivation at this time. The genus is a member of the subtribe *Dendrobiinae*, and both of the species were originally described as Dendrobiums, although they differ radically from that group in both vegetative and floral structure. Pscudobulbous plants, thc bulbs with age become heavily hung with intricate fibres, and bear heavy foliage at their tips. The racemes produce rather numerous, showy, yellow or purple flowers, which appear to offer much to the connoisseur collector. The two species are **Inobulbon munificum** (Finet) Krzl. (*Dendrobium muricatum* Finet var. *munificum* Finet), and **I. muricatum** (Finet) Krzl. (*Dendrobium muricatum* Finet).

Nothing has been ascertained regarding the genetic affinities of this odd group.

CULTURE: Presumably as for the large-pseudobulbed, tropical Dendrobiums. (H)

IONE Ldl.
(*Sunipia* Ldl.)

Ione consists of about seven species, none of them unfortunately present in collections at this time, although most of them are desirable to specialists in the more unusual 'botanical' orchids. A member of the small subtribe *Genyorchidinae*, the plants vegetatively resemble many Bulbophyllums, but differ from that genus in the different structure of the complex flowers. All epiphytic in habit, the Iones range from the higher parts of the Himalayas to Burma and Thailand.

Nothing is known concerning the genetic affinities of *Ione*.

CULTURE: As for *Bulbophyllum*, depending upon the species (or individual, in the case of widespread species) and its place of origin. (I, H)

IONOPSIS HBK
(*Cybelion* Spreng., *Iantha* Hk., *Inopsis* Steud.)

This genus consists of about four mostly very variable species of epiphytic orchids, members of the subtribe *Ionopsidinae*, native over a huge area which extends from South Florida and Mexico to the Galápagos Islands, Bolivia and Paraguay. Only a single species, *I. utricularioides* (Sw.) Ldl., is at all frequent in collections today, and it is often exasperatingly difficult to keep in good condition under artificial greenhouse conditions; a dwarf West Indian species, *I. satyrioides* (Sw.) Rchb.f., has recently been introduced into a few specialized collections. These completely charming little plants are often referred to as the 'Violet Orchids', this name not given them in reference to their colour (though certain forms are shaded with violet!) but rather to the similarity of their typically small blossoms—borne in large numbers on elongate graceful branched sprays—to woodsy flowers such as violets. The blooms in all of the species vary tremendously in size and degree of coloration, ranging in *I. utricularioides* (Sw.) Ldl. from dark violet or lilac to pure white, often in the same colony of plants. The neat appearance of the vegetative portions of these orchids form an almost perfect foil to the panicles of flowers, making them among the most charming of all of the 'botanical' orchids.

Ionopsis has not as yet been taken in hand by the hybridists, and nothing is known of its genetic affinities. It seems distinctly possible, however, in the light of recent experimental breeding, that the group will prove 'crossable' with such genera as *Rodriguezia*, *Comparettia*, and the like.

CULTURE: Ionopsis are generally inhabitants of rather low elevations, hence they require warm or intermediate temperatures under cultivation. Ideally, the plants should be kept on the original twigs or branches on which they occurred in the wild, but this of course is often not possible. Otherwise, small pots, rather tightly packed with perfectly-drained osmunda or chopped tree-fern fibre, seem to suit them rather well. Once well-established and freely-rooting, they may to advantage be transferred and tightly fixed to smallish slabs of tree-fern fibre. Although in nature they often inhabit dry places and are almost xerophytic in habit, under cultivation they seem to benefit by liberal applications of moisture at all times, and high humidity, such as is found in the greenhouse. In sufficiently warm climates, they may be planted on citrus trees, to which they cling with gleeful vigour. They need strong light exposure for best colouring in the flake-like flowers. Excessively intolerant of disturbance, they should be repotted only when absolutely essential, and only then by carefully teasing out the stale medium around their roots and carefully replacing it, moving the root-system as little as possible. The members of the genus *Ionopsis* appear to be short-lived orchids, once they have reached maturity, though no critical research has been done on this subject; under cultivation they generally survive less than five or six years, no matter how theoretically ideal are the conditions under which they are kept. (I, H)

I. utricularioides (Sw.) Ldl. (*Dendrobium utricularioides* Sw., *Epidendrum utricularioides* Sw., *Iantha pallidiflora* Hk., *Ionopsis pallidiflora* Ldl., *I. paniculata* Ldl., *I. tenera* Ldl., *I. zonalis* Ldl. & Paxt.)

Highly variable in vegetative and floral dimensions and details. Pbs. essentially obsolete to about $\frac{1}{2}''$ long, apically leafless or with a diminutive abortive scale-like apicule at tip, borne in the middle of the several sheathing lf.-like bracts, these close together, sometimes almost imbricating, linear-lanceolate to oblong-lanceolate, acute, strongly keeled, fleshily rigid, to 5″ long (rarely more) and about $\frac{1}{3}-\frac{3}{4}''$ wide. Infls. often more than one simultaneously, produced from the lateral or sub-terminal lf.-axils, slender or rather stout, erect to horizontal, few- to very many-fld., simple or more commonly paniculate, to almost 3′ long in exceptionally robust specimens. Fls. highly variable, ranging from less than $\frac{1}{2}''$ long to about $\frac{3}{4}''$ long, the colour varying from plant to plant, from pure white to rich purple, often lilac or

Ionopsis utricularioides (Sw.) Ldl. [BLANCHE AMES]

whitish with purplish veins on the large lip, which is about twice as long as the ss. and usually 2-lbd. at the apex. Winter–spring. (I, H) South Florida and Mexico to the Galápagos Islands, Bolivia, Paraguay, and Brazil.

I. satyrioides (Sw.) Rchb.f. (*Epidendrum satyrioides* Sw., *Dendrobium testiculatum* Sw., *Ionopsis teres* Ldl., *I. testiculata* Ldl.) Pbs. apparently always absent, the lvs. arising directly from the rhiz., terete, subulate, 2–5$\frac{1}{2}''$ long (usually small), often flushed with purplish. Infl. 1–6″ tall (usually small), sometimes branching, usually few-fld., the fls. often all facing upwards. Fls. scarcely expanding, to about $\frac{1}{4}''$ long, whitish or creamy-white, sometimes with pale lilac veins on the proportionately large lip. Spring–autumn. (I, H) Hispaniola; Puerto Rico; Jamaica to Trinidad.

IPSEA Ldl.

The 'Daffodil Orchid', as this fine terrestrial member of the subtribe *Phaiinae* is known in its native Ceylon and South India, is today very scarce in collections, although it is among the most handsome of all ground-dwelling orchidaceous plants. It was formerly rather frequently grown in England and on the Continent— always highly prized by its owners—and should be better known by contemporary orchidists.

No hybrids are known in *Ipsea*, and its generic alliances have not been ascertained. It is in all probability genetically compatible with at least some of its allies, such as *Phaius*, *Calanthe*, *Spathoglottis*, and the like.

CULTURE: As for the tropical species of *Phaius*. Upon completion of the flowering season, a strict resting-period of at least one month is obligatory. (I, H)

I. speciosa Ldl.

Tubers usually subterranean, broadly conical, to $1\frac{1}{2}''$ high. Lvs. few, small, deciduous annually, to about $12''$ long and $\frac{1}{4}''$ wide, plicate, sheathing the st. towards its base. Infls. erect, to almost $2'$ tall, 1- or rarely 2-fld. Fls. about $3''$ in diam., fragrant, rather long-lived, waxy, light golden-yellow, the lip typically somewhat deeper-coloured than the ss. and ps. Lip with short lat. lbs. and a large midlb. Mostly winter. (I, H) Ceylon; Southern India.

ISABELIA B.-R.

Containing but a single scarce species in the damp, humid forests of Brazil, *Isabelia* is a very rare genus in contemporary collections, yet it is among the most enchanting and unusual of all of the myriad 'botanical' members of the subtribe *Laeliinae*. A dwarf, mat-forming epiphytic plant, *Isabelia* is somewhat allied to *Neolauchea* Krzl., but differs from it in the appearance of the vegetative portions as well as in floral structure.

Nothing is known of the genetic affinities of *Isabelia*.

CULTURE: As for *Ornithocephalus*. Because of the creeping, mat-forming habit of the plants, they do best when grown in shallow fern-pans. (I, H)

I. virginalis B.-R.

Pbs. tightly clustered, usually leaning closely against one another and almost prostrate, the rhiz. branching and forming a dense intricate mat on the substratum, the pbs. narrowly ovoid, to about $\frac{3}{8}''$ long, mostly covered by a complex brownish or greyish open network of fibres. Lf. solitary, awl-shaped, $1-3''$ long. Infls. abbreviated, 1-fld. Fls. not opening fully, about $\frac{1}{4}''$ long, snow-white, often not lasting well. Ss. oblong, obtuse, the lat. ss. forming a small sac with the lip-base. Winter. (I, H) Brazil.

ISCHNOCENTRUM Schltr.

A genus comprising a single species, **Ischnocentrum myrtillus** Schltr., this member of the subtribe *Glomerinae* is, like so many components of its aggregation, restricted to New Guinea, where it appears to be an extremely scarce epiphyte, even in the wild state. Vegetatively simulating a small species of *Glossorhyncha* Ridl., this orchid differs in technical details of the flowers, and is unknown in contemporary collections.

Nothing has been ascertained regarding the genetic affinities of this rare genus.

CULTURE: Presumably as for *Glomera*. (C, I)

ISCHNOGYNE Schltr.

Ischnogyne contains but a single known species, this a very rare epiphytic or lithophytic orchid in the mountains of Setschuan, China. **Ischnogyne mandarinorum** (Krzl.) Schltr. (*Coelogyne mandarinorum* Krzl., *Pleione mandarinorum* Krzl.) is evidently unknown in contemporary collections, and is in any case a rather nondescript *Coelogyne*-like plant with small tubular flowers, these of rather unique structure. The genus is closest botanically to *Panisea* Ldl.

Nothing is known of the genetic affinities of this singularly rare orchid.

CULTURE: Probably as for the high-elevation Coelogynes. (C, I)

ISOCHILUS R.Br.
(*Isochilos* Sprgl., *Leptothrium* Kth.)

This is an unusual genus of two species and several varieties, all of them variable in the extreme. Several of these *Isochilus* are relatively frequent in choice contemporary collections, where they are grown as curiosities for their strange grass-like vegetative habit and racemes of attractive, usually brightly-coloured blossoms. A member of the subtribe *Ponerinae*, the components of this genus range from Cuba and Mexico throughout the American tropics to Argentina. In their natural haunts, the plants grow on trees, on rocks, or rarely in the ground in rocky situations; they are often ubiquitous in the wild, forming gigantic colonies cloaking almost every possible spot.

Hybridization has not as yet been attempted with any of the species or variants of the genus *Isochilus*. Its genetic affinities, further, have not as yet been ascertained.

CULTURE: The cultural requirements of *Isochilus* are readily met, even by the beginning orchidist. The plants, once established and with good spreading systems of their odd, disproportionately fleshy roots, thrive in containers of all sorts—pots, baskets, even on slabs or rafts. They do not seem to be particular regarding the type of compost utilized, provided it is adequately drained and does not become stale. The various bark preparations encourage rapid formation of new roots on recently-imported specimens, and flowering seems heavier on clumps kept in these media than those grown in osmunda or tree-fern fibre. Water is necessary at all times, but should the compost become saturated, should be curtailed at once, or basal rotting and leaf-drop may occur. Semi-shaded conditions suit these charming orchids best, and, if kept in a greenhouse, intermediate or warm temperatures should be maintained. In tropical climates, *Isochilus* do very well if attached to trees or to mossy rocks in the garden. Regular applications of weak fertilizing solutions are recommended. (I, H)

I. linearis (Jacq.) R. Br. (*Epidendrum lineare* Jacq., *Cymbidium lineare* Sw., *Leptothrium lineare* Kth., *Isochilus leucanthus* B.-R., *I. linearis* R.Br. var. *leucanthus* Cgn., *I. pauciflorus* Cgn., *I. Langlassei* Schltr., *I. peruvianus* Schltr., *I. brasiliensis* Schltr.)

Sts. forming dense clumps, variable in height (to $2\frac{1}{2}'$ tall at times), variously erect, arching, or pendulous, typically densely leafy throughout (at least when young), the lf.-sheaths verrucose. Lvs. narrowly linear, obliquely retuse at the obtuse apex, to $2\frac{1}{2}''$ long, less than $\frac{1}{4}''$ wide. Fls. one to several, to almost $\frac{1}{2}''$ long, arranged in a loose distichous or sometimes unilateral rac., variable in colour from nearly white to deep rose-purple, the commonest form rosy-magenta, with the lip somewhat darker. Throughout the year, often more than once annually. (I, H) Mexico and Cuba to Argentina.

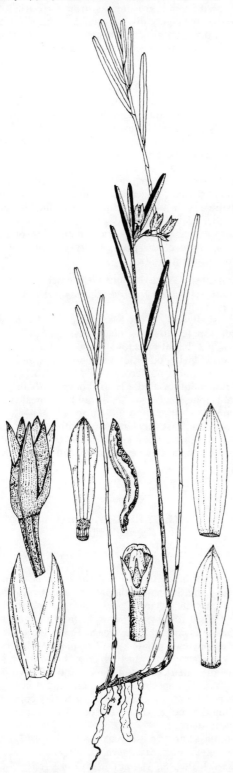

Isochilus linearis (Jacq.) R.Br. [A.D.HAWKES]

I. major Cham. & Schlecht. (*Isochilus latibracteatus* A.Rich. & Gal., *I. chiriquensis* Schltr.)

Distinguished from *I. linearis* (Jacq.) R.Br. principally by the comparatively large unilateral rac., lanceolate lvs., and smooth lf.-sheaths. The upper lvs., which commonly conceal half of the infl., are usually tinged with the same colour as the fls. Fls. to almost ½″ long, white or rose to pink or magenta-purple. Throughout the year, often more than once annually. (I, H) Mexico to Panama; Jamaica.

ISOTRIA Raf.

Two species of *Isotria* are now known, both of them relatively uncommon terrestrial orchids in the United States. The genus is rather closely allied to *Pogonia* Juss., and is placed in synonymy in that group by certain authorities. Odd plants with verticillate foliage and usually solitary flowers, the Isotrias usually occur near streams or in moist areas, mostly in strongly acid soils. Known commonly as 'Whorled Pogonias' or 'Five-Leaved Orchids', they are seldom cultivated today.

No hybrids are known in *Isotria*, and nothing has been ascertained regarding its genetic affinities.

CULTURE: These orchids are very difficult to grow, since the slightest disturbance of the fibrous root-system almost invariably proves fatal. Generally, the Isotrias require conditions such as are suggested for the acid-loving Cypripediums, in a relatively shaded portion of the garden. Pot-culture seems to be impossibly difficult. (C, I)

I. verticillata (Muhl. ex Willd.) Raf. (*Arethusa verticillata* Muhl. ex Willd., *Pogonia verticillata* Nutt.)

St. purplish or reddish-brown, glaucous, hollow, 3½–14″ tall. Lvs. 5 or 6 in a whorl at the st.-top, oblong-lanceolate to broadly obovate or elliptic, obtuse to acute, projecting at right angles to the st., greenish above, somewhat glaucous beneath, to 2″ long. Fls. usually solitary, terminating the st., the pedicellate ovaries 1–2″ long, the fls. about 1¼–2½″ long. Ss. subequal, madder-purple, narrowly lanceolate, acuminate, conduplicate. Ps. much shorter but broader than ss., yellowish-green, elliptic-obovate to elliptic-lanceolate, obtuse to acute. Lip yellowish-green, streaked with purple, oblong-cuneate, 3-lbd. near apex, the lat. lbs. rather erect, the disc with a broad fleshy ridge along its middle. The lvs. of this interesting plant increase noticeably as the flowers expand and form their seed-capsules, sometimes becoming as much as four or five times larger than at first. April–Aug. (C, I) New England to North Florida, west to Michigan and Texas.

I. medeoloides (Pursh) Raf. (*Arethusa medeoloides* Pursh, *Pogonia affinis* Austin ex A.Gray, *Isotria affinis* Rydb.) St. greenish or tinged with purplish, to 10″ tall. Lvs. 5–6 in a whorl at st.-top, pale dusty green, glaucous, drooping, to more than 3″ long. Fls. 1–2, terminating the st., with a short pedicellate ovary, to about 1″ long, the ss. and ps. yellowish-green, the lip almost white, the 2-parted callus elongately warty, pale green. May–June. (C, I) New England south to North Carolina, west to Missouri.

JACQUINIELLA Schltr.

This is a genus of about four species of rather non-descript epiphytic (rarely lithophytic) orchids of the subtribe *Ponerinae*, native in many parts of the American tropics. Closely allied to *Isochilus* R.Br., the species may in time prove referable to that group, though vegetatively they are usually sufficiently distinct to cause no particular confusion. The Jacquiniellas are today uncommon in collections, though in the wild they are often ubiquitous in certain areas, forming huge colonies on trees, usually in the forests at low or medium elevations. They bear erect, often rather zigzag stems, which are furnished with fleshy, distichous, linear leaves. The minute flowers—usually yellowish or greenish in colour—are produced singly or in fascicles at the apex of the stem, and do not open sufficiently to make them of interest to any save the botanically inclined collector.

Nothing has been ascertained concerning the genetic affinities of *Jacquiniella*.

CULTURE: As for the warm-growing, pseudobulbous Epidendrums. These small plants do very well mounted on small tree-fern slabs or cubes. (I, H)

J. globosa (Jacq.) Schltr. (*Epidendrum globosum* Jacq., *Cymbidium globosum* Sw., *Isochilus globosus* Ldl.)

Pls. densely clustered, usually erect, to 6″ tall. Sts. leafy throughout (at least when young), slender, concealed by the lf.-sheaths, sometimes vaguely zigzag. Lvs. distichous, jointed, linear, obliquely obtuse to acute, fleshy, somewhat triangular in cross-section, usually marked with purple, as are the lf.-sheaths. Fls. solitary or fascicled at the tops of the sts., deflexed, less than ¼″ long, usually yellowish, the ss. often red-tipped, not opening well, with some bracts at the base of the pedicellate ovary. Ss. concave, the lat. ones united at base and forming an inflated sac. Ps. elliptic, acute. Lip abruptly geniculate and constricted just below the middle, saccate below the constriction. Mostly spring. (I, H) Mexico throughout the West Indies and Central America to northern South America.

JOSEPHIA Wight
(*Josepha* Bth. & Hk.f.)

Two extremely rare epiphytic orchids make up the genus *Josephia*, these native in Ceylon and India. A member of the very small subtribe *Adrorrhizinae*, the group is closely allied to *Adrorrhizon* Hk.f., but differs in the structure of the extremely small flowers, which are borne in erect, branching panicles. Neither of the species is present in collections at this time.

Nothing is known of the genetic affinities of this genus.

CULTURE: Presumably as for the tropical species of *Bulbophyllum*. (H)

JUMELLEA Schltr.

Jumellea is one of the very numerous segregates from *Angraecum* Bory, from which it is distinguished by reason of technical details of the flowers. As now delimited, the genus consists of about fifty-four species, the vast majority of these endemic to Madagascar, with outlying representatives in the Comoro Islands, the Mascarene Islands, and tropical Africa. Principally epiphytic in the wild, a few of them are also found growing on mossy rocks, and one or two of the species have been found growing as true terrestrials. The Jumelleas are highly diverse orchids, both vegetatively and florally, and although a great many of them are handsome in appearance, only a single species seems to be in cultivation at this time, and it must be classed as a rare plant. This is *Jumellea fragrans* (Thou.) Schltr., an orchid which was well-known in Victorian times as 'Faham Tea', because its dried foliage was imported into England in large quantities for the brewing of a delicately-flavoured beverage.[1] The Jumelleas are deserving of further attention by connoisseur collectors, since many of them are exceptionally handsome plants.

No hybrids have as yet been made in *Jumellea*, and nothing seems known regarding its genetic affinities, although it seems logical to assume that it will prove compatible with at least certain other allied groups of the subtribe *Sarcanthinae*.

CULTURE: As for *Angraecum*, depending upon the place of origin of the particular species or individual under consideration. (I, H)

J. fragrans (Thou.) Schltr. (*Angraecum fragrans* Thou., *Aërobion fragrans* Spreng., *Aëranthus fragrans* Rchb.f.)

Sts. usually leafy to the base, rather slender, to about 12″ tall. Lvs. few to rather numerous, lorate, deeply and unequally 2-lbd. at apex, 3–5″ long, to about ¾″ broad, when dried giving off a pungent odour of vanilla. Infls. 1-fld., often rather numerous at one time, erect or ascending, rather abbreviated. Fls. to about 2″ in diam., waxy, fragrant, long-lasting, white. Ss. and ps. linear, acutish or acuminate, spreading and recurved. Lip about as long as the ss., hastately lanceolate, with a strong groove down the centre; spur slender, longer than the ss., green or greenish. Col. very short. Mostly Jan.–Feb. (H) Mascarene Islands.

KEGELIELLA Mansf.
(*Kegelia* Rchb.f.)

Two extremely rare species comprise the little-known genus *Kegeliella*. These are now known from a very few localities in Costa Rica, Panama, Jamaica, Trinidad, and Suriname, though the genus presumably also occurs in adjacent and intervening territories. Closely allied to *Gongora* R. & P. (and to some other members of the subtribe *Gongorinae*), these strange dwarf epiphytes simulate a seedling plant of that genus, and bear pendulous racemes of a few rather small flowers of remarkable complexity and relatively dull coloration. The species listed below (the other one is **K. Kupperi** Mansf.) is only recently entering collections, and should be better known by specialists because of its botanical interest.

Nothing is known of the genetic affinities of *Kegeliella*.

CULTURE: As for *Stanhopea*. (I, H)

[1] See 'Orchid Tea', by Alex D. Hawkes, in *The Orchid Digest* 8: 146–147. Spring, 1944.

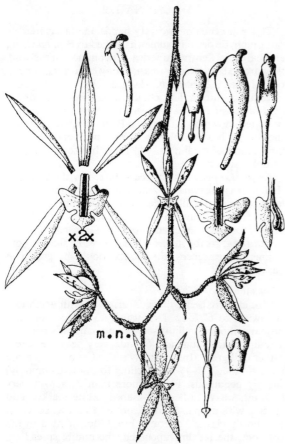

Kegeliella Houtteana (Rchb.f.) L.O.Wms. [Hoehne,
Flora Brasilica]

K. Houtteana (Rchb.f.) L.O.Wms. (*Kegelia Houtteana*
Rchb.f.)

Pbs. ovoid, laterally compressed, rather angular, to
$\frac{3}{4}$" tall. Lvs. 3, to 5" long and 2" wide, folded, elliptic-
lanceolate, acute. Infls. few-fld., pendulous, basal, to 4"
long, the rachis densely covered with tiny reddish
glandular hairs. Fls. not lasting well, about 1" long, the
ss. pale yellow (minutely reddish-hairy outside), the ps.
pale yellow barred with red, the lip yellow, the col.
apple-green. Ss. free, concave, spreading, long-tipped,
mostly lanceolate. Ps. similar in shape, but slightly
smaller. Lip 3-lbd., the lat. lbs. erect, obliquely angular,
the midlb. triangular or subcordate, flat, spreading,
separated from the lats. by emarginate sinuses; disc with
an erect, fleshy, laterally compressed, somewhat 2-lbd.,
tongue-shaped callus. Col. arching, slender below,
broadly winged above. Autumn. (I, H) Panama;
Jamaica; Trinidad; Suriname.

KINGIELLA Rolfe

About five species of *Kingiella* are known, these much
confused with *Doritis* Ldl. and *Phalaenopsis* Bl., though
they are amply distinctive. Smallish epiphytic monopodial orchids, they are found from India to the Philippines and Indonesia, and are singularly scarce in con-

temporary collections, albeit of considerable botanical
interest. The flowers are small, and borne in racemes or
profuse proliferating panicles; they arise from dwarf,
succulent-leaved plants much like a miniature *Phalaenopsis*.

Hybrids between the Kingiellas noted below and
Phalaenopsis have been made, but as of this writing
have not flowered nor been registered.

CULTURE: As for *Phalaenopsis*. Pot-culture is recommended. (I, H)

K. philippinensis (Ames) Rolfe (*Doritis philippinensis*
Ames)

St. freely rooting, abbreviated. Lvs. few in number,
to 7" long and $1\frac{3}{4}$" broad, leathery, usually oblong-
lanceolate. Infl. erect, racemose or paniculate, often
producing accessory branches for several months, many-
fld., to $1\frac{1}{2}$' tall, slender. Fls. not opening fully, about
$\frac{1}{2}$" across, yellow, usually flushed with purple on the lip.
Lip 3-lbd., the proportionately large lat. lbs. each set
with a membranaceous triangular tooth inside near
base, the midlb. emarginate, rather crisp-margined,
the disc with a 2-parted white callus. Mostly autumn.
(I, H) Philippines, widely distributed mostly at rather
low elevations.

K. decumbens (Griff.) Rolfe (*Aërides decumbens* Griff.,
Doritis Wightii Bth., *Phalaenopsis decumbens* Holtt.,
Phalaenopsis Hebe Rchb.f., *Phalaenopsis Wightii* Rchb.f.)
Lvs. rather thin-textured, usually bright green, to about 5"
long and $1\frac{1}{4}$" broad. Infls. erect, sometimes branched, to 8"
tall, with rather numerous fls. facing in all directions. Fls. to
about $\frac{3}{4}$" long, usually somewhat smaller, the ss. and ps.
white, the lat. ss. usually purple-spotted at base, the lip
purple, the midlb. usually the darkest part. Lip rather longer
than ss. and ps., slightly saccate at base, the lat. lbs. slightly
spreading, widening from a narrow base, each with a tooth-
like appendage near the back edge, tips rounded; midlb.
widening from a narrow base, the apex broad and deeply
cleft, at the base with a flattened appendage divided into 2
spreading teeth. Various, often flowering more than once
annually. (I, H) South India and Ceylon throughout South-
east Asia and Malaysia to the Philippines.

KOELLENSTEINIA Rchb.f.

This is a genus of about ten species of very unusual
and rare terrestrial or epiphytic orchids of the subtribe
Zygopetalinae, ranging from Panama throughout the
northern part of South America to Brazil. Only three
of the Koellensteinias appear to be present in choice
collections today, and when well-flowered they are most
attractive, though scarcely showy plants. Two types of
vegetative habit are present in this genus, the plants
either possessing minute terete or four-angled pseudobulbs which are completely enveloped by the imbricating
bases of the leaf-like sheaths, or entirely without pseudobulbous thickenings. In the species without pseudobulbs
(e.g., *K. graminea* (Ldl.) Rchb.f.), the few slender,
plicate leaves resemble those of a *Bletia*, and in the other
species, the foliage is somewhat heavier in texture, less
folded, and often wider. The inflorescences arise from
the bases of the pseudobulbs (or from the bases of the
leaf-clusters), and are erect, slim racemes which are
usually produced from the current season's growth. The

flowers are small and rather simulate a dwarf *Warrea* or *Cyrtopodium*, despite the alliance of the genus with *Paradisianthus* Rchb.f. and *Zygopetalum* Hk.

No hybrids are known in *Koellensteinia*, and nothing is known of its genetic compatibility as yet, though it is presumably 'crossable' with at least some of the allied groups.

CULTURE: As for the tropical Epidendrums with pseudobulbs. *Koellensteinia Kellneriana* Rchb.f. is habitually terrestrial, insofar as is known, and should be grown like a tropical *Bletia*. (I, H)

K. Kellneriana Rchb.f. (*Warrea graveolens* hort.)
Pbs. subterete or 4-angled, tapering, to 1¼″ tall, clustered. Lvs. 1–2, linear-lanceolate, plicate, acute or acuminate, stalked basally, to 2¼′ tall and ¾″ wide. Infls. erect, to 2′ tall, few- to many-fld., bracted. Fls. opening widely, fleshy, slightly fragrant, about 1″ across, the ss. green, the ps. paler green, the lip white transversely barred with lavender or purple. Ss. with the dors. one incurved, concave, elliptic-lanceolate, acute, the lats. oblique, elliptic-lanceolate, acute. Ps. not as fleshy as the ss., similar in shape, slightly smaller. Lip fleshy, 3-lbd., the base short-clawed, jointed to the col.-foot; lat. lbs. obliquely rhombic-triangular, obtuse, erect; midlb. broadly spreading, somewhat concave, rather transversely oblong-reniform; disc with a low, fleshy, warty callus. Mostly spring–early summer. (I, H) Panama; Colombia; Venezuela; British Guiana; Brazil.

K. graminea (Ldl.) Rchb.f. (*Maxillaria graminea* Ldl., *Promenaea graminea* Ldl., *Zygopetalum gramineum* Ldl., *Kefersteinia graminea* Rchb.f., *Aganisia graminea* Bth.) Pbs. absent. Lvs. few, grassy, linear, acute, to 8″ tall and usually less than ⅓″ wide, with a few sheaths at the base. Infls. erect, loosely 3–5-fld., very slender, to 5″ tall. Fls. about 1″ across, rather fleshy, not lasting well, the ss. and ps. oblong, obtuse, yellowish with transverse purplish bars in the lower half, forming rather vague concentric circles, the lip pale purple-marked on the lat. lbs., the larger midlb. golden-yellow. Spring. (I, H) Colombia; Venezuela; Guianas.

K. tricolor (Ldl.) Rchb.f. (*Zygopetalum tricolor* Ldl., *Aganisia tricolor* N.E.Br., *Acacallis cyanea* Ldl. var. *tricolor* N.E.Br.) Rather similar to *K. Kellneriana* Rchb.f., but with smaller lvs. and a more lax, 8–15-fld. infl. Fls. fragrant, rather heavy-textured, about ⅓″ across, the ss. and somewhat broader and shorter ps. greenish-white, the lip white with pale purple transverse lines. Spring. (I, H) Guianas; Brazil.

KUHLHASSELTIA J.J.Sm.

This is a genus of about three known species, all of them extremely rare and little-known terrestrial orchids of the subtribe *Physurinae*, native in the Philippines, the Malay Peninsula, Java, and Borneo. The group is somewhat allied to both *Erythrodes* Bl. and to *Eurycentrum* Schltr., but differs in technical details of the flowers; vegetatively, the several species rather simulate certain types of *Goodyera*. None of them appears to be present in collections at this time.

Nothing is known of the genetic affinities of *Kuhlhasseltia*.

CULTURE: Presumably as for *Anoectochilus*. (H)

LACAENA Ldl.

This is a genus of two very handsome but extremely rare epiphytic orchids, somewhat allied to *Paphinia* Ldl., and native in Central America. Uncommon in the wild, they are today virtually unknown by collectors, though one of them, *Lacaena bicolor* Ldl., has recently been introduced into a few choice assemblages of orchidaceous plants; it is a very striking plant which should be better known by enthusiasts. Pseudobulbous orchids, they bear heavy, folded leaves and pendulous inflorescences of medium-sized, showy blossoms of highly complex structure.

As yet, *Lacaena* has not been utilized by the breeders, though it is presumably genetically compatible with at least some of the allied genera of the subtribe *Gongorinae*. Hybrids between the two Lacaenas would also prove most interesting additions to the roster.

CULTURE: As for *Acineta*. Because of the sharply pendulous inflorescences, the plants should be grown in baskets. (I, H)

L. bicolor Ldl.
Pbs. clustered, egg-shaped, furrowed with age, often yellowish, to 6″ long. Lvs. usually 3 at apex of pbs., broadly elliptic to elliptic-lanceolate, narrowly acute to acuminate, to 2′ long and 6″ wide, very heavy-textured, rather dull green. Infls. usually several at once, to more than 2½′ long, 25–45-fld., arching to (more commonly) sharply pendulous. Fls. to more than 2″ across, very fragrant, waxy, rather bell-shaped, white marked and spotted with purple. Ss. oval, obtuse to acute, concave. Ps. shortly clawed, concave. Lip 3-lbd., jointed to the col.-foot, the lat. lbs. upcurved, the midlb. spreading, deflexed, the disc with a distinctly elevated, densely pubescent maroon callus between the lat. lbs. and a smaller callus on the isthmus. Mostly summer. (I, H) Mexico; Guatemala; Honduras; Nicaragua; Costa Rica.

LAELIA Ldl.
(*Amalias* Hoffmsgg., *Schomburgkia* Ldl.)

The genus *Laelia* Ldl. now contains upwards of seventy-five species, these for the most part epiphytes or lithophytes in the wild. The group has a wide range, which extends from Cuba and Mexico to Argentina, with the largest number of species to be found in Brazil. A member of the subtribe *Laeliinae*, it is closest in its alliance to *Cattleya* Ldl. (from which it differs principally in bearing eight pollinia—in two sets of four each—instead of the four found in that genus) and *Brassavola* R.Br. and *Rhyncholaelia* Schltr. (from both of which it differs in vegetative and floral characters). Contemporary orchidologists, for the most part, also relegate here *Schomburgkia* Ldl., but for horticultural purposes it is often retained as distinct from *Laelia*. Vegetatively the members of this group vary considerably, some of them (notably the Mexican-Guatemalan species) possessing relatively short clustered pseudobulbs, while others (*L. purpurata*, *L. tenebrosa*, etc.) have large elongated pseudobulbs much like a robust *Cattleya*. Those species formerly included in *Schomburgkia* possess two distinct types of bulbs as well: those allied to *L. tibicinis* being very large, usually yellowish,

Glossodia emarginata R.S.Rog. [W. H. NICHOLLS]

Grammatophyllum speciosum Bl. [REV. N. E. G. CRUTT-WELL]

Gomesa crispa (Ldl.) Kl. & Rchb.f. [GEORGE FULLER]

(ABOVE) An unidentified South African species of *Habenaria* shown here as illustrative of this fascinating genus [H. NARRAMORE]

(ABOVE LEFT) *Haemaria discolor* (Ker-Gawl.) Ldl. [GEORGE FULLER]

(LEFT) *Homalopetalum vomeriforme* (Sw.) F. & R. [*Flora of Jamaica*]

Hyalosema grandiflorum (Bl.) Rolfe [GEORGE FULLER]

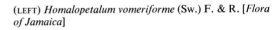

and markedly swollen basally, while those near *L. undulata* simulate a large *Cattleya*, but are distinctly stalked at the base. The inflorescences of several of the Laelias attain heights in excess of six feet, while others bear solitary blossoms on very short peduncles. Florally, the genus is extremely diverse, with most of the blossoms of sufficient dimensions and showiness to warrant their assemblage by collectors. Certain of the smaller Brazilian species (*L. cinnabarina*, *L. flava*, etc.) produce flowers scarcely equalled elsewhere in the subtribe for brilliance of coloration. Many of the Laelias are to be found in collections today, and virtually all of them are worthy of cultivation in even the most modest assemblage of orchidaceous plants.

A great deal of hybridization has been done with the members of this genus, the most notable resultant group being *Laeliocattleya* (*Laelia* × *Cattleya*), of which several hundred crosses are now on record; there are, peculiarly enough, even some natural hybrid Laeliocattleyas, indigenous to Brazil. The Laelias freely interbreed among themselves, and we now have a large series of exceptionally handsome hybrids from such crosses; here again natural hybrids are known, both in Brazil, and in the Mexico-Guatemala area. *Laelia* has also been successfully bred with many other genera of the subtribe *Laeliinae*, such as *Rhyncholaelia*, *Sophronitis*, *Epidendrum*, *Caularthron*, etc., yet despite this, considerable additional experimental breeding yet remains to be done by hybridists who deal in the more unusual kinds of multigeneric orchids.

CULTURE: Generally as for *Cattleya*. Many of the Brazilian Laelias require almost full exposure to the sun to flower successfully, and this most emphatically applies to those species formerly included in the genus *Schomburgkia*. Certain of the species of *Laelia* inhabiting Mexico and Guatemala grow consistently at rather high elevations in the mountains, hence in our collections thrive only when grown under moderately cool temperatures. (C, I, H)

L. albida Batem. ex Ldl. (*Bletia albida* Rchb.f., *Cattleya albida* Beer, *Laelia discolor* A.Rich. & Gal.)

Pbs. clustered, ovoid or subpyriform, becoming wrinkled with age, to 2″ tall. Lvs. paired, rather rigidly leathery, linear-lanceolate, acute, 4–7″ long, usually dark green in colour. Infls. slender, furnished with closely appressed sheathing bracts, 1–2½′ long, terminating in a loose or rather dense rac. of 2–9 fls. Fls. 2″ in diam., fragrant, the ss. and ps. white, often tinged with pale rose, the lip variable in colour. Ss. oblong-lanceolate, acute. Ps. similar to ss, but broader, with a distinct mid-nerve, usually undulate marginally. Lip oblong, 3-lbd., the lat. lbs. erect at the sides of the col., the midlb. reflexed, often vaguely undulate marginally; median part of lip from base to ⅔ of its length traversed by 3 parallel canary-yellow keels, of which the two lateral ones are sometimes spotted with purple; apical part of midlb. bright rose to bright-purple. Col. curving, white, the inner face sometimes flushed with purple. Mostly Dec.–Feb. (C, I) Mexico.

L. anceps Ldl. (*Amalias anceps* Hoffmsgg., *Bletia anceps* Rchb.f., *Cattleya anceps* Beer, *Laelia Barkeriana* Kn. & Westc.)

Pbs. clustered or more commonly borne at some distance from each other on the creeping, rather stout rhiz., ovoid-oblong, compressed, with 2 sharp edges and with broad ribs on each of the flattened sides, glossy, often purple-flushed, 2–3″ tall. Lf. usually solitary, rigidly leathery, sometimes purple-flushed behind, oblong-lanceolate, acutish, 6–8″ long. Infls. rather slender, erect to gracefully arching, 2–4′ long, jointed, with sheathing keeled bracts placed alternately and opposite along its length, ending in a cluster of 2–5 (rarely more) fls., the pedicellate ovaries of which are conspicuously viscous. Fls. 2½–4″ in diam., fragrant or not, lasting rather well, highly variable in colour, in the typical phase with pale rose-purple ss., the ps. usually darker; ss. lanceolate, acuminate, the ps. ovate, acuminate, usually at least half as broad again as ss. Lip 3-lbd., the lat. lbs. infolded over the col., pale rose bordered with purple externally, tawny-yellow striped and margined with purple on inside; midlb. oblong, apiculate, reflexed, vivid purple-crimson or reddish-magenta, the disc bright yellow traversed longitudinally by a thickened ridge and bordered in front with white. Col. semiterete, without wings. There are a great many horticultural variants, based for the most part on rather obscure colour discrepancies; certain of the most highly valued of these have white sepals and petals (and very rarely an almost white lip). Mostly winter, especially Dec.–Jan. (I) Mexico; Honduras.

L. autumnalis Ldl. (*Bletia autumnalis* LaLl. & Lex., *Cattleya autumnalis* Beer, *Laelia Gouldiana* Rchb.f.)

Pbs. clustered or slightly distant on the rhiz., subconical, tapering, becoming ribbed and channelled with age, 4–6″ long. Lvs. 2–3, lanceolate, obtuse, rather rigidly leathery, 5–7″ long. Infls. rather stout, usually with a dull crimson peduncle and rachis, 2–3′ long, bearing a rather loose apical 3–9-fld. rac. Fls. waxy in texture, long-lasting, fragrant, highly variable in colour, 3–4″ in diam., the spreading ss. and ps. bright rose-purple (rarely very vivid magenta-rose, or with apical darker blotches on the ps.), the ss. lanceolate, acuminate, the ps. ovate, acuminate. Lip 3-lbd., the lat. lbs. erect, partially enclosing the col., rounded, white or rose on the outer side; midlb. oblong, acuminate with a recurved tip, whitish at base, the apical part vivid rose-purple or magenta-purple; disc with 2 narrow, longitudinal, parallel raised keels, white spotted with purple along the edge (or bright yellow), with a third yellowish keel which passes between the apical part of these and extends beyond them. Col. clavate, curved, terete and purplish above, concave and white beneath. There is also an extremely rare pure white form. Mostly Oct.–Jan. (C, I) Mexico.

L. cinnabarina Batem. ex Ldl. (*Amalias cinnabarina* Hoffmsgg., *Bletia cinnabarina* Rchb.f., *Cattleya cinnabarina* Beer)

Pbs. 5–12″ tall, cylindric upwards but swollen at the base, when young clothed basally with whitish striped sheaths, often flushed with purple. Lf. usually solitary (rarely paired), to about 12″ long, linear-oblong, acutish, erect, rather rigidly leathery, often flushed with purple. Infls. slender, erect or arching, to 2′ long, with a narrow flattened basal sheath, the rac. 5–15-fld. Fls. to 2½″ in diam., long-lasting, somewhat variable in colour, but usually bright cinnabar-red, the long pedicellate ovaries the same colour as the perianth. Ss. and ps. similar and equal, spreading, linear-lanceolate, acuminate. Lip shorter than other segms., 3-lbd., the lat. lbs. oblong, forming a tube around the col., usually streaked with red on inner side; midlb. narrowly ovate, crisped, reflexed. Col. short, clavate, 3-angled. Mostly Feb.–April. (I, H) Brazil.

L. crispa (Ldl.) Rchb.f. (*Cattleya crispa* Ldl., *Bletia crispa* Rchb.f.)

Pbs. clavate, 7–12″ long, compressed, usually grooved on the flattened sides. Lf. solitary, rigidly erect, oblong-lanceolate, obtuse, 9–12″ long. Infls. issuing from a large, oblong, flattened sheath, rather short, 4–9-fld. Fls. 4–5″ in diam., fragrant, long-lasting, the ss. and ps. white sometimes flushed with purple basally, the ss. obovate-lanceolate, acute, the broader ps. very crisped towards apex and marginally. Lip 3-lbd., the lat. lbs. forming a tube around the col., white outside, yellow inside, the median area between them also yellow streaked longitudinally with purple; midlb. oblong, reflexed, vivid or very dark amethyst-purple to almost black-purple, veined and reticulated with darker hue. Col. clavate, 3-angled, mostly stained on lower face with plum-colour. Mostly summer. (I, H) Brazil.

L. flava Ldl. (*Bletia flava* Rchb.f., *Cattleya flava* Beer, *Laelia fulva* Ldl.)

Pbs. clustered, rather stout, cylindric from a swollen base, usually flushed with dark purple, to 8″ tall. Lf. solitary, lanceolate or linear-lanceolate, very rigidly leathery, dark green, usually flushed purplish or magenta-purple beneath, 4–8″ long. Infls. 1–2′ long, with a narrow compressed basal sheath, apically rather loosely (rarely densely) 5–12-fld. Fls. to almost 2½″ in diam., rather variable in colour from light orange-yellow to vivid golden- or butter-yellow, long-lasting. Ss. and ps. spreading, similar, ligulate, acute, the lat. ss. shorter than other segms., falcate. Lip very narrow, 3-lbd., the lat. lbs. semi-ovate, erect, the midlb. recurving, oblong, crisped, traversed by 4 thickened nerves which are prolonged to the base. Col. short, 3-angled. Mostly spring–early summer. (I, H) Brazil.

L. gloriosa (Rchb.f.) L.O.Wms. (*Schomburgkia gloriosa* Rchb.f., *Schomburgkia crispa* Ldl., *Bletia crispina* Rchb.f., *Bletia gloriosa* Rchb.f.)

Pbs. fusiform, somewhat angled, often flushed with brown or purplish, to 8″ tall. Lvs. normally paired, rigidly leathery, lanceolate, acute, 8–12″ long. Infls. erect, sheathed, to more than 4′ long, the apical rac. densely many-fld., with prominent bracts, forming a large head. Fls. 2–2½″ in diam., waxy, rather short-lived, on elongate white pedicellate ovaries, the linear-oblong, marginally very crisped and undulate ss. and ps. brownish-yellow with darker veins. Lip oblong, vaguely 3-lbd., pale rose-pink, with a darker flush apically, and with 3 raised median lines on the disc. Col. clavate, marginally furnished with wings near apex. Mostly Oct.–Dec. (H) Venezuela; Guianas; Brazil.

L. harpophylla Rchb.f. (*Laelia geraensis* B.-R.)

Pbs. st.-like, clustered, very slender, erect, 5–18″ tall,

furnished with whitish membranaceous sheaths. Lf. solitary, narrowly ligulate, acuminate, leathery, rather rigid, 6–8″ long. Infls. shorter than the lvs., with a pale sheath at their base, apically 4–7-fld. Fls. 2–3″ in diam., long-lasting, vivid cinnabar-red, except for the whitish midlb. of the lip. Ss. and ps. similar, lanceolate, spreading, acute. Lip 3-lbd., the triangular lat. lbs. enfolding the angular, curved col.; midlb. oblong, reflexed, marginally crisped, with 2 raised median lines. Usually Feb.–Mar. (I, H) Brazil.

L. lobata (Ldl.) Veitch (*Cattleya lobata* Ldl., *Bletia Boothiana* Rchb.f., *Bletia lobata* Rchb.f., *Laelia Boothiana* Rchb.f., *Laelia Rivieri* Carr.)

Rhiz. rather stout, creeping. Pbs. fusiform, narrowed basally, the swollen part compressed laterally, 4–8″ long, Lf. solitary, oblong, erect, rigidly leathery, to almost 12″ long. Infl. arising from a large compressed spathe, 2–5-fld., rather short. Fls. fragrant, rather long-lasting, to 5″ in diam., the ss. and ps. pale rose-purple veined for the most part with darker colour. Ss. lanceolate, acute, the margins (especially the basal ones) reflexed. Ps. at least twice as broad as ss., oval, obtuse, wavy and crisped especially near margins. Lip 3-lbd., broadly oval, the lat. lbs. enfolding the col., outside coloured like ss. and ps., inside flushed with yellow and often streaked with purple, the midlb. spreading, very crisped and erose marginally, vivid amethyst-purple with paler streaks radiating from basal middle outwards. Col. rather stout, 3-angled, pale lilac. Spring–early summer. (I, H) Brazil.

L. Perrinii (Ldl.) Batem. (*Cattleya Perrinii* Ldl., *Bletia Perrinii* Rchb.f.)

Pbs. clustered, clavate, 6–10″ long, narrowed markedly below, the swollen part compressed. Lf. usually solitary, rather rigidly leathery, oblong, obtuse or emarginate, to almost 12″ long, often spotted or flushed underneath with brownish-purple. Infls. arising from a compressed sheath, rather abbreviated, few-fld. Fls. to 5½″ in diam., rather long-lasting, the ss. and ps. pale rose-purple, the ligulate, acute dors. sep. erect, the lat. ss. strongly falcate, the slightly broader, undulate-margined ps. spreading horizontally. Lip vaguely 3-lbd., the lat. lbs. enfolding the col. and coloured outside like the ss. and ps., inside yellow streaked with purple; midlb. oblong, acutish with erose apical margins, reflexed, vivid lustrous purple, this hue continuing along the anterior margins of the lat. lbs., the disc straw-yellow to yellow. Col. arching, white flushed with purple. Autumn–winter. (I, H) Brazil.

L. pumila (Hk.) Rchb.f. (*Cattleya pumila* Hk., *Cattleya marginata* Paxt., *Cattleya spectabilis* Paxt., *Cattleya Pinelii* Ldl., *Bletia pumila* Rchb.f.)

Rhiz. creeping. Pbs. borne often at some distance from one another, terete, often curving, 2–4″ long, glossy dark-green. Lf. solitary, very fleshy and rigid, elliptic-oblong, 2–5″ long. Infls. abbreviated, 1-fld., usually shorter than the subtending lf. Fls. long-lasting, fragrant, variable in size and colour, usually 3–4″ in diam., the ss. and ps. usually rose-purple. Ss. spreading, oblong, acute. Ps. ovate-oblong, usually obtuse, often somewhat undulate marginally, mostly twice as broad as the ss. Lip 3-lbd., the lat. lbs. rolled over the col.

and meeting at the edges, outside coloured like the ss. and ps., with the addition of a broad purple blotch at the anterior edge; midlb. oblong, 2-lbd., marginally erose, mostly an odd shade of maroon-purple, sometimes with a paler triangular blotch at apex; disc traversed by 3–5 parallel yellow ridges, the median one longer than the others, and dilated at its extremity. Col. clavate, 3-angled, white. Several variants have been described, of scant botanical importance, being based primarily on coloration of the flowers. Autumn. (I, H) Brazil.

L. purpurata Ldl. & Paxt. (*Laelia Casperiana* Rchb.f., *L. Wyattiana* Rchb.f., *Cattleya Brysiana* Lem., *Cattleya purpurata* Beer, *Bletia Casperiana* Rchb.f.)
Probably the finest of the genus, with literally hundreds of named horticultural variants, the National Flower of Brazil. Pbs. fusiform, stalked basally, the swollen portion rather compressed, glossy, becoming ribbed with age, 2′ tall. Lf. solitary, oblong-ligulate, obtuse, thickly leathery, usually dark green, 12–15″ long. Infls. stout, emerging from a leathery, oblong sheath, 3–7-fld. or more. Fls. fragrant, usually lasting well, 6–8″ in diam., extremely variable in colour, normally with ss. and ps. (which are often darker-coloured) white, or white flushed and veined with pale amethyst-purple, sometimes pale amethyst-purple with darker veins. Ss. oblong-lanceolate, acute, the basal margins usually somewhat reflexed. Ps. usually twice as broad as ss., ovate-oblong, acutish, undulate marginally. Lip rhomboidal when spread out, vaguely 3-lbd., the basal part with an entire margin, enfolding the col. in a tube, outside usually whitish, inside pale to rather bright yellow marked with purple lines, of which the 3 central ones are parallel, the others diverging; midlb. spreading with crisped margins, usually very rich velvety purple, more or less veined with maroon-purple. Col. clavate, 3-angled, curving, greenish. Usually May–July. (I, H) Brazil, especially in the South.

L. rubescens Ldl. (*Laelia acuminata* Ldl., *L. peduncularis* Ldl., *L. violacea* Rchb.f., *Cattleya acuminata* Beer, *Cattleya peduncularis* Beer, *Cattleya rubescens* Beer, *Bletia acuminata* Rchb.f., *Bletia rubescens* Rchb.f.)
Pbs. roundish, ovoid or oblong, strongly compressed, glossy, often purple-flushed, to 2½″ tall and 1¼″ wide, with several membranaceous sheaths at base. Lvs. 1 (rarely 2), glossy, rigidly leathery, oblong-elliptic, obtuse or obliquely retuse, to 8″ long and 1½″ wide. Infls. terete, the peduncle nearly concealed by short papery bracts, with a compact, few- to several-fld. rac. at the apex, to 3′ long (usually shorter). Fls. in some forms not opening well, often closing at night, slightly fragrant or odourless, usually not very long-lived, highly variable in size and colour, 2–3″ in diam., ranging from white to white with the lip-tube red, or in many shades from pink to dark lavender, with the lip-tube usually much darker. Ss. variable, linear-elliptic, linear-lanceolate, oblong-lanceolate or oblanceolate-elliptic, obtuse to narrowly acute, the lats. somewhat oblique. Ps. narrowly or broadly elliptic, obtuse to acute or apiculate. Lip distinctly 3-lbd. near the middle, the lat.

lbs. short, rounded-obtuse, enfolding the col.; midlb. oblong-quadrate to oblong-oval, subtruncate to acute, the margins wavy; disc purplish, red, or carmine, with 2–3 slightly elevated lines. Mostly autumn–winter. (I, H) Mexico; Guatemala; El Salvador; Honduras; Nicaragua; Costa Rica; Panama.

L. speciosa (HBK) Schltr. (*Bletia speciosa* HBK, *Bletia grandiflora* LaLl. & Lex., *Cattleya Grahami* Ldl., *Cattleya majalis* Beer, *Laelia grandiflora* Ldl., *Laelia majalis* Ldl.)
Pbs. clustered, ovoid, pale green or greyish-green, furrowed and wrinkled with age, to more than 2″ tall. Lvs. 1–2, lanceolate, acutish, rather leathery, often soon deciduous, 5–6″ long. Infls. about as long as the lvs., usually 1-fld., rarely 2-fld. Fls. to 6″ in diam., fragrant, rather heavy-textured, long-lived, somewhat variable in colour, but usually with pale rosy-lilac ss. and ps. (these segms. very rarely pure white), the lanceolate ss. half as broad as the oval-oblong, crisped-margined ps. Lip oblong, 3-lbd., the lat. lbs. small, enfolding the col., white flushed with pale lilac towards margins; midlb. spreading, emarginate, traversed longitudinally by a pale yellow raised line which becomes broader towards the base, medially white spotted and mottled with purple, with a more or less broad margin of bright or pale mauve- or rosy-purple. Mostly April–May. (C, I) Mexico, at rather high elevations.

L. superbiens Ldl. (*Bletia superbiens* Rchb.f., *Cattleya superbiens* Beer, *Schomburgkia superbiens* Rolfe)
Very robust and handsome sp., the pbs. oblong-fusiform, somewhat compressed, becoming furrowed with age, to 1½′ tall and 1½″ in diam. Lvs. 1–2, rigidly leathery, oblong to oblong-lanceolate, obtuse to acute, to 12″ long and 2½″ wide. Infls. very stout, to 4′ tall (rarely more), the peduncle with long tubular sheaths, with a many-fld., apical rac., the fls. with pedicellate ovaries to 3″ long. Fls. fragrant, long-lived, to 5″ across, usually rose-purple somewhat paler towards bases of ss. and ps., the lip rich crimson-magenta, the disc yellow or yellowish, covered with 5–6 longitudinal, prominent, crisped, irregular lamellae, the col. white tinged with purple. Ss. spreading, usually undulate, linear-oblong, oblong-lanceolate or narrowly lanceolate, obtuse to acute, the lats. oblique, slightly shorter and broader than the dors. one. Ps. spreading, narrowly oblong to narrowly oblanceolate-oblong, broadly rounded to acute, oblique, the margins usually very undulate. Lip 3-lbd. above the middle, arcuate-decurved, the margins enfolding the col.; lat. lbs. short, oblong, rounded at crisped tip; midlb. much longer than lat. lbs., broadly obovate to obcordate, emarginate, the edges waved and crisped. Winter. (I, H) Mexico; Guatemala; Honduras.

L. tenebrosa Rolfe (*Laelia grandis* Ldl. & Paxt. var. *tenebrosa* Gower)
Similar in habit to *L. purpurata* Ldl. & Paxt., often somewhat less robust in all parts. Fls. few, often not lasting well, fragrant, to almost 6½″ in diam., somewhat variable in colour, but usually with the ss. and undulate, oblong-ligulate, acute, ps. brownish-yellow (rarely

ochre-yellow), the ps. often veined with darker colour. Lip basally tubular, the tube rather narrow and often somewhat flattened from above, whitish to pale rose-red, veined with darker rose-red or purple-red, the flaring midlb. very dark purple-red, often almost black-purple, velvety or not. A very showy sp., which has been widely used by breeders in recent times. Mostly May–June. (I, H) East-central Brazil, from Baía to Rio de Janeiro.

L. tibicinis (Batem. ex Ldl.) L.O.Wms. (*Epidendrum tibicinis* Batem. ex Ldl., *Schomburgkia tibicinis* Batem., *Schomburgkia tibicinis* Batem. var. *grandiflora* Hk., ? *Schomburgkia exaltata* Krzl., *Cattleya tibicinis* Beer, *Bletia tibicinis* Rchb.f.)
Very robust sp., the pbs. densely clustered, elongately fusiform, tapering apically, hollow, to more than 2' long and 3" in diam., often yellowish, in the wild usually inhabited by biting ants. Lvs. several, apical, rigidly leathery, dark green to yellowish, oblong-elliptic, rounded to obtuse, to 1½' long and 3" broad, very rigid and heavy-textured. Infls. simple or branched, the rather dense rac. or panicle at the end of a stout, slow-growing peduncle which in extreme cases reaches 15' in length. Fls. waxy, very fragrant, long-lived, usually opening successively over a long period, 2–3" in diam., highly variable in colour and somewhat so in shape, the ss. and ps. usually vivid purplish-magenta (often flushed with paler or brighter colour), sometimes brownish-orange, the lip whitish-yellow to rich purple, the 5–7-keeled disc usually yellowish. Ss. marginally undulate and twisted, narrowly oblong-elliptic to elliptic-oblanceolate, broadly rounded to obtuse, the lats. somewhat oblique. Ps. marginally undulate and twisted, linear-spatulate to oblanceolate, rounded to subacute. Lip strongly 3-lbd. above the middle, the lat. lbs. enfolding the col., large, roundish, broadly rounded at apex; midlb. small, roundish to rhomboidal, retuse, with a sinus separating it from the lat. lbs., the margins cut-crisped to almost entire. Spring–early summer. (H) Mexico to Costa Rica.

L. undulata (Ldl.) L.O.Wms. (*Schomburgkia undulata* Ldl., *Cattleya undulata* Beer, *Bletia undulata* Rchb.f.)
Pbs. very robust, fusiform, narrowed below, to almost 2' tall, becoming grooved with age, sometimes flushed with brownish or purplish. Lvs. usually 2 (rarely 3), apical, rather heavily leathery, oblong, acutish, to 10" long. Infls. 2–6' tall, erect or arching, with a dense or rather loose, mostly many-fld. rac. at apex, the fls. subtended by long, pendulous, papery bracts, the pedicellate ovaries elongate, usually purplish or whitish-purple. Fls. to almost 2" in diam., fragrant or not, very waxy, often not lasting well, somewhat variable in colour, but usually very dark brown-purple or wine-purple on the spreading or infolding, linear-oblong, very crisped and undulate ss. and ps. Lip 3-lbd. the lat. lbs. erect, oblong; usually pale rose to rose-purple; midlb. spreading, cordate, apiculate, dark purple, with the disc white traversed longitudinally by 5 raised lines. Col. broad, purple. Late winter–spring. (I, H) Colombia; Venezuela.

L. xanthina Ldl. (*Laelia virens* Ldl., *Bletia flabellata* Rchb.f., *Bletia xanthina* Rchb.f.)
Rather similar in vegetative habit to *L. purpurata* Ldl. & Paxt., but smaller, the pbs. usually to about 8" in maximum height, the rigidly leathery lvs. often spotted underneath with dark brown or brown-purple. Infls. issuing from a compressed purplish, sometimes pale green sheath, 3–5-fld. Fls. 2½–3½" in diam., often not opening fully, fragrant or not, rather waxy, bright- or buff-yellow, except the midlb. of the lip, which is white more or less streaked with magenta-purple or red-purple. Ss. and ps. similar and subequal, elliptic-oblong, marginally reflexed. Lip subquadrate, vaguely 3-lbd., the lat. lbs. erect, somewhat enfolding the col., the midlb. acuminate, reflexed apically. Col. almost 3-angled, streaked with red or red-purple on the anterior face. Mostly May–July. (I, H) Brazil.

L. furfuracea Ldl. (*Cattleya furfuracea* Beer, *Bletia furfuracea* Rchb.f.) Pbs. clustered, ovoid, often striped with dull purple or purplish-brown, becoming furrowed with age, 2–3" long. Lf. usually solitary (rarely paired), narrowly oblong, acute, very leathery, 4–6" long. Infls. to almost 12" long, 1–3-fld. or more, rather slender. Fls. fragrant, rather long-lived, opening well, somewhat variable in colour, but usually the ss. and ps. old-rose to pale rose-purple, the ss. lanceolate, acute, the ps. broader, sub-rhomboidal. Lip 3-lbd., the erect lat. lbs. roundish, paler in colour than the ss. and ps., the midlb. oblong, reflexed, usually bright old-rose-purple to rose-purple, with 2 prominent keels on the disc. Col. clavate, terete above, pale rose-purple. Sept.–Nov. (C, I) Mexico: Oaxaca, usually at high elevations.

L. grandis Ldl. & Paxt. (*Bletia grandis* Rchb.f.) Similar in habit to and closely allied to *L. tenebrosa* Rolfe, differing in the dimensions and colour of the fls. Fls. 4–5" in diam., fragrant or not, often not lasting well, the ss. and ps. nankeen-yellow, the former elliptic-lanceolate, wavy, twisted, the broader ps. rhomboid-ovate, often rather crisped marginally. Lip 3-lbd., the lat. lbs. forming a tube around the col., white outside; midlb. roundish, rather crisped marginally, white veined with rose-purple. Mar.–June. (I, H) Brazil, mostly in Baía and Espírito Santo.

L. Humboldtii (Rchb.f.) L.O.Wms. (*Epidendrum Humboldtii* Rchb.f., *Schomburgkia Humboldtii* Rchb.f., *Bletia Humboldtii* Rchb.f.) Robust sp., with a stout rhiz., the pbs. often not very closely placed. Pbs. subcylindric, tapering upwards, rather like those of *L. tibicinis* (Batem. ex Ldl.) L.O.Wms., but smaller, 6–8" at maximum length, becoming furrowed with age, the nodes depressed. Lvs. 2–3, apical, oblong or oblong-cuneate, usually about 6" long, rigidly leathery. Infls. erect, sheathed, 3–4' long, usually paniculate and many-fld., the pedicellate ovaries elongate, purplish. Fls. 2½–3" in diam., lasting well, fragrant, the ss. and ps. pale lilac to almost white, undulate, the former oblong, acute, the latter elliptic-oblong, usually flushed apically with amethyst-purple. Lip 3-lbd., broadly oval, the lat. lbs. triangular, enfolding the col., amethyst-purple outside; midlb. spreading, deeply cleft apically, fringed and crisped marginally, vivid purple streaked with pale purple; disc yellow, traversed longitudinally by 5–7 lamellae, which are rich purple towards base of the lip. Col. terete above, fluted below. Winter–spring. (I, H) Venezuela.

L. Jongheana Rchb.f. (*Bletia Jongheana* Rchb.f.) Pbs. arising from a stout creeping rhiz., often at some intervals from one another, sub-fusiform to ovoid-oblong, compressed, to more than 2" long. Lf. solitary, oval-oblong, obtuse, 3–6" long, rigidly leathery, erect. Infls. abbreviated, usually 1-fld.,

Laeliopsis domingensis (Ldl.) Ldl. [B.S.WILLIAMS]

rather rarely 2-fld. Fls. 4–5″ in diam., heavy-textured, long-lasting, spreading out flat, soft rose-purple, except for the lip which has a yellow disc, in front of which is a white blotch. Ss. lanceolate, acute. Ps. broader than ss., elliptic-oblong, obtuse. Lip 3-lbd., oval-oblong, the lat. lbs. triangular, the midlb. obtuse, emarginate, all segms. crisped and somewhat toothed marginally; disc 7-lamellate. Col. slender, pale rose-purple above. Feb.–Apr. (I, H) Brazil: Minas Gerais, in dry regions.

L. Lyonsii (Ldl.) L.O.Wms. (*Schomburgkia Lyonsii* Ldl., *Schomburgkia carinata* Griseb., *Bletia Lyonsii* Rchb.f.) Rather similar in habit to *L. undulata* (Ldl.) L.O.Wms., often somewhat less robust vegetatively. Infls. erect or arching under the weight of the fls., to 5′ long (rarely more), bracted, the apical rac. rather densely 10–20-fld., with abruptly reflexed, papery bracts subtending each fl. Fls. to 2″ in diam., fragrant, rather waxy, lasting well, white more or less spotted with dark purple or reddish-purple. Ss. oblong-lanceolate, acutish, rather undulate-crisped marginally. Ps. broader than ss., ovate-oblong, acute, undulate-crisped marginally. Lip reflexed, rather small, ovate-oblong, acute, with 5 raised longitudinal lines. Col. short, curving, swollen at base, 2-toothed at apex. Mostly July–Sept. (I, H) Cuba; Jamaica.

L. Thomsoniana (Rchb.f.) L.O.Wms. (*Schomburgkia Thomsoniana* Rchb.f., *Myrmecophila Thomsoniana* Rolfe) Habit much as in *L. tibicinis* (Batem.) L.O.Wms., but generally smaller, the pbs. usually about 6–8″ long, often yellowish. Infl. stout, erect, to 4′ long, frequently branched in upper portions, many-fld., the fls. opening successively over a long period. Fls. to 2¾″ across, cream-white to butter-yellow, the flaring lip apically very dark wine-purple to almost black-purple, undulate marginally. Ps. narrow, very crisped for apical two-thirds. Spring. (H) Cuba; Cayman Islands.

L. Wendlandii Rchb.f. (*Bletia Wendlandii* Rchb.f.) Pbs. fusiform, tapering upwards, longitudinally grooved, to 7″ tall and 1¼″ thick. Lvs. 2–3, apical, rigidly leathery, oblong-elliptic, broadly roundish to acutish, ascending, to 9″ long. Infls. erect, to 7′ tall, rarely branched, few- to many-fld., the sheathing bracts small. Fls. waxy, fragrant, about 2″ in diam., greenish-brown or tan-brown, the lip greenish-white

to pale yellow flushed or striped with purplish, the disc with 3 fringed greenish-yellow, lavender-tinted ridges, the col. light green flushed with lavender. Ss. linear-oblanceolate, obtuse to acute. Ps. crisped, linear to oblanceolate, obtuse or subacute. Lip adnate to col.-base, 3-lbd. above middle, arching; lat. lbs. obtuse, enclosing the col.; midlb. roundish, apically rounded to emarginate, the margins cut. Summer. (H) Guatemala; Honduras; Nicaragua.

LAELIOPSIS Ldl.

Two species of *Laeliopsis* are known to date, one, **L. cubensis** (Ldl.) Ldl. ex Cgn., endemic to Cuba and apparently not presently in cultivation, the other, noted below, being found in a few choice contemporary collections. The genus is a member of the subtribe *Laeliinae*, being closest in its alliance to *Broughtonia* R.Br., from which it differs in the rigidly fleshy, serrate-margined leaves, and the lack of a sepaline tube in the flowers. Both of the *Laeliopsis* are desirable, showy plants, which should be better known by orchidists. Several recent articles on this genus in the popular literature have done nothing but add to the confusion surrounding it and its allies.

A few apparently striking hybrids, in which *Laeliopsis domingensis* figures have been produced to date, mostly in Hawaii, but these are not generally available to collectors.

CULTURE: As for *Broughtonia*. (H)

L. domingensis (Ldl.) Ldl. (*Cattleya domingensis* Ldl., *Bletia domingensis* Rchb.f., *Broughtonia lilacina* Henfr.)

Pbs. clustered, ovoid to fusiform, somewhat compressed, 2–3″ long. Lvs. usually paired, rigidly fleshy, oblong, obtuse, 4–5″ long, marginally saw-toothed. Infls. slender, to almost 2′ long, usually paniculate apically, but sometimes with a cluster of 5–9 fls., these often opening successively over a long period. Fls. 2–2½″

in diam., not expanding fully, often rather short-lived, faintly fragrant or not, the ss. and ps. pale rosy-mauve with purple veins and flushing, the ss. linear-oblong, the ps. oval-oblong, twice as broad as ss., often somewhat undulate and toothed marginally. Lip obscurely 3-lbd., broadly obovate, the lat. lbs. forming a tube which is white outside and pale yellow inside, the disc traversed by pale to rather dark purple lines; midlb. flaring widely, the margins fringed, rose-purple with darker veins and suffusions. Col. clavate, abbreviated, enclosed within the lip-tube. There is a rare albinistic form. Mostly Apr.–June. (H) Hispaniola.

LANIUM Ldl.

The genus *Lanium* includes about four species of dwarf, rather elegant epiphytic or lithophytic orchids. It is one of the components of the subtribe *Laeliinae*, somewhat allied to *Epidendrum* L., but differing from that group in technical details of the small, green or whitish-yellow blossoms. Charming, creeping plants, the Laniums are indigenous to Brazil, the Guianas, and Amazonian Peru, and are today regrettably rare in our collections.

No hybrids have as yet been made utilizing *Lanium*, though its members are presumably genetically compatible with at least certain of the allied genera, and some attractive potentials seem evident through experimental breeding.

CULTURE: Because of the rather elongate, creeping rhizomes, these small orchids should be grown either mounted on tree-fern slabs, or potted in shallow, perfectly-drained fern-pans. A compost of either straight osmunda or a mixture of equal parts of shredded tree-fern and chopped sphagnum moss is suitable. Abundant moisture and high humidity are necessary at all times, coupled with a rather bright spot. Easily grown, they are heartily recommended to all connoisseurs of the graceful 'botanical' orchids. (I, H)

L. avicula Ldl.

Pbs. borne at considerable distances from each other on the creeping rhiz., bright green, oblong, to ¾″ tall. Lvs. normally paired or in 3's. rather rigidly leathery, elliptic, obtuse, to 1¼″ long, bright green. Infls. terminal, rigidly erect, to 6″ tall, the peduncle slender, simple or branched, with rather numerous scattered fls. Fls. mostly less than ½″ in diam., lasting well, opening fully, creamy or yellowish-white. Ss. lanceolate, acute. Ps. linear. Lip ovate, acute, smaller than other segms. Mostly Sept.–Nov. (I, H) Brazil; Amazonian Peru.

L. Berkeleyi Rchb.f.

Similar to *L. avicula* Ldl., but with longer pbs. and larger foliage, to about 8″ tall when in bloom. Fls. very numerous, about ¾″ across, waxy, pale green, sparsely spotted with red or magenta-red. Winter. (I, H) Brazil.

LANKESTERELLA Ames

This is an extraordinary genus of about ten known species, a member of the highly complex subtribe *Spiranthinae*, most closely allied to *Eurystyles* Wawra. Native for the most part in Brazil, a couple of the

Lankesterellas extend into Central America; none appears to be present in cultivation at this time, and it seems improbable that they would thrive under the artificial conditions of our collections, due to their

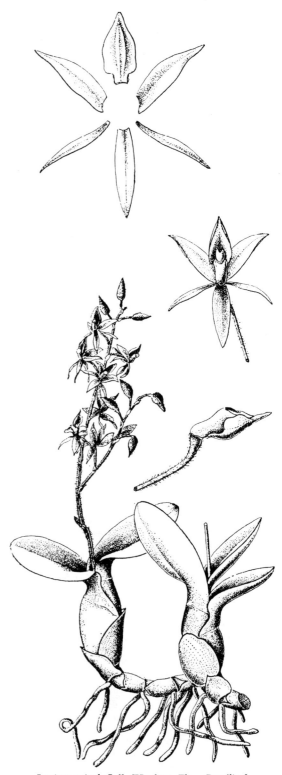

Lanium avicula Ldl. [Hoehne, *Flora Brasílica*]

peculiar habits. These very dwarf orchids are epiphytes, their fleshy fuzzy roots and little rosettes of thick leaves being found commonly on trees even within the cities of Brazil. The flowers are proportionately very large, usually solitary, and are found mostly in shades of emerald-green and white. This is a truly entrancing genus, and one which should be acquired by the connoisseur who is prepared to devote some especial attention to their care.

Nothing is known of the genetic affinities of *Lankesterella*.

CULTURE: Presumably as for *Ornithocephalus*. The plants must never be permitted to dry out at any time. (I, H)

LEAOA C.Porto & Schltr.

A single species of *Leaoa* is known at this time, this the very rare epiphytic **L. monophylla** (B.-R.) C.Porto & Schltr. (*Hexadesmia monophylla* B.-R.), which has been found on a few occasions in Brazil. A member of the subtribe *Ponerinae*, it is closely allied to *Scaphyglottis* P. & E., and will perhaps in future prove referable to that highly polymorphic group. At this time, it is unknown in cultivation.

Nothing is known of the genetic affinities of *Leaoa*.

CULTURE: Probably as for the smaller-growing, tufted species of *Scaphyglottis*. (I, H)

LECANORCHIS Bl.

This is an odd genus of about five species of relatively robust, saprophytic orchids, native in Japan, Malaysia, Indonesia, and New Guinea. Placed in the subtribe *Vanillinae*, its members are unknown in contemporary collections, although some of them seem to be rather common in their native haunts. The thin, brittle stems bear at their tips a raceme of a few or rather numerous complex, vari-coloured flowers, which are unique in possessing a small toothed cup at the top of the pedicellate ovary, just below the sepals.

Nothing is known of the genetic affinities of *Lecanorchis*.

CULTURE: Presumably as for *Corallorrhiza*, though scant success can be anticipated with these refractory saprophytes. (H)

LEMURELLA Schltr.

This is a genus of three known species, all small or medium-sized epiphytic orchids native in Madagascar and the Comoro Islands. Placed in the difficult subtribe *Sarcanthinae*, it is somewhat allied to *Cryptopus* Ldl., but differs in technical details of the tiny, inverted, yellowish blossoms, which are borne in elongate racemes. None of the Lemurellas has as yet been introduced into cultivation.

Nothing is known of the genetic alliances of this rare group.

CULTURE: As for the tropical Angraecums. (H)

LEMURORCHIS Krzl.

Lemurorchis madagascariensis Krzl., the only known member of this rare genus, is an epiphytic monopodial orchid of the subtribe *Sarcanthinae*, somewhat allied to *Listrostachys* Rchb.f., native in the forests of Madagascar. Its rather large, white flowers are attractive, but it has not as yet been introduced into cultivation.

Nothing is known of the genetic affinities of *Lemurorchis*.

CULTURE: Presumably as for the tropical Angraecums. (H)

LEOCHILUS Kn. & Westc.
(*Cryptosaccus* Scheidw. ex Rchb.f., *Cryptosanus* Scheidw., *Leiochilus* Bth., *Rhynchostele* Rchb.f., *Rhynchostelis* Jacks., *Waluewa* Regel)

Leochilus (often mis-spelled *Leiochilus*) contains an estimated fifteen species of closely allied and botanically often rather confused epiphytic or lithophytic orchids ranging from Mexico and the West Indies to northern

Leochilus labiatus (Sw.) O.Ktze. [Fawcett & Rendle, *Flora of Jamaica*]

Argentina. Allied to *Oncidium* Sw., these plants are today very scarce in collections, though at least two species are in cultivation at this time. Usually very dwarf orchids with small pseudobulbs and leaves, they bear short or elongate inflorescences with a few small but unusually intricate flowers. The Leochilus are often found in cultivated plots in nature, growing on twigs or branches in ornamental shrubs or trees, frequently coffee or citrus, and may be very common when encountered in the wild.

No hybrids are known in *Leochilus*. The genus is presumably genetically compatible with at least some of the other members of the subtribe *Oncidiinae*, and some interesting crosses might be made through critical intergeneric breeding.

CULTURE: As for the tropical, pseudobulbous Oncidiums. (I, H)

L. labiatus (Sw.) O.Ktze. (*Epidendrum labiatum* Sw., *Liparis labiata* Spreng., *Rodriguezia cochlearis* Ldl., *Leochilus cochlearis* Ldl., *Oncidium labiatum* Rchb.f.)
Pbs. ellipsoid-oblong, compressed, often reddish-brown, to ¾″ long, with 2–3 leaf-like bracts at the base. Lf. solitary, leathery, elliptic-lanceolate to ligulate, obtuse to subacute, to 2½″ long and ¾″ wide, often reddish-brown, glossy. Infls. solitary or paired, slender, erect, few-fld., sometimes branching, to 10″ tall. Fls. about ½″ across, fleshy, yellow striped and spotted with reddish-brown, the lip yellow with a red or red-brown spot at the base. Dors. sep. elliptic-lanceolate, shortly acuminate, deeply concave; lat. ss. connate to above the middle, the apices rather flaring, with two distinct keels on lower surface. Ps. slightly smaller than the ss., elliptic-oblong, acutish, with distinct central keels on reverse surfaces. Lip entire, slightly concave, oblanceolate, obtuse or sometimes retuse, the blade with a vague median constriction; disc with an erect, 2-grooved. fleshy callus. Summer. (I, H) West Indies; Guatemala throughout Central America to Trinidad and ? Venezuela.

L. scriptus (Scheidw.) Rchb.f. (*Cryptosanus scriptus* Scheidw., *Oncidium scriptum* Rchb.f., *Leochilus major* Schltr., *L. Powellii* Schltr., *L. retusus* Schltr.)
Pbs. oblong-ovoid to ellipsoid-oblong, compressed, truncate apically, to 2″ long, the base with several distichously imbricating bracts, the upper 2–3 of which are lf.-like. Lvs. usually solitary, leathery, ligulate, obtuse or unequally bilobed at apex, slightly folded and stalked at base. Infls. 1 or more, erect or arching, 3–12-fld., sometimes slightly branched, to 10″ tall. Fls. to ¾″ across, greenish-white to greenish-yellow with purple or reddish-brown markings. Ss. spreading, the dors. one elliptic-lanceolate, acute, somewhat concave, the reverse surface with a distinct keel, the lats. often somewhat reflexed. Ps. about as long as the dors. sep., lanceolate, acute. Lip entire, spreading or slightly convex, truncate, obovate-oblong, the narrower base conspicuously thickened and adnate to the col.-base, the broader apex shallowly emarginate, the reverse surface with a distinct central keel; disc with a short, squarish, basal boss which ends in two distinct, parallel, fleshy, pubescent calli. Mostly summer. (I, H) Cuba; Mexico throughout Central America to Panama.

Lepanthes hondurensis Ames [BLANCHE AMES]

LEPANTHES Sw.

Lepanthes is a genus of an estimated sixty-five species of mostly very dwarf epiphytic (rarely lithophytic) orchids, principally inhabiting the mountainous areas of the West Indies, Mexico, Central America, and northern South America. A member of the subtribe *Pleurothallidinae*, its components are very seldom seen in contemporary collections, though they are among the most unusual and daintily attractive of all orchids of this alliance, when one takes the trouble to inspect the diminutive flowers at close range with a magnifying lens. *Lepanthes* is closest in its alliance to *Lepanthopsis* Ames and to the section *Lepanthiformes* of *Pleurothallis* R.Br. (a group of species which should, in all probability, be segregated from the latter genus). They are small, cluster-forming plants with the secondary stems very slender and supporting a single (rarely more) fleshy or rigid leaf at the apex; the solitary or few flower-spikes arise from the base of the leaf, and usually bear several minute blossoms, which are often arranged distichously along the rachis. These wee flowers are of amazing complexity and often of bright hues; unfortunately, in most of the species, they are very short-lived, lasting only two days or so in good condition. In *Lepanthes*, the sepals are about equal, often more or less connate basally, and with the laterals joined nearly to their tips. The petals are typically shorter than the sepals, but are unique in being two-parted or transversely bilobed, thus being quite unlike most other pleurothallids. The lip is two-lobed or rarely three-lobed, adnate to the column, and with the midlobe (if present) small and inconspicuous, while the larger lateral lobes usually appear as wings to the column. The short, footless column is dilated apically, and bears two waxy pollinia in a terminal anther.

No hybrids are known in *Lepanthes*. The genus is presumably inter-fertile with at least some other members of the subtribe *Pleurothallidinae*.

CULTURE: As for the high-elevation species of *Pleurothallis*, *Masdevallia*, etc. (C, I)

L. chiriquiensis Schltr. (*Lepanthes micrantha* Ames)

Pls. clustered, to 4″ tall (usually smaller). Secondary sts. very slender, to about ½″ tall. Lf. solitary, rigidly fleshy, varying from linear-lanceolate to ovate, minutely 3-toothed at the apex, to almost 2″ long and ¾″ wide, often purple-flushed. Infls. few-fld., shorter than the lvs., often appressed against them. Fls. less than ¼″ long, the ss. transparent tan with a dull red median stripe, the ps. rich orange and scarlet, the lip dull red. Dors. sep. oblong-ovate, to lanceolate-ovate, acute, minutely ciliate marginally; lat. ss. ovate-lanceolate, acute, arcuate, sometimes toothed towards the tips. Ps. transverse, ciliate, the lbs. lanceolate to ovate-lanceolate. Lip 3-lbd., the lat. lbs. malleoliform, the midlb. small, apicule-like. Mostly spring. (C, I) Costa Rica; Panama.

L. pulchella (Sw.) Sw. (*Epidendrum pulchellum* Sw.)

Pls. clustered, less than 1″ tall. Secondary sts. about as long as the lvs. Lf. solitary, less than ½″ long, oval, acute, rather fleshy. Infls. usually 2–5 at once, to almost 1″ long, several-fld., with 3–4 fls. open at once. Fls. about ⅛–¼″ long, the ss. yellow, the dors. one crimson medially, the lats. with a crimson basal spot, the ps. crimson shading to yellow marginally, the lip and col. crimson. Dors. sep. ovate, long-acuminate, ciliolate, the lats. connate only at base. Ps. 2-lbd., the posterior lb. subequal to the anterior one, not as wide as the ss., longer than the upper surfaces of the lip, the lbs. subtriangular, the outer edges of the two forming an almost continuous line. Lip 3-lbd., the lat. lbs. embracing the col., the midlb. small, minutely ciliolate. Throughout the year, often more than once annually. (C, I) Jamaica.

L. rotundifolia L.O.Wms.

Pls. to about 3″ tall. Secondary sts. slender, covered with sheaths which are ciliate marginally. Lf. solitary, about 1″ long and ¾–1¼″ wide, orbicular to orbicular-ovate, often broader than long, leathery. Infls. rather many-fld., distichous, shorter than the lvs., somewhat appressed against them. Fls. about ¼″ long, yellow and red. Dors. sep. suborbicular, abruptly acuminate; lat. ss. suborbicular, obtuse or acutish, connate at bases. Ps. 2-lbd., the upper lbs. the longer, lanceolate, acute, oblique; lower lbs. lanceolate, acute, oblique. Lip 2-parted, the lbs. malleoliform. Spring. (C, I) Panama.

LEPANTHOPSIS Ames

According to a recent revision of the genus, that of Leslie A. Garay (in *Orch. Jour.* 2: 467–9, fig. 206. 1953), *Lepanthopsis* consists of ten valid but mostly little-known species, these native from southern Florida and Honduras throughout the West Indies to Brazil and Colombia. The genus is for the most part a segregate from *Pleurothallis* R.Br., but differs materially from that group in the structure of the minute, often extremely complex blossoms. None of the Lepanthopsis, which are epiphytes in small trees and shrubs in nature, appears to be present in collections at this time, and in any event they are strictly of scientific interest.

Nothing is known of the genetic affinities of this odd genus.

CULTURE: As for *Pleurothallis*, depending upon the place of origin of the particular species or individual involved. (I, H)

LEPIDOGYNE Bl.

A member of the extremely complex subtribe *Physurinae*, *Lepidogyne* contains three known species, one (**L. longifolia** Bl.) from Java, the other two

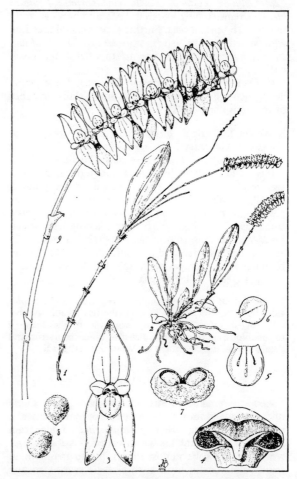

Lepanthopsis floripecten (Rchb.f.) Ames [BLANCHE AMES]

(**L. minor** Schltr. and **L. sceptrum** Schltr.) native in New Guinea. Perhaps the most robust of all physurid orchids, these plants when in flower attain heights in excess of three feet, and bear remarkably (for the alliance) showy inflorescences of complex flowers. Unhappily, none of them is present in contemporary collections, although they offer some intriguing potentialities to the specialist.

Nothing is known of the genetic ties of *Lepidogyne*.

CULTURE: Presumably as for *Erythrodes*. (H)

LEPTOTES Ldl.

Leptotes is a genus of about six extremely attractive dwarf, primarily epiphytic Brazilian and Paraguayan orchids of the subtribe *Laeliinae*, only one of which is at all frequent in our collections at this time. Vegetatively the plants rather simulate a small *Brassavola*, with fleshy, terete foliage produced from diminutive stem-like pseudobulbs. The proportionately large blossoms are freely borne in compact, abbreviated racemes from the leaf-bases. The dried, ripened seed-capsules of *L. bicolor* Ldl. contain vanillin, and are used for flavouring ices and sweets in Brazil.

Only a single hybrid is on record in this genus, this *Leptolaelia x Veitchii* (*Laelia cinnabarina × Leptotes bicolor*), registered by Veitch in 1902, and now evidently unknown by enthusiasts. Further experimental breeding with allied groups, such as *Cattleya*, *Epidendrum*, *Brassavola*, and the like, seems to offer some fascinating potentials.

CULTURE: As for the tropical Cattleyas. These plants do particularly well mounted on small slabs or cubes of tree-fern fibre. (I, H)

L. bicolor Ldl. (*Bletia bicolor* Rchb.f., *Leptotes glaucophylla* Hoffmsgg., *L. serrulata* Ldl., *Tetramicra bicolor* Rolfe, *Tetramicra serrulata* Nichols.)

Pbs. st.-like, usually less than 1″ tall, terete, clustered. Lvs. terete, fleshy, grooved on one side, sharp-pointed apically, to almost 5″ long, usually erect, often rather greyish-green. Infls. 1–6-fld., very abbreviated, borne from base of lvs. Fls. very fragrant, lasting well, sometimes not opening fully, when expanded about 1½–2″ across, the narrow ss. and ps. white, the large lip mostly bright magenta-rose, whitish apically. Mostly winter–spring. (I, H) Brazil; Paraguay.

L. unicolor B.-R. Rather similar vegetatively to *L. bicolor* Ldl., but often very much smaller, the lvs. frequently purplish-tinged. Infls. 2–3-fld., very abbreviated. Fls. nodding to pendulous, entirely bright violet-rose, differing in structural details from the other noted sp. Winter. (I, H) Brazil.

LIMODORUM Sw.

Limodorum, as now restricted, consists of but a single uncommon and rather attractive saprophytic species, a member of the subtribe *Cephalantherinae*. **Limodorum abortivum** Sw. is not known in collections today, and would probably be almost impossible to maintain in good condition for more than a single season, in any event. It inhabits central and southern Europe, and attains a height of somewhat more than two feet, with an apical raceme of rather attractive, mostly violet-purple flowers.

Nothing is known of the genetic affinities of *Limodorum*.

CULTURE: Presumably as for *Corallorrhiza*. (I)

LIPARIS L.C.Rich.
(*Alipsa* Hoffmsgg., *Androchilus* Liebm., *Cestichis* Ldl., *Empusa* Ldl., *Empusaria* Rchb., *Gastroglottis* Bl., *Paliris* Dum., *Platystylis* Ldl., *Pseudorchis* S.F.Gray, *Stichorchis* Thou., *Sturmia* Rchb.f.)

Approximately three hundred and fifty or more species make up the genus *Liparis*, the principal one of the excessively complex and polymorphic subtribe *Liparidinae*. Its members are cosmopolitan in their distribution, although the largest number of them occurs in the Asiatic Tropics, and adjacent areas. Variously terrestrial, lithophytic, or epiphytic orchids, the Liparis are today rather seldom encountered in cultivation, although some of them are singularly attractive plants, well worthy of further attention by collectors. Highly variable in vegetative habit, the majority of the species possess pseudobulbs which are more or less well-developed, leathery or strongly plicate foliage, and erect or pendulous racemes of usually rather numerous flowers. These blossoms are complex in structure, often greenish or purplish in colour, and have the lip the largest part of the bloom in most instances, with the petals typically very narrow and sometimes tightly recurved. The genus is somewhat allied to *Malaxis* Soland. ex Sw., and stands sorely in need of a critical taxonomic revision.

As yet no hybrids are known in *Liparis*, and nothing has been ascertained regarding its genetic affinities. Some unusually interesting potentials seem evident in the realm of interspecific breeding within the genus, particularly among the larger-flowered species indigenous to tropical Africa and Asia.

CULTURE: Since the myriad members of this genus range from the chill temperate zones to the hot tropics, their cultural requirements naturally vary considerably. The Liparis from the North Temperate Zone should be treated much like *Caladenia*, while those from warmer climates which grow terrestrially, require conditions such as those afforded *Phaius*. The few habitually epiphytic species now in cultivation should be grown like the smaller tropical Dendrobiums. (C, I, H)

L. caespitosa (Thou.) Ldl. (*Malaxis caespitosa* Thou., *Liparis pusilla* Ridl.)

Pbs. crowded, ovoid, to about ¾″ tall, becoming wrinkled with age. Lf. solitary, rather leathery, to 8″ long and ½″ wide, narrowing towards base. Infls. erect, to about 9″ tall, the peduncle winged, the many-fld. rac. dense. Fls. inverted, opening gradually over a long period, about ¼″ long when spread out, usually very pale greenish or greenish-yellow. Ss. and much narrower ps. reflexed. Lip fiddle-shaped, the basal part erect, the apical part bent downward, the broad apex with a very short tip. Winter–spring. (I, H) Madagascar; Mascarene Islands; Ceylon and India to Sumatra, Java, Malay Peninsula, and the Philippines.

L. elata Ldl. (*Leptorchis elata* O.Ktze.)

Pbs. clustered, conoidal, to 2″ tall, usually somewhat smaller. Lvs. 3–5, with basal scarious sheaths which envelop pb., plicate, eventually deciduous, ovate to elliptic or elliptic-lanceolate, rounded to acuminate, sheathing the st. at base, 3–12″ long, to 4¾″ broad. Infl. erect, angled and winged above, flushed with madder-purple, the rac. loosely few- to many-fld., the whole structure to 2′ tall at most, usually shorter. Fls. erect or ascending, on stout pedicellate ovaries, to ½″ long, the ss. and ps. greenish streaked with madder-purple, the lip usually wholly madder-purple. Ps. usually spatulate, narrower than the ss., down-thrust. Lip obcordate to oblong-flabellate, emarginate, sometimes with a tiny apicule in the sinus, arcuate-recurved in natural position, vaguely auricled at base on each side, the disc with 2 fleshy tubercles on basal portion. Col. strongly incurved above. Usually summer–autumn. (I, H) South Florida, Cuba, and Mexico throughout Central America and the West Indies to Brazil, Ecuador, and Peru.

L. elegans Ldl. (*Liparis gracilis* Hk.f., *L. stricta* J.J.Sm.)

Rhiz. elongate, creeping. Pbs. borne at intervals of about ¾–1″ apart, ovoid, to 1½″ long, basal sheaths rather large. Lvs. usually paired, to 11″ long and 1¼″ wide in upper half, acute, narrowed gradually below into a broad channelled stalk to 2½″ long. Infl. erect, straight, 10–15″ tall, the rac. densely many-fld., all but the basal fls. crowded. Fls. about ¼″ long when spread out, the reflexed ss. and spreading ps. pale greenish-yellow, the lip salmon-coloured to orange, its basal half parallel to the col., the apical half bent sharply away, sides parallel from middle to apex which is broad, finely toothed, and slightly notched in the middle. Mostly winter. (H) Sumatra; Borneo; Malay Peninsula; Peninsular Thailand; Philippines.

L. ferruginea Ldl. (? *Liparis odorata* Ldl.)

Pbs. very short, swollen, not arising above ground-level. Lvs. 3–4, with sheaths below them, the lf.-blade with a broad stalk about 4″ long, 6–12″ long, ½–1″ broad, plicate, acutish. Infls. with a stout peduncle, erect, 8–12″ tall, the elongate rachis many-fld. Fls. about ⅜″ long, pale yellow-green with a purple lip (rarely entirely purple). Lip rather large, the apex broad, notched, with a small apicule in the sinus. Winter–spring. (H) Cambodia; Malay Peninsula; Sumatra; Java; Borneo; ? India.

L. gibbosa Finet

Rhiz. slender, creeping. Pbs. borne at intervals of about 1¼″ from one another, ovoid, somewhat flattened, to ½″ long. Lf. solitary, lanceolate, acutish, rather leathery, narrowed towards the base, to 8″ long. Infl. to about 6″ long, the peduncle erect at base, curved, flattened, winged, widening near rachis, this portion to ¾″ long, with closely-arranged 2-ranked bracts to ¼″ broad. Fls. rather numerous, but produced singly in succession, varying in colour from salmon to orange-brown, to about ⅜″ long when spread out. Ss. reflexed, the ps. erect and spreading, widened to a short-pointed tip. Lip 4-lbd., the lbs. convex and rounded, the two basal ones slightly larger than apical ones. Summer. (I, H) India; Malay Peninsula; Sumatra; Java; Borneo.

L. lacerata Ridl.

Pbs. clustered, ovoid, sheathed for some time, to 1½″ tall. Lf. solitary, plicate, narrowed to both base and apex, acutish, linear-lanceolate, to 7″ long and 1¼″ wide, with a basal stalk to 1½″ long. Infl. rather slender, to 8″ tall, the 2″ long rac. many-fld. but not crowded. Fls. about ½″ long, usually white with an orange lip, the ps. narrower than the ss. Lip erect basally, with a small transverse callus, hollow in front, then bent sharply away from col., narrowed slightly, the flaring apex deeply 2-lbd., the lbs. diverging, each with about 6 slender teeth. Spring. (H) Malay Peninsula; Sumatra; Borneo.

L. latifolia (Bl.) Ldl. (*Malaxis latifolia* Bl., *Liparis robusta* Hk.f., *L. Scortechinii* Hk.f.)

Pbs. clustered, ovoid, to about 2½″ long, flattened and narrowed upwards, with several large red-brown basal sheaths. Lf. solitary, plicate, oblanceolate, rather broadly pointed, narrowed towards base but scarcely stalked there, to more than 12″ long and almost 3″ wide. Infl. erect, about as long as lf., sheathed basally, many-fld. Fls. to almost ¾″ long when spread out, yellowish, the lip usually orange-brown. Ss. reflexed, the ps. much narrower. Lip large for the fl., the basal half narrow, parallel to the col., with a small 2-lbd. callus, apical half turned down, flaring, deeply 2-lbd., the lbs. rounded and finely toothed. Summer. (H) Malay Peninsula; Sumatra; Java; Borneo.

L. liliifolia (L.) L.C.Rich. ex Ldl. (*Ophrys liliifolia* L., *Malaxis liliifolia* Sw., *Leptorchis liliifolia* O.Ktze.)

Pbs. subterranean, short, corm-like, with spongy roots. Lvs. 2, basal, ovate to elliptic, obtuse to acute, sheathing the st. below, glossy bright green, 1½–7″ long, to 2½″ broad. Infl. 2–10″ tall, angled above, the peduncle often flushed with purplish, the few- to many-fld. rac. rather loose. Fls. on long pedicellate ovaries, to almost 1″ long (often smaller), the ss. pale greenish-white, translucent, the much narrower, pendent-curving ps. madder-purple, the proportionately large lip mauve-purple with a greenish tinge, translucent, usually with 5 prominent branched, dark red-purple veins, the margins apically serrulate-erose. Spring–summer. (C, I) New England west to Minnesota and Iowa, south to Georgia, Alabama, and Tennessee; also China.

L. Loeselii (L.) L.C.Rich. (*Ophrys Loeselii* L., *Leptorchis Loeselii* MacM.)

Pbs. subterranean, globuse, corm-like, rather abbreviated. Lvs. paired, basal, succulent, oblong-elliptic to elliptic-lanceolate, obtuse to acutish, sheathing the infl. below, 1¼–7″ long, to 2½″ broad. Infl. slender, somewhat angled above, to 10″ tall (usually much shorter), loosely few-fld., the fls. opening successively over a long period. Fls. erect or ascending, to about ⅜″ long when spread out, yellowish-green or whitish, usually not lasting well. Dors. sep. erect, the lat. ss. somewhat incurving, the margins involute. Ps. tubular, thread-like. Lip arched-recurved in natural position, the margins finely crenulate-wavy. Spring–autumn. (C, I) Northern North America; Northern and Central Europe; Northern Asia.

L. parviflora (Bl.) Ldl. (*Malaxis parviflora* Bl., *Liparis flaccida* Rchb.f., *Leptorchis flaccida* O.Ktze., *Leptorchis parviflora* O.Ktze.)

Pbs. ovoid, clustered, narrowing upwards from a broad base, 2–4″ long, sheathed at base. Lvs. paired, plicate, rather heavy, to 11″ long and 1¼″ wide, widest near the acute apex, narrowing gradually towards base. Infl. 8–20″ tall, slender, drooping to pendulous from a short erect base, rather densely many-fld. Fls. about ¼″ long when spread out, usually greenish-white with all segms. tipped pink, or all segms. pink basally, reddish apically. Ss. and somewhat narrower ps. curved backwards. Lip with basal half almost parallel to col., concave, with 2 small calli, the apical half sharply bent back so it is parallel to basal half, convex, cleft apically, the margins very short-hairy. Col. with green anther-cap. Summer. (H) Peninsular Thailand; Malay Peninsula; Sumatra; Java; Borneo; Philippines.

L. Rheedii (Bl.) Ldl. (*Malaxis Rheedii* Bl., *Liparis transtillata* Ridl.)

Pbs. rather clustered, often not persisting for many years, ovoid-ellipsoid to conical, to almost 5″ tall, sheathed for some time. Lvs. 4–5, with a basal stalk and sheath about 2″ long, the lf.-blade green, plicate, acute apically, to 8″ long and 4″ wide, unequal at base. Infl. to 15″ tall, the numerous fls. in a rather dense rac. Fls. almost ⅜″ long when spread out, the ss. and considerably smaller ps. greenish to purplish, the lip yellowish to dark purple. Lip strongly bent backwards in middle, basally broad, flaring somewhat to a broadly rounded, slightly notched tip with vaguely wavy margins, the basal lip-callus green, broad, short, concave frontally. Winter–spring. (I, H) Malay Peninsula; Sumatra to New Guinea.

L. tricallosa Rchb.f.

Pbs. clustered, often deteriorating with age, elongate, to almost 5″ long and ¾″ in diam. at base. Lvs. several, short- and broad-stalked at base, to 7″ long and 2½″ broad, plicate, green, the margins usually crisped, sometimes flushed with pinkish. Infl. stout, erect, the peduncle and rachis purple, the many-fld. rac. rather loose. Fls. almost 1½″ long, the ss. pale greenish, the very narrow ps. purple with greenish bases, the lip pale greenish with rose-purple veins, this colour becoming pink with age throughout the segm. Lip broadly ovate, broadly pointed at tip, the margins with tiny teeth towards the apex. Late spring–summer. (H) Sulu Archipelago; Malay Peninsula; Sumatra.

L. viridiflora (Bl.) Ldl. (*Malaxis viridiflora* Bl., *Liparis longipes* Ldl., *Sturmia longipes* Rchb.f.)

Pbs. clustered rather tightly, ovoid, sometimes almost cylindric and thickened basally, 1¼–4″ long, usually flattened. Lvs. paired, ligulate, thickly fleshy, to almost 11″ long and 1½″ wide near acute tip, narrowing gradually towards base. Infls. erect, to 8″ long, the peduncle flattened and narrowly winged, the many fls. very crowded. Fls. less than ¼″ across when spread out, pale greenish, white, or yellowish-white, the lip usually green or orange-yellow. Ss. and narrower ps. reflexed. Lip at top of fl., the basal half erect and concave, the apical half bent at a right angle to it, widest near the

very broadly pointed apex, not toothed nor lobed. Winter. (I, H) China; India; Ceylon; Burma; Thailand; Viet-Nam; Malay Peninsula; Formosa; Philippines; Samoa.

L. atropurpurea Ldl. Pbs. fleshy, cylindrical, clustered, to about 2½″ tall. Lvs. 3–4, apical on the pbs., herbaceous and succulent, shortly stalked, to 5″ long, roundish, shortly acuminate. Infls. erect, to about 1½′ tall, loosely many-fld. Fls. about ¾″ in diam., dark red-purple, the ss. reflexed, the lip cuneate with a recurved apex. Summer. (H) Ceylon.

L. bootanensis Griff. (*Liparis lancifolia* Hk.f.) Pbs. clustered, ovoid, sheathed at base, to ½″ tall. Lf. solitary, rather leathery, to 9½″ long and 1″ wide, narrowed evenly to base and apex, acute at tip, scarcely stalked. Infl. to about 7″ tall, the peduncle flattened and winged, with about 12 fls. Fls. about ½″ across, pale red-brown with a green col. and green lip-calli. Summer. (I, H) Himalayas to Peninsular Thailand and the Langkawi Islands.

L. compressa (Bl.) Ldl. (*Malaxis compressa* Bl., *Cestichis compressa* Ames) Rhiz. slender, elongate, creeping. Pbs. ovoid, compressed, borne about 1¼–4″ apart, to more than 1″ long, with several large basal sheaths. Lf. solitary, to 14″ long and 1¼″ wide, acute, widest in upper half, narrowing gradually towards base. Infl. as in *L. gibbosa* Finet, to 12″ long, the 2-ranked bracts, to ⅜″ wide. Fls. about ⅞″ long, red-brown, the dors. sep. and ps. reflexed. Lip narrow basally, the down-curving blade wider, the apex broadly rounded and with fine marginal teeth. Summer. (H) Philippines; Malay Peninsula; Sumatra; Java; Borneo; Celebes.

L. foliosa Ldl. Pbs. shortly ellipsoidal, clustered, about 1″ tall. Lvs. paired, thickly leathery, lanceolate, acute, to 6″ long. Infls. about 6–7″ long, the rather many-fld. rac. loose. Fls. about ¾″ across, greenish, the lip yellow or yellowish. Autumn. (H) Mascarene Islands.

L. glossula Rchb.f. Rhiz. rather stout, creeping, bearing the pbs. at intervals. Pbs. stout, roundish, about 2″ tall. Lf. solitary, sessile or short-stalked, oblong or linear-oblong, obtuse or acutish, 2–4″ long. Infl. stout, 4–7″ long or more, the rac. rather many-fld. Fls. about ⅝″ across, dull green more or less flushed with purple, the lat. ss. hidden by the large, flat, wavy-margined lip. Summer. (C, I) Himalayas.

L. guineensis Ldl. Rather similar in all parts to *L. elata* Ldl., differing primarily in floral structure. Pbs. as in the other sp. Lvs. ascending, herbaceous, elliptic, to 6″ long. Infl. slightly exceeding the lvs., the rachis angled, the rac. small, densely many-fld. Fls. about ¾″ in diam., greenish. Autumn–early winter. (H) Tropical West Africa.

L. Krameri Franch. (*Leptorchis Krameri* O.Ktze.) Rhiz. creeping, the pbs. corm-like, subterranean, rather small. Lvs. paired, subopposite, orbicular-ovate, obtuse, to 12″ long. Infl. erect or somewhat flexuous, to 6″ tall, with a loose rac. of about 4–12 fls. Fls. about ¼″ long, vaguely fragrant, pale green flushed with purple. Lip clawed basally, obscurely 2-lbd., the lbs. rounded, usually with a tooth in the sinus. Spring–early summer. (C, I) Korea; Japan.

L. perpusilla Hk.f. Pbs. ovoid or oblong, clustered, about ¼″ long. Lvs. 4–5, linear, acutish, leathery, with prominent midrib and recurved margins, curving, ½–1″ long. Infls. 2–4″ long, curving, bearing a short, many-fld. rac. Fls. less than ⅛″ long, yellow, the tiny lip quadrate, 3-lbd., with rounded lat. lbs. and a broad, short midlb. with 2 basal tubercles. A very diminutive orchid, one of the smaller ones known. Summer–autumn. (I) Sikkim.

L. platyglossa Schltr. Pbs. short, succulent, clustered, about 1″ long. Lvs. 3–4, to 4″ long and 2″ wide, rather glossy and leathery, elliptic, acute. Infls. erect, the rac. loosely 4–15-fld. Fls. about 1″ in diam., the oblong ss. and linear ss. greenish, the reniform, ½″ broad lip wine-red. Spring–summer. (H) Cameroons.

L. reflexa Ldl. Rather similar in habit to *L. foliosa* Ldl., but the infl. longer and the rac. more loosely many-fld. Fls. about ¾″ in diam., yellowish-green, the lip usually somewhat darker in colour, the ss. and ps. sharply reflexed. Autumn. (H) Northern Australia.

L. rostrata Rchb.f. Pbs. broadly ovoid, about ¾″ long. Lvs. paired, elliptic-ovate or oblong, narrowed basally, ½–3″ long. Infl. stout, 2–6″ long, erect, with a rather densely many-fld. rac. Fls. about ⅝″ in diam., the ss. and very narrow ps. pale green to purplish, the lip yellowish-green, very broadly cordate, flattened, wavy marginally, pointed at apex, contracted basally. Summer. (C, I) Himalayas.

L. Walkeriae Ldl. Pbs. st.-like, cylindrical, to about 5″ tall. Lvs. 2–3, sheathing basally, to 6″ long, succulently herbaceous, elliptic, acute, plicate. Infls. erect, to about 6″ tall, the few- to many-fld. rac. cylindrical. Fls. about ½″ in diam. when spread out, the ss. and ps. violet, the oblong lip violet with greenish margins. Summer. (H) Ceylon.

L. Wrayi Hk.f. (*Liparis pectinifera* Ridl.) Pbs. clustered, cylindric, fleshy, to about 5″ tall, sheathed towards base. Lvs. 3–4, with a basal sheath and stalk to about 2″ long, the lf.-blade to about 5½″ long and 3″ wide, unequal at base. Infl. to about 8″ tall, with rather numerous well-spaced fls., which open successively. Fls. more than ½″ in diam. when spread out, usually pale green, the lip with 2 small purplish median patches. Dors. sep. recurved, the narrower ps. curving forwards, the lip slightly 2-lbd. and toothed at apex, with a small basal callus. Summer. (H) Malay Peninsula; Sumatra; Java; Borneo.

LISTERA R.Br.
(*Diphryllum* Raf., *Distomaea* Spen., *Polinirhiza* Dulac.)

Listera is a genus of upwards of twenty species of mostly dwarf, terrestrial, rather insignificant orchids which are widespread in the Northern Hemisphere, in North America, Europe, and Asia. They are very rare in contemporary collections, though certain of the North American species (of which there are seven) appear in choice outdoor orchid gardens in the United States, where they are commonly known as 'Twayblades'. The genus is a member of the subtribe *Listerinae*.

No hybrids are known in this genus, and nothing has been ascertained as yet concerning its genetic affinities.

CULTURE: As for *Arethusa*. (C, I)

L. australis Ldl. (*Ophrys australis* House)
Pls. slender, 3–12″ tall, the succulent st. purplish, sometimes clustered. Lvs. 2, opposite at about the middle of the st., ovate to elliptic, deep green, to 1½″ long and ¾″ wide. Rac. loose, few- to many-fld., to 4½″ long. Fls. to about ¼″ long, reddish-purple, the ss. and ps. small, the lip proportionately very large, linear, cleft as much as ¾ of the way to the base, with a slight median basal ridge. Feb.–July. (C, I) Eastern and Southern United States; Canada.

L. ovata (L.) R.Br. (*Ophrys ovata* L., *Diphryllum ovatum* Beck)
Pls. slender or stout, to 2′ tall. Lvs. 2, oval, usually ascending near base of st. Rac. elongated, rigidly erect, many-fld. Fls. less than ½″ long, greenish-yellow, the ss. and ps. small, the hanging lip with spreading diamond-shaped lat. lbs. and elongate, deeply 2-lbd. midlb. Mostly May–July. (C, I) Europe and Asia, above the Arctic Circle and to Siberia and the upper Himalayas from Great Britain.

LISTROSTACHYS Rchb.f.

Two species of *Listrostachys* are known to science, one of them being found in a a few particularly choice contemporary collections. Both are natives of the hot forests of tropical West Africa, and resemble Angraecums, to which genus they are closely related. The genus is, indeed, a segregate from *Angraecum* Bory, differing in technical details of the small flowers. The other species, **Listrostachys Jenischiana** Rchb.f., does not appear to be in cultivation at this time.

No hybrids are known in this genus, and nothing has been ascertained concerning its genetic affinities.

CULTURE: As for the tropical Angraecums. (H)

L. pertusa (Ldl.) Rchb.f. (*Angraecum pertusum* Ldl.)
St. abbreviated. Lvs. narrowly ligulate, unequally 2-lbd. at the apex, rigidly leathery, to 8″ long and 1″ broad. Infls. about as long as the lvs., densely many-fld., often branched. Fls. less than ¼″ across, complex, yellowish-white. Ss. and ps. oblong, obtuse. Lip with a roundish callus, and a cylindrical spur that is thickened apically and is slightly longer than the pedicellate ovary. Spring. (H) Tropical West Africa.

LOCKHARTIA Hk.
(*Fernandezia* R. & P. *sensu* Ldl., in part)

This is a genus, the members of which occur in the region extending from Mexico to Peru and Brazil, of perhaps thirty epiphytic (rarely lithophytic) species, many of which are botanically little-known and taxonomically confused. Somewhat vaguely allied to *Oncidium* Sw. and to other groups of the subtribe *Oncidiinae*, it seems better relegated to a separate subtribe, the *Lockhartiinae*, to be placed next to the *Oncidiinae* in its relationship. These are the delightful, all too infrequently cultivated 'Braided Orchids', so-called because of the remarkably flattened stems, on which the very numerous leaves are closely placed in a distichously imbricating arrangement, thus giving them the appearance of having been braided into place. In many cases, the size and shape of these small leaves seems to be of diagnostic value in the determination of species. The flowers of the Lockhartias are borne singly or (rarely) in airy panicles or small racemes from the leaf-axils near the tops of these stems; each stem may continue to produce blossoms for many years. In certain species, the leafy stems continue to elongate apically for several seasons, thus explaining why these orchids have in the past been placed (erroneously, we believe) in the aggregation *Pseudomonopodiales*, together with *Dichaea*

Ldl., *Pachyphyllum* Ldl., and a few other genera in which this condition prevails. Blossoms in this genus are typically small or very small, usually yellow (often marked with reddish or red-brown), and frequently of remarkable complexity when closely inspected. Despite their often diminutive dimensions, they are delightful little creations, and add the perfect touch to the singulary handsome appearance of the vegetative portions of the plants. We cannot recommend Lockhartias too highly to the orchid enthusiast, since their cultural requirements are met with great ease, and well-grown specimens are uniquely attractive even when not covered with their bright flowers.

No hybrids are known in the genus *Lockhartia*, and nothing has been ascertained as yet concerning its genetic affinities.

CULTURE: These orchids are best grown in pots or smallish baskets filled rather tightly with osmunda or shredded tree-fern fibre; when well-rooting they also do well tightly affixed to small tree-fern slabs. They should, in all cases, be under-potted, since too much extra compost around their roots seems disadvantageous. A spot in warm or intermediate temperatures that is neither too moist nor too dry suits them well, and semi-shade is required to avoid burning or yellowing of the thick foliage. When the leafy stems turn greyish or brownish with age, they should be severed basally—working very carefully with a sharp clean instrument—and removed from the clump, without disturbance of the remainder of the specimen. Lockhartias flower best if not divided, but they should not, conversely, be allowed to grow into excessively large clusters, or blossoming will also be curtailed. Since they have no special moisture-storing structures, water is required at the roots at all times, but if the slightest bit of yellowish colour appears on the leaves, the plants should be examined at once for stale compost or other improper conditions. Weak applications of fertilizers, at regular intervals, are beneficial and induce freer flowering. (I, H)

L. acuta (Ldl.) Rchb.f. (*Fernandezia acuta* Ldl., *Lockhartia pallida* Rchb.f.)

Sts. typically arching or pendulous, to almost 2′ long and ¾″ wide, flattened, densely leafy throughout. Lvs. rather obliquely triangular, acute to sharply apiculate at tip, fleshy, to 1″ long. Infls. produced from upper lf.-axils, often more than one simultaneously, many-fld. for the genus, to 3″ long, profusely branching, with small vaguely heart-shaped bracts at the joints. Fls. less than ½″ across when spread out, white or whitish with a yellow or yellowish lip rather rectangular in outline, the basal half squarish, slightly concave, with narrow, erect, lat. margins, the base stalkless, adnate to the col.-base, the midlb. 4-parted, usually somewhat reflexed. Mostly summer. (I, H) Panama; Colombia; Venezuela; Trinidad.

L. amoena Endr. & Rchb.f. (*Lockhartia costaricensis* Schltr., *L. grandibracteata* Krzl.)

Sts. erect or pendulous, flattened, to 1½′ long and 1″ wide. Lvs. narrowly triangular in profile, subacute at tips, fleshy, to 1″ long. Infls. short, compact, few-fld., panicles up to 1¼′ long. Fls. about ¾″ long, bright yellow,

Lockhartia acuta (Ldl.) Rchb.f. [BLANCHE AMES]

with some reddish-brown markings at the base of the lip, which is much larger than the other segms. Lip complexly 3-lbd., the lat. lbs. linear-ligulate, acute, antrorsely recurving; midlb. squarish, more or less 4-lobulate, undulate marginally, the blunt apex with a deep indentation, the basal lobules strongly reflexed, the disc with a linear, truncate, papillose callus. Spring-summer. (I, H) Costa Rica; Panama.

L. elegans (Lodd.) Hk. (*Fernandezia elegans* Lodd.)

Sts. erect, to about 4″ tall (rarely more), densely leafy. Lvs. obtuse, rather triangular in profile, to about ½″ long. Infls. 1–2-fld., about ½″ long, produced from the upper lf.-axils. Fls. about ½″ long, yellow-green, the bright yellow lip spotted basally with violet-red or purplish-red. Lip with short, spreading, lanceolate lat. lbs., the midlb. obtuse, warted towards the apex. Summer. (I, H) Trinidad; Venezuela; Guianas; Brazil.

L. lunifera (Ldl.) Rchb.f. (*Fernandezia lunifera* Ldl.)

Sts. erect or pendulous, to 8″ tall, densely leafy throughout. Lvs. to almost ¾″ long, fleshy, acutish at tips, triangular in profile. Infls. 1–3-fld., with large bracts, produced from the upper lf.-axils. Fls. about ¾″ long, golden-yellow with a lip that is veined with brown-red. Lip with erect, falcately oblong, obtuse lat. lbs., and a shortly ovate, apically 2-lobuled midlb. which has a warty median area. Summer–autumn. (I, H) Brazil.

L. micrantha Rchb.f. (*Lockhartia chiriquensis* Schltr., *L. Lankesteri* Ames)

Sts. erect or pendulous, flattened, to 1½′ long and about ¾″ wide, leafy throughout. Lvs. fleshy, in profile narrowly triangular with obliquely truncate or retuse tips, to about ¾″ long. Infls. unbranched, 1–2-fld. (rarely more-fld.), to about ¾″ long. Fls. less than ½″ across, often not opening fully, pale yellow or creamy-yellow, the lip with distinct lat. lbs. at the base, 3-lbd., the midlb. with the lateral margins vaguely lobulate. Winter–spring. (I, H) Nicaragua to Suriname.

L. Oerstedii Rchb.f. (*Fernandezia robusta* Batem., *Lockhartia lamellosa* Rchb.f., *L. robusta* Schltr., *L. verrucosa* Rchb.f.)

Sts. usually rigidly erect, clustered, strongly flattened, to 1½′ tall. Lvs. narrowly triangular as seen in profile, acute, to more than 1″ long. Infls. very short, 1–3-fld., produced from the upper lf.-axils. Fls. large for the genus, to almost 1″ long (usually somewhat smaller), bright yellow, the lip marked with red or reddish-brown at the base, the lat. ss. sometimes red-spotted as well. Lip with the midlb. vaguely fiddle-shaped, conspicuously broader at the apex than at base, with a distinct constriction between the apical part and the smaller lat. lobules. Throughout the year, often almost ever-blooming. (I, H) Mexico; Guatemala; Honduras; Costa Rica; Panama.

L. obtusata L.O.Wms. Sts. to more than 12″ tall, erect. Lvs. obliquely oblong in profile, obtuse at tips, to 1″ long. Infls. short, few-fld., from upper lf.-axils. Fls. about ¾″ across, bright yellow, with an orange lip-callus, the lip entire, suborbicular. Autumn. (I) Panama.

L. Pittieri Schltr. (*Lockhartia variabilis* A. & S.) Simulating *L. micrantha* Rchb.f. to a great degree, the lvs. linear-lanceolate to narrowly triangular, obliquely acute to acuminate. Infls. 1-fld., very short. Fls. less than ½″ across, yellow or yellowish, with an orange lip-callus, the lip entire, with a deeply emarginate apex. Mostly spring. (I, H) British Honduras; Costa Rica; Panama.

LOEFGRENIANTHUS Hoehne

Loefgrenianthus Blanche-Amesii (Loefgr.) Hoehne (*Leptotes Blanche-Amesii* Loefgr.) is the only known member of this odd and very attractive genus of the subtribe *Laeliinae*. A pendulous epiphytic plant from the saturated forests of southern Brazil, it bears rather large orange-yellow and white, very complex flowers. Although an extremely interesting and attractive orchid, it is unknown in our collections at this time.

Nothing is known of the genetic affinities of *Loefgrenianthus*.

CULTURE: Possibly as for the intermediate-elevation, non-pseudobulbous Epidendrums, although constantly very high humidity and considerable shade will be required for any success with this apparently very delicate plant. (I)

LUISIA Gaud.

This is a remarkable genus of some thirty-five species of mostly epiphytic orchids, native over a huge region extending from Korea, Japan, and the Ryukyu Islands throughout the Himalayas and South-east Asia to New Guinea and New Caledonia. A member of the sub-tribe *Sarcanthinae*, the group is rather closely allied to *Vanda* R.Br., and its component species, vegetatively, rather simulate the terete-leaved Vandas, such as *V. teres* Ldl., etc. The very short racemes are often produced in considerable numbers, and bear a few, crowded, typically small blossoms of unusual structure and coloration, which are frequently furnished with a most offensive scent. These flowers superficially resemble those of certain kinds of *Ophrys* in many instances, and because of this they have been given the same vernacular name, 'Bee Orchids'. Colour is usually subdued, but when examined closely, these small to medium-sized blossoms exhibit their uniquely intricate formation to the viewer. In many cases the blooms grow in dimensions after they open, often markedly so.

Luisia has to date been used in the production of only one registered hybrid (although, as of this writing, several additional crosses are being raised, notably in the Hawaiian Islands), namely the delightful *Luisanda x Uniwai* (*Luisia teretifolia × Vanda x Miss Joaquim*). Additional experimental hybridization utilizing some of the Luisias is to be strongly recommended.

CULTURE: As for the tropical Vandas, though the Luisias do best in well-drained pots, rather than in baskets. (I, H)

L. Amesiana Rolfe

Habit of the genus, often rather stout and squat, the sts. rarely exceeding 12″ in height. Infls. almost stalkless, densely 2–8-fld., all of the fls. usually open at once. Fls. heavy-textured, rather short-lived, to almost 1″ across, foul-smelling. Ss. and ps. pale yellowish-white, slightly flushed with purple apically, the reverse side often with a few dull purple blotches. Lip whitish-yellow, flushed with purple and with several irregular deep purple blotches, the margins light greenish-yellow. Summer (I, H) Himalayas to Burma and Thailand.

L. Jonesii J.J.Sm.

Sts. curving, stout, terete, usually dull green. Lvs. about 1″ apart, to 7″ long, almost straight, terete. Infls. few-fld., the fls. opening successively, to 1″ long, erect and closely appressed against the st. Fls. to 1½″ across, the cream-white ps. twice as long as the green ss. Lip deep chocolate-purple, blotched, with some longitudinal wrinkles, the margins reflexed. Summer. (H) Malay Peninsula.

L. Psyche Rchb.f. (*Cymbidium scarabaeforme* Rchb.f.)

Sts. to 12″ tall, stout. Lvs. about 1″ apart, ¼″ in diam., usually ascending, blunt-pointed, to 5″ long. Infls. sessile, few-fld. Fls. to 2½″ across, foul-smelling, the oblong, obtuse, concave ss. and much longer, linear-spatulate, obtuse ps. pale greenish-yellow. Lip convex, broadly ovate-oblong, retuse, the base sac-like, nearly 1″ long, violet-brown, marbled with white or yellow, the lat. lbs. erect, embracing the white col. Spring–summer. (I, H) Burma; Thailand.

L. teretifolia Gaud. (*Cymbidium triste* Roxb., *Cymbidium tenuifolium* Wight, *Luisia burmanica* Ldl., *L. brachystachys* Bl. var. *flaviola* Par. & Rchb.f., *L. platyglossa* Rchb.f., *L. tristis* O.Ktze., *L. trichorrhiza* Rchb.f.)
Variable in all parts. Sts. rather slender, to 4′ long, often profusely branching at the base, terete. Lvs. ½–4″ apart, variable in thickness, terete, usually slightly curved, to 6″ long. Infls. mostly less than 1½″ long, few-fld., the fls. mostly all open at once, close against the st. Fls. about ¾″ across, faintly foul-smelling, long-lived or not, rather heavy-textured, the ss. and longer, spreading ps. yellowish or greenish-yellow, the lip about as long as the ss., usually dull purple-brown or chocolate-brown, pubescent, mostly convex, sometimes with a basal irregular yellowish blotch. Ss. oblong to somewhat spatulate, the lats. subacute, with a prominent keel on the reverse surface. Ps. linear-oblong, obtuse. Lip complex, the basal part squarish, saccate, the upper part broadly cordate. Mostly autumn, sometimes more than once annually. (I, H) China, India and Burma throughout Malaysia, Indonesia, and adjacent areas to the Philippines, Marianas Islands, and New Caledonia.

L. Zollingeri Rchb.f. (*Luisia latipetala* J.J.Sm.)
Sts. curving, rather slender, about 8″ long at most. Lvs. to ¾″ apart, slender, rather curving especially towards the apex, to 8″ long. Infls. less than ½″ long, densely several-fld., the fls. not all opening at once. Fls. not expanding fully, about ¾″ across, the dors. sep. and ps. lying close together almost in one plane, the lat. ss. and lip in another plane almost at right angles to the upper one, the ss. and ps. greenish more or less mottled or flushed with purple, the lip dull purple. Mostly autumn. (H) Burma; Thailand; Malay Peninsula; Sumatra; Java.

L. antennifera Bl. Similar in habit to *L. Jonesii* J.J.Sm. Fls. about 1″ across, the ss. and ps. pale green, the lip dark purple. Lip without distinct lat. lbs., the basal part almost square, the apical part ovate, wrinkled. Summer. (H) Malay Peninsula; Sumatra; Java; Borneo.

L. brachystachys Bl. (*Mesoclastes brachystachys* Ldl.) Similar in habit to *L. teretifolia* Gaud., but more slender. Fls. about ¾″ across, the oblong, obtuse ss. usually green outside, rose-purple inside, the linear-oblong, obtuse ps. rose-purple medially, green at tip and base, the lip yellow at base, black-purple for ⅔ of upper part, with strong parallel grooves down the disc, obovate-oblong, almost plane, grooved, scarcely constricted at the base of the broadly ovate upper part. Autumn. (I, H) Himalayas; Burma; Thailand.

L. zeylanica Ldl. Closely allied to *L. teretifolia* Gaud., but differing in the smaller fls. (to only about ½″ across), the stouter, more ascending lvs., shorter sts., and technical characters of the fls., which have yellow-green ss. and ps. and a deep brown-purple lip. Summer–autumn. (H) Ceylon; Lower India.

LYCASTE Ldl.
(*Deppia* Raf.)

The genus *Lycaste* is a group of about thirty-five often perplexing species of mostly epiphytic (sometimes lithophytic or even semi-terrestrial) very handsome orchids in the American Tropics, ranging from Cuba and Mexico to Peru and Brazil. A number of them are in cultivation today, and some are among the most handsome and showy of orchidaceous plants. In many ways the Lycastes resemble *Maxillaria* R. & P. (a genus to which they are only slightly allied), but they may immediately be differentiated by the plicate, not conduplicate foliage and by floral characters. The usually large flowers are produced singly (but often in considerable numbers) on short or rather elongate scapes from the base of the mature pseudobulbs or concurrently with the flush of new growth. In this genus, the petals are often of a different colour from the sepals and frequently parallel the column, arching over the lip. The lovely and highly valued *Lycaste virginalis* (Scheidw.) Lind. (usually grown as *L. Skinneri* Ldl.) is the National Flower of Guatemala.

Lycaste has been utilized by the breeders on a number of occasions, some very fine interspecific hybrids being registered (mostly with *L. virginalis* as one of the parents), and three intergeneric crosses are now on the record. The latter are *Angulocaste* (*Anguloa* × *Lycaste*), *Lycasteria* (*Bifrenaria* × *Lycaste*), and *Zygocaste* (*Zygopetalum* × *Lycaste*). We feel that a tremendous field of experimental hybridization is open to the enthusiast in this alliance, and that in future we may look forward to seeing a large series of fascinating and unusual multigeneric crosses between *Lycaste* and other orchid genera which are genetically allied.

CULTURE: The cultural requirements of *Lycaste* are generally readily met, though there is considerable difference of opinion among learned orchidists regarding their proper and precise treatment. In the wild, these orchids range from near sea-level to high in the mountains, hence temperature requirements must be governed by the particular species or individual involved. Most Lycastes (*L. virginalis* is a rather notable exception) are tolerant of widely ranging temperature variations, but growth and flower-production are often somewhat curtailed if sufficient heat or sufficient coolness is not furnished at the proper season of the year. Various composts have been recommended for the plants, but all of them do very well if grown in straight shredded tree-fern fibre; under many conditions, osmunda does not appear to be quite as acceptable, although certain growers have good success with this medium and use it exclusively. The various bark preparations, particularly if used under glass and in combination with other media, are also used in some instances, though generally with somewhat less success. Other composts contain osmunda and/or tree-fern fibre, often in combination with such materials as chopped leaves (particularly those of oaks, genus *Quercus*) and sphagnum moss; the last-named is frequently used as a surface-topping on the pots. Most Lycastes grow in rather shaded spots in their native haunts, hence this condition must be emulated in the collection. Perfect ventilation and free-

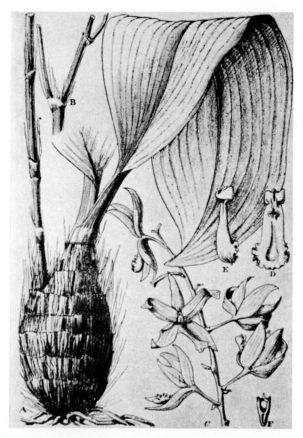

Inobulbon munificum (Finet) Krzl. [KRÄNZLIN]

Laelia undulata (Ldl.) L.O.Wms. [G. C. K. DUNSTERVILLE]

Laelia xanthina Ldl. [GEORGE FULLER]

Leptotes bicolor Ldl. [GEORGE FULLER]

Limodorum abrotivum Sw. [REG S. DAVIS]

Liparis elata Ldl. [H. SCHMIDT-MUMM]

Liparis viridiflora (Bl.) Ldl. [GEORGE FULLER]

Listera ovata (L.) R.Br. [GEORGE FULLER]

moving air are absolutely essential for success with members of this genus; they will never thrive in a stagnant atmosphere. While in active growth, the plants should be watered heavily—assuming that perfect drainage of the compost is available—but upon completion of the new pseudobulbs (when the leaves usually start to fall, and flower-spikes appear in many species), water should be stopped until these new growths harden fully—at least two weeks. Fertilizing at regular intervals is most advantageous and materially augments the number of flowers produced per growth. (C, I, H)

L. aromatica (Grah.) Ldl. (*Maxillaria aromatica* Grah., *Maxillaria consobrina* Beer ex Schltr., *Lycaste consobrina* Rchb.f.)

Pbs. clustered, ovoid, compressed, furrowed with age, to 3½" tall, with some fibrous sheaths at base. Lvs. deciduous, lanceolate, acuminate, plicate, to 1½' long and 4" wide. Scapes usually several at once, to 6" tall, with several inflated brown sheaths. Fls. to almost 3" across, waxy, very fragrant (usually of lemons), yellow (the ps. deeper yellow than the ss.), the lip yellow sparsely dotted with orange on inner surface, the col. yellow, pubescent on anterior surface. Ss. elliptic-oblong to ovate-lanceolate, acute, spreading, slightly pubescent at inner base, the lats. oblique, joined at base to form a blunt mentum. Ps. elliptic to ovate-elliptic, obtuse to acute. Lip hinged to col.-foot, concave below, 3-lbd. above; lat. lbs. elliptic to sublanceolate, obtuse, porrect, somewhat crenulate on apical edge, the lower part forming a tube; midlb. variable from narrowly cuneate-spatulate to elliptic-suborbicular, recurved, usually with wavy margins; disc pubescent, thickened along middle, with a broadly cuneate, truncate, flap-like callus extending over the base of midlb. Mostly spring. (C, I) Mexico; Guatemala; British Honduras; Honduras.

L. Barringtoniae (J.E.Sm.) Ldl. (*Epidendrum Barringtoniae* J.E.Sm., *Dendrobium Barringtoniae* Sw., *Maxillaria ciliata* Ldl., *Maxillaria Barringtoniae* Lodd.)

Pbs. ellipsoidal, furrowed with age, glossy, deep green to yellowish, to 4" tall and 2" thick, clustered. Lvs. deciduous, plicate, narrowly elliptic, stalked at base, narrowing to an acute or acuminate apex, to 1½' long and 5" wide. Scapes usually several at once per growth, erect, to 5" tall, with several loose bracts, the uppermost one about as long as the pedicellate ovary. Fls. drooping, about 2–2½" long, waxy, fragrant, long-lived, the ss. and ps. olive-green, the lip light buff-brown or tan. Ss. oblong-ovate, acute or acuminate, the lats. connate to form a bluntly conical mentum, wider than the dors. one. Ps. similar to the ss. but smaller. Lip long-clawed; lat. lbs. at claw-apex, narrowly falcate; midlb. ovate-oblong, blunt, fimbriate marginally; disc with a broad, deeply furrowed callus. Spring–summer. (I) Cuba; Jamaica.

L. candida Ldl. & Paxt. (*Maxillaria brevispatha* Kl., *Lycaste brevispatha* Kl. ex Ldl., *L. Lawrenceana* hort.)

Pbs. usually ellipsoid-ovoid, rarely almost roundish, laterally compressed, furrowed with age, to 2½" long, with several coarsely fibrous brownish sheaths at base, with 2 conspicuous sharp spines at apex after lvs. have

fallen. Lvs. deciduous, plicate, elliptic-lanceolate, acute or shortly acuminate, to 8" long and 2" wide, usually deep green. Scapes mostly several at once, slender, erect, to 3" tall, usually produced concurrently with the flush of new growth, the several sheathing bracts distant, tubular, the apical one about half the length of the pedicellate ovary. Fls. often not opening fully, somewhat nodding, about 2" across, fragrant of fresh apples, highly variable in colour, the ss. usually pale green to olive-green (rarely rose), usually rose-spotted on inner surface, the ps. white marked with rose (rarely pure white), the lip white marked with rose (rarely pure white). Ss. membranaceous, the dors. one free, erect, elliptic-lanceolate, acute, the apex strongly recurved; lats. adnate to col.-foot, forming a short mentum, the base oblique, elliptic-lanceolate, acute, the tips strongly recurved. Ps. about as large as the ss., elliptic-oblanceolate, the apices recurved. Lip 3-lbd., jointed at base to col.-foot, about as broad as long when spread out; lat. lbs. erect, obscurely emarginate at the subacute apices; midlb. broadly obtuse, the apex somewhat reflexed; disc with an elongate, acute, 2-grooved, tongue-shaped callus. Mostly winter. (I, H) ? Guatemala; Costa Rica; Panama.

L. costata (Ldl.) Ldl. (*Maxillaria costata* Ldl.)

Pbs. ovoid, furrowed with age, to 6" tall, clustered. Lvs. deciduous, usually 1–2, to 15" long and 3" wide, narrowly elliptic-lanceolate, acuminate, plicate, usually rather rigid. Scapes mostly several at once, to 8" tall (rarely taller), with a few inflated sheathing bracts. Fls. to 5" across, greenish-white to ivory-white, usually with a faint blush of yellow around the calli on the lip-disc, lasting for several weeks, very waxy, highly fragrant. Ss. oblong, acutish or subobtuse, the dors. one somewhat arching forward, the lats. usually strongly falcate. Ps. parallel to the col.-sides, ascending, subequal in size to the ss., of rather similar shape. Lip large, the lat. lbs. oblong, obtuse, the midlb. broadly elliptic, marginally dentate, the apical part usually down-curving. Summer. (I) Peru.

L. cruenta Ldl. (*Maxillaria Skinneri* Batem. ex Ldl., *Maxillaria cruenta* Ldl., *Maxillaria balsamea* Beer, *Lycaste balsamea* A.Rich. ex Ldl.)

Pbs. ovoid-oblong, compressed, to 4" long and 2" thick, usually yellowish, furrowed with age, with several fibrous sheaths at base. Lvs. deciduous, plicate, elliptic-lanceolate to broadly elliptic, acute to acuminate, to 15" long and 6" wide. Scapes usually several at once per growth, to 7" tall, with several scarious, somewhat inflated, sheathing bracts. Fls. waxy, very fragrant, long-lived, to about 4" across (usually smaller), the ss. yellow-green, the ps. bright yellow or orange-yellow, the lip yellow flecked with maroon and with a crimson blotch at the base, the col. yellow. Ss. oblong-elliptic to ovate-triangular, somewhat thickened at the apex, concave below, recurved above, often pubescent on inner surface. Ps. broadly elliptic, obtuse or retuse, parallel to the col. Lip hinged to col.-foot, saccate, 3-lbd., usually provided with long whitish hairs in the saccate part; lat. lbs. broadly rounded, erect; midlb. suborbicular to broadly ovate, sometimes notched at apex, decurved, the margins crisped, somewhat pubescent on upper surface; disc corrugated at base, with a small, central, cuneate-squarish, truncate callus. Col. pubescent on anterior face. Spring. (C, I) Mexico; Guatemala; El Salvador; ? Costa Rica.

L. Deppei (Lodd.) Ldl. (*Maxillaria Deppei* Lodd., *Maxillaria chrysoptera* Beer, *Maxillaria leiantha* Beer, *Deppia mexicana* Raf., *Lycaste chrysoptera* Morr., *L. Deppei* (Lodd.) Ldl. var. *punctatissima* Rchb.f., *L. leiantha* Beer)

Pbs. ovoid, compressed, furrowed with age, to 4″ tall and 2″ thick, with scarious sheaths at base. Lvs. deciduous, plicate, elliptic-lanceolate, acuminate, to 1½′ long and 4″ wide. Scapes usually several at once, erect, to 6″ tall, with several red-brown, inflated, sheathing bracts. Fls. to 4½″ across, waxy, fragrant, long-lived, rather variable in colour, the ss. usually pale green flecked with red, the ps. white flecked with red basally, the lip bright yellow with red spots and red lateral stripes in basal portion, the col. white with tiny red dots. Ss. elliptic, obtuse to acutish, concave below, the lats. oblique, joined at base to form a blunt mentum. Ps. obovate-elliptic, obtuse, concave, recurved above. Lip hinged to col.-foot, 3-lbd., arcuate, prominently nervose and granular-ciliate; lat. lbs. bluntly rounded at apex, forming a tube around the col.; midlb. ovate-oblong to oblong-triangular, obtuse, folded and strongly decurved, the margins undulate-crisped; disc thickened along middle, with a free short callus extending over base of midlb., the callus rounded, grooved. Throughout the year, often more than once annually, mostly in spring and autumn. (C, I) Mexico; Guatemala.

L. gigantea Ldl. (*Maxillaria gigantea* Beer, *Maxillaria Heynderycxii* Morr.)

Pbs. ovoid, furrowed with age, to 4½″ tall, with a few scarious sheaths at the base. Lvs. deciduous, plicate, stalked at base, elliptic-lanceolate, acute or acuminate, to 1½′ long and 3½″ wide, rather rigid. Scapes usually few at once, to 12″ tall, erect, with a few rather loose sheathing bracts. Fls. waxy, fragrant, to 7″ long, not as wide, olive-brown, the lip ochre-brown, violet-purple medially, the col. whitish. Ss. lanceolate, acute to acuminate, the lats. mostly strongly falcate. Ps. similar but rather shorter. Lip 3-lbd., somewhat downcurved, the lat. lbs. short, ovate, obtuse; midlb. oval, truncate or retuse, marginally slightly denticulate. Summer. (I) Ecuador; Peru.

L. lasioglossa Rchb.f. (*Maxillaria lasioglossa* Beer)

Pbs. ovoid, compressed, to 4″ tall, about 1½″ thick, furrowed with age. Lvs. deciduous, plicate, elliptic-lanceolate, acute to acuminate, strongly nervose, short-stalked at base, to 1½′ long and 5″ wide. Scapes slender, usually few at once, erect, to 10″ tall, with several inflated sheathing bracts. Fls. to almost 5½″ across, waxy, fragrant, rather variable in colour, the ss. reddish-brown, the ps. yellow, the lip yellow with purple flecks and stripes. Ss. elliptic-lanceolate, acute to apiculate, tomentose on inner surface at base, the lats. slightly oblique, joined at base to form a sharp mentum. Ps. elliptic, rounded and usually mucronate at tip, arching over the col., recurved at tips. Lip hinged to col.-foot. 3-lbd., when spread out obovate, tubular below; lat.

lbs. narrowly semiobcordate, subtruncate and somewhat emarginate at apex; midlb. oblong, obtuse, decurved, the entire surface densely covered with long soft hairs; disc with an ovate-triangular callus that is directed forwards, minutely notched at tip. Col. densely pubescent above the middle on anterior face. Spring. (I) Guatemala; Honduras.

L. locusta Rchb.f.

Rather similar in habit to *L. gigantea* Ldl., the lvs. usually smaller (to about 12″ long and about 2″ wide), and the fls. different. Scapes erect, to about 7″ tall, usually several at once. Fls. to about 4½″ long, waxy, fragrant, the ss. and ps. bluish-green, the lip bordered with white, otherwise dull green, the col. white. Ss. and ps. oblong, obtuse, rather concave, the ps. somewhat smaller. Lip 3-lbd., the large oval midlb. toothed-fimbriate, the smaller lat. lbs. oval, acutish. Col. slender, pubescent on anterior face. Spring. (I) Peru.

L. macrobulbon (Hk.) Ldl. (*Maxillaria macrobulbon* Hk.)

Rather similar in habit to *L. gigantea* Ldl., usually somewhat more robust, the pbs. mostly larger. Scapes erect, to about 7″ tall, with several sheathing loose bracts. Fls. waxy, fragrant, long-lived, to 4″ long, the ss. greenish-yellow, the ps. yellow, the lip yellow. Ss. oblong, obtuse, the lats. somewhat incurved. Ps. slightly shorter than the ss., the apices recurved. Lip 3-lbd., the lat. lbs. very short, blunt, the larger midlb. oval, reflexed apically. Spring–summer. (I) Colombia.

L. macrophylla (P. & E.) Ldl. (*Maxillaria macrophylla* P. & E., *Lycaste Dowiana* Endr. & Rchb.f., *L. Filomenoi* Schltr., *L. macrophylla* Ldl. fma. *Dowiana* P.H.Allen, *L. plana* Ldl.)

Pbs. robust, ovoid, somewhat laterally compressed, often rather angular, to 4″ long and 2¼″ wide, with several leafy bracts at the base, the apices of old pbs. not armed with spines after the lvs. fall. Lvs. 2–3, plicate, deciduous, oblanceolate, acute or acuminate, to 2¼′ long and 5″ wide. Scapes erect or horizontal, usually numerous at one time, to 7″ tall, furnished with several broad, papery, spathaceous bracts. Fls. waxy, fragrant, often somewhat nodding, to 4½″ across, variable in colour (and, somewhat, in size), the ss. usually olive-green, sometimes shaded marginally with reddish-brown, the ps. white often spotted with rose-pink, the lip white, the margins near the apex usually spotted or blotched with rose-red. Ss. broadly spreading, the dors. one free, erect, lanceolate to elliptic-lanceolate, acute, the lats. adnate to the col.-foot to form a short mentum, from the oblique base lanceolate to elliptic-lanceolate, acute. Ps. subequal to the ss., not spreading, more or less parallel to the col., linear-lanceolate to elliptic-oblanceolate, acute, the apices recurved. Lip 3-lbd., usually not equalling the ps , narrowed at base and jointed to the col.-foot; lat. lbs. erect, the apices rather irregularly oblique; midlb. spreading, ovate to subquadrate, acute or obtuse, marginally somewhat ciliate and incurved; disc with a fleshy, lanceolate, acute, concave callus. Mar.–July. (I, H) Costa Rica; Panama; Colombia; Venezuela; Brazil; Guianas; Peru; Bolivia.

L. Powellii Schltr.

Pbs. ellipsoid-ovoid, laterally compressed, smooth to somewhat ridged, to 2½″ long and 1¼″ wide, enveloped at base in 3–4 papery, closely imbricated bracts, the upper 2 of which are usually lf.-like. Lvs. 2–3, plicate, deciduous, lanceolate or elliptic-lanceolate, acute or acuminate, to 15″ long and 3″ wide. Scapes usually few at once, erect, slender, to 5½″ tall, produced from mature pbs. before the lvs. have fallen, with several papery tubular bracts. Fls. very fragrant, waxy, long-lived, to 3½″ across, somewhat variable in colour, the ss. usually pale translucent green, heavily blotched with chestnut-brown, or wine-red with yellow margins, the ps. creamy-yellow to almost white, spotted with rose-pink or wine-red, the lip white, sometimes red-spotted. Ss. wide-spreading, the dors. one free, linear-lanceolate, acute, slightly recurved at apex, the lats. adnate to the col.-foot, forming a short mentum, from the oblique base linear-lanceolate, acute. Ps. subequal to the ss., elliptic-lanceolate, obtuse to subacute, more or less parallel to the col., the tips strongly reflexed. Lip elliptic-obovate, obtuse or subacute, vaguely 3-lbd., the lat. lbs. erect, the midlb. short, spreading, obtuse or subacute, separated from the lats. by plicate folds; disc with a short, fleshy, ligular, obtuse, concave callus. Mostly July–Sept. (I, H) Panama.

L. tricolor (Kl.) Rchb.f. (*Maxillaria tricolor* Kl., *Lycaste Bradeorum* Schltr.)

Closely allied to *L. candida* Ldl. & Paxt., and perhaps only a constant variety of that polymorphic sp. Pbs. to 3½″ tall. Lvs. 3–4, elliptic-lanceolate, plicate, eventually deciduous, acute or acuminate. Scapes usually several at once, erect, to 5″ tall. Fls. often not opening well, fragrant, waxy, to about 2½″ across, the ss. pale green, often pink-spotted, the lip usually white spotted with pink. Differs from *L. candida* Ldl. & Paxt. primarily in having the lip (when spread out) about twice as long as broad (instead of almost as long as broad) and in the basal constriction of the midlb. May–June. (I) Guatemala; Costa Rica; Panama.

Lycaste virginalis (Scheidw). Lind. [VEITCH]

L. virginalis (Scheidw.) Lind. (*Maxillaria virginalis* Scheidw., *Maxillaria Skinneri* Batem. ex Ldl. (1842), *Lycaste alba* Cockerell, *L. Jamesiana* hort., *L. Skinneri* Ldl.)

Doubtless the most popular sp., usually grown under the synonymous name of *L. Skinneri* Ldl. Pbs. ovoid, somewhat compressed, to 4″ tall, 2″ wide, usually furrowed with age, sometimes rather angular. Lvs. several, plicate, deciduous, elliptic-lanceolate, acuminate, to 2¼′ long and 6″ wide. Scapes usually few at once (often solitary), erect, 6–12″ tall, mostly almost concealed by large inflated sheathing bracts. Fls. highly variable in size and colour, to more than 6″ across, very fragrant, waxy, long-lived, the ss. varying from pure white to pale violet-pink, the ps. reddish-violet, paler towards the apex, the lip flecked or veined with reddish-violet (sometimes appearing as a solid colour on the lower side), the disc-callus usually yellow, the column white spotted with crimson at base. Ss. ovate-elliptic to elliptic-oblong, obtuse to subacute, sometimes mucronate, somewhat keeled on back, the lats. joined at base to form a short blunt mentum. Ps. broadly elliptic, reflexed at the apiculate apex. Lip hinged to the col.-foot, 3-lbd.; lat. lbs. pubescent, nearly truncate at apex, erect to form a cymbiform tube around the col.; midlb. suborbicular, obtuse, strongly decurved; disc thickened and somewhat pilose along middle, with a short, fleshy, tongue-like callus projecting from between the lat. lbs. Many horticultural variants have been described, based mostly on floral colour; the most desirable of these have fls. that are pure white in all parts. Autumn–winter. (C, I) Mexico: Chiapas; Guatemala; El Salvador; Honduras.

L. Campbellii C.Schweinf. ex Johnst. Vegetatively rather like *L. candida* Ldl. & Paxt., differing primarily in the much smaller, differently coloured fls. Scapes very slender, to 3″ tall. Fls. rather nodding, bell-shaped, less than 1″ long, fragrant, not lasting well; the ss. green, the ps. yellow-green, the lip yellow. Dors. sep. ovate-elliptic, acute; lats. adnate to the col.-foot, forming a short conical mentum, oblong-ovate, acute. Ps. elliptic-ovate, obtuse, abruptly apiculate, Lip 3-lbd., contracted at base; lat. lbs. erect and somewhat incurved, the tips somewhat obliquely acute; midlb. ovate, subacute, with a recurved apicule; disc with a concave, oblong, obtuse callus. Feb. (H) Panama.

L. ciliata (Pers.) Veitch (*Dendrobium ciliatum* Pers., *Maxillaria ciliata* R. & P.) Pbs. ovoid, rather angled, furrowed with age, to 3″ tall. Lvs. 2, plicate, deciduous, lanceolate-elliptic, acute to acuminate, to 10″ long. Scapes erect, usually rather few at once, to 4″ tall. Fls. fragrant, waxy, long-lived, about 3½″ across, mostly not opening well, erect or ascending, the ss. and ps. green, the lip paler green, the midlb. greenish-yellow. Ss. and ps. oblong, obtuse, the ps. usually paralleling the col.-sides. Lip 3-lbd., the lat. lbs. short, erect, obtuse, the midlb. oval, ciliate-fimbriate marginally. Spring. (C, I) Peru.

L. cochleata Ldl. & Paxt. Rather similar vegetatively to *L. aromatica* (Grah.) Ldl., differing from that sp. in the more deeply orange-coloured fls. and the narrower, thicker lip-callus. Fls. usually under 2″ in diam., waxy, fragrant, the ss. greenish-yellow, the ps. rich orange, the lip rich orange, sparsely red-striped inside below the middle, the col. whitish-yellow. Ss. triangular-ovate to elliptic-lanceolate, acute to apiculate, somewhat pubescent on the inside basal part. Ps. elliptic, obtuse. Lip saccate below the middle and somewhat pubescent there, 3-lbd. above, the lat. lbs. elliptic, obtuse,

incurved below, flaring apically, the midlb. roundish, usually rounded at tip, crisped marginally, the disc with a thick callus that is rounded at the tip and slightly grooved. Spring. (C, I) Guatemala; Honduras.

L. crinita Ldl. (*Maxillaria crinita* Beer). Very close to *L. aromatica* (Grah.) Ldl., but very rare and with the disc of the lip pubescent instead of glabrous. Pbs. and lvs. usually slightly more robust than in the other sp., the scapes mostly longer, the fls. to about 3″ across, fragrant, waxy, yellow or orange-yellow, the ss. and ps. oblong, obtuse, the lip 3-lbd., the callus very prominent, free at tip, rather smaller than that of the other sp. Summer. (C, I) Mexico.

L. Dyeriana Sand. ex Rolfe. A remarkable sp., rather reminiscent of *Cattleya citrina* (LaLl. & Lex.) Ldl., the entire pl. and infl. strongly pendulous. Pbs. sharply angled, glaucous, ovoid, about 1½″ long. Lvs. 2, glaucous-silver or glaucous-blue-green, lanceolate to ligular-lanceolate, acute, about 8″ long. Scapes usually several at once, pendulous, to 5″ long. Fls. waxy, fragrant, long-lived, pendulous, about 2″ long, not opening fully, the ss. light green, the ps. deep grass-green, the lip green. Ss. and the slightly smaller ps. oblong, obtuse. Lip with short, fringed lat. lbs. which upturn at the col.-sides, the midlb. spear-shaped, obtuse at tip, usually fringed marginally along the sides. Summer–autumn. (C, I) Peru.

L. fulvescens Hk. (*Maxillaria fulvescens* Beer, *Lycaste crocea* Lind.) Similar in habit to the closely allied *L. gigantea* Ldl., differing in the shorter scapes (to about 4″ tall), and in the shape of the floral segms. Fls. about 5″ long, waxy, fragrant, long-lived, the ss. and ps. yellowish with a brownish suffusion,

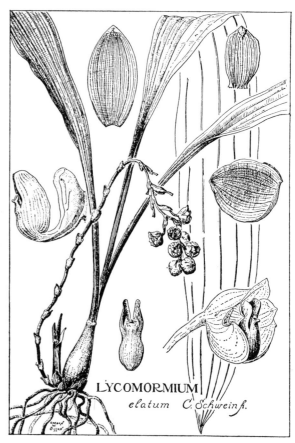

Lycomormium elatum C.Schw. [GORDON W. DILLON]

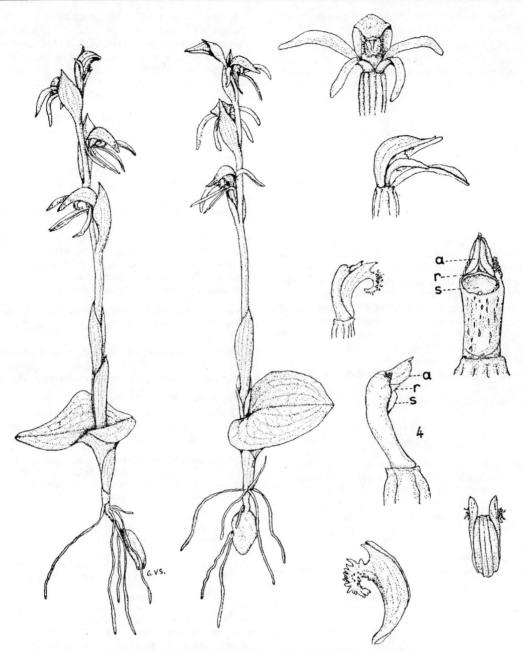

Lyperanthus nigricans R.Br. [Rupp, *Orchids of New South Wales*]

the lip yellow. Ss. and the shorter ps. lanceolate, acute, the lat. ss. rather falcate. Lip with small, acute lat. lbs. and an oval, marginally fimbriate, large midlb., the callus wider towards the front than behind, 2-lbd. Summer. (C, I) Colombia.

L. lanipes (R. & P.) Ldl. (*Maxillaria lanipes* R. & P., *Lycaste mesochlaena* Rchb.f.) Rather closely allied to *L. costata* (Ldl.) Ldl., the pbs. about 2½″ tall. Lvs. 2, long-stalked at base, to about 1½′ long. Scapes usually few at once, to 6″ tall. Fls. about 5″ across, waxy, fragrant, long-lived, greenish-white. Lip white, the lat. lbs. very short, the midlb. basally fringed. Col. hairy at base. Spring–summer. (I) Peru; Ecuador; Brazil.

L. linguella Rchb.f. Allied to and simulating *L. costata* (Ldl.) Ldl., but the fls. smaller, less than 4″ long. Fls. with the ss. and ps. greenish-yellow, oblong, obtuse, the ps. usually shorter and wider; lip usually whitish, the lat. lbs. short, obtuse, the midlb. ovate, acute, fringed marginally, the callus very wide, broadly ovate, emarginate at the apex. Jan.–Feb. (C, I) Peru.

L. Schilleriana Rchb.f. Allied to and rather simulating *L. gigantea* Ldl. in large part. Scapes usually several at once, to 12″ tall, with several prominent sheaths. Fls. waxy, fragrant, long-lived, about 5″ long, the ss. pale olive-green, the ps. white, the lip yellowish with a white midlb. Ss. and ps. oblong, acute or acuminate. Lip 3-lbd., the lat. lbs. small, obtuse, the midlb. ovate, acute, fringed marginally. Spring. (C, I) Colombia.

L. xytriophora Rchb.f. Allied to and rather simulating *L. gigantea* Ldl., the lvs. usually shorter and the fls. different. Scapes very numerous at one time, to 6″ tall, sheathed. Fls. waxy, fragrant, long-lived, to 4″ across, the ss. green shaded or irregularly mottled with brown, the ps. yellow-green in basal half, the apical half white, the lip white flushed with rose inside, the very small callus yellow spotted with red, the slender, anteriorly hairy col. whitish. Ss. wide-spreading, oblong, obtuse, with a small apicule. Ps. shorter and wider than the ss., parallel to the col., the tips out-curved. Lip 3-lbd., the lat. lbs. erect, short, blunt, rather out-curving, the midlb. ovate, down-curved, crisped marginally. Spring–summer. (C, I) Costa Rica; Ecuador.

LYCOMORMIUM Rchb.f.

Lycomormium consists of two very rare and little-known epiphytic orchids of the subtribe *Gongorinae*, both apparently restricted in their distribution to Peru, and not present in contemporary collections. Somewhat allied to *Acineta* Ldl., they are very robust plants with large pendulous racemes of complex, rather cup-shaped, often very beautiful flowers. The genus seems to offer some interesting potentials to the collector, but the species seem, unfortunately, to be excessively scarce even in their native haunts.

Nothing is known of the genetic affinities of *Lycomormium*.

CULTURE: As for *Acineta*. (I, H)

LYPERANTHUS R.Br.
(*Fitzgeraldia* FvM.)

About nine species of *Lyperanthus* are known, all unusual terrestrial orchids of the subtribe *Acianthinae*, native in Australia, New Zealand, and New Caledonia. They are unknown in contemporary collections, though their large, intricate, uniquely coloured blossoms make them of potential interest to connoisseurs. The genus is somewhat allied to *Acianthus* R.Br., but differs in technical floral details.

Nothing is known of the genetic affinities of *Lyperanthus*.

CULTURE: Presumably as for *Caladenia*. (C, I)

MACODES Bl.
(*Argyrorchis* Bl.)

Macodes consists of about seven species of rare but extremely handsome terrestrial orchids in the Malaysian region, especially in Indonesia. One of the groups commonly called 'Jewel Orchids', which are grown not for their relatively insignificant flowers, but rather for the magnificent foliage, they are today seldom seen, although they are assuredly worthy of attention from those specialists willing to attend to their rather complex cultural requirements. Closely allied to *Haemaria* Ldl., the genus differs from it in having the lip at the top of the flower; in both groups the lip and column are markedly twisted.

Macodes petola (Bl.) Ldl. has been crossed with *Haemaria discolor* (A.Rich.) Ldl., to produce the charming *Macomaria x Veitchii*, a hybrid registered by Veitch in 1862, but now apparently lost to cultivation. The genus is probably also genetically compatible with at least certain other members of the alliance.

CULTURE: As for *Anoectochilus*. (H)

M. petola (Bl.) Ldl. (*Neottia petola* Bl., *Anoectochilus petola* hort., *Anoectochilus Veitchianus* hort.)
Dwarf pls., the few lvs. forming a rather loose rosette close against the ground. Lvs. often overlapping, to 3″ long and 2″ wide, acute, ovate, very dark green with 5 longitudinal golden veins and groups of small golden cross-veins, velvety, the under-surface often tingcd with purplish. Infls. erect, 8–15-fld., the stalk fuzzy, to 10″ tall. Fls. small, red-brown with a white lip. Ss. with the dors. one forming a hood with the ps. over the col., the lats. spreading, enclosing the lip-base. Lip twisted, shorter than the lat. ss., the midlb. shortly clawed, the lamina wider than long, saccate at base. Col. twisted. Autumn. (H) Sumatra to the Philippines.

—var. **javanica** (Hk.f.) A.D.Hawkes (*Macodes javanica* Hk.f., *M. petola* (Bl.) Ldl. var. *argenteo-reticulata* J.J.Sm.)
Differs from the typical form in the larger lvs. (to 4½″ long) which are dark velvety-green with innumerable complex, reticulating silvery veins. Autumn. (H) Java.

—var. **robusta** J.J.Sm.
Differs from the typical sp. in the darker velvety-green lvs., which have 7–8 longitudinal, prominent silvery veins. Autumn. (H) Java.

M. dendrophila Schltr. Robust sp., the lvs. obliquely ascending. Lvs. elliptic, acute, stalked basally, to 5″ long and 2″ wide, dark green, with very intricate, fine silvery veins which are most prominent near the margins. Fls. small, brown. Autumn. (H) New Guinea, where it is often epiphytic.

M. Rollinsoni (hort.) Schltr. (*Anoectochilus Rollinsoni* hort.)
Lvs. elliptic, acuminate, basally broadly wedge-shaped, undulate marginally, to 4″ long and 2″ broad, velvety, dark brownish-green, with a wide white band around the margins. Fls. very small, brown. Autumn. (H) ? New Guinea.

M. Sanderiana (hort.) Rolfe (*Anoectochilus Sanderianus* hort.) Lvs. almost round or broadly oval, rounded at base, to 3″ long and 2″ wide, the under-surface purplish, the upper side velvety dark green with innumerable anastomising golden veins, the longitudinal ones of which are particularly prominent. Fls. small, brownish, the lip whitish. Autumn. (H) New Guinea.

MACRADENIA R.Br.
(*Rhynchadenia* A.Rich., *Serrastylis* Rolfe)

Macradenia is a genus of upwards of fifteen species of mostly small, relatively inconspicuous epiphytic orchids, ranging from South Florida and Guatemala to Brazil. Somewhat allied to *Notylia* Ldl., the members of this genus are today extremely scarce in collections, though at least two of them are of sufficient interest to warrant attention by enthusiasts. Pseudobulbous plants with solitary, rather leathery leaves and pendulous, usually few-flowered basal inflorescences, the Macradenias are charming and floriferous plants when well-grown, and grace even the largest of collections.

A few rather interesting hybrids have been produced in recent years utilizing *Macradenia*, these mostly in Hawaii, and not generally available in cultivation. Additional experimental breeding seems to offer some interesting potentials.

CULTURE: Macradenias do equally well either mounted on smallish slabs of tree-fern fibre, or potted (very well-drained) in straight osmunda fibre, or a mixture of equal parts of chopped sphagnum moss and shredded tree-fern fibre. Growing throughout the year, they do not require a rest-period, and should be kept in a moderately humid, semi-shaded spot in the collection. Periodic applications of fertilizers prove most beneficial. (I, H)

M. Brassavolae Rchb.f.

Pbs. cylindrical, slender, to 2″ long, sheathed basally. Lf. solitary, rather fleshy, to 7″ long, linear-elliptic, obtuse to acute, erect. Infls. pendulous, to almost 12″ long, with a loosely or rather densely few- to many-fld. rac. Fls. almost 2″ in diam., chestnut-brown and white-striped, the margins of the ss. and ps. usually translucent green. Ss. and ps. linear-lanceolate, long-acuminate. Lip white, 3-lbd., the lat. lbs. rather incurved around the col., the midlb. filiform-setaceous. Spring. (I, H) Guatemala; Costa Rica; Panama; Colombia; Venezuela.

M. lutescens R.Br. (*Rhynchadenia cubensis* A.Rich.)

Pbs. clustered, narrowly cylindric, somewhat compressed laterally, to 2″ long, rather dull green. Lf. solitary, rather thin-textured, to 7″ long, oblong-lanceolate, acute. Infls. arching or pendulous, loosely few-fld., to 7″ long. Fls. about ¾″ in diam., usually not opening widely, rather short-lived, the ss. and ps. varying from whitish to salmon-pink, often more or less mottled with red-brown or red-purple, the lip mostly whitish. Ss. broadly oblong-elliptic, the lats. rather oblique. Ps. elliptic-oblong, acute. Lip 3-lbd., the lat. lbs. embracing the col., the disc with 3 median keels. Winter. (I, H) South Florida; Cuba; Jamaica; Trinidad; Colombia; Venezuela.

MACROPODANTHUS L.O.Wms.

This is a genus of but a single species of very rare epiphytic orchid, native in the Philippines, which is allied to *Aërides* Lour. and rather resembles that genus in vegetative habit. **Macropodanthus philippinensis** L.O.Wms. is found on the island of Mindanao, and is unknown in contemporary collections. Its small flowers make it of interest largely to specialists.

Nothing is known of the genetic affinities of *Macropodanthus*.

CULTURE: Presumably as for the tropical Vandas, etc. (H)

MALAXIS Soland. ex Sw.

(*Achroanthes* Raf., *Crepidium* Bl., *Dienia* Ldl., *Microstylis* Nutt., *Pedilea* Ldl., *Pterochilus* Hk. & Arn.)

Malaxis is an excessively complex genus of upwards of three hundred species of variously terrestrial, lithophytic, or rarely epiphytic orchids of the subtribe *Liparidinae*, for the most part incompletely-known botanically, and very seldom encountered in contemporary collections. They inhabit virtually all parts of the terrestrial globe, although the largest concentrations of species are found in the tropics, especially in mountainous areas. Highly variable in vegetative form, they somewhat simulate *Liparis* L.C.Rich. in large degree, bearing more or less well-developed pseudobulbs and usually fleshy, often paired leaves—these frequently produced near the middle of the erect flower-spikes. The blossoms are typically very small, yet highly complex, and are often borne in compact, umbel-like, condensed racemes, these usually with long naked peduncles. Floral colour is mostly greenish or whitish, and although individually the blossoms are small, in mass they are often uniquely attractive, and these orchids therefore offer much of interest to the connoisseur collector.

No hybrids are as yet known in *Malaxis*, and nothing seems to have been ascertained regarding its genetic affinities. Since the majority of the species of this genus are principally of scientific interest, no particular benefit in interspecific breeding seems indicated.

CULTURE: Since *Malaxis* occurs in both chilly temperate areas, as well as in the hot, humid tropics, cultural instructions vary according to the particular species under consideration. The temperate-zone species should be grown as *Caladenia*, while those from warm countries desire conditions such as those afforded *Phaius*. A few of the Malaysian and Indonesian species with fleshy, variegated foliage (e.g., *M. calophylla*) should be treated much in the manner of *Anoectochilus*. (C, I, H)

M. calophylla (Rchb.f.) O.Ktze. (*Microstylis calophylla* Rchb.f., *Microstylis Scottii* Hk.f.)

Pbs. st.-like, stout, short, erect, with 2–3 lvs. and some sheaths below them. Lvs. broadly elliptic, acuminate, undulate and crisped marginally, to 6″ long and 1½″ broad, above bronze or pale brown spotted with green or dark bronzy-brown, the margins brownish-red or bright green, usually reddish underneath, the stalk and sheath broad. Infl. to 10″ tall, many-fld., densely cylindric, the fls. opening successively over a rather long period. Fls. inverted, about ¼″ long, the spreading ss. and ps. greenish, pale violet, pale pink, or cream-coloured, the lip usually yellow-green, very variable in shape and dimensions. Mostly spring. (H) Thailand; Malay Peninsula.

M. cylindrostachya (Ldl.) O.Ktze (*Dienia cylindrostachya* Ldl., *Microstylis cylindrostachya* Rchb.f.)

Pbs. st.-like, rather fleshy-thickened at base, clothed with the persistent lf.-sheaths. Lf. solitary, oblong or rounded, 3–4″ long, blunt, rather fleshy, plicate. Infl. slender, rather densely many-fld., cylindrical, 4–18″ tall. Fls. less than ⅛″ in diam., pale yellowish-green, rather short-lived. Ss. narrowly oblong, spreading. Ps. linear, very narrow. Lip ovate, pointed, the margins thickened. Autumn, mostly Aug. (C, I) Himalayas, from Kashmir to Sikkim.

M. latifolia Sm. (*Microstylis latifolia* J.J.Sm., *Microstylis congesta* Rchb.f., *Dienia congesta* Ldl.)

Pbs. prominent, clustered, often in a definite line, to 4″ long, succulent, rather soft, at first leafy. Lvs. usually 4–5 in number, basally with a broad stalk, the sheath on the pb. usually purplish, the lamina elliptic-lanceolate, acutish, undulate marginally, to about 9″ long and 3″ broad. Infl. stout, erect, to 8″ tall, the numerous fls. in a more or less dense cylindrical rac. Fls. about ¼″ long (usually smaller), rather variable in shape and colour, usually yellow-green, more or less flushed with purplish. Ss. and ps. narrow, curving forwards. Lip 3-lbd., the midlb. narrow, the lat. lbs. broad, blunt, without auricles. Mostly autumn–winter. (I, H) South China; India throughout Malaysia to Australia.

M. muscifera Ridl.

Pbs. st.-like, rather small, softly-fleshy, clustered. Lvs. quickly deciduous, paired, sessile or short-stalked, oblong or almost round, blunt apically, rather fleshy, 2–4″ long. Infl. 6–18″ tall, with a densely, many-fld. rac. at apex. Fls. less than ⅛″ across, yellowish-green. Ss. oblong. Ps. linear. Lip ovate, pointed, with thickened margins. Mostly autumn. (C, I) Himalayas, where it is rather widespread from Kashmir to Sikkim.

M. monophyllos (L.) Sw. (*Ophrys monophyllos* L., *Achroanthes monophylla* Greene, *Malaxis diphyllos* Cham., *Microstylis monophyllos* Ldl.)

Highly variable in all parts. St. slender, arising from an ovoid corm surrounded by greyish-white sheaths, normally with 1 long-sheathing lf. near base or about the middle. Lf.-blades abruptly spreading, broadly ovate to elliptic or lanceolate, broadly rounded to narrowly acute at apex, to 4″ long, and 2″ broad. Infl. 2–13″ tall, the loosely many-fld. rac. narrowly cylindric, elongated. Fls. non-resupinate, less than ¼″ in diam., pale greenish-white to greenish or yellowish-green, sometimes marked with red. Ps. linear, strongly reflexed. Lip concave, 3-lbd., triangular-ovate in outline, with the basal part broadly rounded into an ear-like inrolled lobe on each side, sharply contracted above and forming a linear-lanceolate apical lobe which tapers to a sharp point. June–Aug. (C, I) Europe; Northern Asia; Aleutian Islands; Alaska.

M. spicata Sw. (*Achroanthes floridana* Greene, *Malaxis floridana* O.Ktze., *Microstylis floridana* Chapm., *Microstylis spicata* Ldl.)

Pbs. usually very few in number, rather softly fleshy, small, clothed with persistent lf.-sheaths. Lvs. paired, approximate above the middle of the st., ovate to suborbicular, obtuse to acute, glossy and strongly keeled along midrib beneath, 1–4″ long, to more than 2″ broad. Infl. 2¾–15″ tall, the subumbellate to elongate rac. loosely few- to many-fld., ¼–8″ long. Fls. inverted, to about ¼″ long, the ss. and ps. green, the lip pale yellow to orange-vermilion, entire or sub-entire, cordate-ovate, prominently and obtusely on each side at base, with a shallow sac at base, the sac-rim thickened. Autumn–spring. (I, H) Virginia to Florida; Bahamas; West Indies.

Malaxis spicata Sw. [BLANCHE AMES]

M. unifolia Michx. (*Achroanthes unifolia* Raf., *Malaxis ophioglossoides* Muhl. ex Willd., *Microstylis ophioglossoides* Nutt., *Microstylis unifolia* BSP)

Corm bulbous, subterranean, with a solitary lf. from near the middle of the st. Lf. abruptly spreading, bright green, orbicular-ovate to ovate-lanceolate, obtuse to acute, sessile and clasping the st., ¼–3½″ long. Infl. 3–25″ tall, the rac. subumbellate to slender-elongated, densely many-fld. Fls. less than ¼″ long, green, the lip lowermost in the mature fl., highly variable in shape from cordate-deltoid to oblong-quadrate, the ps. very narrow, strongly recurved. Usually Mar.–Aug. (C, I) Newfoundland to Ontario, south to Texas and Florida; Mexico; Guatemala; Cuba; Jamaica.

M. commelinifolia (Zoll.) O.Ktze. (*Microstylis commelinifolia* Zoll.) Pbs. st.-like, often rather irregular, fleshy, to 8″ tall, clustered. Lvs. numerous, elliptic, acutish, undulate marginally, with broad sheathing basal petioles, to more than 1″ long, bright green, usually with a dull purple median stripe. Infl. erect, rather loosely many-fld., to 7″ tall. Fls. about 1/16″ across, pale green, the lip notched marginally. Summer–autumn. (H) Java; Sumatra.

M. discolor (Ldl.) O.Ktze. (*Microstylis discolor* Ldl.) Pbs. small, usually less than 2″ tall, clustered, soon deteriorating.

Lvs. 4–5, about 3″ long, stalked, elliptic, undulate and crisped marginally, metallic-appearing, dark red-brown, the margins vivid green, the undersurface pale magenta-violet. Infl. to about 8″ tall, very densely many-fld. Fls. less than ⅛″ in diam., yellow flushed with orange, complex in structure. Summer, especially July. (H) Ceylon.

M. Josephiana (Rchb.f.) O.Ktze. (*Microstylis Josephiana* Rchb.f.) Pbs. almost obsolete. Lvs. usually about 3 in number, elliptic, olive-green above, the under-side rather reddish, to about 4″ long. Infl. loosely 4–15-fld., to 12″ tall. Fls. about ⅜″ in diam., yellow, the helmet-shaped lip flecked inside with reddish. Spring–summer. (I, H) Himalayas.

M. metallica (Rchb.f.) O.Ktze. (*Microstylis metallica* Rchb.f.) Lvs. 4–5 in number, elliptic, acutish, to 2½″ in length, metallic-appearing, iridescent dark-red, usually purplish beneath. Infl. erect, to about 6″ tall, loosely 10–15-fld. Fls. about ¼″ in diam., brownish-red, the lip rosy-red, notched at apical margin. Spring, mostly in May. (H) Borneo.

M. Soulei L.O.Wms. (*Achroanthes montana* Greene, *Malaxis montana* O.Ktze.) Pb. small, usually solitary, sheathed by lf.-bases. Lf.-blade solitary, abruptly expanded at about middle of st., cordate-ovate to oblong-lanceolate, obtuse, dark bluish-green, usually somewhat marginate, 1–6½″ long. Infl. 4–15″ tall, the very densely many-fld. rac. narrowly cylindric, the fls. closely appressed to the rachis. Fls. inverted, about ⅛″ in diam., yellowish-green, the ps. obliquely linear, obtuse, strongly coiled; lip roundish-ovate to triangular-ovate, the disc 5-nerved, rather deeply concave. Summer–autumn. (I, H) Texas; New Mexico; Arizona; Mexico to Panama.

M. yunnanensis (Schltr.) A.D.Hawkes (*Microstylis yunnanensis* Schltr.) Pbs. tuber-like, short, ovoid. Lvs. 2, usually almost basal on st., oblong or elliptic, the stalks sheathing, 1–2″ long. Infl. 4–9″ tall, the rather densely many-fld. rac. elongate. Fls. about ⅜″ in diam., greenish-yellow, the lip cordate-ovate and eared at base, narrowly lanceolate at tip, with 2 calli at base and thickened nerves on the disc. Mostly July. (C, I) China: Yunnan.

MALLEOLA J.J.Sm. & Schltr.

This is a genus of about thirty species of epiphytic or lithophytic orchids which are widespread from India and Ceylon to New Guinea, the members of which are extremely scarce in contemporary collections. Rather closely allied to *Sarcanthus* R.Br., they vegetatively resemble many members of that genus, but differ in technical details of the flowers, notably in the structure of the lip, column, and pollinia. Because of their relatively small and insignificant flowers, the Malleolas have not been viewed with favour by collectors, though they are interesting and rather attractive when well-grown and in full blossom.

No hybridization has been attempted with the components of this unusual genus as yet, and nothing is known of its genetic affinities.

CULTURE: As for the tropical Vandas, etc. (I, H)

M. penangiana (Hk.f.) J.J.Sm. & Schltr. (*Saccolabium penangianum* Hk.f., *Saccolabium Hendersoni* Carr) Sts. sometimes branched near base, pendulous, to 8″ long, the few lvs. about ½″ apart. Lvs. rigidly fleshy, narrowed gradually to an acute, 2-lbd. tip and suddenly to the slightly twisted base, lanceolate-ligulate, often densely purple-spotted, to 5″ long and ½″ wide. Infls.

stiffly pendulous, short-stalked, densely many-fld., the fls. opening successively for a rather long period, to 1½″ long. Fls. fragrant, waxy, less than ½″ long, the juvenile buds pale yellow, the older buds and fls. with the lat. ss. deep yellow, the dors. sep., ps., and spur pale yellow, the old fls. fading to whitish, the lat. lbs. of the lip with purple-brown margins. Ss. and ps. very small. Lip with erect, fleshy, short lat. lbs., the ends curving inwards to almost meet in front of the midlb., which is very short and fleshy and is extended behind into a fleshy base which nearly closes the spur-entrance; spur pendulous, laterally compressed, the tip narrowed and curved forwards. Spring–summer. (I, H) Malay Peninsula: Perak, Pahang (erroneously described from Penang).

MANNIELLA Rchb.f.

Two species of the genus *Manniella* are now known to science, both of them excessively rare terrestrial orchids of the subtribe *Manniellinae*. **Manniella Gustavi** Rchb.f., an unusual plant with handsomely yellow-blotched foliage, has been found on a very few occasions in the deep forests of tropical West Africa. **Manniella americana** C.Schweinf. is a very recent discovery in the Guayana Highlands of northern South America. Neither of these plants are in cultivation at this time.

Nothing is known of the genetic affinities of this rare genus.

CULTURE: Presumably as for *Anoectochilus*. (H)

MASDEVALLIA R. & P.

Masdevallia is one of the most unique of all orchidaceous genera, containing as it does plants which produce some of the most unusual and extraordinary flowers in the entire family. It consists of approximately three hundred species, which vary in habit from epiphytic or lithophytic to terrestrial. The range of the genus is a large one, extending from Mexico to Brazil and Bolivia, with the greatest development in the high 'cloud forests' of the Andes of Colombia, where about three-quarters of the known species occur. A member of the subtribe *Pleurothallidinae*, *Masdevallia* connects with several other genera through various intermediate species, and certain of the smaller Masdevallias are retained here with some degree of doubt. Mostly easily recognized, even when not in flower, the plants typically consist of tight clusters of very short secondary stems, sheathed for the most part (a few species are repent clamberers), and solitary, glossy-green, usually fleshy leaves which are typically broadest towards the apex and narrowed into a basal stalk. The inflorescences are either borne directly from the obscure rhizome, or from the tiny secondary stems, thus appearing to be basal at all times; they bear, usually, but a single flower, though a few of the species have racemose inflorescences. *Masdevallia* flowers are, as noted above, among the most unusual of all orchids; they vary in size from rather small to gigantic (certain forms of *M. Chimaera* Rchb.f. measure almost a foot from tip to tip!), and mostly have a very characteristic form. The sepals are connate at the base, to the middle, or beyond, into a tube, with the free, spreading portions often elongated and tail-like. The usually narrow petals are much smaller than the sepals, and, with the small jointed lip and erect column, are produced inside the sepaline cup. Colour in these flowers ranges from pure white or greenish to almost black, with some of the finer species brilliant cerise or scarlet. Masdevallias were formerly very popular in England and on the Continent, and fabulous prices were paid on many occasions for particularly choice and rare specimens. In contemporary times, they have largely passed out of vogue, though in recent years a notable renascence of interest has been shown in the genus, and the entrancing Masdevallias are once again appearing in some quantity in a few choice collections.

A large series of hybrids was produced in *Masdevallia* during the late nineteenth century and the very early part of the present one (the last cross was registered in 1904), the *Hybrid Lists* recording a total of forty-seven crosses, a few of which also exist in the wild state, as natural hybrids. The vast majority of these have long since disappeared from our collections, and their re-making should be encouraged, as should additional experimental breeding. Intergeneric crosses in the subtribe *Pleurothallidinae* have not as yet been attempted, and some fascinating results doubtless await the enterprising breeder who tries his hand at hybridizing Masdevallias with members of the allied genera, notably with *Pleurothallis, Scaphosepalum,* etc.

CULTURE: Masdevallias differ somewhat in their cultural requirements from many other orchids, and since a few of them are singularly specialized in the conditions demanded, the genus as a whole has obtained the reputation of being difficult to grow. This is not particularly the case, but it should be noted that attention must be paid to the plants' needs, or scant success with them can be anticipated. Depending upon the species, temperature requirements vary considerably, though the largest number of the Masdevallias do best if afforded 'cool house' treatment. In their natural haunts, these orchids are subjected to almost daily fogs and heavy dews, as well as rains of great intensity from time to time. Under cultivation, it is therefore essential that the plants be kept moist at all times. No resting-period should be given, but care must also be taken that the plants never grow in a soggy or stale compost, as this soon proves very deleterious to their health. Because of the large amounts of moisture which must be furnished them, these plants are always to be kept in a spot where fresh, freely-moving air is readily available. They require a rather bright situation in the collection, but must never be exposed to direct sun, or the fleshy foliage will become burned. A large number of composts have been tried for Masdevallias through the years; these include straight sphagnum moss, a mixture of sphagnum and chopped or shredded osmunda fibre, and a mixture of about equal parts of sphagnum, chopped osmunda, and German peat. The only vital requirement of a compost for these orchids is that it drains thoroughly and rapidly. Masdevallias do best—and are more floriferous in most cases—if potted in small containers. Thus large 'specimen' plants are not often grown, since the central part of the plant-cluster tends frequently to die out if this is attempted. Applications of weak fertilizer at regular intervals seem beneficial. Such species as are included in the 'saccolabiate' section of the genus—*M. Chimaera,*

M. erythrochaete, M. Houtteana, etc.—are better kept in small slatted baskets, due to the sharply pendulous nature of their inflorescences, much in the manner of *Stanhopea.* Masdevallias are particularly susceptible to attacks by thrips and red spider, and steps should be taken to prevent the appearance of these pests in the collection. (C, I)

M. amabilis Rchb.f.

Lvs. leathery, narrowly oblanceolate, acute, 4–6″ long. Scapes slender, 1-fld., erect, to 12″ tall. Fls. about 1″ across the lat. ss., the sepaline tube narrow, bent, orange-yellow longitudinally veined with red, the free portion of the dors. sep. oval, orange-yellow, sometimes deep rose with 5 red veins, the tail 1½–2″ long, dull red; lat. ss. connate to more than half their length, oval-oblong, gradually contracted into slender parallel tails, 1–1½″ long, orange-yellow densely studded with crimson warts, with 3 crimson-purple veins. Ps. and lip oblong, whitish, the former with 1, the latter with several longitudinal red streaks. Dec.–Feb. (C, I) Northern Peru.

M. bella Rchb.f.

Lvs. clustered, leathery, oblong-lanceolate, obtuse, 5–7″ long. Scapes pendulous, 1-fld., to 7″ long, dull purple. Fls. triangular, fragrant, to almost 9″ long, the ss. pale yellow spotted with brownish-crimson, the spots denser on dors. sep., less developed on the lats. and chiefly confined to the outer margins; dors. sep. triangular, contracted into a slender, reddish-brown tail to 4″ long, the lat. ss. larger, connate to beyond the middle, long-tailed like the dors. one. Ps. small, yellow with red spots. Lip white, with a short fleshy claw and concave, shell-like blade, in the hollow of which are numerous raised lines radiating from the claw. Dec.–June. (C) Colombia.

M. Carderi Rchb.f.

Lvs. clustered, leathery, glossy, spatulate-lanceolate, 3–5″ long. Scapes slender, pendulous, to 7″ long, 1-fld., with 2–3 appressed bracts. Fls. bell-shaped, about 2½″ long, cream-white, blotched externally around and near the base of the connate ss. with brown-purple, the inner surface covered with short hairs, and spotted with brown-purple basally, the sepaline tails equidistant, 2″ long, pale yellow, sometimes spotted with brown-purple. Ps. white with a purplish-brown midvein, linear-oblong, reflexed at tip. Lip white, somewhat fiddle-shaped, the basal half with a longitudinal cleft, the apical half shell-like, smooth inside. June–Sept. (C) Colombia.

M. caudata Ldl. (*Masdevallia Shuttleworthii* Rchb.f.)

Lvs. leathery, obovate-oblong to elliptic-oblong, 2–3″ long, narrowed to a slender petiole of about equal length. Scapes 1-fld., as long as or longer than the lvs., slender, erect. Fls. opening fully, slightly fragrant, to almost 8″ long, the sepaline tube short, campanulate-gibbous below. Dors. sep. light yellow spotted with red and with 5–7 red veins, obovate, concave; the tail 2–3″ long, yellow; lat. ss. mauve-purple mottled with white, obliquely ovate, tailed like the dors. one. Ps. white, linear-oblong, very small. Lip pale mauve, small, broadly oblong, reflexed at tip. Nov.–March. (C) Colombia.

M. Chestertoni Rchb.f.

Lvs. leathery, bright glossy-green, narrowly oblanceolate, subacute, 5–7″ long. Scapes pendulous, 1-fld., slender, to 8″ long. Fls. opening widely, to about 3½″ across, the ss. ovate-oblong, keeled behind, the blade greenish-sulphur-coloured, more or less densely spotted with black-purple, the tails about 1″ long, black-purple, rather warty. Ps. tiny, yellowish-red with an apical black callus, oblong. Lip large, pale orange-yellow with numerous radiating raised reddish lines, the claw grooved, the blade transversely reniform, concave. Col. arched, white with a few brownish-red spots near the apex. July–Nov. (C) Colombia.

M. Chimaera Rchb.f.

Lvs. tightly clustered, glossy green, leathery, narrowly oblanceolate, 6–9″ long, narrowed below into a short petiole, this covered with papery sheaths. Scapes slender, erect to sharply pendulous, 6–24″ long, 3–8-fld., jointed, with a small pale green sheath at each joint. Fls. produced singly by successive prolongations of the scape from the joint immediately below the pedicellate ovary, rather foul-smelling, extremely variable in size and colour, but usually to 9″ long, the sepaline tube broadly bell-shaped, very short, the ss. broadly ovate, acuminate, keeled behind, prolonged into slender tails 3–4″ long, the lat. ss. connate to about one-half their length, forming at the suture a deep boat-shaped depression, all more or less pubescent on inside and covered with warty spots, the ground-colour mostly yellow or whitish-yellow, the spots varying from black-red to cinnamon-red or brown-purple, the tails equally variable. Ps. usually white, spatulate, expanded at tip into lobes, on which is a blackish-purple spot. Lip white, sometimes flushed with rose or spotted with orange, red, or yellow, sac-like, the sac with 3 parallel or very slightly divergent raised longitudinal lines and numerous smaller ribs radiating from outside pair to the toothed margin. Col. bent at the apex, usually yellow above and white beneath. There are several dozens of named horticultural variants, differing primarily in size and coloration of the flowers. Nov.–Feb. (C) Colombia.

M. coccinea Lind. (*Masdevallia Harryana* Rchb.f., *M. Lindeni* André)

Lvs. clustered, deep glossy-green, obovate-lanceolate, 6–9″ long, narrowed below into long petioles. Scapes mostly erect, slightly flexuose, to more than 12″ tall, 1-fld., with 3–4 distant joints, at each of which is an appressed spotted sheath. Fls. heavy-textured, waxy, extremely variable in colour and (to a degree) in size, the perianth-tube compressed, bent, slightly gibbous below, white or other colours, the ss. varying from cream-white or pale yellow through orange, scarlet, crimson, magenta-red, to deep rich crimson-purple. Dors. sep. linear, with a triangular base, flexuose above, the lat. ss. connate to about one-third of their length, semi-ovate, oblique, tapering to approximate tips (not tailed), the blades sometimes broadly oval-falcate, the acuminate tips turned towards each other, forming an almost round

body from 1½–3″ in diam. Ps. and lip included in sepaline tube, the ps. with ears at frontal base, the lip tongue-shaped, cordate at base. Mar.–June. (C) Colombia.

M. corniculata Rchb.f. (*Masdevallia calyptrata* Krzl., *M. inflata* Rchb.f.)

Lvs. clustered, oblong-oblanceolate, to 6″ long, including the short petiole. Scapes mostly about 3″ tall, erect, 1-fld., with a large pale green, keeled bract subtending the fl. Fls. not opening widely, about 3″ long, brownish-red mottled with pale yellow, the sepaline tube broadly cylindric, gibbous below, bent. Dors. sep. shortly triangular, suddenly contracted into a slender tail 2″ long; lat. ss. almost oblong, reflexed, contracted into slender tails that are shorter than the upper one and which point straight downwards. Ps. white with yellow tips, ligulate, longer than the col. Lip yellowish spotted with purple, somewhat fiddle-shaped, warty apically. Aug.–Nov. (C, I) Colombia.

M. Davisii Rchb.f.

Lvs. bright glossy-green, thick and leathery, narrowly oblanceolate, 6–8″ long, narrowed into a short basal petiole. Scapes 1-fld., slender, erect, to 10″ long. Fls. heavy-textured, rather fragrant, to 2″ across the lat. ss., the ss. all yellow with some orange marks at the base externally, the sepaline tube sub-cylindric, with a prominent keel above and gibbous beneath at the base, free part of dors. sep. ovate-triangular, ascending, gradually contracted into a slender tail 1″ long; lat. ss. oblong, connate to more than half their length, contracted at apex into slender cusps. Ps. white, very small, concealed within the sepaline tube, oblong, notched at top, eared at base. Lip very small, brownish, with a claw, linear-oblong. May–June. (C) Peru.

M. elephanticeps Rchb.f.

Lvs. very thick and leathery, narrowly spatulate-cuneate, sometimes almost linear-oblong, 6–10″ long. Scapes rather robust, 1-fld., shorter than the lvs., dotted with purple, with 2–3 small, sheathing bracts. Fls. horizontal or deflexed, not opening fully, to about 4″ long, the sepaline tube broadly cylindric, yellowish above, dull purple beneath, the dors. sep. triangular, elongated, keeled above, gradually contracted into a long thick yellowish tail 2–3″ long; lat. ss. reddish-purple on the inner side, dull purple beneath, oblong, connate almost to the middle and contracted into yellowish tails. Ps. yellow, oblong, acute. Lip purple, ligulate, warty above. April–July. (C) Colombia.

M. Ephippium Rchb.f. (*Masdevallia acrochordonia* Rchb.f., *M. Colibri* hort., *M. trochilus* Lind. & André)

Lvs. clustered, leathery, narrowly elliptic-lanceolate, 5–7″ long, narrowed below into a channelled petiole, this half as long as the blade. Scapes rather stout, flexuose, sharply triangular, to more than 12″ tall, 2–3-fld., often spotted. Fls. heavy-textured, very complex, to about 8″ long, the sepaline tube cylindric, short, the dors. sep. yellow stained outside with brown, concave and tawny-yellow within, general shape almost round, contracted into a yellow, reflexed tail to 4″ long; lat. ss. roundish, forming a hemispherical cup, ribbed within and without, reddish or chestnut-brown, contracted like the dors. into long flexuous yellow tails. Ps. white, linear, sometimes 2–3-toothed at apex. Lip reddish-brown, oblong, apiculate, clawed and eared at base, toothed towards the apex. Col. whitish. Mar.–May. (C, I) Colombia; Ecuador.

M. erythrochaete Rchb.f. (*Masdevallia astuta* Rchb.f., *M. Gaskelliana* Rchb.f.)

Lvs. not very fleshy, rather dull green, linear-oblanceolate, 6–12″ long. Scapes slender, erect or sharply pendulous, to 1½′ long, 1-fld. (rarely 2-fld.). Fls. about 4″ across, the sepaline tube short, yellowish-white outside; free part of ss. ovate-triangular, with the connate basal portions yellowish-white spotted with red-purple and furnished with numerous white hairs on inside, the tails reddish-purple, 2″ long. Ps. tiny, brown at the tips. Lip like that of *M. Chimaera* Rchb.f., but smaller, white faintly tinted with rose. Col. white. Sept.–Nov. (C, I) Costa Rica.

M. Estradae Rchb.f. (*Masdevallia ludibunda* Rchb.f.)

Pl. dwarf, densely cluster-forming. Lvs. leathery, elliptic-spatulate, 2–3″ long including the petiole, often 2-toothed at the apex. Scapes slender, erect, 1-fld., longer than the lvs. Fls. opening well, to almost 3″ long, the sepaline tube short, bell-shaped; dors. sep. yellow in basal half, violet-purple in upper half, concave, almost helmet-shaped, suddenly contracted into a yellow thread-like tail 1″ long; lat. ss. oblong, obtuse, almost flat with recurved margins and terminating in long slender tails, 1½–2″ long, basal half and tails yellow, apical half violet-purple. Ps. and lip whitish, linear-oblong. Col. white, spotted and margined with purple. April–May. (C, I) Colombia.

M. floribunda Ldl. (*Masdevallia Galeottiana* A.Rich., *M. myriostigma* Morr.)

Lvs. densely clustered, leathery, dark glossy-green, oblanceolate-oblong, 3–4″ long including the petiole. Scapes numerous, slender, decumbent to erect, 1-fld., usually longer than the lvs. Fls. not opening well, about 1″ long or more, pale buff-yellow dotted with brown-purple, the sepaline tube cylindric, with a small hump at the base on the lower side, the free portion of the ss. very short, that of the upper one triangular, of the lats. almost round; tails (the dors. one is the longest) slender, recurved, reddish. Ps. white, linear-oblong, toothed at the tip. Lip white with an apical red-brown blotch, constricted below the middle. June–Sept. (I, H) Mexico; Guatemala; Honduras; Costa Rica.

M. infracta Ldl. (*Masdevallia longicaudata* Lem.)

Lvs. clustered, lanceolate, leathery, 5–6″ long, bright glossy-green. Scapes 3-angled, twisted, 1-fld., longer than the lvs. Fls. bell-shaped, to 2½″ long, the sepaline tube broadly bell-shaped, bent, with a prominent rib above and a gibbosity below at the base, yellowish-white; free portion of dors. sep. triangular-rotund, concave, yellowish-white, that of the lats. oblong-rotund, connate to below the middle, keeled at the suture, the outer half yellowish-white, the inner half pale violet-purple; tails spreading, 1½–2″ long, pale yellow. Ps. white, linear-oblong, toothed at the apex. Lip

oblong, reflexed at the spotted red-brown apex. May–July. (I, H) Brazil.

M. leontoglossa Rchb.f.

Lvs. clustered, fleshy, bright green, shortly lanceolate-spatulate, to 7″ long. Scapes short, 1-fld., arching, about 1½″ long. Fls. not opening well, with the short tails about 2″ long, outside greenish, inside rose-red, densely red-spotted. Lip broadly ligulate, densely warty. June–Aug. (C, I) Colombia; Venezuela.

M. macrura Rchb.f.

Pls. very robust for the genus, the sts. clustered, about 6″ tall. Lvs. elliptic-lanceolate to elliptic-oblong, 10 12″ long, 2½–3″ broad, very leathery. Scapes to 12″ tall, erect, 1-fld., the pedicellate ovary and base of perianth sheathed by a whitish, membranaceous, keeled bract. Fls. among the largest in the genus, to about 10″ long, opening well, the sepaline tube short, cylindric, ribbed, dull tawny-yellow shaded outside with brown, as are the free portions of the ss., on the inner side both ss. and tube tawny-yellow studded with numerous blackish-purple warts; tails paler and without warts, very long; free portion of dors. sep. lanceolate, acuminate, prolonged into a stoutish tail 4–5″ long; lat. ss. connate to fully 1″ beyond the tube, then tapering into tails as long as the dors. one. Ps. and lip oblong, pale tawny-yellow, the lip with a warty, reflexed tip, and spotted below with purple. Jan.–Mar. (C, I) Colombia.

M. melanopus Rchb.f.

Lvs. fleshy, clustered, 4–5″ long, narrowed below into slender petioles, oblanceolate, 2-toothed at tip. Scapes numerous, longer than the lvs., racemose, 5–7-fld. Fls. not opening fully, about 1″ long, white, sparsely flecked with purple, the sepaline tube shortly bell-shaped, 3-angled, gibbous below; free portion of the ss. almost round, concave within, keeled behind, and contracted into rather short, slender, bright yellow tails. Ps. tiny, linear-oblong. Lip tongue-shaped, dilated at the apex into a round yellow terminal lb. June–Aug. (C, I) North Peru.

M. Mooreana Rchb.f.

Lvs. linear-oblong, 6–8″ long, very leathery, with inflated sheaths at their bases. Scapes 1-fld., rather stout, shorter than the lvs., obscurely angled, green spotted with dull purple, sheathed at base and middle. Fls. horizontal or deflexed, about 3½″ long, not opening fully, the sepaline tube broad, cylindric with a short gibbosity below; dors. sep. triangular, gradually contracted into a linear tail, yellow on the inside, with 3 wine-purple streaks on the paler dilated basal portion; lat. ss. connate to nearly the middle, similar but more acute, the tails parallel, wine-red, covered with innumerable tiny blackish-purple warts on the inner side; tails yellowish towards the tip. Ps. white with a purple mid-line, oblong, acute. Lip blackish-purple, oblong, hairy above. Col. greenish-white, with blackish-purple margins. April–May. (C) Colombia.

M. muscosa Rchb.f. (*Porroglossum muscosum* Schltr.)

Lvs. clustered, elliptic-oblong, about 2″ long or more, minutely 3-toothed at the tip, narrowed below into a slender, grooved petiole shorter than the blade, very leathery, deep green, flushed with purple beneath. Scapes slender, 1-fld., 6–7″ tall, rather tortuous, erect, pale green, clothed with moss-like hairs up to the small appressed bract just below the pedicellate ovary, then glabrous to the ovary-base, this being roughened and bristly, and bent horizontally. Fls. about ¾″ across, the sepaline tube short, compressed, gibbous below; ss. narrowly triangular, 3-veined, prolonged into slender tails 1″ long, pale buff-yellow. Ps. linear, longer than the col., their thickened tips meeting above it, coloured like the ss. Lip sensitive, clawed, the claw adnate to the bent col.-foot, the blade yellow, maroon at the apical edge, triangular, with the broad side at the apex, and with a yellow ridge from the base to the middle. The peculiarly sensitive lip of this species is unique. May–Aug. (C) Colombia.

M. nycterina Rchb.f.

Lvs. clustered, linear-oblanceolate, 6–8″ long, leathery. Scapes 1-fld., pendulous or sprawling, about 5″ long, warty, deep purple, with a small, pale, acute bract at the base of the pedicellate ovary. Fls. spreading, to 6″ long, triangular, the dors. sep. triangular, connate with the lats. at base, these ovate-triangular and connate to below the middle, all keeled behind and contracted into slender, purple-red tails 3″ long, the inner surfaces light yellow spotted with red-purple and studded with short white hairs. Ps. dilated at tip into a round yellowish blade, on which are 3 or 4 blackish spots. Lip with a recurved fleshy claw and concave shell-like blade, in the hollow of which are numerous raised lines radiating from the claw. Col. small, terete, white. May–July. (C) Colombia.

M. pachyantha Rchb.f.

Lvs. clustered, oblanceolate, 6″ long, deep green, leathery. Scapes 1-fld., longer than the lvs., erect. Fls. 2–3″ long, the tails adding an extra 2″ or so; sepaline tube broadly cylindric, slightly bent, pale orange-yellow; dors. sep. triangular, keeled above, pale yellow-green with 3 brown-purple veins, contracted into a rather stout erect tail 1″ long; lat. ss. ovate-oblong, connate to below the middle and prolonged into broad reflexed tails shorter than the upper one, pale yellow-green densely spotted with rose-purple, the spots larger and brighter in colour towards the base; tails bright yellow. Ps. whitish with brown-purple median line, ovate, acute. Lip ligulate, brown basally, blackish at the reflexed apex. Col. terete above, greenish, the margins brown-purple. June–Aug. (C) Colombia.

M. Peristeria Rchb.f.

Lvs. clustered, deep green, leathery, oblanceolate-oblong, 4–6″ long. Scapes 1-fld., shorter than the lvs., with a single bract. Fls. opening widely, 4–5″ across, the sepaline tube broadly cylindric, gibbous at base, with 6 prominent ribs, dull yellowish-green outside; free portion of the ss. triangular, yellow, spotted with purple, contracted into short, tawny-yellow tails 1½″ long. Ps. pale greenish-yellow, linear-oblong, acute. Lip with a narrow claw, the limb oblong, dilated medially and abruptly contracted beyond it, the upper surface studded with

amethyst warts, the tip recurved. Col. white, forming with the ps. a diminutive dove-like image, much like that of *Peristeria elata* Hk. Apr.–June. (C) Colombia.

M. polysticta Rchb.f.

Lvs. leathery, clustered, sub-spatulate, emarginate, 4–6″ long. Scapes 5–7-fld., longer than the lvs., pale green spotted with dull purple. Fls. hooded, about 1½″ long, white spotted with purple, the pedicels short, at the base of each with a rather large, inflated, pale green bract; sepaline tube short; free portion of dors. sep. broadly ovate, concave, that of the lat. ss. narrowly oblong, oblique, convex, with a yellow median line, all with minutely fringed margins, keeled behind, terminating in slender tails that are white and spotted like the blade in basal half, the apical half bright orange-yellow. Ps. and lip tiny; the former spatulate, apiculate, the latter oblong, grooved above. Nov.–Mar. (C) Northern Peru.

M. racemosa Ldl.

Rhiz. creeping, producing the erect sts. (1½–3″ tall) at intervals of ½–1″. Lvs. glossy-green, 2–4″ long, elliptic-oblong, stalked, rather rigidly leathery. Scapes erect or arching, 8–15-fld. or more, slender, 10–15″ long. Fls. to about 2½″ long, brilliant orange-red shaded with crimson, sometimes paler and approaching yellow; sepaline tube cylindric, ribbed, ¾″ long, the free portion of the dors. sep. triangular, acuminate, reflexed; lat. ss. connate into a broadly obcordate, tail-less blade 1–1½″ wide, each segm. with 3 longitudinal veins that are darker in colour than the intervening surface. Ps. and lip tiny, whitish. May–Sept. (C) Colombia.

M. radiosa Rchb.f.

Lvs. not very heavy, oblanceolate, 6–8″ long, clustered. Scapes sprawling, shorter than the lvs., 3- or more-fld., the fls. produced successively. Fls. opening fully, to 7″ long, the sepaline tube broadly bell-shaped; free portion of the ss. similar and subequal, very short, broadly oval, keeled behind, concave, tawny-yellow, fuzzy, densely spotted with blackish-purple, warty papillae in front, with a deep depression at suture of lat. pair; tails 2–3″ long, dull blackish-purple, paler towards the tips. Ps. oblong, keeled, dilated at apex, where there is a blackish spot-like wart. Lip with a fleshy claw and saccate shell-like blade, white with numerous rose-coloured radiating ridges within the sac. Col. yellow medially, with a blackish tip. May–July. (C) Colombia.

M. rosea Ldl.

Lvs. clustered, elliptic-lanceolate, acute, 4–6″ long, narrowed below into erect, grooved petioles. Scapes slender, slightly longer than the lvs., 1-fld. Fls. opening fully, to 3″ long, the sepaline tube 1–1½″ long, angulate, compressed, reddish above, orange-yellow at base; free portion of dors. sep. thread-like, 2″ long, red above, yellow on inner side, the lat. ss. dilated into ovate-lanceolate, concave, rosy-carmine lbs., which are connate to about one-third of their length from the base, and end in short red tails. Ps. and lip very tiny, ligulate, white, the lip with a tuft of blackish apical hairs. Col. arched, white. May–July. (C) Ecuador.

M. Schlimii Rchb.f. (*Masdevallia polyantha* Ldl., *M. sceptrum* Rchb.f.)

Lvs. clustered, leathery, lanceolate-spatulate, to 7″ long. Scapes erect, loosely 4–7-fld., 10–15″ tall. Fls. about 4½″ long, yellowish outside, yellow or cream inside, marbled with brown. Lip ligulate, marbled with red, the apex yellowish. Apr.–May. (C) Venezuela.

M. Schroederiana Sand. (*Masdevallia fulvescens* Rolfe)

Rather similar to *M. Reichenbachiana* Endr., the fls. about 2½″ long, the dors. sep. brownish-red, the lat. ss. bright red in apical half, the lower half white, the tails all yellow. Lip ligulate, whitish-rose. Dec.–June. (C) Peru.

M. simula Rchb.f. (*Masdevallia guatemalensis* Schltr.)

Pls. tiny, clustered, the lvs. linear, 2–3″ long, grooved and bright grass-green above, sometimes tinged with dull purple, vaguely keeled beneath. Scapes 1-fld., including the pedicellate ovary ½–¾″ high, sheathed by papery, pale brown bracts. Fls. hooded, ½″ in diam., the sepaline tube short, the dors. sep. ovate, acuminate, concave on inner side, keeled behind, pale yellow, evenly barred with purple; lat. ss. free, ovate, falcate, acuminate, brighter yellow than the dors. and with small purple spots. Ps. greenish, linear. Lip much larger than ps., broadly tongue-shaped, dull wine-purple. May–July. (C, I) Guatemala; Honduras; Nicaragua; Costa Rica; Panama; Colombia; Ecuador.

M. tovarensis Rchb.f. (*Masdevallia candida* Klotzsch)

Lvs. elliptic-spatulate, clustered, leathery, glossy-green, 5–6″ long, obscurely toothed at apex. Scapes to 7″ long, 2–5-fld., 3-angled, with 2 bracts at apex. Fls. opening widely, waxy, very long-lived, 1″ across, 3″ long, pure white; sepaline tube cylindric, slightly gibbous below; dors. sep. thread-like, 1½″ long, dilated into a triangular base; lat. ss. oval-oblong, 3-nerved, connate to two-thirds their length, rather abruptly contracted at apex into short tails. Ps. and lip oblong, the former unequally 2-lbd., the latter pointed and apically reflexed. Nov.–Feb. (C) Venezuela.

M. troglodytes Morr.

Lvs. clustered, linear-lanceolate, 4–5″ long, with recurved 3-toothed tips. Scapes 1-fld., sprawling, about 3″ long, bracted at each joint. Fls. bell-shaped, slightly more than 1½″ long, reddish-brown inside, white with a few brown spots outside; free portion of ss. very short, almost round, prolonged into thread-like, divergent, red-brown tails 1½″ long. Ps. reddish-brown bordered with white, ligulate. Lip with the claw short, channelled, the saccate limb round, concave, with 1 keel inside, white. May–July. (C) Colombia.

M. Veitchiana Rchb.f.

Lvs. clustered, linear-oblong or linear-oblanceolate, 6–8″ long, subacute at apex. Scapes 1–2-fld., 12–19″ tall, bracted. Fls. to 8″ long, opening widely, long-lived, light cinnabar-red with an iridescent bluish sheen, the sepaline tube bell-shaped, the free portion of ss. broadly ovate, contracted into slender tails, of which the dors. one is narrower and longer than the others, all ss. more or less studded with crimson-purple papillae, the lat. ss.

connate to beyond the middle. Ps. and lip tiny, linear-oblong, white. Col. short, semiterete, white. May–June. (C) Peru, at elevations of 11,000–13,000 feet.

M. velifera Rchb.f.

Lvs. clustered, rigidly erect, linear-elliptic, 6–8″ long, including the petioles. Scapes stoutish, 1-fld., to 4″ long, the pedicellate ovary bent forwards at right angles to the peduncle. Fls. hooded, heavy-textured, foul-smelling, to about 2½–3″ long, the sepaline tube broadly cylindric, gibbous below; dors. sep. triangular, contracted into a rather stout tail 2″ long, ochre-yellow, very smooth and shining outside, minutely dotted with red-brown inside; lat. ss. connate, bent downwards, ending in stoutish tails, coloured like the dors. one. Ps. greenish-white, linear-oblong. Lip almost square, narrow at apex, covered with chocolate-red, closely-set warts. Col. 3-angled, curved, yellowish-green. Nov.–Jan. (C) Colombia.

M. ventricularis Rchb.f.

Lvs. clustered, glossy-green, shortly lanceolate-spatulate, stalked, to 6″ long. Scapes to 4″ long, 1-fld. Fls. to 4½″ long, the sepaline tube large, cylindrical, slightly curved, brownish, the spreading tails thread-like. Lip ligulate, pale violet-purple. Mar.–July. (C) Colombia; Ecuador.

M. Wageneriana Ldl.

Pls. dwarf, tufted, the lvs. spatulate, leathery, about 2″ long. Scapes slender, 1-fld., about 2″ long. Fls. to about 2½″ long, light buff-yellow with numerous tiny red dots sprinkled over the ss. and some crimson lines at bases. Ss. broadly oval-oblong, narrowing very suddenly to slender yellow tails 2″ long, sharply bent backwards from the base, the upper one concave on inner side, keeled behind, the lats. connate to beyond the middle. Ps. hatchet-shaped, 2-toothed at apex. Lip lozenge-shaped, with reflexed, toothed margins, whitish, spotted with red-brown. Col. short, semi-terete, whitish, spotted with red-brown. Mar.–July. (C, I) Venezuela.

M. abbreviata Rchb.f. Lvs. clustered, shortly lanceolate-spatulate, 3–4½″ long. Scapes 6–8-fld., to 8″ tall, arching or erect. Fls. about ¾″ long, white flecked with red, the tails about ½″ long, yellow. Lip small, yellow. Nov.–Feb. (C) Northern Peru.

M. Armini Rchb.f. Lvs. oblong-lanceolate, 1½″ long, narrowed below into a slender petiole as long as the blade. Scapes slender, 1-fld., longer than the lvs. Fls. to about 4″ long, the sepaline tube short, whitish; free portion of ss. crimson-purple, the dors. one roundish, concave; lat. ss. broadly oval-oblong, almost flat, contracted into thread-like, yellowish tails 1–2″ long. Ps. white. Lip reflexed at tip, with a blackish-purple warty blotch there. Oct.–Apr. (C) Colombia.

M. attenuata Rchb.f. (*Masdevallia Laucheana* Krzl.) Lvs. clustered, bright glossy green, rigidly leathery, lanceolate-spatulate, 2½–3½″ long. Scapes 1-fld., usually shorter than lvs., erect. Fls. bell-shaped, waxy, long-lived, about 1″ long, white, the sepaline tube sometimes streaked with red, the tails about ½″ long, orange-yellow or butter-yellow. Lip white with a brown tip. Jan.–Mar. (C, I) Costa Rica; Panama.

M. Barlaeana Rchb.f. Pl. dwarf, tufted, the lvs. elliptic-lanceolate, stalked, to 4″ long. Scapes slender, erect, 1-fld., to 8″ tall. Fls. flaring, the sepaline tube narrow, bent, coral-red above, pinkish beneath; free portion of dors. sep. small, almost square, orange-yellow with a median and marginal red lines, contracted into a threadlike red tail 1½″ long; lat. ss. elliptic-oblong, connate for two-thirds of their length, ending in long points which cross each other, bright carmine shaded with scarlet and with 3 sunken crimson lines. Ps. and lip tiny, white, the lip with an apical purple spot. May–July. (C) Peru.

M. calura Rchb.f. Lvs. oblanceolate, 3″ long, leathery, with a distinct stalk. Scapes 1-fld., erect or arching, to 3″ long. Fls. opening well, deep chocolate-red with a blackish flush, to 3½″ long, the sepaline tube cylindric, bent; free portion of dors. sep. prolonged into a thread-like, orange-yellow tail 1½–2″ long; lat. ss. connate, oval-oblong, reflexed, minutely papillose on inner side, with a small triangular sinus between the parallel, orange-yellow tails. Col. white. June–Aug. (C, I) Costa Rica.

M. civilis Rchb.f. Lvs. linear-oblong, subacute, 5–6″ long. Scapes very short, 1-fld., mottled with blackish-purple. Fls. heavy-textured, the external surface smooth and polished, vaguely foul-smelling, the sepaline tube cylindric, gibbous below at base, greenish-yellow outside, inside deep purple at base, otherwise purple-spotted on a greenish ground; free portion of ss. triangular, prolonged into short recurved tails, greenish-yellow. Ps. white with a deep purple sunken mid-line on inner side. Lip reflexed at apex, mottled and dotted with purple. May–July. (C) Peru.

M. coriacea Ldl. (*Masdevallia Bruchmuelleri* Lind.) Lvs. linear-lanceolate, very leathery, heavy, 5–7″ long, deep green, pale green beneath. Scapes 1-fld., to as long as the lvs., pale green dotted with dull purple. Fls. leathery-textured, opening well, about 3″ long, the sepaline tube broadly cylindric, whitish-yellow with some purple dots along the veins; free portion of dors. sep. triangular, keeled above, coloured like the tube, prolonged into a short, broad tail; lat. ss. oblong, yellowish, prolonged into acuminate points. Ps. white with a purple mid-line. Lip reflexed, hairy above, greenish-yellow, with purple mid-line and marginal dots. May–July. (C) Colombia.

M. cucullata Ldl. Lvs. oblong-lanceolate, 9–12″ long, very leathery, dull green. Scapes 1-fld., to 12″ tall, with a large bract embracing pedicellate ovary and base of sepaline tube. Fls. hooded, about 2″ long, the sepaline tube almost cylindric, with a double gibbosity below; free portion of ss. triangular, keeled, deep maroon-purple; tails 1½″ long, yellowish-green. Ps. white, with a blackish-purple wart on the narrowed tip. Lip deep purple. May–Aug. (C) Colombia.

M. gemmata Rchb.f. (*Masdevallia trichaete* Rchb.f.) Pls. dwarf, clustered, to 2″ tall, the lvs. somewhat fleshy, grooved on face. Scapes thread-like, sprawling, to 2½″ long, 1-fld., bracted. Fls. almost 2″ long, the dors. sep. almost free, triangular basally, brownish-yellow with purple veins, contracted into an orange-yellow, thread-like tail about 1″ long, the lat. ss. larger, joined into an oblong, concave, rather boat-shaped lamina, wine-purple with deeper veins and an orange-yellow tail inserted in each outer margin near the apex. Ps. and lip very tiny, the latter cordate-triangular, purple, like the anterior parts of the ss. crowded with tiny warts. July–Sept. (C) Colombia.

M. Houtteana Rchb.f. (*Masdevallia Benedicti* Rchb.f., *M. psittacina* Rchb.f.) Lvs. clustered, linear-lanceolate, rather like those of a sedge, 5–7″ long. Scapes slender, prostrate, to 4″ long, 1-fld. Fls. ¾″ in diam. (exclusive of tails), the sepaline tube bell-shaped; free portion of ss. short-triangular, cream-white spotted with purple and densely studded with short white hairs; tails spreading, 1½″ long, reddish-purple. Ps. small, dilated at apex, where there is a dense tuft of short blackish hairs. Lip-claw upcurved, the lamina roundish, concave, with several raised radiating lines in the hollow, usually white, sometimes pale pink. May–July. (C, I) Colombia.

M. maculata Klotzsch & Karst. Lvs. linear-lanceolate, 4–5″ long. Scapes few-fld., to 7″ long, 3-angled, upper part sheathed by 2 whitish, papery, opposite bracts. Fls. to about 6″ long, heavy-textured, the sepaline tube short, with a prominent rib above, orange-yellow; free portion of dors. sep. triangular, gradually contracted into a stoutish yellow tail 3″ long; lat. ss. connate to below middle, the inner half brown-purple, the outer half yellow, contracted into pale yellow tails that are either parallel and bent downwards, or cross each other. Ps. white. Lip dull purple, warty and recurved at apex. July–Nov. (C) Venezuela.

M. militaris Rchb.f. (*Masdevallia ignea* Rchb.f.) Lvs. elliptic-lanceolate, rather rigid, to 4″ long, stalked at base. Scapes 1-fld., slender, 12–15″ tall. Fls. to 2½″ across, somewhat variable in colour, usually bright cinnabar-red toned with crimson, the sepaline tube bent, the dors. sep. with a narrow triangular base, prolonged apically into a linear tail that is bent downwards into the sinus between the lat. ss., which are connate to more than half their length, elliptic-oblong, pointed, 3-nerved, the free portions more or less divergent. Ps. linear-oblong, white with a purple median line. Lip similar, recurved at the apex, where there is an orange-red stain. May–July. (C) Colombia.

M. platyglossa Rchb.f. Lvs. oblong-lanceolate, rigid, erect, to 6″ tall. Scapes sprawling, 1-fld., shorter than the lvs. Fls. about 2½″ across, semi-transparent, uniform pale green. Sepaline tube short, cylindric, the free portion of the ss. triangular, contracted to sharp points, each with 3 prominent veins, the ps. ligulate, with a triangular ear above the middle, the lip oval-oblong, reflexed, with numerous tiny warts at the apex. May–June. (C) Colombia.

M. Reichenbachiana Endr. Lvs. clustered, erect, oblanceolate, acute, to 6″ long, with a channelled stalk at base. Scapes slender, 2–4-fld., longer than the lvs., the fls. produced in succession. Fls. almost 3″ long, the funnel-shaped, bent sepaline tube reddish-crimson above, pale yellow beneath, the free portion of dors. sep. triangular, yellowish-white, contracted into a slender tail 1½″ long, the lat. ss. deflexed, connate to one-half their length, then suddenly contracted into slender awn-like tails which cross each other at the tips, yellowish-white. Ps., lip, and col. tiny, white, concealed within the sepaline tube. May–Aug. (C, I) Costa Rica.

M. Rolfeana Krzl. Similar to *M. Reichenbachiana* Endr. in habit, but somewhat smaller in size. Fls. about 2½″ long at most, dark purple, the base of the sepaline tube yellowish, the lip red. April–July. (C, I) Costa Rica.

M. triangularis Ldl. Lvs. elliptic-oblong, 4–6″ long, slender-stalked below. Scapes erect, 1-fld., slender, to 6″ tall, with a small spotted bract at apex. Fls. broadly bell-shaped, when fully open almost 5″ long, the ss. tawny-yellow densely spotted with purple, triangular-oblong, concave, keeled on back, the lats. almost falcate, the tails thread-like, to 3″ long, brownish-purple. Ps. 3-toothed at tip, white. Lip oblong, white, spotted below with red-purple, with a tuft of blackish hairs at reflexed apex. Summer. (C) Venezuela.

M. triaristella Rchb.f. (*Masdevallia tridactylites* Rchb.f.) Pls. dwarf, densely tufted, to about 1½″ high, the lvs. slender, awl-shaped and narrowed at both ends, grooved down the face. Scapes 1–2-fld., slightly longer than the lvs., erect, very slender, rigid, minutely warty, sheathed. Fls. almost 1″ long, red-brown or reddish-yellow with yellow tails. Dors. sep. ovate, concave, suddenly contracted into a flexuous ascending tail about ½″ long, the lat. ss. joined into a boat-shaped lamina which is notched at tip and bears on each margin beyond the middle a thread-like tail about the same length as that of the dors. sep. Ps. 3-toothed at tip. Lip tongue-shaped, deeply 2-lbd. at base, brown. July–Sept. (C, I) Nicaragua; Costa Rica; Colombia.

MAXILLARIA R. & P.

(*Camaridium* Ldl., *Dicrypta* Ldl., *Heterotaxis* Ldl., *Marsupiaria* Hoehne, *Menadena* Raf., *Onkeripus* Raf., *Ornithidium* Salisb., *Pentulops* Raf., *Psittacoglossum* LaLl. & Lex.)

Maxillaria is a genus of an estimated three hundred species of epiphytic, lithophytic, or very rarely terrestrial orchids which range from South Florida and Mexico throughout the West Indies and Central America to Argentina. Particularly well developed in the Andes and in Brazil, it seems increasingly apparent that our knowledge of the genus is still highly incomplete, since new species and variants are being added with remarkable frequency. A rather large number of Maxillarias are sporadic inhabitants of our collections today, but they are far from common orchids, despite the fact that this huge aggregation contains many handsome and spectacular members. 'As would be expected from a large group of plants having a great geographic range, they vary considerably in size and vegetative habit. The species can roughly be separated into two main divisions. In the first division the pseudobulbs are conspicuously present, either as sessile clusters or distributed along the rhizome; while in the second division the pseudobulbs are inconspicuous or entirely absent, the plants usually either erect canes with 2-ranked foliage, or with sessile clusters of leaves in the form of a fan. However, there are many species in which conspicuous pseudobulbs are at first produced at the base, the subsequent growth becoming elongate, often branching or scandent, lacking pseudobulbs, or with pseudobulbs small and hidden by the imbricating leaf bases. Plants of some of these modified types are often indistinguishable from those of *Camaridium* and *Ornithidium*, the first of which in particular is a highly technical and arbitrary generic concept. In accordance with recently accepted usage, both of these are here considered to be Maxillarias.'[1] These orchids always produce solitary flowers, on short to elongate scapes from the bases of the pseudobulbs (or from the leaf-axils, or from certain parts of the flush of new growth, depending upon the species); these one-flowered inflorescences, however, are often produced in considerable quantity, so that in certain types the plants are virtually obscured by the wealth of blossoms. Floral size in *Maxillaria* ranges from very small to more than five inches across (e.g., *M. Sanderiana* Rchb.f.), and colour varies from pure white through a tremendous series of hues to almost black, with browns, reds, yellows, and greens being particularly frequent. Basic floral structure in the genus is much like *Lycaste* and *Bifrenaria*, with the sepals mostly free, or the lateral sepals connate basally, adnate to the base or foot of the column, and often forming a short chin or mentum.

[1] P. H. Allen in *Flora of Panama* 3 (4): 432. 1949.

The petals are usually somewhat smaller than the sepals, and in many cases are extended parallel to the column, over the lip. The lip is concave, varies from distinctly 3-lobed to entire, and is either stalkless or clawed at the base; it is either jointed to or adnate with the column-base or -foot. If present, the lateral lobes of the lip are usually erect and distinct, while the midlobe is spreading or reflexed and often thickened; rarely is the disc without a fleshy callus of some sort. The wingless, curved column has a short foot at the base (or is without one), and bears four waxy pollinia in a terminal one-celled or imperfectly two-celled anther. *Maxillaria* is the principal genus of the subtribe *Maxillarinae*, its closest allies presumably being *Scuticaria* Ldl., *Mormolyca* Fenzl, and *Trigonidium* Ldl.

Despite its potentialities, the genus *Maxillaria* has been virtually untouched by the breeder to date. In the official lists, only one interspecific hybrid is registered, this *Maxillaria x Lyothii* A.D.Hawkes (written, through error, *M. x Lyoth* in the lists) a natural hybrid from the Colombian-Ecuadorean region, which was also artificially produced by Charlesworth in 1930, the parents being *M. Sanderiana* Rchb.f., and *M. venusta* Ldl. Considerable additional experimental breeding within *Maxillaria* should be attempted, since some fascinating possibilities seem evident. As of this date, seedlings of hybrids between this genus and *Bifrenaria*, *Lycaste*, and *Aspasia* are now being grown in several collections throughout the world, thus indicating that *Maxillaria* is (presumably) genetically compatible with at least these groups, and in all probability with many other aggregations as well.

CULTURE: When dealing with a genus as large as the present one, it is naturally difficult to indicate detailed cultural directions without taking up far more space than is at our disposal on the printed pages. Generally speaking, most Maxillarias are relatively easy to grow, and a large number of them (notably those requiring intermediate or warm temperatures) are highly recommended for the amateur collector. Vegetatively *Maxillaria* is an extremely diverse genus, ranging from tiny almost moss-like tufts of succulent foliage less than an inch tall, to huge multi-leaved bulbless plants several feet in length which simulate a *Vanda* or other monopodial orchid! The more delicate, smaller-growing species, especially those without an appreciably elongate rhizome, do very well in smallish, perfectly-drained pots in a compost such as suggested for *Ornithocephalus* and other little 'botanicals'. Species such as *M. tenuifolia*, certain forms of the polymorphic *M. variabilis*, etc., with conspicuously elongate rhizomes (which, however, usually produce roots only at or near the base), need some sort of support, which may be afforded by a 'totem-pole' of tree-fern fibre thrust into the pot or basket in which the specimen is grown; these species do well in a mixture such as that suggested for *Ornithocephalus*, or in straight, preferably tight-packed osmunda fibre, or in smallish chunks of tree-fern fibre, again tightly packed. Certain of the robust species formerly referred to the genus *Camaridium* (= now *Maxillaria* section *Camaridium*), because of their massive leaf-fans, need some sort of trellis or framework up which to clamber, and should generally be treated much

Luisia Jonesii J.J.Sm. [GEORGE FULLER]

Lycaste candida Ldl. & Paxt. [G. C. K DUNSTERVILLE]

Macodes petola (Bl.) Ldl. [GEORGE FULLER]

Macradenia Brassavolae Rchb.f. [H. A. DUNN]

Malaxis latifolia Sm. [REG S. DAVIS]

Masdevallia bella Rchb.f. [GEORGE FULLER]

Masdevallia simula Rchb.f. [GEORGE FULLER]

like a *Vanda*, although considerably cooler temperatures are usually necessary. Finally, certain Maxillarias (e.g., the lovely *M. Camaridii*) are pendulous in habit, and when once established and well-rooting, may advantageously be grown on tree-fern slabs or rafts tightly filled with osmunda fibre. Most members of this large and useful genus require quantities of moisture while in active growth, but benefit by a more or less protracted (up to three weeks or so) rest-period upon completion of flowering, which often takes place from the bases of the just-matured pseudobulbs or stems. Almost without exception, they are highly susceptible to stale conditions at the roots, and repotting (and division, if necessary or desirable) should be done whenever such a situation seems evident. They usually do not do well in highly exposed spots in the collection, since the foliage of many species tends to become sunburned, and hence unsightly. Periodic applications of fertilizer seem most beneficial to all of the Maxillarias in cultivation. Temperature requirements naturally fluctuate from species to species (and, in certain widespread species, from individual to individual), some being strictly tropical inhabitants of lowland regions, while others extend into the high chill mountains of the Andes of South America. (C, I, H)

M. alba (Hk.) Ldl. (*Dendrobium album* Hk., *Broughtonia alba* Spreng.)

Rhiz. usually pendulous, often branching, lengthy, closely covered with imbricating brown, papery bracts. Pbs. inserted at an acute angle to the rhiz., rather distant, narrowly ellipsoidal, very compressed, to 2″ long and 1″ wide, the apex obliquely truncate. Lf. solitary, leathery, ligulate, acuminate, to 15″ long and ¾″ wide, usually glossy-green. Scapes usually rather few, to 2″ long, produced from the bract-axils of the flush of new growth. Fls. about 1½″ across, faintly fragrant, rather waxy, creamy-white, the lip bright yellow. Ss. spreading, ligulate, acuminate, the lats. forming a short rather sharp mentum. Ps. lanceolate. Lip vaguely 3-lbd., concave, slightly arcuate, contracted at base and jointed to the col.-foot, the lat. lbs. erect, the midlb. about one-third the total length, rather thickened; disc with an elongate, ligulate, fleshy callus. Mostly spring. (I, H) Guatemala and Cuba throughout the West Indies and Central America to Brazil.

M. Camaridii Rchb.f. (*Camaridium ochroleucum* Ldl., *Camaridium affine* Schltr., *Cymbidium ochroleucum* Ldl., *Ornithidium album* Hk.)

Rhiz. often pendulous, elongate (sometimes to several feet), giving rise to distant pbs. and infls., rather closely covered with brownish papery bracts. Pbs. ellipsoid-oblong, compressed, smooth, to 2″ long. often yellowish-green, subtended by a pair of lf.-like bracts. Lvs. 2–3 at apex of each pb., to 1½′ long and ½″ wide, rather leathery, linear-lanceolate, obtuse to unequally 2-lbd. at apex, folded and vaguely stalked at base. Scapes to 2″ long, usually few at once, but produced successively from the bract-axils of the flush of new growth (thus flowering 3–4 times per season). Fls. waxy, very fragrant of Narcissus, usually lasting only one day, to 2½″ across, pure white, the outside of the lip white, inside rich yellow, with

reddish-brown or reddish-purple transverse lines, the callus white with a reddish-brown or dark purple, basal blotch. Ss. and ps. wide-spreading, rather concave, acute. Lip 3-lbd., contracted and jointed at base to the col.-foot, the lat. lbs. erect, rounded, the midlb. rather folded to wide-spreading, roundish, acutish; disc with a linear-lanceolate, concave callus, the basal three-quarters of which is densely papillose. Mostly spring. (I, H) Guatemala throughout Central America to the Guianas.

M. coccinea (Jacq.) L.O.Wms. (*Epidendrum coccineum* Jacq., *Cymbidium coccineum* Sw., *Camaridium coccineum* Hoehne, *Ornithidium coccineum* Salisb.)

Rhiz. usually rather elongate, with prominent nodes. Pbs. borne at intervals along the rhiz., with prominently developed basal foliose bracts, ovoid, compressed, to 1¼″ long or more, usually bright glossy-green. Lf. solitary on pb.-apex, leathery, linear-ligulate, acutish, to 12″ long and to 1″ wide. Scapes few to many per new growth, usually produced prior to maturing of the pb., the peduncles slender, to about 2½″ tall or less. Fls. usually less than 1″ in diam., glossy, rather fleshy, pale scarlet-red or rose-red, the lip usually dark red, sometimes with a pale yellowish disc. Ss. and ps. oval, shortly acuminate, the ps. rather the shorter. Lip obscurely 3-lbd., thick-textured, rhombic-oval, with a roundish callus at the base. Summer. (I, H) West Indies; Colombia; Venezuela.

M. crassifolia (Ldl.) Rchb.f. (*Heterotaxis crassifolia* Ldl., *Epidendrum sessile* Sw., *Dicrypta Baueri* Ldl., *Dicrypta crassifolia* Ldl. ex Loud., *Maxillaria sessilis* F. & R., *Maxillaria gatunensis* Schltr.)

Pbs. very inconspicuous (often obsolete), concealed by the imbricating fleshy lf.-like bracts. Lvs., with the basal lf.-sheaths, forming a rather loose and irregular fan, very rigidly fleshy to thinly fleshy, to 1½′ long and about 2″ wide (often much smaller), linear to linear-oblong, obtuse to acute, usually dull green, grooved down the middle. Scapes usually solitary from lower lf.-axils, very short, thick. Fls. not opening fully (rarely somewhat wide-spreading), usually short-lived, fleshy, about ¾″ long, yellow to orange-yellow, the lip often purple-streaked. Ss. oblong-elliptic to broadly lanceolate, acute, the ps. linear-oblanceolate, subacute. Lip obscurely 3-lbd. above the middle, the margins sometimes slightly toothed, the lat. lbs. erect, the midlb. somewhat thickened and minutely warty; disc with a fleshy, thick keel, which is usually tomentose. Mostly late summer, but often rather sporadically throughout the year. (I, H) South Florida; West Indies; Mexico throughout Central America to Venezuela and Brazil.

M. Friedrichsthalii Rchb.f. (*Lycaste aciantha* Rchb.f., *Maxillaria aciantha* Rchb.f., *M. turialbae* Schltr., *M. rhodosticta* Krzl.)

Rhiz. usually arching, pendulous to erect, often rooting only near base. Pbs. approximate, inserted at acute angles on rhiz., elliptic-oblong, rugose, vaguely flattened, to 2″ tall, sheathed basally, the upper pair of sheaths usually lf.-like. Lvs. 2–3 (rarely 1–4), coriaceous, ligular, apically obscurely and unequally 2-lbd., 1½–7″ long, very short-petiolate below. Infls. 1–several, 1-fld., to 1½″ long, sheathed. Fls. variable in size and colour, usually hooded and not opening fully, lasting rather well, to 1¼″ long, the very heavy-textured ss. greenish-yellow to greenish-lavender, linear-lanceolate, acute to acuminate. Ps. similar but often smaller, usually greenish-yellow. Lip entire, linear-oblanceolate, obtuse to acutish, grooved down the middle, usually pale yellowish-green, sometimes marked with almost blackish-brown on the apical sides near margins, this portion conspicuously thickened; disc yellow. Mostly summer. (I, H) Mexico and British Honduras to Panama and Colombia.

M. fucata Rchb.f. (*Maxillaria Hübschii* Rchb.f.)

Pbs. clustered, narrowly ovoid-oblong, 1½–2½″ long, compressed, with acute edges. Lvs. lanceolate, usually obtuse, rather glossy and leathery, 12–18″ long and to about 2½″ broad, narrowed below into a folded petiole about one-third the length of the lamina. Infls. usually numerous at once, rather slender, to 6″ long, with prominently keeled sheathing bracts. Fls. to 2½″ across, heavy-textured, fragrant, the spreading ss. white basally, brick-red medially, tawny-yellow with some red-brown spots at apex, the dors. one ovate-oblong, subapiculate, strongly keeled behind, the lats. much larger, broadly ovate, obtuse. Ps. white basally with some brick-red lines, the apical part yellow, oblong, apiculate, reflexed apically. Lip suborbicular, vaguely lobed, thickened apically, red-brown basally, sulphur-yellow towards apex, the disc plate-like, grooved, bright yellow. Col. triangular, curving, whitish. Spring–early summer. (I) Ecuador.

M. grandiflora (HBK) Ldl. (*Dendrobium grandiflorum* HBK, *Maxillaria Amesiana* hort., *M. eburnea* Ldl., *M. Lehmanni* Rchb.f.)

Pbs. clustered, broadly ovoid-oblong, very compressed, 1½–3″ long. Lf. solitary, rather rigid but not particularly heavy-textured, ligulate, acute, 12–15″ long, 1½–2″ broad, cuneate-conduplicate at base, strongly keeled beneath. Infls. usually few at once, stout, 4–5″ long, erect or horizontal, with boat-shaped, keeled sheathing bracts. Fls. fragrant, heavy-textured, long-lasting, to about 4″ across, the ss. and ps. milk-white (rarely the ps. streaked longitudinally on basal half with rose-pink), ovate-oblong, subacute, the dors. sep. keeled behind, the ps. much smaller than ss., reflexed apically. Lip broadly oval, obscurely 3-lbd., the lat. lbs. incurved, wine-purple, streaked with lighter colour; midlb. reflexed, thickened and crisped marginally, pale buff-yellow, the disc with a grooved, thickened plate that is free at apex. Col. thick, terete, white above, yellow spotted with red on frontal surface. Mostly May–July. (I) Ecuador.

M. Houtteana Rchb.f.

Pbs. clustered on an ascending or pendulous rhiz., narrowly oblong, somewhat compressed, 1½–2″ long, with basal non-leafy sheathing bracts. Lf. solitary, rather leathery, linear-ligulate, acute, 4–6″ long. Infls. abbreviated, usually less than ½″ long, sheathed. Fls. usually about ¾″ in diam., waxy, long-lasting, variable in colour, the typical form with ss. and ps. cinnamon-brown with a narrow yellow margin, paler on reverse

sides, ligulate, acute, the ps. narrower and shorter than the ss., thrust forward over the col. Lip oblong, acute, not lobed, gently reflexed towards the apex, orange-yellow spotted with red-purple or red-brown. Col. semiterete, red spotted with yellow on frontal surface. Mostly winter–spring, but often almost ever-blooming. (I, H) Mexico; Guatemala; Nicaragua.

M. lepidota Ldl. (*Maxillaria pertusa* Rchb.f.)

Pbs. clustered, narrowly ovoid, 1–1½″ long. Lf. solitary, rather glossy and leathery, 9–12″ long, linear-lanceolate, narrowed and conduplicate towards base. Infls. erect, rather slender, to 8″ long, sheathed, the solitary fls. often nodding. Fls. to almost 5″ long when spread out, spidery, rather long-lasting, the ss. linear from a lanceolate basal portion, tail-like, the broader basal part yellow, the tails brown; ps. similar but shorter, entirely yellow. Lip oblong, acute, the lat. margins incurved, the apical half concave, reflexed, yellow spotted with black-purple, the disc with a grooved, pubescent plate. Col. yellow. Mostly May–July. (I) Colombia; Ecuador.

M. longisepala Rolfe

Pbs. clustered, ovoid or ovoid-oblong, rather compressed, 1–1½″ long. Lf. solitary, rather leathery, narrowly ligulate, acute, 6–9″ long. Infls. erect or ascending, to about 6″ long, the sheathing bracts reddish-brown. Fls. to almost 8″ long when spread out, rather long-lived, faintly fragrant, the ss. and slightly shorter ps. very narrow, acuminate, pale purple-brown faintly streaked with a darker hue. Lip ovate-oblong, obtuse or subapiculate, the margins slightly reflexed, light yellowish-green with radiating lines of dark reddish-brown on the margin. Col. pale green, curving. Mostly May–July. (I) Venezuela.

M. luteo-alba Ldl. (*Maxillaria luteo-grandiflora* hort., *M. triloris* E.Morr.)

Pbs. clustered, oblong-ovoid to elliptic-ovoid, somewhat compressed, glossy bright green, 1¼–2″ tall, the bases enveloped with several long, papery, imbricating bracts which become fibrous with age. Lf. solitary, coriaceous, glossy, linear-lanceolate to elliptic-lanceolate, acute, 8–18″ long, narrowed below into conduplicate petioles. Infls. often rather numerous, erect or ascending, 3½–6″ tall, with several papery, tubular bracts. Fls. variable in size and colour, usually long-lasting, often faintly fragrant, to more than 4″ across, the widely spreading ss. white outside and pale yellow inside, ligular, broadly obtuse. Ps. similar in colour to ss., ligular, shortly subacute, the apices incurving, smaller than ss. Lip conspicuously 3-lbd., dark yellow, margined with white, contracted at base and jointed with the col.-foot, the lat. lbs. erect in natural position, the rounded apices somewhat projecting, the midlb. ovate, obtuse, the disc with a tongue-shaped, acute callus. Mostly spring–early summer. (I) Costa Rica; Panama; Colombia; Venezuela; Ecuador.

M. marginata (Ldl.) Fenzl (*Cymbidium marginatum* Ldl., *Maxillaria deflexa* Klotzsch, *M. punctulata* Klotzsch, *M. tricolor* Ldl.)

Pbs. ovoid or ovoid-oblong, clustered, 1½–2″ long. Lf. solitary, rather glossy and leathery, linear-lanceolate,

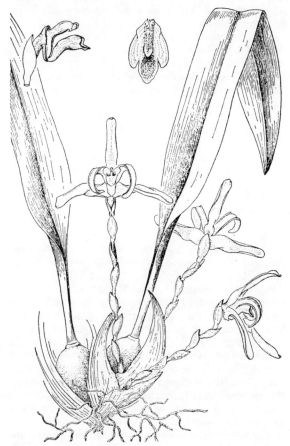

Maxillaria luteo-alba Ldl. [DOROTHY O. ALLEN]

acute, 5–8″ long. Infls. solitary or rather few per growth, 3–4″ long. Fls. about 1½″ long, the ss. thrust forward, pale orange-yellow or straw-yellow usually with a narrow dark red margin and a median red line behind, linear-oblong, acute. Ps. similar but considerably smaller. Lip 3-lbd., the lat. lbs. pale straw-yellow streaked obliquely with red-purple, oblong, erect, the midlb. oblong, acute, reflexed, pale yellow or straw-yellow; disc plate-like, fleshy, with a frontal thickening. Summer–autumn. (I, H) Brazil.

M. neglecta (Schltr.) L.O.Wms. (*Ornithidium neglectum* Schltr., *Ornithidium anceps* Rchb.f.)

Pls. highly variable in vegetative habit, erect or pendulous, the rhiz. usually elongate, branching. Pbs. inserted at an acute angle on the rhiz., the internodes and pb.-bases enveloped in imbricant, papery bracts, the pbs. ligular to roundish, strongly ancipitous to very thick and fleshy, clustered to distant, ½–1½″ long. Lf. solitary, rather leathery, ligular, acute, 2½–7″ long, basally narrowed. Infls. very short, 1-fld., produced in dense clustered fascicles from bases of mature pbs. Fls. not opening fully, about ½″ long, lasting rather well, crystalline in texture, usually with very prominent bracts. Ss. and ps. yellow or white, the lip yellow, geniculate in profile, the long narrow base continuous with the col.-base, the lamina dilated and conspicuously

3-lbd. near apex, the obliquely triangular lat. lbs. erect, with a narrow transverse callus between them, the midlb. inserted at an abruptly deflexed angle below the apices of the lat. lbs. Spring–summer. (I, H) Honduras; Nicaragua; Costa Rica; Panama.

M. picta Hk. (*Maxillaria fuscata* Klotzsch, *M. Kreysigii* Hoffmsgg., *M. leucocheile* Hoffmsgg., *M. monoceras* Klotzsch)

Pbs. clustered or borne at some intervals from each other along a creeping rhiz., ovoid, compressed, becoming furrowed with age, 2–3″ long. Lf. (or rarely 2 lvs.) rather glossy and leathery, narrowly ligulate, acute, 9–15″ long. Infls. erect, rather slender, to 8″ tall. Fls. rather heavy-textured, lasting well, to about 2½″ in diam., fragrant or not. Ss. pale tawny-yellow inside, outside whitish spotted with dull or bright purple, linear-oblong, acute, rather incurving. Ps. similar in shape and colour to ss., but with a red basal streak. Lip oblong, white marked with purple on the narrow, erect lat. lbs., the midlb. reflexed, acute, the disc with a plate-like, oblong, downy callus. Col. terete, blackish-purple. Mostly Jan.–Apr. (I, H) Brazil.

M. porphyrostele Rchb.f.

Pbs. clustered, orbicular-ovoid, compressed, to about 1¾″ tall. Lvs. usually paired, rather leathery, linear, narrowed towards base, obtuse apically, 5–8″ long. Infls. usually multiple per growth, to about 3″ tall. Fls. about 1¼″ across, pale golden-yellow with a purple stripe towards the base of the ps., rather heavy-textured and lasting very well. Ss. incurving, the dors. one linear-oblong, the lats. more lanceolate and much broader at base. Ps. shorter and narrower than the ss., ascending and incurving. Lip 3-lbd., the lat. lbs. auriculate, erect, the margins incurving; midlb. orbicular-oblong, with a rounded tip, almost flat with a tubercular callus at base. Col. slender, bright purple. Late winter–spring. (I, H) Brazil.

M. praestans Rchb.f. (*Maxillaria Kimballiana* hort.)

Pbs. clustered, broadly ovoid, rather glossy, compressed, 1½–2″ long. Lf. solitary, rather leathery, linear-oblong, emarginate, narrowed and conduplicate at base, 7–9″ long. Infls. to 5″ tall, rather ancipitous, the cauline sheaths brown, the larger floral bract inflated, green. Fls. opening rather well, long-lasting, to more than 3½″ in diam., the ss. and ps. tawny-yellow dotted with red-brown at base, narrowly oblong, acute, the dors. sep. strongly keeled at back, the ps. shorter and almost parallel to it. Lip oblong, 3-lbd., the small lat. lbs. rounded, erect, densely spotted with wine-red, the midlb. ovate-oblong, reflexed, brownish-yellow with many reddish warts; disc plate-like, grooved, whitish. Col. semiterete, yellow dotted with red. Spring. (I, H) Mexico; Guatemala.

M. punctata Lodd.

Pl. rather resembling *M. picta* Hk. Pbs. ovoid, clustered, about 1″ long. Lf. solitary, rather leathery, linear-lanceolate, acute, narrowed and conduplicate at base, 7–10″ long. Infls. erect, 3–4″ long, the peduncle pale green. Fls. about 2½″ across, light yellow, paler on the reverse sides with scattered blood-red spots and/or blotches. Ss. linear, acute, the similar ps. narrower and more acute. Lip obscurely lbd., as long as the col., reflexed at the apex, yellow with red longitudinal lines. Col. slender, semiterete, pale yellow, flushed with red at the apex. Spring–summer. (I, H) Brazil.

M. ringens Rchb.f. (*Maxillaria Amparoana* Schltr., *M. Brenesii* Schltr., *M. Rousseauae* Schltr., *M. Tuerckheimii* Schltr.)

Pbs. clustered, elliptic-ovoid, compressed, 1–2¼″ long, with several eventually fibrous sheathing basal bracts. Lf. solitary, glossy and leathery, ligular, obtuse to acute, 6–14″ long, contracted below into a more or less prominent petiole. Infls. 1–more, slender, 2–5″ tall. Fls. rather waxy, lasting well, faintly fragrant, 1–3″ in diam., highly variable in colour, the ligular, obtuse to acuminate ss. spreading, yellow, white, tan, or flushed with pink or lavender, the slightly smaller ps. white or pale yellow. Lip 3-lbd. near apex, white marked with lavender to yellow marked with maroon, contracted basally, the lat. lbs. erect, the obtuse to acute apices projecting, the fleshy midlb. more or less rough-warty on upper surface. Summer. (I, H) Mexico and British Honduras throughout Central America to Colombia and Peru.

M. rufescens Ldl. (*Maxillaria acutifolia* Ldl., *M. articulata* Klotzsch)

Pbs. clustered, ovoid, often rather 4-angled, usually faintly roughened, 1–2″ long. Lf. solitary, rather leathery, ligulate-oblong, acute, 6–8″ long. Infls. erect or horizontal, 1–2″ long, the peduncle purplish, with two dark red-brown sheathing bracts. Fls. usually not lasting well, opening widely or not, fragrant, to about 1¼″ in diam., the ligulate, acutish, spreading ss. pale or rather dark reddish-brown to pinkish-brown, the narrower and shorter ps. usually pale yellow. Lip 3-lbd., yellow spotted with dark or bright red or red-brown, the erect lat. lbs. roundish, the midlb. oblong, slightly reflexed, with the thickened plate-like callus buff-yellow. Col. 3-angled, reddish-brown. Usually early winter, but sometimes more than once annually. (I, H) Cuba and Jamaica, and Guatemala throughout the West Indies and Central America to Brazil, the Guianas, and Peru.

M. Sanderiana Rchb.f.

Probably the finest member of the genus. Pbs. clustered, ovoid, compressed with rather sharp edges, to 2″ long and more. Lf. solitary, narrowly oblong, acute, rather thinly leathery, petioled at base, 7–12″ long. Infls. decumbent or ascending, 5–6″ long, furnished with several sheathing bracts. Fls. 5–6″ in diam., fragrant, rather long-lasting, the ss. ovate-oblong, apiculate, the lats. broader at base than the dors. one (this keeled behind), ivory-white, the dors. one spotted with dark blood-red at the base, the lats. heavily blotched and spotted with blood-red to beyond the middle. Ps. erect, slightly recurving at tips, similar to the lat. ss. and coloured like them, but smaller. Lip fleshy, ovate, 3-lbd., ivory-white with some dark blood-red stains on the lat. lbs., these rounded and incurving; midlb.-margins revolute, crisped, the callus tongue-shaped. Col. 3-angled, dark blood-red above, white spotted with red-purple below the stigmatic surface. Mostly Aug.–Oct. (I) Ecuador, at rather high elevations.

M. setigera Ldl. (*Maxillaria callichroma* Rchb.f., *M. leptosepala* Hk.)

Pbs. clustered, roundish to roundish-ovoid, compressed, 1–1½″ long. Lf. solitary, short-petioled at base, rather leathery, elliptic-oblong, acutish, 6–12″ long. Infls. 3–4″ long, sheathed by alternate and distichous, slightly inflated bracts that are greenish spotted with red. Fls. fragrant, to more than 4″ in diam., the linear, acuminate ss. basally milk-white, apically pale yellow, the ps. similar but smaller and thrust forwards. Lip 3-lbd., the lat. lbs. oblong, incurving, white streaked with purple on the inner side; midlb. oblong, marginally toothed, reflexed, white with a bright yellow, oblong, hairy disc. Col. 3-angled, curving, white above, purple below the stigmatic surface. Mostly summer–autumn. (I, H) Colombia; Venezuela.

M. tenuifolia Ldl.

Rhiz. ascending, usually rooting only near base, sheathed by pale brown or reddish-brown imbricating scales, the pbs. produced at intervals of about 1″, ovoid, compressed, smooth, to about 1″ long. Lf. dark green, linear, acuminate, 12–15″ long, with a depressed median line on the face. Infls. often numerous per growth, to 2″ long. Fls. very heavy-textured, highly fragrant of coconut, 1½–2″ in diam., somewhat variable in colour, usually the ss. and ps. dark red speckled and mottled with pale or dark yellow, the ss. ovate-lanceolate, margins revolute, the ps. similar but shorter, erect and parallel to the col., the tips sometimes flaring outward. Lip oblong, obtuse, reflexed at apex, concave and dark rich blood-red to beyond the middle, the apical part dark yellow with leopard-like red-purple or red-brown spots and blotches; disc with an oblong, pubescent, plate-like callus. Col. clavate, pale yellow above, spotted with dark red in front. Mostly summer–autumn. (I, H) Mexico; British Honduras; Guatemala; Honduras; Nicaragua; ? Costa Rica.

M. variabilis Batem. ex Ldl. (*Maxillaria angustifolia* Hk., *M. chiriquensis* Schltr., *M. Henchmanni* Hk., *M. Lyoni* Ldl., *M. revoluta* Kl.)

Rhiz. erect or pendulous, usually simple, 2–12″ long. Pbs. linear to elliptic-oblong, subcylindric to strongly ancipitous, usually rugose, ½–2½″ long, clustered and inserted at an acute angle on the rhiz., apically truncate, the bases and internodes of rhiz. heavily covered with imbricating, papery bracts. Lf. solitary, coriaceous, ligular, obtuse to 2-lbd. at apex, 1¼–6″ long, contracted into short petioles below. Infls. slender, abbreviated, produced from bract-axils of flush of new growth, or sometimes from base of current mature pbs. Fls. rather heavy-textured, lasting well, to about ¾″ in diam., extremely variable in colour, varying from white or yellow marked with dark red, or with a red lip, or entirely dark red or red-brown. Ss. rather spreading, linear-lanceolate, obtuse or acutish, the ps. smaller, acute, their tips usually reflexed. Lip entirely or vaguely 3-lbd. near apex, the base jointed to col.-foot, the lat. margins rounded and erect, the midlb. subacute to truncate and slightly emarginate, the disc with a ligular, obtuse callus about equalling the lat. lbs. Throughout the year, often almost ever-blooming. (I, H) Mexico and British Honduras throughout Central America to Venezuela and the Guianas.

M. venusta Ldl. ex Rchb.f. (*Maxillaria anatomorum* Rchb.f., *M. Kalbreyeri* Rchb.f.)

Pbs. clustered, oval-oblong, very compressed, 2–3″ long, glossy. Lf. solitary, rather leathery, oblong-lanceolate, acute, 12–15″ long, with a short basal petiole. Infls. nodding or horizontal, 6–12″ long, with large sheathing bracts. Fls. fragrant, waxy, long-lasting, 5–6″ in diam., the white ss. and ps. lanceolate, acuminate, the ss. spreading, the much shorter ps. almost parallel to the col. Lip much shorter than the other segms., fleshy, the upper surface buff-yellow, the lower surface cream-white with scattered red spots, 3-lbd., the lat. lbs. roundish-oblong, the midlb. ovate, obtuse, reflexed, fuzzy, the callus on the disc oblong, plate-like, almost flat. Col. clavate, 3-angled, whitish. Mostly Sept.–Nov. (I) Colombia; Venezuela, at moderately high elevations.

M. acicularis Herb. Pbs. clustered, oblong, furrowed with age, to about 1″ tall. Lvs. paired, awl-shaped, acutish, the longitudinal furrow down the face open, to 3″ long, rather rigid. Infls. very abbreviated. Fls. about ½″ in diam., fragrant or not, glossy dark wine-red. Ss. and ps. oblong, slightly acutish, the ps. thrust forward over the col. Lip obscurely 3-lbd., dark lustrous purple or wine-purple. Col. yellowish. Autumn–early winter. (I, H) Brazil.

M. arachnites Rchb.f. Simulating *M. lepidota* Ldl. in habit, but more compact and robust and with somewhat smaller fls. Fls. about 4″ in diam., fragrant, the ss. and ps. yellow, the ps. rather smaller than the ss., thrust forward and with recurving tips. Lip dark yellow, striped and margined with purple. Spring. (I) Colombia.

M. cerifera (B.-R.) Schltr. (*Ornithidium ceriferum* B.-R.) Rhiz. elongate, the pbs. rather distant from one another, the internodes heavily clothed with sheathing brownish papery bracts. Pbs. oblong, somewhat compressed, about 1″ long. Lvs. paired, linear, obtuse, about 1½″ long, heavy-textured. Infls. erect, slightly exceeding the lvs. in length. Fls. fragrant, to about ½″ in diam., greenish-white, the lip white. Ss. and ps. ligulate, acute. Lip small, oblong, the margins prominently thickened and very waxy in texture. Autumn. (I, H) Brazil.

M. crocea Poepp. Pbs. clustered, ovoid, to 2″ tall. Lf. solitary, rather leathery, ligulate, obtuse, to 6″ long and 1″ wide. Infls. usually multiple per growth, sheathed, to 5″ tall, erect or ascending. Fls. fragrant, long-lasting, to about 2½″ in diam., the ss. and somewhat shorter ps. yellow, reflexed. Lip obscurely lobulate, brown-red, obtuse, shorter than the ps. Late summer–autumn. (I, H) Brazil.

M. cucullata Ldl. (*Maxillaria Lindeniana* A.Rich. & Gal., *M. meleagris* Ldl., *M. obscura* Lind. & Rchb.f., *M. puncto-striata* Rchb.f.) Pbs. usually densely clustered, ovoid to almost rhomboid, usually shiny, to almost 2″ long, somewhat or very compressed, subtended by several prominent, imbricating, long sheaths. Lf. solitary, linear, obtuse or rounded apically, usually rigid, to 15″ long and mostly less than ½″ wide. Infls. from bract-axils of pbs., usually multiple per growth, variable in length but usually short. Fls not opening fully, to 1¾″ in diam., varying from yellowish to almost black-red, usually variously striped and spotted with dark red-brown or maroon, the segms. rather thick and rigid. Lip more or less 3-lbd. about the middle, the lat. lbs. usually triangular, the disc with a grooved spatulate callus on the basal portion. Autumn–

early winter. (I, H) Mexico; British Honduras; Guatemala; Honduras; Nicaragua; Costa Rica; Panama.

M. densa Ldl. (*Ornithidium densum* Rchb.f.) Rhiz. elongate, the pbs. more or less densely clustered on it, covered with imbricating brown or reddish-brown sheathing bracts, usually rooting only near base. Pbs. often yellow-green, ellipsoid-oblong to ovoid-oblong, glossy, compressed-ancipitous, to 3″ long. Lf. solitary, olive-green or yellowish-green, glossy and rather leathery, linear to lanceolate or oblanceolate, obtuse, to 15″ long and almost 2″ wide. Infls. composed of dense fascicles of 1-fld. peduncles in axils of sheaths of new growths. Fls. about ½″ long, hooded, varying in colour from greenish-white and yellowish, white with a purplish tinge, to dark maroon or reddish-brown. Lip 3-lbd., the lat. lbs. rounded, ear-like, upcurving to clasp the col. and to form with the concave plate-like callus a deeply concave base to the lip. Mostly late winter–spring. (I, H) Mexico; British Honduras; Guatemala; Honduras.

M. Fletcheriana Rolfe. Allied to *M. fucata* Rchb.f. and rather similar to it, but much more robust and with fls. of different colour. Pbs. ovoid-oblong, somewhat compressed, about 1½″ long, with 2 basal lf.-like bracts and a single apical one. Lf. stalked basally, oblong or elliptic-oblong, somewhat acuminate, to 8″ long. Infls. to more than 12″ tall, erect or ascending, sheathed. Fls. about 3½″ in diam., fragrant, long-lasting, the ss. white with a prominent purple median line, the ps. similar with several purple lines, the lip yellow, purple-spotted apically, the disc yellow and the lat. lbs. flushed and lined with red-purple. Spring. (I) Peru.

M. Fuerstenbergiana Schltr. Pbs. oval, somewhat compressed, to 2½″ tall. Lf. solitary, ligulate, acutish, rather leathery and glossy, to almost 12″ long. Infls. usually numerous per growth, sheathed, to about 5″ long. Fls. fragrant, long-lasting, rather waxy, to about 4″ across, the ss. wide-spreading, white with a pale orange-yellow apical half, the ps. white, thrust forward over the lip. Lip shortly 3-lbd., whitish, the apex somewhat reflexed. Spring–summer. (I) Colombia.

M. nigrescens Ldl. (*Maxillaria rubro-fusca* Kl.) Pbs. clustered, compressed, roundish, to 2″ tall. Lf. solitary, ligulate, obtuse, to 12″ long. Infls. erect, about 3″ tall. Fls. about 4″ across, very dark purple, sometimes almost black-purple, the lip dark brown-purple. Ss. and ps. linear, obtuse, the ps. the smaller. Lip oblong, obtuse, much shorter than the ps. Col. dark purple, with a white anther. Summer–autumn. (I) Venezuela.

M. Parkeri (Spreng.) Hk. (*Colax Parkeri* Spreng., *Menadena Parkeri* Raf.) Pbs. clustered, ovoid, rather glossy, to 2″ tall. Lf. solitary, ligulate, acutish, to 12″ long and 2″ broad. Infls. erect, sheathed, to 2″ tall. Fls. about 2″ in diam., rather heavy-textured and lasting well, the ss. pale brownish, the ps. whitish, the lip yellowish with violet-purple-marked lat. lbs., the midlb. white marginally, yellow in the middle. Ss. and ps. oblong, rather obtuse. Lip 3-lbd., the lat. lbs. obtuse, the midlb. oval, obtuse, rather undulate. Spring–summer. (H) Guianas; Northern Brazil.

M. pumila Hk. Pbs. clustered, oblong, furrowed with age, to about ½″ long. Lf. solitary, oblong, obtuse, less than 1″ long. Infls. about ¼″ long, erect, sheathed. Fls. about ¼″ long, hooded, dirty dark violet or dark brownish-violet, the lip very dark purple-violet. Ss. and ps. oblong, obtuse. Lip 3-lbd., the lat. lbs. short, the midlb. emarginate. Spring. (H) Guianas.

M. Sophronitis (Rchb.f.) Garay (*Ornithidium Sophronitis* Rchb.f.) Dwarf, creeping pls., the pbs. some distance apart on the rhiz., oval, about ¾″ long. Lvs. usually paired, about 1″ long, oblong, obtuse, rather fleshy. Infls. about 1½″ tall. Fls. less than 1″ in diam., light scarlet-red, the lip golden-yellow. Ss. and ps. oval, acutish, the ps. rather shorter and blunter than other segms. Lip sharply reflexed, the claw rather broad. Spring–autumn. (I) Venezuela.

M. striata Rolfe. Pbs. clustered, oblong-ovoid, to 3″ long. Lf. solitary, narrowly oblong, obtuse, to 1½′ long, petioled basally. Infls. to about 12″ tall, sheathed, erect or ascending. Fls. to almost 5″ in diam., the ss. and ps. yellow with numerous brown longitudinal stripes, the lip white with red veins. Ss. triangular-lanceolate, obtuse. Ps. somewhat shorter than ss., the tips usually yellowish without stripes. Lip obscurely 3-lbd., the midlb. plicate. Late summer–autumn. (I, H) Peru.

M. uncata Ldl. (*Maxillaria Macleei* Batem. ex Ldl., *M. stenostele* Schltr.) Rhiz. erect or pendulous, usually profusely branching and forming dense succulent masses, 1½–14″ long. Pbs. tiny, usually terete, mostly under ½″ long, clustered to rather distant, obliquely inserted on rhiz., enveloped in brown, imbricating, papery sheaths, as are the rhiz.-internodes. Lf. solitary, fleshy, subulate-conduplicate, usually semiterete, ¾–2½″ long, dark green. Infls. short, produced from base of current new growth, to ¾″ long. Fls. translucent, hooded, about ¼″ long, with red, purple or brown stripes. Mostly winter, but at other times of year as well. (I, H) British Honduras and Guatemala to the Guianas, Brazil, and Peru.

M. Valenzuelana (A.Rich.) Nash (*Dicrypta iridifolia* Batem., *Pleurothallis Valenzuelana* A.Rich., *Maxillaria iridifolia* Rchb.f.) Pendulous pls., without pbs., the lvs. distichously arranged in the form of a broad fan, rather fleshy, gladiate, lanceolate, acuminate, usually powdery bluish-green, 3½–12″ long, the broad conduplicate bases closely imbricating. Infls. abbreviated, borne from axils of lvs. near base, usually on side next to the host-tree. Fls. not opening fully, fleshy, to about 1″ across when spread out, the ss. and ps. yellow, the lip entire or vaguely 3-lbd., yellow with more or less definite purple or maroon markings. Summer. (I) Cuba; Honduras and Costa Rica to Colombia, Venezuela, and Brazil.

M. vestita (Sw.) Hoehne (*Epidendrum vestitum* Sw., *Cymbidium vestitum* Sw., *Ornithidium vestitum* Rchb.f.) Rhiz. decumbent or pendulous, branching, closely covered with brownish, papery, imbricating bracts, to more than 12″ long. Pbs. borne at intervals, oblong-ellipsoidal, compressed, to 1¼″ long. Lf. solitary, lanceolate-ligulate, apically acute or obtuse, to 8″ long, rather leathery. Infls. fasciculate in bract-axils just below each pb., abbreviated, strongly sheathed. Fls. not opening widely, about ¼″ long, yellowish or greenish-yellow, sometimes flushed with tan or pale brownish, the clawed lip broadly 3-lbd., the lat. lbs. rounded, the midlb. larger, thickened at the apex. Autumn–spring. (I, H) Cuba; Jamaica; Venezuela; Guianas; Brazil; Peru.

MEDIOCALCAR J.J.Sm.

Mediocalcar is a genus of about twenty species of mostly epiphytic orchids, native primarily in New Guinea, but with outlying representatives in the Moluccas and adjacent insular areas. A rather aberrant member of the subtribe *Glomerinae*, its components are very odd and unusually interesting orchids, often with strange balloon-shaped, usually red blossoms. Although of considerable potential interest to connoisseurs, as yet the Mediocalcars do not appear to be present in our collections. In New Guinea, some of them are very common in the high-elevation 'cloud forests'.

Nothing is known of the genetic affinities of this peculiar group.

CULTURE: Presumably as for the epiphytic kinds of *Bulbophyllum*. (C, I)

MEGALORCHIS Perr.

Megalorchis regalis (Schltr.) Perr. (*Habenaria regalis* Schltr.) is the only species detected to date in this little-known and very rare genus. A member of the subtribe *Habenarinae*, it is placed by H. Perrier de la Bâthie between *Habenaria* Willd. and *Platycoryne* Rchb.f., differing from both of them in structural details of the very large, pure white flowers. It is a showy plant, a terrestrial endemic to Madagascar, which has not as yet been introduced into our collections.

Nothing is known of the genetic affinities of *Megalorchis*.

CULTURE: Presumably as for the tropical Habenarias, Disas, etc. (H)

MEGASTYLIS Schltr.

Megastylis is the sole genus comprising the subtribe *Megastylidinae*, generally placed in alliance with the *Cryptostylidinae*. The eight or so species comprising this terrestrial group, native for the most part in New Caledonia, are very robust, multiflorous orchids of no particular beauty, though they are of considerable botanical interest. None of them have made their appearance in our collections as yet.

Nothing is known of the genetic affinities of *Megastylis*.

CULTURE: Presumably as for the tropical species of *Phaius*. (H)

MEIRACYLLIUM Rchb.f.

This is a genus of two species of very dwarf epiphytic or lithophytic orchids, native in Mexico, El Salvador, and Guatemala, somewhat allied to *Homalopetalum* Rolfe and certain other members of the subtribe *Laeliinae*. They are today virtually unknown in our collections, although both of them are charming little plants with delicate but singularly showy blossoms. Their cultural requirements are readily met, and they scarcely ever fail to produce their flowers in season with remarkable abundance.

No hybrids are known as yet for *Meiracyllium*, which is presumably compatible genetically with at least some other members of the *Laeliinae*. Some unusual and doubtless attractive intergeneric hybrids are potentially available through critical experimental breeding.

CULTURE: Meiracylliums are best grown on flat rafts or slabs of tree-fern fibre or osmunda, once their root-systems are well-established, so that the creeping rhizomes may extend in all directions, as is their natural inclination. Newly imported speciments may conveniently be started in well-sifted, shallow, well-drained pots filled with shredded tree-fern fibre and chopped sphagnum moss. Their general cultural requirements are those of the tropical Cattleyas and Epidendrums. Frequent disturbance or division should be strenuously avoided. (I, H)

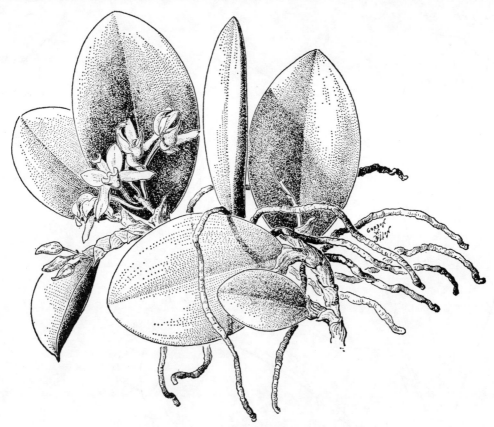

Meiracyllium trinasutum Rchb.f. [GORDON W. DILLON]

M. trinasutum Rchb.f.

Rhiz. elongate, creeping, covered with tubular scarious sheaths. Secondary sts. minute, produced at intervals from the rhiz., 1-lvd., usually covered by sheaths. Lf. stalkless, almost roundish to elliptic-obovate, rounded or obtuse at apex, rigidly fleshy, to 2″ long and 1¼″ wide, often flushed with purplish. Infls. short, 1–6-fld., at apex of secondary sts. Fls. opening rather well, about 1″ across at most, red-purple, the lip often darker. Dors. sep. ovate-elliptic, acute to shortly acuminate; lat. ss. broadly and obliquely triangular-ovate, obliquely acuminate and recurved at apex. Ps. obliquely elliptic, acute. Lip sessile, fleshy, saccate-cucullate, acuminate, with small ears on the lateral basal margins. Col. short, stout, triangular. Spring. (I, H) Mexico: Chiapas; Guatemala.

M. Wendlandi Rchb.f. (*Meiracyllium gemma* Rchb.f.)

Rather similar to *M. trinasutum* Rchb.f. in habit, but usually slightly more robust, differing in the linear-oblanceolate ps., the scoop-shaped lip, and the slender-based col., as well as other characters. Sheaths of the rhiz. usually brownish. Infls. longer than the other sp., few-fld., to 1½″ long. Fls. to more than 1″ across, purple, yellowish at the base. Spring. (I, H) Mexico; Guatemala; El Salvador.

MENADENIUM Raf.

Four species of *Menadenium* are known at this time, all of them exceptionally rare and handsome epiphytic orchids native in Venezuela, the Guianas, and northern Brazil. The genus is rather closely allied to *Zygopetalum* Hk., but differs from it in technical details of the large, showy flowers. Apparently very scarce in their native haunts, the Menadeniums are today little-known by collectors, although the following species is present in a few particularly comprehensive assemblages of choice orchidaceous plants.

No hybrids have as yet been made which utilize the Menadeniums, although it seems highly logical to assume that they will prove genetically compatible with *Zygopetalum*, and doubtless with other orchid groups of this alliance. Some most intriguing potentialities seem evident in this respect, and they should be explored by enterprising breeders.

CULTURE: Generally as for *Zygopetalum*, although the plants are truly epiphytic in habit, and no soil should be added to the compost, as is often suggested for the semi-terrestrial or terrestrial members of that group. Because of the often elongate rhizomes, the Menadeniums do best in slatted baskets or shallow fern-pans. Warm, humid conditions must prevail at all times for best results, although a brief rest-period (of about two weeks' duration) may with benefit be given after flowering. (H)

M. labiosum (L.C.Rich.) Cgn. (*Epidendrum labiosum* L.C.Rich., *Zygopetalum rostratum* Hk., *Zygosepalum rostratum* Rchb.f., *Menadenium rostratum* Raf.)

Rhiz. more or less elongate, often branching and

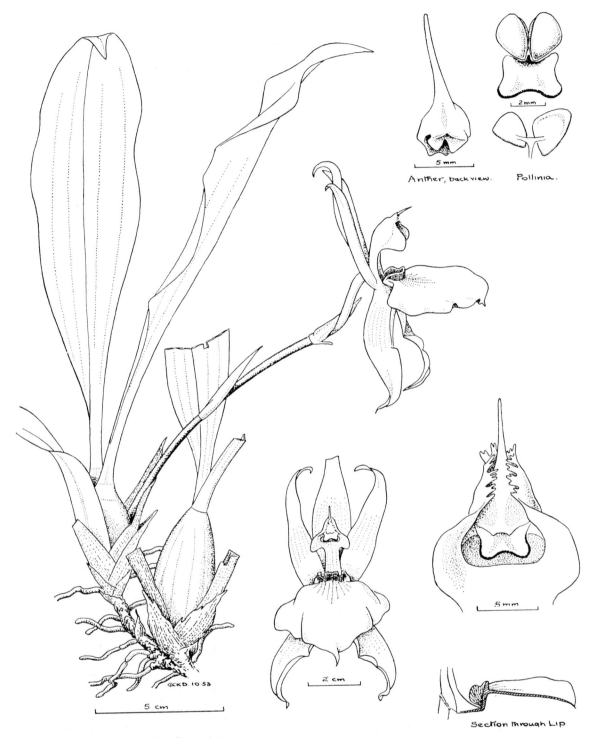

Anther, back view.   Pollinia.

Section through Lip

GCKD. 10·53

5 cm

2 cm

5 mm

Menadenium labiosum (L.C.Rich.) Cgn. [G.C.K. DUNSTERVILLE]

forming large masses. Pbs. borne at rather distant intervals, ovoid-oblong, rather compressed laterally, becoming shrivelled with age, with several basal lf.-like bracts, to 1½″ tall. Lvs. 1–2, usually bright glossy green, rather herbaceous, ligular-lanceolate, acuminate, strongly 5–7-nerved, basally narrowed and almost stalked, to 10″ long and 1½″ broad. Infls. usually shorter than the lvs., erect or ascending, stout, 1–3-fld., the fls. usually open simultaneously. Fls. large and handsome, fragrant, heavy-textured, long-lived, to 4″ long, somewhat variable in colour, usually greenish-yellow more or less suffused with greyish or pinkish, the large lip white

296

with a violet or dark red callus and branching veins from the base, the winged col. usually marked with pale violet veins on its anterior face. Ss. and ps. spreading, usually somewhat reflexed towards tips, narrowly lanceolate, long-acuminate, undulate marginally, somewhat concave. Lip with a thickened basal part, the lamina oval-cordate, slightly toothed on upper margins, the apex acute or abruptly apiculate, the basal callus semicircular, fleshy. Col. with 2 antenna-like prolongations on the clinandrium (as in the male flowers of many Catasetums). Spring–early summer. (H) Venezuela; Guianas; Northern Brazil.

MENDONSELLA A.D.Hawkes
(*Galeottia* A.Rich.)

A genus of three known species, *Mendonsella* is a rare group in contemporary collections, but all of the members are well deserving of attention by the specialist, for their unusual large and flamboyant flowers of great lasting qualities. The genus has been reduced to synonymy under *Zygopetalum* Hk. in the past, but we feel that floral characters warrant its retention as distinct. *Mendonsella* is a new name which has been proposed for the old *Galeottia* of Achille Richard, which was a homonymic epithet.[1] The species range from Mexico and British Honduras to Brazil, and are apparently nowhere frequent in the wild state. All are epiphytic in habit, with more or less prominent pseudobulbs, large folded leaves, and erect inflorescences from the pseudobulb-bases which bear one or more large and highly spectacular blossoms of very intricate structure.

No hybrids have as yet been produced in *Mendonsella*, but it seems to offer some intriguing possibilities to the experimental breeder, since it should, conceivably, prove genetically compatible with such groups as *Zygopetalum*, *Lycaste*, *Aganisia*, *Anguloa*, and several others.

CULTURE: *Mendonsella grandiflora* does best in our collections if kept in well-drained pots, rather tightly filled with osmunda or tree-fern fibre. The plants delight in copious quantities of water while in active growth, but upon completion of the new pseudobulbs should be dried out to a degree until root-action once again commences. The flower-spikes arise from a lower axil of the expanding new shoot, and water must be gradually increased as these appear. A semi-shaded spot suits them best, and like most members of this alliance, they benefit materially by liberal applications of fertilizer when growing well. They are extremely intolerant of stale conditions at the roots, and should be repotted into fresh medium on an average of every two years. This species occurs at rather high elevations (6000 feet in Panama), hence benefits by intermediate, humid temperatures. (I)

M. grandiflora (A.Rich.) A.D.Hawkes (*Galeottia grandiflora* A.Rich., *Batemania grandiflora* Rchb.f., *Zygopetalum grandiflorum* Bth. & Hk.f.)
Pbs. clustered, ovoid, to 3″ long and 1″ in diam., sheathed basally. Lvs. paired, rather heavy, folded, to

[1] See 'The Genus *Mendonsella*', by Alex D. Hawkes, in *Orquidea*. 25:7. 1963.

1½′ long and almost 3″ broad, almost elliptic to lanceolate, abruptly acuminate. Infls. one or more from base of expanding new growth, 2- to several-fld., to 8″ tall, the scape furnished with large inflated sheaths. Fls. to about 3½″ across, fragrant, waxy, long-lived. Ss. and ps. yellowish-green with 5–7 broad red-brown stripes, lanceolate, acuminate, rather curled near the tips. Lip white with longitudinal red streaks, 3-lbd., toothed marginally, very complex, with intricate keels near base. Col. broad and tall, white to pale yellow, with fine red streaks, with small apical wings. Mostly spring–summer. (I) Mexico; British Honduras; Guatemala; Costa Rica; Panama; Colombia.

MESOSPINIDIUM Rchb.f.

This is a genus of four known species of very rare and incompletely known epiphytic orchids, native in Nicaragua, Costa Rica, Panama, and the Andes of northwestern South America. A member of the subtribe *Oncidiinae*, the genus superficially resembles *Brassia* R.Br. in vegetative appearance, while the small flowers are reminiscent of certain Oncidiums, from which group they differ in technical structural details. None of the Mesospinidiums appears to be in our collections at this time.

Nothing is known of the genetic affinities of this odd genus.

CULTURE: Presumably as for the high- and medium-elevation Odontoglossums, depending upon the place of origin of the individual specimen. (C, I)

MICROCOELIA Ldl.
(*Dicranotaenia* Finet, *Gussonaea* A.Rich., *Microcaelia* Hochst. ex A.Rich.)

The remarkable genus *Microcoelia* contains about twenty-five species of epiphytic orchids in tropical Africa, only one of which has to date been introduced into general cultivation, and this on very rare occasions. Singularly interesting and attractive even when not in bloom, they belong to that incredible group of the subtribe *Sarcanthinae* in which the plants are, when mature, totally leafless, being reduced to a cluster of fleshy roots, surrounding a typically minute woody stem, from which the often numerous flower-spikes arise. In this genus the blossoms are bell-shaped and small, but are frequently produced with such profusion that they form a most striking specimen.

Nothing is known of the genetic affinities of *Microcoelia*.

CULTURE: As for *Polyrrhiza*, and other aphyllous epiphytic orchids. (H)

M. Guyoniana (Rchb.f.) Summerh. (*Angraecum Guyonianum* Rchb.f., *Gussonaea globulosa* Ridl.)
Sts. woody, 1–2½″ long. Roots very numerous, wiry, 8–10″ long, dull or bright grey, greenish-grey when wet. Infls. erect, 2–3½″ long, many-fld. Fls. about ¼″ long, bell-shaped, odourless, pure white. Lip slightly longer than other segms., with a spur as long as the lip which curves forward beneath it. Jan.–Mar. (I, H) Eritrea to Northern Rhodesia (& Natal?), across to Belgian Congo and Angola.

M. physophora (Rchb.f.) Summerh. (*Angraecum physo-phorum* Rchb.f., *Gussonaea physophora* Ridl.)

Roots numerous, flattened, to $\frac{3}{16}''$ wide, elongate. Infls. short, 7–15-fld., the rachis flexuous. Fls. very small, white, the lip with a rather lengthy spur. Autumn–winter. (H) Zanzibar; Madagascar.

MICROSACCUS Bl.

Microsaccus is a genus of about five species of rather small epiphytic sarcanthads, native in the region extending from Thailand throughout the Malay Peninsula to Borneo and Java. All are present in a very few choice collections today, but must be classed as singularly rare orchids. Unusual and attractive vegetatively, they are of botanical interest for the structure of the small, typically paired, white flowers. The foliage rather simulates that of many Dendrobiums of the § *Aporum*, being laterally compressed and equitant. The genus is rather vaguely allied to *Adenoncos* Bl. and to *Taeniophyllum* Bl.

No hybrids are known which utilize members of the genus *Microsaccus*, and nothing has been ascertained concerning its genetic affinities.

CULTURE: As for the tropical species of *Vanda*. The dwarf plants do best in smallish, well-drained pots, rather tightly filled with compost. They must never be permitted to dry out at any time. (H)

M. ampullaceus J.J.Sm.

Sts. to 6″ long, to almost 1″ wide (including the lvs.). Lvs. acute, to about $\frac{1}{4}''$ wide. Fls. less than $\frac{1}{4}''$ long, white, the ss. spreading, the ps. wider than the ss. Lip with a transversely compressed spur, in all less than $\frac{1}{4}''$ long, the blade rather narrow, the spur broadened. Summer. (H) Malay Peninsula; Sumatra.

M. brevifolius J.J.Sm.

Sts. to about 4″ long, about $\frac{1}{2}''$ wide (including lvs.). Lvs. very close together, fleshy, with blunt tips, to about $\frac{1}{8}''$ wide. Fls. paired, on very short peduncles, less than $\frac{1}{4}''$ across, white. Lat. ss. not widely spreading. Lip with the blade longer than the spur. Summer. (H) Thailand; Malay Peninsula; Sumatra; Java.

M. javensis Bl. Rather similar in vegetative habit to *M. ampullaceus* J.J.Sm., often with the lvs. more regularly spaced and more horizontal in arrangement. Fls. white, similar to the other sp. in dimensions, but with the ss. and ps. of equal width (rather than the ps. the wider), and the blade of the lip not much narrower than the spur (rather than much narrower). Summer. (H) Malay Peninsula; Java.

M. sumatrana J.J.Sm. Sts. to almost 5″ long, to more than 1″ wide (including the lvs.). Lvs. spreading, the tip narrowed but not sharp-pointed. Fls. white, the lip with a green blotch on the blade, the ss. spreading. Summer. (H) Malay Peninsula; Sumatra.

M. truncatus Carr. Sts. to about 5″ long, the lvs. less than $\frac{1}{2}''$ long, narrowed slightly to a blunt apex. Fls. white with a yellow-green spot on the lip, the ss. scarcely spreading, the spur cylindric. Summer. (H) Malay Peninsula.

MICROTATORCHIS Schltr.

Allied to *Geissanthera* Schltr. and to *Taeniophyllum* Bl., this genus contains upwards of twenty species of predominantly leafless, dwarf epiphytic orchids, native principally in the high, cloud-hung mountain forests of New Guinea. They are extremely complex in structure, and of great interest botanically, but are unknown in our collections at this time, due largely to their unavailability.

Nothing is known of the genetic affinities of *Microtatorchis*.

CULTURE: Depending upon their vegetative appearance (whether aphyllous or with leaves), as for *Polyrrhiza*, and *Ornithocephalus*. (C, I)

Microtatorchis clavicalcarata J.J.Sm. [A.D.HAWKES, AFTER J.J.SMITH]

MICROTIS R.Br.

The genus *Microtis*, a member of the subtribe *Prasophyllinae*, contains about twelve species of rather slender, not particularly attractive terrestrial orchids, the range of which extends from China and the Philippines throughout Indonesia to Australia, New Zealand, and New Caledonia. Like so many of the terrestrial groups of the Orchidaceae, these plants are virtually absent from contemporary collections, though they offer much of interest to the connoisseur. *Microtis* contains plants with globular, subterranean tubers, from which arise erect stems—bearing a solitary cylindrical leaf near the middle—with a terminal, usually dense spike of numerous small green or white, intricate flowers. The dorsal sepal of these blossoms is rather hooded, while the lanceolate to oblong lateral sepals are either spreading or reflexed. The narrower petals are spreading or incurved, while the stalkless lip is simple, blunt at the apex, and bears some raised calli on the upper surface.

No hybrids are known in *Microtis*, and nothing has been ascertained concerning its genetic affinities.

CULTURE: As for *Caladenia*. (C, I)

M. oblonga R.S.Rog. (*Microtis parviflora* Fitzg. not R.Br.)

Variable in habit, from very dwarf to almost $1\frac{1}{2}'$ tall. Lf.-lamina often greatly exceeding the spike in length. Infl. 2–9″ long, usually not very dense. Fls. less than $\frac{1}{4}''$ across, on very slender pedicellate ovaries, usually very pale green, fragrant. Dors. sep. narrow, acute, only slightly hooded; lat. ss. tightly revolute. Ps. narrowly falcate. Lip narrow-oblong, deflexed, with crenulate margins, the disc with several calli. Autumn–winter. (C, I) Australia.

MILTONIA Ldl.
(*Macrochilus* Kn. & Westc.)

About twenty species of *Miltonia*, plus several natural hybrids, are now known to science. These are primarily epiphytic (rarely lithophytic) orchids, widespread in their distribution from Costa Rica and Panama through the Andes to Brazil; centres of development occur in the Colombian and Ecuadorean mountains, and in meridional Brazil. The genus is a member of the subtribe *Oncidiinae*, and is closely allied to *Odontoglossum* HBK, *Oncidium* Sw., and *Brassia* R.Br., from which groups its components differ in often rather tenuous technical floral characters. The genus consists of two basic cultural groups, those from the high elevations being extremely popular with collectors (and being called, as an aggregation, 'Pansy Orchids', because of their handsome large flowers, which often remarkably simulate members of the genus *Viola*), while the warmer-growing, mostly Brazilian species are only recently making their appearance as common inhabitants of our greenhouses. Miltonias vary considerably in all parts—both vegetatively and florally—but in general they bear prominent pseudobulbs and several flexible, rather thin-textured leaves. The flowers are borne singly or in multi-florous racemes from the bases of the most recently-formed pseudobulbs, and in the Andean species are usually white or pinkish, often with median blotches or markings of vivid crimson or magenta, while in the Brazilian members of the group they rather simulate (for the most part) certain kinds of Odontoglossums, with stellate segments, these coloured yellow or greenish, more or less barred or otherwise marked with brown, purple, or magenta-red.

A tremendous number of very complex hybrids have been registered within the genus *Miltonia*, mostly among the relatively few species which inhabit high elevations in the Andes of South America; a few hybrids are also on record which incorporate the handsome Brazilian members of the group. *Miltonia* is apparently freely compatible with most other components of the subtribe *Oncidiinae*, and now we have a wide array of often exceptionally beautiful and floriferous hybrids with *Oncidium* (= *Miltonidium*), *Odontoglossum* (= *Odontonia*), *Cochlioda* (= *Miltonioda*), and more recent, *Brassia* (= *Miltassia*), *Aspasia* (= *Milpasia*), and oddly enough, *Trichopilia* (= *Milpilia*). Considerable additional experimental breeding yet remains to be done with the Miltonias, particularly in the realm of the lesser-known genera of the subtribe to which it belongs.

CULTURE: Since Miltonias occur from sea-level to very high in the chilly mountains of the Andes, two differing sets of cultural conditions are required for these orchids. Those from Brazil and other warm areas do very well when grown in the manner afforded the pseudobulbous, tropical Oncidiums, although since more of them have relatively elongate creeping rhizomes, they are best contained in baskets or fern-pans rather

than in the customary clay pots used for the majority of orchids. Those from high elevations do best in proportionately small, perfectly-drained pots, these rather tightly packed with a compost made up of about equal parts of chopped sphagnum moss and finely chopped tree-fern fibre or osmunda fibre. Since they require constantly high humidity and heavy watering at the roots, the condition of this compost is extremely important, and when the slightest suspicion of its staleness becomes evident, repotting and transplanting should take place. These alpine Miltonias should be grown in relatively shaded spots, and seem to produce their extravagantly handsome, pansy-like flowers best if divided regularly into rather small pieces. Constantly chill conditions are necessary for any sort of success with them, and in general they are not recommended to the beginning hobbyist, unless he is fortunate enough to possess a special air-conditioned or 'cool' greenhouse. (C, I, H)

M. anceps Ldl. (*Odontoglossum anceps* Klotzsch, *Oncidium anceps* Rchb.f.)

Pbs. oblong, somewhat compressed, 2–3″ long. Lvs. 2, linear-oblong, acutish, 4–6″ long. Infls. longer than the lvs., 2-edged, flattened, sheathed by long, alternate, compressed bracts, 1-fld. Fls. 2–2½″ in diam., the ss. and ps. yellow-green, oblong-lanceolate, with recurved obtuse tips. Lip somewhat pandurate, white with 2–3 purple longitudinal streaks on the disc, in front of which are a few purple spots; basal calli 2, with a small tooth between them. Col.-wings purple. April–June. (I, H) Brazil.

M. x Bluntii Rchb.f.

Natural hybrid between *M. spectabilis* Ldl. and *M. Clowesii* Ldl., rather similar in vegetative appearance to the former parent, the lvs. 2, usually larger than those of *M. spectabilis* Ldl. Infls. sheathed by ovate-lanceolate bracts, with 1–few large and very handsome fls. at apex, these usually produced one at a time. Fls. to about 3″ long, fragrant, heavy-textured, the ss. and ps. stellate, whitish-yellow with some red-brown blotches in the midlb., the ss. lanceolate, the ps. broader and less acute. Lip obcordate, with the lat. margins depressed, the apical part much undulated, white, the basal part purplish-crimson as in *M. Clowesii* Ldl. Aug.–Nov. (I, H) Brazil.

—fma. **Lubbersiana** (Rchb.f.) A.D.Hawkes (*Miltonia x Bluntii* Rchb.f. var. *Lubbersiana* Rchb.f.)

Differs from the type in its larger and more brightly-hued fls., which often measure 4″ from tip to tip. Ss. and ps. light yellow with broad close-set purplish-brown bars and blotches, with a purple stain at the base of each segm. Lip purple at the base, with several red-brown lines, the apical area much lighter. Aug.–Nov. (I, H) Brazil.

M. candida Ldl. (*Oncidium candidum* Rchb.f.)

Pbs. narrowly ovoid, somewhat compressed, elongated, 3–4″ long. Lvs. 2, linear-oblanceolate, acute, folded at base, 9–15″ long, glossy light-green. Infls. erect or arching, rather stout, to 2′ long, 3–7-fld. Fls. to 3″ in diam., fragrant, the waxy ss. and ps. chestnut-brown tipped and spotted with yellow, about equal in size,

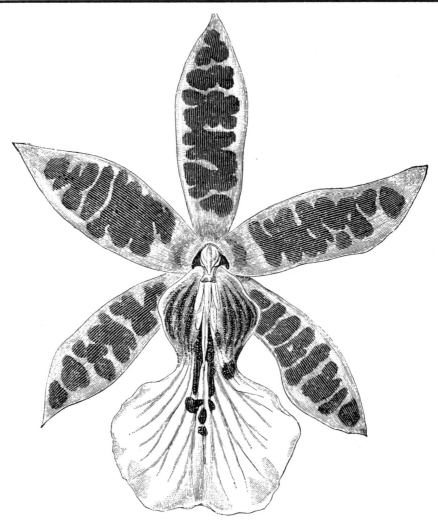

Miltonia x Bluntii Rchb.f. fma. *Lubbersiana* (Rchb.f.) A.D.Hawkes [VEITCH]

narrowly oblong, apiculate, the ps. usually with more yellow, wavy-margined. Lip roundish-obovate with wavy margins, forming a broad funnel-like tube around the col., white with 2 light (rarely dark) violet-purple blotches on the disc, and with 5–7 raised lines that are slightly divergent, of which the 2 next the middle one are more prominent than the others. Col. narrowly winged at apex. Aug.–Nov. (I, H) Brazil.

M. Clowesii Ldl. (*Brassia Clowesii* Ldl., *Odontoglossum Clowesii* Ldl., *Oncidium Clowesii* Rchb.f.)

Pbs. narrowly ovoid-oblong, compressed, narrowed upwards, 3–4″ long, yellowish. Lvs. 2, linear-ligulate, acute, 12–18″ long, glossy. Infls. erect or arching, the scape slender, to about 2′ tall, rather densely 7–10-fld. in upper half. Fls. 2–3″ across, the similar, almost equal ss. and ps. chestnut-brown barred and tipped with yellow, lanceolate, acuminate, glossy. Lip rather pandurate, sharply long-pointed, the basal half violet-purple, the apical half white; crest consisting of 5–7 raised lines of unequal length that vary from white to yellow, of which the middle one is the broadest, the two

next to it the longest. Col.-wings very narrow, entire. Sept.–Nov. (I, H) Brazil.

M. cuneata Ldl. (*Miltonia speciosa* Klotzsch, *Oncidium speciosum* Rchb.f.)

Rhiz. robust, creeping. Pbs. borne at intervals, ovoid-oblong, compressed, 3–4″ long. Lvs. 2, narrowly lanceolate, acute, 9–15″ long. Infls. erect or arching, 5–8-fld., to 2′ tall, furnished with triangular, acute, papery bracts. Fls. 2½–3″ across, the ss. and ps. chestnut-brown tipped with light yellow and sometimes with a few yellow streaks near the base, oblong-lanceolate, acuminate, with recurved tips, undulate marginally. Lip white with a long narrow claw and almost square, wavy lamina, on the disc of which are 2 slightly divergent raised plates that are sometimes spotted with rose. Col.-wings narrow, finely toothed. Feb.–Mar. (I, H) Brazil.

M. Endresii Nichols. (*Miltonia superba* Schltr., *Odontoglossum Warscewiczii* Rchb.f.)

Pbs. concealed by the sheathing lf.-like bracts, ovoid-oblong, strongly compressed, pale green, 1½–2″ long. Lf.

solitary (apical), thin-textured, linear-lanceolate, acute, to 12″ long, pale green. Infls. to 12″ tall, erect or arching, the scape slightly compressed, pale green, 3–5-fld., with small appressed bracts. Fls. flattened, fragile, to 3″ across, on long pedicellate ovaries, white with a light red-purple blotch at the base of each segm. Ss. and ps. similar, almost equal, oval-oblong, acute, the dors. sep. apiculate. Lip broadly pandurate, the basal lbs. small, roundish, the front lb. with a shallow sinus on the anterior margin; crest semi-lunate, produced into 3 short keels in front, pubescent, bright yellow. Col.-wings very narrow, light rose-purple, the anther yellow. Feb.–Apr. (C, I) Costa Rica; Panama.

M. flavescens Ldl. (*Cyrtochilum flavescens* Ldl., *Cyrtochilum stellatum* Ldl., *Oncidium flavescens* Rchb.f., *Miltonia stellata* hort.)

Pbs. borne at intervals on a creeping rhiz., narrowly oval-oblong, strongly compressed, 4–5″ long, yellowish. Lvs. 2, rather soft-textured, often yellowish, linear-ligulate, acutish, to 12″ long and about ¾″ wide. Infls. longer than the lvs., sheathed by distichous, pale brown, membranaceous bracts, the floral bracts linear, acuminate, longer than the pedicellate ovaries, 7–10-fld. in upper part. Fls. star-like, about 3″ across or more, fragrant, the ss. and ps. straw-yellow, the lip white streaked and marked with red-purple on basal half. Ss. linear-oblong, acute. Ps. similar but slightly broader and shorter. Lip shorter than other segms. ovate-oblong, acute, undulate marginally, slightly contracted below the middle, the basal half pubescent, with 4–6 radiating lines. Col.-wings obsolete. June–Oct. (I, H) Brazil; Paraguay.

M. Phalaenopsis Nichols. (*Miltonia pulchella* hort. ex Batem., *Odontoglossum Phalaenopsis* Rchb.f.)

Rather similar in habit to *M. Endresii* Nichols., but smaller and more slender, the pbs. pale green, hidden by the sheathing lf.-like bracts, ovoid, strongly compressed, to 1½″ long. Lf. (apical) solitary, linear, folded at base, tapering apically, to 12″ long, pale green. Infls. shorter than the lvs., the scape somewhat flattened, 3–5-fld. Fls. flattened, 2–2½″ across, the ss. and ps. white, the ss. oval-oblong, acute, the broader ps. elliptic, obtuse. Lip 4-lbd., the basal lbs. white with some light purple streaks, short, roundish, the anterior lbs. larger, squarish, white blotched with light (or dark) purple; crest with 3 small blunt teeth, on each side of which is a yellow spot. Col.-wings very short. Aug.–Nov. (C, I) Colombia.

M. Regnellii Rchb.f. (*Miltonia cereola* Lem., *Oncidium Regnellii* Rchb.f.)

Pbs. yellowish, ovoid-oblong, compressed, narrowed upwards, 3–4″ tall. Lvs. 2, linear-ligulate, acute, to about 12″ long, glossy yellowish-green. Infls. erect, slender, to 2′ tall, loosely 3–7-fld., the fls. opening successively over a rather long period of time. Fls. flattened, 2–3″ long from tip to tip, the ss. and ps. white, sometimes faintly rose-tinted basally, the ss. oblong-lanceolate, apiculate, the broader ps. elliptic-oblong, acute. Lip broadly obcordate, vaguely 3-lbd., light rose streaked with rose-purple and with a white margin; crest consisting of 7–9 radiating pale yellow lines, of which the 3 central ones are the most prominent and most

brilliant. Col.-wings narrow, prolonged upwards. July–Sept. (I, H) Brazil.

M. Roezlii (Rchb.f.) Nichols. (*Odontoglossum Roezlii* Rchb.f.)

Rather similar in habit to *M. Endresii* Nichols., the vegetative parts light bluish-green, the pbs. ovoid-oblong, compressed, almost hidden by the lf.-like basal sheaths, 2–2½″ long. Lf. (apical) solitary, linear, acute, to 12″ long, pale bluish-green. Infls. to about as long as the lvs., slender, 2–5-fld., with small bracts. Fls. very flattened, 3–4″ long, white with a purple blotch at the base of each petal, and an orange-yellow disc at the lip-base. Ss. and broader ps. obovate-oblong, acute. Lip broadly obcordate with an angular sinus in the anterior margin, a small horn-like auricle on each side of the base, and 3 raised lines on the disc with 2 small teeth in front of them. Col.-wings obsolete. Sept.–Nov. (C, I) Panama; Colombia.

M. Russelliana Ldl. (*Oncidium Russellianum* Ldl.)

Pbs. ovoid-oblong, compressed, 2–3″ long. Lvs. 2, narrowly lanceolate, 6–9″ long. Infls. erect or arching, to 2′ long, 5–9-fld., the scape mottled with dull purple, the sheathing bracts brown. Fls. to 2½″ across, the ss. and ps. reddish-brown tipped with pale yellow, oblong-lanceolate, acute. Lip cuneate-oblong, retuse, apiculate, the lateral margins subsinuate, the basal two-thirds rose-lilac, the apical third white or light yellow; disc with 3 raised lines, of which the middle one is the shortest, the lateral pair dilated in front into 2 erect plates. Col.-wings ovate, acute, yellow. July–Aug. (I, H) Brazil.

M. spectabilis Ldl. (*Macrochilus Fryanus* Kn. & Westc., *Oncidium spectabile* Rchb.f.)

Rhiz. robust, creeping, scaly, the pbs. produced at intervals, ovoid-oblong, glossy yellowish-green, compressed, 3–4″ long. Lvs. 2, linear-ligulate, usually yellowish, 4–7″ long. Infls. erect, to about 8″ tall, 1-fld., sheathed by alternate, imbricating, flattened bracts, with a larger one embracing the pedicellate ovary. Fls. almost flat, heavy-textured, long-lived, to 3″ long, variable in colour, the typical form with the ss. and ps. white or cream-white, sometimes tinged with rose towards the base, the lip wine-purple with 6–8 longitudinal veins of deeper hue, the margin white or pale rose, the crest 3-lamellate, the lamellae terminating in small erect plates, usually yellow. Ss. and ps. lanceolate-oblong, acute, the ps. slightly the broader. Lip large, spreading, obovate-orbicular, the margins undulate or somewhat crisped. Col.-wings subtriangular, rose-purple. July–Sept. (I, H) Brazil.

—var. **Moreliana** Henfr. (*Miltonia Moreliana* Warn.)

A very distinct variant, more common in cultivation than the typical phase, from which it differs in having larger fls. (to 4″ long), with plum-purple ss. and ps., the very large flattened lip bright rose-purple with deeper veins and reticulations. July–Sept. (I, H) Brazil.

M. vexillaria (Rchb.f.) Bth. (*Odontoglossum vexillarium* Rchb.f.)

Rather similar in habit to *M. Endresii* Nichols., the entire plant pale bluish-green. Pbs. compressed, scarcely noticeable, to $1\frac{1}{2}''$ tall. Lvs. linear-lanceolate, acute, keeled beneath, imbricate at base, distichous and alternate, usually 6–8 to one growth, the lower two shorter than those above, the pb. with a single apical lf. Infls. usually 2 per growth (sometimes 3–4), slender, arching, 4–7-fld., 12–20″ long. Fls. highly variable in size and colour, 3–4″ long, usually light rose, but often varying from rose-carmine to almost white or white, flushed with light rose. Ss. and ps. similar, almost equal, obovate-oblong, shortly apiculate. Lip flattened, suborbicular, 2-lbd. in front, with a small ovate ascending auricle on each side at base; crest yellow, 2-lbd. at base, prolonged in front into 3 short teeth. Col.-wings obsolete. May–June. (C, I) Colombia; ? Ecuador.

M. Warscewiczii Rchb.f. (*Odontoglossum Warscewiczianum* Hemsl., *Odontoglossum Weltoni* hort., *Oncidium fuscatum* Rchb.f., *Oncidium Weltoni* hort., *Miltonia Warscewiczii* Rchb.f. var. *Weltoni* hort.)
Pbs. clustered, oblong, compressed, 4–5″ long, 1″ broad or more. Lf. solitary, rather leathery, linear-oblong, obtuse, glossy, 5–7″ long. Infls. erect, to 2′ tall or more, usually paniculate, densely many-fld., the fls. usually all opening at once. Fls. fragrant, waxy, about 2″ long, variable in colour, the ss. and ps. brownish-red (sometimes yellow, or sometimes white at tips), similar, almost equal, oblong-spatulate, undulate, broadly spreading. Lip variable in colour and size, rose-purple with a red-brown disc and variably wide white margin, white at the very base where there are 2 small yellow teeth, the lamina broadly oblong with a cleft in anterior margin. Col.-wings rounded, red-purple. Mar.–Apr. (I, H) Panama; Colombia; Ecuador; Peru.

M. laevis (Ldl.) Rolfe (*Odontoglossum laeve* Ldl., *Odontoglossum Karwinskii* Rchb.f., *Cyrtochilum Karwinskii* Ldl., *Oncidium laeve* Beer, *Miltonia Karwinskii* Paxt.) Pbs. ovoid to ovoid-ellipsoid, strongly compressed, becoming furrowed with age, to 5″ long and $2\frac{1}{2}$″ broad. Lvs. 2–3, linear-ligulate to oblong-ligulate, rounded to acutish apically, vaguely leathery in texture, folded basally, to $1\frac{1}{2}$′ long and more than 2″ broad. Infls. erect, robust, typically branched and many-fld., to more than $3\frac{1}{2}$′ tall in most cases. Fls. about $2\frac{1}{2}$″ long in the largest forms, the ss. and ps. yellow or yellowish blotched with reddish-brown, the lip white apically, purplish below the middle. Ss. narrowly elliptic, often apiculate, the lats. strongly keeled on the back, recurved apically, the lateral edges reflexed. Ps. obliquely linear-elliptic. Lip sharply deflexed below the middle, rather elongately fiddle-shaped when spread out, the disc fleshy and grooved, the thick portion ending in 2–5 obscure keels above the bend of the lip. Mostly summer–autumn. (I) Mexico; Guatemala.

M. Reichenheimii (Lind. & Rchb.f.) Rolfe (*Odontoglossum Reichenheimii* Lind. & Rchb.f., *Odontoglossum leucomelas* Rchb.f., *Odontoglossum Schroederianum* Rchb.f., *Miltonia leucomelas* Rolfe, *M. Schroederiana* Veitch). Very closely allied to *M. laevis* (Ldl.) Rolfe and to *M. stenoglossa* Schltr., differing mostly in colour and in the lip not being so prominently deflexed. Fls. numerous, the ss. and ps. yellowish-green barred with purplish-brown, the lip either dark or light purple, usually with a white basal area. Spring. (I) Mexico; Nicaragua; Costa Rica; Panama.

M. stenoglossa Schltr. (*Odontoglossum stenoglossum* L.O. Wms.) Closely allied to and simulating *M. laevis* (Ldl.) Rolfe, differing in the always simple infl., the much smaller fls., and the scarcely dilated apex of the lip. Fls. usually few, about

$1\frac{1}{2}$″ long, the ss. and ps. yellow-green blotched and banded with brown, the lip whitish basally, purple or reddish-purple in the apical half. Spring. (C, I) Mexico; Guatemala; Honduras; Costa Rica.

MISCHOBULBUM Schltr.

Mischobulbum is a genus of about seven or eight species of primarily terrestrial orchids of the subtribe *Collabiinae*, with a range extending from the Himalayas to New Guinea. Allied to *Nephelaphyllum* Bl. and to *Ania* Ldl., they differ from those groups in technical vegetative and floral details, and are very scarce in contemporary collections, although three species are occasionally encountered in cultivation. They are rather unusually handsome plants, and should be far better known by specialists.

No hybrids are known in *Mischobulbum*, and nothing has been ascertained concerning its genetic affinities.

CULTURE: As for the tropical species of *Phaius*. (H)

M. grandiflorum (King & Pantl.) Rolfe (*Tainia grandiflora* King & Pantl.)
Pbs. clustered, cylindrical, to about 3″ tall. Lf. solitary, stalkless, cordate, to 6″ long, green with darker green blotches. Infl. to 8″ tall, almost erect, with an apical, loosely 6–10-fld. rac. Fls. about $1\frac{1}{2}$″ across, very complex, yellow, the lip almost black at the apex. Spring–early summer. (H) Himalayas.

M. scapigerum (Hk.f.) Schltr. (*Nephelaphyllum scapigerum* Hk.f.)
Similar in habit to *M. grandiflorum* (King & Pantl.) Rolfe, but shorter and less robust. Lvs. about 4″ long, ovate, blotched with dark green. Infls. about 5″ tall, the rac. 3–5-fld., rather loose. Fls. about 2″ in diam., the ss. and ps. greenish-yellow striped with brown, the lip white, yellow at the apex, spotted with dark purple, the basal part oval, veined with violet-purple. Spring–summer. (H) Borneo.

M. Wrayanum (Hk.f.) Rolfe (*Ipsea Wrayana* Hk.f., *Nephelaphyllum grandiflorum* Hk.f., *Tainia atropurpurea* Ridl., *Tainia Wrayana* J.J.Sm.)
Pbs. small. Lf. solitary, fleshy, about $5\frac{1}{2}$″ long and $3\frac{1}{2}$″ wide, cordate, the tip shortly acute, not folded. Infls. erect, to 10″ tall, 6–8-fld., the fls. rather crowded. Fls. about $1\frac{1}{4}$″ long, complex, the ss. and ps. greenish with brown-purple veins and somewhat flushed with brown-purple, the lip white with a purple suffusion near the tip, otherwise spotted or veined with pink. Summer. (H) Himalayas to Malay Peninsula.

MOBILABIUM Rupp

Mobilabium consists of but a single known species of very rare epiphytic orchid, known only from a collection or two made in Queensland, Australia. A member of the complex subtribe *Sarcanthinae*, little is at this time known regarding it, and it is not present in cultivation at this time.

Nothing is known regarding the genetic affinities of *Mobilabium*.

CULTURE: Presumably as for the tropical Vandas, etc. (H)

MOERENHOUTIA Bl.

This is a genus of about five species of rare and in-completely-known terrestrial orchids, native in the Pacific Islands, north to the Caroline group. Rather reminiscent of *Goodyera* R.Br. in appearance and floral structure, they are at this time unknown in our collections, and appear to be very rare even in their native haunts. *Moerenhoutia* is a member of the very difficult subtribe *Physurinae*.

Nothing is known of the genetic alliances of this genus.

CULTURE: Presumably as for *Anoectochilus*. (H)

MONADENIA Ldl.

Containing about thirty species of mostly rather in-significant terrestrial orchids, confined to South Africa, *Monadenia* is a member of the very complex subtribe *Disinae*, being segregated from *Disa* Berg. on technical details of the rather small flowers. A single species is present today in a few particularly choice collections, but it is a very rare orchid, and one whose successful cultivation for more than a single season presents serious difficulties.

Nothing is known of the genetic affinities of the genus *Monadenia*.

CULTURE: As for *Disa*, although slightly more warmth may be given the plants than the majority of those orchids. (I)

M. ophrydea Ldl. (*Disa ophrydea* Bolus, *Monadenia lancifolia* Sond.)
Tuber usually solitary, sessile. Lvs. mostly basal, linear-oblong, acute, curled in at the margins, rather fleshy, 2–4″ long. Infl. stout, erect, sheathed, ½–1½′ tall, with a loose rac. about 3–6″ long. Fls. almost ¾″ in diam., glossy, the ss. dark red, the ps. and lip almost crimson-black. Dors. sep. galeate, oblong, blunt; spur filiform, slightly curved, ¾″ long. Lat. ss. ovate-oblong. Ps. obliquely ovate-oblong, emarginate or slightly bidentate, fleshy. Lip oblong, blunt. Sept.–Oct. (I) Cape Colony.

MONOMERIA Ldl.
(*Acrochaene* Ldl.)

Monomeria is a genus of four known species of the small subtribe *Genyorchidinae*, native in the region extending from the Himalayas to Thailand and Viet-Nam. They are extremely rare in collections today, but their unusually-coloured, intricate flowers and attractive, *Bulbophyllum*-like vegetative habit make them desirable to connoisseurs. Three of the species are present in particularly comprehensive contemporary collections.

No hybrids are known in *Monomeria*, and nothing has been ascertained concerning its genetic alliances as yet.

CULTURE: As for the intermediate-growing Bulbo-phyllums. (I)

M. barbata Ldl. (*Epicranthes barbata* Rchb.f., *Monomeria Crabro* Par. & Rchb.f.)
Pbs. ovoid, to 2″ tall, set about 2–3″ apart on the creeping rhiz. Lf. solitary, leathery, ligulate, obtuse, narrowed basally, to almost 12″ long and 1″ wide. Infls. erect or arching, to 15″ tall, the rac. loosely many-fld.

Fls. about 1½″ long, yellow spotted with sepia-brown. Lat. ss. joined together, about twice as long as the dors. one. Ps. very short, triangular, turned inwards, ciliate-toothed marginally. Lip ligulate, with short lat. lbs. Winter. (I) Himalayas; Burma; Thailand.

M. dichroma (Rolfe) Schltr. (*Bulbophyllum dichromum* Rolfe)
Rather resembling *M. barbata* Ldl. in habit, but with longer pbs. and lvs. to 2″ wide. Infls. erect, to 12″ tall, loosely 10–15-fld. Fls. about 2″ long, golden-yellow with red-dotted ps. and a purple-red lip. Lat. ss. slightly longer than the dors. one, joined together. Ps. small, ciliate marginally. Lip short, fleshy, with short lat. lbs. Late winter. (I) Laos; Viet-Nam.

M. punctata (Ldl.) Schltr. (*Acrochaene punctata* Ldl.)
Similar in appearance to *M. barbata* Ldl., but with the rac. rather more dense and more inclined to be sharply pendulous. Fls. about 1″ long, olive-green with small reddish dots and blotches. Ps. a little longer than the col., the foot of which is very short. Winter. (I) Himalayas, mostly in Sikkim.

MONOPHYLLORCHIS Schltr.

Monophyllorchis colombiana Schltr., the only known member of the genus, is an excessively rare and little-known terrestrial orchid of the subtribe *Vanillinae*, which has been collected a few times in the State of Cauca, Colombia. It is evidently a rather attractive plant, somewhat allied to *Pogonia* Juss., but is not present in contemporary collections.

Nothing is known of the genetic affinities of *Monophyllorchis*.

CULTURE: Presumably as for the terrestrial, tropical Habenarias, etc. (I, H)

MONOSEPALUM Schltr.

This is a genus of three known species of very rare epiphytic orchids of the subtribe *Bulbophyllinae*, all endemic to the montane forests of New Guinea, where they were initially detected by Schlechter. Peculiar plants, they are not especially allied to other members of the aggregation. None of the trio is present in collections at this time.

Nothing is known of the genetic affinities of *Monosepalum*.

CULTURE: Presumably as for the 'cloud-forest' species of *Bulbophyllum* and *Dendrobium*. (C, I)

MORMODES Ldl.
(*Cyclosia* Kl.)

The fantastic 'Goblin Orchids', genus *Mormodes*, are today rather widespread and popular with collectors, because of their remarkably intricate flowers, weird coloration, and exotic fragrances, and the relative ease with which they are brought into bloom. This is a genus of some twenty species, with a range extending from Mexico throughout Central and South America to Brazil, with a large number of the known entities occurring in the last-named country. A member of the subtribe *Catasetinae*, *Mormodes* is somewhat allied to

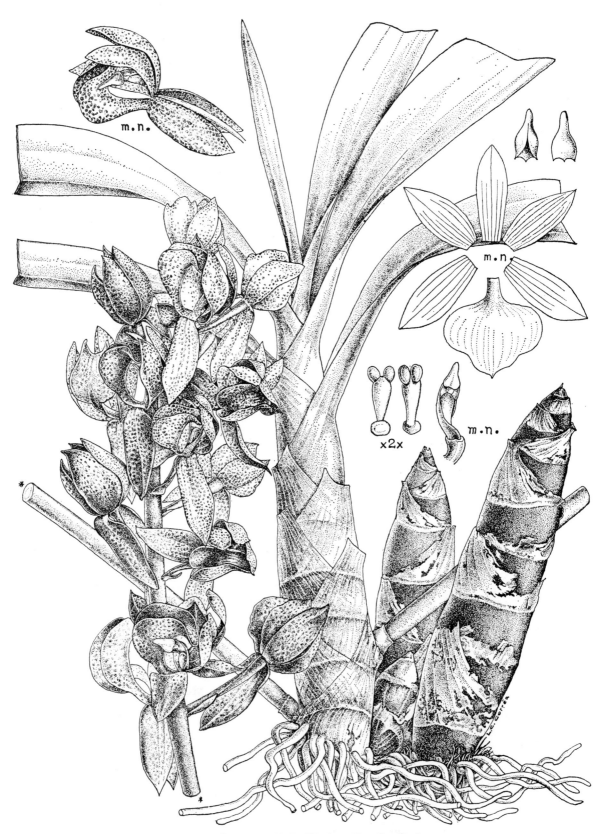

Mormodes tigrinum B.-R. [Hoehne, *Flora Brasílica*]

Maxillaria praestans Rchb.f. [GEORGE FULLER]

Microcoelia species [J. MARNIER-LAPOSTOLLE]

Miltonia Phalaenopsis (Rchb.f.) Nichols. [H. SCHMIDT-MUMM]

Neobenthamia gracilis Rolfe [KARI BERGGRAV]

(ABOVE) *Neogyne Gardneriana* (Ldl.) Rchb.f. [GEORGE FULLER]

(ABOVE LEFT) *Neofinetia falcata* (Thunb.) Hu. One of the very rare variegated forms prized in its native Japan [Y. NAGANO]

Neomoorea irrorata (Rolfe) Rolfe [CHARLES-WORTH & CO.]

Catasetum L.C.Rich. and to Cycnoches Ldl., but its components are readily differentiated from those genera by the consistently perfect flowers (never with the sexes separate), the twisted column, and other characters. These fine orchids are usually epiphytic (frequently on dead or decaying trees), but some of them occasionally occur in the ground, as terrestrials, or even on rock outcroppings. They vegetatively resemble Catasetum (and certain kinds of Cycnoches); the flower-spikes are typically borne from the old, leafless pseudobulbs, most frequently from the middle or upper nodes, and carry from a few to rather many often large and handsome blossoms. The sepals and usually wider petals are either spreading or sharply reflexed, while the lip is variously simple or lobed to a greater or lesser degree, and sometimes more or less hairy. Like the column, the lip is usually very strongly twisted, thus giving to the flowers a characteristic contorted form. Unlike Catasetums, the blossoms of Mormodes have no irritable antennae on the column. Taxonomically, the genus is in a state of considerable confusion, because of the variability of structure within the several species, and the often tremendous colour-range, which has resulted in the establishment of a large number of entities now considered to be mere colour forms of polymorphic taxa. A critical revision of the entire genus is sorely needed.

Thus far only one hybrid is on record in this fascinating group of orchids; this is a rare bigeneric cross, Cycnodes, Mormodes × Cycnoches. Hybrids within the genus itself offer considerable potentials, as do additional crosses with Cycnoches and Catasetum, both of which are presumably allied.

CULTURE: As for Catasetum. Often, the Mormodes seem to be relatively short-lived once they have reached maturity, sometimes perishing—no matter what is done—after about six or eight years following the initial production of flowers. (I, H)

M. Buccinator Ldl. (*Mormodes brachystachyum* Kl., *M. flaveolum* Kl., *M. leucochilum* Kl., *M. Wagenerianum* Kl.)
Pbs. clustered, ellipsoid-ovoid, to 7″ long (rarely more), becoming strongly wrinkled usually after first season. Lvs. strongly-veined, plicate, rather narrow, to about 12″ long, soon deciduous. Infls. erect or arching, to about 15″ long, usually loose, 7–12-fld. Fls. exceedingly polychromatic, among the most variable in the genus, rather heavy-textured, fragrant of spices, twisted, to 2½″ in diam., typically with pale green ss. and ps. and a white or ivory-white lip, in other forms with the ground-colour varying from buff to pale straw-yellow, often striped and spotted with dull red or reddish-brown to varying degrees. Ss. and ps. narrowly oblong, acute, the ss. reflexed, the ps. bent forwards over the col. Lip obovate, trumpet-like, with the sides rolled back and almost meeting at their edges. Col. semiterete, obliquely twisted. Mostly Feb.–Mar. (I, H) Mexico; Venezuela; doubtless also occurring in intermediate countries.

M. colossus Rchb.f. (*Mormodes macranthum* Ldl. & Paxt., *M. Powellii* Schltr., *M. Wendlandii* Rchb.f.)
Pbs. clustered, often elongate, cylindric, tapering upwards, to 12″ tall. Lvs. plicate, deciduous, the per-

sistent imbricating bases unarmed. Infls. to 2′ long, arching, usually produced from near the pb.-bases, usually rather densely many-fld. Fls. fragrant, lasting well, variable in size and colour, to more than 3½″ in diam., contorted, the ss. and ps. olive-green, yellowish-brown, or cream, the lip brown, tan, or yellow. Ss. and somewhat broader ps. spreading, acuminate. Lip elliptic-ovate to rhombic-ovate, acute or acuminate, the lat. margins strongly recurved, shortly clawed at base, the lamina about twice as long as broad. Spring. (I, H) Costa Rica; Panama.

M. Hookeri Lem. (*Mormodes atro-purpurea* Hk., *M. barbatum* Ldl. & Paxt.)
Pbs. small for the genus, usually less than 4″ tall. Lvs. as for other spp. Infls. short, erect, rather few-fld., produced from pb.-bases. Fls. fragrant, about 1½″ in diam., dark reddish-brown or red, the lip often almost black-red. Ss. and somewhat shorter ps. lanceolate, acuminate, strongly reflexed. Lip obovate, truncate, abruptly and minutely apiculate, about as long as broad when expanded, with the lat. lbs. strongly pubescent. Winter, usually Dec.–Jan. (I, H) Costa Rica; Panama; Colombia.

M. igneum Ldl. & Paxt.
Pbs. stout, cylindric, tapering uniformly from the base upwards, to 14″ tall and 2″ in diam. Lvs. 5–15, plicate, distichous, strongly veined, the persistent, closely imbricating, unarmed bases closely enveloping the pbs., the lanceolate, acuminate blades deciduous at end of growing season. Infls. 1–several, erect, arching, to more than 2′ tall, with a few- to many-fld. rac. at the apex. Fls. highly variable in size, colour, and texture, often in the same rac., fragrant, lasting rather well, to more than 2″ in diam., the ss. and ps. yellow, olive-green, tan-brown, or red, often spotted with red, the lip white, yellow, olive-green, tan, brown, or dark reddish-brown, often with tiny brown or reddish-brown spots. Ss. and ps. membranaceous, the dors. sep. erect, lanceolate, acuminate or apiculate, the lat. ss. and ps. usually strongly reflexed, rather similar in shape. Lip almost round when spread out, shortly apiculate, glabrous, the lat. margins strongly reflexed, the base with a conspicuous claw. Spring. (I, H) Costa Rica; Panama; Colombia.

M. luxatum Ldl. (*Catasetum luxatum* Bth., *Mormodes Williamsii* Krzl.)
Pbs. as for the other spp., usually about 8″ tall, the lvs. to almost 2′ long, quickly deciduous. Infls. glaucous, rather stout, to almost 2½′ long, often horizontal, with 12 rather densely-arranged fls. Fls. fragrant, long-lasting, waxy, to 3½″ in diam., the ss. and ps. yellowish-green sometimes spotted with purple, the lip similar in colour, with a brown-purple streak on the inner side (there is also a very rare ivory-white form, with a brown-purple stripe on the inner side of the lip). Ss. ovate, sub-acuminate. Ps. much broader than ss., oval-oblong, acute, concave. Lip shortly clawed, twisted obliquely to one side, vaguely 3-lbd., roundish, concave, almost hemispherical, apiculate. Col. rather triangular. Winter. (I, H) Mexico.

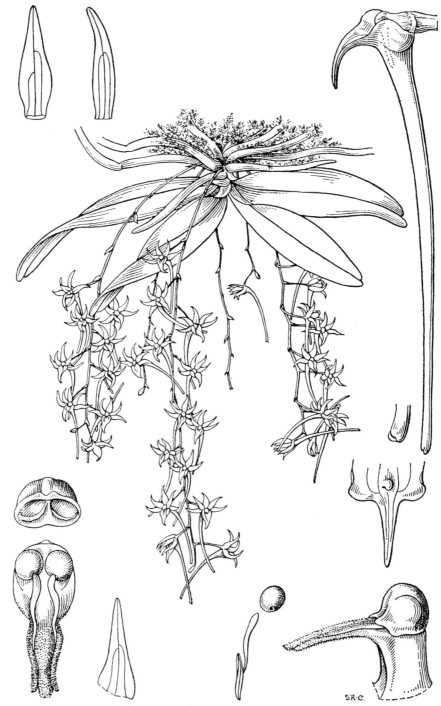

Mystacidium tanganyikense Summerh. [*Icones Plantarum*]

M. maculatum (Kl.) L.O.Wms. (*Cyclosia maculata* Kl.,
Mormodes pardina Batem.)

Pbs. clustered, 5–8″ tall, the quickly deciduous lvs.
12–18″ long. Infls. often horizontal, to 20″ long, densely
many-fld., the fls. often all facing upwards. Fls. heavy-
textured, with a strong rather unpleasant odour, lasting
well, about 1¾″ long, pale tawny-yellow densely spotted
with chocolate-red (entirely bright lemon-yellow in the

fma. **unicolor** hort.). Ss. and ps. similar, subequal, ovate,
acuminate, incurving. Lip slightly smaller than the other
segms., 3-lbd., the lbs. acuminate, the midlb. the largest.
Autumn–early winter. (I, H) Mexico.

M. Greenii Hk.f. Pbs. clustered, 3–4″ long, the lvs. to about
1½′ long. Infls. pendulous, to about 12″ long, densely many-
fld. Fls. to 2½″ in diam., whitish outside, inside the ss. and ps.
light yellow very densely covered with oblong dark red blotches,

the lip basally dark purple, the inner surface yellow streaked with red, the outer surface spotted like the ss. and ps. except on the dilated, dull lilac apex. Ss. and ps. ovate, subacute, concave. Lip curved upwards, gradually dilated from a linear fleshy base to a saccate, incurved, orbicular apex, irregularly toothed marginally. Winter. (I, H) Colombia.

M. ocañae Ldl. & Rchb.f. Pbs. clustered, usually only about 3–4″ long, the lvs. to about 12″ long. Infls. robust, 6–10-fld., to about 12″ long, with prominent boat-shaped bracts. Fls. about 3″ in diam., heavily fragrant, dark orange-yellow closely speckled with red-brown spots and dots. Ss. and ps. similar, lanceolate, acuminate, concave. Lip long-clawed, the lamina 3-lbd., the lat. lbs. short, oblong, rounded at the tip, the midlb. subquadrate, abruptly apiculate, all the lbs. with incurved margins. Winter. (I) Colombia; Venezuela.

MORMOLYCA Fenzl

The seldom-grown genus *Mormolyca* (often misspelled *Mormolyce*) contains but a single species, an unusual epiphytic orchid native in Mexico and Central America. Rather closely allied to *Maxillaria* R. & P., it is distinguished from that group on technical details, and more readily so by the unique appearance of the peculiarly hued flowers, which are odd rather than attractive and of interest primarily to connoisseurs of the 'lesser-known' orchids.

Nothing is known of the genetic affinities of *Mormolyca*. It is presumably genetically compatible with at least certain of the Maxillarias and other members of the subtribe to which it belongs.

CULTURE: As for the pseudobulbous, tropical Maxillarias. Because of the repent rhizomes in most specimens, rather sizeable containers must be provided. (I, H)

M. ringens (Ldl.) Schltr. (*Trigonidium ringens* Ldl., *Mormolyca lineolata* Fenzl)

Pbs. congested or borne some distance apart on the wiry rhiz., roundish to ellipsoid, compressed, often yellowish or brownish, to 2″ long, with basal reddish-brown, scarious imbricated sheaths. Lf. solitary, to 1½′ long, glossy or dull, linear-ligulate to narrowly lanceolate, obtuse to acute, folded at base, fleshy. Infls. usually several at once, slender, erect, 1-fld., to 1½′ tall. Fls. about 2″ across (usually smaller), fleshy, yellowish-green to light lavender, veined with lavender or maroon, the lip lavender or deep maroon. Dors. sep. oblong-elliptic, concave, dorsally carinate at apex; lat. ss. elliptic-oblong, obtuse to mucronate, convex, subfalcate. Ps. linear-elliptic to elliptic-oblanceolate, obtuse to rounded, convex, oblique. Lip 3-lbd., the lat. lbs. tiny, arising below middle of lip, the midlb. large, often dorsally thickened at apex. Mostly summer. (I H), Mexico to Costa Rica.

MYRMECHIS Bl.

A genus of about four known species, two native in Java and Sumatra, two in China and India, *Myrmechis* is not well-understood botanically, and is unknown in contemporary collections. It is somewhat allied to *Zeuxine* Ldl. and certain other members of the subtribe *Physurinae*, but differs from the noted genus in its typically solitary or paired flowers, the technical structure of which is divergent.

Nothing is known of the genetic affinities of this odd genus.

CULTURE: Presumably as for *Anoectochilus*. (H)

MYSTACIDIUM Ldl.

Certain genera of the subtribe *Sarcanthinae* which inhabit Africa and adjacent insular groups are today incompletely known and delimited, despite the admirable studies made on this aggregation by such specialists as Schlechter, Perrier de la Bâthie, Summerhayes, *et al.* The present genus, *Mystacidium*, is one of these. As now considered, it is an aggregation consisting of about five species—only one of .which is cultivated, and that only in the choicest of collections. They are epiphytic orchids inhabiting South-east Africa, mostly in the vicinity of the Cape of Good Hope. The genus is allied to *Aërangis* Rchb.f., and rather simulates many members of that group, but may be distinguished on technical characters of the flowers.

No hybrids are known in *Mystacidium*, and nothing has been ascertained regarding its genetic affinities. It is in all probability 'crossable' with at least some members of the alliance to which it belongs.

CULTURE: As for the tropical Angraecums. (I, H)

M. capense (L.f.) Schltr. (*Angraecum capense* Ldl., *Epidendrum capense* L.f., *Limodorum longicornu* Sw., *Mystacidium filicornu* Ldl., *M. longicornu* Dur. & Schinz)

St. very abbreviated, rather stout, leafy. Lvs. few. leathery, oblong, unequally and obtusely 2-lbd. at apex, to 3″ long. Infls. arching, loosely 10–20-fld., to 6″ long, Fls. opening widely, to 1½″ across, waxy, fragrant, pure white. Ss. and ps. narrowly lanceolate, acute. Lip similar to the other segms., but wider, the spur awl-shaped, to 2″ long, slightly curving. Summer. (I, H) South-east Africa.

NABALUIA Ames

Nabaluia Clemensii Ames, the only known member of the genus, is a very rare epiphytic orchid from Mount Kinabalu, British North Borneo. It is closely allied to *Chelonistele* Pfitz. of the subtribe *Coelogyninae*, and is perhaps referable to that genus. It differs from *Coelogyne* Ldl. in technical details of the lip of the flowers. The plant bears small yellowish or brownish blossoms, and is unknown in our collections at this time.

Nothing is known of the genetic affinities of *Nabaluia*.

CULTURE: Probably as for the tropical species of *Coelogyne*. (I, H)

NAGELIELLA L.O.Wms.
(*Hartwegia* Ldl.)

Nageliella contains but two species, these native in Mexico and Central America, and occasionally encountered in contemporary collections, usually under the synonymous, homonymic name of *Hartwegia* Ldl. They are singularly attractive little epiphytes (rarely lithophytes or semi-terrestrials), with stem-like pseudobulbs, mottled fleshy foliage and tall racemes of small but very brightly-coloured blossoms. The inflorescences continue to produce flowers for several years, hence should not be cut off until they become dry and brittle. Allied to *Hexisea* Ldl. and to *Epidendrum* L., the plants characteristically occur at medium elevations, and are among the more charming of the 'botanical' orchids, being attractive even when not in flower.

No hybrids are known in *Nageliella*, and nothing has been ascertained concerning its genetic affinities.

CULTURE: Nageliellas are very easily grown, and thus are admirably suited for inclusion in every collection. They do particularly well in firmly-packed small, well-drained pots of osmunda fibre, or when tightly affixed to small slabs of tree-fern fibre. They should be kept moderately moist at all times, but never allowed to become wet. Rather bright light brings out the best foliage and floral colour, and frequent fertilizing with a somewhat weakened solution is most beneficial. (I)

N. angustifolia (Booth ex Ldl.) A. & C. (*Hartwegia purpurea* Ldl. var. *angustifolia* Booth ex Ldl.)

Pbs. forming clumps, rather st.-like, terete, often club-shaped above, to 3″ tall. Lf. solitary, thick, erect. linear-lanceolate to oblong-lanceolate, obtuse to acute, green marked with deep brown, reddish, or purplish spots, often purplish underneath, to 4″ long and ¾″ wide, Infls. solitary, at top of sts., stiffly erect, terete, wiry, to 12″ tall, with several tight brownish sheaths, the several fls. appearing successively in one or more congested branches of the paniculate rac. Fls. bell-shaped, bright pink-purple, rather translucent, usually less than ½″ across. Ss. oblong-elliptic or oval-elliptic, rounded or acutish at apex, longitudinally concave, with the midnerve dorsally prominent. Ps. linear to linear-lanceolate, obtuse, usually falcate, minutely denticulate along margins. Lip adnate to col.-base, without a sac-like spur, deeply constricted and geniculate just below the middle; basal part of the constriction running parallel to the col. to form a tubular sac, then dilated above the constriction into a thin, suborbicular, obscurely 3-lbd., deeply concave lamina, the margins of which are crenate or somewhat inrolled, retuse apically. Mostly summer, though often more than once annually. (I) Guatemala.

N. purpurea (Ldl.) L.O.Wms. (*Hartwegia purpurea* Ldl., *Hartwegia comosa* Ldl. ex Pfitz.)

Almost identical vegetatively to *N. angustifolia* (Booth ex Ldl.) A. & C., but the lvs. wider and thinner in texture. Fls. purplish-red, usually slightly larger than those of the other sp., the lip with a protruding sac-like base, conspicuously adnate to the col.-base, the apical part (above the constriction) dilated into a thin cordate-ovate or suborbicular-ovate lamina which is obtuse to acute at the tip and is shallowly concave. Mostly summer. (I) Mexico; Guatemala; Honduras; Nicaragua.

NEOBATHIEA Schltr.

Six species of *Neobathiea* are known to date, all of them rather rare epiphytic orchids which are endemic to the island of Madagascar. Somewhat allied to *Aëranthes* Ldl., they differ from that group of the *Sarcanthinae* in technical details of the often very intricate, frequently rather showy, usually white flowers. At this time, none of the Neobathieas are present in our collections, although they are of considerable potential interest to connoisseurs.

Nothing is known of the genetic affinities of this group.

CULTURE: As for the tropical Angraecums. (H)

NEOBENTHAMIA Rolfe

But a single species of *Neobenthamia* is known to date, this a sporadically cultivated terrestrial orchid of the subtribe *Polystachyinae*, native in tropical East Africa. An unusually handsome plant, its charming clusters of showy flowers, borne at the top of a tall, leafy stem, offer much to the enthusiast, and its cultural requirements are so readily met that it is highly recommended to all orchidists.

No hybrids are known in this aberrant genus, and nothing has been deduced concerning its genetic affinities.

CULTURE: As for *Phaius*. These delightful orchids flower best in full sun, particularly when heavily fertilized. (H)

N. gracilis Rolfe (*Polystachya Neobenthamia* Schltr.)

Sts. slender, often somewhat branching and frequently producing numerous offsets, variable in dimensions, but often to more than 6′ tall in robust specimens, leafy throughout at first, the lvs. basally falling with age. Lvs. rather limp-textured, glossy, linear-lanceolate, acute, to 8″ long. Infls. terminal, densely many-fld., compact, often hemispherical in form, to about 5″ tall. Fls. long-stalked, usually not opening completely, fragrant, long-lived, about 1″ in diam. at most, the ss. and ps. white, the lip white with a golden-yellow middle, with a red spot on each side near base. Winter–spring, often almost ever-blooming. (H) Tropical East Africa.

NEOBOLUSIA Schltr.

Three species of *Neobolusia* are known to date, these rare terrestrial orchids of the subtribe *Habenarinae*, natives of southern Africa. Somewhat related to *Schwartzkopffia* Krzl., none of the trio—**N. ciliata** Summerh., **N. Stolzii** Schltr., and **N. Tysoni** (Bolus) Schltr.—are in cultivation at this time, though their flowers are sufficiently attractive to warrant the attention of the specialist collector.

Nothing is known of the genetic ties of this rare genus.

CULTURE: Presumably as for *Cynorkis* and *Habenaria*. (I, H)

NEOCLEMENSIA Carr

A single exceedingly rare saprophytic orchid makes up the genus *Neoclemensia*, this **N. spathulata** Carr, which has apparently been found on only one occasion in Borneo. A leafless saprophytic plant of the subtribe *Gastrodiinae*, it somewhat simulates *Gastrodia* R.Br., but differs in the virtually free petals, which are much

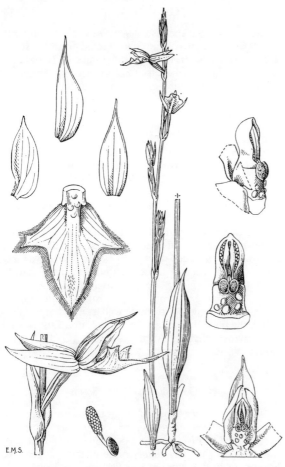

Neobolusia ciliata Summerh. [*Icones Plantarum*]

shorter than the sepals. It is not in cultivation at this time.

Nothing has been ascertained regarding the genetic affinities of *Neoclemensia*.

CULTURE: Possibly as for other saprophytic orchids. (H)

NEOCOGNIAUXIA Schltr.

The genus *Neocogniauxia* consists of two species of very handsome, smallish, epiphytic orchids, one (**N. hexaptera** (Cgn.) Schltr., apparently not in cultivation at this time) in Hispaniola, the other (*N. monophylla* (Griseb.) Schltr.) confined to Jamaica. Usually grown under the synonymous name of *Laelia monophylla* (Griseb.) N.E.Br., the plant described below differs radically from the genus *Laelia*, both in superficial appearance and in technical details. *Neocogniauxia* is today very rare in collections, but is among the most brightly hued and charming of West Indian orchids, and, despite its rather refractory disposition, should be better known by enthusiasts.

Neocogniauxia has not as yet been utilized by the breeders, although it is presumably inter-fertile with some, if not all, of the allied genera of the subtribe *Laeliinae*, such as *Laelia, Brassavola, Cattleya, Epiden-*

drum, etc. Experimental hybridization, in an effort to impart its brilliant coloration to larger flowers, should be encouraged.

CULTURE: Growing mostly in 'cloud forests' at relatively high elevations, this delightful little species requires conditions much like those afforded the alpine Odontoglossums, Masdevallias, and other 'cool' orchids. It is best kept in a pot, in a compost such as that recommended for the mentioned types, and must never be permitted to become dry, although a soggy or stale compost will quickly prove fatal. A shaded, well-ventilated spot is needed for success. (C, I)

N. monophylla (Griseb.) Schltr. (*Trigonidium monophyllum* Griseb., *Octadesmia monophylla* Bth., *Laelia monophylla* N.E.Br., *Epidendrum brachyglossum* Brogn.)

Pbs. reduced to very slender sts. which are more or less covered with cylindrical, speckled sheaths, to 3½" tall (rarely taller). Lf. solitary, to 4" long and ½" wide, linear-oblong, obtuse, not very heavy-textured. Scapes arching, to 8" long, 1-fld., furnished with small sheathing bracts. Fls. ¾–2" across, vivid orange-scarlet except for the purple anther-cap. Ss. and ps. ovate-elliptic, obtuse. Lip obovoid, continuous with the col.-wings below, 3-lbd. near apex, the disc rough, with a sac-like outgrowth along the median line. Autumn–winter. (C, I) Jamaica.

NEODRYAS Rchb.f.

This is a genus of about six species of very rare and little-known epiphytic or sometimes lithophytic orchids, native in the Andean regions of Peru and Bolivia. Allied to *Odontoglossum* HBK and to *Cochlioda* Ldl., they somewhat resemble small Cochliodas with pale reddish flowers that do not open well, differing from their allies in technical details of the lip and column. *Neodryas* is not present in contemporary collections.

Nothing is known of the genetic affinities of this odd group.

CULTURE: Presumably as for the high-elevation Odontoglossums, etc. (C, I)

NEOFINETIA Hu
(*Finetia* Schltr., *Nipponorchis* Masa.)

Neofinetia consists of but a single species, this the rather frequently cultivated and completely delightful orchid from Japan and Korea usually known as *Angraecum falcatum* Ldl. It is an epiphytic, rather dwarf plant somewhat allied to *Angraecopsis* Krzl., from which genus it differs in technical floral details.

A few exceptionally charming hybrids have thus far been registered, in Hawaii, in which *Neofinetia* figures, these crosses with *Ascocentrum* (= *Ascofinetia*) and with *Vanda* (= *Vandofinetia*). Though very pretty, they are not as yet generally available. Additional breeding offers some interesting possibilities.

CULTURE: Generally as for the dwarf Vandas, and the like. *Neofinetia* does particularly well in small, perfectly-drained pots, these tightly filled with either osmunda or shredded tree-fern fibre. (I)

N. falcata (Thunb.) Hu (*Orchis falcata* Thunb., *Angraecum falcatum* Ldl., *Angraecopsis falcata* Schltr., *Finetia falcata* Schltr., *Limodorum falcatum* Sw., *Nipponorchis falcata* Masa., *Oeceoclades falcata* Ldl.)

Sts. frequently branched from near the base, short, usually less than 2½″ tall, densely leafy throughout, at least when young. Lvs. linear, acute, rigidly fleshy, imbricated, often gracefully curving, to 3″ long, usually rather light green, rarely variegated with cream-white longitudinal stripes. Infls. mostly erect, usually shorter than the lvs., with 3–7-fld. rac. near apex. Fls. extremely fragrant (mostly at night), brilliant dead white, to about 1¼″ in diam., mostly longer than wide, the spur curved, awl-like, about 1½″ long, brilliant dead-white. Mostly summer–autumn. (I) Japan; Korea.

NEOGARDNERIA Schltr.

This is a genus of two known species, both natives of the wooded mountains of the State of Rio de Janeiro in Brazil. Rare and little-known in collections, they are attractive epiphytes which warrant further attention by enthusiasts. They were originally described as Zygopetalums, but are amply distinct from that group by reason of technical details of the flowers. Cogniaux has suggested that both are natural hybrids between *Zygopetalum* and *Colax*, but there seems no confirming evidence that this is the case.

No hybrids are known as yet which utilize *Neogardneria*, though it seems probable that the species will prove inter-fertile with *Zygopetalum*, and perhaps with some others of the allied genera. Resultant progeny from such experimental crosses should be very handsome and desirable orchids.

CULTURE: As for the warm-growing Lycastes. (I, H)

N. Binoti (DeWild.) Hoehne (*Zygopetalum Binoti* DeWild.)

Pbs. clustered, ovoid-oblong, somewhat compressed, to 3″ long. Lvs. typically paired, linear-lanceolate, narrowed basally, to more than 12″ long, rather leathery. Infls. elongate, 3–6-fld., erect or arching. Fls. to more than 2″ across, fragrant, waxy, the ss. and ps. greenish or bright green, the lip bright yellow, streaked basally with red and with a bright red callus. Summer. (I, H) Brazil.

N. Murrayana (Gardn.) Schltr. (*Zygopetalum Murrayanum* Gardn., *Eulophia Murrayana* Steud., *Promenaea florida* Rchb.f.)

Pbs. clustered, ovoid, somewhat compressed laterally, to 2½″ long, sheathed basally. Lvs. 2 or more, leathery, ligular-lanceolate, acute or acuminate, to 1½′ long and 1½″ wide, rather glossy. Infls. erect or nodding, mostly less than 12″ long, 3–6-fld., with prominent basal sheathing bracts. Fls. waxy, fragrant, to about 2″ across, the ss. and ps. clear green, the lip white with a yellow callus that has 5 purple-brown stripes and some irregular flushes of the same colour in front of it, the col. yellow-green with deep red streaks on the frontal face. Summer. (I, H) Brazil.

NEOGYNE Rchb.f.

The only known species of *Neogyne* is a very rare but singularly attractive epiphytic orchid (rarely semi-terrestrial), native in the high mountains of Nepal and Southern China. Allied to *Coelogyne* Ldl., the genus differs in the structure of the rather tubular flowers, although the plants vegetatively simulate many members of that large aggregation. *Neogyne* is found occasionally today in particularly specialized collections, but it must be classed as a scarce orchid.

No hybrids are known in this genus, and nothing has been established concerning its genetic affinities.

CULTURE: As for the high-elevation Coelogynes. (C, I)

N. Gardneriana (Ldl.) Rchb.f. (*Coelogyne Gardneriana* Ldl., *Coelogyne trisaccata* Griff.)

Pbs. clustered, roundish, attenuated upwards, often somewhat vaguely angular, to about 6″ tall. Lvs. 2, narrowly elliptic, acutish, rather heavy-textured, vaguely plicate. Infls. at first erect, finally becoming sharply pendulous, to about 8″ long, densely few-fld., the fls. enclosed by large brownish bracts, usually in two ranks. Fls. about 2″ long, not opening well, somewhat tubular, white, the lip with a yellow centre, the tips of the ss. and ps. usually reflexed. Autumn–winter. (C, I) Nepal; China: Yunnan.

NEOKOEHLERIA Schltr.

Neokoehleria is a genus of about three known species, all dwarf, rather strange epiphytic orchids, native in Peru. Allied to *Plectrophora* Focke and other genera of the subtribe *Comparettiinae*, none of them appears to be present in contemporary collections, although they are interesting little 'botanicals' of considerable potential appeal to the connoisseur.

Nothing is known of the genetic affinities of this scarce group.

CULTURE: Presumably as for *Ornithocephalus*. (H)

NEOLAUCHEA Krzl.

This is a genus comprising a single uncommon epiphytic orchid of the subtribe *Laeliinae*, somewhat allied to *Meiracyllium* Rchb.f., native in southern Brazil, and present in only the most comprehensive of contemporary collections. It is a most unusual little plant, with diminutive, terete-leaved pseudobulbs borne at intervals on a long-creeping rhizome, and proportionately large and attractive rosy-red blossoms.

No hybrids are registered in *Neolauchea*, and nothing is known of its genetic affinities.

CULTURE: This dwarf orchid is rather readily grown, once established, but is often difficult to start from propagations, because of the great fragility of all vegetative parts. It does best in a shallow pan or small basket, with perfect drainage, rather tightly packed with chopped osmunda fibre. A shady, perpetually moist situation is necessary, and warm temperatures should prevail at all times. It should be disturbed as infrequently as possible. (I)

N. pulchella Krzl. (*Meiracyllium Wettsteini* Porsch)

Rhiz. very elongated, creeping, bearing the pbs. at intervals of ¾–1″. Pbs. narrowly ovoid, about ¼–½″ tall, slightly less in diam. Lf. solitary, narrowly linear, leathery, often almost terete, to 2¼″ long. Infls. terminal, thread-like, 1-fld., to 2″ tall, erect or arching. Fls. rather hooded, usually about ¼″ long, rosy-red or lilac, brownish toward the lip-base, the dors. sep. concave, the lip concave basally. Nov.–Jan. (I) Southern Brazil.

NEOMOOREA Rolfe
(*Moorea* Rolfe)

Two species of *Neomoorea* are known to date, one of them a highly-prized and magnificent epiphytic or terrestrial orchid, native in Colombia and Panama, which is present in a few comprehensive collections today. Somewhat allied to *Houlletia* Brongn., the plants rather simulate a stout *Stanhopea*, and bear erect or arching racemes of very handsome flowers during the spring months.

Neomoorea has not as yet been taken in hand by the breeders, although it is presumably genetically compatible with *Houlletia*, and doubtless also with other genera of the subtribe *Gongorinae*.

CULTURE: Found in nature either as terrestrials or (perhaps more commonly) as epiphytes, these majestic orchids are best treated with conditions intermediate between the two, being grown in perfectly-drained pots in a compost of about equal parts of shredded osmunda or chopped tree-fern fibre, with some rich loam and gritty sand added. The new bark composts, provided they are carefully sifted to remove all dust, also form a beneficial additive to such a medium. A shaded spot and warm temperatures are necessary, and water should be given in quantity while the growths are maturing, but upon their completion a strict rest is required. The new growths are especially sensitive to over-watering or stale compost. Neomooreas should be disturbed as infrequently as possible for best results. (I, H)

N. irrorata (Rolfe) Rolfe (*Moorea irrorata* Rolfe)

Pbs. robust, egg-shaped, rather laterally compressed, furrowed, often yellowish, to 5″ long. Lvs. 2, ellipticlanceolate, folded, acute or shortly acuminate, strongveined, rather thick and rigid, to almost 3′ long and 6″ wide. Infls. usually erect, to almost 2′ tall. rather densely 10–20-fld. Fls. waxy, fragrant, about 2⅛″ across, the ss. and ps. reddish-brown with white bases, the ss. (and sometimes the ps.) rather concave. Lip deeply 3-lbd., the large lat. lbs. pale yellow banded and marked with brown-purple, the midlb. pale yellow spotted with red, the basal crest winged, stalked. Spring. (I, H) Panama; Colombia.

NEOTINEA Rchb.f.
(*Tinaea* Boiss., *Tinea* Biv.)

Closely allied to *Orchis* [Tournef.] L., this monotypic genus of terrestrial European orchids is very rare in contemporary cultivation, but the structure of the smallish flowers is unusually interesting, and recommends it to specialists. A slender orchid, **Neotinea intacta** (Link) Rchb.f. attains a height of about 10″ at most, and bears a dense raceme of small, greenish, redveined blossoms during the spring and early summer months. It occurs mostly in Southern Europe.

Nothing is known of the genetic affinities of *Neotinea*.

CULTURE: As for the temperate species of *Orchis* and *Habenaria*. (C)

NEOTTIA L.
(*Neottidium* Schlecht., *Synoplectris* Raf.)

About five species of *Neottia* are known to date, all of them scarce saprophytic orchids of the subtribe *Listerinae*. The best-known species is the peculiar 'Bird's Nest Orchid' of Europe (*N. nidus-avis* (L.) Rich.), which is described below, but other species of comparable interest occur in China, India, and the Kamchatka Peninsula of the U.S.S.R. Peculiar plants with fleshy stems, on which the leaves are reduced to tiny sheathing scales, with complex flowers in an apical raceme, the Neottias are—like the majority of the odd saprophytic orchids—extremely rare in our collections, and usually almost impossible to maintain in good condition for more than a single season.

No hybrids are known, and nothing has been ascertained regarding the genetic affinities of the genus.

CULTURE: As for *Corallorrhiza* and other saprophytes. (C, I)

N. nidus-avis (L.) Rich. (*Ophrys nidus-avis* L., *Helleborine nidus-avis* Schm., *Listera nidus-avis* Hk.)

Roots subterranean, matted, rather simulating a bird's-nest (hence the derivation of both the scientific and the vernacular names), small, fleshy, fusiform. St. erect, to about 15″ tall, clothed with a few scale-like bracts, these brown like the st., with an apical rather densely many-fld. rac. Fls. about ⅜″ long, complex, dingy-brown to purplish-brown, the lip deeply cleft at the tip into 2 oblong diverging lbs. with blunt tips. Mostly Apr.–June. (C, I) Europe to western Siberia.

NEOTTIANTHE [Rchb.f.] Schltr.
(*Habenaria* Willd. subgen. *Neottianthe* Rchb.f.)

Seven or eight species of *Neottianthe* are known to science, these rather rare and for the most part incompletely-delimited terrestrial (rarely lithophytic) orchids indigenous to the Himalayas and China. Unknown in our collections at this time, they are members of the subtribe *Habenarinae*, and are principally of scientific interest.

Nothing has thus far been ascertained regarding the genetic affinities of *Neottianthe*.

CULTURE: Presumably as for the cool-growing Habenarias, Orchis, etc. (C, I)

NEO-URBANIA F. & R.

This genus, consisting of a single rare species in Jamaica and Cuba, is a member of the subtribe *Ponerinae*, and is virtually unknown in contemporary collections, despite its being a very handsome foliage plant when well-grown, and its small flowers are uniquely attractive. In the wild, *Neo-Urbania* usually grows epiphytically on trees, its lengthy leafy stems often gracefully pendulous, but occasional specimens occur on rocky hillsides as semi-terrestrials. The genus is closely allied to *Ponera* Ldl., but differs in the axillary flowers and the free, simple pollinia.

Nothing has been ascertained regarding the genetic affinities of this odd genus.

CULTURE: As for the tropical, 'reed-stem' Epidendrums. (I)

N. adendrobium (Rchb.f.) F. & R. (*Ponera adendrobium* Rchb.f., *Pleuranthium adendrobium* Bth. & Hk.f., *Camaridium parviflorum* Fawc.)

Sts. elongate, rooting at the lower internodes, to about 5′ long, semi-erect to very strongly pendulous, leafy almost throughout. Lvs. alternate, linear-lanceolate, subacuminate, to 6″ long, with persistent tightly adpressed sheathing stalks. Infls. very abbreviated, 1-fld., but typically with several fls. produced at once from the lf.-axils, with small scarious bracts at base. Fls. proportionately long-stalked, white, not opening well, about $\frac{1}{5}$″ long. Ss. connivent, the dors. one free, the lats.

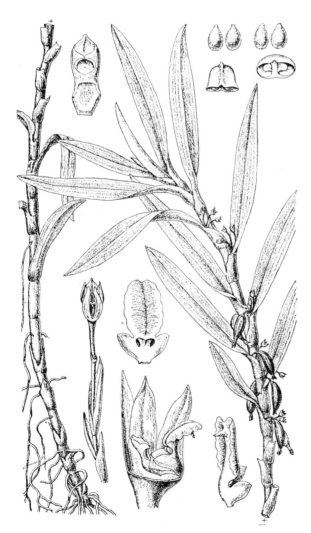

Neo-Urbania adendrobium (Rchb.f.) F. & R. [Fawcett & Rendle, *Flora of Jamaica*]

adnate to the col.-foot, forming a chin under the lip, oblong to oblong-elliptic, subacuminate. Ps. similar, slightly smaller. Lip 3-lbd., jointed to the col.-foot, the lat. lbs. incurved over the col., the midlb. oval, recurved, the disc with 2 calli at the base. Autumn–spring. (I) Jamaica; Cuba: Oriente.

NEPHELAPHYLLUM Bl.

This is a genus of about eight species of seldom-seen terrestrial orchids of the subtribe *Collabiinae*, native in the area extending from the Malay Peninsula and the Philippines throughout Indonesia to Celebes. They are unusually handsome plants, with fleshy variegated foliage on small pseudobulbs, and mostly erect racemes of intricately complex, often brightly coloured flowers. The genus is perhaps closest in its affinity to *Mischobulbum* Schltr., but differs from it in technical details. Rare in cultivation, these plants should be better known by specialist collectors.

No hybrids are known in *Nephelaphyllum*, and its genetic alliances have not as yet been established.

CULTURE: As for the tropical species of *Phaius*. (I, H)

N. pulchrum Bl.

Pbs. borne at intervals along the creeping rhiz., cylindrical, to 1″ tall. Lf. solitary, erect, ovate, basally short; cordate, to 3″ long or more, the upper surface yellow-green with light grey-brown blotches, dark green beneath. Infls. exceeding the lvs. in length, erect, the rac. very densely 3–7-fld., almost head-like. Fls. about 1″ long, the ss. and ps. pink or brownish-green, the large lip pinkish or white at base, otherwise pale yellow, with a dark median yellow bar, on the top of the fl. Spring–summer. (I, H) Malay Peninsula; Java; Sumatra; Borneo.

N. tenuiflorum Bl.

Similar in habit to *N. pulchrum* Bl., but not as robust. Lvs. more triangular-ovate, to almost 3″ long, green with darker blotches. Infls. almost twice as long as the lvs., loosely 5–8-fld. Fls. about $\frac{3}{4}$″ long, rather drooping, not opening fully, the ss. and ps. green, usually more or less flushed with purple, the lip erect, white, furnished near the tip with a few large, succulent, purple hairs. Spring–summer. (H) Malay Peninsula; Sumatra; Java; Borneo.

NEPHRANGIS [Schltr.] Summerh.
(*Tridactyle* Schltr. subgen. *Nephrangis* Schltr.)

But a single species of *Nephrangis* is known to date, this the rare **N. filiformis** (Krzl.) Summerh. (*Listrostachys filiformis* Krzl., *Tridactyle filiformis* Schltr.), an epiphytic orchid of the *Angraecum* alliance (subtribe *Sarcanthinae*) which has been found in several localities in tropical Africa. It is an interesting plant, but regrettably does not seem to be in cultivation at this time.

Nothing is known concerning the genetic ties of *Nephrangis*.

CULTURE: Presumably as for the tropical Angraecums. (H)

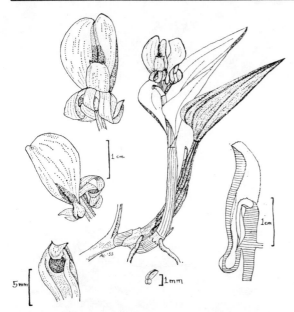

Nephelaphyllum latilabre Ridl. [A.D.HAWKES, AFTER HOLTTUM]

NERVILIA Comm. ex Gaud.
(*Aplostellis* Thou., *Cordyla* Bl., *Haplostellis* Endl., *Roptrostemon* Bl.)

About sixty-five species of *Nervilia* are known, these peculiar primarily terrestrial orchids which have been relegated to a subtribe of their own, the *Nerviliinae*. Inhabiting the subtropical and tropical regions of Africa and Asia, they have solitary, stalked, heart-shaped leaves which are sometimes attractively variegated; these arise from subterranean round tubers. The inflorescences bear a single or a few often relatively large and handsomely complex flowers, mostly white, greenish, or yellowish with purple or reddish markings especially on the lip. Usually the leaves and flowers are produced at different seasons of the year. The genus is incompletely known botanically, and its members are today extremely rare in our collections, although they are largely very desirable orchids for the connoisseur orchidist.

No hybrids have as yet been made in the genus *Nervilia*, and nothing is known of its genetic affinities, although they are possibly with the subtribe *Bletillinae*.

CULTURE: These plants, although attractive, are not particularly easy to maintain in good condition in the collection. Best kept in perfectly drained pots, they will sometimes thrive under conditions such as those suggested for *Phaius* and the like. Annual replenishing of the compost seems advantageous. (I, H)

N. Aragoana Gaud. (*Aplostellis flabelliformis* Ridl., *Pogonia flabelliformis* Ldl., *Pogonia gracilis* Bl., *Pogonia Nervilia* Bl.)
Tubers round, subterranean, producing stolons (these tipped by new tubers) after flowering. Lf. solitary, the petiole to about 8″ tall, the lamina very broadly heart-shaped, shortly acute, marginally rather undulate, green sometimes with dark purplish blotches, the basal

lbs. more or less overlapping, to 4¾″ long and to 6¼″ broad. Infl. produced when lf. has withered, to about 12″ tall, sheathed, 2–15-fld. Fls. opening well, to about 2″ long, the narrow ss. and ps. pale green, the lip shorter than ss., white with purplish or green veins. Lip 3-lbd., the lat. lbs. small, triangular, erect, the tips spreading; midlb. ovate with incurved edges, hairy on the veins. Spring–early summer. (I, H) India throughout Southeast Asia and Indonesia to Samoa.

N. discolor (Bl.) Schltr. (*Cordyla discolor* Bl., *Aplostellis velutina* Ridl., *Pogonia discolor* Bl., *Pogonia velutina* Par. & Rchb.f.) Lf. solitary, the petiole very short, the lamina borne almost at ground-level, heart-shaped, usually not undulate, hairy above and below, brown-purplish, to 4¾″ in diam., with many curving veins raised alternately above and below. Infl. to 4″ tall, 2-fld., bracted. Fls. opening well, to 2¾″ long, the ss. and ps. pale olive-green to dull pale purple, the unlobed lip white at base, with a raised median yellow band, the veins yellow to brown or purple. Spring–early summer. (H) Burma; Thailand; Viet-Nam; Malay Peninsula; Java.

N. nipponica Mak. Lf. cordate-orbicular, rather long-petioled, to 1¾″ in diam. Infl. about 3½″ tall, with a few small sheaths, 1-fld. Fl. nodding, about ⅝″ long, the narrowly lanceolate ss. and ps. purple, the 3-lbd. lip white, spotted with purple. Lip 3-lbd., the lat. lbs. very small, obtuse; midlb. elliptic, obtuse, crisped marginally. Summer. (I) Japan.

N. punctata (Bl.) Schltr. (*Pogonia punctata* Bl., *Aplostellis punctata* Ridl.) Lf.-petiole to 4″ tall, the lamina cordate, 1½–3½″ wide, green, with 7 principal veins, the margin slightly angled at the vein-ends. Infl. about 4″ tall, elongating in fruit, 1-fld. Fl. opening well, about 1½″ long, the ss. and ps. very pale yellowish with numerous dull purple marks. Lip shorter than other segms., the base embracing the col., with small slightly incurved acute lat. lbs., the midlb. retrorse, acute, white or pale mauve with small purple spots. Spring–summer. (H) Langkawi Islands; Malay Peninsula; Sumatra; Java.

NIGRITELLA L.C.Rich.

A single showy terrestrial orchid, native in Central and North Europe, makes up the genus *Nigritella*, a member of the complex subtribe *Habenarinae*, somewhat allied to *Habenaria* Willd. It is a handsome plant when in full flower, but its cultural requirements are not readily met in the average indoor collection, and it should, if possible, be kept in the cool outdoor garden or rockery.

No hybrids are known in *Nigritella*, but it is presumably compatible with certain of the allied genera of the *Habenarinae*.

CULTURE: As for the temperate species of *Habenaria*. A shady spot, in rich, well-drained soil, suits it best. (C)

N. nigra (L.) Rchb.f. (*Satyrium nigrum* L., *Gymnadenia nigra* Rchb.f., *Habenaria nigra* R.Br., *Nigritella angustifolia* L.C.Rich., *Orchis miniata* Crantz, *Orchis nigra* Scop.)
Tubers subterranean, hand-shaped, short and fleshy. Lvs. few to numerous, borne at base of flowering-st., narrowly linear, rather soft-textured. Infl. 2–6″ tall, within a dense head-like rac. of many fls. at the apex. Fls. about ¼″ long, opening widely, very dark purple, often almost black-purple, the lip rhombic-ovate, with

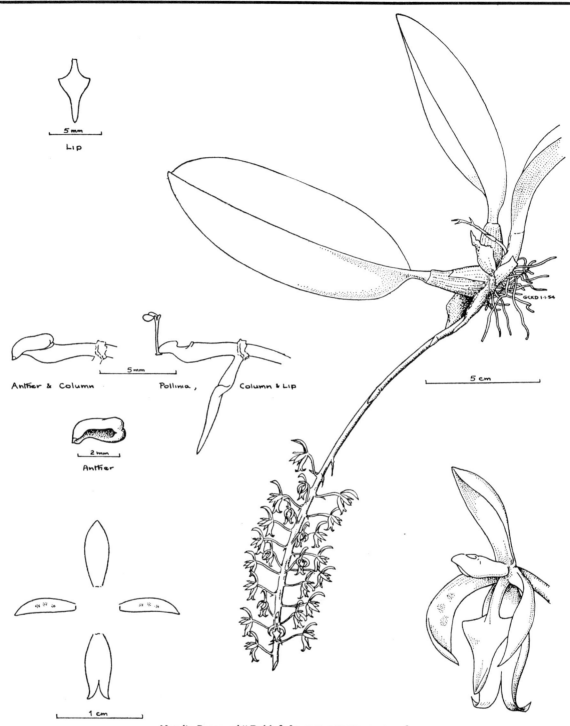

5 mm
Lip

Anther & Column

5 mm

Pollinia,

Column & Lip

2 mm
Anther

5 cm

1 cm

Notylia Bungerothii Rchb.f. [G.C.K.DUNSTERVILLE]

a small spur. Spring–summer. (C) North and Central Europe.

—var. **rubra** (Wettst.) Schltr. (*Nigritella rubra* Wettst.)
Differing from typical *N. nigra* (L.) Rchb.f. in the carmine-red fls., which are borne in a more ellipsoidal head-like rac. Spring–summer. (C) Eastern Alps of Europe.

NOTYLIA Ldl.
(*Macroclinium* B.-R., *Tridachne* Liebm. ex Ldl.)

This is a genus of about forty species of seldom cultivated but unusually interesting epiphytic or lithophytic orchids in the American tropics, extending from Mexico to Brazil and Bolivia. Allied somewhat to *Macradenia* R.Br., the genus is divided into two convenient sections, based on vegetative habit. In the first section (*Eunotylia*), the plants have small but distinct pseudobulbs with a single flat leaf. The second section (*Macroclinium*) consists of plants in which the leaves are equitant and distichously imbricating, with the folded bases sometimes enveloping a small, compressed pseudobulb. Notylias bear (usually) lengthy racemes of very numerous, small flowers, mostly in shades of white, greenish, or yellow. Despite their small size, they are produced in sufficient numbers to be attractive, and recommend the genus to connoisseurs.

No hybrids are known in *Notylia* at this time, and nothing has been ascertained regarding its genetic affinities.

CULTURE: Notylias are best grown in the average collection when tightly affixed to small slabs or cubes of tree-fern fibre. Mostly shade-loving plants, they require abundant moisture and warmth at all times, though naturally care must be taken as regards drainage. They should be disturbed as infrequently as possible. Moderate fertilizing at intervals is beneficial. (I, H)

N. Barkeri Ldl. (*Tridachne virens* Liebm. ex Ldl., *Notylia angustilancea* Schltr., *N. Bernoullii* Schltr., *N. bipartita* Rchb.f., *N. Brenesii* Schltr., *N. guatemalensis* S.Wats., *N. Huegelii* Fenzl, *N. multiflora* Hk., *N. Pittieri* Schltr., *N. tamaulipensis* Rchb.f., *N. Tridachne* Ldl. & Paxt., *N. trisepala* Ldl. & Paxt., *N. turialbae* Schltr.)

Pbs. clustered, oblong, compressed, glossy, to about 1″ long, the bases enveloped in several imbricating bracts, the uppermost ones of which are lf.-like. Lf. (apical) solitary, leathery, ligular, obtuse to acutish, to 7″ long. Infls. 1 or more, arching to sharply pendulous, densely many-fld., to 12″ long, usually somewhat shorter. Fls. about ½″ long (often smaller), faintly fragrant, white, sometimes yellow-spotted. Ss. usually with the lat. ones joined into a single rather obliquely acutish segm., the dors. one free, linear-lanceolate, concave. Ps. downcurving, linear-lanceolate, acute. Lip clawed at base, the blade triangular, acuminate. Mostly spring. (I, H) Mexico to Panama.

N. bicolor Ldl.

Pbs. compressed, disc-shaped, about 1″ tall, with lf.-like bracts at the base. Lf. solitary, rather leathery, sword-shaped, acuminate, about 2″ long. Infls. pendulous, to 4″ long, densely many-fld. Fls. about ¾″ long, the ss. whitish, the ps. white, spotted with dull purple, the lip whitish-purple, with two darker purple spots on the disc. Ss. all free, linear-lanceolate, acutish. Ps. similar but shorter. Lip short-clawed, ligulate, apically wider than at base. Summer. (I, H) Mexico; Guatemala; Nicaragua; Costa Rica.

N. pentachne Rchb.f. (*Notylia gracilispica* Schltr.)

Pbs. oblong, compressed, about 1″ tall, usually somewhat covered by the bases of the lf.-like bracts. Lf. oblong-lanceolate to ligular, obtuse to acutish, rigidly leathery, to 8″ long, stalked below. Infls. 1–2, pendulous, densely many-fld., rarely branched, to more than 12″ long. Fls. almost 1″ long, faintly fragrant, the ss. pale green, the ps. white with 2 tiny orange spots in the centre, the lip white. Dors. sep. lanceolate, acuminate; lat. ss.

joined for more than half their length, the tips wide-spreading and recurved. Ps. rather obliquely lanceolate, short-acuminate. Lip with an elongate, slender claw, the blade abruptly dilated, acuminate. Col. slender, papillose. Spring–autumn. (I, H) Panama.

N. punctata (Ker-Gawl.) Ldl. (*Pleurothallis punctata* Ker-Gawl., *Gomesa tenuiflora* Lodd., *Notylia incurva* Ldl.)

Rather similar in habit to *N. Barkeri* Ldl., the pbs. smaller, the infls. very dense, to 4″ long. Fls. about ½″ long, the ss. yellowish, the ps. whitish with 2–3 yellow median spots, the lip white, sometimes spotted on the disc with yellow. Spring. (I, H) Trinidad; Venezuela.

OAKES-AMESIA Schweinf. & Allen

But a single species of *Oakes-Amesia* is known to date, this restricted, insofar as is known, to the mountainous regions of Panama. **Oakes-Amesia cryptantha** Schweinf. & Allen is a dwarf epiphytic orchid, vegetatively resembling *Ornithocephalus* Hk., but differing radically in the structure of the small, green and white, very complex flowers. It is unknown in collections at this time, and appears to be a very rare plant in the wild.

Nothing is known concerning the genetic affinities of *Oakes-Amesia*.

CULTURE: As for *Ornithocephalus*. (I)

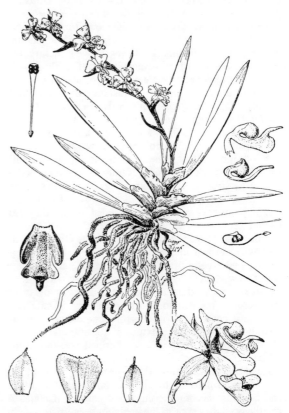

Oakes-Amesia cryptantha Schw. & Allen [GORDON W. DILLON]

OBERONIA Ldl.
(*Titania* Endl.)

Oberonia is a remarkable large genus of an estimated two hundred species of epiphytic (or rarely lithophytic) orchids enjoying a huge range, this extending from East Africa to Samoa, with particularly large representation in Indonesia and New Guinea. A member of the complex subtribe *Liparidinae*, these are without exception very rare plants in cultivation today, though they are —vegetatively rather more than florally—among the most unique and unusual in the entire Orchidaceae. Dr. R. E. Holttum succinctly describes the genus (in *Fl. Malaya* [*Orch. Malaya*] 1: 208. 1953): 'The plants are very easy to recognize, owing to their much-flattened leaves, looking as though they had been put into a press. The leaves are so much laterally flattened that they have practically no upper surface except at the sheathing base. In this they agree with some species of *Dendrobium*, *Bromheadia* and *Microsaccus* [and *Oncidium*, *Ornithocephalus*, *Oakes-Amesia*, etc. in the Americas]; but the peculiar feature of *Oberonia*, shared by none of these, is the slender terminal inflorescence covered with its tiny flowers. The flowers are never more than about 2 mm. long [much less than one eighth of an inch], and often hardly more than 1 mm. . . . The flowers are usually greenish to yellowish, orange or red, sometimes a rich red-brown. They are often beautifully shaped. The inflorescence continues to grow at the base after the middle part is mature; the middle flowers open first, and the basal flowers usually last of all. Usually many fruits are produced." As a member of the subtribe *Liparidinae*, *Oberonia* is most closely in alliance with (and might possibly be confused with) *Hippeophyllum* Schltr., which also has this remarkable vegetative structure, but is readily distinguished—even when not in flower—in that the groups of equitant leaves are borne on a creeping rhizome, at least an inch or so distant from each other, usually at rather greater intervals. Further, *Hippeophyllum* has a long column, whereas that structure in the genus under discussion is always very abbreviated.

Oberonias are, as noted above, very rare orchids in our collections today, hence nothing has been done with them in the way of breeding. If only for the remarkable vegetative structure of the plants (the flowers can scarcely be termed showy!), the myriad members of this fascinating genus offer much to the specialist in the 'botanical' orchids.

CULTURE: Largely dwarf in stature, the Oberonias do best when grown in the warm or intermediate greenhouse, under conditions of high humidity and (except for a few high-elevation species) rather warm temperatures. Since they have no pseudobulbs or other moisture-storing structures, the often very delicate leaf-fans must never be permitted to become dry. They do best in small pots, in a mixture of about equal parts of chopped sphagnum moss and chopped tree-fern fibre. When well-rooting, they can also be mounted on smallish slabs of tree-fern. Drainage must be perfect, as the plants are prone to deteriorate with disconcerting rapidity if the compost becomes even the slightest bit stale. A relatively shaded spot in the greenhouse, with abundant fresh, freely moving air suits them well. Repotting or disturbance of the often fragile root-systems should be done as infrequently as possible. Periodic applications of weakened fertilizing solution are beneficial. (I, H)

O. acaulis Griff.
Stemless pls., the few lvs. linear-ensiform, to 12″ long, fleshy, rather incurving. Infls. erect, very densely many-fld., almost as long as the lvs., about ¼″ in diam., the fls. mostly opening successively. Fls. less than ⅛″ across, golden-yellow, the ps. fringed, the 4-lbd. lip also fringed. Late winter–spring. (I, H) Himalayas.

O. iridifolia (Roxb.) Ldl. (*Cymbidium iridifolium* Roxb., *Malaxis ensiformis* Sm.)
St. very short. Lvs. 4–6, the basal ones the smallest, the largest to 7″ long and about ¾″ wide, jointed at base, apically somewhat incurving. Infls. about 10″ long, the basal part flattened, the fl.-bearing rachis curved, the fls. in rather regular close whorls. Fls. less than ¼″ across, pale greenish or brownish, the sides of the lip with deep teeth, the apex 2-lbd. Winter. (I, H) Himalayas throughout Malaysia to the Pacific Islands (Tahiti, etc.).

O. lunata (Bl.) Ldl. (*Malaxis lunata* Bl., *Oberonia biaurita* Hk.f., *O. porphyrochila* Ridl., *O. subnavicularis* King & Pantl.)
St. short. Lvs. 3–5, to 6½″ long, less than ½″ wide, gradually narrowed to an acute tip. Infls. about as long as the lvs., the fls. in close whorls. Fls. less than ¼″ across, pale pinkish or brownish, the lip dark red-brown, heart-shaped. Winter. (H) Malay Peninsula.

OCTADESMIA Bth.

This is a genus of four known species, natives of the West Indies and Brazil. Rather closely allied to *Neo-Urbania* F. & R. and certain other members of the subtribe *Ponerinae*, two of the Octadesmias are present in a few contemporary collections, although they must be classed as very rare orchids. Epiphytic or rarely semi-terrestrial plants, they bear rather robust stems (not thickened into pseudobulbs) covered with leaves and reaching (in *O. elata* Bth. & Hkf.f.) heights in excess of six feet. The small flowers are produced in terminal, sometimes branched inflorescences, and are rather attractive when examined closely.

Nothing is known of the genetic affinities of this group.

CULTURE: As for the tropical, 'reed-stem' type Epidendrums. (I)

O. elata Bth. & Hk.f.
Sts. clustered, erect, robust, to almost 7′ tall, leafy in upper part, with the fibrous remains of the lf.-sheaths below. Lvs. passing into spathaceous bracts of the infl., the broadly lanceolate rigid lamina to 4½″ long, prominently nervose, jointed to the sheaths. Infls. erect, usually branched, bracted, few-fld., to 10″ tall. Fls. about ¾″ long, fragrant, whitish, the disc of the lip sometimes flushed with yellow. Ss. narrowly oblong, slightly apiculate, the lats. keeled and slightly hooded towards the apex. Ps. narrowly oblong, slightly keeled and hooded. Lip longer than wide, sessile, obovate-oblong; lat. lbs. rounded; midlb. much larger, 3-lobulate, apiculate; disc 2-lamellate below, the lamellae and

prominent mid-nerve extending as distinct lines toward the tip. Spring. (I) Cuba; Jamaica.

O. montana (Sw.) Bth. (*Epidendrum montanum* Sw., *Cymbidium montanum* Sw., *Bletia montana* Rchb.f., *Tetramicra montana* Griseb., *Octadesmia serratifolia* Hk.)

Sts. clustered, to 2' tall, leafy above, the sheaths below striate, minutely warty, brown-spotted. Lvs. oblong-lanceolate, obliquely acutish, rigid, to 4½" long. Infls. simple or branched, few-fld., to 8" tall, bracted. Fls. more than ½" across, cream-white, with the fragrance

Octadesmia montana (Sw.) Bth. [Fawcett & Rendle, *Flora of Jamaica*]

of violets, rather long-lived. Ss. oblong-lanceolate, obtuse, the lats. somewhat the shorter, apically thickened and apiculate. Ps. linear-oblong, tapering to the apiculate tip. Lip about as long as wide, very short-clawed, roundish; lat. lbs. short, obtuse; midlb. much larger, minutely crenulate, apiculate; disc 2-lamellate below, with tiny warty calli along the three nerves from the midlb., the lamellae 2-lbd. Autumn–spring. (I, H) Cuba; Hispaniola; Puerto Rico; Jamaica.

OCTARRHENA Thw.

This genus of the subtribe *Thelasinae* consists of about nineteen species of small, little-known and seldom encountered epiphytic orchids, none of which appears to be present in our collections at this time. Mostly indigenous to New Guinea, outlying representatives of *Octarrhena* occur in such areas as Ceylon, New Caledonia, etc. Simulating *Chitonanthera* Schltr. in vegetative habit, they differ from that group in floral structure, and in the presence of eight pollinia instead of four.

Nothing is known of the genetic affinities of this scarce genus.

CULTURE: Presumably as for the tropical Bulbophyllums. (I, H)

OCTOMERIA R.Br.
(*Aspegrenia* P. & E., *Enothrea* Raf.)

A member of the very complex subtribe *Pleurothallidinae*, *Octomeria* consists of an estimated seventy-five species of epiphytic or lithophytic orchids, for the most part native to Brazil, but with outlying representatives extending to such regions as Honduras, Costa Rica, the West Indies, and the Guianas. Differing from *Pleurothallis* R.Br. primarily in bearing eight pollinia (instead of four), they are highly diverse plants, which are today exceptionally scarce in our collections, although many of them are attractive, mostly dwarf 'botanicals', often with fascicles of white, yellow, or green flowers, these borne at the base of the fleshy or coriaceous leaves.

No hybrids have as yet been registered with *Octomeria*, and nothing is known of its genetic affinities.

CULTURE: As for *Pleurothallis*, depending upon the place of origin of the particular species or individual under consideration. (I, H)

O. graminifolia (L.) Ldl. (*Epidendrum graminifolium* L., *Dendrobium graminifolium* Willd.)

Rhiz. elongate, rooting freely. Sts. borne at intervals along the rhiz., erect or ascending, to 1½" tall. Lf. solitary, rigidly fleshy, linear-lanceolate, acute, to 2½" long, often flushed with reddish. Infls. 1-fld., in the lf.-axils. Fls. not opening fully, faintly fragrant, about ¼" long, pale yellow, the complex lip usually slightly darker in colour, or with a median red spot. Spring or almost throughout the year. (I, H) Lesser Antilles; Trinidad; Tobago.

O. grandiflora Ldl.

Sts. clustered, to 7" tall, slender, sheathed. Lf. solitary, narrowly ligulate, acutish, to 5" long, rigidly leathery,

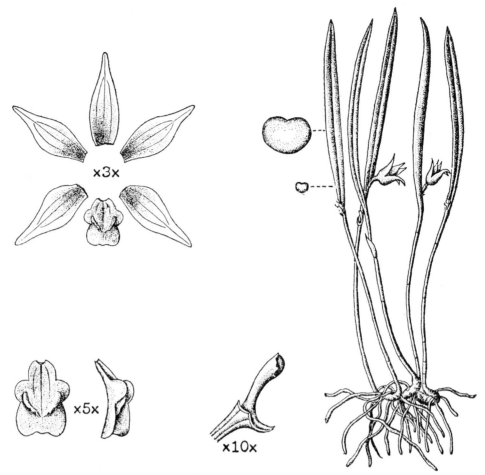

Octomeria caldensis Hoehne [*Flora Brasílica*]

often flushed with purplish or reddish-purple. Infls. clustered at leaf-base, abbreviated, rather numerous, with sheathing papery bracts. Fls. opening rather widely, nodding, to less than 1″ long, yellow or yellowish to greenish-white or white, usually with a red blotch on the base of the lip. Autumn–spring. (I, H) Trinidad; Brazil; Bolivia.

ODONTOCHILUS Bl.

Odontochilus is a genus of fifteen or more species of primarily terrestrial, rather nondescript orchids of the subtribe *Physurinae*, native over an immense region which extends from India throughout South-east Asia, Indonesia, and neighbouring insular groups to the Hawaiian Islands. The group is very closely allied to *Anoectochilus* Bl., and has on occasion been reduced to synonymy under it, but seems distinct in its usually green (not coloured) foliage and lip with only a sac-like base and not a distinct spur. On occasion, some of these scarce but interesting orchids may be found in specialized collections.

No hybrids are known in *Odontochilus*, but it is presumably allied to *Anoectochilus* Bl. genetically, and hybrids between the two should be possible.

CULTURE: As for *Anoectochilus.* (H)

O. crispus (Ldl.) Hk.f. (*Anoectochilus crispus* Ldl.)

Pls. to about 8″ tall when in fl., bearing a few short-stalked, oval, green lvs. to 2″ long near the base of the rather stout st. Infl. rather loosely few-fld., the fls. opening successively over a long period of time Fls. about ¾″ long, not expanding fully, the ss. and ps. greenish, the lip whitish or white. Autumn. (H) Himalayas.

O. Elwesii (King & Pantl.) Clarke (*Anoectochilus Elwesii* King & Pantl.) Rather similar in habit to *O. crispus* (Ldl.) Hk.f., but somewhat larger in all parts, the lvs. velvety, deep brown. Fls. about 1″ long, the ss. and ps. short, greenish, the large green-fringed lip otherwise white. Summer–autumn. (H) Himalayas.

O. grandiflorus (Ldl.) Bth. (*Anoectochilus grandiflorus* Ldl.) A robust pl., up to more than 12″ tall when in bloom, the few lvs. near base of the st., green, elliptic, to about 4″ long. Infl. loosely few-fld., the fls. opening successively. Fls. about 1″ long, the ss. and ps. green with reddish tips, the lip white, with long green fringes. Summer–autumn. (H) Himalayas.

ODONTOGLOSSUM HBK
(*Cuitlauzina* LaLl. & Lex., *Lichterveldia* Lem., *Osmoglossum* Schltr.)

Odontoglossum is an extremely polymorphic genus of approximately three hundred species, a member of the subtribe *Oncidiinae*, allied to *Oncidium* Sw., *Brassia* R.Br., etc. It extends from Mexico to Brazil and Bolivia, with the majority of the known species occurring in the Andean regions of Colombia, Ecuador, Peru, and Venezuela. Highly diverse in vegetative and floral appearance, these orchids are variously epiphytic, lithophytic, or rather rarely terrestrial in the wild. Pseudobulbous plants, they bear one to three apical leaves and are furnished at the pseudobulb-bases with several often leaf-like bracts. The inflorescences are produced from the bases of the pseudobulbs, and are usually erect or arching, although a few species are characterized by strongly pendulous flower-spikes. The flowers are usually rather large and showy, but sometimes are small and relatively insignificant. With spreading sepals and petals, and a rather complex lip (the limb of which is erect or parallel with the column, thus differing from *Oncidium*), floral colour varies tremendously, although white, yellow, and greenish are perhaps the most frequent hues, the segments often being blotched with purple or brown. Complex crests, teeth, lamellae, etc. are found on the disc of the lip, in the vast majority of the species. The column is usually longer and more slender than in *Oncidium*, and apically is either without appendages, or bears marginal lobes, auricles, or teeth. Odontoglossums are today—and have been for many years—extremely popular orchids in cultivation, even though the cultural requirements of many of the high-elevation species (and their multitudinous hybrids) are not especially easy. Many of the species are notably variable in floral form, coloration, and size, and the genus stands sorely in need of a critical revision.

Several thousand hybrids utilizing *Odontoglossum* have been registered to date, and the number continues to grow apace, due largely to the efforts of breeders in England and France, where these plants are grown in huge quantities. Most of the species comprising the genus appear to be freely compatible genetically, and the group has also been found to be readily 'crossable' with most other members of the subtribe *Oncidiinae*, to give rise to such artificial creations as *Odontioda* (× *Cochlioda*), *Odontocidium* (× *Oncidium*), *Odontonia* (× *Miltonia*), *Odontobrassia* (× *Brassia*), etc. Considerable additional experimental hybridization with allied groups should be done, since the products thus far obtained have for the most part been extravagantly showy orchids.

CULTURE: Since the members of the genus range from hot lowlands to well over 10,000 feet in elevation, the cultural requirements of *Odontoglossum* vary markedly, according to the species involved. Those plants from low areas do best when treated in the manner of the tropical, pseudobulbous Oncidiums. Those from high elevations (which make up the bulk of the genus) require somewhat specialized treatment, and usually must be grown in the 'cool house' for any degree of success to be obtained. In the wild, most of these alpine Odontoglossums inhabit forests which are almost constantly bathed in fog or rain, hence under cultivation they need conditions of constant moisture and high humidity. Because of this, a particularly well-drained compost is required, for the plants are highly susceptible to serious damage from stale conditions at the roots.

Most contemporary growers advocate the utilization of a potting-medium made up of about equal parts of chopped osmunda and chopped sphagnum moss. A top-dressing of sphagnum moss is highly recommended, as well. These cool-growing Odontoglossums should be under-potted, unlike most orchids, flowering with greater vigour when their roots are confined to a small pot. For optimum results, repotting and division (if necessary) should be carried out on an annual basis. They benefit by frequent applications of rather weakened fertilizer solution, while in active growth. For most of the species, no appreciable rest-period is needed. Because of the succulent character of both foliage and pseudobulbs, a rather shaded spot in the collection is required, else burning through over-exposure may result. (C, I, H)

O. bictoniense Ldl. (*Cyrtochilum bictoniense* Batem., *Oncidium bictoniense* hort., *Zygopetalum africanum* Hk.)

Pbs. ovoid to ellipsoid, compressed, to 7″ long, more or less concealed by the lf.-sheaths. Lvs. usually 2–3, to 1½′ long, often yellowish-green, elliptic-oblong to linear, acute or acuminate, folded at base. Infls. rigidly erect, usually simple, many-fld., to 3′ tall. Fls. to 1½″ across, fragrant or not, the ss. and ps. pale- or yellowish-green banded with reddish-brown, the large lip white to lavender or pink. Ss. with slightly recurved apices, mostly elliptic-lanceolate, acute or acuminate. Ps. oblique, oblanceolate to elliptic-lanceolate. Lip shortly clawed, mostly broadly heart-shaped, the margins crisped, with a rough callus of 2 erect plates at the base. Winter–spring. (C, I) Mexico; Guatemala; El Salvador.

O. cariniferum Rchb.f. (*Oncidium cariniferum* Beer, *Odontoglossum hastilabium* Ldl. var. *fuscatum* Hk.)

Pbs. ovoid to elliptic-oblong, compressed, usually furrowed, often yellowish, to 5″ long. Lvs. rather leathery, linear-ligular, acute, to 1½′ long and 3″ wide. Infls. many-fld., usually branched, to almost 4′ long, erect or arching. Fls. about 2″ across, brown, the ss. and ps. usually with yellow tips and margins, the lip white aging to pale yellow, the basal disc often red. Ss. and ps. lanceolate, acuminate, the ps. sometimes incurving. Lip vaguely 3-lbd., the narrow basal half elliptic-oblong, the disc with 2 lateral curved wings, the centre with several projecting fleshy teeth. Autumn–spring. (I, H) Costa Rica; Panama; ? Colombia; Venezuela.

O. Cervantesii LaLl. & Lex. (*Odontoglossum membranaceum* Ldl., *O. Cervantesii* LaLl. & Lex. var. *membranaceum* Ldl., *Oncidium Cervantesii* Beer, *Oncidium membranaceum* Beer)

Pbs. ovoid, compressed, clustered, to 2½″ tall. Lf. solitary, ovate-lanceolate to elliptic-lanceolate or oblong-elliptic, rather papery in texture, acute to acuminate, folded at base, to 6½″ long. Infls. erect to somewhat pendulous, 1–6-fld., to more than 12″ long (usually shorter), covered with brownish sheaths. Fls. fragrant, to 2½″ across, white to rose, the ss. and ps. marked on the lower third with reddish-brown transverse concentric spots or lines, the lip concave and purple-striped at base, the rough callus yellowish. Lip short-clawed, the blade mostly heart-shaped, the margins usually toothed. Autumn–spring. (C, I) Mexico; Guatemala.

O. chiriquense Rchb.f. (*Odontoglossum coronarium* Ldl., *O. candelabrum* Lind., *O. miniatum* hort., *Oncidium chiriquense* Beer, *Oncidium coronarium* Beer)

Rhiz. elongate, often clambering, clothed with large usually inflated bracts, these sometimes brown-spotted. Pbs. at intervals of several inches, usually dull purple, oblong-ovoid, compressed, to 4½″ long. Lf. solitary, rather heavy-textured, elliptic-oblong, obtuse or retuse, short-stalked at base, to 12″ long and 4″ wide. Infls. very densely many-fld., the rac. usually cylindrical, erect, robust, to 1½′ tall. Fls. to 2½″ across, bright yellow with large blotches of rich reddish-brown. Ss. and ps. elliptic-oblong to obovate, obtuse, very wavy-margined. Lip 3-lbd., fiddle-shaped, the disc covered with tubercles at base. Mostly spring. (C, I) Costa Rica; Panama; Colombia; Peru.

O. cirrhosum Ldl. (*Oncidium cirrhosum* Beer)

Pbs. ovoid, rather compressed and furrowed with age, to 3″ tall. Lvs. 2, linear-ligulate, acutish, to 12″ long. Infls. densely many-fld., gracefully arching, to 2′ long. Fls. widely spreading, about 4″ across in the largest phases, white with more or less dense blotches of brownish-red, the lip short-clawed, long-acuminate, with 2 horn-like keels on the disc. Ss. and ps. lanceolate, long-acuminate. Spring. (C, I) Ecuador; Colombia.

O. constrictum Ldl. (*Odontoglossum Sanderianum* Rchb.f., *Oncidium constrictum* Beer)

Similar in vegetative appearance to *O. cirrhosum* Ldl. Infls. gracefully arching, usually branched, many-fld., to about 5′ long in largest phases. Fls. about 1½″ across, yellow, the ss. and ps. spotted with sepia-brown towards the bases, the lip mostly yellow, the disc usually rose-spotted. Ss. and ps. spreading, lanceolate, acute. Lip broadly fiddle-shaped, the callus 2-toothed. Autumn–winter. (C, I) Venezuela.

O. × Coradinei Rchb.f.

Natural hybrid between *O. crispum* Ldl. and *O. Lindleyanum* Rchb.f., rather like *O. constrictum* Ldl. in vegetative appearance. Infls. gracefully arching, rather loosely many-fld., to about 3′ long. Fls. about 3″ across, light yellow, spotted with brown, the lip with a rather long claw, oblong, acutish, toothed and undulate marginally, with 2 horn-like yellow calli on the disc. Ss. and ps. spreading, narrowly elliptic, acutish, the margins usually very crisped. Summer. (C) Colombia.

O. cordatum Ldl. (*Odontoglossum Hookeri* Lem., *O. Lueddemanni* Regel)

Pbs. clustered, ovoid-ellipsoid to ellipsoid, compressed, to 3″ long. Lf. solitary, elliptic-lanceolate to elliptic or oblong-ligulate, acuminate to obtuse, folded at the base, rather heavy-textured, to 12″ long. Infls. few- to many-fld., mostly erect or arching, to 1½′ long. Fls. to 3″ across, usually smaller, greenish, whitish, or yellowish blotched and spotted with reddish-brown. Ss. often somewhat recurved, elliptic-lanceolate to linear-lanceolate, long-acuminate, rather concave, the lats. oblique. Ps. spreading, ovate-lanceolate to elliptic-lanceolate, long-acuminate, oblique. Lip short-clawed,

the blade rather wedge-shaped, abruptly long-acuminate, more or less heart-shaped at base, the callus 3-parted. Summer–autumn. (C, I) Mexico; Guatemala; Honduras; Costa Rica.

O. crispum Ldl. (*Odontoglossum Alexandrae* Batem., *O. Edithae* Warn., *O. latimaculatum* hort., *O. Warocqueanum* Lind.)

Among the finest and most variable spp., with many named forms. Pbs. ovoid, compressed, furrowed with age, to 4″ long, subtended by a few lf.-like bracts at the base. Lvs. 2–3, rather soft-textured, linear-ligulate, acutish, to 15″ long. Infls. usually gracefully arching, rather densely 8–20-fld., sometimes branched, to 1½′ long. Fls. extremely variable in size, colour, and degree of crispness of the segm.-margins, usually about 3″ across, mostly white or pale rose, sometimes more or less spotted and blotched with brownish or reddish-brown, widely opening. Ss. and ps. very wide, often overlapping, elliptic, acute to acuminate, variously wavy-margined or toothed and incised there. Lip usually white with a few red spots and a yellow centre, the disc yellow, streaked with brown or red-brown, short-clawed, rather heart-shaped, often long-acuminate, usually very crisped and incised marginally. Mostly autumn–winter. (C) Colombia.

O. cristatum Ldl.

Similar in habit to *O. crispum* Ldl. Infls. usually gracefully arching, often branched, rather many-fld., to 2′ long. Fls. about 2″ across, the ss. and ps. deep brown with a yellow tip and yellow blotch at the base, spreading, ovate-lanceolate, acute. Lip light yellow or yellowish, with a few brown spots, similar in shape to the other segms., the callus with 2 long tooth-like projections. Summer–autumn. (C) Ecuador.

O. Egertoni Ldl. (*Osmoglossum Egertoni* Schltr., *Osmoglossum acuminatum* Schltr., *Osmoglossum anceps* Schltr., *Oncidium Egertoni* Beer)

Pbs. clustered, compressed, tapering, often ridged, narrowly ellipsoid-oblong to ovoid, to 4″ long, usually glossy yellowish-green. Lvs. 2–3, to 1½′ long, usually rigidly erect, rather papery in texture, narrowly linear-ligular, acute or acuminate. Infls. to about 15″ tall, erect, few-fld., slender, the rachis flattened. Fls. less than 1″ long, fragrant or not, white, the disc of the lip yellow with some reddish spots. Ss. not opening widely, concave, the lats. forming a single segm. below the lip, united to beyond the middle. Ps. oblique, about the same size as the dors. sep. Lip entire, elliptic-oblong, acute or acuminate, the disc with 2 low keels. Often confused with *O. convallarioides* (Schltr.) A. & C. and *O. pulchellum* Batem. ex Ldl. Mostly spring. (C, I) Mexico; Guatemala; Honduras; Costa Rica; Panama.

O. grande Ldl.

Pbs. clustered, roundish to ovoid, often rather compressed, furrowed with age, glaucous, to 4″ long and 2½″ wide. Lvs. 1–3, heavy-textured, glaucous, elliptic to lanceolate, acute, stalked at base, to 15″ long and almost 3″ wide. Infls. 4–8-fld., usually erect, robust, to 12″ tall. Fls. wide-spreading, to more than 6″ across, waxy, long-lived, the ss. yellow with broad transverse bars and flecks

Nervilia species, probably undescribed, from Madagascar [J.MARNIER-LAPOSTOLLE]

Neottia nidus-avis (L.) Rich. [GEORGE FULLER]

Oberonia sp. (Philippines) [R.S.DAVIS]

Odontoglossum bictoniense Ldl. [GEORGE FULLER]

Oeoniella polystachys (Thou.) Schltr. [J.MARNIER-LAPOSTOLLE]

Odontoglossum Harryanum Rchb.f. [*The Orchid Journal*]

Odontoglossum pulchellum Batem. ex Ldl. [GEORGE FULLER]

Oncidium chrysodipterum Veitch [H.SCHMIDT-MUMM]

VIII<small>B</small> *Spiranthes speciosa* (Jacq.) A.Rich. [A.D.HAWKES]

VIII<small>A</small> *Oncidium Kramerianum* Rchb.f. [H.A.DUNN]

of reddish-brown, the ps. with the lower half reddish-brown with yellow marginal marks, the upper half bright yellow, the lip white or cream-white flecked with dull reddish-brown. Ss. elliptic-lanceolate to lanceolate, acute to acuminate, marginally undulate. Ps. wider, undulate marginally, mostly oblanceolate-elliptic, obtuse to acute. Lip not clawed, broadly fiddle-shaped, unequally 3-lbd., the midlb. roundish or squarish, blunt at the tip, rather wavy-margined, the disc with a square 2-horned callus. Autumn–spring. (C, I) Mexico; Guatemala.

O. Harryanum Rchb.f.

Pbs. oval, furrowed with age, to 4″ tall, clustered. Lvs. 2, leathery, ligulate-oblong, blunt apically, to 12″ long. Infls. erect or arching, rather densely 4–12-fld., to almost 4′ tall (often shorter). Fls. about 5″ long, widely opening, fragrant, waxy, very handsome, the ss. dark chestnut-brown transversely streaked and margined with rich yellow or greenish-yellow, the narrower ps. dark chestnut-brown, margined with yellow and with some longitudinal purplish-mauve stripes in the basal half. Lip 3-lbd., large, oblong-oval, undulate-margined, the lat. lbs. upcurving, white, heavily streaked with feathery lines of bluish-purple, the much-fringed crest rich yellow, the midlb. white, changing to yellow. Ss. elliptic-oblong, acutish, undulate and crisped, wider than the ps., which are oblong, incurving around the col. Mostly summer–autumn. (I) Colombia.

O. hastilabium Ldl. (*Oncidium hastilabium* Beer)

Rather similar in habit to O. cariniferum Rchb.f. Infls. mostly erect, branched, many-fld., to 5′ tall in robust plants. Fls. about 3″ across, wide-opening, very long-lived, the ss. and ps. pale green with thin transverse bars of purple, the lip purple at base, white apically. Ss. and ps. linear-lanceolate, long-acuminate, wavy-margined. Lip broadly hastate to triangular, the lat. lbs. acute, the midlb. roundish or ovate, acute, the crest 5-parted, irregular. Summer–autumn. (C, I) Colombia.

O. x Humeanum Rchb.f. (*Odontoglossum aspersum* Rchb.f.)

Natural hybrid between O. Rossii Ldl. and O. cordatum Ldl., rather similar in all parts to the first-named parent. Infls. usually 2-fld., rather short, erect. Fls. about 2″ across, the triangular, acuminate ss. yellow striped with bars of cinnamon-brown, the oblong, acuminate, crisped ps. white with 3 sepia-brown basal blotches, the cordate-ovate, acute, rather crisped lip, white, with a 2-lbd. yellow callus which is striped with red. Spring. (C, I) Mexico.

O. Insleayi (Bark.) Ldl. (*Odontoglossum Lawrenceanum* hort., *Oncidium Insleayi* Bark.)

Rather similar in all parts to O. grande Ldl., the pls. often somewhat less robust. Infls. erect, to 12″ tall, 5–10-fld. Fls. about 3″ across, faintly fragrant, the ss. and ps. pale yellow (or golden-yellow), thickly blotched with transverse reddish-brown or chestnut-brown marks, the lip bright yellow, with a row of crimson or brownish-red spots around the margin. Ss. and ps. oblong, obtuse, wavy-margined, wide-spreading. Lip narrowly obovate, retuse, rather small for the size of the fl. Col. with a pair of red subulate horns. Mostly autumn. (C, I) Mexico.

O. Lindleyanum Rchb.f.

Rather similar in vegetative appearance to O. crispum Ldl., the pbs. compressed, ovoid to ovoid-oblong, the lvs. smaller than the other sp., acute. Infls. loosely 3–8-fld., mostly erect, to 15″ tall. Fls. about 2″ across, star-shaped, fragrant, the ss. and ps. yellow with a long bar of cinnamon-brown at base, followed by a large roundish cinnamon-brown spot, the apical part speckled with the same colour, the lip brown with a long yellow tip, the very long, curving lat. lbs. white. Ss. and ps. linear-lanceolate, long-acuminate, cuneate basally. Lip 3-lbd., basally joined to the col., the apical part deflexed, linear-lanceolate. Spring–summer. (C) Colombia.

O. Londesboroughianum Rchb.f.

Rhiz. usually elongate, bearing the pbs. at intervals of several inches. Pbs. greyish-green, oblong-ovoid, somewhat compressed, furrowed with age, about 4″ tall. Lvs. 2–3, deciduous, to 1½′ long, rather soft-textured, narrowly lanceolate, acute. Infls. to 6′ tall, mostly erect, sometimes branched, rather many-fld. Fls. simulating those of an *Oncidium*, to 2″ across, long-lived, the ss. and ps. yellow with concentric rows of reddish-brown spots. Lip bright yellow, the callus often spotted with red-brown; long-clawed, the lat. lbs. small, acute, erect, the very large midlb. flat, kidney-shaped. Ss. oblong, rather concave, acute to acuminate, the ps. wider, undulate marginally, ovate, acutish. Autumn–winter. (C, I) Mexico; Guatemala.

O. luteo-purpureum Ldl. (*Odontoglossum hystrix* Batem., *O. lyratum* Rchb.f., *O. radiatum* Rchb.f., *Oncidium luteopurpureum* Beer)

Highly variable, with many named variants, these based mostly on divergent floral colour. Pbs. usually robust, oval, compressed, to 3″ long. Lvs. rather rigid, ensiform, acute to acuminate, to 2′ long. Infls. rather many-fld., mostly erect, to 3½′ tall, sometimes branched. Fls. 3–4″ across, brilliant chestnut-brown, the margins, tips, and sometimes parts of the bases of the ss. and ps. yellow, the lip yellowish-white with some brown spots, the comb-like crest golden-yellow. Ss. and ps. broadly lanceolate, acute, the ps. usually fringed marginally. Lip long-clawed, the lat. lbs. very small, the kidney-shaped midlb. fringed, emarginate. Spring–summer. (C) Colombia.

O. maculatum LaLl. & Lex. (*Odontoglossum anceps* Lind., *O. Lueddemannianum* Regel, *O. madrense* Rchb.f., *O. maxillare* Ldl., *Oncidium maculatum* Beer)

Similar in all parts to O. cordatum Ldl. Infls. mostly erect, many-fld., rarely branched, to about 2′ tall. Fls. about 2½″ across, the lanceolate-ligulate, acute ss. sepia- or chestnut-brown, rarely violet-purple, sometimes with some green basal transverse bars; ps. elliptic-lanceolate, acuminate, yellow, thickly spotted basally with reddish-brown. Lip similar in colour to the ps., with a short claw, the midlb. rather triangular-rhombic, acuminate, the disc with 2 tall keels. Summer. (C, I) Mexico; Guatemala.

O. nebulosum Ldl. (*Odontoglossum vexativum* Rchb.f.)

Pbs. oblong or ovoid, to about 4″ long, clustered. Lvs. 2, to 8″ long and 3″ wide, rather heavy-textured, ligulate, acute or acuminate. Infls. 5–6-fld., becoming pendulous, arising with the new growth, to 12″ long. Fls. to 3″ across, the ss. and ps. white with spots of red or reddish-brown in the lower half, the lip similar, but the spots larger and the disc tinged with yellow. Ss. lanceolate-elliptic, acutish, the ps. wider, ovate, undulate-margined. Lip ovate, acute, very crisped marginally, short-clawed. Spring. (C, I) Mexico.

O. nobile Rchb.f. (*Odontoglossum Pescatorei* Lind., *Oncidium Pescatorei* Beer)

Closely allied to *O. crispum* Ldl. Pbs. ovoid, furrowed when old, clustered, to 3″ long. Lvs. 2, lorate, acutish, rather soft-textured, to 1½′ long. Infls. many-fld., branching, mostly erect or arching, to 2′ tall. Fls. to 2½″ across, faintly fragrant, variable in colour, white, shaded with pale rose in most instances, the lip white, spotted with rose, the disc golden-yellow, streaked with crimson. Ss. and ps. ovate-oblong, acute, wavy-margined. Lip fiddle-shaped, the midlb. heart-shaped, with an apical cusp. Spring. (C) Colombia.

O. odoratum Ldl. (*Odontoglossum Glonerianum* Lind., *O. gloriosum* Rchb.f., *O. baphicanthum* Rchb.f., *Oncidium odoratum* Beer)

Similar in habit to *O. crispum* Ldl. Infls. erect, many-fld., branched, to more than 3′ tall. Fls. very fragrant and long-lived, to 2″ across, the ss. and ps. golden-yellow, blotched with brownish-red, the lip similarly coloured, white basally, the disc very bright yellow, spotted with crimson or dull red, with 2 pairs of erect teeth. Ss. and ps. narrowly lanceolate, acute or acuminate, wavy-margined. Lip hastate, undulate marginally, the midlb. broadly subulate. Spring. (C, I) Colombia; Venezuela.

O. pardinum Ldl. (*Oncidium pardinum* Beer)

Pbs. ovoid, compressed, to more than 3″ long, furrowed with age. Lvs. rather soft-textured, less than 12″ long, narrowly elliptic-oblong, acute. Infls. many-fld., branched, to 4′ long. Fls. to 3″ across, the ss., ps., and lip golden-yellow, the ps. darker yellow, the lip usually spotted with irregular orange-red marks. Ss. lanceolate, acute. Ps. undulate marginally, somewhat broader and shorter than ss. Lip short-clawed, fiddle-shaped, acute at the tip. Winter. (C) Ecuador; Peru.

O. pendulum (LaLl. & Lex.) Batem. (*Cuitlauzina pendula* LaLl. & Lex., *Odontoglossum citrosmum* Ldl., *Oncidium citrosmum* Beer, *Oncidium Galeottianum* Drapiez, *Lichterveldia Lindleyi* Lem.)

Pbs. dull or glossy, roundish, compressed, becoming wrinkled with age, to 3″ tall. Lvs. 2, oblong-ligulate, obtuse, rather leathery, to 12″ long and 2½″ wide. Infls. sharply pendulous, produced from centre of expanding new shoot, 8–15-fld., with a long, slender peduncle, to 12″ long. Fls. fragrant, waxy, long-lived, about 2″ across, variable in colour, the typical phase white, slightly flushed and sometimes dotted with pale blush-pink, the lip bright or pale mauve-pink with a pale or bright yellow basal claw. Ss. and ps. oblong, obtuse, often undulate-margined. Lip without a crest, kidney-shaped, emarginate. Mostly autumn. (C, I) Mexico.

O. Rossii Ldl. (*Odontoglossum caerulescens* A.Rich. & Gal., *O. rubescens* Ldl., *O. Warnerianum* Rchb.f., *O. Youngii* Gower)

Rather similar in all parts to *O. Cervantesii* LaLl. & Lex., the pbs. often yellowish, becoming very compressed, curving, and wrinkled with age. Infls. erect, 2–4-fld., bracted, to 8″ tall. Fls. to 3″ across, pale yellow, white or pinkish, the ss. and bases of the ps. blotched with reddish-brown, the lip deep yellow, spotted with reddish-brown, sometimes white with the spots only at the base. Ss. spreading, mostly oblong-elliptic, acutish or acuminate, the margins slightly reflexed. Ps. short-clawed, the obtuse or acute apex usually recurved, broadly elliptic to oblong-elliptic, the margins crisped. Lip with a narrow claw, the blade broadly orbicular-subcordate, undulate, the callus 2-winged. Mostly spring. (C, I) Mexico; Guatemala; Honduras; Nicaragua.

O. Schillerianum Rchb.f.

Very similar and allied to *O. Lindleyanum* Rchb.f., the pbs. ovoid, compressed, to 3″ tall, the lvs. to 12″ long. Infls. 7–15-fld., to about 1½′ tall. Fls. about 2″ across, fragrant, wide-opening, the ss. and ps. yellow, spotted inside with purple or purple-brown, the tips of the ps. usually unspotted, the lip white basally, medially purple-brown, the tip yellow. Ss. and ps. elliptic-lanceolate, acute to acuminate. Lip deflexed, clawed, the midlb. ovate, acuminate. Winter–spring. (C, I) Venezuela.

O. Schlieperianum Rchb.f. (*Odontoglossum Insleayi* (Bark.) Ldl. var. *macranthum* Ldl., *O. grande* Ldl. var. *pallidum* hort., *O. Powellii* Schltr., *O. Warscewiczii* Bridges ex Stein)

Similar vegetatively to *O. grande* Ldl. and *O. Insleayi* (Bark.) Ldl. Infls. erect, 2–8-fld., robust, to 8″ tall or more. Fls. to 3″ across, glossy, yellow or greenish-yellow, barred and blotched with reddish-brown. Lip vaguely 3-lbd., somewhat fiddle-shaped when expanded, the basal, narrow claw adnate to the col., the roundish lat. lbs. small, erect, the midlb. about three-quarters the total length of the lip, obtuse to retuse apically, the disc with a short, central keel from the middle and apex of which arise 2 pairs of short, spreading, thick wings. Autumn. (C, I) Costa Rica; Panama.

O. tripudians Rchb.f.

Rather similar in habit to *O. nobile* Rchb.f., often more robust. Infls. unbranched, arching, many-fld., to 2½′ long. Fls. about 2½″ across, outside dull yellow-green, inside the ss. glossy maroon-brown, the bases and tips yellow, the ps. golden-yellow with a few irregular maroon-brown blotches near the base, the lip white, spotted with purplish-red around the 10-keeled calli. Ss. and ps. oblong-elliptic, acuminate, widely opening. Lip constricted medially, oblong-quadrate, crisped basally, the midlb. toothed marginally. Spring. (C) Colombia; Ecuador; Peru.

O. triumphans Rchb.f.

Pbs. large, to 4″ long, ovoid-ellipsoid, compressed, sharp-edged. Lvs. dark green, rather leathery, oblong-lanceolate, acute, to 12″ long. Infls. erect, many-fld., to 1½′ long. Fls. about 3–5″ across, golden-yellow with transverse bars and rows of spots of rich red-brown, the lip white basally, the remainder rich red-brown. Ss. and the broader ps. lanceolate, acute or acuminate, rather wavy-margined. Lip clawed, elongately heart-shaped, acuminate. Spring. (C) Colombia.

O. Uro-Skinneri Ldl.

Closely allied to and simulating *O. bictoniense* (Batem.) Ldl., differing in the larger, slightly differently-coloured fls., and the differently shaped ps. Fls. to about 2½″ across, the ss. and ps. almost entirely dark red or greenish with brown bars and mottling, the lip rose or pinkish-rose, often veined with white. Ps. obliquely ovate-elliptic, obtuse to subacute. Lip short-clawed, the callus puberulent, composed of a pair of erect plates that clasp the col. and are extended at the apex as erect flap-like lbs. Summer–autumn. (C, I) Guatemala.

O. Wallisii Rchb.f. (*Odontoglossum purum* Rchb.f.)

Pbs. ovoid, very compressed, sharp-edged, to 3″ tall. Lvs. linear, acute or acuminate, rather drooping, to 15″ long. Infls. loosely 8–15-fld., arching, to 1½′ long. Fls. about 2½″ across, the ss. pale yellow with a median longitudinal stripe of reddish-brown, the ps. similar but the yellow area larger and the stripe irregular and spotty, the lip white, marked with rose-purple streaks behind the 6-parted crest, the midlb. rose-purple, edged with white, furnished with a semicircular white band. Ss. and ps. oblong-lanceolate, the latter somewhat clawed and usually undulate-margined. Lip clawed, the midlb. ovate, constricted medially, fringed marginally, the tip decurved. Winter. (C) Colombia; Venezuela.

O. brevifolium Ldl. Rhiz. elongate, the ovoid pbs. at some distance from each other, to 3″ tall, 1-lvd., the lvs. stalked at base, to 7″ long and 3″ wide, leathery. Infls. rigidly erect, many-fld., to about 12″ tall. Fls. to 2″ across, the ss. and ps. rich chestnut-brown with a golden-yellow border, undulate-margined, the shorter lip bright golden-yellow, the disc reddish. Spring. (C, I) Ecuador; Peru.

O. convallarioides (Schltr.) A. & C. (*Osmoglossum convallarioides* Schltr.) Closely allied to *O. Egertoni* Ldl. and to *O. pulchellum* Batem. ex Ldl., differing primarily in the much smaller fls. (usually about ¾″ long) which are white sometimes flushed with pink or lavender, the disc of the lip usually yellow, and the concave (rather than curving-deflexed) lip. Spring. (C, I) Mexico; Guatemala; Honduras; Nicaragua; Costa Rica; ? Panama.

O. Edwardii Rchb.f. Pbs. pear-shaped, dark green, to 4″ tall, clustered. Lvs. 2, ligulate, rather leathery, to 2′ long and 1½″ wide. Infls. to 3′ long, usually erect, profusely branched, very many-fld. Fls. fragrant, about 1″ across (rarely larger), bright magenta or reddish-purple, the lip with a bright yellow basal area. Ss. roughened on outer surface, the apices usually incurving. Spring–summer. (C, I) Ecuador.

O. Hallii Ldl. (*Oncidium Hallii* Beer) Allied to *O. luteo-purpureum* Ldl., the pbs. more elongate. Infls. erect or arching, many-fld., to 2′ long. Fls. to about 4″ across, variable in colour, the ovate-lanceolate, acuminate ss. and ps. usually buff-yellow heavily blotched and barred with purplish-brown, the oblong, acuminate, heavily fringed lip white, blotched with purplish-brown, the basal part rich yellow, streaked with orange and white. Spring–summer. (C) Colombia; Ecuador; Peru.

O. Hunnewellianum Rolfe Similar in habit to *O. crispum* Ldl. Infls. loosely 10–25-fld., gracefully arching, to about 1½′ long.

Fls. to 2″ across, pale yellow, densely spotted with brown, the lip yellowish-white, densely spotted with brown, fringed. Autumn–spring. (C) Colombia.

O. Krameri Rchb.f. Dwarf, the clustered pbs. pale green or bluish-green, compressed, roundish or ovoid, to 2″ tall. Lf. solitary, rather rigidly leathery, dull green, elliptic-lanceolate, acute, to 9″ long and 2″ broad. Infls. erect or horizontal (rarely arching), often multiple per growth, loosely 2–3-fld., about 7″ long. Fls. about 1¾″ in diam., very glossy and with a porcelain-like appearance, long-lived, the ss. and ps. pale blush-lilac to ivory-white with a lilac suffusion, the lip vivid violet or pink-violet, marked and spotted with purple and yellow, with two lines of dark rich brown near base. Ss. and ps. spreading, ligulate, obtuse. Lip vaguely reniform, somewhat notched at front edge. Various times of the year, often more than once annually. (I) Costa Rica; Panama.

O. majale Rchb.f. (*Odontoglossum platycheilum* Weath.) Pbs. borne on a creeping rhiz., ovoid, compressed, to 3″ long, the bases mostly concealed by large brown sheaths. Lf. solitary, linear-ligulate, fleshy, folded at base, to 12″ long. Infls. erect, sheathed, 2–4-fld., to 5½″ tall. Fls. about 1½″ long, rose or purplish, the large lip more or less blotched with dark purple or carmine, the midlb. squarish, truncate at apex, minutely toothed on the margins. Spring. (C) Guatemala.

O. naevium Ldl. (*Oncidium naevium* Beer) Dwarf sp., the pbs. small, ovoid, grooved. Lvs. about 8″ long, lanceolate, acutish, narrowed at base. Infls. often branched, rather many-fld., to 3′ tall. Fls. star-shaped, about 2″ across, the long-tipped ss. and ps. undulate marginally, white, irregularly blotched with magenta-rose, the lip white, spotted with magenta-rose, pubescent, the disc yellow. Spring–summer. (I) Colombia; Venezuela; Guianas.

O. nevadense Rchb.f. Very closely allied to *O. cristatum* Ldl., the fls. to about 2½″ across. Ss. and ps. narrowly lanceolate, acuminate, brown, the base with yellow and dark brown longitudinal stripes. Lip white, the erect, crescent-shaped lat. lbs. spotted with brown, the midlb. deeply fringed, usually somewhat recurved. Spring–summer. (C) Colombia.

O. Oerstedii Rchb.f. Rather similar in habit to *O. Krameri* Rchb.f., the pbs. not very compressed, dark green, usually less than 1″ tall. Infls. erect, 1–2-fld., to about 6″ tall. Fls. to 1½″ across, fragrant, waxy, long-lived, white, the base of the lip with a golden-yellow blotch, the callus densely spotted with orange. Lip with a short claw which is adnate to the col., the midlb. broadly spreading and flat, 2-lbd., medially narrow, the margins directly below the col. minutely hairy. Spring. (C, I) Costa Rica; Panama.

O. pulchellum Batem. ex Ldl. (*Osmoglossum pulchellum* Schltr.) Very similar in all parts to *O. Egertoni* Ldl., differing principally in the larger fls. (to 1½″ long), and the sharply deflexed lip. Fls. fragrant, long-lived, white with the outside of the ss. usually pink or purplish, the callus yellowish, spotted with reddish-brown. Autumn–winter (C, I) Mexico; Guatemala; El Salvador; Costa Rica.

O. ramosissimum Ldl. (*Odontoglossum angustatum* Batem., *Oncidium ramosissimum* Beer) Pbs. ovoid, compressed, about 3″ tall, the solitary lf. to 2½′ long or more, narrowly sword-shaped, acute, rather soft-textured. Infls. to 5′ tall, very profusely branched and many-fld., mostly erect. Fls. about 2″ across, faintly fragrant, the narrowly lanceolate, wavy-margined ss. and ps. pure white, the ps. marked at base with lilac-purple, the cordate, undulate, sharp-pointed lip white with a large lilac-purple basal blotch. Spring. (C, I) Colombia.

O. stellatum Ldl. (*Odontoglossum erosum* A.Rich. & Gal., *Oncidium erosum* Beer) Pbs. clustered, sometimes almost cylindrical, to 2″ long. Lf. solitary, distinctly narrowed and folded at base, to 6″ long. Infls. 1–2-fld., short, slender, usually concealed by rather large bracts. Fls. about 2″ across, the narrow, long-tipped ss. and ps. tawny-bronze or purplish with a yellow apex, the ps. sometimes yellowish-white, the lip white or pink, tinged or marked with mauve, marginally strongly and irregularly toothed. Spring. (C, I) Mexico; Guatemala.

O. Williamsianum Rchb.f. (*Odontoglossum grande* Ldl. var. *Williamsianum* Veitch) Closely allied to and simulating in almost all parts *O. grande* Ldl., differing primarily in the much broader, shorter and more obtuse ps., the larger development of yellow and less red-brown blotching of the fls., and the uncinate col.-wings and differently shaped keels on the disc. Spring. (C, I) Mexico; Guatemala; Honduras; Costa Rica.

OEONIA Ldl.
(*Aeonia* Ldl.)

This is a remarkable genus of the subtribe *Sarcanthinae*, with six species known to date, all endemic to Madagascar, except one (**Oeonia volucris** (Thou.) Dur. & Schinz), which also inhabits the Mascarene Islands. Dwarf creeping epiphytes, they bear erect racemes of proportionately large flowers which are typically white —often marked on the deeply lobed lip with red or pink —and which simulate to a large degree those of an *Oncidium*, with which genus the present group naturally has no affinity. Regrettably, these completely delightful little orchids are unknown in contemporary collections, although they offer great potentialities to the connoisseur.

Nothing is known of the genetic affinities of *Oeonia*.
CULTURE: Presumably as for the dwarf angraecoid orchids. (H)

OEONIELLA Schltr.

This genus consists of three species, native in Madagascar, the Mascarenes and the Seychelles Islands. A member of the subtribe *Sarcanthinae*, the Oeoniellas are closely allied to *Oeonia* Ldl., but differ in vegetative appearance and in structural details of the small white, red-spotted flowers. None of them is present in our collections at this time, although they are very desirable as collector's items.

Nothing is known of the genetic affinities of *Oeoniella*.
CULTURE: Presumably as for the dwarf angraecoid orchids. (H)

OLIVERIANA Rchb.f.

A recent paper by Leslie A. Garay (in *Amer. Orch. Soc. Bull.* 32: 18–24. 1963) has discussed this rare genus, and it is there pointed out that it contains two species (one there described as new), both smallish epiphytic orchids endemic to Colombia. Though formerly included in the *Trichopilia* alliance. Garay now relegates it to the subtribe *Oncidiinae*, possibly with good reason. Neither of the Oliverianas appear to be in contemporary cultivation.

Nothing is known of the genetic ties of this odd group.
CULTURE: Presumably as for the high-elevation Odontoglossums, etc. (C, I)

OMMATODIUM Ldl.

Ommatodium Volucris (L.f.) Ldl. (*Pterygodium Volucris* Sw.) is sometimes referred to the closely allied *Pterygodium* Sw., but it appears validly distinct on account of the details of the flowers. A native of South Africa (especially the Cape Peninsula), this medium-sized terrestrial orchid, bearing small, pale greenish-yellow blossoms which give off a rather unpleasant odour, is unknown in cultivation at this time.

Nothing is known of the genetic affinities of *Ommatodium*.
CULTURE: Presumably as for *Caladenia*. (C, I)

OMOEA Bl.
(*Omaea* Schltr.)

Omoea micrantha Bl., the only known member of this rare genus of the subtribe *Sarcanthinae*, is a dwarf epiphytic monopodial orchid, inhabiting the highland forests of Java. At this time, it does not appear to be present in our collections. Somewhat allied to *Saccolabium* Bl., it has short densely leafy stems and solitary, small, pale green flowers of rather intricate structure.

Nothing is known concerning the genetic affinities of *Omoea*.
CULTURE: As for the small, tropical Vandas and their relatives. (I, H)

ONCIDIUM Sw.
(*Baptistonia* B-R., *Coppensia* Dum., *Cyrtochilos* Spreng., *Cyrtochilum* HBK, *Lophiaris* Raf., *Olgasis* Raf., *Papiliopsis* E.Morr., *Psychopsis* Raf., *Tolumnia* Raf., *Xaritonia* Raf., *Xeilyathum* Raf.)

Oncidium is among the larger of orchidaceous genera, with an estimated seven hundred and fifty species being considered valid at this time. This immense assemblage of plants extends from South Florida and Mexico throughout all of tropical America to Argentina; the greatest development of species occurs in Brazil and the Andes of Colombia, Ecuador, and Peru. A large number of Oncidiums are present in contemporary collections, and are often among our most highly prized and ornamental orchids. An extremely technical genus, botanically speaking, many of the described taxa are still not fully understood, and a critical modern revision of the group is sorely needed. Oncidiums grow primarily on trees, as epiphytes, but there are several species which exhibit a predilection for rock outcroppings, or even exist as terrestrials. The genus is closely allied to *Brassia* R.Br., *Odontoglossum* HBK, *Miltonia* Ldl., and several other members of the subtribe *Oncidiinae*. Its components are for the most part extremely variable, and a concise generic description is difficult to compile. Either erect or sharply pendulous plants, they usually have conspicuous, often compressed pseudobulbs, though many species are essentially without pseudobulbous thickenings. In the pseudobulb-bearing species, the bases of these structures are usually enveloped in several papery to leaf-like bracts. One section of the genus (including such charming dwarf plants as *O. crista-galli* Rchb.f., *O. pusillum* (L.) Rchb.f., etc.) is entirely pseudobulb-less and bears the leaves in a distichously imbricating, equitant formation. The leaves vary in texture from papery to very rigidly fleshy, and are found in virtually all forms from equitant to plane, terete or triangular. Usually a single inflorescence is produced from a single growth, but two may be borne from one pseudobulb in certain robust species; these may be very short and one- or two-flowered, or immensely elongate and bearing up to several hundred flowers apiece. They are simple or branched, and in some Oncidiums—mostly those formerly relegated to the segregate genus *Cyrtochilum* HBK—these inflorescences continue to grow and produce flowers for several years; these flower-spikes are normally basal in origin, though in the equitant-leaved species they may be produced from the leaf-axils and thus do not appear to have this type of origin. Floral coloration in *Oncidium* is, for the most part, in shades of yellow and brown, though a few divergent hues occur, such as green, white, red, or magenta. The blossoms vary in size from extremely small to more than five inches in diameter, and are highly diverse in shape and structure. The sepals are characteristically subequal in size, spreading or sharply reflexed, and free—or with the laterals very rarely joined nearly to their tips to form a variously shaped lamina. The petals are in general subequal to the dorsal sepal, or rarely larger than that segment. The lip in most Oncidiums is three-lobed to a greater or lesser degree (rarely almost entire), and often fiddle-shaped; its base is either clawed or sessile, and adnate to the column-base, usually forming a right angle with it. The central part of the lip usually possesses an isthmus, and the disc on the midlobe typically bears conspicuous crests or tubercles of infinite variation; the shape and arrangement of these basal tubercles is customarily of critical importance in the differentiation of species. The usually short and stout column is winged (or not) on the lateral margins near the stigmatic orifice, and the anther bears a pair of waxy pollinia.

Within the past decade, a large number of extravagantly handsome hybrids have been registered within *Oncidium*, due largely to the efforts of W. W. G. Moir, of Honolulu. Despite his notable activities, the field of interspecific breeding in this huge genus is only barely explored, and we may anticipate, in future, the appearance of a multitude of fine new crosses. *Oncidium* has also been hybridized with a number of its allied genera, as well as several from subtribes other than the *Oncidiinae*, notably *Trichocentrum* (= *Trichocidium*), *Rodriguezia* (= *Rodricidium*), etc. Some exciting possibilities seem very evident here, as well.

CULTURE: In a genus as large as *Oncidium*, one must anticipate tremendous variances in cultural requirements, though the basic necessities are much like those of *Cattleya*, Epidendrums of the pseudobulbous group, etc. Pendulous species, such as *O. Jonesianum*, certain forms of *O. longifolium*, etc., should be grown on slabs of tree-fern fibre, or on rafts tightly filled with osmunda fibre and hung vertically. Most of the other Oncidiums do best when grown in pots, though certain of the very

robust species (e.g., *O. sphacelatum*, *O. panamense*, *O. Baueri*, etc.) thrive in wire or slat baskets, filled with composts such as those suggested below. In general, these handsome orchids do best if rather tightly potted, though the medium in which they are grown should not be as firmly packed about the roots as, say, Cattleyas or most Dendrobiums. The majority of Oncidiums thrive in either tree-fern fibre or osmunda. Sphagnum moss can be mixed into these media, in the case of species requiring constant moist conditions. Perfect drainage is always essential for these plants, which are highly intolerant of stale conditions at the roots. While actively growing, all Oncidiums delight in abundant water, but in virtually all cases, upon completion of the new pseudobulbs or leaves, a definite resting-period must be given for proper flower-production, this usually of several weeks' duration. Like all orchids, when the fragile new growths are expanding, caution must be exercised that water does not lodge in the growing tips, or rotting may occur. With notably few exceptions, the Oncidiums do best in a bright, very well-ventilated spot in the collection. They are mostly amenable to adverse conditions, and should form an integral part of even the smallest assemblage of orchidaceous plants, thriving in the 'mixed' collection which typically comprises the amateur's initial acquisitions. Some of the species, such as *O. splendidum*, *O. microchilum*, *O. luridum*, *O. carthagenense*, etc., do very well in almost full sun, and indeed appear to flower better than when kept in a shaded situation. Temperature requirements naturally fluctuate with the different species (and, often, with individual specimens, in the case of a species with particularly widespread dissemination), since the range of these orchids is from tropical, hot, sea-level climes to frigid montane areas; most of the commonly-grown Oncidiums do best under intermediate temperatures. All of the members of this genus benefit by regular and liberal applications of fertilizing solutions, though excessive fertilizing in certain of the very robust species may result only in lush vegetative growth, with but few flowers. (C, I, H)

O. ampliatum Ldl. (*Oncidium Bernoullianum* Krzl.)

Pbs. tightly clustered, usually almost prostrate against the compost or natural tree-trunk, to 5″ tall and 3½″ wide, ovoid to almost round, strongly compressed (rarely angular), usually longitudinally ridged and transversely wrinkled, usually flecked with red or brown. Lvs. 1–3, elliptic-oblanceolate to ligulate, obtuse to acutish, leathery, to 15″ long and almost 5″ wide, short-stalked at base. Infls. solitary (rarely paired), erect or arching, few- to many-fld., sometimes branched, to 4′ long. Fls. highly variable in size, usually about 1″ across, brilliant yellow, nearly white on the reverse sides of the segms., the ss. spotted with reddish-brown, the lip-callus white with red spots. Ss. and ps. much smaller than the proportionately large lip, the ss. spreading, oblong-spatulate, obtuse, the dilated tips deeply concave, the ps. much the broader, clawed basally, the blades flat, suborbicular. Lip 3-lbd., the lat. lbs. rather small, obtuse, the central lip-area shortly constricted, the midlb. abruptly dilated, deeply emarginate and 2-lbd., transversely oblong or kidney-shaped; disc with an erect, fleshy callus which terminates apically in a prominent 3-toothed process. Mostly spring. (I, H) Guatemala to Venezuela, Trinidad, and Peru.

O. ansiferum Rchb.f. (*Oncidium delumbe* Ldl., *O. hieroglyphicum* hort., *O. Lankesteri* Ames, *O. naranjense* Schltr., *O. tenue* Ldl. var. *grandiflorum* Ldl.)

Pbs. very strongly compressed, very thin, smooth, the margins often wavy, ovate-elliptic to oblong-elliptic, 2¼–5″ tall and 1¼–2½″ wide, with 2–3 lf.-like bracts at base. Lvs. usually solitary (rarely 2), rather leathery to light in texture, usually pale or yellowish-green, lanceolate to elliptic-lanceolate, acutish to obtuse, 6–14″ long, to 2¼″ wide. Infls. solitary or paired, erect or arching, paniculate, to 5′ long, few- to rather many-fld. Fls. about 1″ in diam., the ss. and ps. brown or ochre-brown, usually with yellow margins and tips, the midlb. and lat. lbs. of the lip bright yellow, the central isthmus brown with a bright yellow crest. Ss. spreading, elliptic-lanceolate, obtuse to acute, strongly wavy marginally. Ps. somewhat broader, spreading, elliptic-oblong, obtuse to acutish, wavy marginally. Lip fiddle-shaped, the apex transversely kidney-shaped, emarginate, the mid-section abruptly contracted in front into a broad isthmus, the basal parts more or less confluent with the short, roundish lat. lbs.; disc with a 5-lobed puberulous crest, ending in a median porrect tooth. Mostly autumn–winter. (I, H) Guatemala; Nicaragua; Costa Rica; Panama.

O. auriferum Rchb.f.

Pbs. oval, clustered, 1-lvd., 2–2½″ tall. Lf. solitary, linear, acutish, not very heavy-textured, to 10″ long and about ½–¾″ wide. Infls. loosely many-fld., the branches spreading and again panicled, erect or arching, to about 12″ tall. Fls. about 1″ long, the ss. and ps. yellow with two or three transverse brown blotches, the lip golden-yellow with a brown-red blotch on each side of the whitish disc. Ss. and slightly broader ps. spreading, oblong, acutish. Lip golden-yellow with a brown-red blotch on each side of the 2-toothed, whitish callus, the midlb. kidney-shaped, deeply incised. Col. with small, broadly rhombic auricles. Spring, mostly Apr.–May. (I, H) Venezuela.

O. barbatum Ldl. (*Oncidium ciliatulum* Hoffmsgg., *O. ciliatum* Ldl., *O. ciliolatum* Hoffmsgg., *O. fimbriatum* Hoffmsgg., *O. Johnianum* Schltr., *O. microglossum* Kl., *O. subciliatum* Hoffmsgg.)

Pbs. clustered, broadly oval to oval-oblong, compressed, 2–2½″ long. Lf. solitary, linear to oval-oblong, acute or emarginate at apex, glossy, to 4″ long. Infls. slender, the peduncle usually pale green, spotted with red-brown, erect or arching, to about 14″ tall, usually slightly panicled and few-fld. near apex. Fls. 1–1½″ long, waxy, yellow, blotched or spotted with chestnut-brown, the lip vivid yellow, the crest red-dotted. Ss. clawed, oval-oblong, undulate, the lat. pair narrower, connate for about one-third their length. Ps. similar but broader. Lip 3-lbd., the lbs. obovate and almost equal, the lateral two obtuse, the midlb. apiculate; crest placed on a circular disc that is fringed at the margin, 5-toothed, the posterior two teeth divergent, the anterior three

smaller, tuberculose. Col.-wings roundish to almost square. Spring, usually Mar.–May. (I, H) Brazil.

O. Baueri Ldl. (*Epidendrum gigas* L.C.Rich., *Oncidium altissimum* Ldl. not Sw.)

Pbs. clustered, oblong-ovoid, somewhat compressed, rather strongly ridged, 3–7″ long and to 1½″ wide, often yellowish. Lvs. usually paired (rarely 1 or 3) at apex of pb., also some lf.-like bracts at the pb.-bases, linear-ligular to ensiform, acute to acuminate, rather leathery, 1–3½′ long and 1–2½″ broad. Infls. stout, 5–10′ long (rarely more), abundantly branched from near the base (or not), the branches gradually shortening upwards, the lower ones mostly 7–10-fld., the entire infl. erect to rather strongly pendulous through weight of the fls. Fls. to 1″ in diam., rather waxy-textured, long-lived, yellow or yellowish-green, spotted or irregularly barred with brown or reddish-brown, the lip yellow, its claw reddish-brown, the crest whitish. Ss. and ps. linear-lanceolate, undulate, the lat. ss. free and divergent. Lip 3-lbd., the lat. lbs. small, obcordate, the midlb. transversely oblong, emarginate, broadly clawed, the crest (callus) borne on the claw, fleshy, consisting of 3 series of teeth—2 lateral groups of four each and 1 of 3 teeth in front. Col. with short, truncate wings. Often confused with *O. altissimum* Sw. and *O. sphacelatum* Ldl. Mostly spring. (I, H) Puerto Rico; Virgin Islands; Martinique; ? Mexico to Brazil and Peru.

O. bicallosum Ldl.

Very closely allied to and resembling *O. Cavendishianum* Batem., differing primarily in generally having the fls. in a raceme instead of a panicle, the larger and somewhat differently hued fls., the smaller lat. lbs. of the lip, and the form of the col.-wings and callus. Pbs. essentially absent, borne from a robust rhiz. Lvs. 1–2, very heavily leathery, rigid, usually yellowish, oblong-lanceolate, acute, mostly strongly V-shaped, keeled at the back. Infls. erect, to 3′ tall (rarely more), rather robust, very rarely branching, mostly loosely many-fld. Fls. often more than 2″ long, yellow to golden-yellow, often flushed with brownish-green, the lip bright canary-yellow, the callus white, dotted with red. Ss. and ps. similar, obovate-spatulate with undulate margins, the dors. sep. concave, almost hooded, the lats. narrower. Lip 3-lbd., the basal lbs. small, sub-spatulate, the midlb. large, spreading, transversely oblong with a shallow sinus in the anterior margin; callus 2-parted, the posterior part sub-reniform, the anterior part with 3 rounded tubercles. Col.-wings small, decurved. Mostly Aug.–Oct. (I, H) Mexico; Guatemala; El Salvador.

O. bifolium Sims

Pbs. clustered, ovoid, furrowed with age, to almost 3″ tall. Lvs. 2, ligulate, acute, to 6″ long. Infls. loosely 5–10-fld., to 12″ tall and more. Fls. about 1½″ long, the ss. and ps. yellow with more or less dense red-brown spots, oval, blunt at tips, wavy-margined. Lip vivid golden-yellow, the lat. lbs. triangular, the midlb. somewhat kidney-shaped, deeply emarginate. Summer. (I, H) South Brazil; Uruguay.

O. Cabagrae Schltr. (*Oncidium Rechingerianum* Krzl.)

Pbs. clustered, slender, elliptic-ovoid to sub-linear,

strongly compressed, 2–4½″ long, densely brown- or black-spotted, usually ridged with age. Lvs. 2–3, somewhat leathery, ligular, acute, 6–10″ long, narrowed basally into slender stalks. Infls. slender, many-fld., arching, to 3′ long. Fls. long-lived, rather waxy, about 1″ across at most, the ss. and ps. heavily blotched with rich chestnut-brown, usually with yellow margins and tips, the midlb. and lat. lbs of lip bright yellow, with the central isthmus rich reddish-brown, the callus white, spotted with brown. Summer. (I, H) Costa Rica; Panama.

O. carthagenense (Jacq.) Sw. (*Epidendrum carthagenense* Jacq., *Oncidium kymatoides* Krzl., *O. obsoletum* A.Rich. & Gal., *O. Oerstedii* Rchb.f., *O. panduriferum* Kth., *O. undulatum* Salisb.)

Similar to *O. luridum* Ldl. and in certain intermediate forms perhaps too closely approaching it. Pbs. almost obsolescent. Lf. solitary, broadly lanceolate to elliptic-oblong, acute, rigidly fleshy, usually more or less spotted with brown or maroon, 6–24″ long, 1¼–3″ broad, keeled towards base. Infls. erect or arching, many-fld., usually branched, to 5′ tall, rather stout basally. Fls. highly variable in size and colour, averaging about ¾″ in diam., usually more or less heavily blotched and spotted with purplish-rose on a white base-colour, differing from *O. luridum* Ldl. in superficial form and in details of the lip-callus. Mostly May–July. (I, H) South Florida; West Indies; Mexico to Venezuela and Brazil.

O. Cavendishianum Batem. (*Oncidium pachyphyllum* Hk.)

Pbs. essentially absent. Lvs. 1–2, borne from a very robust rhiz., rigidly coriaceous, usually yellow-green, elliptic-oblong, apically subacute, to 2′ long and 8″ wide, keeled. Infl. stout, erect, to 3′ tall, normally a many-fld. panicle. Fls. waxy, fragrant, about 1½″ in diam., the undulate ss. and ps. sometimes entirely yellow, more commonly greenish-yellow, more or less densely spotted and blotched with red, clawed, obovate, the ps. slightly narrower than the ss.; lip bright yellow, 3-lbd., the lat. lbs. obovate, the midlb. transversely oblong with an angular sinus in the anterior margin; the disc-crest with 4 tubercles in the form of a cross, and a fifth central one that is larger and more prominent than the other ones; col.-wings curved, yellow, spotted with red. Winter–early spring. (I) Mexico; Guatemala.

O. cheirophorum Rchb.f. (*Oncidium Dielsianum* Krzl.)

Pbs. tightly clustered, ovoid to suborbicular, compressed, to 1½″ long and 1″ wide, becoming wrinkled with age, with several sheathing bracts at base. Lf. usually solitary, rather thin-textured, linear-ligular, obtuse to subacute, 2–6″ long, stalked below. Infls. 1–2 per growth, slender, erect or arching, densely paniculate, to 12″ long. Fls. numerous, mostly less than ¼″ in diam., vivid yellow, fragrant. Dors. sep. erect, short-clawed basally, the blade deeply concave, the lat. ss. often reflexed. Ps. short-clawed, spreading. Lip conspicuously 3-lbd., the broadly spreading, auriculate lat. lbs. squarish to roundish, usually with reflexed margins, the central portion of lip with an abrupt, narrow constriction; midlb. transversely reniform to 2-lbd., the disc with a prominent, fleshy keel, the upper margins with 2 conspicuous squarish wings, between which at apex is a

short concavity or hood. Mostly autumn–winter. (I) Nicaragua; Costa Rica; Panama; Colombia, mostly in the highlands.

O. chrysomorphum Ldl.

Pbs. clustered, ovoid, to 1½″ long, compressed, smooth, sharp-edged. Lvs. 2–3, linear, subacute to almost acuminate, 7–9″ long, rather leathery. Infls. rather stout, erect, to almost 2′ tall, panicled from the middle, the branches distichously alternate, short and down-curving, with spathe-like bracts, and numerous fls. Fls. crowded, ¾″ in diam., the ss. and ps. golden-yellow, the lip paler yellow. Ss. and ps. similar and subequal, reflexed, spatulate, obtuse. Lip oblong, dilated at apex and at base into two roundish lobes; disc with an almost oblong crest, with 2 teeth in front and 2 on each side. Col.-wings obsolete. Winter. (I) Colombia; Venezuela.

O. citrinum Ldl.

Rather simulating a small *O. altissimum* Sw. in vegetative habit. Infl. slender, usually simple, 4–5-fld., to 15″ tall. Fls. about 1½″ across, greenish-yellow with pale brown blotches, the ss. and ps. spreading, ligulate, acute. Lip vivid yellow, fiddle-shaped, the lat. lbs. short, the midlb. deeply emarginate, with a complex, red-spotted callus. Winter. (H) Trinidad.

O. concolor Hk. (*Cyrtochilum citrinum* Hk.)

Pbs. clustered, oval-oblong, 1½–2″ long, becoming strongly ribbed with age. Lvs. 2–3, bright green, rather leathery, lanceolate-ligulate, acute, to 6″ long. Infls. loosely 6–12-fld., hanging, to 12″ long. Fls. about 2″ long, vivid canary-yellow, the dors. sep. and ascending ps. elliptic-oblong, acute; lat. ss. longer, narrower and more acute, joined for about half their length. Lip clawed, the lamina spreading, roundish to broadly cordate, emarginate; crest 2-lamellate. Col.-wings tooth-like, ascending. Mostly Apr.–May. (I, H) Brazil.

O. crispum Lodd.

Pbs. clustered, oblong, compressed, usually dark brown or almost purplish-brown, ribbed and furrowed on flattened side, 3–4″ long. Lvs. 2–3, coriaceous, oblong-lanceolate, acute, 6–8″ long, 1–2″ broad. Infls. erect or arching under the weight of the 40–80 fls., to 2½′ long, the peduncle glaucescent, mottled with dull crimson, usually strongly branched. Fls. variable in size, 2–3″ in diam., all segms. greatly crisped and undulate, bright chestnut-brown sometimes more or less spotted and margined with vivid yellow, usually with a bright yellow spot in front of the crest. Ss. clawed, oval-oblong, the lat. pair connate to about one-third of their length and hidden behind the lip; ps. broadly oval or almost roundish, short-clawed, crenulate marginally; lip 3-lbd., the lat. lbs. ear-like; the midlb. large, with broad claw and roundish blade; crest 3-lamellate, the front lamella much the largest, horn-like, the posterior 2 multi-toothed. Col.-wings large, toothed. Sept.–Dec. (I) Brazil.

O. crista-galli Rchb.f. (*Oncidium decipiens* Ldl., *O. iridifolium* Ldl.)

Pbs. clustered, ovoid, compressed, to ¾″ tall, usually hidden by the 4–6 conspicuous, lf.-like basal bracts, these with papery blades to 3″ long. Lf. (apical) reduced to a tiny apicule usually less than ¼″ long. Infls. 1–4 per growth, erect or arching, very slender, 1-fld., to 3″ long. Fls. to 1¼″ long, the ss. greenish-yellow, the ps. bright yellow with transverse bands of reddish-brown, the lip bright yellow, marked on the disc with white and reddish-brown irregular blotches. Lip complexly 3-lbd., the large midlb. divided into 4 lobules, all margins crisped. Mostly autumn, sometimes more than once annually. (I, H) Mexico throughout Central America to Colombia, Ecuador, and Peru.

O. dasytyle Rchb.f.

Pbs. clustered, to 2″ long, compressed, sharp-angled and furrowed with age. Lvs. usually paired, 5–6″ long, linear-lanceolate, subacute, rather thin-textured. Infls. slender, to 20″ tall, few-fld., a rac. or sparsely branched panicle. Fls. to 1½″ in diam., pale yellow, blotched with red-brown, the lat. ss. (which are joined to the middle and longer than the dors. one) duller in colour, the clawed, basally eared lip pale yellow, the midlb. large, broadly reniform, with a cordate, 2-lbd. blackish-crimson crest. Col.-wings squarish, the anther beaked. Usually Jan.–Feb., sometimes to July. (I, H) Brazil.

O. divaricatum Ldl.

Pbs. tightly clustered, usually yellowish-green, roundish, very much compressed, to 1½″ in diam. Lf. solitary, rigidly leathery, often yellowish-green, narrowly oblong, to 12″ long and 2″ broad, strongly keeled on reverse side. Infls. 4–6′ long, very profusely branched, many-fld., the peduncle and rachis usually mottled with dull purple. Fls. usually less than 1″ in diam., the clawed ss. and ps. chestnut-brown with a golden-yellow blotch near apex, the dors. one concave, the lats. divaricate, the ps. longer, oblong, obtuse. Lip 3-lbd., the lat. lbs. the largest, roundish, entire, yellow, spotted with chestnut-brown; midlb. transversely oblong, emarginate, yellow with a chestnut spot in front of the cushion-like, 4-lbd. crest. Col.-wings rounded. Mostly autumn. (I, H) Brazil.

O. ensatum Ldl. (*Oncidium cerebriferum* Rchb.f., *O. confusum* Rchb.f.)

Pbs. fleshy, ovoid, somewhat compressed, usually smooth, a rather odd shade of dull bluish-green, 2–3″ tall, the apices very truncate, with 4–6 imbricating basal bracts, 2–3 of which are conspicuously foliaceous, the blades not jointed to the basal parts. Lvs. and bract-blades linear-lanceolate, acuminate, rather thin in texture, to 3′ long and 1¼″ wide, rather rigidly erect, with strong central keel. Infls. 1–2 per growth, erect or noticeably arching, many-fld., the fls. opening a few at a time over a period of months. Fls. about 1″ long, the ss. and ps. greenish to brownish-olive-green, the large lip very vivid yellow. Ss. and ps. spreading, or reflexed, usually undulate marginally. Lip fiddle-shaped, 3-lbd., abruptly contracted at base and adnate to col.-base, the lat. lbs. small, the midlb. 2-lbd., transversely reniform; disc olive-green, with a prominent, fleshy, white, 7-toothed callus. Col. short, with prominent lat. wings. Summer–autumn. (I, H) British Honduras to Panama, normally a terrestrial.

O. falcipetalum Ldl.

Pbs. clustered, ovoid-oblong, 3–4″ long. Lvs. normally paired, ligulate to lanceolate-ligulate, acute, varying in size from 10–15″ long and 1–2″ broad. Infls. stout, flexuous, to more than 10′ long, irregularly branching, each rather short branch 3–5-fld., the fls. opening over a long period of time. Fls. to 3″ long, the ss. rich russet-brown with a narrow yellow margin, strongly clawed, the dors. one roundish, the lat. pair ovate, acute; ps. much smaller, falcate, acute, the margins very wavy, yellow, spotted mostly in basal half with brown; lip linear, reflexed, purplish-brown; crest a narrow ridge, in front of which there is a cluster of sharp tubercles. Col. with a horn-like wing on each side of the stigmatic surface. Autumn–early winter. (I) Venezuela.

O. flexuosum Sims

Rhiz. ascending, robust, clothed with overlapping brownish scales, producing the pbs. often at rather distant intervals, rooting very profusely. Pbs. usually 1–2″ apart on the rhiz., mostly oval-oblong, often yellowish-green, compressed, 1½–3″ long. Lvs. usually 2 (rarely 1), glossy, linear- or linear-lanceolate, acute, 4–9″ long. Infls. 1–more per growth, to 3′ long, the peduncle and rachis usually dull purple, densely and beautifully paniculate towards apex, the branches wiry, mostly many-fld. Fls. varying in size from ¾–1¼″ long, vivid golden-yellow, usually with a red-brown blotch at base of each segm. Ss. and ps. similar, tiny, obovate-oblong, the lat. ss. joined, bifid at apex. Lip clawed, proportionately large, with 2 basal ear-like lobules and a transversely oblong, emarginate lamina; crest 2-parted, the posterior half a downy cushion, the anterior half usually 3–5-toothed. Col.-wings squarish, bent forward. Mostly autumn–winter. (I, H) Brazil; Paraguay; Uruguay.

O. Forbesii Hk.

Pbs. clustered, oblong, compressed, 2–3″ long. Lvs. normally paired, leathery, dark green, oblong-ligulate, acute, 6–12″ long. Infls. erect or arching, to 3′ tall, generally a rather many-fld. panicle. Fls. to 2½″ in diam., all segms. vivid chestnut-brown with a narrow golden yellow border. Dors. sep. broadly oval, the lat. pair narrowly oblong, joined for about one-third their length and concealed by the lip. Ps. clawed, vaguely roundish, marginally crisped. Lip broadly clawed, the lat. lbs. usually bright yellow; midlb. large, fan-shaped, 2-lbd., vivid chestnut-brown with narrow golden-yellow border; crest warty, 5-lbd. Col.-wings roundish, purplish-violet spotted with red. Sept.–Nov. (I, H) Brazil.

O. Gardneri Ldl.

Pbs. clustered, ovoid, 2–3″ long, when old very grooved and compressed. Lvs. 2, linear or oblong-lanceolate, obtuse, dark green above, often flushed with purplish underneath, 6–9″ long. Infls. 2–3′ long, many-fld., paniculate in upper half. Fls. about 2″ in diam., the ss. brown, barred with yellow, clawed, obovate-oblong, the dors. one concave, the lat. pair joined to beyond the middle; ps. much larger, chestnut-brown with numerous yellow markings along the margin, shortly clawed, almost round with wavy margins; lip spreading, fan-shaped, the lat. lbs. small, auriculate.

yellow with red-brown basal markings, the midlb. bright yellow with a broad zone of red-brown confluent spots near the undulate margin; crest fleshy, triangular, with the apex in front studded with red-brown warts, on each side of the tip with 2 warty protuberances; col.-wings narrow, roundish. June–Aug. (I, H) Brazil.

O. incurvum Bark. (*Oncidium albo-violaceum* A.Rich. & Gal.)

Pbs. ovoid, compressed, several-ribbed on flattened sides, 3–4″ long. Lvs. 2–3, linear-ligulate, acute, rather coriaceous, to 1½′ long. Infls. erect to gracefully arching, 3–5′ long, panicled, the branches distichous and alternate, gradually becoming smaller upward, each branch loosely racemose. Fls. about 1″ in diam., fragrant, pink to rose-pink, more or less spotted and blotched with white, the lip-crest vivid yellow, 5-toothed. Ss. and ps. linear-lanceolate, acute to acuminate, undulate marginally; lip 3-lbd., the lat. lbs. small, roundish-oblong; midlb. clawed, spreading, roundish, apiculate, usually with the claw pink, the lamina white. Col.-wings narrow, white. Mostly autumn–winter. (I) Mexico.

O. isthmi Schltr.

Vegetatively similar to *O. panamense* Schltr. and *O. Baueri* Ldl., differing notably in the larger, conspicuously expanded midlb. and much narrower isthmus of the lip. Pbs. to 5″ tall, compressed, longitudinally ridged. Lvs. usually 2 at pb.-apex, with several foliaceous bracts at pb.-base, to 1½′ long and 1¼″ wide, linear-lanceolate, acute, rather heavy. Infls. 1–2 per growth, erect or arching, paniculate, to about 4′ tall, many-fld. Fls. to 1″ long, the ss. and ps. yellow, barred with brown, the panduriform, 3-lbd. lip bright yellow, the small, ear-like lat. lbs. squarish to roundish, the frontal margins abruptly contracted into a narrow central isthmus; midlb. broadly dilated and 2-lbd., transversely reniform, occupying about two thirds the length of the lip, the disc brown, with an erect, compact, 7-toothed basal callus. Col. short, about ⅛″ long, with prominent lat. wings. Mostly autumn. (I, H) Costa Rica; Panama.

O. Jonesianum Rchb.f.

Pbs. so reduced as to appear absent, otherwise vegetatively similar to *O. longifolium* Ldl., the fleshily terete lvs. sharply pendulous. Infls. normally erect, the rather stout peduncle usually purple-mottled, the 10–15 handsome fls. borne in a rac., to 2′ tall. Fls. 2–3″ in diam., long-lasting, the ss. and ps. yellowish-white, spotted with rich chestnut-brown, spreading, obovate-oblong, undulate. Lip clawed, the lat. lbs. reduced to small ear-like lobules at its base, yellow and red; midlb. white with some red spots in front of the crest, transversely oblong with a deep sinus in the anterior margin, undulate; crest consisting of a broad central ridge with lateral processes at each end, muchly tubercled; col.-wings oblong, white, dotted with red. Autumn. (I, H) South Brazil; Paraguay; Uruguay.

O. Kramerianum Rchb.f. (*Oncidium nodosum* E.Morr., *O. Papilio* Ldl. var. *Kramerianum* Ldl., *Papiliopsis nodosus* E.Morr.)

Pbs. tightly clustered, often almost prostrate one on top of the other, roundish to vaguely squarish, usually purplish or dull purple-brown, strongly compressed, 1–1¼″ in diam. Lf. solitary, rigidly leathery, erect, elliptic-oblong, acute, often densely spotted with dull maroon on reverse side, 6–8″ long and to 3″ wide, the upper surfaces sometimes dark green mottled with purple. Infls. erect, persistent for several years and producing fls. at irregular intervals (usually singly) throughout that interval, to more than 3′ tall, strongly jointed, the nodes conspicuously swollen. Fls. very spectacular, lasting rather well, to 5″ long in certain forms, rather similar to *O. Papilio* Ldl., but readily differentiated by technical details of the infl. and the fls. Dors. sep. and ps. similar, erect (at least when fls. first expand), rich reddish-brown, linear-spatulate, undulate strongly towards apex. Lat. ss. oval-oblong, somewhat falcate, orange-red or orange-brown, more or less densely mottled with golden-yellow, the margins undulate, serrulate. Lip sub-pandurate, the smallish lat. lbs. roundish, yellow spotted with rich red-brown; midlb. transversely oblong, with an anterior sinus, vivid canary-yellow with a more or less broad red or red-brown border, very crisped; crest prominent, with 2 basal and 3 front lobes, deep bronze-purple. Col. with 2 horizontal plate-like wings beneath the stigmatic surface, and 2 cirrhi above, each terminating in an odd blackish, glossy gland. Mostly autumn–winter, but sporadic throughout the year. (I, H) Costa Rica; Panama; Colombia; Ecuador.

O. Lanceanum Ldl.

Pbs. very reduced, the rhiz. very stout. Lvs. rigidly erect, heavily coriaceous, elliptic-oblong, acute, to 20″ long and 5″ broad, dark dull green more or less densely spotted with purple or magenta-purple. Infls. erect, often panicled above, few- to rather many-fld., to 1½′ tall. Fls. very waxy and fragrant, long-lasting, to 2½″ long, not as wide, variable in size and colour, the ss. and ps. yellow or yellow-green, more or less densely spotted with chocolate-brown, the very large lip rich magenta or rose-purple, sometimes whitish (very rarely white). Ss. and ps. similar, oval-oblong, obtuse, often rather undulate marginally. Lip 3-lbd., the lat. lbs. triangular-oblong, rather smallish; midlb. broadly clawed, with a transversely oblong lamina, vaguely wavy marginally; crest with an elevated fleshy plate that is obscurely 2-lamellate behind. Col.-wings oblong, oblique, purple or magenta. Mostly summer. (I, H) Colombia; Venezuela; Guianas; Trinidad.

O. leucochilum Batem. (*Cyrtochilum leucochilum* Planch., *Oncidium digitatum* Ldl.)

Pbs. clustered, oval-oblong, usually rather compressed, ribbed with age, 3–5″ long. Lvs. normally 2, ligulate, acute, 8–12″ long, rather dull-green. Infls. 5–12′ long, very profusely branched almost from the base, the slender, distant branches few- to many-fld. Fls. waxy, long-lasting, variable in size and dimensions, to more than 1¼″ long, the ss. and ps. usually pale yellowish-green, more or less densely covered with confluent greenish-brown to rich brown-purple bars, the ornate lip mostly white. Ss. and ps. similar, subequal, elliptic-oblong, acute, often rather wavy-margined. Lip 3-lbd., the lat. lbs. small, oblong, obtuse; midlb. broadly clawed, transversely oblong, emarginate, sometimes wavy marginally; crest usually bright pink-magenta, a narrow raised plate with 2 minute teeth on each side, terminating in one long erect tooth and 2 smaller horizontal ones in front. Col.-wings hatchet-shaped, rose-pink to rosy-magenta, the face below the stigma bright yellow. Mostly winter–spring, sometimes summer, rarely more than once annually. (I, H) Mexico; Guatemala; Honduras.

O. longifolium Ldl. (*Oncidium Cebolleta* Sw. of authors)

Rhiz. stout, the pbs. very small, roundish, scarcely noticeable. Lf. solitary per pb., sub-cylindric to almost terete, elongate, tapering to a sharp, often elongate point, grooved on the face, frequently more or less reddish, or sometimes red-spotted, 6–24″ long, often very robust, highly variable, rigidly erect to sharply pendulous (frequently on the same tree!). Infls. erect, rather stout, to 2½′ long, few- to many-fld., branched or not, the rachis usually reddish-spotted. Fls. variable in all parts, in the finest forms to 1½″ long (usually much smaller), the smallish, undulate ss. and ps. yellow, spotted more or less densely with reddish-brown, often somewhat incurving over the col. Lip large for the fl., canary-yellow to rich golden-yellow, 3-lbd., the lat. lbs. obovate-oblong; midlb. transversely oblong, emarginate; crest an elevated rounded plate, behind which are 2 large teeth and some smaller ones on each side. Col.-wings small. Mostly spring. (I, H) Mexico and West Indies to Paraguay in South America.

O. longipes Ldl. (*Oncidium janeirense* Rchb.f.)

Pbs. clustered, usually rather yellowish, elongate-ovoid, becoming furrowed with age, to about 1″ long, with a rather prominent rhiz. between the pb.-groups on occasion. Lvs. usually 2 (rarely solitary), glossy-green, not very leathery, linear-oblong, mucronate, 4–6″ long, to ½″ wide. Infls. erect, the rachis zigzag, to 6″ tall, 3–5-fld. or more. Fls. lasting well, glossy, 1–1½″ in diam., the ss. and ps. pale red-brown, streaked transversely with yellow and with yellow tips, spatulate or narrowly oblong, undulate, the lat. ss. longer and narrower than the dors. one. Lip 3-lbd., bright canary-yellow, the lat. lbs. roundish-oblong; isthmus or claw often flushed with reddish-brown; midlb. transversely oblong, emarginate; crest an oblong fleshy disc covered with numerous small whitish warts, with 2 prominent teeth in front. Col.-wings very narrow, almost obsolete. Spring–early summer. (I, H) Brazil.

—var. **Croesus** (Rchb.f.) Veitch (*Oncidium Croesus* Rchb.f.)

Differs from the typical sp. in having the fls. somewhat larger (to about 1¾″ in length), and of different coloration: ss. and ps. dark brown-purple, the lip golden-yellow with a brown-purple band around the complex crest. Spring–early summer. (I, H) Brazil.

O. loxense Ldl. (*Cyrtochilum loxense* Krzl.)

Pbs. ovoid to ovoid-pyriform, 3–5″ tall, not overly clustered, vaguely compressed. Lf. solitary, narrowly lanceolate, acute, 9–15″ long and 1½–2″ broad. Infls. rambling, viney, 3½–5′ long, bearing the rather few fls. at irregular intervals. Fls. to 3″ in diam., long-lasting,

very handsome, the ss. broadly clawed, rich cinnamon-brown, barred with light or bright yellow, the lats. free, oval-oblong, obtuse, undulate, with a prominent keel behind; ps. similar to ss. but broader and less prominently keeled behind, bright olive-brown with a few scattered yellow, transverse markings; lip heavy-textured, vivid orange-yellow, the disc somewhat paler, the lat. lbs. reduced to tiny auricles at the base of the broad claw, the midlb. transversely and broadly oblong; crest a fleshy protuberance with 4 shallow plates behind and a raised median fringed plate in front, on each side of which are numerous bristles springing from the protuberance. May–June. (C, I) Ecuador; Peru.

O. luridum Ldl. (*Epidendrum guttatum* L., *Oncidium guttatum* Rchb.f.)

Pbs. essentially absent, the lvs. borne from a robust rhiz., oval-oblong, highly variable in size, rigidly leathery, often with some dull brown or reddish-brown spots on both sides, or completely green, 12–25″ long, conduplicate towards the base. Infls. very robust, to 8′ tall, the rachis dull red-brown, loosely or densely paniculate, the individual branches usually short, 3–5-fld. Fls. ¾–1″ in diam., extremely variable in colour, intergrading with *O. carthagenense* (Jacq.) Sw. in certain forms, usually yellow-brown or red-brown with some yellow irregular (or regular) markings or spots (very rarely entirely lemon-yellow or apple-green). Ss. and ps. clawed, very undulate marginally, the dors. sep. broadly oval to almost roundish, concave, the lat. ss. free, spatulate-oblong; ps. oblong, obtuse. Lip 3-lbd., the lat. lbs. small, rounded, with a revolute margin; midlb. shortly and broadly clawed, transversely oblong, emarginate; crest 5-lbd., the frontal lobe an erect rounded plate, yellow, spotted with red, on each side of this with a smaller, rounded, rose-coloured tubercle, the 2 posterior lobes white, much tuberculated. Col.-wings reniform, pink or white. Mostly spring–autumn. (I, H) South Florida; West Indies and Mexico to British Guiana and Peru.

O. macranthum Ldl. (*Cyrtochilum macranthum* Krzl.)

Pbs. variable in size and shape, usually oval-oblong or ovoid-conical, often vaguely compressed, glossy, 4–6″ long and 2–2½″ in diam., clustered. Lvs. usually paired, narrowly lanceolate, acute, to about 1½′ long, not very heavy-textured. Infls. climbing, viney, to about 12′ long, paniculate, the branches usually short, each bearing 1–4 fls., furnished with boat-shaped bracts. Fls. probably the largest in the genus, highly variable in all parts, in certain forms to more than 4″ across, long-lasting, the clawed ss. yellow, more or less flushed with light brown or cinnabar-brown, orbicular-oblong, undulate; ps. similar to the ss., but the claw shorter and the edges much more crisped-undulate, usually vivid clear yellow, sometimes flushed with pale brown towards the base; lip much smaller than other segms., hastate, the horn-like lat. lbs. mostly violet-purple, the tongue-shaped midlb. white, bordered with violet-purple, narrowing to a reflexed tip; crest cylindric, with 3 large violet-purple teeth in front and 3 smaller white ones behind; col.-wings hatchet-shaped, brownish-purple. Mostly May–July. (C, I) Ecuador; Peru, at high elevations.

O. maculatum Ldl. (*Cyrtochilum maculatum* Ldl., *Odontoglossum Lindleyi* Gal., *Oncidium psittacinum* Lind.)

Extremely variable in all parts, often closely approximating *Odontoglossum* in floral structure. Pbs. tightly clustered, ovoid, often yellowish, very compressed (or not), becoming furrowed with age, 3–5″ long. Lvs. usually paired, rather coriaceous, linear-ligulate, acute, 7–10″ long. Infls. to about 1½′ long, usually racemose and rather densely many-fld., rarely panicled. Fls. to 2″ in diam. (rarely larger), long-lasting, glossy, the ss. and ps. usually yellow-green to yellow, more or less heavily blotched with dark chestnut-brown, subequal, lanceolate-oblong, acute, the tip usually reflexed. Lip rather obscurely 3-lbd., the lat. lbs. reduced to small triangular auricles, the midlb. oblong-ovate, apiculate, white in basal half, apically yellowish (often the entire lip turns yellow with age or after pollination); crest consisting of 4 plates, of which the 2 middle ones are the largest, usually white, streaked with dull or bright red. Col.-wings narrow, horn-like below, sometimes almost obsolete. Winter–early summer. (I) Mexico; Guatemala; Honduras.

O. Marshallianum Rchb.f.

Pbs. clustered, ovoid-oblong, compressed, bright green, 4–6″ long. Lvs. usually 2, oblong-lanceolate, acute, rather leathery, to more than 12″ long, folded at base. Infls. paniculate, many-fld., to more than 5′ tall. Fls. variable in size and colour, in the finest forms to 3″ long, the dors. sep. dull yellow, barred with pale red-brown, obovate-oblong, concave; lat. ss. joined for about one third their length, oblong, almost concealed by the lip, similar to dors. sep. in colour; ps. vivid canary-yellow, irregularly spotted with red-brown in the centre, broadly obovate-oblong, emarginate, noticeably undulate; lip clawed, the lat. lbs. reduced to tiny ears on the claw, the midlb. large, spreading, 2-lbd., bright yellow, broadly oblong, rather wavy-margined, the claw and crest spotted with orange-red; crest consisting of a median triangular erect plate with 2 large teeth on the basal side, 2 smaller ones in front, and 2 minute ones on each side; col.-wings short, squarish, whitish. Apr.–June. (I, H) Brazil.

O. microchilum Batem.

Vegetatively identical to *O. splendidum* A.Rich. Infls. stout, glaucous, to 4′ tall, usually profusely branched, the rather short branches mostly densely many-fld. Fls. to a maximum of 1″ in diam., often smaller, long-lasting, the ss. pale or rather dark brown with sparse yellow markings, elliptic-oblong, keeled behind, the dors. one broader than the lats. and concave; ps. narrower than the ss., chestnut-brown to brown-purple, barred and margined with yellow, oblong, obtuse, undulate, incurving; lip 3-lbd., the midlb. reduced to a small white protuberance, with a purple or red-purple spot; lat. lbs. rounded, convex, white with some purple basal spots; crest somewhat kidney-shaped, tuberculose, white with yellow and brown spots in front, reddish-brown behind; col.-wings triangular, white, the anther beaked. Mostly summer. (I) Mexico; Guatemala.

O. micropogon Rchb.f. (*Oncidium dentatum* Kl., *O. macropterum* Kl.)

Rather closely allied to *O. barbatum* Ldl., differing in the larger fls., with differently shaped ss., ps., and lip-crest. Pbs. clustered, broadly ovoid, compressed with sharp edges, and with 2–3 ribs on each flattened side, 2–2½″ long. Lvs. 1–2, linear-oblong, rather rounded apically, 4–6″ long, glossy-bright green. Infls. arching to almost pendulous, 7–10-fld. or more, to about 1½′ long. Fls. variable in size, the largest forms about 1½″ long, the ss. yellow, barred with red-brown, linear-oblong, acuminate, the lateral pair joined at their base; ps. bright canary-yellow, clawed, roundish; lip with 3 subequal bright-yellow lbs., the lats. round, the midlb. broadly obcordate; crest fleshy, covered with conical yellow and brown tubercles, the margins expanded and with fringe-like teeth; col.-wings deltoid. Summer–autumn. (I, H) Brazil.

O. ornithorhynchum HBK

Pbs. clustered, rather pale greyish-blue-green in most cases, oval-oblong, compressed (often not notably so), to 5″ long, usually smaller, rooting very copiously. Lvs. usually 2, rather thin-textured, coloured much like the pbs., linear-lanceolate, acute, to 12″ long and almost 2″ broad. Infls. often 2 or more per new growth, borne from the axils of the lf.-like bracts which subtend the pbs., arching or pendulous, to 2′ long, panicled, usually very densely many-fld. Fls. about ¾″ long, highly fragrant, long-lived, rose-lilac. Ss. and ps. oblong, the lat. ss. free and divaricate, the ps. broader and undulate. Lip vaguely fiddle-shaped, the lat. lbs. with reflexed margins and sometimes richer in colour than the rest of the fl., the midlb. emarginate; crest consisting of 5 yellow, toothed lamellae, in front of which are 2 horn-like teeth. Col.-wings triangular, minutely dentate; anther beaked. Mostly Oct.–Jan. (C, I) Mexico; Guatemala; El Salvador; Costa Rica.

O. panamense Schltr.

Vegetatively similar to *O. sphacelatum* Ldl. and other allied species. Pbs. approximately placed, oblong-ovoid, compressed, strongly ridged, to 6½″ tall and almost 2½″ wide, with 3–4 foliaceous bracts below. Lvs. 2, linear-lanceolate, acute, rather leathery, to 2½′ long and 1½″ wide, long-petioled below. Infls. 1–2 per growth, erect, arching, pendulous, or sometimes climbing, many-fld. panicles to 12′ long, stout. Fls. about ¾″ across, often rather short-lived, the shortly clawed, vaguely undulate ss. and ps. yellow, heavily barred and blotched with olive-brown; lip obscurely 3-lbd., broadly pandurate, yellow with a large transverse reddish-brown to yellowish-brown blotch below the crest; lat. lbs. rounded or broadly and obtusely triangular, the central lip with a sharp constriction but without a distinct isthmus; midlb. emarginate, obscurely 2-lbd., transversely oblong or subreniform; crest erect, white, fleshy, surmounted by 4 divergent, usually crenulate keels, terminating at the apex in 3 distinct fleshy teeth. Col. short, the wings prominent, spreading, usually serrate. Winter. (H) Panama.

O. Papilio Ldl. (*Psychopsis picta* Raf.)

Pbs. tightly clustered, oval-oblong to almost roundish,

to 2″ long, very compressed, wrinkled, often dull red with darker blotches. Lf. solitary, rigidly erect, dull green, considerably mottled and blotched with purplish-crimson, this coloration most developed on under-surface, elliptic-oblong, acutish, 6–9″ long and 2–2½″ broad. Infls. normally solitary per bulb, 2–5′ tall, prominently jointed, terete from base to beyond the middle, the upper portion flattened and ancipitous, producing a succession of fls. over a period of months. Fls. lasting well, highly variable in size and somewhat so in colour, usually about 5–6″ from tip to tip. Dors. sep. and ps. dull reddish-crimson, often with a few yellow transverse stripes, yellowish-green on reverse side, all three erect together, linear, slightly dilated towards the apex. Lat. ss. oblong, acuminate, decurving, very undulate, bright chestnut-red with some narrow transverse yellow markings. Lip 3-lbd., the lat. lbs. small, rounded, yellow, spotted with red; midlb. broadly clawed, roundish with a shallow sinus in the front margin, canary-yellow to golden-yellow with a more or less broad bright red marginal band; crest a thickened obscurely 3-lbd. raised plate, with 2 small protuberances on the basal side, white, spotted with red. Col.-wings lacerated, much dilated below, and with 2 cirrhi above having a blackish gland at their tip. Almost throughout the year. (I, H) Trinidad; Venezuela; Colombia; Ecuador; Peru.

O. phymatochilum Ldl.

Pbs. clustered, ovoid-oblong, compressed, 3–4″ long, often brownish-purple (or not). Lvs. usually solitary, rather heavy-textured, narrowly elliptic-oblong, acute to acuminate, 9–14″ long, to 1½″ wide. Infls. slender, 3–6′ long, loosely paniculate, many-fld., the peduncle and rachis usually pale green, spotted with dull crimson. Fls. to 2″ long, rather like a smallish *Brassia* in superficial appearance, the more or less reflexed ss. and ps. pale yellow, banded and spotted with brown, or sometimes ivory-white, spotted with orange-red, linear, acuminate, rather wavy-margined, the ps. broader and the free lat. ss. longer than the dors. sep. Lip white, spotted around the crest with red, 3-lbd., the lat. lbs. ear-like, oblong, obtuse, the midlb. trowel-shaped, with a reflexed acuminate tip; crest triangular in outline, with many teeth, the 3 front teeth much the largest. Col.-wings laciniate, white, spotted red. Spring–summer. (I, H) Mexico; Guatemala; Brazil.[1]

O. pubes Ldl. (*Oncidium bicornutum* Hk., *O. puberum* Spreng.)

Pbs. clustered, sub-cylindric, tapering, 2–2½″ long. Lvs. usually paired, glossy dark green, narrowly oblong-lanceolate, acute, 3–5″ long. Infls. to 2′ long, a rather densely many-fld. panicle, the branches distichous and alternate, becoming gradually smaller upwards. Fls. usually less than 1″ in diam., variable in colour, the ss. and ps. usually red-brown, barred and spotted with yellow, the dors. sep. and ps. clawed, obovate, obtuse, incurving, the lat. ss. joined into an oblong blade that is bifid at apex. Lip 3-lbd., the lat. lbs. linear, reflexed, yellow, the midlb. red-brown with a yellow margin,

[1] There seems considerable confusion as to whether the Brazilian plant is the same as the one from Mexico and Guatemala, since they differ radically in vegetative appearance, albeit not too much in floral form.

broadly obovate, emarginate; crest tubercled, fuzzy, toothed in front. Col.-wings oblong, subfalcate, obtuse. Summer–autumn. (I, H) Brazil.

O. pulchellum Hk. (*Tolumnia pulchella* Raf.)

Pbs. absent. Lvs. usually in 2's or 4's, equitant, linear-lanceolate, fleshy, rigid, 3–5″ long and more, acutely keeled behind, often vaguely toothed marginally. Infls. slender, erect, to 15″ tall, 12–20-fld. or more, usually racemose (rarely loosely paniculate). Fls. about 1″ long, extremely variable in colour (and somewhat so in dimensions), white, more or less flushed with rose or lilac-rose on all segms. Dors. sep. ovate, cuneate, concave, the lat. ss. joined into an oblong, spatulate blade, bidentate at tip and concealed by the large lip; ps. similar to the dors. sep. Lip almost square, 4-lbd., the lbs. rounded and almost equal; crest 3-lbd., usually with an ochre-coloured spot in front of it. Col.-wings ovate-oblong, rose-pink. Mostly summer. (I) ? Cuba; Jamaica; Hispaniola; Guianas.

O. pulvinatum Ldl.

Pbs. roundish-oblong, clustered, compressed, to 2″ in diam., often rather yellowish. Lf. solitary, rigidly erect, often yellowish, oblong, acute, 9–12″ long and 2–3½″ broad. Infls. slender, erect or arching, flexuose, loosely panicled, rather many-fld., 5–8′ long. Fls. almost 1″ in diam., the ss. and ps. similar and subequal, basally red-brown, the apical half yellow or yellowish, clawed, oval-oblong, the dors. sep. concave and bent forward. Lip 3-lbd., light yellow, spotted with red, the lat. lbs. roundish, with fimbriate margins, the midlb. transversely oblong, emarginate; crest whitish, spotted with red, a circular papillose cushion. Col.-wings rounded. Differs from the closely allied *O. divaricatum* Ldl. in the differently shaped lip, the crest of which is entire, not lobed. Summer–autumn. (I, H) Brazil.

O. pusillum (L.) Rchb.f. (*Epidendrum pusillum* L., *Cymbidium pusillum* Sw., *Oncidium iridifolium* HBK)

Pbs. absent. Lvs. distichously spreading, forming a broad fan, equitant, linear, often falcate or ensiform, the tips obliquely acute, usually glossy, often yellowish-green, ¾–2½″ long. Infls. 1–6 per lf.-fan, erect or arching, 1-fld., but with usually several fls. being produced in succession from the same infl. Fls. large in proportion to the size of the pl., averaging 1″ long and ¾″ wide, the bright yellow ss. free, the dors. one erect, obtuse, prolonged at the tip into an erect spur, the lats. narrow, acuminate, very closely appressed to under-surface of lip, strongly keeled on reverse sides. Ps. spreading, bright yellow, irregularly barred with reddish-brown, undulate marginally. Lip broadly pandurate, 3-lbd., bright yellow, the lat. lbs. roundish to obovate-spatulate, obtuse, the central portion of lip contracted into a short, broad isthmus, blotched with reddish-brown, the midlb. abruptly dilated, with a deep central sinus, undulate, the disc white, spotted reddish-orange, with a spreading, squarish plate, terminating in a second broad, spreading, roundish plate with a short central keel and undulate margins. Col. with prominent, toothed wings. Almost throughout the year. (I, H) Mexico to Brazil and Bolivia; Trinidad.

O. reflexum Ldl. (*Oncidium pelicanum* Mart. ex Ldl., *O. suave* Ldl., *O. Suttonii* Batem. ex Ldl., *O. Wendlandianum* Rchb.f.)

Pbs. clustered, ovoid, usually glossy yellowish-green, compressed, becoming furrowed with age, to 1½″ long. Lvs. 1–2, usually glossy, linear-lanceolate, acute, 6–8″ long, to ¾″ wide. Infls. slender, straggling, to 3′ long, pale green, mottled with dull crimson, sparsely branched along upper half, few- to rather many-fld. Fls. about 1½″ long, the ss. and ps. light yellow-green, barred with dull red-brown, the lip vivid yellow with some red spots on and around the crest. Ss. and ps. similar and subequal, linear-oblong, acute, undulate marginally, more or less reflexed, the lat. ss. free and divaricate. Lip large and spreading, 3-lbd., the lat. lbs. roundish-oblong, with revolute margins; midlb. broadly clawed, transversely oblong with a sinus in the apical margin; crest with about 10 almost equal tubercles. Col.-wings hatchet-shaped, minutely toothed; anther beaked. Autumn. (I, H) Mexico; Guatemala.

O. sarcodes Ldl. (*Oncidium Rigbyanum* Paxt.)

Pbs. variable in size, clustered, sub-fusiform, somewhat compressed, often glossy brownish-green, 4–6″ long. Lvs. 2 (rarely 3), leathery, rather shiny, oblong, acute, folded at base, to 12″ long and 2″ broad. Infls. slender, the peduncle dull purple, spotted with pale green, erect or arching, 3–6′ long, rather many-fld., shortly branched along upper half. Fls. 1½–2″ in diam., long-lasting, glossy, the ss. and ps. rich chestnut-brown bordered and somewhat marked with yellow, the lip vivid yellow with a few red-brown spots around the crest. Dors. sep. obcordate, concave, the lats. smaller, obovate-oblong, keeled. Ps. obovate, obtuse, undulate marginally. Lip 3-lbd., the lat. lbs. small, oblong with reflexed margins; midlb. transversely oblong with undulate margins; crest an oblong plate, lobed in front, with a tooth on each side near the middle, light yellow, dotted with brown. Col.-wings subtriangular. Spring. (I, H) Brazil.

O. serratum Ldl. (*Cyrtochilum serratum* Krzl., *Oncidium diadema* Ldl.)

Pbs. clustered, ovoid, compressed, to 6″ long and 1¾″ in diam. Lvs. usually 2, narrowly lanceolate, acutish to 1½′ long. Infls. flexuose, clambering, 5–9′ long, distantly branched in upper parts, many-fld. Fls. 3″ long, very handsome, the ss. clawed, chestnut-brown with a narrow yellow border, the dors. one roundish, crisped marginally, the lats. ovate-oblong, deflexed and then curving upwards and sideways like a saddle; ps. similar to lat. ss. but shorter, more crisped and indented at the apex, the basal two-thirds chestnut-brown, the apical third bright yellow. Lip much smaller than other segms., purplish-brown, linear-spatulate, reflexed, with the lat. lbs. small, hatchet-shaped; crest a central white projecting plate with 2 acute teeth in front and a notched plate on each side. Col.-wings dagger-shaped, ascending, red-brown. Winter. (C, I) Ecuador; Peru.

O. sphacelatum Ldl. (*Oncidium Massangei* Morr.)

Pbs. clustered to vaguely distant on the very robust rhiz., usually yellowish, almost oblong, compressed with acute edges, 4–7″ long and 2–3″ wide. Lvs. 2–3, linear-ligulate, rather rigid, to more than 2′ long. Infls. to 6′ long, the peduncle often mottled with dull purple, very branched, the branches short, many-fld. Fls. when in bud very characteristically formed, the tips of the ss. and ps. bent back like recurved horns; fls. when expanded about 1″ across, rather variable, the ss. and ps. usually dark chestnut-brown for basal two-thirds, somewhat barred with yellow, the apical one-third and margins yellow, narrowly oblong, undulate, reflexed at tip. Lip golden-yellow with a more or less developed red-brown area in front of the crest, the entire segm. subpanduriform, the isthmus not well developed, the midlb. marginally usually vaguely undulate; crest a fleshy plate, 3-lbd. in front, toothed on the sides. Col.-wings small, oblong, depressed. This species is often confused with *O. altissimum* Sw. and its allied spp., but may be differentiated by the shape of the lip and the column-wings, among other characters. Mostly Nov.–June. (I, H) Mexico; British Honduras; Guatemala; El Salvador; Honduras; possibly elsewhere in tropical America.

O. sphegiferum Ldl.

Pbs. clustered, broadly oval, often almost round, very compressed, 1–1½″ in diam. Lf. solitary, rigidly erect, elliptic-oblong, acute, 6–8″ long and to almost 1¾″ wide, pale green. Infls. many-fld., paniculate, to about 4½′ long. Fls. almost an inch across, bright orange with a reddish or reddish-brown stain at the base of all segms. Ss. and ps. clawed, the ss. oval, the ps. oblong, apiculate. Lip subpandurate, the rather large lat. lbs. rounded, toothed marginally; midlb. transversely oblong, emarginate, often paler in colour than other segms.; crest oblong, cushion-like, minutely papillose. Col.-wings narrowly oblong. Summer–autumn. (I, H) Brazil.

O. splendidum A.Rich. (*Oncidium tigrinum* LaLl. & Lex. var. *splendidum* Hk.f.)

Pbs. clustered, ovoid to almost round, more or less compressed, usually dull brownish-green or purplish-green, 1½–2″ tall. Lf. solitary, usually coloured like the pbs., rigid, very heavy and thick, oblong or elliptic-oblong, acute to vaguely acuminate, keeled behind, to 12″ long and 3″ broad, often vaguely glaucous. Infls. stout, erect, to 4′ tall, few- to rather many-fld., the peduncle glaucous, sometimes panicled above. Fls. to 3″ long, long-lasting, very handsome, the ss. and ps. similar and subequal, bright yellow, heavily blotched and spotted with rich brown or reddish-brown, narrowly oblong, undulate, usually rather reflexed at tip. Lip very large, vivid golden-yellow, almost flat, the lat. lbs. small and rounded, often with an apical brownish suffusion, the claw of the midlb. broad, the midlb. flaring, transversely and broadly oblong, emarginate; crest consisting of 2 short ridges and a large median one, terminating in 3 blunt teeth. Col.-wings ear-like. Mostly spring–early summer. (I, H) Guatemala; Honduras.

O. stenotis Rchb.f.

Vegetatively almost identical to *O. anthocrene* Rchb.f., sometimes more robust. Infls. 1–2 per growth, erect or arching, to almost 5′ long, panicled, usually rather densely many-fld., the panicle-branches normally not very long. Fls. often rather short-lived, to 1″ in diam., the spreading ss. and ps. yellow, heavily blotched with brown, undulate marginally, with recurved tips, acute. Lip pandurate, 3-lbd., distinctly shorter than the lat. ss., bright yellow with a brown isthmus; lat. lbs. shortly clawed at base, spreading, the blades squarish to roundish, the isthmus narrow; midlb. abruptly dilated, emarginate and 2-lbd., often with a short central apicule, transversely almost kidney-shaped, about equalling the extended lat. lbs. in width; callus erect, fleshy, the sides with 2 or 3 short teeth, the apex abruptly tridenticulate. Col. with 2 rather obscure lat. lbs., the under-surface below the stigma conspicuously thickened into 2 parallel, fleshy lobules. Usually winter, but often more than once annually. (I, H) Nicaragua; Costa Rica; Panama.

O. stipitatum Ldl. (*Oncidium lacerum* Ldl.)

Pbs. almost obsolete, usually less than $\frac{1}{4}''$ long, broadly truncate at apex. Lf. solitary (normally), fleshy, terete, acuminate, longitudinally sulcate, at first horizontal or ascending, becoming pendulous with age, often more or less spotted with reddish-brown, 9–26″ long. Infls. solitary, horizontal or ascending, densely many-fld., paniculate, usually about as long as the lvs. Fls. very variable in size, to about 1″ long, the ss. and ps. yellow, richly marked with reddish-brown, the ss. subequal, shortly clawed, the dors. sep. rather concave, the lats. obliquely obovate; ps. spreading, elliptic-oblong,

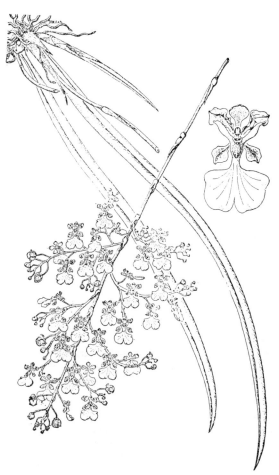

Oncidium stipitatum Ldl. [DOROTHY O. ALLEN]

obtuse, undulate marginally. Lip bright yellow on both front and back surfaces, pandurate, 3-lbd., the basal half of the narrow isthmus reddish-brown; lat. lbs. linear-oblong, obliquely obtuse, often ascending; midlb. abruptly dilated and 2-lbd., transversely semi-orbicular to oblong, often undulate marginally; crest a roundish transverse plate terminating at the apex in a prominent, erect, fleshy, roundish, somewhat laterally compressed tubercle occupying the basal half of the isthmus. Col.-wings narrow, spreading. Mostly summer. (I, H) Honduras; Nicaragua; Panama.

O. tigrinum LaLl. & Lex. (*Odontoglossum tigrinum* Ldl.)

Pbs. rather globular, compressed, 3–4″ in diam. Lvs. 2–3, linear-oblong, obtuse, folded at the base, rather leathery, 9–12″ long. Infls. stout, usually erect, to 3′ tall, loosely panicled, rather many-fld. Fls. about 3″ long, long-lasting, the ss. and ps. bright yellow, more or less heavily blotched with rich brown, similar, subequal, narrowly oblong, undulate marginally, usually reflexed at tip. Lip large, spreading, vivid yellow, sometimes with a brownish suffusion on the broad isthmus, the lat. lbs. small, rounded, the midlb. transversely and broadly oblong, emarginate; crest consisting of 2 short ridges and a large median one, terminating in 3 blunt teeth. Col.-wings ear-like. Autumn–winter. (I, H) Mexico.

—var. **unguiculatum** (Ldl.) Ldl. (*Oncidium unguiculatum* Ldl., *O. ionosmum* Ldl., *Odontoglossum Ghiesbreghtianum* A.Rich. & Gal.)

Differs from the typical sp. in the generally more loose panicles of smaller fls. (seldom more than $2\frac{1}{2}''$ long), the ss. and ps. of which are sometimes spotted (but not barred); and the isthmus of the lip noticeably longer and narrower. Autumn–winter. (I, H) Mexico.

O. triquetrum R.Br.

Pbs. absent. Lvs. in tufts of 3–4 or more, triquetrous, linear, acute, fleshy, the angles very acute, channelled on one side, 3–5″ long. Infls. slender, to about 7″ long, often producing accessory racs. for more than one season, usually 5–15-fld. Fls. about $\frac{1}{2}''$ long, long-lasting, the broadly lanceolate, acute ss. purplish-green, the lats. joined together, bifid at tip; ps. white, tinged with pale green and spotted with purple, ovate, undulate, spreading; lip white, spotted and streaked with purple or reddish-purple, cordate-ovate, the lat. lbs. reduced to rounded ears; crest small, subglobose, orange-yellow; col.-wings oblong, the outer margin crenulate. Mostly summer, but often almost ever-blooming. (I) Jamaica.

O. varicosum Ldl.

Pbs. clustered, oval-oblong, compressed, furrowed with age, often rather yellowish-green, 3–5″ long. Lvs. usually 2 (rarely 3), ligulate-lanceolate, acutish, 6–9″ long. Infls. usually nodding, the peduncle glaucous, 3–5′ long, flexuose and branching beyond the middle, usually very densely many-fld. Fls. variable in size, in the typical sp. seldom more than $1\frac{1}{2}''$ in diam., the ss. and ps. small and inconspicuous, dull yellow, barred with pale red-brown, the dors. sep. oval, concave, the lat. ss. connate to beyond the midlb., obovate; ps. narrowly oblong, crisped marginally. Lip very large, vivid yellow, sometimes with a red-brown blotch in front of the crest, the lat. lbs. roundish; midlb. transversely and broadly reniform, 2–3-lobed; crest consisting of 2 series of 3 teeth standing one before the other, with a little ring of varicose veins on each side; col.-wings oblong, toothed. Autumn–winter. (I, H) Brazil.

—var. **Rogersii** Rchb.f.

Perhaps better treated as a form of the variable species, from which it differs in the larger, more profusely branched panicles of very large fls., the lip of which measures more than 2″ across, the midlb. 4-lbd. by reason of three deep clefts in the anterior margin. Autumn–winter. (I, H) Brazil.

O. Wentworthianum Batem.

Pbs. clustered, robust, ovoid-oblong, somewhat compressed, becoming furrowed with age, to 5″ long, · typically transversely barred with bands of tiny brown spots. Lvs. usually 2, rather leathery, ligulate, acute, to 12″ long. Infls. flexuose, to 7′ long, branched, the branches slender, distant, the longer ones again branched and many-fld. Fls. usually about 1″ in diam., the ss. and ps. yellow, blotched with red-brown (except in apical part), the lip with pale yellow, rounded lat. lbs., the midlb. yellow with some red-brown spots around the crest. Ss. and ps. linear-spatulate, undulate marginally, the lat. ss. free and divergent. Lip 3-lbd., the transversely oblong midlb. 2-lbd., minutely toothed marginally; crest triangular, toothed at each angle, with a smaller tooth on each side and 2 more in front of the apical angle; col.-wings narrow. Summer–autumn. (I, H) Mexico; Guatemala.

O. Aloisii Schltr. Pbs. clustered, ovoid, compressed, with basal lf.-like sheaths, to 4″ tall and 2″ broad. Lvs. 2, erect, strap-shaped, obtuse, rather thin-textured, to 16″ long. Infls. erect or arching, to 4′ long, few-branched, each branch bearing 7–9 fls. Fls. about 1″ across, slightly longer, the spreading ss. and ps. oblong, obtuse, slightly undulate marginally, bright brown with small yellow tips, the ss. slightly clawed at base. Lip pandurate, ½″ long, bright yellow, with a large rich-brown blotch covering the basal half. Summer. (H) Ecuador.

O. altissimum (Jacq.) Sw. (*Epidendrum altissimum* Jacq.) Rather similar to *O. sphacelatum* Ldl., *O. Baueri* Ldl., and several other spp., with which it is often confused, and from which it differs in technical details of the lip and crest. Pbs. ovoid-oblong, compressed, with very acute edges, to about 4″ long and 2½″ wide. Lvs. 1–2, ligulate, acute, rather heavy, to about 12″ long at most. Infls. to about 6′ long, short-branched from below the middle upwards, each branch about 3–5-fld. Fls. to 1″ in diam., rather glossy, the ss. and ps. pale yellow, barred and blotched with pale chestnut-brown along the central area, similar and subequal, narrowly oblong, undulate marginally; lip 3-lbd., the lat. lbs. small, turned backwards, oblong, rounded at the free end, bright yellow; midlb. with a broad saddle-like red-brown claw and transversely oblong emarginate blade, yellow above, white beneath; crest 10-toothed, the teeth arranged in 2 series of 5 each, of which the central one of the front 5 is the largest; col.-wings narrow, rounded. Mostly spring. (I, H) Hispaniola; Lesser Antilles; Guianas; ? Brazil.

O. anthocrene Rchb.f. (*Oncidium Powellii* Schltr.) Pbs. rather distant from one another, oblong-ovoid, compressed, ridged, often brownish, to 6″ long and 2″ wide. Lf. solitary, coriaceous, oblong-lanceolate to ligular, usually obtuse or slightly retuse at apex, narrowed basally, to 15″ long and 2″

broad. Infls. arching, to 4′ long, usually unbranched, many-fld., with conspicuous white papery bracts. Fls. very waxy, 1¼–2½″ in diam., long-lived, the ss. and ps. rich chestnut- or chocolate-brown, barred and margined with yellow, wavy-edged, clawed or the ps. not clawed. Lip pandurate, 3-lbd., the small lat. lbs. yellow, often spotted with brown, the central isthmus red-brown, the broad midlb. bright yellow, 2-lbd.; callus prominent, yellow, many-toothed, terminating at the apex in a broad, transverse, rather roughened plate. Col. without conspicuous lateral wings. Winter–spring. (I, H) Panama; Colombia.

O. aureum Ldl. (*Odontoglossum festatum* Rchb.f., *Odontoglossum hemichrysum* Rchb.f.) Pbs. clustered, ovoid, elongated, to 1½″ long. Lvs. 1–2, rather narrow, 4–5″ long. Infls. to almost 2′ long, erect, terminating in a 5–7-fld. rac. with a zigzag rachis. Fls. about 1¼″ long, the ss. and ps. pale greenish-yellow with a faint purplish tinge near the base, the lat. ss. connate to the middle. Lip vivid golden-yellow, the isthmus short and fleshy, the blade of the midlb. first square when expanded, broadly oblong, undulate, the upper surface finely corrugated; crest a cluster of small upright teeth with a small vertical cleft plate on each side; col.-wings small, toothed. Mostly May–June. (I) Peru.

O. Batemanianum Kn. & Westc. (*Oncidium gallopavinum* C.Morr., *O. Pinellianum* Ldl., *O. ramosum* Ldl., *O. spilopterum* Ldl., *O. stenopetalum* Kl.) Pbs. ovoid to subconical, 3–4″ long, vaguely angled when old. Lvs. 2–3, linear-lanceolate, acute, 7–9″ long. Infls. 3–4′ long, sparsely branched upwards, rather many-fld. Fls. 1¼″ long, the very undulate ss. and ps. light yellow, heavily barred and blotched with chestnut-brown, the dors. sep. ovate, acute, bent forwards, the lat. pair free, clawed, lanceolate, acute, reflexed; ps. broadly ovate, reflexed, twisted. Lip bright yellow, the lat. lbs. narrowly oblong, smallish; midlb. transversely roundish to oblong, with a broad sinus in the anterior margin; crest consisting of 4 series of narrow plates, all more or less toothed. Col.-wings ear-like. Autumn–early winter. (I, H) Brazil; Peru.

O. Boothianum Rchb.f. Pbs. ellipsoidal, compressed, to 3″ tall. Lvs. usually 2, ligulate, acutish, rather leathery, to 12″ long and 3½″ wide. Infl. arching to pendulous, very branched, to 7′ long, many-fld. Fls. about 1¼″ across, the oblong ss. and ps. brown-red, margined with yellow, the lip golden-yellow, with roundish lat. lbs. and a long-clawed, reniform, emarginate, broad midlb.; crest wart-like, shortly-hairy at base. Spring–early summer. (I, H) Venezuela.

O. bracteatum Warsc. & Rchb.f. Pbs. brown, compressed, more or less linear in outline but usually somewhat broader at base and tapering gradually upward, 2½–5″ long. Lvs. 1–2, ligular, obtuse, coriaceous, 6–15″ long, long-petiolate below. Infls. 1–2 per growth, arching, to about 3½′ long, few- to rather many-fld., provided with several conspicuous, elongate, pale brown, spathe-like bracts. Fls. about 1¼″ across, the ss. and ps. greenish-yellow or yellow, heavily blotched and spotted with dark brown or maroon, the apical and lat. lbs. of the lip bright yellow, the central isthmus brown or maroon. Ss. and ps. spreading, undulate marginally; lip panduriform, the isthmus broad, the callus erect, more or less triangular, several-toothed; col.-wings narrow. Winter. (I) Nicaragua; Costa Rica; Panama.

O. Brunleesianum Rchb.f. Pbs. narrowly oblong, compressed, somewhat narrowed upwards, 3–5″ long. Lvs. 2–3, ligulate-oblong, acute, to 7″ long. Infls. to about 1½′ long, mottled with dull crimson, paniculate in upper half, densely many-fld. Fls. ¾″ in diam., the ss. and ps. bent forwards, pale yellow. the ps. with pale red transverse markings on apical half, the dors. sep. oblong, obtuse, the lats. connate into an ovate subacute lamina, bifid at tip. Lip roundish when spread out, 3-lbd., the lat. lbs. incurved towards the col., bright yellow, the midlb. much smaller, reflexed, dark maroon-crimson, almost black; crest a shallow glossy plate, stained with purple, with 2 erect white teeth near the middle; col. terete, with broad, roundish wings, the anther hooded. Spring. (I, H) Brazil.

O. chrysodipterum Veitch (*Cyrtochilum chrysodipterum* Krzl.) Pbs. oblong, compressed, clustered, about 3″ long. Lvs. 1–2, broadly strap-shaped, rather acuminate, cuneate at base, to 2′ long. Infls. flexuose, to 11′ long, with short branches at irregular intervals, each bearing 3–5 or more fls. Fls. 3″ long, very handsome and complex, the ss. with a semiterete claw grooved on the face and slightly reflexed, the dors. sep. cordate-orbicular, undulate marginally, bright chestnut-brown with a narrow yellow border; lat. ss. divergent, broadly ovate, subacute, keeled behind, wholly brown; ps. much smaller, with a shorter claw, ovate-lanceolate, incurved and strongly undulate marginally, bright yellow, spotted in the basal half with brown; lip linear, reflexed, yellow, stained with brown in front of the crest, with 2 triangular auricles at base; crest a semiterete white plate produced in front into numerous yellow teeth in 5 series of 2's and 3's; col. brownish, with a small hastate wing on each side of the stigma and 2 linear deflexed auricles below it. Spring. (C, I) Colombia.

O. chrysopyramis Rchb.f. Pbs. oval-oblong, compressed, with acute edges, 1½–2½″ long. Lvs. 2, linear-ligulate, subacuminate, to 6″ long. Infls. slender, arching, to 2′ long, many-fld., loosely panicled. Fls. about ¾″ long, vivid canary-yellow, the dors. sep. and ps. clawed, oblong, apiculate, concave, keeled behind, the lat. ss. free, linear-oblong, falcate, keeled behind; lip panduriform, with a deep sinus in front margin; crest with 3 projecting teeth in front and 2 2-parted lat. ones between which is a minutely warty cushion; col.-wings falcate, 2-lbd., bent over the anther and denticulate on outer margins. Summer–autumn. (I) Colombia.

O. cornigerum Ldl. Pbs. subcylindric, compressed, 2–3″ long. Lf. solitary, elliptic-oblong, subacute, to 6″ long. Infls. slender, arching or pendulous, pale green, dotted with dull crimson, to 2′ long, paniculate and many-fld. in apical half. Fls. crowded, about ¾″ in diam., the ss. and ps. yellow, spotted and barred with red-brown, the lip bright yellow. Dors. sep. concave, bent forward over the col.; lat. ss. oblong, connate to beyond the middle. Ps. clawed, obovate, obtuse. Lip panduriform, the lat. lbs. small, horn-like, turned upwards and inwards, the midlb. roundish-oblong, marginally crisped; crest 2-parted, the posterior part bilamellate, the anterior part much tubercled. Col.-wings spreading, linear-triangular. Autumn. (I, H) Brazil.

O. cryptocopis Rchb.f. Pbs. narrow, very compressed, 4–5″ long and 1″ broad. Lvs. usually paired, lanceolate, acute, rather leathery, to 12″ long. Infls. branching, rather many-fld., to 5′ long. Fls. 3″ in diam., pale chestnut-brown with golden crisped margins on ss. and ps. and a broad yellow midlb. on the lip. Dors. sep. deltoid-ovate with short broad claw; lat. ss. parallel, much longer than the dors. one, with long claws and an obovate cuneate lamina; ps. ovate-lanceolate, with broad claws. Lip about half as long as the ps., reflexed; lat. lbs. small, hatchet-shaped, recurved; midlb. with a long flat claw and transversely oblong lamina turned completely back; crest tuberculose; col. with small spreading wings and 2 subulate decurved horns in front. Spring. (C, I) Peru; Colombia.

O. cucullatum Ldl. Highly variable in all parts. Pbs. clustered, ovoid, sometimes oval-oblong, compressed, rather dull green, 1½–3″ long. Lvs. 1–2, linear-ligulate, acute, folded at base, 6–8″ long. Infls. slender, erect or nodding, purplish-green in colour, to about 2′ tall, loosely paniculate or racemose, usually about 8–12-fld. Fls. about 1½″ long, variable in colour, the ss. and ps. typically dark chestnut-brown, sometimes greenish or olive-green and rarely with a narrow yellow margin, the lip light rose-purple, more or less spotted with purple-crimson. Ss. and ps. similar, oval-oblong, acute, the lat. ss. connate, bifid at tip, concealed by the lip. Lip 3-lbd., the lat. lbs. small, roundish, the midlb. large and spreading, transversely oblong, emarginate; crest bright orange-yellow, with 2 pairs of tubercles and a fifth smaller one between the posterior pair; col. thick, hooded. Summer–autumn. (C, I) Colombia; Ecuador, usually at high elevations.

—var. **nubigenum** (Ldl.) Ldl. (*Oncidium nubigenum* Ldl.) Differs from the typical sp. in being a much smaller plant, with smaller (about 1¼″ long) fls. Ss. and ps. variable in colour, usually light greenish-brown, sometimes the margins paler; lip white with a violet spot in front of the 3-tubercled crest, narrow basally, the midlb. almost sessile. Summer. (C, I) Ecuador.

—var. **Phalaenopsis** (Rchb.f.) Veitch (*Oncidium Phalaenopsis* Rchb.f.) Pbs. somewhat smaller and more ovoid than the typical sp., the lvs. narrower, the infls. more slender and usually fewer-fld. Fls. about 1½″ long, the ss. and ps. milky-white, more or less barred with dark purple; lip white with a slight flush of rose-purple and with some purple spots around the crest. Summer. (C, I) Ecuador.

O. deltoideum Ldl. Pbs. ovoid, clustered, to about 3″ tall. Lvs. 2–3, linear, acute, rather leathery, to 10″ long and 1″ wide. Infls. paniculate, arching, loosely many-fld., to about 2′ long. Fls. about 1″ across, the ss. and ps. golden-yellow, narrowly ovate-spatulate, clawed, the ps. slightly the shorter. Lip cordate-reniform, golden-yellow; crest pale yellow, surrounded by a red band, complex; col.-wings large. Mostly May–June. (C, I) Peru.

O. ebrachiatum A. & S. Vegetatively identical to *O. stipitatum* Ldl., the lvs. to about 2′ long. Infls. usually solitary, arching, many-fld., paniculate. Fls. about ¼″ long or more, the ss. and ps. yellow, spotted with reddish-brown, the lip yellow on both surfaces. Dors. sep. concave, incurving over the col., the lat. ss. somewhat concave and incurving, the ps. widely spreading. Lip pandurate. 3-lbd., the lat. lbs. subfalcate, obtuse, spreading, or with the tips somewhat antrorse in natural position, the lower margins confluent with the narrow central isthmus; midlb. dilated, emarginate, flabellate-reniform, the minutely papillose disc with a broad, fleshy, flat, lunate, porrect plate below the col., terminating below the apex in a central, vaguely 3-lbd. tubercle, on each side of which are lightly converging keels, terminating in low tuberculate swellings. Col. very short, stout, the lat. wings obsolete. Winter. (I, H) Nicaragua; Panama.

O. excavatum Ldl. (*Oncidium aurosum* Rchb.f.) Pbs. ovoid-oblong, compressed, 3–5″ long, clustered, rather angular with age. Lf. usually solitary, linear-ligulate, acutish, to about 2′ long. Infls. stout, usually stiffly erect, 2–3′ tall, handsomely paniculate in the form of a pyramid, many-fld. Fls. about 1½″ in diam., the very undulate ss. yellow with 2–3 red-brown bars on basal half, the dors. one obovate-oblong, the lat. pair narrower and free, oval-oblong; ps. very undulate, larger than the ss., entirely yellow or with 1–2 red-brown spots near base. Lip 3-lbd., the lat. lbs. small, oblong, convex, red-brown; midlb. transversely oblong, emarginate, vivid canary-yellow; crest convex, studded with small

336

IXᴀ *Pleurothallis hirsuta* Ames [ᴀ.ʜ.ʜᴇʟʟᴇʀ]

IXʙ *Rodriguezia secunda* HBK [ʜ.ʀ.ꜰᴏʟᴋᴇʀsᴍᴀ]

tubercles arranged in 5 lines, with a decurrent shallow plate on each side; col.-wings roundish, retuse. Spring–early summer. (I) Ecuador; Peru.

O. floridanum Ames Pbs. clustered, ovoid, usually smooth, but becoming slightly furrowed with age, to about 4″ long, the sheathing basal bracts foliose. Lvs. 2–3, linear-lanceolate, acute, to more than 2′ long. Infls. stout, usually erect, to more than 7′ tall, paniculate, rather many-fld. in upper parts, the rachis usually dark brown. Fls. ¾–1″ across, rather variable in colour, the ss. and ps. usually greenish-ochre more or less barred with dark brown, the lip bright yellow, marked around the callus with reddish-brown. Ss. and ps. undulate, often rather recurved. Lip rather pandurate, the apical part of the midlb. folded, the lat. lbs. prominent; crest 7-lbd., the bottom pair of lbs. again lobulate; col.-wings yellow, often brown-dotted. Usually summer–autumn. (I, H) South Florida; Bahamas; North Cuba: Archipelago de Camagüey.

O. globuliferum HBK (*Oncidium convolvulaceum* Ldl., *O. scansor* Rchb.f., *O. Wercklei* Schltr.) Rhiz. very elongate, slender, flexuose, scandent, often many feet in length and forming tangled masses. Pbs. produced at considerable intervals, solitary or clustered, usually roundish, compressed, truncate at apex, usually less than 1″ long, with foliose sheathing basal bracts. Lf. solitary, coriaceous, elliptic-oblong, obtuse to subacute, narrowed basally, to 2¼″ long and ¾″ wide. Infls. 1–2 short, 1-fld. scapes about as long as the lvs. Fls. to 1¼″ long and 1″ wide, the ss. and somewhat broader ps. yellow, barred with reddish-brown, the very large lip bright yellow, 3-lbd., the lat. lbs. small, squarish, the isthmus short, broad; midlb. spreading, emarginate, 2-lbd., broadly and transversely reniform; crest more or less triangular, fleshy, 7-toothed; col.-wings spreading. Mostly summer. (I) Costa Rica to Venezuela and Peru.

O. x haematochilum Ldl. Natural hybrid between *O. Lanceanum* Ldl. and *O. luridum* Ldl. Vegetatively identical to the former parent. Infls. to more than 2′ tall, erect or arching, paniculate, many-fld. Fls. 2″ in diam., very fragrant, long-lasting, the clawed ss. and ps. yellow-green, heavily blotched with chestnut-brown, the dors. sep. roundish, the lat. pair free, oblong; ps. obovate-oblong, undulate. Lip broadly clawed, with 2 oblong auricles at base, the lamina transversely oblong, emarginate, these parts with the crest dark rose-purple or magenta-purple, the lamina blood-red, the yellow margin spotted with red; crest 5-parted, with the middle part a raised subtriangular plate, the others very warty; col.-wings kidney-shaped, bent downwards, rose-purple. Winter. (I, H) Colombia; Trinidad.

O. hians Ldl. Pbs. about ¾″ in diam., roundish, slightly compressed and ancipitous. Lf. solitary, varying from oval to linear-oblong, acute, to 2″ long, leathery, slightly glaucous. Infls. very slender, almost thread-like, purplish, to 9″ long, few-fld., erect or arching. Fls. about ½″ in diam., the narrowly oblong ss. and ps. red-brown with a yellow margin; lip vaguely-lbd., linear-spatulate, emarginate, yellow with some red-brown spots; crest very large in proportion to the size of the fl., white, 4-lbd., like the fingers of a partially closed hand, erect, as long as the col., extending parallel to it; col.-wings large, almost square, white. Sept.–Oct. (I, H) Brazil.

O. hyphaematicum Rchb.f. Pbs. oblong, clustered, compressed, 3–4″ long. Lf. usually solitary, ligulate-lanceolate, acute, folded at base, to about 12″ long, rather leathery. Infls. very branched, to more than 5′ long, many-fld., the peduncle usually purplish, the sheathing bracts whitish. Fls. about 1½″ in diam., red-flushed outside, the ss. and ps. red-brown, tipped with yellow, oblong, acute, very undulate; lip bright canary-yellow, flushed beneath with red-purple, with a

broad claw and broadly reniform, apiculate lamina; crest with 5 keels, of which the outside two are the shortest; col. pale yellow, with a hatchet-shaped pale-coloured wing on each side of the stigma. Winter. (I) Ecuador.

O. insculptum Rchb.f. Pbs. clustered, ovoid, compressed, smooth, 3–5″ long, to 2″ in diam. Lvs. 2, ensiform, acute to acuminate, folded at base, to almost 20″ long. Infls. 7–10′ long and more, pale brownish-green, flexuose, paniculate in upper half, the branches distant, short, few-fld. Fls. 1½″ in diam., sepia-brown with an odd metallic lustre, the ss. and ps. with a narrow straw-yellow margin, the crest straw-yellow or white. Ss. and ps. clawed, marginally crisped and undulate, the dors. sep. roundish, the lats. oval-oblong, the ps. broadly oval. Lip narrowly oblong, the lat. margins revolute, the greyish-blue apex reflexed, the lat. lbs. reduced to curving ears below the crest, which is a thickened triangular plate, toothed frontally; col.-wings very narrow. Spring–summer. (C, I) Ecuador.

O. Leiboldii Rchb.f. Pbs. absent. Lvs. few, equitant, curved, ½–1½″ long, conduplicate, the margins denticulate. Infl. slender, erect or arching, rarely few-branched, to 10″ long. Fls. variable, about ½″ long (rarely larger), white or pinkish, the lip marked with dark purple-brown, deeply 3-lbd., the lat. lbs. small, obtuse, the large midlb. reniform, emarginate, separated from the lat. lbs. by a toothed isthmus. Spring. (H) Cuba; Hispaniola; Puerto Rico; Virgin Islands.

O. nanum Ldl. Pbs. essentially absent, the pl. rather resembling a miniature *O. luridum* Ldl., the rigidly fleshy lvs. heavily spotted with dull red, to about 6″ tall. Infls. usually prostrate, panicled, the branches short and few-fld., to about 4″ long. Fls. ¾″ in diam., not opening flat, long-lasting, the similar ss. and ps. yellow, spotted with red-brown, obovate-oblong, obtuse, incurving; lip bright yellow, transversely oblong, the lat. lbs. very small, ear-like; crest proportionately large, 2-lbd., the front lb. at right angles to the back one; col.-wings linear, deflexed, tipped with a clear gland. Summer. (I, H) Guianas; North-west Brazil; East Peru.

O. nebulosum Ldl. (*Oncidium caesium* Rchb.f., *O. Geertianum* Morr., *O. Klotzschianum* Rchb.f.) Pbs. ovoid to roundish, somewhat compressed, to 1½″ long. Lvs. paired, narrowly lanceolate, obtuse to subacute, rather leathery, to 8″ long and 1″ wide, shortly petiolate below. Infls. 1–2 per growth, erect or arching, few-fld., racemose, to about 15″ long. Fls. about 2″ long and 1¼″ wide, the free, usually reflexed ss. and slightly broader, spreading ps. pale yellow to greenish-yellow, shaded or spotted with red or purple; lip 3-lbd., pandurate, bright yellow, the lat. lbs. small, obliquely triangular or squarish, obtuse, the isthmus narrow, the midlb. abruptly and broadly dilated and 2-lbd., transversely reniform; crest short, fleshy, 5-toothed; col.-wings prominent. Winter. (C, I) Mexico; Guatemala; ? Panama.

O. obryzatum Rchb.f. (*Oncidium Brenesii* Schltr., *O. fulgens* Schltr., *O. obryzatoides* Krzl.) Pbs. clustered or slightly distant, roundish, ovoid, or elliptic-oblong, compressed, usually conspicuously ridged, often spotted with dark brown or black, 1–3½″ long, with several lf.-like bracts at base. Lf. solitary, elliptic-oblong, ligular to narrowly linear, subacute, leathery, 4–14″ long, narrowed below. Infls. erect or arching, paniculate, many-fld., 1–4′ long. Fls. very variable, to 1¼″ long and 1″ wide, the spreading ss. and ps. golden-yellow with chestnut-brown blotches near base, obovate-spatulate, usually truncate at apex. Lip pandurate, 3-lbd., golden-yellow with a U-shaped reddish-brown blotch surrounding the yellow basal callus; lat. lbs. squarish to rounded, the isthmus short, narrow, the midlb. dilated, spreading, 2-lbd. with a deep central sinus, often transversely reniform; crest erect, fleshy, sometimes 5-lobulate with 3 distinct apical teeth, or obscurely lobulate with only 2 distinct apical lobes; col.-wings prominent, their tips often converging over the anther. Mostly spring. (I) Costa Rica; Panama; Colombia; Ecuador; Peru.

O. ochmatochilum Rchb.f. (*Oncidium cardiochilum* Ldl.) Pbs. inconspicuous, often almost completely hidden by the sheathing lf.-bases, narrowly ovoid, to 4" long and 1" in diam. Lvs. basally distichously imbricating, forming a complanate petiole, the blades narrowly lanceolate, acute to acuminate, leathery, strong-veined, sometimes conduplicate their entire length, to 2½' long and 2¼" wide. Infls. 1–2 per growth, stout, erect or arching, many-fld., paniculate, to 7' long. Fls. strongly fragrant of lilacs, to 1¼" long and ¾" wide, the free ss. pale green, marked with brown, the dors. one often strongly reflexed; ps. broader than ss., brown or greenish-firown, sometimes mottled white or with paler tips; lip panduriform, 3-lbd., white, spotted with brown or reddish-purple; lat. lbs. squarish, obtuse, projecting; isthmus short but distinct; midlb. abruptly dilated, entire or apiculate, transversely roundish or subcordate; callus prominent, fleshy, multi-tuberculate, terminating at the apex in a short, erect, obtuse, laterally compressed keel, above and below which are 2 pairs of short fleshy teeth; col. wingless. Spring–early summer. (I) Guatemala; Costa Rica; Panama; Colombia; Peru.

O. parviflorum L.O.Wms. Pbs. very flattened, ridged with age, to 3" long and 1" broad, very densely dotted and flushed with lacquered brown, with lf.-like sheathing basal bracts. Lf. usually solitary, to about 6" long, rather narrow and thin-textured, narrowing and folded basally. Infls. to 4' long, slender, gracefully arching, with numerous very short branches. Fls. ½" in diam., lasting well, yellow marked with rich-brown on the ss. and ps., the large pandurate lip vivid lacquered yellow, with a proportionately large, minutely warty basal callus. Autumn. (I) Panama: Coclé and Chiriquí, at 3000 feet and upwards.

O. praetextum Rchb.f. Pbs. clustered, ovoid, compressed, 1½–2" long. Lvs. paired, ensiform, subacute, rather leathery, to 8" long. Infls. to 4' long, arching, paniculate, many-fld. Fls. fragrant, about 1½" in diam., the ss. pale chestnut-brown, barred with yellow, the dors. one clawed, the lat. pair narrower, connate at their base; ps. as broad again as the dors. sep., entirely brown; lip broadly clawed, the lat. lbs. small, yellow; midlb. fan-shaped, yellow with a broad brown margin; crest consisting of 2 lamina that are confluent behind, and 2 projecting lbs. in front, all warty, pale yellow, spotted with brown; col.-wings rounded, yellow and red. Summer. (I, H) Brazil.

O. pumilum Ldl. Pbs. essentially absent. Lvs. from a creeping rhiz., erect, rigidly leathery, oblong, acute, 2–4" long, usually rather bright green. Infls. erect or horizontal, to 6" long, paniculate, the branches short, the fls. very numerous and tightly crowded. Fls. usually less than ¼" across, the tiny ss. and ps. yellow, spotted with red, oblong-spatulate, obtuse, usually incurving; lip 3-lbd., yellow, the lat. lbs. the largest, roundish-oblong, the midlb. subquadrate, truncate; crest 2-parted, the 2 parts divergent, each consisting of two parallel ridges; col.-wings oblong, acute, decurved. Spring–summer. (I, H) Brazil; Paraguay.

O. raniferum Ldl. Pbs. clustered, oblong, tapering upwards, 1–2" long, compressed, furrowed with age. Lvs. paired, linear, grass-like, 5–8" long. Infls. to about 10" long, sparsely branched, many-fld. Fls. more than ½" long, vivid yellow, the crest of the lip orange-red; ss. and ps. reflexed, oblong; lip 3-lbd., the lat. lbs. linear-oblong, spreading, the midlb. broadly obovate with the anterior margin vaguely crenulate;

crest large for the size of the fl., consisting of an oblong vaguely 2-parted cushion that rather resembles a crouching frog; col.-wings very narrow. Spring–early summer. (I, H) Brazil.

O. Retemeyerianum Rchb.f. Habit much like a small example of *O. carthagenense* (Jacq.) Sw., the lvs. usually strongly keeled on reverse side, often dull purplish-green. Infls. to 6' long, many-fld., but the fls. opening a few at a time over a period of several months, few-branched in age. Fls. heavy-textured, waxy, about ¾" in diam., the ss. and ps. pale yellow with more or less dense chocolate-brown spotting and mottling, oblong, apiculate, the ps. slightly the broader. Lip pandurate, dark red-purple to almost black-purple, very glossy, usually flushed with yellow around the crest, which consists of 2 pairs of blunt tubercles and a single median one. Col. with yellow, rounded wings that are bent downwards. Mostly winter. (I, H) Mexico; British Honduras; Honduras.

O. stramineum Ldl. Pbs. essentially absent, the pl. resembling a smallish *O. luridum* Ldl., the lvs. oblong-lanceolate, sub-acute, very rigidly fleshy, narrowed into a stout, short petiole, 6–8" long. Infls. paniculate, inclined or hanging, to about 8" long (usually shorter), rather densely many-fld. Fls. about ¾" across, white or straw-coloured, usually speckled with red or pinky-lilac on the lat. ss., lip and col. Ss. and ps. widely spreading, almost round, the dors. one concave. Lip very shortly clawed, the lat. lbs. oblong, obtuse, falcately recurving; midlb. broadly clawed, kidney-shaped, smaller than the lat. ones; crest warty, 2 warts on each side, more or less confluent; col.-wings broad. Summer. (I) Mexico, near Jalapa and Veracruz.

O. superbiens Rchb.f. Pbs. clustered, elongate-ovoid, 3–4" long, compressed. Lf. usually solitary, broadly linear, almost ensiform, to 1½' long, rather thinly leathery. Infls. flexuose, 4–8' long, branched at irregular intervals, the branches short, few-fld., with large boat-shaped bracts. Fls. 3–3½" in diam., the ss. clawed, waxy, reddish-brown, tipped with light yellow, the dors. one somewhat trulliform with a cordate base, the lats. ovate, obtuse; ps. similar to lat. ss. but smaller with a shorter claw, more undulate and reflexed at apex, pale yellow, barred with brown on basal half; lip plum-purple, eared at base, shortly clawed, with a raised tubercled yellow fleshy crest towards base, and a prominent acute tubercle on each auricle; col. yellow and brown, with a small ascending ear on each side of the stigma. Winter–spring. (C, I) Colombia; Venezuela.

O. teres A. & S. Vegetatively identical to *O. stipitatum* Ldl. Infls. paniculate, densely many-fld., to 1½' long. Fls. to about ½" long, the ss. and ps. yellow, very heavily spotted with reddish-brown, the lip bright yellow on frontal surface, the reverse surface and disc heavily spotted with reddish-brown. Differs principally from the allied sp. in the much shorter lip-isthmus, and the much more prominent and complex basal callus. Winter–spring. (I, H) Panama.

O. tetrapetalum Willd. (*Oncidium pauciflorum* Ldl., *O. quadripetalum* Sw., *O. tricolor* Hk.) Pbs. absent. Lvs. tufted, equitant, usually 3–5 per growth, the rhiz. somewhat creeping, fleshy, triquetrous with acute edges, channelled on one side, 3–6" long. Infls. erect, usually dark purple, to 2' tall, racemose or sparsely branched, rather many-fld., the fls. opening successively over a long period. Fls. about 1" long, the ss. and ps. bright chestnut-red barred and marked with yellow, the lip white with a red or reddish-brown blotch in front of the crest. Ss. and ps. clawed, broadly oblong, subacute, undulate, keeled behind, the lat. ss. connate and hidden by the lip. Lip broadly clawed, with 2 horn-like lat. lbs. and a transversely reniform, emarginate midlb.; crest consisting of 7 tubercles,

3 in front and 4 in two pairs behind, all pointing forwards; col.-wings somewhat scimitar-shaped, pale rose, dotted with yellow. Summer. (I, H) Jamaica through the West Indies to Colombia and Venezuela.

O. unicorne Ldl. (*Oncidium monoceras* Hk.) Pbs. clustered, oval-oblong, compressed, 2–3″ long. Lvs. usually paired, linear-lanceolate, acute, to about 10″ long and 1½″ wide. Infls. erect or horizontal, pale glaucous-green, to almost 2′ long, loosely paniculate and many-fld. above. Fls. ¾″ long, the lanceolate ss. (of which the lat. pair is connate almost to apex) pale greenish or reddish-brown, the broader ps. red-brown, tipped with pale yellow, oblong, undulate, reflexed like the ss.; lip with a fleshy claw and subpanduriform emarginate lamina, of which the basal half is red and the apical half yellow; crest prolonged into an incurved reddish horn as long as the col.; col. slender, wingless, swollen below the stigma. Autumn. (I, H) Brazil.

O. urophyllum Ldl. Pbs. absent. Lvs. equitant, ensiform, curving, 4–6″ long, acuminate, usually dull dark green. Infls. slender, erect or arching, to 2′ long, often paniculate, many-fld., the fls. opening successively over a long period. Fls. usually less than 1″ in diam., the ss. and ps. yellow, blotched with chestnut-brown, the ss. linear-acute, the lats. connate almost to their apex, the ps. obovate, apiculate; lip 3-lbd., canary-yellow, the lat. lbs. small, obovate; midlb. clawed, broadly reniform with a sinus in the anterior margin; crest red and white, consisting of 8 teeth; col.-wings dolabriform, spreading. Summer–autumn. (I, H) Lesser Antilles.

O. variegatum (Sw.) Sw. (*Epidendrum variegatum* Sw., *Oncidium sylvestre* Ldl., *O. velutinum* Ldl.) Rhiz. elongate, sometimes branching, bearing the tufts of essentially pb.-less lvs. at more or less distant intervals, highly variable in all parts. Lvs. equitant, usually 4–6, crowded, distichous, lanceolate and conduplicate, acute, rigid, recurving, the margins saw-toothed, 1¼–3″ long. Infl. slender, racemose or rarely paniculate, few- to many-fld., to almost 12″ tall. Fls. showy, long-lasting, to almost 1″ long, highly variable in colour, usually white or greenish-white, more or less flushed with brown or crimson-purple. Dors. sep. short-clawed, concave, the lat. ss. connate almost to apex and hidden behind the lip. Ps. short-clawed, broadly obovate to suborbicular, usually blunt at apex, undulate. Lip pandurate, 3-lbd., the usually roundish lat. lbs. reflexed, denticulate marginally; isthmus short, broad, yellow-spotted, serrate marginally; midlb. broadly reniform, rather deeply emarginate at apex, with an apicule in the sinus, irregularly crenulate; crest prominent, tuberculate, yellow, with the 3 posterior tubercles larger than the 2 anterior ones; col.-wings conspicuous, these obscurely 2-lbd., marginally toothed. Winter–early summer. (I, H) Cuba; Hispaniola; probably elsewhere in West Indies.

O. Warscewiczii Rchb.f. (*Oncidium bifrons* Ldl.) Pbs. ovoid-oblong, compressed with sharp edges, to more than 3″ tall, the bases enveloped in several foliose bracts. Lvs. usually paired, ligular, obtuse to subacute, leathery, 6–12″ long, narrowed below into slender petioles. Infl. solitary, erect or arching, 4–12-fld., to 1½′ tall, with conspicuous papery, spathaceous bracts. Fls. about 1¼″ in diam., entirely vivid yellow, the dors. sep. free, oblong, obtuse, undulate marginally, the lat. ss. connate almost to apex, bifid at tip; ps. obliquely oblong, obtuse, undulate marginally; lip subpandurate, vaguely 3-lbd., the lat. lbs. inconspicuous auricles, the basal half of the lip almost oblong, the apical half abruptly dilated and 2-lbd., reniform, about twice as wide as basal half; crest narrow, fleshy, the base under the col. semiterete, terminating at the apex in 5 short, divergent teeth; col. dilated apically, with narrow wings. Spring. (C, I) Costa Rica; Panama, at high elevations.

OPHRYS L.C.Rich.
(*Arachnites* F.W.Schmidt, *Myodium* Salisb.)

Ophrys is a genus of somewhat more than twenty species of often handsome terrestrial orchids, native in Central and South Europe, North Africa, Asia Minor, and in Asia to the Caucasus Mountains. A member of the subtribe *Habenarinae*, the group is somewhat allied to *Serapias* L., but is immediately distinguishable on floral characters. These are the attractive 'Bee Orchids', so-named because of the resemblance of the flowers to insects such as bees or flies. They are rare in collections, and are often rather difficult to maintain in good condition for more than a year or so.

A few natural hybrids are known in *Ophrys*. No artificial breeding has been attempted in the genus as yet, and its genetic affinities have not been ascertained.

CULTURE: As for *Orchis* and the temperate Habenarias. (C, I)

O. apifera Huds. (*Arachnites apifera* Tod., *Ophrys insectifera* L. in part)
Infls. to 12″ tall, loosely 4–9-fld. Fls. about 1″ across, the ss. and ps. greenish with reddish centres. Lip slightly convex apically, oblong in outline, shortly and obtusely 5-lbd., purple-brown with yellow blotches. Summer. (C, I) Central Europe; Mediterranean area.

O. arachnites (Leop.) Hoffm. (*Orchis arachnites* Leop., *Orchis fuciflora* Crantz, *Ophrys fuciflora* Rchb.f., *Arachnites fuciflora* Schm.)
To 1½′ tall, the infls. loosely 3–8-fld. Fls. foul-smelling, about 1½″ across, the ss. and ps. rose-red with greenish stripes. Lip mostly brown, complex in structure, densely covered with velvety brown hairs, streaked with pale brown and yellow. Spring–summer. (C, I) Central and South Europe.

O. aranifera Huds. (*Ophrys insectifera* L. in part, *O. rostrata* Ten.)
To 1½′ tall, the infl. loosely 3–9-fld. Fls. to about 1″ across, the ss. and ps. rose-red with greenish stripes. Lip 3-lbd., dull purple-brown, densely covered with velvety purple-brown hairs, with a large irregular yellow blotch on the rather convex midlb. Spring–summer. (C, I) Central and South Europe.

O. Bertoloni (Tod.) Mor. (*Arachnites Bertoloni* Tod., *Ophrys grassensis* Jaur.)
8–12″ tall, the infl. loosely 2–5-fld. Fls. about 1″ across or more, the ss. rose-red or almost white, with 3 red nerves, the ps. smaller, dark rose-red. Lip 3-lbd., black-purple, velvety-hairy, with 2 calli-like areas on the disc, in front of which is a vaguely 3-lbd., mirror-like blue area. Spring–summer. (C, I) South Europe.

O. bombylifera Lk. (*Ophrys canaliculata* Viv., *O. distoma* Viv., *O. pulla* Ten., *O. tabanifera* Willd.)
To 8″ tall, the infl. loosely 1–3-fld. Fls. more than 1″ across, the ss. distinctly 3-nerved, greenish, the ps. green, slightly suffused with purple. Lip 3-lbd., complex, brown, covered with velvety hairs, with a V-shaped, divergent, naked line on the base, the small lat. lbs. furnished with protuberances. Spring. (C, I) South Europe.

O. cornuta Stev.

Similar in habit to *O. scolopax* Cav., to about 15" tall, the infl. loosely 3–6-fld. Fls. about 1½" long, foul-smelling, the ss. rose-red, the ps. rose-red, much smaller. Lip 3-lbd., brown with an irregular white median blotch, the lat. lbs. furnished with long velvety hairs. Spring–early summer. (C, I) Asia Minor; Caucasus Mountains.

O. fusca (Tod.) Lk. (*Arachnites fusca* Tod., *Ophrys funerea* Viv., *O. tricolor* Griseb.)

To 12" tall or more, the infl. loosely 3–6-fld. Fls. about 2" long, the ss. and very narrow ps. green or yellow-green. Lip 3-lbd., the lat. lbs. short, the midlb. 2-lbd., the disc furnished with protuberances, covered with velvety yellow-brown hairs and with 2 small, yellow-bordered, mirror-like areas. Spring. (C, I) South Europe.

O. lutea (Tod.) Cav. (*Arachnites lutea* Tod., *Ophrys vespifera* Brot.)

4–12" tall, the infl. 2–5-fld. Fls. about 1" long, the ss. and ps. yellow-green. Lip 3-lbd., the lat. lbs. short, covered with velvety yellow-brown hairs, towards the front with 2 bluish mirror-like spots, these rimmed with yellow-brown. Spring. (C, I) South Europe.

O. muscifera Huds. (*Arachnites muscifera* Schm., *Ophrys muscaria* Suff., *O. musciflora* Schrk., *O. myodes* Jaeg.)

Pls. robust, to 2' tall, the infl. loosely 3–10-fld. Fls. about 1½" long, musk-scented, the ss. greenish, the ps. narrow, reddish. Lip longer than wide, 3-lbd., covered with velvety black-purple hairs, the almost square midlb. with a 4-angled, white, mirror-like blotch. Spring–early summer. (C, I) Central and South Europe.

O. scolopax Cav. (*Ophrys picta* Lam.)

To more than 15" tall, the infl. loosely 3–8-fld. Fls. about 1" long, the ss. rose-red, the smaller and shorter ps. somewhat darker. Lip 3-lbd., the margins reflexed, covered with velvety purple-brown hairs, with 5 round, yellow-rimmed, mirror-like spots, the lat. lbs. short, humped, the midlb. roundish, with a lanceolate apical filament. Spring. (C, I) South Europe.

O. speculum (Tod.) Lk. (*Arachnites speculum* Tod., *Ophrys vernixia* Brot., *Orchis ciliata* Biv.)

Pls. rather stout, 8–12" tall, the infl. loosely 2–6-fld. Fls. about 1¼" long, the ss. yellowish-green, the shorter ps. violet-brown. Lip 3-lbd., convex, covered with velvety dark-brown hairs, the disc with a glossy, mirror-like, blue spot, the lat. lbs. short, roundish, fringed, the midlb. heart-shaped, obtuse, the margins reflexed. Spring. (C, I) South Europe.

O. sphegodes Miller

Pls. 4–14" tall, the infl. with 2–8 fls. Fls. 1" across, the ss. usually greenish, the ps. similar in colour, much narrower. Lip rounded, the more or less retrorse margins yellow, otherwise brown, with a symmetrical blue hairless mark, otherwise hirsute; lip changes to yellowish-buff with age. Spring–early summer. (C, I) Western, central, and southern Europe, widespread and variable.

ORCHIPEDUM Breda
(*Orchipeda* Breda ex Schltr., *Orchipedium* Bth., *Philippinaea* Schltr. & Ames, *Queteletia* Bl.)

Two extremely rare terrestrial orchids of the subtribe *Physurinae*, one native to Java and the Malay Peninsula, the other apparently endemic to the Philippines, make up the little-known genus *Orchipedum*. Unknown in contemporary collections, these rather robust plants are somewhat allied to *Hylophila* Ldl., from which they are at once distinguished by details of the flower structure.

Nothing is known of the genetic affinities of this scarce group.

CULTURE: Presumably as for *Anoectochilus*. (H)

ORCHIS [Tournef.] L.
(*Orchites* Schur)

The genus *Orchis* is considered the typical one of the Orchidaceae. Consisting of upwards of seventy valid species, plus a number of interspecific hybrids, it reaches its greatest development in Central and Southern Europe, although outlying members extend into Asia (to the Himalayas) and into North America. A rather large number of them are in current cultivation, since their usually densely many-flowered racemes of colourful blossoms are sufficiently showy to attract the interest of the collector. Almost entirely terrestrial in habit (a few of the Asiatic species occasionally occur on moss-laden rocks), the plants are extremely diverse in appearance, and the floral structure often varies markedly within a given species.

A rather large series of handsome natural hybrids exists in *Orchis*, largely among the numerous European species. Natural hybrids with several allied genera of the subtribe *Habenarinae* are also known, among these being *Orchiaceras* (× *Aceras*), *Gymnadeniorchis* (× *Gymnadenia*), *Orchiserapias* (× *Serapias*), and *Orchicoeloglossum* (× *Coeloglossum*). Despite the obvious potentials in artificial breeding with this genus, no hybrids have as yet been officially registered.

CULTURE: These plants, in general, do best if kept in the out-of-doors garden, at least in temperate climates (they are often very difficult to maintain in good condition in the greenhouse, or in the tropics). Soil requirements fluctuate markedly from species to species, some requiring acid conditions, some alkaline, and some thoroughly neutral. A rich compost is always desirable, and one which is sufficiently porous to permit free and rapid drainage, since these plants need quantities of moisture at all times, save for a period of a month or more upon completion of flowering, when they should be rested. The root systems of these plants are often very delicate, and even the slightest bit of disturbance will, in many cases, cause them to die. (C, I)

O. aristata Fisch. ex Ldl.

Roots fibrous and tuberous, the tuberoids fleshy, more or less divided. Lvs. 2–more, becoming bract-like above, oblanceolate to lanceolate, acute to acuminate, clasping the st., 1½–5½" long. Infl. slender, often tinged with purple, over-all to 12" tall, with a few- to many-fld., rather dense rac. Fls. to almost 1" long, varying in colour from light magenta to violet-purple (rarely almost pure white), the ss. erect, concave, the ps. decurrent on the col., adherent to the dors. sep. to form a hood. Lip often spotted with dark purple, roundish to broadly squarish, the basal spur conspicuous, tubular, tapering from a broad base. May–Aug. (C, I) Alaska; Aleutian Islands; Japan; China.

O. coriophora L. (*Orchis fragrans* Poll., *O. Pollini* Spr.)

Tubers 2 or more, sessile, oblong, to 1″ long. St. $\frac{1}{2}$–$1\frac{1}{2}$′ tall, leafy to the top. Lvs. suberect on lower part of st., sheathing above, lanceolate, acute, 1–3″ long. Spike $1\frac{1}{2}$–$4\frac{1}{2}$″ long, densely many-fld. Fls. fragrant, about $\frac{5}{8}$″ long, highly variable in colour, the ss. and ps. striped alternately with red and green, the lip green with a pink, crimson-spotted disc (pure white forms also occur). Ss. united to the middle forming a hood over the col., ovate-lanceolate. Ps. lanceolate, much smaller than the ss. Lip 3-lbd., the lat. lbs. rhombic, rather crenate, the midlb. larger, oblong, entire; spur conical, curved, about $\frac{1}{4}$″ long. May–July. (C, I) Central and Southern Europe; North Africa.

O. incarnata L. (*Orchis lanceolata* Dietr.)

Tubers paired, palmately-lobed. St. 1–3′ tall, stout, hollow, leafy to the top. Lvs. lanceolate, slightly sheathing the st., 3–12″ long. Spike densely many-fld., 2–6″ long. Fls. almost 1″ long, fragrant, rich purple, the disc of the lip usually paler, sometimes yellowish or whitish. Dors. sep. broadly lanceolate, acute, forming with the slightly smaller ps. a hood over the col. Lat. ss. falcately lanceolate, suberect. Lip almost as broad as long, 3-lbd., the lat. lbs. rounded, crenate, the midlb. very small, tooth-like; spur stout, curved, pointing downwards. May–July. (C, I) Europe; North Africa.

O. latifolia L. (*Orchis affinis* Koch, *O. majalis* Rchb., *O. triphylla* Koch)

Tubers usually paired, lobed. St. 1–3′ tall, often hollow, leafy upwards. Lvs. erect, oblong, linear-oblong, or lanceolate, often blotched and spotted with dark purple, or entirely dark green, becoming smaller upwards. Spike cylindrical, densely many-fld., 1–6″ long. Fls. about $\frac{3}{4}$″ long, variable in colour from pink or purple to almost pure white. Ss. ovate, reflexed. Ps. ovate-lanceolate, usually arched over the col. Lip oblong or rhomboid, entire or very obscurely 3-lbd., crenate, the outer lbs. or sides deflexed, the stout spur pendulous. May–July. (C, I) British Isles throughout Europe and Asia to Western China and the Himalayas.

O. laxiflora Lam. (*Orchis ensifolia* Vill., *O. Tabernaemontani* Gmel.)

Tubers 2, somewhat irregular, ovoid or oblong, about 1″ long. St. $\frac{3}{4}$–2′ tall, erect, stout, leafy. Lvs. cauline, suberect, numerous, linear-lanceolate, longest near the middle of the st., 3–9″ long. Spike loosely many-fld., more or less cylindrical, 4–6″ long. Fls. $\frac{3}{4}$–1″ long, reddish-purple or crimson-purple, the lip usually paler centrally. Dors. sep. lanceolate, the lats. lanceolate, slightly falcate towards the tip. Ps. similar to ss., but smaller, forming a loose hood over the col. Lip broadly cuneate, suddenly narrowing towards the base, 3-lbd., the lat. lbs. broad, rounded, crenate, the midlb. very

small, rounded, slightly cleft. Spur stout, cylindrical, curved, suberect, to $\frac{3}{4}$″ long. May–Aug. (C, I) Central and Southern Europe; North Africa.

O. maculata L. (*Orchis basilica* L., *O. Gervasiana* Tod., *O. solida* Moench)

Tubers paired, palmately-lobed. St. $\frac{3}{4}$–2′ tall, rather stout, leafy to the top. Lvs. usually densely brown-mottled, slightly sheathing the st., oblong-lanceolate or lanceolate, 3–6″ long. Spike densely many-fld., 2–5″ long. Fls. about $\frac{3}{4}$″ long, rather variable in colour, usually pale lilac or purple, with semicircular crimson markings on the lip. Dors. sep. ovate, the lat. ss. falcately lanceolate, erect. Ps. similar to ss. but slightly smaller, forming a hood over the col. Lip longer than wide, 3-lbd., the lbs. variable, the midlb. usually narrow and pointed. Spur stout, slightly curved, pendulous, $\frac{3}{8}$″ long. May–June. (C, I) Europe throughout Asia to Siberia; North Africa.

O. madeirensis Summerh. (*Orchis foliosa* Soland.)

Tubers usually paired, rather large, palmately-lobed. St. to 3′ tall, very stout, leafy. Lvs. shining, rich dark green, basal and cauline, ovate, sheathing below, 10–12″ long. Spike densely many-fld., 3–8″ long and as much as $3\frac{1}{2}$″ in diam., very showy. Fls. about 1″ long and $\frac{3}{4}$″ across, purple-red, the lip more or less marked with rich lilac-purple, long-lasting, perhaps the finest in the genus. Dors. sep. ovate-lanceolate, blunt; lat. ss. broadly lanceolate, blunt. Ps. lanceolate, blunt, shorter than the ss., converging over the col. Lip large, broader than long, 3-lbd., the lat. lbs. very broad and blunt, the midlb. small, triangular, blunt. May–Aug. (C, I) Madeira.

O. mascula L. (*Orchis glaucophylla* A.Kern., *O. ovalis* Schm.)

Tubers 2, ovoid, about $\frac{3}{4}$″ long, one of them frequently on a very short stalk. St. $\frac{3}{4}$–2′ tall, stout, leafy below. Lvs. usually forming a tuft at st.-base, sheathing the st. upwards, oblong-lanceolate, suberect, 3–6″ long, blue-green, usually somewhat crimson-purple-spotted near base. Spike oblong in shape, many-fld., 3–5″ long. Fls. about 1″ long, rosy-purple, the lip-disc usually white or pinkish-purple, spotted with rich magenta-purple. Dors. sep. lanceolate, the lats. lanceolate, slightly falcate. Ps. similar to ss. but smaller, forming a loose hood over the col. Lip much longer than wide, 3-lbd., the lat. lbs. large, slightly crenate, the midlb. obovate, bifid at the tip with a sharp tooth in the sinus. Spur stout, cylindrical, about $\frac{1}{4}$″ long. Apr.–June. (C, I) Europe throughout Asia to Siberia; North Africa.

O. militaris L. (*Orchis cinerea* Schrk., *O. galeata* Poir., *O. mimusops* Thunb.)

Tubers 2, somewhat irregular, potato-like, 1″ long or more. St. rather slender to stout, leafy, often sinuous, $\frac{3}{4}$–$1\frac{1}{2}$′ tall. Lvs. mostly basal in a tuft, rather few in number, oblong-lanceolate, concave, 2–4″ long. Spike oblong, or pyramidal, many-fld., 3–5″ long. Fls. about $\frac{3}{4}$″ long, the ss. and ps. pale purple or lilac-crimson, striped with darker colour, the lip vivid crimson-purple, the disc white, spotted with crimson. Dors. sep. lanceolate, the lats. falcate-lanceolate, forming an open hood with the dors. one. Ps. very narrowly lanceolate, curving. Lip 3-lbd., the outer lbs. narrowly linear, slightly diverging, the midlb. cuneate, divided into 2 large diverging lbs. at the tip, with a point between them. Spur stout, curved, $\frac{1}{4}''$ long. May–June. (C, I) Europe throughout Asia to Siberia.

O. morio L. (*Orchis crenulata* Gilib., *O. Nicodemi* Ten.)
Tubers 2, oblong, about 1″ long, with a few thick, short roots above them. St. 6–15″ tall, leafy, rather stout. Lvs. basal and cauline, sheathing the st. upwards, oblong or oblong-lanceolate, 1–2½″ long. Spike rather densely many-fld., 2–4″ long. Fls. about $\frac{3}{4}''$ long, horizontal or suberect, varying from red-violet to reddish-purple or flesh-pink (very rarely white), the lip-disc usually paler, spotted with dark red-purple. Ss. and ps. ovate or lanceolate, forming a hood over the col. Lip variable in shape, usually broader than long, more or less 3-lbd., the midlb. small, notched at the tip. Spur horizontal or ascending, cylindrical, dilated apically, $\frac{1}{4}''$ long. May–June. (C, I) Europe; Western Asia.

O. pallens L. (*Orchis sulphurea* Sims)
Tubers 2, somewhat irregular, oblong, about 1″ long. St. 1–1½′ tall, sparsely leafy, rather stout. Lvs. about 3–4 in number, oblong-lanceolate, rather blunt, sheathing the st. above, and becoming bract-like there, 3–6″ long. Spike 2–5″ long, rather dense, pyramidal to rarely oblong in shape. Fls. about $\frac{3}{4}''$ long, fragrant, rich yellow to cream-coloured. Dors. sep. oblong or ovate, the lats. and ps. lanceolate, the latter smaller than the ss., forming a loose hood over the col. Lip about as broad as long, 3-lbd., the lat. lbs. rounded, the midlb. smaller, rounded or almost square, notched, the entire lip fringed with tiny hairs. Spur stout, cylindrical, suberect, $\frac{1}{2}''$ long. Apr.–July. (C, I) Central and Southern Europe, east to the Caucasus Mountains.

O. palustris Jacq. (*Orchis elegans* Heuff., *O. germanorum* Mor., *O. Heuffeliana* Schur.)
Tubers 2, oblong or ovoid, about 1¼″ long. St. $\frac{3}{4}$–2′ tall, stout, leafy. Lvs. dark green, rather numerous, linear-lanceolate, suberect, sheathing below, narrower and smaller above, 3–6″ long. Spike loose, many-fld., 3–9″ long. Fls. about 1″ long, bright rich purple, the lip spotted with darker purple, the lat. lbs. usually darker. Dors. sep. ovate, the lats. lanceolate, slightly falcate, all erect. Ps. similar, equalling the ss. in length, slightly incurved, forming a loose hood over the col. Lip as broad as long, 3-lbd., the lat. lbs. rounded, the midlb. smaller, rounded, slightly toothed and with a shallow notch in the centre. Spur stout, cylindrical, $\frac{1}{2}''$ long, horizontal or suberect. May–Aug. (C, I) Central and Southern Europe, east to Iran; North Africa.

O. papilionacea L. (*Orchis expansa* Ten., *O. rubra* Jacq.)
Tubers 2, irregular, ovoid, one sessile, the other short-stalked, $\frac{3}{4}''$ in diam. St. 4–8″ tall, rather stout, leafy, usually slightly curving. Lvs. cauline, pale green, linear-lanceolate, usually deeply channelled, 2–3″ long. Spike loose, usually 2–6-fld. Fls. about 1¼″ long and $\frac{5}{8}''$ in diam., pale purple, lilac, or pale pink, the lip usually handsomely veined with crimson. Ss. lanceolate, acute, connivent below, spreading above. Ps. lanceolate, smaller and shorter than the ss., connivent to form a hood over

the col. Lip varying from fan-shaped and rhomboid to roundish, crenately toothed, shallowly lbd., the lat. lbs. somewhat incurved. Spur straight, $\frac{3}{8}''$ long. Apr.–June. (C, I) Mediterranean region, from Portugal to Turkey and Algeria.

O. provincialis Balb. (*Orchis Cyrillii* Ten., *O. leucostachys* Griseb.)
Tubers usually 2, irregular, ovoid, almost sessile, $\frac{1}{2}$–$\frac{3}{4}''$ long. St. $\frac{3}{4}$–1½′ tall, slender. Lvs. mostly near base, few in number, rich green, blotched with dark purple, broadly linear to oblong-lanceolate, rather blunt, becoming bract-like above. Spike many-fld., lax. Fls. about 1″ long, pale yellow, the lip more or less spotted with purple. Dors. sep. cuneate, blunt, the erect lat. ss. ovate, acute. Ps. lanceolate, connate to form a hood over the col. Lip deeply 3-lbd., the lat. lbs. somewhat irregular in shape, usually pointed, the midlb. emarginate, usually with a tooth at the notch. Spur horizontal, stout, dilated at tip, $\frac{5}{8}''$ long. Apr.–June. (C, I) Mediterranean region, from Spain to Asia Minor (Turkey).

O. purpurea Huds. (*Orchis brachiata* Gilib., *O. fusca* Jacq., *O. fuscata* Pall.)
Tubers 2, ovoid or subglobose, to 1¼″ long. St. rather stout, leafy below, $\frac{3}{4}$–2½′ tall. Lvs. mostly basal, in a tuft, oblong or oblong-lanceolate, concave, 6–12″ long. Spike many-fld., oblong or slightly tapering upwards, 3–6″ long. Fls. more than $\frac{3}{4}''$ long, usually pale purple or pinkish-purple, the ss. green-tipped, the large lip with a white, crimson-spotted disc. Dors. sep. ovate-oblong, the lat. ss. lanceolate, conniving with the dors. one in an open hood. Ps. oblong. Lip 3-lbd., the lat. lbs. linear, the midlb. broadly cuneate, widely cleft at the tip, with a small point in the sinus. Spur stout, conical or cylindrical, $\frac{1}{4}''$ long. Mar.–June. (C, I) Europe; Asia Minor.

O. quadripunctata Cyr. (*Anacamptis quadripunctata* Ldl., *Anacamptis Brancifortii* Ldl.)
Tubers paired, somewhat irregular, oblong, about $\frac{3}{4}''$ long. St. rather slender, erect, sparsely leafy, 6–15″ tall. Lvs. cauline, few, oblong or oblong-lanceolate, the uppermost ones clasping the st., 1–3″ long. Spike slender, cylindrical, loose, many-fld., 3–6″ long. Fls. $\frac{3}{4}''$ long, pale reddish-purple, the lip with a white disc, otherwise spotted with red-purple. Dors. sep. oblong or narrowly oval, the lat. ss. lanceolate, slightly falcate at tip. Ps. similar to ss. but smaller, curving over the col. Lip 3-lbd., the lat. lbs. large, rounded, the midlb. almost square or oblong, minutely toothed or notched. Spur slender, curved, cylindrical, $\frac{1}{2}''$ long. Apr.–June. (C, I) Italy; Greece; Crete.

O. rotundifolia Banks ex Pursh (*Habenaria rotundifolia* Richards., *Platanthera rotundifolia* Ldl.)
Pl. stoloniferous, the roots fleshy-fibrous. St. to more than 12″ tall, slender, naked, vaguely angled, provided with a solitary dull green, orbicular to oval or broadly obovate-elliptic, obtuse to rounded lf., 1¼–4″ long. Scape 1–several-fld. (up to about 16), rather congested. Fls. to about $\frac{3}{4}''$ long, the ss. and ps. white to pale mauve-pink, the lip white, spotted with magenta or purple. Dors. sep. and ps. forming a hood over the col., the lat. ss. spreading. Lip longer than the ps., 3-lbd., the midlb.

longer than the others, 2-lbd. or notched at the apex, dilated. Spur slender, shorter than the lip. Mar.-Aug. (C, I) Greenland; Anticosti and Hudson Bay west to Alaska, south to New York and Montana.

O. sambucina L. (*Orchis salina* Fronius, *O. Schleicheri* Sweet)

Tubers 2, palmately-lobed, 1–1½″ long. St. stout, 6–9″ tall, erect, leafy. Lvs. broadly linear to oblong-lanceolate, dark green usually blotched with dark purple, 3–6″ long. Spike compact, many-fld., 2–4″ long. Fls. about ¾″ long, cream-coloured ss. and ps., the lip rather bright yellow with a double ridge of red hairs on the disc. Dors. sep. lanceolate, the lat. ss. lanceolate, slightly falcate. Ps. similar to ss., but smaller and incurved. Lip ovate or ovate-oblong, slightly 3-lbd., the midlb. very small, triangular, tooth-like, the lat. lbs. toothed. Spur very stout, curved, pendulous. May–July. (C, I) Central and Southern Europe, mostly in the mountainous areas.

O. simia Lam. (*Orchis italica* Lam., *O. zoophora* Tuil.)

Tubers 2, oblong, potato-shaped, about 1″ long. St. rather slender, erect or vaguely zigzag, ¾–1½′ tall, leafy below. Lvs. mostly basal, becoming sheathed upwards, lanceolate, deeply channelled, 2–4″ long. Spike oblong or subglobose, rather densely many-fld., 2–3″ long. Fls. about 1¼″ long, the ss. and ps. lilac or pale purple, the lip with crimson-purple lat. lbs., the midlb. white, spotted with crimson. Dors. sep. oblong, erect, the lats. lanceolate, very acute, forming with the dors. one a loose hood over the col. Ps. very narrowly lanceolate or linear. Lip 3-lbd., the lat. lbs. very narrow, linear, the midlb. again divided into 2 narrowly linear lbs., equalling the lat. lbs. in length, with a tooth in the sinus. Spur stout, blunt, ¼″ long. Apr.–June. (C, I) Asia Minor; Central and Southern Asia.

O. spathulata (Ldl.) Rchb.f. (*Gymnadenia spathulata* Ldl.)

Root an elongate underground st., branching into thick fibres. St. stout, often flexuous, sheathed, 2–5″ tall. Lf. solitary, basal, sessile or short-stalked, elliptic, obtuse, fleshy, narrowed towards the base. Spike stout, usually about 2–4-fld. Fls. about ½″ in diam. and ⅝″ long, rosy-purple, the lip usually darker in colour. Dors. sep. ovate, obtuse, the lat ss. oblong, rather acute, spreading or suberect. Ps. elliptic, obtuse, ascending. Lip varying from elliptic to cuneate-obovate, crenulate, obscurely 3-lbd. to entire. Spur stout, blunt. May–June. (C) Himalayas, from Kumaon to Sikkim; Western China: Yunnan, usually at high elevations.

O. spectabilis L. (*Galeorchis spectabilis* Rydb., *Orchis humilis* Michx.)

Roots slender, fleshy, tuberous. St. 3–13″ tall, rather stout, naked, 4–5-angled. Lvs. 2, basal, subopposite, with the petioles sheathing the base of the infl., gradually narrowed into an indistinct petiole, roundish-obovate to broadly elliptic, rounded at the apex, 2–8½″ long, 1¼–4″ wide. Spike 1–15-fld., rather loose, to 4″ long. Ss. and ps. pink to mauve (rarely almost white), the lip pure white. Ss. and ps. ovate or oblong, usually rather concave and forming a tight hood over the col. Lip diverging, oblong or ovate, entire, petaloid. Spur about ⅝″ long, blunt. Apr.–July. (C, I) New Brunswick west to Iowa and Arkansas, south to Georgia and Alabama.

O. tridentata Scop. (*Orchis cercopitheca* Lam., *O. taurica* Ldl., *O. variegata* All.)

Tubers 2, oblong, sessile, about ¾″ long. St. ¾–1½′ tall, rather stout, leafy. Lvs. oblong-lanceolate below, lanceolate above, the uppermost ones acute, degenerating into bracts, 1½–2½″ long. Spike densely many-fld., subglobose, about 2″ long. Fls. about ⅝″ long, the ss. and ps. pale reddish-purple, often flushed with green basally, the lip white or pale purple, more or less spotted with rich crimson. Ss. and ps. lanceolate, acutish, forming a hood over the col. Lip very deeply 3-lbd., the lat. lbs. ribbon-like, truncate and toothed at the apex, the midlb. cuneate, toothed at the tip. Spur conical, curved, ⅜″ long. Apr.–June. (C, I) Central and Southern Europe to Western Asia.

O. ustulata L. (*Himantoglossum parviflorum* Spreng., *Orchis parviflora* Willd.)

Tubers 2, sessile, oblong, about ¾″ long. St. rather stout, leafy or clothed with bracts, 3–12″ tall. Lvs. oblong-lanceolate, becoming bracteose above, these bracts often imbricating, 1–2″ long. Spike oblong or slightly tapering upwards, densely many-fld., about 2″ long usually. Fls. about ½″ long, narrow, the ss. and ps. green, tipped with pink, the lip white, spotted with crimson. Dors. sep. ovate, forming with the lanceolate lat. ss. a hood over the col. Ps. oblong, small. Lip 3-lbd., the lat. lbs. linear, truncate, diverging, the midlb. broadly cuneate or divided into 2 broad blunt lbs. with a tiny tooth in the sinus. Spur thick, cylindrical, curving, ⅛″ long. Mar.–Aug. (C, I) Europe, often in the mountains.

O. anatolica Boiss. St. rather stout, sometimes curving, to 12″ tall. Lvs. mostly near base, oblong or oblong-lanceolate, narrowing upwards, 1–2″ long. Spike 2–4″ long, loosely many-fld. Fls. about ⅝″ long, purple-violet, the lip whitish centrally, unspotted. Ss. and ps. erect, often forming a hood over the col., the ps. smaller than the ss. Lip ovate, slightly 3-lbd., the midlb. very small, slightly notched. May–June. (C, I) Greece to Iraq.

O. brevicalcarata (Finet) Schltr. (*Hemipilia brevicalcarata* Finet, *Gymnadenia brevicalcarata* Finet) Lf. solitary, roundish, membranaceous, contracted into a short petiole. Infl. 3–6″ long, rather stout, the slender rac. 4–8-fld. Fls. ⅜″ long, erect, purplish-rose, the lat. ss. larger than the dors. one, rather oblique. Ps. ovate, oblique, forming a loose hood over the col. with the dors. sep. Lip narrowly cuneate, 3-lbd., the lbs. roundish. Spur reduced to a small sac. Mostly June. (C, I) China: Yunnan, at rather high elevations in the mountains.

O. Delavayi Schltr. St. 3–5″ tall, erect, smooth, with a solitary basal, oblong-ligulate, spreading lf. about 1″ long, and 1–2 pointed sheaths upwards, the rac. 2–5-fld., loose. Fls. about ⅜″ long, the ss. and ps. white or pale purple, the lip spotted with dark purple. Dors. sep. and ps. erect or suberect, the lat. ss. spreading. Lip cuneate below, 3-lbd. above the middle, obliquely ovate-oblong, the lat. lbs. almost square, rounded at the tip, the midlb. square, with an emarginate apex. Spur usually ascending, ½″ long. Mostly June. (C) China: Yunnan, at high elevations.

O. iberica Desf. (*Orchis leptophylla* C.Koch) Tubers 2, fusiform, lobed, about ¾″ long. St. slender, often sinuous, sparsely leafy, 6–15″ tall. Lvs. few, erect, decreasing into bracts upwards, 2–6″ long. Spike 2–4″ long, few- rarely many-fld., loose, very slender. Fls. less than ½″ long, pale purple, the middle of the lip usually almost white. Dors. and lat. ss. lanceolate, the latter slightly hooked at the tips, the ps. linear to narrowly lanceolate, much smaller than ss. Lip ovate, 3-lbd., the lat. lbs. rounded, crenate, the midlb. very small, lanceolate, pointed. Spur rather stout, curved, pointing downwards. May–June. (C, I) Greece to the Caucasus Mountains.

O. Palczewskii Krzl. St. 2½–3½″ tall, leafy, the lvs. mostly basal, narrowly elliptic, blunt, about 2½″ long, rather numerous in a tuft. Spike 2–3-fld. Fls. about ½″ in diam., lilac-pink to purple, the narrow ps. very minutely toothed at tips. Lip shortly clawed, squarish, 3-lbd., the lat. lbs. rounded, the midlb. square, 2-lbd. and retuse at apex, marginally crenulate; disc smooth or covered with minute down. Mostly May. (C, I) Eastern Siberia.

O. patens Desf. St. rather slender, to 1½′ tall, the lvs. few, mostly basal, oblong or lanceolate, dark glaucous green often spotted and blotched with brown or purplish-brown, 2–4″ long. Spike many-fld. and fairly dense, cylindrical, 2–6″ long. Fls. about ½″ long, the ss. and ps. pale purple and green, the lip pale purple medially spotted with dark purple spots, the lat. lbs. dark red-purple. May–June. (C, I) Mediterranean Region; Canary Islands.

O. pauciflora Fisch. St. 4–9″ tall, rather stout, bearing 2 distant lvs., these linear-lanceolate, acute, 2–3″ long. Spike rather densely many-fld., ¾–2″ long. Fls. about ⅝″ across, rich violet-purple or violet-red, the ps. forming a hood over the col., the lip square, pubescent. May–June. (C, I) Manchuria; Korea; Japan.

O. punctulata Stev. (*Orchis Steveniana* Comp.) St. rather stout, 6–15″ tall, the few lvs. oblong or ovate-oblong, blunt, 2–6″ long. Spike loosely many-fld., cylindrical, 2–5″ long. Fls. about ⅝″ long, white or rosy-white more or less spotted with dark rose. Ss. and ps. connivent and forming a hood over the col., the lip 3-lbd., the lat. lbs. ovate, rounded, the midlb. narrow, acutish, much smaller than the lat. ones. Mar.–Apr. (C, I) Turkey; Iraq.

O. salina Turcz. St. 1–2′ tall, erect, rather stout, leafy. Lvs. linear-lanceolate, erect or ascending, acutish, 3–4″ long. Spike loosely few-fld., 3–5″ long. Fls. about ½″ in diam., varying from almost pure white to pale purple. Ps. narrowly lanceolate, incurving. Lip rhomboid, crenate, slightly 3-lbd., the lbs. pointed, vaguely downy, the spur pendulous. May–July. (C, I) Iran through South-west Siberia to Tibet and West China.

OREORCHIS Ldl.

This is a little-known genus of saprophytic orchids, about nine in number, native in the Himalayas, China, and Japan. A member of the subtribe *Cyrtopodiinae*, the group consists of rather insignificant plants with a corm-like rhizome and grassy foliage, the floral structure placing them somewhat in the affinity of *Cremastra* Ldl. None of the species of Oreorchis is present in collections at this time.

Nothing is known of the genetic ties of this rare group.

CULTURE: Presumably as for *Corallorrhiza*. (C, I)

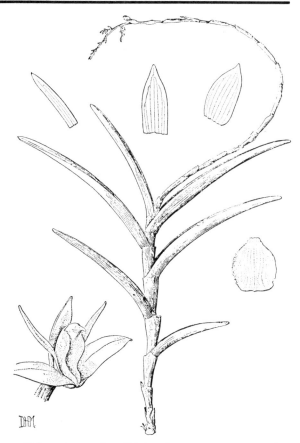

Orleanesia peruviana C.Schw. [DOROTHY H. MARSH]

ORLEANESIA B.-R.

About four or five species now comprise this rare and relatively little-known genus of the subtribe *Ponerinae*, these mostly epiphytic plants indigenous to Peru, Venezuela, and Brazil. Superficially, certain of the Orleanesias rather simulate slender, pseudobulbous Epidendrums, but they differ from that genus in several technical details, and are, in fact, not even incorporated in the same subtribe as that group. Relatively insignificant plants, primarily of scientific interest, none of the members of this genus appears to be generally cultivated at this time.

Nothing is known of the genetic affinities of *Orleanesia*.

CULTURE: Presumably as for the medium-elevation, pseudobulbous Epidendrums. (I)

ORNITHOCEPHALUS Hk.

The principal genus of the subtribe *Ornithocephalinae*, *Ornithocephalus* consists of about thirty-five or so species of epiphytic, most unusual and interesting orchids, these widespread over a huge region extending from Mexico to Trinidad and Brazil. Now relatively frequent in certain choice collections, these delightful dwarf orchids, commonly known as 'Bird's-Head Orchids', because of the unique shape of the tiny, yet incredibly complex green or white, racemose flowers, are highly recommended to all hobbyists, because of their easy cultural requirements and floriferous habits. No pseudobulbs are present in *Ornithocephalus*, the more or less fleshy leaves being arranged in a tight, basally rooting fan, which rather resembles some sort of diminutive *Iris*, rather than an orchid. The often multiple, bracted inflorescences frequently are borne more than once annually, thus adding to their value as subjects for the average orchid collection. The genus is an extremely complicated one, and many of its component taxa are not yet fully delimited.

No hybrids have as yet been made in *Ornithocephalus*, and nothing is known regarding its genetic affinities.

CULTURE: In the wild, these extraordinary plants generally grow on small twigs or branches, in forests where they are constantly bathed in mists or fogs, usually with their roots covered by absorbent mosses and lichens. In our collections, they do well when rooting tightly mounted on small slabs of tree-fern fibre. Otherwise, they should be potted in small, perfectly-drained containers in a firm compost of equal parts of shredded tree-fern fibre and chopped sphagnum moss. Even though in the wild, the leaf-fans are often pendulous, under cultivation they can be mounted or potted in upright fashion. They must never be permitted to dry out, and yet sodden conditions at the roots will rapidly prove fatal to their rather delicate constitutions. Semi-shade is necessary, else the succulent foliage may become

spotted or otherwise unsightly. Periodic applications of a weakened fertilizing solution have been found to be beneficial to foliage and floral production. In certain species, accessory leaf-fans are produced, and when these have a few active roots, they may to advantage be removed from the parent plant and replanted as individuals. (I, H)

O. bicornis Ldl. (*Ornithocephalus diceras* Schltr., *Zygostates costaricensis* Nash)

Lvs. grey-green, equitant, forming a fan, rigid, lanceolate to oblong-lanceolate, acute-apiculate, $\frac{3}{4}$–$3\frac{1}{2}$″ long, the basal sheaths with hyaline margins. Infls. racemose, slender-flexuose, few- to many-fld., densely fuzzy throughout, with large bracts. Fls. cup-shaped, rather long-lived, to about $\frac{3}{16}$″ in diam., the ss. and ps. greenish-white or greenish-yellow, the lip green at its fleshy base. Lip 3-lbd., the lbs. unequal, the inconspicuous lat. lbs. slender, recurved, the midlb. narrowly linear, acute, dorsally keeled, curved forwards. Mostly winter. (I, H) Guatemala to Panama.

O. inflexus Ldl. (*Ornithocephalus elephas* Rchb.f., *O. mexicanus* A.Rich. & Gal., *O. Pottsiae* S.Wats., *O. Tonduzii* Schltr.)

Lvs. equitant, linear-ensiform, acute, to long-acuminate, to 4″ long, the basal sheaths hyaline. Infls. racemose, slender, often rather zigzag, glabrous, loosely many-fld. from the base upwards, to more than 3″ long. Fls. to about $\frac{3}{16}$″ in diam., whitish-green or greenish, sometimes with some darker green markings on the lip. Lip essentially entire, somewhat dilated and fleshy-cordate on lower third, constricted in front of the callus and linear-lanceolate or ligulate above. Winter. (I, H) Mexico and British Honduras to Panama.

O. iridifolius Rchb.f.

Lvs. linear-ensiform, acute to acuminate, 1–3″ long, the basal sheaths hyaline. Infls. slender, often zigzag, spreading, laxly many-fld. from the base upwards, to more than 3″ long, the peduncle and rachis winged, the wings irregularly serrulate. Fls. rather widely opening, to almost $\frac{1}{4}$″ in diam., white, the spreading lip deeply 3-lbd., the lat. lbs. roundish, conspicuous, very fleshy-thickened, the thin midlb. triangular-ovate to sub-orbicular-ovate, obtuse, concave. Summer. (I, H) Mexico; Guatemala.

O. tripterus Schltr.

Lvs. equitant, linear-lanceolate, ensiform, acute to acuminate, $1\frac{1}{2}$–$4\frac{1}{2}$″ long, the basal sheaths hyaline. Infls. slender, somewhat zigzag, loosely many-fld., $2\frac{1}{2}$–6″ long, the peduncle and rachis winged, the wings irregularly serrulate. Fls. to more than $\frac{1}{4}$″ in diam., white-green, rather similar to those of *O. inflexus* Ldl. in shape but differing in the broader lip with a rather roundish concave callus which covers most of the lower half of the entire lip. Lip linguiform, ovate-elliptic, not constricted. Summer. (I, H) Mexico; Guatemala.

O. grandiflorus Ldl. Lvs. narrowly oblong, obtuse, very fleshy for the genus, few in number, 4–6″ long, forming a small pb. in the median axils (?). Infls. longer than the lvs., arching gracefully, rather densely many-fld., bracted. Fls. $\frac{3}{4}$″ in diam., cup-shaped, the ss. and ps. white with a vivid green

Ornithocephalus bicornis Ldl. [BLANCHE AMES]

Ornithophora radicans (Rchb.f.) Pabst & Garay [Hoehne, *Flora Brasilica*]

spot at base, roundish, concave, the smaller lat. ss. reflexed. Lip roundish, saccate and strongly keeled beneath, on the short claw of which is a horseshoe-shaped green callus with a crisped fan-like prolongation in front. Col. curving, white, the rostellum produced into a thread-like appendage parallel with the lip-callus as far as its anterior margin, and then bent upwards and inwards, terminating in a small yellow gland. Mostly summer. (I, H) Brazil.

ORNITHOCHILUS Wall.

Two species of *Ornithochilus* are known to science, both of them very rare epiphytic orchids from the Himalayas and China; one of them is present in a few very choice contemporary collections, but it must be classed as a scarce orchid. The genus is allied to *Phalaenopsis* Bl.—the plants rather resembling certain members of that group—and to *Aërides* Lour., but it is immediately differentiated on technical details of the small flowers, these borne in long arching racemes.

No hybrids are known in *Ornithochilus*, and its genetic affinities have not been ascertained as yet.

CULTURE: As for *Vanda*. (I)

O. fuscus Wall. (*Aërides hystrix* Ldl., *Ornithocephalus eublepharum* Hance)

St. abbreviated, bearing a few oblong-elliptic, rather fleshy lvs. to 5″ long and 2″ wide. Infls. arching to somewhat pendulous, densely many-fld., to 1½′ long. Fls.

small, about ½″ long, the ss. and ps. greenish-yellow with reddish stripes, the lip yellowish with a red midlb. and a rather long yellowish spur. Spring–early summer. (I) Himalayas; Burma; Thailand; Laos; Viet-Nam; Hong Kong.

ORNITHOPHORA B.-R.

Most recent students of the Orchidaceae have considered this genus to be a synonym of *Sigmatostalix* Rchb.f., but in 1951 Garay and Pabst pointed out its distinctness, and it is now recognized as a separate entity, containing but one species, this a rather frequently-cultivated epiphytic plant from southern Brazil. It is a very attractive and floriferous orchid which should be in even the most modest of collections.

No hybrids have as yet been made in *Ornithophora*, and its genetic alliances have not been ascertained.

CULTURE: As for the tropical Oncidiums. Because of the repent rhizomes, cultivation in shallow pots or baskets is suggested. (I, H)

O. radicans (Rchb.f.) Garay & Pabst (*Sigmatostalix radicans* Rchb.f., *Ornithophora quadricolor* B.-R.)

Pbs. narrowly ovoid, rather distant on the slender creeping rhiz., to almost 2″ tall. Lvs. 2, rather thin-textured, narrowly linear, acute, to 7″ long, only about ¼″ wide. Infls. loosely 10–15-fld., slender, arching, usually longer than the lvs. Fls. about ¼″ long or more, the ss. and ps. white, the complex lip yellowish, narrowly clawed, the disc almost square. Col. slender, dark violet-purple. Mostly autumn. (I, H) Brazil.

ORTHOCERAS R.Br.

Orthoceras strictum R.Br. (*O. Solandri* Hk.f.), the only reported member of this genus of the subtribe *Diuridinae*, is a rare terrestrial orchid native in eastern Australia, New Zealand, and New Caledonia. It resembles a *Diuris*, but differs from that genus in technical details of the rather small flowers. *Orthoceras* is not present in contemporary collections.

Nothing is known of the genetic affinities of this rare group.

CULTURE: Presumably as for *Caladenia*. (C, I)

ORTHOPENTHEA Rolfe

Orthopenthea consists of a single species of rare and little-known terrestrial orchid, native in tropical Africa. A member of the subtribe *Disinae*, the genus is a segregate from *Penthea* Ldl., from which it differs in technical floral details. It is unknown in cultivation at this time.

Nothing is known of the genetic ties of *Orthopenthea*.
CULTURE: Presumably as for *Disa*. (I, H)

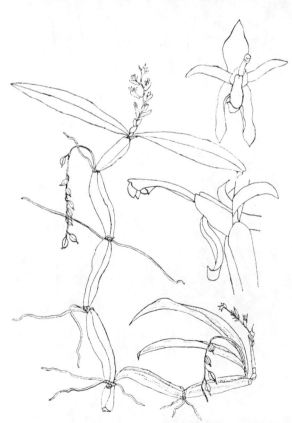

Otochilus alba Ldl. [A.D.HAWKES, AFTER *Orchids of Thailand*]

OTOCHILUS Ldl.
(*Broughtonia* Wall. ex Ldl., *Tetrapeltis* Wall.)

Otochilus is a genus of the subtribe *Coelogyninae*, containing but three species, these all epiphytic (rarely lithophytic) orchids mostly in the mountainous areas extending from the Himalayas to Thailand and Viet-Nam. They are peculiar, rather unattractive plants, with pseudobulbs usually superimposed on top of one another and racemes of small white or brownish flowers. One species has recently been introduced into a few particularly choice collections.

Nothing is known of the genetic ties of *Otochilus*.
CULTURE: Generally as for *Coelogyne*. Because of the awkward habit of the plants, they are best grown attached to tree-fern slabs. They are often prone to rotting if kept the least bit too moist, yet must never be allowed to become completely dry. (I)

O. alba Ldl. (*Broughtonia pendula* Wall., *Coelogyne alba* Rchb.f.)

Pbs. forming sizeable masses to 2′ long and more, erect or pendulous, the individual sections to about 3″ long, becoming 4-winged with age, the new growths arising at or near apex of preceding one. Lvs. usually 2, soon deciduous, rather thin-textured, to 5″ long and 1¼″ broad. Infls. terminal, down-arching to pendulous, very slender, few-fld., to 5″ long. Fls. about ½″ long, narrow, the ss. and ps. white, the narrow lip with a median brown spot. Autumn. (I) Nepal through Himalayas, down to Thailand.

OTOSTYLIS Schltr.

This is a very peculiar genus of four known species of rare terrestrial orchids of the subtribe *Zygopetalinae*, native in Brazil, the Guianas and Trinidad. One of them has recently appeared in our collections from Trinidad, but it must be classed as an extremely scarce orchid. They are handsome pseudobulbous plants vaguely resembling a *Spathoglottis*, with erect inflorescences of mostly white, rather sizeable blossoms of unique formation and great beauty. In the wild, the Otostylis usually inhabit grassy fields or meadows, and are often fully exposed to the tropical sun.

No hybrids are known as yet in this charming genus, and nothing has been ascertained concerning its genetic affinities.
CULTURE: As for the evergreen Calanthes. (I, H)

O. brachystalix (Rchb.f.) Schltr. (*Zygopetalum brachystalix* Rchb.f., *Cyrtopodium Grisebachii* Rolfe, *Aganisia brachystalix* Rolfe, *Koellensteinia brachystalix* Schltr.)

Pbs. tightly clustered, at first scarcely evident because of sheathing lf.-bases, in time becoming ovoid, to almost 1″ tall, often tinged with dull purple. Lvs. 2, rather coriaceous, lanceolate, narrow, acute, folded basally, the blade rather distinctly plicate, 10–18″ long, usually about ¾″ wide. Infls. erect, racemose, the fls. rather numerous but opening only a few at a time over a long period, to 3′ tall and more. Fls. to 1″ across, often cup-shaped, rather short-lived, white or creamy-yellow, the

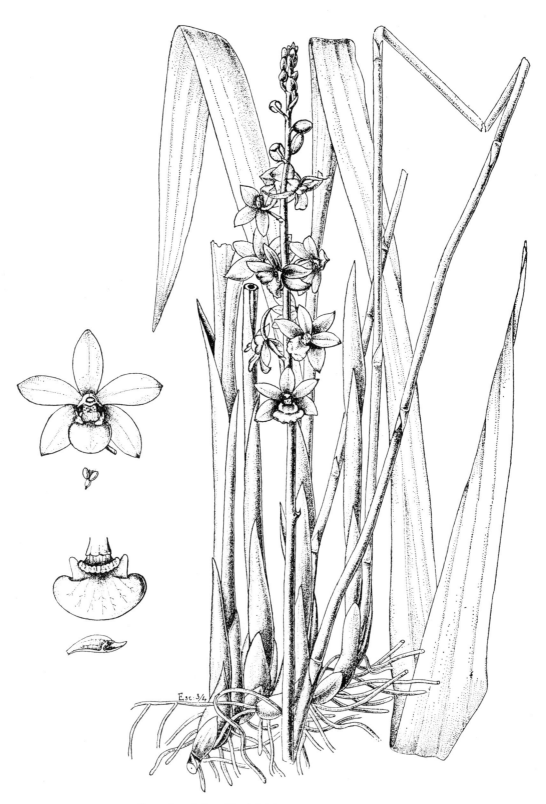

Otostylis paludosa (Cgn.) Schltr. [Hoehne, *Flora Brasílica*]

348

complex lip white, marked with greenish-yellow and pale magenta on the crested disc. Winter–spring, over a period of several months. (I, H) Trinidad.

OXYANTHERA Brongn.

Closely allied to *Thelasis* Bl., with which it is sometimes combined, *Oxyanthera* consists of five rare and little-known species of small, rather insignificant, epiphytic orchids in the region extending from the Malay Peninsula to New Guinea. A single species is present in specialized collections today, but it must be classed as a very rare plant.

No hybrids are reported in *Oxyanthera*, and its genetic affinities are not on record.

CULTURE: As for the tropical Bulbophyllums. (H)

O. micrantha Brongn. (*Oxyanthera decurva* Hk.f., *Thelasis contracta* Bl., *Thelasis decurva* Hk.f., *Thelasis micrantha* J.J.Sm.)

Pbs. flattened, st.-like, sheathed by the lf.-bases. Lvs. linear, to 8″ long, obliquely lobed at the apex, rather soft-textured. Infls. very slender, the apical rac. many-fld., very dense, to about 12″ tall, usually shorter. Fls. less than ¼″ long, tubular, light brownish, the tips of the ss. and ps. whitish, scarcely opening at apex, complex in structure. Mostly summer. (H) Malay Peninsula; Sumatra; Java; Philippines.

Pachyphyllum Cardenasii Smith & Harris
[GRAY HERBARIUM]

PACHITES Ldl.

Two species of *Pachites* are known to date, both of them very rare, slender terrestrial orchids indigenous to Africa's Cape Colony, where they inhabit grassy fields in the south-western area. The genus is allied to *Satyrium* Sw., from which it differs in critical details of the rather small flowers. **Pachites Bodkini** Bolus is not present in our collections at this time, but the species described below has recently been introduced into cultivation.

Nothing is known of the genetic affinities of the genus *Pachites*.

CULTURE: As for *Disa*. (C, I)

P. appressa Ldl.

Tubers finger-like, several, the st. rather stout, erect, wiry, ¾–1½′ tall. Lvs. cauline, diminishing in size upwards and becoming bracteose there, rather numerous, erect, linear, glossy-green, acutish, 3–5″ long. Rac. oblong, rather densely many-fld., to 6″ long. Fls. more than ½″ across, inverted, lilac, the lip with 2 yellow stripes, the col. yellow, margined apically with red. Ss. suberect, elliptic-oblong, the margins incurved. Ps. elliptic-oblong, obtuse, marginally incurving. Lip erect, elliptic-lanceolate, with 2 horn-like processes near the base. Jan.–Feb. (C, I) South-west Cape Colony.

PACHYPHYLLUM Ldl.
(*Orchidotypus* Krzl.)

About twenty species of *Pachyphyllum* are known to date, all of them interesting dwarf epiphytes of the subtribe *Pachyphyllinae*, native in the wet 'cloud-forests' of

the mountainous areas of Colombia, Ecuador, Peru, and Bolivia. They are attractive little plants, with pseudomonopodial habit, their compressed, distichous-leaved stems being somewhat reminiscent of *Dichaea* Ldl. The rather numerous, racemose flowers are usually extremely small and white, but of great complexity when examined closely. Unfortunately, none of these charming orchids seems to be in cultivation at this time.

Nothing is known of the genetic affinities of *Pachyphyllum*.

CULTURE: As for *Ornithocephalus*. The plants must never be permitted to become dry at any time, and are highly intolerant of disturbance at the roots. (C)

PACHYPLECTRON Schltr.

But a single member of the genus *Pachyplectron* is known to date, this, **P. arifolium** Schltr., the only component of the subtribe *Pachyplectroninae*. An extremely rare and apparently handsome 'Jewel Orchid', with variegated foliage and small complex flowers in racemes, it is unknown in cultivation at this time.

Nothing is known of the genetic affinities of *Pachyplectron*.

CULTURE: Presumably as for *Anoectochilus*, etc. (H)

PACHYRHIZANTHE [Schltr.] Nakai
(*Cymbidium* Sw. § *Pachyrhizanthe* Schltr.)

This is a very peculiar genus of the subtribe *Cymbidiinae*, made up of the most part of segregated species from *Cymbidium* Sw., which differ from that group in their saprophytic, usually aphyllous vegetative habit, and in floral characters. Native to northern India,

China, and Japan, they are as yet incompletely known by botanists, and at this time are not present in our collections. They appear to be very rare in the wild.

Nothing is known regarding the genetic affinities of *Pachyrhizanthe*, although it is entirely possible that it will prove 'crossable' with at least certain members of some allied genera.

CULTURE: Possibly as for *Corallorrhiza* and other delicate saprophytes. (C, I)

PACHYSTELE Schltr.

This is a little-known and misunderstood genus of the subtribe *Ponerinae*, which is only dubiously a valid one. All of the species making it up are smallish but rather complex epiphytic plants formerly included in *Scaphyglottis* P. & E., from which they differ in structural details of the very small flowers. Unknown in our collections at this time, the five Pachysteles inhabit Central America, especially Costa Rica.

Nothing is known of the genetic affinities of this rare group.

CULTURE: Presumably as for *Scaphyglottis*. (I)

PACHYSTOMA Bl.

A member of the subtribe *Phaiinae*, *Pachystoma* consists of about eight species, all terrestrials in a region which extends from India and China throughout Malaysia and Indonesia to New Guinea, New Caledonia, and northern Australia. Unknown in contemporary collections, these unusual and often rather attractive orchids produce single, narrow leaves from a fleshy underground rhizome, and bear rather numerous, small flowers in tall inflorescences. Though not large, the blossoms are of attractive form and often brightly coloured.

Nothing is known of the genetic affinities of *Pachystoma*. It is presumably genetically compatible with at least certain of the allied groups.

CULTURE: Presumably as for the tropical species of *Phaius*. (H)

PALMORCHIS B.-R.
(*Jenmania* Rolfe, *Neobartlettia* Schltr., *Rolfea* Zahlbr.)

Forming with *Corymborchis* Thou. ex Bl. the small subtribe *Palmorchidinae*, this unusual genus consists of eight known species of peculiar terrestrial orchids, native from Panama to Brazil. Unknown in contemporary collections, they are botanically most interesting, but scarcely sufficiently showy to warrant attention by any orchidists save specialists. The plants consist of clusters of mostly tall (sometimes several feet in height), bamboo-like stems, large folded leaves, and mostly long-stalked inflorescences of rather small but complex blossoms which usually do not open fully. They appear to be very rare even in their native haunts, and are as yet incompletely known by science.

Nothing is known of the genetic ties of *Palmorchis*.

CULTURE: Presumably as for *Sobralia*, though some difficulty would probably be encountered in transplanting the specimens from the wild into collections. (H)

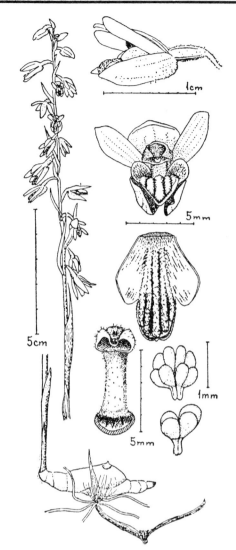

Pachystoma senile (Ldl.) Rchb.f. [*Orchids of Thailand*]

PALUMBINA Rchb.f.

A single excessively rare epiphytic species in Guatemala (reported, dubiously, from Mexico) comprises the genus *Palumbina*, which was formerly encountered in a few particularly choice collections, usually being grown as *Oncidium candidum* Ldl. It differs from *Oncidium* Sw. in the completely united lateral sepals, and in the mode of attachment of the lip to the column. A delightful, free-flowering plant, it should be better known by connoisseurs.

No hybrids have been made utilizing *Palumbina*, and nothing is known of its genetic affinities, though they presumably lie with other groups of the subtribe *Oncidiinae*.

CULTURE: As for the pseudobulbous Oncidiums from moderate elevations. (I)

P. candida (Ldl.) Rchb.f. (*Oncidium candidum* Ldl.)
Pbs. narrowly ellipsoidal, compressed, to 2″ long, with a pair of basal brownish bracts. Lf. solitary, linear-

elliptic to linear-lanceolate, acute to acuminate, strongly folded at base, rather fleshy, to 12″ long. Infls. appearing with the new growths in a sheath-axil, dark purple, slender, mostly erect, to 1½′ tall, few-fld. Fls. rather waxy, slightly more than 1½″ long, fragrant, long-lived, pure white except for several small violet dots usually at the bases of the ps., and a yellow callus on the disc of the lip. Spring. (I) Guatemala; ? Mexico.

PANISEA Ldl.
(*Sigmatogyne* Pfitz.)

Four species of *Panisea* are known to date, all rather rare epiphytic orchids from the Himalayas of India and adjacent areas. A member of the subtribe *Coelogyninae*, the genus is rather close in its relationship to *Coelogyne* Ldl., but differs from it in technical details of the lip and column. Two of the Paniseas are present in our collections today, but both of them must be classed as rare orchids.

No hybrids have been made in this genus as yet, and nothing is known concerning its genetic affinities.

CULTURE: As for the high-elevation, cool-growing Coelogynes. (C, I)

Panisea uniflora Ldl. [A.D.HAWKES, AFTER *Orchids of Thailand*]

P. tricallosa Rolfe (*Sigmatogyne tricallosa* Pfitz.)
Pbs. ovoid, clustered, about ½″ tall. Lf. solitary, short-stalked, linear-lanceolate, to 2″ long. Infls. basal, 1–2-fld., to about 1½″ long. Fls. not opening fully, less than ½″ long, brownish-white, the lip with 3 dull brown calli on the disc, with a prominent S-shaped claw. Spring. (C, I) Himalayas, mostly in Assam; Thailand.

P. uniflora Ldl. (*Coelogyne falcata* Anders., *C. Thuniana* Rchb.f.)
Rather similar in all parts to *P. tricallosa* Rolfe, but with paired, smaller lvs., and somewhat larger fls. (to ¾″ long) which have a distinctly 3-lbd. lip. Spring. (C, I) Himalayas; Burma; Thailand; Laos.

PAPHINIA Ldl.

Paphinia, a rare and seldom-encountered genus of the subtribe *Gongorinae*, contains four species, three of which are occasionally found in particularly choice collections of orchids today. Epiphytic plants of small vegetative stature, they produce proportionately very large and highly spectacular blossoms of great lasting qualities when the specimens are in good cultural condition. The genus is restricted to northern South America, and is recorded to date from Colombia, Venezuela, the Guianas, and northern Brazil. It is somewhat allied to *Lycaste* Ldl., but differs in structural details (and, indeed, in superficial appearance) of the flowers; it may eventually be removed to the subtribe *Lycastinae*.

No hybrids have as yet been made utilizing *Paphinia*, although it is presumably genetically compatible with at least certain of the allied groups, and also possibly with some members of the nearby subtribe *Lycastinae*.

CULTURE: As for the warm-growing Lycastes. Small, perfectly-drained pots should be used for best results. (I, H)

P. cristata (Ldl.) Ldl. (*Maxillaria cristata* Ldl.)
Pbs. clustered, ovoid-oblong to oblong, somewhat compressed, 1–1½″ tall. Lvs. 2–3, lanceolate, acute, rather fleshy, plicate, to 6″ long and about 2″ wide. Infls. pendulous, 1–3-fld., with large, brownish, membranous bracts. Fls. 3–4″ in diam., the spreading ss. and ps. similar, broadly lanceolate, subacuminate, the basal half pale yellow or whitish streaked transversely with chocolate-brown, the apical half usually totally brown, but sometimes with pale yellow longitudinal streaks. Lip shorter than the ss. and ps., clawed, the lamina distinctly 2-parted, dark chocolate-purple; basal hypochil transversely oblong with the front angles acute; epichil subrhomboidal with a tuft of white hairs at the apex; crest an oblong raised plate, 2-toothed at the top, below which are four prominent tubercles. Col. semiterete, with a tooth-like auricle on each side of the stigma, yellowish-green banded with chocolate towards the base, the rostellum beaked. Autumn–early winter. (I, H) Colombia; Venezuela; Trinidad; Guianas.

P. grandiflora B.-R. (*Paphinia grandis* Rchb.f., *P. nutans* Houll.)
Pbs. broadly ovoid or almost roundish, usually somewhat angled, 1–2″ tall, about 1″ in diam. Lvs. 2,

lanceolate-elliptic, acute, to 10″ long, rather heavy, plicate. Infls. pendulous, abbreviated, usually less than 3″ long, 1–3-fld. Fls. to about 5½″ in diam., thin-textured, the ss. and ps. spreading, with the basal half yellowish-white with numerous irregular transverse chocolate-purple bands, the apical half wholly chocolate-purple sometimes with a narrow yellowish-white margin, the lat. ss. sub-falcate, the ps. rather narrowed basally. Lip clawed, distinctly 2-parted, the claw blackish-purple; basal hypochil obovate-oblong, yellowish-white with 2 incurved, linear, light brown auricles; epichil with a narrow claw having 2 dark purple falcate teeth at the base of the roundish fleshy lamina, this covered with whitish shaggy hairs. Col. greenish, spotted with purple. Autumn–early winter. (H) Brazil.

P. rugosa Rchb.f.

Pbs. smooth, ovoid or almost conical, elongated, 1–1½″ long. Lvs. 2, linear-lanceolate, acuminate, rather leathery, plicate, 4–6″ long. Infls. short, pendulous, 2–3-fld. Fls. 2–3″ in diam., the lanceolate, acuminate ss. and ps. light yellow, dotted with red. Lip clawed, the basal hypochil crescent-shaped with 2 subfalcate, erect auricles, red-purple; epichil also red-purple, sub-rhomboidal, re-flexed, with 2 broad auricles and a dense tuft of white bristles at the apex. Col. clavate, curved, greenish-yellow, with a narrow rounded wing on each side of the stigma. Autumn. (I) Colombia.

PAPHIOPEDILUM Pfitz.
(*Cordula* Raf., *Menephora* Raf., *Stimegas* Raf.)

Upwards of fifty species of *Paphiopedilum* are known to date, these often very handsome and horticulturally very popular terrestrial, lithophytic, or rather rarely epiphytic orchids. The genus is widespread over a huge region extending from China and the Himalayas through-out South-east Asia and Indonesia to New Guinea. It is a member of the subtribe *Cypripedilinae*, and is typically erroneously called *Cypripedium* in horticulture, although the members of that group are totally distinct from the present ones. The plants consist of more or less well-developed tufts of often leathery, frequently mottled, attractive foliage. The mostly large and spectacular flowers, commonly called 'Lady's-Slippers' (as are members of the allied genera *Cypripedium*, *Phragmi-pedium*, and *Selenipedium*), are produced singly or in few-flowered racemes on short to elongate inflorescences, all parts of which are often conspicuously hairy. Floral dimensions and formation vary tremendously within the genus, as does colour, although the predominating hues are green, brown, yellow, and white. In a few species, the petals are extraordinarily elongated (e.g., *P. philippinense* (Rchb.f.) Pfitz., *P. Sanderianum* (Rchb.f.) Pfitz.), much as in certain of the South American Phragmipediums.

Literally thousands of hybrids are known in the genus *Paphiopedilum*, these almost universally known under the totally incorrect and very confusing name of *Cypripedium*. Two bigeneric crosses have been registered, under the confused name of *Selenocypripedium*, though they are actually hybrids between *Paphiopedilum* and *Phragmipedium*, and should be known under the name of *Phragmipaphiopedilum*. No additional experimental breeding among the component genera of the subtribe

Cypripedilinae appears to have been done, although some most interesting potentials seem evident in this respect.

CULTURE: A tremendous amount of material has been published concerning the cultural treatment of the Paphiopedilums. Most generally grown in well-drained pots, they are potted in a wide variety of media, although perhaps the most popular in contemporary collections is a mixture of about equal parts of chopped osmunda and chopped sphagnum moss, often with the addition of a small amount of fibrous loam and/or gritty white sand. Many experts advocate the addition of a top-dressing on the compost of fresh, green, actively-growing sphagnum moss. Because these orchids have no thickened storage-structures, such as pseudobulbs, they must be kept con-tinually damp, although the compost should never be permitted to become sodden, or the health of the plant will rapidly and markedly suffer. Paphiopedilums, under most climatic conditions, do better in a greenhouse than out-of-doors, so that the high humidity in which they delight can be maintained. Generally, they require semi-shaded exposure, although excessive shade will reduce the production of the handsome flowers. Weakened fertilizing solutions may be applied with advantage at frequent intervals. Temperature require-ments vary, although the vast majority of the culti-vated species and hybrids do best under relatively cool conditions. (C, I, H)

P. amabile Hall.f.

Similar to *P. Hookerae* (Rchb.f.) Pfitz. in habit, and closely allied to that sp. Lvs. to 6″ long and 1½″ wide, dark green, somewhat irregularly spotted with paler green. Scapes to 12″ tall, with a solitary handsome fl. at the apex. Fls. greatly resembling those of *P. Bullenianum* (Rchb.f.) Pfitz., but the staminode of different shape. Ss. green. Ps. with yellow-green bases and brownish tips, with a few dark brown warts on the margins. Lip greenish at the base of the pouch, brownish-red with darker spots towards the front. Spring–early summer. (H) Borneo.

P. Appletonianum (Gower) Rolfe (*Cypripedium Apple-tonianum* Gower, *Cypripedium Wolterianum* Krzl.)

Lvs. ligulate, obtuse, faintly spotted, to 6″ long and 1½″ wide. Scape 1-fld., to 1½′ tall, erect. Fls. about 4″ in diam. Ss. rather small, yellow-green, striped basally with brownish, ovate, shortly acuminate. Ps. spreading, greenish at the base, rose-red towards the tips, broadly linear, enlarged towards the tips. Lip greenish-brown. Spring. (I, H) Himalayas; Assam; Thailand.

P. Argus (Rchb.f.) Pfitz. (*Cypripedium Argus* Rchb.f., *Cypripedium barbatum* Ldl. var. *Argus* Vos., *Cypri-pedium Pitcherianum* Manda, *Cordula Argus* Rolfe)

Lvs. ligulate, to 7″ long and 1½″ wide, the upper side chequered with light spots. Scape 1-fld., to 15″ tall. Fls. about 4″ in diam. Dors. sep. white except for the darker base, with green and brown longitudinal nerves of un-equal lengths, very broadly ovate, acute. Ps. sharply turned downwards, the base pale, red near the apices and furnished with many black-purple warts, ligulate, acutish. Lip rather broad, dark brown-purple, the lower side paler, veined with light green. Spring–early summer. (I, H) Philippines: Luzon, Negros.

Oncidium Leiboldii Rchb.f. [H. F. LOOMIS]

(RIGHT) *Oncidium varicosum* Ldl.
[G. C. K. DUNSTERVILLE]

(RIGHT) *Ophrys sphegodes* Miller [GEORGE FULLER]

Ophrys apifera Huds. (Albino form on left) [GEORGE
FULLER]

Orchis maculata [L. GEORGE FULLER]

Orchis tridentata Scop. var. lactea Poir. [GEORGE FULLER]

Paphiopedilum insigne (Wall.) Pfitz. [GEORGE FULLER]

Paphinia cristata (Ldl.) Ldl. [H. R. FOLKERSMA]

P. barbatum (Ldl.) Pfitz. (*Cypripedium barbatum* Ldl., *Cordula barbata* Rolfe)

Lvs. shortly ligulate, obtuse, to 6″ long and slightly more than 1″ wide, with rather dark green chequerings. Scape 1-fld., to 10″ tall. Fls. about 4″ across, sometimes smaller. Dors. sep. almost circular, whitish or pale green towards the base, with dark brown-red longitudinal nerves, shortly acuminate at tip. Ps. sharply turned downwards, purple towards the greenish base, with scattered almost black warts, narrowly ligulate, obtuse. Lip purple-brown, about as long as the synsepal, the inflexed lat. lbs. with small purplish warts and spots. Spring–autumn. (I, H) Thailand; Malay Peninsula.

P. bellatulum (Rchb.f.) Pfitz. (*Cypripedium bellatulum* Rchb.f.)

Lvs. narrowly elliptic, sometimes almost ligulate, obtuse, the upper side dark green with lighter spots, the underside dark purple or magenta-purple, to 6″ long, about 1½–2″ wide. Scape very abbreviated, the solitary fl. often touching the foliage. Fls. to 2½″ in diam., white, with numerous (or rather few) dark purple spots. Ss. almost circular. Ps. elliptic, obtuse, large, almost surrounding the lip. Lip rather short, ovoid. Spring. (I, H) Burma; Thailand.

P. Bullenianum (Rchb.f.) Pfitz. (*Cypripedium Bullenianum* Rchb.f.)

Lvs. rather pale blue-green, faintly chequered, usually 5 in number, ligulate, obtuse, to almost 7″ long and 1¼″ wide. Scape 1-fld., to 12″ tall. Fls. 3–3½″ in diam., rather similar to those of *P. Appletonianum* (Gower) Rolfe. Dors. sep. rather small, pale green with a darker median stripe, ovate, acute. Ps. spreading horizontally, with the widened apices somewhat drooping, greenish with purple-brown hairless warts near the basal edge, flushed with purplish or rose-purple in the middle. Lip with a short pouch, dark purplish-red, the inflexed lat. lbs. with large warts. Summer. (H) Borneo; Malay Peninsula.

P. callosum (Rchb.f.) Pfitz. (*Cypripedium callosum* Rchb.f.)

Lvs. few (usually only 4–5), to 10″ long, to almost 2″ wide, rather rigid, the upper side light bluish-green with darker mottling. Scape 1-fld., to 15″ tall. Fls. about 4″ in diam., very showy and long-lived, somewhat variable in colour. Dors. sep. almost circular, white, with 11–13 longitudinal, purple streaks. Ps. acutely deflected downwards, greenish at the base, becoming suffused with purplish near the apex, ligulate, acute. Lip brown-purple, rather large. Mostly spring–summer. (I, H) Thailand; Cambodia.

P. Chamberlainianum (O'Brien) Pfitz. (*Cypripedium Chamberlainianum* O'Brien)

Lvs. ligulate, obtuse, green, to 12″ long and 2″ wide, leathery. Scape to 1½′ tall, 4–8-fld., the fls. produced successively over a rather long period of time. Fls. handsome, about 4″ across. Dors. sep. almost circular, greenish, brownish at base and in the middle. Ps. very spreading, greenish-rose, with many small brown spots, ligulate, undulate marginally, somewhat twisted. Lip light green, occasionally suffused with light brownish, with many red spots. Throughout the year, sometimes more than once annually. (H) Sumatra.

P. Charlesworthii (Rolfe) Pfitz. (*Cypripedium Charlesworthii* Rolfe)

Lvs. broadly linear, green, to 8″ long and about 1″ wide. Scape 1-fld., about 6″ tall. Fls. about 2½″ in diam., very beautiful and long-lasting, waxy in texture. Dors. sep. large, circular, rose-red, often with darker veins radiating from the base. Ps. horizontally spreading, greenish-brown with darker green veins, broadly ligulate, obtuse. Lip coloured like the ps. Staminode white. Autumn. (I) India: Bengal; Burma: Arrakan Mountains.

P. ciliolare (Rchb.f.) Stein (*Cypripedium ciliolare* Rchb.f., *Cordula ciliolaris* Rolfe)

Lvs. usually 4, broadly ligulate, obtuse, the upper side lightly tessellated with paler green, to about 6″ long and 2″ wide. Scape 1-fld., to about 10″ tall. Fls. to 3″ in diam. Dors. sep. very broad, white, striped with green, brownish at the base, ovate, acute. Ps. pendulous, reddish, with many small, round, black-purple spots, broadly ligulate. Lip greenish-brown. Spring–early summer. (I, H) Philippines: Luzon, Dinagat, Mindanao.

P. concolor (Par. & Batem.) Pfitz. (*Cypripedium concolor* Par. & Batem., *Cypripedium tonkinense* Godefr.)

Lvs. usually 4 in number, broadly ligulate, dark green with greyish-green markings, to 6″ long and about 2″ wide, rounded at the tips. Scape 1-fld., to 4″ tall. Fls. to about 3″ in diam., variable, pale yellow with more or less numerous purple spots or dots. Dors. sep. almost circular. Ps. oblong, rounded apically. Lip narrowly egg-shaped. Spring. (I) Thailand; Burma; Cambodia; Laos; Viet-Nam.

P. Curtisii (Rchb.f.) Pfitz. (*Cypripedium Curtisii* Rchb.f.)

Lvs. usually few (4 or more), elliptic, to about 8″ long and 3″ wide, the upper surface indistinctly marbled with darker green. Scape 1-fld., to about 8″ tall. Fls. about 4½″ across. Dors. sep. short, green, edged with white and with some purple longitudinal streaks, broadly ovate, acute. Ps. greenish-rose at the base, becoming paler towards the apex, with many small, dark purple spots. Lip greenish-maroon. Spring–summer. (H) Sumatra.

P. Fairrieanum (Ldl.) Pfitz. (*Cypripedium Fairrieanum* Ldl.)

Lvs. linear, obtuse, light green, to 6″ long and 1″ wide. Scape 1-fld., rather slender, to 10″ tall. Fls. about 2½″ across, very ornate and handsome. Dors. sep. large, white, streaked and intricately netted with violet, broadly elliptic, wavy-margined. Ps. falcate, usually curving outwards at the tips, wavy-margined, whitish with violet stripes. Lip greenish-violet, with purple veins. Summer–early autumn. (C, I) Himalayas; Bhutan; Assam.

P. glaucophyllum J.J.Sm.

Lvs. broadly ligulate, obtuse, bluish-green, to 10″ long and 1½″ wide. Scape to 1½′ tall, bearing several fls. successively over a period of two months or more. Fls. 3″ or more across, rather similar to those of *P. Chamberlainianum* (O'Brien) Pfitz. Dors. sep. almost circular, light green basally, shading to darker green near the tip, with about 12 brown longitudinal stripes, sometimes mottled with light brown. Synsepal mostly green with some brownish marks and blotches. Ps. horizontally spreading, twisted, very pale green or yellowish-green, with scattered dark purple or purple-brown spots and blotches, marginally furnished with long hairs. Lip with a large pouch, pale green at base, becoming mauve or wine-rose above. Mostly spring. (H) Java.

P. Godefroyae (Godefr.) Pfitz. (*Cypripedium Godefroyae* Godefr.)

Lvs. usually 4 in number, linear-oblong, obtuse, the upper surface mottled with whitish-green on a dark green ground, the under side usually purplish, to 6″ long and 1¼″ wide. Scape 1-fld., very short. Fls. much like those of *P. bellatulum* (Rchb.f.) Pfitz., about 2½″ in diam., not opening fully in most cases, creamy-white, spotted and dotted with purple or reddish-purple, the dors. sep. not as wide as in the other sp., the ps. smaller, the lip about as long as the ps., and the teeth at the apex of the staminode larger. Spring–early summer. (I, H) Burma; Thailand; Viet-Nam.

P. Haynaldianum (Rchb.f.) Pfitz. (*Cypripedium Haynaldianum* Rchb.f.)

Lvs. ligulate, rather obtuse at apex, to 10″ long and 1¼″ wide, dull green. Scape 2–6-fld., to 1½′ tall. Fls. to 6″ across, waxy and very handsome, long-lasting. Ss. greenish at base, becoming rose-red towards the tip, with large brown apical spots. Ps. spreading, longer than the ss. Lip rather pinched-in apically, sometimes faintly suffused with brown, otherwise greenish. Mostly spring. (I, H) Philippines: Luzon.

P. hirsutissimum (Ldl.) Pfitz. (*Cypripedium hirsutissimum* Ldl.)

Lvs. linear-oblong, acute, entirely green, to 12″ long and more, to about 1¼″ wide. Scape 1-fld., to about 12″ tall, covered with dark purple hairs, as are the bract, pedicellate ovary, and back of the fl. Fls. about 4″ in diam., with all the segms. ciliated. Dors. sep. broadly cordate, the central and basal parts densely spotted with blackish-purple, the spots often somewhat confluent, the broad marginal area darker or paler green. Synsepal pale green, marked along the veins with purplish. Ps. spreading horizontally, broadly spatulate, slightly twisted, the margins crisped and undulated along basal half, this part green, blotched and spotted with dark purple and studded with many blackish hairs, the dilated apical part bright violet-purple. Lip large, helmet-shaped, dull green, stained with brownish-purple and dotted with tiny blackish warts. Spring. (I, H) Himalayas; Assam; Khasia Hills.

P. Hookerae (Rchb.f.) Pfitz. (*Cypripedium Hookerae* Rchb.f., *Cypripedium barbatum* Ldl. var. *Hookerae* Regel)

Lvs. usually about 4 in number, ligulate, obtuse, the upper side with very noticeable lighter marbling, to 6″ long, to 1½″ wide. Scape slender, 1-fld., 8–12″ tall. Fls. rather resembling those of *P. Appletonianum* (Gower) Rolfe, to about 4″ in diam. Dors. sep. yellowish-white with a green flush towards base and centre, the lattice-like, often connecting radiating nerves usually purplish, cordate-ovate, acute. Ps. inclined downwards, spatulate,

basally undulate, green with blackish spots and a purple margin, the dilated apical part purple. Lip helmet-shaped, brownish-purple, flushed with green, the infolded lbs. yellowish-brown, spotted with red-purple. Staminode large for the size of the fl., brown-purple with a pale yellow-green centre and margin. Spring–early summer. (H) Borneo.

P. insigne (Wall.) Pfitz. (*Cypripedium insigne* Wall.)

Lvs. 5–6 in number, broadly linear or linear-ligulate, acute, 8–12″ long and to 1″ broad, of a uniform usually pale green. Scape 1-fld. (very rarely 2-fld.), to about 12″ tall. Fls. 4–5″ in diam., highly variable in colour, of a varnished appearance. Dors. sep. broadly oval, with the lat. margins slightly revolute and the apical margin bent forwards, the median and basal area apple-green with numerous brownish-purple spots arranged with more or less regularity along the longitudinal green veins, the apical area white. Synsepal smaller, pale green. Ps. spreading, linear-oblong, with undulate margins, pale yellowish-green with brownish-purple longitudinal veins. Lip helmet-shaped, yellowish-green, shaded with brown, the infolded lbs. dark tawny-yellow with paler margins. Staminode squarish, fuzzy, with an orange-yellow tubercle in the centre. There are several dozens of named horticultural variants, these based primarily on divergences in floral coloration. Autumn–spring. (C, I) Himalayas.

P. javanicum (Reinw.) Pfitz. (*Cypripedium javanicum* Reinw.)

Lvs. usually 6–8 in number, elliptic-oblong, 6–8″ long and to 2″ broad, greyish-green above, somewhat sparingly mottled with dark green. Scape mottled pale green and crimson, 1-fld. (rarely 2-fld.), to 12″ tall. Fls. 3–4″ in diam., rather variable in colour, all segms. except the lip ciliolate. Dors. sep. pale green with dark green veins, whitish towards the tip, cordate, acuminate. Ps. broadly ligulate, slightly deflexed, pale green, dotted with tiny blackish warts to two-thirds of their length, the apical third pale dull purple and without warts. Lip sub-cylindric, brownish-green, pale green beneath, the infolded lbs. almost meeting at their edges, pale green, more or less spotted with purple. Summer–autumn. (H) Java; Borneo.

P. Lawrenceanum (Rchb.f.) Pfitz. (*Cypripedium Lawrenceanum* Rchb.f.)

Lvs. usually about 4 in number, oval-oblong, 6–9″ long and to 2½″ broad, tessellated with yellowish-green and dark grass-green. Scape 1–2-fld., 15–18″ tall. Fls. to 5″ in diam., very handsome. Dors. sep. large, almost round, folded at middle, white with broad alternately longer and shorter veins, the median ones usually green at base, the others deep wine-purple. Ps. straight, green with purplish tips, with 5–10 blackish warts on each margin, ligulate, ciliolate. Lip pouch-like, very inflated, dull purple, tinged with brown above, green beneath. Spring–summer. (H) North Borneo.

P. Lowii (Ldl.) Pfitz. (*Cypripedium Lowii* Ldl., *Cypripedium cruciforme* Zoll. & Mir.)

Lvs. ligulate, acutish, 9–15″ long, mucronate or obscurely 2-lbd. at apex, leathery, grass-green. Scape 3–5-fld. (rarely more), 25–40″ tall, usually nodding under the weight of the fls. Fls. with all segms. ciliolate, 3–4″ across, long-lasting. Dors. sep. broadly oval, acute, bent forwards at apex, the sides revolute at base, fuzzy and keeled behind, yellowish-green aging to pale yellow, the basal part veined with brownish-purple. Synsepal similar but smaller, yellowish with green veins. Ps. to 3″ long, spatulate, twisted, deflexed, the narrower basal part yellow with black, circular, scattered spots, some of which are ocellated, the dilated apical part light violet-purple. Lip cylindric-galeate, brown, paler beneath, the narrow infolded lbs. yellowish, the sinus between the sac and infolded lbs. 3-toothed. Staminode bordered with purple hairs. Spring–summer. (H) Sarawak, usually as an epiphyte in tall trees.

P. Mastersianum (Rchb.f.) Pfitz. (*Cypripedium Mastersianum* Rchb.f.)

Lvs. oblong or oval-oblong, acute, 8–10″ long, dark green with pale green tessellation on upper side. Scape dark purple, very hairy, 1-fld., 12–15″ tall. Fls. about 3″ in diam. or more. Dors. sep. almost round, ciliolate marginally, bright green with a broad yellow-white border, and dark green veins. Synsepal much smaller, pale green. Ps. spreading horizontally, spatulate, with ciliolate margins, brownish-red, paler towards the base, where there are numerous small black-purple warts along the upper margin and along the mid-vein. Lip sub-cylindric, very inflated, pale reddish-brown, the infolded lbs. greenish-brown, spotted with dull purple. Spring–summer. (H) Moluccas: Amboina.

P. niveum (Rchb.f.) Pfitz. (*Cypripedium niveum* Rchb.f.)

Lvs. 4–6 in number, oblong, dark dull green above, with greyish-green spots, dark lurid purple beneath, 4–6″ long. Scape erect, 1–2-fld., 6–8″ tall. Fls. to 3″ across, white, more or less dotted with purple towards the base of the dors. sep. and ps. Ss. and ps. ciliolate, the dors. sep. rounded, concave in front, stained with reddish-purple behind. Ps. spreading, slightly deflexed, broadly oblong, obtuse, sometimes almost round. Lip ovoid, with a contracted mouth. Staminode yellow with white margins. Spring–autumn. (H) Langkawi Islands; Peninsular Thailand; Tambilan Islands; Borneo.

P. Parishii (Rchb.f.) Pfitz. (*Cypripedium Parishii* Rchb.f.)

Lvs. oblong-ligulate, 2-lbd. or bifid at apex, leathery, very smooth, bright glossy-green, 9–15″ long and 1½–2½″ broad. Scape suberect, stout, pale green, downy, 4–7-fld., to 2′ tall. Fls. slightly more than 3″ in diam. Dors. sep. pale yellow with green veins, elliptic-oblong, keeled at back, acute, the upper half bent forwards, the lat. margins revolute at base. Ps. 4–5″ long, linear, twisted, first spreading then becoming sharply pendulous, the basal half with undulate margins, green with a few scattered blackish spots, the apical half blackish-purple with a pale margin. Lip slipper-shaped, the infolded lbs. narrow and smooth, dark green, often stained with brown-purple. Staminode pale yellow, mottled with green. Spring–autumn. (I, H) Burma and Thailand, usually epiphytic.

P. philippinense (Rchb.f.) Pfitz. (*Cypripedium philippinense* Rchb.f., *Cypripedium laevigatum* Batem., *Cypripedium Roebelenii* Rchb.f.)

Lvs. ligulate-oblong, obtuse or unequally 2-lbd. at apex, folded at base, 7–12″ long and about 1½″ broad, leathery, with a varnished glossy surface. Scape 3–5-fld. (rarely more), to 2′ tall. Fls. to almost 9″ long. Dors. sep. broadly ovate, acutish, whitish, symmetrically striped with brown-purple. Synsepal similar, white, veined with green. Ps. pendulous, 5–6″ long, ribbon-like, fringed with short hairs, twisted, yellowish at the base where there are some small hairy warts on both margins, and becoming dull reddish-purple along the greater part of their length, apically pale green. Lip helmet-shaped, buff-yellow faintly streaked with brown, the infolded lbs. narrow. Staminode fringed with blackish hairs on each side. Summer–autumn. (H) Philippines: Guimares, Mindanao, Palawan.

P. praestans (Rchb.f.) Pfitz. (*Cypripedium praestans* Rchb.f.)

Lvs. ligulate, obtuse, to 12″ long and 1¼″ broad, rather dull green. Scape to about 1½′ tall, 2–4-fld. Fls. to 4″ in diam. Dors. sep. elliptic, acute, whitish, streaked with red-purple. Ps. linear, twisted, to about 4¾″ long, yellow-green with red-brown veins and with 8–10 blackish warts on the margins near the base. Lip yellow, suffused with red. Spring–autumn. (H) New Guinea.

P. Rothschildianum (Rchb.f.) Pfitz. (*Cypripedium Rothschildianum* Rchb.f., *Cypripedium neo-guineense* Lind.*)

Lvs. ligulate, leathery, glossy green, usually ascending, to 2′ long and 2½–3″ broad. Scape reddish, shortly hairy, to 2½′ tall, 2–5-fld., the fls. rather distant, the ciliate-margined bracts pale yellowish-green with blackish lines. Fls. to 5″ across, very handsome and long-lived. Dors. sep. yellowish with numerous longitudinal dark purple-black stripes, white at the margins, cuneate-oblong, acute. Synsepal similar but smaller. Ps. yellowish-green or pale green, longitudinally striped and somewhat spotted with dark blackish-purple, linear, undulate marginally, horizontal to slightly down-curving, the tips usually upcurving. Lip projecting, slipper-shaped, cinnamon-coloured or purplish-brown, with an ochre margin around the orifice, often yellowish at the apex. Mostly July–Sept. (H) Sumatra; Borneo; ? New Guinea.

P. Spicerianum (Rchb.f.) Pfitz. (*Cypripedium Spicerianum* Rchb.f.)

Lvs. linear-oblong, obtuse, more or less wavy-margined, dark green above, usually spotted with purple underneath towards the base, 6–9″ long, to 1¼″ broad. Scape rather slender, erect, 1–2-fld., 9–12″ tall, the subtending bract whitish, spotted with brownish-purple. Fls. to about 3″ in diam., glossy, lasting well. Dors. sep. broadly obcordate, folded at the middle, with the lat. margins much reflexed basally, the apical margin bent forwards, white except at the fold where there is a crimson-purple band, and at the base where there is a large green, dull-red-speckled blotch. Synsepal greenish-white. Ps. ligulate, deflexed and curved forwards, undulate marginally, yellowish-green, spotted with dull red and with a reddish-crimson median line. Lip rather bell-shaped, with rounded auricles, brown, flushed with crimson. Staminode purplish-crimson, margined with white. Autumn–winter. (C, I) Assam.

Paphiopedilum Stonei (Hk.f.) Pfitz. [VEITCH]

P. Stonei (Hk.f.) Pfitz. (*Cypripedium Stonei* Hk.f.)
Lvs. strap-shaped, obtuse, very leathery, almost fleshy, grass-green, to 15″ long and 1½″ broad. Scape 3–5-fld., to 2′ tall, dull greenish-purple, mostly pubescent below the rachis. Fls. to about 8″ long, often smaller. Dors. sep. cordate, acuminate, white, usually with 2–3 or more blackish-crimson longitudinal streaks, keeled behind. Synsepal similar to dors. and almost equal in size. Ps. linear, 5–6″ long, pendulous, twisted, basally with a few black hairs on each margin, pale tawny-yellow for basal two-thirds of their length, spotted with brownish-crimson, the apical one-third entirely brownish-crimson. Lip projecting, slipper-shaped, dull rose-colour, veined and reticulated with crimson, whitish beneath, the infolded lbs. narrow, whitish. Staminode yellowish-white, mostly fringed with bristle-like hairs. Summer–autumn. (H) North Borneo; Sarawak.

P. tonsum (Rchb.f.) Pfitz. (*Cypripedium tonsum* Rchb.f.)
Lvs. oval-oblong, acutish, tessellated with dark and pale green above, often purple-spotted beneath towards the base, 5–7″ long, to about 1¼″ broad. Scape erect, 1-fld., dull greenish-purple, 12–15″ tall. Fls. polished in appearance, about 4″ in diam. Dors. sep. white, symmetrically veined with green, the alternate shorter veins sometimes purplish, broadly cordate, acute, folded at mid-vein, minutely ciliolate on margins. Ps. spreading, rather broad, sub-spatulate, pale green with darker green veins but sometimes stained with dull purple, with 3–5 blackish warts along the mid-vein, and a few smaller ones along upper margin, both margins almost hairless, except for a few black hairs near apex. Lip large, helmet-shaped, dull green, tinged with brown and crimson, the infolded lbs. broad and warty, almost meeting at their edges. Staminode pale green. Spring–early summer. (H) Sumatra.

P. venustum (Wall.) Pfitz. (*Cypripedium venustum* Wall.)
Lvs. elliptic-oblong to ligulate, acutish, 4–6″ long, to 1½″ broad, dark green, above marbled and blotched with pale greyish-green, beneath rather velvety, heavily mottled with dull purple. Scape erect, 1- (rarely 2-) fld., 6–9″ tall. Fls. to 3″ in diam. Dors. sep. white, veined with dark green, broadly cordate, acute. Ps. spreading, sub-spatulate, marginally ciliate, the basal part green with some blackish warts borne chiefly near the margins and on the mid-vein, the apical part dull purple, flushed with brown. Lip sub-cylindric, pale yellow-green, tinged with rose, veined and reticulated with green, the infolded lbs. tawny-yellow, almost meeting at their edges. Winter–spring. (C, I) Himalayas.

P. villosum (Ldl.) Pfitz. (*Cypripedium villosum* Ldl.)
Lvs. linear-ligulate, acutish, 10–18″ long, to 1½″ broad, grass-green above, paler beneath and spotted with purple towards base. Scape very hairy, 1-fld., to 12″ tall. Fls. varnished in appearance, 5–6″ in diam., variable in colour. Dors. sep. ciliolate, broadly oval, slightly hooded at apex, the margins revolute towards base, with a hairy keel on back, brown-purple basally and centrally, the remainder green, with a narrow white marginal band. Synsepal similar but smaller, pale yellow-green. Ps. ciliolate, spatulate, with some purple hairs at the base, undulate, bent forward, with a broad brown-purple mid-vein, the upper half yellow-brown, the lower half paler. Lip large, slipper-shaped, brownish-yellow with a tawny-yellow margin at the orifice, the infolded lbs. broad, tawny-yellow. Staminode tawny-yellow. Autumn–spring. (C, I) Assam; Burma; Thailand.

P. Dayanum (Rchb.f.) Pfitz. (*Cypripedium Dayanum* Rchb.f.)
Lvs. usually 4–5 in number, ligulate, acutish, 5–7″ long, variable in colour, sometimes pale green with some oblong spots of dark green scattered on upper surface, sometimes tessellated with dark and light green. Scape 1-fld., to more than 12″ tall. Fls. 4–5″ in diam., the dors. sep. white, symmetrically veined with green. Ps. slightly deflexed, fringed with long black hairs, basal half brownish-green, apical half dull rose-purple. Lip subconical and compressed at apex, brownish-purple veined with green, the infolded lbs. densely spotted with small purplish warts. Spring. (H) North-east Borneo.

P. Druryi (Beddome) Pfitz. (*Cypripedium Druryi* Beddome)
Rhiz. stout, creeping. Lvs. ligulate, acute, to 10″ long, bright green. Scape 1-fld., to 12″ tall. Fls. about 3″ in diam. Dors. sep. broadly oval, inflexed above, greenish-yellow with

broad blackish median band, with numerous black hairs on reverse surface. Synsepal similar but smaller and paler, often with 2 median black stripes. Ps. ligulate, incurving, undulate, ochre-yellow to almost golden-yellow, with a broad blackish median line and some blackish warts towards the base, furnished with many black hairs below median line inside. Lip helmet-shaped, bright yellow, spotted with red-purple on inside, the infolded lbs. not meeting at their edges. Spring. (I, H) South India: Travancore.

P. exul (O'Brien) Pfitz. (*Cypripedium exul* O'Brien) Lvs. broadly linear, obtuse, to 8″ long and ¾″ broad, green. Scape 1-fld., to about 5″ tall. Fls. resembling those of *P. insigne* (Wall.) Pfitz., but smaller, only about 3″ in diam. at most. Dors. sep. greenish, edged with white, more or less spotted with brown. Ps. yellow, with purple lines in the middle part. Lip bright yellow. Mostly June–July. (I, H) Peninsular Thailand.

P. nigritum (Rchb.f.) Pfitz. (*Cypripedium nigritum* Rchb.f.) Lvs. oblong, acutish, dark green with lighter marbling above, to 6″ long and 1¼″ broad. Scape about 8″ tall, 1-fld. Fls. to 2½″ in diam. Dors. sep. oblong, acute, red at base, becoming white at apex, densely brown-streaked. Ps. greenish at base, becoming brown-red towards the apex, with darker warts, acutely spreading. Lip brown-purple. Spring–summer. (H) Borneo.

P. purpuratum (Ldl.) Pfitz. (*Cypripedium purpuratum* Ldl., *Cypripedium sinicum* Hance) Lvs. usually about 4 in number, elliptic-oblong, obtuse, 3–5″ long, tessellated above with dark and pale green, the latter shade usually predominating. Scape 1-fld., 5–7″ tall. Fls. about 3–3½″ in diam. Dors. sep. roundish, cuspidate-acute, folded at the mid-vein, the sides basally revolute, white with a greenish stain in the centre and with 8–10 symmetrically curving brown-purple stripes. Synsepal small, greenish. Ps. sub-spatulate, spreading, wavy, purplish-crimson with sometimes dark purple, sometimes green veins, and with numerous small blackish warts towards the base. Lip sub-cylindric, brownish-purple with darker veins and reticulations, the infolded lbs. purple with numerous small warts. Staminode dull green, stained with purple. Summer–autumn. (I, H) Hongkong and adjacent Chinese coast.

P. Sanderianum (Rchb.f.) Pfitz. (*Cypripedium Sanderianum* Rchb.f.) Lvs. broadly ligulate, obtuse, to more than 12″ long, keeled beneath, heavily leathery. Scape to 2′ tall, 3–5-fld. or more, dark purple, pubescent. Fls. the largest in the genus, about 4″ from tip of dors. sep. to tip of lip, the ps. very elongate. Dors. sep. broadly lanceolate, acute, concave, ciliolate, pale yellow-green with broad longitudinal brown stripes, hairy and keeled behind. Synsepal similar but somewhat smaller. Ps. to more than 2′ long, narrow, ribbon-like, pendulous, somewhat twisted, ciliate and broader at base, pale-yellow, bordered with brown-purple for about 2–3″ of their length, then spotted with brown-purple for a comparable length, the remainder dull purple with scattered yellow bars or spots. Lip slipper-shaped, brownish-purple above, pale yellow beneath, the infolded lbs. narrow, pale buff-yellow. Staminode pale yellow and purple, very hairy at the sides. Summer–early autumn. (H) Philippines.

P. superbiens (Rchb.f.) Pfitz. (*Cypripedium superbiens* Rchb.f., *Cypripedium Veitchianum* Lind.) Lvs. elliptic-oblong, 5–7″ long, to 2¼″ broad, variable in colour, usually pale yellowish-green tessellated with dull dark green, often very pretty. Scape 1-fld., to about 12″ tall. Fls. with all segms. ciliolate, to 4″ in diam. Dors. sep. broadly ovate, acute, white, symmetrically striped with green. Ps. deflexed, ligulate, fringed on both margins with black hairs, white, veined with green and

much spotted with blackish warts, the spots at the margins usually the largest. Lip large, somewhat helmet-shaped, brownish-purple in front, pale green beneath, the infolded lbs. flushed with crimson, warty. Spring–summer. (H) Islands of the Straits of Malacca.

P. Victoriae-Mariae (Hk.f.) Rolfe (*Cypripedium Victoriae-Mariae* Hk.f.) Resembling *P. Chamberlainianum* (O'Brien) Pfitz. in habit and foliage, but the scape to more than 2′ tall, the fls. smaller. Fls. similar to the other noted sp., to about 3½″ in diam. Dors. sep. almost circular, green, brown-streaked. Ps. horizontally spreading, green, margined with red. Lip purple-brown, green at the orifice-opening. Spring–summer. (H) Sumatra.

P. Volonteanum (Sand.) Pfitz. (*Cypripedium Volonteanum* Sand.) Lvs. 4–5 in number, ligulate, acutish, the upper side with pale green mottlings on a dark green ground, about 8″ long and 2″ broad. Scape 1-fld., to 10″ tall. Fls. about 3½″ in diam. Dors. sep. ovate, acute, yellow-green, with slightly darker nerves. Ps. down-curving, shortly ligulate, obtuse, slightly broader apically than at base, twisted once, the edges slightly undulate, the base green, becoming rose-red at the apex, the upper edge with black warts. Lip pale green, slightly suffused with rose. Summer–autumn. (H) Borneo.

PAPPERITZIA Rchb.f.

Papperitzia Leiboldii Rchb.f., the only known member of the genus, is an extremely rare dwarf epiphytic orchid which has been collected a very few times in the States of Oaxaca and Vera Cruz in Mexico. It has been

Papperitzia Leiboldii Rchb.f. [GORDON W. DILLON]

placed in a subtribe of its own, the *Papperitziinae*, but Louis O. Williams, who has studied the available specimens, puts it into the *Oncidiinae*, next to *Leochilus* Kn. & Westc. An unusual little plant, it has not as yet been introduced into our collections.

Nothing is known of the genetic affinities of this odd group.

CULTURE: Presumably as for *Ornithocephalus*. (I, H)

PAPUAEA Schltr.

The genus *Papuaea* contains a single species of exceedingly rare and incompletely known terrestrial orchid from New Guinea. A member of the complex subtribe *Physurinae*, it is somewhat allied to *Platylepis* Bl. and to *Moerenhoutia* Bl., from which it differs in technical details of the small flowers. At this time, *Papuaea* is unknown in our collections, and in any event it is primarily of scientific interest.

Nothing is known of the genetic affinities of this scarce genus.

CULTURE: Presumably as for *Anoectochilus*, etc. (H)

PARACALANTHE Kudo

The Japanese botanist Kudo has removed about six species from the genus *Calanthe* R.Br. for his group *Paracalanthe*, perhaps for good reason, although the group has not generally been recognized by most contemporary orchidologists. These plants, all terrestrial, are native to Japan, and are apparently unknown in our collections at this time. The genus is placed in the subtribe *Phaiinae*.

Nothing is known of the genetic affinities of *Paracalanthe*.

CULTURE: Presumably as for the temperate-zone Calanthes. (C, I)

PARADISIANTHUS Rchb.f.

This genus of four known species is restricted in its dissemination to Brazil, mostly along the coastal areas from Baía southward. Placed in the subtribe *Zygopetalinae*, they are relatively unspectacular, mostly terrestrial orchids which certainly do not live up to their pompous botanical name, which means 'Paradise Flower'! Bearing small pseudobulbs and tufts of plicate foliage, the smallish flowers of *Paradisianthus* are mostly greenish-white, often mottled with red or reddish-brown. They are today extremely rare in our collections, and in any event are primarily of interest to specialists.

Nothing has been ascertained regarding the genetic affinities of this group, though it will presumably prove to be 'crossable' with at least certain other members of its subtribe, and possibly with other groups as well, such as the *Lycastinae*, etc.

CULTURE: As for *Peristeria elata*, or the evergreen Calanthes. (H)

P. Mosenii Rchb.f.

Pbs. at first hidden by the strongly sheathing lf.-bases, eventually exposed, clustered, forming large clumps, to 1½″ long, rather fusiform. Lvs. several, basal and on pb.-apices, highly variable in size and shape, lanceolate-

oblong, acuminate apically and narrowed into a pseudostem basally, the lamina strongly 5-veined, to 1½′ long and 3″ wide. Infls. erect, rarely sparsely branched, to 1½′ tall, with 8–15 rather laxly arranged fls., which usually open in succession over a long period. Fls. to more than ¾″ in diam., rather fragile in texture, mostly short-lived, the spreading ss. and ps. in basal half yellowish-green irregularly barred with purplish-red stripes, the apical half without the bars, the complex lip white or whitish with darker reddish-purple streaks. Mostly autumn. (H) Brazil, especially near the coast.

PARAPHALAENOPSIS A.D.Hawkes

I have recently erected the genus *Paraphalaenopsis* to accommodate three rare and very attractive orchids which have long been considered to be highly aberrant components of *Phalaenopsis* Bl. These are terete-leaved epiphytes, all endemics to a relatively restricted area in western Borneo (officially Kalimantan, of Indonesia), which have in recent times been taken in hand to some degree by hybridists. Its relationship seems closer to *Vanda* than to true *Phalaenopsis*, and it seems peculiar that the group has been retained in the latter genus for such a long period—*P. Denevei* having been described in 1925.

When crossed with *Vanda*, *Paraphalaenopsis* gives *Paravanda*. When crossed with *Arachnis*, we have *Pararachnis*, and when bred with *Renanthera*, we have *Pararenanthera*. It seems probable that the genus will prove to be rather freely compatible with other allied genera of the subtribe *Sarcanthinae*, though as of this writing no hybrids with true *Phalaenopsis* have been effected.

CULTURE: As for *Phalaenopsis*. The plants are difficult to import, and often moderately refractory in the average collection, albeit very desirable. (H)

P. Denevei (J.J.Sm.) A.D.Hawkes (*Phalaenopsis Denevei* J.J.Sm.)

St. short, erect or hanging. Lvs. usually 3–6 in number, upright or more or less pendulous, terete, acute or obtuse at apex, usually dark bluish-green, to 2½′ long and basally about ½″ in diam., often much smaller. Infls. arising from below the lvs., to 6″ long, usually ascending, serially arising from virtually the same point on the stem, 3–15-fld. Fls. faintly fragrant, lasting upwards of 3 weeks, opening well, somewhat variable in size and colour, usually about 2″ across, heavy-textured, the often somewhat reflexed ss. and ps. light greenish-yellow to dark yellow-brown, usually with a conspicuous paler border, usually very undulate. Lip distinctly 3-lbd., its median part white, the apical parts of the lobes crimson or violet with a yellow border, the other parts spotted or striped with red or violet, the rather square callus orange with erratic transverse red lines; lat. lbs. erect, falcate, triangular, incurving, the tip very shortly subulate-acuminate; midlb. clawed, fleshy, decurved or not, narrowly spatulate, convex, the apex rounded or vaguely lobulate. Col. very short and thick, papillose, white. Mostly March–July. (H) Western Borneo (Kalimantan).

P. Laycockii (M.R.Henders.) A.D.Hawkes (*Phalaenopsis Laycockii* M.R.Henders.) Much like *P. Denevei* (J.J.Sm.)

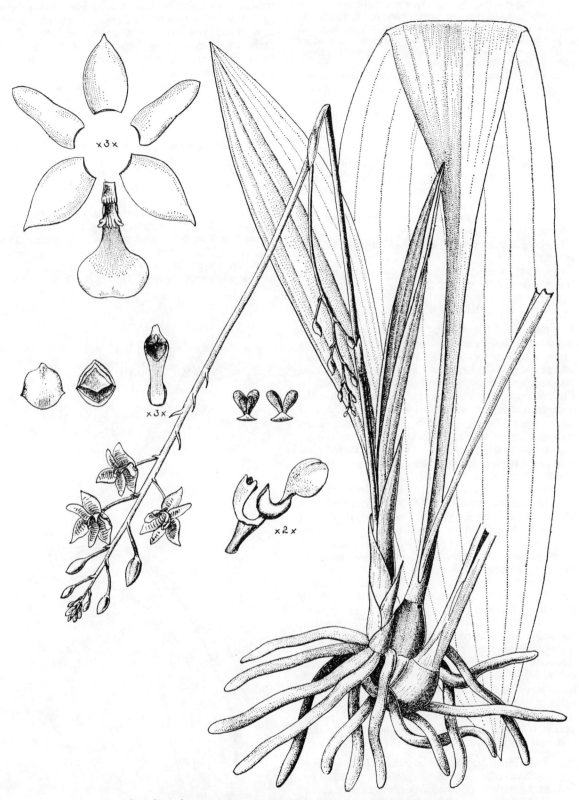

Paradisianthus micranthus (B.-R.) Schltr. [Hoehne, *Flora Brasílica*]

359

A.D.Hawkes in habit, the fls. with a peculiar fragrance, to 3″across, the ss. and ps. white, more or less suffused with pale pinkish-mauve. Lip 3-lbd., the erect lat. lbs. oblong, incurved and somewhat twisted, inside more or less brown-spotted on white ground, outside white, shading to pale brown, lower half pale lilac; midlb. pale pinkish-mauve at tip, shading to reddish-brown, then changing abruptly into reddish-brown irregular markings, the calli pale yellow striped irregularly with reddish-brown. Col. thick, rather S-shaped, white. Summer. (H) Western and south-western Borneo (Kalimantan).

PARHABENARIA Gagnep.

About two species of very little-known terrestrial orchids make up this genus. They are natives of Cambodia and Viet-Nam, and are unknown in our collections at this time. *Parhabenaria* is a member of the complex subtribe *Habenarinae*, and the components are rather interesting but scarcely showy plants.

Nothing is known of the genetic affinities of this rare group.

CULTURE: Presumably as for the warm-growing Habenarias and their allies. (I, H)

PECTEILIS Raf.

A member of the subtribe *Habenarinae*—and often included in *Habenaria* Willd.—the six or so species of *Pecteilis* are very spectacular, leafy, terrestrial or rarely lithophytic orchids, native in China and Japan, Southeast Asia, and Indonesia. Their roots consist of medium-sized oblong or irregular tubers, almost sessile on the underground part of the stem, which is usually leafy and rather stout. The few-flowered racemes bear large, usually white or pale green blossoms, in most species with extravagantly fringed lips. Two of the Pecteilis are now in cultivation, but both are relatively rare orchids in our collections.

Pecteilis Susannae (L.) Raf. has been crossed with *Habenaria rhodocheila* Hance to give *Pectabenaria x Original*, registered by A. Regnier about 1912, as a *Habenaria*. It is presumed that *Pecteilis* is freely compatible with at least most of the Habenarias (and other allied genera), and some fascinating potentials seem possible through additional experimental breeding.

CULTURE: Generally as for *Caladenia*. Holttum[1] remarks: 'This is a very beautiful species, and not difficult to cultivate if care is taken to rest the tuber in dry earth after the leafy stem has died. After about four months, the bud at the top of the tuber will begin to grow, when it should be repotted. It will take about four months to flowering, and then will live for another two months before dying back. It is important to tend the plant carefully even after flowering, as during this period the new tuber is being formed. Well-grown cultivated plants, manured carefully during their most active growing period, will attain a size rarely seen in the wild plants, and bear a large number of flowers.' (I, H)

P. radiata (Sprgl.) Raf. (*Orchis radiata* Sprgl., *Hemihabenaria radiata* Finet, *Platanthera radiata* Ldl.)
Tubers ovoid to globose, with fibrous roots above. St. 6–12″ tall, slender, leafy, often rather zigzag. Lvs. borne on st., linear, sharp-pointed, 3–6″ long, slightly

[1] In *Fl. Malaya* (*Orch. Malaya*)1: 81. 1953.

twisted in many cases. Rac. usually 2-fld., rarely 3-fld. Fls. about 1″ across, the ss. and ps. yellowish-green, often tinted with purple, the lip pure white to yellow. Dors. sep. erect, the lats. similar but larger, spreading. Ps. ovate, pointed, erect. Lip clawed basally, 3-lbd., the lat. lbs. wedge-shaped, deeply lacerate into narrow segms., the midlb. tongue-shaped, pointed. Spur more than 1″ long, slender, cylindrical, pendulous, curving. Usually July–Aug. (I) Korea; Japan, usually in the mountains.

P. Susannae (L.) Raf. (*Orchis Susannae* L., *Habenaria Susannae* R.Br., *Platanthera Susannae* Ldl.)
Tubers usually paired, irregular, 3–4″ long. St. to more than 4′ tall, robust, leafy almost throughout, the largest lvs. mostly below the middle. Lvs. to 5″ long and 2″ wide, sessile, ovate-oblong, the uppermost ones cucullate. Infl. loose, to about 8″ long, 3–10-fld. Fls. 3–4″ across, snow-white or greenish-white, fragrant. Dors. sep. erect, almost round, the lats. spreading, raised above the horizontal, their edges reflexed. Ps. small, very narrow. Lip about 2″ across, 3-lbd. to the base, with very

Pedilochilus Clemensiae L.O.Wms. [GORDON W. DILLON]

large lat. lbs. and narrow midlb., the lat. lbs. fringed
with long narrow teeth, the midlb. usually linear,
blunt apically. Spur slender, long. Aug.–Sept. (I, H)
South China; India; Malay Peninsula, often at rather
high elevations in the mountains.

PEDILOCHILUS Schltr.

Pedilochilus consists of more than fifteen species of
strange epiphytic orchids, all of them inhabiting the
upland forests of New Guinea. Somewhat allied to
Bulbophyllum Thou. and other members of the subtribe
Bulbophyllinae, they differ from that genus in floral
structure and are, for the most part, still incompletely
known to science. None of the Pedilochilus is to be
found in our collections at this time.

Nothing is known concerning the genetic affinities of
this odd group.

CULTURE: Presumably as for the tropical Bulbophyllums, etc. (I)

PELATANTHERIA Ridl.

Pelatantheria includes three known species of rare
epiphytic monopodial orchids, native in India, Burma,
Laos, Viet-Nam, and the Malay Peninsula. A single
species is present in a few particularly comprehensive
contemporary collections, but is a very scarce orchid.
These plants 'have the vegetative appearance of
Camarotis rather than *Sarcanthus*, but the flowers have
the lip in the normal position. The structure of the spur
with its back callus is exactly as in *Sarcanthus*, and the
shape of the lip generally, except that the midlobe is
always long-pointed; in one species (**P. ctenoglossa**
Ridl.) the point is fringed with hairs. The horned
column resembles *Trichoglottis*, but the horns are
pointed and smooth. There are four pollinia, united in
two bodies, exactly as in *Sarcanthus*, not two as stated
by Ridley.'[1] The stems of the Pelatantherias are rather
elongate and clambering; they bear a few oblong,
apically bilobed, fleshy leaves and give rise to relatively
short simple racemes of fleshy, usually small flowers of
no particular beauty. The genus is primarily of botanical
interest.

No hybrids are known in *Pelatantheria*, and our knowledge of the genus's genetic affinities is nil.

CULTURE: As for the tropical Vandas and allies. (H)

P. cristata (Ridl.) Ridl. (*Cleisostoma cristatum* Ridl.)

Sts. to more than 12″ long, the internodes almost 1″
long. Lvs. fleshy, to 3″ long, slightly narrowed about ½″
from the tip, lbs. of the apex with points curved towards
each other. Infls. to about 4″ long, crowded. Fls. about
10, sweet-scented, less than ½″ long, the ss. and ps.
yellowish, closely veined with red-brown, the lip white
with pink markings. Ss. strongly keeled on back, the
keels toothed towards the tips, concave, the lat. ss.
rising above the horizontal. Ps. spreading, blunt, almost
as long as the lat. ss. Lip with triangular lat. lbs., the
apex acute, incurved; midlb. arrow-shaped, with a low
median ridge and higher lateral ridges joining the ends
of the lat. lbs., the tip suddenly narrowed and turned
down; spur conical, with longitudinal septum in apical

[1] Holttum in *Fl. Malaya* (*Orch. Malaya*)1: 645. 1953.

part, the back callus very massive and long, short-
hairy beneath, lying right across the mouth of the spur
and touching the lat. keels on the midlb. Summer. (H)
Malay Peninsula: Pahang, Negri Sembilan, Perak.

PELEXIA [Poit.] L.C.Rich.
(*Adnula* Raf., *Collea* Ldl.)

Pelexia is a large genus (containing about sixty-five
species) of complex terrestrial orchids, widespread in
tropical America, from Mexico southward, with the
centre of dispersal in Brazil, where about two-thirds of
the known entities occur. A member of the extremely
complicated and polymorphic subtribe *Spiranthinae*, the
genus has been reduced to *Spiranthes* L.C.Rich. by some
orchidologists, but appears amply distinct on floral

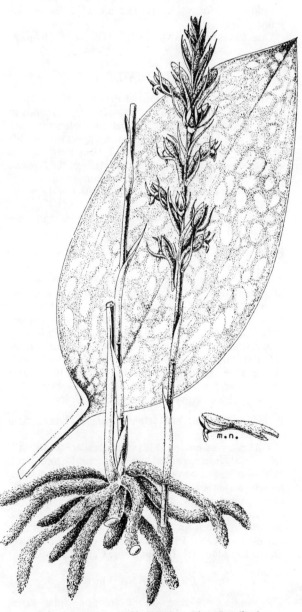

Pelexia maculata Rolfe [Hoehne, *Flora Brasilica*]

characters. These are attractive ground orchids of considerable ornamental value, but appear to be unknown in collections at this time.

Nothing is known of the genetic affinities of *Pelexia*. CULTURE: Presumably as for *Cynorkis*. (I, H)

PENNILABIUM J.J.Sm.

This is a genus of about four species of small epiphytic orchids, mostly with the habit of a *Sarcochilus*, but with yellowish or whitish, sometimes red-spotted, flowers of distinct structure. Dwarf plants, they reach their greatest development in Malaya, with a single species (**P. Angraecum** (Ridl.) J.J.Sm.) extending into Burma. None of the Pennilabiums is found in contemporary collections, and they are strictly of botanical importance, due to the short-lived habit of the small but complicated blossoms.

Nothing is known of the genetic affinities of this genus.

CULTURE: Presumably as for the dwarf, tropical Vandas, etc. (H)

PENTHEA Ldl.

Upwards of eleven species of *Penthea* are known at this time, all of them rather scarce terrestrial orchids in South and South-central Africa, two of which are present in a few particularly choice collections at this time. The genus is a close ally of *Disa* Berg., but is segregated by reason of structural details of the flowers, which vary from rather small to medium-sized.

Nothing is known of the genetic affinities of the genus *Penthea*.

CULTURE: As for *Caladenia* and other temperate terrestrial orchids. (C, I)

P. filicornis (L.) Ldl. (*Orchis filicornis* L., *Disa filicornis* Thunb.)
Tubers usually solitary, subterranean, oblong-ovoid. St. rather stout, to 1½′ tall, the few lvs. linear to linear-lanceolate, to 1½″ long, narrowing upwards into sheathing bracts. Infl. 4–10″ long, covered with narrow sheathing bracts, the few to numerous fls. in a loosely subcorymbose spike. Fls. ⅝″ across, pink, the lat. ss. suffused with purple, the other segms. spotted with purple. Dors. sep. galeate, the spur reduced to a nearly obsolete sac, the lat. ss. oblong. Ps. falcate-oblong. Lip narrowly linear. Nov.–Dec. (C, I) Cape Colony.

P. patens (Thunb.) Ldl. (*Ophrys patens* Thunb., *Disa patens* Sw.)
Tubers ovoid-oblong. St. rather slender, to 10″ tall. Lvs. basal, linear, rather numerous, to 1″ long. Infl. clothed with numerous narrow sheaths, the 4–6-fld. loosely corymbose rac. bracted. Fls. to more than 1″ across, vivid yellow, the dors. sep. broadly ovate or cordate-ovate, almost flat, the spur obsolete; lat. ss. narrowly ovate from a broad oblique base, their tips narrowly falcate. Ps. falcate-oblong. Lip narrowly linear. Oct.–Dec. (C, I) South-west Cape Colony.

PERGAMENA Finet

A single very rare orchid comprises the genus *Pergamena*, this, **P. uniflora** Finet, a small terrestrial

which rather resembles *Calypso bulbosa* (L.) Oakes in appearance. Indigenous to Japan, where it grows in montane forests, it is unknown in our collections at this time; it is a member of the subtribe *Calypsoinae*, being somewhat allied to *Calypso* Salisb.

Nothing is known of the genetic ties of *Pergamena*. CULTURE: Possibly as for *Calypso*. (C)

PERISTERANTHUS T.E.Hunt
(*Fitzgeraldiella* Schltr.)

This genus is a very recent segregate from *Ornithochilus* Wall., containing but a single uncommonly grown Australian epiphytic species of some beauty, though the flowers are small. From *Ornithochilus*, the present genus is distinguished by the sessile (instead of long-clawed) lip, the absence of the midlobe of the lip, the lack of a flap over the spur-orifice, the presence of a column-foot, and the pollinia, which number four, in two groups of two each. *Peristeranthus* vegetatively simulates many others of the sarcanthad orchids, and produces its blossoms in long, multiflorous racemes.

Nothing is known of the genetic affinities of *Peristeranthus*.

CULTURE: As for the tropical Vandas, etc. (H)

P. Hillii (FvM.) T.E.Hunt (*Saccolabium Hillii* FvM., *Ornithochilus Hillii* Bth.)
Sts. irregular, to 6″ long, rigid, covered with persistent lf.-bases. Lvs. 5–6, distichous, rather papery in texture, flat, strongly nerved, oblong-lanceolate, acute, unequally 2-lbd. at tip, to 5″ long and 1½″ wide. Infls. long, mostly pendulous, loosely many-fld., to 8″ long, often more than one simultaneously from a single spot on the st. Fls. about ¼″ long, greenish richly spotted with crimson, thick, short-stalked. Ss. and ps. similar, ligulate-spatulate, the ps. slightly narrower, the lat. ss. and ps. somewhat falcate, all incurved. Lip stalkless, movable, the lat. lbs. relatively large, erect, triangular; midlb. absent; sac with a long, finger-like callus projecting upwards from the base of the anterior wall, the spur bent forwards. Sept.–Oct. (H) Australia: New South Wales, Queensland.

PERISTERIA Hk.
(*Eckardia* Endl.)

Peristeria is a genus of about six species of epiphytic or terrestrial orchids in the American tropics, ranging from Costa Rica to Suriname, Brazil, and Peru. Best known for the remarkably beautiful *P. elata* Hk.—the 'Holy Ghost Orchid', or 'Dove Orchid' which is the national flower of Panama, the group also contains several attractive epiphytic members with pendulous inflorescences of fleshy, fragrant, rather cup-shaped flowers of unique appearance and unusual coloration. Allied to and rather simulating *Acineta* Ldl., the Peristerias—with the exception of *P. elata* Hk., which is often cultivated—are today relatively rare in collections, although all of them are sufficiently handsome to warrant attention by enthusiasts.

No hybrids have been made utilizing these orchids as yet, although interspecific breeding should prove most interesting and profitable. *Peristeria* is also presumably inter-fertile with at least some other genera of the sub-tribe *Gongorinae*.

CULTURE: *Peristeria elata* requires rather specialized conditions in order to induce flowering. It typically, in the wild, inhabits heavily shaded to semi-sunny areas on the borders of wooded tracts, the plants resting on a thick layer of rotted leaves, with the roots scarcely penetrating into the ground beneath. A loose, very well-aerated compost is thus required; one consisting of equal parts of leaf-mould and rich humus, with the addition of some chopped tree-fern fibre, liberally interspersed with broken crock, seems a suitable one, with at least half of the pot filled with crock to aid in drainage. Abundant water should be given while the plants are actively growing, but upon maturation of the new pseudobulbs, moisture should be strictly curtailed until root-action again starts. Warm temperatures should prevail with this species, and likewise with all the other Peristerias, which should be grown like Acinetas, in baskets or on rafts. Periodic heavy feedings are beneficial to all members of the genus, and the plants should be disturbed as infrequently as possible. (I, H)

P. cerina Ldl.

Pbs. robust, ovoid, to 5″ tall and 2″ in diam. Lvs. 3–4, deciduous before flowering, elliptic, acute, 1–1½′ long. Infls. short pendulous 8–15-fld. racs. to 6″ long. Fls. mostly facing upwards, very fragrant and fleshy, about 1½″ across, yellow or golden-yellow. Ss. broadly obtuse. Ps. oval, almost rhombic, obtuse. Lip with the epichil orange-coloured, the hypochil concave, the lat. lbs. short, ovate, the epichil ovate, obtuse, concave. Summer. (H) Guianas; ? Brazil.

P. elata Hk.

Pbs. robust, clustered, ovoid, to 6″ tall and 4″ in diam. Lvs. deciduous, to 4′ long and almost 12″ wide, lanceolate, acuminate, strongly folded. Infls. solitary, rigidly erect, to 4½′ tall, produced simultaneously beside the new growth and developing with it, flowering when the pb. has matured but typically prior to the falling of the lvs., with 10–20 handsome fls. in a loose or rather dense rac., fls. opening successively over a long period. Fls. not expanding fully, cup-shaped, about 2″ in diam., very fragrant, waxy, pure white, sometimes flushed outside with brownish. Ss. broadly concave, the dors. one free, ovate, obtuse, the lats. somewhat connate basally, ovate or suborbicular, shortly acute. Ps. elliptic-obovate, obtuse. Lip very fleshy, the claw (hypochil) broad, its lateral margins with ascending wings which are white, heavily spotted with rose-red, the inner basal surface thickened into a fleshy lobule; apical lobe (epichil) white, jointed to the front margin of the hypochil, entire, squarish, retuse, nearly truncate, with a central glabrous, fleshy, pure white crest. The national flower of Panama. Mostly July–Aug. (I, H) Costa Rica; Panama; Colombia; Venezuela.

P. pendula Hk. (*Peristeria lentiginosa* Lodd., *P. maculata* hort.)

Similar in habit to *P. cerina* Ldl., but the rac. more loose, 4–7-fld., the fls. to 2″ across, white, blotched and mottled with dull or bright red. Ss. and ps. broad,

obtuse. Lip with oval, obtuse lat. lbs. and a curved, ovate epichil that is larger. Winter–spring. (H) Panama; Guianas.

PERISTYLUS Bl.

About thirty species of *Peristylus* are known to date, these primarily terrestrial orchids of the complex subtribe *Habenarinae*, often included in *Habenaria* Willd., but in actuality closer in their relationship to *Herminium* R.Br. Rather widely dispersed in the North Temperate Zone, some of them extend into the tropics, where they typically inhabit the higher mountainous areas. Slender, deciduous plants, they bear globular or oval underground tubers, and small, green or white blossoms in loose or dense, usually bracted spikes. Five species appear to be in cultivation at this time, but they are all rare plants in our collections, and because of their insignificant flowers, primarily of interest to the specialist.

Nothing is known of the genetic alliances of *Peristylus*.

CULTURE: As for *Caladenia*. (C, I)

P. Steudneri (Rchb.f.) Rolfe (*Herminium Steudneri* Rchb.f.)

St. to 15″ tall, leafy above, below clothed with narrow, black-spotted sheaths. Lvs. few, oblong, sharp-pointed, distant, becoming bract-like above, ½–1¼″ long. Infl. with a dense cylindrical rac. to 3″ long. Fls. $\frac{3}{16}$″ across, green and white, the lip 3-lbd., the lat. lbs. triangular, the midlb. narrower, with a longitudinal keel; spur subglobose, obscurely 2-lbd. at apex. May–July. (C, I) Ethiopia, in the high mountains.

P. Volkensianus (Krzl.) Rolfe (*Platanthera Volkensiana* Krzl.)

Tuber ovoid to oblong, about ¾″ long. St. 2–3′ tall, very slender, leafy medially, with a few sheaths below. Lvs. oblong, pointed, narrowed basally, to 6″ long. Infl. to 10″ long, dense. Fls. less than $\frac{3}{16}$″ across, greenish-yellow, the spur curved, slightly flattened, blunt. Mostly autumn. (C, I) Tanganyika Territory, at high elevations.

P. Lefebureanus A.Rich. (*Habenaria Lefeburiana* Dur. & Schinz) St. 3–6″ tall, leafy in the middle, with sheaths below. Lvs. broadly ovate-oblong, blunt, ¾–1½″ long. Infl. with a dense rac. to 1½″ long. Fls. $\frac{3}{16}$″ across, pale green, the lip as broad as long, 3-lbd. at apex, the midlb. triangular-ovate with a fleshy disc; spur saccate, very tiny. May–Aug. (C, I) Ethiopia, on high mountains.

P. Petitianus A.Rich. (*Habenaria Petitiana* Dur. & Schinz) St. to 1¾′ tall, several-sheathed near base. Lvs. few, ovate to broadly elliptic-oblong. Infl. with a dense or rather loose rac. to 5½″ long. Fls. about $\frac{3}{16}$″ across, pale green, the lip deeply 3-lbd., the lat. lbs. linear, falcate, slightly longer than the linear midlb.; spur tiny, oblong. July–Sept. (C, I) Ethiopia, in high mountains.

P. Quartinianus A.Rich. (*Habenaria Roemeriana* Dur. & Schinz, *Platanthera Quartiniana* Engl.) St. about 15″ tall, sheathed basally. Lvs. 2–3, yellowish-green, borne rather near base of st., oblong to lanceolate-oblong, pointed, 2–3″ long. Infl. with a loose rac. 4–5″ long. Fls. about ¼″ across, green and white, the ss. with hairy margins; lip 3-lbd., the lat. lbs. linear, blunt, the midlb. linear, incurved, blunt, slightly longer than lat. ones; spur cylindrical, ¼″ long. Aug.–Sept. (C, I) Ethiopia, in the higher mountains.

PERRIERELLA Schltr.

But a single species of *Perrierella* is known to science, this an extremely rare epiphytic monopodial orchid of the subtribe *Sarcanthinae*, endemic to Madagascar. **Perrierella madagascariensis** Schltr. is somewhat allied to *Sobennikoffia* Schltr. and to *Lemurella* Schltr., but differs from both groups in structural details of the small, inverted, green flowers. It is unknown in contemporary collections, and appears to be very rare even in its native forests.

Nothing is known of the genetic affinities of this scarce genus.

CULTURE: Presumably as for the dwarf angraecoid orchids. (H)

PESCATOREA Rchb.f.

The genus *Pescatorea* consists of about a dozen spectacular, bulbless epiphytes, native in the region extending from Costa Rica to Ecuador and Colombia, a few of which are occasionally encountered in particularly choice contemporary collections. Allied to *Huntleya* Ldl. and to *Chondrorhyncha* Ldl., they vegetatively simulate those plants, and, like them, bear large, waxen, fragrant flowers, singly, on relatively short basal inflorescences. *Pescatorea* may be distinguished from the related groups on technical characters of the lip and its basal callus.

No hybrids have as yet been produced in *Pescatorea*, although interspecific breeding should certainly be attempted, as it appears to offer considerable interesting potentialities. Intergeneric hybridization with allied groups, such as *Huntleya*, *Chondrorhyncha*, *Bollea*, and possibly *Zygopetalum* and even *Lycaste* is also recommended as a distinct possibility. (See Appendix.)

CULTURE: As for *Chondrorhyncha*. (C, I)

P. cerina (Ldl. & Paxt.) Rchb.f. (*Huntleya cerina* Ldl. & Paxt., *Zygopetalum cerinum* Rchb.f.)
Without pbs., the pls. consisting of rather clustered tufts of lvs., arranged in a loose fan. Lvs. usually erect, rather fleshy, to 2′ long and 2″ wide, mostly linear-lanceolate, acute or acuminate. Scapes basal, to 4″ tall, erect or horizontal (rarely semi-pendulous). Fls. to 3″ across, very waxy, heavily fragrant, the ss. white (lats. usually with a greenish-yellow basal blotch), the ps. white, all segms. obtuse apically. Lip 3-lbd., rich yellow, the callus very large, grooved, usually marked with reddish-brown. Col. short and stout, white, with a lavender anther. Autumn. (C, I) Costa Rica; Panama.

P. Klabochorum Rchb.f. (*Zygopetalum Klabochorum* Rchb.f.)
Similar in habit to *P. cerina* (Ldl. & Paxt.) Rchb.f., but rather more robust. Fls. very heavy-textured, to 3½″ across. Ss. white with a deep chocolate-purple tip, oblong, obtuse. Ps. shorter, similar in colour, rather wedge-shaped. Lip trowel-shaped, 3-lbd., ochre-yellow or white, with the entire surface except the margins closely covered with short purple-tipped papillae, ranged in lines; callus 19-keeled, sulphur-yellow with the apical parts brown. Col. short, yellowish, flushed with brown and purple. Summer. (C) Colombia; Ecuador.

P. bella Rchb.f. (*Zygopetalum bellum* Rchb.f.) Similar in habit to the other spp., the fls. rather like those of *P. cerina* (Ldl. & Paxt.) Rchb.f., but to 3½″ across, the ss. and ps. pale or whitish violet, with a broad band of deep purple-violet near tips. Lip rather hooded, whitish-yellow, with an apical purplish-violet blotch; callus large, 21-keeled, purplish. Col. purplish with a triangular yellowish-white basal blotch, covered with numerous purplish spots. Spring. (C) Colombia.

P. Dayana Rchb.f. (*Zygopetalum Dayanum* Rchb.f.) Similar to *P. cerina* (Ldl. & Paxt.) Rchb.f. in habit, but slightly more robust. Scapes to 2½″ tall. Fls. to more than 3″ across, very fragrant, long-lived, the oblong-obovate ss. and roundish or rhomboidal ps. milk-white, the ss. green-tipped. Lip angulate basally, oblong, retuse, emarginate, white, more or less flushed with purplish-violet, with rays of this colour extending from the base of the large, keeled, rich magenta-violet callus. Col. yellow with a broad reddish basal band. Winter. (C) Colombia.

P. Lehmanni Rchb.f. (*Zygopetalum Lehmanni* Rchb.f.) Similar in habit to the other spp., the lvs. rather narrower, to 1½′ tall, acute apically. Scapes to about 6″ tall, often horizontal. Fls. very waxy, fragrant, long-lived, to 3½″ across, the ss. and ps. somewhat concave, broadly cuneate-oblong, acute, white, with numerous close, curved, parallel lines of reddish-purple extending almost to the margins. Lip deep mauve-purple, the larger part oblong, revolute, retuse, covered with purple bristle-like papillae, the crest 11-keeled, chestnut-brown. Spring–autumn, often more than once annually. (C) Colombia; Ecuador.

PETALOCHILUS R.S.Rog.

Two species of *Petalochilus* are known to date, both of them rare terrestrial orchids native in New Zealand. A member of the subtribe *Caladeniinae*, the group is highly aberrant in that the lip simulates to large degree the other floral segments. **P. calyciformis** R.S.Rog. and **P. saccatus** R.S.Rog., the former with greenish flowers, the latter with pink flowers, are the two species, neither of which appears to be in cultivation in collections outside their native haunts at this time.

Nothing is known of the genetic affinities of *Petalochilus*.

CULTURE: Possibly as for *Caladenia*, etc. (C, I)

PHAIUS Lour.
(*Pachyne* Salisb., *Pesomeria* Ldl., *Phajus* Hassk., *Tankervillea* Lk.)

A member of the subtribe *Phaiinae*, this genus consists of approximately thirty species of often large and spectacular, principally terrestrial orchids, several of which are popular with collectors today. The range of *Phaius* is a large one, extending from East Africa and Madagascar, throughout tropical Asia and Indonesia to the Himalayas, New Caledonia, and the Fiji Islands. Somewhat allied to *Calanthe* R.Br., they often simulate certain members of that genus in habit, or bear elongated stem-like pseudobulbs, well set with folded, often sizeable foliage. The inflorescence is lateral on the pseudobulb and typically erect. The frequently numerous flowers usually open successively, so that the plants remain in bloom for a long period of time. The tubular lip is rather characteristic of the blossoms, which occur in a wide variety of hues, many of them unusual for orchids.

Phaius has been rather widely utilized to date by the breeders. Hybrids are registered with *Calanthe* (= *Phaiocalanthe*), with *Cymbidium* (= *Phaiocymbidium*), with *Gastorchis* (= *Gastophaius*), and with *Spathoglottis* (= *Spathophaius*). Hybrids within the genus are also recorded, most of them having been produced in England many years ago and not currently in cultivation. Additional experimental breeding with allied groups should be attempted, since these plants offer so much to the enthusiast.

CULTURE: All of the species of this genus now in our collections should be treated as terrestrials. In warm climates they may advantageously be grown out-of-doors in specially-prepared beds of rich compost such as those recommended for *Arachnis* and other clambering sarcanthads. If kept in pots, these should be especially well-drained, since all of the Phaius are intolerant of stale conditions at the roots. A potting-medium consisting of about one-third rich loam, one-third well-rotted manure, and one-sixth each shredded osmunda and chopped tree-fern fibre is recommended. Additional fertilizing should be done at regular and frequent intervals, since these plants are heavy feeders. Upon completion of the new growths, a resting-period of about three weeks or so should be arranged, for better production of the flower-spikes. Phaius do best in brightly lighted spots, but care must be taken that the rather thin foliage does not become burned through over-exposure. Temperatures should be high at all times for best results, although the popular and widely grown *P. Tankervilliae* will often withstand exposure to about 40 degrees Fahrenheit for short periods. Repotting should be attended to immediately after flowering, when it is deemed advisable to split the clumps of pseudobulbs into rather small groups, since it seems evident that the plants flower more freely if this is done each year. (I, H)

P. amboinensis (Zipp.) Bl. (*Bletia amboinensis* Zipp., *Phaius papuanus* Schltr., *P. Zollingeri* Rchb.f.)

Pls. to almost 3′ tall. Pbs. st.-like, to about 1½′ tall, leafy throughout. Lvs. eventually deciduous, elliptic, rather thin in texture, folded, dull green. Infls. loosely 3–7-fld., rather elongate, borne from the lower half of the pbs. Fls. to almost 4″ across, delicately fragrant, the ss. and ps. snow-white, the lip bright yellow. Ss. and ps. oblong, acutish. Lip 3-lbd. towards the apex, almost spurless. Autumn. (H) Java throughout Indonesia to the Moluccas and New Guinea.

P. callosus (Bl.) Ldl. (*Limodorum callosum* Bl., *Phaius Hasseltii* Rchb.f.)

Pbs. clustered, to about 3″ tall and in diam. Lvs. 3–4, to 2′ long, narrowly elliptic, acuminate, narrowed into a basal stalk, folded. Infls. erect, to more than 2′ tall, with about 7–10 fls., the bracts deciduous. Fls. to about 4″ across, fragrant, long-lived, the ss. and ps. usually reddish-brown on the back and yellowish-brown on front, the lip yellowish with purple markings towards the apex. Ss. and ps. oblong, sharply acute. Lip tubular, 3-lbd., the short spur not or slightly 2-lbd. Spring–summer. (I, H) Malay Peninsula; Sumatra; Java.

P. flavus (Bl.) Ldl. (*Limodorum flavum* Bl., *Bletia Woodfordii* Hk., *Phaius bracteosus* Rchb.f., *P. crispus* Bl., *P. indigoferus* Rchb.f., *P. flexuosus* Bl., *P. maculatus* Ldl., *P. platychilus* Miq.)

Pbs. conical or cylindric, to 4″ tall, narrowing upwards. Lvs. 3–8, their sheaths overlapping, to form a false st. to 2′ tall, the blades to 1½′ long and 4½″ wide, lanceolate, acuminate, often irregularly spotted or blotched with yellow. Infls. borne from the pb.-base, erect, many-fld., to 3′ tall. Fls. fragrant, long-lived, to 3″ across, light yellow with some brown or red-brown markings on the lip. Ss. oblong. Ps. oblong, slightly smaller than the ss., narrowed towards the base. Lip tubular, hairy and with 3 keels on the disc, the spur very short, conical. Col. hairy on front. Spring. (I, H) North-east India; Thailand; Malay Peninsula; Sumatra; Java; Philippines.

P. Tankervilliae (Ait.) Bl. (*Limodorum Tankervilliae* Ait., *Limodorum Incarvillei* Pers., *Bletia Incarvillei* R.Br., *Phaius Blumei* Ldl., *P. grandifolius* Ldl. not Lour., *P. Incarvillei* O.Ktze., *P.Wallichii* Hk.f., *P. bicolor* Thw.)

Pbs. tightly clustered, rather irregular, dull green, to about 3″ high and in diam. Lvs. 3–4, to 3′ long, folded, narrowly elliptic, acuminate, rather heavy. Infls. stout, borne from the pb.-base, to more than 4′ tall, 10–20-fld., several fls. usually open at once, the bracts large, falling prior to expansion of the fls. Fls. fragrant, heavy-textured, long-lived, to more than 4½″ across, the ss. and ps. powdery-white outside, more or less red-brown inside, often with yellowish margins, the large lip mostly whitish outside, the blade dark wine-red inside, purplish apically and somewhat so at base. Ss. and ps. oblong, acute, all spreading in a horizontal plane with the lip below them. Lip embracing the col., trumpet-shaped, the edges of apical part rather crisped and recurved, the spur small, more or less forked at tip. Mostly spring–summer. (I, H) South China; North India throughout Malaysia and Indonesia to Australia and the Pacific Islands; introduced and naturalized in Cuba, Jamaica, Panama, and Hawaii.

P. longipes (Hk.f.) Holtt. (*Calanthe gracilis* Ldl., *Calanthe longipes* Hk.f.) Pbs. st.-like, to about 12″ tall. Lvs. several, on upper part of st., folded, the blade about 8″ long and 1½″ wide. Infls. arising from lower leafless part of st., erect, to 1½′ tall, few-fld., the fls. opening successively. Fls. about 1″ across, the ss. and ps. white, the lip white with 2 yellow ridges on the disc. Ss. hairy outside. Lip not spurred, but slightly saccate at base, the lat. lbs. erect, the midlb. crisped marginally. Summer. (I, H) South China and Sikkim to the Malay Peninsula.

P. pauciflorus (Bl.) Bl. (*Limatodis pauciflora* Bl.) Pbs. st.-like, to almost 4′ tall, the basal part angled and sheathed. Lvs. about 5 in apical part of st., often stalked, to 12″ long and 4″ wide, folded. Infls. borne from st. below lvs. or from axils of lowest lvs., often several at once, elongating gradually to about 7″ long, bearing a succession of 8–15 fls., the bracts persistent. Fls. to about 2½″ across, the ss. pale yellow, the ps. white with violet spots, the lip orange-yellow with red spots arranged in lines, the slender spur to ¾″ long, pink. Summer. (I, H) Malay Peninsula; Sumatra; Java.

PHALAENOPSIS Bl.
(*Polychilus* Kuhl & v.Hass., *Polystylus* v.Hass., *Stauritis* Rchb.f., *Stauroglottis* Schau., *Synadena* Raf.)

The fabulous 'Moth Orchids', as members of the genus *Phalaenopsis* are commonly called, are today among the most popular cultivated plants of this entire family. Many of the hybrids in particular are grown in great quantities for the cut-flower trade, the blossoms of the white forms being especially utilized for wedding bouquets, etc. They are considered by many enthusiasts, perhaps with reason, to be among the handsomest of all orchids. About seventy species are included in *Phalaenopsis*, the range extending from the Himalayas through Malaysia and Indonesia to Formosa, the Philippines, Australia (Queensland), and New Guinea. Botanically the genus is not entirely well understood nor delimited, and many of the described entities have been collected only once or on a very few occasions. These fine orchids have a rather characteristic vegetative appearance, and are unlikely to be confused with other genera, even when not in bloom. The thick stems are very abbreviated, and the few broad, usually drooping, leathery leaves are closely clustered in a distichous arrangement. The inflorescence is either short or very elongate, drooping to rigidly erect, and bears from one to very numerous handsome, mostly large flowers; in a few species, the rachis is flattened and furnished with two rows of alternating prominent bracts. Floral colour varies considerably, but in the most frequently cultivated species is either white (with some yellow markings on the lip), or different shades of pink. The sepals and petals in the genus are rather similar and spreading, with the petals in many instances far the wider of the segments. The lip is joined (without a hinge) to the column foot, and is without a spur; it is more or less distinctly three-lobed. One or more appendages or calli are usually present at the base of the midlobe—or between the lateral lobes— one of which is typically forked, with slender spreading antennae. With the removal of *Doritis* Ldl., *Kingiella* Rolfe, and *Paraphalaenopsis* A.D.Hawkes, *Phalaenopsis* seems a better organized genus, yet there are still many taxonomic problems existing within its confines.

Many hybrids are on record within the genus *Phalaenopsis*, and in relatively recent times some fascinating experimental crosses have been made. These utilize the relatively rare species with barred or striped blossoms—*P. Mannii, P. cornu-cervi, P. violacea*, and the like—and the results range from yellows through a whole series of exciting 'novelty' colour combinations. Several of the 'Moth Orchids' have also been successfully crossed with allied genera of the subtribe *Sarcanthinae*, giving rise to such groups as *Vandaenopsis* (× *Vanda*), *Renanthopsis* (× *Renanthera*), *Arachnopsis* (× *Arachnis*), etc. The field of multigeneric hybridization with this genus still offers much of potential interest, and should be further explored.

CULTURE: Phalaenopsis are, almost entirely, tropical orchids, and hence require warm temperatures at all times. Since they are without pseudobulbs (all moisture-storing is done in the fleshy foliage), they must never be permitted to dry out, yet the compost in which they are grown must be sufficiently porous to permit perfect drainage, or the health of the plants will suffer materially and irreparably. Most of the species and hybrids grow throughout the year—though very slowly, after they have reached maturity—and caution must always be exercised that water does not lodge in the growing apex, or rotting and the possible death of the plant may result. Instructions for potting vary from grower to grower, but almost all experts agree that a firm compost (either tree-fern or osmunda chunks) is necessary for success, with perfect drainage obligatory. Most of the Phalaenopsis grow best in a semi-shaded spot, since excessive sun will burn the coriaceous foliage; too much shade, however, causes the leaves to grow long and flaccid, and flowering to be curtailed. While in especially active growth, all members of this genus benefit materially by liberal and regular applications of fertilizers of various sorts, preferably given in liquid form. Repotting or transferral to other media should be done only when absolutely essential, as the members of the group are singularly intolerant of disturbance. (I, H)

P. amabilis (L.) Bl. (*Epidendrum amabile* L., *Cymbidium amabile* Roxb., *Phalaenopsis grandiflora* Ldl., *P. Rimestadiana* hort., *P. amabilis* (L.) Bl. var. *papuana* Schltr.)

Lvs. few, broadly ovate-oblong, blunt apically, rather fleshy and leathery, dull green above and below, to 12″ long (rarely longer) and about 5″ wide. Infls. slender, gracefully arching, to 3′ long, usually loosely 6–20-fld. Fls. to 4″ across, variable in size and dimensions of the segms., white, flushed with yellow on the lip and more or less marked and striped with red around the calli there. Ss. oblong, blunt at tips. Ps. clawed, mostly broadly rhombic-cuneate, blunt and somewhat emarginate apically. Lip shorter than the ps.; lat. lbs. erect, usually striped with red at base, half-rhombic, oblong; midlb. rhombic-ligulate, ending in 2 elongate antenna-like cirrhi, the disc with 2 prominent red-striped calli, yellow to almost orange-yellow. Mostly Oct.–Jan. (I, H) Indonesia; Northern Australia; New Guinea; New Britain.

P. Aphrodite Rchb.f. (*Phalaenopsis gloriosa* Rchb.f., *P. Sanderiana* Rchb.f.)

Simulating *P. amabilis* (L.) Bl. in almost all respects, differing chiefly in the smaller fls. (to 3″ across or less), the deeper red markings on the lip-disc, and the rather shorter midlb. of almost triangular shape. Winter–early spring. (I, H) Philippines.

P. cornu-cervi (Breda) Bl. & Rchb.f. (*Polychilus cornu-cervi* Breda)

Lvs. few, leathery, green, to slightly less than 12″ long, usually shorter, about 1½″ wide, oblong, obtuse, narrowed basally. Infls. to 8″ long, the rachis branched, much flattened, furnished with conspicuous alternating bracts which are arranged in 2 rows. Fls. expanding singly or a few at a time, fragrant, waxy, long-lived, the ss. and ps. pale yellow-green, barred and blotched with red-brown, the lip mostly white and yellow. Ss. and ps. spreading, oblong, rather acute. Lip small, complex; lat. lbs. erect, pale yellow or white; midlb. with the basal part white or yellow with orange side markings, narrowing to the white middle part, suddenly expanded to a white, shortly pointed apical part; base with 3 appendages in series, yellow, white, and violet in colour. Spring–autumn. (H) Malay Peninsula; Sumatra; Java; Borneo.

P. equestris Rchb.f. (*Phalaenopsis rosea* Ldl., *Stauroglottis equestris* Schauer)

Lvs. mostly oval in shape, obtuse apically, rather leathery, to 6″ long and 3″ wide, dull green, sometimes flushed beneath with dull purple. Infls. gracefully arching, to 12″ long, rather densely 10–15-fld. Fls. to almost 1″ across, pale rose-red, the lip magenta-rose, marked with deep red. Ss. and ps. narrowly elliptic, obtuse. Lip with oval, obtuse lat. lbs. and an ovate-ligulate, obtuse midlb. which has an oblong, furrowed callus on the disc. Autumn–winter. (I, H) Philippines.

P. fuscata Rchb.f. (*Phalaenopsis Denisiana* Cgn., *P. Kunstleri* Hk.f., *P. viridis* J.J.Sm.)

Lvs. rather thin, to 12″ long and 4″ wide, basally very much narrowed. Infls. to 12″ long, often laterally branched, the fls. usually 1–3 on each branch, facing in all directions, often opening successively over a long period of time. Fls. fragrant, waxy, to about 1½″ across, pale yellow-green, more or less blotched and suffused with chocolate-brown near the bases of the ss. and ps.; lip white, marked with red-brown. Ss. and ps. oblong, obtuse, spreading. Lip shorter than the ss.; lat. lbs. rather short and broad, twisted so they touch, white spotted and lined with red-brown; midlb. flat with a median ridge and a forked basal appendage, widening from base to near apex, broadly and bluntly pointed, cream-colour striped with red-brown. Spring. (H) Malay Peninsula; Sumatra; Borneo.

P. Lowii Rchb.f.

Lvs. rather fleshy, usually deciduous for at least part of the year, to 4″ long and 1″ wide, narrowly elliptic, acutish. Infls. erect, loosely 3–6-fld., to 12″ tall. Fls. rather fleshy, fragrant, to about 2″ across, whitish-rose, the lip with pale rose-red lat. lbs., the midlb. magenta-red of varying intensity. Ss. and ps. oblong, obtuse, spreading. Lip with erect lat. lbs. that are rather incurved apically, the midlb. oblong, obtuse, keeled. Summer–autumn. (I) Burma.

P. Lueddemanniana Rchb.f.

Lvs. bright waxy yellow-green, rather rigid, elliptic, obtuse (somewhat variable in shape), to 10″ long and about 5″ wide, often much shorter and narrower. Infls. usually not exceeding the lvs. in length, irregularly zigzag, often flattened upwards, 2–7-fld., the fls. usually produced singly over a long period of time. Fls. variable in size and in colour, usually less than 2″ in diam., highly fragrant and long-lived, waxy, iridescent in most forms, in the typical phase with the ss. chestnut-brown with some rather narrow, pale yellow streaks, the margins whitish and the basal half heavily suffused with amethyst, narrowly elliptic, obtuse to acutish; ps. similar in shape to ss. but smaller, mostly bright amethyst with more scattered chestnut-brown streaks, the margins whitish. Lip 3-lbd., the erect lat. lbs. with 2 unequal tips, white, flushed with light purple or pale magenta, the frontal lobule brilliant yellow; midlb. much larger, oblong, obtuse, bright amethyst with a paler edge, with numerous

white, erect, bristle-like hairs along the raised median keel; col. white, more or less flushed with pale·purple or pale magenta. Several horticultural colour variants have been described. Spring. (I, H) Philippines.

P. Mannii Rchb.f.

Lvs. rather flaccid to rigid, ovate-oblong or shortly lanceolate, short-acuminate, to 10″ long and 2½″ wide. Infls. gracefully arching, slender, usually shorter than the lvs., 4–6-fld., the fls. usually all open at once. Fls. waxy, fragrant, long-lasting, about 1½″ in diam., yellowish, thickly spotted and transversely barred with light or dark brown, the lip white, rather similar in shape to that of *P. cornu-cervi* (Breda) Bl. & Rchb.f. Ss. and ps. waxy, spreading, ligulate-oblong, acutish. Lip shorter than the ps. Spring–autumn. (I, H) North India, especially Assam.

P. Schilleriana Rchb.f.

Vegetatively similar to *P. amabilis* (L.) Bl., but the lvs. usually more flaccid and dull dark green mottled with silver-grey, often magenta underneath. Infls. erect to gracefully arching, to more than 3′ long, few- to many-fld., usually branched. Fls. variable in size, usually less than 2½″ across, and somewhat so in colour, the typical phase pale pinkish-rose, the disc of the lip golden-yellow, marked with scarlet, the basal part of the midlb. red-dotted. Ss. oblong, blunt at the tips, wide-spreading, sometimes slightly reflexed. Ps. clawed, usually broadly rhombic-cuneate, blunt apically and sometimes emarginate. Lip with spreading-erect, oblong, obtuse lat. lbs., the midlb. elliptic, constricted near the tip, and then flaring into 2 semi-triangular processes, the whole structure rather anchor-shaped. Mostly spring. (I, H) Philippines.

P. Stuartiana Rchb.f.

Vegetatively much like *P. Schilleriana* Rchb.f., the lvs. often smaller and narrower. Infls. erect or gracefully arching, usually rather many-fld., to 3′ long, simple or branched. Fls. opening flat, to 2″ across, similar in shape to the other noted sp., the ss. and ps. white, the lower halves of the lat. ss. spotted with brown or reddish-brown, the lip 3-lbd., the basal part of the lat. lbs. yellow, spotted with red-purple, the apical part whitish with fewer spots, the midlb. usually light yellow or white, spotted with red-purple. Ss. elliptic-oblong, obtuse to acutish; ps. clawed, much larger than the ss., sub-rhomboidal, rarely with a few tiny purple spots over basal half. Lip with the lat. lbs. obliquely obovate-oblong, the midlb. narrow at base, abruptly dilated into a sub-rhomboidal blade with 2 anchor-like appendages at the apex; crest short, thick, golden-yellow often spotted with red-purple, divided at the summit into 2 oblong lobes. Autumn–spring. (I, H) Philippines.

P. Mariae Burb. Lvs. deflexed, narrowly obovate-oblong, 6–10″ long, bright glossy-green. Infls. usually exceeding the lvs. in length, mostly branched, rather few-fld. Fls. 1½–2″ in diam., the ss. and ps. similar and almost equal, yellowish-white, with 4–5 broad, chestnut-brown transverse bands and an amethyst stain at the base. Lip shorter than other segms., 3-lbd., the erect lat. lbs. incurving, white with a median purple stain, and a yellow appendage on the anterior side; midlb. fleshy, vivid amethyst-purple, with a recurved spur at base,

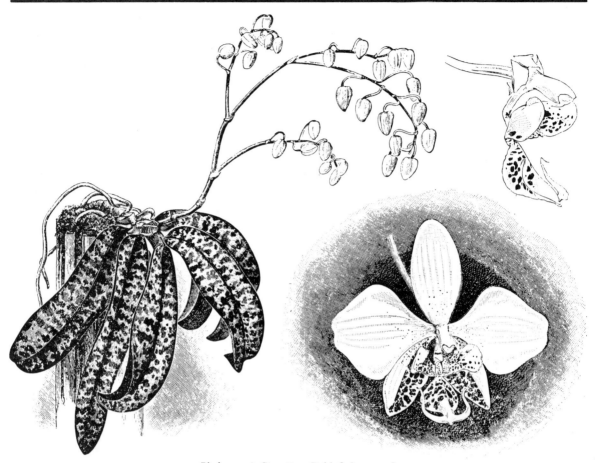

Phalaenopsis Stuartiana Rchb.f. [VEITCH]

keeled above, the keel covered with white hairs. Col. terete, with a beaked anther. Summer, mostly June–July. (I, H) Philippines: Mindanao; Sulu Archipelago; Borneo.

P. Parishii Rchb.f. Lvs. elliptic or elliptic-oblong, 2–4″ long, dark green. Infls. racemose, about as long as the lvs., 5–9-fld. Fls. usually under ¾″ in diam., the ss. and ps. white, the complex lip 3-lbd., the lat. lbs. yellow, spotted with purple, the midlb. bright rose-purple. Dors. sep. oblong, the lats. broader, ovate-oblong. Ps. obovate. Lip with a short claw bent at right angles to the blade, the lat. lbs. very small, horn-like, bent backwards; midlb. almost triangular; crest semi-lunate, with a fimbriate outer margin, white with a yellowish-brown centre, below which is a linear appendage, projecting forwards and divided to near the base into 4 slender filaments. Col. white, spotted on anterior face with purple. Spring. (I) Assam; Burma.

P. speciosa Rchb.f. Lvs. drooping, obovate-oblong, bright glossy-green, 7–12″ long and 2½–3″ wide. Infls. drooping, longer than the lvs., sometimes branched, 9–12-fld. or more. Fls. 2″ in diam., fragrant, the ss. and ps. spreading in a star-like fashion, amethyst-purple with a pale margin, the lat. ss. with a yellowish mucro, the ss. oval-oblong, the ps. narrower, elliptic-oblong, acute. Lip shorter than the other segms., 3-lbd., the lat. lbs. erect, with an orange-yellow protuberance on the inner side, purple at base, orange medially, white at apex, oblong, truncate; midlb. fleshy, amethyst-purple, oblong, with an acute, pubescent keel above. Col. white, dilated at the toothed apex. Spring. (H) Andaman Islands.

P. sumatrana Korth. & Rchb.f. Lvs. obovate or obovate-oblong, subacute, rather heavy-textured, 6–10″ long. Infls. ascending, to about 12″ long, 5–9-fld. Fls. about 2″ in diam., the similar, subequal ss. and ps. cream-white, barred with red-brown, the lat. lbs. of the lip white with some orange spots on the inner side, the midlb. white with some purple or reddish-purple streaks on each side of the keel. Ss. ovate-oblong, acute, the ps. slightly narrower and more cuneate. Lip shortly clawed, 3-lbd., the lat. lbs. ligulate-oblong, erect, truncate, the tip prolonged backwards into a protruding tooth; midlb. fleshy, oblong, with a prominent keel on the disc, with 2 small erect teeth at the base and a dense tuft of short, hispid hairs at apex. Col. semi-terete, notched at the apex. Mostly spring. (I, H) Sumatra; Borneo; Malay Peninsula.

P. tetraspis Rchb.f. Lvs. obovate, cuneate, 8–9″ long and 2–3″ broad. Infls. much shorter than the lvs., 3–5-fld. Fls. 1½–2″ in diam., ivory-white, the lat. lbs. flushed with yellow outside. Ss. and ps. similar, spreading, oval-oblong, acute, the lat. ss. broader than the dors. one. Lip fleshy, 3-lbd., the lat. lbs. ligulate, curved upwards and inwards, truncate at the free end; midlb. sub-rhomboidal, with a tuft of bristles at the apex; crest sub-conic. Col. swollen basally. Spring. (H) Andaman Islands.

P. violacea Teijsm. & Binn. Lvs. variable in size and somewhat so in shape, broadly oval or elliptic-oblong, to 9″ long and 4″ broad, bright shiny-green. Infls. rather stout, jointed, usually about 4–5″ long, 2–7-fld., the fls. usually opening successively over a long period. Fls. 2–3″ in diam., very

Paphiopedilum Spicerianum (Rchb.f.) Pfitz.
[GEORGE FULLER]

Paraphalaenopsis Denevei (J.J.Sm.) A.D.Hawkes [M. R. HENDERSON]

Peristeria pendula Hk. [H. A. DUNN]

Pescatorea Dayana Rchb.f. [H. SCHMIDT-MUMM]

Phaius Tankervilliae (Ait.) Bl. [AMERICAN ORCHID SOCIETY]

Phalaenopsis gigantea J.J.Sm. [G. F. J. BLEY]

Phalaenopsis violacea Teijsm. & Binn. [GEORGE FULLER]

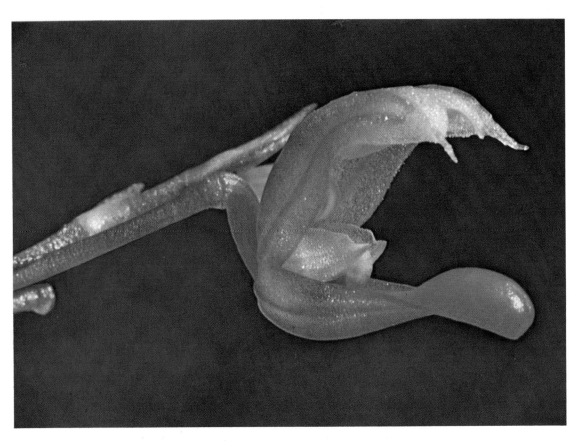

Xᴀ   *Scaphosepalum elasmotopus* Schltr. [ᴀ.ʜ.ʜᴇʟʟᴇʀ]

Xʙ   *Scuticaria Steelii* (Hk.) Ldl. [ꜰ.ʟ.sᴛᴇᴠᴇɴsᴏɴ]

variable in colour, the dors. sep. and ps. similar, ovate-oblong, mucronate, greenish-white with a bright violet-purple basal blotch which sometimes spreads to beyond the middle; lat. ss. oblong, acute, subfalcate, with a depressed mid-line and keel behind, the inner half violet-purple to two-thirds of the length, the apical third whitish, the outer half greenish-white. Lip shortly clawed, 3-lbd., the lat. lbs. oblong, erect, truncate, golden-yellow, with a small yellow crest between them that is prolonged in front into a narrow, apically bifid plate; midlb. vivid violet-purple, obovate-oblong, apiculate, keeled above, with 2 small bristles at the basal end of the keel, concave beneath. Col. thickened basally, terete above, dark purple. Spring–summer. (I, H) Sumatra; Borneo; Malay Peninsula.

PHLOEOPHILA Hoehne & Schltr.

Rather closely allied to *Cryptophoranthus* B.-R., the two known species of *Phloeophila*—**P. paulensis** Hoehne & Schltr. and **P. echinata** (B.-R.) Hoehne & Schltr.—are very rare, creeping, mat-forming little epiphytes which have been found a few times in Brazil. Very odd in appearance, they differ from *Cryptophoranthus* primarily in having the sepal-tips completely free from one another. Neither species is in cultivation at this time.

Nothing is known of the genetic affinities of *Phloeophila*.

CULTURE: Possibly as for the dwarf, mat-forming *Pleurothallis*. (I, H)

PHOLIDOTA Ldl.
(*Acanthoglossum* Bl., *Camelostalix* Pfitz., *Chelonanthera* Bl., *Crinonia* Bl., *Ptilocnema* D.Don)

Pholidota is a little-known and seldom-cultivated genus of about forty species of mostly epiphytic, usually rather insignificant orchids allied to *Coelogyne* Ldl., but differing materially from that group in floral characters. They range from southern China and the Himalayas throughout South-east Asia, Indonesia, and the Philippines, to northern Australia, New Caledonia, and New Guinea. Bearing clustered or distantly spaced one or two-leaved prominent pseudobulbs on a rather stout rhizome, they produce numerous, small, usually dull-coloured flowers in long, mostly two-ranked racemes, in which the rachis is often conspicuously irregular and zigzag. The persistent or deciduous, large, concave bracts which occur in most species—often almost hiding the blossoms—give the common name of 'Rattlesnake Orchid' to at least some of the cultivated Pholidotas.

The genus has not as yet been taken in hand by the breeders, though it is presumably genetically compatible with at least some of the allied genera of the subtribe *Coelogyninae*. Some unusual and doubtless attractive multigeneric crosses seem possible in this respect.

CULTURE: As for *Coelogyne*, depending upon the place of origin of the particular species or individual. (C, I, H)

P. articulata Ldl. (*Coelogyne articulata* Rchb.f., *Coelogyne khasiana* Rchb.f., *Pholidota decurva* Ridl., *P. khasiana* Rchb.f.)

Pbs. to about 4″ long, 2-lvd., cylindric, rather slender, each arising from the apex of the last (as in some species

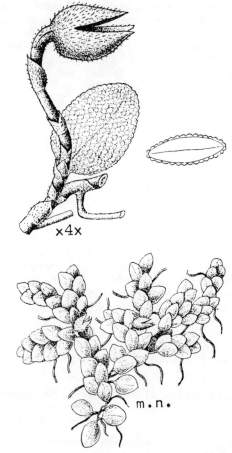

Phloeophila paulensis Hoehne & Schltr. [Hoehne, *Flora Brasílica*]

of *Scaphyglottis* and *Hexisea*), the whole structure often pendulous. Lvs. with a short stalk, rather leathery, to 4″ long and 1½″ wide, elliptic, acute. Infls. about 6″ long, slender, drooping, the bracts about ½″ long, broad, brownish, falling as the fls. expand. Fls. numerous, often not opening well, to ½″ across, musk-scented, pinkish to dull tan-brown, the hollow basal part of the lip with 5 low longitudinal yellow ridges, the base of the lamina orange. Ss. and ps. nearly equal, ovate-elliptic, acutish. Lip with the basal cavity narrowing towards its end, where the blade is borne, this broader than long, slightly twisted, vaguely 2-lbd. Spring–summer. (I, H) Himalayas; Burma; Thailand; Laos; Viet-Nam; Malay Peninsula; Java.

P. imbricata (Roxb.) Ldl. (*Cymbidium imbricatum* Roxb., *Coelogyne imbricata* Rchb.f., *Coelogyne conchoidea* Rchb.f., *Pholidota conchoidea* Ldl., *Ptilocnema bracteatum* D.Don)

Pbs. to 2½″ long, broadly conical, sometimes vaguely angled, dull grey-green. Lf. solitary, rigidly leathery, erect, similar in colour to the pbs., stalked at the base, to 12″ long and 2½″ wide, plicate, elliptic, acute. Infls. synanthous, rather sharply drooping from an erect bare peduncle, the whole to 12″ long, the persistent floral bracts brown, almost hiding the fls., closely packed together in 2 ranks. Fls. not expanding well, to under ½″ across, musk-scented or odourless, tan to pale fleshy-pink, the midlb. of the lip often with a yellow spot, the anther brown. Ss. broadly elliptic, concave, the lat. ones keeled outside. Ps. shorter and narrower, acute. Lip with a saccate base, the sides of which rise on either side of the col. like lat. lbs., the midlb. often 2-lbd., spreading downwards. Mostly spring–summer. (I, H) South China and the Himalayas throughout all of tropical Asia, Indonesia, and the Philippines to Northern Australia and New Guinea.

P. ventricosa (Bl.) Rchb.f. (*Chelonanthera ventricosa* Bl., *Coelogyne ventricosa* Rchb.f., *Pholidota grandis* Ridl.)
Pbs. clustered, to 4″ long, narrowly ovoid, ribbed. Lvs. 2, rather rigidly leathery, to 2′ long, the stalk about 6″ long, the narrowly elliptic, acute, plicate lamina to 4″ wide. Infls. erect, proteranthous, to 1½′ tall, the peduncle stout, about 8″ long, the fls. very numerous and close together, the bracts large, deciduous. Fls. about ½″ across, opening rather well, the ss. greenish, the ps. almost white, the lip white. Ss. concave, ovate, acutish. Ps. reflexed, smaller, acute. Lip with the basal sac-like part longer than wide, the edge slightly reflexed, the blade spreading, deeply lobed at the end and slightly so on each side. Col. with very broad wings. Throughout the year, often more than once annually. (I, H) Malay Peninsula; Sumatra; Java; Borneo.

P. carnea (Bl.) Ldl. (*Crinonia carnea* Bl.) Pbs. to about 2″ apart on the creeping rhiz., to 1½″ long, ovoid, becoming wrinkled with age, the rhiz. between them with large brown sheaths. Lvs. 2, to about 12″ long and ½″ wide, stalked, rather leathery, elliptic-lanceolate, acutish. Infls. synanthous, down-curving, to about 8″ long, the bracts deciduous. Fls. to ¼″ across, pinkish, the lip with a yellow median spot. Ss. ovate-elliptic, blunt apically. Ps. much smaller than ss., blunt at tips. Lip S-curved along its mid-line, widening from a narrow sac-like base to a broadly rounded down-turned blade, this with 2 broad fleshy ridges at the base. Summer. (I, H) Malay Peninsula; Sumatra; Borneo; Philippines.

P. gibbosa (Bl.) deVr. (*Chelonanthera gibbosa* Bl.) Pbs. distant on a stout rhiz. that is sheathed by large brown bracts, to about 4″ apart, to 3″ tall, ovoid, often rather angular. Lvs. 2, rigidly leathery, short-stalked, to about 12″ long, the elliptic, acute blade to 2″ wide. Infls. synanthous, pendulous from an erect slender peduncle, the whole to 12″ long, the rachis zigzag, the small bracts deciduous. Fls. widely opening, about ½″ across, pale pinkish or greenish, the lip pale pink. Ss. and ps. reflexed, obtuse, the tips of the ps. rolled backwards. Lip with the blade 3-lbd., the lat. lbs. small, the midlb. broad, deeply cleft, the halves overlapping in front. Mostly summer. (I, H) Malay Peninsula; Sumatra; Java; Borneo.

PHRAGMIPEDIUM Rolfe
(*Phragmopedilum* Rolfe, *Uropedium* Ldl.)

About twelve or so species of *Phragmipedium* are known to date, these often very handsome and justifiably popular terrestrial, or rarely lithophytic or truly epiphytic orchids in the American tropics, ranging from southern Mexico (Chiapas) to Peru, Bolivia, and Brazil. A member of the subtribe *Cypripedilinae*, the members of this genus are commonly known in cultivation under the completely erroneous and very confusing name of *Selenipedium* (no true Selenipediums are in our collections at this time), or even worse, under the name of *Cypripedium*! They differ from the allied genera of the subtribe in technical details of the flowers and their pedicellate ovaries, and are usually quite distinctive even when not in blossom, with their tightly ranked, usually leathery, gracefully arching foliage. Certain forms of the polymorphic and widespread *P. caudatum* (Ldl.) Rolfe are among the largest of all orchids, as regards the dimensions of their fantastically elongate flowers. These 'long-tailed' Phragmipediums are often known as 'Mandarin Orchids', because of the supposed Oriental faces, with accompanying drooping 'mustache' apparent in the blossoms.

A large series of *Phragmipedium* hybrids are on record at this time, all of them listed in the official registries under the erroneous and confusing epithet of *Selenipedium*. The status of many of these often handsome crosses—many of which are present in contemporary collections—is rather vague. The two hybrids between this genus and *Paphiopedilum*, known under the peculiar name of *Selenocypripedium*, are discussed under the latter genus. Additional experimental breeding both within the genus *Phragmipedium*, and with its allied groups, offers some fascinating potentials.

CULTURE: The Phragmipediums vary in habit from truly epiphytic (*P. caudatum*) to lithophytic on mossy rocks, or truly terrestrial, usually on grassy banks. *P. caudatum* is best grown in well-drained pots, in firmly-packed osmunda fibre mixed with chopped sphagnum moss. The other species (and the hybrids) do well in smallish, perfectly-drained pots, filled with a mixture of about equal parts of chopped sphagnum moss, shredded tree-fern fibre, and fibrous loam or rich garden soil. Since they have no moisture-storing structures, they must be kept damp at all times, though excessive moisture (and imperfect drainage) can cause rapid cultural difficulties. Most of the Phragmipediums benefit by rather bright light-exposure, short of burning the typically heavy foliage. Liberal applications of fertilizers at relatively frequent intervals are beneficial. Although some of these orchids in the wild extend to rather high elevations, all of them under cultivation do best in the intermediate house. (I)

P. caudatum (Ldl.) Rolfe (*Cypripedium caudatum* Ldl., *Cypripedium Humboldtii* Warsc. ex Rchb.f., *Cypripedium Warszewiczianum* Rchb.f., *Paphiopedilum caudatum* Pfitz., *Phragmopedilum Warszewiczianum* Schltr.)
Lf.-fans borne very close together, the lvs. usually about 6, distichously clustered, broadly lorate, obtuse, the apex shallowly and unequally 2-lbd., rather rigidly leathery, to 2′ long and more than 2″ broad, often rather yellowish-green when grown in bright exposure. Infl. vaguely velvety, naked, erect, to more than 2′ tall, very loosely 1–6-fld. in upper parts. Fls. largest of the genus, among the most elongate of all orchids, to more than 2½′ long (counting the extremely lengthy ps.). Dors. sep. 6–7″ long, pale yellow or whitish with longitudinal yellow-green veins in front, pubescent behind, lanceolate, acuminate, the synsepal similar but broader, con-

cave at the base. Ps. linear, ribbon-like, pendulous, elongating as the fl. expands, to more than 2′ long (rarely to more than 2½′ long), yellowish basally, otherwise dull brownish-crimson. Lip slipper-shaped, thrust forward, 2–2½″ long, brownish-green, passing to bronze-green around the orifice, the veins and reticulations dark green, pale yellow-green beneath, the infolded lbs. meeting at their edges, ivory-white, spotted with purple inside the yellow-brown border around the orifice. Staminode triangular, yellowish, the auricles fringed with brown-purple hairs. Several horticultural forms are known, based mostly on minor structural or coloration details of the flowers. Spring–autumn. (I) Mexico (Chiapas) to Panama, Colombia, Venezuela, Ecuador, and Peru.

P. longifolium (Warsc. & Rchb.f.) Rolfe (*Cypripedium longifolium* Warsc. & Rchb.f., *Selenipedium longifolium* Rchb.f., *Cypripedium Hincksianum* Rchb.f., *Paphiopedilum Hincksianum* Pfitz., *Paphiopedilum longifolium* Pfitz.)

Lf.-tufts very close together, the lvs. narrowly linear or linear-ligulate, acute, canaliculate, distichous, to 2¾′ long and 1½″ broad, usually rather dark but bright green. Infl. erect, stoutish, dark purple or green, often vaguely pubescent towards base, 6–10-fld. or more, the fls. usually produced singly over a long period of time. Fls. waxy, long-lasting, to almost 8″ in diam., not as long. Dors. sep. usually erect or somewhat thrust forward, pale green with rose veins and whitish margins, ovate-lanceolate, undulate or not marginally. Synsepal almost twice as broad as dors. sep., ovate, acuminate, pale green with dark green veins. Ps. spreading almost horizontally, linear-lanceolate, often slightly twisted, pale yellow-green with rose margins, these margins becoming whitish towards the base. Lip slipper-shaped, yellow-green, tinged with brown in front, the infolded lbs. yellow-green, dotted with rose-purple, with an angular auricle between the sac and the lat. lbs. Staminode pale yellow-green with a blackish fringe on the rear margin, and a blunt, deflexed tooth on the front one. Mostly autumn, but often more than once annually. (I) Costa Rica; Panama; Colombia.

P. Boissierianum (Rchb.f.) Rolfe (*Cypripedium Boissierianum* Rchb.f., *Selenipedium Boissierianum* Rchb.f., *Paphiopedilum Boissierianum* Pfitz.) Lvs. distichously clustered, lorate, acute, to more than 3′ long and 1¾″ wide, heavily leathery. Infl. erect, 3–15-fld., to 3¼′ tall. Fls. to 6″ long, pale yellow-green, veined and reticulated with dark emerald-green, the ss. and ps. usually margined with white. Dors. sep. lanceolate, acuminate, crisped marginally. Synsepal twice as broad as dors. sep. Ps. spreading horizontally, 4–5″ long, broad basally, narrowing towards apex, twisted, the margins crisped. Lip prominent, the sac sub-cylindric, brownish in front, the infolded lbs. broad, spotted copiously with greenish-brown. Autumn. (I) Ecuador; Peru.

P. caricinum (Ldl. & Paxt.) Rolfe (*Cypripedium caricinum* Ldl. & Paxt., *Selenipedium caricinum* Rchb.f., *Selenipedium Pearcei* Rchb.f.) Rhiz. creeping, bearing the lf.-tufts at intervals from one another. Lvs. usually 3–6, distichously imbricating, narrowly linear, sedge-like, to 1½′ long, usually less than ½″ wide. Infl. erect, to 2′ tall, 3–7-fld., the peduncle usually purplish-green. Fls. to 6½″ long. Dors. sep. greenish-white, veined with pale yellow-green, lanceolate, acute, undulate, mostly erect. Synsepal rather large, whitish. Ps. pendulous, twisted, linear, 3–5″ long, white, tinged towards the tips with rose, veined with light green. Lip slipper-shaped, pale yellow-green with darker green veins, the infolded lbs. ivory-white, spotted marginally with green and purple. Staminode green with a purple fringe on the basal side. Spring. (I) Peru; Bolivia.

P. Hartwegii (Rchb.f.) L.O.Wms. (*Cypripedium Hartwegii* Rchb.f., *Selenipedium Hartwegii* Rchb.f., *Paphiopedilum Hartwegii* Pfitz.) Lvs. heavily leathery, broadly lorate, narrowed basally, to more than 2′ long. Infl. to 3′ tall, with several spathe-like red-brown bracts near base, loosely 7–9-fld. Fls. to about 5″ long, greenish-yellow, the veins usually darker green. Dors. sep. attenuate above, undulate marginally. Ps. pendulous, linear-lanceolate, attenuate above, slightly twisted, vaguely crisped on the margins. Lip vaguely slipper-shaped, the lbs. retuse, squarish. Spring. (I) Ecuador; Peru.

P. Lindleyanum (Schomb.) Rolfe (*Cypripedium Lindleyanum* Schomb., *Selenipedium Lindleyanum* Rchb.f., *Paphiopedilum Lindleyanum* Pfitz.) Lvs. tufted, strap-shaped, vivid grass-green, often with yellowish margins, to more than 2′ long and 2½″ wide. Infls. to almost 4′ tall, stiffly erect, pubescent, green, the rachis reddish, 3–7-fld. Fls. to about 3″ long. Dors. sep. oblong, acute, pubescent, undulate marginally, light green with alternating longer and shorter longitudinal red-brown veins. Synsepal broader, concave, pale green, veined with red-brown. Ps. deflexed, linear-oblong, the margins undulate and ciliate, pale green, veined with red-brown. Lip helmet-shaped, green with red-brown veins and reticulations, the inflexed lbs. broad, densely spotted with red-brown. Staminode pubescent, yellow-green. Autumn–winter. (I) British Guiana, mostly near Mount Roraima; Venezuela.

P. Schlimii (Batem.) Rolfe (*Cypripedium Schlimii* Batem., *Selenipedium Schlimii* Rchb.f., *Paphiopedilum Schlimii* Pfitz.) Lvs. clustered, ligulate, acute, to 12″ long, about ¾″ wide, bright grass-green above, often purplish beneath. Infl. erect, rarely branched, to almost 2′ tall, 5–8-fld., pubescent, the peduncle usually greenish-purple. Fls. to 2″ in diam., all segms. covered with a soft velvety down, variable in colour. Dors. sep. concave, arching, greenish-white flushed with pale rose-pink, oval-oblong, acute, keeled behind. Synsepal broader, concave, whitish, veined with pale green. Ps. oval-oblong, spreading, white, spotted and stained with rose-purple, mostly near the base. Lip inflated, broadly ovoid in form, contracted at the orifice, rose-carmine, whitish beneath, the infolded lbs. streaked alternately with white and rose-carmine. Staminode bright yellow, flushed in front with brownish. Mostly spring, but sometimes more than once annually. (I) Colombia.

PHRAGMORCHIS L.O.Wms.

But a single species of *Phragmorchis* is known to date, this the excessively rare **P. teretifolia** L.O.Wms., an unusual epiphytic monopodial orchid from Luzon, in the Philippines. Most closely allied to *Schoenorchis* Bl. of the subtribe *Sarcanthinae*, it is today not present in our collections, and because of the diminutive dimensions of the complex flowers, is primarily of scientific interest.

Nothing is known of the genetic affinities of *Phragmorchis*.

CULTURE: Possibly as for the medium-elevation Vandas and their allies. (I)

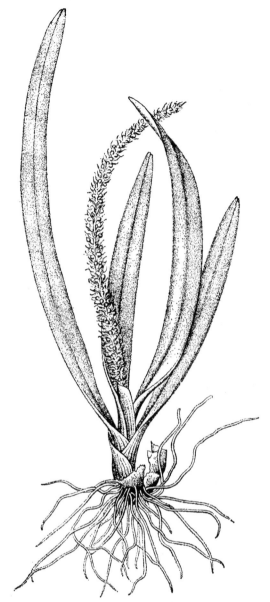

Phreatia goliathensis J.J.Sm. [J.J.SMITH]

PHREATIA Ldl.

This is a remarkable genus comprising more than one hundred and fifty species, of which only one or two appear to be present in contemporary collections, and these must be classed as exceptionally rare orchids. A member of the subtribe *Thelasinae*, *Phreatia* is a highly polymorphic group with both pseudobulbous and pseudobulb-less species. The genus ranges from the Himalayas of India to Samoa, with a huge number of species in New Guinea; none of the components bear flowers of sufficient dimensions to warrant serious attention by any save orchidists interested in the 'botanical' orchids. Typically small epiphytes or lithophytes, the Phreatias have very numerous, intricate, tiny blossoms on mostly elongate, dense spikes. Many

of the members of this genus are botanically little-known, and require considerable additional study by the taxonomists.

No hybrids have been attempted in *Phreatia*, and nothing is known of the genus's genetic ties.

CULTURE: As for the tropical Bulbophyllums, generally. A compost made up of about equal parts of shredded tree-fern fibre and chopped sphagnum moss is excellent, though straight osmunda may also be utilized. The Phreatias are largely strictly tropical plants, requiring warm temperatures and high humidity. (I, H)

P. densiflora (Bl.) Ldl. (*Dendrolirium densiflorum* Bl.)

Sts. very short, not pseudobulbous, with up to about 12 lvs. Lvs. glossy-green, to about 12″ long and more than $\frac{1}{2}$″ wide, linear-lanceolate, very unequally rounded at tip, basally sheathing, rather thinly leathery. Infls. to 14″ long, slender, the densely many-fld. rac. to about 8″ long. Fls. scarcely opening, white, about $\frac{1}{8}$″ long or less, the dors. sep. broadly ovate, the lats. forming a broad mentum; lip widened from base with the end broad and down-curving. Winter. (I, H) Sumatra; Malay Peninsula; Philippines.

P. secunda (Bl.) Ldl. (*Dendrolirium secundum* Bl., *Phreatia microtidis* Ldl., *P. minutiflora* Ldl.)

Sts. not pseudobulbous, with usually 9 lvs. These fleshily leathery, bright green, to 2″ long and slightly more than $\frac{1}{8}$″ wide, linear-lanceolate, the bases short, wider, sheathing. Infls. to about 2$\frac{1}{2}$″ long, the numerous crowded fls. opening well, all directed to one side of the infl. Fls. pale green, about $\frac{1}{8}$″ long, the lip broad basally, almost oblong, deeply channelled towards tip, the extreme apex white. Autumn–winter. (I, H) Sumatra; Malay Peninsula; Philippines.

PHYMATIDIUM Ldl.

Phymatidium is a peculiar genus of about six species of very small epiphytic orchids, all native in the humid woods of Brazil. A member of the subtribe *Ornithocephalinae*, the group is vaguely allied to *Platyrhiza* B.-R., but differs from it in technical details. They are strange little plants with diminutive leaves, copious roots, and tiny, pale-coloured but very complex blossoms. None of the Phymatidiums appears to be in collections at this time.

Nothing is known of the genetic affinities of this rare genus.

CULTURE: As for *Ornithocephalus*. The plants are very fragile, and should be retained on the branch on which they occur if at all possible. (H)

PHYSOCERAS Schltr.

Physoceras is a genus of about five known species, all endemic to Madagascar, where they are variously epiphytic, lithophytic, or terrestrial in the forests. It is a member of the subtribe *Habenarinae*, and is usually placed between *Platycoryne* Rchb.f. and *Cynorkis* Thou., from which it is distinguished on technical characters. The complex, white or rose, rather large flowers are borne in erect few-flowered racemes. Unfortunately, this genus is unknown in contemporary collections, but it appears to offer some very intriguing possibilities for the specialist.

Nothing is known of the genetic affinities of *Physoceras*.

CULTURE: As for *Cynorkis*. (I, H)

PHYSOSIPHON Ldl.

Physosiphon consists of about seven species or more of epiphytic orchids, widespread from Mexico to Brazil. A member of the subtribe *Pleurothallidinae*, it is closely allied to *Stelis* Sw. and to certain species of *Masdevallia* R. & P., and its precise delimitations are not as yet known. It has been suggested that perhaps several of the species do not correctly belong in *Physosiphon*. Vegetatively, they mostly resemble *Pleurothallis*, bearing elongate racemes of small but complex flowers from the leaf-axils. The sepals in this genus are joined for more than half of their length, to form a rather angular, inflated tube, in which the petals, lip and column are borne. *Physosiphon* is rare in contemporary collections, but the species are for the most part attractive little plants with unusual blossoms produced in great profusion.

No hybrids have been made in this genus, and as yet its genetic affinities have not been established.

CULTURE: The several species of *Physosiphon* occur at elevations ranging from near sea-level to more than 9000

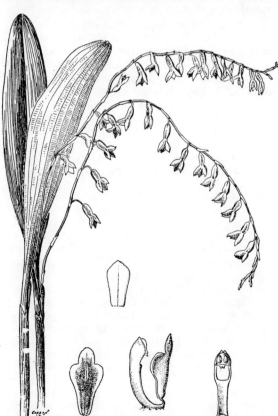

Physosiphon tubatus (Lodd.) Rchb.f. [GORDON W. DILLON]

feet elevation, hence temperature requirements vary. Basically, cultural conditions such as those afforded *Pleurothallis* are needed, although the plants typically do best in small, well-drained pots, in a firm mixture of equal parts of chopped sphagnum moss and shredded tree-fern fibre. When rooting well, the plants also thrive when mounted on smallish tree-fern slabs or cubes. They must never be allowed to become completely dry, nor permitted to stay wet at the roots. Diffused light is needed, since the fleshy foliage has a tendency to burn. (C, I, H)

P. tubatus (Lodd.) Rchb.f. (*Stelis tubatus* Lodd., *Physosiphon carinatus* Ldl., *P. guatemalensis* Rolfe, *P. Lindleyi* Rolfe, *P. Loddigesii* Ldl., *P. ochraceus* A.Rich. & Gal., *P. Moorei* Rolfe)
Sts. clustered, erect, sheathed, to almost 5″ long. Lf. solitary on each st., fleshy, rather rigid, to 6″ long, elliptic to oblanceolate, often yellowish-green. Infls. often several from each lf.-axil, 3–14″ long, densely many-fld., usually arching or horizontal, the fls. often rather regularly ranked. Fls. nodding, highly variable in colour, from greenish-yellow to brick red, to about ¾″ long (often smaller), the sepaline tube strongly angled. Mostly summer. (I, H) Mexico; Guatemala.

PHYSOTHALLIS Garay

A single very rare epiphytic orchid from the mountains of Ecuador makes up this little-known, newly described genus. A member of the subtribe *Pleurothallidinae*, **Physothallis Harlingii** Garay is not present in our collections today, and appears to have been collected on only one occasion. It is indicated as being intermediate between *Physosiphon* Ldl. and *Pleurothallis* R.Br., but differs in technical details of the flowers.

Nothing is known of the genetic affinities of *Physothallis*.

CULTURE: Presumably as for the highland species of *Stelis*, *Pleurothallis*, etc. (I)

PILOPHYLLUM Schltr.

Two species of this incompletely known terrestrial genus are recorded, neither of which appears to. be present in contemporary collections. A segregate from *Chrysoglossum* Bl., *Pilophyllum* differs in several respects from that group, both in vegetative and floral characters. The plants inhabit Java and New Guinea.

Nothing is known of the genetic ties of *Pilophyllum*.

CULTURE: Presumably as for the tropical species of *Phaius*. (H)

PINELIA Ldl.

Among the smallest members of the subtribe *Laeliinae*, *Pinelia* consists of about two or three species of very diminutive epiphytic orchids, native in Brazil, Colombia, and the Guianas. Not especially allied to any other genus of the subtribe, except possibly *Pygmaeorchis* Brade, they seldom exceed one half-inch in height, and bear proportionately large, rather complex flowers. The genus is unknown in collections at this time.

Nothing has been ascertained regarding the genetic affinities of *Pinelia*.

CULTURE: Possibly as for *Ornithocephalus*, although the little plants should receive considerably more shade, and must never be permitted to become dry. (I)

PITYPHYLLUM Schltr.

Two species of *Pityphyllum* are known to date, both of them extremely rare in the wild, and at this time apparently unknown in our collections. The genus is a member of the subtribe *Maxillarinae*, and is relatively close in its alliance to *Maxillaria* R. & P., from which it differs in structural details. Rather small, pseudobulbous epiphytes, **Pityphyllum antioquiense** Schltr. is from Colombia, while **P. laricinum** (Krzl.) Schltr. (*Maxillaria laricina* Krzl.) is from Peru.

Nothing is known of the genetic alliances of this rare genus.

CULTURE: Probably as for the medium-elevation Maxillarias. (I)

PLATANTHERA L.C.Rich.

(*Bicchia* Parl., *Blephariglottis* Raf., *Hemihabenaria* Finet, *Lindblomia* Fries, *Limnorchis* Rydb., *Mecosa* Bl., *Neolindleya* Krzl., *Piperia* Rydb.)

Consisting of approximately two hundred and fifty species, this primarily terrestrial group is sometimes included in *Habenaria* Willd., from which it is separated on technical details. A rather large number of them are now in cultivation, primarily by specialists dealing in the 'hardy' orchids. Distribution of *Platanthera* is very large, with the majority of the species inhabiting the north temperate zones, and a few outlying representatives extending into the tropics of South America and Africa. Their root-system consists of rounded or sometimes lobed tubers, these sessile on the underground portion of the stem. The scapes are usually stout and clothed with variously formed leaves, which become more numerous towards the base. The flowers vary considerably in size, but all are of interesting construction; some are markedly showy, when well-flowered, and well deserve better attention by collectors.

Some natural hybrids are known in *Platanthera*, but otherwise nothing has been ascertained regarding the genetic affinities of the genus.

CULTURE: Generally as for *Caladenia*, although most of the cultivated species of *Platanthera* require relatively cool temperatures at all times. (C, I)

P. bifolia (L.) L.C.Rich. (*Orchis bifolia* L., *Gymnadenia bifolia* Mey., *Habenaria bifolia* Sw., *Lysias bifolia* Salisb., *Platanthera solstitialis* Bom.)

Tubers 2, fusiform, 1–2″ long, with several thick fibres above them. Lvs. 2 (rarely more), basal, usually opposite, ovate-lanceolate, blunt or acute apically. Infl. to 1¾′ tall, bracted, robust, erect or curving slightly, the rac. loosely many-fld., 4–8″ long. Fls. about ¾″ long, white, the lip and slender, cylindrical, curved, 1″ long spur greenish. Dors. sep. ovate, with a blunt apical point; lat. ss. lanceolate, curved towards the tip. Ps. narrowly oblong, curved and forming a hood over the col. Lip entire, linear, tongue-shaped. Mostly Apr.–June. (C, I) Europe; North Asia to China.

P. blephariglottis (Willd.) Hk.f. (*Blephariglottis blephariglottis* Willd., *Habenaria blephariglottis* Ldl.)

Root a cluster of thick fleshy fibres. Lvs. mostly cauline, linear-oblong to oblong-lanceolate, rather pointed, becoming smaller upwards, 3–7″ long. Infl. to almost 3′ tall, leafy, rather stout, the rather loose, usually many-fld. rac. to 4″ long. Fls. about ½″ across, pure white, fragrant. Ss. suborbicular to orbicular-ovate, blunt at tips. Ps. similar to ss., but smaller, toothed or fringed at apex. Lip oblong, entire, mostly deeply cut into many narrow fringe-like segms. June–Aug. (C, I) Eastern and Central Canada to South-east United States.

P. borealis (Cham.) Rchb.f. (*Habenaria borealis* Cham.)

Tubers 2, ovoid, about 1″ long, with few roots above them. Lvs. cauline, numerous, the lowermost oblong-lanceolate, blunt, the uppermost lanceolate, acute to acuminate, becoming bracteose on the rachis, 2–6″ long. Infl. 1–2½′ tall, stout, the many-fld., rather dense rac. 4–8″ long. Fls. about ⅝″ across, white or greenish-white. Dors. sep. ovate, obtuse. Lat. ss. and ps. lanceolate. Lip ovate-oblong, dilated basally. Spur club-shaped, about ⅜″ long. June–July. (C) Alaska south to Washington.

P. ciliaris (L.) Ldl. (*Orchis ciliaris* L., *Habenaria ciliaris* R.Br.)

Tubers usually absent, the root-system thick, cord-like, fibrous. Lvs. mostly cauline, oblong to lanceolate, acute, narrowing upwards, 4–8″ long. Infl. to 2½′ tall, leafy, rather stout, the rac. oblong, densely many-fld., 1½–4½″ long. Fls. rather long-lasting for the genus, ½″ across by 1″ long, brilliant orange. Ss. roundish or obovate, entire. Ps. smaller than ss., linear or oblong-linear, usually somewhat toothed. Lip large, oblong, divided from below the middle into numerous very narrow spreading filaments. Spur slender, about ⅛″ long. Usually July–Aug. (C, I) North-east Canada southward to Tennessee, Mississippi, and Florida.

P. cristata (Michx.) Ldl. (*Orchis cristata* Michx., *Habenaria cristata* R.Br., *Blephariglottis cristata* Raf.)

Roots a cluster of thick, narrowly fusiform fibres. Lvs. few to numerous, linear to linear-lanceolate, becoming smaller upwards. 2–8″ long. Infl. 6–24″ tall, rather stout, leafy, the fairly dense, cylindrical rac. 2–4″ long. Fls. about ¼″ across, white or greenish-white, fragrant. Ss. orbicular-ovate. Ps. similar in shape to ss., but fringed marginally in a comb-like fashion. Lip oblong, very deeply cut into narrow segms. Spur about ¼″ long. Mostly July–Aug. (C, I) Eastern and Central United States, north to Massachusetts, south to Florida.

P. densa (Wall.) Ldl. (*Habenaria densa* Wall., *Platanthera clavigera* Ldl.)

Tuber large, ovoid. Lvs. numerous, ovate or oblong, acute to acuminate, sheathing at base, 3–5″ long. Infl. 1–3′ tall, very robust, leafy upwards, the narrow, densely many-fld. rac. to 15″ long. Fls. erect, ¼″ across, greenish-white, the ss. subequal, ovate, obtuse, puberulous; ps. almost as long as ss., fleshy, obliquely ovate, obtuse; lip linear, obtuse, as long as the clavate, $\frac{1}{4}''$ long spur. June–July. (C) Himalayas, usually at high elevations.

P. dilatata (Pursh) Ldl. ex Beck (*Orchis dilatata* Pursh, *Habenaria dilatata* Hk., *H. fragrans* Niles, *H. graminifolia* Henry)

Root of thick, fleshy fibres. Lvs. cauline, linear-lanceolate, blunt or rounded at apex, 3–8″ long. Infl. 1–2′ tall, rather fleshily stout, leafy, the narrow, many-fld. rac. 2–9″ long. Fls. about $\frac{1}{2}''$ across, snow-white, delicately fragrant, the ss. ovate, blunt, the ps. lanceolate, obtuse, the lip entirely or vaguely 3-lbd., dilated at base, blunt apically, the spur blunt, clavate, incurved, about $\frac{3}{8}''$ long. June–Sept. (C) Newfoundland, Labrador and Alaska south to New Jersey and California.

P. diphylla Rchb.f. (*Gymnadenia diphylla* Link, *Habenaria cordata* R.Br.)

Tuber potato-shaped, about 1″ long, with few fibrous roots above it. Lvs. 2, basal, elliptic-cordate, with prominent rich dark green reticulate venation, 1–2″ long, sometimes borne some distance up the st. and widely separated. Infl. slender, usually curved, to 12″ tall, the rather loosely many-fld., secund rac. 2–4″ long. Fls. about $\frac{1}{4}''$ long, pale green, fragrant, the ss. and ps. lanceolate, suberect; lip 3-lbd. to the middle, the lbs. subequal, lanceolate; spur tiny. Feb.–May. (I) South Europe; North Africa; Canary Islands; Madeira.

P. elegans Ldl. (*Gymnadenia longispica* Durand, *Habenaria elegans* Bolander)

Tubers usually paired, oblong or ovoid, potato-shaped. Lvs. basal, usually 2, ovate or oblong, 3–7″ long, withering as soon as infl. is formed. Infl. to $2\frac{1}{2}'$ tall, rather slender, almost naked, the loosely many-fld. rac. 4–12″ long. Fls. about $\frac{1}{2}''$ across, fragrant, greenish-white. Dors. sep. ovate-lanceolate, the lats. lanceolate. Ps. narrowly lanceolate. Lip 3-lbd., the lat. lbs. small, recurved, spreading, the midlb. oblong-lanceolate. Spur filiform, to $\frac{3}{4}''$ long. Usually July–Aug. (C, I) British Columbia to California.

P. fimbriata (Dryand.) Ldl. (*Orchis fimbriata* Dryand., *Habenaria fimbriata* R.Br.)

Roots tufted, thick, coarse, fibrous. Lvs. mostly cauline, usually erect, becoming smaller upwards, lanceolate to oblong-obovate, 4–12″ long. Infl. 1–4′ tall, stout, leafy, the rather densely many-fld. rac. 4–16″ long. Fls. about $1\frac{1}{4}''$ long and $\frac{3}{4}''$ across, fragrant, varying from rich lilac-purple to white. Ss. ovate, obtuse. Ps. oblong, usually more or less toothed apically. Lip deeply divided into 3 lbs., these fan-shaped, all deeply cut and fringed marginally. Spur slender, about $1\frac{1}{4}''$ long. June–Aug. (C, I) Newfoundland and Quebec south to North Carolina and Tennessee.

P. hologlottis Maxim. (*Habenaria neuropetala* Miq.)

Tubers 2, oblong or fusiform. Lvs. cauline, lanceolate or linear-lanceolate, decreasing in size upwards, to 9″ long. Infl. $1\frac{1}{2}$–$3\frac{1}{2}'$ tall, stout, leafy, the densely many-fld. rac. 6–9″ long. Fls. about $\frac{3}{8}''$ across, bright or dull green, fragrant. Dors. sep. oblong, obtuse, the lats. similar,

deflexed. Ps. shorter than the ss., ovate, obtuse. Lip linear, obtuse, noticeably fleshy. Spur filiform, incurved, $\frac{5}{8}''$ long. May–July. (C) Siberia; North China; Japan.

P. Hookeri (Torr.) Ldl. (*Habenaria Hookeri* Torr., *Lysias Hookeriana* Rydb.)

Roots fibrous, rather thick, fleshy. Lvs. cauline, spreading or ascending, oval, orbicular or obovate, fleshy, glossy bright green, 3–6″ long. Infl. 8–16″ tall, rather stout, leafy, the rather loose, many-fld. rac. 4–8″ long. Fls. more than $\frac{1}{2}''$ across, fragrant, greenish-yellow. Ss. lanceolate, acute, spreading. Ps. narrowly linear or awl-shaped, acute. Lip entire, linear-lanceolate, acute, about $\frac{3}{8}''$ long. Spur slender, about $\frac{3}{4}''$ long. June–Sept. (C, I) Nova Scotia and Ontario to Minnesota and Pennsylvania.

P. hyperborea (L.) Ldl. (*Orchis hyperborea* L., *Habenaria hyperborea* R.Br.)

Roots fibrous, thick, fleshy, fibrous. Lvs. cauline, lanceolate, usually acute to acuminate, 2–12″ long. Infl. $\frac{3}{4}$–2′ tall, rather stout, leafy, the narrow, cylindrical, many-fld. rac. 2–8″ long. Fls. about $\frac{1}{2}''$ across, fragrant, pale green to yellowish-green, the ss. and ps. ovate, obtuse; lip lanceolate, entire, obtuse, about $\frac{3}{8}''$ long; spur clavate, incurving, about $\frac{1}{4}''$ long. May–Aug. (C) Newfoundland and Labrador west to British Columbia, south to Utah and Pennsylvania; Greenland; Iceland.

P. integra (Nutt.) A.Gray (*Orchis integra* Nutt., *Habenaria integra* Spreng.)

Roots thickened, fibrous, almost tuberous. Lvs. mostly near base of st., broadly linear or linear-lanceolate, becoming smaller upwards, 2–8″ long. Infl. 1–2′ tall, rather stout, the oblong, densely many-fld. rac. 1–3″ long. Fls. about $\frac{3}{8}''$ across, honey-scented, very vivid orange. Ss. oval or obovate, obtuse. Ps. ovate, usually larger than ss. Lip oblong or ovate-oblong, irregularly toothed or crenulate, longer than the ps. Spur straight, about $\frac{3}{8}''$ long. July–Sept. (C, I) New Jersey to Florida, west to Texas.

P. japonica (Thunb.) Ldl. (*Orchis japonica* Thunb., *Habenaria japonica* A.Gray, *Platanthera manubriata* Krzl., *P. setchuanica* Krzl.)

Tubers narrowly oblong or fusiform. Lvs. few, variable from cuneate to roundish or oblong, usually about 4″ long at most, becoming bracteose above. Infl. rather stout, 18–20″ tall, the loose or dense, few- to many-fld. rac. 3–6″ long. Fls. about $\frac{7}{8}''$ across, highly fragrant, pale green. Dors. sep. cucullate, acute; lat. ss. obliquely oblong, acute, deflexed. Ps. linear, acutish to obtuse, straight. Lip entire, linear, the margins reflexed, the base almost saccate. Spur filiform, 2″ long. Mostly July. (C) China; Japan, usually in the higher mountains.

P. lacera (Michx.) D.Don (*Orchis lacera* Michx., *Habenaria lacera* Lodd.)

Tubers slender, fusiform, with thick fleshy fibres. Lvs. mostly cauline, oblong to oblong-lanceolate, becoming smaller above, 3–8″ long. Infl. to almost 3′ tall, the rather slender rac. 3–12″ long. Fls. about $\frac{3}{8}''$ across, yellow, suffused with green. Ss. ovate or suborbicular, obtuse. Ps. linear, almost as long as the ss. Lip divided to below the middle into 3 very deeply fringed lbs. Spur clavate, about ⅝″ long. June–Aug. (C, I) Newfoundland west to Manitoba, south to Missouri and Alabama.

P. leucophaea (Nutt.) Ldl. (*Orchis leucophaea* Nutt., *Habenaria leucophaea* A.Gray)

Root of stout fibres. Lvs. cauline, elliptic, ovate to ovate-lanceolate, becoming smaller towards top of st., 2–10″ long. Infl. 1–3′ tall, stout, erect, leafy, the rather few-fld. rac. 2–8″ long. Fls. about ¾″ across, pure white, fragrant, the ss. broadly ovate, almost membranous; ps. obovate or spatulate, irregularly toothed on tip and margins; lip very deeply divided into 3 crenate lbs., these cut into fine-toothed segms., forming a spreading fringe; spur about ¼″ long. June–Aug. (C, I) North-east Canada; East and Central United States.

P. minor (Miq.) Rchb.f. (*Platanthera japonica* (Thunb.) Ldl. var. *minor* Miq., *P. interrupta* Maxim.)

Tubers usually 2, small, globular. Lvs. 2–3, oblong and blunt, or oblong-lanceolate and pointed, 2–3″ long, decreasing in size upwards. Infl. 6–9″ tall, slender, the few- or many-fld. rac. rather short. Fls. about ⅜″ across, green and white, the dors. sep. ovate, pointed, the lat. ss. semi-ovate, falcate, erect; ps. narrowly ovate, acute to sub-acuminate; lip simple, linear, as long as the ss.; spur cylindrical, fleshy, to ⅜″ long. June–July. (C, I) Korea; China; Japan.

P. montana (Bach.) Schltr. (*Platanthera bifolia* (L.) L.C.Rich. var. *montana* Bach., *Platanthera chlorantha* Custer, *Habenaria chlorantha* Bab.)

Tubers usually paired, oblong or fusiform, to about 1″ long. Lvs. usually paired, basal, oblong, obtuse, 3–4″ long. Infl. ¾–2′ tall, rather slender, clothed with a few narrow bracts, the loosely many-fld. rac. 4–6″ long. Fls. about ¾″ long, white, tinged with green, fragrant, the dors. sep. almost triangular, the lats. obliquely lanceolate, spreading; ps. linear, forming a hood with the dors. sep. over the col.; lip lanceolate, tongue-shaped; spur rather stout, cylindrical, about 1⅛″ long. May–June. (C, I) Central and Southern Europe; North Africa, usually in the mountains.

P. nivea (Nutt.) Ldl. (*Gymnadenia nivea* Nutt., *Gymnadeniopsis nivea* Rydb., *Habenaria nivea* Ldl.)

Roots stout, almost tuberous. Lvs. mostly basal, becoming much reduced in size upwards, linear or linear-oblong, 2–8″ long. Infl. ¾–1¾′ tall, usually slender, leafy, the cylindric, usually very dense rac. ¾–4″ long. Fls. about ⅜″ across, very fragrant, usually pure white (rarely pinkish), the dors. sep. ovate, concave, the lat. ss. ovate, considerably dilated on the inner side of the base; ps. broadly linear or linear-oblong, smaller than the ss.; lip linear, sometimes dilated towards the tip, with 2 small teeth near its base; spur filiform, about ⅜″ long. May–Aug. (C, I) New Jersey to Florida, west to Texas and Arkansas.

P. obtusata (Pursh) Ldl. (*Orchis obtusata* Pursh, *Habenaria obtusata* Richards.)

Roots rather long, fibrous. Lf. solitary, basal, obovate, tapering below, 2–4″ long. Infl. 3–8″ tall, slender, naked, noticeably 4-angled, the lax rac. about 1½–2½″ long. Fls. about ¼″ long, pale green and white, fragrant; ss. oblong, the dors. one elliptic-ovate, erect, the lats. spreading, dilated or obtusely 2-lbd. at the base; lip entire, linear-lanceolate, blunt, deflexed; spur slender, curved, blunt, about 3/16″ long. July–Sept. (C, I) Canada; Alaska; North-east and North Central United States; Norway.

P. orbiculata (Pursh) Ldl. (*Orchis orbiculata* Pursh, *Habenaria orbiculata* Torr.)

Roots, thick, fleshy, fibrous. Lvs. usually 2, basal, with their blades flat on the ground, orbicular or oval, undulate marginally, silvery beneath, 4–9″ long. Infl. 1–2¼′ tall, stout, erect, almost naked, the many-fld. rac. 4–9″ long. Fls. about ¾″ across, greenish-white, fragrant, the dors. sep. suborbicular or reniform, the lat. ss. oblong, falcate; ps. smaller than ss., falcate; lip linear, narrow, entire, curved; spur slender, about ¼″ long. June–Aug. (C, I) Canada; Alaska; Northern United States.

P. peramoena (A.Gray) A.Gray (*Habenaria peramoena* A.Gray)

Tubers clustered, narrow, tapering. Lvs. mostly cauline, oblong or lanceolate, becoming smaller towards top of st., 3–8″ long. Infl. ¾–2½′ tall, erect, leafy, the oblong, many-fld. rac. 1½–6″ long. Fls. about ½″ across, rich violet-purple, fragrant, the ss. suborbicular or orbicular-ovate, the dors. one sometimes smaller than the lats.; ps. orbicular-ovate, contracted into a stalk at the base, entire or toothed, smaller than the ss.; lip deeply divided into 3 cuneate lbs., the lat. lbs. sharply toothed, the midlb. deeply notched at apex; spur slender. June–Aug. (C, I) Pennsylvania south to Alabama, west to Illinois and Missouri.

P. psycodes (L.) Ldl. (*Orchis psycodes* L., *Habenaria psycodes* Spreng.)

Roots of thick fibres. Lvs. ovate, elliptic or oblong-lanceolate, becoming smaller upwards, 2–10″ long. Infl. ¾–2¾′ tall, stout, leafy, the usually many-fld. rac. 2–6″ long. Fls. about ⅝″ across, lilac (rarely white), fragrant, the ss. ovate, blunt, the dors. one narrower than the lats.; ps. oblong or oblong-lanceolate, with a few teeth on the outer margins; lip very deeply divided into 3 fan-shaped lbs., these deeply cut to fringed on their margins; spur slender, clavate at tip, about ⅝″ long. June–Aug. (C, I) Newfoundland to Quebec, south to Minnesota and North Carolina.

P. stenostachya Ldl. (*Habenaria stenostachya* Bth., *Habenaria peristyloides* Wight)

Tuber usually solitary, irregular. Lvs. nearly all near base, erect, lanceolate, sheathing at the base, 1–4″ long. Infl. ½–2½′ tall, usually slender, with numerous small sheaths above the lvs., the few- to many-fld. rac. 3–5″ long. Fls. less than ⅜″ across, yellowish-green or white; ss. subequal, linear, concave, pointed; ps. fleshy, triangular, ovate or oblong; lip divided into 3 long, narrow lbs., almost saccate at base; spur straight, stout. May–July. (C, I) China; India; Burma, mostly at high elevations.

P. stricta Ldl. (*Habenaria gracilis* S.Wats., *Habenaria saccata* Greene, *Habenaria stricta* Rydb., *Limnorchis stricta* Rydb.)

Tubers 2, ovoid or oblong, about 1″ long. Lvs. cauline

Platanthera nivea (Nutt.) Ldl. [BLANCHE AMES]

377

and basal, linear-oblong, blunt below, lanceolate and pointed on upper part of the st., gradually becoming bracteose on rachis, 3–9″ long. Infl. $\frac{3}{4}$–$2\frac{1}{4}$′ tall, rather stout, leafy, the loosely many-fld. rac. 6–12″ long. Fls. about $\frac{3}{8}$″ across, pale greenish-yellow, fragrant, the dors. sep. broadly ovate; lat. ss. ovate, blunt, spreading; ps. narrowly lanceolate; lip linear-lanceolate, pointed; spur clavate, about $\frac{1}{4}$″ long. June–Aug. (C, I) Alaska and Alberta south to California and Arizona.

P. albo-marginata (King) Krzl. (*Habenaria albo-marginata* King) Tuber globular, depressed, about $\frac{3}{4}$″ in diam. Lvs. 2, oblong-lanceolate, about $1\frac{1}{2}$″ long. Infl. to 6″ tall, fleshy, 8–10-fld. Fls. about $\frac{1}{2}$″ across, the ss. green with white margins, the ps. and lip white, the cylindrical, upcurved spur green, $\frac{5}{8}$″ long. June. (C) Sikkim, at high elevations.

P. algeriensis Batt. Tubers usually paired, fusiform, to $1\frac{1}{4}$″ long. Lvs. basal, 2 or rarely 3, opposite, oblong-lanceolate, 6–12″ long. Infl. 1–$2\frac{3}{4}$′ tall, stout, furnished with a few lanceolate, large, lf.-like bracts, the very densely many-fld., erect, cylindrical rac. 4–9″ long. Fls. about 1″ long, yellowish-green, fragrant, the ovate dors. sep. and narrowly oblong ps. forming a hood over the col.; lat. ss. lanceolate, curved, spreading; lip entire, oblong-lanceolate; spur curved, slender, clavate towards tip, $1\frac{1}{4}$″ long. Mar.–May. (I) North Africa, especially Algeria.

P. arcuata Ldl. (*Habenaria arcuata* Hk.f.) Roots branched, thickened, tuberous, fibrous. Lvs. basal and cauline, oblong or lanceolate, pointed, narrowing towards apex of st., sheathing at base, 3–4″ long. Infl. very stout and leafy, to 15″ tall, the stout rac. many-fld. Fls. about $\frac{3}{4}$″ across, green and white, fragrant, the dors. sep. cucullate, beaked, the lat. ss. oblong, blunt, deflexed, the ps. small, linear, membranous; lip linear, large, twice as long as the ss., with incurved margins; spur incurved, pointed, to $2\frac{1}{2}$″ long. May–June. (C, I) Western Himalayas, at high elevations.

P. Bakeriana (King) Krzl. (*Habenaria Bakeriana* King) Tubers oblong or ovoid. Lf. usually solitary, rarely paired, oblong-lanceolate, pointed, 2–3″ long. Infl. slender, about 12″ tall, the many-fld. rac. about 4″ long. Fls. about $\frac{1}{4}$″ across, green, fragrant; dors. sep. oblong; lat. ss. oblong-lanceolate, subfalcate, pointed; ps. ovate, suboblique, forming a hood over the col. with the dors. sep.; lip entire, narrowly linear, as long as the ss.; spur filiform, incurved, about $\frac{3}{8}$″ long. Mostly July. (C, I) Sikkim, at high elevations.

P. Chorisiana (Ldl.) Rchb.f. (*Peristylus Chorisianus* Ldl., *Platanthera Matsudai* Mak.) Tubers 2, ovoid or oblong. Lvs. cauline, ovate or ovate-lanceolate, pointed, 2–4″ long. Infl. to 2′ tall, rather stout, bearing 2 lvs., the loose, few-fld. rac. 3–5″ long. Fls. about $\frac{3}{8}$″ across, pale green; ss. ovate, acute or obtuse, membranous, spreading; ps. rounded-ovate, curving over the col., somewhat fleshy; lip ovate, hooded towards tip; spur cylindrical, rather short. June–Aug. (C, I) North Japan; Aleutian Islands.

P. Dyeriana (King) Krzl. (*Habenaria Dyeriana* King) Tubers 2, oblong. Lvs. basal and cauline, numerous, oblong, blunt, 1–$1\frac{1}{2}$″ long, becoming smaller upwards. Infl. about 10″ tall, very leafy, the rac. few- to many-fld., 1–$2\frac{1}{2}$″ long. Fls. about $\frac{1}{2}$″ across, green and white; dors. sep. ovate-triangular, blunt; lat. ss. similar, crenulate; ps. narrowly ovate-triangular, the tip minutely toothed; lip triangular and linear towards tip, with thickened lines on the disc; spur filiform, thickened at tip, about $\frac{1}{4}$″ long. Mostly Aug. (C) Sikkim, at elevations of about 12,000 feet.

P. Finetiana Schltr. (*Habenaria stenantha* Finet var. *auriculata* Finet) Roots elongated, filiform, possibly tuberous in time. Lvs. 3–4, oblong-elliptic or elliptic-lanceolate, 4–6″ long. Infl. to 2′ tall, sparsely leafy, the rather dense 15–20-fld. rac. to 6″ long. Fls. about $\frac{3}{8}$″ across, green and white, fragrant; dors. sep. oblong-elliptic, concave, blunt, erect; lat. ss. obliquely broadly ovate, blunt, deflexed; ps. obliquely ligulate, erect; lip linear-subulate, the margins reflexed; spur filiform, incurved, $\frac{5}{8}$″ long. July–Aug. (C, I) China: Szechuan, at high elevations.

P. Freynii Krzl. (*Platanthera densa* Freyn) Tubers 2, ovoid or fusiform, shortly 2-lbd. Lvs. 2, near base of st., elliptic, sheathing below, about 3″ long. Infl. 8–10″ tall, sheathed basally, the densely many-fld. rac. 2–3″ long. Fls. about $\frac{1}{2}$″ across, white or greenish-white; dors. sep. cordate; lat. ss. obliquely elliptic, obtuse, as long as dors. sep.; ps. obliquely lanceolate, shorter than the ss.; lip broadly linear, slightly ascending, about $\frac{1}{2}$″ long. June–July. (C, I) Siberia, mostly near Lake Baikal.

P. Henryi (Rolfe) Rolfe (*Habenaria Henryi* Rolfe) Root of 2 oblong or ovoid tubers and numerous fibres. Lvs. cauline, oblong or elliptic-oblong, pointed to rather obtuse, $1\frac{1}{2}$–4″ long. Infl. 1–2′ tall, leafy, the lax, usually few-fld. rac. 4–9″ long. Fls. about $\frac{1}{2}$″ across, pale green, faintly fragrant; dors. sep. erect, ovate, concave, rather blunt; lat. ss. spreading, oblong, blunt; ps. obliquely ovate-lanceolate, pointed, forming a hood with the dors. sep.; lip entire, oblong-linear, blunt, fleshy; spur slender, cylindrical, curved, $\frac{5}{8}$″ long. June–Aug. (C) Western China, at high elevations.

P. Heyneana (Ldl.) Ldl. (*Habenaria Heyneana* Ldl., *Habenaria glabra* A.Rich.) Tuber usually solitary, oblong or ovoid. Lvs. ovate, erect or recurved, subimbricate, shortly sheathing, pointed. Infl. to 12″ tall, stout, leafy upwards, the secund, many-fld. rac. 2–4″ long. Fls. about $\frac{1}{2}$″ across, greenish-yellow; dors. sep. ovate-oblong; lat. ss. oblong-lanceolate ps. linear-oblong; lip divided into 3 linear segms. almost to the base, the median one broader than the others; spur subclavate, $\frac{3}{8}$″ long. Mostly July. (C, I) South India.

P. juncea (King) Krzl. (*Habenaria juncea* King) Tubers small, ovoid or oblong. Lf. solitary, basal, oblong-lanceolate, pointed, short-stalked, 2–3″ long. Infl. slender, 12–15″ tall, with 2–3 linear-lanceolate distant bracts, the rac. very loose, slender. Fls. $\frac{3}{16}$″ across, green; dors. and lat. ss. ovate-triangular; ps. narrowly oblong, blunt; lip entire, ovate-lanceolate, pointed; spur cylindrical, incurved, $\frac{1}{8}$″ long. Usually July. (C) Sikkim, at high elevations.

P. Makinoi Yatabe Tubers several, oblong. Lvs. basal and cauline, ovate-oblong or elliptic, about $2\frac{1}{2}$″ long. Infl. about 12″ tall, stout, leafy, the densely many-fld. rac. about $2\frac{1}{2}$″ long. Fls. about $\frac{3}{8}$″ across, yellowish-green to white, fragrant; dors. sep. ovate or oblong, obtuse; lat. ss. subobliquely ovate, blunt; ps. falcate-ovate or narrowly triangular, small; lip oblong-ovate, dilated medially, short; spur cylindrical, incurved, $\frac{3}{16}$″ long. July–Aug. (C, I) Japan.

P. mandarinorum Rchb.f. (*Platanthera Keiskei* Franch., *P. oreades* Franch.) Tubers usually paired, ovoid, about $\frac{3}{4}$″ long. Lvs. usually 1–6, oblong or linear-lanceolate, pointed, 2–3″ long. Infl. slender, 9–15″ tall, somewhat leafy, the loosely few- to many-fld. rac. 2–3″ long. Fls. about $\frac{3}{4}$″ across, green and white, fragrant; dors. sep. oblong, small; lat. ss. narrowly oblong, blunt, reflexed; ps. falcately ovate-lanceolate, blunt; lip narrowly linear, blunt; spur filiform, $1\frac{1}{4}$″ long. June–July. (C, I) China; Japan, usually growing under coniferous trees.

P. Maximowicziana Schltr. Tubers paired, small, rounded. Lvs. cauline, few in number, oblong-lanceolate, pointed, 2–3″ long, becoming smaller and narrower upward. Infl. 5–10″ tall, slender, the few-fld. rac. short. Fls. about ⅜″ across, yellowish-green, fragrant; dors. sep. ovate, pointed; lat. ss. narrowly ovate, often slightly hooked at the tip, all erect; ps. narrowly ovate, pointed; lip entire, broadly linear, obtuse; spur cylindrical, fleshy, about ½″ long. July–Aug. (C, I) Korea; Japan.

P. neglecta Schltr. Tubers usually paired, oblong. Lf. solitary, suberect, oblong, obtuse, cuneate basally, 4½″ long or less. Infl. to 15″ tall, with 1 leaf below the middle, with lf.-like sheaths above, slender, smooth, the loose, 6–12-fld. rac. 4–5″ long. Fls. about ⅜″ long, reddish-purple; dors. sep. almost round, blunt, concave, erect; lat. ss. deflexed, oblong, blunt; ps. narrowly ligulate, pointed, oblique, spreading; lip linear, blunt, decurved, somewhat dilated at the base; spur slender, dilated medially, pointed, ⅜″ long. July–Aug. (C, I) Korea; North-east China.

P. nipponica Mak. (*Platanthera Matsumurana* Schltr.) Tubers 2, ovoid or oblong. Lf. solitary, basal, ligulate, blunt or pointed, erect, slightly narrowed towards the base. Infl. 12–15″ tall, slender, smooth, with 4–6 lanceolate sheaths above, the loosely 3–8-fld. rac. 1½–2½″ long. Fls. about ¼″ across, pale green, fragrant, the dors. sep. oblong, blunt, concave, smooth, erect; lat. ss. oblong-ligulate, blunt, oblique and deflexed; ps. oblong, subfalcate, blunt, erect; lip ligulate, blunt, dilated at base; spur filiform, ascending, ⅝″ long. June–Aug. (C, I) Japan.

P. ophrydioides F.Schmidt. Tubers plural, narrowly oblong. Lvs. 1–2, ovate or elliptic, blunt or pointed, about 2″ long, becoming linear-lanceolate and bracteose above. Infl. 8–10″ tall, slender, the loose rac. 5–10-fld. Fls. about ½″ across, pale green, fragrant; dors. sep. ovate, pointed; lat. ss. similar, somewhat narrower, reflexed; ps. ovate, pointed, erect; lip entire, narrowly oblong; spur filiform, about ½″ long. Mostly Aug. (C, I) Japan; Sakhalin Island.

P. sachalinensis F.Schmidt. Tubers 2, small, ovoid. Lvs. 2–3, distant, oblong or ovate, blunt, about 6″ long. Infl. to 2′ tall, rather stout, densely many-fld., 4–8″ long. Fls. about ¼″ across, white, fragrant; dors. sep. oblong, blunt; lat. ss.

subfalcate; ps. ovate, blunt, spreading; lip entire, linear; spur green, filiform, curved, about ⅜″ long. July–Aug. (C, I) North Japan; Sakhalin Island.

PLATYCORYNE Rchb.f.

Platycoryne is a genus of the subtribe *Habenarinae*, somewhat allied to *Habenaria* Willd., of about nine species of rather slender, few-flowered terrestrial orchids, native in tropical Africa, with a single representative in Madagascar. They are rather showy little plants with brilliantly-hued blossoms, but unfortunately are unknown in contemporary collections.

Nothing is known concerning the genetic affinities of *Platycoryne*.

CULTURE: As for *Cynorkis*. (I, H)

PLATYGLOTTIS L.O.Wms.

Platyglottis coriacea L.O.Wms., the only described member of this peculiar genus of the subtribe *Ponerinae*, is an extremely rare epiphytic orchid known to date only from the immediate vicinity of El Valle de Antón, Coclé Province, Panama. A rather large, mostly pendulous, leafy-stemmed plant with racemose flowers which are big for the alliance, it is unfortunately unknown in contemporary collections, although it is an unusually interesting orchid, well worth attention by the specialist.

Nothing is known of the genetic affinities of *Platyglottis*.

CULTURE: Presumably as for the tropical 'reed-stem' type Epidendrums, though because of its pendulous habit, it should probably be grown on a tree-fern slab. (I)

PLATYLEPIS A.Rich.
(*Coralliocyphos* Fleischm. & Rech., *Diplogastra* Welw., *Notiophrys* Ldl.)

Platylepis is an incompletely understood genus of about fourteen species of mostly insignificant terrestrial

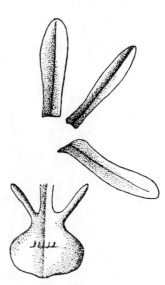

Platyrhiza quadricolor B.-R. [Hoehne, *Flora Brasilica*]

379

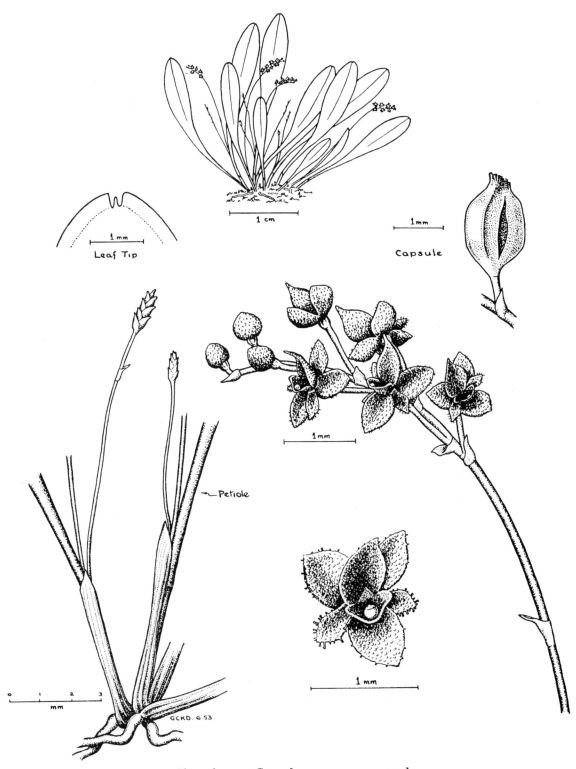

1 cm

Leaf Tip

1 mm

Capsule

1 mm

Petiole

1 mm

o   1   2   3
mm

GCKD. 6·53

1 mm

Platystele ornata Garay [G.C.K.DUNSTERVILLE]

380

orchids with a wide distribution, ranging from tropical Africa and the Mascarene Islands to New Guinea, the New Hebrides, Samoa, and Tahiti. A member of the subtribe *Physurinae*, it is somewhat allied to *Moerenhoutia* Bl. and *Lepidogyne* Bl., from which it differs in structural details of the rather small but extremely complex flowers. None of the species is in cultivation at this time.

Nothing is known concerning the genetic affinities of *Platylepis*.

CULTURE: Possibly as for *Anoectochilus*. (H)

PLATYRHIZA B.-R.

The only known member of this genus, **Platyrhiza quadricolor** B.-R., is a very rare epiphytic inhabitant of the Brazilian forests. A member of the subtribe *Ornithocephalinae*, it is apparently not present in contemporary collections, though it is an attractive dwarf plant, rather reminiscent of *Hofmeisterella* Rchb.f. in habit, with small but brightly coloured and remarkably intricate blossoms.

Nothing is known of the genetic affinities of *Platyrhiza*.

CULTURE: Presumably as for *Ornithocephalus*. (H)

PLATYSTELE Schltr.

Platystele is a genus of perhaps two species, one of these from Costa Rica, the other in Venezuela. They are dwarf epiphytes, mostly inhabiting 'cloud forest' formations, of the complex subtribe *Pleurothallidinae*. The tiny flowers, at least in the Venezuelan species, are amazingly intricate. Neither of the Platysteles appears to be in cultivation at this time.

Nothing is known of the genetic affinities of this rare genus.

CULTURE: Presumably as for the high-elevation species of *Pleurothallis*, etc. (C, I)

PLECTRELMINTHUS Raf.
(*Leptocentrum* Schltr.)

The solitary member of this genus is a segregate from both *Angraecum* Bory and *Aërangis* Rchb.f., by reason of the very complicated and unusual structure of the column and the pollinia. A very showy plant while in flower, it is regrettably rare in contemporary collections. A rather widespread epiphyte in tropical West Africa, it is among the most interesting of all the myriad angraecoid orchids.

As yet, *Plectrelminthus* has not been taken in hand by the breeders. It is presumably genetically compatible with at least some of the other members of the '*Angraecum* alliance'. Experimental hybridization should produce some extraordinary results.

CULTURE: As for the tropical Angraecums, etc. (H)

P. caudatus (Ldl.) Summerh. (*Angraecum caudatum* Ldl., *Plectrelminthus bicolor* Raf., *Listrostachys caudata* Rchb.f., *Leptocentrum caudatum* Schltr.)

St. erect, usually less than 12″ tall, densely leafy to the base typically, giving off numerous heavy roots to several feet in length, the growing tips of which are distinctly glaucous. Lvs. close together, recurved, closely imbri-

cating basally, rather heavily leathery, broadly strap-shaped, unequally 2-lbd. at apex, 12–15″ long, to 1½″ wide. Infls. horizontally arranged to somewhat drooping, to 2′ long, the peduncle and rachis brownish-green, bearing 5–9 (rarely more) fls. in apical two-thirds, the rachis of which is conspicuously zigzag. Fls. distant, inverted, fragrant, long-lasting, heavy-textured, to 3″ in length, almost as wide, the ss. and ps. olive-green, flushed with tan or pale brown, the lip white, the apical awl-shaped mucro green, the oddly twisted spur 8–9″ long, pale brown to brownish-green. Ss. and ps. spreading, rather similar, linear-lanceolate, acuminate, the margins revolute, the tips incurving. Lip with a basal claw which is channelled towards the spur entrance, the lamina obcordate-cuneate, with rather prominent veins and crisped, undulate margins. Col. terete, brown, the rostellum prolonged into an awl-shaped red-brown beak; anther also with a beak, this shorter than that of the rostellum and appressed against it. Aug.–Oct. (H) Tropical West Africa, especially Sierra Leone.

PLECTROPHORA Focke

Four members of this rare and little-known genus of the subtribe *Comparettiinae* are known at this time, all of them epiphytes in Brazil, where they are rare even in the wild state. They rather simulate a robust *Ornithocephalus* in vegetative habit, but differ radically in the structure and dimensions of the proportionately large, very unusually complex flowers. None of the Plectrophoras is present in collections at this time, though they are of potential interest to connoisseurs.

Nothing is known of the genetic affinities of *Plectrophora*.

CULTURE: Presumably as for *Ornithocephalus*. (I, H)

PLEIONE D.Don
(*Bolborchis* Zoll. & Mor., *Gomphostylis* Endl.)

Pleione is a genus as yet little-known by collectors in the United States, although its members—of which about twenty or so are known to date—have been highly popular and widely-grown in England and on the Continent for generations. They are among the most delightful of all cool-growing orchids (some of the species also thrive under intermediate temperatures), and their cultural requirements are easily met even in the most modest of collections. Closely allied to *Coelogyne* Ldl. (and, indeed, sometimes included as a section of that genus), they are unique in habit, being cluster-forming, mostly rather dwarf plants found growing in the ground, or on rocks or trees, with peculiar flask-shaped, irregular pseudobulbs, deciduous folded foliage, and solitary, often proportionately very large and handsome flowers which typically arise concurrently with the new growths. These blossoms, often with ornately frilled and incised tubular labellums, rather simulate those of Cattleyas, and when produced in abundance—as they usually are on well-grown specimens—are singularly attractive. The range of the genus *Pleione* is principally in the Himalayan regions of India, although some of the representatives extend into Burma, Thailand, and China, and several very fine species occur in Formosa.

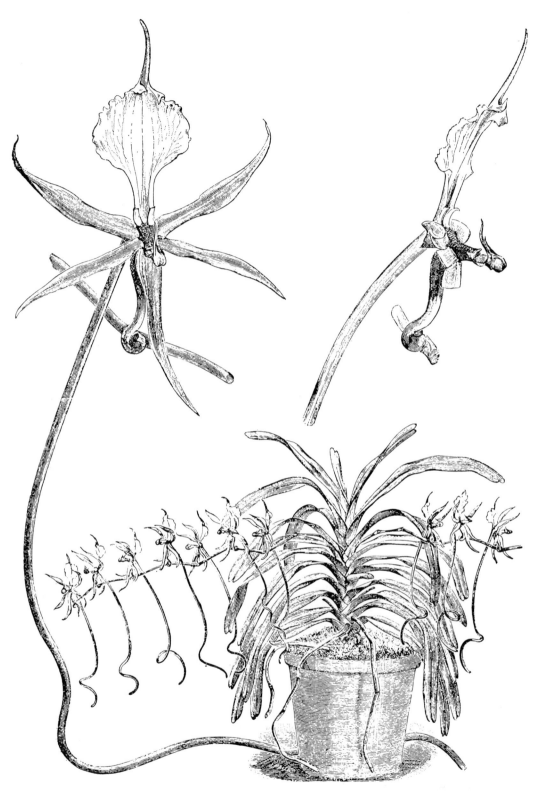

Plectrelminthus caudatus (Ldl.) Summerh. [VEITCH]

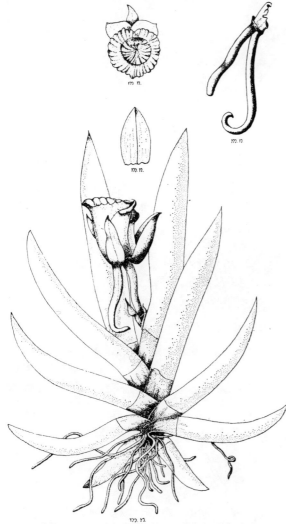

Plectrophora calcarhamata Hoehne [Hoehne, *Flora Brasílica*]

A single hybrid has recently been made in *Pleione*, in France. Additional crosses within the genus, and with such presumed allies as Coelogyne, seem to offer some unusually interesting potentials.

CULTURE: The Pleiones do best under cultivation when grown in shallow pots or fern-pans, these to be perfectly drained for optimum results, as the plants are very intolerant of stale conditions at the roots. A compost made up of about equal parts of fibrous loam, chopped sphagnum moss, gritty white sand, and chopped tree-fern fibre; the addition of a top-dressing of sphagnum moss is often recommended. While actively growing, the plants do best in the cool-house or intermediate-house, in rather humid conditions, with copious water and abundant fertilizer applied; unsightly spotting of the rather delicate, quickly deciduous foliage often results from watering late in the day, hence this should be avoided. When the pseudobulbs are fully matured, and the leaves begin to fall, water should be sharply curtailed—giving the plants only enough to avoid shrivelling

of the pseudobulbs—but as the flower-buds appear from the (typically) bare pseudobulbs, water may be resumed, to better expand the handsome blossoms. Repotting and division into single pseudobulbs is urged on an annual basis, this to be done immediately after the flowers fade. Water should be gradually increased as the new shoots appear, after a rest-period sometimes lasting as long as two months. A rather bright spot in the collection suits them well, although excessive exposure will cause burning of the foliage. (C, I)

P. Delavayi (Rolfe) Rolfe (*Coelogyne Delavayi* Rolfe)
Pbs. clustered, globular or slightly flattened, about 1″ long. Lvs. appearing after the fls. fade, plicate, elliptic-oblong or elliptic-lanceolate, acutish, 3–6″ long. Scape sheathed, 3–3½″ long. Fl. solitary, about 3″ in diam., bright rose-purple, the lip marked with darker rose-purple. Ss. and ps. narrowly lanceolate, acutish. Lip rhomboid, obscurely 3-lbd., the midlb. fimbriate, with 3 rows of teeth down the middle of the disc. Mostly May–July. (C, I) China: Yunnan, at rather high elevations.

P. Hookeriana D.Don (*Coelogyne Hookeriana* Ldl.)
Rhiz. rather creeping. Pbs. not particularly clustered, narrowly ovoid, ¾–1″ long. Lvs. 1–2, elliptic-lanceolate, acutish, plicate, 2–4″ long, often arising with the infl. Scape arising from apex of pb., slender, sheathed, to 2″ long. Fl. solitary, about 2″ in diam., rather fragile in character, the ss. and ps. pale rose-purple, the lip white, more or less blotched with pale reddish-brown, the disc with 5 yellow, fringed keels down its centre. Ss. and ps. subequal, spreading, oblong-lanceolate, acutish. Lip large, concave, very obscurely 3-lbd., the margin toothed and/or undulate, the disc with 5 ciliate ridges. Spring–early summer. (C, I) Himalayas, especially Sikkim; Burma; Thailand.

P. humilis (Sm.) D.Don (*Epidendrum humile* Sm., *Cymbidium humile* Sm., *Coelogyne humilis* Ldl.)
Pbs. flagon-shaped, clustered or somewhat distant from one another, 1–1½″ long. Lvs. sheathed at the base and springing from the pb.-apices, elliptic or lanceolate, plicate, quickly deciduous, 2–6″ long. Scape 2–3″ long, borne from pb.-base, 1–rarely 2-fld., sheathed. Fls. 1–2″ in diam., faintly fragrant, highly variable in colour, ranging from almost pure white to pale purple, usually with some reddish-purple, orange, or brown markings on the lip. Ss. and ps. spreading, subequal, lanceolate, rather narrow. Lip obovate, forming a vague tube around the col. at its base, the apical margins fringed, the disc furnished with several fringed keels. Usually Sept.–Nov. (C, I) Nepal to Sikkim, usually at high elevations (about 6000–10,000 feet above sea-level).

P. praecox (Sm.) D.Don (*Epidendrum praecox* Sm., *Cymbidium praecox* Sm., *Coelogyne praecox* Ldl., *Coelogyne Wallichiana* Ldl., *Pleione Wallichiana* Ldl.)
Pbs. highly variable, usually rather tightly clustered, bottle-shaped to very shortly cylindric, strongly depressed at the apex, to more than 1½″ tall, often blotched with dark red-purple on a rich green ground. Lvs. 1–2, quickly deciduous, rather fragile in texture, elliptic or lanceolate, acutish, sheathed at base, 2–9″ long. Scapes

Pleione humilis (Sm.) D.Don [VEITCH]

1-fld. (rarely 2-fld.), 3–4″ long, sheathed. Fls. rather variable in size and coloration, ranging from 2½–4″ in diam., fragrant, the ss. and ps. rich rose-purple, the lip usually darker, the keels on the disc white and yellow. Ss. and ps. narrowly lanceolate, pointed, often somewhat recurving. Lip bifid at apex, usually deeply fimbriate, the crests very fringed. Autumn, mostly Sept.–Oct. (C, I) Southern China; Himalayas; Burma.

P. Reichenbachiana T.Moore (*Coelogyne Reichenbachiana* Veitch)

Pbs. cylindric, 2–2½″ tall, lobed, and with a conical protuberance at the apex, green, spotted and mottled with blackish-brown. Lvs. similar to the other spp., soon deciduous. Scapes 1-fld. (rarely 2-fld.). Fls. about 2″ in diam., the ligulate ss. light rosy-lilac striated and stained with amethyst-purple in the middle and towards

XIᴮ *Stenoglottis fimbriata* Ldl. [A.D.HAWKES]

XIᴬ *Stenocoryne racemosa* (Hk.) Krzl. [A.D.HAWKES]

the apex; ps. narrower and paler in colour than ss. Lip oblong, emarginate, the basal half rolled around the col., white, the apical half flaring, ciliate marginally, white, spotted, with purple; disc with 3 fringed, yellow keels. Col. slender, with 3 notched wings at the apex. Autumn. (C, I) Burma.

P. Forrestii Schltr. Pbs. pear-shaped, with several ridges near the apex, about 1″ long. Lvs. absent at flowering-time, ovate-lanceolate, rather fragile. Scapes erect, 1-fld., to about 6″ tall. Fls. about 3″ across, vivid orange, marked on the lip with brown. Ss. and ps. oblong-ligulate, blunt, smooth. Lip rhomboid, obscurely 3-lbd., the lat. lbs. rounded, short, with toothed margins, the midlb. much larger, almost square, marginally toothed or fringed, the nerves thickened and somewhat toothed at the base down the centre. Apr.–June. (C, I) China: Western Yunnan.

P. grandiflora Rolfe Pbs. ovoid or ovoid-oblong, about 1½″ long. Lvs. absent at flowering-time, oblong-lanceolate, plicate, rather fragile, in texture. Scapes sheathed at base, 1 fld., 4–5″ long. Fls. about 4″ in diam., fragrant, pure white, sometimes with some crimson-purple markings on the lip. Ss. and ps. subequal, lanceolate-oblong. Lip vaguely 3-lbd., broadly elliptic-oblong, with deep marginal fringes, the disc with 5 rows of fringe-like teeth. Spring–early summer. (C, I) China: Western Yunnan.

P. Henryi Rolfe (*Coelogyne Henryi* Rolfe, *Coelogyne pogonioides* Rolfe, *Pleione pogonioides* Rolfe) Pbs. narrowly ovoid, about ¾″ long. Lf. solitary, produced simultaneously with the fls., elliptic-lanceolate, obtuse, 4–7½″ long. Scapes 1–2-fld., sheathed at base, 3–6″ long. Fls. about 3″ in diam., rich magenta-rose, with some dark magenta markings on the lip. Ss. and ps. narrowly lanceolate, acutish. Lip obscurely 3-lbd., the lat. lbs. rounded, the midlb. orbicular-oblong, fringed marginally, with 3 rows of sharp teeth down the centre of the disc. Mostly June. (C, I) China: Yunnan, Hupeh, Szechuan.

P. lagenaria Ldl. (*Coelogyne lagenaria* Ldl.) Pbs. about 1″ long, somewhat bottle-shaped, with a rounded protuberance about midway between base and apex, green, mottled with blackish-brown. Lvs. narrowly oblanceolate, 7–10″ long, quickly deciduous. Scapes 1-fld., about 2″ long, strongly sheathed. Fls. 2–3″ in diam., fragrant, the narrowly lanceolate ss. and ps. rose-lilac, often flushed darker medially and apically. Lip oblong, emarginate, the basal half infolded over the col., pale rose-lilac externally, striped inside with purple, the distal half open with undulate margins, purple with paler transverse streaks and blotches and with a white margin, the disc yellow and red with 5 longitudinal fringed keels. Col. clavate, winged at apex. Autumn, mostly Oct.–Nov. (C, I) Assam; Burma.

P. maculata (Ldl.) Ldl. (*Coelogyne maculata* Ldl., *Coelogyne diphylla* Ldl., *Coelogyne candida* Ldl., *Coelogyne Arthuriana* Rchb.f., *Pleione Arthuriana* Rchb.f.) Pbs. almost bottle-shaped, about 1″ long, the basal two-thirds cylindric, the apical third conical. Lvs. lanceolate, acute, plicate, 6–9″ long, quickly deciduous. Scapes short, 1-fld., sheathed at the base with small greenish scales and with a large membranaceous bract above. Fls. more than 2″ in diam., rather variable in shape and colour, fragrant, the spreading similar, subequal ss. and ps. white, the ps. rarely streaked with purple, lanceolate, acute. Lip oval-oblong, 3-lbd., the lat. lbs. narrow, erect, white, streaked obliquely on the inner side with purple, the midlb. spreading, undulate, white with large purple marginal spots (these sometimes confluent to form a solid marginal band) and yellow disc, this with 5 fringed keels that

extend to the base. Col. slender, terete, white. Autumn, mostly Oct.–Nov. Northern India; Himalayas; Assam; Thailand.

P. yunnanensis Rolfe Pbs. spherical, very flattened, pumpkin-shaped, less than 1″ tall. Lvs. absent at flowering-time, lanceolate, acutish, rather small. Scapes slender, sheathed, 1-fld., 4–5″ long. Fls. about 3″ in diam., variable in colour from rosy-lilac to bright pink or reddish-purple, the lip usually marked with darker shades. Ss. and ps. almost equal, oblong-lanceolate, acutish. Lip obovate-orbicular, sometimes obscurely 3-lbd., blunt, fringed towards the tip, the disc with 5 lamellae. Spring, mostly April. (C, I) China: Western Yunnan.

PLEUROBOTRYUM B.-R.

Two species of *Pleurobotryum* are known to science, both of them rare epiphytic orchids of the subtribe *Pleurothallidinae*, endemic to Brazil. Pendulous plants, they rather simulate an *Octomeria* (or even a slender *Brassavola*), and are closest in taxonomic alliance to *Pleurothallis* R.Br. Although they are very pretty orchids when in bloom—with their racemes of rather intricate flowers—they appear to be unknown in our collections at this writing.

Nothing is known of the genetic affinities of *Pleurobotryum*.

CULTURE: Presumably as for *Pleurothallis*, although because of the pendulous habit of the plants, they will need to be grown on a tree-fern slab or raft. (I, H)

PLEUROTHALLIS R.Br.

(*Acianthera* Scheidw., *Acronia* Presl, *Anathallis* B.-R., *Brenesia* Schltr., *Centranthera* Scheidw., *Crocodilanthe* Rchb.f., *Duboisia* Karst., *Dubois-Reymondia* Karst., *Humboldtia* R. & P., *Kraenzlinella* O.Ktze., *Myoxanthus* P. & E., *Otopetalum* Krzl., *Restrepia* HBK, *Rhynchopera* Kl., *Specklinia* Ldl., *Talpinaria* Karst.)

Pleurothallis is without a doubt the largest genus of the Orchidaceae in the New World, the latest estimate of its number of component species running in excess of one thousand. In their native haunts they are often among the most ubiquitous of all orchidaceous plants, it being a not uncommon event to encounter a dozen or more different species on a single tree-trunk in the luxuriant 'cloud-forests' of Central or South America, where these enchanting plants reach their greatest development. Outlying representatives extend as far as South Florida and Argentina, with the greatest centres of dispersal occurring in Brazil, the Colombian Andes, and Costa Rica. Typically epiphytes (there are a few species of *Pleurothallis* which grow as terrestrials or on rocks as lithophytes), they are extremely diverse in vegetative habit, ranging from minute moss-like plants to peculiar bushy structures several feet in height. Pseudobulbs are never present, but the secondary stems are on rare occasions somewhat thickened; they for the most part bear a solitary leaf, of highly variable dimensions and appearance. The inflorescence is terminal or rarely lateral, fasciculate, racemose, or sometimes a solitary flower at the end of an elongate peduncle. The flowers for the most part are small, of extremely diverse colour and shape, usually with the sepals larger than the other

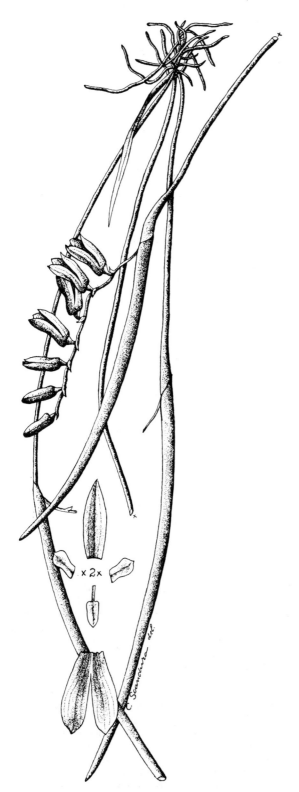

Pleurobotryum atropurpureum B.-R. [Hoehne, *Flora Brasílica*]

segments. Despite their often diminutive dimensions, these blossoms are among the most intriguing of all orchids, and when carefully studied—preferably with a magnifying hand-lens—the tremendous intricacy and variation in their structure becomes evident. Many of the species are confused botanically, and several of them are highly polymorphic, thus adding to the difficulty of working with the group. The sepals in particular are very variable, especially as to size, while the lip and petals are for the most part remarkably constant as to morphology and size. A rather large number of Pleurothallis are to be found in specialized collections of 'botanical' orchids today, since few of them are sufficiently showy to warrant attention by others than the connoisseur. Almost all of these myriad plants, however, have a great deal of charm when examined closely, and they are becoming more and more popular with orchidists throughout the world as attractive oddities, well deserving of a spot in even the most modest of collections.

No hybrids have been made in *Pleurothallis* as yet, and nothing is known concerning its genetic compatibilities. A vast field of endeavour is open to the enterprising breeder here, particularly in hybridization with allied groups, such as *Masdevallia*, *Stelis*, and other members of the huge subtribe *Pleurothallidinae*.

CULTURE: In an aggregation of plants as tremendous as this one, it is difficult to give terse cultural instructions for the group as a whole. For the most part, the Pleurothallis are of singularly easy culture, though there are a few which are notably refractory little plants which never really thrive in the collection, no matter how strictly their wants are met. All of the Pleurothallis should be treated as epiphytes, being grown in small pots (they must never be 'over-potted') rather tightly filled with osmunda or tree-fern fibre; they do very well, for the most part, mounted on small tree-fern slabs, as well. Highly intolerant of disturbance, these orchids should be repotted only when absolutely necessary, though strict attention must be paid to the compost, for they will soon perish if it becomes stale around their roots. Perfect drainage is necessary, since they grow almost throughout the year in most species, and require constantly damp—but never wet—conditions. Semishade is most satisfactory, and care must always be exercised that the often fleshy foliage does not become sunburned through over-exposure to the sun's rays. Regular applications of fertilizers—at about one-half normal strength—increase the vigour of the growths. When the plants become too large for their container, or the centre of the clump (in the case of the tufted species) dies out, they may be divided into smaller specimens to good advantage. They often require as much as two years to become completely re-established after this is done. The clambering or moss-like species should be grown on slabs of tree-fern fibre or on specially made rafts of osmunda, and while becoming established must be tended carefully, as regards the amount of water furnished them. Temperature requirements naturally differ from species to species, depending upon the place of origin of the particular plant. Pleurothallis occur from hot, sea-level areas to elevations in excess of 10,000 feet in the Colombian Andes. (C, I, H)

P. Amesiana L.O.Wms.

Sts. to 8″ tall, produced from a rather creeping rhiz., covered with whitish sheaths. Lf. solitary, slightly stalked, ovate-elliptic, heavily fleshy, to 3″ long. Fls. solitary, but usually several borne at once, about 2″ long, yellowish, variously flushed and spotted with red-brown or purple. Dors. sep. lanceolate, elongate and caudate apically, the tail thread-like. Lat. ss. free or joined into an oblanceolate-oblong, 2-toothed lamina. Ps. similar to the dors. sep. Mostly summer. (I) Guatemala; Costa Rica.

P. Barberiana Rchb.f.

Pls. to about 4″ tall, the sts. rudimentary. Lf. solitary, fleshy, elliptic-spatulate, to about $\frac{3}{4}$″ long. Infls. erect, very slender, loosely 3–6-fld., to about 4″ tall. Fls. about 1″ long, yellowish, spotted with violet-purple, the lip deeper violet-purple. Spring–summer. (I, H) Brazil.

P. Blaisdellii S.Wats. (*Pleurothallis peraltensis* Ames)

Pls. to 6″ tall, usually somewhat shorter. Sts. covered with closely appressed, apically flaring, hairy-margined sheaths, very slender. Lvs. usually very fleshy, typically purplish, ovate-oblong to narrowly lanceolate, oblique and 3-toothed at tip. Infls. racemose, 1–several-fld., often more than one produced simultaneously, generally much shorter than the lf. Fls. less than $\frac{1}{2}$″ long, not opening widely, purplish-red or bronze-green, usually with a deep wine-purple, fuzzy lip. Ss. and ps. often ciliate marginally. Late spring–summer. (I, H) Mexico to Costa Rica and Panama.

P. Brighamii S.Wats. (*Pleurothallis acrisepala* A. & S., *P. barboselloides* Schltr., *P. periodica* Ames)

Pls. less than 4″ tall, the sts. almost obsolete, white-sheathed. Lf. bright lustrous green, rigidly erect, oblanceolate to elliptic-oblong, obtuse to acute and 3-toothed at the apex, to 3″ long and more than $\frac{1}{4}$″ wide. Infls. erect, the peduncle filiform, to 3″ tall, with a congested, few-fld. rac. at the apex, the fls. opening one at a time over a long period of time. Fls. delicate, usually expanding well, to about $\frac{3}{4}$″ long, yellowish with reddish-brown stripes or marked with green and brown. Ss. slightly united at base, the lat. ones united to above the middle. Lip ciliate on apical margin, mobile. Mostly summer. (I, H) Guatemala and British Honduras to Panama.

P. cardiothallis Rchb.f. (*Pleurothallis acutipetala* Schltr., *P. costaricensis* Schltr., *P. Schlechteriana* Ames)

Pls. slender, to $2\frac{1}{4}$′ tall, the sts. rigid, to more than $1\frac{1}{2}$′ long, sheathed, the sheaths deciduous. Lf. leathery, broadly cordate-ovate to cordate-lanceolate, long-tailed apically, spreading or almost horizontal, 4–9$\frac{1}{2}$″ long, $1\frac{1}{4}$–4″ wide below the middle. Fls. ringent, fasciculate, appearing one at a time, rather fleshy, the pedicellate ovaries rather long and slender, subtended by papery tubular bracts, the whole infl. enclosed at base in a papery, flattened spathe to more than 1″ long; individual fls. not opening widely, more than $\frac{1}{2}$″ long, varying from deep red to greenish-yellow, the ss. warty on outer surface, the lats. entirely united. Mostly summer. (I, H) Mexico to Costa Rica.

P. cardium Rchb.f. (*Pleurothallis Lansbergii* Regel)

Pls. to 8″ tall, the sts. slender, to about $6\frac{1}{2}$″ tall. Lf. rigidly leathery, oblong-lanceolate, acuminate, basally somewhat cordate, about 3″ long. Fls. solitary or fasciculate in lf.-axil, fleshy, about $1\frac{1}{4}$″ long, yellowish-red, with a dark red lip. Lat. ss. united. Ps. spreading, linear. Autumn–winter. (I) Venezuela.

P. circumplexa Ldl. (*Pleurothallis mesophylla* A.Rich. & Gal.)

Pls. slender, 4–14″ tall, the clustered sts. 3-winged, 2–9$\frac{1}{2}$″ long. Lf. tapering into and continuous with the st., broadly ovate to lanceolate, obtuse to retuse at the apex, dorsally keeled along the mid-vein, 2$\frac{1}{4}$–5$\frac{1}{2}$″ long, $\frac{3}{4}$–2″ wide, often becoming somewhat wrinkled with age. Infl.-peduncle united its entire length with lf., to 1$\frac{1}{2}$″ long, composed of one or more fasciculate racs. which bear a few fls. and reach a length of about 1″. Fls. distichous, the pedicellate ovaries roughened, as are the ss. outside, reddish-brown or brownish-yellow, not opening fully, to about $\frac{1}{4}$″ long, the lat. ss. united and forming a concave lamina. Spring–summer. (I, H) Mexico and Guatemala to Costa Rica.

P. compacta (Ames) A. & S. (*Platystele compacta* Ames, *Stelis compacta* Ames)

Pls. densely cluster-forming, to 4″ tall, the sts. almost obsolete. Lf. linear-lanceolate to linear-oblanceolate, obtuse and obliquely 3-toothed at apex, leathery, $\frac{1}{4}$–2″ long. Infl. solitary, filiform, exceeding the lf., densely many-fld., the rac. cylindrical, the whole infl. to 4″ tall. Fls. not opening well, mostly less than $\frac{1}{16}$″ across, usually with some purple spots. Ps. as long as or longer than ss., rather narrow. Summer. (I) Guatemala; Honduras; Costa Rica.

P. dolichopus Schltr. (*Pleurothallis lamprophylla* Schltr.)

Pls. erect, slender, clustered, 6–16″ tall, the sts. to 8″ tall, sheathed. Lf. erect, oblong to oblong-elliptic, broadly rounded or obtuse apically, stalked basally, leathery, 2–5$\frac{1}{2}$″ long, to 1$\frac{1}{4}$″ wide. Infls. several, clustered in lf.-axil, rather densely many-fld., all of the fls. open at once, to 8″ long, several-sheathed at base. Fls. roughened on outer surface, suberect, not opening well, $\frac{1}{4}$–$\frac{3}{4}$″ long, the ss. pale yellow or greenish-yellow, the much smaller ps. translucent, the lip red-brown with 3 purple stripes at base. Spring–summer. (I, H) Mexico to Costa Rica.

P. elegans (HBK) Ldl. (*Dendrobium elegans* HBK)

Pls. to 15″ tall. Sts. clustered, slender, erect, to 6″ tall. Lf. coriaceous, oblong, obtuse, narrowed basally into a petiole. Infls. erect, gracefully arching, to more than 12″ long, rather densely many-fld., the fls. secund. Fls. not expanding fully, fleshy, faintly fragrant, long-lasting, about $\frac{1}{4}$″ long, pale yellow. Autumn. (I) Colombia.

P. gelida Ldl. (*Pleurothallis chiriquensis* Schltr.)

Pls. cluster-forming, robust, to almost 2′ tall, the sts. to more than 12″ long, partly covered with papery sheaths. Lf. solitary (very rarely paired), glossy bright green, 3–9″ long and $\frac{1}{2}$–3″ broad, elliptic-oblong to oblong-ovate, obtuse or acute, narrowed basally. Infls. 1–several at once, erect or arching, densely many-fld., racemose, as long as or shorter than the lvs. Fls.

typically nodding, not opening fully, pale yellow to greenish-yellow, delicately fragrant. Ss. warty within, especially towards the tips. Mostly spring–summer. (I, H) South Florida; West Indies; Panama; South America.

P. Ghiesbreghtiana A.Rich. & Gal. (*Pleurothallis incompta* Rchb.f., *P. longissima* Ldl., *P. lyroglossa* Schltr., *P. Niederleini* Schltr., *P. racemiflora* Ldl.)

Pls. slender, clustered, $4\frac{1}{2}$–24″ tall, highly variable in all parts. Sts. $1\frac{1}{2}$–7″ tall, sheathed. Lf. rather leathery, glossy bright green, oblong-elliptic, linear, or oblanceolate, retuse and obtuse at apex, to almost 7″ long, to $1\frac{1}{4}$″ wide. Infls. solitary, sheathed at base, furnished with several tubular bracts, loosely many-fld., slender, to about 15″ long. Fls. nodding, fragrant, long-lasting, about $\frac{1}{4}$–$\frac{1}{2}$″ long, translucent, yellow or greenish-yellow, not opening fully, the lat. ss. united almost their entire length. Mostly summer. (I, H) West Indies; Mexico to Panama.

P. glandulosa Ames (*Pleurothallis vittariaefolia* Schltr.)

Pls. densely clustered, $\frac{3}{4}$–2″ tall, the sts. almost obsolete. Lf. erect, very narrowly linear to linear-oblanceolate, obtuse, obliquely 3-toothed at apex, fleshy, $\frac{3}{4}$–$1\frac{1}{2}$″ long. Infls. 1–2-fld., thread-like, warty, to almost 2″ long. Fls. not expanding fully, to about $\frac{1}{2}$″ long, greenish-yellow or reddish-yellow, the ss. warty outside on nerves and margins. Summer. (H) Mexico to Panama.

P. glumacea Ldl.

Pls. about 8″ tall, the sts. very short. Lf. fleshy, lanceolate–spatulate, blunt apically, to about $2\frac{1}{2}$″ long. Infls. erect or gracefully arching, slender, densely many-fld., the fls. in 2 ranks, long-stalked, to 8″ long. Fls. not opening well, fragrant, waxy, to about $\frac{1}{4}$″ long or more, yellowish, with short obtuse ps. Winter. (I, H) Brazil.

P. Grobyi Batem. (*Pleurothallis choconiana* S.Wats., *P. dryadum* Schltr., *P. integrilabia* AHS, *P. marginata* Ldl., *P. panamensis* Schltr., *P. pergracilis* Rolfe, *P. picta* Ldl.)

Pls. rather variable, densely clustered, $1\frac{1}{4}$–6″ tall, the sts. almost obsolete, concealed by a white scarious sheath. Lf. rigidly leathery, obovate to oblanceolate, rounded or obtuse and retuse apically, conspicuously marginate, usually purplish or at least purple-mottled on underside, to almost 3″ long (usually much smaller), short-stalked. Infls. erect, thread-like, loosely few-fld., somewhat zigzag, 1–6″ long, the peduncle usually reddish. Fls. not opening fully, often nodding, to more than $\frac{1}{4}$″ long, greenish-white or yellow, marked (often striped longitudinally) with reddish-purple, the lat. ss. united to form a 2-toothed lamina. Spring–summer. (I, H) West Indies; Mexico throughout Central America to northern South America.

P. Hawkesii E.A.Flickinger (*Restrepia striata* Rolfe)

Pls. densely cluster-forming, to about $4\frac{1}{2}$″ tall, the sts. covered by inflated, papery, purple-spotted sheaths. Lf. rigidly leathery, glossy dark green, broadly elliptic, acute, to about $3\frac{1}{2}$″ long. Infl. erect, thread-like, 1-fld., to about 5″ tall. Fls. opening fully, rather long-lived, to $2\frac{1}{4}$″ long, the dors. sep. erect, thread-like, the end abruptly widened, yellowish with a dark maroon longitudinal stripe down each side of the mid-vein, the lat. ss. joined

for about half their length, yellow, striped with maroon, the ps. thread-like, with widened tips, coloured like the dors. sep., the small lip yellow, striped with maroon. Winter–spring. (I) Colombia.

P. immersa Lind. & Rchb.f. (*Pleurothallis calerae* Schltr., *P. Krameriana* Rchb.f., *P. lasiosepala* Schltr.)

Pls. variable, cluster-forming, 7–18″ tall, the sts. short, stout, concealed by 2 brown tubular sheaths. Lf. fleshy, rigid, glossy bright green, oblong-oblanceolate, broadly, rounded to obtuse and retuse at apex, 4–8″ long, $\frac{3}{4}$–$1\frac{1}{2}$″ wide. Infls. with the basal part of the peduncle imbedded in the lf., upwards becoming free, the rac. loosely many-fld., conspicuously zigzag, $6\frac{1}{2}$–14″ long. Fls. mostly nodding, heavy-textured, not opening fully, $\frac{1}{4}$–$\frac{1}{2}$″ long, dusky greenish-yellow or purplish-brown with dark nerves, sometimes almost orange-yellow with brown nerves, the lat. ss. united almost to apex. Mostly summer. (I, H) Mexico; Guatemala; Honduras; Nicaragua; Costa Rica; Panama; Colombia; Venezuela.

P. inflata Rolfe

Pls. 8–12″ tall, the sts. clustered, slender, to about $4\frac{1}{2}$″ long. Lf. narrowly elliptic, about $4\frac{1}{2}$″ long, rigidly leathery. Infls. pendulous, loosely 1–2-fld. Fls. fleshy, opening well, about $1\frac{1}{4}$″ long, whitish-yellow, with violet-black spots and streaks, the lat. ss. coherent, the ps. rather large, lanceolate. Spring–summer. (I) Colombia.

P. insignis Rolfe (*Pleurothallis glossopogon* Nichols.)

To almost 12″ tall, the sts. clustered, slender, to about 6″ long. Lf. narrowly elliptic, rigidly leathery, to about 4″ long. Infls. loosely 2–3-fld., to almost 12″ long, mostly erect. Fls. fleshy, opening rather well, faintly fragrant, about $\frac{1}{2}$″ long or more, yellowish, streaked with red, the lip brown or reddish-brown, furnished with white hairs on its apex. Winter. (I) Venezuela.

P. Johnsoni Ames (*Brenesia costaricensis* Schltr.)

Pls. ascending or spreading, cluster-forming, to more than 10″ tall, the sts. rather stout, rigid, $1\frac{1}{2}$–$5\frac{1}{2}$″ long, concealed by loose overlapping sheaths. Lf. fleshy, oblong-lanceolate to oblong-elliptic, acute, conduplicate below middle, 3–5″ long, 1–$2\frac{1}{4}$″ wide. Infls. lateral and terminal, the rac. few-fld., the terminal one arising from lf.-base, to $1\frac{1}{2}$″ long, the lat. one arising at base of sts., flexuous, to $2\frac{3}{4}$″ long, provided with short inflated sheaths. Fls. fleshy, rather foul-smelling, not opening well, reddish, blotched with purple, the ss. glandular-warty on all surfaces, the lat. ones free to below the middle, the ps. glandular-warty on all surfaces, with long hairs on upper margins. An extraordinary plant! Winter. (I, H) Mexico (Chiapas); Guatemala; Honduras.

P. muricata Schltr. (*Kraenzlinella muricata* Rolfe, *Pleurothallis diuturna* Schltr., *P. sororoa* Schltr.)

Pls. rather stout, cluster-forming, 7–20″ tall, the sts. usually maroon-tinged, $\frac{3}{4}$–3″ long. Lf. erect or suberect, linear-oblong to elliptic, obtuse at apex, sessile, fleshy, 3–7″ long, $\frac{1}{2}$–$1\frac{1}{2}$″ wide. Infls. erect, a loosely many-fld. rac., usually solitary, long-peduncled, to about $1\frac{1}{2}$′ long. Fls. erect-spreading, $\frac{1}{4}$–$\frac{3}{4}$″ long, reddish-brown and maroon marked with green-yellow, the ss. minutely warty on outer surface, the lat. ss. free. Ovary densely muricate, about $\frac{1}{4}''$ long. Summer–autumn. (I) Guatemala to Panama.

P. ophiocephala Ldl. (*Pleurothallis puberula* Klotzsch, *P. stigmatoglossa* Rchb.f., *Restrepia ophiocephala* Rchb.f.)

Pls. stiffly erect, cluster-forming, $5\frac{1}{2}$–16″ tall, the sts. terete, rather stout, $2\frac{1}{2}$–10″ long. Lf. short-stalked, oblong to lanceolate, obtuse to shortly acute, often oblique, leathery, usually bright glossy yellowish-green, 3–8″ long, $\frac{1}{2}$–$1\frac{1}{2}''$ wide. Fls. 1–3, ringent, in a terminal fascicle, with prominent sheathing bracts, fleshy, not opening well, foul-smelling to odourless, yellow, more or less densely spotted with magenta, purple, or brown-purple. Ss. concave below middle, fleshy-thickened and convex above middle, papillose with irregularly broken transverse ridges on inner surface, outside scurfy with brownish stellate scales, the lats. at first connate, in time separating almost to base. Ps. with a white marginal fringe. Lip loosely hinged on col.-foot, usually deep maroon-purple. Winter–spring. (I, H) Mexico; Guatemala; Costa Rica.

P. pansamalae Schltr.

Pls. slender, densely clustered, $3\frac{1}{2}$–$9\frac{1}{2}''$ tall, the sts. rigid, 2–$6\frac{1}{2}''$ long. Lf. leathery, cordate-ovate to narrowly cordate-lanceolate, acuminate, $\frac{1}{4}$–$1\frac{1}{4}''$ wide below middle. Fls. fasciculate, with slender thread-like pedicels, subtended by scarious somewhat cup-shaped bracts, the infl.-base subtended by a spathe-like sheath, fls. not opening well, less than $\frac{1}{4}''$ long, greenish, marked with yellow, red, or brown, the lat. ss. joined, the ps. marginally toothed, the lip very crisped marginally. Summer–autumn. (I) Mexico; Guatemala; British Honduras; Honduras.

P. platystylis Schltr. (*Pleurothallis Bernoullii* Schltr.)

Pls. slender, cluster-forming, 6–13″ tall, the sts. sheathed, $1\frac{1}{2}$–$7\frac{1}{4}''$ long. Lf. erect, leathery, oblong-ligulate to oblanceolate, broadly rounded or obtuse at apex, tapering into stalk at base, 2–$4\frac{1}{2}''$ long, to $1\frac{1}{4}''$ wide. Infls. 1–2, slender, loosely many-fld., the fls. secund, short-stalked, 4–8″ long. Fls. erect-spreading, to about $\frac{1}{2}''$ long or more, yellow or greenish-yellow, the ss. often recurved above the middle with the apical margins somewhat involute, the lats. united for about half their length. Mostly summer. (I) Mexico; Guatemala; Honduras.

P. Roezlii Rchb.f.

Pls. very large for the genus, to 2′ tall, the sts. clustered, slender, to 6″ long. Lf. leathery, rigid, almost linear, to 9″ long. Infls. loosely 8–12-fld., gracefully arching, to about 12″ long. Fls. pendent, not opening fully, rather foul-smelling, to more than $1\frac{1}{4}''$ long, deep purple or wine-purple, the ss. concave, oblong-ovate, the lat. ones joined, the ps. shortly acuminate, the lip fleshy, obtuse. Winter. (I) Colombia.

P. rubens Ldl. (*Humboldtia ringens* O.Ktze.)

Rather similar in habit to *P. Ghiesbreghtiana* A.Rich. & Gal., but usually somewhat smaller, the lf. oblong, obtuse. Infl. densely many-fld., secund, usually longer than the lvs. Fls. not opening well, pendent, about $\frac{1}{4}''$

long, yellow, the ss. all free, oblong, the somewhat shorter ps. oblong-spatulate, the lip oblong, 2-keeled. Spring–summer. (I, H) Brazil.

P. ruscifolia (Jacq.) R.Br. (*Epidendrum ruscifolium* Jacq., *Dendrobium ruscifolium* Sw., *Pleurothallis glomerata* Ames)

Pls. large for the genus, cluster-forming, 4–20″ tall, the sts. rigid, 2–16″ long, slender. Lf. leathery, oblong-elliptic to lanceolate, acute to acuminate and obliquely 3-toothed at apex, often somewhat falcate, strong-veined, $2\frac{1}{2}$–$7\frac{1}{2}''$ long, $\frac{1}{2}$–$1\frac{1}{4}''$ wide, short-stalked at base. Infls. few–many-fld., a dense cluster subtended by a membranaceous sheath, the rather long pedicels thread-like. Fls. delicately fragrant, rather fragile, opening widely, $\frac{1}{4}$–$\frac{3}{4}''$ long, pale green to pale yellow, the lat. ss. united to form an ovate-lanceolate to lanceolate, long-acuminate lamina, the ps. horizontally spreading, the lip fleshy, the col. with a prominent pulverulent foot. Mostly summer. (I, H) West Indies; Guatemala; Costa Rica; Panama; Northern South America.

P. segoviensis Rchb.f. (*Pleurothallis amethystina* Ames, *P. bifalcis* Schltr., *P. falcatiloba* Ames, *P. Johannis* Schltr., *P. Wagneri* Schltr., *P. Wercklei* Schltr.)

Pls. densely cluster-forming, rather variable, particularly in size and colour of fls., 3–9″ tall, the sts. slender, $\frac{1}{2}$–2″ long, concealed by sheaths. Lf. erect, rigidly leathery, light glossy-green, oblanceolate-ligulate, obtuse and retuse (with tiny teeth) at apex, 2–5″ long, to about $\frac{1}{2}''$ wide at most. Infls. solitary, slender, usually erect, loosely few–many-fld., to $6\frac{1}{2}''$ long, including the thread-like peduncle, mostly exceeding the lf. in length. Fls. highly variable, nodding to horizontal, not opening well, mostly about $\frac{1}{4}''$ long, yellow-green with brown markings (usually irregular longitudinal stripes) to deep purplish-red, the lat. ss. united, the elliptic lamina 2-toothed at apex. Spring–summer. (I, H) Mexico to Panama.

P. stenostachya Rchb.f. (*Pleurothallis dubia* A.Rich. & Gal., *P. Lankesteri* Rolfe, *P. minutiflora* S.Wats., *P. myriantha* Lehm. & Krzl., *P. stenostachya* Rchb.f. var. *Lankesteri* Ames)

Pls. densely cluster-forming, $1\frac{1}{4}$–$3\frac{1}{2}''$ tall, the sts. slender, $\frac{1}{2}$–$1\frac{1}{4}''$ long, concealed by several tubular whitish papery sheaths. Lf. with a rather long, slender petiole, obovate to linear-spatulate, obtuse, leathery, conspicuously marginate, $\frac{1}{2}$–3″ long, about $\frac{1}{4}''$ wide. Infls. 1–several at once, fasciculate, thread-like, few–many-fld., to $\frac{1}{2}''$ long. Fls. opening widely, about $\frac{1}{8}''$ long or slightly more, greenish or orange-yellow, marked with purple, the lat. ss. almost free, the fleshy lip minutely warty on margins and on disc. Summer–autumn. (I, H) Mexico; British Honduras; Guatemala; Honduras; Costa Rica; Panama.

P. tribuloides (Sw.) Ldl. (*Epidendrum tribuloides* Sw., *Dendrobium tribuloides* Sw., *Cryptophoranthus acaulis* Krzl., *Pleurothallis fallax* Rchb.f., *P. spathulata* A.Rich. & Gal.)

Pls. densely cluster-forming, to 3″ tall, the sts. almost obsolete, concealed by white, papery, imbricating sheaths. Lf. somewhat leathery, obovate to oblanceolate, broadly rounded or obtuse and retuse at apex, to 2¾″ long or more, usually about ½″ wide. Infls. very abbreviated, 1–3-fld., less than ¼″ long, provided with loose white papery sheaths and bracts. Fls. fleshy, scarcely opening, about ¼″ long, brick-red or deep maroon, the ss. minutely granular-warty on outer surface, the lats. united, the ps. fleshy-thickened above middle, the lip fringed along margin especially at apex, the caps. globose, densely and profusely echinate. Late summer–autumn. (I, H) West Indies; Mexico to Panama.

P. Tuerckheimii Schltr. (*Pleurothallis megachlamys* Schltr.)

Pls. erect, 6–25″ tall, the sts. rather stout, to 10″ long, provided with 2 large, tubular, glossy-brown sheaths. Lf. solitary, oval, oblong-elliptic or lanceolate, obtuse, 1½–10″ long, ¾–2¾″ wide. Infls. solitary, loosely many-fld., to more than 12″ long, the peduncle stout, with a large tubular sheath at the base, this reddish-brown, glossy, rather leathery. Fls. not opening fully, fleshy, to 1″ long, reddish-brown (rarely magenta-brown) and white, the brown or reddish-brown ss. roughened on outer surfaces, the lats. united almost to the apex, the ps. white with 3 prominent brown nerves, the fleshy lip brown or reddish-brown. Summer. (I, H) Mexico; Guatemala; Honduras; Nicaragua; Costa Rica; Panama.

P. xanthophthalma (Rchb.f.) L.O.Wms. (*Restrepia xanthophthalma* Rchb.f., *Restrepia Lansbergii* 'Rchb.f.' ex Hk.)

Pls. densely clustered, 2½–8″ tall, the sts. slender, 1¼–5″ long, entirely concealed by papery sheaths, these sharp-keeled, whitish, the lowermost purple-flecked. Lf. solitary, bright green, often purplish beneath or mottled with purple, rigidly leathery, ovate-lanceolate to linear-oblong, obtuse and obliquely 3-toothed at apex, 1½–3″ long, ½–1″ wide. Infls. 1–several, thread-like, 1-fld., to about ½″ long, enclosed at base by uppermost st.-sheath. Fls. nodding but opening well, faintly fragrant, to about 1″ long, white or pale greenish-yellow, more or less spotted with purple or red-purple. Dors. sep. and ps. long-tailed, the tips of the tails fleshy, the lat. ss. united almost to the apex, the lip 3-lbd., the lat. lbs. terminated by thread-like tails. Mostly summer. (I, H) Mexico; Guatemala; Honduras; Nicaragua; Costa Rica; Panama.

P. Broadwayi Ames Pls. to 4½″ tall, the often flexuous sts. concealed by inflated, ciliate-margined sheaths. Lvs. suberect, scattered along the st., obovate to elliptic-oblong, obtuse and retuse at the apex, coriaceous, to about ¾″ long. Infls. terminal or lateral, filiform, to 2″ long, loosely few-fld. Fls. usually nodding, not opening fully, to about ¼″ long, yellow-green, more or less marked with purple. Summer. (I) West Indies; Mexico to Panama and Venezuela.

P. ciliaris (Ldl.) L.O.Wms. (*Specklinia ciliaris* Ldl.) Sts. clustered, slender, rather zigzag, 1–3¼″ long, with prominent inflated, marginally ciliate sheaths. Lf. solitary, oblong-elliptic to linear-lanceolate, blunt or toothed apically, leathery, purplish-green, ¾–2½″ long. Infls. usually several at once, clustered from the lf.-base, filiform, few-fld., to 1″ long. Fls. nodding, not opening fully, to almost ¼″ long, purplish-red to yellowish-green, often flushed with darker colour, the ss. and ps. ciliate marginally, the curving lip also ciliate marginally. Mostly spring. (I) Mexico; Guatemala; Honduras; Nicaragua; Costa Rica.

P. comayaguensis Ames Pls. closely appressed to bark of trees, the sts. almost obsolete, borne at close intervals from a creeping rhiz. Lf. solitary, elliptic or lens-shaped, fleshy, to ¼″ long, conspicuously marginate. Infls. solitary in lf.-axils, about ¼″ long, bearing about 4 fls. successively. Fls. opening rather well, red, the lip usually darker. Dors. sep. oblong, very concave, the lats. joined almost to their tips, this lamina concave at base. Ps. with several marginal hairs. Lip with margins of basal half strongly inrolled, the margins of apical half deflexed, rather densely elongate-hairy, auricled at base. Summer. (I, H) Guatemala; Honduras.

P. corniculata (Sw.) Ldl. (*Epidendrum corniculatum* Sw., *Pleurothallis jocolensis* Ames) Sts. almost obsolete, with several brown papery sheaths. Lf. solitary, obovate to oblong-elliptic, obtuse and with 3 minute apical teeth, leathery, ½–1½″ long. Infls. erect, filiform, 1-fld., to 1¾″ long. Fls. rather similar to those of *P. Brighamii* S.Wats., but more delicate in texture, to ½″ long, pale green or yellow, the lat. ss. coherent almost to apex, the lip curving, canaliculate with basal dilated margins upturned, apically with tiny papillae and hairs. Summer. (I, H) West Indies; Mexico; Guatemala; Honduras; Costa Rica; British Guiana.

P. fuegi Rchb.f. Sts. almost obsolete, with papery tubular sheaths. Lf. solitary, obovate to oblanceolate, obtuse and 3-toothed apically, rather leathery, to ¾″ long. Infls. solitary, filiform, with a loose few-fld. rac., to 1¾″ long. Fls. opening rather well, about ½″ long, pale bronzy-green or whitish-green, often marked with purple. Dors. sep. long-caudate, concave at base, the lats. slightly united at base, obliquely lanceolate, then long-caudate. Lip 3-lbd., down-curving, the

Pleurothallis Ospinae R.E.Schultes [VEITCH]

erect lat. lbs. roundish, the midlb. obtuse, somewhat convex. Summer. (I) Guatemala; Honduras; Nicaragua; Panama.

P. hirsuta Ames Sts. slender, 3-angled above, sheathed, to 4¼″ long. Lf. solitary, elliptic-oblong, 3-toothed at obtuse apex, rigidly leathery, to 2″ long and ¾″ broad. Infls. 1–3, filiform, longer than the lf., the rac. loosely few-fld. Fls. ringent, about ½″ long, not opening fully, greenish-yellow with spots or blotches of purple, hairy. Dors. sep. deeply concave below, reflexed apically, hirsute inside near margin; lat. ss. decurving, united on lower half to form a mentum, spreading above, hirsute inside towards apex. Ps. fleshy apically. Lip with a slender claw, curved at base and again at apex, the lamina oblong, rounded apically. Winter. (I) Mexico; Guatemala; Honduras.

P. Ospinae R.E.Schultes (*Restrepia antennifera* HBK) Sts. slender, to 4″ long, with brownish-grey, black-dotted flattened sheaths. Lf. solitary, elliptic-lanceolate, rather heavy, to 3″ long. Infls. numerous, 1-fld., thread-like, to 3″ long. Fls. to 1¼″ long, the narrow ascending dors. sep. translucent-yellow with 3 longitudinal dark purple veins; lat. ss. joined almost to tips, forming a broad structure that is yellow, heavily spotted with dark purple or reddish-purple. Ps. ¾″ long, yellow, very slender, with an apical enlarged area. Lip shorter than ps., pink or rose, spotted with dark brown, warty. A remarkable orchid. Spring. (C) Colombia: at high elevations in very wet places.

P. pachyglossa Ldl. (*Pleurothallis formosa* Schltr.) Sts. slender, to 6″ long, with 2 brownish sheaths. Lf. solitary, erect-spreading, elliptic-oblong to lanceolate, blunt to short-acuminate, tapering into the short sulcate petiole, 2–5½″ long, to 1″ wide. Infls. often zigzag, 1-fld. or with few scattered fls., to 10″ long. Fls. opening well, to 1¾″ long, reddish or dull purplish. Dors. sep. cymbiform, somewhat ciliate marginally, the lats. united almost to the apex, concave, with free tips. Ps. roughened above the middle on outer surface, inside apically papillose-ciliate. Lip short-clawed, warty above the middle, the callus warty and crested. Autumn–winter. (I, H) Mexico to Costa Rica.

P. sertularioides (Sw.) Spreng. (*Epidendrum sertularioides* Sw.) Rhiz. slender, creeping, covered with papery-fibrous sheaths, the sts. almost obsolete, borne at intervals. Lf. solitary, grass-green on both surfaces, linear-oblanceolate to linear-spatulate, obtuse, narrowed below, to 1½″ long and ³⁄₁₆″ broad above middle. Infls. usually paired, filiform, 1–2-fld. Fls. not opening fully, about ¼″ long, yellowish. Lat. ss. slightly united at base. Ps. falcate-lanceolate, acuminate. Lip fleshy, linear, narrowed at fleshy obtuse apex, with a tiny upcurved lobule just above base. Spring. (I, H) Cuba; Jamaica; Mexico; Guatemala; Honduras; Nicaragua.

P. stenopetala Ldl. Much like *P. Ghiesbreghtiana* A.Rich. & Gal. in habit, and perhaps better considered a form of this widespread plant. Infls. very many-fld., usually erect. Fls. to ½″ long, whitish-yellow, the lip often with a median bright yellow mark, the ss. narrowly linear, free from one another. Autumn. (I, H) Brazil.

PLEUROTHALLOPSIS C.Porto & Brade

Pleurothallopsis nemorosa (B.-R.) C.Porto & Brade (*Lepanthes nemorosa* B.-R.), the only known member of its genus, is a very rare epiphytic orchid native to Brazil. A *Pleurothallis*-like plant, it differs from that group in technical details of the rather small, complexly formed flowers, which are borne singly on rather elon-

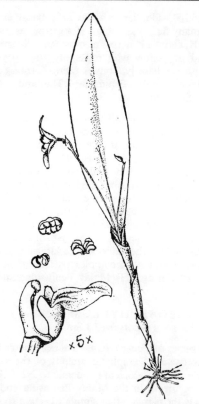

Pleurothallopsis nemorosa (B.-R.) C.Porto & Brade
[Hoehne, *Flora Brasílica*]

gate peduncles from the leaf-bases. *Pleurothallopsis* is not in cultivation at this time.

Nothing is known of the genetic affinities of this rare group.

CULTURE: Presumably as for *Pleurothallis*. (I, H)

PLOCOGLOTTIS Bl.

This is a genus of about thirty species of terrestrial orchids of the subtribe *Phaiinae*, very scarce and seldom seen in present-day collections, with a range which extends from Malaya and the Philippines to New Guinea. They are rather attractive, small-flowered orchids, vaguely allied to *Spathoglottis* Bl., which are well worthy of further attention from orchidists. Bearing mostly cylindrical, clean pseudobulbs topped by one (rarely two) folded, stalked leaves, the blossoms are produced on elongate inflorescences from the bulb-bases, and open in succession over a long period of time, often lasting in good condition for more than a month. The small lip is peculiarly arranged, and, when touched, springs closed against the column.

No hybrids are known in this genus, and its exact genetic affinities have not been established as yet.

CULTURE: As for the tropical species of *Phaius*. (H)

P. javanica Bl.

Pbs. cylindric, usually light green, to about 4″ tall and ½″ in diam., sheathed when young. Lf. solitary, plicate, slender-stalked at base, the blade to more than

15″ long and 5″ wide, the tip acute. Infls. basal, erect, to 2½′ tall, many-fld., the rachis elongating as the fls. expand. Fls. about 1¼″ across at most (usually smaller), the ss. and ps. yellow with red spots, the lip yellow, flushed with red basally, convex there, forming a sac. Spring–summer. (H) Peninsular Thailand; Malay Peninsula; Sumatra; Java.

P. Lowii Rchb.f. (*Plocoglottis porphyrophylla* Ridl.)

Pbs. cylindric, tapering upwards, often purple-flushed, to 3½″ tall and ⅛″ in diam. at base, sheathed when young, the sheaths usually purple-flushed. Lvs. solitary or paired, short-stalked, the blade to 12″ long and 3½″ wide, plicate, usually flushed underneath with dull or rather bright purple or red-purple. Infls. basal, soft-hairy, to more than 3′ tall, elongating, producing the rather numerous fls. singly or in pairs over a period of several weeks. Fls. about 1″ across, the hairy-backed dors. sep. and ps. dull yellow, the hairy-backed lat. ss. red, the lip yellow to orange, with a complex pattern of dull red-brown spots. Spring. (H) Malay Peninsula; Sumatra; Borneo.

POAEPHYLLUM Ridl.
(*Lectandra* J.J.Sm.)

Three species of *Poaephyllum* have been described to date, all very scarce epiphytic orchids of the subtribe *Glomerinae*, two of which are endemic to New Guinea, the third occurring in the Malay Peninsula and Java. Vegetatively the plants rather simulate certain species of *Appendicula* Bl., a genus to which they are only vaguely allied, the flowers being distinct in structural details. None of the Poaephyllums is present in our collections today, though they are rather attractive plants, albeit with very small blossoms.

Nothing is known of the genetic affinities of this rare genus.

CULTURE: Presumably as for *Appendicula*, etc. (I)

PODANDRIA Rolfe

A solitary species of *Podandria* is known to date, this a rare terrestrial orchid of the *Habenaria* alliance, native to Upper and Lower Guinea in tropical Africa. Unknown in contemporary collections, **Podandria macrandra** (Ldl.) Rolfe (*Habenaria macrandra* Ldl.) appears to be a rather showy plant with racemes of large, very complex flowers. It is allied to both *Habenaria* Willd. and to *Platanthera* L.C.Rich., but is readily differentiated from them in the floral structure.

Nothing is known of the genetic affinities of *Podandria*.

CULTURE: Presumably as for the tropical Habenarias, etc. (H)

PODANGIS Schltr.

The only known species of *Podangis*, **P. dactyloceras** (Rchb.f.) Schltr. (*Listrostachys dactyloceras* Rchb.f., *Listrostachys forcipata* Krzl.) is a rare and little-known epiphytic orchid of the angraecoid alliance of the subtribe *Sarcanthinae*, which seems to be rather widespread in tropical Africa. An interesting plant with white flowers, it is evidently not in cultivation at this time.

Nothing is known concerning the genetic ties of *Podangis*.

CULTURE: Presumably as for the warm-growing Angraecums. (H)

PODOCHILUS Bl.
(*Apista* Bl., *Cryptoglottis* Bl., *Hexameria* R.Br., *Placostigma* Bl., *Platysma* Bl.)

Podochilus is a genus of about seventy-five species of mostly small, often moss-like epiphytic orchids of the subtribe *Podochilinae*, which have a wide range extending from Ceylon to New Guinea. They are virtually unknown in collections today, but are for the most part delightful plants of most unusual vegetative appearance, bearing solitary or racemose, typically tiny blossoms of charming structure. The genus is close in its relationship to *Chilopogon* Schltr. and to *Appendicula* Bl.

No hybrids have as yet been made in *Podochilus*, and nothing is known concerning its genetic affinities.

CULTURE: These mostly dwarf epiphytes do best if given the general treatment afforded the tropical species of *Bulbophyllum*, etc. Pot-culture seems most preferable for all, though certain of the arching or pen-

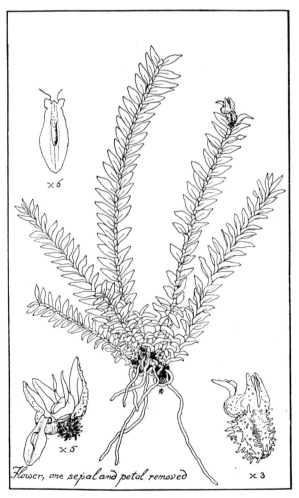

Podochilus hystricinus Ames [BLANCHE AMES]

dulous species may be grown on tree-fern slabs or in smallish baskets. (I, H)

P. microphyllus Ldl. (*Podochilus confusus* J.J.Sm.)

Pls. usually arching, the slender sts. clustered, to about 8″ long, densely covered with 2-ranked lvs. Lvs. close together, rather fragile-textured, spreading, to about ¼″ long and more, sharp-pointed, basally twisted, often purplish. Infls. terminal and lateral, few-fld., bracted. Fls. not opening well, about ⅛″ long, white, the ss. often with a purple median line, the ps. with a purple median blotch, the lip-disc often with 2 purple blotches. Mostly summer. (I, H) Malay Peninsula; Sumatra; Java; Borneo.

P. muricatus (Teijsm. & Binn.) Schltr. (*Appendicula muricata* Teijsm. & Binn.)

Pls. usually pendulous, the sts. slender, clustered, to about 6″ long, very densely leafy, the lvs. 2-ranked, about ⅛″ long or less, ovate, blunt, slightly notched at the tip. Infls. terminal, usually 1-fld., very abbreviated. Fls. about ¼″ long, white with some purple marks on ps. and lip, the ss. stiffly hairy outside, the col.-arms deep purple. Caps. conspicuously hairy. Summer–autumn. (H) Malay Peninsula; Sumatra; Java.

POGONIA Juss.

As currently delimited, *Pogonia* consists of about ten species of terrestrial, rather small orchids, with a wide distribution in both hemispheres, principally in the temperate regions. A member of the subtribe *Vanillinae*, these plants are extremely rare in contemporary collections, although the pretty North American 'Rose Pogonia', **P. ophioglossoides** (L.) Ker-Gawl., may on occasion be encountered in a few highly specialized aggregations of native orchids. Several genera are often included in *Pogonia*, among them *Triphora* Nutt., *Isotria* Raf., *Cleistes* L.C.Rich., etc.; these are considered distinct in the present treatment.

Nothing appears to be known of the genetic affinities of the genus *Pogonia* at this time.

CULTURE: The species described below is sometimes indicated as easily grown in the out-of-door garden, but such is definitely not the case, since it is a singularly refractory and temperamental orchid! A bed of sandy, rich humus is necessary, one in which a high acid content is present, with perfect drainage. Water must be almost constantly supplied, and this water must be completely free from lime. Cool or intermediate temperatures are required. The plant apparently will not grow if confined in pots. (C, I)

P. ophioglossoides (L.) Ker-Gawl. (*Arethusa ophioglossoides* L.)

Pl. slender, the roots rather fleshy, hairy, the st. green or brownish-green, 3–25″ tall. Lf. solitary, about halfway up the st., ovate to broadly ovate-lanceolate, obtuse to subacute, ¾–4¾″ long, with a lf.-like bract subtending the normally solitary fl. Fls. lasting several days, fragrant, opening rather well, very pretty, rose to white, the lip-disc with short fleshy yellow-white bristles along the 3 central veins. Ps. thrust forward mostly along the sides of the col., broader than the spreading ss. Lip narrowly oblong-spatulate, narrowed at the base, lacerate-toothed along the apical margin. Col. toothed apically. Mar.–Aug. (C, I) Newfoundland and Nova Scotia south to South Florida, west to Minnesota and Missouri.

POGONIOPSIS Rchb.f.

Pogoniopsis is a genus of two very rare and little-known saprophytic orchids, both native to Brazil, and a member of the subtribe *Vanillinae*. Dwarf plants, they are completely unknown in collections at this time, and are in any event primarily of interest to botanical students of the alliance.

Nothing is known of the genetic affinities of this odd group.

CULTURE: Presumably as for *Corallorrhiza*, though little success may be anticipated in keeping the plants alive for more than a single season. (H)

POLYCYCNIS Rchb.f.

About seven rather polymorphic species make up the oddly interesting epiphytic genus *Polycycnis*. A member of the subtribe *Gongorinae*, they are very rare in our collections at this time, but like all members of this aggregation, offer considerable interest to connoisseurs. Vegetatively most of these orchids, which are normally epiphytic in the wild, simulate a *Stanhopea*—to which genus they are somewhat allied. The flowers, however, are borne in considerable numbers in often elongate, pendulous inflorescences, and differ radically in structure from all other gongoroid orchids. Their formation is very complex, often so much so that their facile description is very difficult. *Polycycnis* ranges from Costa Rica to Brazil and Peru, and at this time only a single species seems to be in cultivation.

No hybrids have as yet been produced in this genus, although it seems entirely probable that it will prove freely compatible with at least certain other members of the subtribe *Gongorinae*. The results from such intergeneric hybrids should be extraordinarily unusual and interesting orchids, and such experimental crosses are to be encouraged.

CULTURE: As for *Stanhopea*, *Acineta*, etc. (I, H).

P. barbata (Ldl.) Rchb.f. (*Cycnoches barbatum* Ldl., *Polycycnis gratiosa* Endr. & Rchb.f.)

Pbs. clustered, ovoid, ridged, to 1¾″ tall and 1″ in diam. Lf. solitary, rather heavy-textured, plicate, elliptic-lanceolate, acute or acuminate, 10–15″ long and 1½–4″ wide. Infls. usually sharply pendulous, rather loosely few- to many-fld., to more than 12″ long, the rachis pubescent. Fls. membranaceous, often short-lived, on elongate pedicellate ovaries, about 2″ long, pale translucent yellow, spotted with red. Ss. spreading or reflexed, concave, lanceolate, acuminate, the lat. ss. connate at base. Ps. vaguely stalked at base, narrowly oblanceolate, spreading or reflexed. Lip with a 3-lbd. basal claw (hypochil) adnate to the col.-base, white, spotted with red, the lat. lbs. acute, erect, the apex with a central, densely pubescent, carinate projection; epichil vaguely 3-lbd., white, spotted with purple, ovate, acuminate, the

Polycycnis muscifera (Ldl. & Paxt.) Rchb.f. [Hoehne, *Flora Brasilica*]

base of this epichil inserted about midway on the under-surface of the hypochil, producing the effect of a double lip, one slightly above and behind the other; disc densely pubescent. Col. slender, green, gracefully arching, terete below, dilated and truncate above, the anther purple. Spring. (I, H) Costa Rica; Panama; Colombia; Venezuela; Brazil.

POLYOTIDIUM Garay

The genus *Polyotidium* was established in 1958, being based on *Hybochilus Huebneri* Mansf., an extremely rare, insignificant epiphytic orchid from Amazonian Colombia. **P. Huebneri** (Mansf.) Garay, the only known species, is a dwarf, delicate but botanically very interesting plant, unknown to date in our collections. Garay places it in the small subtribe *Papperitziinae*.

Nothing is known of the genetic affinities of this genus.

CULTURE: Possibly as for *Ornithocephalus* and other fragile epiphytic orchids, (H)

POLYRRHIZA Pfitz.

This is a strange genus of about four species, natives of the West Indies, with a single spectacular representative extending into South Florida. A member of the subtribe *Campylocentrinae*, *Polyrrhiza* contains some of the most extraordinary of the so-called 'leafless' orchids, in which the plants consist merely of an abbreviated perennial rhizome-like stem, a tangled cluster of greyish roots (which carry on the processes of photosynthesis for the organism), and inflorescences. In this genus, the flowers are singularly large and handsome for the alliance, this making them admirably suited to the collector. Two species of *Polyrrhiza* are in sporadic cultivation, but neither of them is common, and their cultural requirements are often rather refractory.

No hybrids have as yet been attempted with this peculiar genus, and nothing is known concerning its genetic affinities. Some unusual experimental breeding seems possible here, and should be tried by some enterprising enthusiasts.

CULTURE: As for the leafless Campylocentrums. (H)

P. funalis (Sw.) Pfitz. (*Limodorum funale* Sw., *Aëranthes funalis* Rchb.f., *Dendrophylax funalis* Fawc., *Oeceoclades funalis* Ldl.)

Pls. leafless, the sts. very reduced, rhiz.-like, emitting a few slender, rather bright grey, somewhat compressed roots, to about 12" long or so, many of them not attached to the substratum but hanging free. Infls. produced from the central st., 2–4" tall, 1–2-fld., erect. Fls. to about 2" long, waxy, fragrant, rather long-lived, the ss. and ps. somewhat reflexed, greenish-yellow, the large, complexly lbd. lip pure glittering white. Spur more than 2" long, yellowish. Feb.–April. (H) Cuba; Cayman Islands; Jamaica.

P. Lindeni (Ldl.) Cgn. (*Angraecum Lindeni* Ldl., *Aëranthus Lindeni* Rchb.f., *Dendrophylax Lindeni* Bth. ex Rolfe)

Pls. leafless, the sts. very reduced, emitting long, flexuous, grey-green roots to several feet in length, these mostly closely appressed to the bark of trees. Infls. rather stout, brownish-black, furnished with tubular sheathing bracts, 2½–9" long, producing several fls. which open successively. Fls. showy, fragrant, waxy, long-lived, to almost 5" long from tip to tip, the dors. sep. and ps. reflexed, white, more or less flushed with cream-yellow or green, the lat. ss. down-out-curving, similar in colour. Lip very large and complex, pure white, boat-shaped at base, the lat. lbs. short, the midlb. suddenly dilated into a pair of very long antenna-like lbs. which spread outward and then downward and end in curly tips. Feb.–July. (H) South Florida; Cuba.

POLYSTACHYA Hk.
(*Encyclia* P. & E., *Epiphora* Ldl.)

Upwards of one hundred and thirty species of *Polystachya* are now known to date. Their distribution is a peculiar disjunct one, with the majority of the components inhabiting tropical Africa, although we find scattered representatives extending into the Americas—from Florida and Mexico southward to Brazil—and into South-east Asia and Indonesia. The principal genus of the subtribe *Polystachyinae*, the group is relatively little known in contemporary collections, although it contains a great many charming and showy epiphytic members. Highly diverse in vegetative form, the small to medium-sized flowers (which occur in a wide variety of hues) are normally inverted and hood-shaped; their complexity needs to be studied under a lens to best appreciate the blossoms. For the orchidist interested in the more unusual 'botanical' orchids, this genus offers much of interest, and should be more widely grown and appreciated.

As yet no hybrids have been made within *Polystachya*, although some fascinating possibilities in the field of critical interspecific breeding seem evident. Nothing is known of the genetic ties of the group.

CULTURE: Polystachyas are for the most part very readily grown, hence are heartily recommended even to the beginning hobbyist. Largely epiphytic in the wild, they require the general cultural conditions of *Dendrobium*, being best grown in proportionately small, well-drained pots, in a tightly packed compost of either straight osmunda, or a mixture of equal parts of shredded tree-fern fibre and chopped sphagnum moss. When rooting well, they thrive on slabs or cubes of tree-fern fibre. They do well in a rather bright spot in the collection, and benefit by liberal water and high humidity while actively growing, but usually require a brief rest-period upon completion of the new growths. Frequent and liberal applications of fertilizing materials have proved beneficial. (I, H)

P. Adansoniae Rchb.f.

Pbs. oblong, green to yellow, clustered or in rows, small. Lvs. 2–4, narrowly elliptic, 1½–2½" long, to ½" broad, bright green. Infls. stiffly erect, with a very dense many-fld. rac. Fls. inverted, ¼" long, not opening well, white or greenish-white with mauve elongate tips to the ss. and ps. Lip triangular, with very short lateral lbs., the midlb. sharply acute, the inner surface fluffy. Col. with a vivid mauve anther-cap. Apr.–June. (H) Tropical

Polyrrhiza Lindeni (Ldl.) Cgn. [BLANCHE AMES]

Africa, from Uganda and Kenya across to Guinea and Angola, often on Baobab trees (*Adansonia digitata*).

P. affinis Ldl. (*Polystachya bracteosa* Ldl.)
Pbs. almost round, disc-shaped, flattened sharply from above, usually flushed with purplish, very close together, to 2″ in diam. Lvs. 2, borne from middle of pb.-apex, leathery, elliptic-lanceolate, acute, to 8″ long, narrowed basally, the under-surface usually purple. Infls. arching to sharply pendulous, loosely many-fld., to 12″ long, densely covered with short, mostly orange hairs. Fls. not opening fully, covered outside with short orange hairs, about ½″ across, golden-yellow or orange-yellow, more or less striped with brown, the ss. ovate, incurving. July–Aug. (H) Sierra Leone to Belgian Congo.

P. cucullata (Afzel) Dur. & Schinz (*Limodorum cucullatum* Afzel, *Dendrobium galeatum* Sw., *Bulbophyllum galeatum* Ldl., *Polystachya galeata* Rchb.f., *P. grandiflora* Ldl.)
Pbs. clustered, cylindric, to 2″ tall. Lf. solitary, linear-lanceolate, acute, to 6″ long. Infls. erect, 1–2-fld., to 4″ tall. Fls. not opening fully, rather heavy-textured, about 1½″ across, green, more or less spotted and dotted with rose-red. Midlb. of the lip white. Oct.–Dec. (H) Sierra Leone.

P. Hislopii Rolfe
Pbs. in rows, ovoid or fusiform-oblong, to 2″ long, the sheaths purple-striped. Lvs. 3–4, lanceolate-oblong, 2–6″ long. Infls. erect or arching, to 6″ long, hairy, few-fld., the pedicellate ovaries woolly. Fls. hairy outside, about 1¼″ long, hooded, the ss. and ps. light green, the lip white, veined and spotted with light purple. Aug.–Oct. (H) Southern Rhodesia.

P. Lawrenceana Krzl.
Pbs. oblong, clustered, often in rows, to 2″ tall. Lvs. 2–4, rather leathery, linear-ligulate, obtuse, to 4″ long. Infls. erect or arching, loosely 6–12-fld., about 6″ long, densely covered with short hairs. Fls. about ¾″ long, hooded, olive-green, striped on the outside with brown, the lip 3-lbd., rose-red. July–Aug. (H) Nyasaland.

P. luteola (Sw.) Hk. (*Cranichis luteola* Sw., *Dendrobium polystachyon* Sw., *Dendrorchis minuta* O.Ktze., *Epidendrum minutum* Aubl., *Polystachya minuta* Frapp.)
Pbs. clustered, often regularly ranked, tapering from a thickened base, usually less than ½″ tall. Lvs. 1–several, rather leathery, oblong-elliptic to linear-lanceolate or oblong-lanceolate, obtuse to acute, usually bright yellowish-green, 1½–12″ long, ¼–1½″ broad. Infl. erect, sheathed, producing one or more compact racs. near the apex, often producing these successively for a long period, often unilateral; racs. densely many-fld. Fls. fragrant, inverted, pale yellowish-green, the lip usually whitish-yellow. Ps. much narrower than the ss. Lip deeply 3-lbd. above the middle, the midlb. undulate-crisped marginally; disc covered with tiny glandular hairs. Throughout the year, often more than once annually. (I, H) South Florida and Mexico throughout tropical America; also in the Old World tropics and subtropics.

P. Ottoniana Rchb.f. (*Polystachya capensis* Sanderson)
Pbs. clustered, ovoid, ½″ long, prolonged at apex into a slender compressed st. 1–1½″ long. Lvs. produced from summit of the st., 2, linear, emarginate, grassy, of unequal length, the longer one to 4″ long, the shorter about 2″ long. Infls. borne from between the lvs., about 2″ long, slender, 1-fld. Fls. ½″ in diam., white, the ss. with a median purple line on the outside, the lip with a yellow blotch on the disc. Dors. sep. oblong, acute; lat. ss. ovate, acute, adnate to the col.-foot, forming a mentum with it and the lip-base. Lip oval-oblong, vaguely lbd., reflexed apically. Col. semiterete, with a purple anther. Sept.–Nov. (I, H) South Africa; Natal.

P. puberula Ldl. (*Polystachya odorata* Ldl.)
Pbs. clustered, ovoïd, to 2″ long. Lvs. 2–4, rather leathery, lanceolate to elliptic-lanceolate, to 8″ long. Infls. arching, loosely many-fld., to 10″ long, covered with short hairs and small warts. Fls. about ¼″ long, not opening fully, light yellow, hairy and warty on outside of ss. Sept.–Nov. (H) Sierra Leone to Cameroons.

P. pubescens (Ldl.) Rchb.f. (*Epiphora pubescens* Ldl., *Polystachya Lindleyana* Sanderson)
Pbs. crowded, about ½″ in diam., elongated. Lvs. 2–3, oblong-lanceolate, 3–4″ long, the first or lowermost one much smaller than the others. Infls. erect, arising from between the lvs., to 5″ long, flattened below, fuzzy, 12–20-fld. above. Fls. inverted, about ¾″ across, bright yellow, the lip and inferior half of the ss. red-streaked. Ss. ovate, acute. Ps. somewhat smaller, obovate-oblong, obtuse. Lip smaller than the other segms., 3-lbd., the lat. lbs. roundish-oblong, fuzzy inside, the midlb. ovate reflexed at apex. May–June. (I, H) South-east Africa.

POMATOCALPA Breda

About thirty species of primarily epiphytic, monopodial orchids make up the genus *Pomatocalpa*, only one or two of which are found in contemporary collections. Holttum (in *Fl. Malaya* 1: 622. 1953) makes some pertinent comments concerning the Malayan components of the group: 'The shape of the flowers is very constant, notably in the saccate form of the lip with the tongue on its back wall, the latter being quite distinct from the callus at the back of the spur of *Sarcanthus*. The short simple usually downcurved midlobe is also distinct from the arrow-head shape usual in *Sarcanthus*. The plants are often larger, and the inflorescences denser, than in *Sarcanthus*. . . . The tongue at the back of the lip of *Pomatocalpa* shows a resemblance to *Trichoglottis*; but in *Pomatocalpa* the tongue is much deeper in the sac, and the whole structure of the flower is much simpler than in most species of *Trichoglottis*. It seems likely, however, that *Pomatocalpa*, *Acampe* and *Trichoglottis* are related genera, and *Gastrochilus* also.' The range of the genus extends from the Himalayas and Ceylon throughout Malaya, Indonesia, and the Philippines to Samoa. The Pomatocalpas are primarily of value to connoisseurs, due to their scarcity and the generally small dimensions of the blossoms.

No hybrids are known as yet, either within *Pomatocalpa* or with allied groups, and nothing has been

Polystachya luteola (Sw.) Hk. [BLANCHE AMES]

ascertained concerning the genetic affinities of the genus.

CULTURE: As for the tropical species of *Vanda*. Most Pomatocalpas will stand considerable exposure to sunlight, and flower better when so treated. (I, H)

P. spicatum Breda (*Cleisostoma uteriferum* Hk.f., *Saccolabium Hobsoni* Ridl., *Saccolabium uteriferum* Ridl.)

St. thick, abbreviated, leafy. Lvs. ligulate, the apices broadly and unequally rounded, leathery, to 7" long and 1½" wide, the margins wavy, the spreading basal sheaths closely overlapping. Infls. simple or sparsely branched, hanging to pendulous, the numerous fls. crowded on a stout rachis, to 7" long. Fls. opening successively (but many expanded at one time), rather cup-shaped, about ½" long, the ss. and ps. pale yellow, marked with pink at the base, the lat. ss. with irregular pink markings over most of the surface, the lip with pale yellow, sometimes purple-spotted lat. lbs., the tongue yellowish with a purple flush, the edge white, toothed, the midlb. short, fleshy, down-curved, white, sometimes pink-spotted. Spring–summer. (H) Malay Peninsula; Sumatra; Java; Borneo.

P. Wendlandorum (Rchb.f.) J.J.Sm. (*Cleisostoma Wendlandorum* Rchb.f.)

St. short, rather thick, leafy. Lvs. ligulate, at the tips unequally and obtusely 2-lbd., leathery, usually hanging, to 8" long and 1½" wide. Infls. shorter than the lvs., to 5" long, hanging, densely many-fld. Fls. about ¼" across, light brownish-yellow, the lip often dull yellow. Ss. and ps. oblong, obtuse. Lip with a conical spur and a small ovate midlb. Spring. (I, H) Himalayas; Burma; Andaman Islands.

PONERA Ldl.
(*Nemaconia* Kn. & Westc.)

Six species of *Ponera* are now known to science, none of them apparently present in our collections except the widespread and often locally common *P. striata* Ldl., which is sometimes grown for its handsome, arching leafy stems—which more simulate a small bamboo rather than an orchid. The genus, the typical one of the subtribe *Ponerinae*, includes epiphytic or lithophytic orchids whose range extends from Mexico to Brazil. Highly diverse in vegetative dimensions and structure, the Poneras bear mostly small (to exceedingly small), rather dull-coloured blossoms, thus making them primarily of interest to the connoisseur collector.

No hybrids have as yet been produced in this genus, and nothing is known regarding its genetic affinities.

CULTURE: The only species currently in cultivation, because of its usually strongly down-arching, often very elongate stems must be grown on slanted baskets tightly filled with osmunda fibre, or—once the root-system is very active—on a slab of fresh tree-fern. Mostly found in shaded situations in the wild, they suffer when exposed to too much bright light, and should never be allowed to become completely dry, although perfect drainage is essential, else the handsome glossy foliage will become spotted and unsightly. *Ponera striata* benefits by rather liberal and frequent applications of fertilizer, provided the plants are well-established. The other members of

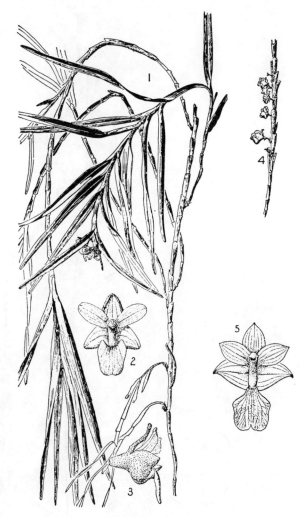

Ponera longipetala Correll & *P. subquadrilabia* Correll
[GORDON W. DILLON]

the genus probably require similar cultural treatment, except for the very dwarf species, which should be grown in small pots in osmunda. (I, H)

P. striata Ldl. (*Ponera australis* Cgn., *Sobralia polyphylla* Krzl.)

Pls. forming large, usually hanging masses, the slender sts. to 4' long (often shorter), leafy above, concealed by close-fitting lf.-sheaths, these tan or brownish. Lvs. distichous, glossy dark green, usually drooping, narrowly linear-lanceolate, tapering to the obliquely 2-toothed apex, 2½–8" long. Infls. usually borne opposite lf.-axils along leafless st. (sometimes terminal on st.), 1–4 in a fasciculate cluster, sessile, 1-fld. Fls. not opening well, rather short-lived, about ½" in diam., the ss. and ps. pale green or greenish-tan with lavender or pale reddish-brown stripes, the large lip white usually striped with lavender. Autumn–early winter. (I, H) Mexico and British Honduras throughout Central America to Brazil and Venezuela.

Ponthieva racemosa (Walt.) Mohr [BLANCHE AMES]

PONTHIEVA R.Br.
(*Calorchis* B.-R., *Schoenleinia* Klotzsch)

Ponthieva consists of about twenty-five species of terrestrial (rarely epiphytic or lithophytic) orchids, which are widespread from Virginia (United States) to Chile, with perhaps the largest assemblage occurring in Ecuador. Seldom encountered in contemporary collections, several of the species are of sufficient beauty to warrant attention by specialists, though their cultivation is often somewhat difficult. The genus is a member of the subtribe *Cranichidinae*, and is somewhat allied to *Cranichis* Sw., differing in details of the flowers, which are for the most part larger and showier than most of the congeners.

Nothing is known of the genetic affinities of *Ponthieva*.

CULTURE: As for *Habenaria*, *Spiranthes*, *Calopogon*, and the like. Most of the species require a semi-acid soil for best results, and none is particularly easy to maintain in good condition for very long. The few epiphytic species should be grown like *Cynorkis*. (I, H)

Pholidota imbricata (Roxb.) Ldl. [REG S. DAVIS]

Phragmipedium caudatum (Ldl.) Rolfe [GEORGE FULLER]

Phymatidium delicatulum Ldl. [E. COOPER]

Platanthera bifolia (L.) L.C.Rich. [GEORGE FULLER]

Pleurothallis stenopetala Ldl. [GEORGE FULLER]

Pogonia ophioglossoides (L.) Ker-Gawl.
[W. M. BUSWELL]

Pterostylis curta R.Br. [P. A. GILBERT]

Pomatocalpa vitellinum (Rchb.f.) Ames [REG S. DAVIS]

P. racemosa (Walt.) Mohr (*Arethusa racemosa* Walt., *Neottia glandulosa* Sims, *Ponthieva Brittonae* Ames, *P. glandulosa* R.Br.)

Lvs. mostly in a basal rosette, succulent, bright dark-green above, dull beneath, oblong-elliptic to rather lanceolate, obtuse to acutish, ¾–7″ long, to more than 2″ wide. Infls. fuzzy, rigidly erect, 6–24″ tall, few–many-fld., the fls. opening successively over a long period. Fls. inverted, to more than ¼″ long and broad, whitish-green, usually veined with emerald-green, with distinctly clawed ps. Autumn–spring. (I) South-east United States to Mexico, southward through West Indies and Central America to South America.

P. maculata Ldl. Mostly epiphytic sp. Lvs. usually 2, basal, elliptic-lanceolate, long-hairy throughout. Infls. 12–18″ tall, loosely 15–20-fld., long-hairy. Fls. almost 1¼″ in diam., spreading, the dors. sep. reddish, the lat. ss. white with black-violet spots, the ps. and small lip golden-yellow with brown stripes. Spring. (I, H) Colombia; Venezuela.

POROLABIUM Tang & Wang

Habenaria biporosum Maxim. was, some years ago, made the type of this new genus by Tang & Wang, its current name being **Porolabium biporosum** (Maxim.) Tang & Wang. Indigenous to Japan, it is a rather small terrestrial orchid of the subtribe *Habenarinae*, which is not present in our collections at this time, and is in any event primarily of scientific importance.

Nothing is known of the genetic affinities of this odd group.

CULTURE: Presumably as for the temperate-zone Habenarias, etc. (C, I)

PORPAX Ldl.

This is a genus of about eight species of very dwarf, epiphytic or lithophytic orchids of the subtribe *Dendrobiinae*, closely allied to *Eria* Ldl., and sometimes included in that group, from which it differs in the vegetative structure of the plants, and floral details, principally in that the sepals are connate into a distinct tube, in which the petals and lip are borne. The *Porpax* are today extremely scarce in collections, but they are among the most charmingly distinctive of all small 'botanical' orchids. The genus occurs in the Himalayas, India, Burma, Thailand, and the Malay Peninsula.

No hybrids are known in *Porpax*, and nothing seems to have been ascertained regarding its genetic affinities, although they presumably lie with *Eria*, etc.

CULTURE: As for the small-growing, tropical Bulbophyllums. (I, H)

P. meirax (Par. & Rchb.f.) King & Pantl. (*Cryptochilus meirax* Par. & Rchb.f., *Eria meirax* N.E.Br.)

Pbs. tightly clustered, round, very flattened, less than ½″ in diam. (usually only slightly more than ¼″ in diam.), closely appressed against the tree or rock on which they grow. Lvs. paired, narrowly elliptic, acute, about 1″ long, eventually deciduous. Infls. very abbreviated, 1-fld., borne from the apex of leafless pbs. Fls. about ½″ long, dull brown, with only the tips of the ss. free and spreading slightly. Ps. shorter than the ss., entirely enclosed in the sepaline tube. Lip short, rather indistinctly 3-lbd., the

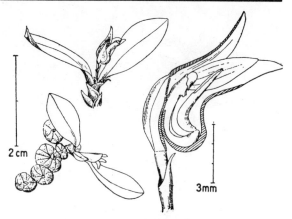

Porpax meirax (Par. & Rchb.f.) King & Pantl. [*Orchids of Thailand*]

lat. lbs. erect and rounded, the midlb. oblong, blunt-pointed. Col. short, with a very long curved foot. Summer. (I, H) Himalayas; Sikkim; Burma; Thailand; Malay Peninsula.

PORPHYRODESME Schltr.

A member of the subtribe *Sarcanthinae*, **Porphyrodesme papuana** Schltr., the only known species of this rare genus, is somewhat allied to *Uncifera* Ldl., and is not present in collections at this time. It inhabits the high mountain forests of New Guinea, and is a rather small monopodial plant with tiny reddish flowers, these borne on a slender red inflorescence.

Nothing is known of the genetic affinities of *Porphyrodesme*.

CULTURE: Presumably as for the cool-growing Vandas and Aërides. (C, I)

PORPHYROGLOTTIS Ridl.

Containing but a single very rare epiphytic species, *Porphyroglottis* is a remarkable genus of the subtribe *Cymbidiinae*, native in Sarawak, Dutch Borneo (now Kalimantan), and the Malay Peninsula. Unknown in collections outside of its native haunts, **P. Maxwelliae** Ridl. is a most unusual plant, vegetatively identical to a small specimen of *Grammatophyllum speciosum* Bl., but with totally different, complex, rosy flowers with a dark purple-brown and yellow lip.

Holttum (*Fl. Malaya* 1: 513. 1953) notes that seed-capsules have been produced between *Porphyroglottis* and *Grammatophyllum multiflorum* Ldl., but no hybrids have been registered.

CULTURE: As for the tropical species of *Dendrobium*. (H)

PORPHYROSTACHYS Rchb.f.

A genus comprising but a single species, **Porphyrostachys pilifera** (HBK) Rchb.f. (*Altensteinia pilifera* HBK, *Stenoptera cardinalis* Ldl.), native in the Andes of Ecuador and Peru, it should perhaps be referred to *Altensteinia* HBK or to *Pseudocentrum* Ldl., but differs somewhat from these groups in technical details of the

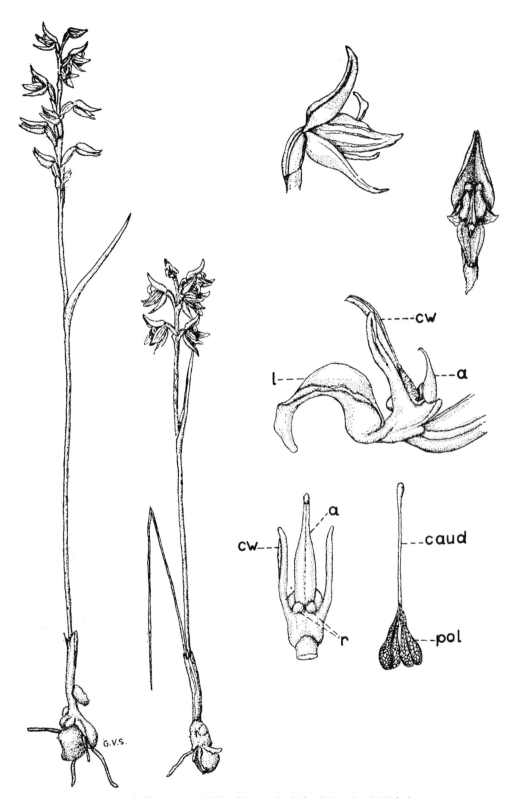

Prasophyllum striatum R.Br. [Rupp, *Orchids of New South Wales*]

flowers. A terrestrial orchid, this spectacular plant attains heights of almost two feet, and bears a dense raceme of light or rather brilliant scarlet flowers of great beauty. Unfortunately, it is essentially unknown in contemporary cultivation, though it is available from Ecuadorean sources.

Nothing is known of the genetic affinities of *Porphyrostachys*.

CULTURE: Presumably as for the cool-growing Habenarias, etc. (C, I)

PRASOPHYLLUM R.Br.
(*Genoplesium* R.Br.)

A genus of more than eighty species, the unusual Prasophyllums are restricted to Australia for the most part, with a few outlying representatives in New Zealand, and one in New Caledonia. Virtually unknown in collections outside of their native haunts, these complex and often botanically confused terrestrial orchids typically bear rather dull-coloured, inconspicuous flowers—often of unusual structure—in erect dense or lax racemes. Almost all of the species of this genus of the subtribe *Prasophyllinae* are highly variable, exhibiting great extremes of formation in various individuals.

Although natural hybrids are recorded in this genus, no artificial breeding has been attempted, and nothing is known of its genetic compatibility with allied groups.

CULTURE: As for *Caladenia*. (C, I)

P. striatum R.Br.

Tubers subterranean, irregular in shape. Lf. solitary, sheathing the base of the infl., the lamina terete, short. Infl. to 12″ tall, slender, with 2–10 inverted fls. in a loose rac. Fls. less than ½″ long, white, striped with green, the lip white apically, undulate marginally. Apr.–June. (C, I) Australia: New South Wales.

PRESCOTTIA Ldl.
(*Decaisnea* Brongn., *Galeoglossum* A.Rich. & Gal., *Prescotia* Ldl.)

This is a complex genus of about thirty species of mostly terrestrial (rarely epiphytic on mossy trees in cloud-forests) orchids, widespread from South Florida and Mexico to Brazil and Peru, with the centre of development in Brazil. A genus of the subtribe *Cranichidinae*, it is somewhat allied to *Stenoptera* Presl and to *Altensteinia* HBK, but differs in structural details of the tiny, usually green blossoms, which are borne in erect, very dense spikes above a rosette of somewhat flaccid foliage. None of the Prescottias appears to be present in contemporary collections, although some of them are rather attractive and should appeal to specialists.

Nothing is known of the genetic affinities of this group.

CULTURE: Presumably as for the tropical *Spiranthes*, etc. (I, H)

PRISTIGLOTTIS Cretz & J.J.Sm.

The genus *Pristiglottis* now contains about twenty species of the subtribe *Physurinae*, most of which were formerly incorporated in *Cystopus* Bl. Terrestrial orchids of the vague 'Jewel Orchid' category—certain of them

have handsomely variegated or mottled foliage—they are largely inhabitants of the Indonesian region, and at this time do not appear to be present in our collections, although some of them are of potential interest to connoisseur collectors.

Nothing has been discovered regarding the genetic alliances of *Pristiglottis*.

CULTURE: Presumably as for *Anoectochilus*. (H)

PROMENAEA Ldl.

This is a genus of about fifteen rather variable species of primarily epiphytic (rarely lithophytic) orchids, all apparently restricted to Brazil, where they are often rather common in the wild state. A member of the subtribe *Zygopetalinae*, these charming mostly dwarf plants have in the past been reduced to *Zygopetalum* Hk., but they appear distinct from that group, on the basis of floral characters. Now uncommon in collections, they have been in the past among the more popular of the so-called 'botanical' orchids, especially in England. Compact, prominently pseudobulbous plants, they produce—when well-grown—a veritable mass of proportionately large and bright flowers of unique form and coloration, which makes them of considerable potential value to all orchidists.

Two hybrids, now very rare, are registered in *Promenaea*, viz. *P. x Colmaniana* (*P. xanthina* × *P. x Crawshayana*), registered in 1935, and *P. x Crawshayana* (*P. stapelioides* × *P. xanthina*), registered by Crawshay in 1905. Additional critical breeding within the genus should be attempted, as well as possible inter-generic hybrids with members of certain allied groups, such as *Zygopetalum*, *Menadenium*, etc.

CULTURE: The Promenaeas are singularly easy to grow, and are recommended even to the beginning hobbyist. Best kept in smallish, perfectly-drained pots, filled with a compost made up of mixed chopped sphagnum moss and shredded tree-fern fibre. While actively growing, they benefit by liberal applications of water and rather high humidity (they should be kept in the warm or intermediate greenhouse for best results), but as soon as the flowers fade, a rest-period of about three weeks or so should be afforded them. A relatively bright, but not excessively sunny spot suits them well, though care should be taken not to allow the usually coriaceous foliage to become burned. While in active growth, they benefit by regular and frequent applications of fertilizing materials. Highly intolerant of stale conditions at the roots, they should be repotted and transferred to fresh compost at about biennial intervals. (I, H)

P. microptera Rchb.f. (*Zygopetalum micropterum* Rchb.f.)

Pbs. clustered, roundish, somewhat laterally compressed, about 1″ tall at most. Lvs. ligulate, greyish-green, about 2″ long and ½″ wide. Infls. slightly arching, 1–3-fld., to 2″ long. Fls. about 2″ in diam., waxy, fragrant, light yellow or whitish, sometimes more or less spotted with red. Ss. and ps. ovate, acutish. Lip usually yellowish-white with carmine-red streaks, basally dotted with red, the lat. lbs. small, the midlb. oblong-lanceolate. Summer. (I, H) Brazil.

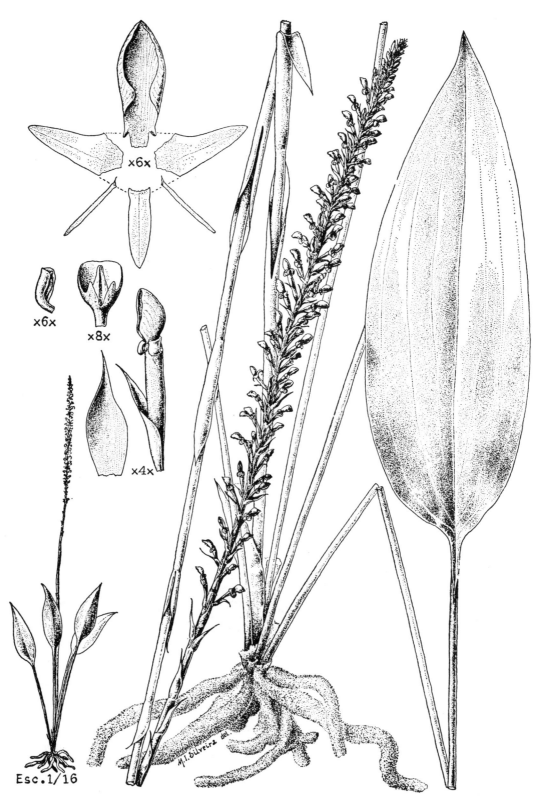

Esc.1/16

×6×

×6×

×8×

×4×

Prescottia stachyodes Ldl. [Hoehne, *Flora Brasílica*]

Promenaea xanthina (Ldl.) Ldl. [VEITCH]

P. Rollinsoni (Ldl.) Ldl. (*Maxillaria Rollinsoni* Ldl., *Zygopetalum Rollinsoni* Rchb.f.)

Rather similar to the preceding sp. in habit. Fls. to about 1½″ in diam., pale yellow. Ss. and ps. elliptic, short-acuminate. Lip 3-lbd., yellow, dotted with dark violet-purple, the lat. lbs. small, oblong, the midlb. oval, short-acuminate. Late summer. (I, H) Brazil.

P. stapelioides (Ldl.) Ldl. (*Maxillaria stapelioides* Ldl., *Zygopetalum stapelioides* Rchb.f.)

Resembling the other spp. in habit. Fls. to almost 2″ across, the ss. and ps. greenish-yellow, densely barred and blotched with lurid purple. Lip dark lurid purple, the midlb. almost round, spotted with black-purple, the lat. lbs. paler in colour, with some dark blotches. Summer–autumn. (I, H) Brazil.

P. xanthina (Ldl.) Ldl. (*Maxillaria xanthina* Ldl., *Maxillaria citrina* Don, *Promenaea citrina* Don, *Maxillaria guttata* hort., *Zygopetalum citrinum* Nichols., *Zygopetalum xanthinum* Rchb.f.)

Similar to the other described spp. in habit. Fls. about 2″ in diam., very fragrant, heavy-textured, long-lasting, citron-yellow. Lip with an obovate yellow midlb. and oblong, obtuse, red-dotted lat. lbs. Col. dotted with red on the frontal surface. Late summer. (I, H) Brazil.

PSEUDACORIDIUM Ames

A single species of *Pseudacoridium* is known to date, this an extremely rare but rather attractive epiphytic orchid, native to Luzon in the Philippines. Closely allied to *Dendrochilum* Bl., it differs from that group in technical details of the inflorescence and flowers, and is not in cultivation at this time.

Nothing is known of the genetic affinities of *Pseudacoridium*.

CULTURE: Presumably as for the smaller-growing, tropical Coelogynes. (I, H)

PSEUDERIA Schltr.

Pseuderia consists of about nineteen species of very unusual orchids of the subtribe *Dendrobiinae*, somewhat allied to *Eria* Ldl., but differing from that genus materially in both vegetative appearance and in floral structure. Apparently unknown in our collections at this time, they are primarily epiphytic plants (often commencing life as terrestrials at the bases of trees, and becoming true epiphytes as the basal portions of the stem decay with age), mostly indigenous to New Guinea, but with outlying representatives in the Moluccas, Caroline Islands, Santa Cruz Islands, Samoa, and the Fiji Islands. The flowers are usually rather small and insignificant, and the genus is primarily of scientific interest.

Nothing is known of the genetic affinities of *Pseuderia* at this time.

CULTURE: Probably as for the tropical Vandas, because of the habit of the plants. (H)

PSEUDOCENTRUM Ldl.

This is a genus of the subtribe *Cranichidinae*, with about five terrestrial species in Costa Rica and the West Indies. Unknown in contemporary collections, it is incompletely delimited botanically, and is perhaps not a valid taxon. The plants are rather reminiscent of certain species of *Spiranthes* L.C.Rich.

Nothing is known of the genetic ties of *Pseudocentrum*.

CULTURE: Presumably as for the tropical Spiranthes, etc. (I, H)

PSEUDOCTOMERIA Krzl.

Only a single species of *Pseudoctomeria* is known to science, this an extremely rare rather small epiphytic orchid endemic to Costa Rica, where it has been found on only a very few occasions. A member of the subtribe *Pleurothallidinae*, it differs from the somewhat allied genus *Octomeria* R.Br. in critical details. At this time, it is unknown in our collections, and in any event is primarily of scientific interest.

Nothing is known of the genetic affinities of *Pseudoctomeria*.

CULTURE: Presumably as for the cool-growing Pleurothallis, Masdevallias, etc. (C, I)

PSEUDOLAELIA Porto & Brade

Two species of *Pseudolaelia* are known to date, both of them very rare epiphytic or lithophytic orchids of the subtribe *Laeliinae*, native to Brazil. Rather simulating certain species of the section *Schomburgkia* of *Laelia* Ldl., the two species, **Pseudolaelia corcovadensis** Porto & Brade and **P. vellozicola** (Hoehne) Porto & Brade (*Schomburgkia vellozicola* Hoehne) are peculiar plants which offer considerable potentials to the specialist collector, but unfortunately neither of them appears to be in general cultivation at this time.

Nothing has been ascertained regarding the genetic affinities of *Pseudolaelia*, although it is entirely possible that they will prove 'crossable' with at least certain other members of the alliance to which they belong.

CULTURE: As for the Brazilian lithophytic Laelias. *Pseudolaelia vellozicola* habitually, insofar as we know,

grows on the trunks of the peculiar Vellozias, and it is possible that its removal will prove fatal to the orchid. (I, H)

PSEUDOLIPARIS Finet

Only a single species of *Pseudoliparis* is known to date; this is a most unusual and very little-known rarity, **P. epiphytica** (Schltr.) Finet (*Microstylis epiphytica* Schltr.), from New Guinea. The group is a member of the subtribe *Liparidinae*, and is apparently not in cultivation at this time.

Nothing has been ascertained regarding the genetic ties of this odd group.

CULTURE: Possibly as for the tropical, small-growing Bulbophyllums. (I)

PSEUDOMAXILLARIA Hoehne

Containing but a single species, this odd group—a segregate from *Maxillaria* R. & P., of the subtribe *Maxillarinae*—is restricted to South-eastern Brazil, where **P. chloroleuca** (B.-R.) Hoehne is a reasonably frequent epiphyte in wooded areas. The genus differs from *Maxillaria* in having the lateral sepals connate for some distance from the base, and in the lip's being firmly inserted on the column-foot, instead of freely movable. The species is extremely scarce in contemporary collections, and being rather unspectacular, is primarily of interest to specialists.

Nothing is known of the genetic affinities of *Pseudomaxillaria*, but they are probably closest to *Maxillaria*.

CULTURE: A pendulous plant, this orchid must be grown (once well-rooted) either on a vertically-hung raft of tightly-packed osmunda, or on a slab of tree-fern fibre. Otherwise its cultural requirements are those of the tropical Maxillarias. (I, H)

P. chloroleuca (B.-R.) Hoehne (*Ornithidium chloroleucum* B.-R.)

Rhiz. st.-like, branching rather freely, pendulous, rooting only at base, 2–12″ long, rather thoroughly clothed with imbricating small bracts, producing pbs. at irregular intervals. Pbs. $\frac{3}{4}$–2″ apart, strongly bracted basally, compressed laterally, to more than 1″ tall and $\frac{1}{2}$″ in diam., becoming grooved with age, dark green. Lf. solitary, rather coriaceous, ligular-lanceolate, acuminate apically, narrowed into a pseudo-petiole basally, to 6″ long. Infls. fasciculate in bract-axils below the most recent pb., often being re-produced for two or three years from the same position on the rhiz., the peduncles typically 1-fld. (rarely 2-fld.), short sheathed, the perianth partially hidden by the sheathing bracts. Fls. not expanding fully, less than $\frac{1}{2}$″ in length, greenish-white, the lip yellowish or yellowish-green, rather complex, the lat. ss. slightly joined to the base of the dors. one, these lats. connate for upwards of one-third to one-half of their total length, concave. Late winter–spring. (I, H) Brazil.

PSEUDOSTELIS Schltr.

Two species of *Pseudostelis* are known at this time, both of them relatively rare epiphytic orchids endemic to Brazil. Neither **Pseudostelis derregularis** (B.-R.)

Pseudostelis Bradei Schltr. [Hoehne, *Flora Brasilica*]

Schltr. nor **P. Bradei** Schltr. are present in our collections at this time, though they are interesting plants, rather simulating a *Stelis* or a *Physosiphon*, to both of which groups they are in close affinity, differing, however, in structural details of the tiny racemose flowers.

Nothing is known of the genetic affinities of *Pseudostelis*.

CULTURE: As for *Pleurothallis*, *Stelis*, etc. (I, H)

PSILOCHILUS B.-R.

Psilochilus is a monotypic genus of medium-sized terrestrial orchids, the single species being widespread in the West Indies, Guatemala and elsewhere in Central America, and much of northern South America. A member of the subtribe *Vanillinae*, it is a rare plant even in its native haunts, and but seldom encountered in collections at this time, though it is sufficiently attractive to warrant attention by the specialist.

Nothing is known concerning the genetic affinities of *Psilochilus*.

CULTURE: As for *Anoectochilus*. (H)

P. macrophyllus (Ldl.) Ames (*Pogonia macrophylla* Ldl.)

Pls. coarse, purplish, from a creeping rhiz., 4–14″ tall, the thick st. leafy. Lvs. fleshy, ovate-cordate to ovate-oblong, acute or acuminate, usually rich magenta-purple beneath and somewhat purple-flushed above, to 4½″ long and 1½″ wide, the bases loosely sheathing the st. Infl. short, sometimes branched, 2–8-fld., 1–3″ long, with large bracts, the rachis purple. Fls. not opening fully, about ¾″ long, the ss. dark greenish-purple, the ps. greenish-white, the lip greenish-yellow or white with a purple tip, the apical margins crisped. Summer. (H) West Indies; Guatemala to northern South America.

PTERICHIS Ldl.
(*Acraea* Ldl.)

A genus of about twelve species of extremely rare terrestrial orchids, *Pterichis* is a member of the complex subtribe *Cranichidinae*. None of these plants, found for the most part in the Andes of Colombia, Ecuador, and Peru, have been introduced into our collections, and they are typically solely of botanical interest. The intricate flowers, usually white in colour, are borne in dense racemes above a solitary, ground-hugging leaf.

Nothing is known of the genetic affinities of the genus *Pterichis*.

CULTURE: Presumably as for *Spiranthes* and the like, though rather cool conditions must naturally prevail at all times. (C, I)

PTEROGLOSSA Schltr.

Pteroglossa is a genus of two known species of robust, rather showy terrestrial orchids, native in Brazil, Paraguay, and Argentina. A member of the exceedingly complex subtribe *Spiranthinae*, they are segregated from *Spiranthes* L. C. Rich. on perhaps untenable grounds, though they seem to have sufficient divergent characters to warrant their relegation to a separate group. The genus is probably closer to *Centrogenium* Schltr. than to typical *Spiranthes*. Unfortunately, neither of the two species, **P. macrantha** (Rchb.f.) Schltr. or **P. regia** (Krzl.) Schltr., are present in contemporary collections, although they are among the showiest of all the myriad spiranthoid orchids.

Nothing is known of the genetic affinities of *Pteroglossa*.

CULTURE: Presumably as for the tropical Spiranthes, Habenarias, etc. (I, H)

PTEROGLOSSASPIS Rchb.f.
(*Triorchos* Small & Nash)

About ten species of *Pteroglossaspis* are known to date, most of them indigenous to tropical Africa, but with two American representatives. The genus is allied to *Eulophia* R.Br., but is differentiated on technical details of the flowers. Terrestrial plants with usually subterranean, corm-like pseudobulbs and erect racemes of often rather attractive blossoms, one species is present today in a very few specialized collections, although it must be classed as a rarity.

Nothing is known of the genetic affinities of *Pteroglossaspis*.

CULTURE: As for *Phaius*. (I, H)

P. ecristata (Fern.) Rolfe (*Cyrtopodium ecristatum* Fern., *Eulophia ecristata* Ames, *Triorchos ecristatus* Small)
Pbs. corm-like, subterranean, fibrous-rooting. Lvs. several, clustered at the base of the pl., linear-lanceolate, long-acuminate, the lower part sheathing the infl., plicate, eventually deciduous, ½–2¼′ long, to 1¼″ broad. Infl. rather stout, sheathed strongly throughout, to 4′ tall, with a prominently bracted, loosely or densely few- to many-fld. rac. at the apex. Fls. nodding, usually less than 1″ long, brown variously tinged and marked with dark purple. Lip concave, below, deeply 3-lbd., naked, slightly crenate-erose on the margins, varying from pale brown to dark purple, strongly veined, the roundish, rather small lat. lbs. incurved, the midlb. roundish, strongly involute at apex. Col. short and blunt. June–Sept. (I, H) North Carolina; Louisiana; Florida; Cuba.

PTEROSTEMMA Lehm. & Krzl.

Pterostemma antioquiensis Lehm. & Krzl., the only known member of the genus (and of the aberrant sub-tribe *Pterostemmatinae*), is an exceedingly rare, dwarf, epiphytic orchid which has been encountered on a very few occasions in the high Andes of Colombia. A most unusual little plant, it is not in collections at this time, and is still not fully understood by the botanists.

Nothing is known of the genetic alliances of this peculiar orchid.

CULTURE: Presumably as for *Ornithocephalus*, though cool conditions should prevail at all times. (C)

PTEROSTYLIS R.Br.
(*Diplodium* Sw.)

A member of the complex subtribe *Pterostylidinae*, this group now contains upwards of seventy species, the majority of which are native to Australia, with outlying representatives in New Zealand, New Guinea, and New Caledonia. Primarily terrestrial orchids, they are as yet very infrequent in collections outside of their native haunts, though these 'Greenhoods', as they are known in Australia, are exceptionally interesting plants, albeit seldom highly showy when in blossom. Deciduous plants, they produce large, incredibly shaped flowers singly or in loose few-flowered racemes, the floral colour primarily green or greenish, but often with delicate tints and suffusions of red and red-brown. The structure of the blooms of the different species is often excessively complicated, and frequently rather difficult to describe.

Some natural hybrids are known in *Pterostylis* in Australia, but other than this nothing has been ascertained regarding its genetic affinities.

CULTURE: As for *Caladenia*. (C, I)

P. Banksii R.Br. (*Pterostylis australis* Ldl.)
Tubers small, on slender fleshy fibres. St. 6–18″ tall, relatively stout, leafy at base and on st. Lvs. alternate, sheathing entire st., linear-lanceolate, to 12″ long. Fl.

solitary, terminal, to 3″ long, vivid bright green. Dors. sep. and ps. crossing and forming a beaked hood; lat. ss. elongate, filiform, ascending; lip linear, its tip exerted from the hood, the disc-appendage curved, fuzzy at top. July–Nov. (C, I) New Zealand.

P. Baptistii Fitzg.
Pl. slender, the st. from 8–20″ tall. Lvs. usually in basal rosette of 5–8, short-petiolate, conspicuously reticulate-veined, oblong to broadly lanceolate. Fl. to 3″ long or more, light green with fawn-coloured bands and markings, or occasionally darker green with correspondingly darker markings. Dors. sep. erect for more than half its length, the curving to a short point slightly exceeding the broad ps.; lat. ss. erect below, united for about one-third of their length, the free portions sharply narrowing and retracted across the hood. Usually Aug.–Oct. (C, I) Australia, from South Queensland to East Victoria.

P. curta R.Br.
Lvs. basal, in a compact rosette, ovate to ovate-elliptic, stalked, to 1½″ long. Infl. about 6″ tall (rarely to 10″), 1–2-fld. Fls. to 1½″ long, green, often tinted with brown. Hood formed by dors. sep. and ps. curving forward at about half its length, the lat. ss. erect, united for about half their length, the free end not prolonged into filiform points but acuminate, curving slightly backwards and crossing the hood but scarcely exceeding it. Mostly July–Sept., but also at other times of year. (C, I) Australia.

P. nutans R.Br.
Pl. highly variable in height, from 1¾–20″ tall, slender. Lvs. stalked, in a basal rosette of about 5, ovate to oblong, often wavy marginally. Fl. usually single, to almost 1½″ long, green, conspicuously bent forward so that the interior faces the ground. Dors. sep. greatly curved for almost its whole length, sometimes slightly longer than ps. Lat. ss. joined for one-third to half their length, the free tails linear, slightly exceeding the hood. Apr.–Oct. (C, I) Australia.

PTERYGODIUM Sw.

About thirty-six species make up this unusual genus of principally terrestrial orchids of the subtribe *Disperidinae*, these native to the hilly and mountainous areas of southern Africa. Often very beautiful plants, with dense or loose racemes of white or yellow flowers of frequently complicated structure, they are regrettably scarce in our collections today, and should be better known by orchidists. Bearing subterranean tubers, the fairly stout or sometimes flexuose stems are clothed with oblong or lanceolate, suberect leaves which become bract-like upwards, particularly in the raceme. In the wild, the Pterygodiums are usually found in moist, open grasslands.

No hybrids are known as yet in *Pterygodium*, and nothing has been ascertained regarding its genetic affinities, although they certainly lie with such groups as *Ceratandra* Eckl. and *Disperis* Sw.

CULTURE: As for *Caladenia*. (I)

P. acutifolium Ldl.

St. stout, flexuous, to 2′ tall and more. Lvs. cauline, oblong-lanceolate, 3–7″ long. Infl. 1½–4″ long, rather dense, usually many-fld. Fls. almost 1″ in diam., dark golden-yellow, very handsome, lasting rather well. Dors. sep. ovate-lanceolate, subconcave, with a rounded sac behind the sharply reflexed apex; lat. ss. obliquely ovate, widely spreading. Ps. cohering with the dors. sep. into a spreading, broadly semi-obovate, very oblique limb. Lip broadly triangular-ovate, sharply reflexed, undulate, the appendage triangular-oblong, erect, recurved apically. Mostly Nov.–Dec. (I) Cape Colony.

P. catholicum (L.) Sw. (*Ophrys catholica* L., *Ophrys alaris* L., *Arethusa alaris* Thunb.)

St. rather stout, somewhat flexuous, ½–12″ tall. Lvs. cauline, distant, oblong or elliptic-oblong, sessile, sheathing at the base, 1–5″ long. Infl. ½–12″ tall, usually about 3–8-fld. Fls. about ¾″ across, pale sulphur-yellow, the ps. and lip sometimes orange-red. Dors. sep. ovate-lanceolate, subconcave; lat. ss. ovate, curved at the apex, spreading. Ps. cohering with the dors. sep. into an expanded limb, broadly elliptic-oblong, very oblique. Lip broadly rhomboid-orbicular, very undulate, reflexed, the appendage ovate-oblong, obscurely 3-lbd., blunt, recurved apically. Aug.–Oct. (I) Cape Colony.

P. magnum Rchb.f. (*Corycium magnum* Rolfe)

St. stout, furnished with short basal sheaths, to almost 4′ tall. Lvs. usually about 6, oblong-lanceolate, sessile, sheathing at the base, 4–9″ long. Infl. 6–18″ long, cylindrical, dense. Fls. about ½″ long, green, more or less striped or streaked with red. Dors. sep. oblong-lanceolate, concave; lat. ss. ovate-lanceolate, subconcave, spreading. Ps. obliquely suborbicular-oblong, the outer margin strongly fringed. Lip cuneate-obovate or flabellate, fringed at apex, the appendage vaguely 3-lbd. Nov.–Jan. (I) Cape Colony; Griqualand East; Natal; Orange Free State; Transvaal.

P. alatum (Thunb.) Sw. (*Ophrys alata* Thunb.) St. rather stout, to about 6″ tall. Lvs. basal and cauline, oblong-lanceolate, ¾–1¾″ long. Infl. 1–2½″ long, many-fld., rather dense. Fls. about ½″ across, pale sulphur-yellow. Dors. sep. lanceolate-oblong, the lats. similar, spreading. Ps. cohering with the dors. sep. into an obovate-orbicular limb, outer margin crisped and crenulate. Lip 3-lbd., the midlb. broadly triangular, the lat. lbs. rounded, crenulate, the appendage rather 3-lbd., clavate, erect. Autumn, mostly Sept. (I) South-west Cape Colony.

P. nigrescens (Sond.) Schltr. (*Corycium nigrescens* Sond.) St. rather stout, to 2′ tall. Lvs. cauline, spreading, lanceolate, acutish, sheathing basally, 2–6″ long. Infl. 2–6″ long, cylindrical, dense. Fls. about ¼″ long, globular, dark brown or dark purple. Dors. sep. suborbicular, concave, blunt, the lats. joined into a very concave suborbicular limb. Ps. obliquely orbicular, deeply saccate, the outer margin broadly dilated. Lip pandurate-oblong, concave, the appendage borne on lip-claw, spur-like. Dec.–Jan. (I) Cape Colony; Orange Free State; Transvaal; Natal.

P. tricuspidatum Schltr. (*Corycium tricuspidatum* Bolus) St. stout, to 15″ tall. Lvs. dull green, spreading, lanceolate, to 3½″ long. Infl. 4–6″ long, densely many-fld. Fls. globular, about ¼″ long, green and brown. Dors. sep. broadly ovate, concave, the lats. broadly elliptic-oblong, blunt, concave. Ps.

forming a globose hood with the dors. sep., obliquely ovate or suborbicular, very concave. Lip broadly clawed, cuneately 3-lbd., the lat. lbs. oblong-lanceolate, diverging, the midlb. narrowly subulate, the small appendage oblong. Feb–May. (I) East Cape Colony; Griqualand East; Natal.

PYGMAEORCHIS Brade

Pygmaeorchis brasiliensis Brade, the only known member of this rare and rather little-known genus of the subtribe *Laeliinae*, is a very tiny epiphytic plant which has been collected on a very few occasions in Brazil. It is somewhat allied to *Pinelia* Ldl., but differs in technical details of the diminutive flowers. One of the smallest of all epiphytic orchids, it is unknown in our collections at this time.

Nothing is known of the genetic affinities of *Pygmaeorchis*.

CULTURE: Possibly as for *Pinelia*. (I)

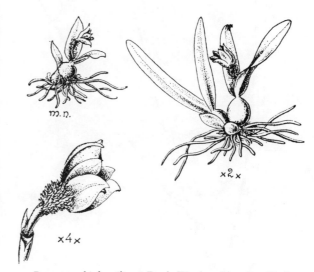

Pygmaeorchis brasiliensis Brade [Hoehne, *Flora Brasilica*]

QUEKETTIA Ldl.

Quekettia microscopica Ldl., the only known member of this genus of the subtribe *Capanemiinae*, is an exceptionally rare dwarf epiphytic orchid from the misty forests of Brazil. It is rather incompletely known botanically, and is not at this time present in our collections.

Nothing has been ascertained concerning the genetic affinities of *Quekettia*.

CULTURE: Presumably as for *Ornithocephalus*. (I)

RANGAËRIS [Schltr.] Summerh.

The genus *Rangaëris* consists of about six species of principally epiphytic orchids of the complex angraecoid aggregation of the subtribe *Sarcanthinae*, all of them indigenous to tropical Africa. They are rather unusual plants, apparently not in our collections at this

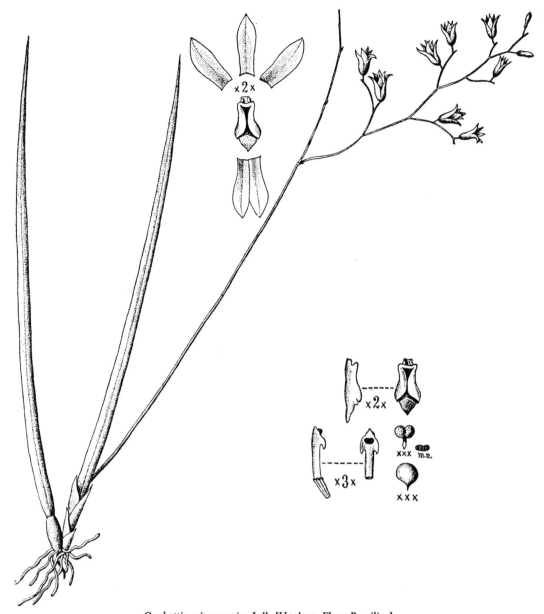

Quekettia microscopica Ldl. [Hoehne, *Flora Brasílica*]

time, although they seem to offer some potential interest to the connoisseur orchidist.

Nothing is known of the genetic affinities of *Rangaëris*.

CULTURE: Presumably as for the Angraecums from similar regions. (I, H)

REICHENBACHANTHUS B.-R.

But a single very rare epiphytic species makes up the genus *Reichenbachanthus*, **R. modestus** B.-R., which has been collected on a few occasions in the moist forests of the Brazilian State of São Paulo. Allied to *Scaphyglottis* P. & E., and to several other members of the complex subtribe *Ponerinae*, it is a peculiar, rather nondescript, fleshy-leaved, branching orchid, with small but com-

plex flowers of no especial beauty. *Reichenbachanthus* appears to be unknown in collections at this time.

Nothing is known concerning the genetic ties of this group.

CULTURE: Possibly as for the intermediate-elevation, non-pseudobulbous Epidendrums. (I)

RENANTHERA Lour.
(*Nephranthera* Hassk.)

About twelve species of *Renanthera* are currently accepted as valid by the botanists. These range from China and the Himalayas throughout South-east Asia, the Philippines, and Indonesia to New Guinea; over this huge area, they are customarily epiphytic, but on occasion are found to adopt a terrestrial or lithophytic habit. Vegetatively the genus consists of two basic sections, one of rather short-stemmed plants somewhat simulating certain Vandas (a genus to which *Renanthera* is rather closely allied), the other of often very elongate, vine-like plants, sometimes attaining heights in excess of twenty feet. Botanically, *Renanthera* is closest to *Vandopsis* Pfitz. and *Arachnis* Bl., from both of which it differs in superficial (and more detailed) structure of the usually scarlet, orange, or crimson flowers, which are frequently produced in tremendous numbers in huge, horizontally spreading, usually branched sprays. Renantheras have been in cultivation for a very long time (*R. coccinea* Lour. was one of the first epiphytic orchids to flower in England), and even today they are justly prized by collectors for their spectacular, very hand-

some flowers, produced in such extravagant quantities.

Renanthera has, mostly during the past decade or so, been taken in hand by many orchid breeders. As a result, and because the genus is rather freely compatible with most allied groups of the subtribe *Sarcanthinae*, there are today many extraordinarily handsome hybrids, these including *Renantanda* (× *Vanda*), *Renanopsis* (× *Vandopsis*), *Renanthopsis* (× *Phalaenopsis*), *Aranthera* (× *Arachnis*), etc. Considerable additional hybridization with such allied groups should be attempted, and more interspecific crossing within the genus itself (a few exceptionally handsome interspecific Renantheras are now registered) is recommended. Often these hybrids utilizing *Renanthera* in their parentage are, under optimum conditions, almost ever-blooming, thus making them of immeasurable value to the collector.

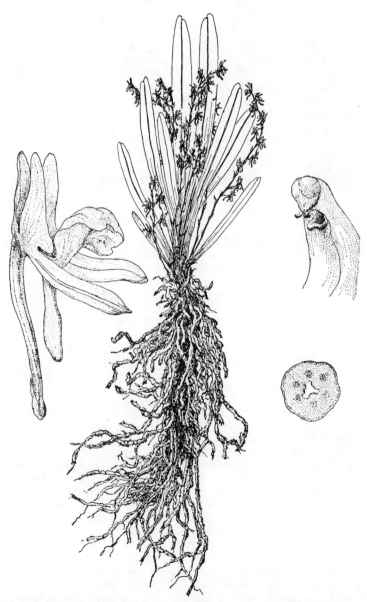

Rangaëris brachyceras (Summerh.) Summerh. [*Flora of the Belgian Congo*]

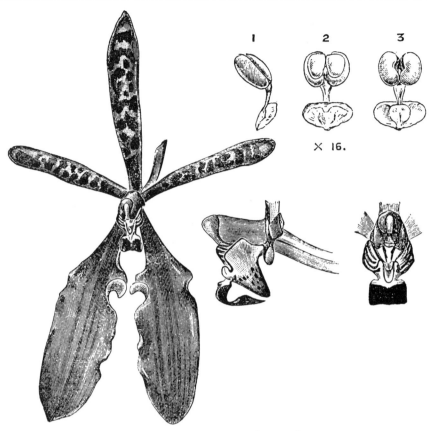

Renanthera coccinea Lour. [VEITCH]

CULTURE: The small-growing Renantheras should be grown like Vandas. Those such as *R. coccinea*, *R. Storiei*, etc., with prominently elongate stems, should be treated like *Arachnis*. Most of these orchids require almost full sun-exposure, plus liberal fertilizing, to produce their full quota of majestic flowers. (I, H)

R. coccinea Lour. (*Epidendrum Renanthera* Raeusch., *Gongora phillippica* Llanos)

Sts. clambering, usually erect, freely rooting, rather woody with age, to 15′ long (rarely more), sometimes sparsely branched near base. Lvs. very numerous, horizontally spreading, oblong, sheathing the st. at base, apically obliquely emarginate, rather rigidly leathery, usually yellowish-green, 4–6″ long. Infls. produced from the st. opposite one of the upper lvs., usually branched and bearing in some cases more than 150 fls., to 4′ long. Fls. about 3½″ long, long-lasting, changing in colour as they age, the dors. sep. and ps. linear-spatulate, vivid red, spotted with yellow, the ps. slightly the narrower and shorter; lat. ss. dark vermilion-red, glossy, clawed at base, oblong, lobate on inner side near base. Lip small, sessile on the col.-base, with a conical saccate spur beneath, 3-lbd., the lat. lbs. erect, truncate, pale yellow, streaked on inner side with bright or dull red; midlb. ovate, acuminate, reflexed, dark red with a pale yellow 2-lamellate callus at base. Col. terete, without wings, dark red. Spring–autumn. (H) South China to Thailand.

R. Imschootiana Rolfe (*Renanthera Papilio* King & Pantl.)

St. usually solitary, becoming woody with age, usually less than 3′ tall, densely leafy. Lvs. fleshy, rather rigid, dark green, oblong, obtuse and shortly 2-lbd. at apex, usually less than 4″ long and ¾″ broad. Infls. horizontally spreading, branched, rather loosely many-fld., to 1½′ long. Fls. to more than 2¼″ long, lasting a month and more, the dors. sep. and ps. linear-ligulate, yellow, the ps. mostly spotted with scarlet-red, the lat. ss. elliptic, clawed basally, light scarlet-red, obtuse at tip, towards base undulate marginally, much larger than other segms. Lip about ¼″ long, scarlet-red, the keels yellow, the lat. lbs. small, triangular, the midlb. roundish, the spur short, obtuse. Summer, especially June–July. (I) Assam; Laos; Viet-Nam.

R. Storiei Rchb.f. (*Vanda Storiei* Storie)

An exceedingly robust sp., sometimes to more than 20′ tall, the usually solitary st. very thick, becoming woody with age, rooting freely. Lvs. linear-ligulate, unequally 2-lbd. at apex, with an apicule between the lbs., to almost 12″ long and 1½″ broad. Infl. horizontally spreading, rather densely many-fld., often with more than 150 fls., to more than 4′ long, freely branching. Fls. long-lasting, about 2½″ long, the dors. sep. and ps. yellowish-red with dark red spots and blotches, narrowly ligulate, the lat. ss. vivid scarlet-red, with more or less numerous darker, roundish blotches, much larger than other segms., clawed at base, elliptic, undulate marginally. Lip mostly scarlet-red, the lat. lbs. erect, broadly oblong, the midlb. larger, somewhat reflexed, with yellow keels on the disc, the spur short, obtuse. Summer, mostly June–July. (H) Philippines.

R. elongata Ldl. (*Renanthera micrantha* Bl., *Saccolabium reflexum* Ldl.) St. elongate, often branched near the base, to about 5′ long, usually erect, freely rooting. Lvs. horizontally spreading, rather leathery and rigid, dark green, oblong-ligulate, unequally 2-lbd. at apex, to 4″ long and 1¼″ broad. Infls. erect or ascending, very branched, rather densely many-fld., to 2′ long (rarely longer). Fls. about ¾″ long (usually somewhat smaller), long-lasting, yellow, more or less densely spotted with bright red. Ss. and ps. oblong, obtuse, the ps. smaller than the ss. Lip red with yellow keels on the disc, the lat. lbs. very small, the midlb. oblong, reflexed towards apex, the spur oblong, obtuse. Winter, mostly Dec.–Jan. (H) Java; Sumatra; Borneo; Malay Peninsula.

R. matutina (Bl.) Ldl. (*Aërides matutina* Bl., *Renanthera angustifolia* Hk.f.) St. clambering and hanging, to 6′ tall (rarely more), sometimes branching from base. Lvs. numerous, thickly fleshy, rigid, dark grey-green, linear-oblong, obliquely emarginate or 2-lbd. at apex, channelled above, 4–8″ long, to about ½″ broad, the lf.-sheaths dark-coloured. Infls. sparsely branched, often flexuose, many-fld., to 2½′ long, the branches elongating for some time, almost horizontal. Fls. about 2¼″ long, rather narrow, bright reddish-crimson or light crimson with dark red spots, sometimes flushed with yellow, changing with age to orange-yellow. Ss. and ps. similar, linear, acute, the lat. ss. at first parallel, then usually divergent. Lip much smaller than the other segms., the lat. lbs. with narrow curved tips, orange-yellow and white with red spots; midlb. very short, reflexed, blunt, red-brown; spur much longer than midlb., cylindric, blunt. Col. yellow, spotted with dark crimson. Autumn. (H) Malay Peninsula; Sumatra; Java.

R. monachica Ames Rather similar in habit to *R. matutina* (Bl.) Ldl., but considerably shorter in size, the robust st. usually less than 2′ tall, typically leafy throughout. Lvs. very fleshy and rigid, dull green, sometimes flushed with dull brown or dull purple when grown in full sun, to about 5″ long, to almost ½″ thick. Infl. erect to arching, loosely or rather densely 6–30-fld., to about 1½′ long. Fls. long-lasting, 1–1½″ in diam., much longer than wide, the spreading ss. and ps. bright orange with blood-red spots, the small lip mostly blood-red. Dors. sep. and ps. narrow, pointed, the lat. ss. downthrust, wider medially than other segms., narrowing basally. Mostly late winter–spring. (I, H) Philippines: Luzon.

R. pulchella Rolfe Rather similar to *R. Imschootiana* Rolfe. St. normally solitary, leafy, usually only about 7–12″ tall at most. Lvs. distinctly 2-ranked, narrowly oblong, shortly 2-lbd. at apex, leathery, to 3½″ long. Infl. usually horizontal, to about 12″ long, rather densely many-fld., branched. Fls. slightly more than 1″ long, yellow, the upper half of the ps. carmine-red, the lat. lbs. of the lip marked with the same colour. Autumn. (I) Assam; Burma.

RENANTHERELLA Ridl.

A single species of rare epiphytic or lithophytic orchid in the Malay Peninsula makes up the little-known genus *Renantherella*, often considered to be synonymous with *Renanthera* Lour., from which it differs in the sharp-pointed foliage, the inverted flowers, and the elongated column. It is very scarce in contemporary collections,

but is a handsome and highly floriferous orchid which should be better appreciated by specialists.

A recent hybrid between *Renanthera* and *Renantherella* has been registered, and it has been recommended (by this writer) that the hybrid epithet be altered in the registry to read *Ellanthera*, to avoid confusion which presently exists.

CULTURE: As for *Arachnis* and *Renanthera*. (H)

R. histrionica (Rchb.f.) Ridl. (*Renanthera histrionica* Rchb.f.)

Sts. clambering, often hanging, to 3′ long and more, leafy throughout, the roots very robust. Lvs. very fleshy, curved, gradually narrowed to a sharp tip, to about 4″ long. Infls. horizontal, freely produced, to about 4″ long, few-fld., the fls. opening singly or in pairs as the rachis elongates. Fls. inverted, about 1″ long, the ss. and ps. lemon-yellow with some small crimson spots near the margins and tips, the lip yellow with red spots, the long col. yellow, red-spotted. Mostly summer. (H) Malay Peninsula.

RHINERRHIZA Rupp

Rhinerrhiza is a rather recently established genus, containing but a single species, this a singularly attractive but little-known epiphytic orchid from Australia. A member of the subtribe *Sarcanthinae*, it was formerly included in *Sarcochilus* R.Br., but was removed from that group for technical details of the plants (notably the roots) and flowers. Speaking of it in his book, *The Orchids of New South Wales* (1943), page 132, the late Rev. H. M. R. Rupp writes: 'This plant, which is quite amenable to cultivation, is unlike any other Australian species of *Sarcochilus*. Its thick raspy roots give it a singular appearance. The buds of the racemes remain very small and inconspicuous until within a few days of flowering, when they suddenly begin to swell and to elongate. As a rule, almost all of the racemes, of which there may be 7 or 8, some with as many as 45 buds, open their flowers simultaneously at night, transforming a somewhat unattractive plant by morning into a blaze of orange and red flowers, white-centred. Within a day or two, every flower is withered.' At this time, *Rhinerrhiza* is a very rare orchid in collections outside of its native haunts, but it is assuredly of interest to connoisseurs who specialize in the more unusual 'botanical' orchids.

Nothing is known concerning the genetic affinities of this peculiar genus.

CULTURE: As for the smaller-growing Vandas. (I, H)

R. divitiflora (FvM. ex Bth.) Rupp (*Sarcochilus divitiflorus* FvM. ex Bth.)

Sts. mostly very short, sometimes to 3″ long, the roots copious and very rough-textured. Lvs. few, to 4½″ long, rigid, oblong to broadly lanceolate, shallowly grooved above. Infls. racemose, 1–8 produced simultaneously, to 15″ long, the numerous fugacious fls. lasting only a day or two. Fls. about 2½″ long, bright orange with red spots, the midlb. of the lip with a conspicuous white sac. Ss. and ps. narrowly linear, tapering to elongate filiform points, the lat. ss. broader at base than other segms. Lip very short, the lat. lbs. larger than the midlb.,

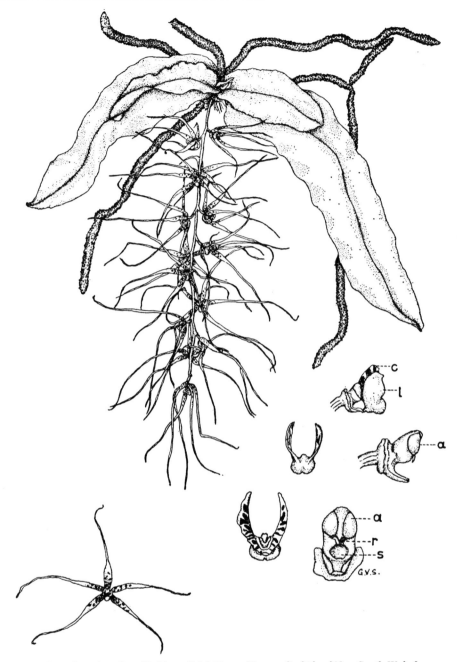

Rhinerrhiza divitiflora (FvM. ex Bth.) Rupp [Rupp, *Orchids of New South Wales*]

embracing the very abbreviated col. Autumn. (I, H) Australia: New South Wales, Queensland.

RHIPIDOGLOSSUM Schltr.

The little-known genus *Rhipidoglossum* contains four described species of epiphytic orchids, all of these native to tropical Africa, with none of them present in our collections at this time. The group is a member of the angraecoid alliance of the subtribe *Sarcanthinae*, and its components bear smallish but complex green or orange-flushed little flowers in racemes.

Nothing is known of the genetic affinities of this rare genus.

CULTURE: Presumably as for *Angraecum*, depending upon the place of origin of the particular species or individual under consideration. (I, H)

RHIZANTHELLA R.S.Rog.

A single species of *Rhizanthella* is known to date, this one of the very extraordinary 'subterranean' orchids thus far detected. **R. Gardneri** R.S.Rog. has been found on a few occasions in West Australia, and is doubtless more

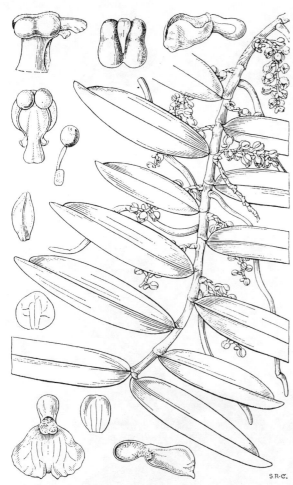

Rhipidoglossum densiflorum Summerh. [*Icones Plantarum*]

frequent than we now realize, since its discovery is almost invariably accidental. It is a member of the small subtribe *Rhizanthellinae*, and differs from the allied genus *Cryptanthemis* Rupp in several technical details. It is not in cultivation at this time.

Nothing is known concerning the genetic affinities of this unusual genus.

CULTURE: See *Cryptanthemis*. (H)

RHYNCHOLAELIA Schltr.

The two known species of *Rhyncholaelia* are both relatively frequent in our collections at this time, almost invariably being known as Brassavolas, in which genus they were formerly included. They differ from that group, however, in the *Cattleya*-like vegetative appearance of the plants, and in several structural details of the very large and spectacular flowers. Principally epiphytic plants in Mexico and Central America, they are handsome orchids which should be in every collection, no matter how modest.

As Brassavolas, both species of *Rhyncholaelia* have been used on a large number of occasions in the production of handsome hybrids. *R. Digbyana* figures

prominently in the make-up of the vast majority of contemporary Brassocattleyas, Brassolaeliocattleyas, etc. These orchids have also been successfully crossed with *Sophronitis*, *Epidendrum*, and *Diacrium* (= now referred to *Caularthron*).

CULTURE: These fine orchids require the general cultural conditions afforded Cattleyas, Laelias, and the like. In the wild, they typically inhabit stunted trees in relatively dry regions, hence in the collection must not be kept overly moist at any time. They do best when potted, tightly, in straight osmunda fibre or shredded tree-fern fibre, or when well-rooted, on slabs of tree-fern fibre. Like most of these plants, the Rhyncholaelias benefit materially by liberal and frequent applications of fertilizers. They should be grown, for best results, in bright, sunny spots. (I, H)

R. Digbyana (Ldl.) Schltr. (*Brassavola Digbyana* Ldl., *Laelia Digbyana* Bth. ex. Jacks.)

Pbs. club-shaped, compressed, concealed by whitish sheaths, to 6″ tall and more, glaucous. Lf. solitary, rigidly fleshy, elliptic, obtuse, glaucous-grey-green, to 8″ long and more than 2″ wide. Infls. 1-fld., terminal, concealed by a large spathe-like sheath. Fls. extremely fragrant (particularly at night), long-lived, heavy-textured, glossy, to almost 7″ across, pale yellowish-green, the very large lip usually cream-white more or less flushed with greenish, often with a vivid emerald-green area in the throat. Ss. elliptic-lanceolate to oblong-ligulate, obtuse, the lats. rather oblique. Ps. obliquely elliptic-oblanceolate, broadly obtuse at apex, the margins somewhat undulate, much wider than the ps. Lip very large, vaguely 3-lbd., the apical margins deeply and intricately fringed and cut, the disc with several short prominent lamellae. Spring–summer. (I, H) Mexico: Yucatán, Quintana Roo; British Honduras; Guatemala.

—fma. **fimbripetala** (Ames) A.D.Hawkes (*Laelia Digbyana* Bth. var. *fimbripetala* Ames, *Brassavola Digbyana* Ldl. var. *fimbripetala* H.G.Jones)

Differs from the typical plant in having the petals marginally fringed to a greater or lesser degree. Mostly spring. (I, H) Honduras.

R. glauca (Ldl.) Schltr. (*Brassavola glauca* Ldl., *Bletia glauca* Rchb.f., *Laelia glauca* Bth.)

Pbs. oblong-spindle-shaped, not too close together on the creeping rhiz., glaucous, compressed, to 4″ long and more. Lf. solitary, rigidly leathery, glaucous, oblong-elliptic, obtuse, to 4½″ long and 1¼″ wide. Infls. 1-fld., subtended by a large compressed spathe-like sheath, terminal. Fls. to almost 5″ across, heavy in texture, fragrant, long-lived, olive-green to white or lavender (the ps. usually paler), the lip white or yellowish with a rose-pink spot or several reddish stripes in the throat. Ss. linear-elliptic to oblong-lanceolate, subobtuse to subacuminate. Ps. obliquely linear-elliptic, usually sharp-pointed, slightly undulate, usually slightly wider than the ss. Lip vaguely 3-lbd., the basal part of the lat. lbs. enfolding the col., the whole segm. roundish or almost square when expanded, the apex very blunt or apiculate. Mostly spring. (I, H) Mexico; Guatemala; Honduras; ? Panama.

Rhynchostylis coelestis Rchb.f. [VEITCH]

Ryncholaelia glauca (Ldl.) Schltr. [GEORGE FULLER]

Rodriguezia venusta (Ldl.) Rchb.f. [*The Orchid Journal*]   *Sarcanthus bifidus* (Ldl.) Ames [REG. S. DAVIS]

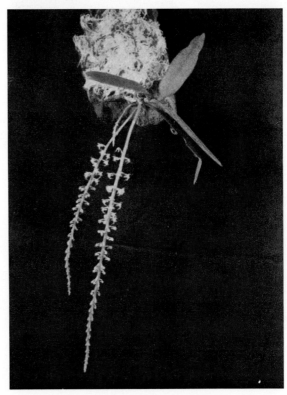

Sarcochilus Hartmanni FvM. [GEORGE FULLER]

Sarcochilus pallidus (Bl.) Rchb.f. [REG S. DAVIES]

RHYNCHOSTYLIS Bl.
(*Anota* Schltr.)

As presently limited, four species of *Rhynchostylis* are recognized, all of them present to greater or lesser extent in our collections, usually under the extremely confusing and highly erroneous name *Saccolabium*, which applies to a completely distinct aggregation of orchids. A member of the subtribe *Sarcanthinae*, the group is vaguely allied to such groups as *Aërides* Lour., *Vanda* R.Br., etc. Usually stout, rather short-stemmed epiphytic (or rarely lithophytic) orchids, the Rhynchostylis inhabit the Indo-Malaysian region, extending to the Philippines. Because of the densely multiflorous racemes, they are often known commonly as the 'Fox-tail Orchids'.

Several hybrids have to date been registered in which *Rhynchostylis* appears, and additional ones are now out of the flask stage. Unfortunately, almost all of those registered to date have been listed under erroneous and confusing names in the official lists, and repeated efforts to correct this on the part of the author and others have been in vain. Since these lovely orchids appear to be rather freely inter-fertile with at least some of the allied groups, it is to be hoped that ere long accuracy in their hybrid listings will be reached.

CULTURE: Generally as for *Vanda*. These fine orchids are singularly intolerant of being disturbed, hence when the compost requires changing, it should—if at all possible—be carefully teased out from around the roots, and replaced, rather than completely removing the plant from its original container. (I, H)

R. coelestis Rchb.f. (*Saccolabium coeleste* Rchb.f.)

St. stout, to about 8″ tall (rarely more), freely emitting large cord-like roots below. Lvs. few to rather numerous, rather closely spaced, rigidly fleshy, ligulate, closely imbricating at base, unequally lbd. and toothed at apex, channelled above, acutely keeled beneath, 4–8″ long, about ¾″ broad at most. Infls. erect, very densely many-fld. along apical half, the rac. cylindrical. Fls. about ¾″ in diam., waxy, fragrant, the pedicellate ovaries furrowed, twisted, white or pale blue, the dors. sep. and ps. white, the broader lat. ss. white with an indigo-blue apical blotch, the lip basally white, the apical half vivid indigo-blue. Ss. and ps. similar and subequal, oval-oblong, obtuse. Lip obovate-oblong, with a very compressed, slightly curved, sac-like spur. Col. very short, with a beaked dark blue anther. Summer–autumn. (I, H) Thailand.

R. gigantea (Ldl.) Ridl. (*Saccolabium giganteum* Ldl., *Saccolabium densiflorum* Ldl., *Anota densiflora* Schltr., *Rhynchostylis densiflora* L.O.Wms., *Vanda densiflora* Ldl.)

St. robust, very short, usually less than 4″ tall, densely leafy, producing numerous very stout roots. Lvs. very heavily leathery, ligulate, unequally and acutely 2-lbd. at apex, frequently with prominent longitudinal pale striations, to 12″ long and 2¼″ broad. Infls. to 15″ long, pendulous, very densely many-fld. Fls. waxy, long-lasting, highly fragrant, about 1″ in diam., the ss. and ps. pure white, more or less spotted with red-violet or magenta, often with a well-defined apical blotch of this colour, the lip red-violet or magenta, usually whitish

towards the middle and base. Ss. and ps. elliptic-oblong, acutish, spreading, often rather undulate. Lip ovate-spatulate, with small roundish lat. lbs., the spur compressed, short, obtuse. Autumn–early winter. (I, H) Burma; Thailand; Laos.

R. retusa (L.) Bl. (*Epidendrum retusum* L., *Saccolabium retusum* Voigt, *Saccolabium Blumei* Ldl., *Saccolabium guttatum* Ldl., *Rhynchostylis praemorsa* Bl.)

St. robust, to 2′ tall, usually much shorter, typically completely hidden by the imbricating lf.-bases, emitting copious very stout white roots. Lvs. ligulate, spreading or gracefully arching, very close together, to more than 12″ long, very rigidly leathery, imbricate at base, at apex obliquely 2-lbd. or truncate, often with paler longitudinal streaks on both surfaces. Infls. pendulous, to 2′ long, typically very densely many-fld. and cylindrical. Fls. fragrant, waxy, short- or long-lived, variable in colour, about ¾″ in diam., the ss. and ps. white, more or less copiously spotted with amethyst-purple, the lip entirely amethyst-purple. Ss. oval-oblong, acute, the lats. considerably broader than the dors. one. Ps. narrowly oblong, acute. Lip deeply saccate at base, the sac very compressed, the lamina obovate-oblong, channelled above, reflexed apically. Col. short, the anther beaked. Summer–autumn. (I, H) India; Ceylon; Burma; Thailand; Laos; Viet-Nam; Malay Peninsula; Java; Borneo; Philippines.

R. violacea (Ldl.) Rchb.f. (*Vanda violacea* Ldl., *Saccolabium violaceum* Rchb.f., *Anota violacea* Schltr.)

Rather similar in all floral parts to *R. retusa* (L.) Bl., differing primarily in technical details of the fls., which are often less densely arranged in the arching or pendulous racemose infl.; vegetatively resembling *R. gigantea* (Ldl.) Ridl. Fls. about ¾″ in diam., white, more or less dotted with violet-red, the lip entirely violet-purple or violet-red, with 5 close basal keels, the apex distinctly 3-lbd. Winter. (I, H) Philippines.

RIDLEYELLA Schltr.

A single genus and species, **Ridleyella paniculata** Schltr., makes up the extremely scarce and little-known subtribe *Ridleyellinae*. Vegetatively and florally somewhat simulating a *Bulbophyllum*, this epiphyte from the high mountain forests of New Guinea is actually closer in alliance to *Thelasis* Bl., differing in the unusual structure of its dark purplish-blue blossoms. It is not present in collections at this time.

Nothing is known of the genetic affinities of *Ridleyella*.

CULTURE: Presumably as for the high-elevation Dendrobiums. (C, I)

RIMACOLA Rupp

Rimacola elliptica (R.Br.) Rupp (*Lyperanthus ellipticus* R.Br., *Caladenia elliptica* Rchb.f.) is the only known member of this genus. It is an extremely rare (even in the wild) terrestrial or lithophytic orchid native in the state of New South Wales, Australia, where it typically occurs on moist sandstone cliffs. It was formerly included in *Lyperanthus* R.Br., but it differs radically from that group in many ways; it is now placed in the sub-tribe *Caladeniinae*. It is unknown in collections at this time.

Nothing is known regarding the genetic affinities of *Rimacola*.

CULTURE: Possibly as for *Caladenia*, although it seems evident that a lime-rich soil would be requisite for any success. (C, I)

RISLEYA King & Pantl.

This rare and little-known genus of the subtribe *Liparidinae* consists of but a single species, **Risleya atropurpurea** King & Pantl., a small and insignificant orchid from the high Himalayas. The group appears to be a very distinctive one, with no especially close allies, and is not in cultivation at this time.

Nothing is known of the genetic affinities of *Risleya*.

CULTURE: Probably as for the cooler-growing species of *Liparis*, *Malaxis*, etc. (C)

ROBIQUETIA Gaud.

This is a genus of about fourteen species of pendulous, monopodial epiphytes, native in the region extending from India and Malaya throughout Indonesia and the Philippines to New Guinea. Allied to *Malleola* J.J.Sm. & Schltr., the plants simulate these orchids to a large extent, but differ in the thin two-lobed appendages within the spur, and in the shape of the column. Mostly rather robust plants, Robiquetias bear pendulous ra-cemes of small, often brightly coloured flowers. They are very rare in contemporary collections, but several of the species are sufficiently attractive to warrant further attention from enthusiasts.

The members of *Robiquetia* have not as yet been utilized in hybridization, and nothing is known of the genetic affinities of the group.

CULTURE: As for the tropical Vandas. (I, H)

R. hamata Schltr.
Sts. lengthy, pendulous, rather thicker than most other spp., leafy. Lvs. erect-spreading, oblong-ligulate, ob-tusely and unequally bilobed apically, to 10" long and more than 1½" wide. Infls. pendulous, often exceeding the lvs. in length, the rac. cylindrical, elongate, about 1" in diam. Fls. about ½" across, numerous, brownish-red with darker spots and blotches on the ss. and ps. Ss. oblong, obtuse, the lats. oblique. Ps. obliquely elliptic, obtuse, slightly shorter than the ss. Lip with the lbs. as long as the ps., the lat. lbs. oblique, roundish, erect, very blunt; midlb. ovate-triangular, subacute; spur cylindrical, apically hooked, obtuse, about ½" long. Dec.–Jan. (I) New Guinea, in the mountains at rather high elevations.

R. Mooreana (Rolfe) J.J.Sm. (*Saccolabium Mooreanum* Rolfe, *Saccolabium Kerstingianum* Krzl., *Sacco-labium Sayerianum* FvM. & Krzl., *Saccolabium Sanderianum* Krzl.)
Sts. pendulous, to about 12" long, leafy. Lvs. to 7" long and 2" wide, oblong-ligulate, obliquely and obtusely 2-lbd. at apex. Infls. pendulous, stalked, to 8" long,

densely many-fld. Fls. about ½" across, varying from rose-red to purple or white. Ss. and ps. oval, obtuse. Lip obscurely 3-lbd., oblong, much larger than the ss. and ps., obtuse; spur obtuse, somewhat constricted medially. Jan.–Feb. (I, H) New Guinea.

R. spathulata (Bl.) J.J.Sm. (*Cleisostoma spathulatum* Bl., *Cleisostoma spicatum* Ldl., *Saccolabium densi-florum* Ldl.)
Sts. pendulous, to more than 1½' long, stout. Lvs. to 8" long and 2" wide, widest above the middle, twisted at the base to bring the blades into a single plane, broad and very unequally 2-lbd. apically. Infls. drooping, to 10" long, very densely many-fld. Fls. less than ½" across, the ss. and ps. red-brown with dull yellow margins and a median band of the same hue, the lip dull yellow. Dors. sep. concave, the lats. slightly wider. Ps. smaller and narrower. Lip with triangular lat. lbs., the back edges of which are adjacent to and as tall as the col. and the front edges of which are thickened; midlb. pointing obliquely upwards, triangular, thickened and narrowed to the tip; spur at an acute angle to the pedicellate ovary, somewhat transversely widened towards the blunt apex, about ¼" long. Summer. (I, H) Burma throughout Malaysia to the Philippines.

RODRIGUEZIA R. & P.
(*Burlingtonia* Ldl., *Physanthera* Bert. ex Steud.)

Rodriguezia is a genus of about thirty species of very attractive epiphytes or lithophytes in the American tropics, ranging from Nicaragua to Peru and Brazil, with the greatest representation in the last-named country. Allied to *Ionopsis* HBK, they are usually small plants with rather prominent pseudobulbs which may be clustered or borne at considerable intervals from each other on elongate, wiry rhizomes. Usually sheathed basally with large, leaf-like bracts, these pseudobulbs produce one or more erect or arching racemes—mostly many-flowered—from the bract-axils. The blossoms are often rather large and occur in many different hues, certain of the species being notably attractive when well-flowered. Some Rodriguezias are so extremely floriferous that the plants are almost obscured by the blossoms. Because of their easily met cultural requirements, these fine orchids are thoroughly recommended to all enthusiasts.

As of this date, few hybrids have been registered in which *Rodriguezia* figures. These few, however, are strikingly handsome crosses, largely with *Oncidium* (= *Rodricidium*) and *Comparettia* (= *Rodrettia*), made almost entirely by the indefatigable W. W. G. Moir, of Honolulu. One hybrid within the genus itself is also on record. Though these new crosses are not generally avail-able, they are very floriferous and give ample evidence of future critical breeding in which this valuable genus figures.

CULTURE: Rodriguezias may be grown with facility either in pots, in baskets, or on slabs of tree-fern once the root-systems are well developed. A perfectly drained compost—usually osmunda or tree-fern fibre, the latter mostly shredded—is required, since these orchids are highly intolerant of stale conditions at the roots. Since they mostly grow throughout the year, they need liberal supplies of water at all times, assuming drainage is perfect. A rather bright spot and warm or intermediate temperatures are needed for the majority of the cultivated species. Applications of fertilizers prove beneficial during particularly active growth periods. The Brazilian species with lengthy, wire-like rhizomes (e.g., *R. decora*) should be mounted on elongate tree-fern 'totem poles' for best results, since they are difficult to confine to a container. Such species as *R. secunda, R. venusta*, etc., do best if not disturbed too often, being grown into handsome and spectacular 'specimen' plants. (I, H)

R. Batemani P. & E. (*Burlingtonia rubescens* Ldl.)

Pbs. clustered, oval, compressed, about 1½–2″ tall. Lf. solitary, rigidly leathery, oblong-ligulate, acute, to 4″ long. Infls. densely 3–8-fld., arching. Fls. about 2½″ long, the ss. and ps. white, flushed with rose, the lip white, flushed and veined with rose-red, the 2 keels on the disc yellow. Ss. ovate, the ps. falcate, shorter than the ss. Lip cuneate, wider at the tip than at the base, shortly and bluntly 2-lbd., the basal spur short, conical. Spring–summer. (I) Peru.

R. decora (Ldl.) Rchb.f. (*Burlingtonia decora* Ldl.)

Rhiz. wire-like, very elongate, to several feet in length. Pbs. about 4″ apart, flattened, to 1″ tall. Lf. solitary, rather rigidly leathery, oblong, acute, to 4″ long and 1″ broad. Infls. loosely 6–12-fld., often branching later, wire-like, gracefully arching, to 2′ long. Fls. about 1½″ long, faintly fragrant, the ss. and ps. white or yellowish outside, white or yellowish with dark red-purple spots inside, the very large lip white with some red-spotted keels on the disc. Ss. and ps. oblong, acute, the lat. ss. forming a slight spur. Lip kidney-shaped from a narrow base. Autumn–winter. (I, H) Brazil.

R. granadensis (Ldl.) Rchb.f. (*Burlingtonia granadensis* Ldl.)

Pbs. about 1″ tall, almost hidden by the lf.-like bracts, ovoid, compressed. Lf. solitary, lanceolate, acute, leathery, to 4″ long. Infls. rather loosely 5–8-fld., to 6″ long. Fls. about 2″ long, white with a yellow blotch at the base of the lip. Ss. and ps. ovate, acutish. the lat. ss. joined. Lip stalked, shortly ovate, emarginate, much larger than the other segms. Autumn. (I) Colombia.

R. maculata (Ldl.) Rchb.f. (*Burlingtonia maculata* Ldl.)

Pbs. about 1″ tall, ovoid, compressed. Lf. solitary, leathery, linear-lanceolate, acute, to 5″ long and ½″ wide. Infls. loosely 6–10-fld., to 6″ long, pendulous. Fls. about 1¼″ long, the ss. and ps. yellow with brown spots, the large lip brownish-yellow with darker brown blotches, the whitish basal area with irregular keels. Ss. and ps. oblong, acutish, the lat. ss. joined. Lip 2-lbd., wider at the apex than below. Spring. (I, H) Brazil.

R. secunda HBK (*Pleurothallis coccinea* Hk., *Rodriguezia lanceolata* Lodd., *R. secunda* HBK var. *panamensis* Schltr.)

Pbs. oblong-elliptic, compressed, clustered, furrowed with age, about 1½″ long, almost completely obscured by the bases of the large, lf.-like bracts. Lvs. several, usually rigidly leathery, linear-ligulate to elliptic-oblong, obtuse to emarginate, to 9½″ long and 1¼″ wide.

Infls. 1–6 at a time per new growth, usually arching, simple, densely many-fld., the fls. all facing upwards, to more than 12″ long (usually much shorter). Fls. about 1″ long in largest phases, varying from brilliant rose-red to (very rarely) almost white, through several shades of pink, the ss. and ps. forming a hood over the entire, slightly clawed, wavy-margined lip. Dors. sep. concave, ovate, obtuse with a minute apicule, the lat. ss. joined, with a distinct angle at the base. Ps. obovate, acute or apiculate. Throughout the year, often more than once annually. (I, H) Panama; Colombia; Venezuela; Guianas; Trinidad; Brazil.

R. venusta (Ldl.) Rchb.f. (*Burlingtonia venusta* Ldl., *Burlingtonia fragrans* Ldl., *Rodriguezia fragrans* hort.)

Rather similar in habit to *R. secunda* HBK, but the rhiz. more elongate and the pbs. smaller. Infls. loosely few-fld., arching, to 7″ long. Fls. about 1½″ long, very fragrant, white with a rich golden-yellow disc on the lip. Ss. and ps. narrowly elliptic, acute, the lat. ss. joined, concave. Lip fan-shaped from a narrow base, wavy-margined. Autumn. (I, H) Brazil; Peru.

R. candida (Ldl.) Rchb.f. (*Burlingtonia candida* Ldl.) Closely allied to and simulating *R. Batemani* P. & E., differing primarily in the more elongate lat. ss. and the shape of the lip, which has up to 4 keels on the disc. Fls. about 2″ long, fragrant, white, the lip with golden-yellow veins. Spring. (I, H) Brazil.

R. compacta Schltr. Pbs. oblong-elliptic, compressed, about 1″ long. Lf. solitary, rather rigidly leathery, oblong-ligular to ligular, obtuse, to 6″ long. Infls. 1–2 at a time, slender, few-fld., deflexed, about 3″ long. Fls. about 2″ long, fragrant, pale yellow or greenish-yellow, the lip yellow, the mid-nerve of which is thickened and projects between the apical lbs. as a short apicule, the base produced into a short, curved, subulate spur. Autumn. (I, H) Nicaragua; Costa Rica; Panama.

R. pubescens (Ldl.) Rchb.f. (*Burlingtonia pubescens* Ldl., *Rodriguezia Lindeni* Cgn.) Similar to and closely allied to *R. granadensis* (Ldl.) Rchb.f., the infls. loosely 10–15-fld., to 9″ long. Fls. about 1¾″ across, fragrant, white with a yellow spot on the lip-base, the col. hairy. Spring. (I, H) Brazil.

RODRIGUEZIOPSIS Schltr.

Two species of *Rodrigueziopsis* are known to date, both of them rather scarce epiphytic orchids, endemic to Brazil. Unusual plants with clambering rhizomes, at intervals along which the small pseudobulbs are borne, they bear rather attractive smallish flowers in apical racemes. Neither **R. eleutherosepala** (B.-R.) Schltr. nor **R. microphyta** (B.-R.) Schltr. appear to be in cultivation at this time, although they are potentially of interest to the connoisseur. The genus is placed in the subtribe *Capanemiimae.*

Nothing is known of the genetic affinities of *Rodrigueziopsis.*

CULTURE: As for *Ornithocephalus*, although the plants require some sort of support for their clambering wire-like rhizomes. Growing in humid forests, they should never be permitted to become totally dry at any time. (I, H)

Rodriguezia pubescens (Ldl.) Rchb.f. [*Gardeners' Chronicle*]

ROEPEROCHARIS Rchb.f.

About seven species of *Roeperocharis* are known to date, all of them rare and little-known terrestrial orchids of the subtribe *Habenarinae*, indigenous to the mountainous parts of tropical Africa. Generically rather close to *Habenaria* Willd., these plants are at this time unknown in our collections, and in most cases are incompletely defined botanically.

Nothing has been ascertained regarding the genetic affinities of *Roeperocharis*.

CULTURE: Possibly as for the tropical species of *Habenaria*. (I, H)

ROLFEËLLA Schltr.

A member of the subtribe *Habenarinae*, and endemic to Madagascar, this monotypic genus, consisting solely of **Rolfeëlla glaberrima** (Ridl.) Schltr. (*Benthamia glaberrima* H.Perr., *Habenaria glaberrima* Schltr., *Holothrix glaberrima* Ridl., *Platanthera glaberrima* Schltr.), appears to be closer in its alliance to *Schizochilus* Sond. than to *Benthamia* A.Rich., to which it has been referred by Perrier de la Bâthie, *et al.* A relatively common terrestrial plant in its native haunts, it is unfortunately not present in collections at this time.

Nothing is known of the genetic affinities of *Rolfeëlla*.

CULTURE: Presumably as for *Cynorkis*. (I, H)

RUDOLFIELLA Hoehne
(*Lindleyella* Schltr., *Schlechterella* Hoehne)

A segregate from the genus *Bifrenaria* Ldl. on technical grounds, *Rudolfiella* is a group of about six species of rare and unusual epiphytic or lithophytic orchids, these mostly inhabiting Brazil, but with outlying representatives extending into the Guianas, Trinidad, Venezuela, Colombia, and Panama. Vegetatively much like Bifrenarias in appearance, the small to medium-sized, often vividly-coloured flowers of *Rudolfiella* are arranged in often elongate, usually erect racemes. Although desirable orchids, at this time the members of this genus are extremely rare in our collections.

Nothing has been ascertained regarding the genetic affinities of *Rudolfiella*, although they presumably lie with *Bifrenaria*, etc. Some unusually interesting and

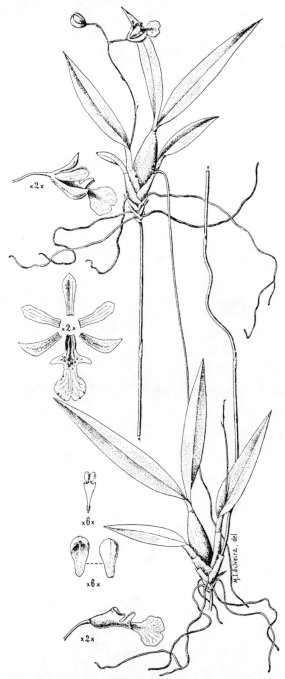

stalked, narrowly elliptic, acuminate, the under side sparsely flecked with reddish, to 6″ long, and about 2″ broad. Infls. slender, erect or arching, to 8″ tall, loosely 7–15-fld. Fls. about 1¼″ long, the ss. and ps. orange-yellow, spotted on the inner surface with dull purple, the lip complex, yellow, spotted with purple, the disc crest-like, paler yellow. Autumn. (I, H) Trinidad; Guianas; Venezuela; Colombia.

RUSBYELLA Rolfe

A member of the subtribe *Capanemiinae*, **Rusbyella caespitosa** Rolfe, the only known member of this very rare genus, is a small epiphytic orchid, indigenous to Bolivia. It is allied to, and rather simulates *Trizeuxis* Ldl., but bears larger flowers of divergent structure. The genus is incompletely known botanically, and is not present in collections at this time.

Nothing is known of the genetic affinities of *Rusbyella*.

CULTURE: Possibly as for *Ornithocephalus*. (I, H)

SACCOGLOSSUM Schltr.

Saccoglossum is a genus of two known species, both excessively rare and incompletely described epiphytic orchids, native in the highland forests of New Guinea. A member of the subtribe *Bulbophyllinae*, the group is notable for the great complexity of the strange flowers, and is not at this time present in collections.

Nothing is known of the genetic affinities of this very scarce genus.

CULTURE: Presumably as for the tropical Bulbophyllums. (C, I)

SACCOLABIOPSIS J.J.Sm.

A single species of *Saccolabiopsis* is known, this the rare and little-known **S. Bakhuizenii** J.J.Sm., which has been found on a few occasions in the montane forests of the island of Java. A member of the subtribe *Sarcanthinae*, the genus is unknown in our collections at this time, and because of the small size of the plant and its diminutive yet complexly formed flowers, it is primarily of scientific importance.

Nothing is known of the genetic affinities of *Saccolabiopsis*.

CULTURE: Presumably as for the dwarf Vandas and their allies. (I, H)

SACCOLABIUM Bl.

As now delimited, *Saccolabium* consists of about twelve species of mostly rather small epiphytic orchids of the subtribe *Sarcanthinae*, native over the region extending from the Himalayas throughout Indonesia to New Guinea. Small, fugacious-flowered, they are apparently unknown in contemporary collections; for other so-called Saccolabiums, see the index of this work. The genus is somewhat allied botanically to *Sarcochilus* R.Br.

Rodrigueziopsis eleutherosepala (B.-R.) Schltr. [Hoehne, *Flora Brasílica*]

attractive hybrids seem possible utilizing the members of this genus.

CULTURE: As for *Bifrenaria*. (I, H)

R. aurantiaca (Ldl.) Hoehne (*Bifrenaria aurantiaca* Ldl., *Lindleyella aurantiaca* Schltr., *Schlechterella aurantiaca* Hoehne)

Pbs. rather clustered, ovoid, somewhat laterally compressed, vaguely 4-angled, to 2″ tall. Lf. solitary, shortly

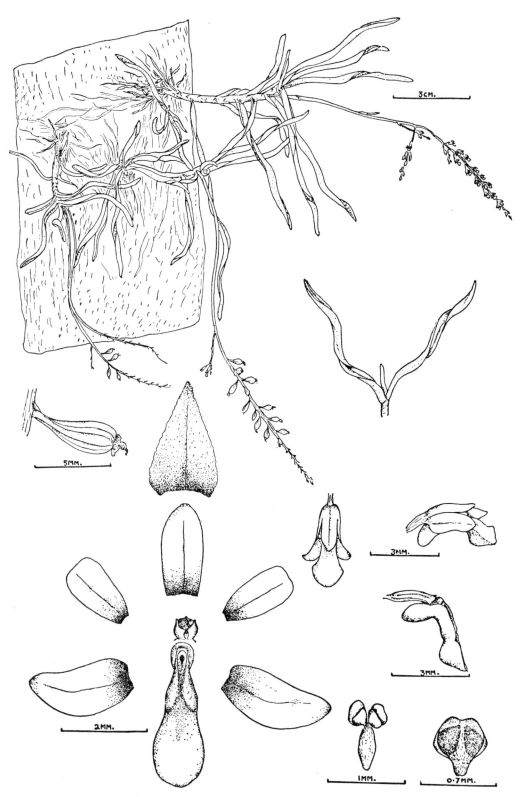

Saccolabium tortifolium Jayaweera [DON M. A. JAYAWEERA]

422

No hybrids are registered in true *Saccolabium*, and nothing has been ascertained regarding its genetic affinities.

CULTURE: Presumably as for the tropical Vandas. (H)

SANDERELLA O.Ktze.

But a single very rare species of *Sanderella* is known to date, this **S. discolor** (B.-R.) Cgn. (*Parlatorea discolor* B.-R.), a very small but interesting epiphytic orchid which has been collected on a few occasions in Brazil. Somewhat allied to *Trizeuxis* Ldl. of the subtribe *Capanemiinae*, it is a pseudobulbous plant with racemes of diminutive, but very complex flowers. At this time,

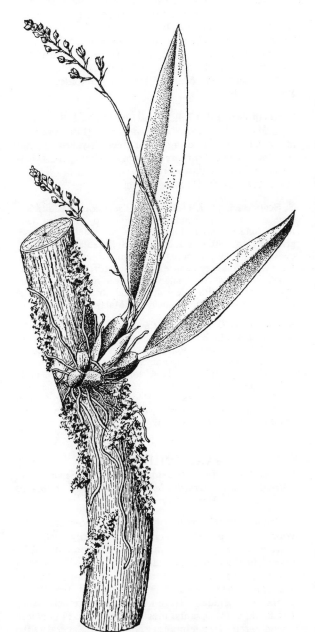

Sanderella discolor Cgn. [Hoehne, *Flora Brasilica*]

Sanderella does not appear to be present in our collections.

Nothing is known concerning the genetic affinities of this rare group.

CULTURE: Possibly as for *Ornithocephalus*. (I)

SARCANTHUS Ldl.
(*Echioglossum* Bl.)

Almost ninety mostly epiphytic species of *Sarcanthus* are currently considered to be valid, but very few of them are present in our collections today, and the vast majority of them are incompletely described. The range of the genus—which is a member of the subtribe *Sarcanthinae*, and somewhat allied to *Pomatocalpa* Breda and to *Gastrochilus* D.Don—is an extensive one, from the Indian Himalayas and Ceylon throughout South-east Asia, the Philippines, and Indonesia to New Guinea. Holttum (in *Fl. Malaya* 1: 646–7. 1953) remarks: 'This is the largest genus of the small-flowered orchids of this group. The flowers are always rather fleshy and last several days. Their most distinctive feature is the large callus at the back of the spur, just within the entrance. This often has a groove on its lower surface, the groove resting on the top edge of the septum which divides the bottom of the spur. The back callus also sometimes interlocks with the front callus. In one way or another the entrance to the spur is very restricted. To what extent this aids in guiding visiting insects so that they effect pollination is unknown in most cases, and any observations of visiting insects would be of interest. The spur often has plenty of nectar.' The flowers, as is evident from the above comments, are remarkably complex, and it is often difficult to describe them with any degree of accuracy. Despite their dimensions, they are for the most part rather showy plants, and of interest to the connoisseur collector.

No hybrids have as yet been made in *Sarcanthus*, and nothing is known of its genetic affinities. We may, however, assume that it will prove compatible with at least some of the allied members of the *Sarcanthinae*. The generally small blossoms would perhaps deter its utilization as a parent in most instances.

CULTURE: As for the tropical (or subtropical) Aërides, Vandas, and the like. Since some of the species are strongly pendulous in habit, they should be grown in baskets, while the erect-stemmed types do well in pots. All of the Sarcanthus should be disturbed as infrequently as possible, since they are highly intolerant of having their generally fleshy roots moved. (I, H)

S. appendiculatus (Ldl.) Hk.f. (*Aërides appendiculatum* Ldl.)

Pls. pendulous, to more than 1½′ long. Lvs. numerous, pendulous, terete, obtuse, to 5″ long. Infls. usually rather numerous at once, curved and drooping, stalked, rather densely 10–15-fld., the fls. borne only on last third, to more than 15″ long. Fls. about ¾″ long, lasting well, waxy, yellowish with dull red-brown stripes, the lip yellow and purple, with some red-brown stripes behind on the spur. Ss. and ps. oblong, obtuse, spreading and reflexed, almost equal. Lip 3-lbd., the midlb. pointed, the spur conical. Summer. (I) Himalayas; Burma.

S. bifidus (Ldl.) Ames (*Saccolabium bifidum* Ldl., *Gastrochilus bifidus* O.Ktze.)
St. about 3″ long, set with a few heavy-textured oblong or elliptic lvs. to 5″ long and 1″ broad. Infls. sharply pendulous, to 8″ long, many-fld. Fls. about ½″ in diam., white or cream-coloured, often marked with dull purple on the 3-lbd., short-spurred lip. Autumn–winter. (H) Philippines, where it is widespread.

S. erinaceus Rchb.f. (*Aërides dasypogon* hort., *Sarcanthus Stowellianus* Batem.)
Sts. abbreviated, only a few inches long. Lvs. ligulate or lanceolate, obtuse to acutish, to 3½″ long and ¾″ broad, leathery. Infls. loosely many-fld., the stalk short-hairy, 3–6″ long. Fls. hairy outside, about ½″ wide and long, cream-white, the ss. and ps. flushed with rose and with a deeper blotch of the same colour on each segm.-tip. Lip rose-red, with small lat. lbs. and an oval midlb. which is incurved, the spur broadly conical, obtuse, short. Pedicellate ovary and seed-caps. rose-red or reddish, with short rigid hairs. Autumn–early winter. (I, H) Burma.

S. filiformis Ldl.
Sts. pendulous, thin, to several feet long, cylindrical. Lvs. narrowly cylindrical, obtuse, rather far apart on the st., to 10″ long, only about ⅛″ in diam. Infls. rather densely many-fld., 6–10″ long, curved. Fls. about ⅓″ in diam., the ss. and ps. dark purple with green margins and median stripe. Lip fleshy, white, basally broad, yellow, the midlb. white, the spur with a narrow lamina from midlb.-base downwards, and a very large-lbd. fuzzy callus below the very broad, thick, yellow col. Summer–autumn. (I, H) Himalayas; Burma; Thailand; Viet-Nam.

S. Parishii Hk.
Similar to *S. erinaceus* Rchb.f. in habit. Infls. 6–16″ long. Fls. about ⅙″ in diam., golden-yellow, the ss. and ps. striped with dull red or brownish-red, the ps. smaller than the ss. Lip with small lat. lbs. and a broadly triangular, obtuse midlb., yellow, with the spur almost ¼″ long, rose-red. Autumn. (I, H) Burma.

S. racemifer (Wall.) Rchb.f. (*Aërides racemiferum* Wall., *Saccolabium racemiferum* Ldl., *Sarcanthus pallidus* Ldl., *S. tricolor* Rchb.f.)
Sts. erect, robust, often more than ½″ in diam., producing very stout roots, to several feet tall. Lvs. very thick and leathery, ligulate, unequally 2-lbd. at apex, to 12″ long and 2″ broad. Infls. erect, to 3′ long, with several long, slender branches, loosely many-fld., the peduncle stout. Fls. about ⅓″ in diam., the ss. and ps. dark purple or dull brown with yellow margins, oblong, rather blunt. Lip white, with small triangular lat. lbs. that are flushed with red at tips, and a short kidney-shaped midlb. Spur shorter than the pedicellate ovary, oblong, obtuse, whitish. Spring. (I, H) Himalayas; Burma; Thailand; Laos.

S. rostratus (Lodd.) Ldl. (*Vanda recurva* Hk., *Vanda rostrata* Lodd.)
Sts. elongated, pendulous, to almost 12″ long, leafy. Lvs. thick, fleshy, lanceolate, acutish, to almost 4″ long, about ½″ broad. Infls. pendulous, densely many-fld.,

about 3½″ long. Fls. less than ½″ across, fleshy, the spreading, oblong, obtuse ss. and ps. yellow-green with brown veins. Lip whitish, with short lat. lbs. and a violet-rose, acute midlb. Autumn. (I) China, mostly in the south.

S. subulatus (Bl.) Rchb.f. (*Cleisostoma subulatum* Bl., *Saccolabium secundum* Ridl., *Sarcanthus secundus* Griff.)
Sts. pendulous, to more than 12″ long, rather slender. Lvs. rather far apart, fleshy, to 12″ long and about ½″ broad, the sides parallel, constricted about 1″ from the tip, which is sharp-pointed. Infls. sharply pendulous, very densely many-fld., elongating for some time, to 6″ long. Fls. opening well, about ¼″ long or more, fleshy, the ss. and ps. dark purple-brown with pale green margins and median stripe, the lip lilac on spur and midlb., fading to white at base, yellow at base of lat. lbs., very complex. Spur very large, tapering to tip. Summer–autumn. (I, H) Himalayas; Burma; Thailand; Cambodia; Viet-Nam; Malay Peninsula; Sumatra; Java; Borneo; Celebes.

S. teretifolius (Ldl.) Ldl. (*Vanda teretifolia* Ldl.)
Similar in habit to *S. appendiculatus* (Ldl.) Hk.f. in almost all parts, differing in the greenish-yellow ss. and ps., these veined with red-brown, and the yellowish-white lip with a more broadly conical, short, obtuse spur. Autumn. (I, H) Hong Kong.

S. Scortechinii Hk.f. (*Saccolabium Scortechinii* Ridl.) Sts. elongate, sometimes pendulous, prominently sheathed. Lvs. to 4½″ long and more than ¾″ wide, flat, stalked at base, gradually narrowed at acute apex. Infls. stiffly pendulous, densely many-fld., to more than 6″ long. Fls. almost ½″ long, fleshy, the dors. sep. and ps. almost entirely dark purple-brown, the lat. ss. with pale yellow-green median stripe and margins, the lip with pale yellowish lat. lbs., the midlb. pale mauve, arrow-shaped. Summer. (H) Malay Peninsula.

S. tridentatus (Ldl.) Rupp (*Cleisostoma tridentatum* Ldl., *Saccolabium calcaratum* FvM., *Sarcochilus calcaratus* FvM., *Sarcochilus tridentatus* Rchb.f.) Sts. sometimes branched, to about 12″ long, producing numerous hanging (usually free) roots. Lvs. rather fleshy, 1½–4″ long, rather narrow, often vaguely curving. Infls. 3–10-fld., shorter than the lvs., slender. Fls. fragrant, less than ¼″ long, the segms. brown and green, or light and dark green, with the lip sometimes whitish. Autumn–winter. (I) Australia.

SARCOCHILUS R.Br.
(*Cylindrochilus* Thw., *Grossourdya* Rchb.f., *Gunnia* Ldl., *Micropera* Ldl., *Ornitharium* Ldl. & Paxt., *Pteroceras* Hass., *Stereochilus* Ldl.)

Sarcochilus is a genus of somewhat more than fifty component species, which are primarily epiphytic (rarely lithophytic or semi-terrestrial) orchids widespread in the region extending from India throughout Malaya, Indonesia, and adjacent insular areas to Australia, New Zealand, and certain of the Pacific Islands. It includes a large number of extremely handsome and showy plants, most of which are but seldom encountered in contemporary collections. Several of the Australian species, such as *S. australis* (Ldl.) Rchb.f.,

XIIB *Xylobium Powellii* Schltr. [A.D.HAWKES]

XIIA *Trichocentrum albo-coccineum* Lind. [A.D.HAWKES]

S. Ceciliae FvM., and *S. falcatus* R.Br., are rather popular with collectors in that country, and many other members of the group are well worthy of attention from enthusiasts, since the plants are easily grown and are floriferous in the extreme in most cases. *Sarcochilus* is allied to *Thrixspermum* Lour. and is similar in the typically short-lived flowers, but the plants in the present genus never possess elongate stems, the lip is hinged to the column-foot (with the junction between the two parts distinct), the lip often bears a tubular spur instead of a sac, and the stipes of the paired pollinia is not particularly short. The plants themselves are petite and neat in appearance, and the flowers—usually of relatively sizeable dimensions—occur in colours that are, for the most part, very attractive. These blossoms are rather more simplified in superficial structure than most of the allied sarcanthad genera.

Only a single hybrid is registered as of this writing for *Sarcochilus*, this the handsome *Sarcothera x Kona*, a cross between *Sarcochilus pallidus* (Bl.) Rchb.f. and *Renanthera monachica* Ames, produced in the Hawaiian Islands. Additional experimental breeding with allied genera is to be encouraged, and some fascinating prospects seem evident through critical interspecific hybridization as well. The genus is presumably genetically compatible with at least some of the allied groups, such as *Vanda, Phalaenopsis, Aërides,* etc.

CULTURE: As for *Vanda*, depending upon the species under consideration. (I, H)

S. australis (Ldl.) Rchb.f. (*Gunnia australis* Ldl., *Sarcochilus parviflorus* Ldl., *S. Gunnii* FvM., *S. Barklyanus* FvM., *Thrixspermum australe* Rchb.f., *Thrixspermum parviflorum* Rchb.f.)

Pls. dwarf, the sts. abbreviated, the roots profuse, mostly creeping (some aerial). Lvs. 3–6, broadly or narrowly lanceolate, often slightly twisted, sometimes falcate, to 3″ long. Infls. racemose, to 6″ long, 5–14-fld. Fls. about ½″ across, fragrant, varying from brownish to pale yellow-green, the lip white, flushed with yellow and with purple blotches and streaks. Ss. and ps. similar, the ps. slightly the shorter. Lip with several conspicuous calli on the midlb. Autumn–winter. (I) Australia: New South Wales, Queensland, Victoria, Tasmania.

S. Ceciliae FvM. (*Thrixspermum Ceciliae* Rchb.f.)

Pls. dwarf, usually gregarious on cliffs or rocks (sometimes on trees). Sts. erect, usually abbreviated, sometimes to 5″ tall. Lvs. brownish-green, obscurely spotted, mostly linear, to 3½″ long. Infls. racemose, erect, very slender, often longer than the lvs. Fls. borne above the middle of the peduncle, 3–8 in number, bright pink, bell-shaped, about ½″ across. Ss. and ps. not widely expanding, the ps. the narrower. Lip short, the midlb. very short, thick and densely pubescent above, the calli more or less adnate to the lat. lbs. Late autumn–winter. (I, H) Australia: New South Wales, Queensland.

S. falcatus R.Br. (*Thrixspermum falcatum* Rchb.f.)

Sts. to 3″ long. Lvs. few, to 6″ long, oblong-lanceolate, pale green, rather thick, falcate. Infls. racemose, from below the lvs., longer or shorter than them, very rarely rigidly erect. Fls. 3–12, to about 1¼″ across, white or rarely cream-coloured, very fragrant. Ss. and ps.

almost equal, spreading, narrowed basally, varying from broadly ovate to almost lanceolate, more or less concave, often with a purplish-red median line on the reverse side. Lip with the lat. lbs. broad, erect, usually stained inside with orange and traversed by bright or dark red lines; midlb. very short, upturned, yellowish, with a large protuberance or spur below which it is sometimes purple-blotched. Mostly Oct.–Nov. (I, H) Australia: New South Wales, Queensland, Victoria.

S. Fitzgeraldii FvM.

Robust, extensively branching pl., the sts. to more than 3′ long, usually growing on rocks. Lvs. numerous, to 7″ long, narrowly oblong, falcate or straight. Infls. racemose, numerous at once, to 9″ long, 4–15-fld. Fls. white or pink with crimson blotches or spots near the centre, or the segms. entirely blotched, or the whole fl. crimson with darker blotches (or very rarely pure white), to 1½″ across. Ss. and ps. similar, almost equal, very narrow at base, broadening to ovate-lanceolate, usually with the basal third blotched with crimson. Lip less than half as long as the other segms., the lat. lbs. large, erect, falcate, streaked with light crimson, the midlb. yellow or orange, small, with several large calli. Winter. (I, H) Australia: New South Wales, Queensland.

S. Hartmanni FvM.

Rather similar in habit to *S. Fitzgeraldii* FvM., but erect and more robust, the lvs. thicker and more or less deeply channelled. Infls. racemose, long-peduncled, the fls. smaller than those of the related sp., rather crowded near the summit of the infl. Fls. to 1¼″ across, pure white, or white with deep maroon spots near the centre. Lip very small, the lat. lbs. often striped with deep red on inside, the midlb. small, conical. Col.-foot deep red or red-spotted. Winter. (I, H) Australia: New South Wales, Queensland.

S. Hillii (FvM.) FvM. (*Dendrobium Hillii* FvM., *Thrixspermum Hillii* Rchb.f.)

Very dwarf, epiphytic on trees, the root-system very extensive. Sts. abbreviated. Lvs. to 2″ long, linear, spotted. Infls. racemose, usually not exceeding the lvs., very slender. Fls. 2–6, less than ½″ across, white or pink, very fragrant. Ss. and ps. widely spreading, ovate to almost orbicular, concave. Lip very short, the lat. lbs. almost triangular, the midlb. broader than long, retuse, densely white-pubescent above, the lamina with several large calli. Summer. (I, H) Australia: New South Wales, Queensland.

S. olivaceus Ldl. (*Thrixspermum olivaceum* Rchb.f.)

Vegetatively similar to *S. falcatus* R.Br., but the lvs. of thinner texture, darker green in colour, and less commonly falcate. Infls. racemose, often shorter than the lvs., sometimes to 5½″ long. Fls. 2–11, about 1″ across, olive-green or old-gold colour, with a delicate fragrance. Ss. and ps. almost equal, the basal third very narrow, then ovate-lanceolate and usually obtuse at apex. Lip white with red markings, the lat. lbs. oblong-falcate and incurved, the midlb. very short, orbicular, the spur below it large and almost square. Late autumn–winter. (I, H) Australia: New South Wales, Queensland.

S. pallidus (Bl.) Rchb.f. (*Dendrocolla pallida* Bl., *Sarco-chilus aureus* Hk.f., *S. cladostachys* Hk.f., *S. unguiculatus* Ldl., *Thrixspermum unguiculatum* Rchb.f.)

Pl. rather simulating a robust sp. of *Phalaenopsis*, the sts. short, few-lvd. Lvs. fleshy, oblong, obtuse, to 9″ long and 2″ wide, somewhat narrowed basally. Infls. mostly sharply pendulous, to about 8″ long, few-fld. at the apex, but densely so, the rachis thickened. Fls. opening singly or a few at a time, to 2″ across (usually somewhat smaller), waxy-textured and rather strongly fragrant, white to cream-yellow, the lip with purple-barred lat. lbs., the midlb. and spur more or less purple-spotted. Ss. and ps. narrowly elliptic, acutish, wide-spreading. Lip much shorter than the other segms., composed of a spur continuing more or less in the line of the col.-foot, with lat. lbs. curved upwards and back-wards towards the col. A variable but very handsome sp. Throughout the year, often more than once annually. (H) Malay Peninsula; Sumatra; Java; Borneo; Philippines.

S. virescens Ridl.

St. rooting freely, to about 1″ long. Lvs. few, to 3″ long and ½″ wide, fleshy, slightly twisted at base, ovate-elliptic, the apex acutely 2-lbd. Infls. short, usually pendulous, the rachis flattened, irregular, elongating to about 3″ as the fls. open successively. Fls. to about 12 in number, borne in 2 ranks, strongly fragrant of vanilla, lasting one day, waxy, the ss. and ps. pale yellowish-green, the lip white, with an orange callus on the midlb. Dors. sep. concave, with a short narrow tip, the lats. joined to the col.-foot for half its length. Ps. smaller than ss., rounded at tips. Lip saccate but without a spur, the lat. lbs. ascending and diverging, rounded, the midlb. represented by the very fleshy bluntly conical, short end of the lip. Autumn. (H) Malay Peninsula.

S. appendiculatus (Bl.) J.J.Sm. (*Dendrocolla appendiculata* Bl., *Ascochilus hirtulus* Ridl., *Sarcochilus hirtulus* Hk.f.) Sts. short. Lvs. few, leathery, elliptic, the apex pointed and very unequally bilobed, to 3″ long and ½″ wide. Infls. to about 2″ long, the peduncle with tiny prickles, the few-fld. rachis thickened. Fls. fleshy, short-lived, about ½″ across, pale or dark yellow, densely spotted with red-brown, the lat. lbs. of the lip purplish. Ss. and ps. reflexed against the pedicellate ovary, the ps. slightly the smaller. Lip spurred, complex. Summer–autumn. (H) Malay Peninsula; Java.

S. Berkeleyi (Rchb.f.) Rchb.f. (*Thrixspermum Berkeleyi* Rchb.f.) Sts. to more than 2″ long, very thin, with about 7 lvs. at the apex. Lvs. to 6″ long and ¾″ wide, widest near tip, narrowing gradually to the base, leathery. Infls. pendulous, to 10″ long, the rachis not the numerous fls. mostly all open at once. Fls. about 1″ across, the ss. and ps. pale yellow, thickly spotted with orange-brown (or not spotted), the midlb. of the lip lilac-spotted, the spur brown-spotted, the col. pale greenish-yellow. Dors. sep. very concave; lat. ss. running halfway along the col.-foot. Ps. as wide as dors. sep., but shorter. Lip almost at right angles to col.-foot, the lat. lbs. erect, the midlb. very fleshy, with 3 short acute erect points, 2 median, 2 on the sides. Winter. (H) Malay Peninsula; Andaman Islands; Nicobar Islands.

S. hirsutus Hk.f. (*Ascochilus hirsutus* Ridl., *Sarcochilus Burchardianus* Schltr.) Sts. very short. Lvs. few, pendulous, leathery, to 8″ long and 1¼″ wide, elliptic, widest near apex

and obtusely 2-lbd. there. Infls. almost horizontal, the peduncle densely covered with tiny prickles, the rachis about 8–10-fld. (fls. several open together, lasting for several days), thickened, the floral bracts and pedicellate ovaries shortly stiff-hairy. Fls. about ½″ across, the ss. and ps. yellow, barred and spotted with crimson, the ss. hairy outside, the lip with erect lat. lbs. which are white with an apical purple blotch, the midlb. white, with low raised much-toothed lat. lobules, the hairy spur white with purple spots in front. Autumn. (H) Malay Peninsula; Sumatra; Borneo.

S. stenoglottis Hk.f. Lvs. to 10″ long and more than 2″ wide, often flushed with purple, widest in upper half, the tip broad. Infls. pendulous, to more than 3″ long, the rachis thickened, elongating as the fls. open, in time becoming 6″ long. Fls. very crowded, opening successively, about ½″ across, the ss. and ps. spreading, pale yellowish to almost white, transversely

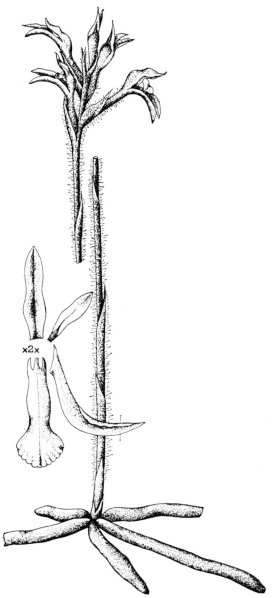

Sarcoglottis Cogniauxiana (B.-R.) Schltr. [Hoehne. *Flora Brasilica*]

spotted with purple near the base. Lip joined to the very short col.-foot, larger than the ss. and ps., bent almost at right angles in the middle, most of its area consisting of a narrow spur which is constricted by a fleshy thickening about the middle, the tip with a blunt point, the lat. lbs. with purple streaks, the midlb, very short, usually whitish. Summer. (H) Malay Peninsula; Sumatra; Borneo.

SARCOGLOTTIS Presl

A member of the exasperatingly complex subtribe *Spiranthinae*, *Sarcoglottis* contains upwards of twenty-five species of often very showy, usually large-flowered terrestrial orchids, native for the most part in Brazil, with outlying representatives extending to other areas of the American tropics. The group, which is unfortunately unknown in contemporary collections, is perhaps referable to *Spiranthes* L.C.Rich., but seems to have several characters which warrant its retention as distinct.

Nothing is known of the genetic affinities of *Sarcoglottis*.

CULTURE: Probably as for the tropical *Spiranthes*. (I, H)

SARCORHYNCHUS Schltr.

Three species of *Sarcorhynchus* are known to date, one from the Cameroons, the second from the Belgian Congo and Uganda, the third from Tanganyika Territory. The genus is a member of the very complex angraecoid group of the subtribe *Sarcanthinae*, and at this time none of them is to be found in our collections, although they are rather attractive epiphytic, lithophytic, or rarely terrestrial monopodials, much simulating many of their allies in vegetative habit, but differing in technical details of the numerous small flowers, which are usually borne in dense arching racemes.

Nothing is known at this time regarding the genetic affinities of *Sarcorhynchus*.

CULTURE: Presumably as for the tropical Angraecums. (H)

SARCOSTOMA Bl.

Sarcostoma is a genus of two known species, one of which is found in a very few specialized collections; the other, **S. celebicum** Schltr., from Celebes, is incompletely known and does not appear to have been introduced into cultivation. The genus is a member of the subtribe *Glomerinae*, and is closest in its alliance to *Ceratostylis* Bl., differing from it in technical details of the small flowers. The plants are typically epiphytic in their natural habitat.

No hybrids have been made from *Sarcostoma*, and nothing is known of its genetic affinities as yet.

CULTURE: As for the tropical Bulbophyllums. (H)

S. javanica Bl. (*Ceratostylis cryptantha* Ridl., *Ceratostylis linearis* Ridl., *Sarcostoma linearis* Carr)
Sts. short, closely packed together. Lvs. 1–2, narrow, to 4″ long. Infls. short, bearing 1 fl. at a time, terminal, less than ¼″ long. Fls. cup-shaped, about ¼″ across, lasting one day, the ss. white, the ps. with a narrow

white apical half, the borders of basal half deep crimson, the lip cream-coloured. Summer–autumn. (H) Malay Peninsula; Sumatra; Java.

SATYRIDIUM Ldl.

But a single species of *Satyridium* is known to date, this a rare and rather pretty terrestrial orchid of the subtribe *Satyriinae*, native to south-western Cape Colony in Africa. Allied to *Satyrium* L., it is today to be found in a very few choice collections, but must be considered among the rarer of cultivated orchids.

Nothing is known of the genetic affinities of *Satyridium*.

CULTURE: As for *Caladenia*. (C, I)

S. rostratum Ldl. (*Satyrium rhynchanthum* Bolus)
Roots fibrous. St. 9–21″ tall, clothed with many lanceolate sheaths. Lvs. usually basal, oblong or lanceolate, rather membranaceous, spreading, 1–2½″ long. Infl. 1–6″ long, many-fld., rather dense. Fls. about ⅜″ in diam., lilac, the lip spotted with purple, the anther vivid carmine. Dors. sep. oblong, blunt, the lats. falcate-oblong, spreading. Ps. elliptic-oblong, sometimes minutely toothed at the apex. Lip slightly hooded, ovate, beaked at the apex, the spur oblong, very stout, blunt, ¼″ long. Autumn–winter. (C, I) South-west Cape Colony.

SATYRIUM L.
(*Aviceps* Ldl., *Diplectrum* Endl.)

Approximately one hundred and fifty-five species of *Satyrium* are known to science, these primarily terrestrial orchids (rarely lithophytic) mostly inhabiting South Africa, but with extra-territorial representatives extending into tropical Africa and Madagascar, to Java, China, and Australia. Often rather robust plants, they bear dense spikes of rather handsome, often brightly coloured and complex flowers, which offer much to the collector, although as a rule the Satyriums are seldom seen in cultivation at this time. The flowers are inverted, and bear two spurs. The root system consists of several ovoid or globular tubers with numerous fleshy roots where the stem and the tubers join; the large tuber perishes when it has produced a flower-stem and seed-capsules, whereupon the smaller tubers gradually increase in dimensions and produce flower-stems. In some species the stout stems are clothed at the base with a few large leaves which often lie prone on the soil-surface, while in others the leaves are cauline and decrease upwards into bracts, these subtending each flower. In the wild, the Satyriums typically inhabit rather constantly moist grasslands, often growing in rocky fields or meadows. The genus is a member of the small subtribe *Satyriinae*, with *Satyridium* Ldl. its closest botanical ally.

No hybrids have as yet been produced in this genus, and nothing has been ascertained regarding its genetic affinities. Some most attractive interspecific hybrids seem possible here, and should be attempted by enterprising breeders.

CULTURE: As for *Caladenia*. (C, I)

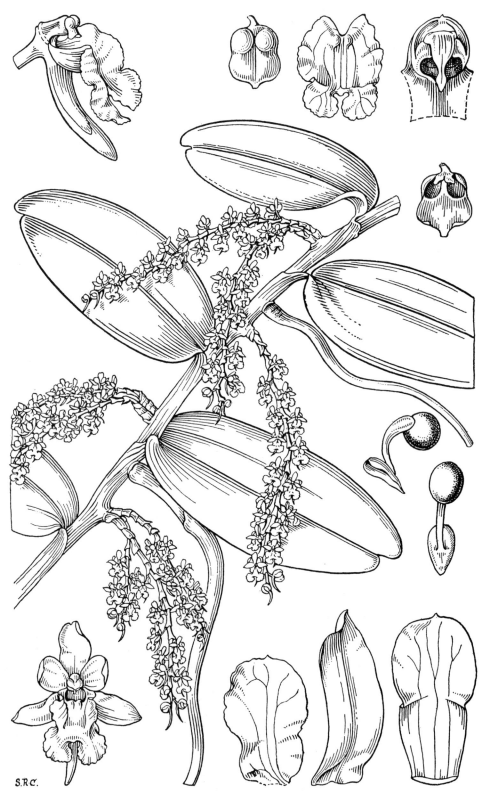

Sarcorhynchus bilobatus Summerh. [*Icones Plantarum*]

S. bifolium A.Rich.

St. stout, 1¼–1¾′ tall. Lvs. basal, usually paired, suborbicular, horizontally arranged, 2–4″ long and wide, often with several cauline ones as well, these oblong-lanceolate, rather sheath-like. Infl. rather densely many-fld., 2½–4½″ long. Fls. about 1¼″ in diam., hooded, greenish-yellow, fragrant. Dors. sep. cuneate-oblong, blunt, the lats. broadly oblong. Ps. narrowly oblong, united to the ss. at their bases. Lip hooded, marginally reflexed, the apex broad, blunt, crenulate, erect, the spur linear, ¾″ long. Autumn, mostly Aug.–Sept. (C, I) Ethiopia, in the mountains.

S. cristatum Sond. (*Satyrium pentadactylum* Krzl.)

St. stout, ¾–1½′ tall, clothed with several sheaths. Lvs. basal, 2–3, dull green, fleshy, ovate-oblong to broadly elliptic, rather pointed, 3–6″ long. Infl. densely many-fld., 2–6″ long. Fls. about ½″ in diam., white, more or less streaked with vivid red. Dors. sep. oblong or elliptic-oblong, blunt, the lats. broadly elliptic-oblong. Ps. oblong or elliptic-oblong, blunt. Lip helmet-shaped, broadly elliptic-oblong, with a crenulate, reflexed apex, the spur stout, curved, about ½″ long. Mostly Feb.–Mar. (I) East South Africa.

S. membranaceum Sw. (*Satyrium cucullatum* Thunb.)

St. stout, ¾–1½′ tall, clothed with numerous lanceolate sheaths. Lvs. basal, rather fleshy, orbicular, blunt, 1½–4″ long. Infl. dense, 3–8″ long. Fls. about ⅝″ in diam., bright pink, very handsome, rather thin-textured but lasting well, fragrant. Dors. sep. oblong, pointed, the lats. broadly oblong, spreading. Ps. oblong, blunt, the margins fringed. Lip broadly helmet-shaped, with a reflexed, fringed apex, the spurs slender, curved, 1″ long. Autumn–early winter. (C, I) East Cape Colony.

S. nepalense D.Don (*Satyrium albiflorum* A.Rich., *S. pallidum* A.Rich., *S. Perrottetianum* A.Rich., *S. Wightiorum* Ldl.)

St. usually very stout, ½–2½′ tall, sheathed above. Lvs. mostly basal, few, varying from oblong to linear-oblong, rather fleshy, sessile, sheathing basally, to 8″ long. Infl. densely many-fld., 3–6″ long. Fls. about ⅝″ in diam., varying from dark pink to pure white, fragrant. Dors. sep. narrowly oblong, recurved, the lats. linear-oblong, spreading. Ps. almost linear. Lip broadly oblong, concave, with a pronounced keel on the back, the spurs usually stout, about ¾″ long. Autumn, mostly Sept. (C, I) Nepal; India; Southern China; Burma.

S. parviflorum Sw. (*Satyrium cassideum* Ldl., *S. densiflorum* Ldl., *S. eriostomum* Ldl., *S. lydenburgense* Rchb.f., *S. tenuifolium* Krzl., *Diplectrum parviflorum* Pers.)

St. stout, clothed with sheaths, 1–2½′ tall, the lower sheaths lf.-like. Lvs. almost basal, usually 2–4, spreading, dull green, broadly ovate or elliptic-oblong, rather fleshy, 3–8″ long. Infl. densely many-fld., 4–8″ long. Fls. about ¼″ in diam., green or yellowish-green. Dors. sep. spatulate-oblong, obtuse, the lats. falcate-oblong, obtuse. Ps. spatulate-oblong, united to the middle with the ss. Lip helmet-like, broadly ovoid or obovate-globose, the margins and apex reflexed and crenulate, the spurs curved, at times diverging, about ½″ long. Autumn–winter. (C, I) South Africa.

S. speciosum Rolfe (*Satyrium Buchanani* Rolfe)

St. stout, to more than 2′ tall, with 2–3 lvs. near the middle, sheathed above and below. Lvs. broadly elliptic-oblong or ovate-oblong, rather pointed, 3–6″ long. Infl. usually many-fld., 4–7″ long. Fls. about ¾″ in diam., dark red. Dors. sep. oblong-lanceolate, blunt, the lats. broadly lanceolate, spreading. Ps. oblong-lanceolate, united with the ss. for half their length. Lip hooded, subcompressed, the orifice rather narrow, the tip broadly ovate, reflexed, the base united to the lat. ss. for about one-quarter of its length, the spurs narrow, curved, ½″ long. Sept.–Nov. (C, I) Nyasaland.

S. sphaerocarpum Ldl. (*Satyrium Beyrichianum* Krzl., *S. militare* Ldl.)

St. stout, 1–1¾′ tall, clothed with a few large sheaths. Lvs. mostly basal, 2–4, dull green, rather fleshy, ovate-oblong or elliptic-oblong, acutish, 2–6″ long. Infls. densely many-fld., 2–8″ long. Fls. fragrant, about ¾″ long, white, blotched and suffused with bright red. Ss. united almost to the middle, the dors. one lanceolate-oblong, the lats. broadly oblong. Ps. lanceolate-oblong. Lip helmet-shaped, broadly elliptic-ovate, the apex reflexed, the spurs stout, curved, about ½″ long. Autumn–winter. (I) East Cape Colony; Griqualand East; Natal.

S. Atherstonei Rchb.f. (*Satyrium monopetalum* Krzl., *S. trinerve* Schltr., *S. triphyllum* Krzl.) St. slender, 1–2′ tall, with a few narrow sheaths. Lvs. cauline, oblong or linear-oblong, rather fleshy, dark green, 3–6″ long. Infls. very densely many-fld., to 4½″ long. Fls. about $\frac{3}{16}$″ across, white or white and yellow. Ss. and ps. united to the middle, the lat. ss. somewhat spreading. Lip ovoid-globose, helmet-shaped, slightly reflexed at tip, the spurs rather stout, curved, ⅛″ long. Oct.–Feb. (C, I) East Cape Colony; Transvaal; Natal.

S. candidum Ldl. (*Satyrium utriculatum* Sond.) St. rather stout, to 1½′ tall, sheathed. Lvs. usually paired, basal, prostrate on the ground, roundish, to 4″ long and broad. Infl. about 3″ long, densely many-fld. Fls. about ¼″ across, white, flushed with rosy-red. Lip almost round, the spurs rather long. June–July. (I) South Africa.

S. carneum (Dryand.) R.Br. (*Orchis carnea* Dryand.) St. stout, to 2¼′ tall, sheathed. Lvs. paired, basal, usually almost prostrate on the ground, roundish-elliptic, to 4″ long, almost as broad. Infl. very densely many-fld., about 2–3″ long. Fls. about ½″ across, fragrant, pale rosy-red or almost flesh-coloured. Autumn. (I) South Africa.

S. densum Rolfe. St. stout, clothed with rather numerous sheaths, 2–2¼′ tall. Lvs. cauline, paired, oblong-lanceolate or obovate-oblong, rather blunt, 6–7″ long. Infl. very densely many-fld., 7–9″ long. Fls. about ⅝″ across, yellowish-green, fragrant. Dors. sep. narrowly oblong, reflexed, the lat. ss. spreading. Ps. reflexed, united to the ss. for about one third of their length. Lip hooded, subcompressed, broad, the apex pointed, reflexed, the spurs elongate-linear, slightly curved, ¾″ long. Autumn–early winter. (C, I) Nyasaland.

S. humile Ldl. St. to 9″ tall, stout, clothed with sheaths. Lvs. 2, spreading, fleshy, dull green, ovate or suborbicular, rather blunt, sessile, 1¼″ long. Infl. loosely many-fld., to 2½″ long. Fls. about ⅜″ across, yellow or yellowish-green. Lip helmet-shaped, with a very broad, blunt, reflexed apex, the spurs slender, curved, about ⅝″ long. Autumn–winter. (C, I) South west Cape Colony.

S. macrophyllum Ldl. St. very stout, sheathed, to 2¼′ tall. Lvs. 2–4, basal, dark green, rather fleshy, ovate-oblong to

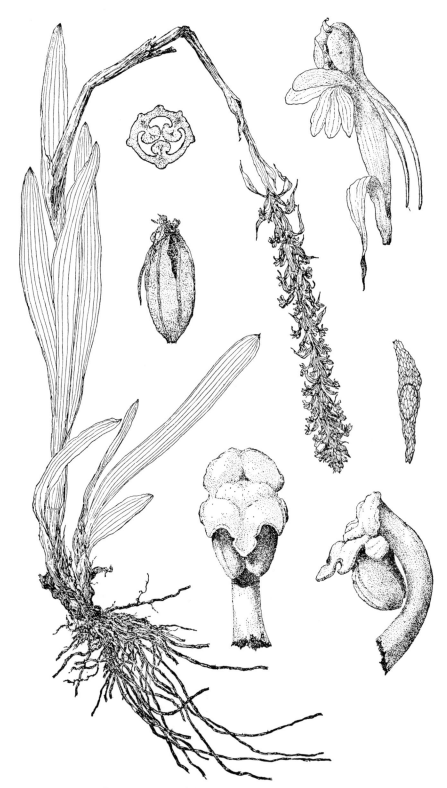

Satyrium crassicaule Rendle [*Flora of the Belgian Congo*]

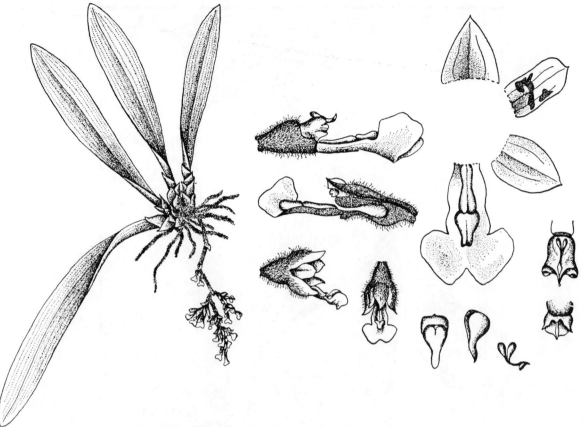

Saundersia paniculata Brade [Hoehne, *Flora Brasilica*]

broadly elliptic, blunt, subsessile, 4–12″ long. Infl. rather densely many-fld., 4–10″ long. Fls. about ½″ across, pale or dark pink, fragrant. Ss. and ps. linear, blunt, the lat. ss. oblong, shorter than the dors. one. Lip helmet-shaped, broadly ovate, with a reflexed tip, the spurs slender, curved, 1″ long. Feb.–May. (C, I) East Cape Colony; Griqualand East; Transkei; Natal.

S. maculatum Burch. (*Satyrium longicolle* Ldl.) St. rather stout, clothed with numerous imbricating sheaths. Lvs. paired, thickly fleshy, dull green, basal, ovate or ovate-orbicular, blunt, sessile, to 3″ long. Infl. loosely or densely many-fld., 2–6″ long. Fls. about ⅝″ across, white or pale pink, more or less spotted with purple. Lip helmet-shaped, oblong or ovate-oblong, reflexed at tip, the spurs slender, curved, about 1¼″ long. Autumn, mostly Oct.–Nov. (C, I) South Cape Colony.

S. Woodii Schltr. St. to 1¾′ tall, clothed with numerous imbricate sheaths. Lvs. basal or on short lateral sts. at the base of the flowering-st., oblong or elliptic, rather blunt, 4–6″ long. Infl. densely many-fld., 3–6″ long. Fls. about ⅝″ across, pink to orange-red, very pretty. Lip helmet-shaped, broadly elliptic-ovate with a reflexed, pointed apex, the spurs slender, curved, about ¾″ long. Oct.–Dec. (C, I) Natal; Orange Free State.

SAUNDERSIA Rchb.f.

Saundersia mirabilis Rchb.f., the only known member of this genus of the small subtribe *Saundersiinae*, is an extremely rare and little-known epiphytic orchid from Brazil. A unique and delightfully strange orchid, it is unfortunately unknown in our collections today, although it offers much of interest to the specialist in the 'botanicals'.

Nothing is known concerning the genetic affinities of *Saundersia*.

CULTURE: As for *Ornithocephalus*. (I, H)

SAUROGLOSSUM Ldl.

Sauroglossum is a genus of three known species of robust, small-flowered terrestrial orchids, native in Brazil and Argentina. A segregate from *Spiranthes* L.C.Rich., the group is possibly not distinct from that polymorphic genus, but technical details of the blossoms seem to give sufficient evidence to warrant its retention. None of the three species is known in collections today, and the small dimensions of their flowers offer little of interest to any save the specialist.

Nothing is known of the genetic affinities of *Sauroglossum*.

CULTURE: Presumably as for the tropical Habenarias, Spiranthes, etc. (H)

SCAPHOSEPALUM Pfitz.

About forty species of *Scaphosepalum* are known to date, these very odd, primarily epiphytic orchids found in mossy 'cloud forests' over a wide region extending from Guatemala to Ecuador and Peru. Rather closely

431

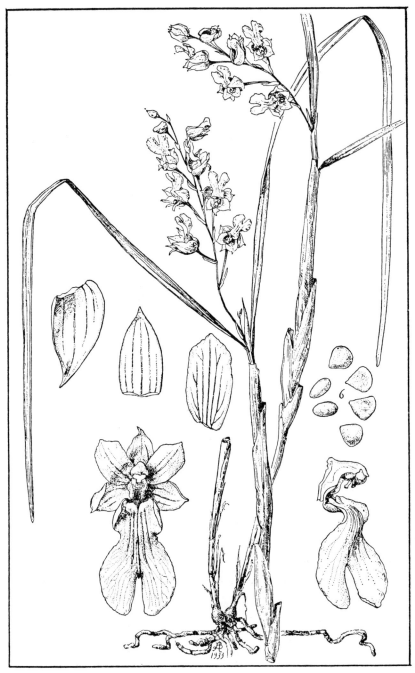

Scaphyglottis hondurensis (Ames) L.O.Wms. [BLANCHE AMES]

allied to *Pleurothallis* R.Br. and to *Masdevallia* R. & P., they are today extremely scarce in our collections, although they are most interesting plants, with racemes of small but extremely intricate flowers, in which the joined lateral sepals typically bear a fleshy protuberance at their tips, thus giving to the often vividly hued blossoms a most fantastic appearance, quite unlike most of their relatives.

No hybrids have as yet been made with *Scaphosepalum*, and nothing appears to be on record regarding its genetic affinities, although they presumably lie with *Pleurothallis* and *Masdevallia*.

CULTURE: As for *Pleurothallis* and *Masdevallia*, depending upon the place of origin of the particular species or individual involved. (C, I)

S. Standleyi Ames

Sts. clustered, sheathed, very short. Lf. solitary, erect, narrowly elliptic to oblanceolate, 3-toothed at obtuse apex, rigidly leathery, narrowing below, to more than

4½″ long. Infls. lateral from lowermost node of secondary st., filiform, sheath-bracted, bearing an apical, multiflorous rac., the fls. opening successively over a long period of time. Fls. not opening fully, to more than ¼″ long, dark purple-red or purplish-green. Lat. ss. joined together almost throughout their length, strongly concave, with a warty callus above the middle. Lip tongue-shaped, obtuse, with 2 keels on the disc. Autumn. (I) Guatemala; Honduras; Costa Rica; Panama.

S. anchoriferum (Rchb.f.) Rolfe (*Masdevallia anchorifera* Rchb.f.) Rather similar in habit to *S. Standleyi* Ames, but smaller, the lvs. to 4″ long, lanceolate-spatulate. Infls. to 4″ tall, erect or ascending, 5–7-fld., usually with only 1 fl. open at one time. Fls. not opening fully, rather short-lived, about ⅜″ long, yellowish-brown, the lat. ss. united to about the middle, the fleshy-thickened apical parts spreading. Autumn–winter. (I) Costa Rica.

SCAPHYGLOTTIS P. & E.
(*Cladobium* Ldl., *Hexadesmia* Brongn., *Hexopia* Batem. ex Ldl., *Reichenbachanthus* B.-R., *Tetragamestus* Rchb.f.)

Scaphyglottis is a most interesting but seldom-cultivated genus of orchids, most of which are epiphytic plants (sometimes lithophytic) which range from Mexico and the West Indies throughout Central America and much of South America, to southern Brazil and Bolivia. The exact confines of the group have not as yet been established by the botanists, but there seem to be at least fifty valid species contained herein, and possibly many more. A member of the subtribe *Ponerinae*, these unique orchids, highly variable in vegetative habit and typically bearing very small but attractive flowers in great profusion, are now becoming popular with collectors of the so-called 'botanical' orchids, because of their relative abundance in the wild (in many cases), ease of importation and cultivation, and extreme floriferousness. Perhaps the majority of the Scaphyglottis possess a remarkable growth-habit (which is equalled in the Asiatic coelogynids *Pholidota articulata* Ldl. and the genus *Otochilus* Ldl., as well as the American *Hexisea* Ldl.), in that the pseudobulbs are typically borne one on top of the other, each successive growth appearing from the apex of the former one. Other members of the group have distinct (often stalked) fat pseudobulbs, and all species bear terminal inflorescences at the apex of the pseudobulb or segment-like pseudobulbous growth. Although small, the flowers are usually of attractive coloration and intricate formation when carefully inspected, preferably with a magnifying lens, since few of them reach any appreciable dimensions.

No hybrids have as yet been attempted in *Scaphyglottis*, and its genetic alliances have not been ascertained. Interspecific (or, preferably, inter-sectional) breeding should help to clarify many of the critical taxonomic problems in this complex alliance of orchids, and is to be recommended to interested hybridists.

CULTURE: The cultural requirements of almost all members of the genus *Scaphyglottis* are very readily met. In general, it may be stated that they require conditions such as those furnished for the pseudobulbous, tropical and subtropical species of *Epidendrum*. Since the components of this genus are found at altitudes ranging from near sea-level to high in the South American Andes, temperature requirements are based on the particular plant under consideration, some of them needing hot conditions, some intermediate, and even a few, cool. While the plants are actively growing, copious quantities of water should be supplied, but upon completion of the new growths—and, in most cases, after flowering—moisture should be strictly curtailed for some time, until root-action and breaking of the new shoots again commences. A sunny spot in the collection seems to suit all of the cultivated species rather well, and—depending upon the size of the plants—they may be grown either in well-drained pots or in baskets filled with osmunda fibre or shredded tree-fern fibre. Many of them thrive when mounted on smallish tree-fern slabs or cubes. Certain of the more delicate South American members of the genus benefit by application of a top-dressing of fresh, live sphagnum moss, for better moisture retention. (C, I, H)

S. Behrii (Rchb.f.) Bth. & Hk.f. (*Ponera Behrii* Rchb.f., *Ponera albida* Rchb.f., *Scaphyglottis albida* Schltr., *S. guatemalensis* Schltr., *S. pauciflora* Schltr.)
Pls. often pendulous, forming dense clumps, the pbs. rather thin, stalked, superposed one above the other or in small fascicles, 2–8″ long. Lvs. 2, grass-like, 3–11″ long, often rather thin-textured. Fls. small, less than ¼″ across, borne in fascicles at the apex of each successive pb., not opening fully, white, the lip larger than the other segms., 3-lbd. above the middle, sometimes faintly flushed with pale lilac. Mostly spring. (I, H) Guatemala and British Honduras throughout Central America to Panama and Colombia.

S. Lindeniana (A.Rich. & Gal.) L.O.Wms. (*Hexadesmia Lindeniana* A.Rich. & Gal., *Hexadesmia fasciculata* Brongn., *Hexadesmia pachybulbon* Schltr.)
Robust pls., among the stoutest in the entire genus, the clustered pbs. stalked basally, more or less spindle-shaped and compressed above, 2–12″ tall, to 1″ wide. Lvs. normally 2, leathery, dull green, 2–10″ long. Infls. terminal, 2–several-fld., short, subtended by numerous small papery sheathing bracts. Fls. varying from ⅛–¾″ in diam., yellow-green or reddish-green, usually more or less flushed or veined with purplish, often rather hooded and not opening well. Mostly spring. (I, H) Mexico throughout Central America to Panama and possibly Colombia.

SCELOCHILUS Klotzsch

About four species of small epiphytic orchids make up the little-known genus *Scelochilus*, a member of the subtribe *Comparettiinae*, somewhat allied to *Plectrophora* Focke and *Neokoehleria* Schltr. They are peculiar little plants of no notable beauty, but one of them has made its way into a few particularly choice collections.

Nothing is known of the genetic affinities of this peculiar genus.

CULTURE: As for *Ornithocephalus*. (H)

S. Tuerckheimii Schltr.
Pls. composed of a slender short rhiz. which produces small 1-lvd. pbs. and elongated infls., the pbs.

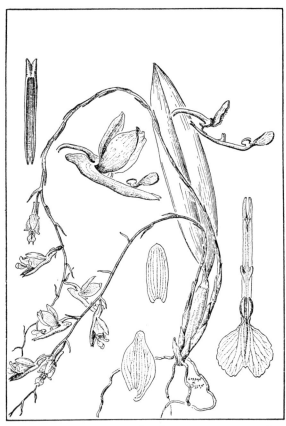

Scelochilus latipetalus C.Schw. [GORDON W. DILLON]

cylindrical, $\frac{1}{2}$–1″ long, concealed by large greyish, papery sheaths. Lf. leathery, erect-spreading, elliptic, usually abruptly acuminate, folded at base, 2$\frac{3}{4}$–5″ long, to 1$\frac{1}{4}$″ wide. Infl. a simple or somewhat branched rac., lateral from pb.-base, slender, 2$\frac{1}{2}$–12″ long, mostly erect. Fls. not opening well, about $\frac{1}{2}$″ long, bright yellow, often with light green veins, the lat. ss. united almost to apex, with a prominent saccate mentum at base, the lip very complex, produced at base into a didymous spur that is enclosed in the mentum of lat. ss. Summer. (I, H) Guatemala; Honduras; Nicaragua; Costa Rica.

SCHIZOCHILUS Sond.

A member of the complex subtribe *Habenarinae*, about fourteen species of *Schizochilus* are now known to science, of which a couple are now present in particularly choice collections. Terrestrial plants with small but rather pretty flowers, usually in one-sided racemes, they inhabit tropical and South Africa.

Nothing is known of the genetic affinities of *Schizochilus*, and no hybrids have as yet been attempted.

CULTURE: As for the tropical Habenarias, etc. (I, H)

S. Bulbinella (Rchb.f.) Bolus (*Brachycorythis Bulbinella* Rchb.f., *Platanthera Bulbinella* Schltr.)

Roots usually 2 ovoid tubers. Lvs. mostly near base, linear or linear-oblong, acute, 2–3$\frac{1}{2}$″ long. Infl. 6–12″ tall, sheathed, the rather many-fld. rac. dense. Fls. about

$\frac{3}{16}$″ in diam., vivid golden-yellow, fragrant, the ss. broadly ovate, rather blunt, the ps. broadly ovate, rather blunt; lip as long as the ss., obscurely or shortly 3-lbd., vaguely downy; lat. lbs. rounded or very blunt and very short; midlb. oblong or ovate-oblong, rather blunt; disc with 3 nerves or obscure keels at base; spur saccate, very tiny. Winter. (I, H) Transvaal; Griqualand East.

S. Zeyheri Sond. (*Brachycorythis Zeyheri* Rchb.f., *Platanthera Zeyheri* Schltr.)

Roots usually 2, ovoid, tuberous. Lvs. mostly basal, linear to linear-oblong, 1–4$\frac{1}{2}$″ long. Infl. 6–15″ tall, sheathed, the rather dense, many-fld. rac. to 2″ long. Fls. almost $\frac{1}{2}$″ in diam., yellow, or porcelain-white with a yellow lip. Ss. ovate-oblong, prominently 3-nerved; ps. narrowly ovate, half as long as the ss., 1-nerved; lip fuzzy, 3-lbd., as long as the ss., the lat. lbs. falcate-ovate, blunt, the midlb. linear-oblong, twice as long as the lat. ones; disc with a small erect tubercle at base; spur cylindrical or rather compressed, oblong. Winter–early spring. (I. H) Transvaal; Orange Free State; Natal; Cape Colony.

SCHIZODIUM Ldl.

A member of the subtribe *Disinae*, *Schizodium* consists of about fifteen species of terrestrial orchids, apparently confined in their distribution to the southwestern part of Africa's Cape Colony, where they usually occur in open meadows, often at considerable elevations in the mountains. A segregate from *Disa* Berg., because of the complexly 2-parted lip (which consists of both a basal hypochil and an apical epichil), they are very little-known and exceptionally rare in contemporary collections, due in large part to the difficulty of obtaining them, and otherwise because of their rather small, not overly showy blossoms.

Nothing is known of the genetic affinities of *Schizodium*.

CULTURE: Primarily as for *Disa*, etc. Because of their semi-alpine habitats, they do best in the cool house, in shallow, well-drained pans filled with a very porous mixture of about equal parts of fibrous loam, shredded peat-moss, and gritty white sand. A rather sunny, damp situation suits them well, but they are far from easy to maintain in good condition for more than a single season under average greenhouse arrangements. (C, I)

S. clavigerum Ldl. (*Disa clavigera* Bolus)

Tuber usually solitary, rather irregular, oblong. Lvs. basal, spatulate, forming a tuft, about $\frac{1}{2}$″ long or more. Infl. slender, flexuous, to about 12″ tall, the 4-fld. or more rac. rather lax. Fls. about $\frac{1}{4}$″ in diam., flesh-pink, spotted more or less densely with carmine. Dors. sep. elliptic-oblong, erect, the spur clavate or subclavate, blunt, $\frac{3}{16}$″ long. Lat. ss. oblong. Ps. narrowly oblong, shortly bifid at apex, with a rounded basal lb. in front. Lip 2-parted, the basal hypochil concave, the epichil pandurate-oblong. Mostly Sept.–Oct. (C, I) South-west Cape Colony.

S. obtusatum Ldl. (*Schizodium bifidum* Schltr.)

Tuber usually solitary, irregular, oblong. Lvs. basal, forming a tuft or vague rosette, spoon-shaped, about $\frac{1}{2}$″

Schlimia trifida Rchb.f. [*Gardeners' Chronicle*]

long. Infl. slender, flexuous, about 3–5″ tall, sheathed, loosely 1–4-fld. Fls. about $\frac{1}{4}$″ in diam., bright pink. Dors. sep. elliptic-oblong, concave, erect, the spur clavate. Lat. ss. oblong. Ps. narrowly oblong, with prominent rounded angles in front. Lip with a somewhat curved hypochil, the epichil subpandurate. July–Nov. (C, I) South-west Cape Colony.

SCHLIMIA Planch. & Lind.

Schlimia contains two little-known species of unusually handsome epiphytic orchids of the subtribe *Gongorinae*, one of which is today to be encountered in a very few choice collections, although it is a very rare orchid. The other species, **Schlimia jasminodora** Planch., does not appear to be cultivated at this time. Smallish pseudobulbous plants, the incredibly complex, hooded flowers indicate the affinity of the group with *Stanhopea* Frost.

Nothing is known of the genetic affinities of *Schlimia*, although the group is probably 'crossable' with at least certain other members of the alliance, and some extraordinary multigeneric hybrids seem possible.

CULTURE: As for *Stanhopea*, although considerably cooler conditions are required than for most of those orchids. Additions of chopped sphagnum moss to the compost is recommended, since these plants usually grow throughout the year (hence do not require a rest-period), and need constantly moist conditions at the roots. They are extremely intolerant of stale compost, and should be transferred to fresh potting-material immediately when such a condition seems evident. (C, I)

S. trifida Rchb.f.

Pbs. clustered, sub-fusiform, about 1″ long. Lf. solitary, shortly petiolate, elliptic-oblong, acute, 4–6″ long, to about $1\frac{3}{4}$″ wide, strongly veined, often undulate marginally. Infls. drooping to almost pendulous, the peduncle usually dull purple, with a secund 4–6-fld. rac., the fls. inverted. Fls. waxy, very fragrant, about 2″ long, white, spotted on the dors. sep. with purple. Dors. sep. oblong, obtuse. Lat. ss. forming a large, helmet-shaped sac. Ps. linear, acute, reflexed towards their tips. Lip shorter than the other segms., 3-parted, the basal hypochil sub-pandurate, usually with an orange-yellow blotch, the epichil lanceolate. Col. semiterete, with 2 squarish fleshy wings. Winter. (C, I) Colombia, at relatively high elevations.

SCHOENORCHIS Bl.

This is a genus of about fifteen species of rare and seldom-cultivated, but unusually attractive epiphytic sarcanthad orchids, native in the region extending from the Himalayas to New Guinea. The group is somewhat allied to *Gastrochilus* D.Don and several other aggregations of the subtribe *Sarcanthinae*, but the floral structure—particularly that of the anther and rostellum—is very characteristic and easily distinguishes *Schoenorchis*. Vegetatively, the plants are variable, some possessing strap-shaped leaves and others bearing very narrow, almost terete foliage. The flowers, produced in large numbers in small simple or branched inflorescences, are among the smallest of all orchids, thus making these plants of interest primarily to the connoisseur.

No hybrids are recorded in *Schoenorchis*, and nothing is known as yet regarding its genetic affinities.

CULTURE: As for the tropical Vandas, etc. (I, H)

S. gemmata (Ldl.) J.J.Sm. (*Saccolabium gemmatum* Ldl., *Cleisostoma gemmatum* King & Pantl.)

Sts. slender, pendulous, to 12″ long. Lvs. slender, awl-shaped, acute, to 6″ long. Infls. branching, slender, rather loosely many-fld., to 8″ long. Fls. secund, less than ¼″ long. Ss. and ps. oblong, obtuse, purple-red, the lat. ss. with whitish apices. Lip obscurely 3-lbd., rose-red, the midlb. oval, obtuse; spur oblong, obtuse, shorter than the purple-red pedicellate ovary. July–Aug. (I, H) Himalayas.

S. juncifolia Bl. (*Saccolabium juncifolium* J.J.Sm.)

Sts. slender, pendulous, to more than 12″ long. Lvs. slender, terete, acute, to 5″ long. Infls. to 4″ long, densely many-fld. Fls. about ½″ long, blue-violet with a paler lip. Ss. and ps. oblong, shortly acuminate. Lip longer than the other segms., with an oblong-ligulate disc and a proportionately elongate, helmet-like spur. Col. whitish, the anther purple-red. Early summer. (H) Sumatra; Java.

S. micrantha Bl. (*Saccolabium chionanthum* Ldl., *Saccolabium perpusillum* Hk.f.)

Sts. much branched and densely clustered, rooting at base only, to about 6″ long, slender. Lvs. subterete, thickly fleshy, grooved above, curved away from the st., to 1½″ long, bent and slightly constricted at a point near the apex. Infls. horizontal, to 2″ long, densely many-fld., the fls. all pointing forwards. Fls. scarcely opening, about ⅛″ long, white, turning yellow with age. Ps. close to the ss., slightly smaller. Lip with a large ellipsoidal spur that is curved forwards. Summer. (H) Malay Peninsula; Java.

S. haianensis (Rolfe) Schltr. (*Saccolabium hainanense* Rolfe) Rather simulating *S. gemmata* (Ldl.) J.J.Sm., but distinguished from it in having the lvs. twice as wide and flattened underneath, the infls. denser and the fls. more than ¼″ long. Ss. and

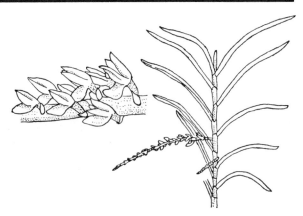

Schoenorchis micrantha Bl. [A.D.HAWKES, AFTER HOLTTUM]

ps. oblong, obtuse, dark purple, the lat. ss. tipped with white. Lip white, longer than the ss., with a very shortly ovate disc and a more conical, blunt-tipped spur. March–Apr. (H) Hainan; Hong Kong.

SCHWARTZKOPFFIA Krzl.

A genus of two known species, *Schwartzkopffia* is a member of the subtribe *Habenarinae*, and is perhaps closest in its alliance to *Brachycorythis* Ldl. Very small terrestrial orchids from tropical Africa, neither **Schwartzkopffia pumilio** (Ldl.) Schltr., nor **S. Lastii** (Rolfe) Schltr. is known in contemporary collections.

Nothing is known of the genetic affinities of this rare group.

CULTURE: Presumably as for *Cynorkis*. (H)

SCUTICARIA Ldl.

Scuticaria is a genus of three known species, native in Brazil, the Guianas, and Venezuela. They are extraordinarily interesting and handsome epiphytic orchids, with long, whip-like, strictly pendulous foliage in the two cultivated species, while in the very rare Brazilian **S. strictifolia** Hoehne, the leaves are erect. Large and showy flowers are produced at the base of the plant. The genus is a member of the subtribe *Maxillarinae*, but is readily distinguishable from the other groups in that alliance by vegetative and floral characters. Neither of the cultivated Scuticarias is a common plant in collections, though both are very desirable orchids.

No hybrids have as yet been made with *Scuticaria*, and nothing is known of its genetic affinities. It seems logical to assume that it would breed with *Maxillaria*.

CULTURE: Because of the pendulous habit of the plants, these orchids must be grown on rafts, tree-fern slabs, or in baskets hung sideways. They do best in a tightly packed compost of osmunda or tree-fern fibre, and should be kept in a rather bright, sunny spot, short of burning of the foliage through excessive exposure. During the season of active growth, they benefit by liberal applications of water, but after the flowers have faded the plants should be given a decided rest-period of about two weeks' duration or so. (I, H)

S. Hadweni (Ldl.) Hk. (*Bifrenaria Hadweni* Ldl.)

Pbs. pendulous, clustered, to about 2½″ long, cylindrical, furrowed, prominently jointed. Lvs. sharply pendulous, solitary on the pbs., rather soft-textured, dark green, to almost 2′ long, whip-like, attenuated at the apex, with a deep longitudinal groove. Infls. borne from pb.-bases or on special leafless pb.-like growths, 1½–8″ long, pendulous or arching, often several borne at once. Fls. solitary, waxy, fragrant, long-lived, to 3″ across, the ss. and ps. yellow with large blotches of bright brown, the somewhat tubular lip white or cream-white, irregularly spotted with bright red, the face of the col. flushed with red. Spring–autumn. (I, H) Brazil; Guianas.

S. Steelii (Hk.) Ldl. (*Maxillaria Steelii* Hk., *Maxillaria flagellifera* Ldl., *Scuticaria de Keyseriana* hort., *S. Keyseriana* hort.)

Rather similar in habit to *S. Hadweni* (Ldl.) Hk., but differing in the lvs., which attain lengths in excess of 4′. Infls. 1–3-fld., pendulous. Fls. fragrant, waxy, long-lived, to more than 3″ in diam., the ss. and ps. yellow, irregularly blotched (mostly in transverse zones) with reddish-brown, the somewhat flaring-tubular lip pale yellow, irregularly blotched with red, especially on the lat. lbs. Autumn. (I, H) Brazil; Guianas; Venezuela.

SELENIPEDIUM Rchb.f.
(*Selenipedilum* Pfitz., *Solenipedium* Beer)

Three species of *Selenipedium* are known at this time, all of them exceptionally rare and highly unusual terrestrial members of the subtribe *Cypripedilinae*. Despite the frequent appearance of this name in horticulture, and in lists of orchid hybrids, no true Selenipediums appear to be in cultivation at this time, the name being erroneously applied by orchidists to members of the genus *Phragmipedium* Rolfe (which see for additional comments on this confused matter). Very tall-growing, almost bamboo-like plants with reedy stems and prominent plicate foliage, they bear small, rather nondescript flowers in a terminal raceme, and are primarily of scientific interest. **Selenipedium chica** Rchb.f. inhabits the lowlands of Panama; **S. palmifolium** (Ldl.) Rchb.f. (*Cypripedium palmifolium* Ldl.) is known from the Guianas and northern Brazil; and **S. Isabelianum** B.-R. has been collected in the Brazilian States of Pará and Amazonas.

No hybrids have been made utilizing the true Selenipediums, and nothing appears to be known concerning its genetic affinities.

CULTURE: Possibly as for *Sobralia*, although it seems rather doubtful that the peculiar plants would thrive in our collections for more than a single season. (H)

SEMIPHAJUS Gagnep.

Two species of *Semiphajus* are known to date, both of them apparently very rare in their native Viet-Nam (especially Annam). Peculiar plants without pseudobulbs, the medium-sized, rose or greenish-purple, racemose flowers are borne before the full development of the plicate, canaliculate leaves. At this time,

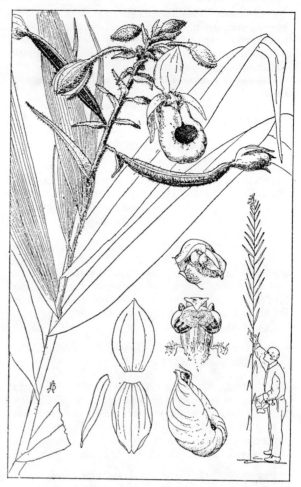

Selenipedium chica Rchb.f. [BLANCHE AMES]

neither of the Semiphajus is known in our collections, although they seem to be relatively attractive orchids of some potential interest to the specialist.

Nothing is known of the genetic affinities of the genus *Semiphajus*.

CULTURE: Possibly as for the tropical *Phaius*. (I, H)

SEPALOSACCUS Schltr.

Sepalosaccus humilis Schltr., the only known member of this rare genus, is a small epiphytic orchid of the subtribe *Maxillarinae*, which has been found a few times in the forests of Costa Rica. It is unknown in contemporary collections, and is in any event a singularly inconspicuous plant, primarily of botanical interest.

Nothing is known of the genetic ties of *Sepalosaccus*.

CULTURE: Presumably as for the medium-elevation Maxillarias, Oncidiums, etc. (I)

SEPALOSIPHON Schltr.

A single species, **Sepalosiphon papuanum** Schltr., comprises this exceedingly rare genus of epiphytic orchids from New Guinea. Vegetatively simulating

Glossorhyncha Ridl., the group is allied to it and is hence a member of the subtribe *Glomerinae*. A plant with small olive-green blossoms—whose structure differs somewhat from *Glossorhyncha*—it is unknown in collections today.

Nothing is known of the genetic affinities of *Sepalosiphon*.

CULTURE: Presumably as for the tropical Bulbophyllums, etc. (H)

SERAPIAS L.
(*Helleborine* Tournef.)

This is a genus of about a dozen species of terrestrial, often handsome orchids, native mostly in southern Europe, about the Mediterranean, with some of them extending into Asia Minor. The genus is allied to *Orchis* [Tournef.] L., differing primarily in its spurless flowers and details of the column. The Serapias are attractive plants, but unfortunately are very rare in contemporary collections outside of their native haunts.

A few natural hybrids are known in this genus. No artificially induced hybrids are on record, and little is known concerning the group's genetic affinities.

CULTURE: As for *Orchis*. (C, I)

S. cordigera (Pers.) L. (*Helleborine cordigera* Pers., *Serapias ovalis* L.C.Rich.)
Pls. 8–15″ tall, leafy, the lvs. linear-lanceolate, acute. Infls. 3–8-fld., rather dense, furnished with rather large bracts which are reddish with purple veins. Fls. about 1″ long, the ss. pale reddish, the smaller ps. somewhat darker. Lip 3-lbd., about twice as long as the ss., the lat. lbs. roundish, purple, the midlb. elliptic, acuminate, dark purple. Spring. (C, I) South Europe.

S. lingua (Pers.) L. (*Helleborine lingua* Pers., *Helleborine oxyglottis* Pers., *Serapias glabra* Lap.)
Similar in habit to *S. cordigera* (Pers.) L., to about 15″ tall. Infl.-bracts elliptic-lanceolate, often slightly longer than the fls., violet-rose with darker veins. Fls. about 1″ long, the ss. violet-red sometimes marbled with greenish, the ps. smaller and often darker. Lip 3-lbd., about twice as long as the ss., with an oblong thickening on the disc, the roundish lat. lbs. dark purple, the midlb. elliptic-lanceolate, acuminate, covered with short hairs, clear violet-red. Spring. (C, I) South Europe.

S. longipetala (Ten.) Poll. (*Helleborine longipetala* Ten., *Helleborine pseudocordigera* Seb., *Serapias hirsuta* Lap., *S. lancifera* St.Am., *S. oxyglottis* Rchb., *S. pseudocordigera* Moric)
Similar in habit to *S. cordigera* (Pers.) L., to almost 2′ tall. Infl.-bracts twice as long as the fls., which number 4–8, in a rather loose rac. Fls. about 1″ long, the ss. coherent, lanceolate, violet-red, paler outside. Ps. smaller and shorter. Lip 3-lbd., about half as long as the ss., with 2 thickenings on the disc, the roundish lat. lbs. dark purple, the midlb. elliptic-lanceolate, hairy, not as broad as other lbs., brownish-red, with a yellowish centre. Spring. (C, I) South Europe.

S. neglecta DeNot.
Similar in habit to *S. cordigera* (Pers.) L., to about 12″ tall. Bracts of the infl. shorter than the fls., oval, acute,

greenish, often flushed with violet or almost purple. Fls. 2–6, large, about 1½″ long or more, the ss. lanceolate, light violet-purple, the ps. much smaller. Lip 3-lbd., twice as long as the ss., with 2 linear thickenings on the disc, the lat. lbs. roundish, dark purple, the oval, acuminate midlb. about as wide, covered with fine hairs, cinnabar-red with an ochre-red middle. Spring. (C, I) South Europe.

S. occultata Gay (*Serapias laxiflora* Chaub., *S. parviflora* Parl.)
Similar to the other spp. in habit, but more slender and shorter. Infl. loose, 4–8-fld., the bracts lanceolate, often slightly longer than the fls., reddish or sometimes green. Fls. small for the genus, about ½″ long or more, the ss. lanceolate, pale violet-red with greenish nerves, the ps. smaller, greenish or reddish. Lip 3-lbd., scarcely longer than the ss., with 2 round humps on the disc, the lat. lbs. roundish, dark purple, the midlb. larger, yellow-red, lanceolate, acute, furnished with brownish hairs. Spring. (C, I) South Europe.

SIEVEKINGIA Rchb.f.

About four species of *Sievekingia* are known to science, of which two are present today in a very few highly specialized collections of 'botanical' orchids. Dwarf epiphytic plants, rather simulating a seedling *Stanhopea*, they produce pendulous or strongly arching racemes of smallish but very complex and interesting blossoms. The genus is a member of the subtribe *Gongorinae*, and its component species are among the rarest of all cultivated orchidaceous plants. They also appear to be excessively scarce in their native habitats, and have seldom been collected by botanical explorers.

Nothing is known of the genetic affinities of *Sievekingia*, although it seems entirely possible that the group will prove 'crossable' with at least certain of the allied genera.

CULTURE: As for *Stanhopea*. The plants, because of their small dimensions, should be kept in little slatted baskets, through the interstices of which their often sharply pendulous inflorescences may be produced. A compost of equal parts of chopped sphagnum moss and shredded tree-fern fibre should be used, this to be confined within the basket through the use of thin slabs of tree-fern or sheets of osmunda placed against the sides and bottom of the container. Mostly inhabiting moist tropical forests, these plants should never be permitted to dry out completely, although even a semblance of stale conditions at the roots can rapidly prove fatal. They require semi-shaded exposures, and should be lightly fertilized at regular intervals. The Sievekingias are often rather difficult to grow for more than a single season, and are not recommended for the amateur collector. (I, H)

S. suavis Rchb.f.
Pbs. clustered, ovoid, rather angular, to 1¼″ tall, with several papery basal bracts. Lf. solitary, lanceolate or elliptic-lanceolate, acute or shortly acuminate, plicate, vaguely leathery, to 10″ long and 1¼″ wide. Infls. abbreviated, pendulous, 3–6-fld. Fls. usually less than 1″ in diam., complex, the ss. pale lemon-yellow, the ps.

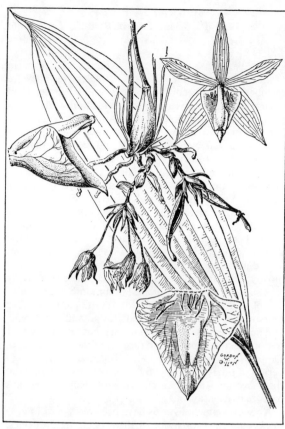

Sievekingia peruviana Rolfe ex C.Schw. [GORDON W. DILLON]

orange, the lip orange, spotted with reddish-purple, the col. green, with broad orange wings. Ss. subequal, spreading, the dors. one concave, the lats. concave. Ps. lanceolate, acute. Lip ovate or obovate-rhombic when expanded, rather boat-like, the lat. margins erect, the apex acute; disc with 3 prominent or obscure, erect keels, the central keel prolonged and ending in an inconspicuous 2-lbd. scale. Mostly June. (I, H) Costa Rica; Panama.

S. **peruviana** Rolfe. Rather similar to *S. suavis* Rchb.f. in habit, the pendulous infl. 4–6-fld., very short. Fls. about 1″ across, pale yellow, furnished outside with brownish scale-like hairs. Ss. and ps. elliptic, acute. Lip broadly rhombic, slightly 3-lbd., usually golden-yellow, obtuse at apex, with an apically 2-lbd. keel on the disc, and 9 ranked papillae-rows on each side. Feb.–Mar. (I) Peru.

SIGMATOSTALIX Rchb.f.

About twelve species of *Sigmatostalix* are known to date, all rather small but extremely unusual and interesting epiphytic plants, distributed from Mexico to Brazil. A member of the subtribe *Oncidiinae*, this group differs from allied genera in the unique structure of the small blossoms, which often rather superficially—with their typically elongate, arcuate columns—resemble those of a *Cycnoches*! Two species appear to be present in our collections at this time, both of them very rare orchids.

Nothing is known of the genetic affinities of *Sigmatostalix*, but presumably they are with *Oncidium* and other related genera.

CULTURE: These neat-growing little plants are best kept in smallish, well-drained pots, in a compost made up of equal parts of chopped sphagnum moss and shredded tree-fern fibre. The rather leathery foliage is susceptible to burning through too much exposure to bright light. Upon completion of the new pseudobulbs, a rest-period of about two weeks may be given the plants with benefit. Otherwise they should be kept continuously moist, and in conditions of high humidity. Periodic weakened applications of fertilizer seem beneficial. (I, H)

S. **guatemalensis** Schltr. (*Sigmatostalix costaricensis* Rolfe, *S. poikilostalix* Krzl.)

Pbs. rather clustered, bright green, elliptic-oblong, compressed, to $1\frac{1}{2}$″ long, with several foliose bracts at base. Lf. solitary, rather thinly leathery, ligular to elliptic-lanceolate, acute, contracted into a short petiole at base, $1\frac{1}{2}$–5″ long. Infls. 1–2 per growth, erect, slender, few- to many-fld., 5–12″ long, sometimes producing accessory branching racs. after the main rac. has finished flowering. Fls. to about $\frac{1}{2}$″ in diam. when spread out, the usually reflexed ss. and ps. pale green to yellow, more or less marked with brown. Lip usually reddish-brown with a dark yellow tip, rarely entirely yellow,

Sigmatostalix mexicana L.O.Wms. [GORDON W. DILLON]

439

with a distinct, narrow, fleshy claw at base, produced in front into a short, sharp-pointed spur, the blade of the lip abruptly dilated, rather obscurely 3-lbd., spreading or slightly convex, usually cordate, the lat. lobules small, usually with incurving projections from the posterior margin. Col. elongate, slender, rather curved, the apex shortly dilated on either side of the stigma. Mostly winter. (I, H) Mexico; Guatemala; Nicaragua; Costa Rica; Panama.

S. hymenantha Schltr.

Rather similar vegetatively to *S. guatemalensis* Schltr. Infls. slender, erect, shortly branched, to about 5½″ long, the branches usually very short and densely bracteate. Fls. tiny, usually less than ¼″ long, greenish and tan or pale brown, the ss. and ps. usually reflexed, oblong, acute; lip obscurely 3-lbd., the basal claw short, the blade ovate, obtuse, spreading or slightly convex, the disc with a fleshy, 2-lbd., transversely subreniform callus, with an obscure rounded tubercle in the centre of each of the lat. lobules. Col. stout, terete, erect, slightly dilated at apex. Winter–spring, often almost ever-blooming. (I, H) Costa Rica; Panama.

SILVORCHIS J.J.Sm.
(*Sylvorchis* J.J.Sm. ex Schltr.)

This is a genus comprising but a single known species, **Silvorchis colorata** J.J.Sm., a small saprophytic orchid from Java. It is a rather aberrant and very little-known member of the subtribe *Habenarinae*, which is not presently in cultivation, and in any event it seems to be primarily of scientific interest.

Nothing is known of the genetic ties of *Silvorchis*.

CULTURE: Possibly as for *Corallorrhiza*, although success with it under the artificial conditions of our collections seems rather doubtful. (H)

SMITHORCHIS Tang & Wang

A single rare species, **Smithorchis calceoliformis** (W.W.Sm.) Tang & Wang (*Herminium calceoliformis* W.W.Sm.) makes up this little known terrestrial genus. A member of the subtribe *Habenarinae*, indigenous to China, it is at this time not present in our collections.

The genetic affinities of *Smithorchis* have not as yet been ascertained.

CULTURE: Presumably as for the cool-growing Habenarias, etc. (C, I)

SOBENNIKOFFIA Schltr.

Three species of *Sobennikoffia* are known to date, all rare epiphytic orchids endemic to Madagascar. The genus is somewhat allied to *Perrierella* Schltr. and to *Oeoniella* Schltr., differing from them in technical details of the rather showy white blossoms. None of them appears to be in contemporary collections, though they are handsome plants, well deserving of attention by specialists.

Nothing is known of the genetic affinities of *Sobennikoffia*.

CULTURE: Presumably as for the tropical Angraecums. (H)

SOBRALIA R. & P.
(*Cyathoglottis* P. & E., *Fregea* Rchb.f., *Lindsayella* A. & S.)

Sobralias are only gradually assuming the place in orchid collections which they so richly deserve. They are members of an exceedingly complex and misunderstood genus of about thirty-five species which are widespread from Mexico throughout Central America to Brazil and Peru. A member of the subtribe *Sobraliinae*, the group is allied to *Elleanthus* Presl, but differs from that interesting but rather nondescript aggregation in its typically large spectacular flowers, which in many instances simulate—or even excel in beauty—those of a *Cattleya*. Variously terrestrial, epiphytic, or lithophytic, the species are strange orchids, vegetatively, with their reed-like stems supporting a few to rather many papery or leathery, heavily plaited leaves at intervals along their lengths. In some species, these stems reach sizeable dimensions, while others are dwarf in habit. The mostly large and showy flowers are borne either singly (but successively, over a period of a month or so), or in complex terminal racemes or even panicles. The blossoms of *Sobralia* are usually large and handsome, and occur in a wide range of colours, but unhappily they seldom persist in perfection for more than a day or two. Despite this failing, they are produced over a long period of time—often when flowers are at a premium in the collection—and their extravagant beauty never fails to attract attention.

About seventeen hybrids have been registered to date in *Sobralia*, two or more of them being natural ones, occurring in the wild state. Insofar as we are able to ascertain, none of these hybrids are still in cultivation, hence a tremendous field lies open to some enterprising breeder who wishes to work with these singularly handsome orchids. No intergeneric hybridization has as yet been attempted with *Sobralia*, and nothing is known concerning its genetic compatibilities.

CULTURE: Sobralias—despite an often-voiced comment to the contrary—are not particularly difficult to grow, provided one attends to their requirements with care. Their importation is extremely discouraging, since the plants seem particularly susceptible to the toxic gases used as fumigants by many countries today (including the United States), but if seedlings or mature plants can be obtained, success can almost be guaranteed. Although some of them are epiphytic in nature, under cultivation Sobralias should be treated as semi-terrestrials, being grown in a compost such as that recommended for Cymbidiums. Thorough drainage is extremely important, since these orchids are particularly intolerant of stale or sour conditions at the roots; as much as one-third of the pot or tub in which they are kept should ideally be filled with broken crock or brick to assure this. While actively growing, Sobralias need quantities of water, but when the new leafy stems have reached their full development, moisture should be somewhat lessened for a month or more to give them a bit of a rest-period. During the major growth-period, they benefit materially by liberal applications of weak manure-water or other moderate fertilizer. In the wild, many of them grow fully exposed to the tropical sun, and in the artificial climates of our greenhouses they do best if kept in a relatively bright spot; excessive shade will result in beautiful growth, but few—if any—flowers, since the stems have not had an opportunity to ripen thoroughly. One of the most important points to remember, when dealing with Sobralias, is not to disturb them any more than is absolutely necessary. Even repotting will in many cases set the plants back so far, that it will take several years for them to flower again. As a rule, these orchids are more floriferous if allowed to grow into large, 'specimen' plants, rather than divided regularly. Most of the Sobralias occur in warm areas, hence they require intermediate or warm temperatures at all times. (I, H)

S. decora Batem.

Sts. clustered, 12–30″ tall, with the lower surfaces of the lvs. and their sheaths more or less black-warty or fuzzy. Lvs. 2–9″ long, oblanceolate to narrowly lanceolate, long-acuminate. Infls. very abbreviated, 1–2-fld., terminal. Fls. fragrant, lasting one day, about 3–4″ across, the ss. (which have strongly recurved apices) and ps. usually white or blush-white, the large tubular lip rose-purple or lavender, streaked with yellow and brown on the disc, this covered with numerous branched veins, provided with many tiny lamellae which traverse it longitudinally. Spring–summer. (I, H) Mexico; British Honduras; Guatemala; Honduras; Nicaragua; Costa Rica.

—var. **aërata** Allen & Wms.

Differs from the type in technical details of the fls., which are often somewhat larger and differently coloured: ss. greenish outside, almost brick-red inside; ps. flushed brick-red with lighter margins and dorsal median line, inner surface brick-red with a white border; lip-disc brick-red with a median white stripe and the lat. margins white towards the base, lip-base deep red within. Mostly summer. (I, H) Panama.

S. dichotoma R. & P. (*Cattleya dichotoma* Beer, *Sobralia Mandoni* Rchb.f.)

One of the largest spp., the clustered, simple or sparsely branched sts. 6–12′ tall (rarely even more). Lvs. heavy-textured, oblong to oblong-lanceolate, long-acuminate, prominently nerved, rather rigid, 7–15″ long, 1½–3″ wide, Infls. axillary, ascending, dichotomously branched, slender, many-fld., the fls. opening successively over a long period of time, to about 8″ long. Fls. fleshy, fragrant, to more than 4″ across, outer surfaces whitish, inside varying from reddish to violet-red, sometimes whitish-rose or intense purple-red or red, the lip usually darker, its midlb. very undulate-crisped. Summer–autumn. (I) Colombia; Ecuador; Peru.

S. fragrans Ldl. (*Sobralia eublepharis* Rchb.f.)

Sts. smooth, flattened, rather slender, 7–15″ tall. Lvs. few, rigidly papery, oblong-lanceolate to narrowly lanceolate, acute or acuminate, somewhat toothed at tip, 2½–9½″ long. Infls. long-stalked, bearing 1–2 fls. at the apex, which is furnished with 2–3 bracts. Fls. fragrant, short-lived, 2¼–3″ across, yellowish-white, tinged with pink, the apical lip-margin crisped and deeply fringed, the disc with 9 raised lamellae that become fringed towards the lip-apex. Spring. (I) Guatemala to Panama and Colombia.

S. leucoxantha Rchb.f. (*Sobralia Powellii* Schltr.)

Sts. clustered, to more than 4′ tall. Lvs. elliptic to lanceolate, acuminate, smooth above, more or less scurfy on underside, 3–9″ long, the sheaths usually furnished with small dark warts. Infls. short, 1-fld., terminal. Fls. fragrant, short-lived, 4–6½″ across, the ss. and ps. white, the lip white with the throat yellow to orange, the margins wavy. Summer–early autumn. (I, H) Costa Rica; Panama.

S. liliastrum Ldl. (*Cattleya liliastrum* Beer, *Epidendrum liliastrum* Salzm., *Sobralia Elisabethae* Schomb.)

Sts. clustered, mostly naked below, smooth, 3–7′ tall and more. Lvs. narrowly lanceolate, acuminate, strong-nerved, 4½–8″ long and ½–1″ wide. Infls. terminal, gradually elongating, the rachis zigzag, bracted, producing about 10 fls. in succession. Fls. usually erect, opening well, fleshy, fragrant, short-lived, to about 4″ across, white veined with yellow, or rose veined with white, the flaring lip undulate-crisped marginally, chrome-yellow on disc, otherwise mostly rose or white, flushed with rose. Summer–early autumn. (I, H) Guianas; Brazil. ·

S. Lindleyana Rchb.f.

Sts. slender, to about 2′ tall. Lvs. elliptic-lanceolate to ovate-lanceolate, acuminate, 2–5″ long and to 2″ wide, the sheaths smooth. Infls. 1-fld., bracted. Fls. fragrant, fleshy, short-lived, about 3½–4″ across, the ss. and ps. white (often turning yellowish with age), the lip white with some irregular red spots on the disc, which is yellow basally, the apical part lacerate or crisped. Mostly summer. (I, H) Costa Rica; Panama.

S. macrantha Ldl.

Sts. tightly clustered, from a large mass of roots, 2–8′ tall or more, the lf.-sheaths smooth or rough-warty. Lvs. narrowly to broadly lanceolate, long-acuminate, rigid, 5–12″ long, ¾–3″ wide. Infls. several-fld., the fls. produced singly over a long period, this subtended by a large lf.-like bract. Fls. rather fleshy, short-lived, fragrant, highly variable in size and colour, 6–10″ across, usually rose-purple (a pure white form is known), with the very large, ornate, flaring-tubular lip white on the inside of tubular basal part, tinged centrally with yellow, the marginal area usually deeper than other segms. Spring–autumn. (I, H) Mexico to Costa Rica.

S. macrophylla Rchb.f. (*Cattleya chlorantha* Beer, *Cyathoglottis macrantha* C.Lem., *Sobralia chlorantha* Hk.)

Sts. clustered, compressed above, smooth, 3½–5″ tall. Lvs. rigidly papery, broadly oblong, acute or somewhat acuminate, strong-nerved, bright glossy-green, 6–8″ long and 2–3″ wide, the smooth sheaths somewhat angular, rather inflated in upper part of st. Infls. 1-fld., the fl. subtended by a single rather large lf.-like bract. Fls. sessile, not opening well, short-lived, fragrant, fleshy, pale yellow, the lip with crisped margins and a deep golden-yellow disc. Summer–early autumn. (I, H) ? Costa Rica; Panama; Brazil.

S. panamensis Schltr.

Sts. simple, branched, or producing new plants at nodes, furnished with red-brown scurfy material, to about 5' tall. Lvs. elliptic to broadly elliptic-lanceolate, acuminate, glabrous or vaguely furfurescent at base dorsally, 2–8″ long and $\frac{3}{4}$–2$\frac{1}{2}$″ wide. Infls. 1-fld., terminal, the fl. subtended by an often large lf.-like bract. Fls. fragrant, fleshy, short-lived, to about 4$\frac{1}{2}$″ across, purple to white, the large flaring, crisp-margined lip yellow in the throat. Summer. (I, H) Panama.

S. Rolfeana Schltr.

Sts. slender, to about 4' tall. Lvs. oblong-elliptic to elliptic-lanceolate, acute to acuminate, smooth, borne mostly near middle of st., reduced in size upwards, 2$\frac{1}{2}$–8″ long, $\frac{3}{4}$–3″ wide. Infls. 1-fld., terminal or sub-terminal. Fls. fragrant, fleshy, short-lived, often not opening fully, to about 5″ across when expanded, cream-yellow, the lacerate-margined lip with a lemon-yellow throat. Summer. (I, H) Panama.

S. rosea P. & E. (*Sobralia Rueckeri* Lind.)

Sts. robust, leafy throughout, near apex somewhat zigzag, to about 7' tall, smooth. Lvs. cartilaginous, oblong-lanceolate, long-acuminate, narrowed basally, strong-veined, 8–14″ long, 2–3″ wide, the sheaths somewhat roughened. Infls. terminal, erect, few–many-fld., the fls. opening successively (but several open at once), the rachis angled, 6–10″ long. Fls. opening well, fleshy, fragrant, longer-lasting than most other spp., 7–9″ across, pale rosy-lilac or purplish-rose, the large flaring lip crisped marginally, bordered with deep purple-rose, the throat yellowish-white. Summer–early autumn. (I, H) Colombia; Ecuador; Peru; ? Brazil.

S. violacea Lind. (*Cattleya odoratissima* P.N.Don, *Cattleya violacea* Beer)

Sts. clustered, 2–6' tall. Lvs. rather narrowly lanceolate, rigidly papery, long-acuminate, to 12″ long. Infls. several-fld., the fls. opening singly, subtended by several acuminate bracts. Fls. fragrant, fleshy, short-lived, about 6″ across at most, the usually reflexed ss. mostly deep rosy-purple, the broad, frilled ps. paler, the large flaring lip little-crisped marginally, rosy-purple there, the throat deep orange, with a zone of yellow beyond this. Mostly summer. (I, H) Colombia; Venezuela; Bolivia.

S. xantholeuca hort. ex Wms.

Sts. rather stout, leafy throughout, the lf.-sheaths pale green speckled with red-brown, to more than 6' tall. Lvs. oblong-lanceolate, long-acuminate, spreading and drooping, 6–12″ long, 1–3″ wide. Infls. 1-fld., subtended by several large compressed bracts. Fls. fragrant, fleshy, short-lived, 6–9″ across, yellow, the tubular lip with crisped margins, the throat golden-yellow, streaked with darker yellow. Summer. (I, H) Mexico (Chiapas); Guatemala.

S. callosa L.O.Wms. (*Lindsayella amabilis* A. & S.) Sts. slender, to about 1$\frac{1}{2}$' tall. Lvs. few, narrowly elliptic to linear-lanceolate, acute or obtuse, toothed apically, strongly folded, very glossy deep-green, 1$\frac{1}{2}$–4″ long, mostly less than $\frac{1}{2}$″ wide, the sheaths striate. Infls. usually 1-fld., from axis of uppermost lf. Fls. odourless, rather fragile, short-lived, to 2″ across, opening well, entirely vivid cerise. Summer. (I) Panama.

S. Lindeni W.Wats. Very similar in all parts, and perhaps referable to *S. liliastrum* Ldl., the fls. about 3″ across, rich rose-red. Spring–summer. (I, H) Ecuador.

S. sessilis Ldl. (*Cattleya sessilis* Beer, *Sobralia Galeottiana* Ldl.) Sts. clustered, leafy throughout, rarely branched, brown-red-granular, to 5' tall and more. Lvs. thinly cartilaginous, broadly oblong-lanceolate, acuminate, narrowed towards base, 4–9″ long, the sheaths roughened, the lf.-laminas brownish-grey beneath. Infls. terminal, producing several fls. over a long period of time, made up of numerous narrow, brown-spotted bracts. Fls. fragrant, fleshy, short-lived, to more than 4″ across, pale rose-red, the ss. and ps. somewhat reflexed, the funnel-shaped lip with the apical part frilled, recurving, intense rose-red, with a whitish tip. Autumn. (I, H) Guianas; Brazil.

S. suaveolens Rchb.f. (*Sobralia epiphytica* Schltr.) Sts. clustered, rigidly erect, to about 1$\frac{1}{2}$' tall. Lvs. elliptic to elliptic-lanceolate, acute, 2–8″ long, the sheaths glabrous. Infls. usually 2–3-fld., from axil of uppermost lf., bracted. Fls. fragrant, waxy, hooded, about 2$\frac{1}{2}$″ long, yellow, the darker yellow lip fringed, furnished with several lacerated, branching lamellae on the disc. Summer. (I, H) Panama.

SODIROËLLA Schltr.

A single species of *Sodiroëlla* is known to date, this the excessively rare **S. ecuadorensis** Schltr., which has apparently been collected on only one occasion on Mount Chimborazo, in Ecuador. A very peculiar epiphytic orchid, it rather simulates a *Stelis* or *Pleurothallis*, but upon examination of the racemose, inverted, fragile flowers, it is seen to be a member of the subtribe *Telipogoninae*, closest in its alliance to *Stellilabium* Schltr. At this time, *Sodiroëlla* is not present in our collections.

Nothing is known of the genetic affinities of this very rare genus.

CULTURE: Presumably as for *Telipogon*. (C)

SOLENANGIS Schltr.

Two species of *Solenangis* are known, **S. scandens** (Schltr.) Schltr. (*Angraecum scandens* Schltr.) and **S. clavata** (Rolfe) Schltr. (*Angraecum clavatum* Rolfe), neither of which appears to be in cultivation at this time. These are rather unusual and interesting epiphytic orchids of the subtribe *Sarcanthinae*, both native to tropical West Africa, with small white to greenish-yellow flowers. The genus seems to offer some possibilities to the connoisseur orchidist.

Nothing is known of the genetic affinities of *Solenangis*.

CULTURE: Presumably as for *Angraecum*. (H)

SOLENIDIUM Ldl.

Two species of *Solenidium* are known to date, both of them extremely rare epiphytic orchids, today to be encountered only in a very few specialized collections. Closely allied to *Oncidium* Sw., and rather simulating certain members of that genus, the Solenidiums produce rather numerous attractive flowers in most erect racemes, these produced from the bases of prominent pseudobulbs. One species appears to be endemic to Colombia, the other is from the Guianas.

Nothing is known regarding the genetic affinities of *Solenidium*, although they presumably lie with other members of the subtribe *Oncidiinae*.

CULTURE: As for pseudobulbous Oncidiums. *S. lunatum* is a lowland plant, while *S. racemosum* requires considerably cooler temperatures at all times. (C, I, H)

S. lunatum (Ldl.) Schltr. (*Oncidium lunatum* Ldl.)

Pbs. clustered, oval, rather compressed, to about 1½″ tall. Lvs. usually paired, ligulate or linear-ligulate, obtuse, rather leathery, 2½–5″ long, about ¾″ wide. Infl. usually erect, rather loosely many-fld., to about 10″ tall. Fls. about ¾″ in diam., the spreading ss. and ps. yellow, more or less mottled with brown, shortly ovate-spatulate, very blunt at tips. Lip about as long as the other segms., white, spotted with brown, with a basal, narrow claw, the lamina reniform, basally shortly hairy; crest 4-lbd., covered with papillose hairs. Summer. (I, H) Guianas.

S. racemosum Ldl. (*Oncidium racemosum* Rchb.f.)

Pbs. clustered, very compressed, ovoid, usually dull green, 2–3″ long. Lvs. usually paired, linear or linear-lanceolate, acute, rather thinly leathery, to 8″ long and about ½″ broad. Infl. erect, loosely 10–15-fld., to about 12″ tall. Fls. spreading, about 1″ in diam., long-lasting, yellow, more or less barred and blotched with brown. Ss. and ps. shortly ovate-oblong, shortly apiculate, the ps. somewhat the smaller. Lip with a broadly cuneate claw, the blade shortly ovate, obtuse; crests paired, oblong, whitish, hairy. Col. short and thick. Winter. (C, I) Colombia, at relatively high elevations.

SOLENOCENTRUM Schltr.

This is a very small genus of three or so species of rather nondescript terrestrial orchids of the subtribe *Cranichidinae*, the members of which are indigenous to Costa Rica and the Andes of South America. Structurally of considerable botanical interest, they are apparently very rare in the wild, and are not at this time in our collections.

Nothing is known of the genetic affinities of *Solenocentrum*.

CULTURE: Possibly as for *Spiranthes*. (I)

SOPHRONITELLA Schltr.

A single species makes up this genus, a segregate from *Sophronitis* Ldl., from which group it differs in vegetative structure and in details of the showy flowers. Occasionally represented today in choice collections, it is however a relatively rare orchid outside of its native Brazil, where it is a frequent and often almost ubiquitous epiphyte.

Sophronitella violacea has been used on only one recorded occasion in the production of a hybrid, this with *Epidendrum x O'Brienianum* to give rise to *Epiphronitella x Orpetii*, registered by Thayer in 1901. Always a rare hybrid, this now seems to have disappeared from our collections. Considerable potentials utilizing *S. violacea* with other allied genera of the subtribe *Laeliinae*, with most of which it is presumably freely compatible, seem evident to the enterprising breeder.

CULTURE: As for *Ornithocephalus*. The plants do especially well when kept in proportionally small, well-drained pots, in a shaded, constantly moist and humid spot. If allowed to grow into large specimens, they are spectacular in the extreme. (I, H)

S. violacea (Ldl.) Schltr. (*Sophronitis violacea* Ldl., *Sophronia violacea* O.Ktze., *Cattleya violacea* Beer)

Pbs. tightly clustered, erect, ovoid or narrowly ovoid, ½–1¼″ long. Lf. solitary, leathery, glossy, linear, acute, 1¼–3¼″ long. Infls. short-peduncled, 1–2-fld. Fls. opening fully, rather long-lived, somewhat variable in size and colour, usually about 1″ in diam., dark violet-rose, often suffused somewhat paler on the ss. and ps., the lip often darker, the anther-cap dark purple-red. Ss. and ps. spreading, narrowly oblong, acutish. Lip oblong, obtuse, about as long as the ps. Nov.–Feb. (I, H) Brazil.

SOPHRONITIS Ldl.
(*Lophoglottis* Raf., *Sophronia* Ldl.)

With the removal of the plant usually known as *Sophronitis violacea* Ldl. to the segregate group *Sophronitella* Schltr., true *Sophronitis* now contains six apparently valid species, all of them smallish epiphytic or lithophytic orchids, endemic to Brazil. The genus is a member of the subtribe *Laeliinae*, and at least two of its members are in cultivation today, although neither of them is a common plant. Rather dwarf, pseudobulbous plants, they vary considerably in appearance within the genus, bearing either small flowers in clusters, or proportionately very large, solitary ones. Under cultivation, the *Sophronitis* are often annoyingly refractory to maintain in good condition for any length of time.

One of the cultivated Sophronitis, *S. coccinea*, has been utilized on a great many occasions by the hybridists, to impart its exceptionally vivid scarlet coloration to the progeny in many instances, when crossed with such allied groups as *Cattleya* (= *Sophrocattleya*), *Laelia* (= *Sophrolaelia*), *Epidendrum* (= *Epiphronitis*), etc. Many of the finest of contemporary orchid hybrids contain *Sophronitis* in their make-up, in greater or lesser degrees. Considerable additional experimental breeding, with certain other allied genera of the subtribe, remains to be done, and the results promise to be fascinating in the extreme.

CULTURE: In the wild, *Sophronitis coccinea* usually inhabits trees in moss-hung, extremely humid, rather shady forests, at medium elevations. Under cultivation, it does best if grown in proportionately small, perfectly-drained pots, in a mixture of about equal parts of chopped sphagnum moss and finely shredded tree-fern fibre. A top-dressing of sphagnum moss is often used to good advantage. The plants—which are rather frail and often difficult to keep in good condition for very long—grow throughout the year, hence should never be given a rest-period. Because they need constantly high humidity, and quantities of water at the roots, it is extremely important that the compost drains thoroughly and readily; the slightest degree of staleness at the roots will cause the rapid deterioration of the plant. A rather shaded spot in the collection is suggested, although too much shade will result in poorly coloured blossoms. Periodic applications of weakened fertilizer are beneficial. *Sophronitis cernua*, a very dwarf plant, does well under approximately the same conditions, although it will stand almost full sun exposure, and delights in a brief rest-period upon completion of the new growths. (I, H)

S. cernua Ldl. (*Cattleya cernua* Beer, *Sophronia cernua* Ldl., *Sophronitis modesta* Ldl., *Sophronitis pendula* Hoffmsgg.)

Pbs. subcylindric, often somewhat flattened from the top, tightly clustered, usually forming large mats, about ½″ long, usually greyish-green. Lf. solitary, rigidly leathery, usually greyish-green, oval-oblong, obtuse, to 1″ long, often lying flat against the neighbouring pbs. Infls. terminal, abbreviated, 2–5-fld. Fls. to more than 1″ in diam., opening flat, variable in colour, usually vivid cinnabar-red, with the base of the lip and the col. orange-yellow. Ss. elliptic, acute. Ps. ovate, broader than the ss. and usually more vividly coloured. Lip ovate, acuminate, partly convolute over the col. at base. Autumn–winter. (I, H) Brazil.

S. coccinea (Ldl.) Rchb.f. (*Cattleya coccinea* Ldl., *Cattleya grandiflora* Beer, *Sophronitis grandiflora* Ldl., *Sophronitis militaris* Rchb.f., *Sophronitis rosea* Mort.)

Pbs. fusiform or rather cylindric-ovoid, 1–1½″ long, tightly clustered. Lf. solitary, oblong-lanceolate, rigidly leathery, usually dark glossy-green, short-stalked or sessile, 2½–3″ long. Infls. terminal, abbreviated, 1-fld. (very rarely 2-fld.). Fls. highly variable in size and coloration, 1½–3″ in diam., usually vivid glittering scarlet, with the base and lat. lbs. of the lip orange-yellow streaked with scarlet (forms with vivid carmine-purple or bright rose-purple fls. are known). Ss. elliptic-oblong, obtuse. Ps. about twice as broad as ss., oval or rhombic, obtuse. Lip 3-lbd., the lat. lbs. erect or partially infolding the col., the midlb. oblong, acute, concave. Col. usually white. Autumn–winter. (I) Brazil.

SPATHOGLOTTIS Bl.
(*Paxtonia* Ldl.)

Spathoglottis is a genus of about forty species, these widespread from southern China and the Himalayas throughout Malaysia and Indonesia to the Philippines, New Caledonia, and Samoa; the centre of development is in New Guinea, where more than twenty species are known. Allied to *Calanthe* R.Br., *Phaius* Lour., and other members of the subtribe *Phaiinae*, these are handsome, typically terrestrial orchids which are gradually gaining the recognition with collectors which they justifiably deserve. The plants bear prominent, usually ovoid, sometimes depressed pseudobulbs, these giving rise to a few folded, often narrow leaves. The tall, slender inflorescences arise from a basal leaf-axil, and bear a succession of small to rather large and handsome flowers over a period of many months. The structure of the blossoms is a characteristic one, not to be readily confused with any other related genus; the lip is strongly 3-lobed, with narrow lateral lobes (these lacking in one species) which are oblong and upcurved, the midlobe very narrowly clawed, and with two small ovoid calli at the base, and with two small laterally spreading teeth as accessories. The end of the lip-blade is more or less widened and sometimes cleft. The slender, curved column is footless. Floral colour in *Spathoglottis* is very extensive, ranging from brilliant yellow and pure white to crimson and several shades of magenta, purple, and mauve. Individually, the blossoms often are not particularly long-lived, but the profusion with which they are produced and the length of the blooming-season make these among the most charming and satisfactory of all terrestrial orchids. Several of the species are deciduous, losing their foliage during the dry season in their native haunts and blossoming when virtually leafless.

A large and beautiful series of interspecific hybrids has been raised in this genus, principally in Malaya, Thailand, and the Hawaiian Islands. Holttum comments:[1] 'All *Spathoglottis* species are freely inter-fertile, but most hybrids are very nearly sterile, when either selfed or crossed with a parent or other species. This has resulted in difficulty in raising second generation hybrids, where variation may be expected. Many crossings have proved seedless, or produced one or two seeds only in a capsule, and the seeds are then difficult to isolate. The fruits ripen in about six weeks after pollination. They are still green when they ripen, and must be watched carefully every day, or all seeds will be lost. The seedlings grow quickly, and should be ready to plant out in pots 4–6 months from sowing in flasks. Seedlings sometimes flower in 18 months from seed, and should not take much longer than 2 years if they are carefully tended.' The genus has also been bred with *Phaius*, the resultant hybrid being known as *Spathophaius*. It seems logical that *Spathoglottis* is also genetically compatible with such groups as *Calanthe* and possibly even *Cymbidium*, and some fascinating potentials are evident in critical breeding along these lines.

CULTURE: In warm areas, these handsome orchids do very well in specially prepared beds out-of-doors, in a compost such as that recommended for *Arachnis* and certain other climbing sarcanthad plants. When planting, care must be taken that the pseudobulbs remain above the ground-level. If grown in pots, perfect drainage is one of the most important factors. A rich mixture such as that suggested for *Phaius* is eminently satisfactory, with perhaps a little more chopped osmunda or shredded tree-fern fibre added especially for the occasionally refractory hybrids. After new growth is begun, frequent applications of fertilizer are of considerable benefit. The plants do best in full sun, or at least in a very bright situation. (I, H)

S. affinis DeVr.

Pbs. small, flattened, wider than high, irregular in shape, resting leafless during the dry season. Lvs. folded, to about 12″ long and ¾″ wide, sharp-pointed. Infls. erect, fine-hairy, many-fld., the fls. facing in all directions, slender, to more than 12″ tall. Fls. slightly more than 1″ across, yellow, with some purple streaks on the widened part of the lat. ss., the lip often purple-marked, with a broadened, notched end on midlb. Summer. (I, H) Burma; Thailand; Malay Peninsula; Java.

[1] In *Fl. Malaya* (*Orch. Malaya*)1: 166. 1953.

S. aurea Ldl. (*Spathoglottis Wrayi* Hk.f.)

Pbs. small, rather irregular. Lvs. narrowly lanceolate, acute, to 2' long and 1½" wide, the stalks 4–8" long, the sheaths (and sometimes also. the lvs.) purple-tinged. Infls. smooth, to more than 2' tall, loosely 4–10-fld., the fls. opening successively. Fls. to 2¾" across, rich deep golden-yellow, the lat. lbs. of the lip more or less flushed or spotted with crimson, the calli and midlb.-base with small crimson spots arranged in streaks. Ss. and ps. oblong, obtuse, about equal in length. Lip with small, narrow lat. lbs. and a narrow midlb. which is scarcely expanded near the pointed tip. Spring. (I) Malay Peninsula; Sumatra; Java.

S. Fortunei Ldl.

Pbs. small. Lvs. several, rather fragile, tightly folded, 6–8" long, to ¾" wide. Infls. slender, loosely 4–8-fld., to 12" tall, fine-hairy, with small bracts. Fls. about 1¼" across, the ss. and ps. golden-yellow. Lip 3-lbd., complex, the lat. lbs. red-spotted, the midlb. somewhat longer, with 2 thick calli on the disc. Winter. (I, H) Hong Kong.

S. ixioides (D.Don) Ldl. (*Cymbidium ixioides* D.Don, *Pachystoma Josephi* Rchb.f.)

Similar in habit to *S. Fortunei* Ldl., differing in the very narrow (less than ¼" wide) grass-like lvs. and the shorter, 1–3-fld. infls. Fls. about 1¼" across, the ss. and ps. golden-yellow, the lip golden-yellow with some red spots on the short lat. lbs. Summer–autumn. (I) Himalayas, often at relatively high elevations.

S. Kimballiana hort. Sand.

Similar in habit to *S. aurea* Ldl., but more slender and taller. Fls. to 3" across, the ss. and ps. pale clear yellow, the ss. strongly purple-flushed on reverse sides, the lip with some red dots on the midlb.-base. Lat. lbs. of the lip very wide, the apices rounded. Spring. (H) Borneo.

S. plicata Bl. (*Bletia angustata* Gaud., *Bletia angustifolia* Gaud., *Paxtonia rosea* Ldl. *Phaius Rhumphii* Bl., *Spathoglottis lilacina* Griff., *S. spicata* Ldl.)

Pbs. tightly clustered, ovoid to rather conical, often irregular, to 1½" tall, bright or dull green, strongly ringed. Lvs. sheathing basally, linear-lanceolate, acute or acuminate, to more than 2' long, 2–3" wide, folded. Infls. rather rigidly erect, to 2½" tall, the rac. rather densely 5–25-fld., with large, often pinkish bracts which are typically persistent, the fls. opening successively over a very long period. Fls. often self-pollinating, extremely variable in size, to a maximum of about 1½" across, the ss. and ps. violet-red or pinkish-purple, the lip with bright yellow basal calli, sometimes magenta-spotted medially. Ss. and ps. narrowly elliptic, acute, the ps. often somewhat incurved. Lip with small, semi-rhombic lat. lbs. and a long-clawed, linear midlb, which is strongly widened apically. There are many horticultural variants, differing largely in colour and size of the fls. Throughout the year, often almost ever-blooming. (I, H) Formosa; Philippines; Malay Peninsula; Indonesia; New Guinea; Caroline Islands; naturalized in Hawaii and to a degree adventive in South Florida.

S. Bensoni Hk.f. Pbs. small, clustered. Lvs. narrowly lanceolate, acute, folded, to 12" long. Infls. to about 20" tall, few-fld., the fls. rather distant, opening gradually over a long period of time. Fls. roughened outside, about 1" across, lilac, the lip with short, broad lat. lbs., the calli yellow, proportionately large, very close together. Summer. (I, H) Burma.

S. chrysantha Ames Pbs. small, ovoid, about ½" in diam. Lvs. narrow, to 2' long and ½" broad, rather persistent. Infls. erect, smooth, to more than 2' tall, the several fls. opening successively over a long period. Fls. to 2" across, dark rich yellow, the ss. and ps. about equal. Lip narrow, tapering towards base, dotted with red basally, the blunt lat. lbs. narrow, reddish-maroon basally, the midlb. apically retuse and obscurely apiculate. Spring. (I) Philippines: Luzon, at high elevations.

S. confusa J.J.Sm. Similar in habit to *S. Kimballiana* hort. Sand., the lvs. long-stalked (stalk to 12" long), the blades rather narrow, folded, to more than 2' long and 2½" wide. Fls. rather like the allied sp., to 2¾" across, yellow, the lat. lbs. narrower, the midlb. ¾" long and about ¼" wide near the apex. Summer. (H) Borneo.

S. Elmeri Ames Pbs. small, to about ½" in diam. Lvs. lanceolate, to 3' long and 3" wide, folded, deciduous before blooming-season. Infls. erect, few-fld. Fls. to almost 2" across, rich yellow, the ss. and ps. equal, the ps. obtuse at tips. Lip with oblong, rounded lat. lbs. and midlb. that is reniform at tip. Spring. (I) Philippines: Mindoro, Negros, at moderate elevations in the mountains.

S. grandifolia Schltr. Pbs. clustered, about 1¼" in diam. Lvs. 2–4, folded, elliptic, acuminate, stalked below, to 5' long and 10" wide at the middle. Infls. mostly erect, to about 6' tall, the rac. gradually elongating, rather densely many-fld., the bracts deciduous. Fls. more than 1½" across, violet-rose, the lat. lbs. of the lip darker, the calli on midlb. yellow. Winter–summer, perhaps almost ever-blooming. (H) New Guinea.

S. Hardingiana Par. & Rchb.f. Specific epithet often misspelled *Handingiana*. Pbs. clustered, small, rather conical. Lvs. paired, lanceolate, acute, to 7" long and ¾" wide. Infls. erect, to about 12" tall, the loose rac. about 8–10-fld., borne from pb.-base, the rachis red, soft-hairy. Fls. almost 1" across, the buds when unopened greenish, the expanded ss. and ps. clear white. faintly tinged with rose at the tips, the lip-calli marked with red and yellow, the col. rose, the anther-cap deep red-purple. Ps. much narrower than the ss., like them sharply recurved. Lip long, narrow, awl-shaped, without lat. lbs., the 2 calli borne at about the middle, proportionately large. Col. long, slender, strongly arched. Autumn–winter. (I, H) Burma.

S. Lobbii Rchb.f. Pbs. often subterranean, irregular, clustered. Lvs. paired, to more than 1½' long, linear-lanceolate, acuminate. Infls. erect, slender, 3–5-fld., to 2' tall. Fls. about 1½" across, yellow, the lip-calli darker yellow. Ss. and ps. broad, almost equal. Lip 3-lbd., the lat. lbs. obovate-oblong, the midlb. longer, narrow-clawed, suddenly dilated into an obcordate, flabelliform, smooth blade. Summer–autumn. (I, H) Burma; ? Borneo.

S. x Parsonsii Ames A natural hybrid, the parents presumed to be *S. plicata* Bl. and *S. Vanoverberghii* Ames. Rather similar to the latter parent in habit, the infls. with only a few fls. open at once. Fls. slightly smaller than in *S. plicata*, rather deep orange-salmon colour when first open, fading on second day to a paler shade. Ps. distinctly wider than ss., with very wide base. Lip with short midlb., this wide apically. Throughout the year, often almost ever-blooming. (I) Philippines: Luzon, in the mountains.

S. Petri Rchb.f. Pbs. conical, to 2″ tall, mostly greyish-green. Lvs. to 1½′ long and 2″ wide. Infls. erect, densely 10–15-fld., to more than 2′ tall, the bracts deciduous. Fls. about 1½″ across, light or dark rose-purple, the lip-disc dark purple, the callus large, hairy, yellow, spotted with red. Ss. and ps. broad, elliptic, apiculate. Lip 3-lbd., the lat. lbs. oblong, the very short-clawed midlb. oval. Spring. (I, H) Fiji Islands.

S. tomentosa Ldl. Habit as in *S. plicata* Bl., the lvs. narrower. Infls. to about 1½′ tall, the few-fld. racs. rather loose, the scape, bracts, and buds finely velvety-hairy. Fls. about 1¾″ across, purple-mauve (rarely almost white or yellow), the lip-lbs. darker, the tip of the midlb. with 2 widely spreading narrow halves, the calli and midlb.-base yellow with small dark purple or red spots. Autumn. (I, H) Philippines: Mindanao.

S. Vanoverberghii Ames Pbs. ovoid to rather cylindric, to 1½″ long. Lvs. folded, lanceolate, to 15″ long and 2″ broad. Infls. shorter than the lvs., produced after lvs. have fallen, minutely hairy, erect, 4–6-fld. Fls. to 1½″ across, vivid lemon-yellow, often with a few sparse dark red spots on the midlb. of the lip, the ss. soft-fuzzy outside. Lip clawed, the lat. lbs. hatchet-shaped, the midlb. flaring and retuse apically. Late winter–spring. (I) Philippines: Luzon, at high elevations.

S. Vieillardii Rchb.f. Similar to and closely allied to *S. plicata* Bl., but larger in all parts, the fls. to almost 2″ across, light pinkish-purple or mauve-purple, the lip-callus yellow, often red-spotted. Lip with broad lat. lbs., the midlb. broadly elliptic, the calli borne on the claw, small. Autumn. (I, H) New Caledonia.

SPHYRARHYNCHUS Mansf.

A single species of *Sphyrarhynchus* has been described to date, **S. Schliebenii** Mansf., a very rare epiphytic member of the subtribe *Sarcanthinae*. It is a rather interesting plant from Tanganyika Territory, which is not as yet present in our collections.

Nothing is known of the genetic affinities of *Sphyrarhynchus*.

CULTURE: Presumably as for *Angraecum*. (H)

SPHYRASTYLIS Schltr.

A genus consisting of but a single exceedingly rare epiphytic species, *Sphyrastylis* is today unknown in collections, and is in any event of principally botanical interest. **Sphyrastylis oberonioides** Schltr., a native of the Department of Antioquia, in Colombia, is a smallish plant rather simulating a member of *Oberonia* Ldl., although the genus is placed in the subtribe *Ornithocephalinae*.

Nothing is known concerning the genetic affinities of this group.

CULTURE: Presumably as for *Ornithocephalus*. (C, I)

SPICULAEA Ldl.
(*Arthrochilus* FvM.)

Sometimes referred to *Drakaea* Ldl., to which it is closely allied, *Spiculaea* is a genus of three species of rather uncommon terrestrial orchids—unknown in contemporary cultivation outside of their native Australia. Bearing very complex and unusually interesting flowers in loose racemes, they are of especial note

because of the freely mobile lip, which moves about in even the slightest breath of breeze.

Nothing is known of the genetic affinities of this interesting genus.

CULTURE: Presumably as for *Caladenia*. (C, I)

SPIRANTHES L.C.Rich.
(*Aristotelea* Lour., *Cyclopogon* Presl, *Cycloptera* Endl., *Dothilis* Raf., *Gyrostachys* Pers., *Helictonia* Ehrh., *Ibidium* Salisb., *Monustes* Raf., *Narica* Raf., *Sacoila* Raf., *Stenorynchus* L.C.Rich., *Stenorrhynchus* Rchb., *Synassa* Ldl.)

Approximately three hundred species are currently contained in the genus *Spiranthes* by most contemporary students, although certain of these are segregated by other orchidologists into a formidable number of other groups. These primarily terrestrial (rarely lithophytic or epiphytic) orchids constitute a group which is among the more exasperatingly complex and technical in the entire family, and almost every authority on the Orchidaceae exercises his own particular opinions concerning taxa in this aggregation; this has, perforce, resulted in an extraordinarily large synonymy for the various species, and since many of them are very incompletely known botanically, *Spiranthes* as a group stands in a condition of rather frightful confusion! Primarily indigenous to the temperate zones, many of them occur as well in the tropical regions, extending southward to Australia, Tasmania, New Zealand, and Chile. With tuberous or heavily fibrous roots, the leaves are usually rather insignificant; tremendous variability is found in the flowers, which are mostly borne in elongate racemes (these often notably arranged in an odd spiral fashion), and often it is exceedingly difficult to differentiate between the species when they are closely allied. The blossoms are usually rather small, typically tubular, and generally appear in shades of white or green, although a few subtropical and tropical species bear rather large flowers in shades of scarlet, orange, or yellow. Floral structure is remarkably complex, the formation of the column in particular being of primary diagnostic importance. The genus is the principal member of the subtribe *Spiranthinae*, differing from other groups primarily in technical floral details. Despite the size of the aggregation, remarkably few of the Spiranthes are to be found in any contemporary collections except a very few specialized ones which deal in the often refractory temperate-zone 'ground orchids'.

Several natural hybrids are known in *Spiranthes*, but otherwise nothing has been ascertained regarding the genus' genetic affinities. It seems possible that through interspecific breeding of some of the larger, brightly coloured, tropical species, some most interesting results could be obtained.

CULTURE: Most members of this highly polymorphic, cosmopolitan genus are excessively difficult to maintain in good condition for more than a brief period. Often the soil in which an individual specimen occurs is all-important, and unless this can be precisely approximated in the collection, scant success can be anticipated. Usually a well-drained, rather sandy soil is required, and when pot-grown in the greenhouse, the addition of chopped sphagnum moss and finely chopped tree-fern fibre often seems most beneficial. Perfect drainage is always obligatory, whether the specimens are being grown in pots in an enclosure, or outside in the garden or rockery. Acid conditions are often necessary for many of the North American species. Certain of the showier, tropical species may be grown with some moderate degree of success in a mixture consisting of equal parts of loam, chopped sphagnum moss, chopped tree-fern fibre, and gritty white sand. In almost all cases, a strict resting-period is required after the inflorescences die down, in order for the flowers to be produced with any degree of regularity. Temperature requirements naturally fluctuate markedly in this large genus, which ranges from snow-bound regions to hot tropical jungles. (C, I, H)

S. cernua (L.) L.C.Rich. (*Ophrys cernua* L., *Gyrostachys cernua* O.Ktze., *Gyrostachys constricta* Small, *Ibidium cernuum* House, *Spiranthes constricta* K.Schum.)

Pl. occasionally stoloniferous, the roots slender, fibrous. Lvs. mostly basal, often absent at flowering-time, linear to linear-lanceolate, acute to acuminate, 1½–10″ long. Infl. erect, downy-pubescent above, to almost 2′ tall, slender, the rac. densely fld., compact, spirally-arranged in most specimens, the bracts large. Fls. to about ⅜″ long, fragrant, rather short-lived, somewhat fuzzy outside, white. Ps. adhering to the dors. sep. Lip ovate-oblong, arcuate-recurved, usually constricted at about the middle and dilated at the apex, the margins crisped or erose, basal calli prominent, pubescent. July–Dec. (C, I) Eastern Canada (Nova Scotia southward) to South Florida, west to Texas and the Dakotas.

S. cinnabarina (LaLl. & Lex.) Hemsl. (*Neottia cinnabarina* LaLl. & Lex., *Stenorrhynchus cinnabarinus* Ldl., *Gyrostachys cinnabarina* O.Ktze.)

Roots tuberous, several in number, rather fusiform, large. Lvs. borne near base of st., distichous, conduplicate, oblanceolate to linear-lanceolate, subobtuse to shortly acuminate, to 9″ long and 1¼″ wide, rather heavy-textured. Infl. erect, fuzzy above with brown or white jointed hairs, to more than 3′ tall, the usually short rac. densely many-fld., with prominent bracts. Fls. tubular, rather long-lasting, to almost 1″ long, varying in colour from yellowish-orange to yellowish-scarlet, the segms. conspicuously recurved and flaring near apex, the ss. and ps. minutely papillose, the ss. sparsely pubescent on outer surface. Lip sessile, obovate-lanceolate to elliptic-lanceolate, narrowly long-acuminate above the middle, expanded and shallowly concave below the middle, thickened at apex, the disc with a longitudinal flat callus on each side at the base. Summer–autumn. (I, H) Texas; Mexico; Guatemala.

S. gracilis (Bigel.) Beck (*Neottia gracilis* Bigel., *Gyrostachys gracilis* O.Ktze., *Ibidium gracile* House, *Spiranthes lacera* Raf.)

Roots fasciculate, stout, short fleshy. Lvs. basal, fugacious, broadly ovate to elliptic or ovate-lanceolate, short-petioled, the lamina, ½–2½″ long and to almost 1″ wide. Infl. slender, sparsely pubescent above in some cases, 7–26″ tall, densely or loosely fld., strongly spiraled

Spiranthes cernua (L.) L.C.Rich. [BLANCHE AMES]

or sometimes secund. Fls. in a single rank, to ¼″ long, vaguely fragrant, white with a more or less bright green stripe on the centre of the lip. Lip oblong-quadrate to elliptic-oblong, with the apical margins crenulate to somewhat fringed-erose, the slightly grooved central portion conspicuously green; calli basal, short, erect. Spring–late autumn. (C, I) Nova Scotia west to Manitoba, Minnesota and Iowa, south to Texas and south-central Florida.

S. orchioides (Sw.) A.Rich. (*Satyrium orchioides* Sw., *Stenorrhynchus orchioides* L.C.Rich., *Spiranthes jaliscana* S.Wats.)

Roots fleshy, tuberous, mostly clavate, rather large. Lvs. basal, appearing after the fls., narrowly oblong to oblong-lanceolate, occasionally oblong-oblanceolate, obtuse to acute, glabrous, rather heavy-textured, 4–14″ long, 1–2″ wide. Infl. stout, glandular-pubescent, the rachis (including the fls.) usually covered with white scurfy scales, 1–3′ tall, the loosely or densely many-fld.

rac. often to about 2¼″ in diam. Fls. flaring-tubular, usually suberect, to 1″ long, varying in colour from almost white to brick-red or dark crimson. Ps. connate to dors. sep. Lip sessile, entire, sac-like in natural position with a pair of linear submarginal calli; disc pubescent below the middle and on the margins. Spring–autumn. (I, H) Florida; Bahamas; West Indies; Mexico throughout Central America to South America.

S. sinensis (Pers.) Ames (*Neottia sinensis* Pers., *Neottia australis* R.Br., *Spiranthes australis* Ldl.)

Lvs. few, basal, quickly withering, to about 3½″ long and ¼″ wide, linear-lanceolate, acutish. Infl. slender, to about 10″ tall, the densely many-fld. rac. spirally arranged. Fls. tubular, about ³⁄₁₆″ long or more, translucent white or tinged with rosy-mauve, the lip white with an apical flush of mauve, the col. green, the anther brown. Lip as long as the ss., apically rounded, the base concave, containing 2 spherical glands. Autumn. (I, H) Subtropical and tropical Asia to Australia and New Zealand.

S. speciosa (Jacq.) A.Rich. (*Neottia speciosa* Jacq., *Stenorrhynchus speciosus* Ldl.)

Roots clavate, clustered, rather large. Lvs. rather heavy-textured, elliptic, acute, stalked at base, to almost 7″ long and 2½″ broad. Infls. stout, erect, to about 2′ tall, sheathed, the erect, dense, somewhat one-sided rac. usually many-fld., with large bracts, the rachis red. Fls. tubular, the segms. with flaring tips, to ¾″ long, crimson or rosy-pink. Lip 7-nerved, fuzzy on the disc, shortly pubescent on lower face, concave, slightly saccate at each side on the base. Col. pubescent below the stigma. Autumn–winter. (I, H) Cuba; Jamaica; Hispaniola; Puerto Rico; Guatemala south to Colombia and Venezuela.

S. tortilis (Sw.) L.C.Rich. (*Neottia tortilis* Sw., *Ibidium tortile* House)

Roots long, slender, clustered. Lvs. (often absent) basal, semiterete to narrowly linear, 3–12″ long. Infl. erect, slender, to 2½′ tall, the dense rac. spiraled, formed of a single row of tiny fls. Fls. often fragrant, to about ¼″ long, white, marked on the central part of the lip-disc with green or yellowish-green. Lip variable in shape, often conspicuously constricted just above the middle, the apical margin crenulate-undulate, strongly recurved in natural position, the callosities slender or stout, mammillate. Nov.–July. (I) Florida; Louisiana; West Indies; Guatemala; Trinidad.

S. vernalis Engelm. & Gray (*Gyrostachys vernalis* O.Ktze.)

Roots coarse, fusiform, clustered. Lvs. basal or extending part way up st., usually ascending, linear to narrowly lanceolate, acuminate, often strongly keeled or semiterete, to more than 12″ long and ¼″ wide. Infl. stout or slender, copiously pubescent above, 7–36″ tall, the rac. densely many-fld., spiraled, the rachis and ovaries usually covered with a dense mat of reddish-brown hairs. Fls. usually fragrant, usually in a single rank, to ⅜″ long or more, yellowish or white, rarely marked on the lip with green, fuzzy outside, the lip fleshy-thickened, recurving in natural position, somewhat dilated and crenulate-wavy at apex, the basal callosities stout, incurved, pubescent. Jan.–Aug. (C, I) North-east Canada; south to South Florida; west to Texas and Mexico and Guatemala.

S. aestivalis A.Rich. (*Gyrostachys aestivalis* Dumort.) Roots usually 2, hairy, fusiform. Lvs. numerous, basal and cauline, linear-lanceolate, sheathing, almost distichous, 2–4″ long. Infl. leafy, rather stout, 6–12″ tall, the spiral, lax, many-fld. rac. about 3–5″ long. Fls. about ¼″ long, fragrant, pure translucent white, the lip oblong-ovate, the margins near tip slightly dentate. Summer. (I) Europe.

S. exigua Rolfe (*Hetaeria exigua* Schltr.) Roots tuberous, oblong. Lvs. obsolete. Infl. about 2½″ tall, very slender, clothed with a single imbricating sheath, the loosely few-fld. rac. about 1″ long. Fls. more than ¼″ long, pale green, faintly fragrant. Lip oblong, pointed, with tiny hastate lbs., the base with 2 tubercles. Mostly Aug. (I) China.

S. spiralis (Sw.) C.Koch (*Neottia spiralis* Sw., *Spiranthes autumnalis* A.Rich.) Roots several, oblong, or fusiform, hairy. Lvs. usually forming a rosette at base of st., numerous, ovate or ovate-oblong, tapering towards base, to 2″ long and ¾″ wide, rather dark green. Infl. to about 12″ tall, usually gracefully curving, rather slender, bracted, the spirally-twisted many-fld. rac. about 2–5″ long. Fls. about ¼″ long, fragrant, translucent white, the lip usually flushed with pale or rather bright green. Lip cuneate, usually entire at the tip. Autumn–early winter. (C, I) Europe; Asia Minor; North Africa.

STANHOPEA Frost ex Hk.
(*Ceratochilus* Ldl., *Stanhopeastrum* Rchb.f.)

Estimates of the total number of valid entities contained in the genus *Stanhopea* range from about eight to twenty-five or more, with something in excess of one hundred names having been proposed in the past. These incredible orchids are notably variable in colour, and floral shape, and students have long segregated many colour variants as distinct species. The range of this fascinating genus—one of the most extraordinary in the entire Orchidaceae—extends from Mexico to Peru and Brazil. Many of the species are still confused taxonomically, and virtually all of the plants in cultivation are mis-named from time to time. *Stanhopea* is a member of the subtribe *Gongorinae*, and is somewhat allied to *Paphinia* Ldl., *Houlletia* Brongn., etc. They are, in the main, easily grown and flowered, and when in bloom their remarkably large, waxy blossoms never fail to evince astonished comment. Unfortunately, in most cases, these frequently massive, highly fragrant flowers rarely persist for more than three days. Like many members of this subtribe, they are produced from the pseudobulb-bases and hang sharply downwards; the huge inflated flower-buds typically open with an audible snapping sound. Most Stanhopeas are epiphytic in habit, but a few species exhibit a predilection for rock outcroppings, and still others may be found growing in rocky soil on hillsides.

Hybrids are known in *Stanhopea*, but they are few in number, and extremely scarce in contemporary collections. According to the *Hybrid Lists*, seven are now registered, but one of these is indicated as *S. devoniensis*, an entity which we now consider a good species (not a

Serapias occultata Gay [GEORGE FULLER]

Sobralia leucoxantha Rchb.f. [H. A. DUNN]

Spathoglottis × *Parsonsii* Ames [REG S. DAVIS]

Sophronitis coccinea (Ldl.) Rchb.f. [GEORGE FULLER]

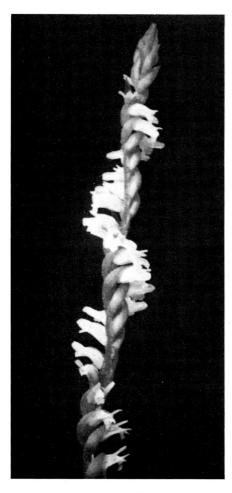

Spiranthes spiralis (Sw.) C. Koch
[GEORGE FULLER]

(ABOVE RIGHT) *Stelis cascajalensis* Ames
[GEORGE FULLER]

Symphyglossum sanguineum (Rchb.f.)
Schltr. [GEORGE FULLER]

natural hybrid), allied to *S. Hernandezii*. The others are *S. x assidensis* (*S. Hernandezii* × *S. Wardii*), *S. x bellaerensis* (*S. insignis* × *S. oculata*), *S. x Shinjik* (*S. saccata* × *S. Hernandezii*), *S. x Spindleriana* (*S. oculata* × *S. Hernandezii*), *S. x Wolteriana* (*S. Martiana* × *S. Hernandezii*), and *S. x Hesperides* (*S. inodora* × *S. Hernandezii*). Because of the confusion which has existed in the past regarding the identity of certain of the cultivated Stanhopeas (and which still exists to a large degree!), it seems probable that some of the parentages indicated may be erroneous. No hybrids have as yet been made between *Stanhopea* and allied genera of the *Gongorinae*, but a fascinating and doubtless profitable field of experimental breeding seems available in this direction, and should be explored.

CULTURE: The basic cultural requirements of Stanhopeas are readily met, even by the novice, hence these orchids are heartily recommended to all enthusiasts who delight in the unusual. Because of the strictly pendulous nature of the inflorescences, the plants must be grown in baskets or on rafts or tree-fern slabs; if they are kept in pots, the flower-spikes still grow downward, from the bases of the pseudobulbs, and may even attempt to open their mammoth buds within the compost, with naturally unsatisfactory results. Stanhopeas, for the most part, revel in intermediate temperatures, though warmer ones are not disadvantageous to any species save the very few from high elevations. While in active growth, the plants should be kept moist at all times, but upon completion of the new pseudobulbs, a resting-period of about a month—when no water is given at the roots—should be afforded them, to assure flower-production. A perfectly-drained compost is required, usually osmunda or tree-fern fibre. The plants should be kept in semi-shade at all times, since the foliage is rather prone to burning or yellowing if over-exposed to the sunlight. While growing, regular liberal applications of fertilizer prove beneficial. If the pseudobulb-clumps become excessively large, flowering is usually curtailed, so 'specimen' plants should in the main be avoided in this genus. (I, H)

S. devoniensis Ldl. (*Stanhopea Cavendishii* Ldl. ex Baxt., *S. maculosa* Kn. & Westc., *S. nigroviolacea* Morr. ex Beer)

Pbs. ovoid-conical, oblique, to 2½″ long and 1¼″ thick, with papery, fibrous sheaths at the base. Lf. solitary, rigidly leathery, plicate, oblong to elliptic-lanceolate, acuminate, stalked at base, including stalk to 1½′ long and 2½″ wide. Infls. pendulous, stout, 2–3-fld., with several papery spotted sheathing bracts. Fls. very fragrant, waxy, to about 4″ long and across, very intricate and variable in colour, the ss. and ps. pale yellow or yellowish-orange, spotted with reddish-brown, the huge lip ivory-white, stained and blotched with purple, the col. white, spotted with crimson. Lip very fleshy, the hypochil subrotund-globose, the inner surface with radiating granulated lines; mesochil with a pair of sharp, incurved, somewhat sulcate horns about 1″ long which meet at the base in a broad fleshy tubercle that projects at the base of the epichil and closes up the entrance to the hypochil-cavity; epichil ovate, somewhat canaliculate,

rather 3-toothed at apex, the teeth rather blunt. Col. with or without wings, if present very small. Summer. (I, H) Mexico; ? Guatemala.

S. ecornuta Lem. (*Stanhopeastrum ecornutum* Rchb.f.)

Pbs. ovoid, grooved, densely clustered, to 2½″ long, with several papery fibrous basal sheaths. Lf. solitary, plicate, rigidly leathery, broadly elliptic to oblong-elliptic, acute to subacuminate, stalked at base, the entire lf. to about 2′ long and 7″ wide. Infls. pendulous, 1–3-fld., the floral bracts large, inflated, deeply concave. Fls. very fragrant, waxy, to 4½″ across, the ss. cream-white, the ps. cream-white usually with some purple spots at base, the lip yellow, becoming orange-yellow at base and inside, the col. yellow. Dors. sep. oblong-squarish, truncate and thickened at top, convex, the lat. ss. oblique, deeply concave below. Ps. obtuse, convex. Lip simple, without horns, cymbiform-calceolate, compressed, obtuse, thick and very waxy, with several tumor-like swellings inside at the base and at apical margin of the interior. Col. rigid, cymbiform, grooved. Summer. (I) Guatemala; Honduras; Nicaragua; Costa Rica.

S. graveolens Ldl. (*Stanhopea costaricensis* Rchb.f., *S. inodora* Rchb.f., *S. oculata* (Lodd.) Ldl. var. *constricta* Klinge, *S. Warscewicziana* Kl.)

Pbs. ovoid to subconic, 1–1½″ long, clustered, becoming grooved and somewhat wrinkled with age. Lf. firm, plicate, lanceolate to elliptic-lanceolate, acute, 11–24″ long and 2½–4½″ wide. Infls. short, pendulous, with 1–6 fls., the rachis enveloped in several papery, spathe-like bracts. Fls. very fragrant, waxy, to 5″ long, variable in colour and somewhat so in structural details, varying from white to pale yellow or yellow with reddish-brown or purple dots, the ss. and ps. often with more or less circular rings of dark colour, the base of the hypochil with or without 2 lateral dark purple 'eyes' or blotches. Ss. and ps. rather membranaceous, the dors. sep. erect, concave, the lat. ss. and ps. reflexed, the ps. wavy-margined. Lip fleshy, complexly 3-parted, the short mesochil inserted on concave apex of hypochil, the lat. margins with 2 elongate, falcate, acuminate, incurved horns, the epichil jointed with mesochil-apex, its margins more or less reflexed. Spring–early summer. (I, H) Mexico to Brazil.

S. Hernandezii (Kth.) Schltr. (*Anguloa Hernandezii* Kth., *Stanhopea tigrina* Batem. ex Ldl.)

Closely allied to *S. devoniensis* Ldl., differing in the fls. to twice as large (to about 8″ across); in this sp. the inner surface of the hypochil is lamellated (not warty), the mesochil-horns arise from two roughened calli (not from a broad fleshy tubercle), the epichil is rhombic-ovoid with sharp apical teeth (instead of small, ovoid, with blunt teeth), and the col. is broadly winged near the middle (instead of slightly winged towards the apex, if at all). Summer. (I, H) Mexico.

S. insignis Frost

Pbs. clustered, ovoid to almost spherical, 1½–3″ long. Lf. rigidly leathery, plicate, oblong, acute at apex, narrowed into a stalk at base, 12–18″ long, 2¼–4″ wide. Infls. pendulous, loosely 2–3-fld. (rarely more), to 10″

long, with large bracts. Fls. pendulous, heavy-textured, very fragrant, to about 5″ long at most, the rather membranaceous ss. and ps. reflexed, yellowish-white to dull orange-yellow, more or less densely covered with round violet-purple blotches, the ps. wavy-margined. Lip pendulous below the other segms., very fleshy, the hypochil ivory-white, flushed, dotted, and blotched with dull black-purple and reddish-purple, the mesochil and epichil more or less spotted with same colour. Col. broadly winged towards apex, greenish with ivory-white wings, the whole organ more or less spotted with red-purple. Autumn. (I, H) Peru; Brazil.

S. oculata (Lodd.) Ldl. (*Ceratochilus oculatus* Lodd., *Stanhopea Bucephalus* Ldl., *S. cymbiformis* Rchb.f., *S. guttata* Koch, *S. guttulata* Ldl., *S. Lindleyi* Zucc., *S. oculata* (Lodd.) Ldl. var. *Barkeriana* Ldl., *S. oculata* (Lodd.) Ldl. var. *geniculata* Klinge, *S. ornatissima* Lem.)

Closely allied to, and mostly resembling *S. Wardii* Lodd. ex Ldl. Infls. 5–8-fld., pendulous, with several distichous inflated bracts. Fls. fragrant of vanilla, waxy, to more than 5″ across, variable in colour, the ss. and ps. usually yellow with large reddish-purple spots (rarely the ground colour is almost white), the lip-hypochil with a large reddish-purple blotch on each side, otherwise coloured like the ss. and ps. Distinguished from *S. Wardii* in having the hypochil transversely cleft below, thus forming a prominent hump just below the mesochil; lower part of hypochil cymbiform, the margins smooth and straight (not angular or toothed). Summer. (I, H) Mexico; British Honduras; Guatemala; Honduras; Nicaragua; ? Costa Rica; Panama.

S. Wardii Lodd. ex Ldl. (*Stanhopea amoena* Kl., *S. aurea* Lodd. ex Ldl., *S. Purpusii* Schltr., *S. venusta* Ldl., *S. Wardii* Lodd. ex Ldl. var. *aurea* Ldl.)

Pbs. clustered, ovoid-conical to rhomboidal, sulcate, somewhat compressed and angled, to 3″ long and 1½″ in diam., with fibrous papery sheaths at base. Lf. rigidly leathery, plicate, broadly obovate-elliptic to elliptic-lanceolate, abruptly acute, to 1½′ long and 6½″ wide, with a slender basal stalk. Infls. usually 3–9-fld., the fls. rather crowded, the sheathed peduncle long. Fls. very fragrant, to 5″ across, the ss. and ps. pale yellow, cream-white, or greenish-white, blotched or dotted with brownish-purple or reddish-purple, the hypochil of the lip orange-yellow or maroon with a large purple-brown spot on each side, the mesochil and epichil pale yellow. Ss. membranaceous, concave, the dors. one erect, the lats. reflexed, as are the wavy-margined ps. Lip very fleshy, the hypochil inflated, subsaccate, geniculate in profile, with a deeply emarginate, central constriction, with a more or less pronounced gibbose swelling about the middle of the lower surface, the lateral margins with falcate, acuminate thickenings; mesochil short, inserted on hypochil-apex, with 2 elongate, acuminate, incurved, falcate horns; epichil jointed to mesochil-apex, ovate, acute, concave, the margins somewhat reflexed. Col. broadly winged above. Differs from the closely allied *S. oculata* (Lodd.) Ldl. in the characters noted under that sp. Mostly autumn. (I, H) Mexico to Panama and possibly into South America.

S. eburnea Ldl. (*Ceratochilus grandiflorus* Lodd., *Stanhopea calceolatus* Drap., *S. calceolus* hort. ex Rchb.f., *S. grandiflora* Ldl.) Similar in habit to *S. devoniensis* Ldl. Infls. sharply pendulous, 2–3-fld., furnished with several large inflated sheathing bracts. Fls. extremely fragrant, very waxy, to more than 6″ long, ivory-white, the up-curving ps. often purple-dotted marginally, as are parts of the very complex lip. Col. very slender, with apical wings, greenish. Autumn. (I, H) Trinidad; Guianas; Northern Brazil.

S. grandiflora (HBK) Rchb.f. (*Anguloa grandiflora* HBK, *Epidendrum grandiflorum* HBK) Similar in habit to *S. devoniensis* Ldl. Infls. pendulous, loosely 4–5-fld., rather elongate. Fls. fragrant, to about 6″ long, the reflexed ss. and ps. orange-yellow sparsely dotted with purple-red, the pendent, extremely complex lip with an orange-yellow hypochil, on each side of which is a deep purple blotch, the remainder of the lip mostly orange-yellow. Autumn. (I, H) Ecuador; Peru.

S. Hasseloviana Rchb.f. Similar in habit to the other spp., the infls. 2–3-fld., including the peduncle to 10″ long. Fls. fragrant, heavy-textured, to more than 5″ long, the reflexed ss. and ps. pale rose-red, blotched with deeper rose-red, these blotches marginally even darker, the pendulous, complex, very heavy lip pale rose-red, dotted with purple, the broadly-winged col. pale rose-red, dotted with purple. Summer–early autumn. (I, H) Northern Peru.

S. Lewisae A. & C. Similar in habit to the other spp. Infls. 3–5-fld., drooping to pendulous. Fls. fragrant, waxy, to 4½″ across, the ss. and ps. cream-white flecked with purple or reddish-purple, the lip with the basal half deep yellow with rows of purple flecks, the densely red-flecked upper half whitish, the col. white. Differs from all other spp. in the extremely short lat. horns on the lip, which are terete and free only at the tips, as well as the rigid apical part of the lip. Summer. (I) Guatemala.

S. Martiana Ldl. (*Stanhopea implicata* Westc., *S. velata* Morr.) Rather similar to the other spp. in vegetative habit, the infls. pendulous, almost always 2-fld., short, furnished with several large sheathing bracts. Fls. pendulous, fragrant, to about 4½″ long, the ss. and ps. sharply reflexed, light yellow or almost white, sparsely blotched with purple, the lip-hypochil short, saccate, basally violet-purple, with warts inside, the mesochil with 2 rather broad acuminate horns, the epichil oblong. Col. narrowly winged. Autumn. (I, H) Mexico (Guerrero, Oaxaca).

S. platyceras Rchb.f. Habit as in the other spp. Infls. pendulous, 3–7-fld., rather long. Fls. sharply pendulous, fragrant, heavy-textured, to more than 6″ long, the sharply reflexed ss. and ps. pale yellow densely dotted with dark brown-purple, the lip pendulous, its epichil almost semiglobular, basally flushed with light violet-purple, spotted with darker violet-purple, the mesochil with 2 rather broad, large horns, the epichil broadly ovoid, obtuse. Summer. (I) Colombia.

S. pulla Rchb.f. Pbs. often almost black, usually wrinkled, ovoid, subconic, to 1¼″ long. Lf. plicate, rigidly leathery, elliptic-lanceolate, acute or acuminate, long-stalked, to 2′ long and 4″ wide. Infls. very short, usually 2-fld., the fls. facing each other, the bracts very large. Fls. the smallest in the genus, about 2½″ across, fragrant, the ss. pale yellow, the ps. slightly darker yellow, the lip tan marked and margined with red-brown, with a reddish-brown keel on the inner disc. Lip very fleshy and waxy, simple, the body composed of the hypochil, which is broadly inflated at the base and adnate to the col.-base, the lateral margins rather erect, the ventral surface of the hypochil broadly concave, the inner disc with

Stanhopea eburnea Ldl. [Hoehne, *Flora Brasílica*]

an elongate, rather prominent keel, terminating at the apex in a short, subcordate, acute, fleshy protuberance confluent with the hypochil-apex. Col. without broad lateral wings. Summer. (I) Costa Rica; Panama.

S. quadricornis Ldl. Vegetatively like the other spp. Fls. large, yellowish-orange, spotted with crimson, the lip with a large crimson basal blotch. Dors. scp. ovate-oblong, obtuse and minutely retuse at the tip; lat. ss. obliquely ovate, obtuse. Ps. elliptic-oblong, obtuse, undulate. Lip fleshy, the hypochil concave-saccate, with a pair of short horns arising under the col. and projecting forward over the saccate part (thus distinguishing itself from all other spp. in the genus); mesochil with a long pair of lateral falcate horns arising near the constriction and curved over the upper half of the lip; epichil broadly ovate, obtuse. Summer. (I) Mexico; Guatemala; Colombia.

S. saccata Batem. (*Stanhopea Marshii* Rchb.f., *S. radiosa* Lem.) Habit as in the other spp. Infls. 2–3-fld., pendent, the peduncle longer than that of most spp., the bracts spotted. Fls. fleshy, fragrant of orange-peel or cinnamon, to 4″ across, the ss. and ps. greenish-white or cream-colour, finely flecked with purple and brown, the lip with the deeply saccate base (hypochil) orange, the remainder coloured like the other segms. Ps. marginally undulate-crisped. Lip fleshy, waxy, the base terminating in 2 long narrow horns and a somewhat conduplicate 3-lobulate lamina; the horns arising on each side of the mesochil above the pouch linear-lanceolate, acute, falcate, bent slightly inwards; lamina (epichil) ovate-subquadrate, conduplicate, 3-lobulate at tip, the middle apiculate lobule shorter than the projecting obtuse lateral ones. Summer. (I, H) Mexico; Guatemala; El Salvador.

STELIS Sw.
(*Humboldtia* R. & P., *Dialissa* Ldl.)

Almost five hundred species of *Stelis* are known to date, all of them small epiphytic or lithophytic orchids of the subtribe *Pleurothallidinae*, distributed from Cuba and Mexico to Brazil and Peru, with particularly large development in southern Central America and in the Andes mountains of South America. This is among the most highly technical of all orchidaceous genera, and because of the customarily very small dimensions of the flowers, the fleshiness and pliability of the usually critically important petals, and the variability of the individual taxa, the group is still very incompletely known. These interesting, strictly 'botanical' orchids typically inhabit moist forests at moderate to high elevations, often being found in considerable numbers on mossy trees or, more rarely, on damp rocks. Many of the species have light-sensitive flowers, which open only when exposed to sunlight and which close more or less tightly during the night. Vegetatively, they rather simulate many members of the closely allied genus *Pleurothallis* R.Br., being as diverse as are those incredible orchids. In the majority of the species, the flowers (usually borne in elongate, dense racemes) are definitely triangular in shape, the sepals being markedly more developed than the tiny petals, lip, and column. In the section *Dialissa*, the blossoms considerably more simulate those of certain Pleurothallis, from which group they differ in technical details of the floral parts. Because of the generally very small dimensions of the flowers, most species of *Stelis* are seldom grown by enthusiasts. Almost all of them are, however, perfect little jewels when studied under a magnifying lens, and since they

are for the most part of facile culture, the very numerous members of the genus should be better known by specialists who deal with the myriad 'botanical' orchids.

No hybrids are known in *Stelis*, and nothing has been ascertained regarding its genetic affinities.

CULTURE: As for *Pleurothallis*, depending upon the place of origin of the individual specimen. (C, I, H)

S. bidentata Schltr.

Sts. abbreviated, clustered, sheathed. Lf. solitary, erect, linear or narrowly oblanceolate, obtuse and with 2–3 tiny apical teeth, somewhat oblique, basally narrowing, $1\frac{1}{4}$–3″ long, to $\frac{3}{8}$″ wide. Infls. erect, to $4\frac{1}{2}$″ long, loosely few-fld. slender, filiform. Fls. usually opening only at night (closing during the day), less than $\frac{1}{4}$″ in diam., purplish or white with a greenish, purplish, or reddish-brown suffusion. Ss. orbicular-ovate, obtuse, concave, 3-nerved, the lat. ss. coherent below the middle. Ps. cuneate to roundish-rhombic, broadly obtuse, concave, apically thickened. Lip fleshy, triangular-ovate, obtuse, 2-teethed apically, deeply concave in front and at base. Summer. (I, H) Mexico: Guatemala; Honduras.

S. ciliaris Ldl. (*Stelis atropurpurea* Hk., *S. Bruchmuelleri* Rchb.f., *S. confusa* Schltr., *S. Jimenezii* Schltr.)

Sts. to $1\frac{1}{4}$″ long, stout, sheathed. Lf. solitary, linear to elliptic-oblanceolate, obtuse and obliquely 3-toothed or retuse apically, tapering into a short petiole basally, erect, leathery, $1\frac{1}{4}$–6″ long, to $1\frac{1}{4}$″ wide. Infls. erect, loosely many-fld., slender, exceeding the lvs., with obliquely tubular reddish floral bracts. Fls. to about $\frac{3}{8}$″ in diam., often lasting rather well, extremely variable in shape, varying from deep maroon to purplish. Ss. broadly ovate to roundish-elliptic, rounded to acutish, mostly conspicuously ciliate on margins. Ps. broadly cuneate, flabellate or subreniform, thickened along solitary central vein and above, from a narrow base. Lip oval or ovate, subtruncate or obtuse and recurved at apex, fleshy, the lower margins upturned; disc with a mammillate callus on each side at base. Mostly spring. (I) Mexico and British Honduras to Costa Rica.

S. Endresii Rchb.f. (*Stelis parvibracteata* Ames)

Sts. slender, sheathed, to 2″ long. Lf. elliptic-ligulate to oblanceolate, obtuse to rounded at apex, leathery, usually without a petiole, 3–$4\frac{3}{4}$″ long, to $\frac{3}{4}$″ broad above the middle. Infls. loosely fld., to $9\frac{1}{2}$″ long, the infundibuliform, acute floral bracts shorter than pedicellate ovaries. Fls. opening well, lasting rather well, to about $\frac{3}{8}$″ in diam., varying from pinkish to reddish-green or purplish-red, rather similar to those of *S. leucopogon* Rchb.f., but differing in the lat. ss. with only 3 veins (not 5), and the differently shaped lip. Spring–summer. (I) Mexico to Panama, Brazil, and Peru.

S. hymenantha Schltr. (*Stelis cuspidilabia* Schltr., *S. seleniglossa* Schltr.)

Sts. densely clustered, often forming fascicles, rather stout, covered by 2 long tubular sheaths, $\frac{1}{2}$–3″ long. Lf. solitary, rather leathery, erect, linear-oblanceolate, obtuse and obliquely 3-toothed at apex, narrowed basally, $1\frac{1}{2}$–4″ long, to about $\frac{3}{8}$″ broad. Infl. solitary, loosely few- to many-fld., to 6″ long, the floral bracts tubular-cucullate, subobtuse to acuminate. Fls. slightly nodding, less than $\frac{1}{16}''$ long, pale greenish-white or greenish-yellow. Ss. connate near base, shallowly concave, 3-nerved. Ps. cuneate-obovate, thickened and subtruncate at apex, somewhat concave. Lip suborbicular-obovate with a prominent deltoid acuminate apicule, concave, the margins and apicule curved upward. Summer. (I) Mexico to Panama.

S. leucopogon Rchb.f. (*Stelis Bernoullii* Schltr., *S. cascajalensis* Ames, *S. eximia* Ames)

Large sp., the sts. stout, sheathed, $\frac{1}{2}$–6″ long. Lf. solitary, very thickly leathery, usually with a short broad petiole, narrowly elliptic to elliptic-oblanceolate, obtuse and retuse apically, sometimes oblique, $2\frac{3}{4}$–$6\frac{1}{2}''$ long, to $1\frac{1}{4}''$ broad. Infls. 1–2, stout, loosely many-fld., to 12″ tall, the floral bracts funnel-shaped. Fls. large for the genus, to about $\frac{1}{2}''$ in diam., appearing almost simultaneously and remaining open for only a short period during the day, but re-opening for several successive days, varying from purplish to greenish, the veins often darker. Ss. deltoid-ovate to rhombic-ovate, obtuse, fleshy, 5-nerved. Ps. broadly flabellate to cuneate, very thickened at apex, glabrous or somewhat glandular-puberulent. Lip squarish to subquadrate-obovate, somewhat obliquely truncate at apex, rounded beneath, with a tiny erect apiculate process on front margin, fleshy. Mostly summer, but sometimes more than once annually. (I, H) Guatemala; Nicaragua; Costa Rica; Panama.

S. purpurascens A.Rich. & Gal. (*Stelis Bourgeavii* Schltr., *S. Carioi* Schltr., *S. curvata* Schltr., *S. fulva* Schltr., *S. Purpusii* Schltr., *S. thecoglossa* Schltr.)

Large sp., the erect or ascending sts. clustered, $1\frac{1}{2}$–$7\frac{1}{2}''$ long. Lf. solitary, rather leathery, linear-oblanceolate, oblong to oblong-lanceolate, obtuse and retuse at apex, usually without petioles, usually oblique, 2–8″ long, to $1\frac{1}{4}''$ broad. Infls. 1–2, to 13″ long, loosely many-fld., the floral bracts ovate-cucullate, clasping the rachis. Fls. opening rather well, on curved pedicellate ovaries, to about $\frac{3}{8}''$ in diam., reddish-brown to purplish or purplish-green. Ss. orbicular-ovate to subrhombic, obtuse to subacute, adherent to about the middle, 3–6-nerved with the nerves mostly keeled on the outside. Ps. small, the apical margin thickened and more or less roughened. Lip fleshy, roundish to subreniform, broadly rounded or obtuse at apex. Winter. (I, H) Mexico; Guatemala; Honduras; El Salvador; Costa Rica.

S. rubens Schltr. (*Stelis Liebmannii* Rchb.f. ex Hemsl., *S. Tuerckheimii* Schltr.)

Sts. clustered, very slender, $\frac{1}{4}$–$1\frac{1}{4}''$ long. Lf. erect, rather leathery, narrowly linear-oblong, obtuse and minutely 3-toothed at apex, tapering into the petiole, $1\frac{1}{2}$–5″ long, to more than $\frac{1}{4}''$ broad. Infl. filiform, somewhat flexuose, to $8\frac{1}{2}''$ long, the floral bracts ovate-cucullate. Fls. tiny, about $\frac{3}{16}''$ in diam., on curved pedicellate ovaries, opening well, white or yellowish-green, tinged with purple. Ss. coherent below the middle, minutely papillose-puberulent on inner surface, the dors. one often somewhat recurved. Ps. fleshy, thickened on apical margin. Lip vaguely 3-lbd., arcuate with a sharply upturned acute tip, the lat. lbs. rounded and erect, the

midlb. narrowly lanceolate or triangular-cymbiform. Winter. (I) Mexico; British Honduras; Guatemala.

S. Alleni L.O.Wms. Large sp., the sheathed sts. $2\frac{1}{2}$–6″ long. Lf. solitary, leathery, elliptic to elliptic-oval, acute or obtuse, short-petioled at base, to $7\frac{1}{2}''$ long and almost 3″ broad. Infls. to 12″ long, bearing fls. to the base, often multiple, with large cucullate sheaths, the bracts infundibuliform. Fls. largest of the genus, nodding, not opening fully, to more than $\frac{1}{2}''$ long, almost black. Dors. sep. hooded, the lats. connate to their apices, cucullate and gibbous at apex. Ps. apically very thickened. Lip much like the ps., but smaller. Spring. (I) Panama.

S. crescentiicola Schltr. (*Stelis isthmii* Schltr., *S. praemorsa* Schltr.) Sts. clustered, less than $\frac{3}{4}''$ long. Lf. solitary, leathery, oblanceolate, acute or obtuse, narrowed into a petiole, to $3\frac{1}{4}''$ long and $\frac{1}{4}''$ broad. Infls. erect, somewhat flexuous, to 7″ long, very densely many-fld., the floral bracts infundibuliform. Fls. opening well, about $\frac{3}{16}''$ in diam., greenish or yellowish-green. Ss. covered inside with tiny warts. Ps. flabellate, not thickened at apex. Lip with a transverse callus through middle, the short apex incurved. Winter. (I, H) Costa Rica; Panama.

S. despectans Schltr. (*Stelis chiriquensis* Schltr., *S. nutantiflora* Schltr.) Sts. clustered, $\frac{3}{4}$–$4\frac{3}{4}''$ long. Lf. petiolate at base, the lamina $\frac{3}{4}$–$4\frac{3}{4}''$ long, to about $\frac{1}{4}''$ broad, linear-elliptic to linear-oblanceolate, the slender petiole to $1\frac{1}{4}''$ long. Infls. as long as or exceeding lvs. in length, loosely many-fld., sometimes multiple. Fls. on arcuate-decurved pedicellate ovaries, nodding, to about $\frac{1}{4}''$ long or less, pale green to yellow. Ss. adherent at base, the lower half of the dors. one concave, recurved above the middle, much longer than the strongly concave lats. Ps. concave, fleshy-thickened along apical margin. Lip with a thin membranous callus stretched across the lower half to form a hood. Summer. (I) Guatemala; Costa Rica; Panama.

S. gracilis Ames Sts. slender, erect or ascending, to $1\frac{1}{4}''$ long. Lf. rigid, pale green, linear-oblong to linear-oblanceolate, obtuse, somewhat oblique, 2–$5\frac{1}{4}''$ long, to more than $\frac{1}{4}''$ broad. Infls. very slender, filiform, rather flexuous, to 6″ long, with numerous rather scattered fls., the floral bracts tubular. Fls. often nodding, on slender pedicellate ovaries, usually less than $\frac{3}{16}''$ in diam., greenish-white. Ss. ovate, acutish, with revolute margins. Ps. cuneate, fleshy. Lip fleshy, somewhat concave in front; disc with 2 approximate calli in the middle. Summer. (I, H) Mexico; Guatemala; Honduras; Nicaragua; Costa Rica.

S. Hennisiana Schltr. Rather similar in habit to *S. ciliaris* Ldl., the lvs. with longer petioles, to almost 5″ long, rather leathery. Infls. erect, to 6″ long, rather densely many-fld., the fls. secund. Fls. opening rather well, about $\frac{3}{8}''$ in diam., very dark purple, often suffused with darker colour on lip. Ps. semicircular. Lip almost square. Spring. (I) Colombia.

S. micrantha (Sw.) Sw. (*Epidendrum micranthum* Sw., *Dendrobium micranthum* Sw.) Sts. $\frac{3}{4}$–6″ long, clustered, with striped sheaths. Lf. rather leathery, lanceolate-oblong to ligulate, obtuse or minutely toothed at apex, $2\frac{3}{4}$–$6\frac{1}{2}''$ long, to $\frac{1}{2}''$ broad. Infls. solitary or paired, to 6″ long, densely many-fld. Fls. not opening fully, about $\frac{3}{8}''$ in diam., the elliptical ss. pale green, the sub-quadrangular ps. dark purple. Lip dark purple, rather like the ps. in shape. Col. dark purple. Throughout the year, often almost ever-blooming. (I, H) Jamaica.

S. microchila Schltr. (*Stelis barbata* Rolfe, *S. bryophila* Schltr., *S. cinerea* Schltr., *S. costaricensis* Schltr.) Pls. small, the sts. to $\frac{3}{4}''$ long. Lf. erect, linear-oblanceolate to narrowly spatulate, obtuse and minutely 3-cusped at apex, tapering into a very short petiole, to 2″ long, usually oblique. Infls. rather densely many-fld., 2–4 times as long as lvs., filiform. Fls. opening well, about ¼″ in diam., reddish-brown or bronze-green. Ss. adherent at base, usually coarsely glandular-pubescent. Ps. thickened along apical margin. Lip small, fleshy, with 2 median and marginal falcate calli or lobes curving inward towards the centre of the disc. Autumn. (I) Guatemala; Costa Rica; Panama.

S. Miersii Ldl. Sts. clustered, sheathed, to about 2″ tall. Lf. leathery, shortly lanceolate-linear, to 2¾″ long and about ½″ broad. Infls. to about 6″ long, densely many-fld., usually rigidly erect. Fls. usually secund, about ⅛″ in diam., not opening fully, green or yellowish-green. Ps. small, almost reniform. Lip with an apicule at the tip. Winter. (I, H) Brazil.

S. ophioglossoides (Jacq.) Sw. (*Epidendrum ophioglossoides* Jacq., *Dendrobium ophioglossoides* Sw., *Stelis polystachya* Cgn.) Rather similar in habit to *S. micrantha* (Sw.) Sw., differing in the lf. being longer than the st. (to 4¼″ long). Infls. much longer than the lf., 1–3 in number, to almost 9″ long, rather densely many-fld. Fls. not opening well, to about ¼″ in diam. at most, 3-cornered when closed, the ss. greenish-yellow, tinged basally with purple, the ps. and lip dark purple. Throughout the year. (I. H) Cuba; Jamaica.

S. ovatilabia Schltr. (*Stelis cyclopetala* Schltr.) Sts. clustered, ¼–4¼″ long. Lf. erect, linear to linear-spatulate, obtuse apically, ¾–5″ long, to about ⅜″ broad. Infl. slender, to 4″ long, peduncled, rather densely many-fld. above, the bracts ovate-cucullate, clasping the rachis. Fls. small, opening well, about 3/16″ in diam., greenish-white. Ss. fleshy, broadly ovate to oval, obtuse. Ps. roundish to subreniform, oblique, fleshy-thickened at obtuse apex. Lip trulliform, subtruncate and usually auriculate at base, shallowly concave in front. Col. dilated at tip, almost twice as long as ps. Autumn. (I) Mexico; Guatemala; Costa Rica, usually at rather high elevations.

S. parvula Ldl. Sts. ascending or erect, to 1¼″ long, concealed by tubular loosely appressed brownish sheaths. Lvs. with a rather long petiole, ¾–2½″ long, the lamina linear to linear-oblanceolate, obtuse and 3-toothed at apex, abruptly tapering into the petiole. Infls. densely many-fld., slender, to 4″ long, the floral bracts proportionately large, amplexicaul-peltiform, the margins revolute. Fls. tiny, not opening fully, to about ⅜″ in diam., white, greenish-white to purplish. Ss. deltoid-ovate, adherent at base. Ps. truncate to obtuse and fleshy-thickened at obscurely warty apex. Lip ovate-subcordate or rhombic with obtuse angles and upturned lateral margins; disc with a tuberous callus on each side below middle, the calli coherent to form a transverse ridge. Summer. (I, H) Guatemala; Nicaragua; Costa Rica.

STELLILABIUM Schltr.

Stellilabium astroglossum (Rchb.f.) Schltr. (*Telipogon astroglossus* Rchb.f.) is the only known member of this rare and incompletely understood genus, restricted in its dissemination to the high Peruvian Andes. A segregate from *Telipogon* HBK, it vegetatively resembles certain members of that odd genus, but differs in the unique structure of the very small flowers. *Stellilabium* is not known to be in cultivation at this time.

Nothing is known of the genetic affinities of this exceedingly rare genus.

CULTURE: Presumably as for *Telipogon*. (C)

STENIA Ldl.

This is a very rare genus consisting of but a single species, **Stenia pallida** Ldl., a native of the Guianas and Trinidad, a member of the subtribe *Huntleyinae*, but perhaps not correctly placed there because of certain rather aberrant characteristics of the flowers. An epiphytic orchid, *Stenia* bears no pseudobulbs, the plants being composed of a rather folded series of thin, short leaves arranged in a loose fan, and short, one-flowered inflorescences. The blossoms are small, short-lived, rather waxy, and pale yellow in colour, the lip usually a darker yellow with some red spots on the inside. It is not an especially showy plant, but is of interest to collectors who specialize in the rarer 'botanical' orchids. It does not seem to be in cultivation at this time.

Nothing is known of the genetic affinities of *Stenia*.

CULTURE: As for *Huntleya*, *Bollea*, etc., although warmer temperatures are required. (I, H)

STENOCORYNE Ldl.
(*Adipe* Raf.)

A segregate from *Bifrenaria* Ldl., *Stenocoryne* consists of about twelve species of epiphytic or rarely lithophytic orchids of the subtribe *Lycastinae*, for the large part endemic to Brazil. The genus is perhaps closer in its alliance to *Rudolfiella* Hoehne and *Xylobium* Ldl. than to true *Bifrenaria*, though a few of the component species are occasionally grown in choice collections under the latter name. Attractive, pseudobulbous orchids with erect sprays of usually rather showy, complex flowers, the Stenocorynes should be better known by enthusiasts.

No hybrids have as yet been attempted in this genus, and nothing is known of its genetic affinities. It is probably compatible with such allies as *Lycaste*, *Bifrenaria*, and the like, and doubtless some most intriguing hybrids could be produced through critical experimental breeding.

CULTURE: As for the warm-growing Lycastes. (I, H)

S. leucorrhoda (Rchb.f.) Krzl. (*Bifrenaria leucorrhoda* Rchb.f., *Bifrenaria vitellina* Ldl. var. *leucorrhoda* Rchb.f.)

Pbs. borne at intervals along a creeping rhiz., conical-oblong, in age becoming markedly angular, to almost 3″ tall. Lf. solitary, stalked basally, the petiole to 6″ long, the lamina oblanceolate, acute, rather leathery, prominently veined, to 12″ long and 3″ broad. Infls. mostly erect, with 5–8 fls. near the apex, to more than 12″ tall. Fls. not opening fully, waxy, rather long-lasting, about ¾″ long, whitish-rose, the complex lip spurred. Summer. (I, H) Central Brazil.

S. racemosa (Hk.) Krzl. (*Adipe fulva* Raf., *Adipe racemosa* Raf., *Bifrenaria racemosa* Ldl., *Colax racemosus* Spreng., *Maxillaria racemosa* Hk.)

Pbs. clustered, egg-shaped, strongly angular, often mottled with dull brownish, to 2″ long. Lf. elliptic-lanceolate, acute, to 6″ long, glossy green, rather heavily leathery. Infls. with a slender peduncle, loosely 4–10-fld., erect, to 10″ tall. Fls. not opening widely, about ¾″ long, faintly fragrant, the ss. and ps. yellowish

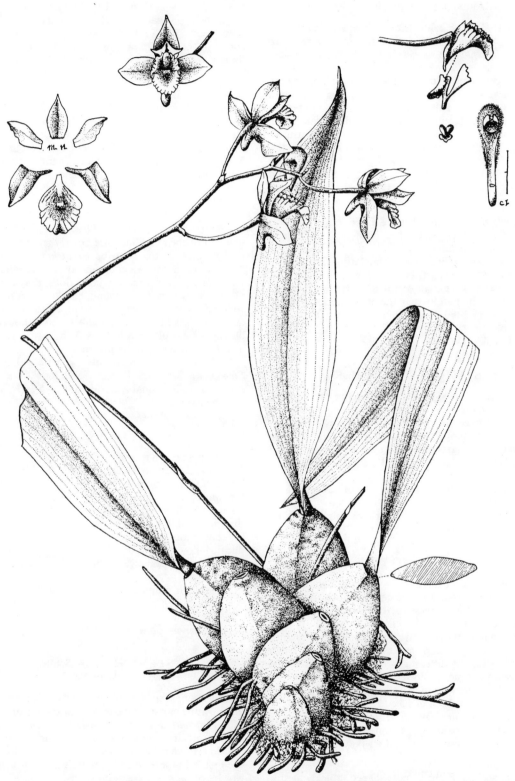

Stenocoryne racemosa (Hk.) Krzl. [Hoehne, *Flora Brasílica*]

to rich yellow, the lip white with reddish veins, wavy marginally. Autumn. (I, H) Brazil.

S. secunda (Vell.) Hoehne (*Epidendrum secundum* Vell., *Bifrenaria aureo-fulva* Ldl., *Maxillaria aureo-fulva* Hk., *Maxillaria stenopetala* Kn. & Westc., *Steno-coryne aureo-fulva* Krzl.)

Pbs. tightly clustered, prominently angled, often very dark brownish-green, to 1½″ tall, and almost as much in diam. at base. Lf. solitary, stalked basally, the petiole to 1½′ long, the lamina to 10″ long, oblong-lanceolate, acute, rather leathery, prominently veined. Infls. usually erect, 3–15-fld. in upper third, to about 12″ tall, slender. Fls. nodding, not opening well, to about 1″ long, brownish-yellow, sometimes more or less flushed and lined with dull red. Spring. (I, H) Brazil.

S. vitellina (Ldl.) Krzl. (*Maxillaria vitellina* Ldl., *Maxillaria barbata* Kn. & Westc., *Bifrenaria Harrisoniae* (Hk.) Rchb.f. var. *vitellina* Stein, *Bifrenaria vitellina* Ldl.)

Rather closely allied to and simulating *S. racemosa* (Hk.) Krzl. in large part. Infls. with slender peduncles, erect, loosely 5–8-fld., to about 8″ tall. Fls. about ¾″ long, opening more fully than the other species, orange-yellow, the lip 3-lbd., hairy inside, yellow, with a dark purple blotch in the throat. Col. whitish. Summer. (I, H) Brazil.

STENOGLOSSUM HBK

Stenoglossum coriophoroides HBK, the only known member of the genus, is a native of the mountains of Ecuador. It is nowhere common, and is evidently unknown in contemporary collections. Allied to *Epidendrum* L., it rather simulates a pseudobulbous member of that genus, but differs in structural details of the small flowers.

The genetic affinities of *Stenoglossum* have not been ascertained.

CULTURE: Presumably as for the high-elevation, pseudobulbous Epidendrums. (C, I)

STENOGLOTTIS Ldl.

This is a genus of three known species, two of which are occasionally found in choice collections today (the third, **Stenoglottis zambesiaca** Rolfe, from Nyasaland, is extremely rare and little-known botanically). They are charming terrestrial (rarely semi-epiphytic) orchids of the subtribe *Habenarinae*, somewhat allied to *Orchis* [Tournef.] L., but differing in technical details of the complex and attractive flowers.

No hybrids are known in *Stenoglottis*, and its genetic affinities have not been deduced.

CULTURE: As for *Cynorkis*. These orchids should be disturbed as infrequently as possible, and must be allowed a strict resting-period after flowering. (C, I)

S. fimbriata Ldl.

Roots subterranean, spindle-shaped, thickly fleshy, clustered. Lvs. 3–6, forming a loose rosette, oblong-lanceolate, green, usually with dark brown-purple irregular flecks over most of the surface, 2¼–4″ long,

often rather crisped and undulate marginally. Infl. erect, to 10″ tall, bearing a loosely 10–25-fld. rac. at the apex, the fls. opening gradually over a long period of time. Fls. less than ½″ long, pale or bright rosy-red, with some purplish spots on the lip. Ss. and ps. forming a hood over the long, three-tailed lip. Autumn. (C, I) South and south-central Africa.

S. longifolia Ldl.

Similar in habit to the other sp., but more robust, the entirely green or sparsely spotted lvs. larger, the infl. to more than 12″ tall, the rac. dense, many-fld. Fls. larger than those of the other sp., similar in colour, the lip 5–7-parted. Possibly only a stout variant of *S. fimbriata* Ldl. Autumn. (C, I) Natal; Zululand.

STENOPTERA Presl

About twenty species of *Stenoptera* are known to date, all of them medium-sized or rather robust terrestrial orchids of the subtribe *Cranichidinae*, native in Central and South America, mostly in the mountains. Unknown in contemporary collections, they consist of fibrous roots under the ground, basal clusters of mostly wide and leathery foliage, and tall, erect, usually very dense racemes of small but highly complex flowers. The blossoms typically measure less than one-quarter of an inch in diameter, and are inverted.

Nothing is known of the genetic affinities of *Stenoptera*.

CULTURE: Presumably as for *Spiranthes*, *Habenaria*, and the like. (C, I)

STEREOSANDRA Bl.

The only known member of this genus of the subtribe *Epipogoninae*, **Stereosandra javanica** Bl., inhabits the floors of forests in Sumatra, Java, Borneo, and parts of the Malay Peninsula. A rather small saprophyte (to about 1½′ tall at most), it is unknown in collections at this time, and, because of its habit, probably not suitable for cultivation. It is an interesting little orchid with complicated flowers—white, violet, and yellow in colour. *Stereosandra* is somewhat allied to *Epipogum* [Gmel.] L.C.Rich.

The genetic affinities of this peculiar genus have not been ascertained as yet.

CULTURE: Presumably as for other tropical saprophytes, such as *Galeola*, etc. (H)

STEVENIELLA Schltr.
(*Stevenorchis* Wankow & Krzl.)

Only a single species of *Steveniella* is known to date, this a rather nondescript terrestrial orchid of the subtribe *Habenarinae*, native to Asia Minor, the Caucasus region, and Iran. Rarely encountered in collections at this time, it is a rather slender plant which has in the past been placed in several different genera, but which seems worthy of rank as a separate genus.

No hybrids are as yet known in *Steveniella*, and nothing has been ascertained regarding its genetic affinities.

CULTURE: As for *Orchis*. (C, I)

S. satyrioides (Steven) Schltr. (*Orchis satyrioides* Steven, *Coeloglossum satyrioides* Nym., *Himantoglossum satyrioides* Spreng., *Peristylus satyrioides* Rchb.f., *Platanthera satyrioides* Rchb.f.)

Tubers usually paired, oval or oblong, about 1″ long. St. slender, about 12″ tall, clothed with a few sheaths. Lvs. paired, basal, elliptic or ovate-oblong, 2–4″ long. Infl. 2–4″ long, loosely few-fld. Fls. about ½″ long (exclusive of the spur), the ss. and ps. dull green, flushed with purple, the lip green, shaded with brown, covered with fine hairs. Dors. sep. oblong, blunt; lats. lanceolate, blunt, curved. Ps. narrowly lanceolate, curved, forming an open hood with the dors. sep. Lip 3-lbd., the lat. lbs. oblong, the midlb. spatulate, all lbs. finely toothed marginally; spur slender, curved, about 1″ long. Apr.–June. (C, I) Asia Minor; Caucasus Mountains; Iran.

STIGMATODACTYLUS Maxim.
(*Pantlingia* Prain)

This is a very rare and little-known genus of about four species of terrestrial, rather insignificant orchids of the subtribe *Acianthinae*, native in the Himalayas, China, and Japan. Somewhat allied to *Acianthus* R.Br. and to *Townsonia* Cheesem., none of the Stigmatodactylus appears to be present in collections at this time.

Nothing is known of the genetic ties of this obscure group.

CULTURE: Presumably as for *Caladenia*. (C)

STOLZIA Schltr.

A genus of four known species to date, *Stolzia* is an odd and exceedingly rare group of the subtribe *Stolziinae* (florally like the subtribe *Polystachyinae*, although the plants superficially resemble small Bulbophyllums), all very dwarf epiphytic orchids known only from very restricted localities in Tanganyika and elsewhere in adjacent central Africa. Insignificant little plants, they are exclusively of botanical importance, and are to date unknown in our collections.

Nothing is known of the genetic affinities of the genus *Stolzia*.

CULTURE: Presumably as for the very dwarf, tropical species of *Bulbophyllum*. (H)

SYMPHYGLOSSUM Schltr.

A single species of *Symphyglossum* is known at this time, a very attractive plant which has recently been introduced into cultivation. A native of the mountains of Ecuador, it has been grown in the past under its synonymous name of *Cochlioda sanguinea* Bth. It differs from true *Cochlioda* in technical details of the delicate flowers, these produced on a neat pseudobulbous plant which is normally epiphytic.

Symphyglossum sanguineum has been used by the breeders on six different occasions to date, under the name *Cochlioda*; several additional crosses are now in at least the flask stage with various persons. I have proposed the following hybrid epithets to accommodate these crosses accurately:[1] *Symphyglossonia* (*Symphy-*

[1] In *The Orchid Weekly* 4: 121. 1963.

glossum × *Miltonia*), *Symphodontioda* (× *Odontioda*), and *Symphodontoglossum* (× *Odontoglossum*). Additional experimental hybridizing with this unusual orchid would seem to be in order.

CULTURE: As for the high-elevation Odontoglossums, the cool-growing Miltonias, and the like. It seems to thrive under somewhat more intermediate temperatures than are usually requisite for these fine orchids. (C, I)

S. sanguineum (Rchb.f.) Schltr. (*Cochlioda sanguinea* Bth., *Mesospinidium sanguineum* Rchb.f.)

Pbs. clustered, ovoid, somewhat compressed laterally, usually rather pale green, to 1½″ tall, with some lf.-like basal bracts. Lvs. 1–2, linear, obtuse, rather soft-textured, to 10″ long and more than ½″ broad. Infls. arching to almost pendulous, rather slender, to 4′ long, often with more than 100 fls., the branches usually secund, producing fls. for more than one year in some instances. Fls. short- or rather long-lived, to more than 1″ long, rose-red, the col. and lip-base usually white or whitish. Ss. and ps. lanceolate-oval, acutish to obtuse, the lat. ss. joined for about half their length. Lip proportionately small, vaguely triangular, scarcely lobed, with 2 oblong lamellae on the disc. Col. partially adnate to the lip-base. Autumn–spring. (C, I) Ecuador.

SYMPHYOSEPALUM Hand.-Mazz.

The single known species of *Symphyosepalum*, **S. gymnadenioides** Hand.-Mazz., is an extremely rare terrestrial orchid, which has apparently been found on only a single occasion in China. It is a member of the subtribe *Habenarinae*, incompletely known by the botanists, and not present in our collections at this time.

Nothing is known of the genetic ties of this rare group.

CULTURE: Possibly as for the cool-growing Orchis, Habenarias, etc. (C, I)

SYSTELOGLOSSUM Schltr.

Two species of *Systeloglossum* are known to date, both rare and seldom collected, grass-like epiphytic orchids which are apparently endemic to Costa Rica. **Systeloglossum acuminatum** A. & S. and **S. costaricense** Schltr. have been described. The genus is a member of the subtribe *Oncidiinae*, near *Aspasia* Ldl., but seems rather aberrant in that aggregation. Neither of the species is known in cultivation at this time.

The genetic affinities of this rare genus are unknown.

CULTURE: Presumably as for the medium-elevation species of *Scaphyglottis*. (I)

TAENIOPHYLLUM Bl.

Taeniophyllum forms, together with *Geissanthera* Schltr., *Microtatorchis* Schltr., *Dendrophylax* Rchb.f., *Polyrrhiza* Pfitz., certain species of *Campylocentrum* Bth., and such African groups as *Microcoelia* Ldl., etc., a most remarkable aggregation of orchids. In these

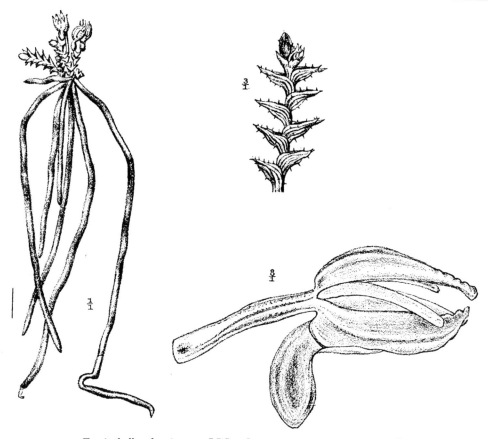

Taeniophyllum breviscapum J.J.Sm. [J.J.SMITH AND NATADIPURA]

plants the leaves (if they may be called that) are generally reduced to infinitesimal brownish scales, clustered on or around the often obscure prostrate or ascending tiny stem which is found at the centre of the radiating cluster of roots, which frequently extend several feet from the median axis of the plant. In these extraordinary 'leafless' orchids the processes of photosynthesis are carried out by the elongate roots which, unlike the vast majority of flowering plants, contain definite chloroplasts with their all-essential chlorophyll. Scarcely any research has been done on the physiological phenomena of these amazing orchids, and it is to be hoped that in future students will attack the problems which are evident in this respect. Approximately 200 species of *Taeniophyllum* have been described, most of them occurring in New Guinea, with outlying representatives extending as far distant as China and Japan, Tahiti, and Australia. A member of the complex subtribe *Sarcanthinae*, it is particularly allied to *Geissanthera* Schltr. and to *Microtatorchis* Schltr., from both of which it is differentiated by technical characters. *Taeniophyllum* is a very difficult genus, and one which is but little known by specialists. In the wild the plants are seldom common in a given locality, and it is usually difficult to find their diminutive root-clusters in any event, since many of them exhibit a predilection for the smaller twigs and branchlets of trees, where they grow among the dense foliage. Many of the species are known from only one

or two collections by botanists, hence the members of this group are extremely rare in cultivation at this time. Their cultural requirements, like those of most 'leafless' orchids, are not met with ease, and they are to be recommended only to the specialist who is willing to devote considerable attention to their rather refractory requirements.

No hybrids are known in *Taeniophyllum*, and its genetic affinities have not as yet been ascertained.

CULTURE: As for the leafless species of *Campylocentrum*. (H)

T. filiforme J.J.Sm. (*Taeniophyllum macrorhizum* Ridl.)

Roots long, more or less cylindric, often hanging free, slender, with distinct white spots beneath, to several feet in length, radiating. Infls. very slender, to 2½″ long, the rachis with 2-ranked, very close, overlapping bracts. Fls. produced successively, lasting one day, not opening widely, pale yellowish, about ⅛″ long. Ss. and ps. almost equal. Lip longer than the other segms., the blade slightly longer than the spur, slightly 3-lbd., concave, blunt; spur very slender at mouth, then swollen, the tip pointed. Mostly summer. (H) Malay Peninsula; Sumatra; Java; Celebes.

TAENIORRHIZA Summerh.

This remarkable genus consists of but a single species, **Taeniorrhiza gabonensis** Summerh., a leafless epiphytic orchid from Gabon, in tropical West Africa. Vaguely allied to *Chauliodon* Summerh. and to *Microcoelia* Ldl., it is a member of the complex subtribe *Sarcanthinae*. It bears flattened green roots, rather like those of a *Phalaenopsis*, and rather small, very complicated brown flowers on short inflorescences. It is as yet unknown in our collections.

Nothing is known of the genetic alliances of *Taeniorrhiza*.

CULTURE: Presumably as for *Polyrrhiza* and other aphyllous epiphytes from hot areas. (H)

TAINIA Bl.

Tainia is a rather confused genus of the subtribe *Collabiinae*, a group from which the genera *Ania* Ldl. (now placed in the subtribe *Phaiinae*) and *Nephelaphyllum* Bl. have been in large part removed. As now delimited, *Tainia* consists of about a dozen primarily terrestrial (rarely lithophytic or epiphytic) orchids which range from Formosa and Malaya to New Guinea. They are pseudobulbous plants, with petioled, plicate or rarely fleshy foliage, and often tall, erect inflorescences of frequently handsome flowers, of exotic coloration and unusual formation. These characters combine to make the Tainias of potential interest to collectors, yet but a single member of the genus appears to be present in cultivation at this time, and it is a singularly rare orchid. A critical revision of this entire aggregation of taxa is sorely needed, since the nomenclature has become almost incredibly confused during the past few decades.

Nothing appears to be known regarding the genetic affinities of *Tainia*, and no hybrids are on register at this time.

CULTURE: As for the tropical species of *Phaius*. (H)

T. latilingua Hk.f.

Pbs. clustered, often partially buried in the soil, narrowly cylindric, to about 2″ tall. Lf. solitary, with a slender petiole to about 6″ long or more, the lamina to 12″ long and 4″ wide, elliptic, acutish, plicate. Infl. basal, erect, to 2′ tall and more, with a many-fld. apical rac., the fls. usually all open at once. Fls. long-lasting, to 2″ across or less, the ss. and ps. greenish, flushed with purple, the lip 3-lbd., very pale yellow, usually pink basally, the lat. lbs. triangular, erect, the midlb. proportionately large, with vaguely dentate margins, 3-keeled. Col. with 2 reddish spots on the anther. Spring. (H) Malay Peninsula; Sumatra.

TAPEINOGLOSSUM Schltr.

A genus of but two known species, **Tapeinoglossum centrosemiflorum** Schltr. and **T. nannodes** Schltr., this group is restricted to the high montane forests of New Guinea, and is unknown at this time in collections. Allied to *Bulbophyllum* Thou., it is at once distinguishable by the unique structure of the flowers.

Nothing has been made known concerning the genetic ties of *Tapeinoglossum*.

CULTURE: Presumably as for the 'cloud-forest' species of *Bulbophyllum*, *Dendrobium*, etc. (C, I)

TELIPOGON HBK

Upwards of fifty species of *Telipogon* have been described to date, none of which is to be found in our collections at this time, since the plants appear virtually impossible to grow under artificial conditions. Inhabiting the high mountain 'cloud forests' of the region extending from Costa Rica to Peru, the largest number of species appears in Colombia. *Telipogon* is the principal genus of the subtribe *Telipogoninae*; its members are usually dwarf, delicate epiphytes without pseudobulbs, consisting of clustered or rather distant, often speedily deciduous little leaves, from the axils of which arise slender few-flowered racemes of extremely fragile but lovely blossoms, sometimes several inches across. The sepals are considerably smaller than the expanded petals and lip, and are often completely hidden by them, so that the flower appears to be an almost perfect triangle, consisting of only three parts. The petals and lip are broad and beautifully veined, these being often vividly coloured and roughened with hairs or other projections. The short column is typically covered with small barbs or spine-like protuberances. Colour is often brilliant, varying from golden-yellow to almost blue in the different species.

Nothing is known of the genetic affinities of this odd genus, at this time.

CULTURE: Since the swirling, chill mists of the tropical 'cloud forest' are almost impossible to emulate in the

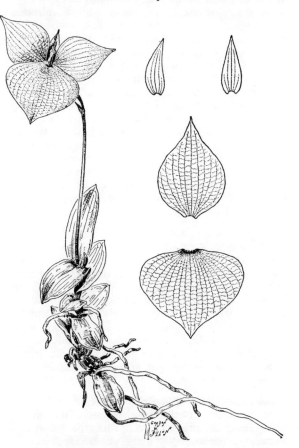

Telipogon Vargasii C.Schw. [GORDON W. DILLON]

collection, but scant success may be expected with these singularly refractory little orchids. They have occasionally been kept alive, for a year or so, in tiny pots filled with chopped osmunda fibre and chopped green sphagnum moss, in a special enclosure in the cool greenhouse, in which almost constant spray falls on them, and the humidity is saturated. They need considerable shade from bright light, as well. (C, I)

TETRAMICRA Ldl.

Tetramicra consists of about twelve known species, all found in the West Indies, where they range from the Bahamas to Trinidad. In the wild they usually occur as lithophytes on rocks, or grow in sandy places as terrestrials. A member of the subtribe *Laeliinae*, the group is very little known in contemporary collections, though several of its components are showy when in bloom. Small-bulbed (or bulbless) plants, usually with distinctly elongated, branched rhizomes, they mostly bear very fleshy and rigid leaves, often in small fans, at some distance from one another. The Tetramicras bear their often very attractive—and proportionately sizeable—blossoms on tall, wire-like, erect inflorescences. Coloration varies often within a single species, but is generally pretty.

Hybrids in which *Tetramicra* figures have been made in Hawaii with several genera of the *Laeliinae*, but as of this writing none of these have been registered.

CULTURE: Because of the usually elongate rhizomes of the plants, the Tetramicras are best cultivated in shallow pots or fern-pans, perfectly drained. A very porous compost of about equal parts of shredded tree-fern and small bits of gravel is suitable, or straight osmunda fibre can be used. Often xerophytic in the wild, these pretty orchids do not require as great quantities of moisture as do many of their allies—indeed, over-watering can quickly prove fatal. After flowering, they benefit by a rest-period of upwards of a month, though undue shrivelling of the vegetative parts must naturally be avoided. They do best in a bright spot, so that the succulent foliage turns reddish or purplish in colour. If well-rooting, they can be mounted on tree-fern slabs. Periodic applications of fertilizer are beneficial during times of active growth. (I, H)

T. canaliculata (Aubl.) Urb. (*Tetramicra rigida* Ldl., *Bletia rigida* Rchb.f.)

St. basally with several short, papery bracts. Lvs. few, heavily leathery, usually recurving, awl-shaped to semi-cylindric, canaliculate, to 6½″ long and only ⅜″ in diameter. Infls. erect, to 2′ tall, loosely many-fld. in upper part, the fls. opening successively over a lengthy period. Fls. showy, under 1″ in diam., lasting well, faintly fragrant, the ss. and ps. mostly greenish, flushed with purple, the very deeply 3-lbd. lip vivid rose striped on narrow-based midlb. with violet-purple. Spring. (H) Hispaniola to Trinidad.

T. eulophiae Rchb.f. (*Bletia eulophiae* Rchb.f.)

Pbs. obsolete. Lf.-tufts borne at rather distant intervals on the creeping, wire-like rhiz., the lvs. linear-cylindric, acuminate, 2½–8″ long. Infls. slender, erect, to more than 16″ tall, rather few- to many-fld., sometimes branched. Fls. about ⅓″ in diam. or more, the ss. and ps. greyish-red, the lip usually vivid rose-purple. Lip 3-lbd., the lat. lbs. ear-like, the midlb. long-clawed, rather broad apically, with an apicule. Spring–summer. (I, H) Cuba, where it is widespread.

T. parviflora Ldl. ex Rchb.f. (*Bletia parviflora* Rchb.f.)

Rhiz. elongate, wiry, bearing the lf.-tufts at rather distant intervals. Lvs. usually 2–3 per growth, linear, fleshy, semiterete, ½–1½″ long, ascending. Infls. terminal from the abbreviated stem, erect, slender, rigid, 7–16″ tall, with a rather loose few-fld. rac. in upper portion. Fls. about ⅕″ long, rather long-lasting, faintly fragrant, the ss. green, sometimes striped inside with fine lines of purplish-brown, the ps. usually pinkish-brown, the lip pink, or sometimes white, flushed with pink. Ss. 5-nerved, oblong, acute to obtuse. Ps. 3-nerved, linear-lanceolate, somewhat obtuse. Lip 3-lbd., much larger than other segms., the lat. lbs. broadly elliptic-ovate, the midlb. obovate. Col. erect, with 2 broad wings at sides of the stigma. Feb.–Apr. (I, H) Bahamas; Jamaica; Dominican Republic.

TEUSCHERIA Garay

This is a recently described genus of two species of very unusual and notably rare epiphytic orchids, one extending from Panama to Ecuador, the other apparently endemic to Venezuela. An aberrant member of the subtribe *Phaiinae*, it is noted as being somewhat vaguely related to the Asiatic genus *Acanthephippium* Bl. ex Endl., from which it differs in a great many details. Neither of the Teuscherias is as yet in general cultivation, though they are interesting plants.

Nothing is known of the genetic ties of this odd genus.

CULTURE: As for *Ornithocephalus*. Because of the creeping rhizomes, the plants should be kept in sizeable, shallow fern-pans or baskets. (I, H)

THECOSTELE Rchb.f.

Thecostele is a genus of about four or five species of seldom-seen epiphytic pseudobulbous orchids inhabiting the area from the Himalayas throughout Malaysia to the Philippines. Somewhat allied to *Acriopsis* Reinw., the species are today very rare in collections, and because of the small dimensions of the flowers, are of interest primarily to connoisseurs. 'The structure of the flower in this genus is very complex. The lip is attached to the short column-foot, and its edges are joined to an outgrowth from the column parallel to the foot and above it (the outgrowth is longer than the foot); the free blade of the lip curves upward at its base, closing the entrance to the tube, with the side lobes rising on either side; the column is curved right over so that its tip is above the entrance to the tube, and in *T. secunda* its arms bend downwards between the side lobes of the lip. At the bottom of the tube is a nectary, which presumably some insect is able to reach, and the end of the column is so placed that the insect will touch the anther, being partly guided by the side lobes of the lip and the column-arms.'[1] Two species of *Thecostele* may be found

[1] R. E. Holttum in *Fl. Malaya* (*Orch. Malaya*) 1: 553. 1953.

Thelasis sphaerocarpa J.J.Sm. [J.J.SMITH]

in particularly comprehensive collections, but they must be classed as very rare orchids.

Nothing has been ascertained concerning the genetic affinities of this odd genus.

CULTURE: As for the tropical Bulbophyllums. (H)

T. alata (Roxb.) Par. & Rchb.f. (*Cymbidium alatum* Roxb., *Thecostele Zollingeri* Rchb.f., *T. maculosa* Ridl., *Collabium Wrayi* Hk.f.)

Pbs. clustered, ovoid, flattened, with a few ridges, to $2\frac{1}{2}''$ tall and $1''$ wide. Lvs. 2–4, to $12''$ long and $2''$ wide, stalked at base, the apex suddenly narrowed to a broad point, linear, rather leathery. Infls. slender, arching or pendulous, to $1\frac{1}{2}'$ long, many-fld., branched. Fls. about $\frac{3}{4}''$ across, erect, the ss. and ps. pale yellow at base, white in the middle, light purple apically, with a few irregular purple or crimson spots, the lat. lbs. of the lip white, the midlb. white with a purple tip and large purple blotches in the middle. Ss. oblong, obtuse, the lat. ss. usually a little shorter than the dors. one. Ps. slightly shorter and narrower than ss., obtuse. Lip with a tube at the base, the narrow, erect, curved, convex lat. lbs. with 2 short keels between them, the midlb. convex, bent downwards,

finely hairy, the apex broad, slightly 2-lbd. Mostly autumn. (H) Himalayas throughout Malaysia to the Philippines and Borneo.

T. secunda Ridl. Pbs. flattened, about $1\frac{1}{2}''$ long. Lvs. shaped like those of the other sp., to $8''$ long and $1\frac{1}{4}''$ wide. Infls. rigidly down-pointing, up to 17-fld., the fls. all facing the same direction, to $6''$ long. Fls. about $1''$ across, pale greenish-yellow with purple markings, the ss. flushed with purple at tips and on mid-line near base, the ps. edged with purple and with purple on basal mid-line, the lip with the lat. lbs. purplish-brown, the midlb. finely hairy, with a purple V-shaped mark in the middle and some other irregular purple marks, the strongly curved col. deep purple-crimson. Autumn. (H) Malay Peninsula; Borneo.

THELASIS Bl.

Thelasis is a genus of upwards of ten species of rarely grown and rather insignificant but most interesting epiphytic orchids, native largely in Malaysia and Indonesia. A member of the small subtribe *Thelasinae*, the group is usually placed between *Oxyanthera* Brongn. and *Phreatia* Ldl., but differs from those genera in technical details. Only a single species seems to be present in cultivation at this time, and it is found in only the most comprehensive of collections.

The genetic ties of *Thelasis* are not known at this time.

CULTURE: As for the tropical Bulbophyllums. (H)

T. carinata Bl. (*Thelasis elata* Hk.f.)

Pbs. obsolete, the stems very short, clustered. Lvs. usually about 5 in number, to more than 12″ long, oblong, 2-lbd., sheathing at base. Infls. slender, erect or arching, with the rac. bent at an angle, densely many-fld. Fls. not opening widely, less than ¼″ long, white, suffused with greenish at segment bases. Summer. (H) Philippines; Malay Peninsula; Sumatra; Borneo.

THELYMITRA Forst.
(*Macdonaldia* Gunn. ex Ldl.)

This is a genus of somewhat more than fifty species of frequently spectacular terrestrial orchids, indigenous principally to Australia, but with outlying representatives in such areas as Java, the Philippines, Timor, New Zealand, New Guinea, and New Caledonia. Known in Australia and New Zealand as the 'Sun Orchids'—because of their habit of expanding the flowers only when exposed to the bright light of an especially sunny day—the Thelymitras are very rare in cultivation outside of their native haunts, though many of them are exceptionally showy plants, well deserving of greater attention. Producing generally tall racemes of handsome, wide-opening blossoms on graceful stems from subterranean tubers, these orchids are singularly 'unorchid-like' in appearance, all parts of the perianth being relatively similar in shape and size. Only the column is complex, being short and stout, with prominent lateral wings, the wings being united in front at the base and then either extending upward behind the anther (over which they form a hood) or else extending behind —but not above—the anther, or extending only on the sides of the anther. These column-wings are in all known cases furnished with a side lobe, which in many of the species terminates in a conspicuous tuft of hairs. Floral hue in *Thelymitra* is variable—even in a single species—but certain of the commoner Australian types produce blossoms which in many cases are a vivid blue, one of the rarest colours in the Orchidaceae. Like so many of the terrestrial groups, this is a genus which should be far better known by collectors.

No artificially induced hybrids are known in *Thelymitra*, and apparently natural breeding has not occurred. Genetic compatibility with other groups has not been explored, although it seems possible that multigeneric crossing should prove profitable and most interesting with other genera in the subtribe *Thelymitrinae*.

CULTURE: As for *Caladenia*. (C, I)

T. aristata Ldl. (*Thelymitra angustifolia* Hk.f. not R.Br., *T. grandis* FvM. ex Bth., *T. megacalyptra* Fitzg.)

Pls. usually about 12″ tall, rather slender. Lf. solitary, often very long and not very deeply channelled. Fls. in a rac., 3–8, to 1½″ across, pale mauve, fragrant. Hood of the col. smooth and yellow on top, shading to brown behind, emarginate or bifid in front, the tufts of hair white or pale pink. Autumn–winter. (C, I) Australia.

T. ixioides Sw. (*Thelymitra iridioides* Sieb. ex Bth., *T. juncifolia* Ldl., *T. lilacina* FvM. ex Ldl.)

Pls. slender to rather robust, to more than 2′ tall. Lf. rather large and broad, acute to acuminate. Fls. solitary, few, to numerous, to 2″ across, bright blue (rarely pink or white). Dors. sep. and ps. usually dotted with dark blue. Col.-hood 3-parted, with stick-like glands forming a double crest, the margins yellow; tufts of hair white; anther obtuse, its apex just above the bases of the penicillate lbs. Autumn–winter. (C, I) Australia; New Zealand.

T. venosa R.Br. (*Macdonaldia venosa* Ldl.)

Pls. slender, to 1½′ tall, the solitary lf. rather broad, scarcely reaching the infl. Fls. 1–10, about 1″ across, blue with conspicuous darker veins. Lip often prominently undulate on margins. Col.-wings not produced behind the anther, their lat. lbs. not penicillate nor dentate, but more or less spirally involute; anther very prominent, with a bifid apex. Late spring–summer. (C, I) Australia; New Zealand.

T. carnea R.Br. (*Thelymitra Elizabethae* FvM.) Pls. very slender, to 1½′ tall, the sts. dark. Lf. solitary, almost terete. Fls. expanding only in hot weather, rarely more than ½″ across, flesh-pink or pale red. Col.-wings not as high as the anther and not forming a hood, their lat. lbs. devoid of hair-tufts, but with a broad denticulate apex. Autumn–early winter. (C, I) Australia.

T. flexuosa Endl. (*Macdonaldia Smithiana* Gunn. ex Ldl., *Macdonaldia concolor* Ldl., *Thelymitra Smithiana* Hk.f.) Pls. very slender, to 7″ tall, the st. flexuous, the solitary lf. with a terete lamina. Fls. 1–3, very small, pale lemon-yellow. Col.-wings not forming a hood, their lat. lbs. short and dentate or occasionally entire. Autumn, mostly Aug.–Sept. (C, I) Australia, mostly in South and West.

T. pauciflora R.Br. Pls. variable, from 6″ to 1½′ tall, the lf. solitary, leathery. Fls. variable in size, often solitary or paired, sometimes more numerous, usually small and opening only in bright weather, the colour ranging from white to blue, pink, purple, or maroon. Col.-hood quite smooth, yellow on top, dark brown below, deeply bifid in front, the hair-tufts white, very abruptly bent upwards; stigma low on col., the anther prominent. Spring–early summer. (C, I) Australia; New Zealand.

THRIXSPERMUM Lour.
(*Dendrocolla* Bl., *Orsidice* Rchb.f., *Ridleya* Hk.f.)

Thrixspermum is a fascinating and complex genus of about sixty species of primarily epiphytic, monopodial orchids which are widespread in the area extending from Ceylon to Samoa, with particularly extensive representation in Malaya, the Philippines, and Indonesia. Some pertinent comments on the genus in Malaya are given by Holttum (in *Fl. Malaya* (*Orch. Malaya*) 1: 594–5. 1953): 'The principal distinguishing characters of the genus [from *Adenoncus* Bl. and *Arachnis* Bl.] are the column-foot and its firm junction with the lip, the saccate shape of the lip with the callus on the front wall of the sac, and the unequal pollinia on their very short stipes. . . . This genus includes a number of common Malayan species, many of them with graceful and attractive, though not very large, flowers. The flowers are unfortunately always very short-lived. Once an inflorescence has begun to bear flowers, it continues to produce them at intervals for several weeks or months, except in *T. calceolus*. In some species the flower-buds are certainly responsive to the stimulus of a sudden fall in temperature, like *Dendrobium crumenatum*, but the response seems not to be so regular, or perhaps to a slightly different stimulus. It is certain, however, that *T. calceolus*, *T. amplexicaule*, *T. arachnites* and other species are gregarious in flowering in the same neighbourhood. . . . The genus *Thrixspermum* is naturally divided into two sections according to the form of the inflorescence. These sections have been raised to the rank of separate genera, but they are so closely related in flower-structure that it is more natural to unite them. They are distinguished as follows: Section 1. *Orsidice*. Flowers two-ranked; Section 2. *Dendrocolla*. Flowers facing all ways. In the first section, *Orsidice*, most species . . . are easily distinguished by the large closely alternating laterally compressed bracts of their inflorescences', which rather resemble those of *Bromheadia palustris*. Two flower-types are found in this section, one with the sepals and petals long and narrow, the other with short, relatively broad sepals and petals; the flowers of this second group are much like those of many members of *Dendrobium*. Vegetatively the various species exhibit extremes of variation, some being rather elongate vine-like plants, while others possess abbreviated, leafy stems. Members of this genus—many of which are well deserving of attention by specialists—are today very scarce in collections outside of their native haunts. This is due, principally, to the lack of sources for specimens, and also due to the difficulty with which the plants are imported. When brought into the United States, for example, where they are subjected to fumigation on entry, it seems virtually impossible to bring them through in any semblance of good condition.

A single hybrid has been produced in Singapore, but seems to be unknown outside of Malaya; it is called *Thrixspermum x Eric Holttum*, named in honour of the learned author of *The Orchids of Malaya* and many other important studies on Orchidaceae; the parents are *T. amplexicaule* and *T. scopa*. It is presumed that these plants will prove freely inter-fertile with certain other genera of the subtribe *Sarcanthinae*, such as *Vanda*, *Arachnis*, *Renanthera*, etc. Resultant progeny should be of great horticultural interest.

CULTURE: As for *Vanda*, dependent upon the original habitat of the plant. (I, H)

T. acuminatissimum (Bl.) Rchb.f. (*Dendrocolla acuminatissima* Bl., *Sarcochilus notabilis* Hk.f., *Thrixspermum notabile* Ridl.)

Sts. to about 2″ long, the internodes short. Lvs. to 4″ long and less than 1″ wide, widest near tip which is bluntly pointed and slightly 2-lbd., narrowed gradually to the base. Infls. slender, to 5″ long, 1–4 from each nodes on the st.; rachis to 3″ long, about ¼″ across the two rows of bracts. Fls. about 2½″ across, the ss. and ps. yellow, flushed with red at the base, the ps. shorter than the ss., the lip pale yellow, red-spotted, the midlb. thread-like, with a white tip; lat. lbs. small, blunt, white-tipped; inside of sac spotted with red. Summer. (H) Malay Peninsula; Sumatra; Borneo; Philippines.

T. amplexicaule (Bl.) Rchb.f. (*Dendrocolla amplexicaulis* Bl., *Aërides amplexicaulis* Ldl., *Orsidice amplexicaulis* Rchb.f., *Orsidice lilacina* Rchb.f., *Sarcochilus amplexicaulis* Rchb.f., *Sarcochilus lilacinus* Griff., *Thrixspermum lilacinum* Rchb.f.)

Sts. to almost 3′ long, erect or clambering, slender, pale yellow-green, often with purple spots, with numerous long, flexuous, white roots, the internodes to 2″ apart. Lvs. to 2½″ long, usually less than 1″ wide, the base broad, cordate and amplexicaul, gradually tapered to a blunt notched tip, yellow-green, the sheaths much shorter than the internodes. Infls. slender, to 10″ long; rachis elongating to 5″ long, with prominent blunt or sharp-pointed bracts. Fls. wide-opening, about 1½″ across, varying from white to pale lilac, the lip-sac with a small yellow callus and an orange-red hairy patch below it, the lat. lbs. blotched with white and mauve, the midlb. white. Lat. ss. ovate, slightly decurrent on the col.-foot, broader than the dors. one. Ps. shorter than the ss., with rounded tips. Lip shorter than the ss., the sac prominent, the lat. lbs. small, pointed, with the ends curved forwards, the midlb. fleshy, blunt. Summer. (H) Malay Peninsula; Sumatra; Java; Borneo; Philippines.

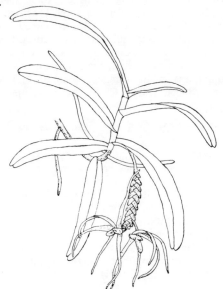

Thrixspermum arachnites (Bl.) Rchb.f. [A.D.HAWKES, AFTER HOLTTUM]

T. arachnites (Bl.) Rchb.f. (*Dendrocolla arachnites* Bl., ? *Thrixspermum papillosum* Carr)

Sts. to 8″ long, the internodes about ¾″ long. Lvs. fleshy, the young ones with some purple spots, especially on the sheaths, to 5″ long and ¾″ wide, usually widest in the upper half, narrowed to the base, the tip rounded and unequally 2-lbd. Infls. to 4″ long; rachis elongating to 6″ in length, with flattened, curved, imbricated bracts. Fls. about 3″ across, pale yellow, the lip white, spotted with orange-red near base. Ps. shorter than the ss. Lip proportionately small (about ½″ long), the lat. lbs. curved forward, blunt, the midlb. fleshy, laterally flattened, the sac purple-spotted inside, with a few hairs at the base only. Summer. (H) Malay Peninsula; Sumatra; Java; Borneo.

T. calceolus (Ldl.) Rchb.f. (*Sarcochilus calceolus* Ldl.)

Sts. elongate, to more than 4′ long, creeping or pendulous, slightly flattened, the internodes about ¾″ long. Lvs. fleshy, at right angles to the st., to 4″ long and 1¼″ wide, oblong, narrowed to the twisted base and to the unequally 2-lbd. apex. Infls. 1–3 at a node, to about 1½″ long, few-fld., the bracts overlapping, about ¼″ long. Fls. fleshy, fragrant, about 2″ across, white, the lip orange-yellow with a white tip and lat. lbs., the callus at front of lip white, with a yellow, orange-spotted patch below it. Ss. and ps. broader than in most spp., acute, the ps. slightly the smaller. Lip proportionally large, with a short, rounded sac, the lat. lbs. narrow, erect, the ends curved forward, the midlb. fleshy, bluntly pointed. More or less throughout the year. (H) Malay Peninsula; Sumatra; Borneo.

T. carinatifolium (Ridl.) Schltr. (*Sarcochilus carinatifolius* Ridl., *Dendrocolla carinatifolia* Ridl., *Thrixspermum batuense* J.J.Sm.)

Sts. to 7″ long, flattened, the internodes abbreviated. Lvs. to 2½″ long and ¾″ wide, the apex broadly rounded and unequally 2-lbd., the base narrowed almost to a short stalk. Infls. to 5″ long; rachis to 2″ long, the bracts acute, not very close together. Fls. about ½″ across, white or faintly yellowish. Ss. and ps. rather narrow, the lat. ss. with the lower edge suddenly curved upwards above the much widened base. Lip with the sac curved, conical, the lat. lbs. narrow, curved, the midlb. shorter, broad and blunt, the callus rounded. Summer. (H) Malay Peninsula; Sumatra; Java; Christmas Island; apparently always near the sea.

T. hainanense (Rolfe) Schltr. (*Sarcochilus hainanensis* Rolfe)

Sts. erect, to 12″ tall, rather densely leafy. Lvs. to 5″ long, ligulate, obtuse. Infls. erect or arching, to about 8″ long, the bracts closely compressed, the fls. rather numerous. Fls about 3½″ across, the ss. and ps. light yellow, the lip white, spotted with yellow. Ss. and ps. long-acuminate from a lanceolate base. Lip about ¾″ long, with a yellow transverse stripe at the apex of the sac and below it, the sac rather long, the lat. lbs. short, finely papillose, the midlb. also slightly papillose, ovate, obtuse. Summer–autumn. (H) Hainan Island.

T. pardale (Ridl.) Schltr. (*Dendrocolla pardalis* Ridl.)

Sts. slender, to 10″ long, the internodes to about ¾″ long. Lvs. to 3″ long and rarely as wide as ¾″, narrowed to base and the unequally 2-lbd. apex. Infls. slender, to 10″ long; rachis elongating to 2″, the bracts very close together, narrowed to a slender tip, ascending (except the lowest ones). Fls. about ½″ across, cream or nearly white with deep purple spots. Dors. sep. widest in upper half, the lat. ss. slightly wider. Ps. smaller than the ss. Lip deeply saccate, the lat. lbs. erect, rounded, merging forwards into the short rounded midlb.; the whole inside and edges of the lip conspicuously hairy. Summer. (H) Malay Peninsula; Sumatra; Borneo.

T. Raciborskii J.J.Sm.

Rather similar in habit to *T. hainanense* (Rolfe) Schltr., but somewhat more robust, the infls. to 8″ long. Fls. to almost 8″ across, pale yellow, the lip light yellow, spotted with red-brown in the middle and on the sac. Ss. and ps. linear, long-caudate, the ps. somewhat the shorter. Lip similar in structure to that of *T. hainanense* (Rolfe) Schltr., the sac oblong, obtuse, the lat. lbs. very short, dentiform, the midlb. oblong, obtuse, fleshy, open in the middle, with a short apicule. Spring–autumn. (H) Sumatra.

T. scopa (Hk.f.) Holtt. (*Sarcochilus scopa* Hk.f.)

Sts. long, climbing, the internodes to 2″ long. Lvs. to 3″ long and 1″ wide, oblong or widest near the base, the apex rounded and 2-lbd. Infls. very variable, from 2–8″ long; rachis with bracts about ½″ wide, the internodes about ¼″ long, the bracts strongly curved. Fls. to almost 6″ across, pale yellow, the lip similar to that of *T. arachnites* (Bl.) Rchb.f. Ss. longer than the thread-tipped ps. Summer. (H) Malay Peninsula.

T. trichoglottis (Hk.f.) O.Ktze. (*Sarcochilus trichoglottis* Hk.f., *Dendrocolla trichoglottis* Ridl.)

Sts. to 10″ long, slender, the internodes to about ½″ long. Lvs. leathery, to 2½″ long and less than ½″ wide, widest near the rounded, unequally 2-lbd. apex. Infls. many, often 2 to a node, the peduncles to 2½″ long, the rachis to 1½″ long, the bracts close, stiff, less than ¼″ long. Fls. about ½″ across, pale yellowish, with some yellow-brown or orange spots on the lat. lbs. (and sometimes on the outside of the midlb.) of the lip, the callus orange. Dors. sep. widest above the middle; lat. ss. slightly wider, widest below the middle. Ps. narrower than the ss. Lip with the sac less than ¼″ deep, the lat. lbs. erect, rounded, the midlb. very short, triangular; edges of the lbs. and the interior of the sac clubbed-hairy, the longest hairs on the lat. lbs.; callus broad, low. Summer. (H) Malay Peninsula; Sumatra; Java; Borneo.

T. aberrans Schltr. Sts. very dwarf, less than 1″ long, densely leafy. Lvs. erect-spreading, ligulate, to 1½″ long. Infls. to 3″ long, filiform, the bracts of the rachis compressed, imbricate. Fls. among the smallest in the genus, less than ½″ across, whitish, flecked with orange-yellow. Spring. (H) New Guinea.

T. album (Ridl.) Schltr. (*Dendrocolla alba* Ridl.) Sts. to 4″ long. Lvs. to 4″ long, narrowed a little to the 2-lbd. tip, the lvs. acute. Infls. to 6″ long, the rachis very abbreviated, the bracts acutely pointed. Fls. 1–4 together, to ¾″ across, white or pale yellowish, the callus with a small orange spot, the sac brown-spotted inside; lip rather long-hairy. Summer. (H) Malay Peninsula; Sumatra.

T. brevibracteatum J.J.Sm. Sts. to 2′ long. Lvs. to 3″ long, oblong, unequally 2-lbd. Infls. 1–4″ long, the rachis to more than 1″ long, the bracts rather small. Fls. about 1″ across, pale or bright yellow, the lip similar to that of *T. amplexicaule* (Bl.) Rchb.f., but the lat. lbs. broader, yellow with red markings, the midlb. white. Summer. (H) Malay Peninsula; Sumatra.

T. collinum Schltr. Sts. slightly compressed, to 8″ tall. Lvs. ligulate, unequally and obtusely 2-lbd. at apex, to 6″ long. Infls. to about 6″ long, the rachis with compressed, conduplicate, falcate bracts. Fls. about 3″ across, yellow-white, the lip with brown dots, the apex of the sac with a brownish-yellow apicule. Spring–summer. (H) New Guinea.

T. crassifolium Ridl. Sts. to 6½″ long, the internodes short. Lvs. to 5″ long, shaped like those of *T. arachnites* (Bl.) Rchb.f., the sheaths and sometimes the young lf.-blades purple. Infls.

Tetramicra parviflors Ldl. ex Rchb.f. [*Flora of Jamaica*]

Thelymitra Sargentii R.S.Rog. [W. H. NICHOLLS]

Trichoglottis rosea (Ldl.) Ames [REG S. DAVIS]

Trichoglottis fasciata Rchb.f. [JOHN FREDERICKS]

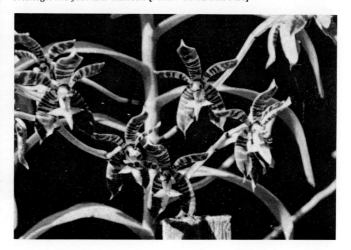

Trichopilia fragrans (Ldl.) Ldl. [H. SCHMIDT-MUMM]

Trichopilia tortilis Ldl. [GEORGE FULLER]

Vanda insignis Bl. [GEORGE FULLER]

to 5″ long, the rachis as long again, the bracts large. Fls. about 1½–2″ across, the ss. and ps. deep yellow, the lip shaped like that of *T. arachnites* (Bl.) Rchb.f., basally orange, the tip cherry-red, distinctly hairy outside. Summer. (H) Malay Peninsula.

T. leucarachne Ridl. Sts. to 6″ long, the internodes short. Lvs. to almost 6″ long and ¾″ wide, unequally 2-lbd. at tip. Infls. to 7″ long, the rachis stout, about ½″ across the bracts. Fls. to 5½″ across when expanded, the ss. and ps. white or faintly greenish-yellow, the lip white with crimson-purple spots on the lat. lbs. and base of the midlb., the midlb. hairy towards the base and within the spur. Spring. (H) Peninsular Thailand; Langkawi Islands.

THUNIA Rchb.f. ·

This is a genus of about 8 apparently valid—but all closely allied—species of very handsome terrestrial or semi-epiphytic orchids, native in the mountains of India, Burma, and nearby regions. A member of the small subtribe *Thuniinae*, the group is justifiably popular with collectors, the tall leafy plants being attractive even when not in spectacular flower. *Thunia* was once included in *Phaius*, and the blossoms superficially resemble certain members of that genus, but differ in critical details. They are borne in drooping, large-bracted racemes at the tips of the cane-like pseudobulbs, and are often several inches in diameter. The foliage is deciduous for much of the year in this genus.

Two fine hybrids are known in *Thunia* as of this writing, both now decidedly rare in collections. These are *T. x gattonensis* (*T. marjorensis* × *T. Winniana*), registered by Colman in 1917, and *T. x Veitchiana* (*T. Bensoniae* × *T. Marshalliana*), registered by Veitch in 1885. Additional breeding within the genus, and with members of possibly allied groups, offers some extremely interesting potentialities.

CULTURE: Thunias are very easily grown and brought into flower, even by the amateur, hence they are strongly recommended to all collectors. They do best in pots, rather tightly filled with a compost such as that suggested for *Phaius*, with copious broken crock in the bottom to assure the perfect drainage which is essential for their success. While actively growing, the plants should be kept in a sunny spot (but not so bright that the rather frail foliage becomes burned), and given quantities of water and fertilizing materials. As soon as the flowers have faded and the foliage starts to yellow and fall, lower temperatures should be afforded, and moisture considerably curtailed. Repotting and division may be attended to when the leaves have completely fallen; annual repotting seems most beneficial to these orchids. Upon the reappearance of the new growths (usually in the spring), water may gradually be increased, but a lengthy and very strict resting-period is most essential for the production of good growths and flowers. The plants may be divided at the base, or the bare canes may be cut into lengths of about six inches, and propagated in moist sand or sphagnum moss; new plantlets will sprout from most of the nodes. Thunias are susceptible to the attacks of thrips and red spider, and these pests should be watched for at all times when the foliage is present on the plants. (I)

T. alba (Wall.) Rchb.f. (*Phaius albus* Wall.)

Pbs. st.-like, terete, to about 2′ tall (rarely more), leafy throughout. Lvs. scaly at base of pbs., becoming to 8″ long at middle, oblong-lanceolate, acute, glaucous beneath, rather papery in texture. Infls. terminal, bracted, loosely 5–10-fld., mostly hanging. Fls. often not expanding fully, to 2½″ long, the ss. and ps. pure white, the lip bell-shaped, white, marked on the disc and midlb. with purple and lilac, usually veined with golden-yellow, the apical margins toothed and crisped. Mostly June–Aug. (I) North India; Burma; Thailand.

T. Bensoniae Rchb.f.

Similar in habit to *T. alba* (Wall.) Rchb.f., often slightly more robust in all vegetative parts. Fls. to 3″ across, delightfully fragrant, rather longer-lived than most of the spp., the spreading ss. and ps. bright magenta, becoming white towards the base, the large, open lip magenta frontally, white at base; lat. lbs. rolled over the col. to form a tube; midlb. frilled marginally, rich magenta-purple, with several crisped keels of brilliant golden-yellow on the disc. Mostly June–Aug. (I) Burma.

T. Marshalliana Rchb.f.

Similar to the other spp. in habit, but usually more robust vegetatively, to 3′ tall (rarely more). Lvs. pale green above, glaucous and rather powdery beneath. Infls. drooping, 3–12-fld., with large white bracts. Fls. fragrant, long-lived, to 5″ across, the spreading ss. and ps. white, the large tubular-flaring lip white, the midlb. crisped marginally, golden-yellow, with numerous forked deep orange-red veins, the tubular part usually streaked with yellow and purple, the disc with 5 yellow raised keels and 5 shorter ones on each side, all fringed with crystalline hairs. June–Aug. (I) Burma.

Thunia Marshalliana Rchb.f. [B.S.WILLIAMS]

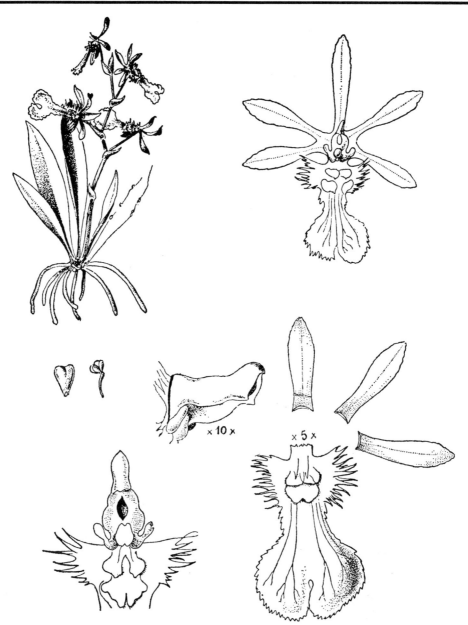

Thysanoglossa jordanensis C.Porto & Brade [Hoehne, *Flora Brasilica*]

THYLACIS Gagnep.

Thylacis consist of two species of dwarf, epiphytic orchids of rather peculiar appearance and structure, whose precise affinities do not seem to have been ascertained. Both of them, **T. Fleuryi** Gagnep. and **T. Poilanei** Gagnep., are natives of Viet-Nam, the former from Tonkin, the latter from Annam. They produce small white or yellow flowers in erect, laterally borne inflorescences, and because of their dimensions are principally of scientific interest. At this time, neither of the Thylacis is in cultivation.

Nothing is known of the genetic ties of this odd group.

CULTURE. Unknown.

THYSANOGLOSSA C.Porto & Brade

Two species of *Thysanoglossa* are known to date, both of them—**T. jordanensis** C.Porto & Brade and **T. organensis** Brade—very rare, dwarf epiphytic orchids which have been found on a few occasions in the humid forests of Brazil. A member of the subtribe *Ornithocephalinae*, this genus seems to have no very close allies in the aggregation, producing proportionately large, *Oncidium*-like flowers from a small tuft of rather fleshy leaves. Neither of the Thysanoglossas appears to be in cultivation at this time.

Nothing is known of the genetic affinities of this peculiar group.

CULTURE: Possibly as for *Ornithocephalus*. (I)

Tipularia discolor (Pursh) Nutt. [BLANCHE AMES]

TIPULARIA Nutt.

A member of the subtribe *Calypsoinae*, *Tipularia* consists of three species, one of which is occasionally grown by specialists in temperate-zone terrestrial orchids. The

other two, **T. japonica** Matsum. from Japan, and **T. Josephi** Ldl. from the Himalayas, do not appear to be grown at this time. They are odd, relatively inconspicuous plants, with subterranean series of corms, solitary rather colourful leaves, and erect racemes of small but unusually complicated flowers. The common name of 'Crippled Crane-Fly' has been given to *T. discolor* (Pursh) Nutt.; it is, insofar as we know, the only orchid in which the petals are arranged asymmetrically in the perianth, one of these segments overlapping the dorsal sepal for about half its width, thus giving to the blossoms a peculiar appearance.

No hybrids are known in *Tipularia*, and nothing has been ascertained regarding its genetic alliances.

CULTURE: Generally as for *Caladenia*. A relatively acid compost, rich in humus, is suggested. (C, I)

T. discolor (Pursh) Nutt. (*Orchis discolor* Pursh, *Tipularia unifolia* BSP)

Corms forming a series below ground, flattened, rather irregular. St. naked except for a long tubular basal sheath, brownish-green flushed with bronze or purple. Lf. produced in autumn months, solitary, cordate to ovate-elliptic, acute to acuminate, slender-stalked, dull green above and often blotched with purple, purplish beneath, 2–4″ long, 1–3¼″ wide. Infl. very slender, erect, 4–18″ tall, the rac. loosely many-fld., without floral bracts. Fls. to about ½″ in diam., nodding, varying in colour from greenish or lemon-yellow to rusty bronze or purplish, sometimes mottled with darker colour, the spur strongly upcurving, to almost 1″ long. Summer–early autumn. (C, I) Massachusetts to Central Florida.

TOWNSONIA Cheesem.

Two species of *Townsonia* are known to date, one, **T. deflexa** Cheesem. a native of New Zealand, the other **T. viridis** Schltr., from Tasmania. The genus is somewhat allied to *Acianthus* R.Br., differing from it in technical characters of the foliage and the column. These rather insignificant terrestrial orchids are unknown in cultivation at this time.

Nothing is known of the genetic ties of the genus *Townsonia*.

CULTURE: Presumably as for *Caladenia*. (C, I)

TRAUNSTEINERA Rchb.

This genus consists of a single species of rather showy terrestrial orchid, this widespread and often common in meadows in Central and Northern Europe. *Traunsteinera* is close in its alliance to *Orchis* [Tournef.] L. and to *Nigritella* L.C.Rich., from both of which it differs in technical details of the densely crowded flowers. At this time, it is a rare plant in collections outside of its native haunts, but is sufficiently showy to warrant attention by connoisseurs.

No hybrids seem known in *Traunsteinera* at this time, although its genetic affinities are presumably with *Orchis*, etc.

CULTURE: As for *Orchis*. (C, I)

T. globosa (L.) Rchb. (*Orchis globosa* L., *Orchis Halleri* Crantz, *Orchis sphaerica* M.B., *Nigritella globosa* Rchb.)

Tubers paired, oblong, lobed, about 1¼″ long. St. rather stout, sparingly leafy, usually flexuous, ¾–1½′ tall. Lvs. few, lanceolate or oblong, erect and more or less

sheathing the st., 2–6″ long. Rac. pyramidal or sub-globose, densely many-fld., 1–2″ long. Fls. about ⅜″ long, the ss. and ps. usually pale pinkish-purple, the lip pale, vivid crimson, spotted with dark crimson-purple. Dors. sep. lanceolate, narrowing towards the often-club-shaped tip, the lat. ss. similar but obliquely twisted near tip. Ps. similar to dors. sep. but smaller, all sub-erect. Lip 3-lbd., cuneate, the lbs. subequal, the central one with a slender apical tooth; spur slender, ⅛″ long. May–June. (C, I) Central and Northern Europe.

TREVORIA F.C.Lehm.

Three species of *Trevoria* are known to date, all exceptionally rare and spectacular epiphytic orchids of the subtribe *Gongorinae*, native in the high mountains of Colombia and Ecuador. None of them appears to be present in our collections at this time, although they are magnificent orchids, well worthy of attention by the connoisseur. The genus is somewhat allied to *Sievekingia* Rchb.f., but is immediately distinct by characters of the large flowers, which are borne in pendulous racemes.

Nothing is known concerning the genetic affinities of *Trevoria*, although it seems probable that they will prove freely compatible with at least certain other members of the subtribe.

CULTURE: As for *Stanhopea*, although cooler conditions should prevail. (I)

TRIAS Ldl.

Trias contains but two species, both of them rare and seldom-seen epiphytic orchids native in Burma. Both species are in sporadic cultivation today, usually as Bulbophyllums, to which genus they are very closely allied, but from which they are differentiated by technical characters of the flowers. Though relatively small plants, the two species of *Trias* are uniquely attractive when in bloom, and should be better known by connoisseurs.

Nothing is known of the genetic affinities of this genus.

CULTURE: As for the intermediate-growing, pseudo-bulbous Bulbophyllums. (I)

T. oblonga Ldl. (*Bulbophyllum oblongum* Rchb.f., *Dendrobium tripterum* Wall.)

Pbs. angular, rather clustered, to ¾″ in diam., slightly longer than thick. Lf. solitary, to 1¼″ long, elliptic or oblong, obtuse, rather leathery. Infls. very slender, erect or arching, to 1″ tall, 1-fld., produced from the pb.-base. Fls. about 1″ across, heavy-textured, not lasting well, the ss. and ps. brownish-green or yellow, the lip maroon or purple. Ss. spreading, ovate, subacute, the lats. adnate to the col.-foot. Ps. ovate, acutish. Lip trulliform, grooved down the middle, mobile, subacute, the basal auricles erect. Col. with the anther-horn notched at tip. Spring. (I) Burma; Thailand.

T. picta (Par. & Rchb.f.) Bth. (*Bulbophyllum pictum* Par. & Rchb.f.)

Pbs. ovoid, about ½″ tall, to ¾″ in diam. Lf. solitary, lanceolate to ovate, narrowed at both ends, to 2½″ long, leathery. Infls. short, 1-fld., slender. Fls. ¾″ across,

Trevoria Lehmanni Rolfe [A.D.HAWKES, AFTER *Botanical Magazine*]

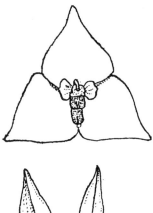

Trias picta (Par. & Rchb.f.) Bth. [A.D. HAWKES, AFTER *Orchids of Thailand*]

greenish-white, spotted with purple. Ss. ovate, acutish. Ps. obovate, deflexed, acutish. Lip mobile, not grooved down the middle, the surface convex, granulate, the tip rounded. Col. with the anther-horn entire. Spring. (I) Burma; Thailand.

TRICERATORHYNCHUS Summerh.

This is a recently described genus of the subtribe *Sarcanthinae*, comprising but a single species to date, **Triceratorhynchus viridiflorus** Summerh., a small epiphytic angraecoid orchid from Uganda and Kenya Colony. The genus is allied to *Sphyrarhynchus* Mansf., differing from it in technical characters, and is unknown at this time in our collections.

The genetic affinities of *Triceratorhynchus* have not been determined.

CULTURE: Presumably as for the tropical Angraecums. (H)

TRICHOCENTRUM P. & E.
(*Acoidium* Ldl.)

This is a genus of an estimated eighteen species or so of rather ill-defined plants, botanically, mostly smallish but singularly showy epiphytic (rarely lithophytic) orchids extending from Mexico to southern Brazil, with most of the species in the last-named country. *Trichocentrum* is a member of the subtribe *Trichocentrinae*, but is at once distinguished from all other orchids of this and other alliances by the very peculiar structure of the floral spur, which is formed much in the manner of that of *Habenaria* Willd., in that it is strictly a part of the lip, and not a prolongation of the column-foot. The Trichocentrums which are in cultivation, although they are

far from numerous and are not commonly grown, are attractive compact plants, with proportionately large and handsome flowers of typically unique coloration, in which the lip usually far exceeds the other floral segments in dimensions. Further, all of these plants are readily grown, even under relatively adverse cultural conditions, and they seldom fail to produce their delightful blossoms in profusion.

One hybrid within the genus *Trichocentrum* has been registered to date. Oddly enough, several hybrids with *Oncidium* are also known (= *Trichocidium*), though the genera are supposedly not close relatives. Additional experimental breeding with this group of charming small orchids seems definitely to be in order.

CULTURE: These small epiphytes are variously cultivated in pots, or on slabs or cubes of tree-fern fibre. If kept in pots, these containers should be rather small and perfectly drained, filled with a compost of equal parts of chopped sphagnum moss and shredded tree-fern fibre; tight-packed osmunda fibre can also be used. They require considerable moisture at all times—although the compost must never be permitted to become sodden, or the plants will rapidly deteriorate—high humidity, and a moderately bright situation, although excessive sun will cause burning of the succulent foliage. Best grown in a very airy place in the intermediate or warm greenhouse, they are relatively slow-growing orchids, highly intolerant of being disturbed. Periodic applications of mild fertilizing solutions are most beneficial when growth is active. (I, H)

T. albo-coccineum Lind. (*Trichocentrum albo-purpureum* Lind. ex Rchb.f., *T. albo-violaceum* Rchb.f. ex Schltr., *T. amazonicum* B.-R., *T. atropurpureum* Lind. ex Regel)

Typical vegetatively of most of the spp. Pbs. almost absent, very small, usually hidden by the copious fibrous roots. Lf. solitary (rarely paired), rigidly leathery, sometimes reddish-spotted or flushed beneath with purplish, oblong-lanceolate, acute to somewhat acuminate, narrowed towards the base but not stalked there, to about 4″ long and 1½″ wide, somewhat channelled down the middle, persisting for many years. Infls. basal, usually creeping and horizontal, bearing 1–5 fls. or·sometimes more, these successive (usually one at a time) over a period of several months, the infl. elongating to about 2½–3″ long, rather irregular, slender. Fls. about 2″ long (occasionally longer), usually opening widely, long-lived, heavy-textured, variable in colour, the spreading ss. and ps. usually greenish-yellow outside, inside brownish-yellow or olive-brown, the large lip white with a pale or dark purplish or reddish-purple blotch and bright or dull yellow keels on the disc. Lip often almost square, frequently with wavy margins, apically somewhat 2-lbd., the spur short. Mostly late summer–autumn. (I, H) Ecuador; Peru; Brazil.

T. fuscum Ldl. (*Acoidium fuscum* Ldl.)

Similar to the first-named sp. in habit, the lvs. often somewhat broader and frequently slightly longer. Fls. to about 1½″ across, long-lived, the ss. and ps. olive-brown, the large lip white with a pale violet irregular basal blotch and two yellowish keels on the disc. Ss. and ps.

oblong, shortly apiculate. Lip cuneately oblong, bluntly 2-lbd., the spur sharp-pointed, rather large. Autumn. (I, H) Brazil.

T. panamense Rolfe

Similar to the first-named sp. in habit, the lvs. usually darker green, often flushed with purple, often smaller. Infls. frequently pendulous, elongating for many months, sometimes branched. Fls. produced singly, about ½″ long, fleshy, usually rather short-lived, the ss. and ps. pale green to greenish-yellow, the lip often concave, white with a reddish-brown or reddish-purple basal blotch, the spur vaguely 4-lbd. Summer–autumn. (I, H) Panama.

T. Pfavii Rchb.f. Similar to the other spp. in habit, the lvs. often somewhat more acute apically. Infls. usually shorter than the lvs., often 2-fld. Fls. about 1½″ in diam., the ss. and ps. white, usually with a more or less well-developed basal blotch or spot of brownish at or near the base. Lip white, with a reddish blotch near the base, vaguely wedge-shaped, apically bluntly 2-lbd., wavy-margined, with a very short and blunt spur. Autumn–early winter. (I, H) Costa Rica; Panama.

T. tigrinum Lind. & Rchb.f. Similar to the other spp., the lvs. obtuse apically. Fls. to about 2¼″ long, the ss. and ps. yellow, more or less heavily spotted with brown, the large lip white with a rose-red base, broadly ovate, apically shortly and bluntly 2-lbd., with 3 yellow keels on the disc, the spur very short and blunt. Spring–early summer. (I, H) Ecuador.

TRICHOCEROS HBK

Trichoceros contains about six species of small, rare epiphytic orchids of the subtribe *Telipogoninae*, natives of the Andean regions of Colombia, Ecuador, Peru, and Bolivia. Allied to *Telipogon* HBK, the species noted below has recently been introduced into a few choice collections from Ecuador. These are unique plants—differing primarily from *Telipogon* in the presence of small pseudobulbs, elongate clambering rhizomes, and differently shaped flowers—which offer much to the specialist orchidist.

Nothing is known of the genetic affinities of *Trichoceros*.

CULTURE: This small plant should be grown in a well-drained pot filled with a compost made up of about equal parts of chopped sphagnum moss and shredded tree-fern fibre. A 'totem pole' of tree-fern fibre should be inserted into the pot, up which the clambering rhizomes can extend. Intermediate temperatures are suitable, and the plants should be kept in a rather shaded situation. Care must be taken that the compost never becomes stale—though the plants require quantities of moisture at all times—cr the rather delicate pseudobulbs will rot quickly. Well-rooted specimens may also successfully be mounted on tree-fern slabs. (I)

T. parviflorus HBK (*Trichoceros armillatus* Rchb.f., *T. muscifer* Krzl.)

Extremely variable in all parts, the rhiz. usually elongate and clambering, often to several feet in length, bearing tiny pbs. topped by several distichous leathery lvs. and clusters of thick roots at distant intervals from one another. Infl. often paired per new growth, usually

erect, to 10″ long, 3–20-fld., the fls. expanding successively over a long period. Fls. widely opening, lasting well, to slightly under 1″ across, the ss. and ps. greenish to pale yellow, lined with brown, the middle part and usually hair-like lip-appendages dark red to almost black-red. Mostly autumn. (I) Ecuador; Peru; Bolivia.

TRICHOGLOTTIS Bl. emend. Rchb.f.
(*Oeceoclades* Ldl., *Sarothrochilus* Schltr., *Staurochilus* Ridl., *Stauropsis* Rchb.f.)

Trichoglottis, as now delimited (albeit rather vaguely), is a moderate-sized genus of upwards of thirty-five species, mostly epiphytic in habit, ranging from the Himalayas throughout the Asiatic tropics, the Philippines, and Indonesia to New Guinea, with the centre of development apparently in the Philippines. The genus is a variable one, somewhat allied to *Vandopsis* Pfitz., *Sarcanthus* Ldl., *Acampe* Ldl., and *Pomatocalpa* Breda, differing from all of them in details of the floral structure. The plants range in stature from rather small to robust, and in general the flowers (often produced in large numbers) are sufficiently large and showy to warrant their cultivation by orchidists. Several of the species are in sporadic cultivation today, but the bulk of the genus is worthy of attention and should be better known.

Two or three exceptionally handsome hybrids have been produced to date, all with the genetically allied genus *Vanda*. The most noteworthy of these is *Trichovanda x Ulaula* (*Trichoglottis brachiata* × *Vanda Sanderiana*), a Hawaiian production which is among the most spectacular of all the sarcanthad hybrids. Additional experimental breeding with the allied groups is to be strongly recommended; the results should prove fascinating and most valuable to connoisseurs.

CULTURE: As for the tropical Vandas. Certain of the species are clambering epiphytes, and require some sort of support for the elongating stems. (I, H)

T. brachiata Ames (*Trichoglottis philippinensis* Ldl. var. *brachiata* Ames)

Sts. sparsely branching from near base, rooting freely, erect or hanging, to 2′ tall, leafy throughout. Lvs. distichous, rigidly leathery, rather close together, bright green, to about 2″ long or less, oblong-elliptic, retuse and apiculate at tip, ascending and with the sides upcurving noticeably. Infls. 1-fld. (very rarely 2-fld.), short, produced from opposite the lf.-bases. Fls. faintly fragrant, heavily waxy, long-lived, to almost 2″ in diam., variable in colour, but usually vivid rich red-purple, margins with a narrow yellow or whitish area (and often with a median streak of same hue), the hairy lip complex, mostly white with some purple basal streaks, a median area of vivid yellow, and some red-purple near the apex. Spring–summer. (H) Philippines: Biliran, Mindanao.

T. Dawsoniana (Rchb.f.) Rchb.f. (*Cleisostoma Dawsonianum* Rchb.f., *Sarothrochilus Dawsonianus* Schltr., *Staurochilus Dawsonianus* Schltr.)

Sts. erect, stout, 1–2′ tall, rather densely leafy. Lvs. narrowly ligulate, unequally 2-lbd. at apex, leathery, 3–6″ long. Infls. erect, branched, loosely many-fld., to

1½′ tall. Fls. 1–1½″ in diam., the rather fleshy ss. and ps. green or yellowish-green, spotted with brown or purple, the lip yellow with dense brown hairs in the middle. Ss. and ps. spreading, oblong, obtuse, narrowed basally. Lip 5-lbd., shorter than the ss., the lbs. oblong, obtuse. Col. hairy. Summer–autumn. (I) Thailand; Burma.

T. fasciata Rchb.f. (*Staurochilus fasciatus* Ridl., *Stauropsis fasciata* Ridl.)

Rather similar in habit to *T. Dawsoniana* (Rchb.f.) Rchb.f., the robust clambering sts. to 7′ tall, often branching near base. Infls. rather horizontal or ascending, simple, usually rather numerous at once, to about 5″ long, the 2–4 fls. opening successively. Fls. about 2″ across, longer than wide, fragrant, fleshy, very long-lived, the large ss. and ps. white on backs, the frontal surfaces pale lemon-yellow or yellow with broad transverse brown bands. Lip white with a few brown spots, the midlb. mostly hairy. Ss. and ps. spreading, oblong, acute. Lip complex, the lat. lbs. erect, the median lbs. spreading sideways, the fleshy midlb. somewhat downcurved. Mostly spring. (I, H) Philippines; Thailand; Laos; Viet-Nam; Malay Peninsula; Sumatra; Langkawi Islands.

T. ionosma (Ldl.) J.J.Sm. (*Cleisostoma ionosmum* Ldl., *Staurochilus ionosma* Schltr.)

Similar in habit to *T. Dawsoniana* (Rchb.f.) Rchb.f. Lvs. 8–10″ long, to 1½″ wide, leathery. Infls. erect, branched, loosely many-fld., to about 1¼′ tall. Fls. about 1¼″ across, fleshy, fragrant, long-lived, the ss. and ps. yellowish, blotched with brown, the lip white, veined with red. Lip smaller than the ss., hairy, the small lat. lbs. triangular, the ovate midlb. small, blunt. Spring. (I, H) Philippines; ? Formosa.

T. philippinensis Ldl. (*Stauropsis philippinensis* Rchb.f.)

Rather similar to *T. brachiata* Ames, but the lvs. more distant on the st., more glossy in appearance, and much more flattened and spreading outward and downward. Infls. often 2-fld., abbreviated. Fls. fragrant, long-lived, to about 1½″ in diam., the segms. much narrower than those of the allied sp., the flaring ss. and ps. dull red-brown with broad yellowish or whitish-yellow margins. Lip narrower than that of the allied sp., red-brown, yellow, and whitish. Spring–summer. (H) Philippines: Luzon, Negros, Mindanao.

T. rosea (Ldl.) Ames (*Cleisostoma roseum* Ldl., *Pomatocalpa roseum* J.J.Sm., *Trichoglottis flexuosa* Rolfe)

Sts. pendulous, branching from the base and above, forming large complex masses, to 4′ long (usually shorter), densely leafy. Lvs. glossy green, ligulate, acutish, to 3″ long, rather heavily leathery. Infls. stalkless, 1–3-fld., many produced all along the sts. Fls. not opening fully, long-lived, waxy, about ¼″ in diam., the ss. and ps. yellowish-brown, the lip white, often marked with pale magenta. Throughout the year, often almost ever-blooming. (I, H) Philippines.

T. lanceolaria Bl. Sts. pendulous, to almost 3′ long, slender, leafy. Lvs. to 4″ long, leathery, narrowly elliptic, acute, twisted basally. Infls. very short, in a tight row of 3–6 at each node. Fls. 2–4, about ¼″ across, the ss. and ps. pale yellow with a broad red-brown or crimson stripe down the middle (sometimes spotted, rarely plain), the lip with a transverse deep yellow stripe at base of the midlb. and 2 low hairy calli, the spur very prominent. Throughout the year. (H) Malay Peninsula; Sumatra; Java.

T. luzonensis Ames (*Staurochilus luzonensis* Ames) St. usually solitary, erect, rather stout, to 2′ tall (rarely more). Lvs. distant from one another, heavily and rigidly leathery, dark green, lorate, apically unequally and obtusely 2-lbd., to more than 8″ long and 1¼″ broad. Infl. usually solitary from opposite lf.-bases on median or upper part of st., to 3′ long, amply branched, stout, rather densely 20–50-fld. Fls. fleshy, long-lasting, faintly fragrant, to about 1½″ in diam., the spreading, spatulate, obtuse ss. and ps. dull yellow, closely spotted and blotched transversely with red-brown. Lip complex, mostly yellow, with a flush of red-brown on the median part of the bristle-covered midlb. Summer–autumn, often more than once annually. (H) Philippines: Luzon, Mindanao.

T. retusa Bl. Sts. long-climbing, to several feet in length, leafy. Lvs. to almost 3″ long, leathery, the tips unequally 2-lbd. Infls. 1-fld., 1–3 at a node, rather short. Fls. fragrant, fleshy, about 1″ across, the ss. and ps. pale greenish-yellow, spotted with red-brown, the spots rather large, the lip with the lat. lbs. purple-spotted, the midlb. greenish-yellow, brown-spotted apically, with a small hairy yellow basal callus, the middle covered with long white hairs. Mostly summer. (H) Malay Peninsula; Sumatra; Java; Borneo.

TRICHOPILIA Ldl.
(*Leucochyle* Klotzsch, *Leucohyle* Rchb.f., *Pilumna* Ldl., *Trichophilia* Pritz.)

Trichopilia is a genus of possibly thirty known species of epiphytic, lithophytic, or sometimes terrestrial orchids, widespread from Mexico and Cuba to Brazil. A member of the subtribe *Trichopiliinae*, it is not too closely allied to any other genus. Many of the entities contained here are of dubious value, and will perhaps eventually be reduced to synonymy under a relatively small number of taxa. About a dozen of the Trichopilias are present in our collections today, several of them common and justifiably popular, the others scarce and seldom-seen. They are, without exception, handsome and free-flowering orchids, with attractive, neat, pseudobulbous habit, and basal, few-flowered racemes of mostly large and spectacular blossoms. These flowers occur in a wide range of colours, and superficially resemble a *Cattleya*, with their spreading sepals and petals and trumpet-shaped or tubular lips. Often deliciously fragrant, they are for the most part long-lived, and make excellent material for corsages and the like.

A single hybrid within the genus is on record, this *Trichopilia x Gouldii* (*T. fragrans* × *T. suavis*), registered by Charlesworth in 1911; it has apparently disappeared from cultivation. Recently, some unusual hybrids have been made in Hawaii with *Miltonia* (= *Milpilia*), which causes us to believe that the group is genetically compatible with at least some members of the subtribe *Oncidiinae*. Additional experimental breeding should certainly be undertaken with these lovely and floriferous orchids.

CULTURE: Trichopilias are, for the most part, readily grown, even by the novice, hence they are heartily recommended to all orchid collectors. They do best in pots, filled rather tightly with osmunda or tree-fern fibre, and with copious broken crock in the bottom to assure the perfect drainage which is all-essential to their success. Because the basal flower-spikes in many of the species are somewhat deflexed, it is recommended that the pseudobulb-clump be raised slightly at the centre of the container. They also do well, when well-rooted, on rafts of osmunda fibre or slabs of tree-fern. While actively growing, these fine orchids require quantities of moisture at the roots, but upon maturation of the new pseudobulbs, they should be given a rest-period of several weeks, or until the incipient new shoots start to expand. Most of the species grow in the wild in semi-shaded situations, and this condition should obtain in the greenhouse as well; the rather thick foliage is very prone to burning through over-exposure. Limited applications of weak fertilizer are beneficial. Most of the Trichopilias seem to flower more profusely if divided regularly into rather small clumps, rather than permitted to grow into 'specimen' plant dimensions. Although some of them occur at relatively high elevations in the Andes, all of the cultivated species thrive under intermediate or warm temperatures. (I, H)

T. fragrans (Ldl.) Ldl. (*Pilumna fragrans* Ldl., *Trichopilia albida* Wendl., *T. Backhouseana* Rchb.f., *T. candida* Lind., *T. Lehmanni* Regel)

Pbs. narrowly oblong, somewhat compressed, 4–5″ tall, sheathed basally. Lf. solitary, rather leathery, glossy, oblong-elliptic, acuminate, narrowed basally, to 6½″ long and 1½″ wide. Infls. down-arching, loosely 2–5-fld., to about 12″ long. Fls. very fragrant, rather waxy, long-lived, to 4½″ across, variable, the oblong-linear, acute ss. and ps. greenish-white, with undulate margins, the tubular lip snow-white, with a golden-yellow blotch in the throat, the apex slightly incised. Winter. (I, H) Cuba; Jamaica; Colombia.

T. laxa (Ldl.) Rchb.f. (*Pilumna laxa* Ldl., *Trichopilia Reichenheimii* Kl.)

Pbs. very compressed, almost globular to broadly oval, 1½–2″ high. Lf. leathery, elliptic-oblong, acuminate, underneath often spotted with red, 4½–6½″ long, about 1½″ wide. Infls. horizontal to somewhat pendulous, loosely 4–7-fld., to 10″ long. Fls. fragrant, waxy, not opening fully, when expanded to about 2½″ across, the linear-ligulate ss. and ps. olive-green to olive-brown, the flaring lip snow-white, with some prominent keels on the disc. Autumn–early winter. (I, H) Colombia; Venezuela; Ecuador; Brazil.

T. maculata Rchb.f. (*Trichopilia Powellii* Schltr.)

Pbs. clustered, elliptic-oblong, strongly compressed, ¾–2″ long, to 1″ wide, inserted at an acute angle to the rhiz., the bases enveloped in several, densely spotted, papery bracts. Lf. rather leathery, dull green, elliptic-lanceolate, acute, 2–5″ long. Infls. slender, 1-fld., arching or pendulous, to 2½″ long. Fls. fragrant, rather waxy, to about 2½″ across, the ss. and ps. pale yellow or greenish-yellow, the lip white (becoming pale yellow in age), the throat yellow with numerous fine red lines. Ss. and ps. lanceolate, acuminate, often somewhat twisted, the ps. often undulate marginally. Lip tubular, the flaring apical part vaguely crisped and incised. Mostly winter. (I, H) Guatemala; Panama.

T. marginata Henfr. (*Trichopilia coccinea* Warsc., *T. crispa* Ldl., *T. lepida* hort.)

Pbs. strongly compressed, clustered, linear, broadly truncate, 2¼–5½″ long, the bases enveloped in several papery, usually strongly blotched sheaths. Lf. leathery, elliptic-lanceolate to lanceolate, acute to acuminate, 4½–12″ long, to 2″ wide, basally narrowed. Infls. short, arching to pendulous, 2–3-fld. Fls. rather fragrant, heavy-textured, to 4″ across, highly variable in colour, mostly with the ss. and ps. reddish with paler margins, the lip usually white on outer surface (rarely red), the inner tube deep rose-red, the reflexed margins of midlb. often white-margined. Ss. and ps. usually not twisted, but often with undulate margins. Lip tubular, the apical margins crisped or tightly undulate. Spring. (I, H) Guatemala; Costa Rica; Panama; Colombia.

T. suavis Ldl. & Paxt. (*Trichopilia Kienastiana* Rchb.f.)

Pbs. rather fleshy, crowded, somewhat compressed laterally, usually dull greyish-green, oblong-ovoid to almost round, to 3″ long, the bases enveloped in several thin, papery bracts. Lf. rather leathery, elliptic-lanceolate, acute, 4–14″ long and 1¼–3″ wide, narrowed below into a short stalk. Infls. short, 2–5-fld., arching or pendulous. Fls. very fragrant, to 4″ across, variable in colour, the ss. and ps. white or cream-white, sometimes spotted with pale rose-pink or red, the very large lip white or cream-white, usually heavily spotted with rose-pink, the throat usually marked with yellow or orange, very rarely red-blotched. Ss. and ps. lanceolate, acute, usually undulate marginally. Lip tubular, the flaring midlb. usually crisped marginally, the disc with a prominent, erect, central keel. Mostly Mar.–Apr. (I) Costa Rica; Panama; Colombia.

T. subulata (Sw.) Rchb.f. (*Epidendrum subulatum* Sw., *Cymbidium subulatum* Sw., *Leucohyle subulata* Schltr., *Leucohyle Warscewiczii* Kl., *Trichopilia hymenantha* Rchb.f., *T. jamaicensis* F. & R.)

Pls. 4–10″ tall, with short, inconspicuous, clustered, cylindric pbs. to 1″ long, the bases enveloped in several papery, brown bracts. Lf. fleshy, linear-lanceolate to semiterete, acuminate, 3½–8½″ long, mostly less than ¼″ wide, contracted at base. Infls. pendulous, 3–8-fld., 1–2½″ long, subtended by and furnished with large, papery bracts. Fls. fragrant, about 1½″ across, the ss. and ps. pure white to pale yellow, the lip white, usually irregularly spotted with rose-purple, concave (not tubular), the margins often deeply lacerate. Autumn. (I, H) Jamaica; Panama; Colombia.

T. tortilis Ldl.

Pbs. clustered, narrowly ovoid to oblong-cylindrical, compressed, 1½–4½″ long, more or less enveloped by papery, brown-spotted sheaths. Lf. suberect, leathery, glossy, elliptic-lanceolate to elliptic-oblanceolate, acute to shortly acuminate, folded at base, 3½–9″ long, 1–1½″ wide. Infls. slender, 1–2-fld., mostly pendulous, 2–4″ long. Fls. fragrant, waxy, when flattened out to 6″ across, the narrow, conspicuously twisted ss. and ps. brownish-purple to light lavender, with an irregular yellowish or greenish border, the large tubular lip white to yellowish-white, spotted in the yellow throat with brown or crimson, the margins crisped-undulate.

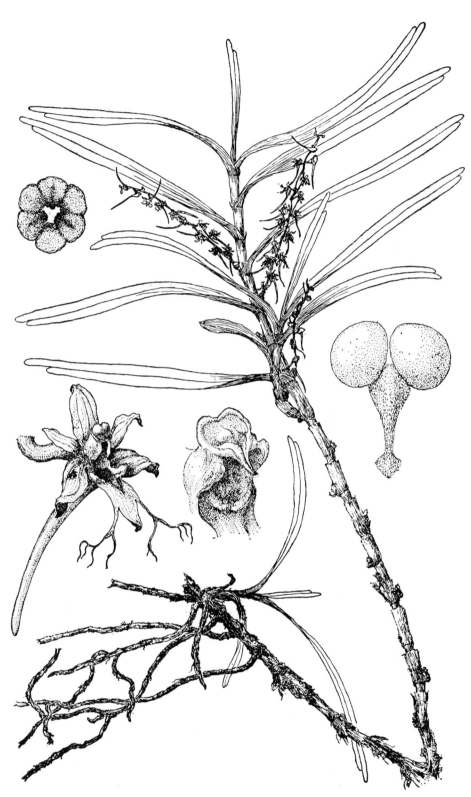

Tridactyle bicaudata (Ldl.) Schltr. [*Flora of the Belgian Congo*]

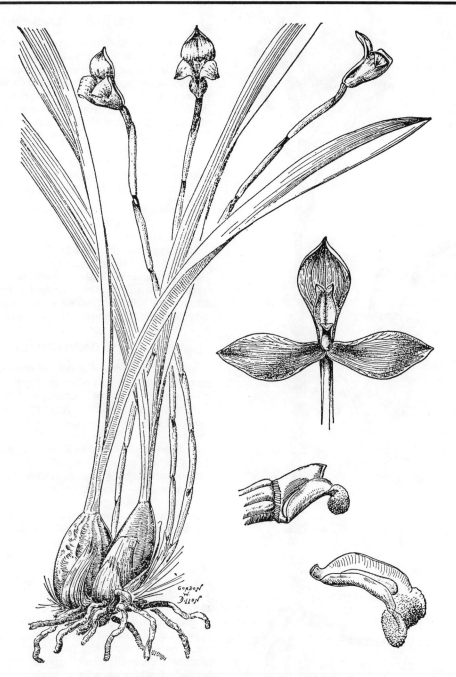

Trigonidium Egertonianum Batem. [GORDON W. DILLON]

Winter. (I, H) Mexico; Guatemala; El Salvador; Honduras.

T. brevis Rolfe Pbs. cylindric-conical, somewhat compressed, clustered, 3–5″ long. Lf. elliptic-lanceolate, acute, about 6″ long. Infls. 2–3-fld., pendulous, abbreviated. Fls. about 3″ across, fragrant, the ss. and ps. greenish-yellow, sparsely blotched with chocolate-brown, the bell-shaped lip white, slightly flushed and veined with yellow on the midlb. and disc. Autumn. (I) Peru.

T. Galeottiana A.Rich. (*Trichopilia picta* Lem.) Similar in

habit to *T. tortilis* Ldl., the 1-fld. infls. usually numerous, hanging to pendulous. Fls. fragrant, long-lived, to about 5″ across, the ss. and ps. olive-brown with pale green margins, the tubular lip barred and lined with crimson-purple, the margins of the midlb. white, the throat pale yellow. Mostly Aug.–Sept. (I) Mexico.

T. Hennisiana Krzl. Very closely allied to *T. fragrans* Ldl., and possibly only a form of that highly variable sp., differing primarily in the lip, which is much broader apically, and has deep incisions all along the apical margin. Spring–early summer. (I) Colombia.

475

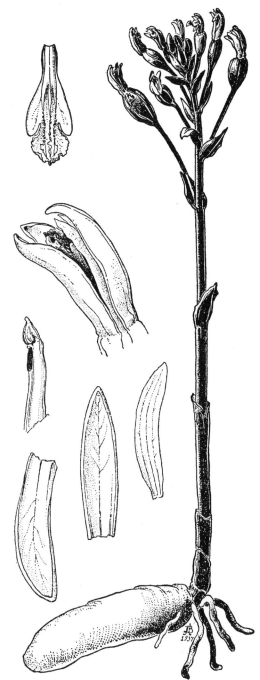

Triphora cubensis (Rchb.f.) Ames [BLANCHE AMES]

T. leucoxantha L.O.Wms. Rather similar in habit to *T. suavis* Ldl. & Paxt. Infls. 1–4-fld., arching to pendulous, to 3″ long. Fls. fragrant, very handsome, to about 2½″ across, white with a pale yellow blotch at base of the rather bell-shaped lip, which is tightly crisped marginally. Summer. (I) Panama.

T. turialbae Rchb.f. Very closely allied to *T. tortilis* Ldl., and perhaps only a constant form of that variable sp. Fls. fragrant, to 2½″ across, the ss. and ps. pure white, the tubular lip white with some pale orange lines in the throat, the midlb. undulate-margined, the disc with an elongate, central keel. Summer. (I, H) Costa Rica; Panama.

TRIDACTYLE Schltr.

A genus of about twelve epiphytic or lithophytic monopodial orchids in tropical and South Africa, *Tridactyle* is uncommon in contemporary collections, although a single species is present in particularly choice greenhouses at this time, usually erroneously named. Allied to several genera of the complex *Angraecum* alliance of the subtribe *Sarcanthinae*, these are small-flowered orchids of no especial beauty, but great botanical interest.

No hybrids are known in *Tridactyle*, and its genetic affinities have not been ascertained as of this writing.

CULTURE: As for the tropical Angraecums, etc. (H)

T. bicaudata (Ldl.) Schltr. (*Angraecum bicaudatum* Ldl., *Eulophia angustifolia* Eckl. & Zeyh., *Listrostachys bicaudata* Finet)

Sts. elongated, to more than 12″ long, leafy throughout. Lvs. spreading, to 4″ long and 1″ wide, ligulate, obliquely 2-lbd. at the apex, leathery. Infls. densely many-fld., spreading, usually shorter than the lvs. Fls. less than ½″ across, brownish-white, with a cylindric spur as long as the rest of the fl. Summer. (H) Congo to South Africa.

TRIGONIDIUM Ldl.

About a dozen rather ill-defined species make up the genus *Trigonidium*, and of these only two appear to be present in contemporary collections. They range from Mexico to Brazil, with the majority of known entities indigenous to the latter-named country. The genus is a member of the subtribe *Maxillarinae* and hence somewhat allied to *Maxillaria* R. & P., though when in flower they are immediately distinguishable from the components of that group. In *Trigonidium* the relatively large blossoms—borne on elongate, bracted, usually erect, one-flowered scapes—consist mostly of the sepals, these being greatly developed and virtually obscuring the much smaller petals, lip, and column. The sepals are connivent at their bases, to form a tube, and have the apical portions spreading or rather strongly reflexed. In several of the species the small petals bear an unusual brightly coloured glandular thickening towards the apex. The Trigonidiums are, almost without exception, epiphytic plants, though on rare occasions they are found growing on rock-outcroppings as lithophytes.

No hybrids are known in this genus, and nothing has been deduced concerning its genetic affinities. It seems probable that multigeneric hybrids, with other genera of the *Maxillarinae*, would produce some intriguing progeny.

CULTURE: As for the low-elevation, warm-growing Maxillarias. Because of the clambering habit of *T. Lankesteri*, some sort of support is required. (I, H)

T. Egertonianum Batem. (*Trigonidium Seemanni* Rchb.f.)

Pbs. clustered, ovoid to elliptic-ovoid, ridged, to 3″ tall and 1½″ thick, usually rather compressed laterally, often yellowish. Lvs. 2, long-stalked below, to 2′ long and 1¼″ wide, glossy, rather leathery, linear-lanceolate, acute. Infls. often several at once, erect, 1-fld. scapes to 1½′ tall, enveloped with tubular, papery bracts. Fls. about 1½″ long at most, long-lived, the ss. varying from

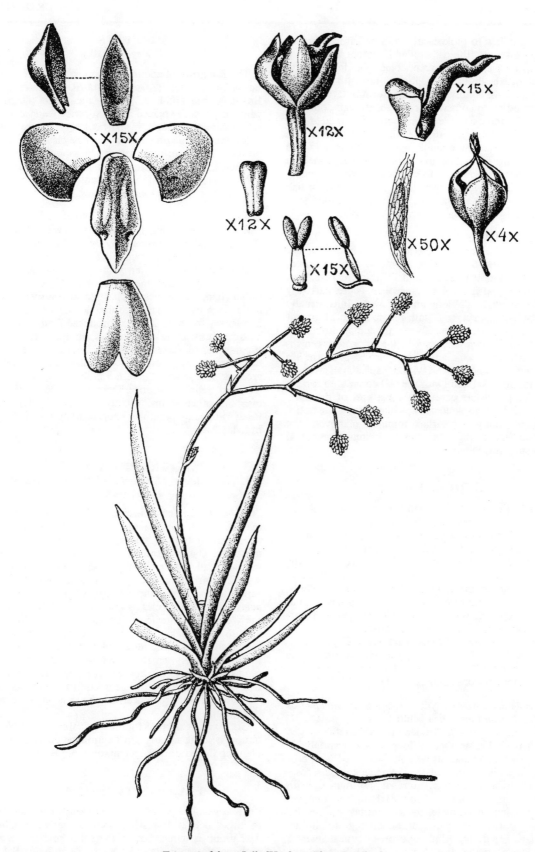

Trizeuxis falcata Ldl. [Hoehne, *Flora Brasilica*]

477

greenish-yellow to pinkish-tan, with or without brown or purple stripes, the ps. similar in colour but with a brown, purple, or iridescent blue glandular apical thickening, the lip usually yellowish-tan with brown or red stripes. Ss. connivent at base, forming a tube, the tips spreading to somewhat reflexed, the lats. oblique. Ps. mostly lanceolate, the apices sharply recurved or not. Lip 3-lbd., contracted at base, the lat. lbs. erect and parallel to the col., the midlb. ovate, acute, mostly pale yellow, rather fleshy, the tip recurved and roughened on both upper and lower surfaces, the disc with a tongue-shaped callus. Mostly spring. (I, H) Mexico; British Honduras; Guatemala; El Salvador; Honduras; Nicaragua; Costa Rica; Panama; Colombia.

T. Lankesteri Ames

Rhiz. very elongate, enveloped in tubular, papery bracts, the pbs. 6–15″ apart. Pbs. ovoid, compressed, ridged, to more than 3″ tall and 1¼″ thick at base. Lvs. 3–5, rather leathery, oblong-lanceolate, acute, narrowly stalked below, to 11″ long and 1½″ wide. Infls. usually solitary, 1-fld., erect, to 6″ tall. Fls. to about 2″ long at most, the ss. light greenish-tan to cinnamon-brown, veined with brown or purplish, the ps. pale greenish-tan with brown veins and some purple spots, the lip white with brown spots. Ss. with the apical half strongly reflexed, the basal half (with the ps.) connate to form a tube, the ps. visible between the margins of the dors. and lat. ss. Ps. conspicuously apiculate or aristate at tip. Lip 3-lbd., the upper surface minutely glandular, the under-surface strongly verrucose. Spring–summer. (I, H) Costa Rica; Panama.

TRIPHORA Nutt.

This is a genus of about ten species of relatively inconspicuous terrestrial orchids in temperate and tropical America. Closely allied to *Pogonia* Juss., it is a member of the subtribe *Vanillinae*, and is virtually unknown in contemporary collections, although several of the species are attractive little plants well worthy of attention by connoisseurs. Like so many terrestrial orchids, their cultural requirements are not met with ease, but at least one species, noted below, may be grown if particular attention is paid to the conditions.

Nothing is known of the genetic ties of *Triphora*.

CULTURE: As for *Arethusa*, though certain of the tropical species will require a greater degree of heat than those temperate-zone orchids. (C, I)

T. trianthophora (Sw.) Rydb. (*Arethusa trianthophoros* Sw., *Triphora mexicana* Schltr.)

Pls. to almost 12″ tall, slender and fragile, often tinged with maroon. Lvs. to about 1″ long, stalkless, variable in shape, clasping the st., usually purple-tinged. Fls. produced in axils of upper lvs., 1–3, pale pink or rose-magenta to almost white, more or less marked with white, green, and purple, about ½″ long, nodding. Ss. linear to linear-lanceolate, the lats. rather falcate. Ps. falcate, obtuse or acute, linear-oblong to linear-spatulate. Lip deeply 3-lbd., obovate or cuneate, with 3 green keels on the disc. Spring. (C, I) Eastern and Central United States; Mexico; Guatemala; Panama.

TRIZEUXIS Ldl.
(*Trixeuxis* Ldl.)

This is a genus of about three species of dwarf epiphytic orchids, ranging from Costa Rica to Trinidad, Brazil, Bolivia, and Peru. A single member of the group, which is generally placed in the subtribe *Capanemiinae*, is occasionally found in particularly comprehensive collections at this time, but it must be classed as a rare orchid. Because of the very tiny blossoms, *Trizeuxis* is of interest primarily to the specialist in the 'botanicals'.

Nothing is known of the genetic affinities of *Trizeuxis*.

CULTURE: As for *Ornithocephalus*. (I, H)

T. falcata Ldl. (*Trizeuxis andina* Schltr.)

Pls. variable in size from 1–4″ tall, with short sts., the imbricating lf.-bases usually enveloping a tiny, squarish, compressed, 1-lvd. pb. Lvs. falcate or gladiate, acute or acuminate, often yellowish or tan-green, the blades ½–3″ long and mostly less than ¼″ wide, glossy, rather rigid, the imbricating bases distichously arranged in the form of an open fan. Infls. slender, erect, paniculate scapes to about 3″ long, produced from pb.-bases, conspicuously exceeding the lvs. in most cases. Fls. subglobose, very small, in dense, head-like or elongate racs. terminating the panicle-branches, the ss. and ps. green or pale yellow, the rather fleshy lip-apex, which is recurved, yellow or orange. Dors. sep. concave, arching over the other segms. Mostly summer. (I, H) Costa Rica; Panama; Colombia; Venezuela; Trinidad; Brazil; Bolivia; Peru.

TROPIDIA Bl.
(*Chloidia* Ldl. in part, *Cnemidia* Ldl. *Govindooia* Wight, *Decaisnea* Ldl.)

Upwards of thirty-five species of *Tropidia* are known to date, these for the most part rather nondescript terrestrial orchids of no especial value, save to connoisseurs. The distribution of the group is a rather odd one, with all but one of the species indigenous to the Asiatic subtropics and tropics, ranging from China and Japan to Indonesia; the solitary American species, **T. polystachya** (Sw.) Ames, is known from South Florida, the West Indies, Mexico, and parts of Central America, and the Galápagos Islands. Vegetatively the plants rather simulate a broad-leaved bambusoid grass, and the mostly very small flowers—greenish, white, or reddish in colour—are borne in compact panicles. None of the Tropidias appear to be in cultivation at this time.

Nothing is known concerning the genetic affinities of this group.

CULTURE: Possibly as for the tropical species of *Phaius*, although scant success can be anticipated when transplanting these rather fragile plants from the wild. (I, H)

TSAIORCHIS Tang & Wang

Tsaiorchis is a genus of but two known species, both of these slender terrestrial orchids, native in China. The group is a member of the subtribe *Habenarinae*, perhaps closest in its alliances to *Neottianthe* Schltr., and is at present unknown in our collections.

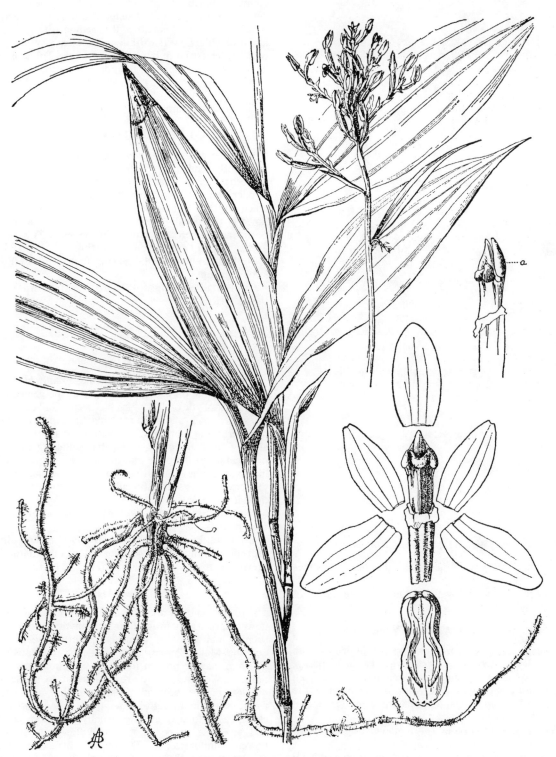

Tropidia polystachya (Sw.) Ames [BLANCHE AMES]

Tylostigma foliosum Schltr. [*Flore de Madagascar*]

of Celebes and Buru, in Indonesia. A member of the complex subtribe *Physurinae*, the affinity of the group is with *Myrmechis* Bl. and *Odontochilus* Bl., from which it differs in structural details of the medium-sized (for the alliance) white flowers. Although apparently very pretty orchids, terrestrial in habit, neither of the Tubilabiums has made its way into contemporary collections.

Nothing is known of the genetic affinities of this rare genus.

CULTURE: Presumably as for *Anoectochilus*. (H)

TYLOSTIGMA Schltr.

Seven species of *Tylostigma* are known, all of them apparently endemic to the island of Madagascar. Terrestrial or lithophytic on mossy rocks, they are slender plants of the subtribe *Habenarinae*, somewhat allied to *Diplacorchis* Schltr. The small but complex flowers are usually yellowish or greenish, and are borne in dense erect racemes. No species of *Tylostigma* appear to be in cultivation at this time.

Nothing is known of the genetic affinities of this little-known group.

CULTURE: Possibly as for the tropical Habenarias and the like. (I, H)

ULEIORCHIS Hoehne

Uleiorchis Cogniauxiana Hoehne (*Wullschlaegelia Ulei* Cgn.), the only known member of the genus, is a frail, saprophytic orchid which has been found on a very few occasions in the State of Santa Catarina, Brazil. A member of the subtribe *Cranichidinae*, it is closest in its alliance to *Wullschlaegelia* Rchb.f., differing in technical details of the plant and of the larger flowers. It is, like many of the saprophytes, unknown in collections at this time, and its successful cultivation seems problematical at any event.

Nothing is known of the genetic alliances of *Uleiorchis*.

CULTURE: Presumably as for *Corallorrhiza* and other saprophytes, though tropical conditions must naturally prevail, as regards temperature. (H)

UNCIFERA Ldl.

This is a genus of about four known species of small-flowered, relatively insignificant, epiphytic, monopodial orchids, native in the Himalayas, Burma, Viet-Nam, and the Malay Peninsula. A single representative of *Uncifera* may be present in a very few choice contemporary collections. They are of interest to specialists because of the unusual floral structure, and when well-grown, are attractive vegetatively. The plants bear clean, fleshy foliage on long, usually pendulous stems, and give rise to pendulous many-flowered (or few-flowered) inflorescences. Despite the small dimensions of the blossoms, they are of interestingly intricate structure and, when viewed with a lens, are rather pretty.

No hybrids have as yet been made in *Uncifera*, and nothing is known of its genetic alliances.

CULTURE: As for the tropical Vandas. (I, H)

Nothing is known of the genetic affinities of this rare aggregation.

CULTURE: Presumably as for the temperate species of *Orchis*, etc. (C)

TUBEROLABIUM Yamamoto

The genus *Tuberolabium* is a rather ill-defined and incompletely known one, containing but a single species, this **T. kotoense** Yamamoto, an epiphytic orchid from the island of Formosa. The group is a member of the subtribe *Sarcanthinae*, and at this time is not present in our collections.

The genetic affinities of *Tuberolabium* are not known at this time.

CULTURE: Possibly as for the smaller Vandas, etc. (I)

TUBILABIUM J.J.Sm.

Two species of *Tubilabium* are known to date, both of them exceptionally rare 'Jewel Orchids' from the islands

Vanda Watsoni Rolfe [GEORGE FULLER]

Ypsilopus longifolia Summerh. [GEORGE FULLER]

Zeuxine strateumatica (L.)
Schltr. [JACK BRANT, JR.]

Zygopetalum intermedium Lodd. [GEORGE FULLER]

Zygopetalum intermedium Lodd. [JOHN W. BLOWERS]

U. tenuicaulis (Hk.f.) Holtt. (*Saccolabium tenuicaule* Hk.f.)

Sts. slender, pendulous, to more than 12″ long. Lvs. narrowed gradually to an acute tip, to 5″ long, rather leathery. Infls. numerous, very short, 1–3-fld., more than one borne per node. Fls. less than ½″ long, yellow, the tip of the lip and the col. white. Lip with the lat. lbs. having an erect back edge, the forward edges sloping downwards and incurved; midlb. narrowly elliptic, concave, pointing upwards in front of the col., as long as the spur, with 2 small diverging curved horns at the tip; spur directed obliquely backwards from the mouth, widening in the middle to a broad forward-curved tip, with long hairs on the front wall closing the narrowest part; stipes of pollinia very large. Summer. (H) Malay Peninsula; Langkawi Islands.

VANDA Jones
(*Papilionanthe* Schltr.)

The more than seventy species of *Vanda*, together with their myriad interspecific hybrids, multigeneric hybrids, and horticultural forms, make up one of the most prominent of groups of cultivated orchids today. A description of the Vandas seems almost redundant, since they—like the Cattleyas, Dendrobiums, Cymbidiums, Oncidiums, and the like—are so extremely popular with contemporary orchidists, but certain things should be noted here. Initially, they are all monopodial orchids, mostly epiphytic in habit, although some lithophytes and true terrestrials are also known. All of them are Asiatic in origin, the range of the genus extending from China, the Himalayas, Ceylon, and the Philippines throughout South-east Asia, Indonesia, and adjacent insular groups to New Guinea and northern Australia. Vegetatively the plants are somewhat diverse, though all have relatively elongate—sometimes very long—frequently climbing or clambering stems of varying degrees of thickness. For horticultural and cultural purposes the leaves of Vandas designate two important categories, namely the terete-leaved species and the strap-leaved species.[1] Terete leaves (basically roundish when viewed in cross-section) are found in only four species; the apices of these terete leaves vary from sharp-pointed to rather blunt. The strap-leaved species (which include the vast majority of those described) have relatively flattened, plane leaves which may be more or less channelled above and keeled beneath; the apices of these vary from sharp-pointed to rounded and distinctly lobed (often obliquely so) to more or less strongly toothed or cut. In *Vanda* the inflorescence is normally simple and erect or approximately so; it usually arises from near the upper part of the plant, but not from its apex—from the leaf-axils, or in the terete-leaved species (and hybrids) from opposite the leaf-bases. A few to rather many medium-sized to large, mostly fleshy, heavy-textured flowers are pro-

[1] Semi-terete-leaved Vandas are, for the most part, hybrids between these two categories, hence they form a third, artificially produced class of foliar habit. *V. Amesiana* Rchb.f. and *V. Kimballiana* Rchb.f. technically have semi-terete leaves as well.

duced, these lasting for several days to upwards of two months in perfection. Floral colour is tremendously varied in Vandas—particularly in the more advanced and complex hybrid forms—although browns, purples, yellows, magentas, and blues perhaps predominate. In this genus, formation of the flower is remarkably constant (now that the aberrant *Euanthe Sanderiana* (Rchb.f.) Schltr. has been removed), and are almost always readily recognized, even by the casual observer, when they are produced.

Vanda has, during the past couple of decades, figured in the production of an amazing number of hybrid orchids. A great many of these have been made through interspecific breeding, but now the total of intergeneric crosses, making use of *Vanda* for at least one parent, is almost as impressive. Vandas appear to be very freely inter-fertile with a large number of allied groups of the subtribe *Sarcanthinae*, among these being *Arachnis* (= *Aranda*), *Ascocentrum* (= *Ascocenda*), *Neofinetia* (= *Vandofinetia*), *Renanthera* (= *Renantanda*), *Vandopsis* (= *Opsisanda*), *Aërides* (= *Aëridovanda*), etc. Despite the large number of hybrids now on record (these include, by the way, a series of well-established natural crosses, notably indigenous to Burma and the lesser islands of Indonesia), there are still tremendous fields of experimental endeavour awaiting the breeder in this varied and large alliance of orchidaceous plants.

CULTURE: Most Vandas are easily grown by collectors everywhere, even though their cultural requirements may be slightly different from those required by certain other orchids, such as Cattleyas, Oncidiums, Dendrobiums, etc. Culturally, the genus is conveniently divided into three categories: (1) terete, (2) semi-terete, and (3) strap-leaf. In general neither of the first two categories (species and/or hybrids) are as well suited to indoor (i.e., under glass or lath) cultivation in temperate climes as are the strap-leaved forms; these terete and semi-terete Vandas may grow luxuriantly, but usually no flowers are produced under such conditions unless the plants are allowed to scramble up against the glass or lath and thus be exposed to very bright light, which seems requisite for production of blossoms. Almost all of the strap-leaved species and hybrids form admirable subjects for the greenhouse or lath-house collection (or for cultivation as house plants, in the home, for that matter), their cultural requirements being easily met, and their spectacular flowers often being borne more than once annually. All Vandas benefit by as much light as possible, short of burning of the foliage through excessive exposure to the sun's rays. In the strap-leaved types, if the leaves are being produced close together and are hard and durable in texture, it may be assumed that the plants are enjoying good cultural conditions; if, however, the plants are receiving too little light (often coupled with too much water), the leaf-bases are typically not particularly close together and do not overlap on the stem as they should, and the leaves themselves are proportionately too long, often somewhat loosely pendulous and flaccid, and are dark green instead of the more preferable yellowish-green. Ideal light conditions often make Vandas less attractive in appearance than those grown in less light, but the plants will flower far more easily if they are treated in this fashion. Most Vandas (except for the majority of the strictly tropical terete and semi-terete kinds mentioned above) may with success be grown in a mixed greenhouse with Cattleyas and other orchids requiring intermediate temperatures. Certain of the species (and their hybrids), such as *V. coerulea*, *V. Amesiana*, *V. Kimballiana*, etc., in general require somewhat cooler conditions for proper flower production, than do the majority of the others, since in the wild they are inhabitants of rather high elevations. These orchids require high humidity at all times for best results, and since they grow throughout the year, they must never be given a rest-period of any sort. Vandas need large amounts of water at all times, although caution must always be exercised that they do not become soggy or stale at the base, where most of the roots occur in the compost. Through care in potting and the use of proper compost and drainage materials, this potential difficulty may be avoided. A particularly important point to be noted is that water must never lodge in the growing stem-apex of these plants, or rotting of the entire terminal growing-point may occur. Like most cultivated orchids, members of this genus must have quantities of freely circulating fresh air at all times. Vandas are not particular about the compost in which they are grown. In Hawaii, where some of the finest Vandas of the world are cultivated, almost every conceivable potting-medium is utilized, although relatively large chunks of tree-fern fibre, liberally mixed with broken crock and/or charcoal is preferred by most enthusiasts. Other growers successfully maintain them in straight broken crock or cracked brick, vermiculite, volcanic pumice-stone, or even straight gritty sand; when such materials are utilized, fertilizing should be attended to with more care than under ordinary conditions. In recent times, the addition of bark preparations (particularly the larger chunks, from which all dust and detritus have been removed) are widely used by growers throughout the world, often in combination with such materials as tree-fern or chopped osmunda. Vandas do well in either pots or baskets; no matter what potting-material is used, however, particular attention must be paid to the thorough drainage which is so essential for success with these orchids. Because of their habit, the plants should be potted rather high up in the container, with only the basal parts of the stem and the roots buried in the compost. Most Vandas produce copious aerial roots from the upper portions of the stem; these should be allowed to hang free, since they are highly specialized accessory moisture-absorbing structures. Like the majority of monopodial orchids, Vandas benefit by liberal and frequent applications of fertilizing materials of various sorts; without the addition of these, vegetative growth and floral production is often rather unsatisfactory. (C, I, H)

V. alpina (Ldl.) Ldl. (*Luisia alpina* Ldl., *Luisia Griffithii* Krzl., *Vanda Griffithii* Ldl.)

Sts. rather thick, densely leafy, short. Lvs. 4–5″ long, about ½″ wide, typically down-curving or horizontal, thickly leathery, linear or ligulate, apically prominently and unequally 2-lbd. Infls. very short, 1–4-fld., mostly horizontal, distinctly jointed, often somewhat zigzag. Fls. nodding, faintly fragrant, waxy, 1–1½″ across, long-

lived. Ss. and ps. pale yellow-green to almost emerald-green, the lat. lbs. of the lip blackish-purple inside and pale yellow or greenish-yellow outside; midlb. longitudinally striped with black-purple and pale yellow, usually green marginally. Lip fleshy, saccate basally, the erect lat. lbs. triangular, somewhat concave, the midlb. slightly reflexed, cordate at base, with 2 horn-like cirrhi at apex. Col. short, whitish or cream-yellow. Spring–summer. (C, I) Himalayas, mostly at elevations of 3000–5000 feet.

V. Amesiana Rchb.f.

St. short, thick, densely leafy, producing very numerous extremely thick roots, especially near the base. Lvs. to almost 12″ long, about ½″ in diam., very fleshy, almost semi-terete, the upper side with a deep groove (so that they appear tear-drop-shaped in cross-section). Infls. erect or suberect, to 2½′ tall, peduncle usually pale green, spotted with bright red or magenta-red, with 12–35 fls. in apical portion. Fls. to 2″ across, very fragrant, extremely variable in colour, the ss. and ps. typically white flushed with delicate rose, the lip amethyst-purple to dark rose, sometimes striped with darker colour, often paler marginally. Lip rather larger than the ss., the erect lat. lbs. short, roundish, the midlb. broadly cuneate, very obtuse, undulate marginally, with a very short obtuse spur. Mostly summer, but often sporadic throughout the entire year, sometimes flowering more than once annually. (C, I) Viet-Nam; Laos; Cambodia; Thailand, at elevations of about 4000–5000 feet.

V. coerulea Griff. ex Ldl.

St. robust, eventually to 4′ and more tall in old specimens, very densely leafy, the lvs. usually strictly horizontal in arrangement. Lvs. rigidly leathery, usually yellow-green, to 10″ long and about 1″ wide, linear-ligulate, deeply channelled above and keeled beneath, irregularly cut and toothed at apex. Infls. mostly erect or gracefully arching, to 2′ tall, mostly 5–15-fld. Fls. highly variable in shape, colour, and size, to 4″ across in the larger phases, the ss. and ps. typically pale blue with darker reticulating markings (varying to pure white and pink in certain very rare forms), the small lip mostly very dark purple-blue, with whitish lat. lbs. Ss. and ps. spreading, broadly ovate-spatulate, obtuse, the ps. frequently entirely or partially twisted so that the rear surface is foremost. Lip with small, triangular, acute lat. lbs. and an oblong, convex midlb. furnished with 2–3 keels. Mostly autumn–winter. (C, I) Himalayas; Burma; Thailand, at rather high elevations.

V. coerulescens Griff.

St. short, rather slender, few-lvd. Lvs. to 10″ long, ¾″ wide, linear, channelled above and strongly keeled beneath, bilobed at the apex, the lbs. ending in spiny tips. Infls. slender, erect or suberect, to 2′ tall, many-fld. Fls. to 1½″ across, 15 or more, extremely variable in colour, fragrant, rather light in texture but lasting well. Ss. and ps. usually pale blue or mauve-blue (rarely white), the lip dark violet-blue. Ss. and ps. obovate-spatulate, obtuse, spreading. Lip about as long as the ps., 3-lbd.; lat. lbs. small, oblong; midlb. obovate, emarginate, with deflexed margins and 2 thickened median ridges on the disc; spur incurved, short, blue. Col. blue, the anther yellowish. Spring–summer. (I, H) Burma.

V. concolor Bl. (*Vanda Roxburghii* R.Br. var. *unicolor* Hk.)

St. to 2′ tall and more, densely leafy, erect. Lvs. linear, to 10″ long and 1″ wide, sharply 2–3-toothed at apex. Infls. erect to arching, to about 8″ long, rather loosely 7–10-fld. Fls. about 2″ across, rather fragrant, fleshy, long-lasting, the ss. and ps. greenish-brown, often mottled with darker colour, the lip with white lat. lbs. and a white midlb. which has median reddish streaks or lines. Ss. and ps. almost cuneate-spatulate, very blunt apically, undulate marginally. Lip with small roundish lat. lbs.; midlb. oblong, narrowed medially, 5-keeled, the spur short, blunt, compressed laterally. Winter–spring. (I) China.

V. cristata (Wall.) Ldl. (*Aërides cristatum* Wall., *Vanda striata* Rchb.f.)

St. to about 8″ tall, erect, rather stout, densely leafy. Lvs. to 6″ long, mostly horizontally arranged, leathery, linear or ligulate, blunt and with three distinct teeth at the apex. Infls. usually sharply erect, short, 3–7-fld. Fls. about 2″ across, waxy, fragrant, long-lived, rather variable in coloration. Ss. and ps. mostly yellow-green (sometimes almost cream-yellow), the ss. oblong, obtuse, incurving, the narrower ps. rather falcate, otherwise similar. Lip green underneath, above dark tawny-yellow, marked with blood-red longitudinal irregular stripes and spots, the lat. lbs. inside dark blood red; this segm. is rather complex, with small, erect, blunt, almost reniform lat. lbs., and a large cuneate-ovate midlb. which is divided at the extreme apex into 3 narrow, acutish, diverging lobules. Spring–summer, mostly Mar.–July. (C, I) Nepal; Bhutan; Sikkim, at rather high elevations.

V. Denisoniana Bens. & Rchb.f.

St. rather abbreviated, stoutish, densely leafy throughout. Lvs. rather leathery, linear, to 12″ long and less than 1″ wide, sharply bilobed at apex. Infls. arching or horizontal, to 6″ long, with about 4–6 fls. Fls. variable, deliciously fragrant, waxy in texture, very long-lived, about 2″ long from tip to tip, the ss. and ps. typically varying from greenish-white to pure white or ivory-white, the lip white with a yellow or yellowish basal blotch. Ss. and ps. elliptic, expanded from a broad basal clawed portion, obtuse at apex, mostly rather recurved, the lat. ss. generally the broadest. Lip slightly longer than the ss., rather complex, the small lat. lbs. obliquely oval, the midlb. large, broadly fiddle-shaped, becoming almost kidney-shaped towards the apex, where it is distinctly forked, the lobules being sharply outstretched, the disc with 4–5 erect, irregular keels, the spur laterally compressed, oblong, obtuse, about ¼″ long. Mostly spring. (I, H) Burma: Arrakan Mountains, at about 2000–2500 feet elevation.

—fma. **hebraica** (Rchb.f.) A.D.Hawkes (*Vanda hebraica* hort., *V. Denisoniana* Bens. & Rchb.f. var. *hebraica* Rchb.f.)

Commoner in cultivation than the typical form of the species, similar to it in all parts, differing only in the floral coloration. Ss. and ps. sulphur-yellow on both surfaces, on the inside more or less densely covered with numerous spots and short transverse bars of brown or brown-purple, these mottlings often simulating certain letters of the Hebraic alphabet, hence the name. Lip yellow, olive-green at apex, spur orange inside. Mostly spring. (I, H) Burma: Arrakan Mountains.

V. Hookeriana Rchb.f.

Sts. clambering, often branched basally (sometimes above), terete, to many feet in length, emitting thick white roots at right angles to the lf.-bases. Lvs. terete, almost straight, with a constriction about ¾″ from the tip, to 4″ long. Infls. produced from opposite upper lf.-bases, usually erect, to almost 12″ long, bearing 2–10 fls. which open in succession. Fls. to more than 2″ across, lasting well, somewhat variable in colour (very rarely pure white), the dors. sep. very pale mauve with a network of slightly darker purplish-mauve, sometimes with a few faint purplish spots, mostly arching over the col., elliptic, obtuse, crisped marginally; lat. ss. horizontally spreading, almost white, similar in colour to the dors. one. Ps. coloured like the dors. sep., twisted at base, broadly oval, obtuse, crisped or undulate marginally. Lip with the spreading to semi-erect lat. lbs. rich purple, becoming darker near the base, almost triangular; midlb. pale mauve with rich purple markings which are transverse near base, spreading on either side of an unmarked median line, grading into smaller irregular spots near margins, this part widening from a narrow base, the outer edge almost semicircular, 3-lbd., rather crisped and wavy; calli 2, at spur-entrance, rounded, small, curved towards each other and touching; spur very short. Col. rather long, hairy at base and on the edges of the stigmatic surface. Mostly autumn, but almost ever-blooming in the tropics. (H) Malay Peninsula; Sumatra; Borneo.

V. insignis Bl.

Vegetatively similar to *V. Denisoniana* Bens. & Rchb.f. Infls. usually about 7-fld., to almost 12″ long, horizontal to suberect. Fls. lasting six weeks or more, about 2½″ across, waxy, highly fragrant, the ss. and ps. somewhat reflexed, wavy-margined, greenish-yellow with dark warm brown blotches which coalesce towards the edges, shortly spatulate-ovate, obtuse to acutish. Lip 3-lbd., notably longer than the ss., the rather incurving lat. lbs. white, roundish-quadrate, the very large midlb. clear mauve to almost red-magenta, broad, flat, widest near the vaguely upcurved broadly rounded tip, broadly kidney-shaped, obtuse, undulate marginally; spur oblong, obtuse, compressed on the sides. Mostly autumn, but sometimes as often as 3 times annually. (H) Moluccas; Timor; Alor Islands.

V. Kimballiana Rchb.f.

Rather similar in habit to *V. Amesiana* Rchb.f., the st. usually less than 12″ tall, with numerous very thick roots produced mostly near the base. Lvs. to 9″ long, channelled down the face, dark green usually tinged with purplish, very fleshy. Infls. mostly stiffly erect, to 1½′ tall, with up to 20 fls. which are often all open at once, the pedicellate ovaries very pale purple. Fls. fragrant, long-lived, about 2″ across. Ss. and ps. white, sometimes flushed with pale purple, narrowed at bases, oblong-elliptic, obtuse, the dors. sep. and the ps. undulate marginally, the lat. ss. somewhat sickle-shaped. Lip 3-lbd., the small acuminate lat. lbs. yellow, spotted with purple or reddish-brown, the midlb. almost roundish, crisped marginally, brilliant amethyst-purple; spur pale purple, almost 1" long, obtuse, somewhat compressed from the sides. Mostly Sept.–Dec. (C, I) China: Yunnan; Burma: Shan States; Thailand, always at elevations in excess of 4000 feet.

V. lamellata Ldl. (*Vanda clitellaria* Rchb.f., *V. Cumingii* Ldl. ex Paxt., *V. Vidalii* Boxall)

St. rather robust, very densely leafy, to 1½' tall. Lvs. narrower than most other spp., often vaguely yellowish, folded, recurved, leathery, to 10" long and ¾" wide, linear, irregularly toothed and cut at tip. Infls. erect to horizontal, with up to 25 rather crowded fls., mostly less than 12" long, rarely branching and paniculate. Fls. very fragrant, waxy, long-lived, highly variable in colour, to 1¼" across. Ss. and ps. typically yellowish or greenish with more or less prominent brown spots and longitudinal irregular stripes, broadly elliptic-spatulate from a narrow base, obtuse, the margins (especially of the ps.) undulate. Lip shorter than the ss., 3-lbd., the whitish or yellowish lat. lbs. erect, roundish, the midlb. white or yellow with some dark brown streaks down the middle, with 2–3 large basal keels, the apex almost truncate, oblong. Mostly Nov.–Jan., but sometimes more than once annually. (I, H) Philippines; ? Marianas Islands.

—var. **Boxallii** (Rchb.f.) Rchb.f. (*Vanda Boxallii* Rchb.f., *V. superba* Lind. & Rodig.)

Differing from the typical form of the sp. in its more robust, more open growth, with larger lvs. Fls. usually more numerous (up to 30 or more per infl.), to 1½" in diam., the ss. and ps. whitish or cream-white with a few purplish or reddish-purple streaks, the inner halves of the lat. ss. almost entirely reddish-purple or brownish-purple. Lip vivid rose-purple. Mostly autumn–winter. (I, H) Philippines: Luzon.

V. parviflora Ldl. (*Aërides testaceum* Ldl., *Aërides Wightianum* Ldl., *Vanda testacea* Rchb.f., *V. vitellina* Krzl.)

St. rather abbreviated, usually under 6" tall, rather densely leafy. Lvs. about 4–8" long, rather rigidly leathery, lorate, unequally 2-lbd. at apex with a mucro in the sinus. Infls. with stout peduncle, erect, to 7" long, rather loosely 5–12-fld. Fls. ½–¾" in diam., the ss. and ps. usually flesh-coloured, flushed with greenish (or yellowish with a vague pinkish tinge), the lip usually white, with raised keels on the disc, this area stained and spotted with purple or reddish-purple. Ss. and ps. similar and subequal, obovate-spatulate, obtuse. Lip 3-lbd., the lat. lbs. small, incurved, the midlb. large, broadly oblong, dilated and crenate at the apex; spur rather long, obtuse, incurving. Summer, mostly June–July. (I, H) Himalayas and India to Ceylon and Burma.

V. teres (Roxb.) Ldl. (*Dendrobium teres* Roxb., *Papilionanthe teres* Schltr.)

St. terete, often profusely branching from near base and above and forming dense tangled masses frequently many feet in length. Lvs. terete, similar to the st., 4–8"

long, distichously and alternately arranged at an acute angle to the st., erect or rather sharply ascending. Infls. 6–12" long, borne opposite the lf.-bases from upper parts of the st., bearing 3–6 fls. which are rather loosely arranged. Fls. 3–4" in diam., rather long-lasting, variable in colour, fragrant, borne on ribbed, strong-twisted pedicellate ovaries. Ss. and ps. pale rose-purple more or less suffused with white, the ss. spreading vertically, the ps. horizontally; dors. sep. ovate, obtuse; lat. ss. sub-rhomboidal, obtuse, with a hooked apicule on the under side near the apex; ps. suborbicular, slightly larger than the dors. sep. and usually strongly undulate marginally. Lip 3-lbd., the lat. lbs. roundish, infolded over the col., tawny-yellow with rather irregular bands of dull or vivid red spots on the inner side; midlb. broadly clawed, the broadly obcordate lamina deeply cleft at the apex, and with the lateral margins revolute, pale rose-purple; spur prominent, funnel-shaped, compressed laterally. Col. white, with a beaked anther. Almost ever-blooming in the tropics, otherwise usually May–July. (H) Himalayan foothills to Burma and Thailand.

V. tessellata (Roxb.) Hk. (*Aërides tessellatum* Roxb., *Cymbidium tessellatum* Sw., *Cymbidium tesselloides* Roxb., *Epidendrum tessellatum* Roxb., *Vanda Roxburghii* R.Br., *V. tesselloides* Rchb.f.)

St. usually 1–2' tall, rather densely leafy. Lvs. rather closely arranged, curving, very leathery, rather rigid, 5–7" long, ½–¾" broad, 3-toothed at the apex. Infls. ascending or suberect, usually longer than the lvs., 5–8-fld., the pedicellate ovaries white, grooved, slightly twisted. Fls. to 2" in diam., fragrant, rather long-lasting, very variable in colour, the typical form with the ss. and ps. white outside, inside pale green, tessellated with brown, oval-oblong, sometimes almost elliptic-spatulate, usually undulate marginally. Lip 3-lbd., the lat. lbs. small, lanceolate, acute, white; midlb. roundish at base, becoming quadrate in apical portion, with a notch in anterior margin, convex above, violet-purple, becoming paler towards base; spur conical, obtuse. Col. white. Mostly autumn–early winter. (I, H) Ceylon; India; Burma.

V. tricolor Ldl. (*Limodorum suaveolens* Herb., *Vanda suaveolens* Bl.)

St. often branching rather profusely from at or near the base, freely rooting well upwards, often densely leafy throughout. Lvs. gracefully curving, imbricating at base, heavily leathery, ligulate, unequally 2-lbd. at apex, to 1½' long and 1½" broad. Infls. with rather stout peduncles, horizontally arranged or ascending, usually shorter than the lvs., about 7–12-fld., the pedicellate ovaries angled, strongly twisted, 2–3" long, white, usually flushed with pale magenta-purple near base. Fls. 2–3" long, waxy and long-lasting, very fragrant, variable in shape and very much so in coloration, in the typical phase the ss. and ps. similar, obovate-oblong to orbicular-obovate, narrowed into a short claw at base, the basal margins often reflexed, the ps. frequently twisted almost completely around, undulate marginally towards apex, light yellow more or less densely spotted with bright (or dull) red-brown, the spots arranged in longitudinal rows

Vanda teres (Roxb.) Ldl. [VEITCH]

and often confluent, sometimes covering the greater part of the surface, white on outer surfaces. Lip 3-lbd., rather large, the smallish lat. lbs. white, subquadrate, curving inwards, the midlb. sub-panduriform, deeply emarginate, convex above, with 3 ridges, two of which extend to the apical margin, whitish at the base with some red-brown streaks, the remaining area bright or dull magenta-purple; spur short, compressed, white. Col. short, very dilated laterally at base. Autumn–winter. (H) Java; Bali.

—var. **suavis** (Ldl.) Veitch (*Vanda suavis* Ldl.)

Differs from the typical form in usually bearing longer infls., containing more numerous fls., these exceedingly heavy-scented, the ground-colour of ss. and ps. white, the fewer spots vivid red-purple or magenta-purple; midlb. of lip slightly narrower than in the typical sp., the margins often more strongly reflexed, the basal half dark magenta-purple, the apical half paler. Autumn–winter. (H) Java.

V. Bensoni Batem. St. erect, to about 1½′ tall, densely leafy. Lvs. linear, obliquely truncate and toothed at apex, 7–12″ long and ½–¾″ broad. Infls. erect or ascending, usually longer than the lvs., 10–15-fld. Fls. to 2″ in diam., fragrant, long-lived, the ss. and ps. similar and subequal, pale rose or whitish outside, inside yellow or yellowish-green, veined and reticu-

lated with chestnut-brown, shortly clawed basally, the blade broadly ovate, obtuse. Lip broadly clawed, the claw yellowish above and with a small triangular, ear-like, white lat. lb. on each side; midlb. light rose-purple, fleshy, convex with 3 raised median lines, cordate-oblong, expanding at the apex into 2 oblong-falcate lobules; spur short, funnel-shaped, compressed. Col. pale rose-purple. Mostly Aug.–Oct. (I, H) Burma.

V. Dearei Rchb.f. Very robust sp. to 8′ tall in old specimens, the st. stout. Lvs. close together, broad, usually yellowish-green, slightly twisted. Infl. very short, the peduncle often not more than 4″ long, few-fld. Fls. about 2″ across, heavy-textured, fragrant, long-lasting, cream-coloured, usually flushed towards tips of segms. with pale brownish, the broad ss. and ps. overlapping. Lip 3-lbd., the small white lat. lbs. inflexed towards each other, the large midlb. cream-coloured, shading to lemon-yellow at apex, which is deeply incised; disc with dark crimson streaks. Summer, but also at intervals throughout the year. (H) Borneo, at low elevations.

V. foetida J.J.Sm. Very stout sp., much like *V. Dearei* Rchb.f. in habit. Infl. short, usually 2–3-fld. Fls. about 1¾″ across, with a strong unpleasant odour, waxy, the rather broad ss. and ps. usually pale mauve at edges shading to cream at base, more or less netted with darker mauve. Lip 3-lbd., the lat. lbs. yellowish, the midlb. purplish or mauve-purple. Mostly summer. (H) Sumatra.

V. limbata Bl. Rather similar in habit to *V. lamellata* Ldl., the numerous lvs. 6–8″ long and ¾–1¼″ broad, rather close together, rigidly leathery. Infls. erect or ascending, to about 10″ long, 10–12-fld. Fls. to 2″ in diam., fragrant, long-lasting, the subequal and similar ss. and ps. broadly clawed at base, the blade elliptic, bright cinnamon-brown tessellated with darker hue, the margins usually golden-yellow, outside paler in colour and often flushed with lilac. Lip 3-lbd., pale lilac, the lat. lbs. small, rounded, the midlb. quadrate, vaguely pandurate, obscurely mucronate at truncate tip, the fleshy disc with 5–7 parallel grooves, marginally reflexed; spur short, conical, obtuse. Mostly July–Aug. (H) Java.

V. luzonica Loher ex Rolfe Similar in vegetative appearance to *V. tricolor* Ldl., often rather rank-growing, to about 4′ tall, sometimes branching profusely from base. Infls. horizontal to ascending, to about 16″ long, usually 10–25-fld. Fls. 2½–3″ in diam., heavily waxy, long-lasting, very fragrant, the somewhat clawed ss. and ps. white with more or less well-developed irregular blotches of vivid crimson or magenta-purple near the tips. Lip 3-lbd., vivid magenta-red or magenta-purple. Usually spring, but sometimes more than once annually. (I, H) Philippines: Luzon.

V. Merrillii Ames & Quis. Robust sp., rather similar in habit to *V. tricolor* Ldl., to 6′ tall in old specimens, often branching from near base, rooting freely. Infls. often rather numerous at one time, horizontal to ascending, to about 10″ long, usually about 10–15-fld. Fls. 1½–2″ in diam., very waxy and lacquered in appearance, long-lasting, with a rather peculiar odour, the clawed, very undulate ss. and ps. usually cream-yellow, heavily blotched with dark mahogany-red or blood-red, much paler outside. Lip large, flaring, mostly yellowish, sometimes with some vague dark red streaks and marks. Mostly spring, especially Apr. (I, H) Philippines: Luzon; Negros.

V. pumila Hk.f. Similar in habit to *V. cristata* (Wall.) Ldl., but the st. usually shorter and the lvs. somewhat longer and broader. Infls. to about 6″ long, loosely 2–4-fld. Fls. to about 2¼″ in diam., fragrant, heavy-textured, the narrowly oblong, obtuse ss. and ps. whitish-green, spotted and dotted with brown. Lip 3-lbd., the lat. lbs. short, triangular, obtuse, erect; midlb. oval, apically shortly acuminate, several-keeled, rather large, yellowish, streaked with red; spur shortly conical, obtuse. Mostly June–July. (I, H) Himalayas, at rather low elevations.

V. Roeblingiana Rolfe St. erect, to several feet tall, usually not branching, densely leafy. Lvs. linear, unequally bilobed and acuminate at apex, rather leathery, to about 8″ long and 1″ broad. Infls. horizontal to ascending, 7–12″ long, usually about 8–15-fld. Fls. lasting rather well, fragrant, to about 2″ in diam., the oblong, obtuse ss. and ps. clawed towards base, yellow or yellowish with irregular, usually interrupted reddish-brown longitudinal stripes, the margins yellow. Lip about as long as the ps., 3-lbd., the small, quadrangular lat. lbs. yellowish or whitish streaked with red or red-brown, the midlb. broadly clawed at base, flaring to two roundish, fringed lobules, mostly red-brown, with some yellow markings; spur conical, rather short. Usually autumn, but also often in the spring as well. (I) Philippines: Luzon, at elevations of 4000–5000 feet.

V. spathulata Spreng. St. climbing, often several feet in length, rooting freely, rather like an *Arachnis*, the lvs. to 5″ long, rather distant from one another, often purplish. Infls. erect or arching, to 15″ long, many-fld., the fls. opening a few at a time over a long period. Fls. heavy-textured, fragrant or not, to 1¼″ across, flattened, bright yellow, the lat. lbs. of the lip

usually marked with reddish-brown. Almost ever-blooming when well-established in bright sun. (H) South India; Ceylon.

V. sumatrana Schltr. Much like *V. Dearei* Rchb.f. in habit, very robust. Infls. short, few-fld. Fls. almost 2″ across, creosote-scented, waxy, glossy, usually shading from olive-brown at tips to reddish-brown basally on ss. and ps. Lip basally white, the apex flushed with pale brown, rounded and turned down at tip. Col. stout, pure white. Summer. (H) Sumatra.

V. tricuspidata J.J.Sm. Much like *V. teres* Ldl. in habit. Infls. erect, long-stalked, bearing a few fls. in succession over a long period. Fls. to about 2¼″ long, opening well, the dors. sep. and ps. similar, usually pale mauve or pink-mauve, the broad rounded lat. ss. deflexed, usually white. Lip 1¼″ long, dark purple, the lat. lbs. narrow, sharp-pointed, spreading; midlb. large, ovate, with 3 long slender points. Almost ever-blooming when well-established. (H) Lesser Sunda Islands, especially Alor.

V. Watsoni Rolfe Similar in habit to *V. Kimballiana* Rchb.f., but the st. shorter and the lvs. almost terete, with a deep groove on upper face, to about 12″ long, usually rather few in number. Infls. erect, slender, to 1½′ long, densely many-fld. Fls. about 1¾″ in diam., the ss. and ps. like those of the other noted sp., snow-white, slightly undulate marginally. Lip as long as the lat. ss., white, yellow towards the base, the lat. lbs. very small, triangular, obtuse, the midlb. almost circular, slightly concave, the margins fine-toothed; spur saccate, short, obtuse. Mostly Feb.–Apr. (I) Viet-Nam: Annam.

VANDOPSIS Pfitz.
(*Fieldia* Gaud.)

Vandopsis is a genus of about twelve species of typically very robust and spectacular epiphytic or lithophytic orchids of the subtribe *Sarcanthinae*, whose range extends from China and the Ryukyu Islands to New Guinea, the majority of the described components occurring in the last-named island. At least five of the species are in contemporary cultivation, being among the most prized of vandaceous orchids. The genus is allied to *Renanthera* Lour. and to *Arachnis* Bl., but is differentiated by structural details of the usually very showy blossoms. Most of the cultivated Vandopsis are grown under erroneous names.

· Two species of the genus, *V. lissochiloides* (Gaud.) Pfitz. and *V. gigantea* (Ldl.) Pfitz., have thus far been utilized by the breeders, with extraordinarily handsome results. When crossed with *Vanda*, *Opsisanda* is the name bestowed on the progeny; with *Renanthera*, *Renanopsis*, and with *Arachnis*, *Vandachnis*. A tremendous amount of potentially important hybridization still awaits the enterprising breeder with this genus, particularly with other allied groups of the *Vandeae*.

CULTURE: Mostly as for the tropical species of *Vanda*. Vandopsis are usually large orchids, and will, for the most part, stand more exposure to full sun than many Vandas. Regular applications of fertilizer seem most beneficial in this genus. (I, H)

V. gigantea (Ldl.) Pfitz. (*Vanda gigantea* Ldl., *Vanda Lindleyana* Griff., *Fieldia gigantea* Rchb.f., *Stauropsis gigantea* Bth.)
Sts. usually very abbreviated, rarely to 12″ tall, robust. Lvs. few, tongue-shaped, unequally 2-lbd. at the apex,

usually yellowish-green, to 2′ long and 2½″ wide, extremely heavy and rigidly leathery. Infls. pendulous to strongly arching, loosely 6–18-fld., to 12″ long. Fls. to about 3″ in diam., often lasting for several months in perfection, vaguely fragrant at times, very thick and heavy-textured, the ss. and ps. yellow with concentric rings of light brown markings, the lip yellow, with a high white keel down the middle. Mostly spring–summer. (I, H) Burma; Thailand.

V. lissochiloides (Gaud.) Pfitz. (*Fieldia lissochiloides* Gaud., *Grammatophyllum pantherinum* Zipp., *Stauropsis lissochiloides* Pfitz., *Vanda Batemani Ldl.*, *Vanda lissochiloides* Ldl.)

Sts. very robust, to 6′ tall (sometimes taller), occasionally sparsely branched from at or near the base, leafy throughout. Lvs. arranged horizontally, very heavy and rigidly leathery, to 2′ long and 2″ broad, ligulate, unequally 2-lbd. at apex. Infls. robust, rigidly erect, to 8′ tall, loosely 12–30-fld., the fls. opening successively over a period of many months. Fls. very heavy-textured, extremely long-lived, sweetly fragrant, to about 3″ across, rather variable in colour, the typical phase with the outside of the ss. and ps. densely spotted with rich magenta (sometimes wholly magenta), the inside yellow, blotched with magenta-purple, the lip yellow and magenta-red. Mostly summer, but in the tropics sometimes ever-blooming. (H) Philippines; Moluccas.

V. Parishii (Rchb.f.) Schltr. (*Vanda Parishii* Rchb.f.)

Sts. abbreviated, rather robust, erect, usually about 6–8″ tall at most. Lvs. few, heavily leathery, oblong-elliptic, unequally 2-lbd. at the apex, to 10″ long and 2½″ broad. Infls. arching to semi-erect, loosely 5–7-fld., to 1½′ long. Fls. to about 2½″ in diam., fragrant, heavy-textured, long-lived, the wide ss. and ps. greenish-yellow with brown blotches, the smaller lip pale yellow with rose-red spots. Summer–autumn. (I, H) Burma; Thailand.

—var. **Mariottiana** (Rchb.f.) Schltr. (*Vanda Mariottiana* Rchb.f.)

More frequent in cultivation than the type, from which it differs primarily in the colour of the fls., these lustrous rosy-magenta, the ss. and ps. brownish apically, white in the middle, the lip brilliant magenta. Summer. (I, H) Burma; Thailand.

V. undulata (Ldl.) J.J.Sm. (*Vanda undulata* Ldl., *Stauropsis undulata* Bth.) Pls. long-climbing, rather vine-like, rooting freely, to more than 2′ tall. Lvs. numerous, horizontally spreading, oblong, leathery, to about 3½″ long. Infls. long-stalked, the rachis thickened, rather densely few-fld., to 12″ long or less. Fls. 8–15, to more than 1¼″ across, waxy,

Vandopsis Parishii (Rchb.f.) Schltr. var. *Mariottiana* (Rchb.f.) Schltr. [VEITCH]

487

fragrant, the ss. and ps. white, often pink-flushed, the complex lip greenish-yellow, margined with red. Summer. (I) Himalayas, mostly in Assam.

V. Warocqueana (Rolfe) Schltr. (*Stauropsis Warocqueana* Rolfe) St. very robust, densely leafy, to more than 2' long. Lvs. leathery, tongue-shaped, to 15" long and 2" broad. Infls. rigidly erect, loosely many-fld., to almost 2' tall. Fls. rather nodding, to about 1½" across, fragrant, long-lived, the ss. and ps. heavy-textured, yellow, densely spotted with brown-red, the lip fleshy, yellowish, marked with magenta, the keels whitish. Summer–autumn. (H) New Guinea.

VANILLA Sw.
(*Myrobroma* Salisb., *Vanillophorum* Neck.)

In a remarkable study concerning the genus *Vanilla*,[1] one hundred and ten species are recognized as being valid. These are vine-like orchids—variously terrestrial, lithophytic, or truly epiphytic—of the subtribe *Vanillinae*, closest in their taxonomic alliance to *Galeola* Lour. They are widespread in almost all of the tropical (and sub-tropical) portions of the globe, though they reach their greatest development in Brazil, tropical Africa, and the West Indies. These are unusual plants, some of them having large handsome leathery leaves, while the viney stems in others are essentially leafless, the leaves being reduced to diminutive scale-like bracts. The flowers are for the most part large and showy, though they usually do not last very well, in some cases fading after only a few hours of expansion; these blossoms are, however, produced in succession from abbreviated inflorescences, over a rather long period of time, hence a blossoming *Vanilla* is attractive for several weeks or even months. These flowers are fleshy and very difficult to preserve, hence the genus contains many still-confused taxa. The members of the genus are most noteworthy in that several of them bear seed-capsules which, when suitably dry and cured, contain the alkaloid vanillin, from which commercial vanilla extract is derived. Despite the appearance of synthetic products, the growing of Vanilla is still an important industry in some parts of the world, notably Mexico, Madagascar, and Tahiti, where entire plantations are devoted to the cultivation of these unusual economically important orchids. A great many contemporary orchid collections have at least one specimen of *Vanilla*, these usually grown as curiosities, since all too often in the average greenhouse they do not produce their attractive flowers. If, however, attention is paid to the cultural needs of the plants (see cultural instructions below), members of this genus are usually not difficult to bring into bloom with regularity.

No hybrids have as yet been registered utilizing members of the genus *Vanilla*, although several appear to have been made by scientific experimenters. Doubtless some unusually interesting and attractive hybrids could be made through critical experimental breeding, and this is to be recommended to interested orchidists.

CULTURE: When mature, most of the Vanillas are very lengthy, often freely branching vines. Because of this, when grown in our collections, they must be given

[1] *Le Vanillier et la Vanille dans le Monde*, by Gilbert Bouriquet and collaborators. Éditions Paul Lechevalier, Paris, 1954.

some sort of support, such as a trellis or lattice-work, The stems produce a basal root-system, but also give off rather numerous roots from the nodes up the stems, hence it is recommended that these aerial roots be put sufficiently close to some medium that they can attach themselves. The base of the plant may to advantage be put in a well-drained pot, in a compost such as that suggested for *Phaius* (this applies even to the strictly epiphytic species of the genus), with the viney stems trained upwards. Usually, even in the tropics, Vanillas do not produce their flowers until they are rather large, and when the apical parts of the growing stems can hang freely from their support. Flowering is also definitely encouraged if the plants are grown in a very bright situation, some of the species, in fact, producing their blooms only when they are exposed to full sun; this particularly applies to the so-called 'leafless' Vanillas. Members of this genus grow throughout the year, hence they need never be allowed a rest-period. Quantities of moisture and as high humidity as possible are requisite at all times, and the majority of the species benefit by frequent and liberal applications of fertilizing materials. Propagation in this genus is remarkable easy: the fleshy stems are merely cut up into sections each of which comprises from three to five leaf- (or bract-) nodes; if these sections bear a root or two, so much the better, but if they are placed in moist sand mixed with chopped sphagnum moss, they will quickly root by themselves, and produce adventitious shoots from the still extant leaf-axils, especially in the upper parts of the stem-section. When grown in a sodden compost, even large specimens of most of the Vanillas are highly suscepible to various types of fatal bacterial rots and other ills, hence such conditions need to be strenuously avoided. (I, H)

V. barbellata Rchb.f. (*Vanilla articulata* Northrop)
St. elongate, often bronze-tinged through exposure to the sun, clambering and rather profusely branched, fleshy, often many feet long and forming huge entangled masses, producing at the nodes bracts or abortive lvs. and aerial roots, the internodes to about 12" long. Infls. short, axillary, racemose, with up to about 12 fls. Fls. very fleshy, fragrant, not lasting well, the ss. and ps. somewhat incurving, green, the lip greenish below, dark red shading to white on the edge, attached to the lower two-thirds of the col., the midlb. strongly reflexed, pleated and distinctly 3-lbd. at broadly truncate apex; disc hairy and furnished with wart-like protuberances. Mostly May–July. (I, H) South Florida; Bahamas; Cuba; ? elsewhere in West Indies.

V. Dilloniana Correll
Rather similar in habit to *V. barbellata* Rchb.f., but often less robust, the internodes usually shorter (seldom more than 5" long), the infls. as in the other-noted sp. Fls. not opening fully, fugacious, fragrant, fleshy, almost 2½" long, the ss. and ps. greenish, the large complex lip white and purple, tubular below, the apical part reflexed and dilated, marginally very frilled and crisped, the disc with ornate and very complex hairs and wart-like papillae, these usually arranged in definite coloured serial ranks. Mostly Mar.–June. (I, H) South Florida. Cuba; Hispaniola.

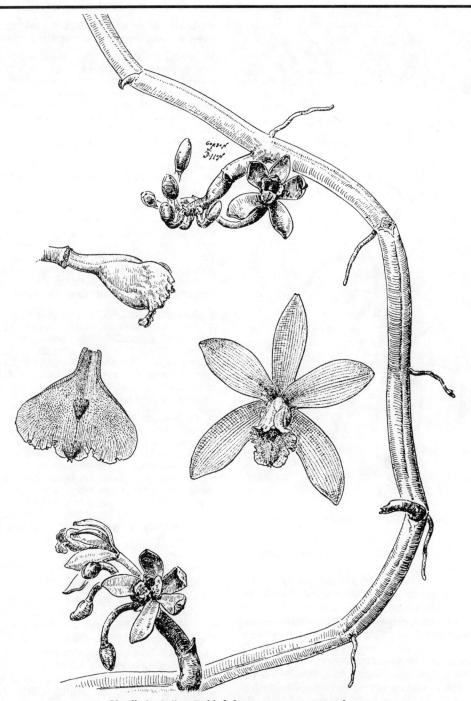

Vanilla barbellata Rchb.f. [GORDON W. DILLON]

V. planifolia Andrews (*Myrobroma fragrans* Salisb., *Vanilla fragrans* Ames)

St. elongate, often many feet in length, sparsely or profusely branching, slender or robust, leafy, rooting at most nodes. Lvs. subsessile, fleshy-succulent, oblong-elliptic to narrowly lanceolate, acute to short-acuminate, in robust forms to almost 9″ long and 3″ broad. Infls. axillary, to about 3″ long, the 20 or so fls. produced usually singly but in succession. Fls. not opening very well, fragrant, fleshy but short-lived, less than 2½″ long, greenish-yellow, the complex tubular lip often whitish on the disc, the lamina irregularly fringed on the re-curved margins. Throughout the year, often almost ever-blooming in well-established specimens. (I, H) South Florida; West Indies; Mexico through Central America well into South America; also cultivated in both hemi-spheres, and sometimes appearing as an escape plant in other areas.

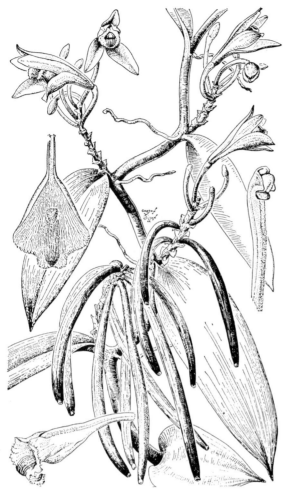

Vanilla planifolia Andr. [GORDON W. DILLON]

V. pompona Schiede (*Vanilla grandiflora* Ldl., *V. guianensis* Splitg.)

Rather similar in habit to *V. planifolia* Andrews, but considerably more robust, forming a very stout, frequently unbranched vine, to many feet long. Lvs. very thick and succulent, basally abruptly contracted and subcordate, with very short petioles, to 12″ long and 4½″ broad. Infls. abbreviated, rarely under 7″ long, the rachis very stout, the numerous fls. crowded. Fls. not opening well, fleshy, to 3¾″ long, rather fragrant, fugacious, the ss. and ps. greenish-yellow, the lip white to orange-yellow. Lip undulate-crisped marginally, the disc is smooth except for a crest of recurved, cuneate, overlapping appendages beneath the upper part of the col. Mostly summer, but sometimes in well-established specimens almost ever-blooming. (I, H) Mexico throughout Central America to Peru, Bolivia, and Brazil.

V. africana Ldl. Slender vine to many feet in length, branched. Lvs. oblong-lanceolate to narrowly ovate, acuminate, rounded and short-petioled at base, strong-veined, to almost 5″ long and 1¼″ broad. Infls. sometimes branched, abbreviated, rather densely many-fld. Fls. hooded, fragrant, white,

marked on the lip with purple. Lip 3-lbd., the disc made up of 4–5 lamellae. Summer–autumn. (H) Tropical West Africa.

V. aphylla (Roxb.) Bl. (*Limodorum aphyllum* Roxb.) Sts. slender, somewhat flattened, essentially leafless, the internodes 2–5″ long, rooting at the nodes, where tiny bract-like abortive lvs. are often produced on new growth. Infls. very short, usually about 3-fld. Fls. opening well, to almost 2″ in diam., the ss. and ps. pale greenish, often reflexed and curling back, the lat. lbs. of the lip erect on the sides of the col., pale green, the midlb. rounded, with reflexed slightly toothed edges, almost entirely covered with pale pinkish hairs, flushed with rose on a greenish-white ground. Mostly summer. (H) Viet-Nam and Cambodia through Malay Peninsula to Java.

V. Humblotii Rchb.f. Sts. robust and often rather elongate, branched, essentially leafless, glaucous-green, usually brownish-spotted and rough-warty, rooting at the nodes. Infls. axillary, many-fld., the fls. produced in succession, to 12″ long. Fls. opening well, very showy and lasting rather well, to 5½″ in diam., canary-yellow, the handsome flaring lip marked with intricate radiating brown or reddish-brown fringed lines. Summer. (H) Comoro Islands.

V. phaeantha Rchb.f. Rather similar in habit to *V. planifolia* Andrews, the lvs. fleshy, to 5½″ long and 1¾″ broad. Infls. abbreviated, about 12–fld. Fls. opening rather well, fragrant, fleshy, to almost 5″ in diam., greenish, the lip often whitish in the tube, with some yellow fringed scales on the disc, the tube of the lip upcurving, with the apex flaring, this part undulate-crisped. Mostly Apr.–June. (I, H) South Florida; Bahamas; West Indies.

V. Phalaenopsis Rchb.f. Rather similar in habit and appearance to *V. Humblotii* Rchb.f., differing in its stout long-peduncled infl. with the fls. arranged in a corymb, in fl.-colour, and in several details of floral structure, notably in the very prominent, recurved papillae on the disc of the lip. Fls. to about 3″ in diam., not opening as widely as those of the other-noted sp., the ss. and ps. white, often flushed basally with brownish, the lip outside (on the tubular part) white, flushed with wine-pink, inside yellow-orange, this hue becoming much darker in the throat. Summer. (H) Seychelles Islands.

VARGASIELLA C.Schweinf.

Vargasiella peruviana C.Schweinf., the only known member of the genus (and, indeed of the subtribe *Vargasiellinae*), is an excessively rare terrestrial or epiphytic orchid which has been found on a few occasions in the Cuzco area of Peru, usually at high elevations. Unknown in contemporary collections, it is a very peculiar plant, somewhat vaguely allied to the subtribe *Liparidinae*, with membranaceous leaves on ascending stems, and erect racemes of medium-sized, rather fleshy, hooded white and pink flowers of no especial attraction.

Nothing is known of the genetic affinities of *Vargasiella* at this time.

CULTURE: Possibly as for the more fragile species of *Sobralia*, although from the appearance of the plant, scant success should be anticipated growing it in the collection. (C)

VEXILLABIUM Maekawa

But a single species of *Vexillabium* is known to date, this a very rare terrestrial orchid from the upland forests of Japan. A member of the complex subtribe *Physurinae*, it is incompletely known botanically, and is not present in our collections at this time.

Nothing has been ascertained regarding the genetic affinities of *Vexillabium*.

CULTURE: Possibly as for *Anoectochilus*, although somewhat cooler temperatures would seem to be indicated, because of the native habitat of the plant. (I)

VIEILLARDORCHIS Krzl.

Vieillardorchis is a genus consisting of but a single species, this an excessively rare and incompletely known terrestrial orchid which has been found a few times in New Caledonia. A member of the subtribe *Listerinae*, this genus is as yet not found in our collections, and in any event appears to be primarily of botanical interest.

Nothing is known of the genetic ties of this rare group.

CULTURE: Presumably as for *Anoectochilus* and its allies. (H)

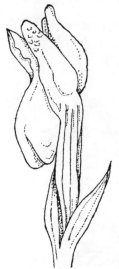

Vrydagzynea argyrotaenia Schltr. [A.D.HAWKES, AFTER
J.J.SMITH]

VRYDAGZYNEA Bl.
(*Vrydagzenia* Bl. ex Schltr.)

A member of the subtribe *Physurinae*, this genus contains upwards of twenty-five species, widespread over a tremendous area which extends from North India to the Fijis and the Hawaiian Islands. Vaguely allied to *Anoectochilus* Bl. and to *Zeuxine* Ldl., none of the component species appears to be present in collections at this time, and most of them are in any event of strictly scientific interest. The small, densely clustered flowers are of unique structural complexity.

Nothing is known of the genetic alliances of *Vrydagzynea*.

CULTURE: Presumably as for *Anoectochilus*. (H)

WARMINGIA Rchb.f.

Three species of *Warmingia* are known at this time, all of them rare epiphytic orchids from the humid forests of southern and south-central Brazil. They rather closely simulate *Macradenia* R.Br., but differ in technical details of the very fragile, usually snow-white flowers, which are borne in dense racemes. Relatively showy little plants, the Warmingias are unfortunately not in cultivation today.

Nothing is known of the genetic affinities of this genus.

CULTURE: Probably as for *Ornithocephalus*. (I, H)

WARREA Ldl.

About six rather incompletely known terrestrial (rarely lithophytic) orchids make up this genus, a member of the subtribe *Cyrtopodiinae*, without any particularly close generic allies. Ranging from Costa Rica and Panama to Colombia, Venezuela, Brazil, and Peru. Handsome, pseudobulbous plants (somewhat simulating certain of the African Eulophias in vegetative appearance), they bear tall racemes of usually large and showy flowers of great complexity, in a rather wide range of colours. Unfortunately, at this time the Warreas are excessively rare in cultivation, although the genus as a whole should be better known by collectors.

No hybrids have been produced as yet which utilize *Warrea*, and nothing is known of its genetic affinities. It seems vaguely possible that it will prove, through experimental hybridization, to be genetically compatible with at least certain members of the subtribes *Zygopetalinae* and *Lycastinae*.

CULTURE: As for *Phaius*. Some of the Warreas grow at rather high elevations, hence require intermediate temperatures. (I, H)

W. costaricensis Schltr.

Pbs. often not very well-developed, if present short, cylindric, tapering upward, usually rather hidden by the persistent lf.-sheaths. Lvs. plicate, strong-veined, lanceolate, acute or acuminate, to 2′ long and 3″ wide, narrowed at base into a short, stout, sheathing petiole. Infls. produced from sheathing petiole-base, erect, rather stout, to more than 2′ tall, with a few rather crowded fls. Fls. to more than 2½″ across, reddish-bronze, the lip paler in colour, with dark reddish-bronze markings. Dors. sep. concave, the lats. oblique, forming a short rounded mentum with the col.-foot. Ps. oblique. Lip entire, roundish when spread out, the basal callus narrow. Col. slender, curving, with a foot at base. Summer. (I, H) Costa Rica; Panama.

W. Warreana (Lodd. ex Ldl.) C.Schweinf. (*Maxillaria Warreana* Lodd. ex Ldl., *Warrea tricolor* Ldl., *Warrea unijugata* Regel, *Aganisia tricolor* Bois)

Pbs. clustered, subcylindric, rather irregular, narrowed upwards, 4–5″ long, often with portions of the persistent lf.-sheaths attached. Lvs. plicate, rather heavy-textured, oblong-lanceolate, acuminate, narrowed into a vague petiole at base, to almost 2′ long and almost 5″ broad. Infls. erect, robust, to about 2½′ long, jointed,

Warmingia Eugenii Rchb.f. [Hoehne, *Flora Brasílica*]

usually purplish, the apical rather dense rac, 4–10-fld. or more. Fls. not opening fully, faintly fragrant, lasting well, about 1½″ across, heavy-textured, the ss. and ps. white, tinged outside with yellowish, the lip white, marked inside with vivid yellow and rich purple. Ss. and ps. similar, roundish, ovate, concave, acute, the two lat. ss. ending below in an obtuse spur. Lip obovate, the basal half concave with 3 raised ridges, the apical half spreading, obscurely lobed and crisped, with several crisped lamellae. Col. short, almost cylindric. Autumn, especially Aug. (I, H) Colombia; Venezuela; Guianas; Brazil.

WARREËLLA Schltr.

This is a genus of but a single species, **Warreëlla cyanea** (Ldl.) Schltr. (*Aganisia cyanea* Bth. not Rchb.f., *Maxillaria cyanea* Beer, *Warrea cinerea* Bth., *Warrea cyanea* Ldl.), a native of Amazonian Colombia and possibly also adjacent parts of Brazil. A member of the subtribe *Zygopetalinae*, it is a segregate from *Warrea* Ldl. A very unusual terrestrial orchid, it consists of small pseudobulbs—enveloped by the sheathing, folded, strongly veined foliage, and erect racemes of rather showy, bluish-white flowers in which the lip is a bright sea-blue. It is, unhappily, not present in our collections at this time, but is assuredly a suitable item for the connoisseur.

Nothing is known of the genetic affinities of *Warreëlla*.

CULTURE: Presumably as for the tropical species of *Phaius*, etc. (H)

WULLSCHLAEGELIA Rchb.f.

A member of the subtribe *Cranichidinae*, *Wullschlaegelia* consists of three very scarce and incompletely known species of saprophytic orchids, native in the West Indies, Central America, and South America. All of them are rare even in the wild, and the genus is unknown in contemporary collections. They are insignificant, very slender, small-flowered orchids of scant merit save as botanical curiosities.

Nothing is known of the genetic affinities of *Wullschlaegelia*.

CULTURE: Possibly as for *Corallorrhiza* and other delicate saprophytic genera. (I, H)

XERORCHIS Schltr.

This is an extremely rare and little-known genus, comprising but a single species, native in the Amazonian regions of Brazil, a member of the subtribe *Vanillinae*. **Xerorchis amazonica** Schltr. is known only from a very few collections, made mostly in the vicinity of Manáos, and is not present in contemporary greenhouses. Vegetatively and florally, it rather resembles a *Pogonia*, and indeed it is somewhat allied to that genus.

Nothing has been deduced concerning the genetic affinities of *Xerorchis*.

CULTURE: Presumably as for the smaller-growing, tropical Sobralias. (H)

Wullschlaegelia aphylla (Sw.) Rchb.f. [Fawcett & Rendle, *Flora of Jamaica*]

XYLOBIUM Ldl.
(*Onkeripus* Raf., *Pentulops* Raf.)

Xylobium is a genus of about twenty species of primarily epiphytic (rarely lithophytic or terrestrial) orchids, which range from Mexico and Cuba to Brazil and Peru. Somewhat allied to *Lycaste* Ldl. and other members of the subtribe *Lycastinae*, the plants vegetatively rather resemble certain species of the aforementioned genus (and also some Bifrenarias), but they are readily distinguished by the structure of the flowers, which are borne in often abbreviated, more or less dense racemes. With few exceptions, these handsome orchids are little grown by enthusiasts, although most of them possess a certain charm, even when not in blossom, being of neat appearance, with both pseudobulbs and foliage of singular attractiveness. Their cultural requirements are easily met, and the plants flower with pleasant regularity once they are established in the collection.

No hybrids are as yet known in *Xylobium*, though the genus is presumably freely inter-fertile with *Lycaste* and other members of the alliance, and also possibly with such groups as *Maxillaria*, etc. Some fascinating experimental breeding is doubtless possible when this aggregation is critically considered.

CULTURE: As for *Lycaste*. (I, H)

X. elongatum (Ldl. & Paxt.) Hemsl. (*Maxillaria elongata* Ldl. & Paxt.)

Pbs. terete, finely grooved with age, to 10″ long and ½″ in diam., glossy, sheathed at the base. Lvs. 2, apical, glossy, plicate, rather rigid, linear-lanceolate to broadly elliptic, plicate, to 1½′ long and 4″ wide, thick-stalked at base. Infls. erect, 5–15-fld., rather dense, 2–12″ tall, with several brownish-red sheaths which often partially enclose the fls. Fls. to 1½″ across, often not expanding fully, the ss. and ps. white or pale yellow, the lip white or pale yellow, striped with purple or maroon. Lip with the midlb. densely warty. Sept.–Mar. (I, H) Mexico; Guatemala; Nicaragua; Costa Rica; Panama.

X. foveatum (Ldl.) Nichols. (*Maxillaria foveata* Ldl., *Maxillaria concava* Ldl., *Maxillaria stachyobiorum* Rchb.f., *Xylobium concavum* Hemsl., *X. Filomenoi* Schltr., *X. stachyobiorum* Hemsl.)

Pbs. robust, ovoid to subconic, tapering upwards, smooth to strongly ridged, to 4″ long and 1½″ in diam., with brown fibrous sheaths at the base. Lvs. 2–3, usually deciduous after the second year, plicate, rather rigidly leathery, lanceolate, to 15″ long and 3″ wide. Infls. erect or arching, to 12″ long, rather densely many-fld., with several broad papery bracts below. Fls. faintly fragrant, waxy, usually not opening well, about ¾″ long, creamy-white to pale yellow, the lip creamy-white with reddish veins on the disc. Nov.–Mar. (I, H) Mexico to Peru and British Guiana; Jamaica.

X. palmifolium (Sw.) Fawc. (*Epidendrum palmifolium* Sw., *Dendrobium palmifolium* Sw., *Maxillaria decolor* Ldl., *Maxillaria palmifolia* Ldl.)

Pbs. ovoid to broadly cylindric, usually deep dull green, mostly smooth, glossy, to 3″ tall. Lf. solitary, rigidly leathery, broadly lanceolate, plicate, to 1½′ long and 3″ wide. Infls. loosely few-fld., usually arching, to 4″ long, sheathed at base. Fls. about ¾″ long, usually not opening widely, faintly fragrant, the ss. and ps. yellowish-white, the lip ivory-white, with a warty midlb. Autumn. (I, H) Cuba; Dominican Republic; Jamaica.

X. Powellii Schltr. (*Xylobium sublobatum* Schltr.)

Pbs. slender, subterete (rarely cylindric-tapering), to 3″ long and ½″ in diam., basally sheathed. Lf. usually solitary (rarely 2), plicate, lanceolate, leathery, to 2′ long and 2″ wide. Infls. erect, few- to many-fld., to 6″ tall, with several papery bracts below the fl.-bearing

portion. Fls. faintly fragrant, usually not opening widely, to ½″ long, yellow or tan, sometimes tinged with light green, the lip usually lighter, with the lat. lbs. often absent. July–Aug. (I, H) Nicaragua; Costa Rica; Panama.

YOANIA Maxim.

This is a genus of two known species of uncommon and relatively unattractive saprophytic orchids of the subtribe *Calypsoinae*, one native in Japan, the other Himalayan. Neither is known in contemporary collections, and they are primarily of botanical interest in any case. *Yoania* has been placed in alliance with *Eulophia* R.Br. (subtribe *Eulophiinae*), in the past, but floral structure seems to indicate more affinity with *Calypso* Salisb. and its relatives. These plants have prominent jointed rhizomes, the leaves being reduced to mere scales on the inflorescence, and the relatively small flowers have similar sepals and petals (which expand widely) and a boat-shaped lip which bears a sac-like protuberance near its apex.

Nothing is known of the genetic affinities of the genus *Yoania*.

CULTURE: Presumably as for *Corallorrhiza* and other saprophytes. (C, I)

YOLANDA Hoehne

Yolanda restrepioides Hoehne, the only known member of this rare and most unusual genus, is known to date from only a very few collections made in the Serra de Paranapiacaba, in Brazil. A component of the subtribe *Pleurothallidinae*, it is a strange creeping epiphyte with very peculiarly shaped yellowish-green flowers. At this time, *Yolanda* does not appear to be present in our collections.

Nothing is known of the genetic affinities of this genus.

CULTURE: Probably as for the repent-stemmed Pleurothallis, although constantly moist conditions must prevail. (H)

YPSILOPUS Summerh.

Two species of *Ypsilopus* are known to date, both of them very rare epiphytic orchids, at this time not present in our collections. Both species are rather small, narrow-leaved, monopodial plants of the *Angraecum* alliance, their closest affinity seeming to be with *Rangaëris* [Schltr.] Summerh. Indigenous to tropical Africa, they are primarily of scientific interest.

Nothing is known of the genetic affinities of this unusual group.

CULTURE: Presumably as for the tropical Angraecums, etc. (H)

ZETAGYNE Ridl.

Zetagyne albiflora Ridl., the only known member of its genus, is a very rare and little-known epiphytic orchid which has apparently been collected on only one occasion in Annam. A small pseudobulbous plant with tiny white blossoms, its exact generic affiliations seem not to have been decided. At this time it is not present in our collections.

Nothing is known of the genetic ties of *Zetagyne*.

CULTURE: Unknown.

ZEUXINE Ldl.
(*Adenostylis* Bl., *Haplochilus* Endl., *Monochilus* Wall., *Psychechilus* Breda, *Strateuma* Raf., *Tripleura* Ldl.)

A member of the complex subtribe *Physurinae*, this genus consists of an estimated thirty-five or so species of primarily terrestrial orchids, whose range extends from tropical Africa and Madagascar throughout tropical Asia to the Fiji Islands in the Pacific. A single species, the pretty little **Z. strateumatica** (L.) Schltr., has become naturalized in most of the State of Florida, having been introduced into the area as an adventive with Centipede Grass (*Eremochloa ophiuroides*) from China. A few of the Zeuxines—notably those whose ornamentally coloured foliage places them in the 'Jewel Orchid' category—are found today in a very small group of choice collections, but they must be considered as rare plants. Rather simulating narrow-leaved species of *Anoectochilus* in most instances, they differ from the allied genera—*Eucosia* Bl. and *Myrmechis* Bl.—in technical details of the typically very small, but complicated flowers.

No hybrids are known in *Zeuxine*, and nothing has been ascertained concerning its genetic alliances.

CULTURE: As for *Anoectochilus*, for the most part. There is rather conclusive evidence that *Z. strateumatica* is an annual (the only orchidaceous annual known!), and its cultivation is extremely difficult, although it often comes up spontaneously in orchid pots in a collection into which it has been introduced. (H)

Z. abbreviata (Ldl.) Hk.f. (*Etaeria abbreviata* Ldl.)
St. basally creeping and rooting, the leafy part about 3″ long, with 5 lvs., these sheathed at base, the blade to 3″ long and 1¼″ wide, green. Infls. to 5″ tall, usually about 15-fld., bracted. Fls. hooded, about ¼″ long, white, the ss. with brownish or pink bases, the lip saccate in basal half, very complex. Winter. (H) Sikkim; Sumatra; Malay Peninsula.

Z. affinis (Ldl.) Bth. (*Monochilus affinis* Ldl.)
Flowering pl. to 12″ tall, the lvs. borne about to its middle. Lvs. lanceolate, to about 1½″ long, green. Infl. rather densely many-fld. Fls. about ½″ long, hooded, green or greenish, with a golden-yellow lip-disc, the lip very complex in structure. Spring–summer. (H) Himalayas, usually at low elevations.

Z. flava (Wall.) Bth. (*Monochilus flavus* Wall., *Etaeria flava* Ldl.)
Rather similar in habit to *Z. affinis* (Ldl.) Bth., but more slender, and with differently shaped fls., often leafless at flowering-time. Fls. hooded, complex, about ¼″ long or less, olive-green with a yellowish lip. May–June. (H) South India; Ceylon.

Z. goodyeroides Ldl. (*Monochilus galeatus* Ldl.)
Flowering pls. to 8″ tall, the st. bearing lvs. mostly above the middle. Lvs. ovate, acutish, about 1½″ long, very dark velvety green with an almost white mid-nerve, the underside often purplish. Infls. loose, few-fld. Fls. about ½″ long, hooded, reddish outside, white inside, very complex. Summer–autumn. (H) Himalayas.

Z. nervosa (Wall.) Trimen (*Monochilus nervosus* Wall., *Etaeria nervosa* Ldl.)
Rather similar in all parts to *Z. goodyeroides* Ldl., to about 12″ tall when in bloom. Lvs. pale green above, paler beneath. Infls. loose, few-fld. Fls. about ¾″ long, hooded, yellowish, the lip often whitish. Autumn. (H) Himalayas to Ceylon, usually at rather low elevations.

Z. regia (Ldl.) Trimen (*Monochilus regius* Ldl.)
Pls. in fl. 6–8″ tall. Lvs. mostly borne below the middle of the st., few in number, to 2½″ long, about 1″ wide or less, dark velvety green with a prominent median white or cream-white stripe. Infls. loose, rather few-fld. Fls. hooded, complex in structure, about ¾″ long, green, the proportionately long lip snow-white. Summer–autumn. (H) South India; Ceylon.

Z. strateumatica (L.) Schltr. (*Orchis strateumatica* L., *Adenostylis sulcata* Bl., *Zeuxine sulcata* Ldl.)
Pls. highly variable in dimensions, often tightly colonial, 1–7″ tall, the st. rather stout, often purplish. Lvs. several, not stalked, the narrow grassy blade to 1½″ long, keeled beneath, often purple-flushed, the upper ones partly embracing the very dense, usually somewhat cylindrical rac. Fls. quickly self-pollinating, bracted, hooded, less than ½″ long, the ss. and ps. glittering white, the ss. usually greenish at base. the lip with shortly saccate base, the small blade vivid yellow-green to almost butter-yellow. Jan.–Mar. (H) Afghanistan to South China, throughout South-east Asia to Malay Peninsula; widely naturalized in Central and South Florida.

Z. violascens Ridl. (*Hetaeria purpurascens* Bl.)
St. basally crawling, the erect part to about 7″ tall, the few lvs. mostly borne near base. Lf.-blade about ¾″ long by ¼″ wide, stalked, dark purplish with a pale mid-rib. Infl. slender, to 4″ long, short-hairy, few-fld. Fls. small, hooded, white (rarely pink), about ½″ long, the lip usually with a small yellow median area. Autumn–winter. (H) Sumatra; Java; ? Borneo; Malay Peninsula.

Z. clandestina Bl. Pls. to 11″ tall, rather leafy. Lvs. about 6, to 1½″ long, shortly stalked. Infl. slender, the scape hairy, to 5″ long, the fls. not crowded, bracted. Fls. hooded, about ¼″ long, greenish, the ss. hairy, the lip-blade white with a greenish base. Autumn. (H) Malay Peninsula; Java.

Z. gracilis (Breda) Bl. (*Psychechilus gracile* Breda) St. creeping at base, ascending, the lvs. fading at flowering-time, the leafy st. about 4″ long. Lvs. with thin blades, to 2″ long, short-pointed, scarcely stalked. Infl. to more than 7″ long, hairy, the rac. few- to many-fld. Fls. more than ¼″ long, hooded, the hairy ss. greenish, the ps. greenish with white tips, the lip yellowish basally, white apically, complex in structure. Summer–autumn. (H) Sumatra; Java; Borneo: Malay Peninsula.

ZYGOCOLAX Rolfe

This is a natural hybrid genus between a species of *Zygopetalum* Hk. and a species of *Colax* Ldl., which is known from a few localities in the humid forests of south-central Brazil. An exceptionally interesting epiphytic orchid, it is today very rare in our collections, although it has also been produced artificially on several occasions, notably by English orchidists. Vegetatively and florally, the genus is rather intermediate between the two parent groups.

Several other Zygocolax are on record in the hybrid lists, these having been produced artificially.

CULTURE: As for *Zygopetalum*. (I)

Z. x Veitchii Rolfe

Natural (and artificial) hybrid between *Zygopetalum crinitum* Lodd. and *Colax jugosus* (Ldl.) Ldl., rather intermediate in all parts between the parents. Pbs. broader and shorter than the *Colax* parent, the lvs. narrower, and the racs. shorter and fewer-fld. than in the *Zygopetalum* parent. Fls. about 3″ in diam., fragrant, very handsome, long-lived, the ss. and ps. similar and subequal, broader than the *Zygopetalum* but narrower than the *Colax* parent, yellow-green copiously spotted and blotched with brown-purple. Lip roundish, with 2 basal auricles, the central area white with radiating lines of violet-purple papillae, the marginal area streaked with violet-purple. Col. yellow-green, spotted with brown-purple. Spring–early summer. (I) Brazil.

ZYGOPETALUM Hk.
(*Zygopetalon* Rchb.)

About eighteen species of *Zygopetalum* are now considered valid, the majority of these terrestrial, or rarely epiphytic or lithophytic, very handsome orchids native in Brazil; additional members of the group occur in Paraguay, Peru, Bolivia, Venezuela, and the Guianas. A few of them are now present in our collections, and all of them are well worthy of attention by the specialist, being showy plants with large racemes of big, very ornamental blossoms. Strongly pseudobulbous plants, they have attractive, usually glossy foliage, which eventually becomes deciduous; the sizeable flowers are borne, often in considerable numbers, in erect or arching racemes, and frequently persist in perfection for more than a month. In California and elsewhere in the United States, one species of *Zygopetalum* (*Z. intermedium*, grown habitually as *Z. Mackayi*, which is a distinct, much rarer plant) is grown commercially, in rather large quantities, for cut-flowers, which enjoy considerable popularity on the market.

Zygopetalum has been utilized by the breeders on several occasions, in the production of such groups as *Chondropetalum* (× *Chondrorhyncha*), *Zygobatemania* (× *Batemania*), *Zygocaste* (×*Lycaste*), *Zygocolax* (× *Colax*)[1] and *Zygonisia* (× *Aganisia*). It also seems entirely probable that the group will prove genetically compatible with several other groups, in the light of recently acquired knowledge regarding this matter, such as *Maxillaria, Bifrenaria, Neomoorea, Huntleya,*

[1] *Zygocolax x Veitchii* Rolfe is also a natural hybrid, in Brazil, and is treated above.

Pescatorea, Anguloa, and others. A tremendous field of hybridization endeavour seems to be present in connection with this aggregation of orchids.

CULTURE: Most of the Zygopetalums are easily grown in our collections, when treated basically like the evergreen Calanthes, the tropical species of *Phaius*, etc. They delight in an airy, rather sunny situation, and require a brief resting-period upon completion of the new growths, for best production of the handsome flowers. Like most terrestrial orchids (even the epiphytic Zygopetalums—except for those noted below—are best treated as terrestrials under cultivation), they benefit by frequent and liberal applications of fertilizing materials. Two species, both sporadically encountered in highly comprehensive collections, require very specialized conditions, namely *Z. graminifolium* Rolfe and *Z. maxillare* Lodd. In the wild in its native Brazil, the first-named species habitually inhabits the trunks of small tree-ferns, in humid swamps, while *Z. maxillare* almost always is found on the trunk of the tree-fern *Dicksonia Sellowiana*, or species of *Cyathea* or *Alsophila*. If removed from their tree-fern-trunk home, or if the 'host' fern is permitted to die, the orchids usually soon deteriorate and perish. It seems possible that if these two species were grown from seed, and established on living tree-ferns (preferably of the particular species involved) in the greenhouse, some degree of success might be obtained, but otherwise this does not seem possible in most instances. (I, H).

Z. brachypetalum Ldl.

Rather similar in habit to *Z. intermedium* Lodd. and *Z. Mackayi* Hk., the pbs. with more strongly developed basal fibres, the lvs. longer and more flaccid in texture, the infls. more slender and taller, the fls. spaced farther apart and of different coloration and shape. Infls. usually rigidly erect, to almost 3′ tall, the 4–10 or more fls. far apart in upper portions. Fls. fragrant, waxy, rather long-lived, to slightly more than 3″ apart, the spreading ss. and ps. dirty green outside, inside pale green basally and marginally, otherwise dark or rather pale purplish- or wine-red, the lip white, with irregular purplish-red streaks radiating from the base, the many-grooved basal callus rather fuzzy, dark purple, the short col. bright apple-green. Mostly autumn–winter. (I, H) Brazil, usually in the higher mountainous areas.

Z. crinitum Lodd. (*Zygopetalum Crepauxi* Carr, *Z. Mackayi* Hk. var. *crinitum* Ldl., *Z. pubescens* Hoffmsgg., *Z. stenochilum* Lodd.)

Rather similar to *Z. intermedium* Lodd. and *Z. Mackayi* Hk., but usually less robust vegetatively and often with horizontally spreading infls., rather than rigidly erect ones. Pbs. ovoid to elongate-ovoid, somewhat compressed laterally, becoming wrinkled and grooved with age, to 4″ tall. Lvs. (apical) 2–3, rather fleshily coriaceous, lanceolate, glossy, acuminate apically and narrowed basally, to 1½′ long and almost 2″ broad. Infls. rather robust, to 1½′ long, sheathed, the 3–10 large fls. usually all arranged on one side only (unlike the allied spp.). Fls. waxy, very fragrant, long-lasting, widely opening, to almost 3½″ across, the ss. and ps. greyish-green or apple-green, irregularly

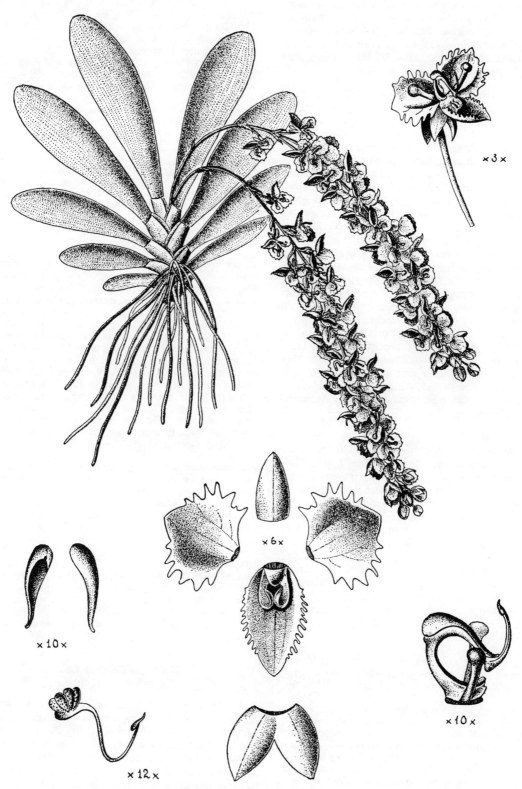

×3×

×6×

×10×

×12×

×10×

Zygostates lunata Ldl. [Hoehne, *Flora Brasílica*]

blotched and streaked with dull red or brown, the large, frilled lip white with more or less extensive branched veins radiating from the base, these dark red to rosy-red, the veins densely furnished with erect short hairs of the same colour. Summer–autumn. (I, H) Brazil, rather widely dispersed.

Z. intermedium Lodd. (*Zygopetalum Mackayi* Paxt. not Hk., *Z. Roezlii* Rchb.f., *Z. velutinum* Hoffmsgg.)

The most frequent sp. in cultivation, typically confused with *Z. Mackayi* Hk. Pbs. usually ovoid-conical, tightly clustered, slightly compressed laterally, at first with prominent basal sheaths, these breaking down into fibres with age, bright-green, becoming sulcate with age, to 3½″ tall and 2″ in diam. Lvs. (apical) 3–5, glossy bright-green, rather fleshily coriaceous, lanceolate-elliptic to lanceolate-ligulate, acute or acuminate, narrowed towards base, paler beneath, to 18″ long and 2¼″ wide. Infls. arising from axils of basal lf.-like bracts, robust, usually erect, strongly sheathed, to more than 2′ tall, with 4–5 fls. or more, usually all open at once. Fls. very fragrant, waxy, long-lived, to 3″ in diam., widely opening, the ss. and ps. bright green or yellowish-green, blotched with reddish-brown, the lip frilled, white, with radiating branched veins from the base, these violet-red. Differs principally from *Z. Mackayi* Hk. in having the ps. approximately the same length as the dors. sep. (rather than considerably shorter than it), the inner part of the lip noticeably fuzzy (instead of only vaguely roughened), and the col. fuzzy on its inner face (rather than glabrous). Autumn–winter. (I, H) Brazil.

Z. Mackayi Hk.

Rare in contemporary cultivation, usually confused with the much commoner *Z. intermedium* Lodd., from which it differs principally in the characters noted under that sp. Infls. to more than 3′ tall, often rather tortuous, with 5–10 large fls. which often expand simultaneously, with very prominent bracts subtending the pedicellate ovaries of each fl., these to more than 1″ long. Fls. waxy, very fragrant, long-lasting, to a maximum of 3¼″ in diam., the ss. and ps. often incurving apically, yellowish-green, with large irregular blotches of reddish-brown or maroon, the lip white with very intricate branching veins radiating from the base, these veins dark red to almost blue, furnished with tiny erect hairs of the same colour, these often almost absent. Autumn–winter. (I, H) Brazil.

Z. bolivianum Schltr. (*Zygopetalum intermedium* Lodd. var. *peruvianum* Rolfe) Rather similar in all parts to *Z. intermedium* Lodd., differing in technical details of the fls., notably in the differently shaped lip which is completely glabrous and smooth. Fls. rather few, showy, waxy, fragrant, to almost 3½″ across, the spreading ss. and ps. pale green with rather sparse rich dark maroon blotches, these mostly arranged in longitudinal series. Lip large, frontally truncate or rounded, deeply excised, the margins slightly undulate, white with radiating branched veins from the base, these vivid reddish-magenta. Winter. (I, H) Bolivia; Peru.

Z. Burkei Rchb.f. Pbs. clustered, narrowly oblong, furrowed with age, to 3″ long. Lvs. usually paired, to almost 2′ long, narrowly lanceolate, acuminate, strongly nervose. Infls.

erect, to 1½′ tall, with 4–5 fls. which typically all expand simultaneously. Fls. waxy, fragrant, long-lived, to more than 2″ in diam., the ss. and ps. ovate-lanceolate, green, densely marked with longitudinal bands of brown, which here and there break up into spots or blotches. Lip clawed, obovate, marginally rather frilled, white, the branched veins crimson or purplish-red, very brilliant. Autumn–winter. (H) Venezuela; British Guiana; Suriname; Brazil: Amazonas.

Z. graminifolium Rolfe Rhiz. usually rather elongate, the pbs. often some distance apart, relatively small for the genus (usually 2″ tall), strongly sheathed basally. Lvs. (apical) usually 2–3, rather flaccid, narrowly linear-lanceolate, to 1½′ long and only about ½″ wide at broadest point. Infls. to about 1½′ tall, the rather crowded 6–10 fls. usually all open at once. Fls. to slightly more than 2″ across, the ss. and ps. greenish, very densely mottled and blotched (the markings often confluent) with dark greyish-brown or greyish-maroon, the lip mostly blue-purple with radiating branched veins of darker intensity, and usually an apical whitish zone. Mostly summer. (I, H) Brazil.

Z. maxillare Lodd. (*Zygopetalum Hasslerianum* Krzl., *Z. mandibulare* Rchb.f.) Rhiz. flexuose, creeping, rather thin. Pbs. often several inches apart, 2–3″ long, ovoid-oblong, more or less compressed and often markedly angular. Lvs. narrowly lanceolate, subacuminate, prominently venose, narrowed basally, to 15″ long and slightly more than 1″ wide. Infls. erect or arching, to about 15″ long, furnished with large usually brownish sheathing bracts, 5–8-fld. Fls. about 2½″ long, fragrant, waxy, long-lived, the ps. and dors. sep. ascending, the lat. ss. down-curving, all light green, this background almost entirely obscured by bronzy-brown, the lip 3-lbd., the lat. lbs. narrowly oblong, erect, joined to the semilunate violet-purple, fleshy crest that is ridged and furrowed on the inner side; midlb. almost round, marginally crisped, this margin paler than the other violet-blue or purplish-blue segm. Winter–spring. (I, H) Brazil; Paraguay.

Z. Mosenianum B.-R. Highly aberrant, rather simulating a loose-leaved *Vanda*, being of markedly monopodial habit! Pbs. absent, the scrambling, freely rooting leafy st. to almost 7′ tall, rarely branching. Lvs. distichously arranged, jointed to the lf.-bases and eventually deciduous, rather flaccid in texture, strongly nerved, the lamina linear-lanceolate, acuminate, arching, to 10″ long and 1¼″ wide. Infls. arising from near tip of growing apex, axillary, 3–7-fld., 6–15″ tall. Fls. rather distant, to 2″ across, waxy, fragrant, rather long-lived, whitish-green, spotted and irregularly blotched with bright brown or maroon, the ss. and ps. apically often somewhat recurving, the lip rather fleshy, white with branched veins from the base of a bright or rather dull red or purplish-red hue. Winter–spring. (I, H) Brazil, usually growing in swampy areas.

ZYGOSTATES Ldl.
(*Dactylostylis* Scheidw.)

A member of the subtribe *Ornithocephalinae*, *Zygostates* contains three species of small epiphytic orchids in Brazil, **Z. Alleniana** Krzl., **Z. cornuta** Ldl., and **Z. lunata** Ldl. None of these charming little plants appears to be present in collections at this time. They rather simulate certain species of *Ornithocephalus* Hk. in vegetative appearance, but differ in technical details of the flowers.

Nothing is known of the genetic affinities of *Zygostates*.

CULTURE: Presumably as for *Ornithocephalus*. (H)

THE ORCHID AUTHORITIES

When a person names an orchid (or, for that matter, any other plant) his name—or, more usually, an accepted abbreviation thereof—is correctly affixed to the name which he has given. For example, we have *Cattleya labiata* Ldl. This fine and popular *Cattleya* species was given its name in the year 1821 by John Lindley, who was a noted student of the Orchidaceae (in fact, he is often called the 'Father of Orchidology'). This particular orchid's name is correctly always written in this manner, with the word 'Ldl.' after the actual botanical names—generic and specific—of the plant. This 'Ldl.' is the most generally accepted abbreviation for 'Lindley', and from it we can thereby readily ascertain by whom the species was originally described. In horticultural usage, in speaking, and in most popular publications, these authors' abbreviations are generally not utilized, and it is because of this that confusion frequently occurs, since the same name may have been given by two different orchidologists (or even by the same orchidologist in some exceptional cases!) to orchids which we now know to be completely distinct.

For example, the orchid *Oncidium altissimum* was originally described by Olaf Swartz in the year 1800. Yet, thirty-three years later, evidently being unaware of Swartz's use of the same name, or perhaps believing that he had the same plant under consideration, John Lindley used the epithet *altissimum* again—but this time for an *Oncidium* which we now know to be correctly *O. Baueri* Ldl. Thus, in the literature we encounter at least two entirely different orchids with this identical name of *Oncidium altissimum*. One of these is the true *O. altissimum* of Swartz, which was the first-described of the pair, and hence has precedence under our contemporary rules of botanical nomenclature. The other, *O. altissimum* Ldl.—established by Lindley more than thirty years after Swartz applied his name to an orchid—is now considered to be a synonym of *Oncidium Baueri* Ldl.

A great many students of plants have worked with the orchids. Linnaeus was the first of these who is recognized as being authoritative by contemporary botanists. In our time perhaps five or more persons are actively engaged, throughout the world—in England, in the United States, in Brazil, and elsewhere—in attempting to better our understanding of the intricacies of the Orchidaceae and the interrelationships of the component genera and species. All of these orchidologists —whether from the dead past or our contemporaries —have abbreviations for their names which are accepted by their colleagues. These are applied to new genera, new species, new combinations, or other new taxonomic categories which they have propounded.

A list of these authorities of the orchid family, past and present, with the customarily accepted abbreviations for their names, follows. These abbreviations are made use of in the pages of this encyclopaedia, and should, we feel, appear as a regular part of every botanical name wherever or whenever it is utilized in the literature.

A. & C. = Oakes Ames and Donovan Stewart Correll
A. & S. = Oakes Ames and Charles Schweinfurth
Adans. = Michael Adanson
A.Gray = See **Gray, A.**
AHS = Oakes Ames, F. Tracy Hubbard, and Charles Schweinfurth
Ait. = William Aiton
All. = Carlo Allioni
Allen & Williams = See **Allen & Wms.**
Allen & Wms. = Paul H. Allen and Louis O. Williams
Allen, P.H. = Paul H. Allen
Ames = Oakes Ames
Ames & Corr. = See **A. & C.**
Ames, Hubb. & Schweinf. = See **AHS**
Ames & Schltr. = Oakes Ames and Rudolph Schlechter
Anderson = Jacob Peter Anderson
André = René André
Andrews, A.L. = Albert LeRoy Andrews
Andrews, H.C. = Henry C. Andrews
A.Rich. & Gal. = See **Rich., A., & Gal.**
Aubl. = J.B.C.F. Aublet
Auct. = Authors; referring to usage by various or by many authors
Austin = Coe F. Austin
Auth. = See **Auct.**
Banks = Sir Joseph Banks
Barb.-Rdr. = See **B.-R.**
Barb.-Rodr. = See **B.-R.**
Barnh. = John Hendley Barnhart
Bat. = See **Batem.**
Batem. = James Bateman
Bauer = Franz Andreas Bauer
Beck = Lewis Caleb Beck
Beer = Johann Georg Beer
Benth. = See **Bth.**
Benth. & Hook.f. = See **Bth. & Hk.f.**
B.-R. = João Barbosa-Rodrigues
Bth. = George Bentham
Bth. & Hk.f. = George Bentham and Joseph Dalton Hooker
Bigel. = Jacob Bigelow
Bl. = Karl Ludwig Blume
Blake = Sidney Fay Blake
Blume = See **Bl.**
Bolander = Henry Nicholas Bolander
Bongard = August Heinrich Gustav Bongard
Bonpl. = Aimé Bonpland
Br., N.E. = Nathaniel E. Brown
Br., R. = Robert Brown
Britt. = Nathaniel Lord Britton
Brongn. = Adolphe Théodore Brongniart
BSP = Nathaniel Lord Britton, Emerson Ellick Sterns, and Justus Ferdinand Poggenberg
Bull = William Bull
Camp = Wendell Holmes Camp
Cgn. = Alfred Céléstin Cogniaux
Cgn. & Rolfe = Alfred Céléstin Cogniaux and Robert Allen Rolfe

Cham. = Adalbert von Chamisso
Chapm. = Alvan Wentworth Chapman
Chat. = Jean Jacques Chatelain
Cockerell = Theodore Dru Alison Cockerell
Cogn. = See **Cgn.**
Corr. = Donovan Stewart Correll
Correll = See **Corr.**
Crantz = Heinrich Johann Nepomuk von Crantz
Cunn. = Richard Cunningham
Cunn., A. = Allan Cunningham
DC = Augustin Pyramus De Candolle
Don, D. = David Don
Don, G. = George Don
Dressler = Robert L. Dressler
Druce = George Claridge Druce
Dryander = Jonas Dryander
du Petit-Thouars = See **Thou.**
Eames = Edward A. Eames
Eat., A. = Amos Eaton
Eat., A.A. = Alvah Augustus Eaton
Eat., H.H. = Hezekiah Hilbert Eaton
Ed.Morr. = See **Morr., E.**
Ell. = Stephen Elliott
E.Morr. = See **Morr., E.**
Endl. = Stephan Ladislaus Endlicher
Engelm. = George Engelmann
Engl. = Heinrich Gustav Adolf Engler
F. & R. = William Fawcett and Alfred Barton Rendle
Fawc. = William Fawcett
Fawc. & Rendle = See **F. & R.**
F.C.Lehm. = See **Lehm., F.C.**
Fern. = Merritt Lyndon Fernald
Fernald = See **Fern.**
Fisch. = Friedrich Ernst Ludwig von Fischer
Flick. = Edward Arthur Flickinger
Frapp. = Charles Frappier
FvM = Ferdinand von Mueller
Gagnep. = François Gagnepain
Gal. = Henri Galeotti
Garay = Leslie A. Garay
Gaud. = Charles Gaudichaud-Beaupré
Gmel. = Samuel Gottlieb Gmelin
Goldie = John Goldie
Gr. = See **Griseb.**
Gray, A. = Asa Gray
Greene = Edward Lee Greene
Greenm. = Jesse More Greenman
Griff. = William Griffith
Gris. = See **Griseb.**
Griseb. = Heinrich Rudolph August Grisebach
Gronov. = Johann Friedrich Gronovius
Guill. = See **Guillaum.**
Guillaum. = Auguste Guillaumin
Hall. = Albrecht von Haller
Hawkes, A.D. = Alex Drum Hawkes
HBK = Friedrich Wilhelm Heinrich Alexander von Humboldt, Aimé Jacques Alexandre Bonpland, and Karl Sigismund Kunth
Heller = Amos Arthur Heller
Heller, A.H. = Alfonse H. Heller
Hemsl. = William Botting Hemsley
Hk. = William Jackson Hooker
Hk.f. = Joseph Dalton Hooker

Hook. = See **Hk.**
Hook.f. = See **Hk.f.**
Hoehne = Federico Carlos Hoehne
Holtt. = Richard Eric Holttum
hort. = *Hortorum*, literally 'of the gardens'. Placed after names current among horticulturists, but not necessarily all horticulturists. Often used with less exactitude than names of authors, frequently indicating of garden or unknown origin; many of these plants have never been adequately described.
H.Perr. = See **Perr., H.**
Hubb. = Frederick Tracy Hubbard
Hult. = Eric Hultén
Hunt, T.E. = Trevor E. Hunt
Jacq. = Nickolaus Joseph von Jacquin
Jennings = Otto Emery Jennings
Jeps. = Willis Linn Jepson
Jepson = See **Jeps.**
Juss. = Antoine Laurent de Jussieu
Karst. = Gustav Karl Wilhelm Hermann Karsten
Karw. = Wilhelm Karwinsky von Karwin
Ker = See **Ker-Gawl.**
Ker-Gawl. = John Bellenden Ker (John Gawler)
Kl. = See **Klotzsch**
Klotzsch = Johann Friedrich Klotzsch
Kränzl. = See **Krzl.**
Kraenzl. = See **Krzl.**
Krzl. = Fritz Kraenzlin
Kth. = Karl Sigismund Kunth
Ktze., O. = Otto Kuntze
Kunth = See **Kth.**
Kuntze = See **Ktze., O.**
L. = Carl von Linné (Carolus Linnaeus)
L. & K. = Friedrich C. Lehmann and Fritz Kraenzlin
LaLl. = Pablo de La Llave
LaLl. & Lex. = Pablo de La Llave and Juan José Martinez de Lexarza
Lam. = Jean-Baptiste Antoine Pierre Monet, Chevalier de Lamarck
L.C.Rich. = See **Rich., L.C.**
Ldl. = John Lindley
Ldl. & Bauer = John Lindley and Franz Andreas Bauer
Ldl. & Paxt. = John Lindley and William Paxton
Lehm., F.C. = Friedrich C. Lehmann
Lehm. & Kränzl. = See **L. & K.**
Lem. = Charles Lemaire
Lex. = Juan José Martinez de Lexarza
L'Her. = C. L. L'Héritier de Brutelle
L'Herit. = See **L'Her.**
Lind. & Rod. = Lucién Linden and Émile Rodigas
Lind. & Rodig. = See **Lind. & Rod.**
Lind. = Jean Linden
Lind., L. = Lucién Linden
Lind. & Rchb.f. = Lucién Linden and Heinrich Gustav Reichenbach
Linden = See **Lind.**
Lindl. = See **Ldl.**
Lindl. & Paxt. = See **Ldl. & Paxt.**
Link = Heinrich Friedrich Link
Linn. = See **L.**
Lodd. = Conrad Loddiges
Lodd., G. = George Loddiges
Loddiges = See **Lodd.**

Loud. = John Claudius Loudon
Lour. = João Loureiro
L.Wms. = See **Wms., L.O.**
Macbr. = James Francis Macbride
Mak. = Tomitaro Makino
Makino = See **Mak.**
Mans. = See **Mansf.**
Mansf. = Richard Mansfeld
Mart. = Karl Friedrich Philipp von Martius
Martius = See **Mart.**
Mast. = Maxwell T. Masters
Matsum. = Jinzo Matsumura
Maxim. = Karl Johann Maximowicz
Merr. = Elmer Drew Merrill
Michx. = André Michaux
Mill. = Philip Miller
Miq. = Friedrich Anton Wilhelm Miquel
Moench = Konrad Moench
Mohr = Charles Theodor Mohr
Moore = Thomas Moore
Morong = Thomas Morong
Morr., E. = Charles Jacques Édouard Morren
Morris = Frank Morris
Muell., F. = See **FvM**
Muhl. = Gotthilf Ernst Heinrich Muhlenberg
Nash = George Valentine Nash
N.E.Br. = See **Br., N.E.**
Nees = Christian Gottfried Nees von Esenbeck
Nichols. = George Nicholson
Nicholson = See **Nichols.**
Niles = Grace Greylock Niles
Northr. = Alice Belle (Rich) Northrop
Northrop = See **Northr.**
Nutt. = Thomas Nuttall
Oakes = William Oakes
O'Brien = James O'Brien
O.Ktze. = See **Ktze., O.**
Otto = Friedrich Otto
Pabst = Guido F. J. Pabst
Par. = Samuel Bonsal Parish
Par. & Rchb.f. = Samuel Bonsal Parish and Heinrich
Gustav Reichenbach
Parish = See **Par.**
Parl. = Filippo Parlatore
Parlat. = See **Parl.**
Pav. = José Antonio Pavón
Pavon = See **Pav.**
Paxt. = Joseph Paxton
Peck = Morton Eaton Peck
Perr., H. = Henri Perrier de la Bâthie
Pers. = Christian Hendrick Persoon
Pfitz. = Ernst Hugo Heinrich Pfitzer
Pfitzer = See **Pfitz.**
P.H.Allen = See **Allen, P.H.**
Phil. = Rudolph Amandus Philippi
Planch. = Jules Émile Planchon
Poir. = Jean Louis Marie Poiret
Prain = Sir David Prain
Prantl = Karl Prantl
Presl = Karel Boriweg Presl
Pursch = See **Pursh**
Pursh = Frederick T. Pursh (Pursch)
Raf. = Constantino Samuel Rafinesque-Schmaltz

R.Br. = See **Br., R.**
Rchb.f. = Heinrich Gustav Reichenbach
Regel = Eduard von Regel
Reichb.f. = See **Rchb.f.**
Rendle = Alfred Barton Rendle
Rich., A. = Achille Richard
Rich., A. & Gal. = Achille Richard and Henri Galeotti
Rich., L.C. = Louis Claude Marie Richard
Ridl. = Henry Nicholas Ridley
Ridley = See **Ridl.**
Rod. = Émile Rodigas
Rodig. = See **Rod.**
Rodr. = See **B.-R.**
Rog., R.S. = Robert S. Rogers
Rolfe = Robert Allen Rolfe
Roxb. = William Roxburgh
Roxbg. = See **Roxb.**
R. & P. = Hipólito Ruiz López and José Antonio
Pavón
Ruiz = Hipólito Ruiz López
Ruiz & Pav. = See **R. & P.**
Ruschi = Augusto Ruschi
Rydb. = Per Axel Rydberg
S. & Z. = Philipp Franz von Siebold and Joseph
Gerhard Zuccarini
Salisb. = Richard Anthony Salisbury
Salvin = Osbert Salvin
Sand. = Frederick K. Sander
Sander = See **Sand.**
Scheidw. = Michael Joseph Scheidweiler
Schlecht. = Diedrich Franz Leonhard von Schlechten-
dahl
Schlechtend. = See **Schlecht.**
Schltr. = Friedrich Richard Rudolph Schlechter
Schrad. = Heinrich Adolph Schrader
Schult. = Joseph August Schultes
Schultes, R.E. = Richard Evans Schultes
Schum. = Karl Moritz Schumann
Schw., C. = Charles Schweinfurth
Schw. & Allen = Charles Schweinfurth and Paul H.
Allen
Schw. & Corr. = Charles Schweinfurth and Donovan
Stewart Correll
Schweinf., C. = See **Schw., C.**
Schweinf. & Corr. = See **Schw. & Corr.**
Seem. = Berthold Seemann
Sieb. & Zucc. = See **S. & Z.**
Sims = John Sims
Small = John Kunkel Small
Sm., J.J. = Johann Joseph Smith
Smith, J.J. = See **Sm., J.J.**
Soland. = Daniel Solander
Spreng. = Kurt Sprengel
Standl. = Paul Carpenter Standley
Steud. = Ernest Gottlieb Steudel
Steyerm. = Julian Steyermark
St.Hil. = Auguste de Saint-Hilaire
Summ. = See **Summerh.**
Summerh. = Victor S. Summerhayes
Sw. = Olaf Swartz
Swartz = See **Sw.**
Thou. = Aubert DuPetit-Thouars
Thouars = See **Thou.**

Thunb. = Carl Peter Thunberg
Torr. = John Torrey
Turcz. = Nicholaus Turczaninow
Urb. = Ignatius Urban
Urban = See **Urb.**
Van Houtte = Louis Van Houtte
Veitch = John Gould Veitch
Wall. = Nathanael Wallich
Walp. = Wilhelm Gerhard Walpers
Walt. = Thomas Walter
Warcz. = See **Warsc.**
Warsc. = Joseph Warscewicz

Warsz. = See **Warsc.**
Wats., S. = Sereno Watson
Wendl. = Hermann Wendland
Wherry = Edgar Theodore Wherry
White = Marcus W. White
White, C.T. = Cyril Tennyson White
Wight = Robert Wight
Willd. = Karl Ludwig Willdenow
Wms., B.S. = Benjamin Samuel Williams
Wms., L.O. = Louis Otho Williams
Woolw. = Frances Woolward
Zucc. = Joseph Gerhard Zuccarini

CHECK-LIST OF ORCHID GENERA

In compiling a listing such as the present one, based on the available literature, coupled with taxonomic and bibliographic research, the writer must take into consideration a series of factors. Certainly not the least of these is the human factor or element. All plant taxonomists—orchidologists not excluded—are human, and hence have diverse interpretations regarding differing entities, or taxa such as those of the genera of the Orchidaceae incorporated in the following lists.

Since the author, as compiler—not as 'final authority' —is merely here suggesting the group of taxa which he believes to be of sound validity, and his is a strictly individual interpretation, perforce such interpretation will quite naturally vary considerably among other students of the Orchid Family. It is hoped that this check-list will be of assistance to both contemporary and future orchidologists, and will hasten the time when we can state with certainty that we know *all* of the genera comprising the Orchidaceae.

In the check-list which follows, genera which I consider to be of valid standing are designated by being printed in bold-face type (**Abdominea**), while those I believe to be synonymous with other taxa are indicated in italic type (*Abola*); such synonymous genera are referred to the apparently correct genus. An approximate count of the known number of species in each valid genus is appended, parenthetically, together with the subtribal grouping of the Orchidaceae in which the genus is currently included.

Aa Rchb.f., Xen. Orch. 1: 18. 1858. = **Altensteinia** HBK
Abdominea J.J.Sm. in Bull. Jard. Bot. Buitenz. II, 14: 52. 1914. (1 sp., subtribe Sarcanthinae)
Abola Ldl., Fol. Orch. Abola [1]. 1853. = **Caucaea** Schltr.
Abrochis Neck., Elem. 3: 130. 1790. = **Orchis** [Tourn.] L.
Acacallis Ldl., Fol. Orch. Acacallis [1]. 1853. (1 sp., subtribe Zygopetalinae)
Acampe Ldl., Fol. Orch. Acampe [1]. 1853. (13 spp., subtribe Sarcanthinae)
Acanthephippium Bl. ex Endl., Gen. 200. 1837. (15 spp., subtribe Phaiinae)
Acanthoglossum Bl., Bijdr. 381. 1825. = **Pholidota** Ldl.
Acanthophippium Bl., Bijdr. 353, pl. 47. 1825. = **Acanthephippium** Bl. ex Endl.
Aceras R.Br. in Ait., Hort. Kew., ed. 2, 5: 191. 1813. (1 sp., subtribe Habenarinae)

Aceratorchis Schltr. in Fedde, Repert. Sp. Nov., Beih. 13: 328. 1922. (2 spp., subtribe Habenarinae)
Achroanthes Raf. in Med. Repos. N.Y. 5: 352. 1808, without description; & in Jour. Phys. 89: 261. 1819. = **Malaxis** Soland. ex Sw.
Acianthera Scheidw. in Otto & Dietr., Allgem. Gartenz. 10: 292. 1842. = **Pleurothallis** R.Br.
Acianthus R.Br., Prodr. Fl. Nov. Holl. 321. 1810. (20 spp., subtribe Acianthinae)
Acineta Ldl. in Bot. Reg., Misc. 67. 1847. (12 spp., subtribe Gongorinae)
Aclinia Griff., Notul. 3: 320. 1851. = **Dendrobium** Sw.
Acoidium Ldl. in Bot. Reg., under pl. 1951. 1837. = **Trichocentrum** P. & E.
Acoridium Nees & Meyen in Nov. Act. Nat. Cur. 19, Suppl. 1: 131. 1843. = **Dendrochilum** Bl.
Acostaea Schltr. in Fedde, Repert. Sp. Nov., Beih. 19: 22, 283. 1923. (2 spp., subtribe Pleurothallidinae)
Acraea Ldl. in Bth., Pl. Hartweg. 155. 1845. = **Pterichis** Ldl.
Acriopsis Reinw. ex Bl., Catal. Gew. Buitenz. 97. 1823; & Bl., Bijdr. 376. 1825. (6 spp., subtribe Thecostelinae)
Acroanthes Raf. in Jour. Phys. 89: 261. 1819. = **Malaxis** Soland. ex Sw.
Acrochaene Ldl., Fol. Orch. Acrochaene [1]. 1853. = **Monomeria** Ldl.
Acrolophia Pfitz. in Engl. & Prantl, Natür. Pflanzenfam. II, 6: 133. 1888. (9 spp., subtribe Polystachyinae)
Acronia Presl, Rel. Haenk. 1: 103. 1827. = **Pleurothallis** R.Br.
Acropera Ldl., Gen. & Sp. Orch. 172. 1833. = **Gongora** R. & P.
Acrostylia Frapp. ex Cordem., Fl. Île Réunion 227. 1895. = **Cynorkis** Thou.
Ada Ldl., Fol. Orch. Ada [1]. 1853. (2 spp., subtribe Oncidiinae)
Adelopetalum Fitzg. in Jour. Bot. 29: 152. 1891. = **Bulbophyllum** Thou.
Adeneleuterophora B.-R., Orch. Nov. 2: 179. 1881. = **Elleanthus** Presl
Adeneleuthera O.Ktze. in Post & Ktze., Lexic. 9. 1903. = **Elleanthus** Presl
Adenochilus Hk.f., Fl. New Zeal. 1: 246, pl. 56. 1853. (2 spp., subtribe Caladeniinae)
Adenoncos Bl., Bijdr. 381. 1825. (10 spp., subtribe Sarcanthinae)

Adenostyles Bth. & Hk.f., Gen. Plant. 3: 599. 1883, *sphalm.* = **Zeuxine** Ldl.

Adenostylis Bl., Bijdr. 414. 1825. = **Zeuxine** Ldl.

Adipe Raf., Fl. Tellur. 2: 101. 1836. = **Stenocoryne** Ldl.

Adnula Raf., Fl. Tellur. 2: 87. 1836. = **Pelexia** [Poit.] L.C.Rich.

Adrorrhizon Hk.f. in Trimén, Fl. Ceylon 4: 161. 1898. (1 sp., subtribe Adrorrhizinae)

Aeceoclades Duch. in Orb. Dict. 9. 1849, *err. typ.* = **Trichoglottis** Bl.

Aeëridium Salisb. in Trans. Hort. Soc. 1: 295. 1812. = **Aërides** Lour.

Aeonia Ldl. in Bot. Reg., under pl. 817. 1824. = **Oeonia** Ldl.

Aërangis Rchb.f. in Flora 48: 190. 1865. (70 spp., subtribe Sarcanthinae)

Aëranthes Ldl. in Bot. Reg., pl. 817. 1824. (30 spp., subtribe Sarcanthinae)

Aëranthus Bartl., Ord. 57. 1830. = **Aëranthes** Ldl.

Aëranthus Rchb.f. in Walp., Ann. 6: 899. 1861. = several genera of subtribe Sarcanthinae, mostly **Angraecum** Bory

Aërides Lour., Fl. Cochin-Chin. 525. 1790. (60 spp., subtribe Sarcanthinae)

Aëridium Pfeiff., Nom. 1: 67. 1873. = **Aërides** Lour.

Aërobion Kaempf. ex Spreng., Syst. 3: 679. 1826. = **Angraecum** Bory

Aetheria Endl., Gen. 214. 1837. = **Hetaeria** Bl.

Aganisia Ldl. in Bot. Reg. 25: Misc. 45. 1839; & *l.c.*, 32. 1840. (1 sp., subtribe Zygopetalinae)

Aggeianthus Wight ex Schltr., Die Orchid. 278. 1914, *sphalm.* = **Porpax** Ldl.

Aggeranthus Wight, Icon. 5: 18, pl. 1737. 1852. = **Porpax** Ldl.

Aglossorhyncha Schltr. in K.Schum. & Lauterb., Nachtr. Fl. Deutsch Südsee 133. 1905. (6 spp., subtribe Glomerinae)

Agrostophyllum Bl., Bijdr. 368, pl. 53. 1825. (60 spp., subtribe Glomerinae)

Alamania LaLl. & Lex., Nov. Veg. Descr. 2 (Orch. Opusc.): 31. 1825. (1 sp., subtribe Laeliinae)

Alamannia Ldl., Orch. Scel. 14. 1826, *sphalm.* = **Alamania** LaLl. & Lex.

Alipsa Hoffmsgg., Preis.-Verz. Orch. 20. 1840; cf. Linnaea 16: Litt. 228. 1842. = **Liparis** L.C.Rich.

Alismorchis Thou., Orch. Îles Afr., pl. 35. 1822. = **Calanthe** R.Br.

Alismorkis Thou. in Nouv. Bull. Soc. Philom., no. 19: 318. 1809. = **Calanthe** R.Br.

Allochilus Gagnep. in Bull. Mus. Hist. Nat. Paris II, 4: 591. 1932. (1 sp., subtribe Phaiinae)

Altensteinia HBK, Nov. Gen. & Sp. 1: 382, pls. 72, 73. 1815. (20 spp., subtribe Cranichidinae)

Alvisia Ldl., Fol. Orch. Alvisia [1]. 1859. = **Eria** Ldl.

Alwisia Thw. ex Ldl. in Jour. Linn. Soc. 3: 42. 1838, in obs. = **Taeniophyllum** Bl.

Amalia Rchb., Nomen. 52. 1841. = **Laelia** Ldl.

Amalias Hoffmsgg., Preis.-Verz. Orch. 20. 1840; cf. Linnaea 16: Litt. 228. 1842. = **Laelia** Ldl.

Amaridium hort. ex Lubbers, Cat. Pl. Rar. San Donato 15. 1880, *sphalm.* = **Maxillaria** R. & P.

Amblostoma Scheidw. in Otto & Dietr., Allgem. Gartenz. 6: 383. 1838. (3 spp., subtribe Laeliinae)

Amblyglottis Bl., Bijdr. 369, pl. 64. 1825. = **Calanthe** R.Br.

Ambrella H. Perr. in Bull. Soc. Bot. France 81: 655. 1934. (1 sp., subtribe Sarcanthinae)

Amesia Nels. & MacBr. in Bot. Gaz. 61: 472. 1913. = **Epipactis** [Zinn., in part] Sw.

Amitostigma Schltr. in Fedde, Repert. Sp. Nov., Beih. 4: 91. 1919. (24 spp., subtribe Habenarinae)

Amparoa Schltr. in Fedde, Repert. Sp. Nov., Beih. 19: 64. 1923. (2 spp., subtribe Oncidiinae)

Amphigena Rolfe in Dyer, Fl. Cap. 5(2): 197. 1913. (2 spp., subtribe Disinae)

Amphiglottis Salisb. in Trans. Hort. Soc. 1: 294. 1812. = **Epidendrum** L.

Amphorchis Thou., Orch. Îles Afr., Tabl. Synopt. 1822. = **Cynorkis** Thou.

Amphorkis Thou. in Nouv. Bull. Soc. Philom., no. 19: 316. 1809. = **Cynorkis** Thou.

Anacamptis A.Rich. in Mém. Mus. Paris 4: 47, 55. 1818. (1 sp., subtribe Habenarinae)

Anacheilium Hoffmsgg., Preis.-Verz. Orch. 21. 1840; cf. Linnaea 16: Litt. 229. 1842. = **Epidendrum** L.

Anaectochilus Ldl., Gen. & Sp. Orch. 498. 1840, *sphalm.* = **Anoectochilus** Bl.

Anaphora Gagnep. in Bull. Mus. Hist. Nat. Paris II, 4: 592. 1932. (1 sp., subtribe Liparidinae)

Anathallis B.-R., Orch. Nov. 1: 23. 1877. = **Pleurothallis** R.Br.

Ancistrochilus Rolfe in Dyer, Fl. Trop. Afr. 7: 44. 1897. (2 spp., subtribe Phaiinae)

Ancistrorhynchus Finet in Bull. Soc. Bot. France 54, Mém. 9: 44. 1907. (12 spp., subtribe Sarcanthinae)

Androchilus Liebm. in Bot. Notis. 101. 1844. = **Liparis** L.C.Rich.

Androcorys Schltr. in Fedde, Repert. Sp. Nov., Beih. 4: 52. 1919. (4 spp., subtribe Androcorydinae)

Androgyne Griff., Notul. 3: 279. 1851. = **Panisea** Ldl.

Anecochilus Bl., Bijdr. 411, pl. 15. 1825. = **Anoectochilus** Bl.

Anectochilus Bl., Orch. Archip. Ind. 44. 1858. = **Anoectochilus** Bl.

Angorchis Nees in R.Br., Verm. Schrift. 2: 423, *in adnot.* 1826. = **Angraecum** Bory

Angorchis Thou. in Nouv. Bull. Soc. Philom., no. 19: 314–19. 1809. = **Angraecum** Bory

Angorkis Thou. in Nouv. Bull. Soc. Philom., no. 19: 318. 1809. = **Angraecum** Bory

Angraecopsis Krzl. in Engl., Bot. Jahrb. 27: 171. 1900. (14 spp., subtribe Sarcanthinae)

Angraecum Bory, Voy. 1: 359, pl. 19. 1804. (200 spp., subtribe Sarcanthinae)

Anguloa R. & P., Prodr. Fl. Peruv. & Chil. 118, pl. 26. 1794. (10 spp., subtribe Lycastinae)

Ania Ldl. in Wall., Catal., no. 3740–1. 1828. (4 spp., subtribe Phaiinae)

Anisopetalum Hk., Exot. Fl., pl. 149. 1825. = **Bulbophyllum** Thou.

Anistylis Raf., Neogen. 4. 1825. = **Liparis** L.C.Rich.

Ankylocheilos Summerh. in Bot. Mus. Leafl. Harv. Univ. 11: 168. 1943. (1 sp., subtribe Sarcanthinae)

Anocheile Hoffmsgg. ex Rchb., Nomencl. 235. 1841. = **Epidendrum** L.

Anochilus Rolfe in Dyer, Fl. Cap. 5(2): 280. 1913. (2 spp., subtribe Disperidinae)

Anoectochilus Bl., Bijdr. 411, pl. 15. 1825. (20 spp., subtribe Physurinae)

Anota Schltr., Die Orchid. 587. 1914. = **Rhynchostylis** Bl.

Ansellia Ldl. in Bot. Reg. 30: under pl. 12. 1844. (1 sp., subtribe Polystachyinae)

Anthericlis Raf. in Amer. Monthly Mag. 195. 1819; & in Jour. Phys. 89: 261. 1819. = **Tipularia** Nutt.

Anthogonium Wall. ex Ldl., Introd. Nat. Syst., ed. 2, 1: 341. 1836. (1 sp., subtribe Phaiinae)

Anthosiphon Schltr. in Fedde, Repert. Sp. Nov., Beih. 7: 182. 1920. = **Cryptocentrum** Bth.

Anticheirostylis Fitzg., Austral. Orch. 2(4). 1891. = **Corunastylis** Fitzg.

Aopla Ldl. in Bot. Reg., under pl. 1701. 1835. = **Herminium** L.

Apation Bl. ex Ridl. in Jour. Linn. Soc. 23: 279. 1886, in syn. = **Liparis** L.C.Rich.

Apatura Ldl., Gen. & Sp. Orch. 130. 1831. = **Pachystoma** Bl.

Apetalon Wight, Icon. 5: 22, pl. 1758. 1852. = **Didymoplexis** Griff.

Aphyllorchis Bl., Bijdr. pl. 77. 1825. (12 spp., subtribe Cephalantherinae)

Apista Bl., Bijdr. 296. 1825. = **Podochilus** Bl.

Aplectra Raf., Catal. 13. 1824. = **Aplectrum** Torr.

Aplectrum Torr., Comp. Fl. St. 322. 1826. (1 sp., subtribe Corallorrhizinae)

Aplostellis Thou., Orch. Îles Afr., pl. 24. 1822. = **Nervilia** Gaud.

Aporostylis Rupp & Hatch in Proc. Linn. Soc. N.S. Wales 70: 60. 1946. (1 sp., subtribe Caladeniinae)

Aporum Bl., Bijdr. 334, pl. 39. 1825. = **Dendrobium** Sw.

Appendicula Bl., Bijdr. 297, pl. 40. 1825. (40 spp., subtribe Podochilinae)

Arachnanthe Bl., Rumphia 4: 33, pl. 196. 1828. = **Arachnis** Bl.

Arachnis Bl., Bijdr. 365. 1825. (17 spp., subtribe Sarcanthinae)

Arachnites F.W.Schmidt, Fl. Boëm. 1: 74. 1793. = **Ophrys** L.

Arethusa [Gronov.] L., Sp. Pl., ed. 1, 2: 950. 1753. (2 spp., subtribe Bletillinae)

Arethusantha Finet in Bull. Soc. Bot. France 44: 179. 1897. (1 sp., subtribe ? Bletillinae)

Argyrorchis Bl., Orch. Archip. Ind. 12, 31, 36. 1858. = **Macodes** Ldl.

Arhynchium Ldl. & Paxt., Flow. Gard. 1: 142. 1850–1. = **Armodorum** Breda

Arietinum Beck, Bot. N. & Mid. U.S. 352. 1833. = **Cypripedium** L.

Arisanorchis Hay., Icon. Pl. Formos. 4: 109. 1914. = **Cheirostylis** Bl.

Aristotelea Lour., Fl. Cochin-Chin. 522. 1790. = **Spiranthes** L.C.Rich.

Armodorum Breda, Orch. Kuhl & v.Hass. [p. 6.] 1827. (3 spp., subtribe Sarcanthinae)

Arnedina Rchb., Nomencl., no. 1984. 1841. = **Arundina** Bl.

Arnottia A.Rich. in Mém. Soc. Hist. Nat. Paris 4: 29. 1828. (2 spp., subtribe Habenarinae)

Arophyllum Endl., Gen. Pl. 193, no. 1376. 1837. = **Arpophyllum** LaLl. & Lex.

Arpophyllum LaLl. & Lex., Nov. Veg. Descr. 2 (Orch. Opusc.): 19. 1825. (2 spp., subtribe Ponerinae)

Arrhynchium Ldl. & Paxt., Flow. Gard. 1: 142. 1850–1. = **Armodorum** Breda

Arthrochilum G.Beck, Fl. Nied. Oest. 212. 1890. = **Epipactis** [Zinn., in part] Sw.

Arthrochilus FvM., Fragm. Bot. 1: 42. 1858. = **Spiculaea** Ldl.

Arundina Bl., Bijdr. 401. 1825. (1 sp., subtribe Thuniinae)

Asarca Poepp. ex Ldl. in Quart. Jour. Roy. Inst. 1: 32. 1827. = **Chloraea** Ldl.

Ascocentrum Schltr. in Fedde, Repert. Spec. Nov., Beih. 1: 975, in obs. 1913. (9 spp., subtribe Sarcanthinae)

Ascochilopsis Carr in Gard. Bull. Straits Settlem. 5: 21. 1929. (1 sp., subtribe Sarcanthinae)

Ascochilus Bl., Fl. Java Praef. vi. 1828. = **Geodorum** Jacks.

Ascochilus Ridl. in Jour. Linn. Soc. 32: 374. 1896. = subtribe Sarcanthinae, principally to **Sarcanthus** Ldl., and **Sarcochilus** R.Br.

Ascoglossum Schltr. in Fedde, Repert. Spec. Nov., Beih. 1: 974. 1913. (2 spp., subtribe Sarcanthinae)

Ascotainia Ridl., Mat. Fl. Malay Penins. 1: 115. 1907. = **Ania** Ldl.

Aspasia Ldl., Gen. & Sp. Orch. 139. 1833. (10 spp., subtribe Oncidiinae)

Aspegrenia P. & E., Nov. Gen. & Sp. 2: 12, pl. 116. 1837. = **Octomeria** R.Br.

Aspla Rchb., Nomencl. 50. 1841, *err. typ.* = **Herminium** L.

Astroglossus Rchb.f. ex Bth. & Hk.f., Gen. Pl. 3: 588. 1883. = **Stellilabium** Schltr.

Ate Ldl., Gen. & Sp. Orch. 326. 1835. = **Habenaria** Willd.

Auliza Salisb. in Trans. Hort. Soc. London 1: 294. 1812. = **Epidendrum** L.

Aulizeum Ldl. ex Stein, Orchideenb. 539. 1892, in syn. = **Epidendrum** L.

Aulostylis Schltr. in Fedde, Repert. Spec. Nov., Beih. 1: 392. 1912. = **Calanthe** R.Br.

Auxopus Schltr., Westafr. Kautschuk-Exped. 275. 1900. (2 spp., subtribe Gastrodiinae)

Aviceps Ldl., Gen. & Sp. Orch. 345. 1838. = **Satyrium** L.

Baptistania B.-R. ex Pfitz. in Engl. & Prantl, Natürl. Pflanzenfam. II, 6: 220. 1889, *sphalm.* = **Oncidium** Sw.

Baptistonia B.-R., Orch. Nov. 1: 95. 1877. = **Oncidium** Sw.

Barbosella Schltr. in Fedde, Repert. Spec. Nov. 15: 259. 1918. = **Pleurothallis** R.Br.

Barkeria Kn. & Westc., Flor. Cab. 2: 7, pl. 49. 1838. = **Epidendrum** L.

Barlaea Rchb.f. in Linnaea 41: 54. 1877. = **Cynorkis** Thou.

Barlia Parlat., Nouv. Gen. Plant. Monocot. 5. 1858; & Fl. Ital. 3: 445. 1858. = **Himantoglossum** Spreng.

Barombia Schltr., Die Orchid. 600. 1914. (1 sp., subtribe Sarcanthinae)

Bartholina R.Br. in Ait., Hort. Kew., ed. 2, 5: 194. 1813. (3 spp., subtribe Habenarinae)

Basigyne J.J.Sm. in Bull. Jard. Bot. Buitenz. II, 25: 4. 1917. = **Dendrochilum** Bl.

Basiphyllaea Schltr. in Fedde, Repert. Spec. Nov. 17: 77. 1921. (3 spp., subtribe Laeliinae)

Baskervillea Ldl., Gen. & Sp. Orch. 505. 1840. (2 spp., subtribe Cranichidinae)

Batemania Ldl. in Bot. Reg., pl. 1714. 1834. (2 spp., subtribe Zygopetalinae)

Bathiea Schltr. in Beih. Bot. Centralbl. 33(2): 440. 1915; & l.c., 36(2): 180. 1918. = **Neobathiea** Schltr.

Beadlea Small, Fl. S.E. U.S. 319. 1903. = **Spiranthes** L.C.Rich.

Beclardia A.Rich. in Mém. Soc. Hist. Nat. Paris 4: 69. 1828. = **Cryptopus** Ldl.

Beloglottis Schltr. in Beih. Bot. Centralbl. 37(2): 364. 1920. = **Spiranthes** L.C.Rich.

Benthamia A.Rich. in Mém. Soc. Hist. Nat. Paris 4: 37, pl. 7. 1828. (26 spp., subtribe Habenarinae)

Bicchia Parlat., Fl. Ital. 3: 396. 1858. = **Habenaria** Willd.

Bicornella Ldl. in Bot. Reg., under pl. 1701. 1835. = **Cynorkis** Thou.

Bieneria Rchb.f. in Bot. Zeit. 11: 3, pl. 1. 1853. = **Chloraea** Ldl.

Biermannia King & Pantl. in Jour. As. Soc. Beng. 66: 591. 1897. (1 sp., subtribe Sarcanthinae)

Bifolium Petiver, Opera II, Herb. Brit., pl. 70, figs. 10–12. 1764; cf. Nieuwl. in Amer. Midl. Natural. 3: 128. 1913. = **Listera** R.Br.

Bifrenaria Ldl., Gen. & Sp. Orch. 152. 1833. (11 spp., subtribe Lycastinae)

Bilabrella Ldl. in Bot. Reg., under pl. 1701. 1835. = **Habenaria** Willd.

Binotia Rolfe in Orch. Rev., 296. 1905. (1 sp., subtribe Cochliodinae)

Bipinnula Comm. ex Juss., Gen. 65. 1789. (8 spp., subtribe Chloraeinae)

Birchea A.Rich. in Ann. Sci. Nat. II, 15: 66, pl. 10. 1841. = **Luisia** Gaud.

Blephariglottis Raf., Fl. Tellur. 2: 38. 1836. = **Habenaria** Willd.

Bletia R. & P., Prodr. Fl. Peruv. & Chil. 119, pl. 26. 1794. (50 spp., subtribe Bletiinae)

Bletiana Raf. in Amer. Monthly Mag. 268. 1818. = **Bletia** R. & P.

Bletilla Rchb.f. in Fl. des Serres, I, 8: 246. 1851–3. (7 spp., subtribe Bletillinae)

Bogoria J.J.Sm., Fl. Buitenz. 5 (Orch. Java): 566. 1905. (3 spp., subtribe Sarcanthinae)

Bolbidium Ldl., Veg. Kingd. 181. 1847, *nomen.* = **Dendrobium** Sw.

Bolbophyllaria Rchb.f. in Bot. Zeit. 10: 934. 1852. = **Bulbophyllum** Thou.

Bolbophyllopsis Rchb.f. in Bot. Zeit. 10: 933. 1852. = **Bulbophyllum** Thou.

Bolbophyllum Spreng., Syst. 3: 681, 732. 1826. = **Bulbophyllum** Thou.

Bolborchis Zoll. & Mor., Syst. Verz. Zoll. 89. 1845–6. = **Pleione** D.Don

Bolborchis Ldl. ex Schltr., Die Orchid. 130. 1914. = **Coelogyne** Ldl.

Bollea Rchb.f. in Bot. Zeit. 10: 667. 1852. (6 spp., subtribe Zygopetalinae)

Bolusiella Schltr. in Beih. Bot. Centralbl. 36(2): 103. 1918. (6 spp., subtribe Sarcanthinae)

Bonatea Willd., Spec. Plant. 4: 43. 1805. (20 spp., subtribe Habenarinae)

Bonniera Cordem. in Rev. Gén. de Bot. 11: 416. 1899. (2 spp., subtribe Sarcanthinae)

Bothriochilus Lem., Jard. Fleur. 3: pl. 325. 1852–3; & Illus. Hortic. 3: Misc. 30, 31. 1856. (4 spp., subtribe Ponerinae)

Brachionidium Ldl., Fol. Orch. Brachionidium [1]. 1859. (6 spp., subtribe Pleurothallidinae)

Brachtia Rchb.f., in Linnaea 22: 853. 1849. (4 spp., subtribe Brachtiinae)

Brachycorythis Ldl., Gen. & Sp. Orch. 363. 1838. (10 spp., subtribe Habenarinae)

Brachystele Schltr. in Beih. Bot. Centralbl. 36(2): 370. 1920. = **Spiranthes** L.C.Rich.

Brachystepis Pritz., Ind. Icon. 162. 1855. = **Oeonia** Ldl.

Bracisepalum J.J.Sm. in Engl., Bot. Jahrb. 65: 464. 1933. (1 sp., subtribe Coelogyninae)

Brassavola R.Br. in Ait., Hort. Kew., ed. 2, 5: 216. 1813. (15 spp., subtribe Laeliinae)

Brassavolaea P. & E., Nov. Gen. & Sp. 2: 3. 1838. = **Brassavola** R.Br.

Brassavolea Spreng., Syst. 3: 744. 1826. = **Brassavola** R.Br.

Brassia R.Br. in Ait., Hort. Kew., ed. 2, 5: 215. 1813. (30 spp., subtribe Oncidiinae)

Brenesia Schltr. in Fedde, Repert. Spec. Nov., Beih. 19: 199, 200. 1923. = **Pleurothallis** R.Br.

Bromheadia Ldl. in Bot. Reg., App. 90. 1841. (11 spp., subtribe Polystachyinae)

Broughtonia R.Br. in Ait., Hort. Kew., ed. 2, 5: 217. 1813. (1 sp., subtribe Laeliinae)

Broughtonia Wall. ex Ldl., Gen. & Sp. Orch. 35. 1830. = **Otochilus** Ldl.

Brownleea Harv. ex Ldl. in Hk., Lond. Jour. Bot. 1: 16. 1842. (10 spp., subtribe Disinae)

Bryobium Ldl., Introd. Nat. Syst., ed. 2: 446. 1836. = **Eria** Ldl.

Bucculina Ldl. in Hk., Comp. Bot. Mag. 2: 209. 1836. = **Holothrix** L.C.Rich.

Buchtienia Schltr. in Fedde, Repert. Sp. Nov. 27: 33. 1929. (1 sp., subtribe Spiranthinae)

Buesiella C. Schweinf. in Bot. Mus. Leafl. Harv. Univ. 15: 153, pl. 48. 1952. (1 sp., subtribe Bulbophyllinae)

Bulbophyllaria S.Moore in Baker, Fl. Maurit. 344. 1877, *sphalm.* = **Bulbophyllum** Thou.

Bulbophyllum Thou., Orch. Îles Afr., Tabl. Esp. 3, & Icon., pls. 93–7. 1822. (2000 spp., subtribe Bulbophyllinae)

Bulleyia Schltr. in Notes Roy. Bot. Gard. Edinb. 24: 108. 1912. (1 sp., subtribe Coelogynine)

Burlingtonia Ldl. in Bot. Reg., pl. 1927. 1837. = **Rodriguezia** R. & P.

Burnettia Ldl., Gen. & Sp. Orch. 517. 1840. (1 sp., subtribe Acianthinae)

Cadetia Gaud. in Freyc., Voy., Bot. 422, pl. 33. 1826. (60 spp., subtribe Dendrobiinae)

Caelia G.Don in Sweet, Hort. Brit., ed. 3, 637. 1839. = **Coelia** Ldl.

Caeloglossum Steud., Nom., ed. 2, 1: 247. 1847. = **Coeloglossum** Hartm.

Caelogyne Wall. ex Steud., Nom., ed. 2, 1: 247. 1847. = **Coelogyne** Ldl.

Caladenia R.Br., Prodr. Fl. Nov. Holl. 323. 1810. (70 spp., subtribe Caladeniinae)

Calanthe R.Br. in Bot. Reg., under pl. 573. 1821. (150 spp., subtribe Phaiinae)

Calanthidium Pfitz. in Engl. & Prantl, Natürl. Pflanzenfam. II, 6: 153. 1888. = **Calanthe** R.Br.

Calcearia Bl., Bijdr. 417, pl. 33. 1825. = **Corybas** Salisb.

Calceolaria Heist., Syst. 5. 1748. = **Cypripedium** L.

Calceolus [Tournef.] Adans., Fam. 2: 70. 1763. = **Cypripedium** L.

Calceolus Mill., Gard. Dict., Abridg. Ed. 4. 1754; cf. Druce in Rep. Bot. Exch. Club Brit. Is. 3: 430. 1913. = **Cypripedium** L.

Caleana R.Br., Prodr. Fl. Nov. Holl. 329. 1810. (5 spp., subtribe Drakaeinae)

Caleya R.Br. in Ait., Hort. Kew., ed. 2, 5: 204. 1813. = **Caleana** R.Br.

Calipogon Raf., Att. Jour. 148. 1832. = **Calopogon** R.Br.

Calista Ritg. in Marb. Ges. Schrift. 2: 128. 1828. = **Dendrobium** Sw.

Calliphylon Bub., Fl. Pyr. 4: 56. 1901. = **Epipactis** [Zinn., in part] Sw.

Callista Lour., Fl. Cochinch. 519. 1790 = **Dendrobium** Sw.

Callithronum Ehr., Beitr. 4: 48. 1789. = **Cephalanthera** L.C.Rich.

Callostylis Bl., Bijdr. 340, pl. 74. 1825. = **Eria** Ldl.

Calochilus R.Br., Prodr. Fl. Nov. Holl. 320. 1810. (10 spp., subtribe Thelymitrinae)

Caloglossum Schltr. in Fedde, Repert. Spec. Nov. 15: 212. 1918. = **Cymbidiella** Rolfe

Calopogon R.Br. in Ait., Hort. Kew., ed. 2, 5: 204. 1813. (4 spp., subtribe Bletillinae)

Calorchis B.-R., Orch. Nov. 1: 44. 1877. = **Ponthieva** R.Br.

Calostylis O.Ktze., Rev. Gen. Pl. 2: 679. 1891, in syn., *sphalm.* = **Eria** Ldl.

Calymmanthera Schltr. in Fedde, Repert. Spec. Nov., Beih. 1: 955. 1913. (5 spp., subtribe Sarcanthinae)

Calypso Salisb., Parad. Lond., pl. 89. 1806. (1 sp., subtribe Calypsoinae)

Calypsodium Link, Handb. 1: 252. 1829. = **Calypso** Salisb.

Calyptrochilum Krzl. in Engl., Bot. Jahrb. 22: 30. 1895. (6 spp., subtribe Sarcanthinae)

Camaridium Ldl. in Bot. Reg., under pl. 844. 1824. = **Maxillaria** R. & P.

Camarotis Ldl., Gen. & Sp. Orch. 219. 1833. (14 spp., subtribe Sarcanthinae)

Camelostalix Pfitz. in Engl. & Prantl, Das Pflanzenr. IV, 50 (Coelog.) : 159. 1907. = **Pholidota** Ldl.

Cameridium Rchb.f. in Linnaea 22: 857. 1849, *sphalm.* = **Maxillaria** R. & P.

Camilleugenia Frapp. ex Cordem., Fl. Île Réunion 234. 1895. = **Cynorkis** Thou.

Campylocentron Bth. in Bth. & Hk.f., Gen. Plant. 3: 585. 1883, *sphalm.* = **Campylocentrum** Bth.

Campylocentrum Bth. in Jour. Linn. Soc. 18: 337. 1881. (65 spp., subtribe Campylocentrinae)

Capanemia B.-R., Orch. Nov. 1: 337. 1877. (12 spp., subtribe Capanemiinae)

Cardiophyllum Ehr., Beitr. 4: 148. 1789. = **Listera** R.Br.

Carteretia A.Rich., Sert. Astrol. 10, pl. 4. 1834. = **Sarcanthus** Ldl.

Carteria Small in Torreya 10: 187. 1910. = **Basiphyllaea** Schltr.

Catachaetum Hoffmsgg., Preis-Verz. Orch. 22. 1842. = **Catasetum** L.C.Rich.

Catasetum L.C.Rich. ex Kth., Syn. Pl. Aequin. 1: 330. 1822. (110 spp., subtribe Catasetinae)

Cathea Salisb. in Trans. Hort. Soc. Lond. 1: 300. 1812. = **Calopogon** R.Br.

Cattleya Ldl., Collect. Bot., pls. 33, 37. 1824. (65 spp., subtribe Laeliinae)

Cattleyopsis Lem., Jard. Fleur. 4: misc. 59. 1854. (3 spp., subtribe Laeliinae)

Caucaea Schltr. in Fedde, Repert. Spec. Nov., Beih. 7: 189. 1920. (1 sp., subtribe Oncidiinae)

Caularthron Raf., Fl. Tellur. 2: 40. 1836. (6 spp., subtribe Laeliinae)

Centranthera Scheidw. in Otto & Dietr., Allgem. Gartenz. 10: 293. 1842. = **Pleurothallis** R.Br.

Centrochilus J.C.Schau. in Nov. Act. Nat. Cur. 19, Suppl. 1: 435, pl. 113. 1843. = **Habenaria** Willd.

Centrogenium Schltr. in Fedde, Repert. Spec. Nov., Beih. 6: 54. 1919. (15 spp., subtribe Spiranthinae)

Centroglossa B.-R., Orch. Nov. 2: 234. 1881. (7 spp., subtribe Trichocentrinae)

Centropetalum Ldl., Sert. Orch., under pl. 21. 1839. (7 spp., subtribe Pachyphyllinae)

Centrosia A.Rich. in Mém. Soc. Hist. Nat. Paris 4: 39. 1828. = **Calanthe** R.Br.

Centrosis Sw., Summ. Vegetab. Scand. 32. 1814, without descr.; & Adnot. Bot. 52. 1829. = ? **Cephalanthera** L.C.Rich.

Centrosis Thou., Orch. Îles Afr., pls. 35, 36. 1822. = **Calanthe** R.Br.

Centrostigma Schltr. in Engl., Bot. Jahrb. 53: 521. 1915. 6 spp., subtribe Habenarinae)

Cephalangraecum Schltr. in Beih. Bot. Centralbl. 36(2): 135. 1918. = **Ancistrorhynchus** Finet

Cephalanthera L.C.Rich. in Mém. Mus. Paris 4: 51. 1818. (12 spp., subtribe Cephalantherinae)

Ceraia Lour., Fl. Cochinch. 518. 1790. = **Dendrobium** Sw.

Ceratandra Eckl. ex Bauer, Illus. Gen. Orch., pl. 16. 1837. (2 spp., subtribe Disperidinae)

Ceratandropsis Rolfe in Dyer, Fl. Cap. 5(3): 266. 1913. (1 sp., subtribe Disperidinae)

Ceratium Bl., Bijdr. 314, pl. 46. 1825. = **Eria** Ldl.

Ceratochilus Bl., Bijdr. 358, pl. 25. 1825. (1 sp., subtribe Sarcanthinae)

Ceratochilus Ldl. in Lodd., Bot. Cab., pl. 1414. 1828. = **Stanhopea** Frost ex Hk.

Ceratopsis Ldl., Gen. & Sp. Orch. 383. 1840. = **Epipogum** [Gmel.] L.C.Rich.

Ceratostylis Bl., Bijdr. 304, pl. 56. 1825. (70 spp., subtribe Glomerinae)

Cereia Lour., Fl. Cochinch. 518. 1790, *sphalm.* = **Dendrobium** Sw.

Cerochilus Ldl. in Gard. Chron., 87. 1854. = **Hetaeria** Bl.

Cestichis Thou., Orch. Îles Afr., pl. 90. 1822. = **Liparis** L.C.Rich.

Chaenanthe Ldl. in Bot. Reg., Misc. 38. 1838. (1 sp., subtribe Comparettiinae)

Chaetocephala B.-R., Orch. Nov. 2: 37. 1881. (2 spp., subtribe Pleurothallidinae)

Chamaeangis Schltr. in Beih. Bot. Centralbl. 32(2): 426. 1915. (8 spp., subtribe Sarcanthinae)

Chamaeanthus Schltr. in J.J.Sm., Fl. Buitenz. 5 (Orch. Java) : 552. 1915. (8 spp., subtribe Sarcanthinae)

Chamaegastrodia Mak. & Maek. in Bot. Mag. Tokyo 49: 596. 1935; & Icon. Pl. As. Or. 2: 163. 1937. (1 sp., subtribe Gastrodiinae)

Chamaeorchis Koch, Syn. Fl. Germ. 692. 1837. = **Herminium** R.Br.

Chamaerepes Spreng., Syst. 3: 702. 1826. = **Herminium** R.Br.

Chamorchis A.Rich. in Mém. Mus. Paris 4: 49. 1818. = **Herminium** R.Br.

Changnienia Chien in Contrib. Biol. Lab. Sc. Soc. China, Bot. Ser. 10: 89. 1935. (1 sp., subtribe unknown)

Chaseëlla Summerh. in Kirkia 1: 88. 1961. (1 sp., subtribe Bulbophyllinae)

Chaubardia Rchb.f. in Bot. Zeit. 10: 671. 1852. (1 sp., subtribe Huntleyinae)

Chauliodon Summerh. in Bot. Mus. Leafl. Harv. Univ. 11: 163. 1943. (1 sp., subtribe Sarcanthinae)

Cheiradenia Ldl., Fol. Orch. Cheiradenia [1]. 1853. (2 spp., subtribe Huntleyinae)

Cheiropterocephalus B.-R., Orch. Nov. 1: 28. 1877. = **Malaxis** Soland. ex Sw.

Cheirorchis Carr in Gard. Bull. Straits Settlem. 7: 40. 1932. (5 spp., subtribe Sarcanthinae)

Cheirostylis Bl., Bijdr. 413, pl. 16. 1825. (15 spp., subtribe Physurinae)

Chelonanthera Bl., Bijdr. 384, pl. 51. 1825. = **Pholidota** Ldl.

Chelonistele Pfitz. in Engl. & Prantl, Das Pflanzenr. IV, 50 (Coelogyn.): 136. 1907; Carr in Gard. Bull. Straits Settlem. 8: 216. 1935. (5 spp., subtribe Coelogyninae)

Chelrostylis Pritz., Icon. Ind. 255. 1855, *sphalm*. = **Cheirostylis** Bl.

Chiloglottis R.Br., Prodr. Fl. Nov. Holl. 322. 1810. (10 spp., subtribe Drakaeinae)

Chilopogon Schltr. in Fedde, Repert. Spec. Nov., Beih. 1: 332. 1912. (3 spp., subtribe Podochilinae)

Chiloschista Ldl. in Bot. Reg., under pl. 1522. 1832. (2 spp., subtribe Sarcanthinae)

Chitonanthera Schltr. in K.Schum. & Lauterb., Nachtr. Fl. Deutsch Südsee 193. 1905. (7 spp., subtribe Thelasinae)

Chitonochilus Schltr. in K.Schum. & Lauterb., Nachtr. Fl. Deutsch Südsee 134. 1905. (1 sp., subtribe Glomerinae)

Chloidia Ldl., Gen. & Sp. Orch. 484. 1840. = **Corymborchis** Thou. ex Bl.

Chloraea Ldl. in Brand, Quart. Jour. Roy. Inst., n.s., 1: 47. 1827. (100 spp., subtribe Chloraeinae)

Chlorosa Bl., Bijdr. 420, pl. 31. 1825. (2 spp., subtribe Cryptostylidinae)

Choeradoplectron Schau. in Nov. Act. Nat. Cur. 19, Suppl. 1: 436. 1843. = **Habenaria** Willd.

Chondradenia Maxim. ex Mak. in Bot. Mag. Tokyo 16: 8. 1902. = **Orchis** [Tournef.] L.

Chondrorhyncha Ldl., Orch. Linden. 12. 1846. (12 spp., subtribe Huntleyinae)

Chroniochilus J.J.Sm. in Bull. Jard. Bot. Buitenz. II, 26: 81. 1918. (2 spp., subtribe Sarcanthinae)

Chrysobaphus Wall., Tent. Fl. Nepal. 37, pl. 27. 1826. = **Anoectochilus** Bl.

Chrysocycnis Lind. & Rchb.f. in Bonplandia 2: 280; 1854. (2 spp., subtribe Maxillarinae)

Chrysoglossum Bl., Bijdr. 337, pl. 7. 1825. (10 spp., subtribe Collabiinae)

Chusua Nevski in Komarov, Fl. URSS 4: 670, 753. 1935. (2 spp., subtribe Habenarinae)

Chysis Ldl. in Bot. Reg. 23: pl. 1937. 1837. (2 spp., subtribe Chysinae)

Chytroglossa Rchb.f. in Hamb. Gartenz. 19: 546. 1863. (3 spp., subtribe Ornithocephalinae)

Cionisaccus Breda, Orch. Kuhl & Hass. [pl. 8]. 1827. = **Goodyera** R.Br.

Ciripedium Zumag, Fl. Pedem. 1: 18. 1829. = **Cypripedium** L.

Cirrhaea Ldl. in Bot. Reg., under pl. 930. 1825. (4 spp., subtribe Gongorinae)

Cirrhopetalum Ldl. in Bot. Reg., under pl. 832. 1824. = **Bulbophyllum** Thou.

Cistella Bl., Bijdr. 293, pl. 55. 1825. = **Geodorum** Jacks.

Claderia Hk.f., Fl. Brit. India 5: 810. 1885. (2 spp., subtribe Thuniinae)

Cladobium Ldl., Introd. Nat. Syst., ed. 2, 446. 1836. = **Scaphyglottis** P. & E.

Cladobium Schltr. in Beih. Bot. Centralbl. 37(2): 431. 1920. = **Lankesterella** Ames

Cladorhiza Raf., Med. Fl. 1: 145. 1828, in obs., as syn. = **Corallorrhiza** [Hall.] R.Br.

Cleisocentron Bruhl, Guide Orch. Sikkim 136. 1926. = **Gastrochilus** D.Don

Cleisostoma Bl., Bijdr. 362. 1825. = subtribe Sarcanthinae, mostly **Sarcanthus** Ldl. and **Pomatocalpa** Breda.

Cleistes L.C.Rich. in Mém. Mus. Paris 4: 31. 1818. (80 spp., subtribe Vanillinae)

Clinhymenia A.Rich. & Gal. in Compt.-Rend. Acad. Sci. Paris 18: 512. 1844. = **Cryptarrhena** R.Br.

Clowesia Ldl. in Bot. Reg. 29: Misc. 25, pl. 39. 1843. = **Catasetum** L.C.Rich.

Clynhymenia A.Rich. & Gal. in Ann. Sci. Nat. III, 3: 24. 1845, in syn. = **Cryptarrhena** R.Br.

Cnemidia Ldl. in Bot. Reg., under pl. 1618. 1833. = **Tropidia** Ldl.

Coccineorchis Schltr. in Beih. Bot. Centralbl. 37(2): 434. 1920. = **Spiranthes** L.C.Rich.

Cochleanthes Raf., Fl. Tellur. 2: 45. 1836. = **Zygopetalum** Hk.

Cochlia Bl., Bijdr. 320, pl. 59. 1825. = **Bulbophyllum** Thou.

Cochlioda Ldl., Fol. Orch. Cochlioda [1]. 1853. (5 spp., subtribe Cochliodinae)

Codonorchis Ldl., Gen. & Sp. Orch. 410. 1840. (1 sp., subtribe Caladeniinae)

Codonosiphon Schltr. in Fedde, Repert. Spec. Nov., Beih. 1: 893. 1913. (3 spp., subtribe Bulbophyllinae)

Coelandria Fitzg., Austral. Orch. 1(7): pl. 2. 1882. = **Dendrobium** Sw.

Coelia Ldl., Gen. & Sp. Orch. 36. 1830. (1 sp., subtribe Ponerinae)

Coeliopsis Rchb.f. in Gard. Chron. 9. 1872. (1 sp., subtribe Gongorinae)

Coeloglossum Hartm., Handb. Skand. Fl., ed. 1, 329. 1820. (4 spp., subtribe Habenarinae)

Coelogyne Ldl., Collect. Bot., under pl. 33. 1825. (125 spp., subtribe Coelogyninae)

Cogniauxiocharis [Schltr.] Hoehne in Arq. Bot. Estad. S. Paulo, n.s., *form. maior*, 1: 132. 1944. = **Spiranthes** L.C.Rich.

Cohnia Rchb.f. in Bot. Zeit. 10: 928. 1852. = **Cohniella** Pfitz.

Cohniella Pfitz. in Engl. & Prantl, Natürl. Pflanzenfam. 2(6): 194. 1889. (1 sp., subtribe Capanemiinae)

Coilochilus Schltr. in Engl., Bot. Jahrb. 39: 36. 1906. (1 sp., subtribe Cryptostylidinae)

Coilostylis Raf., Fl. Tellur. 4: 37. 1836. = **Epidendrum** L.

Colax Ldl. ex Spreng., Syst. 3: 727. 1826; & in Bot. Reg., Misc. 50. 1843. (3 spp., subtribe Zygopetalinae)

Collabium Bl., Bijdr. 357. 1825. (5 spp., subtribe Collabiinae)

Collaea Endl., Gen. Suppl. 2: 20. 1842, in syn. = **Centrogenium** Schltr.

Collea Ldl. in Bot. Reg., under pl. 760. 1823. = **Centrogenium** Schltr.

Cologyne Griff., Notul. 3: 280. 1851, *err. typ.* = **Coelogyne** Ldl.

Commersorchis Thou., Orch. Îles Afr., Tab. Synopt. 1. 1822. = **Dendrobium** Sw.

Comparettia P. & E., Nov. Gen. & Sp. 1: 42, pl. 73. 1835. (12 spp., subtribe Comparettiinae)

Comperia C.Koch in Linnaea 22: 287. 1849. = **Orchis** [Tournef.] L.

Conchidium Griff., Notul. 3: 321, pl. 310. 1851. = **Eria** Ldl.

Conchochilus Hassk. in Hoev. & DeVr., Tijdschr. 9: 146. 1842. = **Appendicula** Bl.

Conopsidium Wallr. in Linnaea 14: 147. 1840. = **Orchis** [Tournef.] L., **Habenaria** Willd.

Constantia B.-R., Orch. Nov. 1: 78. 1877. (4 spp., subtribe Laeliinae)

Coppensia Dum. in Mém. Acad. Brux. 9: 10. 1835, in note. = **Oncidium** Sw.

Coralliorrhiza Aschers, Fl. Brandenb. 697. 1864. = **Corallorrhiza** [Hall.] R.Br.

Corallorrhiza [Haller] R.Br. in Ait., Hort., Kew., ed. 2, 5: 209. 1813. (12 spp., subtribe Corallorrhizinae)

Cordanthera L.O.Wms. in Lilloa 6: 241. 1941. (1 sp., subtribe Ornithocephalinae)

Cordiglottis J.J.Sm. in Bull. Jard. Bot. Buitenz. III, 5: 95. 1922. (1 sp., subtribe Sarcanthinae)

Cordula Raf., Fl. Tellur. 4: 46. 1836. = **Paphiopedilum** Pfitz.

Cordyla Bl., Bijdr. 416. 1825. = **Nervilia** Comm. ex Gaud.

Cordylostylis Falc. in Hk., Jour. Bot. 4: 74. 1842. = **Goodyera** R.Br.

Corisanthes Steud., Nomen., ed. 2, 1: 474, 1840, in syn. = **Cypripedium** L.

Corunastylis Fitzg., Austral. Orch. 1(2): pl. 2. 1888. (1 sp., subtribe Prasophyllinae)

Coryanthes Hk. in Bot. Mag., pl. 3102. 1831. (15 spp., subtribe Gongorinae)

Corybas Salisb., Parad. Lond., pl. 83. 1803. (60 spp., subtribe Corybasinae)

Corycium Sw. in Vet. Akad. Nya Handl. Stockh. 21: 220. 1800. (8 spp., subtribe Disperidinae)

Corydandra Rchb., Nomen. 53. 1841. = **Galeandra** Ldl.

Corymbis Thou., Orch. Îles Afr., pls. 37, 38. 1822. = **Corymborchis** Thou. ex Bl.

Corymborchis Thou. ex Bl., Orch. Ind. Archip. 125. 1855. (18 spp., subtribe Tropidiinae)

Corymborkis Thou. in Nouv. Bull. Soc. Philom., no. 19: 318. 1809. = **Corymborchis** Thou. ex. Bl.

Corynanthes Rchb.f. in Bot. Zeit. 6: 65. 1848, *sphalm.* = **Coryanthes** Hk.

Corysanthes R.Br., Prodr. Fl. Nov. Holl. 328. 1810. = **Corybas** Salisb.

Corythanthes Lem. in Orb. Diet. 4: 259. 1849. = ? **Coryanthes** Hk.

Costaricaea Schltr. in Fedde, Repert. Spec. Nov., Beih. 19: 30. 1923. = **Hexisea** Ldl.

Cottonia Wight, Icon. 5(1): 121, pl. 1875. 1852. (1 sp., subtribe Sarcanthinae)

Cranichis Sw., Prodr. Veg. Ind. Occ. 120. 1788. (50 spp., subtribe Cranichidinae)

Cremastra Ldl., Gen. & Sp. Orch. 172. 1833. (2 spp., subtribe Cyrtopodiinae)

Crepidium Bl., Bijdr. 387. 1825. = **Malaxis** Soland. ex Sw.

Crinonia Bl., Bijdr. 338. 1825. = **Pholidota** Ldl.

Criosanthes Raf. in Amer. Monthly Mag. 268. 1818. = **Cypripedium** L.

Crocodeilanthe Rchb.f. & Warsc. in Bonplandia 2: 113. 1854. = **Pleurothallis** R.Br.

Crossangis Schltr. in Beih. Bot. Centralbl. 36(2): 141. 1918. = **Diaphananthe** Schltr.

Crybe Ldl., Introd. Nat. Syst., ed. 2, 446. 1836. (1 sp., subtribe Bletillinae)

Cryptanthemis Rupp in Proc. Linn. Soc. N.S.Wales 57: 58. 1932. (1 sp., subtribe Rhizanthellinae)

Cryptarrhena R.Br. in Bot. Reg. 2: pl. 153. 1816. (3 spp., subtribe Notyliinae)

Cryptocentrum Bth. in Jour. Linn. Soc. 18: 325. 1881. (15 spp., subtribe Maxillarinae)

Cryptochilos Spreng., Gen. 2: 676. 1832, *sphalm.* = **Cryptochilus** Wall.

Cryptochilus Wall., Tent. Fl. Nepal 36, pl. 36. 1822. (2 spp., subtribe Dendrobiinae)

Cryptoglottis Bl., Bijdr. 296, pl. 42. 1825. = **Podochilus** Bl.

Cryptophoranthus B.-R., Orch. Nov. 2: 79. 1881. (20 spp., subtribe Pleurothallidinae)

Cryptopus Ldl. in Bot. Reg., under pl. 817. 1824. (3 spp., subtribe Sarcanthinae)

Cryptosaccus Rchb.f., Xen. Orch. 1: 15. 1858, in syn. = **Leochilus** Kn. & Westc.

Cryptosanus Scheidw. in Otto & Dietr., Allgem. Gartenz. 11: 101. 1843. = **Leochilus** Kn. & Westc.

Cryptostylis R.Br., Prodr. Fl. Nov. Holl. 317. 1810. (20 spp., subtribe Cryptostylidinae)

Ctenorchis Schum. in Just, Bot. Jahresb. 1: 467. 1901. = **Angraecum** Bory

Cuculina Raf., Fl. Tellur. 4: 49. 1836. = **Catasetum** L.C.Rich.

Cuitlanzina Ldl., Orch. Scel. 15. 1826. = **Odontoglossum** HBK

Cuitlauzina LaLl. & Lex., Nov. Veg. Descr. 2 (Orch. Opusc.): 32. 1825. = **Odontoglossum** HBK

Cuitlauzinia Rchb., Nomen. 54. 1841. = **Odontoglossum** HBK

Cyanaeorchis B.-R., Orch. Nov. 1: 112. 1877. (1 sp., subtribe Polystachyinae)

Cyanorchis Thou. ex Steud., Nomen., ed. 2, 1: 457. 1840. = **Phaius** Lour.

Cyanorkis Thou. in Nouv. Bull. Soc. Philom., no. 19: 317. 1809. = **Phaius** Lour.

Cyathoglottis P. & E., Nov. Gen. & Sp. 1: 55, pl. 94. 1835. = **Sobralia** R. & P.

Cybele Falc. in Ldl., Veg. Kingd. 183. 1847. = **Herminium** L.

Cybelion Spreng., Syst. 3: 679, 721. 1826. = **Ionopsis** HBK

Cyclopogon Presl, Rel. Haenk. 1: 93, pl. 13. 1827. = **Spiranthes** L.C.Rich.

Cycloptera Endl., Ench. 113. 1841. = **Spiranthes** L.C. Rich.

Cyclosia Klotzsch in Otto & Dietr., Allgem. Gartenz. 6: 305. 1838. = **Mormodes** Ldl.

Cycnauken Lem. in Fl. des Serres 1: 207. 1845. = **Cycnoches** Ldl.

Cycnoches Ldl., Gen & Sp. Orch. 154. 1833. (7 spp., subtribe Catasetinae)

Cylindrochilus Thw., Enum. Pl. Zeyl. 307. 1861. = **Sarcochilus** R.Br.

Cylindrolobus Bl., Praef. Fl. Java 6. 1828. = **Eria** Ldl.

Cymbidiella Rolfe in Orch. Rev. 26: 58. 1918. (3 spp., subtribe Cymbidiinae)

Cymbidium Sw. in Nov. Act. Soc. Sc. Upsal. 6: 70. 1799. (70 spp., subtribe Cymbidiinae)

Cynorchis Thou., Orch. Îles Afr., Tabl. Synopt., & pi. 13. 1822. = **Cynorkis** Thou.

Cynorkis Thou. in Nouv. Bull. Soc. Philom., no. 19: 317. 1809. (125 spp., subtribe Habenarinae).

Cynosorchis Thou., Orch. Îles Afr., Tabl. Synopt., & pls. 14, 15. 1822. = **Cynorkis** Thou.

Cyperocymbidium A.D.Hawkes in Orch. Rev. 72: 420. 1964.

Cyperorchis Bl., Rumphia 4: 47. 1848, in obs.; & Mus. Bot. Lugd.-Bat. 1: 48. 1849. (6 spp., subtribe Cymbidiinae)

Cyphochilus Schltr. in Fedde, Repert. Spec. Nov., Beih. 1: 358. 1912. (7 spp., subtribe Glomerinae)

Cypripedium L., Sp. Plant., ed. 1, 2: 951. 1753. (50 spp., subtribe Cypripedilinae)

Cyrtidium Schltr. in Fedde, Repert. Spec. Nov., Beih. 27: 178. 1924. (2 spp., subtribe Maxillarinae)

Cyrtochilos Spreng., Syst. 3: 729. 1826. = **Oncidium** Sw.

Cyrtochilum HBK, Nov. Gen. & Sp. 1: 349. 1815. = **Oncidium** Sw.

Cyrtoglottis Schltr. in Fedde, Repert. Spec. Nov., Beih. 7: 181. 1920. (1 sp., subtribe Maxillarinae)

Cyrtopera Ldl. in Wall., Catal., nos. 7362–4. 1821; & Gen. & Sp. Orch. 189. 1833. = **Eulophia** R.Br.

Cyrtopodium R.Br. in Ait., Hort. Kew., ed. 2, 5: 216. 1813. (35 spp., subtribe Cyrtopodiinae)

Cyrtorchis Schltr., Die Orchid. 596. 1914. (15 spp., subtribe Sarcanthinae)

Cyrtosia Bl., Bijdr. 396, pl. 6. 1825. = **Galeola** Lour.

Cyrtostylis R.Br., Prodr. Fl. Nov. Holl. 322. 1810. = **Acianthus** R.Br.

Cystopus Bl., Orch. Archip. Ind. 82. 1858. (16 spp., subtribe Physurinae)

Cystorchis Bl., Orch. Archip. Ind. 87, pls. 24, 36. 1858. (8 spp., subtribe Physurinae)

Cytherea Salisb. in Trans. Hort. Soc. Lond. 1: 301. 1812. = **Calypso** Salisb.

Cytheris Ldl. in Wall., Catal., no. 3750. 1830. = **Calanthe** R.Br.

Dactylorchis [Klinge] Verm., Steud. Dactylorch. 64. 1947. = **Orchis** [Tournef.] L.

Dactylorhiza Neck., Elem. 3: 129. 1790. = **Orchis** [Tournef.] L.

Dactylorhynchus Schltr. in Fedde, Repert. Spec. Nov., Beih. 1: 890. 1913. (1 sp., subtribe Bulbophyllinae)

Dactylostalix Rchb.f. in Bot. Zeit. 36: 74. 1878. = **Cremastra** Ldl.

Dactylostylis Scheidw. in Otto & Dietr., Allgem. Gartenz. 7: 405. 1839. = **Zygostates** Ldl.

Decaisnea Brongn. in Duperr., Voy. Coq., Bot. 192, pl. 39. 1829. = **Prescottia** Ldl.

Decaisnea Ldl. in Wall., Catal., no. 7388. 1831. = **Tropidia** Ldl.

Deiregyne Schltr. in Beih. Bot. Centralbl. 36 (2): 426. 1920. = **Spiranthes** L.C.Rich.

Dendrobium Sw. in Nov. Act. Soc. Sc. Upsal. 6: 82. 1799. (1600 spp., subtribe Dendrobiinae)

Dendrobrium Ag., Aphor. 188. 1823, *sphalm.* = **Dendrobium** Sw.

Dendrochilum Bl., Bijdr. 398, pl. 52. 1825. (150 spp., subtribe Coelogyninae)

Dendrocolla Bl., Bijdr. 286, pl. 67. 1825. = **Thrixspermum** Lour.

Dendrolirium Bl., Bijdr. 343, pl. 69. 1825. = **Eria** Ldl.

Dendrophylax Rchb.f. in Walp., Ann. 6: 903. 1861. (5 spp., subtribe Campylocentrinae)

Dendrorchis Thou. in Nouv. Bull. Soc. Philom., no. 19: 314. 1809. = **Polystachya** Hk.

Dendrorchis Thou., Orch. Îles Afr., Tabl. Synopt. 1822. = ? **Aërides** Lour.

Dendrorkis Thou. in Nouv. Bull. Soc. Philom., no. 19: 318. 1809. = ? **Aërides** Lour.

Denslovia Rydb. in Brittonia 1: 85. 1931. = **Habenaria** Willd.

Deppia Raf., Fl. Tellur. 2: 51. 1836. = **Lycaste** Ldl.

Deroemeria Rchb.f., Poll. Orch. Comm. 29. 1852. (3 spp., subtribe Habenarinae)

Desmotrichum Bl., Bijdr. 329, pl. 35. 1825. = **Flickingeria** A.D.Hawkes

Diacrium Bth. in Jour. Linn. Soc. 18: 312. 1881. = **Caularthron** Raf.

Diadenium P. & E., Nov. Gen. & Sp. 1: 41, pl. 71. 1835. (1 sp., subtribe Comparettiinae)

Dialissa Ldl. in Ann. & Mag. Nat. Hist., I, 15: 107. 1845. = **Stelis** Sw.

Diaphananthe Schltr. in Engl., Bot. Jahrb. 53: 600. 1915. (25 spp., subtribe Sarcanthinae)

Diceratostele Summerh. in Kew Bull. 151. 1938. (1 sp., subtribe Sobraliinae)

Dicerostylis Bl., Orch. Archip. Ind. 1: 116. 1858. = **Hylophila** Ldl.

Dichaea Ldl., Gen. & Sp. Orch. 208. 1833. (40 spp., subtribe Dichaeinae)

Dichaeopsis Pfitz. in Engl. & Prantl, Natürl. Pflanzenfam. 2(6): 207. 1889. = **Dichaea** Ldl.

Dichopus Bl., Mus. Bot. Lugd.-Bat. 2: 176. 1856. = **Dendrobium** Sw.

Dickasonia L.O.Wms. in Bot. Mus. Leafl. Harv. Univ. 9: 37. 1941. (1 sp., subtribe Coelogyninae)

Dicranotaenia Finet in Bull. Soc. Bot. France 54, Mém. 9: 47. 1907. = **Microcoelia** Ldl.

Dicrophyla Raf., Fl. Tellur. 9: 39. 1836. = **Haemaria** Ldl.

Dicrypta Ldl., Gen. & Sp. Orch. 44, 152. 1830. = **Maxillaria** R. & P.

Didactyle Ldl., Fol. Orch. Didactyle [1]. 1852. = **Bulbophyllum** Thou.

Didiciea King & Pantl. in Jour. As. Soc. Beng. 65: 118. 1896. (1 sp., subtribe Calypsoinae)

Didothion Raf., Fl. Tellur. 4: 39. 1836. = **Epidendrum** L.

Didymoplexis Griff. in Calc. Jour. Nat. Hist. 4: 383, pl. 17. 1844. (10 spp., subtribe Gastrodiinae)

Dienia Ldl. in Bot. Reg., under pl. 825. 1824. = **Malaxis** Soland. ex Sw.

Diglyphis Bl., Praef. Fl. Jav. vi. 1828. = **Chrysoglossum** Bl.

Diglyphosa Bl., Bijdr. 336, pl. 60. 1825. = **Chrysoglossum** Bl.

Diglyphys Spach., Hist. Veg. Phan. 12: 176. 1846. = **Chrysoglossum** Bl.

Dignathe Ldl. in Jour. Hort. Soc. 4: 268. 1849. = **Leochilus** Kn. & Westc.

Digomphotis Raf., Fl. Tellur. 2: 37. 1836. = **Habenaria** Willd.

Dikylikostigma Krzl. in Notizbl. Bot. Gart. Berlin 7: 321. 1919. = **Spiranthes** L.C.Rich.

Dilochia Ldl., Gen. & Sp. Orch. Pl. 38. 1830. (5 spp., subtribe Thuniinae)

Dilochus Miq., Fl. Ind. Bat. 3: 669. 1858. = **Dilochia** Ldl.

Dilomilis Raf., Fl. Tellur. 4: 43. 1836. = **Octadesmia** Bth.

Dimerandra Schltr. in Fedde, Repert. Spec. Nov., Beih. 17: 43. 1922. = **Epidendrum** L.

Dimorphorchis Rolfe in Orch. Rev. 27: 149. 1919. (2 spp., subtribe Sarcanthinae)

Dinema Ldl., Orch. Scel. 16. 1826; & Gen. & Sp. Orch. 111. 1831. = **Epidendrum** L.

Dinklageëlla Mansf. in Fedde, Repert. Spec. Nov. 36: 63. 1934. (1 sp., subtribe Sarcanthinae)

Diothonaea Ldl. in Hk., Jour. Bot. 1: 12. 1834. (5 spp., subtribe Ponerinae)

Dipera Spreng., Syst. 3: 696. 1826. = **Disperis** Sw.

Diperis Wight, Icon. 5: pl. 1719. 1852. = **Disperis** Sw.

Diphryllum Raf. in Med. Repos. N.Y. 5: 357. 1808. = **Listera** R.Br.

Diphyes Bl., Bijdr. 310, pl. 66. 1825. = **Bulbophyllum** Thou.

Diphylax Hk.f., Icon. Pl. 19: pl. 1865. 1889. = **Habenaria** Willd.

Diplacorchis Schltr. in Beih. Bot. Centralbl. 37(2): 129. 1929. (1 sp., subtribe Habenarinae)

Diplecthrum Pers., Syn. 2: 508. 1807. = **Satyrium** L.

Diplectraden Raf., Fl. Tellur. 2: 90. 1836. = **Habenaria** Willd.

Diplectrum Endl., Gen. 211. 1837. = **Satyrium** L.

Diplocaulobium [Rchb.f.] Krzl. in Engl., Das Pflanzenr. IV, 50, ii, B, 21: 331. 1910. (40 spp., subtribe Dendrobiinae)

Diplocentrum Ldl. in Bot. Reg., under pl. 1522. 1832. (2 spp., subtribe Sarcanthinae)

Diplochilus Ldl. in Bot. Reg., under pl. 1499. 1832. = **Diplomeris** D.Don

Diploconchium Schau. in Nov. Act. Nat. Cur. 19, Suppl. 1: 428. 1843. = **Agrostophyllum** Bl.

Diplodium Sw. in Ges. Nat. Fr. Berl. Mag. 4: 84, pl. 3. 1810. = **Pterostylis** R.Br.

Diplogastra Welw. ex Rchb.f. in Flora 48: 183. 1865. = **Platylepis** A.Rich.

Diplolabellum Mak. in Jour. Jap. Bot. 11: 305. 1935. (1 sp., subtribe Corallorrhizinae)

Diplomeris D.Don, Prodr. Fl. Nepal 26. 1825. (4 spp., subtribe Habenarinae)

Diploprora Hk.f., Fl. Brit. Ind. 6(1): 26. 1890. (5 spp., subtribe Sarcanthinae)

Diplorhiza Ehr., Beitr. 4: 147. 1789. = **Habenaria** Willd.

Dipodium R.Br., Prodr. Fl. Nov. Holl. 330. 1810. (12 spp., subtribe Cymbidiinae)

Dipteranthus B.-R., Orch. Nov. 2: 232. 1881. (3 spp., subtribe Ornithocephalinae)

Dipterostele Schltr. in Fedde, Repert. Spec. Nov., Beih. 8: 106. 1921. (1 sp., subtribe Telipogoninae)

Disa Berg, Fl. Cap. 348. 1767. (200 spp., subtribe Disinae)

Discyphus Schltr. in Fedde, Repert. Spec. Nov. 15: 417. 1919. = **Spiranthes** L.C.Rich.

Diseris Wight, Icon. 5: 17, pl. 1719, in text. 1852. = **Disperis** Sw.

Disperis Sw. in Vet. Akad. Handl. Stockh. 21: 218. 1800. (50 spp., subtribe Disperidinae)

Dissorhynchium Schau. in Nov. Act. Nat. Cur. 19, Suppl. 1: 434, pl. 13. 1843. = **Habenaria** Willd.

Distichis Thou. ex Ldl., Veg. Kingd. 181. 1847. = **Liparis** L.C.Rich.

Diteilis Raf., Herb. Raf. 73. 1833. = **Liparis** L.C.Rich.

Dituilis Raf., Fl. Tellur. 4: 49. 1836. = **Liparis** L.C.Rich.

Ditulima Raf., Fl. Tellur. 4: 41. 1836. = **Dendrobium** Sw.

Diuris Sm. in Trans. Linn. Soc. 4: 222. 1798. (40 spp., subtribe Diuridinae)

Domingoa Schltr. in Urb., Symb. Antill. 7: 496. 1913. (2 spp., subtribe Laeliinae)

Donacopsis Gagnep. in Bull. Mus. Hist. Nat. Paris II, 4: 593. 1932. (1 sp., subtribe unknown)

Doritis Ldl., Gen. & Sp. Orch. 178. 1833. (1 sp., subtribe Sarcanthinae)

Dorycheile Rchb., Nomen. 56. 1851. = **Cephalanthera** L.C.Rich.

Dossinia C.Morr. in Ann. Soc. Gand. 4: 123. 1848. (1 sp., subtribe Physurinae)

Dothilis Raf., Fl. Tellur. 2: 60. 1836. = **Spiranthes** L.C.Rich.

Dothilophis Raf., Fl. Tellur. 4: 39. 1836. = **Epidendrum** L.

Doxosma Raf., Fl. Tellur. 4: 9. 1836. = **Epidendrum** L.

Drakaea Ldl., Swan River App. 55. 1839. (4 spp., subtribe Drakaeinae)

Drakea Endl. Ench. 114. 1841. =**Drakaea** Ldl.

Dryadorchis Schltr. in Fedde, Repert. Spec. Nov., Beih. 1: 976. 1913. (2 spp., subtribe Sarcanthinae)

Drymoda Ldl., Sert. Orch., pl. 8c. 1838. (2 spp., subtribe Genyorchidinae)

Drymonanthus Nicholls in Victor. Natural. 59: 173. 1943. (1 sp., subtribe Sarcanthinae)

Dryopeia Thou., Orch. Îles Afr., pls. 1–3. 1822. = **Disperis** Sw.

Dryopria Thou., Orch. Îles Afr., Tabl. des Espéc. 1. 1822. = **Disperis** Sw.

Dryorkis Thou. in Nouv. Bull. Soc. Philom. no. 19: 316. 1809. = **Disperis** Sw.

Duboisia Karst. in Otto & Dietr., Allgem. Gartenz. 15: 394. 1847. = **Pleurothallis** R.Br.

Dubois-Reymondia Karst. in Bot. Zeit. 6: 397. 1848. = **Pleurothallis** R.Br.

Duckeëlla C.Porto & Brade in An. Prim. Réun. Sul-Amer. Bot. 1938, 3: 31. 1940. (1 sp., subtribe Vanillinae)

Earina Ldl. in Bot. Reg., under pl. 1699. 1834. (7 spp., subtribe Glomerinae)

Eburophyton Heller in Muhlenbergia 1: 48. 1904. = **Cephalanthera** L.C.Rich.

Echinoglossum Rchb., Nomen. 54. 1841. = **Trichoglottis** Bl.

Echioglossum Bl., Bijdr. 364, pl. 28. 1825. = **Sarcanthus** Ldl., **Trichoglottis** Bl.

Eckardia Endl., Gen. Suppl. 2: 17. 1842, in syn. = **Peristeria** Hk.

Eggelingia Summerh. in Bot. Mus. Leafl. Harv. Univ. 14: 235. 1951. (2 spp., subtribe Sarcanthinae)

Eicosia Bl., Fl. Jav. Praef. vii. 1828, *nomen.* = **Eucosia** Bl.

Elasmatum Dulac, Fl. Hautes Pyr. 121. 1867. = **Goodyera** R.Br.

Eleorchis Mak. in Jour. Jap. Bot. 11: 297. 1935. (2 spp., subtribe Bletillinae)

Elleanthus Presl, Rel. Haenk. 1: 97. 1827. (70 spp., subtribe Sobraliinae)

Eltroplectris Raf., Fl. Tellur. 2: 51. 1836. = **Pelexia** [Poit.] L.C.Rich.

Empusa Ldl. in Bot. Reg., under pl. 825. 1824. = **Liparis** L.C.Rich.

Empusaria Rchb., Consp. 69. 1828. = **Liparis** L.C.Rich.

Encheiridion Summerh. in Bot. Mus. Leafl. Harv. Univ. 11: 161. 1943. (1 sp., subtribe Sarcanthinae)

Encyclia Hk. in Bot. Mag., pls. 2831, 3013. 1828. = **Epidendrum** L.

Encyclia P. & E., Nov. Gen. & Sp. 2: 10. 1838. = **Epidendrum** L., **Polystachya** Hk.

Encyclium Neum. in Rev. Hortic. II, 4: 137. 1845–6. = **Epidendrum** L.

Endeisa Raf., Fl. Tellur. 2: 51. 1836. = **Dendrobium** Sw.

Endresiella Schltr. in Fedde, Repert. Spec. Nov. 17: 13. 1921. (1 sp., subtribe Gongorinae)

Enothrea Raf., Fl. Tellur. 4: 43. 1836. = **Octomeria** R.Br.

Entaticus S.F.Gray, Nat. Arr. Brit. Pl. 2: 198. 1821. = **Habenaria** Willd.

Ephippianthus Rchb.f. in F.Schmidt, Reisen Amurl. 180, pl. 5. 1868. (1 sp., subtribe Calypsoinae)

Ephippium Bl., Bijdr. 308, pl. 65. 1825. = **Bulbophyllum** Thou.

Epiblastus Schltr. in K.Schum & Lauterb., Nachtr. Fl. Deutsch Südsee 136. 1905. (20 spp., subtribe Glomerinae)

Epiblema R.Br., Prodr. Fl. Nov. Holl. 315. 1810. (1 sp., subtribe Thelymitrinae)

Epicladium Small, Fl. Miami 56. 1913. = **Epidendrum** L.

Epicranthes Bl., Bijdr. 306, pl. 9. 1825. = **Bulbophyllum** Thou.

Epicrianthes Bl., Fl. Jav. Praef. vii. 1828. = **Bulbophyllum** Thou.

Epidanthus L.O.Wms. in Bot. Mus. Leafl. Harv. Univ. 8: 148. 1940. (3 spp., subtribe Epidanthinae)

Epidendrum L., Sp. Pl., ed. 2: 1347. 1763. (1000 spp., subtribe Laeliinae)

Epidorchis Thou. in Nouv. Bull. Soc. Philom., no. 19: 314. 1809. = **Angraecum** Bory, **Mystacidium** Ldl.

Epidorkis Thou. in Nouv. Bull. Soc. Philom., no. 19: 318. 1809. = **Dendrobium** Sw.

Epigeneium Gagnep. in Bull. Mus. Hist. Nat. Paris II, 4: 593. 1932. (35 spp., subtribe Dendrobiinae)

Epigogum Koch, Syn. Fl. Germ., ed. 1, 693. 1837, *sphalm.* = **Epipogum** [Gmel.] L.C.Rich.

Epilyna Schltr. in Beih. Bot. Centralbl. 36(2): 374. 1918. = **Elleanthus** Presl

Epipactis Haller, Enum. Stirp. Helv. 1: 277. 1742. = **Goodyera** R.Br.

Epipactis [Zinn, in part] Sw. in Vet. Akad. Handl. Stockh. 21: 232. 1800; emend. L.C.Rich. in Mém. Mus. Hist. Nat. Paris 4: 51, 60. 1818. (25 spp., subtribe Cephalantherinae)

Epipactum Ritg. in Marb. Schrift. 2: 125. 1831. = **Epipactis** [Zinn., in part] Sw.

Epiphanes Bl., Bijdr. 421, pl. 4. 1825. = **Gastrodia** R.Br.

Epiphanes Rchb.f. in Seem., Fl. Vit. 295. 1868. = **Didymoplexis** Griff.

Epiphora Ldl. in Hk., Comp. Bot. Mag. 2: 201. 1836. = **Polystachya** Hk.

Epipogium R.Br., Prodr. Fl. Nov. Holl. 330, 331. 1810. = **Epipogum** [Gmel.] L.C.Rich.

Epipogon Sw., Summ. Veg. Scand. 32. 1814. = **Epipogum** [Gmel.] L.C.Rich.

Epipogum [Gmel.] L.C.Rich. in Mém. Mus. Paris 4: 58. 1818. (5 spp., subtribe Epipogoninae)

Epistephium Kth., Syn. Pl. Aequin. 1: 340. 1822. (20 spp., subtribe Vanillinae)

Epithecia Kn. & Westc., Flor. Cab. 2: 167. 1838. = **Dichaea** Ldl.

Epithecium Bth. & Hk.f., Gen. Plant. 3: 529, 1239. 1883. = **Dichaea** Ldl.

Eria Ldl. in Bot. Reg., pl. 904. 1825. (550 spp., subtribe Dendrobiinae)

Eriaxis Rchb.f. in Linnaea 41: 63. 1877. = **Galeola** Lour.

Eriochilos Spreng., Syst. 3: 714. 1826. = **Eriochilus** R.Br.

Eriochilum Ritg. in Marb. Schrift. 2: 121. 1831, *sphalm.* = **Eriochilus** R.Br.

Eriochilus R.Br., Prodr. Fl. Nov. Holl. 323. 1810. (5 spp., subtribe Caladeniinae)

Eriochylus Steud., Nom., ed. 2, 1: 586. 1840, *sphalm.* = **Eriochilus** R.Br.

Eriodes Rolfe in Orch. Rev. 23: 326. 1915. = **Tainia** Bl.

Eriopsis Ldl. in Bot. Reg., pl. 18. 1847. (6 spp., subtribe Gongorinae)

Erioxantha Raf. in Loud., Gard. Mag. 8: 247. 1832. = **Eria** Ldl.

Erporkis Thou. in Nouv. Bull. Soc. Philom., no. 19: 317. 1809. = **Platylepis** A.Rich.

Erycina Ldl., Fol. Orch. Erycina [1]. 1833. (2 spp., subtribe Oncidiinae)

Erythrodes Bl., Bijdr. 410, pl. 72. 1825. (100 spp., subtribe Physurinae)

Erythrorchis Bl., Rumphia 1: 200, pl. 70. 1835. = **Galeola** Lour.

Esmeralda Rchb.f., Xen. Orch. 2: 38. 1878. = **Arachnis** Bl.

Etaeria Bl., Bijdr. 409, pl. 14. 1825. = **Hetaeria** Bl.

Euanthe Schltr., Die Orchid. 567. 1914. (1 sp., subtribe Sarcanthinae)

Eucnemis Ldl., Gen. & Sp. Orch. 161. 1833. = **Govenia** Ldl.

Eucosia Bl., Bijdr. 415, pl. 18. 1825. (3 spp., subtribe Physurinae)

Eulophia R.Br. ex Ldl. in Bot. Reg. 8: pl. 686. 1823. (300 spp., subtribe Eulophiinae)

Eulophidium Pfitz. in Engl. & Prantl, Natürl. Pflanzenfam. II, 6: 188. 1889. (10 spp., subtribe Eulophidiinae)

Eulophiella Rolfe in Lindenia 7: 77. 1891. (4 spp., subtribe Cyrtopodiinae)

Eulophiopsis Pfitz., Entworf. Natur. Anordn. Orch. 105. 1887; & in Engl. & Prantl, Natürl. Pflanzenfam. 2(6): 183. 1889. = **Graphorkis** Thou.

Eulophus R.Br. in Bot. Reg. 7: under pl. 573. 1821, *sphalm.* = **Eulophia** R.Br.

Euothonaea Rchb.f. in Bot. Zeit. 10: 772. 1852. = **Hexisea** Ldl.

Euphroboscis Wight, Icon. 5: pl. 1732. 1852. = **Thelasis** Bl.

Eurycentrum Schltr. in K.Schum. & Lauterb., Nachtr. Fl. Deutsch Südsee 89. 1905. (4 spp., subtribe Physurinae)

Eurychone Schltr. in Beih. Bot. Centralbl. 36(2): 134. 1918. (2 spp., subtribe Sarcanthinae)

Eurystyles Wawra in Oestr. Bot. Zeitschr. 13: 223. 1863. (7 spp., subtribe Spiranthinae)

Eveleyna Steud., Nom., ed. 2, 1: 620. 1820. = **Elleanthus** Presl

Evelyna P. & E., Nov. Gen. & Sp. 1: 32, pl. 56. 1835. = **Elleanthus** Presl

Evota Rolfe in Dyer, Fl. Cap. 5(3): 268. 1913. (3 spp., subtribe Disperidinae)

Evrardia Gagnep. in Bull. Mus. Hist. Nat. Paris II, 4: 596. 1932. (1 sp., subtribe Cephalantherinae)

Exeria Raf., Fl. Tellur. 4: 49. 1836. = **Eria** Ldl.

Exophya Raf., Fl. Tellur. 2: 63. 1836. = **Epidendrum** L.

Eydisanthema Neck., Elem. 3: 133. 1794. = **Epidendrum** L.

Fernandezia Ldl., Gen. & Sp. Orch. 207. 1833. = **Lockhartia** Hk.

Fernandezia R. & P., Prodr. Fl. Peruv. & Chil. 123, pl. 27. 1794. = **Dichaea** Ldl., **Centropetalum** Ldl., **Pachyphyllum** HBK

Fieldia Gaud. in Freyc., Voy., Bot. 424, pl. 36. 1826. = **Vandopsis** Pfitz.

Finetia Schltr. in Beih. Bot. Centralbl. 36(2): 140. 1918, in obs. = **Neofinetia** Hu

Fissipes Small, Fl. S.E. U.S. 311. 1903. = **Cypripedium** L.

Fitzgeraldia FvM. in Wing, South. Sc. Rec. 56. 1882, in obs. = **Lyperanthus** R.Br.

Flickingeria A.D.Hawkes in Orch. Weekly 2: 451. 1961. (35 spp., subtribe Dendrobiinae)

Forbesina Ridl. in Jour. Bot. 63: Suppl. 120. 1925. (1 sp., subtribe Coelogyninae)

Forficaria Ldl., Gen. & Sp. Orch. 362. 1838. (1 sp., subtribe Disinae)

Forsythmajoria Krzl. ex Schltr., Die Orchid. 73. 1914, in syn. = **Cynorkis** Thou.

Fractiunguis Schltr. in Anex. Mem. Inst. Butantan 1(4): 35. 1922. (2 spp., subtribe Laeliinae)

Fregea Rchb.f. in Bot. Zeit. 10: 712. 1852. = **Sobralia** R. & P.

Froscula Raf., Fl. Tellur. 4: 44. 1836. = **Dendrobium** Sw.

Fuertesiella Schltr. in Urb., Symb. Antill. 7: 492. 1913. (3 spp., subtribe Cranichidinae)

Funkiella Schltr. in Beih. Bot. Centralbl. 37(2): 430. 1920. = **Spiranthes** L.C.Rich.

Gabertia Gaud. in Freyc., Voy., Bot. 425. 1826. = **Grammatophyllum** Bl.

Galeandra Ldl. in Bauer, Illustr. Orch. Pl., pl. 8. 1832. (25 spp., subtribe Polystachyinae)

Galearis Raf., Fl. Tellur. 2: 39. 1836. = **Orchis** [Tournef.] L., **Habenaria** Willd.

Galeoglossum A.Rich. & Gal. in Ann. Sci. Nat. III, 3: 31. 1845. = **Prescottia** Ldl.

Galeola Lour., Fl. Cochinch. 2: 520. 1790. (80 spp., subtribe Vanillinae)

Galeorchis Rydb. in Britt., Man. Fl. N. U.S. 292. 1901. = **Orchis** [Tournef.] L.

Galeottia A.Rich. in Ann. Sci. Nat. III, 3: 25. 1845. = **Mendonsella** A.D.Hawkes

Galeottiella Schltr. in Beih. Bot. Centralbl. 37(2): 360. 1920. = **Spiranthes** L.C.Rich.

Galera Bl., Bijdr. 415, pl. 3. 1825. = **Epipogum** [Gmel.] L.C.Rich.

Gamaria Raf., Fl. Tellur. 4: 49. 1836. = **Disa** Berg.

Gamoplexis Falc. in Proc. Linn. Soc. 1: 320. 1847; & in Trans. Linn. Soc. 20: 293, pl. 13. 1847. = **Gastrodia** R.Br.

Gamosepalum Schltr. in Beih. Bot. Centralbl. 37(2): 429. 1920. = **Spiranthes** L.C.Rich.

Gastorchis Thou., Orch. Îles Afr., Tabl. Genres, & Prem. Tabl. Espéc. 1822. (6 spp., subtribe Phaiinae)

Gastridium Bl., Fl. Jav. Praef. vii. 1828. = **Dendrobium** Sw.

Gastrochilus D.Don, Prodr. Fl. Nep. 32. 1825. (15 spp., subtribe Sarcanthinae)

Gastrodia R.Br., Prodr. Fl. Nov. Holl. 330. 1810. (20 spp., subtribe Gastrodiinae)

Gastroglottis Bl., Bijdr. 397. 1825. = **Liparis** L.C.Rich.

Gastropodium Ldl. in Ann. & Mag. Nat. Hist. I, 15: 107. 1845. = **Diothonaea** Ldl.

Gastrorchis Schltr. in Fedde, Repert. Spec. Nov., Beih. 33: 166. 1924. = **Gastorchis** Thou.

Gastrorkis Thou. in Nouv. Bull. Soc. Philom., no. 19: 317. 1809. = **Gastorchis** Thou.

Gavillea P. & E. ex Steud., Nom., ed. 2, 1: 166. 1840. = **Chloraea** Ldl.

Geissanthera Schltr. in K.Schum. & Lauterb., Nachtr. Fl. Deutsch Südsee 231. 1905. (17 spp., subtribe Sarcanthinae)

Gennaria Parlat., Fl. Ital. 3: 404. 1858. (1 sp., subtribe Habenarinae)

Genoplesium R.Br., Prodr. Fl. Nov. Holl. 319. 1810. = **Prasophyllum** R.Br.

Genyorchis Schltr., Westafr. Kautschuk-Exped. 280. 1900. (5 spp., subtribe Genyorchidinae)

Geobina Raf., Fl. Tellur. 4: 49. 1836. = **Goodyera** R.Br.

Geoblasta B.-R., Vellosia, ed. 2, 133. 1891. = **Chloraea** Ldl.

Geodorum Jacks. in Andr., Bot. Rep., pl. 626. 1810. (10 spp., subtribe Eulophiinae)

Georchis Ldl. in Wall., Catal., no. 7379. 1831. = **Goodyera** R.Br.

Gersinia Neraud in Gaud., Freyc., Voy., Bot. 27. 1826. = **Bulbophyllum** Thou.

Ghiesbrechtia Ldl., Veg. Kingd. 182. 1847. = **Calanthe** R.Br.

Ghiesbreghtia A.Rich. & Gal. in Ann. Sci. Nat. III, 3: 28. 1845. = **Calanthe** R.Br.

Ghiesebreghtia Ldl., Fol. Orch. Ghiesebreghtia [1]. 1854. = **Calanthe** R.Br.

Gigliolia B.-R., Orch. Nov. 1: 25. 1877. = **Octomeria** R.Br.

Giulianettia Rolfe in Hk., Icon. Plant., pl. 2616. 1899. (2 spp., subtribe Glomerinae)

Glomera Bl., Bijdr. 372, pl. 68. 1825. (50 spp., subtribe Glomerinae)

Glossaspis Spreng., Syst. 3: 675, 694. 1826. = **Habenaria** Willd.

Glossodia R.Br., Prodr. Fl. Nov. Holl. 323. 1810. (5 spp., subtribe Caladeniinae)

Glossorhyncha Ridl. in Jour. Linn. Soc. 33: 341. 1891. (60 spp., subtribe Glomerinae)

Glossula Ldl. in Bot. Reg., pl. 862. 1824. = **Habenaria** Willd.

Goadbyella R.S.Rog. in Trans. & Proc. Roy. Soc. S.Austral. 51: 294. 1927. (1 sp., subtribe Prasophyllinae)

Goldschmidtia Dammer in Orchis 4: 86. 1910. = **Dendrobium** Sw.

Gomesa R.Br. in Bot. Mag., pl. 1748. 1815. (10 spp., subtribe Oncidiinae)

Gomesia Spreng., Syst. 3: 729. 1826. = **Gomesa** R.Br.

Gomeza Ldl., Orch. Scel. 15. 1826. = **Gomesa** R.Br.

Gomezia Bartl., Ord. Nat. 58. 1830. = **Gomesa** R.Br.

Gomphichis Ldl., Gen. & Sp. Orch. 446. 1840. (10 spp., subtribe Cranichidinae)

Gomphostylis Wall. ex Ldl., Gen. & Sp. Orch. 43. 1830. = **Pleione** D.Don

Gonatostylis Schltr. in Engl., Bot. Jahrb. 39: 56. 1906. (1 sp., subtribe Physurinae)

Gongora R. & P., Prodr. Fl. Peruv. & Chil. 117, pl. 25. 1794. (12 spp., subtribe Gongorinae)

Gonogona Link, Enum. Hort. Berol. 2: 369. 1822. = **Goodyera** R.Br.

Goodiera Koch, Syn. Fl. Germ., ed. 2, 802. 1844. = **Goodyera** R.Br.

Goodyera R.Br. in Ait., Hort. Kew., ed. 2, 5: 191. 1813. (25 spp., subtribe Physurinae)

Gorgoglossum F.C.Lehm. in Gard. Chron. III, 21: 346. 1897. (1 sp., subtribe Gongorinae)

Govenia Ldl. in Lodd., Bot. Cab., pl. 1709. 1831. (8 spp., subtribe Cyrtopodiinae)

Govindooia Wight, Icon. 6: 34, pl. 2090. 1853. = **Tropidia** Ldl.

Govindovia C.Muell. in Walp., Ann. 6: 158. 1861. = **Tropidia** Ldl.

Grammangis Rchb.f. in Hamb. Gartenz. 16: 520. 1860; & Xen. Orch. 2: 17. 1873. (5 spp., subtribe Cymbidiinae)

Grammatophyllum Bl., Bijdr. 377, pl. 20. 1825. (8 spp., subtribe Cymbidiinae)

Graphorchis Thou. in Nouv. Bull. Soc. Philom., no. 19: 314, 319. 1809. = **Graphorkis** Thou.

Graphorkis Thou. in Nouv. Bull. Soc. Philom., no. 19: 318. 1809. (5 spp., subtribe Eulophiinae)

Grastidium Bl., Bijdr. 333. 1825. = **Dendrobium** Sw.

Grobya Ldl. in Bot. Reg., pl. 1740. 1835. (4 spp., subtribe Grobyinae)

Grossourdya Rchb.f. in Bot. Zeit. 22: 297. 1864. = **Thrixspermum** Lour.

Gunnia Ldl. in Bot. Reg., under pl. 1699. 1834. = **Sarcochilus** R.Br.

Gussonaea A.Rich. in Mém. Soc. Hist. Nat. Paris 4: 67. 1828. = **Microcoelia** Ldl.

Gussonia Spreng., Gen. 2: 664. 1831. = **Microcoelia** Ldl.

Gyaladenia Schltr. in Beih. Bot. Centralbl. 38(2): 124. 1921. = **Habenaria** Willd.

Gyas Salisb. in Trans. Hort. Soc. 1: 299. 1812. = **Bletia** R. & P.

Gymnadenia R.Br. in Ait., Hort. Kew., ed. 2, 5: 191. 1813. (15 spp., subtribe Habenarinae)

Gymnadeniopsis Rydb. in Britt., Man. Fl. N. U.S. 293. 1901. = **Habenaria** Willd.

Gymnochilus Bl., Orch. Archip. Ind. 107, pl. 32. 1858. (2 spp., subtribe Physurinae)

Gynizodon Raf., Fl. Tellur. 4: 40. 1836. = **Miltonia** Ldl.

Gynoglottis J.J.Sm. in Rec. Trav. Bot. Néerl. 1: 49. 1904. (1 sp., subtribe Coelogyninae)

Gyrostachys Pers., Syn. 2: 511. 1807. = **Spiranthes** L.C.Rich.

Habenaria Willd., Sp. Plant. 4: 44. 1805. (750 spp., subtribe Habenarinae)

Habenella Small, Fl. S.E. U.S. 316. 1903. = **Habenaria** Willd.

Habenorkis Thou. in Nouv. Bull. Soc. Philom., no. 19: 317. 1809. = **Habenaria** Willd.

Haemaria Ldl., Orch. Scel. 9. 1826. (1 sp., subtribe Physurinae)

Haematorchis Bl., Rumphia 4: pl. 200 B. 1848. = **Galeola** Lour.

Hakoneaste Mak. in Bot. Mag. Tokyo 49: 598. 1935. (1 sp., subtribe Calypsoinae)

Hallackia Harv., Thes. Cap. 2: 2, pl. 102. 1863. = **Huttonaea** Harv.

Hammarbya O.Ktze., Rev. Gen. Pl. 2: 665. 1891. (1 sp., subtribe Liparidinae)

Hancockia Rolfe in Jour. Linn. Soc. 36: 20. 1903. (1 sp., subtribe Collabiinae)

Hapalorchis Schltr. in Fedde, Repert. Spec. Nov., Beih. 6: 52. 1919. = **Spiranthes** L.C.Rich.

Haplochilus Endl., Ench. 113. 1841; & Gen., Suppl. 2: 28. 1842. = **Zeuxine** Ldl.

Haplostellis Endl., Gen. 219. 1837. = **Nervilia** Comm. ex Gaud.

Haraëlla Kudo in Jour. Soc. Trop. Agric., Taiwan 2: 26. 1930. (2 spp., subtribe Sarcanthinae)

Harrisella F. & R. in Jour. Bot. 47: 265. 1909. = **Campylocentrum** Bth.

Hartwegia Ldl. in Bot. Reg., under pl. 1970. 1837. = **Nageliella** L.O.Wms.

Hecabe Raf., Fl. Tellur. 4: 44. 1836. = **Phaius** Lour.

Hederorkis Thou. in Nouv. Bull. Soc. Philom. Paris 1: 319. 1809. =? **Polystachya** Hk.

Helcia Ldl. in Bot. Reg., Misc. 17. 1845. (2 spp., subtribe Trichopiliinae)

Helictonia Ehr., Beitr. 4: 148. 1789. = **Spiranthes** L.C. Rich.

Helleborine Martyn, Hist. Pl., pl. 50. 1736. = **Calopogon** R.Br.

Helleborine Hill, Brit. Herb., pl. 477. 1736. = ? **Epipactis** [Zinn., in part] Sw.

Helleborine Tournef. ex Hall., Enum. Stirp. Helv. 1: 274. 1742; Pers., Syn. 2: 512. 1807. = ? **Serapias** L.

Helleborine Mill., Gard. Dict., abridg. ed., 4. 1754; Druce in Rep. Bot. Exch. Club. Br. Isles 3: 432. 1913. = **Serapias** L.

Hellerorchis A.D.Hawkes in Orch. Jour. 3: 275. 1959. (6 spp., subtribe Oncidiinae)

Helorchis Schltr. in Fedde, Repert. Spec. Nov., Beih. 33: 35. 1924. = **Cynorkis** Thou.

Hemihabenaria Finet in Rev. Gén. de Bot. 13: 532. 1902. = **Habenaria** Willd.

Hemiperis Frapp. ex Cordem., Fl. Île Réunion 235. 1895. = **Habenaria** Willd.

Hemipilia Ldl., Gen. & Sp. Orch. 296. 1835. (8 spp., subtribe Habenarinae)

Hemiscleria Ldl., Fol. Orch. Hemiscleria [1]. 1853. = **Diothonaea** Ldl.

Henosis Hk.f., Fl. Brit. Ind. 5: 771. 1890; & l.c., 6: 1890. = **Bulbophyllum** Thou.

Herminium R.Br. in Ait., Hort. Kew., ed. 2, 5: 191. 1813. (20 spp., subtribe Habenarinae)

Herpysma Ldl. in Wall., Catal., no. 7389. 1831; & in Bot. Reg., under pl. 1618. 1833. (2 spp., subtribe Physurinae)

Herschelia Ldl., Gen. & Sp. Orch. 362. 1838. (19 spp., subtribe Disinae)

Hetaeria Bl., Bijdr. 409, pl. 14. 1825, as *Etaeria*; & Fl. Jav. Praef. vii. 1828. (30 spp., subtribe Physurinae)

Heterotaxis Ldl. in Bot. Reg., pl. 1028. 1826. = **Maxillaria** R. & P.

Hexadesmia Brongn. in Ann. Sci. Nat. II, 17: 14. 1842. = **Scaphyglottis** P. & E.

Hexalectris Raf., Neogen. 4. 1825. (6 spp., subtribe Corallorrhizinae)

Hexameria R.Br. in Bl., Pl. Jav. Rar. 26, pl. 7. 1838. = **Podochilus** Bl.

Hexisea Ldl. in Hk., Jour. Bot. 1: 7. 1834. (6 spp., subtribe Laeliinae)

Hexopia Batem. ex Ldl. in Bot. Reg., Misc. 46. 1840, *nomen*; & l.c., Misc. 2. 1844. = **Scaphyglottis** P.& E.

Himanthoglossum Koch, Syn. Fl. Germ., ed. 1, 689. 1837. = **Himantoglossum** Spreng.

Himantoglossum Spreng., Syst. 3: 675, 694. 1826. (4 spp., subtribe Habenarinae)

Hintonella Ames in Bot. Mus. Leafl. Harv. Univ. 6: 186. 1938. (1 sp., subtribe Ornithocephalinae)

Hippeophyllum Schltr. in K.Schum. & Lauterb., Nachtr. Fl. Deutsch Südsee 107. 1905. (4 spp., subtribe Liparidinae)

Hippoglossum Breda, Orch. Kuhl & Hass. [pl. 14]. 1827. = **Bulbophyllum** Thou.

Hipporchis Thou. in Nouv. Bull. Soc. Philom., no. 19: 317. 1809. = ?

Hoehneëlla Ruschi, Orq. Nov. Estad. Espíritu Santo 3. 1945. (3 spp., subtribe Huntleyinae)

Hofmeistera Rchb.f., Poll. Orch. 30. 1852. = **Hofmeisterella** Rchb.f.

Hofmeisterella Rchb.f. in Walp., Ann. 3: 563. 1852. (1 sp., subtribe Oncidiinae)

Holcoglossum Schltr. in Fedde, Repert. Spec. Nov., Beih. 4: 285. 1919. (1 sp., subtribe Sarcanthinae)

Hologyne Pfitz. in Engl. & Prantl, Das Pflanzenr. IV, 50 (Coelogyn.): 131. 1907. = **Coelogyne** Ldl.

Holopogon Kom. & Nev. in Komarov, Fl. URSS 4: 620, 750. 1935. (1 sp., subtribe Listerinae)

Holothrix L.C.Rich. in Mém. Mus. Hist. Nat. Paris 4: 55. 1818. (20 spp., subtribe Habenarinae)

Homalopetalum Rolfe in Hk., Icon. Plant., pl. 2461. 1896. (4 spp., subtribe Laeliinae)

Hormidium Ldl. ex Heynh., Nom. 1: 880. 1840. = **Epidendrum** L.

Houlletia Brongn. in Ann. Sci. Nat., II, 15: 37. 1841. (10 spp., subtribe Gongorinae)

Huebneria Schltr. in Beih. Bot. Centralbl. 42(2): 96. 1925. (1 sp., subtribe Ponerinae)

Humboldtia R. & P., Prodr. Fl. Peruv. & Chil. 121, pl. 27. 1794. = **Pleurothallis** R.Br.

Huntleya Batem. ex Ldl. in Bot. Reg., under pl. 1991. 1837; & l.c., pl. 14. 1839. (4 spp., subtribe Huntleyinae)

Huttonaea Harv., Thes. Cap. 2: 1, pl. 101. 1863. (5 spp., subtribe Huttonaeinae)

Huttonia Bolus in Jour. Linn. Soc. 19: 339. 1882. = **Huttonaea** Harv.

Hyacinthorchis Bl., Mus. Bot. Lugd.-Bat. 1: 48, pl. 16. 1849. = **Cremastra** Ldl.

Hyalosema [Schltr.] Rolfe in Orch. Rev. 27: 130. 1919. (20 spp., subtribe Bulbophyllinae)

Hybochilus Schltr. in Fedde, Repert. Spec. Nov. 16: 429. 1920. (1 sp., subtribe Capanemiinae)

Hydranthus Kuhl & v.Hass. ex Rchb.f., Xen. Orch. 2: 20. 1862. = **Dipodium** R.Br.

Hygrochilus Pfitz. in Engl. & Prantl, Natürl. Pflanzenfam., Nachtr. 1: 112. 1897. = **Vanda** Jones

Hylophila Ldl. in Wall., Catal., no. 7896. 1831; & Bot. Reg., under pl. 1618. 1833. (5 spp., subtribe Physurinae)

Hymanthoglossum Tod., Orch. Sic. 67. 1842. = **Himantoglossum** Spreng.

Hymenorchis Schltr. in Fedde, Repert. Spec. Nov., Beih. 1: 994. 1913. (7 spp., subtribe Sarcanthinae)

Hypodema Rchb., Nom. 56. 1841. = **Cypripedium** L.

Hypodematium A.Rich., Tent. Fl. Abyss. 2: 286, pl. 83. 1850. = **Eulophia** R.Br. ex Ldl.

Hysteria Reinw. ex Bl., Cat. Gew. Buitenz. 99. 1823, *nomen.* = **Corymborchis** Thou. ex Bl.

Iantha Hk., Exot. Fl., pl. 113. 1825. = **Ionopsis** HBK

Ibidium Salisb. in Trans. Hort. Soc. Lond. 1: 291. 1822. = **Spiranthes** L.C.Rich.

Iebine Raf., Fl. Tellur. 4: 39. 1836. = **Liparis** L.C.Rich.

Imerinaea Schltr. in Fedde, Repert. Spec. Nov., Beih. 33: 151. 1924. (1 sp., subtribe Liparidinae)

Inobulbon Schltr. & Krzl. ex Krzl. in Engl., Das Pflanzenr. 4, 50, ii, B, 21: 316. 1910. (2 spp., subtribe Dendrobiinae)

Inopsis Steud., Nom., ed. 1, 432. 1821. = **Ionopsis** HBK

Ione Ldl., Fol. Orch. Ione [1]. 1853. (7 spp., subtribe Genyorchidinae)

Ionopsis HBK, Nov. Gen. & Sp. 1: 348. pl. 83. 1815. (4 spp., subtribe Ionopsidinae)

Ionorchis G.Beck, Fl. Nied. Oest. 2(1): 215. 1890. = **Limodorum** [Tournef.] L.

Ipsea Ldl., Gen. & Sp. Orch. 124. 1831. (1 sp., subtribe Phaiinae)

Iridorchis Bl., Orch. Archip. Ind. 90, pl. 26. 1858. = **Cymbidium** Sw.

Iridorchis Thou. in Nouv. Bull. Soc. Philom., no. 19: 314. 1809. = **Oberonia** Ldl.

Iridorchis Thou., Orch. Îles Afr., Tabl. Synopt. 1. 1822. = **Oberonia** Ldl.

Iridorkis Thou. in Nouv. Bull. Soc. Philom., no. 19: 319. 1809. = **Oberonia** Ldl.

Isabelia B.-R., Orch. Nov. 1: 75. 1877. (1 sp., subtribe Laeliinae)

Ischnocentrum Schltr. in Fedde, Repert. Spec. Nov., Beih. 1: 918. 1912. (1 sp., subtribe Glomer... ..ae)

Ischnogyne Schltr. in Fedde, Repert. Spec. 1 ...v. 12: 106. 1913. (1 sp., subtribe Coelogyninae)

Isias DeNot in Mem. Acc. Sc. Tonn., II, 7: 413. 1844. = **Serapias** L.

Isochilos Spreng., Syst. 3: 734. 1826. = **Isochilus** R.Br.

Isochilus R.Br. in Ait., Hort. Kew., ed. 2, 5: 209. 1813. (2 spp., subtribe Ponerinae)

Isotria Raf. in Med. Repos. N.Y. 5: 357. 1808. (2 spp., subtribe Vanillinae)

Itaculumia Hoehne in Bol. Mus. Nac. Rio de Janeiro 12(3–4): 79. 1836. = **Habenaria** Willd.

Jacquiniella Schltr. in Fedde, Repert. Spec. Nov., Beih. 7: 123. 1920. (4 spp., subtribe Ponerinae)

Jansenia B.-R., Vellosia, ed. 2, 1: 124. 1891. = **Plectrophora** Focke

Jantha Steud., Nom., ed. 2, 1: 797. 1840. = **Ionopsis** HBK

Jenmania Rolfe in Kew Bull. 198. 1898. = **Palmorchis** B.-R.

Jensoa Raf., Fl. Tellur. 4: 38. 1836. = **Cymbidium** Sw.

Jimenesia Raf., Fl. Tellur. 4: 38. 1836. = **Bletilla** Rchb.f.

Jone Ldl. ex Schltr., Die Orchid. 334. 1914. = **Ione** Ldl.

Jonorchis G.Beck, Fl. Nied. Oest. 1: 215. 1890. = **Limodorum** Sw.

Josepha Bth. & Hk.f., Gen. Plant. 3: 516. 1883, *sphalm.* = **Josephia** Wight

Josephia Wight, Icon. 5: 19, pls. 1742–3. 1851. (2 spp., subtribe Adrorrhizinae)

Jumellea Schltr., Die Orchid. 609. 1914. (54 spp., subtribe Sarcanthinae)

Katherinea A.D.Hawkes in Lloydia 19: 94. 1956. = **Epigeneium** Gagnep.

Kefersteinia Rchb.f. in Bot. Zeit. 10: 633. 1852. = **Chondrorhyncha** Ldl.

Kegelia Rchb.f. in Bot. Zeit. 10: 670. 1852. = **Kegeliella** Mansf.

Kegeliella Mansf. in Fedde, Repert. Spec. Nov. 36: 60. 1934. (2 spp., subtribe Gongorinae)

Keranthus Lour. ex Endl., Gen. 193. 1836, in syn. = **Dendrobium** Sw.

Kingiella Rolfe in Orch. Rev. 25: 196. 1917. (5 spp., subtribe Sarcanthinae)

Kochiophyton Schltr. ex Cgn. in Mart., Fl. Bras. 3(6): 574. 1906. = **Acacallis** Ldl.

Koellensteinia Rchb.f. in Bonplandia 2: 17. 1854. (10 spp., subtribe Zygopetalinae)

Kraenzlinella O.Ktze. in Post & Ktze., Lexic. 310. 1903. = **Pleurothallis** R.Br.

Kuhlhasseltia J.J.Sm., Icon. Bogor., pl. 301. 1910. (3 spp., subtribe Physurinae)

Lacaena Ldl. in Bot. Reg., Misc. 18. 1843. (2 spp., subtribe Gongorinae)

Laelia Ldl., Gen. & Sp. Orch. 115. 1831. (75 spp., subtribe Laeliinae)

Laeliopsis Ldl. in Ldl. & Paxt., Flow. Gard. 3: 155, pl. 105. 1852–3. (2 spp., subtribe Laeliinae)

Lanium Ldl. ex Bth. & Hk.f., Icon. Plant., pl. 1334. 1881. (4 spp., subtribe Laeliinae)

Lankesterella Ames, Sched. Orch. 4: 3. 1923. (10 spp., subtribe Spiranthinae)

Larnandra Raf., Neogen. 4. 1825. = **Epidendrum** L.

Lathrisa Sw., Anot. Bot. 48. 1829. = **Bartholina** R.Br.

Latourea Bth. & Hk.f., Gen. Plant. 3: 501. 1883. = **Dendrobium** Sw.

Latouria Bl., Rumphia 4: 41, pls. 195, 199. 1850. = **Dendrobium** Sw.

Leaoa Schltr. & C.Porto in Arch. Jard. Bot. Rio de Janeiro 3: 292. 1922. (1 sp., subtribe Ponerinae)

Lecanorchis Bl., Mus. Bot. Lugd.-Bat. 2: 188. 1856. (5 spp., subtribe Vanillinae)

Lectandra J.J.Sm. in Bull. Dép. Agric. Ind. Néerl. 13: 55. 1907. = **Poaephyllum** Ridl.

Ledgeria FvM, Fragm. Bot. 1: 238. 1859. = **Galeola** Lour.

Leiochilus Bth. in Jour. Linn. Soc. 18: 328. 1881. = **Leochilus** Kn. & Westc.

Lemuranthe Schltr. in Fedde, Repert. Spec. Nov., Beih. 33: 84. 1924. = **Cynorkis** Thou.

Lemurella Schltr. in Fedde, Repert. Spec. Nov., Beih. 33: 366. 1925. (3 spp., subtribe Sarcanthinae)

Lemurorchis Krzl. in Engl., Bot. Jahrb. 17: 58. 1893. (1 sp., subtribe Sarcanthinae)

Leochilus Kn. & Westc., Flor. Cab. 2: 143. 1838. (15 spp., subtribe Oncidiinae)

Leopardanthus Bl., Rumphia 4: 47. 1848; & Mus. Bot. Lugd.-Bat. 1: 47, pl. 15. 1849. = **Dipodium** R.Br.

Lepantes Sw. in Schrad., Jour. 2: 249. 1799. = **Lepanthes** Sw.

Lepanthes Sw. in Nov. Act. Soc. Sc. Upsal. 6: 85. 1799. (65 spp., subtribe Pleurothallidinae)

Lepanthos St. Lag. in Ann. Soc. Bot. Lyon 7: 56. 1880. = **Lepanthes** Sw.

Lepanthopsis Ames in Bot. Mus. Leafl. Harv. Univ. 1(9): 3. 1933. (10 spp., subtribe Pleurothallidinae)

Lepervenchea Cordem. in Rev. Gen. de Bot. 11: 415. 1899. = **Angraecum** Bory

Lepidogyne Bl., Orch. Archip. Ind. 93, pl. 25. 1858. (3 spp., subtribe Physurinae)

Leptocentrum Schltr., Die Orchid. 600. 1914. = **Plectrelminthus** Raf.

Leptoceras Ldl., Swan River App. 53. 1839. = **Caladenia** R.Br., **Lyperanthus** R.Br.

Leptorchis Thou. in Nouv. Bull. Soc. Philom., no. 19: 149. 1809. = **Liparis** L.C.Rich.

Leptorkis Thou. in Nouv. Bull. Soc. Philom., no. 19: 317. 1809. = ?**Malaxis** Soland. ex Sw.

Leptotes Ldl. in Bot. Reg., pl. 1625. 1833. (6 spp., subtribe Laeliinae)

Leptotherium D.Dietr., Syn. Pl. 1: 398. 1839. = **Isochilus** R.Br.

Leptothrium Kth. in HBK, Nov. Gen. & Sp. 1: 340. 1815. = **Isochilus** R.Br.

Lequeetia Bub., Fl. Pyren. 4: 57. 1901. = **Limodorum** [Tournef.] L.

Leucochyle Klotzsch, Ind. Sem. Hort. Berol., App. 1. 1854. = **Trichopilia** Ldl.

Leucohyle Rchb.f. in Walp., Ann. 6: 679. 1861, *sphalm.* = **Trichopilia** Ldl.

Leucolaena Ridl. in Jour. Linn. Soc. 28: 340. 1891. = **Didymoplexis** Griff.

Leucorchis Bl., Mus. Bot. Lugd.-Bat. 1: 31. 1849. = **Didymoplexis** Griff.

Leucorchis E.Mey., Preuss. Pflanzeng. 50. 1839. = **Habenaria** Willd.

Leucostachys Hoffmsgg., Preis-Verz. Orch. 26. 1842. = **Goodyera** R.Br.

Lichenora Wight, Icon. 5: pl. 1738. 1852. = **Eria** Ldl.

Lichinora Wight, Icon. 5: 18. 1852, *sphalm.* = **Eria** Ldl.

Lichterveldia Lem., Illustr. Hortic. 2: pl. 59. 1855. = **Odontoglossum** HBK

Limatodes Ldl., Gen. & Sp. Orch. 252. 1833. = **Calanthe** R.Br.

Limatodis Bl., Bijdr. 375. 1825. = **Calanthe** R.Br.

Limnas Ehr., Beitr. 4: 146. 1789. = **Malaxis** Soland. ex Sw.

Limnorchis Rydb. in Mem. N.Y. Bot. Gard. 1: 104. 1900. = **Habenaria** Willd.

Limodoron St. Lag. in Ann. Soc. Bot. Lyon 7: 129. 1880. = **Limodorum** [Tournef.] L.C.Rich.

Limodorum [Tournef.] L.C.Rich. in Mém. Mus. Paris 4: 50. 1818. (1 sp., subtribe Cephalantherinae)

Limodorum Ludw., Def. 120. 1737. = **Epipactis** [Zinn., in part] Sw., **Cephalanthera** L.C.Rich.

Limonias Ehr., Beitr. 4: 147. 1789. = **Epipactis** [Zinn., in part] Sw.

Lindblomia Fries in Lindbl., Bot. Notiser 134. 1843. = **Habenaria** Willd.

Lindleyella Schltr., Die Orchid. 414. 1914. = **Rudolfiella** Hoehne

Lindsayella Ames & Schweinf. in Bot. Mus. Leafl. Harv. Univ. 5: 33. 1937. = **Sobralia** R. & P.

Liparis L.C.Rich. in Mém. Mus. Hist. Nat. Paris 4: 43, 52. 1818. (350 spp., subtribe Liparidinae)

Lissochilos Bartl., Ord. 37. 1830. = **Eulophia** R.Br. ex. Ldl.

Lissochilus R.Br. ex Ldl., Bot. Reg., pl. 573. 1821; & Ldl., Coll. Bot., pl. 31. 1822. = **Eulophia** R.Br. ex Ldl.

Lissoschilus Hornsch in Synn. Ratisb. 1: 125. 1825. = **Eulophia** R.Br. ex Ldl.

Listera R.Br. in Ait., Hort. Kew., ed. 2, 5: 201. 1813. (20 spp., subtribe Listerinae)

Listeria Spreng., Anleit. 2(1): 293. 1817. = **Listera** R.Br.

Listrostachys Rchb.f. in Bot. Zeit. 10: 930. 1852. (2 spp., subtribe Sarcanthinae)

Lobogyne Schltr. in Mém. Herb. Boiss., no. 21: 85. 1900. = **Appendicula** Bl.

Lockhartia Hk. in Bot. Mag. pl. 2715. 1827. (30 spp., subtribe Lockhartiinae)

Loefgrenianthus Hoehne in Bol. Inst. Bras. Sc. 2: 352. 1927; & in Arch. Bot. Estad. S.Paulo 1: 592. 1927. (1 sp., subtribe Laeliinae)

Lonchitis Bub., Fl. Pyren. 4: 50. 1901. = **Serapias** L.

Lophiaris Raf., Fl. Tellur. 4: 40. 1836. = **Oncidium** Sw.

Lophoglottis Raf., Fl. Tellur. 4: 49. 1836. = **Sophronitis** Ldl.

Lorchophyllum Ehr., Beitr. 4: 148. 1789. = **Cephalanthera** L.C.Rich.

Loroglossum L.C.Rich. in Mém. Mus. Hist. Nat. Paris 4: 47. 1818. = **Orchis** [Tournef.] L., **Aceras** R.Br.

Lothiana Krzl. in Gard. Chron. III, 75: 173. 1924. = **Masdevallia** R. & P.

Louisia Rchb.f., Xen. Orch. 2: 204. 1858, *sphalm.* = **Luisia** Gaud.

Luddemania Rchb.f. in Lind., Pescatorea 1: pl. 22. 1860. = **Acineta** Ldl.

Ludisia A.Rich. in Dict. Clas. Nat. 7: 437. 1825. = **Haemaria** Ldl., **Dossinia** C.Morr.

Lueddemannia Rchb.f. in Bonplandia 2: 281. 1854. = **Acineta** Ldl.

Luedemannia Bth. in Bth. & Hk.f., Gen. Plant. 3: 552. 1883. = **Acineta** Ldl.

Luisia Gaud. in Freyc., Voy., Bot. 426, pl. 37. 1826. (35 spp., subtribe Sarcanthinae)

Lycaste Ldl. in Bot. Reg. n.s., 6: Misc. 14. 1843. (35 spp., subtribe Lycastinae)

Lycomormium Rchb.f. in Bot. Zeit. 10: 833. 1852. (2 spp., subtribe Gongorinae)

Lyperanthus R.Br., Prodr. Fl. Nov. Holl. 325. 1810. (9 spp., subtribe Acianthinae)

Lyraea Ldl., Gen. & Sp. Orch. 46. 1830. = **Bulbophyllum** Thou.

Lyroglossa Schltr. in Beih. Bot. Centralbl. 37(2): 448. 1920. = **Spiranthes** L.C.Rich.

Lysias Salisb. in Trans. Hort. Soc. Lond. 1: 288. 1812. = **Habenaria** Willd.

Lysiella Rydb. in Mem. N.Y. Bot. Gard. 1: 104. 1900. = **Habenaria** Willd.

Lysimnia Raf., Fl. Tellur. 4: 43. 1836. = **Brassavola** R.Br.

Macdonaldia Gunn ex Ldl., Swan River App. 50, pl. 9. 1839. = **Thelymitra** Forst.

Macodes Ldl., Gen. & Sp. Orch. 496. 1840. (7 spp., subtribe Physurinae)

Macradenia R.Br. in Bot. Reg., pl. 612. 1822. (15 spp., subtribe Notyliinae)

Macrocentrum Phil., Sert. Mend. Arl. 42. 1871. = **Habenaria** Willd.

Macrochilus Kn. & Westc., Flor. Cab. 1: 93. 1837. = **Miltonia** Ldl.

Macroclinium B.-R. ex Pfitz. in Engl. & Prantl, Natürl. Pflanzenfam. 2(6): 220. 1889. = **Notylia** Ldl.

Macroplectrum Pfitz. in Engl. & Prantl, Natürl. Pflanzenfam. 2(6): 214. 1889. = **Angraecum** Bory

Macropodanthus L.O.Wms. in Bot. Mus. Leafl. Harv. Univ. 6: 103. 1938. (1 sp., subtribe Sarcanthinae)

Macrostomium Bl., Bijdr. 335, pl. 37. 1825. = **Dendrobium** Sw.

Macrostomum Bth. & Hk.f., Gen. Plant. 3: 499. 1883, *sphalm.* = **Dendrobium** Sw.

Macrostylis Breda, Orch. Kuhl & Hass. [pl. 2]. 1827. = **Corymborchis** Thou. ex Bl.

Maelenia Dum. in Mém. Acad. Sc. Brux. 9: Bot. 10. 1834. = **Cattleya** Ldl.

Malachadenia Ldl. in Bot. Reg., Misc. 67. 1839. = **Bulbophyllum** Thou.

Malaxis Soland. ex Sw., Prodr. Veg. Ind. Occ. 119. 1778. (300 spp., subtribe Liparidinae)

Malleola J.J.Sm. & Schltr. ex Schltr. in Fedde, Repert. Spec. Nov., Beih. 1: 979. 1913. (30 spp., subtribe Sarcanthinae)

Maniella Schltr., Die Orchid. 91. 1914, *sphalm.* = **Manniella** Rchb.f.

Manniella Rchb.f., Otia Bot. Hamb. 109. 1881. (2 spp., subtribe Manniellinae)

Mariarisqueta Guinea, Ensayo Geobot. Guin. Cont. Españ. 268. 1946; & in An. Jard. Bot. Madrid 6(2): 470. 1946. = **Cheirostylis** Bl.

Marsupiaria Hoehne in Arq. Bot. Estad. S.Paulo, n.s., *form. maior*, 2: 69. 1947. = **Maxillaria** R. & P.

Masdevallia R. & P., Prodr. Fl. Peruv. & Chil. 122, pl. 27. 1794. (300 spp., subtribe Pleurothallidinae)

Maxillaria R. & P., Prodr. Fl. Peruv. & Chil. 116, pl. 25. 1794. (300 spp., subtribe Maxillarinae)

Mecosa Bl., Bijdr. 403, pl. 1. 1825. = **Habenaria** Willd.

Mediocalcar J.J.Sm. in Bull. Inst. Buitenz. 7: 3. 1900. (20 spp., subtribe Glomerinae)

Megaclinium Ldl. in Bot. Reg., pl. 989. 1826. = **Bulbophyllum** Thou.

Megalorchis H.Perr. in Bull. Soc. Bot. France 83: 579. 1937. (1 sp., subtribe Habenarinae)

Megastylis Schltr., Die Orchid. 93. 1914. (8 spp., subtribe Megastylidinae)

Meiracyllium Rchb.f., Xen. Orch. 1: 12, pl. 6. 1854. (2 spp., subtribe Laeliinae)

Melaxis Steud., Nom., ed. 2, 1: 118. 1841, *sphalm.* = **Liparis** L.C.Rich.

Meliclis Raf., Fl. Tellur. 2: 99. 1836. = **Coryanthes** Hk.

Menadena Raf., Fl. Tellur. 2: 98. 1836. = **Maxillaria** R. & P.

Menadenium Raf., Fl. Tellur. 4: 45. 1836. (4 spp., subtribe Zygopetalinae)

Mendonsella A.D.Hawkes in Orquidea 25: 7. 1963. (3 spp., subtribe Zygopetalinae)

Menephora Raf., Fl. Tellur. 4: 46. 1836. = **Cypripedium** L.

Mesadenella Pabst & Garay in Arq. Jard. Bot. Rio de Jan. 12: 207. 1952. = **Spiranthes** L.C.Rich.

Mesadenus Schltr. in Beih. Bot. Centralbl. 37(2): 367. 1920. = **Spiranthes** L.C.Rich.

Mesicera Raf., Neogen. 4. 1825. = **Habenaria** Willd.

Mesoclastes Ldl., Gen. & Sp. Orch. 44. 1830, = **Luisia** Gaud.

Mesoptera Raf., Fl. Tellur. 4: 49. 1836. = **Liparis** L.C.Rich.

Mesospinidium Rchb.f. in Bot. Zeit. 10: 929. 1852. (4 spp., subtribe Oncidiinae)

Metachilum Ldl., Gen. & Sp. Orch. 74. 1830. = **Appendicula** Bl.

Microcaelia Hochst. ex A.Rich., Tent. Fl. Abyss. 2: 285. 1851. = **Microcoelia** Ldl.

Microchilus Presl, Rel. Haenk. 1: 94. 1827. = **Erythrodes** Bl.

Microcoelia Ldl., Gen. & Sp. Orch. 60. 1830. (25 spp., subtribe Sarcanthinae)

Micropera Ldl. in Bot. Reg., under pl. 1522. 1832. = **Sarcochilus** R.Br.

Microsaccus Bl., Bijdr. 367. 1825. (5 spp., subtribe Sarcanthinae)

Microstylis Nutt., Gen. Amer. 2: 196. 1818. = **Malaxis** Soland. ex Sw.

Microtatorchis Schltr. in K.Schum. & Lauterb., Nachtr. Fl. Deutsch Südsee 224. 1905. (20 spp., subtribe Sarcanthinae)

Microtheca Schltr. in Fedde, Repert. Spec. Nov., Beih. 33: 76. 1924. = **Cynorkis** Thou.

Microtis R.Br., Prodr. Fl. Nov. Holl. 320. 1810. (12 spp., subtribe Prasophyllinae)

Miltonia Ldl. in Bot. Reg. 23: under pl. 1976. 1837. (20 spp., subtribe Oncidiinae)

Mischobulbum Schltr. in Fedde, Repert. Spec. Nov., Beih. 1: 98. 1911. (8 spp., subtribe Collabiinae)

Mitopetalum Bl., Praef. Fl. Jav. viii. 1828. = **Ania** Ldl.

Mitostigma Bl., Mus. Bot. Lugd.-Bat. 2: 189. 1856. = **Amitostigma** Schltr.

Mobilabium Rupp in Queensl. Natural. 13, no. 78: 2. 1946. (1 sp., subtribe Sarcanthinae)

Moerenhoutia Bl., Orch. Archip. Ind. 99, pls. 28, 42. 1858. (5 spp., subtribe Physurinae)

Monacanthus G.Don in Sweet, Hort. Brit., ed. 3, 644. 1839. = **Catasetum** L.C.Rich.

Monachanthus Ldl. in Bot. Reg. 18: under pl. 1538. 1832. = **Catasetum** L.C.Rich.

Monadenia Ldl., Gen. & Sp. Orch. 356. 1838. (30 spp., subtribe Disinae)

Monixus Finet in Bull. Soc. Bot. France 54, Mém. 9: 15. 1907. = **Angraecum** Bory

Monochilus Wall. ex Ldl., Gen. & Sp. Orch. 486. 1840. = **Hetaeria** Bl., **Zeuxine** Ldl., **Cheirostylis** Bl.

Monomeria Ldl., Gen. & Sp. Orch. 61. 1830. (4 spp., subtribe Genyorchidinae)

Monophyllorchis Schltr. in Fedde, Repert. Spec. Nov., Beih. 7: 39. 1920. (1 sp., subtribe Vanillinae)

Monorchis Ehr., Beitr. 4: 147. 1789. = **Herminium** R.Br.

Monosepalum Schltr. in Fedde, Repert. Spec. Nov., Beih. 1: 682, 893. 1912–13. (3 spp., subtribe Bulbophyllinae)

Monotris Ldl. in Bot. Reg., under pl. 1701. 1834. = **Holothrix** L.C.Rich.

Montolivaea Rchb.f., Otia Bot. Hamb. 107. 1881. = **Habenaria** Willd.

Monustes Raf., Fl. Tellur. 2: 87. 1836. = **Spiranthes** L.C.Rich.

Moorea Rolfe in Gard. Chron. III, 8(2): 7. 1890. = **Neomoorea** Rolfe

Mormodes Ldl., Introd. Nat. Syst., ed. 2, 446. 1826. (20 spp., subtribe Catasetinae)

Mormolyca Fenzl in Denkschr. Acad. Wien, Math. Nat. 1: 253. 1850. (1 sp., subtribe Maxillarinae)

Myanthus Ldl. in Bot. Reg. 18: under pl. 1538. 1832. = **Catasetum** L.C.Rich.

Mycaranthes Bl., Bijdr. 352, pl. 57. 1825. = **Eria** Ldl.

Mycaranthus Bth. & Hk.f., Gen. Plant. 3: 510. 1883, *sphalm.* = **Eria** Ldl.

Myoda Ldl. in Wall., Catal., no. 7390. 1830. = **Haemaria** Ldl.

Myodium Salisb. in Trans. Hort. Soc. Lond. 1: 289. 1812. = **Ophrys** L.

Myoxanthus P. & E., Nov. Gen. & Sp. 1: 50, pl. 88. 1835. = **Pleurothallis** R.Br.

Myrmechis Bl., Orch. Archip. Ind. 76, pl. 21. 1858. (4 spp., subtribe Physurinae)

Myrmecophila Rolfe in Orch. Rev. 25: 50. 1917. = **Laelia** Ldl.

Myrobroma Salisb., Parad. Lond., pl. 82. 1807. = **Vanilla** Sw.

Myrosmodes Rchb.f., Xen. Orch. 1: 19, pl. 8. 1854. = **Altensteinia** HBK

Mystacidium Ldl. in Hk., Comp. Bot. Mag. 2: 205. 1836. (5 spp., subtribe Sarcanthinae)

Nabaluia Ames, Orchid. 6: 70. 1920. (1 sp., subtribe Coelogyninae)

Nageliella L.O.Wms. in Bot. Mus. Leafl. Harv. Univ. 8: 144. 1940. (2 spp., subtribe Ponerinae)

Nanodes Ldl. in Bot. Reg., pl. 1541. 1832. = **Epidendrum** L.

Narica Raf., Fl. Tellur. 2: 87. 1836. = **Spiranthes** L.C.Rich.

Nasonia Ldl. in Bth., Pl. Hartweg. 150. 1844. = **Centropetalum** Ldl.

Nauenia Klotzsch in Otto & Dietr., Allgem. Gartenz. 21: 193. 1853. = **Lacaena** Ldl.

Navenia Klotzsch ex Bth. & Hk.f., Gen. Plant. 3: 547. 1883. = **Lacaena** Ldl.

Neippergia C.Morr. in An. Soc. Bot. Gand. 5: 375, pl. 282. 1849. = **Acineta** Ldl.

Nemaconia Kn. & Westc., Flor. Cab. 2: 127. 1838. = **Ponera** Ldl.

Nematoceras Hk.f., Fl. N. Zel. 1: 249, pl. 57. 1855. = **Corybas** Salisb.

Nemuranthes Raf., Fl. Tellur. 2: 61. 1836. = **Habenaria** Willd.

Neobartlettia Schltr. in Fedde, Repert. Spec. Nov. 16: 440. 1920. = **Palmorchis** B.-R.

Neobathiea Schltr. in Fedde, Repert. Spec. Nov., Beih. 33: 369. 1925. (6 spp., subtribe Sarcanthinae)

Neobenthamia Rolfe in Bot. Mag., pl. 7221. 1892; & in Gard. Chron. (2): 272, fig. 33. 1894. (1 sp., subtribe Polystachyinae)

Neobolusia Schltr. in Engl., Bot. Jahrb. 20, Beibl. 50: 5. 1895. (1 sp., subtribe Habenarinae)

Neoclemensia Carr in Gard. Bull. Straits Settlem. 8: 180. 1935. (1 sp., subtribe Gastrodiinae)

Neocogniauxia Schltr. in Urb., Symb. Antill. 7: 495. 1913. (2 spp., subtribe Laeliinae)

Neodryas Rchb.f. in Bot. Zeit. 10: 834. 1852. (6 spp., subtribe Oncidiinae)

Neofinetia Hu in Rhodora 27: 107. 1925. (1 sp., subtribe Sarcanthinae)

Neogardneria Schltr. in Notizbl. Bot. Gart. Berlin 7: 471. 1921, in obs. (2 spp., subtribe Zygopetalinae)

Neogyne Rchb.f. in Bot. Zeit. 10: 931. 1853. (1 sp., subtribe Coelogyninae)

Neokoehleria Schltr. in Fedde, Repert. Spec. Nov. 10: 390. 1912. (3 spp., subtribe Comparettiinae)

Neolauchea Krzl. in Bull. Herb. Boiss. 5: 110. 1897. (1 sp., subtribe Laeliinae)

Neolehmannia Krzl. in Engl., Bot. Jahrb. 26: 478. 1899. = **Epidendrum** L.

Neolindleya Krzl., Orch. Gen. & Sp. 1: 651. 1899. = **Habenaria** Willd.

Neomoorea Rolfe in Orch. Rev. 12: 30. 1904. (2 spp., subtribe Gongorinae)

Neotia Scop., Ann. 4, Hist. Nat. 99. 1770, *sphalm.* = **Neottia** Sw.

Neotinea Rchb.f., Poll. Orch. Comm. 18, 29. 1852. (1 sp., subtribe Habenarinae)

Neottia Sw. in Vet. Akad. Handl. Stockh. 21: 224. 1800. (5 spp., subtribe Listerinae)

Neottianthe [Rchb.f.] Schltr. in Fedde, Repert. Spec. Nov. 16: 290. 1919. (8 spp., subtribe Habenarinae)

Neottidium Schlecht., Fl. Berol. 1, p. lxv, 454. 1823. = **Neottia** Sw.

Neo-Urbania F. & R. in Jour. Bot. 47: 125. 1909. (1 sp., subtribe Ponerinae)

Nephelaphyllum Bl., Bijdr. 372, pl. 22. 1825. (8 spp., subtribe Collabiinae)

Nephelephyllum Bl., Fl. Jav. Praef. vii. 1828, *sphalm.* = **Nephelaphyllum** Bl.

Nephrangis [Schltr.] Summerh. in Kew Bull. 301. 1948. (1 sp., subtribe Sarcanthinae)

Nephranthera Hassk. in Hoev. & DeVr., Tijdschr. 9: 145. 1842. = **Renanthera** Lour.

Nerissa Raf., Fl. Tellur. 2: 89. 1836. = **Ponthieva** R.Br.

Nervilia Comm. ex Gaud. in Freyc., Voy., Bot. 422, pl. 35. 1826, *nom. conserv.* (50 spp., subtribe Nerviliinae)

Nidema Britt. & Millsp., Fl. Baham. 94. 1920. = **Epidendrum** L.

Nidus Riv., Icon. Pl. 3–7. 1760. = **Neottia** Sw.

Nienokuea Chev., Expl. Bot. Afr. Occ. Franç. 1: 622. 1920, *nomen*; & in Compt. Rend. Acad. Sci. Paris 220: 634. 1945. = **Polystachya** Hk.

Nigritella L.C.Rich. in Mém. Mus. Hist. Nat. Paris 4: 48. 1818. (1 sp., subtribe Habenarinae)

Nipponorchis Masamune in Mem. Fac. Sci. & Agr. Taihoku Imp. Univ. 11, Bot. 4: 592. 1934. = **Neofinetia** Hu

Norna Wahlenb., Fl. Suec., ed. 2, 561. 1826. = **Calypso** Salisb.

Notiophrys Ldl. in Jour. Linn. Soc. 1: 189. 1857. = **Platylepis** A.Rich.

Notylia Ldl. in Bot. Reg. 11: under pl. 930. 1825. (40 spp., subtribe Notyliinae)

Nychosma Raf., Fl. Tellur. 2: 9. 1836. = **Epidendrum** L.

Oakes-Amesia C.Schweinf. & Allen in Bot. Mus. Leafl. Harv. Univ. 13: 133. 1948. (1 sp., subtribe Ornithocephalinae)

Oberonia Ldl., Gen. & Sp. Orch. 15. 1830. (200 spp., subtribe Liparidinae)

Ocampoa A.Rich. & Gal. in Ann. Sci. Nat. III, 3: 31. 1845. = Cranichis Sw.

Octadesmia Bth. in Jour. Linn. Soc. 18: 311. 1881. (4 spp., subtribe Ponerinae)

Octarrhena Thw., Enum. Pl. Zeyl. 305. 1861. (19 spp., subtribe Thelasinae)

Octomeria D.Don, Prodr. Fl. Nepal. 31. 1825. = Eria Ldl.

Octomeria R.Br. in Ait., Hort. Kew., ed. 2, 5: 211. 1813. (75 spp., subtribe Pleurothallidinae)

Odonectis Raf., in Med. Repos. N.Y. 5: 357. 1808. = Isotria Raf.

Odontochilus Bl., Orch. Archip. Ind. 79, pls. 29, 36. 1858. (15 spp., subtribe Physurinae)

Odontoglossum HBK, Nov. Gen. & Sp. 1: 350, pl. 85. 1815. (300 spp., subtribe Oncidiinae)

Odontorrhynchus M.N.Correa in Darwiniana 10: 157. 1953. = Spiranthes L.C.Rich.

Odontostyles Breda, Orch. Kuhl & Hass. [pl. 4]. 1827. = Bulbophyllum Thou.

Oeceoclades Ldl. in Bot. Reg., under pl. 1522. 1832; & Gen. & Sp. Orch. 235. 1833. = Trichoglottis Bl.

Oecoeclades Franch. & Sav., Enum. Pl. Jap. 2: 28. 1879, sphalm. = Trichoglottis Bl.

Oeonia Ldl., Orch. Scel. 14. 1826. (6 spp., subtribe Sarcanthinae)

Oeoniella Schltr. in Beih. Bot. Centralbl. 33(2): 439. 1915. (3 spp., subtribe Sarcanthinae)

Oerstedella Rchb.f. in Bot. Zeit. 10: 932. 1852. = Epidendrum L.

Olgasis Raf., Fl. Tellur. 2: 51. 1836. = Oncidium Sw.

Oliveriana Rchb.f. in Linnaea 41: 111. 1877. (1 sp., subtribe Trichopiliinae)

Omaea Schltr., Die Orchid. 573. 1914, sphalm. = Omoea Bl.

Ommatodium Ldl., Gen. & Sp. Orch. 363. 1838. (1 sp., subtribe Disperidinae)

Omoea Bl., Bijdr. 359. 1825. (1 sp., subtribe Sarcanthinae)

Oncidium Sw. in Vet. Akad. Handl. Stockh. 21: 239. 1800. (750 spp., subtribe Oncidiinae)

Oncodia Ldl., Fol. Orch. Oncodia [1]. 1853. = Brachtia Rchb.f.

Onkeripus Raf., Fl. Tellur. 4: 42. 1836. = Xylobium Ldl.

Onychium Bl., Bijdr. 323, pl. 10. 1825. = Dendrobium Sw.

Ophris L., Syst., ed. 1. 1735. = Ophrys L.

Ophris Mill., Dict. Gard., abridg. ed., 4. 1754; cf. Druce in Rep. Bot. Exch. Club Brit. Isles 3: 434. 1913. = Listera R.Br.

Ophrys L., Sp. Pl. 945. 1753. (20 spp., subtribe Habenarinae)

Orchidion Mitch. in Act. Phys. Med. Acad. Nat. Cur. 8: App. 218. 1748. = Arethusa [Gronov.] L.

Orchidium Sw., Summ. Veg. Scand. 32. 1814; & in Svensk. Bot., pl. 518. 1819. = Calypso Salisb.

Orchidofunckia A.Rich. & Gal. in Ann. Sci. Nat., III, 3: 24. 1845. = Cryptarrhena R.Br.

Orchidotypus Krzl. in Engl., Bot. Jahrb. 37: 383. 1906. = Pachyphyllum HBK

Orchiodes Trew. in Act. Phys. Med. Caes. Leop. Nat. Cur. 3: 406, pl. 6, fig. 7. 1736. = Epipactis [Zinn., in part] Sw., Goodyera R.Br.

Orchipeda Breda ex Schltr., Die Orchid. 114. 1914, sphalm. = Orchipedum Breda

Orchipedium Bth. in Jour. Linn. Soc. 18: 344. 1881. err. typ. = Orchipedum Breda

Orchipedum Breda, Orch. Kuhl & Hass. [pl. 10]. 1827. (2 spp., subtribe Physurinae)

Orchis [Tournef.] L., Sp. Pl. 939. 1753. (70 spp., subtribe Habenarinae)

Orchites Schur, Enum. Pl. Trans. 5: 942. 1866. = Orchis [Tournef.] L.

Oreorchis Ldl. in Jour. Linn. Soc. 3: 26. 1859. (9 spp., subtribe Cyrtopodiinae)

Orestias Ridl. in Jour. Linn. Soc. 24: 197. 1887; & in Bol. Soc. Broter. 5: 201. 1887. = Liparis L.C.Rich.

Orleanesia B.-R., Orch. Nov. 1: 62. 1877. (5 spp., subtribe Ponerinae)

Ormostema Raf., Fl. Tellur. 4: 38. 1836. = Dendrobium Sw.

Ornitharium Ldl. & Paxt., Flow. Gard. 1: 188, fig. 117. 1850–1. = Sarcochilus R.Br.

Ornithidium Salisb. in Trans. Hort. Soc. Lond. 1: 293. 1812. = Maxillaria R. & P.

Ornithocephalus Hk., Exot. Fl. 2: pl. 127. 1825. (35 spp., subtribe Ornithocephalinae)

Ornithochilus Wall. ex Ldl., Gen. & Sp. Orch. 242. 1838. (2 spp., subtribe Sarcanthinae)

Ornithophora B.-R., Orch. Nov. 2: 225. 1881. (1 sp., subtribe Oncidiinae)

Orsidice Rchb.f. in Bonplandia 2: 93. 1854. = Thrixspermum Lour.

Orthoceras R.Br., Prodr. Fl. Nov. Holl. 316. 1810. (1 sp., subtribe Diuridinae)

Orthochilus Hochst. ex A.Rich., Tent. Fl. Abyss. 2: 284, pl. 82. 1851. = Eulophia R.Br. ex Ldl.

Orthopenthea Rolfe in Dyer, Fl. Cap. 5(3): 179. 1912. (1 sp., subtribe Disinae)

Ortmannia Opiz. in Flora 17: 592. 1834. = Geodorum Jacks.

Orxera Raf., Fl. Tellur. 4: 37. 1836. = Aërides Lour.

Osmoglossum Schltr. in Orchis 10: 162. 1916. = Odontoglossum HBK

Osyricera Bl., Bijdr. 307, pl. 58. 1825. = Bulbophyllum Thou.

Otandra Salisb. in Trans. Hort. Soc. Lond. 1: 298. 1812. = Geodorum Jacks.

Otochilus Ldl., Gen. & Sp. Orch. 35. 1830. (3 spp., subtribe Coelogyninae)

Otopetalum Lehm. & Krzl. in Engl., Bot. Jahrb. 26: 457. 1899. = Pleurothallis R.Br.

Otostylis Schltr. in Orchis 12: 38. 1918. (4 spp., subtribe Zygopetalinae)

Oxyanthera Brongn. in Duperr., Voy. Coq., Bot. 197, pl. 37. 1829. (5 spp., subtribe Thelasinae)

Oxysepalum Wight, Icon. 5: 17, pl. 1736. 1852, as Oxysepala. = Bulbophyllum Thou.

Oxystophyllum Bl., Bijdr. 335, pl. 38. 1825. = Dendrobium Sw.

Pachiphyllum LaLl. & Lex., Nov. Veg. Descr., fasc. 2 (Orch. Opusc).: 42. 1825, sphalm. = Pachyphyllum HBK

Pachites Ldl., Gen. & Sp. Orch. 301. 1835. (2 spp., subtribe Satyriinae)

Pachycentron Schltr., Die Orchid. 17. 1914, *sphalm,* = **Pachyplectron** Schltr.

Pachychilus Bl., Fl. Jav. Praef. 7. 1828. = **Pachystoma** Bl.

Pachyne Salisb. in Trans. Hort. Soc. Lond. 1: 299. 1812. = **Phaius** Lour.

Pachyphyllum HBK, Nov. Gen. & Sp. 1: 338, pl. 77. 1815. (20 spp., subtribe Pachyphyllinae)

Pachyplectron Schltr. in Engl., Bot. Jahrb. 39: 51. 1906. (1 sp., subtribe Pachyplectroninae)

Pachyrhizanthe [Schltr.] Nakai in Bot. Mag. Tokyo 45: 109. 1931. (5 spp., subtribe Cymbidiinae)

Pachystele Schltr. in Fedde, Repert. Spec. Nov., Beih. 19: 28. 1923. (5 spp., subtribe Ponerinae)

Pachystoma Bl., Bijdr. 376. 1825. (8 spp., subtribe Phaiinae)

Paliris Dum., Fl. Belg. 134. 1827. = **Liparis** L.C.Rich.

Palmoglossum Klotzsch ex Rchb.f., Xen. Orch. 1: 174. 1856. = **Pleurothallis** R.Br.

Palmorchis B.-R., Orch. Nov. 1: 169. 1877. (8 spp., subtribe Palmorchidinae)

Palumbina Rchb.f. in Walp., Ann. 6: 699. 1861. (1 sp., subtribe Oncidiinae)

Panisea Ldl., Fol. Orch. Panisea [1]. 1854. (4 spp., subtribe Coelogyninae)

Panstrepis Raf., Fl. Tellur. 4: 41. 1836. = **Coryanthes** Hk.

Pantlingia Prain in Jour. As. Soc. Beng. 65: 107. 1896. = **Stigmatodactylus** Maxim.

Paphinia Ldl. in Bot. Reg., Misc. 14. 1843. (4 spp., subtribe Gongorinae)

Paphiopedilum Pfitz., Entwurf. Natürl. Anordn. Orch. 95. 1887. (50 spp., subtribe Cypripedilinae)

Papilionanthe Schltr. in Orchis 9: 78. 1915. = **Vanda** Jones

Papiliopsis E.Morr. ex Cgn. & Marchal, Pl. Feuill. Ornem. 2: under pl. 55. 1874. = **Oncidium** Sw.

Papperitzia Rchb.f. in Bot. Zeit. 10: 670. 1852; descr. ampl. L.O.Wms. in Bot. Mus. Leafl. Harv. Univ. 9: 123. 1923. (1 sp., subtribe Papperitziinae)

Papuaea Schltr. in Fedde, Repert. Spec. Nov. 16: 105. 1919. (1 sp., subtribe Physurinae)

Paracalanthe Kudo in Jour. Soc. Trop. Agric. Taiwan 2: 235. 1930, *in adnot.* (6 spp., subtribe Phaiinae)

Paradisianthus Rchb.f. in Bot. Zeit. 10: 930. 1852. (4 spp., subtribe Zygopetalinae)

Paragnathis Spreng., Syst. 3: 695. 1826. = **Diplomeris** D.Don

Paraphalaenopsis A.D.Hawkes in Orquidea 25: 212. 1963. (3 spp., subtribe Sarcanthinae)

Parhabenaria Gagnep. in Bull. Mus. Hist. Nat. Paris II, 4: 597. 1932. (2 spp., subtribe Habenarinae)

Parlatorea B.-R., Orch. Nov. 1: 141. 1877. = **Sanderella** O.Ktze.

Pattonia Wight, Icon. 5: pl. 1750. 1852. = **Grammatophyllum** Bl.

Paxtonia Ldl. in Bot. Reg., Misc. 61. 1838. = **Spathoglottis** Bl.

Pecteilis Raf., Fl. Tellur. 2: 37. 1836. (6 spp., subtribe Habenarinae)

Pectinaria Cordem. in Rev. Gén. de Bot. 11: 472. 1899. = **Angraecum** Bory

Pedilea Ldl., Orch. Scel. 27. 1826. = **Malaxis** Soland. ex Sw.

Pedilochilus Schltr. in K.Schum. & Lauterb., Nachtr. Fl. Deutsch Südsee 218. 1905. (15 spp., subtribe Bulbophyllinae)

Pedilonum Bl., Bijdr. 320, pl. 36. 1825. = **Dendrobium** Sw.

Pedocheilus Wight, Icon. 5: pl. 1748, fig. 2. 1852, *sphalm.* = **Podochilus** Bl.

Pelatantheria Ridl. in Jour. Linn. Soc. 32: 371. 1896. (3 spp., subtribe Sarcanthinae)

Pelexia [Poit.] L.C.Rich. in Mém. Mus. Hist. Nat. Paris 4: 59. 1818. (65 spp., subtribe Spiranthinae)

Pelma Finet in Lecomte, Not. Syst. 2: 112. 1909. = **Bulbophyllum** Thou.

Pennilabium J.J.Sm. in Bull. Jard. Bot. Buitenz. II, 13: 47. 1914, in obs.; & l.c., 14: 45. 1915. (4 spp., subtribe Sarcanthinae)

Penthea Ldl., Introd. Nat. Syst., ed. 2, 446. 1836. (11 spp., subtribe Disinae)

Pentulops Raf., Fl. Tellur. 4: 42. 1836. = **Xylobium** Ldl.

Peramium Salisb. in Trans. Hort. Soc. Lond. 1: 301. 1812. = **Goodyera** R.Br.

Pergamena Finet in Bull. Soc. Bot. France 47: 263. 1900. (1 sp., subtribe Calypsoinae)

Peristeranthus T.E.Hunt in Queensl. Nat. 15: 17. 1954. (1 sp., subtribe Sarcanthinae)

Peristeria Hk. in Bot. Mag. pl. 3116. 1831. (6 spp., subtribe Gongorinae)

Peristylis Bth. ex Bth. & Hk.f., Gen. Plant. 3: 625. 1883, *sphalm.* = **Peristylus** Bl.

Peristylus Bl., Bijdr. 404, pl. 30. 1825. (30 spp., subtribe Habenarinae)

Perrierella Schltr. in Fedde, Repert. Spec. Nov., Beih. 33: 365. 1925. (1 sp., subtribe Sarcanthinae)

Perularia Ldl. in Bot. Reg., under pl. 1701. 1835. = **Habenaria** Willd.

Pescatorea Rchb.f. in Bot. Zeit. 10: 667. 1852. (12 spp., subtribe Huntleyinae)

Pesomeria Ldl. in Bot. Reg., Misc. 5. 1838. = **Phaius** Lour.

Petalocentrum Schltr. in Fedde, Repert. Spec. Nov. 15: 144. 1918. = **Sigmatostalix** Rchb.f.

Petalochilus R.S.Rog. in Jour. Bot. 62: 65. 1924. (2 spp., subtribe Caladeniinae)

Petronia B.-R., Orch. Nov. 1: 106. 1877. = **Batemania** Ldl.

Petrostylis Pfitz., Icon. Ind. 1: 828. 1855, *sphalm.* = **Pterostylis** R.Br.

Phadrosanthus Neck., Elem. 3: 153. 1790. = **Epidendrum** L.

Phaius Lour., Fl. Cochinch. 529. 1790. (30 spp., subtribe Phaiinae)

Phajus Hassk., Cat. Hort. Bogor. Alt. 42. 1844. = **Phaius** Lour.

Phalaenopsis Bl., Bijdr. 294. 1825. (70 spp., subtribe Sarcanthinae)

Phaniasia Bl. ex Miq. in Ann. Mus. Bot. Lugd.-Bat. 2: 206. 1865–6, in obs. = **Habenaria** Willd.

Philippinaea Schltr. & Ames in Ames, Orchid. 6: 278. 1920. = **Orchipedum** Breda

Phloeophila Hoehne & Schltr. in Arch. Bot. Estad. S.Paulo 1: 199. 1926. (2 spp., subtribe Pleurothallidinae)

Pholidota Ldl. in Hk., Exot. Fl. 2: pl. 138. 1825. (40 spp., subtribe Coelogyninae)

Phormangis Schltr. in Beih. Bot. Centralbl. 36(2): 103. 1918. = **Ancistrorhynchus** Finet

Phragmipedium Rolfe in Orch. Rev. 4: 331. 1896. (12 spp., subtribe Cypripedilinae)

Phragmopedilum Pfitz. in Engl., Bot. Jahrb. 25: 527. 1898, as subgenus. = **Phragmipedium** Rolfe

Phragmorchis L.O.Wms. in Bot. Mus. Leafl. Harv. Univ. 6: 52. 1938. (1 sp., subtribe Sarcanthinae)

Phreatia Ldl., Gen. & Sp. Orch. 63. 1830. (150 spp., subtribe Thelasinae)

Phyllomphax Schltr. in Fedde, Repert. Spec. Nov., Beih. 4: 118. 1919. = **Brachycorythis** Ldl.

Phyllorchis Thou. in Nouv. Bull. Soc. Philom., no. 19: 314, 319. 1809. = **Bulbophyllum** Thou.

Phyllorkis Thou. in Nouv. Bull. Soc. Philom., no. 19: 319. 1809. = **Bulbophyllum** Thou.

Phymatidium Ldl., Gen. & Sp. Orch. 209. 1833. (6 spp., subtribe Ornithocephalinae)

Physanthera Bert. ex Steud., Nom., ed. 2, 2: 463, 830. 1831. = **Rodriguezia** P. & E.

Physarus Steud., Nom., ed. 2, 2: 330. 1831, *sphalm.* = **Erythrodes** Bl.

Physinga Ldl. in Bot. Reg., Misc. 32. 1838. = **Epidendrum** L.

Physoceras Schltr. in Fedde, Repert. Spec. Nov. Beih. 33: 78. 1924. (5 spp., subtribe Habenarinae)

Physosiphon Ldl. in Bot. Reg. 21: under pl. 1797. 1835. (7 spp., subtribe Pleurothallidinae)

Physothallis Garay in Svensk. Bot. Tidskr. 47: 199. 1953. (1 sp., subtribe Pleurothallidinae)

Physurus L.C.Rich. in Mém. Mus. Hist. Nat. Paris 4: 55. 1818, *nomen nudum.* = **Erythrodes** Bl.

Pierardia Raf., Fl. Tellur. 4: 41. 1836. = **Dendrobium** Sw.

Pilophyllum Schltr., Die Orchid. 128. 1914. (2 spp., subtribe Collabiinae)

Pilumna Ldl. in Bot. Reg. n.s., 7: Misc. 73. 1844. = **Trichopilia** Ldl.

Pinalia Buch.-Ham. ex D.Don, Prodr. Fl. Nepal. 31. 1825, in syn. = **Eria** Ldl.

Pinelia Ldl., Fol. Orch. Pinelia [1]. 1853. (3 spp., subtribe Laeliinae)

Piperia Rydb. in Bull. Torrey Bot. Club, 269. 1901. = **Habenaria** Willd.

Pittierella Schltr. in Fedde, Repert. Spec. Nov. 3: 80. 1906. = **Cryptocentrum** Bth.

Pityphyllum Schltr. in Fedde, Repert. Spec. Nov., Beih. 7: 162. 1920. (2 spp., subtribe Maxillarinae)

Placostigma Bl., Fl. Jav. Praef. vi. 1828. = **Podochilus** Bl.

Platanthera L.C.Rich. in Mém. Mus. Hist. Nat. Paris 4: 48. 1818. (250 spp., subtribe Habenarinae)

Platyclinis Bth. in Jour. Linn. Soc. 18: 295. 1881. = **Dendrochilum** Bl.

Platycoryne Rchb.f. in Bonplandia 3: 212. 1855. (9 spp., subtribe Habenarinae)

Platyglottis L.O.Wms. in Ann. Mo. Bot. Gard. 29: 345. 1942. (1 sp., subtribe Ponerinae)

Platylepis A.Rich., Orch. Îles France et Bourbon 39. 1828. (14 spp., subtribe Physurinae)

Platypus Small & Nash in Small, Fl. S.E. U.S. 329. 1903. = **Eulophia** R.Br. ex Ldl.

Platyrhiza B.-R., Orch. Nov. 2: 230. 1881. (1 sp., subtribe Ornithocephalinae)

Platysma Bl., Bijdr. 295, pl. 43. 1825. = **Podochilus** Bl.

Platystele Schltr. in Fedde, Repert. Spec. Nov. 8: 565. 1910. (1 sp., subtribe Pleurothallidinae)

Platystylis Ldl., Gen. & Sp. Orch. 18. 1836. = **Liparis** L.C.Rich.

Plectrelminthus Raf., Fl. Tellur. 4: 42. 1836. (1 sp., subtribe Sarcanthinae)

Plectrophora Focke in Tijdschr. Nat. Wetensch. 1: 212. 1848. (4 spp., subtribe Comparettiinae)

Plectrurus Raf., Neogen. 4. 1825. = **Tipularia** Nutt.

Pleione D.Don, Prodr. Fl. Nepal. 36. 1825. (20 spp., subtribe Coelogyninae)

Pleuranthium Bth. in Jour. Linn. Soc. 18: 312. 1881. = **Epidendrum** L.

Pleurobotryum B.-R., Orch. Nov. 1: 20. 1877. (2 spp., subtribe Pleurothallidinae)

Pleurothallis R.Br. in Ait., Hort. Kew., ed. 2, 5: 211. 1813. (1000 spp., subtribe Pleurothallidinae)

Pleurothallopsis C.Porto & Brade in Arch. Inst. Biol. Veg. Rio de Janeiro 3: 133. 1937. (1 sp., subtribe Pleurothallidinae)

Plexaure Endl., Prodr. Fl. Norf. 30. 1833. = **Phreatia** Ldl.

Plocaglottis Steud., Nom., ed. 2, 2: 356. 1841. = **Plocoglottis** Bl.

Plocoglottis Bl., Bijdr. 380. 1825. (30 spp., subtribe Phaiinae)

Poaephyllum Ridl., Mat. Fl. Malay Penins. 1: 108. 1907. (3 spp., subtribe Glomerinae)

Podandria Rolfe in Dyer, Fl. Trop. Afr. 7: 205. 1898. (1 sp., subtribe Habenarinae)

Podangis Schltr. in Beih. Bot. Centralbl. 36(2): 81. 1918. (1 sp., subtribe Sarcanthinae)

Podanthera Wight, Icon. 5: 22, pl. 1759. 1851. = **Epipogum** [Gmel.] L.C.Rich.

Podochilus Bl., Bijdr. 295, pl. 12. 1825. (75 spp., subtribe Podochilinae)

Pogochilus Falc. in Hk., Jour. Bot. 4: 33. 1832. = **Galeola** Lour.

Pogoina Griff. ex B.Grant, Orch. Burma 355. 1895, *sphalm.* = **Pogonia** Juss.

Pogonia Juss., Gen. 65. 1789. (10 spp., subtribe Vanillinae)

Pogoniopsis Rchb.f., Otia Bot. Hamb. 82. 1881. (2 spp., subtribe Vanillinae)

Pollinirhiza Dulac, Fl. Hautes Pyren. 120. 1867. = **Listera** R.Br.

Polychilos Breda, Orch. Kuhl & Hass. [pl. 20]. 1827. = **Phalaenopsis** Bl.

Polycycnis Rchb.f. in Bonplandia 3: 218. 1855. (7 spp., subtribe Gongorinae)

Polyotidium Garay in Bot. Mus. Leafl. Harv. Univ. (1 sp., subtribe Papperitziinae)

Polyrrhiza Pfitz. in Engl. & Prantl, Natürl. Pflanzenfam. 2(6): 215. 1895. (4 spp., subtribe Campylocentrinae)

Polystachya Hk., Exot. Fl. 2: pl. 103. 1825. (130 spp., subtribe Polystachyinae)

Pomatocalpa Breda, Orch. Kuhl & Hass. [pl. 15]. 1827. (30 spp., subtribe Sarcanthinae)

Ponera Ldl., Gen. & Sp. Orch. 113. 1831. (6 spp., subtribe Ponerinae)

Ponerorchis Rchb.f. in Linnaea 25: 227. 1852. = **Habenaria** Willd.

Pongonia Griff. ex B.Grant, Orch. Burma 351. 1895, *sphalm.* = **Pogonia** Juss.

Ponthieva R.Br. in Ait., Hort. Kew., ed. 2, 5: 199. 1813. (25 spp., subtribe Cranichidinae)

Porolabium Tang & Wang in Bull. Fan Mem. Inst. Biol. Peiping, Bot. Ser., 10: 36. 1940. (1 sp., subtribe Habenarinae)

Porpax Ldl. in Bot. Reg., Misc. 62. 1845. (8 spp., subtribe Dendrobiinae)

Porphyrodesme Schltr. in Fedde, Repert. Spec. Nov., Beih. 1: 982. 1913. (1 sp., subtribe Sarcanthinae)

Porphyroglottis Ridl. in Jour. Linn. Soc. 31: 290. 1896. (1 sp., subtribe Cymbidiinae)

Porphyrostachys Rchb.f., Xen. Orch. 1: 18. 1858. (1 sp., subtribe Cranichidinae)

Porroglossum Schltr. in Fedde, Repert. Spec. Nov., Beih. 7: 82. 1920. = **Masdevallia** R. & P.

Prasophyllum R.Br., Prodr. Fl. Nov. Holl. 317. 1810. (80 spp., subtribe Prasophyllinae)

Preptanthe Rchb.f. in Fl. des Serres 8: 245. 1852–3. = **Calanthe** R.Br.

Prescottia Ldl. in Hk., Exot. Fl. 2: pl. 115. 1825, as *Prescotia*. (30 spp., subtribe Cranichidinae)

Pristiglottis Cretz & J.J.Sm. in Acta Faun. Fl. Univ. Bucar., II, Bot. 1(14): 4. 1934. (20 spp., subtribe Physurinae)

Promenaea Ldl. in Bot. Reg., Misc. 13. 1843. (15 spp., subtribe Zygopetalinae)

Prosthechea Kn. & Westc., Flor. Cab. 2: 111. 1838. = **Epidendrum** L.

Pseudacoridium Ames, Orchid. 7: 79. 1922. (1 sp., subtribe Coelogyninae)

Pseudepidendrum Rchb.f. in Bot. Zeit. 10: 733. 1852. = **Epidendrum** L.

Pseuderia Schltr. in Fedde, Repert. Spec. Nov., Beih. 1: 644. 1912. (19 spp., subtribe Dendrobiinae)

Pseuderiopsis Rchb.f. in Linnaea 22: 852. 1849. = **Eriopsis** Ldl.

Pseudocentrum Ldl. in Jour. Linn. Soc. 3: 63, 64. 1859. (5 spp., subtribe Cranichidinae)

Pseudoctomeria Krzl. in Kew Bull. 116. 1925. (1 sp., subtribe Pleurothallidinae)

Pseudodiphryllum Nevski in Komarov, Fl. URSS 4: 649, 752. 1935. = **Habenaria** Willd.

Pseudoeurystyles Hoehne in Arq. Bot. Estad. S.Paulo, n.s., *form. maior*, 1: 129. 1944. = **Eurystyles** Wawra

Pseudogoodyera Schltr. in Beih. Bot. Centralbl. 36(2): 369. 1920. = **Spiranthes** L.C.Rich.

Pseudolaelia C.Porto & Brade in Arch. Inst. Biol. Veg. Rio de Janeiro 2: 209. 1935. (2 spp., subtribe Laeliinae)

Pseudoliparis Finet in Bull. Soc. Bot. France 54: 536. 1907. (1 sp., subtribe Liparidinae)

Pseudomacodes Rolfe in Kew Bull. 127. 1892. = **Macodes** Ldl.

Pseudomaxillaria Hoehne in Arq. Bot. Estad. S.Paulo, n.s., *form. maior*, 2: 71. 1947. (1 sp., subtribe Maxillarinae)

Pseudorchis S.F.Gray, Nat. Arr. Brit. Pl. 2: 213. 1821. = **Liparis** L.C.Rich.

Pseudostelis Schltr. in Anex. Mem. Inst. Butantan 1(4): 36. 1922. (2 spp., subtribe Pleurothallidinae)

Psilanthemum Klotzsch ex Stein, Orchideenb. 532. 1892, in syn. = **Epidendrum** L.

Psilochilus B.-R., Orch. Nov. 2: 272. 1881. (2 spp., subtribe Vanillinae)

Psittacoglossum LaLl. & Lex., Nov. Veg. Descr., fasc. 2 (Orch. Opusc.): 29. 1825. = **Maxillaria** R. & P.

Psychechilus Breda, Orch. Kuhl & Hass. [pl. 9]. 1827. = **Zeuxine** Ldl., **Hetaeria** Bl.

Psychilis Raf., Fl. Tellur. 4: 40. 1836. = **Epidendrum** L.

Psychopsis Raf., Fl. Tellur. 4: 40. 1836. = **Oncidium** Sw.

Pterichis Ldl., Gen. & Sp. Orch. 444. 1840. (12 spp., subtribe Cranichidinae)

Pteroceras Hasse ex Hassk. in Flora 25(2), Beibl. 6. 1842. = **Sarcochilus** R.Br.

Pterochilus Hk. & Arn., Bot. Beech. Voy., pl. 17. 1832. = **Malaxis** Soland. ex Sw.

Pteroglossa Schltr. in Beih. Bot. Centralbl. 37(2): 450. 1920. (2 spp., subtribe Sarcanthinae)

Pteroglossaspis Rchb.f., Otia Bot. Hamb. 67. 1878. (10 spp., subtribe Eulophiinae)

Pterostemma Krzl. in Engl., Bot. Jahrb. 26: 489. 1899. (1 sp., subtribe Pterostemmatinae)

Pterostylis R.Br., Prodr. Fl. Nov. Holl. 326. 1810. (70 spp., subtribe Pterostylidinae)

Pterygodium Sw. in Vet. Akad. Nya Handl. Stockh. 21: 217, pl. 3. 1800. (36 spp., subtribe Disperidinae)

Pterypodium Rchb.f. in Flora 50: 117. 1867, *sphalm.* = **Pterygodium** Sw.

Ptichochilus Bth. in Jour. Linn. Soc. 18: 341. 1881. = **Tropidia** Ldl.

Ptilocnema D.Don, Prodr. Fl. Nepal. 33. 1825. = **Pholidota** Ldl.

Ptychochilus Schau. in Nov. Act. Nat. Cur. 19, Suppl. 1 (Pl. Meyen): 431, pl. 12B. 1843. = **Tropidia** Ldl.

Ptychogyne Pfitz. in Engl., Das Pflanzenr. IV, 50 (Coelogyn.): 18. 1907. = **Coelogyne** Ldl.

Pygmaeorchis Brade in Arq. Serv. Florest. Rio de Janeiro 1(1): 42. 1939. (1 sp., subtribe Laeliinae)

Quekettia Ldl. in Bot. Reg., Misc. 3. 1839. (1 sp., subtribe Capanemiinae)

Queteletia Bl., Orch. Archip. Ind. 117, pl. 37. 1858. = **Orchipedum** Breda

Radinocion Ridl. in Bol. Soc. Broter. 5: 200. 1877. = **Aërangis** Rchb.f.

Ramonia Schltr. in Fedde, Repert. Spec. Nov., Beih. 19: 294. 1923. = **Scaphyglottis** P. & E.

Ramphidia Miq., Fl. Ind. Bat. 3: 730. 1858. = **Hetaeria** Bl.

Rangaëris [Schltr.] Summerh. in Hutch. & Dalz., Fl. W. Trop. Afr. 2: 404. 1936, in key (English); & in Kew Bull. 227. 1936. (6 spp., subtribe Sarcanthinae)

Regnellia B.-R., Orch. Nov. 1: 81. 1877. = **Bletia** R. & P.

Reichenbachanthus B.-R., Orch. Nov. 2: 164. 1881. (1 sp., subtribe Ponerinae)

Renanthera Lour., Fl. Cochinch. 521. 1790. (12 spp., subtribe Sarcanthinae)

Renantherella Ridl. in Jour. Linn. Soc. 32: 354. 1896. (1 sp., subtribe Sarcanthinae)

Repandra Ldl., Orch. Scel. 12. 1826. = **Disa** Berg.

Restrepia HBK, Nov. Gen. & Sp. 1: 366, pl. 94. 1815. = **Pleurothallis** R.Br.

Rhamphidia Ldl. in Jour. Linn. Soc. 1: 181. 1857. = **Hetaeria** Bl.

Rhaphidorhynchus Finet in Bull. Soc. Bot. France 54, Mém. 9: 32. 1907. = **Microcoelia** Ldl.

Rhinerrhiza Rupp in Vict. Nat. 67: 206. 1951. (1 sp., subtribe Sarcanthinae)

Rhipidoglossum Schltr. in Beih. Bot. Centralbl. 36(2): 80. 1918. (4 spp., subtribe Sarcanthinae)

Rhizanthella R.S.Rog. in Jour. Roy. Soc. W. Austral. 15: 1. 1928. (1 sp., subtribe Rhizanthellinae)

Rhizocorallon Haller in Rupp, Fl. Jen. 301. 1745. = **Corallorrhiza** [Haller] R.Br.

Rhomboda Ldl. in Jour. Linn. Soc. 1: 181. 1857. = **Hetaeria** Bl.

Rhophostemon Wittst., Etymol. Handw. 763. 1856. = **Pogonia** Juss.

Rhynchadenia A.Rich., Fl. Cub. Fanerog. 2: 248, pl. 85. 1853. = **Macradenia** R.Br.

Rhynchanthera Bl., Bijdr., Tabell. 78. 1826. = **Corymborchis** Thou. ex Bl.

Rhyncholaelia Schltr. in Beih. Bot. Centralbl. 36(2): 477. 1918. (2 spp., subtribe Laeliinae)

Rhynchopera Klotzsch in Lk., Kl. & Otto, Icon. Pl. Rar., 103, pl. 41. 1850. = **Pleurothallis** R.Br.

Rhynchophreatia Schltr. in Engl., Bot. Jahrb. 56: 488. 1921. = **Phreatia** Ldl.

Rhynchostele Rchb.f. in Bot. Zeit. 10: 770. 1852. = **Leochilus** Kn. & Westc.

Rhynchostylis Bl., Bijdr. 285, pl. 49. 1825, as *Rhyncostylis*. (4 spp., subtribe Sarcanthinae)

Rhyncostylis Steud., Nom., ed. 2, 2: 457. 1841, *sphalm.* = **Rhynchostylis** Bl.

Ridleya Schum. in Just, Jahresb. 26(1): 338. 1900, *sphalm.* = **Risleya** King & Pantl.

Ridleyella Schltr. in Fedde, Repert. Spec. Nov., Beih. 1: 948. 1913. (1 sp., subtribe Ridleyellinae)

Rimacola Rupp in Victor. Natural. 58: 188. 1942. (1 sp., subtribe Caladeniinae)

Risleya King & Pantl. in Ann. Bot. Gard. Calcutta 8: 246. 1898. (1 sp., subtribe Liparidinae)

Ritaia King & Pantl. in Ann. Bot. Gard. Calcutta 8: 156. 1898. = **Ceratostylis** Bl.

Robiquetia Schltr. in Fedde, Repert. Spec. Nov., Beih. 1: 983. 1913. (14 spp., subtribe Sarcanthinae)

Rodriguezia R. & P., Prodr. Fl. Peruv. & Chil. 115, pl. 25. 1794. (30 spp., subtribe Comparettiinae)

Rodrigueziopsis Schltr. in Fedde, Repert. Spec. Nov. 16: 427. 1920. (2 spp., subtribe Capanemiinae)

Roeperocharis Rchb.f., Otia Bot. Hamb. 104. 1881. (7 spp., subtribe Habenarinae)

Roezliella Schltr. in Fedde, Repert. Spec. Nov. 15: 146. 1918. = **Sigmatostalix** Rchb.f.

Rolfea Zahlbr. in Jour. Bot. 36: 493. 1898. = **Palmorchis** B.-R.

Rolfeëlla Schltr. in Fedde, Repert. Spec. Nov., Beih. 33: 18. 1924. (1 sp., subtribe Habenarinae)

Rophostemon Endl., Gen. 21. 1837, *sphalm.* = **Pogonia** Juss.

Rophostemum Rchb., Nomen. 55. 1841. = **Pogonia** Juss.

Roptrostemon Bl., Fl. Jav. Praef. vi. 1828. = **Nervilia** Comm. ex Gaud.

Rudolfiella Hoehne in Arq. Bot. Estad. S.Paulo, n.s., 2: 14. 1944. (6 spp., subtribe Lycastinae)

Rusbyella Rolfe ex Rusby in Mem. Torrey Bot. Club 6: 122. 1896. (1 sp., subtribe Capanemiinae)

Rynchostylis Bl., Bijdr. 285, pl. 49. 1825. = **Rhynchostylis** Bl.

Saccidium Ldl., Gen. & Sp. Orch. 301. 1835. = **Holothrix** L.C.Rich.

Saccochilus Bl., Fl. Jav. Praef. viii. 1828. = **Thrixspermum** Lour.

Saccoglossum Schltr. in Fedde, Repert. Spec. Nov., Beih. 1: 683. 1912. (2 spp., subtribe Bulbophyllinae)

Saccolabiopsis J.J.Sm. in Bull. Jard. Bot. Buitenz. II, 26: 93. 1918. (1 sp., subtribe Sarcanthinae)

Saccolabium Bl., Bijdr. 292. 1825. (12 spp., subtribe Sarcanthinae)

Sacodon Raf., Fl. Tellur. 4: 45. 1836. = **Cypripedium** L.

Sacoila Raf., Fl. Tellur. 2: 86. 1836. = **Spiranthes** L.C.Rich.

Salacistis Rchb.f. in Bonplandia 5: 36. 1857. = **Hetaeria** Bl.

Sanderella O.Ktze., Rev. Gen. Pl. 649. 1891. (1 sp., subtribe Capanemiinae)

Sanopodium hort. ex Rchb.f. in Flora 71: 156. 1888, *sphalm.* = **Epigeneium** Gagnep.

Sarcanthus Ldl., Coll. Bot., pl. 39B. 1821. (90 spp., subtribe Sarcanthinae)

Sarchochilus Vidal, Phan. Cuming. Philipp. 150. 1885. = **Sarcochilus** R.Br.

Sarcobodium Beer, Prakt. Orch. 306. 1854. = **Epigeneium** Gagnep.

Sarcochilus R.Br., Prodr. Fl. Nov. Holl. 332. 1810. (50 spp., subtribe Sarcanthinae)

Sarcoglossum Beer, Prakt. Orch. 306. 1854. = **Cirrhaea** Ldl.

Sarcoglottis Presl, Rel. Haenk. 1: 95, pl. 15. 1827. (25 spp., subtribe Spiranthinae)

Sarcopodium Ldl. & Paxt. in Paxt., Flow. Gard. 1: 136. 1853. = **Epigeneium** Gagnep.

Sarcorhynchus Schltr. in Beih. Bot. Centralbl. 36(2): 104. 1918. (3 spp., subtribe Sarcanthinae)

Sarcostoma Bl., Bijdr. 339, pl. 45. 1825. (2 spp., subtribe Glomerinae)

Sarothrochilus Schltr. in Fedde, Repert. Spec. Nov. 3: 50. 1906. = **Trichoglottis** Bl.

Satirium Neck., Delic. Gallo-Belg. 2: 372. 1768. = **Satyrium** L.

Satorkis Thou. in Nouv. Bull. Soc. Philom., no. 19: 316. 1809. = **?**

Satyridium Ldl., Gen. & Sp. Orch. 345. 1838. (1 sp., subtribe Satyriinae)

Satyrium Sw. in Vet. Akad. Handl. Stockh. 21: 214. 1800. (155 spp., subtribe Satyriinae)

Saundersia Rchb.f. in Bot. Congr. Hon. 120. 1866; & Beitr. Orch. 17, pl. 6. 1869. (1 sp., subtribe Saundersiinae)

Sauroglossum Ldl. in Bot. Reg., pl. 1618. 1833. (3 spp., subtribe Spiranthinae)

Sayeria Krzl. in Oestr. Bot. Zeitschr. 44: 298. 1894. = **Dendrobium** Sw.

Scandederis Thou., Orch. Îles Afr., 3ᵐᵉ Tabl. 1822. = **Dendrobium** Sw.

Scaphosepalum Pfitz. in Engl. & Prantl, Natürl. Pflanzenfam. 2(7): 139. 1888. (40 spp., subtribe Pleurothallidinae)

Scaphyglottis P. & E., Nov. Gen. & Sp. 1: 58. 1835. (50 spp., subtribe Ponerinae)

Scaredederis Thou., Orch. Îles Afr., pl. 91. 1822. = **Dendrobium** Sw.

Scelochilus Klotzsch in Otto & Dietr., Allgem. Gartenz. 9: 261. 1841. (4 spp., subtribe Comparettiinae)

Schiedeëlla Schltr. in Beih. Bot. Centralbl. 37(2): 379. 1920. = **Spiranthes** L.C.Rich.

Schismoceras Presl, Rel. Haenk. 1: 96, pl. 13, fig. 2. 1827. = **Dendrobium** Sw.

Schizochilus Sond. in Linnaea 19: 78. 1847. (14 spp., subtribe Habenarinae)

Schizodium Ldl., Gen. & Sp. Orch. 358. 1838. (15 spp., subtribe Disinae)

Schlechterella Hoehne in Arq. Bot. Estad. S.Paulo, n.s., 2: 12, in obs., 13, in key. 1944. = **Rudolfiella** Hoehne

Schlimia Planch. & Lind. in Lind., Catal. 1852; ex Ldl. & Paxt., Flow. Gard. 3: 115. 1852–3. (2 spp., subtribe Gongorinae)

Schoenleinia Klotzsch ex Ldl., Veg. Kingd. 182. 1847. = **Ponthieva** R.Br.

Schoenorchis Reinw., Cat. Gew. Buitenz. 100. 1823, *nomen*; & ex Bl., Bijdr. 361. 1825. (15 spp., subtribe Sarcanthinae)

Schomburgkia Ldl., Sert. Orch., pls. 10, 13. 1838. = **Laelia** Ldl.

Schwartzkopffia Krzl. in Engl., Bot. Jahrb. 28: 177. 1900. (2 spp., subtribe Habenarinae)

Scleropteris Scheidw. in Otto & Dietr., Allgem. Gartenz. 7: 407. 1839. = **Cirrhaea** Ldl.

Scoliochilus Rchb.f., Xen. Orch. 2: 118. 1872, in obs. = **Appendicula** Bl.

Scopularia Ldl. in Bot. Reg., under pl. 1701. 1834. = **Holothrix** L.C.Rich.

Scuticaria Ldl. in Bot. Reg., Misc. 14. 1843. (3 spp., subtribe Maxillarinae)

Scyphoglottis Pritz., Icon. Ind. 1: 1012. 1855, *sphalm.* = **Scaphyglottis** P. & E.

Selenipedilum Pfitz. in Engl. & Prantl, Natürl. Pflanzenfam. 2(6): 84. 1888. = **Selenipedium** Rchb.f.

Selenipedium Rchb.f. in Bonplandia 2: 116. 1854; & Xen. Orch. 1: 3, pls. 2, 27, 44, 62, 181. 1854. (3 spp., subtribe Cypripedilinae)

Semiphajus Gagnep. in Bull. Mus. Hist. Nat. Paris II, 4: 598. 1932. (2 spp., subtribe ? Phaiinae)

Sepalosaccus Schltr. in Fedde, Repert. Spec. Nov., Beih. 19: 244. 1923. (1 sp., subtribe Maxillarinae)

Sepalosiphon Schltr. in Fedde, Repert. Spec. Nov., Beih. 1: 317. 1912. (1 sp., subtribe Glomerinae)

Seraphyta Fisch. & Mey. in Bull. Sci. Acad. St. Petersb. 8: 24. 1840. = **Epidendrum** L.

Serapias L., Sp. Pl. 949. 1753 partim emend. Sw. in Vet. Akad. Handl. Stockh. 21: 225. 1800. (12 spp., subtribe Habenarinae)

Serapiastrum O.Ktze., Rev. Gen. Pl. 3(2): 141. 1898. = **Serapias** L.

Serrastylis Rolfe in Kew Bull. 158. 1894; & in Gard. Chron. (2): 726, fig. 91. 1894. = **Macradenia** R.Br.

Sertifera Ldl. ex Rchb.f. in Linnaea 41: 63. 1877. = **Elleanthus** Presl

Sestochilos Breda, Orch. Kuhl & Hass. [pl. 3]. 1827. = **Bulbophyllum** Thou.

Siagonanthus P. & E., Nov. Gen. & Sp. 1: 40, pl. 69. 1835. = **Maxillaria** R. & P.

Sieberia Spreng., Anleit. 2: 282. 1817. = **Habenaria** Willd.

Sievekingia Rchb.f., Beitr. Syst. Pfl. 3. 1871. (4 spp., subtribe Gongorinae)

Sigmatochilus Rolfe in Jour. Linn. Soc., Bot. 42: 155. 1914. = **Coelogyne** Ldl.

Sigmatogyne Pfitz. in Engl., Das Pflanzenr. IV, 50 (Coelogyn.): 133. 1907. = **Panisea** Ldl.

Sigmatostalix Rchb.f. in Bot. Zeit. 10: 769. 1852. (12 spp., subtribe Oncidiinae)

Silvorchis J.J.Sm. in Bull. Dép. Agric. Ind. Néerl. 13: 2. 1907. (1 sp., subtribe Habenarinae)

Sirhookera O.Ktze., Rev. Gen. Plant. 2: 681. 1891. = **Josephia** Wight

Smallia Nieuwl. in Amer. Midl. Natural. 3: 158. 1913, in obs. = **Eulophia** R.Br. ex Ldl.

Smithorchis Tang & Wang in Bull. Fan Mem. Inst. Biol. Peiping, Bot. Ser., 7: 139. 1936. (1 sp., subtribe Habenarinae)

Sobennikoffia Schltr. in Fedde, Repert. Spec. Nov., Beih. 33: 361. 1925. (3 spp., subtribe Sarcanthinae)

Sobralia R. & P., Prodr. Fl. Peruv. & Chil. 120, pl. 26. 1794. (35 spp., subtribe Sobraliinae)

Sodiroëlla Schltr. in Fedde, Repert. Spec. Nov., Beih. 8: 107. 1921. (1 sp., subtribe Telipogoninae)

Solenangis Schltr. in Beih. Bot. Centralbl. 36(2): 133. 1918. (2 spp., subtribe Sarcanthinae)

Solenidium Ldl., Orch. Linden. 15. 1846. (2 spp., subtribe Oncidiinae)

Solenipedium Beer, Prakt. Orch. 310. 1854, *sphalm.* = **Selenipedium** Rchb.f.

Solenocentrum Schltr. in Fedde, Repert. Spec. Nov. 9: 163. 1911. (3 spp., subtribe Cranichidinae)

Sophronia Ldl., in Bot. Reg., pl. 1129. 1828. = **Sophronitis** Ldl.

Sophronitella Schltr. in Fedde, Repert. Spec. Nov., Beih. 35: 76. 1925. (1 sp., subtribe Laeliinae)

Sophronitis Ldl. in Bot. Reg., under pl. 1147. 1828. (6 spp., subtribe Laeliinae)

Spathiger Small, Fl. Miami 55. 1913. = **Epidendrum** L.

Spathoglottis Bl., Bijdr. 400. 1825. (40 spp., subtribe Phaiinae)

Specklinia Ldl., Gen. & Sp. Orch. 8. 1830. = **Pleurothallis** R.Br.

Sphyrarhynchus Mansf. in Notizbl. Bot. Gart. Berlin 12: 706. 1935. (1 sp., subtribe Sarcanthinae)

Sphyrastylis Schltr. in Fedde, Repert. Spec. Nov., Beih. 7: 194. 1920. (1 sp., subtribe Ornithocephalinae)

Speiranthes Hassk., Cat. Hort. Bogor. Alt. 47. 1844, *sphalm.* = **Spiranthes** L.C.Rich.

Spiculaea Ldl., Swan River App. 56. 1839. (3 spp., subtribe Drakaeinae)

Spiranthes L.C.Rich. in Mém. Mus. Hist. Nat. Paris 4: 50. 1818, *nomen conserv.* (300 spp., subtribe Spiranthinae)

Spiranthos St. Lag. in Ann. Soc. Bot. Lyon 7: 56. 1880. = **Spiranthes** L.C.Rich.

Stachyobium Rchb.f. in Gard. Chron., 785. 1869. = **Dendrobium** Sw.

Stanhopea Frost ex Hk. in Bot. Mag. pls. 2948, 2949. 1829. (25 spp., subtribe Gongorinae)

Stanhopeastrum Rchb.f. in Bot. Zeit. 10: 927. 1852. = **Stanhopea** Frost ex Hk.

Stauritis Rchb.f. in Hamb. Gartenz. 18: 34. 1862. = **Phalaenopsis** Bl.

Staurochilus Ridl. in Jour. Linn. Soc. 32: 351. 1896. = **Trichoglottis** Bl.

Stauroglottis Schau. in Nov. Act. Nat. Cur. 19, Suppl. 1: 432. 1843. = **Phalaenopsis** Bl.

Stauropsis Rchb.f. in Hamb. Gartenz. 16: 117. 1860. = **Trichoglottis** Bl.

Stelis Sw. in Schrad., Jour. 2: 239. 1799. (500 spp., subtribe Pleurothallidinae)

Stellilabium Schltr., Die Orchid. 530. 1914. (1 sp., subtribe Telipogoninae)

Stellorkis Thou. in Nouv. Bull. Soc. Philom. no. 19: 317. 1809. = ?

Stenia Ldl. in Bot. Reg., under pl. 1991. 1837. (1 sp., subtribe Huntleyinae)

Stenocoryne Ldl. in Bot. Reg., Misc. 53. 1843. (12 spp., subtribe Lycastinae)

Stenoglossum HBK, Nov. Gen. & Sp. 1: 355, pl. 87. 1815. (1 sp., subtribe Laeliinae)

Stenoglottis Ldl. in Hk., Comp. Bot. Mag. 2: 209. 1836. (3 spp., subtribe Habenarinae)

Stenopolen Raf., Fl. Tellur. 4: 49. 1836. = **Stenia** Ldl.

Stenoptera Presl, Rel. Haenk. 1: 95, pl. 14. 1827. (30 spp., subtribe Cranichidinae)

Stenorhynchos Ldl. in Ann. & Mag. Nat. Hist., I, 15: 386. 1845. = **Spiranthes** L.C.Rich.

Stenorhyncus Ldl., in Bth., Pl. Hartweg. 92. 1842. = **Spiranthes** L.C.Rich.

Stenorrhynchos Spreng., Gen. 2: 660. 1831. = **Spiranthes** L.C.Rich.

Stenorrhynchum Rchb., Nomen. 55. 1841. = **Spiranthes** L.C.Rich.

Stenorrhynchus Rchb., Consp. 67. 1828. = **Spiranthes** L.C.Rich.

Stenorynchus L.C.Rich. in Mém. Mus. Hist. Nat. Paris 4: 59. 1818. = **Spiranthes** L.C.Rich.

Stereochilus Ldl. in Jour. Linn. Soc. 3: 38. 1859. = **Sarcochilus** R.Br.

Stereosandra Bl., Mus. Bot. Lugd.-Bat. 2: 176. 1856. (1 sp., subtribe Epipogoninae)

Steveniella Schltr. in Fedde, Repert. Spec. Nov. 15: 292, 295. 1918. (1 sp., subtribe Habenarinae)

Stevenorchis Wankow & Krzl. in Fedde, Repert. Spec. Nov., Beih. 15: 45. 1931. = **Steveniella** Schltr.

Stichorchis Thou., Orch. Îles Afr., Tabl. 1ᵉʳ. 1822. = **Liparis** L.C.Rich.

Stichorkis Thou. in Nouv. Bull. Soc. Philom., no. 19: 318. 1809. = **Liparis** L.C.Rich.

Stigmatodactylus Maxim. ex Mak., Il. Fl. Jap. 1: pl. 43. 1891; & in Bot. Mag. Tokyo 19: 68. 1905. (4 spp., subtribe Acianthinae)

Stimegas Raf., Fl. Tellur. 4: 45. 1836. = **Cypripedium** L.

Stolzia Schltr. in Engl., Bot. Jahrb. 53: 564. 1915. (4 spp., subtribe Stolziinae)

Strateuma Raf., Fl. Tellur. 2: 89. 1836. = **Zeuxine** Ldl.

Strateuma Salisb. in Trans. Hort. Soc. Lond. 1: 290. 1812. = **Orchis** [Tournef.] L.

Sturmia Rchb. in Moessl., Handb., ed. 2, 2: 1576. 1828. = **Liparis** L.C.Rich.

Styloglossum Breda, Orch. Kuhl & Hass. [pl. 7]. 1827. = **Calanthe** R.Br.

Sulpitia Raf., Fl. Tellur. 4: 37. 1836. = **Epidendrum** L.

Sunipia Buch.-Ham. ex Sm. in Rees, Cycl. 34, Art. Stelis., no. 11: 13. 1816; & Ldl., Orch. Scel. 14. 1826. = **Ione** Ldl.

Sutrina Ldl. in Ann. & Mag. Nat. Hist., I, 10: 184. 1842. = **Rodriguezia** R. & P.

Sylvorchis J.J.Sm. ex Schltr., Die Orchid. 61. 1914, *sphalm.* = **Silvorchis** J.J.Sm.

Symphyglossum Schltr. in Orchis 13: 8. 1919. (1 sp., subtribe Oncidiinae)

Symphyosepalum Hand.-Mazz., Symb. Sin. 7: 1327. 1936. (1 sp., subtribe Habenarinae)

Synadena Raf., Fl. Tellur. 4: 9. 1836. = **Phalaenopsis** Bl.

Synassa Ldl., Orch. Scel. 9. 1826; & in Bot. Reg., under pl. 1618. 1833. = **Spiranthes** L.C.Rich.

Synmeria Nimmo in J.Grah., Cat. Pl. Bomb. Addent., *sine numero.* 1839. = **Habenaria** Willd.

Synoplectris Raf., Fl. Tellur. 2: 89. 1836. = **Neottia** Sw.

Synptera Llanos, Fragm. 98. 1851. = **Trichoglottis** Bl.

Systeloglossum Schltr. in Fedde, Repert. Spec. Nov., Beih. 19: 251. 1923. (2 spp., subtribe Oncidiinae)

Taeniophyllum Bl., Bijdr. 355, pl. 70. 1825. (200 spp., subtribe Sarcanthinae)

Taeniorrhiza Summerh. in Bot. Mus. Leafl. Harv. Univ. 11: 166. 1943. (1 sp., subtribe Sarcanthinae)

Tainia Bl., Bijdr. 354. 1825. (12 spp., subtribe Collabiinae)

Tainiopsis Hay., Icon. Pl. Formos. 4: 63. 1914, in obs. = **Ania** Ldl.

Tainiopsis Schltr. in Orchis 9: 10. 1915. = **Tainia** Bl.

Talpinaria Karst., Fl. Columb. 1: 153, pl. 76. 1859. = **Pleurothallis** R.Br.

Tankervillia Link, Handb. 1: 251. 1829. = **Phaius** Lour.

Tapeinoglossum Schltr. in Fedde, Repert. Spec. Nov., Beih. 1: 892. 1913. (2 spp., subtribe Bulbophyllinae)

Taurostalix Rchb.f. in Bot. Zeit. 10: 933. 1852. = **Bulbophyllum** Thou.

Telipogon HBK, Nov. Gen. & Sp. 1: 335, pl. 75. 1815. (50 spp., subtribe Telipogoninae)

Telopogon Mutis ex Spreng., Anleit. 2(1): 291. 1817, *sphalm.* = **Telipogon** HBK

Tetragamestus Rchb.f. in Bonplandia 2: 21. 1854. = **Scaphyglottis** P. & E.

Tetramicra Ldl., Gen. & Sp. Orch. 119. 1831. (12 spp., subtribe Laeliinae)

Tetrapeltis Wall. ex Ldl., Gen. & Sp. Orch. 212. 1832. = **Otochilus** Ldl.

Teuscheria Garay in Amer. Orch. Soc. Bull. 27: 820, pl. 1958. (2 spp., subtribe Phaiinae)

Thecostele Rchb.f. in Bonplandia 5: 37. 1857. (5 spp., subtribe Thecostelinae)

Thelasis Bl., Bijdr. 385, pl. 75. 1825. (10 spp., subtribe Thelasinae)

Thelychiton Endl., Prodr. Fl. Norf. 32. 1833. = **Dendrobium** Sw., **Bulbophyllum** Thou.

Thelymitra Forst., Char. Gen. 97, pl. 49. 1776. (50 spp., subtribe Thelymitrinae)

Thelypogon Spreng., Syst. 3: 682. 1826. = **Telipogon** HBK

Theodorea B.-R., Orch. Nov. 1: 14. 1877. = **Hellerorchis** A.D.Hawkes

Thicuania Raf., Fl. Tellur. 4: 47. 1836. = **Dendrobium** Sw.

Thiebautia Colla in Mém. Soc. Linn. Paris 3: 161, pl. 4. 1823. = **Bletia** R. & P.

Thisbe Falc. in Ldl., Veg. Kingd. 183. 1847. = **Herminium** L.

Thorvaldsenia Liebm. in Lindbl., Bot. Notiser 103. 1844. = **Chysis** Ldl.

Thorwaldsenia Rchb.f. in Bot. Zeit. 4: 396. 1846, *sphalm.* = **Chysis** Ldl.

Thrixspermum Lour., Fl. Cochinch, 519. 1790. (60 spp., subtribe Sarcanthinae)

Thunia Rchb.f. in Bot. Zeit. 10: 764. 1852. (8 spp., subtribe Thuniinae)

Thylacis Gagnep. in Bull. Mus. Hist. Nat. Paris II, 4: 599. 1932. (2 spp., subtribe Sarcanthinae)

Thysanochilus Falc. in Proc. Linn. Soc. 1: 14. 1839. = **Eulophia** R.Br. ex Ldl.

Thysanoglossa C.Porto & Brade in An. Prim. Réun. Sul-Amer. Bot. 1938, 3: 42. 1940. (2 spp., subtribe Ornithocephalinae)

Tinaea Boiss., Fl. Orient. 5: 58. 1884, *sphalm.* = **Neotinea** Rchb.f.

Tinea Bivona in Giorn. Sci. Sicil., 149. 1833. = **Neotinea** Rchb.f.

Tipularia Nutt., Gen. Amer. 2: 195. 1818. (3 spp., subtribe Calypsoinae)

Titania Endl., Prodr. Fl. Norf. 31. 1833. = **Oberonia** Ldl.

Todaroa A.Rich. & Gal. in Ann. Sci. Nat., III, 3: 28. 1845. = **Campylocentrum** Bth.

Tolumnia Raf., Fl. Tellur. 2: 101. 1836. = **Oncidium** Sw.

Tomitris Raf., Fl. Tellur. 2: 89. 1836. = **Corymborchis** Thou. ex Bl.

Townsonia Cheesem., Man. N. Zeal. Fl. 691. 1906. (2 spp., subtribe Acianthinae)

Trachelosiphon Schltr. in Beih. Bot. Centralbl. 37(2): 423. 1920. = **Spiranthes** L.C.Rich.

Traunsteinera Rchb., Nom. 50. 1841; & Fl. Sax. 87. 1844. (1 sp., subtribe Habenarinae)

Trevoria F.C.Lehm. in Gard. Chron. (1): 345. 1897. (3 spp., subtribe Gongorinae)

Trias Ldl. in Wall., Catal., no. 1977. 1829; & Gen. & Sp. Orch. 60. 1830. (2 spp., subtribe Bulbophyllinae)

Tribrachia Ldl. in Bot. Reg., under pl. 832. 1824; & Coll. Bot., pl. 41. 1825. = **Bulbophyllum** Thou.

Tribrachium Bth. ex Bth. & Hk.f., Gen. Plant. 3: 501. 1883, *sphalm.* = **Bulbophyllum** Thou.

Triceratorhynchus Summerh. in Bot. Mus. Leafl. Harv. Univ. 14: 232. 1951. (1 sp., subtribe Sarcanthinae)

Trichocentrum P. & E., Nov. Gen. & Sp. 2: 11, pl. 115. 1838. (18 spp., subtribe Trichocentrinae)

Trichoceras Spreng., Anleit. 2(1): 291. 1817. = **Trichoceros** HBK

Trichoceros HBK, Nov. Gen. & Sp. 1: 337, pl. 76. 1815. (6 spp., subtribe Telipogoninae)

Trichochilus Ames in Jour. Arnold Arboret. 13: 142. 1932. = **Dipodium** R.Br.

Trichoglottis Bl., Bijdr. 359. 1825, in part; emend. Rchb.f. (35 spp., subtribe Sarcanthinae)

Trichophila Pritz., Icon. Ind. 1115. 1855, *sphalm.* = **Trichopilia** Ldl.

Trichopilia Ldl., Introd. Nat. Syst., ed. 2, 446. 1836. (30 spp., subtribe Trichopiliinae)

Trichorhiza Ldl. ex Steud., Nom., ed. 2, 2: 702. 1841. = **Luisia** Gaud.

Trichosia Bl., Bijdr., Tabell. 11. 1825. = **Eria** Ldl.

Trichosma Ldl. in Bot. Reg., pl. 21. 1842. = **Eria** Ldl.

Trichostosia Griff., Notul. 3: 331. 1851, *sphalm.* = **Eria** Ldl.

Trichotosia Bl., Bijdr. 342. 1825. = **Eria** Ldl.

Tridachne Liebm. ex Ldl. & Paxt., Flow. Gard. 3: 45. 1852. = **Notylia** Ldl.

Tridactyle Schltr., Die Orchid. 602. 1914. (12 spp., subtribe Sarcanthinae)

Trigonidium Ldl. in Bot. Reg. pl. 1923. 1837. (12 spp., subtribe Maxillarinae)

Triorchis Millan, Jac. Pet. Opera, pl. 68, fig. 7. 1765. = ? **Spiranthes** L.C.Rich.

Triorchos Small & Nash in Small, Fl. S.E. U.S. 329. 1903. = **Pteroglossaspis** Rchb.f.

Triphora Nutt., Gen. Amer. 2: 192. 1818. (10 spp., subtribe Vanillinae)

Tripleura Ldl. in Wall., Catal., no. 7391. 1832; & in Bot. Reg., under pl. 1618. 1833. = **Zeuxine** Ldl.

Triplorhiza Ehr., Beitr. 4: 149. 1789. = **Habenaria** Willd.

Tritelandra Raf., Fl. Tellur. 2: 85. 1836. = **Epidendrum** L.

Trixeuxis Ldl., Orch. Scel. 15. 1826. = **Trizeuxis** Ldl.

Trizeuxis Ldl., Coll. Bot., pl. 2. 1823. (3 spp., subtribe Capanemiinae)

Trophianthus Scheidw. in Otto & Dietr., Allgem. Gartenz. 12: 218. 1844. = **Aspasia** Ldl.

Tropidia Ldl. in Wall., Catal., no. 7386. 1831; & in Bot. Reg., under pl. 1618. 1833. (35 spp., subtribe Tropidiinae)

Tropilis Raf., Fl. Tellur. 2: 95. 1836. = **Dendrobium** Sw.

Tryphia Ldl. in Bot. Reg., under pl. 1701. 1835. = **Holothrix** L.C.Rich.

Tsaiorchis Tang & Wang in Bull. Fan Mem. Inst. Biol. Peiping, Bot. Ser., 7: 131. 1936. (2 spp., subtribe Habenarinae)

Tuberolabium Yamamoto in Bot. Mag. Tokyo 38: 209. 1924. (1 sp., subtribe Sarcanthinae)

Tubilabium J.J.Sm. in Bull. Jard. Bot. Buitenz. III, 9: 446. 1928. (2 spp., subtribe Physurinae)

Tulexis Raf., Fl. Tellur. 4: 42. 1836. = **Brassavola** R.Br.

Tulotis Raf., Fl., Tellur. 2: 37. 1836. = **Habenaria** Willd.

Tussaca Raf., Prec. Decour. 42. 1814; & in Jour. Phys. 89: 261. 1819. = **Goodyera** R.Br.

Tylochilus Nees in Verh. Gartenb. Ges. Berl. 8: 194, pl. 3. 1832. = **Cyrtopodium** R.Br.

Tylostigma Schltr. in Beih. Bot. Centralbl. 34(2): 297. 1916. (7 spp., subtribe Habenarinae)

Tylostylis Bl., Fl. Jav. Praef. vi. 1828. = **Eria** Ldl.

Ulantha Hk. in Bot. Mag., under pl. 2990, and Index. 1830. = **Chloraea** Ldl.

Uleiorchis Hoehne in Arq. Bot. Estad. S.Paulo 1: 129. 1944. (1 sp., subtribe Cranichidinae)

Uncifera Ldl. in Jour. Linn. Soc. 3: 39. 1859. (4 spp., subtribe Sarcanthinae)

Uropedilum Pfitz. in Engl. & Prantl, Natürl. Pflanzen-fam. 2(6): 84. 1888, in obs. = **Phragmipedium** Rolfe

Uropedium Ldl., Orch. Linden. 28. 1846. = **Phragmipedium** Rolfe

Vainilla Salisb., Parad. Lond. 2(2): under pl. 82. 1807. = **Vanilla** Sw.

Vanda Jones in As. Res. 4: 302. 1795; & R.Br. in Bot. Reg., pl. 506. 1820. (70 spp., subtribe Sarcanthinae).

Vandea Griff., Notul. 3: 352. 1851, *sphalm.* = **Vanda** Jones

Vandopsis Pfitz. in Engl. & Prantl, Natürl. Pflanzenfam. 2(6): 210. 1889. (12 spp., subtribe Sarcanthinae)

Vanilla Sw. in Nov. Act. Soc. Sci. Upsal. 6: 66, pl. 5. 1799; & in Schrad., Jour. 2: 208. 1799. (110 spp., subtribe Vanillinae)

Vanillophorum Neck., Elem. 3: 134. 1790. = **Vanilla** Sw.

Vargasiella C.Schweinf. in Bot. Mus. Leafl. Harv. Univ. 15: 150, pl. 47. 1952. (1 sp., subtribe Vargasiellinae)

Vexillabium Maekawa in Jour. Jap. Bot. 11: 457. 1935. (1 sp., subtribe Physurinae)

Vieillardorchis Krzl. in Lecomte, Not. Syst. 4: 143. 1928. (1 sp., subtribe Listerinae)

Vonromeria J.J.Sm. in Bull. Dép. Agric. Ind. Néerl. 39: 21. 1910. = ?**Chitonanthera** Schltr.

Vrydagzenia Bl. ex Schltr., Die Orchid. 123. 1914, *sphalm.* = **Vrydagzynea** Bl.

Vrydagzynea Bl., Orch. Archip. Ind. 71, pls. 17, 19, 20. 1858. (25 spp., subtribe Physurinae)

Wailesia Ldl. in Jour. Hort. Soc. Lond. 4: 261. 1849. = **Dipodium** R.Br.

Walnewa Regel ex hort. in Gard. Chron. (1): 307. 1891, *sphalm.* = **Leochilus** Kn. & Westc.

Waluewa Regel in Act. Hort. Petrop. 11: 309. 1890. = **Leochilus** Kn. & Westc.

Warczewiczella Rchb.f. in Bot. Zeit. 10: 635. 1852. = **Chondrorhyncha** Ldl.

Warczewitzia Skinner in Ldl. & Paxt., Flow. Gard. 1: 45. 1850–1. = **Catasetum** L.C.Rich.

Warmingia Rchb.f., Otia Bot. Hamb. 87. 1881, *nom. conserv.* (3 spp., subtribe Notyliinae)

Warrea Ldl. in Bot. Reg., n.s., 6: Misc. p. 14. 1843. (6 spp., subtribe Cyrtopodiinae)

Warreëlla Schltr., Die Orchid. 424. 1914. (1 sp., subtribe Zygopetalinae)

Warscewiczella Rchb.f., Xen. Orch. 1: 61. 1858, in obs. = **Chondrorhyncha** Ldl.

Warszewiczella Bth. & Hk.f., Gen. Plant. 3: 543. 1883, *sphalm.* = **Chondrorhyncha** Ldl.

Wullschlaegelia Rchb.f. in Bot. Zeit. 21: 131. 1863. (3 spp., subtribe Cranichidinae)

Xaritonia Raf., Fl. Tellur. 4: 9. 1836. = **Oncidium** Sw.

Xeilyathum Raf., Fl. Tellur. 2: 62. 1836. = **Oncidium** Sw.

Xerorchis Schltr. in Fedde, Repert. Spec. Nov. 11: 44. 1912. (1 sp., subtribe Vanillinae)

Xiphizusa Rchb.f. in Bot. Zeit. 11: 919. 1852. = **Bulbophyllum** Thou.

Xiphophyllum Ehr., Beitr. 4: 148. 1789. = **Cephalanthera** L.C.Rich.

Xiphosium Griff. in Calcutta Jour. Nat. Hist. 5: 364. 1843. = **Eria** Ldl.

Xylobium Ldl. in Bot. Reg. 11: under pl. 897. 1825. (20 spp., subtribe Lycastinae)

Yoania Maxim. in Bull. Acad. St. Petersb. 18: 68. 1873. (2 spp., subtribe Calypsoinae)

Yolanda Hoehne in Arch. Mus. Nac. Rio de Janeiro 22: 72. 1919. (1 sp., subtribe Pleurothallidinae)

Ypsilopus Summerh. in Kew Bull. 439. 1949. (2 spp., subtribe Sarcanthinae)

Zeduba Buch.-Ham. ex Meissn., Gen. Comm. 280. 1842. = **Calanthe** R.Br.

Zetagyne Ridl. in Jour. Nat. Hist. Soc. Siam 4: 118. 1921. (1 sp., subtribe Coelogyninae)

Zeuxine Ldl., Orch. Scel. 9. 1826, as *Zeuxina.* (35 spp., subtribe Physurinae)

Zoduba Buch-Ham. ex D.Don, Prodr. Fl. Nepal. 30. 1825. = **Calanthe** R.Br.

Zoöphora Bernh., Syst. Verz. Erf. 308. 1800. = **Orchis** [Tournef.] L.

Zosterostylis Bl., Bijdr. 418, pl. 32. 1825. = **Cryptostylis** R.Br.

Zygoglossum Reinw. ex Bl., Cat. Gew. Buitenz. 100. 1823, *nomen.* = **Bulbophyllum** Thou.

Zygopetalon Rchb., Consp. 69. 1828. = **Zygopetalum** Hk.

Zygopetalum Hk. in Bot. Mag., pl. 2748. 1827. (18 spp., subtribe Zygopetalinae)

Zygosepalum Rchb.f. in Walp., Ann. 6: 665. 1863. = **Menadenium** Raf.

Zygostates Ldl. in Bot. Reg., under pl. 1927. 1837. (3 spp., subtribe Ornithocephalinae)

MULTIGENERIC ORCHID HYBRID GROUPS

As of July 1st, 1963,[1] the following groups utilizing more than one genus of orchids have been registered. In several instances, inaccuracies or inconsistencies present in the 'official' international orchid hybrid lists are pointed out. Doubtless these will be corrected in due course by The Registrar of Orchid Hybrids. An index of genera utilized in these multigeneric groups is appended, commencing on page 530 of this book. Phonetic pronunciations for the hybrid groups are included in the final index of the book.

[1] See Appendix to this work.

Adaglossum (*Ada* × *Odontoglossum*), McBean 1913

Adioda (*Ada* × *Cochlioda*), Graire 1911

Aëridachnis (*Aërides* × *Arachnis*), Singapore Botanic Gardens 1957

Aëridofinetia (*Aërides* × *Neofinetia*), Iwanaga 1961

Aëridolabium (*Aërides* × *Saccolabium* = *Rhynchostylis*), O. M. Kirsch 1959 = **Aëridostylis**

Aëridopsis (*Aërides* × *Phalaenopsis*), Shinjiku, no date

Aëridostylis (*Aërides* × *Rhynchostylis*), Hawkes 1960

Aëridovanda (*Aërides* × *Vanda*), Colman 1918

Angulocaste (*Anguloa* × *Lycaste*), DeBievre 1903

Anoectomaria (*Anoectochilus* × *Haemaria*), Veitch 1865

Arachnopsis (*Arachnis* × *Phalaenopsis*), van Brero 1941

Aranda (*Arachnis* × *Vanda*), Singapore Botanic Gardens 1937

Aranthera (*Arachnis* × *Renanthera*), Singapore Botanic Gardens 1937

Armodachnis (*Armodorum* × *Arachnis*), Hawkes 1957

Ascocenda (*Ascocentrum* × *Vanda*), Sideris 1949

Ascofinetia (*Ascocentrum* × *Neofinetia*), Yamada 1961

Aspasium (*Aspasia* × *Oncidium*), Moir 1959

Bardendrum (*Barkeria* = *Epidendrum* × *Epidendrum*), Earl J. Small 1962 = **Epidendrum**

Beaumontara (*Brassavola* × *Laelia* × *Cattleya* × *Schomburgkia*), Moir 1961

Brapasia (*Brassia* × *Aspasia*), Moir 1959

Brassidium (*Brassia* × *Oncidium*), O. M. Kirsch 1948

Brassocattleya (*Brassavola* × *Cattleya*), Veitch 1889

Brassodiacrium (*Brassavola* × *Diacrium*), Colman 1909

Brassoepidendrum (*Brassavola* × *Epidendrum*), Pitt 1906

Brassolaelia (*Brassavola* × *Laelia*), Veitch 1898

Brassolaeliocattleya (*Brassavola* × *Laelia* × *Cattleya*), Lawrence 1897

Brassonitis (*Brassavola* × *Sophronitis*), Dr. Clarence Shaw 1962 = **Brassophronitis**

Brassophronitis (*Brassavola* × *Sophronitis*), Germany ca. 1935

Brassotonia (*Brassavola* × *Broughtonia*), E. W. Charles 1960

Burrageara (*Cochlioda* × *Miltonia* × *Odontoglossum* × *Oncidium*), Black & Flory 1927

Cattleytonia (*Broughtonia* × *Cattleya*), Moir 1957

Charleswortheara (*Cochlioda* × *Miltonia* × *Oncidium*), Charlesworth 1919

Chondrobollea (*Chondrorhyncha* × *Bollea*), Natural hybrid

Chondropetalum (*Chondrorhyncha* × *Zygopetalum*), Sanders 1908

Colmanara (*Miltonia* × *Odontoglossum* × *Oncidium*), no data

Cycnodes (*Cycnoches* × *Mormodes*), Charles P. Slocum 1961

Cyperocymbidium (*Cyperorchis* × *Cymbidium*), Hawkes 1962

Dekensara (*Brassavola* × *Cattleya* × *Schomburgkia*), Flandria 1955

Diabroughtonia (*Broughtonia* × *Diacrium*), Moir 1956

Diacattleya (*Diacrium* × *Cattleya*), Colman 1908

Dialaelia (*Diacrium* × *Laelia*), Veitch 1905

Dialaeliocattleya (*Cattleya* × *Diacrium* × *Laelia*), Colman 1908

Doritaenopsis (*Doritis* × *Phalaenopsis*), L. C. Vaughn 1961

Dossinimaria (*Dossinia* × *Haemaria*), Veitch 1861

Ellanthera (*Renanthera* × *Renantherella*), Hawkes 1963

Epicattleya (*Epidendrum* × *Cattleya*), Veitch 1897

Epidiacrium (*Epidendrum* × *Diacrium*), Colman 1905

Epigoa (*Epidendrum* × *Domingoa*), Moir 1957

Epilaelia (*Epidendrum* × *Laelia*), Sanders 1894

Epilaeliocattleya (*Epidendrum* × *Laelia* × *Cattleya*), Moir 1960

Epilaeliopsis (*Epidendrum* × *Laeliopsis*), L. Ariza-Julia 1959

Epiphronitella (*Epidendrum* × *Sophronitella*), Hawkes 1959

Epiphronitis (*Epidendrum* × *Sophronitis*), Veitch 1890

Epitonia (*Epidendrum* × *Broughtonia*), O. M. Kirsch 1960

Fujiwarara (*Brassavola* × *Cattleya* × *Laeliopsis*), Dr. T. Fujiwara 1963

Gastocalanthe (*Gastorchis* × *Calanthe*), Hawkes 1952

Gastophaius (*Gastorchis* × *Phaius*), Hawkes 1952

Grammatocymbidium (*Grammatophyllum* × *Cymbidium*), Germany ca. 1940

Gymnadeniorchis (*Gymnadenia* × *Orchis*), Natural hybrid

Gymnaglossum (*Gymnadenia* × *Coeloglossum*), Natural hybrid

Gymnanacamptis (*Gymnadenia* × *Anacamptis*), Natural hybrid

Gymnigritella (*Gymnadenia* × *Nigritella*), Natural hybrid

Hawaiiara (*Renanthera* × *Vanda* × *Vandopsis*), Fujio 1959

Holttumara (*Arachnis* × *Renanthera* × *Vanda*), Singapore Botanic Gardens 1958

Iwanagara (*Brassavola* × *Cattleya* × *Diacrium* × *Laelia*), E. Iwanaga 1960

Kirchara (*Cattleya* × *Epidendrum* × *Laelia* × *Sophronitis*), Moir 1959

Laeliocattleya (*Laelia* × *Cattleya*), Veitch 1863

Laelonia (*Laelia* × *Broughtonia lilacina* = *Laeliopsis domingensis*), Chen 1957 = **Opsilaelia**

Leptolaelia (*Leptotes* × *Laelia*), Veitch 1902

Liaopsis (*Laeliopsis* × *Laelia*), Moir 1961 = **Opsilaelia**

Limara (*Arachnis* × *Renanthera* × *Vandopsis*), Lim 1960

Lioponia (*Broughtonia* × *Laeliopsis*), Moir 1959

Lowiara (*Brassavola* × *Laelia* × *Sophronitis*), Low 1912

Luisanda (*Luisia* × *Vanda*), University of Hawaii, no date

Lycasteria (*Bifrenaria* × *Lycaste*), McBean 1954

Lyfrenaria (*Bifrenaria* × *Lycaste*), In literature 1954 = **Lycasteria**

Lyonara (*Cattleya* × *Laelia* × *Schomburgkia*), Moir 1959

Macomaria (*Macodes* × *Haemaria*), Veitch 1862

Milpasia (*Miltonia* × *Aspasia*), Moir 1959

Milpilia (*Miltonia* × *Trichopilia*), Moir 1960

Miltassia (*Miltonia* × *Brassia*), Moir 1961

Miltoncidium (*Miltonia* × *Oncidium*), In literature, various dates = **Miltonidium**

Miltonidium (*Miltonia* × *Oncidium*), Mansell & Hatcher 1940

Miltonioda (*Miltonia* × *Cochlioda*), Charlesworth 1909

Moirara (*Paraphalaenopsis* × *Renanthera* × *Vanda*), Moir 1963

Odontioda (*Odontoglossum* × *Cochlioda*), Vuylsteke 1904

Odontobrassia (*Odontoglossum* × *Brassia*), Germany, no date

Odontocidium (*Odontoglossum* × *Oncidium*), Charlesworth 1911

Odontonia (*Miltonia* × *Odontoglossum*), Lairesse 1905

Oncidettia (*Oncidium* × *Comparettia*), Moir 1963

Oncidioda (*Cochlioda* × *Oncidium*), Charlesworth 1910

Opsilaelia (*Laelia* × *Laeliopsis*), Hawkes 1960

Opsisanda (*Vanda* × *Vandopsis*), Tanaka 1947

Orchiaceras (*Aceras* × *Orchis*), Natural hybrid

Orchicoeloglossum (*Coeloglossum* × *Orchis*), Natural hybrid

Orchiserapias (*Orchis* × *Serapias*), Natural hybrid

Pararachnis (*Paraphalaenopsis* × *Arachnis*), Hawkes 1963

Pararenanthera (*Paraphalaenopsis* × *Renanthera*), Hawkes 1963

Paravanda (*Paraphalaenopsis* × *Vanda*), Hawkes 1963

Pectabenaria (*Pecteilis* × *Habenaria*), Hawkes 1960

Pescarhyncha (*Pescatorea* × *Chondrorhyncha*), Moir 1960

Pescoranthes (*Pescatorea* × *Cochleanthes* = *Chondrorhyncha*), Moir 1962 = **Pescarhyncha**

Phaiocalanthe (*Phaius* × *Calanthe*), Veitch 1867

Phaiocymbidium (*Phaius* × *Cymbidium*), Moore 1902

Phalaerianda (*Aërides* × *Phalaenopsis* × *Vanda*), Tanaka 1951 = **Tanakara**

Phalandopsis (*Phalaenopsis* × *Vandopsis*), O. M. Kirsch 1960

Phragmipaphiopedilum (*Phragmipedium* × *Paphiopedilum*), Hawkes 1956

Potinara (*Brassavola* × *Cattleya* × *Laelia* × *Sophronitis*), Charlesworth 1922

Renades (*Aërides* × *Renanthera*), O. M. Kirsch 1955

Renanda (*Arachnis* × *Renanthera* × *Vanda*), Rivermont 1961 = **Holttumara**

Renanopsis (*Renanthera* × *Vandopsis*), O. M. Kirsch 1948

Renanstylis (*Renanthera* × *Rhynchostylis*), Richella Orchids (F. Takakura) 1960

Renantanda (*Renanthera* × *Vanda*), Vacherot-Lecoufle 1935

Renanthopsis (*Renanthera* × *Phalaenopsis*), Vacherot-Lecoufle 1931

Rhynchanthera (*Renanthera* × *Rhynchostylis*), Hawkes 1962 = **Renanstylis**

Rhynchocentrum (*Rhynchostylis* × *Ascocentrum*), Sagarik 1963

Rhyncorades (*Rhynchostylis* × *Aërides*), Orchid Registrar 1962 = **Aëridostylis**

Rhyncovanda (*Vanda* × *Rhynchostylis*), Fantastic Gardens 1958 = **Vandacostylis**

Ridleyara (*Arachnis* × *Trichoglottis* × *Vanda*), Singapore Botanic Gardens 1956

Rodrassia (*Rodriguezia* × *Brassia*), Moir 1960

Rodrettia (*Rodriguezia* × *Comparettia*), R. & T. Okubo 1958

Rodricidium (*Rodriguezia* × *Oncidium*), Okubo (Moir) 1957

Rodridenia (*Macradenia* × *Rodriguezia*), Moir 1962

Rodritonia (*Miltonia* × *Rodriguezia*), Moir 1958

Rolfeara (*Brassavola* × *Cattleya* × *Sophronitis*), Thwaites 1919

Saccanthera (*Renanthera* × *Saccolabium* = *Rhynchostylis*), O. M. Kirsch 1961 = **Renanstylis**

Sanda (*Saccolabium* × *Vanda*), no data

Sanderara (*Brassia* × *Cochlioda* × *Odontoglossum*), Sanders 1937

Sarcothera (*Renanthera* × *Sarcochilus*), Bryan 1954

Schombocattleya (*Schomburgkia* × *Cattleya*), Dallemagne 1903

Schombodiacrium (*Schomburgkia* × *Diacrium*), Moir 1959

Schomboepidendrum (*Schomburgkia* × *Epidendrum*), Moir 1957

Schombolaelia (*Schomburgkia* × *Laelia*), Charlesworth 1913

Schombonia (*Schomburgkia* × *Broughtonia*), Moir 1962

Selenocypripedium (*Selenipedium* = *Phragmipedium* × *Cypripedium* = *Paphiopedilum*), Boullet 1912 = **Phragmipaphiopedilum**

Shipmanara (*Broughtonia* × *Diacrium* × *Schomburgkia*), Yamada 1963

Sophrocattleya (*Cattleya* × *Sophronitis*), Veitch 1886

Sophrolaelia (*Sophronitis* × *Laelia*), Veitch 1894

Sophrolaeliocattleya (*Cattleya* × *Laelia* × *Sophronitis*), Charlesworth 1900

Spathophaius (*Spathoglottis* × *Phaius*), Malaya, no date

Staurachnis (*Arachnis* × *Stauropsis fasciata* = *Trichoglottis fasciata*), Sorapure 1950 = **Trichachnis**

Symphodontioda (*Symphyglossum* × *Odontoglossum* × *Cochlioda*), Hawkes 1963

Symphodontoglossum (*Symphyglossum* × *Odontoglossum*), Hawkes 1963

Symphyglossonia (*Symphyglossum* × *Miltonia*), Hawkes 1963

Tanakara (*Aërides* × *Phalaenopsis* × *Vanda*), Tanaka 1951

Tenranara (*Brassavola* × *Cattleya* × *Laeliopsis*), Dr. T. Fujiwara (Yamada) 1962 = **Fujiwarara**

Trevorara (*Arachnis* × *Paraphalaenopsis* × *Vanda*), Trevor 1963

Trichachnis (*Arachnis* × *Trichoglottis*), Hawkes 1960

Trichocidium (*Oncidium* × *Trichocentrum*), R. B. Livingston (Fountain) 1955

Trichovanda (*Trichoglottis* × *Vanda*), Foster 1948

Vancampe (*Acampe* × *Vanda*), Moir 1958

Vandachnis (*Arachnis* × *Vandopsis*), Lyon 1948

Vandacostylis (*Rhynchostylis* × *Vanda*), Guillaumin 1935

Vandaecum (*Angraecum falcatum* = *Neofinetia falcata* × *Vanda*), Yamada 1960 = **Vandofinetia**

Vandaenopsis (*Phalaenopsis* × *Vanda*), de Saram 1931

Vandofinetia (*Neofinetia* × *Vanda*), Hawkes 1960

Vandopsides (*Aërides* × *Vandopsis*), McCoy 1958

Vuylstekeara (*Cochlioda* × *Miltonia* × *Odontoglossum*), Hye 1912

Wilsonara (*Cochlioda* × *Odontoglossum* × *Oncidium*), Charlesworth 1916

Yamadara (*Brassavola* × *Cattleya* × *Epidendrum* × *Laelia*), Yamada 1960

Zygobatemania (*Batemania* × *Zygopetalum*), Linden 1899

Zygocaste (*Lycaste* × *Zygopetalum*), Sanders 1945

Zygocolax (*Colax* × *Zygopetalum*), Veitch 1886 (also natural hybrid)

Zygonisia (*Aganisia* × *Zygopetalum*), Sanders 1902

INDEX TO MULTIGENERIC ORCHID HYBRID GROUPS

The following is a cross-index of all orchid genera utilized in the preceding roster of multigeneric hybrid groups.

Certain discrepancies in nomenclature will be at once evident, when compared with the system followed elsewhere in this book. Examples are found in *Brassavola* versus *Rhyncholaelia*, *Schomburgkia* as a genus separate from *Laelia*, *Euanthe* as a genus included in *Vanda*, *Diacrium* as the name for *Caularthron*, etc. These are instances of casual horticultural nomenclature versus accurate botanical nomenclature, a remarkable and extraordinarily erratic system which is all too prevalent in the Orchidaceae.

Though beginning attempts have been made, in very recent times, by the Advisory Committee of The International Authority for the Registration of Orchid Hybrids, even their proposals to date have done little to clarify the hundreds of examples of inconsistency which permeate the entire structure of names of orchid hybrids.

In the formulae for the multigeneric hybrid groups indexed here, the component genera are listed in alphabetical sequence, for easier reference.

Acampe × *Vanda* = **Vancampe**
Aceras × *Orchis* = **Orchiaceras**
Ada × *Cochlioda* = **Adioda**
Ada × *Odontoglossum* = **Adaglossum**
Aërides × *Arachnis* = **Aëridachnis**
Aërides × *Neofinetia* = **Aëridofinetia**
Aërides × *Phalaenopsis* = **Aëridopsis**
Aërides × *Phalaenopsis* × *Vanda* = **Tanakara**
Aërides × *Renanthera* = **Renades**
Aërides × *Rhynchostylis* = **Aëridostylis**
Aërides × *Saccolabium** (= *Rhynchostylis*) = **Aëridostylis**
Aërides × *Vanda* = **Aëridovanda**
Aërides × *Vandopsis* = **Vandopsides**
Aganisia × *Zygopetalum* = **Zygonisia**
Anacamptis × *Gymnadenia* = **Gymnanacamptis**
Anguloa × *Lycaste* = **Angulocaste**
Anoectochilus × *Haemaria* = **Anoectomaria**
Arachnis × *Aërides* = **Aëridachnis**
Arachnis × *Armodorum* = **Armodachnis**
Arachnis × *Paraphalaenopsis* = **Pararachnis**
Arachnis × *Paraphalaenopsis* × *Vanda* = **Trevorara**
Arachnis × *Phalaenopsis* = **Arachnopsis**
Arachnis × *Renanthera* = **Aranthera**
Arachnis × *Renanthera* × *Vanda* = **Holttumara**
Arachnis × *Renanthera* × *Vandopsis* = **Limara**
Arachnis × *Trichoglottis* = **Trichachnis**
Arachnis × *Trichoglottis* × *Vanda* = **Ridleyara**
Arachnis × *Vanda* = **Aranda**
Arachnis × *Vandopsis* = **Vandachnis**
Armodorum × *Arachnis* = **Armodachnis**
Ascocentrum × *Neofinetia* = **Ascofinetia**
Ascocentrum × *Rhynchostylis* = **Rhynchocentrum**
Ascocentrum × *Vanda* = **Ascocenda**
Aspasia × *Brassia* = **Brapasia**
Aspasia × *Miltonia* = **Milpasia**

Aspasia × *Oncidium* = **Aspasium**
*Barkeria** (= *Epidendrum*) × *Epidendrum* = **Epidendrum**
Batemania × *Zygopetalum* = **Zygobatemania**
Bifrenaria × *Lycaste* = **Lycasteria**
Bollea × *Chondrorhyncha* = **Chondrobollea**
Brassavola × *Broughtonia* = **Brassotonia**
Brassavola × *Cattleya* = **Brassocattleya**
Brassavola × *Cattleya* × *Diacrium* × *Laelia* = **Iwanagara**
Brassavola × *Cattleya* × *Epidendrum* × *Laelia* = **Yamadara**
Brassavola × *Cattleya* × *Laelia* = **Brassolaeliocattleya**
Brassavola × *Cattleya* × *Laelia* × *Schomburgkia* = **Beaumontara**
Brassavola × *Cattleya* × *Laelia* × *Sophronitis* = **Potinara**
Brassavola × *Cattleya* × *Laeliopsis* = **Fujiwarara**
Brassavola × *Cattleya* × *Schomburgkia* = **Dekensara**
Brassavola × *Cattleya* × *Sophronitis* = **Rolfeara**
Brassavola × *Diacrium* = **Brassodiacrium**
Brassavola × *Epidendrum* = **Brassoepidendrum**
Brassavola × *Laelia* = **Brassolaelia**
Brassavola × *Laelia* × *Sophronitis* = **Lowiara**
Brassavola × *Sophronitis* = **Brassophronitis**
Brassia × *Aspasia* = **Brapasia**
Brassia × *Cochlioda* × *Odontoglossum* = **Sanderara**
Brassia × *Miltonia* = **Miltassia**
Brassia × *Odontoglossum* = **Odontobrassia**
Brassia × *Oncidium* = **Brassidium**
Brassia × *Rodriguezia* = **Rodrassia**
Broughtonia × *Brassavola* = **Brassotonia**
Broughtonia × *Cattleya* = **Cattleytonia**
Broughtonia × *Diacrium* = **Diabroughtonia**
Broughtonia × *Diacrium* × *Schomburgkia* = **Shipmanara**
Broughtonia × *Epidendrum* = **Epitonia**
*Broughtonia** × *Laelia* = **Laelonia** (= **Opsilaelia**)
Broughtonia × *Laeliopsis* = **Lioponia**
Broughtonia × *Schomburgkia* = **Schombonia**
Calanthe × *Gastorchis* = **Gastocalanthe**
Calanthe × *Phaius* = **Phaiocalanthe**
Cattleya × *Brassavola* = **Brassocattleya**
Cattleya × *Brassavola* × *Diacrium* × *Laelia* = **Iwanagara**
Cattleya × *Brassavola* × *Epidendrum* × *Laelia* = **Yamadara**
Cattleya × *Brassavola* × *Laelia* = **Brassolaeliocattleya**
Cattleya × *Brassavola* × *Laelia* × *Schomburgkia* = **Beaumontara**
Cattleya × *Brassavola* × *Laelia* × *Sophronitis* = **Potinara**
Cattleya × *Brassavola* × *Laeliopsis* = **Fujiwarara**
Cattleya × *Brassavola* × *Schomburgkia* = **Dekensara**
Cattleya × *Brassavola* × *Sophronitis* = **Rolfeara**
Cattleya × *Broughtonia* = **Cattleytonia**
Cattleya × *Diacrium* = **Diacattleya**
Cattleya × *Diacrium* × *Laelia* = **Dialaeliocattleya**
Cattleya × *Epidendrum* = **Epicattleya**
Cattleya × *Epidendrum* × *Laelia* = **Epilaeliocattleya**
Cattleya × *Epidendrum* × *Laelia* × *Sophronitis* = **Kirchara**
Cattleya × *Laelia* = **Laeliocattleya**
Cattleya × *Laelia* × *Schomburgkia* = **Lyonara**
Cattleya × *Laelia* × *Sophronitis* = **Sophrolaeliocattleya**
Cattleya × *Schomburgkia* = **Schombocattleya**

Cattleya × *Sophronitis* = **Sophrocattleya**
Chondrorhyncha × *Bollea* = **Chondrobollea**
Chondrorhyncha × *Pescatorea* = **Pescarhyncha**
Chondrorhyncha × *Zygopetalum* = **Chondropetalum**
Cochlioda × *Ada* = **Adioda**
Cochlioda × *Brassia* × *Odontoglossum* = **Sanderara**
Cochlioda × *Miltonia* = **Miltonioda**
Cochlioda × *Miltonia* × *Odontoglossum* = **Vuylstekeara**
Cochlioda × *Miltonia* × *Odontoglossum* × *Oncidium* = **Burrageara**
Cochlioda × *Miltonia* × *Oncidium* = **Charleswortheara**
Cochlioda × *Odontoglossum* = **Odontioda**
Cochlioda × *Odontoglossum* × *Oncidium* = **Wilsonara**
Cochlioda × *Odontoglossum* × *Symphyglossum* = **Symphodontioda**
Cochlioda × *Oncidium* = **Oncidioda**
Coeloglossum × *Gymnadenia* = **Gymnaglossum**
Coeloglossum × *Orchis* = **Orchicoeloglossum**
Colax × *Zygopetalum* = **Zygocolax**
Comparettia × *Oncidium* = **Oncidettia**
Comparettia × *Rodriguezia* = **Rodrettia**
Cycnoches × *Mormodes* = **Cycnodes**
Cymbidium × *Cyperorchis* = **Cyperocymbidium**
Cymbidium × *Grammatophyllum* = **Grammatocymbidium**
Cymbidium × *Phaius* = **Phaiocymbidium**
Cyperorchis × *Cymbidium* = **Cyperocymbidium**
Cypripedium* (= *Paphiopedilum*) × *Selenipedium** (= *Phragmipedium*) = **Phragmipaphiopedilum**
Diacrium × *Brassavola* = **Brassodiacrium**
Diacrium × *Brassavola* × *Cattleya* × *Laelia* = **Iwanagara**
Diacrium × *Broughtonia* = **Diabroughtonia**
Diacrium × *Broughtonia* × *Schomburgkia* = **Shipmanara**
Diacrium × *Cattleya* = **Diacattleya**
Diacrium × *Cattleya* × *Laelia* = **Dialaeliocattleya**
Diacrium × *Epidendrum* = **Epidiacrium**
Diacrium × *Laelia* = **Dialaelia**
Diacrium × *Schomburgkia* = **Schombodiacrium**
Domingoa × *Epidendrum* = **Epigoa**
Doritis × *Phalaenopsis* = **Doritaenopsis**
Dossinia × *Haemaria* = **Dossinimaria**
Epidendrum × *Barkeria** (= *Epidendrum*) = **Epidendrum**
Epidendrum × *Brassavola* = **Brassoepidendrum**
Epidendrum × *Brassavola* × *Cattleya* × *Laelia* = **Yamadara**
Epidendrum × *Broughtonia* = **Epitonia**
Epidendrum × *Cattleya* = **Epicattleya**
Epidendrum × *Cattleya* × *Laelia* × *Sophronitis* = **Kirchara**
Epidendrum × *Diacrium* = **Epidiacrium**
Epidendrum × *Domingoa* = **Epigoa**
Epidendrum × *Laelia* = **Epilaelia**
Epidendrum × *Laelia* × *Cattleya* = **Epilaeliocattleya**
Epidendrum × *Laeliopsis* = **Epilaeliopsis**
Epidendrum × *Schomburgkia* = **Schomboepidendrum**
Epidendrum × *Sophronitella* = **Epiphronitella**
Epidendrum × *Sophronitis* = **Epiphronitis**
Gastorchis × *Calanthe* = **Gastocalanthe**
Gastorchis × *Phaius* = **Gastophaius**
Grammatophyllum × *Cymbidium* = **Grammatocymbidium**
Gymnadenia × *Anacamptis* = **Gymnanacamptis**
Gymnadenia × *Coeloglossum* = **Gymnaglossum**

Gymnadenia × *Nigritella* = **Gymnigritella**
Gymnadenia × *Orchis* = **Gymnadeniorchis**
Habenaria × *Pecteilis* = **Pectabenaria**
Haemaria × *Anoectochilus* = **Anoectomaria**
Haemaria × *Dossinia* = **Dossinimaria**
Haemaria × *Macodes* = **Macomaria**
Laelia × *Brassavola* = **Brassolaelia**
Laelia × *Brassavola* × *Cattleya* = **Brassolaeliocattleya**
Laelia × *Brassavola* × *Cattleya* × *Diacrium* = **Iwanagara**
Laelia × *Brassavola* × *Cattleya* × *Epidendrum* = **Yamadara**
Laelia × *Brassavola* × *Cattleya* × *Schomburgkia* = **Beaumontara**
Laelia × *Brassavola* × *Cattleya* × *Sophronitis* = **Potinara**
Laelia × *Brassavola* × *Sophronitis* = **Lowiara**
Laelia × *Broughtonia** (= *Laeliopsis*) = *Laelonia* (= **Opsilaelia**)
Laelia × *Cattleya* = **Laeliocattleya**
Laelia × *Cattleya* × *Diacrium* = **Dialaeliocattleya**
Laelia × *Cattleya* × *Epidendrum* = **Epilaeliocattleya**
Laelia × *Cattleya* × *Epidendrum* × *Sophronitis* = **Kirchara**
Laelia × *Cattleya* × *Schomburgkia* = **Lyonara**
Laelia × *Cattleya* × *Sophronitis* = **Sophrolaeliocattleya**
Laelia × *Diacrium* = **Dialaelia**
Laelia × *Epidendrum* = **Epilaelia**
Laelia × *Laeliopsis* = **Opsilaelia**
Laelia × *Leptotes* = **Leptolaelia**
Laelia × *Schomburgkia* = **Schombolaelia**
Laelia × *Sophronitis* = **Sophrolaelia**
Laeliopsis × *Brassavola* × *Cattleya* = **Fujiwarara**
Laeliopsis × *Broughtonia* = **Lioponia**
Laeliopsis × *Epidendrum* = **Epilaeliopsis**
Laeliopsis × *Laelia* = **Opsilaelia**
Leptotes × *Laelia* = **Leptolaelia**
Luisia × *Vanda* = **Luisanda**
Lycaste × *Anguloa* = **Angulocaste**
Lycaste × *Bifrenaria* = **Lycasteria**
Lycaste × *Zygopetalum* = **Zygocaste**
Macodes × *Haemaria* = **Macomaria**
Macradenia × *Rodriguezia* = **Rodridenia**
Miltonia × *Aspasia* = **Milpasia**
Miltonia × *Brassia* = **Miltassia**
Miltonia × *Cochlioda* = **Miltonioda**
Miltonia × *Cochlioda* × *Odontoglossum* = **Vuylstekeara**
Miltonia × *Cochlioda* × *Odontoglossum* × *Oncidium* = **Burrageara**
Miltonia × *Cochlioda* × *Oncidium* = **Charleswortheara**
Miltonia × *Odontoglossum* = **Odontonia**
Miltonia × *Odontoglossum* × *Oncidium* = **Colmanara**
Miltonia × *Oncidium* = **Miltonidium**
Miltonia × *Rodriguezia* = **Rodritonia**
Miltonia × *Symphyglossum* = **Symphyglossonia**
Miltonia × *Trichopilia* = **Milpilia**
Mormodes × *Cycnoches* = **Cycnodes**
Neofinetia × *Aërides* = **Aëridofinetia**
Neofinetia × *Ascocentrum* = **Ascofinetia**
Neofinetia × *Vanda* = **Vandofinetia**
Nigritella × *Gymnadenia* = **Gymnigritella**
Odontoglossum × *Ada* = **Adaglossum**
Odontoglossum × *Brassia* = **Odontobrassia**
Odontoglossum × *Brassia* × *Cochlioda* = **Sanderara**
Odontoglossum × *Cochlioda* = **Odontioda**

Odontoglossum × *Cochlioda* × *Miltonia* = **Vuylstekeara**
Odontoglossum × *Cochlioda* × *Miltonia* × *Oncidium* = **Burrageara**
Odontoglossum × *Cochlioda* × *Oncidium* = **Wilsonara**
Odontoglossum × *Cochlioda* × *Symphyglossum* = **Symphodontioda**
Odontoglossum × *Miltonia* = **Odontonia**
Odontoglossum × *Miltonia* × *Oncidium* = **Colmanara**
Odontoglossum × *Oncidium* = **Odontocidium**
Odontoglossum × *Symphyglossum* = **Symphodontoglossum**
Oncidium × *Aspasia* = **Aspasium**
Oncidium × *Brassia* = **Brassidium**
Oncidium × *Cochlioda* = **Oncidioda**
Oncidium × *Cochlioda* × *Miltonia* = **Charleswortheara**
Oncidium × *Cochlioda* × *Miltonia* × *Odontoglossum* = **Burrageara**
Oncidium × *Cochlioda* × *Odontoglossum* = **Wilsonara**
Oncidium × *Comparettia* = **Oncidettia**
Oncidium × *Miltonia* = **Miltonidium**
Oncidium × *Miltonia* × *Odontoglossum* = **Colmanara**
Oncidium × *Odontoglossum* = **Odontocidium**
Oncidium × *Rodriguezia* = **Rodricidium**
Oncidium × *Trichocentrum* = **Trichocidium**
Orchis × *Aceras* = **Orchiaceras**
Orchis × *Coeloglossum* = **Orchicoeloglossum**
Orchis × *Gymnadenia* = **Gymnadeniorchis**
Orchis × *Serapias* = **Orchiserapias**
Paphiopedilum × *Phragmipedium* = **Phragmipaphiopedilum**
Paraphalaenopsis × *Arachnis* = **Pararachnis**
Paraphalaenopsis × *Arachnis* × *Vanda* = **Trevorara**
Paraphalaenopsis × *Renanthera* = **Pararenanthera**
Paraphalaenopsis × *Renanthera* × *Vanda* = **Moirara**
Paraphalaenopsis × *Vanda* = **Paravanda**
Pecteilis × *Habenaria* = **Pectabenaria**
Pescatorea × *Chondrorhyncha* = **Pescarhyncha**
Phaius × *Calanthe* = **Phaiocalanthe**
Phaius × *Cymbidium* = **Phaiocymbidium**
Phaius × *Gastorchis* = **Gastophaius**
Phaius × *Spathoglottis* = **Spathophaius**
Phalaenopsis × *Aërides* = **Aëridopsis**
Phalaenopsis × *Aërides* × *Vanda* = **Tanakara**
Phalaenopsis × *Arachnis* = **Arachnopsis**
Phalaenopsis × *Doritis* = **Doritaenopsis**
Phalaenopsis × *Renanthera* = **Renanthopsis**
Phalaenopsis × *Vanda* = **Vandaenopsis**
Phalaenopsis × *Vandopsis* = **Phalandopsis**
Phragmipedium × *Paphiopedilum* = **Phragmipaphiopedilum**
Renanthera × *Aërides* = **Renades**
Renanthera × *Arachnis* = **Aranthera**
Renanthera × *Arachnis* × *Vanda* = **Holttumara**
Renanthera × *Arachnis* × *Vandopsis* = **Limara**
Renanthera × *Paraphalaenopsis* = **Pararenanthera**
Renanthera × *Paraphalaenopsis* × *Vanda* = **Moirara**
Renanthera × *Phalaenopsis* = **Renanthopsis**
Renanthera × *Renantherella* = **Ellanthera**
Renanthera × *Rhynchostylis* = **Renanstylis**
Renanthera × *Sarcochilus* = **Sarcothera**
Renanthera × *Vanda* = **Renantanda**
Renanthera × *Vanda* × *Vandopsis* = **Hawaiiara**
Renanthera × *Vandopsis* = **Renanopsis**

Renantherella × *Renanthera* = **Ellanthera**
Rhynchostylis × *Aërides* = **Aëridostylis**
Rhynchostylis × *Ascocentrum* = **Rhynchocentrum**
Rhynchostylis × *Renanthera* = **Renanstylis**
Rhynchostylis × *Vanda* = **Vandacostylis**
Rodriguezia × *Brassia* = **Rodrassia**
Rodriguezia × *Comparettia* = **Rodrettia**
Rodriguezia × *Macradenia* = **Rodridenia**
Rodriguezia × *Miltonia* = **Rodritonia**
Rodriguezia × *Oncidium* = **Rodricidium**
Saccolabium* (= *Rhynchostylis*) × *Aërides* = **Aëridostylis**
Saccolabium* (= *Rhynchostylis*) × *Vanda* = **Vandacostylis**
Sarcochilus × *Renanthera* = **Sarcothera**
Schomburgkia × *Brassavola* × *Cattleya* = **Dekensara**
Schomburgkia × *Brassavola* × *Cattleya* × *Laelia* = **Beaumontara**
Schomburgkia × *Broughtonia* = **Schombonia**
Schomburgkia × *Broughtonia* × *Diacrium* = **Shipmanara**
Schomburgkia × *Cattleya* = **Schombocattleya**
Schomburgkia × *Diacrium* = **Schombodiacrium**
Schomburgkia × *Epidendrum* = **Schomboepidendrum**
Schomburgkia × *Laelia* = **Schombolaelia**
Schomburgkia × *Laelia* × *Cattleya* = **Lyonara**
Selenipedium* (= *Phragmipedium*) × *Cypripedium** (= *Paphiopedilum*) = **Phragmipaphiopedilum**
Serapias × *Orchis* = **Orchiserapias**
Sophronitella × *Epidendrum* = **Epiphronitella**
Sophronitis × *Brassavola* = **Brassophronitis**
Sophronitis × *Brassavola* × *Cattleya* = **Rolfeara**
Sophronitis × *Brassavola* × *Cattleya* × *Laelia* = **Potinara**
Sophronitis × *Brassavola* × *Laelia* = **Lowiara**
Sophronitis × *Cattleya* = **Sophrocattleya**
Sophronitis × *Cattleya* × *Epidendrum* × *Laelia* = **Kirchara**
Sophronitis × *Cattleya* × *Laelia* = **Sophrolaeliocattleya**
Sophronitis × *Epidendrum* = **Epiphronitis**
Sophronitis × *Laelia* = **Sophrolaelia**
Spathoglottis × *Phaius* = **Spathophaius**
Symphyglossum × *Cochlioda* × *Odontoglossum* = **Symphodontioda**
Symphyglossum × *Miltonia* = **Symphyglossonia**
Symphyglossum × *Odontoglossum* = **Symphodontoglossum**
Trichocentrum × *Oncidium* = **Trichocidium**
Trichoglottis × *Arachnis* = **Trichachnis**
Trichoglottis × *Arachnis* × *Vanda* = **Ridleyara**
Trichoglottis × *Vanda* = **Trichovanda**
Trichopilia × *Miltonia* = **Milpilia**
Vanda × *Acampe* = **Vancampe**
Vanda × *Aërides* = **Aëridovanda**
Vanda × *Aërides* × *Phalaenopsis* = **Tanakara**
Vanda × *Arachnis* = **Aranda**
Vanda × *Arachnis* × *Paraphalaenopsis* = **Trevorara**
Vanda × *Arachnis* × *Renanthera* = **Holttumara**
Vanda × *Arachnis* × *Trichoglottis* = **Ridleyara**
Vanda × *Ascocentrum* = **Ascocenda**
Vanda × *Luisia* = **Luisanda**
Vanda × *Neofinetia* = **Vandofinetia**
Vanda × *Paraphalaenopsis* = **Paravanda**
Vanda × *Paraphalaenopsis* × *Renanthera* = **Moirara**

Vanda × Phalaenopsis = **Vandaenopsis**
Vanda × Renanthera = **Renantanda**
Vanda × Renanthera × Vandopsis = **Hawaiiara**
Vanda × Rhynchostylis = **Vandacostylis**
Vanda × Trichoglottis = **Trichovanda**
Vanda × Vandopsis = **Opsisanda**
Vandopsis × Aërides = **Vandopsides**
Vandopsis × Arachnis = **Vandachnis**
Vandopsis × Arachnis × Vanda = **Limara**

Vandopsis × Phalaenopsis = **Phalandopsis**
Vandopsis × Renanthera = **Renanopsis**
Vandopsis × Renanthera × Vanda = **Hawaiiara**
Vandopsis × Vanda = **Opsisanda**
Zygopetalum × Aganisia = **Zygonisia**
Zygopetalum × Batemania = **Zygobatemania**
Zygopetalum × Chondrorhyncha = **Chondropetaluu**
Zygopetalum × Colax = **Zygocolax**
Zygopetalum × Lycaste = **Zygocaste**

GLOSSARY

In the phonetic pronunciations appended to the terms in this listing, the accent falls on the syllable in italics.

aberrant (ah-*ber*-ant) = Varying from typical; unusual or exceptional.

abortive (ah-*bor*-tiv) = Imperfectly formed or developed; rudimentary.

abrupt (ah-*brupt*) = Suddenly ending, as a leaf or floral segment which narrows quickly to a point; suddenly changing in shape and size.

acaulescent (ah-kaw-*less*-ent) = Having no true stem.

accrescent (ah-*kress*-ent) = Increasing in size or length with age, or after fertilization, as in the perianth-segments and/or pedicellate ovary in certain species of *Phalaenopsis, Taeniophyllum, Corybas, Didymoplexis*, etc.

acicular (ah-*sik*-yu-lar) = Needle-shaped.

acotyledonous (ah-kot-i-*lee*-do-nus) = Without cotyledons, as the seedlings of orchids when they have initially germinated, to differentiate them from true monocotyledons or dicotyledons.

aculeate (ah-*kyu*-lee-ate) = Prickly; sharp-pointed.

acuminate (ah-*kyu*-mi-nate) = Tapering to a slender point.

acute (ah-*kyute*) = Ending sharply and abruptly, in an angle of less than 90°.

adnate (*ad*-nate) = Grown to; said of parts that are attached throughout their entire length to parts of a different series.

adventitious (ad-ven-*ti*-shus) = Produced out of the usual or normal place.

adventive (ad-*ven*-tiv) = Referring to an introduced plant which is not yet entirely established in its new environment.

aerial (ah-*er*-ee-al) = Living without connection with the ground.

agglutinate (ah-*gloo*-ti-nate) = To fuse together.

aggregate (*ag*-re-gate) = Clustered; clumped together.

alate (*ah*-late) = Winged; having wings or wing-like parts or extensions.

alternate (*al*-ter-nate) = The arrangement of leaves or other parts placed first one and then another (not opposite to each other nor in pairs) on a stem or axis.

amplexicaul (am-*plex*-i-kol) = With leaves or bracts clasping the stem.

anastomosing (ah-*nas*-toe-mow-sing) = Netted; interveined.

ancipitous (an-*sip*-i-tus) = Bearing two edges, these usually rather sharp.

angraecoid (an-*grye*-koid) = Orchids of the *Angraecum* group.

annual (*an*-yu-al) = A plant which survives only a single year or season.

anomalous (ah-*nom*-a-lus) = Deviating from the general rule or type; abnormal; irregular.

anterior (an-*ter*-ee-or) = The side in front.

anther (*an*-ther) = The sac containing the pollen, i.e. the essential portion of the stamen or male part of the flower.

anthesis (*an*-the-sis) = The period or action when the flower expands, the pollen is ripe, and the stigma is receptive.

antrorse (an-*trors*) = Directed forwards or upwards.

apetalous (ah-*pet*-a-lus) = Without petals.

aphyllous (ah-*fil*-us) = Without leaves.

apiculate (ah-*pik*-yu-late) = Ending in a short, sharp, abrupt, rather soft tip.

apicule (a-*pi*-kyule) = The short, sharp, abrupt, rather soft projection sometimes extending beyond the terminus of the lamina in such parts as leaves, sepals, petals, lips, etc.

appendage (ah-*pen*-daj) = An attached subsidiary or secondary part, as a projecting or hanging portion or supplement; an extension or extra part or process.

appendiculate (ah-pen-*dik*-yu-late) = Bearing or possessing an appendage.

approximate (ah-*prox*-i-mate) = Placed or situated close together, but not united.

arachnoid (ah-*rak*-noyd) = Spider-like; in orchidology, applying to plants which simulate members of the genus *Arachnis* in some fashion.

arcuate (*ar*-kyu-ate) = Shaped or similar to a bow in form.

aristate (*ah*-ris-tate) = Provided with an awn or bristle-like appendage, especially on the floral bracts.

articulate (ar-*tik*-yu-late) = Jointed; possessing a node or joint.

ascending (ah-*sen*-ding) = Upcurved; growing or directed upwards.

asepalous (ah-*see*-pa-lus) = Without sepals.

asexual (ah-*sex*-yu-al) = Without sex; sexless.

asymmetrical (ah-si-*met*-ri-kal) = Not symmetrical; with no regular shape.

attenuate (ah-*ten*-yu-ate) = Becoming slender or very narrow; slenderly long-tapering.

auricle (*aw*-ri-kl) = An ear-like appendage.

auriculate (aw-*rik*-yu-late) = Bearing auricles.

awl-shaped (*awl*-shaped) = Gradually tapering down from the base to a narrow stiff point.

awn (on) = A bristle-like, usually rather stiff appendage, especially found on the floral bracts.

axil (*ax*-il) = Upper angle formed between the stem or branch and any other branch, leaf, tubercle or other organ arising from them.

axile (*ax*-ile) = Borne in or on the axis; referring to the axis.

axillary (*ax*-il-ah-ri) = Situated in, rising from, or pertaining to an axil.

axis (*ax*-is) = The stem on which organs are arranged.

barbate (*bar*-bate) = Bearded; barbed.

basifixed (*bas*-i-fixd) = Attached by the base.

beak (beek) = A pointed projection ending the fruit or other parts of a plant; as in the beaked anther in *Ornithocephalus*, etc.

bifid (*bi*-fid) = Two-split to the middle; divided into two equal lobes.

bifoliate (by-*foe*-lee-ate) = With two leaves.

bigeneric (by-je-*ner*-ik) = Applied to hybrids made between members of two genera.

bilobate (by-*low*-bate) = Two-lobed; parted into two lobes.

bilobed (*by*-lobed) = Synonym for **bilobate**.

bilocular (by-*lok*-yu-lar) = Two-celled; with two locules or compartments.

bisexual (by-*sex*-yu-al) = Two-sexed; with both stamens and pistils.

blade (blade) = Expanded portion of a leaf or petal.

brachiate (*brak*-ee-ate) = Branches or parts spreading at nearly right angles and placed alternately.

bract (brakt) = A much-reduced leaf-like or scale-like organ subtending a flower or aggregation of flowers; a modified inflorescence leaf.

bracteate (*brak*-tee-ate) = Bearing bracts.

bulbose (bul-*bows*) = Inflated at the base; with a bulb.

bulbous (*bul*-bus) = Bulb-like.

caespitose (*ses*-pi-tows) = Growing in tufts or dense clumps.

calcarate (*kal*-kah-rate) = Furnished with a spur; spurred.

calceolate (kal-*see*-oh-late) = Slipper-like; with the form of a round-toed shoe.

calli (*kal*-eye) = Plural of **callus**.

callosity (ka-*los*-i-ti) = Thickened and hardened part or protuberance.

callus (*kal*-us) = A hard prominence or protuberance.

campanulate (kam-*pan*-yu-late) = Bell-shaped.

canaliculate (kan-ah-*lik*-yu-late) = Channelled or grooved lengthwise.

capitate (*kap*-i-tate) = Head-like or head-shaped; gathered into a head or dense cluster.

capitulum (ka-*pit*-yu-lum) = A head or very dense cluster of sessile flowers.

capsule (*kap*-sool) = A dry splitting seed-vessel composed of two or more carpels; the 'seed-pods' of orchids are correctly termed capsules.

carinate (*kah*-ri-nate) = Keeled; provided with a projecting central longitudinal line or ridge on the lower or under surface.

carnose (kar-*nows*) = Fleshy; pulpy.

cataphyll (*kat*-ah-fil) = Undeveloped leaf, as at the beginning of a growth; the sheathing leaf-like bracts found at the pseudobulb-bases of certain orchids.

cauda (*kaw*-da) = A more or less elongate tail-like growth or projection.

caudae (*kaw*-dye) = Plural of **cauda**.

caudate (*kaw*-date) = Furnished with a tail or tails.

caudicle (*kaw*-di-kl) = Little stem; stemlet; in orchids, the stalk of the pollinium.

caulescent (kaw-*less*-ent) = Producing a stem or stems above ground or above the substratum.

cauline (*kaw*-leen) = Of or pertaining to the stem.

cespitose (*ses*-pi-tows) = Alternate spelling of **caespitose**.

chartaceous (kar-*tay*-shus) = Thin, hard and stiff; with the texture of writing-paper.

ciliate (*sil*-ee-ate) = Fringed with usually small hairs.

cirrhi (*seer*-eye) = Plural of **cirrhus**.

cirrhus (*seer*-us) = A tendril.

clasping (*klas*-ping) = Partly or wholly surrounding another structure; as a leaf clasping a stem.

clavate (*kla*-vate) = Club-shaped; thickened towards the top.

claw (klaw) = Long, narrow, stalk-like base of petals or sepals or lips found in some orchid flowers.

clawed (klawd) = Furnished with a claw.

cleistogamous (klys-*tog*-ah-mus) = With fertilization taking place within the unopened flower.

clinandrium (kli-*nan*-dree-um) = The usually rather cup-shaped area of the column of the orchid flower in which the anther lies.

clone (kloan) = A plant derived by vegetative propagation from one original specimen.

coalesce (koe-ah-*less*) = To grow together, referring to similar parts of a flower.

coherent (koe-*he*-rent) = Two or more similar parts or organs joined together.

cohesion (koe-*hee*-zhun) = Union of two or more organs of the same kind.

column (*kol*-um) = The specialized central body of the orchid flower, formed by the union of the stamens and pistils; **gynostemium**.

compressed (kom-*presd*) = Flattened, especially laterally.

concave (kon-*kave*) = Hollow, as the inside of a saucer.

conduplicate (kon-*doo*-pli-kate) = Two parts folded together lengthwise.

congeneric (kon-je-*ner*-ik) = Belonging to the same ·genus.

congested (kon-*jes*-ted) = Crowded very close together.

conical (*kon*-i-kal) = Cone-shaped.

connate (*kon*-ate) = United or joined congenitally, firmly; especially similar structures joined as one body or organ.

connivent (*kon*-i-vent) = Coming into contact or converging.

convex (kon-*vex*) = Arched or rounded, as the outside of a saucer.

convolute (kon-vo-*loot*) = Rolled up, the edges overlapping.

cordate (*kor*-date) = Heart-shaped.

coriaceous (koe-ree-*ay*-shus) = Leathery in texture.

corm (korm) = A solid, bulb-like structure, usually subterranean.

costate (*kos*-tate) = Ribbed; strongly nerved or veined.

cotyledon (kot-i-*lee*-don) = Seed-leaf; primary leaf or leaves in an embryo.

crenate (*kre*-nate) = With the margins notched, scalloped, or in rounded projections.

crenulate (*kren*-yu-late) = Minutely crenate; somewhat scalloped marginally.

crest (krest) = An elevated and irregular or toothed ridge, in orchids found on the lip.

crested (*kres*-ted) = Furnished with a crest or crests.

cristate (*kris*-tate) = Crested; comb-like.

cruciate (*kroo*-see-ate) = Cross-shaped.

cucullate (*kyu*-kyu-late) = Hooded.

cuneate (*kyu*-nee-ate) = Wedge-shaped; triangular, with the narrow end at the point of attachment.

cupular (*kup*-yu-lar) = Cup-like or cup-shaped.

cymbiform (*sim*-bi-form) = Boat-shaped.

cytology (sy-*tol*-oh-jee) = The section of biology dealing with cells in reference to their structure, functions, multiplication, and life history.

dactylose (*dak*-ti-lows) = Finger-shaped.

damping off = The collapse of seedlings, usually caused by infestations of the fungi *Botrytis vulgaris* or *Pythium Debaryanum*.

deciduous (de-*sid*-yu-us) = Falling off.

decumbent (de-*kum*-bent) = Reclining or lying on the ground, but with an ascending apex or extremity.

decurrent (de-*ku*-rent) = Running or extending downwards.

decurved (de-*kurvd*) = Curved downwards.

deflexed (de-*flexd*) = Bent or turned down or away, usually rather abruptly so.

dehiscence (de-*hiss*-ens) = Spontaneous opening of a ripe fruit to discharge its seeds.

dehiscent (de-*hiss*-ent) = Splitting along definite lines to discharge seeds in a fruit.

deltoid (*del*-toyd) = Triangular.

dentate (*den*-tate) = With sharp-pointed teeth on the margins which are directed outwards.

denticulate (den-*tik*-yu-late) = Minutely dentate.

diandrous (dy-*an*-drus) = With two stamens, as members of the orchid subtribe *Cypripedilinae*.

dicotyledon (dy-kot-i-*lee*-don) = A plant with two cotyledons.

didymous (*did*-ee-mus) = Twin; growing or occurring in pairs.

dimorphic (dy-*mor*-fik) = Having two unlike or dissimilar forms or shapes.

dimorphy (*dy*-mor-fee) = A condition in which two unlike or dissimilar forms or shapes occur.

dioecious (dy-*ee*-shus) = Unisexual; with the male (staminate) and female (pistillate) flowers on different individual plants.

disc (disk) = A more or less rounded, flattened structure; in orchids, particularly referring to the median or basal portion of the lip (usually the midlobe).

discoid (*dis*-koyd) = Shaped like a disc.

disk = Synonym for **disc**.

distichous (*dis*-ti-kus) = Arranged in two ranks or rows.

diurnal (dy-*ur*-nal) = Referring to the daytime; in reference to flowers, signifying those which open only during the day.

divaricate (dy-*vah*-ri-kate) = Spreading; widely diverging.

divergent (dy-*ver*-jent) = Widely spreading.

dorsal (*dor*-sal) = Relating to the back or outer surface.

double (*dub*-l) = Used in reference to flowers that have more than the usual or normal number of floral parts, particularly petals.

ebracteate (ee-*brak*-tee-ate) = Without bracts.

ecalcarate (ee-*kal*-ka-rate) = Without a spur or spurs.

echinate (*ek*-i-nate) = Furnished with prickles or bristles.

ecology (ee-*kol*-oh-jee) = The section of biology which deals with the mutual relationships between organisms (plants or animals) and their environment.

ellipsoid (ee-*lip*-soyd) = A compressed sphere; an elliptic solid.

elliptic (ee-*lip*-tik) = A flat part or body that is oval and narrowed to rounded ends.

emarginate (ee-*mar*-ji-nate) = With a shallow notch in the apical margin.

endemic (en-*dem*-ik) = Confined to a certain, usually rather restricted area, and not found elsewhere.

ensiform (*en*-si-form) = Sword-shaped or -formed.

ephemeral (e-*fem*-er-al) = Lasting only one day when in flower; evanescent.

epichil (*ep*-i-kil) = The upper part of the jointed, complex lip of certain orchids, as in the genus *Stanhopea*.

epiphyte (*ep*-i-fite) = A plant which grows on another plant, but is not nourished by it (hence, not parasitic); an 'air-plant'.

epiphytic (ep-i-*fit*-ik) = Pertaining to **epiphyte**.

equitant (*ek*-wi-tant) = Leaves which are conduplicate and which stand inside each other, in two ranks, in the manner of an *Iris*.

erose (ee-*rows*) = With the margin irregularly notched, as if gnawed.

evanescent (ev-ah-*ness*-ent) = Short-lived; not lasting for a long period.

evergreen (*ev*-er-green) = Remaining green or retaining foliage throughout the year.

exotic (ex-*ot*-ik) = Not native; foreign.

exserted (ex-*ser*-ted) = Extending or projecting beyond some enclosed organ or part.

falcate (*fal*-kate) = Sickle-shaped; scythe-shaped.

fascicle (*fass*-ik-el) = A dense or close bundle, clump, or cluster, particularly of similar organs or structures having a common source.

fetid (*fet*-id) = Synonym for **foetid**.

filiform (*fil*-i-form) = Thread-like; long, slender, and terete.

fimbriate (*fim*-bree-ate) = Fringed.

fimbrillate (*fim*-bri-late) = With minute fringes.

flabellate (fla-*be*-late) = Fan-shaped.

flaccid (*fla*-sid) = Soft and limp; flabby.

flexuose (flex-yu-*ose*) = Bending or curving gently in opposite directions; wavy.

flora (*flo*-rah) = The vegetation or plant life of a given region; also a book describing this vegetation.

floriferous (flo-*ri*-fer-us) = Free-flowering; easily brought into flower.

foetid (*fet*-id) = With a disagreeable odour.

foliaceous (foe-lee-*ay*-shus) = Leaf-like; used particularly in reference to sepals or bracts which simulate small or large leaves in texture, size, or colour.

fornicate (*for*-ni-kate) = Arched; curved.

fringed (frinjd) = Furnished with hair-like appendages on the margins.

fruit (froot) = The ripened ovary of a seed plant, with its contents and various accessory surrounding envelopes or parts.

fugacious (fyu-*gay*-shus) = Withering quickly; falling off soon after anthesis (in reference to a flower).

furcate (*fur*-kate) = Forked.

fusiform (*fyu*-si-form) = Spindle-shaped; tapering at both ends.

galeate (*gal*-ee-ate) = Helmet-shaped.

geminate (*jem*-i-nate) = Twin; in pairs.

genera (*jen*-er-ah) = Plural of **genus**.

generic (je-*ner*-ik) = Of or pertaining to a genus.

genetics (je-*net*-iks) = The science which deals with heredity and hereditary variations.

geniculate (je-*nik*-yu-late) = Bent abruptly, like a knee.

genus (*jee*-nus) = A subdivision of a family, consisting of one or more species which show similar characteristics and appear to have a common ancestry.

glabrate (*glab*-rate) = Becoming glabrous, or nearly so, with age.

glabrous (*glab*-rus) = Smooth; devoid of hair or pubescence.

gladiate (*glad*-ee-ate) = Sword-shaped.

glaucous (*glaw*-kus) = Covered with a bluish-grey, bluish-green, or whitish bloom which will not rub off.

glomerate (*glom*-e-rate) = Grouped together in a dense or compact cluster or clusters.

gregarious (gre-*gah*-ree-us) = Growing together in clusters or colonies.

gynostemium (jin-oh-*stee*-mee-um) = Synonym for **column**.

habitat (*hab*-i-tat) = The natural abode of an organism.

herbaceous (er-*bay*-shus) = Herb-like; not woody.

herbarium (er-*bah*-ree-um) = A collection of dried (or otherwise preserved) plant specimens, annotated and determined.

hirsute (heer-*soot*) = Pubescent, the hairs being rather coarse and stiff; hairy.

homonym (*hoe*-moe-nim) = A scientific name which is preoccupied by its earlier application to a different entity of the same category, and hence untenable under the rules of taxonomic priority.

hyaline (*hy*-ah-leen) = Resembling glass; transparent or translucent.

hypochil (*hy*-po-kil) = Lower or basal part of the lip in some orchids, as in *Stanhopea*.

imbricate (*im*-bri-kate) = Overlapping, like shingles on a roof.

incised (in-*sized*) = With the margins cut into sharp, deep, irregular teeth.

included (in-*kloo*-ded) = Inclosed in and not protruding from the surrounding parts or organs.

incumbent (in-*kum*-bent) = Resting upon or lying against some other object.

indehiscent (in-dee-*hiss*-ent) = Not splitting open at maturity; opposite of dehiscent.

indigene (in-*di*-je-nee) = Native of.

indigenous (in-*di*-je-nus) = Native; not introduced; not exotic.

inflexed (in-*flexd*) = Bent or turned abruptly inwards or downwards.

inflorescence (in-floe-*ress*-ens) = The general arrangement and disposition of the flowers on an axis; mode of flower-bearing; much more frequently used in the sense of a flower-cluster.

infundibuliform (in-fun-*dib*-yu-li-form) = With the form of a funnel or cone.

internode (*in*-ter-node) = Portion of a stem situated between the nodes or joints.

introduced (in-tro-*doosed*) = Brought from another region; not native.

introduction (in-tro-*duk*-shun) = An exotic plant introduced by man or other agency from its native region to another area.

introrse (in-*troars*) = Facing inwards or towards the axis of growth.

involute (in-voe-*loot*) = Inrolled; with both edges rolled in towards the middle, each edge presenting a spiral appearance in cross-section.

isthmus (*isth*-mus) = A narrowed portion of a part or segment of a flower.

keel (keel) = A projecting ridge on a surface, basically rather similar to the keel of a boat.

keeled (keeld) = Provided with a keel or keels.

keiki (*kay*-kee) = Hawaiian term, used by orchidists to signify an offshoot or offset from a plant.

labellum (lah-*bel*-um) = Lip, particularly that of an orchid flower.

labiate (*lah*-bee-ate) = Lipped; furnished with a lip.

lacerate (*la*-ser-ate) = Deeply and irregularly cut along the margins.

laciniate (la-*sin*-ee-ate) = Narrowly incised or slashed, particularly along the margins.

lageniform (*la*-gen-i-form) = Flagon-shaped.

lamella (la-*mel*-ah) = A thin flat scale or plate.

lamellae (la-*mel*-eye) = Plural of **lamella**.

lamellate (*la*-mel-ate) = Furnished with a lamella or lamellae.

lamina (*lam*-i-na) = The blade or expanded part of a leaf, petal, or other structure.

lanceolate (*lan*-see-oh-late) = Lance-shaped; several times longer than broad and tapering from near the base to the pointed apex.

lateral (*lat*-er-al) = Of or pertaining to the side of an organism or of its parts.

lax (laks) = Loose; not dense.

lenticular (len-*tik*-yu-lar) = Lentil-shaped; lens-shaped.

ligneous (*lig*-nee-us) = Woody.

ligulate (*lig*-yu-late) = Strap-shaped.

limb (lim) = Used to distinguish the broad expanded part in a clawed segment from the narrower basal part.

linear (*lin*-ee-ar) = Narrow and comparatively long, with parallel margins.

lineate (*lin*-ee-ate) = Marked with lines or stripes.

linguiform (*lin*-gwi-form) = Tongue-shaped.

lingulate (*lin*-gyu-late) = Tongue- or strap-shaped.

lithophyte (*lith*-oh-fite) = A plant which inhabits rocks or stone outcroppings.

lithophytic (*lith*-oh-fit-ik) = Pertaining to **lithophyte**.

lobate (*loe*-bate) = Furnished with lobes.

lobe (lobe) = A part of a segment that represents a division to about the middle.

lobed (lobed) = Furnished with a lobe or lobes.

lobulate (*low*-byu-late) = Furnished with lobules.

lobule (*low*-byool) = A small lobe.

lorate (*low*-rate) = Strap-shaped.

lunate (*loo*-nate) = Crescent-shaped.

lyrate (*lye*-rate) = Shaped like a lyre; with an enlarged apical lobe and smaller lower ones.

maculate (*mak*-yu-late) = Spotted; blotched; stained.

marginate (*mar*-ji-nate) = With a distinct border or margin.

membranaceous (mem-bra-*nay*-shus) = Thin and more or less translucent.

mentum (*men*-tum) = The chin-like protuberance occurring in certain orchid flowers, formed usually by the bases of the lateral sepals with the elongated column-foot.

mesochil (*mes*-oh-kil) = The intermediate or middle part of the lip of orchids when this structure is separated into three distinct parts, as in *Stanhopea*.

midrib (*mid*-rib) = Main vein or rib of a leaf or leaf-like part.

monandrous (mo-*nan*-drus) = With one stamen.

monocotyledon (mon-oh-kot-i-*lee*-don) = With a single cotyledon or seed-leaf.

monoecious (mo-*nee*-shus) = With the male (staminate) flowers and female (pistillate) flowers borne in separate inflorescences but on the same plant.

monopodial (mon-oh-*poe*-dee-al) = Growing only from the apex of the plant (from its terminal bud); characteristic of all orchids of the subtribe *Sarcanthinae*.

morphology (more-*fol*-oh-jee) = The science that treats of forms or the transformation of organs or parts.

mucro (*moo*-krow) = A short and sharply abrupt tip.

mucronate (*moo*-krow-nate) = Furnished with a mucro.

multigeneric (mul-ti-je-*ner*-ik) = Of many genera; usually used in reference to hybrids combining many genera.

muricate (*moo*-ri-kate) = Roughened with short, hard prominences.

myrmecophilous (meer-me-*ko*-fi-lus) = Ant-loving; inhabited by ants.

nephroid (*nef*-royd) = Kidney-shaped.

nerve (nurv) = A rib or vein, when unbranched and more or less parallel to other veins, used particularly in reference to leaves.

nerved (nurvd) = Furnished with nerves.

nocturnal (nok-*tur*-nal) = Of the night; used in reference to flowers which open after dark.

node (node) = A joint or knot.

nodose (noe-*dose*) = Furnished with nodes; knotty; knobbed.

nomenclature (*noe*-men-klay-chur) = The system of naming.

nutant (*noo*-tant) = Nodding; drooping.

obcordate (ob-*kor*-date) = Inversely cordate; heart-shaped with the attachment at the apex.

oblanceolate (ob-*lan*-see-oh-late) = Inversely lanceolate, with the point of attachment at the more tapering end.

oblique (ob-*leek*) = With unequal sides; asymmetrical.

oblong (*ob*-long) = Two to four times as long as broad, the sides being almost parallel.

obovate (ob-*oh*-vate) = Inversely ovate; egg-shaped, with the narrow end downwards.

obtuse (ob-*toos*) = Blunt; wider than a right angle.

orbicular (or-*bik*-yu-lar) = Spherical.

orbiculate (or-*bik*-yu-late) = Circular.

orchidist (*or*-ki-dist) = One who collects or is interested in orchids horticulturally.

orchidologist (or-ki-*dol*-oh-jist) = A botanist who specializes in the technical study of orchids.

orchidology (or-ki-*dol*-oh-jee) = The branch of technical botany which deals with orchids and their study.

oval (*oh*-val) = Broadly elliptical; slightly contracted upwards.

ovate (*oh*-vate) = Egg-shaped, with the broader end downwards.

ovoid (*oh*-voyd) = Egg-shaped, the larger end towards the stem or axis; used in a three-dimensional sense, as opposed to ovate.

palmate (*pal*-mate) = Lobed or divided in a palm-like or hand-like manner.

pandurate (*pan*-doo-rate) = Fiddle-shaped.

panicle (*pa*-ni-kl) = A compound raceme; a compound, more or less open inflorescence in which the lower branches are longer and blossom earlier than the upper ones.

paniculate (pa-*nik*-yu-late) = Arranged in a panicle.

papillae (pa-*pil*-eye) = Small nipple- or pimple-like projections on a segment.

papillose (pa-pi-*loes*) = Bearing or producing papillae.

parasite (*pa*-rah-site) = An organism which derives its sustenance from another (host) plant; not to be confused with an epiphyte (which see); no true parasites are known in the Orchidaceae.

parasitic (pa-ra-*si*-tik) = Pertaining to parasite.

parthenogenetic (par-the-no-je-*ne*-tik) = Seed which develops without fertilization or fecundation, but by stimulus only.

parthenogenesis (par-the-no-*je*-ne-sis) = The act by which a seed develops without fertilization or fecundation, but by stimulus only.

partite (*par*-tite) = Divided very nearly to the base.

patent (*pa*-tent) = Spreading; opening widely.

pathology (path-*ol*-oh-jee) = The science of diseased or morbid conditions, in plants dealing with diseases, their causes, results, and cures.

pectinate (*pek*-ti-nate) = Shaped like a comb, with narrow parallel projections.

pedicel (*ped*-i-sel) = The stalk of an individual flower or fruit in an inflorescence which is composed of more than one flower or fruit.

pedicellate ovary (ped-*i*-se-late *oh*-va-ree) = In orchids, the combined pedicel with the ovary of the flower.

peduncle (pe-*dun*-kel) = Stalk of a flower-cluster or of a solitary flower.

pedunculate (pe-*dun*-kyu-late) = Growing on a peduncle.

pellucid (pe-*loo*-sid) = Transparent; clear, so that it can almost be seen through.

peloric (pe-*loe*-rik) = An abnormal formation of a flower, in which some perianth-part simulates another part.

peltate (*pel*-tate) = Shaped like a shield, with the stem or stalk attached near the centre instead of at the margin.

pendulous (*pen*-doo-lus) = Inclined or hanging downwards.

perfect (*per*-fekt) = With both stamens and pistils in the same flower; neither male (staminate) nor female (pistillate), but combining both sexes in the same flower.

perfoliate (per-*foe*-lee-ate) = With the leaf surrounding the stem.

perianth (*per*-ee-anth) = Floral envelope, consisting of the calyx and corolla (even if not all parts are present); the perianth of an orchid flower consists of the sepals, petals, and lip.

persistent (per-*sis*-tent) = Remaining attached, instead of falling off at the usual time.

petal (*pet*-al) = One of the separate modified leaves of the corolla of a flower, usually coloured, making up the inner and upper series of a floral envelope or flower. In orchids, one of the petals is normally modified into a **lip** or **labellum** (which see).

petaloid (*pet*-ah-loyd) = Like a petal.

petiolate (*pet*-ee-oh-late) = With a leaf-stalk; petioled.

petiole (*pet*-ee-ole) = The stalk by which a leaf is attached to a stem.

pilose (pye-*lose*) = Shaggy with soft, slender hairs.

pistil (*pis*-til) = The female or seed-producing organ of a flower, consisting usually of the ovary, style, and stigma; in orchids, the pistil becomes part of the column (or gynostemium) and pedicellate ovary.

pistillate (*pis*-ti-late) = Referring to pistil; bearing a pistil.

plaited (*plate*-ed) = Folded lengthwise, like a closed fan.

plane (plane) = Evenly flat, rather than wrinkled, folded, grooved, or otherwise.

pleurothallid (ploo-row-*thah*-lid) = An orchid of the subtribe *Pleurothallidinae*, the *Pleurothallis* group.

plicate (*ply*-kate) = Folded like a fan.

plumose (ploo-*mose*) = Feathery; feather-like; with fine hairs on each side, like the plume of a feather.

pollen (*pol*-en) = Spores or grains borne by the anther, containing the male element; in orchids, it is usually not granular, as in most other plants.

pollination (pol-i-*nay*-shun) = Mechanical or physical operation of transferral of pollen from the stamen to the pistil.

pollinia (paw-*lee*-nee-ah) = In orchids, the coherent masses of pollen found in the anthers.

pollinium (paw-*lee*-nee-um) = Singular form of **pollinia**.

polymorphic (pol-ee-*mor*-fik) = Occurring in several distinct forms.

porrect (poe-*rekt*) = Extended horizontally; stretched out; widely expanded.

posterior (pos-*ter*-ee-or) = At or towards the back; opposite the front; towards the axis.

praemorse (*pry*-morse) = Jagged, as if bitten off.

process (*pro*-sess) = An extension of any surface or part beyond the main outline.

procumbent (pro-*kum*-bent) = Prostrate: lying on the surface of the ground but not rooting.

prostrate (*pros*-trate) = Lying flat on the ground.

pruinose (proo-i-*nose*) = Covered with a whitish, frost-like bloom of fine vegetable wax; excessively glaucous.

pseudobulb (*soo*-doe-bulb) = Thickened or bulb-like stems of certain orchids, the part being solid and borne above the ground or substratum.

puberulent (pyu-*ber*-yu-lent) = Finely pubescent or downy.

puberulous (pyu-*ber*-yu-lus) = Somewhat pubescent or downy.

pubescent (pyu-*bess*-ent) = Hairy, the hairs short, soft, and downy.

pulvinate (*pul*-vi-nate) = Resembling a cushion.

punctate (*punk*-tate) = Dotted with tiny spots of colour or holes.

pyriform (*pye*-ri-form) = Shaped like a pear.

quadrangular (kwad-*ran*-gyu-lar) = With four angles.

quadrate (*kwad*-rate) = Squared.

quadrigeneric (kwad-ri-je-*ner*-ik) = Pertaining to four genera; used particularly in reference to hybrids combining members of four genera.

raceme (rah-*seem*) = A simple, elongated, indeterminate cluster with stalked flowers.

racemose (rah-se-*mose*) = Growing in the form of a raceme.

rachis (*rah*-kis) = The axis of a spike, raceme, or branch of a panicle.

radiate (*ray*-dee-ate) = Standing on and spreading out from a common centre.

radical (*rad*-i-kal) = Belonging or pertaining to the root or base.

ramification (ram-i-fi-*kay*-shun) = The mode or style of branching of a plant.

ramose (rah-*mose*) = Branched.

reclinate (*rek*-li-nate) = Bent down or falling back from the perpendicular.

recurved (re-*kurvd*) = Curved in a direction opposite to the usual one; curved backwards.

reflexed (re-*flexd*) = Turned backwards; bent or folded back.

remote (re-*mote*) = Separated by spaces longer than typical.

reniform (*ren*-i-form) = Kidney-shaped.

repand (*re*-pand) = With a gently wavy or fluted margin; undulate.

repent (*rep*-ent) = Creeping, and typically rooting at the joints.

resupinate (re-*soo*-pi-nate) = Upside-down; turned over; inverted in position by a twist of the axis or, in orchids, by a twist of the pedicellate ovary.

reticulate (re-*tik*-yu-late) = Forming a network, as the veins of a leaf.

retrorse (re-*trorse*) = Turned backwards or downwards.

retuse (re-*toos*) = With the apex rounded or obtuse and shallowly notched.

revolute (*rev*-oh-loot) = Rolled backwards from the margin upon the lower surface.

rhachis (*rah*-kis) = Archaic spelling of **rachis**.

rhizome (*ry*-zome) = A rootstock that is actually a stem or branch, but grows entirely beneath the surface of the ground, or, in most orchids, creeps along the substratum.

rhombic (*rom*-bik) = Somewhat lozenge-shaped; like the shape of a top.

rhomboid (*rom*-boyd) = Somewhat lozenge-shaped, but in a three-dimensional sense.

rib (rib) = Primary vein of a leaf; one of a plurality of parallel or equally diverging ridges.

ringent (*rin*-jent) = Gaping; said of lipped flowers with an open throat or mouth.

rootstock (*root*-stok) = A subterranean stem; rhizome.

rosette (row-*zet*) = A more or less dense basal cluster of leaves.

rostrate (*ros*-trate) = Provided with a beak.

rosulate (*row*-zoo-late) = In a rosette.

rotate (*row*-tate) = Wheel-shaped; with the flowers flattened and widely spreading.

rotund (row-*tund*) = Nearly circular; orbicular, inclining to be oblong.

rudimentary (roo-di-*men*-ta-ree) = Incomplete; very little developed.

rugose (roo-*gose*) = Roughened by wrinkles.

rugulose (*roo*-gyu-lose) = Minutely rugose; finely wrinkled.

rupicolous (roo-*pi*-koe-lus) = Dwelling in or on rocks or stones.

saccate (*sak*-ate) = Bag-like; sac-like.

sagittate (*sa*-ji-tate) = Shaped like an arrow-head.

saprophyte (*sap*-row-fite) = An organism which lives on dead organic matter.

saprophytic (sap-row-*fit*-ik) = Pertaining to **saprophyte**.

sarcanthad (sar-*kan*-thad) = A member of the orchid subtribe *Sarcanthinae*, the *Vanda-Phalaenopsis* alliance.

saxicolous (sax-*i*-koe-lus) = Dwelling in or near rocky places; growing on rocks.

scabrous (*skab*-rus) = Rough or gritty to the touch.

scape (skape) = A leafless peduncle or main flower-stalk arising from the underground or sub-surface parts of a plant; it may bear scales or bracts, but no foliage-leaves, and it may be one- or many-flowered. Often used erroneously as a synonym for raceme, rachis, or peduncle.

scapose (skah-*pose*) = Bearing a scape or scapes.

scarious (*ska*-ree-us) = Thin, dry, membranous, and not green.

secund (se-*kund*) = Borne on one side only; unilateral.

seed (seed) = An ovule when fertilized and matured.

segment (*seg*-ment) = One of the parts of a leaf, petal, sepal, or perianth that is divided but not truly compound; also used as a synonym for 'a part', usually when speaking of the parts of a flower.

self-fertilization = Fertilization secured by pollen from the same flower.

self-pollination = Transferral of pollen from stamen to pistil of the same flower.

semi-epiphyte (*sem*-i-*ep*-i-fite) = A term applied to certain plants which are found growing in pockets of humus which has collected in the crotches of tree-branches, hence which are not truly epiphytic; partly or somewhat epiphytic.

sepal (*see*-pal) = One of the modified leaves forming the outer and lower series of a floral envelope or flower.

sepaline (*see*-pa-leen) = Pertaining to the sepals.

septate (*sep*-tate) = Partitioned; divided by partitions.

septum (*sep*-tum) = A dividing wall or partition.

serrate (*ser*-ate) = Saw-toothed marginally, with the teeth pointing towards the apex of the part.

serrulate (*ser*-yu-late) = Minutely or somewhat serrate.

sessile (*ses*-il) = Without a stem or stalk; stalkless.

sheath (sheeth) = Any long more or less tubular structure surrounding an organ or part.

simple (*sim*-pl) = Not branched or otherwise divided; entire.

sinuate (*sin*-yu-ate) = Wavy-margined; in this condition the indentations are deeper than in an undulate or repand one.

sinus (*sy*-nus) = A depression between the lobes of a leaf or flower or other expanded organ.

spathaceous (spa-*thay*-shus) = Furnished with a sheath; sheath-like.

spatulate (*spat*-yu-late) = Shaped like a spoon or spatula.

species (*spee*-sheez) = A group of organisms showing inter-gradation among its individuals or races, and one or more characteristics in common which definitely separate it from any other group; this is the singular and plural form.

specific (spe-*sif*-ik) = Pertaining to a species; definite.

spermatophyte (sper-*mat*-oh-fite) = A seed-producing plant.

spicate (*spy*-kate) = In the form of a spike.

spike (spike) = An elongated flower-cluster in which the flowers are devoid of pedicels and are sessile on the main peduncle; often erroneously used as a synonym for raceme.

spreading (*spred*-ing) = Standing outward or horizontally.

spur (spur) = A hollow tubular or sac-like extension of a floral organ, as of a sepal or petal; it usually contains nectar-producing glands.

stamen (*stay*-men) = The male floral organ which bears the pollen.

staminate (*stam*-i-nate) = Male; bearing stamens only.

staminode (*stam*-i-node) = A sterile or abortive stamen, or a structure resembling such and borne in the staminal part of a flower; staminodes occur in the flowers of the orchid subtribe *Cypripedilinae*.

staminodium (stam-i-*no*-dee-um) = Synonym for **staminode**.

standard (*stan*-dard) = In orchids of the subtribe *Cypripedilinae*, used to designate the large, showy, usually erect dorsal sepal.

stellate (*stel*-ate) = Resembling a star; star-like.

sterile (*ster*-il) = Barren; imperfect.

stigma (*stig*-ma) = The tip of a pistil; the part which receives the pollen for the fertilization of the ovule; in orchids it is a sticky cavity or excavation, usually situated on the under-surface of the upper part of the column.

stipe (stipe) = A slender, stalk-like base, such as the stipe of certain orchid pollinia.

stipitate (*stip*-i-tate) = Provided with a stipe or stalk.

striate (*stry*-ate) = Marked with longitudinal lines, grooves, or ridges; striped.

strict (strikt) = Narrow and often rigidly erect; straight and upright.

striolate (*stry*-oh-late) = Somewhat or faintly striped.

subacute (*sub*-ah-kyute) = Somewhat or partially acute.

subcordate (sub-*kor*-date) = Almost heart-shaped.

subcoriaceous (sub-koe-ree-*ay*-shus) = Somewhat or approaching leathery in texture.

suberect (*sub*-ee-rekt) = Nearly or almost erect.

subgenus (sub-*jee*-nus) = One of the divisions into which large genera are sometimes taxonomically divided.

subsessile (sub-*ses*-il) = Almost stalkless.

substratum (sub-*strah*-tum) = The material upon which a plant grows.

subtended (sub-*ten*-ded) = Included in an axil; enclosed beneath.

subterete (sub-*ter*-ete) = Somewhat terete.

subulate (*sub*-yu-late) = Awl-shaped.

succulent (*suk*-yu-lent) = Fleshy; juicy.

sulcate (*sul*-kate) = Grooved, especially with deep, longitudinal furrows.

superposed (soo-per-*posed*) = One on top of another.

symmetrical (si-*met*-ri-kal) = Capable of division into similar halves.

sympodial (sim-*poe*-dee-al) = Axial growth continued by successive lateral shoots, instead of by the terminal bud; the opposite of **monopodial** (which see).

synsepal (*sin*-see-pal) = In orchids of the subtribe *Cypripedilinae*, the (typically) cohering lateral sepals.

taxonomy (tax-*on*-oh-mee) = The science of classification, dealing with the arrangement of plants into groups according to natural relationships.

teratology (ter-ah-*tol*-oh-jee) = The study of monstrosities or of abnormal and aberrant forms and malformations.

terete (te-*reet*) = Circular in transverse section; elongate and pencil-shaped.

terminal (*ter*-mi-nal) = Apical; produced at the end.

terminology (ter-mi-*nol*-oh-jee) = The subject which deals with names and naming.

terrestrial (te-*res*-tree-al) = Of the earth; growing in the soil.

tessellate (*tes*-e-late) = Marked or divided into small squares, like a mosaic.

tetragonal (tet-*ra*-goe-nal) = With four angles or corners.

throat (throat) = In orchids with a tubular lip, used to designate the lower part of the tube.

tomentose (toe-men-*tose*) = Covered with woolly, matted hairs.

tooth (tooth) = A sharp-pointed marginal projection.

tortuous (*tor*-tyu-us) = Twisted; with irregular bending or crooking.

triandrous (try-*an*-drus) = With three stamens.

tribe (tribe) = A group of related genera forming a natural division within a family.

tridentate (try-*den*-tate) = With three teeth.

trigeneric (try-je-*ner*-ik) = Of three genera; usually used in reference to hybrids combining members of three genera.

trilobate (try-*low*-bate) = With three lobes.

truncate (*trun*-kate) = Square at the apex, as if cut off.

tuber (*too*-ber) = A thickened, usually underground stem.

tubercle (*too*-ber-kul) = A small, more or less conical protuberance or projection.

tuberculate (too-*ber*-kyu-late) = Furnished with tubercles.

tuberous (*too*-ber-us) = Tuber-like; furnished with tubers.

turbinate (*tur*-bi-nate) = Inversely conical; shaped like a top.

umbel (*um*-bel) = An indeterminate, convex or flat-topped inflorescence in which the pedicels of the cluster arise from a common point.

umbellate (*um*-bel-ate) = Furnished with or pertaining to an umbel.

undulate (*un*-dyu-late) = Wavy; with wavy margins.

unguiculate (un-*gwik*-yu-late) = Clawed; narrowed to a stalk-like base.

unguicule (*un*-gwi-kyool) = A claw.

unilateral (yu-ni-*la*-ter-al) = One-sided; arranged on a single side only.

unisexual (yu-ni-*sex*-yu-al) = With flowers of one sex only.

urceolate (*ur*-see-oh-late) = Urn-shaped.

utriculate (yu-*trik*-yu-late) = Bladder-like; inflated.

vaginate (*va*-ji-nate) = Provided with or surrounded by a sheath.

varietal (va-*rye*-eh-tal) = Of or pertaining to a variety.

variety (va-*rye*-eh-tee) = A division of a species, differing from the species in one or more characteristics which are not sufficiently strong to warrant erection of another, distinct species.

venose (ve-*nose*) = Veined; full of veins.

ventral (*ven*-tral) = The front; used in reference to the anterior or inner face or part of an organ or structure; opposite to the back, or dorsal, part.

ventricose (*ven*-tri-kose) = Swollen on one side; unevenly inflated.

verrucose (*ver*-yu-kose) = Covered with or furnished with wart-like projections.

verticel (*ver*-ti-sel) = A whorl.

verticillate (ver-*ti*-si-late) = Whorled; arranged in circles around an axis, similar to the spokes of a wheel.

vesicle (*ves*-i-kul) = A little bladder or bladder-like cavity.

villous (*vil*-us) = Pubescent with soft, straight hairs; shaggy.

virgate (*veer*-gate) = Rod-like; long, slender, and straight; twiggy.

viscid (*viss*-id) = Sticky; glutinous.

vittate (*vi*-tate) = Striped lengthwise.

whorl (worl) = An arrangement of three or more leaves or other organs in a circle about an axis.

wing (wing) = Any more or less thin expansion from a surface, typically at a decided angle to the surface.

winged (wingd) = Bearing or producing wings.

xerophyte (*zer*-oh-fite) = A plant which is adapted to live on a limited supply of moisture.

xerophytic (*zer*-oh-fit-ik) = Relating or belonging to **xerophyte**.

zonate (*zo*-nate) = Banded or zoned in definite areas.

zygomorphic (zye-go-*mor*-fik) = Capable of being divided into two symmetrical halves only by a single longitudinal plane passing through the axis; all orchid flowers are normally zygomorphic.

APPENDIX

The following comments are pertinent to this *Encyclopaedia*, having come to my attention after the body of the volume had been set up in type. As noted elsewhere, orchids introduced into general cultivation after the compilation of the work will be taken up in detail in the periodic *Supplements*.

Bletilla Rchb.f. = An artificially produced hybrid in this genus was registered in Japan in 1956.

Cadetia Gaud. = A complete list of valid taxa, with synonymy and distribution, for this genus has been published in my continuing serial, 'Index of Orchidaceous Plants', in *Orquidea* 23: 178–84. 1961; and l.c., 24: 10–11. 1962.

Chondrorhyncha Ldl. = A couple of hybrids have been registered recently for this genus, under the name *Cochleanthes* Raf.

Comparettia P. & E. = W. W. G. Moir has utilized the members of this genus extensively in recent years in the production of obviously unusual hybrids with components of the subtribe *Oncidiinae*.

Cycnoches Ldl. = Several hybrids have been registered in this genus recently, almost without exception with erroneously named parents indicated. The continued acceptance of the identification of *Cycnoches chlorochilon* Klotzsch (= *C. ventricosum* Batem. var. *chlorochilon* (Klotzsch) P.H.Allen) for the common, large-flowered 'Swan Orchid', is indeed regrettable, since it is *C. ventricosum* Batem. var. *Warscewiczii* (Rchb.f.) P.H.Allen. See my publication of the annual list of *Orchid Hybrids 1962*: 96. 1963, for a discussion.

Dendrobium Sw. = All members of this important genus, and its allies of the subtribe *Dendrobiinae*, are being taken up in my serial, 'Index of Orchidaceous Plants', which commenced publication in *Orquidea* 23: 176. 1961, and is continuing, with nine parts in print as of this writing. A great many hybrids are still being accepted for registration under erroneous or misspelled names in this group, though these mistakes have been pointed out on several occasions to the Official Orchid Hybrid Registrar.

Diplocaulobium [Rchb.f.] Krzl. = In my annual list of *Orchid Hybrids 1962*: 96. 1963, I have pointed out that a hybrid registered by Limberlost Nursery of Australia between *Dendrobium aureicolor* and *D. Phalaenopsis* (= *D. bigibbum* Ldl. var. *Phalaenopsis* (Fitzg.) F.M.Bail.) probably represents a bigeneric group. This since *Dendrobium aureicolor* J.J.Sm. is correctly *Diplocaulobium aureicolor* (J.J.Sm.) A.D. Hawkes—assuming that the initial parent is correctly identified. No name has as yet been proposed for hybrids between these two genera.

Epidendrum L. = Several recent articles have proposed the reinstatement of *Encyclia* Hk. as a genus separate from *Epidendrum* L. But the same authors who make this proposal, confusingly continue to utilize the name *Epidendrum* when referring to their supposed 'genus' *Encyclia*!

Epidendrum alatum Batem. = Carl L. Withner has pointed out (in *Orch. Weekly* 5: 44–6. 1964) the apparently correct identity of this long-confused species. *Epidendrum belizense* Rchb.f. is also discussed in this important paper.

Epidendrum ionophlebium Rchb.f. = Garay has relegated this species to synonymy under **E. chacaoense** Rchb.f. (in Dunsterville & Garay, *Venez. Orch. Illus.* 2: 108, pl. 1961), without any explanation for his action.

Epidendrum oncidioides Ldl. = R. A. Dressler has pointed out (in *Fla. Orchidist*, May–June 1962) the apparently correct identity of this long-confused species, which is actually exceedingly rare in contemporary collections.

Eulophia R.Br. = V. S. Summerhayes has pointed out, in a remarkable article in *Orch. Rev.* 72: 88. 1964, that several of my proposed new combinations in this genus are not valid, because of studies issued by him at a previous date. Since I have never seen his papers, I must refer any interested readers to them, provided they have access to particularly extensive reference libraries.

Glossodia R.Br. = Two Western Australian species previously referable to this genus have become the new group **Elythranthera** [Endl.] A.S.George (*fide* L. Cady in *The Orchadian*, no. 4: 37. 1964).

Hofmeisterella Rchb.f. = *H. eumicroscopica* (Rchb.f.) Rchb.f. has recently been recorded from Venezuela by G. C. K. Dunsterville (in *Orch. Rev.* 72: 84, fig. 48. 1964). The type came from Ecuador (not Brazil), and the species is also known from Peru.

Ionopsis HBK = Henry P. Butcher, of Volcán, Chiriquí, Republic of Panama, pointed out (in *Orch. Weekly* 5: 27. 1964) that *I. utricularioides* (Sw.) Ldl. apparently has a far longer life-span than I noted in the discussion of it in this *Encyclopaedia*, mentioning that he has found specimens 'that I know are at least ten years old'. He also (l.c.) records *I. satyrioides* (Sw.) Rchb.f. from Panama; this species is illustrated in l.c., 4: 467. 1964.

Leochilus Kn. & Westc. = *L. labiatus* (Sw.) O.Ktze. has been reported from South Florida (see *Orch. Weekly* 4: 448. 1964), but as of this writing I have not seen any authentic specimens.

Mormodes Ldl. = A rather large series of articles, variously popularized or scientific, has appeared in the past year or two in several orchid magazines, dealing with this complex genus. These papers, by several different authors, express opinions regarding taxonomic components of this group which are highly divergent from those used in this *Encyclopaedia*, and regrettably in most instances only add to the already considerable confusion existing here.

Oncidium Cavendishianum Batem. = This attractive, frequently grown species is also known from Honduras.

Oncidium variegatum (Sw.) Sw. = This species was recorded from South Florida by Oakes Ames in the early 1900's. It does not appear to exist here, and our indigenous plant is possibly an undescribed one. The name *Oncidium 'miamiense'* has been used on several occasions in the popular literature for this Florida orchid, but apparently has never been validly published. In any event, the epithet is inappropriate, since the plant does not occur within about one hundred miles of Miami!

Orchis [Tournef.] L. = An artificially produced hybrid in this genus was registered by a Japanese orchidist in 1956.

Pescatorea Rchb.f. = A member of this genus, crossed with *Chondrorhyncha* Ldl. gives *Pescarhyncha*, registered by Moir in 1961. This has now been referred to *Pescoranthes*, confusingly.

Plectrophora Focke = **P. cultrifolia** (B.-R.) Cgn., a Brazilian species, has been found in Venezuela, and recorded by G. C. K. Dunsterville. Henry P. Butcher has also discovered a member of the genus in Panama.

Pleurothallis R.Br. = Since the original manuscript of this *Encyclopaedia* was set up in type, a notable number of previously uncultivated members of this genus have been made available on the general orchid market. These will be taken up in detail in the periodic *Supplements* to this work.

Pleurothallis Ghiesbreghtiana A.Rich. & Gal. = Garay has relegated this widespread species to synonymy under **P. quadrifida** (LaLl. & Lex.) Ldl. (in Dunsterville & Garay, *Venez. Orch. Illus.* 2: 298, pl. 1961), without any explanation for his action.

Polystachya Hk. = A hybrid, artificially produced, was registered in this genus in 1955. The widespread *P. luteola* (Sw.) Hk. has been called **P. extinctoria** Rchb.f. by V. S. Summerhayes and A. A. Bullock (see *Orch. Weekly* 4: 383. 1964).

Sarcochilus R.Br. = Two artificially produced hybrids have been registered in this interesting genus to date (see *Orch. Weekly* 5: 19. 1964).

Scaphyglottis P. & E. = *Hexadesmia* Brongn., previously referred to synonymy in this complex genus, has recently been reinstated as valid, perhaps with good reason.

Schomburgkia Ldl. = Several recent articles have proposed the reinstatement of this genus, and have also reinstated taxa previously considered synonyms of widespread or variable entities. The continuing use of this genus as a valid one in horticulture causes exceptional confusion for all concerned, especially since it is recognized with remarkable inconsistency.

Scuticaria Ldl. = *S. Steelii* (Hk.) Ldl. has recently been introduced into American collections in considerable quantities from Amazonian Peru.

Selenipedium Rchb.f. = S. **Steyermarkii** Foldats was added to this notably rare genus in 1961, from materials collected at the 'Lost World' of Auyántepuí, in the Guayana Highlands of Venezuela (see Dunsterville in *Orch. Rev.* 71: 384, *ff.* 1963).

NEW LOCALITY NAMES = In recent times, many new nations have come into being throughout the world. Especially is this true in Africa, where scarcely a month seems to pass without the recognition of one or more. The majority of these are not as yet generally known on an international scale, hence they have not, by and large, been utilized in this study. Notable examples might be cited in the Malagasy Republic (Madagascar), Taiwan (Formosa), Malawi (Nyasaland), West Irian (part of New Guinea), Kalimantan (Indonesian Borneo), and Sabah (North Borneo).

MULTIGENERIC ORCHID HYBRID GROUPS

The following groups of hybrids utilizing more than one genus of orchids have been registered during the period extending from July 1st, 1963, through August 31st, 1964. See pages 527 to 529 for the initial list of these groups.

Aëridoglossum (*Aërides* × *Ascoglossum*), E. Iwanaga 1963
Aliceara (*Brassia* × *Miltonia* × *Oncidium*), E. Iwanaga 1964
Colmanara (*Miltonia* × *Odontoglossum* × *Oncidium*), Moir[1] 1963
Hookerara (*Brassavola* × *Cattleya* × *Diacrium*), Moir 1963
Nakamotoara (*Ascocentrum* × *Neofinetia* × *Vanda*), W. K. Nakamoto 1964

[1] This name was used in the *Sanders' Complete List of Orchid Hybrids* to January 1st, 1946, in the 'Alphabetical List of Generic Parents', but no entry is given within the body of the work.

Phalanetia (*Neofinetia* × *Phalaenopsis*), W. K. Nakamoto 1964
Recchiara (*Brassavola* × *Cattleya* × *Laelia* × *Schomburgkia*), Brazil 1950[2]
Renanthoglossum (*Ascoglossum* × *Renanthera*), E. Iwanaga 1963
Schombavola (*Brassavola* × *Schomburgkia*), Moir 1964
Vascostylis (*Ascocentrum* × *Rhynchostylis* × *Vanda*), F. Takakura 1964[3]
Warneara (*Comparettia* × *Oncidium* × *Rodriguezia*), Moir 1964

[2] This is a prior name for *Beaumontara*, of Moir, registered in 1961, *fide* Garay in *Orch. Rev.* 72: New Orch. Hybr. list [p. 4]. July 1964.

[3] In the interests of consistency in registration of multigeneric orchid hybrids, it would seem much more appropriate if the designating suffix *-ara* had been utilized for this trigeneric group. Another example of this inconsistency is *Epilaeliocattleya* (*Cattleya* × *Epidendrum* × *Laelia*), registered in 1960.

INDEX

Bold face numerals indicate an illustration in the text, or on facing or adjacent plate. Roman numerals indicate a colour plate. Typographical errors which have been published in the literature, as indexed here, are listed but are not given phonetic pronunciations, since these would be of no particular use to my readers.

543